This is what you must remember: the ending of one story is just the beginning of another. This has happened before, after all. People die. Old orders pass. New societies are born. When we say "the world has ended," it's usually a lie, because *the planet* is just fine.

But this is the way the world ends.

This is the way the world ends.

This is the way the world ends.

For the last time.

Praise for

THE INHERITANCE TRILOGY

"A complex, edge-of-your-seat story with plenty of funny, scary, and bittersweet twists."

—*Publishers Weekly* (Starred Review)

"An offbeat, engaging tale by a talented and original newcomer."

—*Kirkus*

"An astounding debut novel... the world-building is solid, the characterization superb, the plot complicated but clear."

—*RT Book Reviews* (Top Pick!)

"A delight for the fantasy reader."

—*Library Journal* (Starred Review)

"*The Hundred Thousand Kingdoms*... is an impressive debut, which revitalizes the trope of empires whose rulers have gods at their fingertips."

—io9.com

"N. K. Jemisin has written a fascinating epic fantasy where the stakes are not just the fate of kingdoms but of the world and the universe."

—sfrevu.com

"Many books are good, some are great, but few are truly important. Add to this last category *The Hundred Thousand Kingdoms*, N. K. Jemisin's debut novel... In this reviewer's opinion, this is the must-read fantasy of the year."

—*BookPage*

"A similar blend of inventiveness, irreverence, and sophistication—along with sensuality—brings vivid life to the setting and other characters: human and otherwise... *The Hundred Thousand Kingdoms* definitely leaves me wanting more of this delightful new writer."
—*Locus*

"A compelling page-turner." —*The Onion A.V. Club*

"An absorbing story, an intriguing setting and world mythology, and a likable narrator with a compelling voice. The next book cannot come out soon enough." —fantasybookcafe.com

"*The Broken Kingdoms*... expands the universe of the series geographically, historically, magically and in the range of characters, while keeping the same superb prose and gripping narrative that made the first one such a memorable debut."
—*Fantasy Book Critic*

"*The Kingdom of Gods* once again proves Jemisin's skill and consistency as a storyteller, but what sets her apart from the crowd is her ability to imagine and describe the mysteries of the universe in language that is at once elegant and profane, and thus, true."
—*Shelf Awareness*

Praise for the
DREAMBLOOD DUOLOGY

"Ah, N. K. Jemisin, you can do no wrong." —Felicia Day

"*The Killing Moon* is a powerhouse and, in general, one hell of a story to read. Jemisin has arrived." —*Bookworm Blues*

"The author's exceptional ability to tell a compelling story and her talent for world-building have assured her place at the forefront of fantasy." —*Library Journal* (Starred Review)

"Jemisin excels at world-building and the inclusion of a diverse mix of characters makes her settings feel even more real and vivid." —*RT Book Reviews* (Top Pick!)

"The novel also showcases some skillful, original world-building. Like a lucid dreamer, Jemisin takes real-world influences as diverse as ancient Egyptian culture and Freudian/Jungian dream theory and unites them to craft a new world that feels both familiar and entirely new. It's all refreshingly unique."
—*Slant Magazine*

"Read this or miss out on one of the best fantasy books of the year so far." —*San Francisco Book Review*

"N. K. Jemisin is playing with the gods again—and it's just as good as the first time." —io9.com

THE FIFTH SEASON

Also by N. K. Jemisin

THE INHERITANCE TRILOGY
The Hundred Thousand Kingdoms
The Broken Kingdoms
The Kingdom of Gods
The Awakened Kingdom (novella)

The Inheritance Trilogy (omnibus edition)

DREAMBLOOD
The Killing Moon
The Shadowed Sun

THE BROKEN EARTH
The Fifth Season

THE FIFTH SEASON

THE BROKEN EARTH: BOOK ONE

N. K. JEMISIN

www.orbitbooks.net

The characters and events in this book are fictitious. Any similarity to real persons, living or dead, is coincidental and not intended by the author.

Orbit
Hachette Book Group
1290 Avenue of the Americas, New York, NY 10104
www.orbitbooks.net

Printed in the United States of America

LSC-C

First Edition: August 2015

20 19 18

Orbit is an imprint of Hachette Book Group, Inc. The Orbit name and logo are trademarks of Little, Brown Book Group Limited.

Library of Congress Cataloging-in-Publication Data

Jemisin, N. K.
The fifth season / N. K. Jemisin.—First edition.
pages ; cm.—(The broken earth ; Book One)
ISBN 978-0-316-22929-6 (trade pbk.)—ISBN 978-0-316-22930-2 (e-book)—ISBN 978-1-4789-0083-2 (audio book download)
I. Title.
PS3610.E46F54 2015
813'.6—dc23

2015002138

For all those who have to fight for the respect that everyone else is given without question

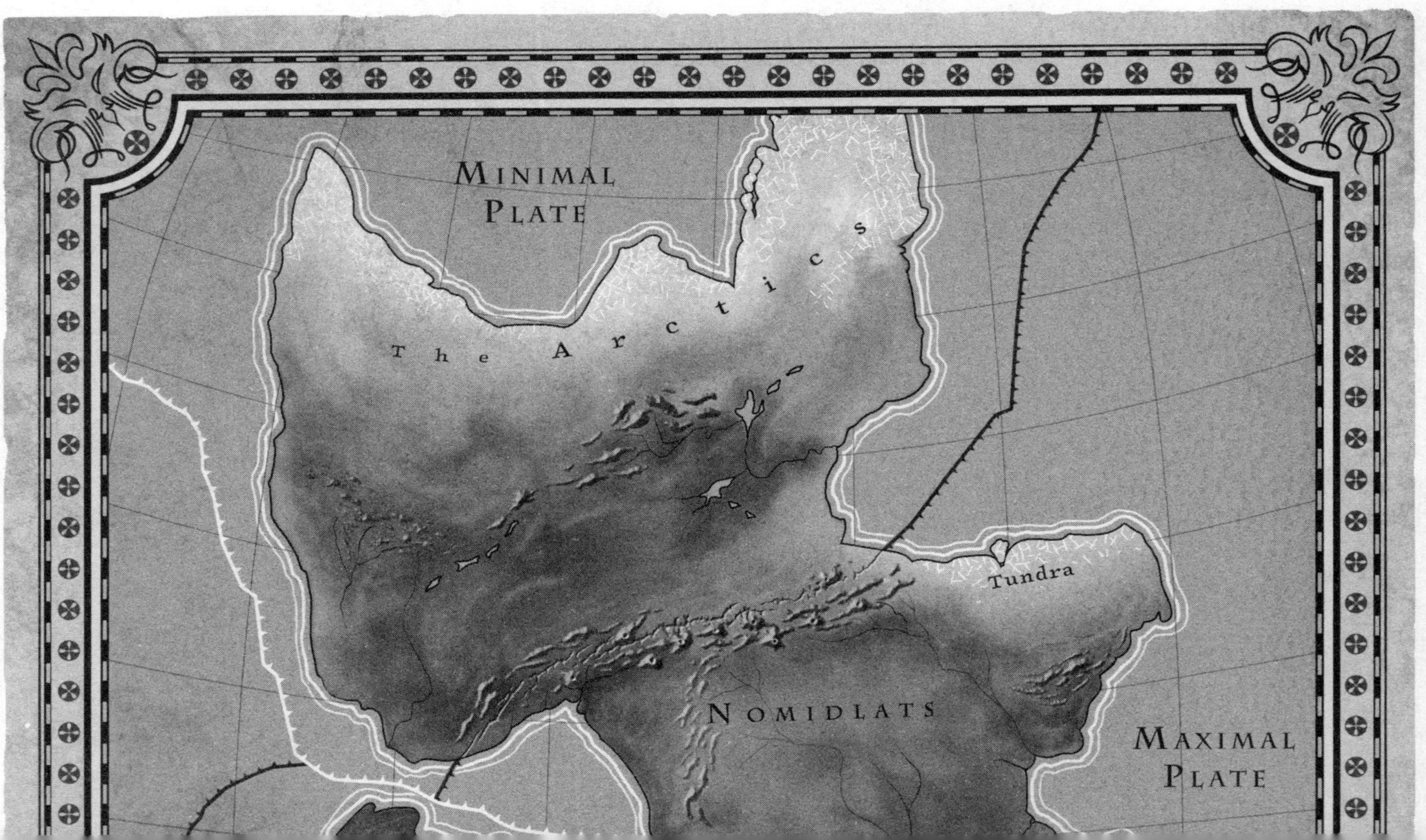
Minimal Plate
The Arctics
Tundra
Nomidlats
Maximal Plate

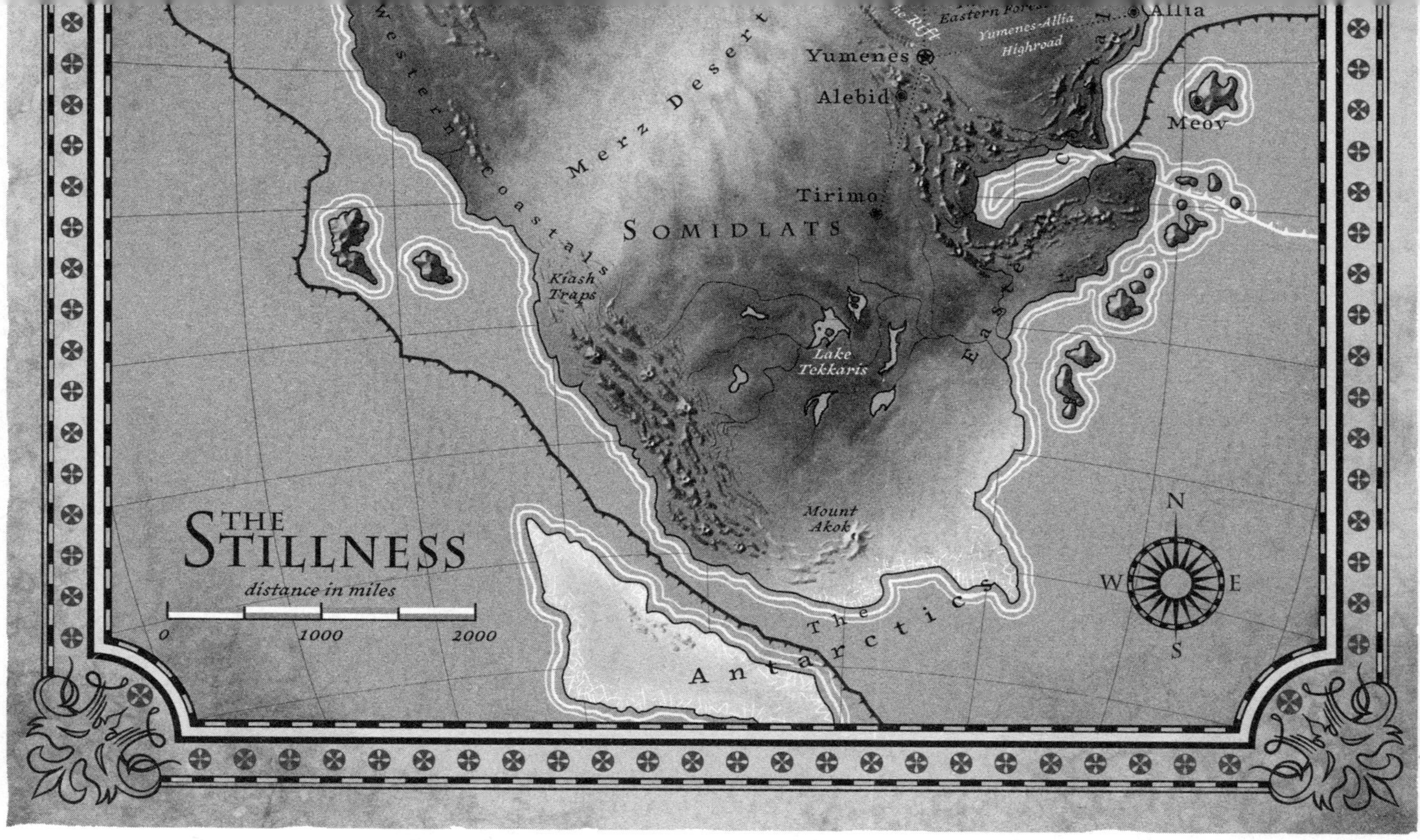

The Stillness
distance in miles
0
1000
2000
Yumenes
Alebid
Tirimo
Eastern Forest
Yumenes-Allia Highroad
Allia
Meov
Merz Desert
Western Coastals
Somidlats
Kiash Traps
Lake Tekkaris
Mount Akok
The Antarctics
N
S
E
W

PROLOGUE

you are here

Let's start with the end of the world, why don't we? Get it over with and move on to more interesting things.

First, a personal ending. There is a thing she will think over and over in the days to come, as she imagines how her son died and tries to make sense of something so innately senseless. She will cover Uche's broken little body with a blanket—except his face, because he is afraid of the dark—and she will sit beside it numb, and she will pay no attention to the world that is ending outside. The world has already ended within her, and neither ending is for the first time. She's old hat at this by now.

What she thinks then, and thereafter, is: *But he was free.*

And it is her bitter, weary self that answers this almost-question every time her bewildered, shocked self manages to produce it:

He wasn't. Not really. But now he will be.

* * *

But you need context. Let's try the ending again, writ continentally.

Here is a land.

It is ordinary, as lands go. Mountains and plateaus and canyons and river deltas, the usual. Ordinary, except for its size and its dynamism. It moves a lot, this land. Like an old man lying restlessly abed it heaves and sighs, puckers and farts, yawns and swallows. Naturally this land's people have named it *the Stillness.* It is a land of quiet and bitter irony.

The Stillness has had other names. It was once several other lands. It's one vast, unbroken continent at present, but at some point in the future it will be more than one again.

Very soon now, actually.

The end begins in a city: the oldest, largest, and most magnificent living city in the world. The city is called Yumenes, and once it was the heart of an empire. It is still the heart of many things, though the empire has wilted somewhat in the years since its first bloom, as empires do.

Yumenes is not unique because of its size. There are many large cities in this part of the world, chain-linked along the equator like a continental girdle. Elsewhere in the world villages rarely grow into towns, and towns rarely become cities, because all such polities are hard to keep alive when the earth keeps trying to eat them... but Yumenes has been stable for most of its twenty-seven centuries.

Yumenes is unique because here alone have human beings dared to build not for safety, not for comfort, not even for beauty, but for bravery. The city's walls are a masterwork of delicate mosaics and embossing detailing its people's long and brutal history. The clumping masses of its buildings are punctuated by great high towers like fingers of stone, hand-wrought lanterns powered by the modern marvel of hydroelectricity, delicately arching bridges woven of glass and audacity, and architectural structures called *balconies* that are so simple, yet so breathtakingly foolish, that no one has ever built them before in written history. (But much of history is unwritten. Remember this.) The streets are paved not with easy-to-replace cobbles, but with a smooth, unbroken, and miraculous substance the locals have dubbed *asphalt*. Even the shanties of Yumenes are daring, because they're just thin-walled shacks that would blow over in a bad windstorm, let alone a shake. Yet they stand, as they have stood, for generations.

At the core of the city are many tall buildings, so it is perhaps unsurprising that one of them is larger and more daring than all the rest combined: a massive structure whose base is a star pyramid of precision-carved obsidian brick. Pyramids are the most stable architectural form, and this one is pyramids times five because why not? And because this is Yumenes, a vast geodesic sphere whose faceted walls resemble translucent amber sits at the pyramid's apex, seeming to balance there lightly—though in truth, every part of the structure is channeled toward the sole purpose of supporting it. It *looks* precarious; that is all that matters.

The Black Star is where the leaders of the empire meet to do their leaderish things. The amber sphere is where they keep their emperor, carefully preserved and perfect. He wanders its golden halls in genteel despair, doing what he is told and dreading the day his masters decide that his daughter makes a better ornament.

None of these places or people matter, by the way. I simply point them out for context.

But here is a man who will matter a great deal.

You can imagine how he looks, for now. You may also imagine what he's thinking. This might be wrong, mere conjecture, but a certain amount of likelihood applies nevertheless. Based on his subsequent actions, there are only a few thoughts that could be in his mind in this moment.

He stands on a hill not far from the Black Star's obsidian walls. From here he can see most of the city, smell its smoke, get lost in its gabble. There's a group of young women walking along one of the asphalt paths below; the hill is in a park much beloved by the city's residents. (*Keep green land within the walls*, advises stonelore, but in most communities the land is fallow-planted with legumes and other soil-enriching crops. Only in Yumenes is greenland sculpted into prettiness.) The women laugh at something one of them has said, and the sound wafts up to the man on a passing breeze. He closes his eyes and savors the faint tremolo of their voices, the fainter reverberation of their footsteps like the wingbeats of butterflies against his sessapinae. He can't sess all seven million residents of the city, mind you; he's good, but not that good. Most of them, though, yes, they are there. *Here.* He breathes deeply and becomes a fixture of the earth. They tread upon the filaments of his nerves; their voices stir the fine hairs of his skin; their breaths ripple the air he draws into his lungs. They are on him. They are in him.

But he knows that he is not, and will never be, one of them.

"Did you know," he says, conversationally, "that the first stonelore was actually *written* in stone? So that it couldn't be changed to suit fashion or politics. So it wouldn't wear away."

"I know," says his companion.

"Hnh. Yes, you were probably there when it was first set down, I forget." He sighs, watching the women walk out of sight. "It's safe to love you. You won't fail me. You won't die. And I know the price up front."

His companion does not reply. He wasn't really expecting a response, though a part of him hoped. He has been so lonely.

But hope is irrelevant, as are so many other feelings that he knows will bring him only despair if he considers them again. He has considered this enough. The time for dithering is past.

"A commandment," the man says, spreading his arms, "is set in stone."

Imagine that his face aches from smiling. He's been smiling for hours: teeth clenched, lips drawn back, eyes crinkled so the crow's feet show. There is an art to smiling in a way that others will believe. It is always important to include the eyes; otherwise, people will know you hate them.

"Chiseled words are absolute."

He speaks to no one in particular, but beside the man stands a woman—of sorts. Her emulation of human gender is only superficial, a courtesy. Likewise the loose drapelike dress that she wears is not cloth. She has simply shaped a portion of her stiff substance to suit the preferences of the fragile, mortal creatures among whom she currently moves. From a distance the illusion would work to pass her off as a woman standing still, at least for a while. Up close, however, any hypothetical observer would notice that her skin is white porcelain; that is not a metaphor. As a sculpture, she would be beautiful, if too relentlessly realistic for local tastes. Most Yumenescenes prefer polite abstraction over vulgar actuality.

When she turns to the man—slowly; stone eaters are slow aboveground, except when they aren't—this movement pushes her beyond artful beauty into something altogether different. The man has grown used to it, but even so, he does not look at her. He does not want revulsion to spoil the moment.

"What will you do?" he asks her. "When it's done. Will your kind rise up through the rubble and take the world in our stead?"

"No," she says.

"Why not?"

"Few of us are interested in that. Anyway, you'll still be here."

The man understands that she means you in the plural. *Your kind. Humanity.* She often treats him as though he represents his whole species. He does the same to her. "You sound very certain."

She says nothing to this. Stone eaters rarely bother stating the obvious. He's glad, because her speech annoys him in any case; it does not shiver the air the way a human voice would. He doesn't know how that works. He doesn't *care* how it works, but he wants her silent now.

He wants *everything* silent.

"End," he says. "Please."

And then he reaches forth with all the fine control that the world has brainwashed and backstabbed and brutalized out of him, and all the sensitivity that his masters have bred into him through generations of rape and coercion and highly unnatural selection. His fingers spread and twitch as he feels several reverberating points on the map of his awareness: his fellow slaves. He cannot free them, not in the practical sense. He's tried before and failed. He can, however, make their suffering serve a cause greater than one city's hubris, and one empire's fear.

So he reaches deep and takes hold of the humming tapping bustling reverberating rippling vastness of the city, and the quieter bedrock beneath it, and the roiling churn of heat and pressure beneath that. Then he reaches wide, taking hold of the great sliding-puzzle piece of earthshell on which the continent sits.

Lastly, he reaches up. For power.

He takes all that, the strata and the magma and the people and the power, in his imaginary hands. Everything. He holds it. He is not alone. The earth is with him.

Then *he breaks it.*

* * *

Here is the Stillness, which is not still even on a good day.

Now it ripples, reverberates, in cataclysm. Now there is a line, roughly east–west and too straight, almost neat in its manifest unnaturalness, spanning the girth of the land's equator. The line's origin point is the city of Yumenes.

The line is deep and raw, a cut to the quick of the planet. Magma wells in its wake, fresh and glowing red. The earth is good at healing itself. This wound will scab over quickly in geologic terms, and then the cleansing ocean will follow its line to bisect the Stillness into two lands. Until this happens, however, the wound will fester with not only heat but gas and gritty, dark ash—enough to choke off the sky across most of the Stillness's face within a few weeks. Plants everywhere will die, and the animals that depend on them will starve, and the animals that eat those will starve. Winter will come early, and hard, and it will last a long, long time. It *will* end, of course, like every winter does, and then the world will return to its old self. Eventually.

Eventually.

The people of the Stillness live in a perpetual state of disaster preparedness. They've built walls and dug wells and put away food, and they can easily last five, ten, even twenty-five years in a world without sun.

Eventually meaning in this case *in a few thousand years.*

Look, the ash clouds are spreading already.

* * *

While we're doing things continentally, *planetarily*, we should consider the obelisks, which float above all this.

The obelisks had other names once, back when they were first built and deployed and used, but no one remembers those names or the great devices' purpose. Memories are fragile as slate in the Stillness. In fact, these days no one really pays much attention to the things at all, though they are huge and beautiful and a little terrifying: massive crystalline shards that hover amid the clouds, rotating slowly and drifting along incomprehensible flight paths, blurring now and again as if they are not quite real—though this may only be a trick of the light. (It isn't.) It's obvious that the obelisks are nothing natural.

It is equally obvious that they are irrelevant. Awesome, but purposeless: just another grave-marker of just another civilization successfully destroyed by Father Earth's tireless efforts. There are many other such cairns around the world: a thousand ruined cities, a million monuments to heroes or gods no one remembers, several dozen bridges to nowhere. Such things are not to be admired, goes the current wisdom in the Stillness. The people who built those old things were weak, and died as the weak inevitably must. More damning is that they *failed*. The ones who built the obelisks just failed harder than most.

But the obelisks exist, and they play a role in the world's end, and thus are worthy of note.

* * *

Back to the personal. Need to keep things grounded, ha ha.

The woman I mentioned, the one whose son is dead. She was not in Yumenes, thankfully, or this would be a very short tale. And you would not exist.

She's in a town called Tirimo. In the parlance of the Stillness a town is one form of *comm*, or community—but as comms go Tirimo is barely large enough to merit that name. Tirimo sits in a valley of the same name, at the foot of the Tirimas Mountains. The nearest body of water is an intermittent creek the locals call Little Tirika. In a language that no longer exists except in these lingering linguistic fragments, *eatiri* meant "quiet." Tirimo is far from the glittering, stable cities of the Equatorials, so people here build for the inevitability of shakes. There are no artful towers or cornices, just walls built out of wood and cheap brown local bricks, set upon foundations of hewn stone. No asphalted roads, just grassy slopes bisected by dirt paths; only some of those paths have been overlaid with wooden boards or cobblestones. It is a peaceful place, although the cataclysm that just occurred in Yumenes will soon send seismic ripples southward to flatten the entire region.

In this town is a house like any other. This house, which sits along one of these slopes, is little more than a hole dug into the earth that has been lined with clay and bricks to make it waterproof, then roofed over with cedar and cut sod. The sophisticated people of Yumenes laugh (laughed) at such primitive digs, when they deign (deigned) to speak of such things at all—but for the people of Tirimo, living in the earth is as sensible as it is simple. Keeps things cool in summer and warm in winter; resilient against shakes and storms alike.

The woman's name is Essun. She is forty-two years old. She's like most women of the midlats: tall when she stands, straight-backed and long-necked, with hips that easily bore two children and breasts that easily fed them, and broad, limber hands. Strong-looking, well-fleshed; such things are valued in the Stillness. Her hair hangs round her face in ropy fused locks, each perhaps as big around as her pinky finger, black fading to brown at the tips. Her skin is unpleasantly ocher-brown by some standards and unpleasantly olive-pale by others. Mongrel midlatters, Yumenescenes call (called) people like her—enough Sanzed in them to show, not enough to tell.

The boy was her son. His name was Uche; he was almost three years old. He was small for his age, big-eyed and button-nosed, precocious, with a sweet smile. He lacked for none of the traits that human children have used to win their parents' love since the species evolved toward something resembling reason. He was healthy and clever and he should still be alive.

This was the den of their home. It was cozy and quiet, a room where all the family could gather and talk or eat or play games or cuddle or tickle one another. She liked nursing Uche here. She thinks he was conceived here.

His father has beaten him to death here.

* * *

And now for the last bit of context: a day later, in the valley that surrounds Tirimo. By this time the first echoes of the cataclysm have already rippled past, although there will be aftershakes later.

At the northernmost end of this valley is devastation: shattered trees, tumbled rock faces, a hanging pall of dust that has not dissipated in the still, sulfur-tinged air. Where the initial shock wave hit, nothing remains standing: it was the sort of shake that jolts everything to pieces and rattles those pieces into pebbles. There are bodies, too: small animals that could not run away, deer and other large beasts that faltered in their escape and were crushed by rubble. A few of the latter are people who were unlucky enough to be traveling along the trade road on precisely the wrong day.

The scouts from Tirimo who came this way to survey the damage did not climb over the rubble; they just looked at it through longeyes from the remaining road. They marveled that the rest of the valley—the part around Tirimo proper, several miles in every direction forming a near-perfect circle—was unscathed. Well, really, they did not *marvel*, precisely. They looked at each other in grim unease, because everyone knows what such apparent fortune means. *Look for the center of the circle,* stonelore cautions. There's a rogga in Tirimo, somewhere.

A terrifying thought. But more terrifying are the signs coming out of the north, and the fact that Tirimo's headman ordered them to collect as many of the fresher animal carcasses as they could on the circuit back. Meat that has not gone bad can be dried, the furs and hides stripped and cured. Just in case.

The scouts eventually leave, their thoughts preoccupied by *just in case.* If they had not been so preoccupied, they might have noticed an object sitting near the foot of the newly sheared cliff, unobtrusively nestled between a listing gnarlfir and cracked boulders. The object would have been notable for its size and shape: a kidney-shaped oblong of mottled chalcedony, dark green-gray, markedly different from the paler sandstone tumbled around it. If they had gone to stand near it, they would have noticed that it was chest-high and nearly the length of a human body. If they had touched it, they might have been fascinated by the density of the object's surface. It's a heavy-looking thing, with an ironlike scent reminiscent of rust and blood. It would have surprised them by being warm to the touch.

Instead, no one is around when the object groans faintly and then splits, fissioning neatly along its long axis as if sawed. There is a loud scream-hiss of escaping heat and pressured gas as this happens, which sends any nearby surviving forest creatures skittering for cover. In a near-instantaneous flicker, light spills from the edges of the fissure, something like flame and something like liquid, leaving scorched glass on the ground around the object's base. Then the object grows still for a long while. Cooling.

Several days pass.

After a time, something pushes the object apart from within and crawls a few feet before collapsing. Another day passes.

Now that it has cooled and split, a crust of irregular crystals, some clouded white and some red as venous blood, line the object's inner surface. Thin pale liquid puddles near the bottom of each half's cavity, though most of the fluid the geode contained has soaked away into the ground underneath.

The body that the geode contained lies facedown amid the rocks, naked, his flesh dry but still heaving in apparent exhaustion. Gradually, however, he pushes himself upright. Every movement is deliberate and very, very slow. It takes a long time. Once he is upright, he stumbles—slowly—to the geode, and leans against its bulk to support himself. Thus braced, he bends—slowly—and reaches within it. With a sudden, sharp movement he breaks off the tip of a red crystal. It is a small piece, perhaps the size of a grape, jagged as broken glass.

The boy—for that is what he resembles—puts this in his mouth and chews. The noise of this is loud, too: a grind and rattle that echoes around the clearing. After a few moments of this, he swallows. Then he begins to shiver, violently. He wraps his arms around himself for a moment, uttering a soft groan as if it has suddenly occurred to him that he is naked and cold and this is a terrible thing.

With an effort, the boy regains control of himself. He reaches into the geode—moving faster now—and pulls loose more of the crystals. He sets them in a small pile atop the object as he breaks them loose. The thick, blunt crystal shafts crumble beneath his fingers as if made of sugar, though they are in fact much, much harder. But he is in fact not actually a child, so this is easy for him.

At last he stands, wavering and with his arms full of milky, bloody stone. The wind blows sharply for an instant, and his skin prickles in response. He twitches at this, fast and jerky as a clockwork puppet this time. Then he frowns down at himself.

As he concentrates, his movements grow smoother, more evenly paced. More *human*. As if to emphasize this, he nods to himself, perhaps in satisfaction.

The boy turns then, and begins walking toward Tirimo.

* * *

This is what you must remember: the ending of one story is just the beginning of another. This has happened before, after all. People die. Old orders pass. New societies are born. When we say "the world has ended," it's usually a lie, because *the planet* is just fine.

But this is the way the world ends.

This is the way the world ends.

This is the way the world ends.

For the last time.

1

you, at the end

You are she. She is you. You are Essun. Remember? The woman whose son is dead.

You're an orogene who's been living in the little nothing town of Tirimo for ten years. Only three people here know what you are, and two of them you gave birth to.

Well. One left who knows, now.

For the past ten years you've lived as ordinary a life as possible. You came to Tirimo from elsewhere; the townsfolk don't really care where or why. Since you were obviously well educated, you became a teacher at the local creche for children aged ten to thirteen. You're neither the best teacher nor the worst; the children forget you when they move on, but they learn. The butcher probably knows your name because she likes to flirt with you. The baker doesn't because you're quiet, and because like everyone else in town he just thinks of you as Jija's wife. Jija's a Tirimo man born and bred, a stoneknapper of the Resistant use-caste; everyone knows and likes him, so they like you peripherally.

He's the foreground of the painting that is your life together. You're the background. You like it that way.

You're the mother of two children, but now one of them is dead and the other is missing. Maybe she's dead, too. You discover all of this when you come home from work one day. House empty, too quiet, tiny little boy all bloody and bruised on the den floor.

And you . . . shut down. You don't mean to. It's just a bit much, isn't it? Too much. You've been through a lot, you're very strong, but there are limits to what even you can bear.

Two days pass before anyone comes for you.

You've spent them in the house with your dead son. You've risen, used the toilet, eaten something from the coldvault, drunk the last trickle of water from the tap. These things you could do without thinking, by rote. Afterward, you returned to Uche's side.

(You fetched him a blanket during one of these trips. Covered him up to his ruined chin. Habit. The steampipes have stopped rattling; it's cold in the house. He could catch something.)

Late the next day, someone knocks at the house's front door. You do not stir yourself to answer it. That would require you to wonder who is there and whether you should let them in. Thinking of these things would make you consider your son's corpse under the blanket, and why would you want to do that? You ignore the door knock.

Someone bangs at the window in the front room. Persistent. You ignore this, too.

Finally, someone breaks the glass on the house's back door. You hears footsteps in the hallway between Uche's room and that of Nassun, your daughter.

(Nassun, your daughter.)

The footsteps reach the den and stop. "Essun?"

You know this voice. Young, male. Familiar, and soothing in a familiar way. Lerna, Makenba's boy from down the road, who went away for a few years and came back a doctor. He's not a boy anymore, hasn't been for a while, so you remind yourself again to start thinking of him as a man.

Oops, thinking. Carefully, you stop.

He inhales, and your skin reverberates with his horror when he draws near enough to see Uche. Remarkably, he does not cry out. Nor does he touch you, though he moves to Uche's other side and peers at you intently. Trying to see what's going on inside you? *Nothing, nothing.* He then peels back the blanket for a good look at Uche's body. *Nothing, nothing.* He pulls the blanket up again, this time over your son's face.

"He doesn't like that," you say. It's your first time speaking in two days. Feels strange. "He's afraid of the dark."

After a moment's silence, Lerna pulls the sheet back down to just below Uche's eyes.

"Thank you," you say.

Lerna nods. "Have you slept?"

"No."

So Lerna comes around the body and takes your arm, drawing you up. He's gentle, but his hands are firm, and he does not give up when at first you don't move. Just exerts more pressure, inexorably, until you have to rise or fall over. He leaves you that much choice. You rise. Then with the same gentle firmness he guides you toward the front door. "You can rest at my place," he says.

You don't want to think, so you do not protest that you have your own perfectly good bed, thank you. Nor do you declare that you're fine and don't need his help, which isn't true. He walks you outside and down the block, keeping a grip on your elbow the whole time. A few others are gathered on the street outside. Some of them come near the two of you, saying things to which Lerna replies; you don't really hear any of it. Their voices are blurring noise that your mind doesn't bother to interpret. Lerna speaks to them in your stead, for which you would be grateful if you could bring yourself to care.

He gets you to his house, which smells of herbs and chemicals and books, and he tucks you into a long bed that has a fat gray cat on it. The cat moves out of the way enough to allow you to lie down, then tucks itself against your side once you're still. You would take comfort from this if the warmth and weight did not remind you a little of Uche, when he naps with you.

Napped with you. No, changing tense requires thought. *Naps.*

"Sleep," Lerna says, and it is easy to comply.

* * *

You sleep a long time. At one point you wake. Lerna has put food on a tray beside the bed: clear broth and sliced fruit and a cup of tea, all long gone to room temperature. You eat and drink, then go into the bathroom. The toilet does not flush. There's a bucket beside it, full of water, which Lerna must have put there for this purpose. You puzzle over this, then feel the imminence of thought and have to fight, fight, *fight* to stay in the soft warm silence of thoughtlessness. You pour some water down the toilet, put the lid back down, and go back to bed.

* * *

In the dream, you're in the room while Jija does it. He and Uche are as you saw them last: Jija laughing, holding Uche on one knee and playing "earthshake" while the boy giggles and clamps down with his thighs and waggles his arms for balance. Then Jija suddenly stops laughing, stands up—throwing Uche to the floor—and begins kicking him. You know this is not how it happened. You've seen the imprint of Jija's fist, a bruise with four parallel marks, on Uche's belly and face. In the dream Jija kicks, because dreams are not logical.

Uche keeps laughing and waggling his arms, like it's still a game, even as blood covers his face.

You wake screaming, which subsides into sobs that you cannot stop. Lerna comes in, tries to say something, tries to hold you, and finally makes you drink a strong, foul-tasting tea. You sleep again.

* * *

"Something happened up north," Lerna tells you.

You sit on the edge of the bed. He's in a chair across from you. You're drinking more nasty tea; your head hurts worse than a hangover. It's nighttime, but the room is dim. Lerna has lit only half the lanterns. For the first time you notice the strange smell in the air, not quite disguised by the lanternsmoke: sulfur, sharp and acrid. The smell has been there all day, growing gradually worse. It's strongest when Lerna's been outside.

"The road outside town has been clogged for two days with people coming from that direction." Lerna sighs and rubs his face. He's fifteen years younger than you, but he no longer looks it. He has natural gray hair like many Cebaki, but it's the new lines in his face that make him seem older—those, and the new shadows in his eyes. "There's been some kind of shake. A big one, a couple of days ago. We felt nothing here, but in Sume—" Sume is in the next valley over, a day's ride on horseback. "The whole town is . . ." He shakes his head.

You nod, but you know all this without being told, or at least you can guess. Two days ago, as you sat in your den staring at the ruin of your child, something came toward the town: a convulsion of the earth so powerful you have never sessed its like. The word *shake* is inadequate. Whatever-it-was would have collapsed the house on Uche, so you put something in its way—a breakwater of sorts, composed of your focused will and a bit of kinetic energy borrowed from the thing itself. Doing this required no thought; a newborn could do it, although perhaps not so neatly. The shake split and flowed around the valley, then moved on.

Lerna licks his lips. Looks up at you, then away. He's the other one, besides your children, who knows what you are. He's known for a while, but this is the first time he's been confronted by the actuality of it. You can't really think about that, either.

"Rask isn't letting anyone leave or come in." Rask is Rask Innovator Tirimo, the town's elected headman. "It's not a full-on lockdown, he says, not yet, but I was going to head over to Sume, see if I could help. Rask said no, and then he set the damn miners on the wall to supplement the Strongbacks while we send out scouts. Told them specifically to keep *me* within the gates." Lerna clenches his fists, his expression bitter. "There are people out there on the Imperial Road. A lot of them are sick, injured, and that rusty bastard won't let me *help*."

"First guard the gates," you whisper. It is a rasp. You screamed a lot after that dream of Jija.

"What?"

You sip more tea to soothe the soreness. "Stonelore."

Lerna stares at you. He knows the same passages; all children learn them, in creche. Everyone grows up on campfire tales of wise lorists and clever geomests warning skeptics when the signs begin to show, not being heeded, and saving people when the lore proves true.

"You think it's come to that, then," he says, heavily. "Fire-under-Earth, Essun, you can't be serious."

You are serious. It has come to that. But you know he will not believe you if you try to explain, so you just shake your head.

A painful, stagnating silence falls. After a long moment, delicately, Lerna says, "I brought Uche back here. He's in the infirmary, the, uh, in the coldcase. I'll see to, uh... arrangements."

You nod slowly.

He hesitates. "Was it Jija?"

You nod again.

"You, you saw him—"

"Came home from creche."

"Oh." Another awkward pause. "People said you'd missed a day, before the shake. They had to send the children home; couldn't find a substitute. No one knew if you were home sick, or what." Yes, well. You've probably been fired. Lerna takes a deep breath, lets it out. With that as forewarning, you're almost ready. "The shake didn't hit us, Essun. It passed around the town. Shivered over a few trees and crumbled a rock face up by the creek." The creek is at the northernmost end of the valley, where no one has noticed a big chalcedony geode steaming. "Everything in and around town is fine, though. In almost a perfect circle. Fine."

There was a time when you would have dissembled. You had reasons to hide then, a life to protect.

"I did it," you say.

Lerna's jaw flexes, but he nods. "I never told anyone." He hesitates. "That you were... uh, orogenic."

He's so polite and proper. You've heard all the uglier terms for what you are. He has, too, but he would never say them. Neither would Jija, whenever someone tossed off a careless *rogga* around him. *I don't want the children to hear that kind of language,* he always said—

It hits fast. You abruptly lean over and dry-heave. Lerna starts, jumping to grab something nearby—a bedpan, which you haven't needed. But nothing comes out of your stomach, and after a moment the heaves stop. You take a cautious breath, then another. Wordlessly, Lerna offers a glass of water. You start to wave it away, then change your mind and take it. Your mouth tastes of bile.

"It wasn't me," you say at last. He frowns in confusion and you realize he thinks you're still talking about the shake. "Jija. He didn't find out about me." You think. You shouldn't think. "I don't know how, what, but Uche—he's little, doesn't have much control yet. Uche must have done something, and Jija realized—"

That your children are like you. It is the first time you've framed this thought completely.

Lerna closes his eyes, letting out a long breath. "That's it, then."

That's not it. That should never have been enough to provoke a father to murder his own child. Nothing should have done that.

He licks his lips. "Do you want to see Uche?"

What for? You looked at him for two days. "No."

With a sigh, Lerna gets to his feet, still rubbing a hand over his hair. "Going to tell Rask?" you ask. But the look Lerna turns on you makes you feel boorish. He's angry. He's such a calm, thoughtful boy; you didn't think he could get angry.

"I'm not going to tell Rask anything," he snaps. "I haven't said anything in all this time and I'm not going to."

"Then what—"

"I'm going to go find Eran." Eran is the spokeswoman for the Resistant use-caste. Lerna was born a Strongback, but when he came back to Tirimo after becoming a doctor, the Resistants adopted him; the town had enough Strongbacks already, and the Innovators lost the shard-toss. Also, you've claimed to be a Resistant. "I'll let her know you're all right, have her pass that on to Rask. *You* are going to rest."

"When she asks you why Jija—"

Lerna shakes his head. "Everyone's guessed already, Essun. They can read maps. It's clear as diamond that the center of the circle was this neighborhood. Knowing what Jija did, it hasn't been hard for anyone to jump to conclusions as to *why*. The timing's all wrong, but nobody's thinking that far." While you stare at him, slowly understanding, Lerna's lip curls. "Half of them are appalled, but the rest are glad Jija did it. Because *of course* a three-year-old has the power to start shakes a thousand miles away in Yumenes!"

You shake your head, half startled by Lerna's anger and half unable to reconcile your bright, giggly boy with people who think he would—that he could—But then, Jija thought it.

You feel queasy again.

Lerna takes another deep breath. He's been doing this throughout your conversation; it's a habit of his that you've seen before. His way of calming himself. "Stay here and rest. I'll be back soon."

He leaves the room. You hear him doing purposeful-sounding things at the front of the house. After a few moments, he leaves to go to his meeting. You contemplate rest and decide against it. Instead you rise and go into Lerna's bathroom, where you wash your face and then stop when the hot water coming through the tap spits and abruptly turns brown-red and smelly, then slows to a trickle. Broken pipe somewhere.

Something happened up north, Lerna said.

Children are the undoing of us, someone said to you once, long ago.

"Nassun," you whisper to your reflection. In the mirror are the eyes your daughter has inherited from you, gray as slate and a little wistful. "He left Uche in the den. Where did he put you?"

No answer. You shut off the tap. Then you whisper to no one in particular, "I have to go now." Because you do. You need to find Jija, and anyway you know better than to linger. The townsfolk will be coming for you soon.

* * *

The shake that passes will echo. The wave that recedes will come back. The mountain that rumbles will roar.

—*Tablet One, "On Survival," verse five*

2

Damaya, in winters past

THE STRAW IS SO WARM that Damaya doesn't want to come out of it. Like a blanket, she thinks through the bleariness of half-sleep; like the quilt her great-grandmother once sewed for her out of patches of uniform cloth. Years ago and before she died, Muh Dear worked for the Brevard militia as a seamstress, and got to keep the scraps from any repairs that required new cloth. The blanket she made for Damaya was mottled and dark, navy and taupe and gray and green in rippling bands like columns of marching men, but it came from Muh Dear's hands, so Damaya never cared that it was ugly. It always smelled sweet and gray and a bit fusty, so it is easy now to imagine that the straw—which smells mildewy and like old manure yet with a hint of fungal fruitiness—is Muh's blanket. The actual blanket is back in Damaya's room, on the bed where she left it. The bed in which she will never sleep again.

She can hear voices outside the straw pile now: Mama and someone else talking as they draw closer. There's a rattle-creak as the barn door is unlocked, and then they come inside.

Another rattle as the door shuts behind them. Then Mother raises her voice and calls, "DamaDama?"

Damaya curls up tighter, clenching her teeth. She hates that stupid nickname. She hates the way Mother says it, all light and sweet, like it's actually a term of endearment and not a lie.

When Damaya doesn't respond, Mother says: "She can't have gotten out. My husband checked all the barn locks himself."

"Alas, her kind cannot be held with locks." This voice belongs to a man. Not her father or older brother, or the comm headman, or anyone she recognizes. This man's voice is deep, and he speaks with an accent like none she's ever heard: sharp and heavy, with long drawled *o*'s and *a*'s and crisp beginnings and ends to every word. Smart-sounding. He jingles faintly as he walks, so much so that she wonders whether he's wearing a big set of keys. Or perhaps he has a lot of money in his pockets? She's heard that people use metal money in some parts of the world.

The thought of keys and money makes Damaya curl in on herself, because of course she's also heard the other children in creche whisper of child-markets in faraway cities of beveled stone. Not all places in the world are as civilized as the Nomidlats. She laughed off the whispers then, but everything is different now.

"Here," says the man's voice, not far off now. "Fresh spoor, I think."

Mother makes a sound of disgust, and Damaya burns in shame as she realizes they've seen the corner she uses for a bathroom. It smells terrible there, even though she's been throwing straw down as a cover each time. "Squatting on the ground like an animal. I raised her better."

"Is there a toilet in here?" asks the child-buyer, in a tone of polite curiosity. "Did you give her a bucket?"

Silence from Mother, which stretches on, and belatedly Damaya realizes the man has *reprimanded* Mother with those quiet questions. It isn't the sort of reprimand Damaya is used to. The man hasn't raised his voice or called anyone names. Yet Mother stands still and shocked as surely as if he'd followed the words with a smack to the head.

A giggle bubbles up in her throat, and at once she crams her fist into her mouth to stop it from spilling out. They'll hear Damaya laugh at her mother's embarrassment, and then the child-buyer will know what a terrible child she really is. Is that such a bad thing? Maybe her parents will get less for her. That alone almost makes the giggles break free, because Damaya hates her parents, she *hates* them, and anything that will make them suffer makes her feel better.

Then she bites down on her hand, hard, and hates herself, because *of course* Mother and Father are selling Damaya if she can think such thoughts.

Footsteps nearby. "Cold in here," says the man.

"We would have kept her in the house if it was cold enough to freeze," says Mother, and Damaya almost giggles again at her sullen, defensive tone.

But the child-buyer ignores Mother. His footsteps come closer, and they're... strange. Damaya can sess footsteps. Most people can't; they sess big things, shakes and whatnot, but not anything so delicate as a footfall. (She has known this about herself all her life but only recently realized it was a warning.) It's harder to perceive when she's out of direct contact with the ground, everything conveyed through the wood of the barn's frame and the metal of the nails holding it together—but still, even from a story up, she knows what to expect. *Beat* beat, the step and then its reverberation into the depths, *beat* beat, *beat* beat. The child-buyer's steps, though, go nowhere and do not echo. She can only hear them, not sess them. That's never happened before.

And now he's coming up the ladder, to the loft where she huddles under the straw.

"Ah," he says, reaching the top. "It's warmer up here."

"DamaDama!" Mother sounds furious now. "Get down here!"

Damaya scrunches herself up tighter under the straw and says nothing. The child-buyer's footsteps pace closer.

"You needn't be afraid," he says in that rolling voice. Closer. She feels the reverberation of his voice through the wood and down to the ground and into the rock and back again. Closer. "I've come to help you, Damaya Strongback."

Another thing she hates, her use name. She doesn't have a strong back at all, and neither does Mother. All "Strongback" means is that her female ancestors were lucky enough to join a comm but too undistinguished to earn a more secure place within it. *Strongbacks get dumped same as commless when times get hard*, her brother Chaga told her once, to tease her. Then he'd laughed, like it was funny. Like it wasn't true. Of course, Chaga is a Resistant, like Father. All comms like to have them around no matter how hard the times, in case of sickness and famine and such.

The man's footsteps stop just beyond the straw pile. "You

needn't be afraid," he says again, more softly now. Mother is still down on the ground level and probably can't hear him. "I won't let your mother hurt you."

Damaya inhales.

She's not stupid. The man is a child-buyer, and child-buyers do terrible things. But because he has said these words, and because some part of Damaya is tired of being afraid and angry, she uncurls. She pushes her way through the soft warm pile and sits up, peering out at the man through coils of hair and dirty straw.

He is as strange-looking as he sounds, and not from anywhere near Palela. His skin is almost white, he's so paper-pale; he must smoke and curl up in strong sunlight. He has long flat hair, which together with the skin might mark him as an Arctic, though the color of it—a deep heavy black, like the soil near an old blow—doesn't fit. Eastern Coasters' hair is black like that, except fluffy and not flat, but people from the east have black skin to match. And he's big—taller, and with broader shoulders, than Father. But where Father's big shoulders join a big chest and a big belly, this man sort of *tapers*. Everything about the stranger seems lean and attenuated. Nothing about him makes racial sense.

But what strikes Damaya most are the child-buyer's eyes. They're *white*, or nearly so. She can see the whites of his eyes, and then a silvery-gray disc of color that she can barely distinguish from the white, even up close. The pupils of his eyes are wide in the barn's dimness, and startling amid the desert of colorlessness. She's heard of eyes like these, which are called *icewhite* in stories and stonelore. They're rare, and always an ill omen.

But then the child-buyer smiles at Damaya, and she doesn't

even think twice before she smiles back. She trusts him immediately. She knows she shouldn't, but she does.

"And here we are," he says, still speaking softly so that Mother won't hear. "DamaDama Strongback, I presume?"

"Just Damaya," she says, automatically.

He inclines his head gracefully, and extends a hand to her. "So noted. Will you join us, then, Damaya?"

Damaya doesn't move and he does not grab her. He just stays where he is, patient as stone, hand offering and not taking. Ten breaths pass. Twenty. Damaya knows she'll have to go with him, but she likes that he makes it *feel* like a choice. So at last, she takes his hand and lets him pull her up. He keeps her hand while she dusts off as much of the straw as she can, and then he tugs her closer, just a little. "One moment."

"Hnh?" But the child-buyer's other hand is already behind her head, pressing two fingers into the base of her skull so quickly and deftly that she doesn't startle. He shuts his eyes for a moment, shivers minutely, and then exhales, letting her go.

"Duty first," he says, cryptically. She touches the back of her head, confused and still feeling the lingering sensation of his fingers' pressure. "Now let's head downstairs."

"What did you do?"

"Just a little ritual, of sorts. Something that will make it easier to find you, should you ever become lost." She cannot imagine what this means. "Come, now; I need to tell your mother you'll be leaving with me."

So it really is true. Damaya bites her lip, and when the man turns to head back to the ladder, she follows a pace or two behind.

"Well, that's that," says the child-buyer as they reach Mother on the ground floor. (Mother sighs at the sight of her, perhaps in exasperation.) "If you could assemble a package for her—one or two changes of clothing, any travel food you can provide, a coat—we'll be on our way."

Mother draws up in surprise. "We gave away her coat."

"Gave it away? In winter?"

He speaks mildly, but Mother looks abruptly uncomfortable. "She's got a cousin who needed it. We don't all have wardrobes full of fancy clothes to spare. And—" Here Mother hesitates, glancing at Damaya. Damaya just looks away. She doesn't want to see if Mother looks sorry for giving away the coat. She especially doesn't want to see if Mother's *not* sorry.

"And you've heard that orogenes don't feel cold the way others do," says the man, with a weary sigh. "That's a myth. I assume you've seen your daughter take cold before."

"Oh, I." Mother looks flustered. "Yes. But I thought..."

That Damaya might have been faking it. That was what she'd said to Damaya that first day, after she got home from creche and while they were setting her up in the barn. Mother had raged, her face streaked with tears, while Father just sat there, silent and white-lipped. Damaya had hidden it from them, Mother said, hidden everything, pretended to be a child when she was really a monster, that was what monsters *did*, she had always known there was something *wrong* with Damaya, she'd always been such a little *liar*—

The man shakes his head. "Nevertheless, she will need some protection against the cold. It will grow warmer as we approach the Equatorials, but we'll be weeks on the road getting there."

Mother's jaw flexes. "So you're really taking her to Yumenes, then."

"Of course I—" The man stares at her. "Ah." He glances at Damaya. They both look at Damaya, their gazes like an itch. She squirms. "So even thinking I was coming to kill your daughter, you had the comm headman summon me."

Mother tenses. "Don't. It wasn't, I didn't—" At her sides, her hands flex. Then she bows her head, as if she is ashamed, which Damaya knows is a lie. Mother isn't ashamed of anything she's done. If she was, why would she do it?

"Ordinary people can't take care of...of children like her," says Mother, very softly. Her eyes dart to Damaya's, once, and away, fast. "She almost killed a boy at school. We've got another child, and neighbors, and..." Abruptly she squares her shoulders, lifting her chin. "And it's any citizen's duty, isn't it?"

"True, true, all of it. Your sacrifice will make the world better for all." The words are a stock phrase, praise. The tone is uniquely not. Damaya looks at the man again, confused now because child-buyers don't kill children. That would defeat the point. And what's this about the Equatorials? Those lands are far, far to the south.

The child-buyer glances at Damaya and somehow understands that she does not understand. His face softens, which should be impossible with those frightening eyes of his.

"To Yumenes," the man says to Mother, to Damaya. "Yes. She's young enough, so I'm taking her to the Fulcrum. There she will be trained to use her curse. Her sacrifice, too, will make the world better."

Damaya stares back at him, realizing just how wrong she's

been. Mother has not sold Damaya. She and Father have *given* Damaya away. And Mother does not hate her; actually, she *fears* Damaya. Is there a difference? Maybe. Damaya doesn't know how to feel in response to these revelations.

And the man, the man is not a child-buyer at all. He is—

"You're a Guardian?" she asks, even though by now, she knows. He smiles again. She did not think Guardians were like this. In her head they are tall, cold-faced, bristling with weapons and secret knowledge. He's tall, at least.

"I am," he says, and takes her hand. He likes to touch people a lot, she thinks. "I'm *your* Guardian."

Mother sighs. "I can give you a blanket for her."

"That will do, thank you." And then the man falls silent, waiting. After a few breaths of this, Mother realizes he's waiting for her to go fetch it. She nods jerkily, then leaves, her back stiff the whole way out of the barn. So then the man and Damaya are alone.

"Here," he says, reaching up to his shoulders. He's wearing something that must be a uniform: blocky shoulders and long, stiff lines of sleeve and pant leg, burgundy cloth that looks sturdy but scratchy. Like Muh's quilt. It has a short cape, more decorative than useful, but he pulls it off and wraps it around Damaya. It's long enough to be a dress on her, and warm from his body.

"Thank you," she says. "Who are you?"

"My name is Schaffa Guardian Warrant."

She's never heard of a place called Warrant, but it must exist, because what good is a comm name otherwise? "'Guardian' is a use name?"

"It is for Guardians." He drawls this, and her cheeks grow warm with embarrassment. "We aren't much use to any comm, after all, in the ordinary course of things."

Damaya frowns in confusion. "What, so they'll kick *you* out when a Season comes? But..." Guardians are many things, she knows from the stories: great warriors and hunters and sometimes—often—assassins. Comms need such people when hard times come.

Schaffa shrugs, moving away to sit on a bale of old hay. There's another bale behind Damaya, but she keeps standing, because she likes being on the same level with him. Even sitting he's taller, but at least not by so much.

"The orogenes of the Fulcrum serve the world," he says. "You will have no use name from here forth, because your usefulness lies in what you are, not merely some familial aptitude. From birth, an orogene child can stop a shake; even without training, you are orogene. Within a comm or without one, *you are orogene*. With training, however, and with the guidance of other skilled orogenes at the Fulcrum, you can be useful not merely to a single comm, but all the Stillness." He spreads his hands. "As a Guardian, via the orogenes in my care, I have taken on a similar purpose, with a similar breadth. Therefore it's fitting that I share my charges' possible fate."

Damaya is so curious, so full of questions, that she doesn't know which to ask first. "Do you have—" She stumbles over the concept, the words, the acceptance of herself. "Others, l-like me, I," and she runs out of words.

Schaffa laughs, as if he senses her eagerness and it pleases him. "I am Guardian to six right now," he says, inclining his head to let Damaya know that this is the right way to say it, to think it. "Including you."

"And you brought them all to Yumenes? You found them like this, like me—"

"Not exactly. Some were given into my care, born within the Fulcrum or inherited from other Guardians. Some I have found since being assigned to ride circuit in this part of the Nomidlats." He spreads his hands. "When your parents reported their orogenic child to Palela's headman, he telegraphed word to Brevard, which sent it to Geddo, which sent it to Yumenes—and they in turn telegraphed word to me." He sighs. "It's only luck that I checked in at the node station near Brevard the day after the message arrived. Otherwise I wouldn't have seen it for another two weeks."

Damaya knows Brevard, though Yumenes is only legend to her, and the rest of the places Schaffa has mentioned are just words in a creche textbook. Brevard is the town closest to Palela, and it's much bigger. It's where Father and Chaga go to sell farmshares at the beginning of every growing season. Then she registers his words. Two more weeks in this barn, freezing and pooping in a corner. She's glad he got the message in Brevard, too.

"You're very lucky," he says, perhaps reading her expression. His own has grown sober. "Not all parents do the right thing. Sometimes they don't keep their child isolated, as the Fulcrum and we Guardians recommend. Sometimes they do, but we get the message too late, and by the time a Guardian arrives a mob has carried the child off and beaten her to death. Don't think unkindly of your parents, Dama. You're alive and well, and that is no small thing."

Damaya squirms a little, unwilling to accept this. He sighs. "And sometimes," he continues, "the parents of an orogene will try to hide the child. To keep her, untrained and without a Guardian. That always goes badly."

This is the thing that's been in her mind for the past two weeks, ever since that day at school. If her parents loved her, they would not have locked her in the barn. They would not have called this man. Mother would not have said those terrible things.

"Why can't they—" she blurts, before she realizes he has said this on purpose. To see if *why can't they just hide me and keep me here* is something she's been thinking—and now he knows the truth. Damaya's hands clench on the cape where she's holding it closed around herself, but Schaffa merely nods.

"First because they have another child, and anyone caught harboring an unregistered orogene is ejected from their comm as a minimum punishment." Damaya knows this, though she resents the knowledge. Parents who cared about her would *risk*, wouldn't they? "Your parents could not have wanted to lose their home, their livelihood, and custody of both their children. They chose to keep something rather than lose everything. But the greatest danger lies in what you are, Dama. You can no more hide that than you can the fact that you are female, or your clever young mind." She blushes, unsure if this is praise. He smiles so she knows it is.

He continues: "Every time the earth moves, you will hear its call. In every moment of danger you will reach, instinctively, for the nearest source of warmth and movement. The ability to do this is, to you, as fists are to a strong man. When a threat is imminent, of course you'll do what you must to protect yourself. And when you do, people will die."

Damaya flinches. Schaffa smiles again, as kindly as always. And then Damaya thinks about that day.

It was after lunch, in the play-yard. She had eaten her bean roll while sitting by the pond with Limi and Shantare as she usually did while the other children played or threw food at each other. Some of the other kids were huddled in a corner of the yard, scratching in the dirt and muttering to each other; they had a geomestry test that afternoon. And then Zab had come over to the three of them, though he'd looked at Damaya in particular as he said, "Let me cheat off you."

Limi giggled. She thought Zab liked Damaya. Damaya didn't like *him*, though, because he was awful—always picking on Damaya, calling her names, poking her until she yelled at him to stop and got in trouble with their teacher for doing it. So she said to Zab, "I'm not getting in trouble for you."

He'd said: "You won't, if you do it right. Just move your paper over—"

"*No*," she'd said again. "I'm not going to do it right. I'm not going to do it *at all*. Go away." She'd turned back to Shantare, who had been talking before Zab interrupted.

Next thing Damaya knew, she was on the ground. Zab had shoved her off the rock using both hands. She tumbled head over heels literally, landing on her back. Later—she'd had two weeks in the barn to think about it—she would recall the look of shock on his face, as if he hadn't realized she would go over so easily. But at the time, all she had known was that she was on the ground. The *muddy* ground. Her whole back was cold and wet and foul, everything smelled of fermenting bog and crushed grass, it was in her *hair* and this was her best *uniform* and Mother was going to be *furious* and *she* was furious and so she'd grabbed the air and—

Damaya shivers. *People will die.* Schaffa nods as if he has heard this thought.

"You're firemountain-glass, Dama." He says this very softly. "You're a gift of the earth—but Father Earth hates us, never forget, and his gifts are neither free nor safe. If we pick you up, hone you to sharpness, treat you with the care and respect you deserve, then you become valuable. But if we just leave you lying about, you'll cut to the bone the first person who blunders across you. Or worse—you'll shatter, and hurt many."

Damaya remembers the look on Zab's face. The air had gone cold for only an instant, billowing around her like a burst balloon. That was enough to make a crust of ice on the grass beneath her, and to make the sweatdrops go solid on Zab's skin. They'd stopped and jerked and stared at each other.

She remembers his face. *You almost killed me,* she had seen there.

Schaffa, watching her closely, has never stopped smiling.

"It isn't your fault," he says. "Most of what they say about orogenes isn't true. There's nothing you did to be born like this, nothing your parents did. Don't be angry with them, or with yourself."

She begins to cry, because he's right. All of it, everything he says, it's right. She hates Mother for putting her in here, she's hated Father and Chaga for letting Mother do it, she hates herself for being born as she is and disappointing them all. And now Schaffa knows just how weak and terrible she is.

"Shh," he says, standing and coming over to her. He kneels and takes her hands; she starts crying harder. But Schaffa squeezes her hands sharply, enough to hurt, and she starts and draws breath and blinks at him through the blur. "You mustn't, little one. Your mother will return soon. Never cry where they can see you."

"Wh-what?"

He looks so sad—for Damaya?—as he reaches up and cups her cheek. "It isn't safe."

She has no idea what this means.

Regardless, she stops. Once she's wiped her cheeks, he thumbs away a tear that she's missed, then nods after a quick inspection. "Your mother will probably be able to tell, but that should do for everyone else."

The barn door creaks and Mother is back, this time with Father in tow. Father's jaw is tight, and he doesn't look at Damaya even though he hasn't seen her since Mother put her in the barn. Both of them focus on Schaffa, who stands and moves a little in front of Damaya, nodding thanks as he accepts the folded blanket and twine-wrapped parcel that Mother gives him.

"We've watered your horse," Father says, stiffly. "You want provender to carry?"

"No need," says Schaffa. "If we make good time, we should reach Brevard just after nightfall."

Father frowns. "A hard ride."

"Yes. But in Brevard, no one from this village will get the fine idea to come seek us out along the road, and make their farewells to Damaya in a ruder fashion."

It takes a moment for Damaya to understand, and then she realizes: People from Palela want to kill Damaya. But that's wrong, isn't it? They can't really, can they? She thinks of all the people she knows. The teachers from creche. The other children. The old ladies at the roadhouse who used to be friends with Muh before she died.

Father thinks this, too; she can see that in his face, and he frowns and opens his mouth to say what she's thinking: *They wouldn't do something like that.* But he stops before the words leave his mouth. He glances at Damaya, once and with his face full of anguish, before remembering to look away again.

"Here you are," Schaffa says to Damaya, holding out the blanket. It's Muh's. She stares at it, then looks at Mother, but Mother won't look back.

It isn't safe to cry. Even when she pulls off Schaffa's cloak and he wraps the blanket around her instead, familiar-fusty and scratchy and perfect, she keeps her face completely still. Schaffa's eyes flick to hers; he nods, just a little, in approval. Then he takes her hand and leads her toward the barn door.

Mother and Father follow, but they don't say anything. Damaya doesn't say anything. She does glance at the house once, catching a glimpse of someone through a gap in the curtains before the curtains flick shut. Chaga, her big brother, who taught her how to read and how to ride a donkey and how to skip rocks on a pond. He doesn't even wave goodbye... but this is not because he hates her. She sees that, now.

Schaffa lifts Damaya onto a horse bigger than any she's ever seen, a big glossy bay with a long neck, and then Schaffa's in the saddle behind her, tucking the blanket around her legs and shoes so she won't chafe or get chilblains, and then they are away.

"Don't look back," Schaffa advises. "It's easier that way." So she doesn't. Later, she will realize he was right about this, too.

Much later, though, she will wish that she had done it anyway.

* * *

[obscured] the icewhite eyes, the ashblow hair, the
filtering nose, the sharpened teeth, the salt-split tongue.

—Tablet Two, "The Incomplete Truth," verse eight

3

you're on your way

You're still trying to decide who to be. The self you've been lately doesn't make sense anymore; that woman died with Uche. She's not useful, unobtrusive as she is, quiet as she is, ordinary as she is. Not when such extraordinary things have happened.

But you still don't know where Nassun is buried, if Jija bothered to bury her. Until you've said farewell to your daughter, you have to remain the mother that she loved.

So you decide not to wait for death to come.

It *is* coming for you—perhaps not right now, but soon. Even though the big shake from the north missed Tirimo, everyone knows it *should* have hit. The sessapinae do not lie, or at least not with such jangling, nerve-racking, mind-screaming strength. Everyone from newborns to addled elders sessed that one coming. And by now, with refugees wandering down the road from less fortunate towns and villages—refugees who are all heading southward—the folk of Tirimo will have begun to hear stories. They will have noticed the sulfur on the wind.

They will have looked up at the increasingly strange sky, and seen the change there as an ill omen. (It is.) Perhaps the headman, Rask, has finally sent someone over to see about Sume, the town in the next valley over. Most Tirimos have family there; the two towns have been trading goods and people for generations. Comm comes before all else, of course, but as long as nobody's starving, kin and race can mean something, too. Rask can still afford to be generous, for now. Maybe.

And once the scouts return and report the devastation that you know they'll find in Sume—and the survivors that you know they *won't* find, or at least not in any great number—denial will no longer be possible. That will leave only fear. Frightened people look for scapegoats.

So you make yourself eat, this time carefully not thinking of other times and other meals with Jija and the kids. (Uncontrollable tears would be better than uncontrollable vomiting, but hey, you can't choose your grief.) Then, letting yourself quietly out through Lerna's garden door, you go back to your house. No one's around, outside. They must all be at Rask's waiting for news or duty assignments.

In the house, one of the storecaches hidden beneath the rugs holds the family's runny-sack. You sit on the floor in the room where Uche was beaten to death, and there you sort through the sack, taking out anything you won't need. The set of worn, comfortable travel-clothing for Nassun is too small; you and Jija put this pack together before Uche was born, and you've been neglectful in not refreshing it. A brick of dried fruit has molded over in fuzzy white; it might still be edible, but you're not desperate enough for that. (Yet.) The sack contains papers that prove you and Jija own your house, and other papers showing that you're current on your quartent taxes and were both registered Tirimo comm and Resistant use-caste members. You leave this, your whole financial and legal existence for the past ten years, in a little discarded pile with the moldy fruit.

The wad of money in a rubber wallet—paper, since there's so much of it—will be irrelevant once people realize how bad things are, but until then it's valuable. Good tinder once it's not. The obsidian skinning knife that Jija insisted upon, and which you're unlikely to ever use—you have better, natural weapons—you keep. Trade goods, or at least a visual warn-off. Jija's boots can also be traded, since they're in good condition. He'll never wear them again, because soon you will find him, and then you will end him.

You pause. Revise that thought to something that better befits the woman you've chosen to be. Better: You will find him and ask him why he did what he did. *How* he could do it. And you will ask him, most importantly, where your daughter is.

Repacking the runny-sack, you then put it inside one of the crates Jija used for deliveries. No one will think twice of seeing you carry it around town, because until a few days ago you did so often, to help out Jija's ceramics and tool-knapping business. Eventually it will occur to someone to wonder why you're filling delivery orders when the headman is probably on the brink of declaring Seasonal Law. But most people will not think of it *at first,* which is what matters.

As you leave, you pass the spot on the floor where Uche lay for days. Lerna took the body and left the blanket; the blood splatters are not visible. Still, you do not look in that direction.

Your house is one of several in this corner of town, nestled between the southern edge of the wall and the town greenland. You picked the house, back when you and Jija decided to buy it, because it's isolated on a narrow, tree-shrouded lane. It's a straight run across the green to the town center, which Jija always liked. That was something you and he always argued about: You didn't like being around other people more than necessary, while Jija was gregarious and restless, frustrated by silence—

The surge of absolute, grinding, head-pounding rage catches you by surprise. You have to stop in the doorway of your home, bracing your hand against the door frame and sucking in deep breaths so that you don't start screaming, or perhaps stabbing someone (yourself?) with that damn skinning knife. Or worse, making the temperature drop.

Okay. You were wrong. Nausea isn't so bad as a response to grief, comparatively speaking.

But you have no time for this, no *strength* for this, so you focus on other things. Any other things. The wood of the doorsill, beneath your hand. The air, which you notice more now that you're outside. The sulfur smell doesn't seem to be getting worse, at least for now, which is perhaps a good thing. You sess that there are no open earth vents nearby—which means this is coming from up north, where the wound is, that great suppurating rip from coast to coast that you *know* is there even though the travelers along the Imperial Road have only brought rumors of it so far. You hope the sulfur concentration doesn't get much worse, because if it does people will start to retch and suffocate, and the next time it rains the creek's fish will die and the soil will sour…

Yes. Better. After a moment you're able to walk away from the house at last, your veneer of calm back firmly in place.

Not many people are out and about. Rask must have finally declared an official lockdown. During lockdown the comm's gates are shut—and you guess by the people moving about near one of the wall watchtowers that Rask has taken the preemptive step of putting guards in place. That's not supposed to happen till a Season is declared; privately you curse Rask's caution. Hopefully he hasn't done anything else that will make it harder for you to slip away.

The market is shut down, at least for the time being, so that no one will hoard goods or fix prices. A curfew starts at dusk, and all businesses that aren't crucial for the protection or supply of the town are required to close. Everyone knows how things are supposed to go. Everyone has assigned duties, but many of these are tasks that can be done indoors: weaving storage baskets, drying and preserving all perishable food in the house, repurposing old clothing and tools. It's all Imperially efficient and lore-letter, following rules and procedures that are simultaneously meant to be practical and to keep a large group of anxious people busy. Just in case.

Still, as you walk the path around the green's edge—during lockdown no one walks on it, not because of any rule but because such times remind them that the green is *cropland to be* and not just a pretty patch of clover and wildflowers—you spy a few other Tirimo denizens out and about. Strongbacks, mostly. One group is building the paddock and shed that will segregate a corner of the green for livestock. It's hard work, building something, and the people doing it are too engrossed in the task to pay much heed to a lone woman carrying a crate. A few faces you vaguely recognize as you walk, people you've seen before at the market or via Jija's business. You catch a few glances from them, too, but these are fleeting. They know your face enough that you are Not Stranger. For now, they're too busy to remember that you may also be *rogga's mother.*

Or to wonder from which parent your dead rogga child might have inherited his curse.

In the town center there are more people about. Here you blend in, walking at the same pace as everyone else, nodding if nodded to, trying to think about nothing so that your face falls into bored, disengaged lines. It's busy around the headman's office, block captains and caste spokespeople coming in to report what lockdown duties have been completed before heading back out to organize more. Others mill about, clearly hoping for word on what's happened in Sume and elsewhere—but even here, no one cares about you. And why should they? The air stinks of broken earth and everything past a twenty-mile radius has been shattered by a shake greater than any living person has ever known. People have more important matters to concern them.

That can change quickly, though. You don't relax.

Rask's office is actually a small house nestled between the stilted grain-caches and the carriageworks. As you stand on tiptoe to see above the crowd, you're unsurprised to see Oyamar, Rask's second, standing on its porch and talking with two men and a woman who are wearing more mortar and mud than clothing. Shoring up the well, probably; that's one of the things stonelore advises in the event of a shake, and which Imperial lockdown procedure encourages, too. If Oyamar is here, then Rask is elsewhere either working or—knowing Rask—sleeping, after having worn himself out in the three days since the event. He won't be at home because people can find him too easily there. But because Lerna talks too much, you know where Rask hides when he doesn't want to be disturbed.

Tirimo's library is an embarrassment. The only reason they have one is that some previous headwoman's husband's grandfather raised a stink and wrote letters to the quartent governor until finally the governor funded a library to shut him up. Few people have used it since the old man died, but although there are always motions to shut it down at the all-comm meetings, those motions never get quite enough votes to proceed. So it lingers: a ratty old shack not much bigger than the den of your house, packed nearly full with shelves of books and scrolls. A thin child could walk between the shelves without contorting; you're neither thin nor a child, so you have to slip in sideways and sort of crabwalk. Bringing the crate is out of the question: You set it down just inside the door. But that doesn't matter, because there's no one here to peek inside it—except Rask, who's curled up on a tiny pallet at the back of the shack, where the shortest shelf leaves a space just wide enough for his body.

As you finally manage to push your way between the stacks, Rask starts out of a snore and blinks up at you, already beginning to scowl at whoever has disturbed him. Then he *thinks*, because he's a levelheaded fellow and that's why Tirimo elected him, and you see in his face the moment when you go from being Jija's wife to Uche's mother to *rogga*'s mother to, oh Earth, rogga, too.

That's good. Makes things easier.

"I'm not going to hurt anyone," you say quickly, before he can recoil or scream or whatever he has tensed to do. And to your own surprise, at these words Rask blinks and *thinks* again, and the panic recedes from his face. He sits up, leaning his back against a wooden wall, and regards you for a long, thoughtful moment.

"You didn't come here just to tell me that, I assume," he says.

You lick your lips and try to hunker down in a crouch. It's awkward because there's not much room. You have to brace your butt against a shelf, and your knees encroach more than you like on Rask's space. He half-smiles at your obvious discomfort, then his smile fades as he remembers what you are, and then he frowns to himself as if both reactions annoy him.

You say, "Do you know where Jija might have gone?"

Rask's face twitches. He's old enough to be your father, just, but he's the least paternal man you've ever met. You've always wanted to sit down somewhere and have a beer with him, even though that doesn't fit the ordinary, meek camouflage you've built around yourself. Most of the people in town think of him that way, despite the fact that as far as you know he doesn't drink. The look that comes into his face in this moment, however, makes you think for the first time that he would make a good father, if he ever had children.

"So that's it," he says. His voice is gravelly with sleep. "He kill the kid? That's what people think, but Lerna said he wasn't sure."

You nod. You couldn't say the word *yes* to Lerna, either.

Rask's eyes search your face. "And the kid was . . . ?"

You nod again, and Rask sighs. He does not, you note, ask whether *you* are anything.

"Nobody saw which way Jija went," he says, shifting to draw his knees up and rest one arm on them. "People have been talking about the—the killing—because it's easier than talking about—" He lifts and drops his hands in a helpless gesture. "Lots of gossip, I mean, and a lot of it's more mud than stone. Some people saw Jija load up your horse cart and go off with Nassun—"

Your thoughts stutter. "*With* Nassun?"

"Yeah, with her. Why—" Then Rask understands. "Oh, shit, she's one, too?"

You try not to start shaking. You do clench your fists in an effort to prevent this, and the earth far below you feels momentarily closer, the air immediately around you cooler, before you contain your desperation and joy and horror and fury.

"I didn't know she was alive," is all you say, after what feels like a very long moment.

"Oh." Rask blinks, and that compassionate look returns. "Well, yeah. She was when they left, anyway. Nobody knew anything was wrong, or thought anything of it. Most people figured it was just a father trying to teach his firstborn the business, or keep a bored child out of trouble, the usual. Then that shit up north happened, and everybody forgot about it till Lerna said he'd found you and . . . and your boy." He pauses here, jaw flexing once. "Never would've figured Jija for the type. He hit you?"

You shake your head. "Never." It might have been easier to bear, somehow, if Jija had been violent beforehand. Then you could have blamed yourself for poor judgment or complacency, and not just for the sin of reproducing.

Rask takes a deep, slow breath. "Shit. Just...shit." He shakes his head, rubs a hand over the gray fuzz of his hair. He's not a born-gray, like Lerna and others with ashblow hair; you remember when his hair was brown. "You going after him?" His gaze flickers away and back. It is not quite hope, but you understand what he is too tactful to say. *Please leave town as soon as possible.*

You nod, happy to oblige. "I need you to give me a gate pass."

"Done." He pauses. "You know you can't come back."

"I know." You make yourself smile. "I don't really want to."

"Don't blame you." He sighs, then shifts again, uncomfortable. "My...my sister..."

You didn't know Rask had a sister. Then you understand. "What happened to her?"

He shrugs. "The usual. We lived in Sume, then. Somebody realized what she was, told a bunch of other somebodies, and they came and took her in the night. I don't remember much about it. I was only six. My folks moved here with me after that." His mouth twitches, not really smiling. "S'why I never wanted kids, myself."

You smile, too. "I didn't, either." Jija had, though.

"Rusting Earth." He closes his eyes for a moment, then abruptly gets to his feet. You do, too, since otherwise your face will be entirely too close to his stained old trousers. "I'll walk you to the gate, if you're going now."

This surprises you. "I'm going now. But you don't have to." You're not sure this is a good idea, really. It might draw more attention than you want. But Rask shakes his head, his jaw set and grim.

"I do. Come on."

"Rask—"

He looks at you, and this time you are the one who winces. This isn't about you anymore. The mob that took his sister from him wouldn't have dared to do so if he'd been a man at the time.

Or maybe they'd have just killed him, too.

He carries the crate as you walk down Seven Seasons, the town's main street, all the way up to Main Gate. You're twitchy, trying to look confident and relaxed even though you feel anything but. It would not have been your choice to walk this route, through all these people. Rask draws all the attention at first, as people wave or call out to him or come over to ask him if there's any news... but then they notice you. People stop waving. They stop approaching and start—at a distance, in twos and threes—watching. And occasionally following. There's nothing to this except the usual small-town nosiness, at least on the surface. But you see these knots of people also *whispering*, and you feel them *staring*, and that sets all your nerves a-jangle in the worst way.

Rask hails the gate guards as you approach. A dozen or so Strongbacks who are probably miners and farmers under ordinary circumstances are there, just milling about in front of the gate with no real organization. Two are up in the crow's nests built atop the wall, where they can overlook the gate; two are standing near the gate's eyeholes at ground level. The rest are just there, looking bored or talking or joking with one another.

Rask probably chose them for their ability to intimidate, because all of them are Sanzed-big and look like they can handle themselves even without the glassknives and crossbows they carry.

The one who steps forward to greet Rask is actually the smallest of them—a man you know, though you don't remember his name. His children have been in your classes at the town creche. He remembers you, too, you see, when his eyes fix on you and narrow.

Rask stops and sets the crate down, opening it and handing you the runny-sack. "Karra," he says to the man you know. "Everything okay here?"

"Was till now," Karra says, not taking his eyes off you. The way he's looking at you makes your skin tighten. A couple of the other Strongbacks are watching, too, glancing from Karra to Rask and back, ready to follow someone's lead. One woman is openly glaring at you, but the rest seem content to glance at you and away in quick slashes.

"Good to hear," Rask says. You see him frown a little, perhaps as he reads the same signals you're picking up on. "Tell your people to open the gate for a minute, will you?"

Karra doesn't take his eyes off you. "Think that's a good idea, Rask?"

Rask scowls and steps sharply up to Karra, getting right in his face. He's not a big man, Rask—he's an Innovator, not a Strongback, not that it really matters anymore—and right now he doesn't need to be. "Yeah," Rask says, his voice so low and tight that Karra focuses on him at last with a stiffening of surprise. "I do. Open the gate, if you don't *mind.* If you're not too rusting *busy.*"

You think of a line from stonelore, Structures, verse three. *The body fades. A leader who lasts relies on more.*

Karra's jaw flexes, but after a moment he nods. You try to look absorbed in shrugging on the runny-sack. The straps are loose. Jija was the last one to try it on.

Karra and the other gate-minders get moving, working on the system of pulleys that helps to winch the gate open. Most of Tirimo's wall is made of wood. It's not a wealthy comm with the resources to import good stone or hire the number of masons needed, although they're doing better than poorly managed comms, or newcomms that don't even have a wall yet. The gate, though, is stone, because a gate is the weakest point of every comm wall. They only need to open it a little for you, and after a few slow, grinding moments and calls from those hauling to those spotting for approaching intruders, they stop.

Rask turns to you, plainly uncomfortable. "Sorry about—about Jija," he says. Not about Uche, but maybe that's for the best. You need to keep your head clear. "About all of it, shit. Hope you find the bastard."

You only shake your head. Your throat is tight. Tirimo has been your home for ten years. You only started to think of it as such—home—around the time of Uche's birth, but that's more than you ever expected to do. You remember chasing Uche across the green after he first learned to run. You remember Jija helping Nassun build a kite and fly it, badly; the kite's remmants are still in a tree somewhere on the eastern side of town.

But it is not as hard to leave as you thought it would be. Not now, with your former neighbors' stares sliding over your skin like rancid oil.

"Thanks," you mutter, meaning for it to cover many things, because Rask didn't have to help you. He has damaged himself by doing so. The gate-minders respect him less now, and they'll talk. Soon everyone will know he's a rogga-lover, which is dangerous. Headmen can't afford that kind of weakness when a Season's coming on. But for the moment what matters most to you is this moment of public decency, which is a kindness and an honor you never expected to receive. You aren't sure how to react to it.

He nods, uncomfortable as well, and turns away as you start toward the gap in the gate. Perhaps he does not see Karra nod to another of the gate-minders; perhaps he does not see the latter woman quickly shoulder her weapon and orient it on you. Perhaps, you will think later, Rask would have stopped the woman, or somehow prevented everything to come, if he had seen.

You see her, though, mostly out of the periphery of your vision. Then everything happens too fast to think. And because you *don't* think, because you've been trying *not* to think and this means you're out of the habit, because thinking means you will remember that your family is *dead* and everything that meant happiness is now *a lie* and thinking of that will make you *break* and start screaming and screaming and screaming

and because once upon a time and in another life you learned to respond to sudden threats in a very particular way, you

reach for the air around you and *pull* and

brace your feet against the earth beneath you and *anchor* and *narrow* and

when the woman fires the crossbow, the bolt blurs toward

you. Just before the bolt hits, it bursts into a million glittering, frozen flecks.

(*Naughty, naughty*, chides a voice in your head. The voice of your conscience, deep and male. You forget this thought almost the instant it occurs. That voice is from another life.)

Life. You look at the woman who just tried to kill you.

"What the—Shit!" Karra stares at you, as if stunned by your failure to fall down dead. He crouches, hands balled into fists, nearly jumping up and down in his agitation. "Shoot her again! Kill her! Shoot, Earth damn it, before—"

"What the fuck are you doing?" Rask, finally noticing what's happening, turns back. It's too late.

Down below your feet and everyone else's, a shake begins.

It's hard to tell, at first. There is no warning jangle of sesuna, as there would be if the movement of the earth came *from* the earth. That's why people like these fear people like you, because you're beyond sense and preparation. You're a surprise, like a sudden toothache, like a heart attack. The vibration of what you're doing rises, fast, to become a rumble of tension that can be perceived with ears and feet and skin if not sessapinae, but by this point it's too late.

Karra frowns, looking at the ground beneath his feet. Crossbow Woman pauses in the middle of loading another bolt, eyes widening as she stares at the shivering string of her weapon.

You stand surrounded by swirling flecks of snow and disintegrated crossbow bolt. Around your feet, there is a two-foot circle of frost riming the packed earth. Your locks waft gently in the rising breeze.

"You can't." Rask whispers the words, his eyes widening at

the look on your face. (You don't know what you look like right now, but it must be bad.) He shakes his head as if denial will stop this, taking a step back and then another. "Essun."

"You killed him," you say to Rask. This is not a rational thing. You mean you-plural, even though you're speaking to you-specific. Rask didn't try to kill you, had nothing to do with Uche, but the attempt on your life has triggered something raw and furious and cold. *You cowards. You animals, who look at a child and see prey*. Jija's the one to blame for Uche, some part of you knows that—but Jija grew up here in Tirimo. The kind of hate that can make a man murder his own son? It came from everyone around you.

Rask inhales. "Essun—"

And then the valley floor splits open.

The initial jolt of this is violent enough to knock everyone standing to the ground and sway every house in Tirimo. Then those houses judder and rattle as the jolt smooths into a steady, ongoing vibration. Saider's Cart-Repair Shop is the first to collapse, the old wooden frame of the building sliding sideways off its foundation. There are screams from inside, and one woman manages to run out before the door frame crumples inward. On the eastern edge of town, closest to the mountain ridges that frame the valley, a rockslide begins. A portion of the eastern comm wall and three houses are buried beneath a sudden grinding slurry of mud and trees and rocks. Far below the ground, where no one but you can detect, the clay walls of the underground aquifer that supplies the village wells are breached. The aquifer begins to drain. They will not realize for weeks that you killed the town in this moment, but they will remember when the wells run dry.

Those who survive the next few moments will, anyhow. From your feet, the circle of frost and swirling snow begins to expand. Rapidly.

It catches Rask first. He tries to run as the edge of your torus rolls toward him, but he's simply too close. It catches him in mid-lunge, glazing his feet and solidifying his legs and eating its way up his spine until, in the span of a breath, he falls to the ground stone-stiff, his flesh turning as gray as his hair. The next to be consumed by the circle is Karra, who's still screaming for someone to kill you. The shout dies in his throat as he falls, flash-frozen, the last of his warm breath hissing out through clenched teeth and frosting the ground as you steal the heat from it.

You aren't just inflicting death on your fellow villagers, of course. A bird perched on a nearby fence falls over frozen, too. The grass crisps, the ground grows hard, and the air hisses and howls as moisture and density is snatched from its substance... but no one has ever mourned earthworms.

Fast. The air swirls briskly all down Seven Seasons now, making the trees rustle and anyone nearby cry out in alarm as they realize what's happening. The ground hasn't stopped moving. You sway with the ground, but because you know its rhythms, it is easy for you to shift your balance with it. You do this without thinking, because there is only room left in you for one thought.

These people killed Uche. Their hate, their fear, their unprovoked violence. They.

(He.)

Killed your son.

(Jija killed your son.)

People run out into the streets, screaming and wondering why there was no warning, and you kill any of them who are stupid or panicked enough to come near.

Jija. They are Jija. The whole rusting town is *Jija.*

Two things save the comm, however, or at least most of it. The first is that most of the buildings don't collapse. Tirimo might be too poor to build with stone, but most of its builders are ethical and well paid enough to use only techniques that stonelore recommends: the hanging frame, the center beam. Second, the fault line of the valley—which you're currently peeling apart with a thought—is actually a few miles to the west. Because of these things, most of Tirimo will survive this, at least until the wells die.

Because of these things. And because of the terrified, bouncing scream of a little boy as his father runs out of a madly swaying building.

You pivot toward the sound instantly, habitually, orienting on the source with a mother's ears. The man clutches the boy with both arms. He doesn't even have a runny-sack; the first and only thing he took the time to grab was his son. The boy looks nothing like Uche. But you stare as the child bounces and reaches back toward the house for something the man has left behind (favorite toy? the boy's mother?), and suddenly, finally, you *think.*

And then you stop.

Because, oh uncaring Earth. Look what you've done.

The shake stops. The air hisses again, this time as warmer, moister air rushes into the space around you. The ground and your skin grow instantly damp with condensation. The rumble of the valley fades, leaving only screams and the creak of falling wood and the shake-siren that has only belatedly, forlornly, begun to wail.

You close you eyes, aching and shaking and thinking, *No. I killed Uche. By being his mother.* There are tears on your face. And here you thought you couldn't cry.

But there's no one between you and the gate now. The gate-minders who could, have fled; besides Rask and Karra, several more were too slow to get away. You shoulder the runny-sack and head for the gate opening, scrubbing at your face with one hand. You're smiling, too, though, and it is a bitter, aching thing. You just can't help acknowledging the irony of the whole thing. Didn't want to wait for death to come for you. Right.

Stupid, stupid woman. Death was always here. Death is you.

* * *

Never forget what you are.

—*Tablet One, "On Survival," verse ten*

4

Syenite, cut and polished

This is shit, Syenite thinks, behind the shield of her pleasant smile.

She doesn't let the affront show on her face, however. Nor does she shift even minutely in the chair. Her hands—four fingers ringed respectively in plain bands of carnelian, white opal, gold, and onyx—rest on her knees. They're out of sight below the edge of the desk, from Feldspar's perspective. She could clench them with Feldspar none the wiser. She doesn't.

"Coral reefs *are* challenging, you realize." Feldspar, her own hands occupied with the big wooden cup of safe, smiles over its rim. She knows full well what's behind Syenite's smile. "Not like ordinary rock. Coral is porous, flexible. The fine control required to shatter it without triggering a tsunami is difficult to achieve."

And Syen could do it in her sleep. A two-ringer could do this. A grit could do it—though, admittedly, not without substantial collateral damage. She reaches for her own cup of safe, turning the wooden hemisphere in her fingers so that they will not shake, then taking a sip. "I appreciate that you have assigned me a mentor, senior."

"No, you don't." Feldspar smiles, too, and sips from her cup of safe, ringed pinky in the air while she does so. It's as if they're having a private contest, etiquette versus etiquette, best shit-eating grin take all. "If it's any consolation, no one will think less of you."

Because everyone knows what this is really about. That doesn't erase the insult, but it does give Syen a degree of comfort. At least her new "mentor" is a ten-ringer. That, too, is comforting, that they thought so much of her. She'll scrape whatever morsels of self-esteem she can out of this.

"He recently completed a circuit in the Somidlats," Feldspar says, gently. There's no actual gentleness to the conversation's subject matter, but Syen appreciates the older woman's effort. "Ordinarily we'd allow him more time to rest before setting him back on the road, but the quartent governor was insistent that we do something about Allia's harbor blockage as soon as possible. You're the one who'll do the work; he's just there to supervise. Getting there should take a month or so, if you don't make many detours and travel at an easy pace—and there's no hurry, given that the coral reef isn't exactly a sudden problem."

At this, Feldspar looks fleetingly, but truly, annoyed. The quartent governor of Allia, or possibly Allia's Leadership, must have been especially irritating. In the years since Feldspar became her assigned senior, Syen has never seen the old woman show any expression worse than a brittle smile. They both know the rules: Fulcrum orogenes—Imperial orogenes, blackjackets, the ones you probably shouldn't kill, whatever people want to call them—must be always polite and professional. Fulcrum orogenes must project confidence and expertise whenever they are in public. Fulcrum orogenes must never show anger because it makes the stills nervous. Except Feldspar would never be so improper as to use a slur like *the stills*—but that is why Feldspar is a senior and has been given supervisory responsibilities, while Syenite merely grinds her own edges alone. She'll have to demonstrate more professionalism if she wants Feldspar's job. That, and she'll apparently have to do a few other things.

"When do I meet him?" Syenite asks. She takes a sip of safe so this question will seem casual. Just a bit of conversation between old friends.

"Whenever you like." Feldspar shrugs. "He has quarters in the seniors' hall. We did send him a briefing and a request that he attend this meeting..." Again she looks mildly irritated. This whole situation must be terrible for her, just terrible. "...but it's possible he missed the message, since as I said he's been recovering from his circuit. Traveling the Likesh Mountains alone is difficult."

"Alone?"

"Five-ringers and above are no longer required to have a partner or Guardian when traveling outside the Fulcrum." Feldspar sips from her cup of safe, oblivious to Syenite's shock. "At that point we are judged stable enough in our mastery of orogeny to be granted a modicum of autonomy."

Five rings. She has four. It's bullshit that this has anything to do with orogenic mastery; if a Guardian has doubts about an orogene's willingness to follow the rules, that orogene doesn't make it to the first ring, let alone the fifth. But… "So it'll be just him and me."

"Yes. We've found that arrangement to be most effective in circumstances like this."

Of course.

Feldspar continues. "You'll find him in Shaped Prominence." That's the complex of buildings that houses most of the Fulcrum's complement of seniors. "Main tower, top floor. There are no set-aside quarters for the most senior orogenes because there are so few—he is our only ten-ringer, at present—but we could at least spare him a bit of extra space up there."

"Thank you," Syen says, turning her cup again. "I'll go see him after this."

Feldspar pauses for a long moment, her face going even more pleasantly unreadable than usual, and that is Syenite's warning. Then Feldspar says: "As a ten-ringer, he has the right to refuse any mission short of a declared emergency. You should know that."

Wait. Syen's fingers stop turning the cup, and her eyes flick up to meet those of the older woman. Is Feld saying what it sounds like she's saying? Can't be. Syen narrows her eyes, no longer bothering to conceal her suspicion. And yet. Feldspar has given her a way out. Why?

Feldspar smiles thinly. "I have six children."

Ah.

Nothing more to be said, then. Syen takes another sip, trying not to grimace at the chalky grit near the bottom of the cup. Safe is nutritious, but it's not a drink anyone enjoys. It's made from a plant milk that changes color in the presence of any contaminant, even spit. It's served to guests and at meetings because, well, it's safe. A polite gesture that says: *I'm not poisoning you. At least, not right now.*

After that Syen takes her leave of Feldspar, then heads out of Main, the administrative building. Main sits amid a cluster of smaller buildings at the edge of the sprawling, half-wild expanse that comprises the Ring Garden. The garden is acres wide, and runs in a broad strip around the Fulcrum for several miles. It's just that huge, the Fulcrum, a city in itself nestled within the greater body of Yumenes like . . . well. Syenite would've continued the thought with *like a child in a woman's belly*, but that comparison seems especially grotesque today.

She nods to her fellow juniors in passing as she recognizes them. Some of them are just standing or sitting around in knots and talking, while others lounge on patches of grass or flowers and read, or flirt, or sleep. Life for the ringed is easy, except during missions beyond the Fulcrum's walls, which are brief and infrequent. A handful of grits tromp through along the wending cobbled path, all in a neat line overseen by juniors who've volunteered as instructors, but grits aren't permitted to enjoy the garden yet; that is a privilege reserved only for those who've passed their first-ring test and been approved for initiation by the Guardians.

And as if the thought of Guardians summons them, Syen spies a few burgundy-uniformed figures standing in a knot near one of the Ring's many ponds. There's another Guardian on the other side of the pond, lounging in an alcove surrounded by rosebushes, appearing to listen politely while a young junior sings to a small seated audience nearby. Perhaps the Guardian *is* just listening politely; sometimes they do that. Sometimes they need to relax, too. Syen notes this Guardian's gaze lingering on one of the audience members in particular, however: a thin, white youth who doesn't seem to be paying much attention to the singer. He's looking at his hands, instead, which are folded in his lap. There's a bandage around two of his fingers, holding them together and straight.

Syen moves on.

She stops first at Curving Shield, one of many clusters of buildings that house the hundreds of junior orogenes. Her roommates aren't home to see her fetch a few necessary items from her chest, for which she is painfully grateful. They'll hear about her assignment soon enough through the rumor mill. Then she heads out again, eventually reaching Shaped Prominence. The tower is one of the older buildings of the Fulcrum complex, built low and wide of heavy white marble blocks and stolid angles atypical of the wilder, fanciful architecture of Yumenes. The big double doors open into a wide, graceful foyer, its walls and floor embossed with scenes from Sanzed history. She keeps her pace unhurried, nodding to the seniors she sees whether she recognizes them or not—she *does* want Feldspar's job, after all—and taking the wide stairways gradually, pausing now and again to appreciate the artfully arranged patterns of light and shadow cast by the narrow windows. She's not sure what makes the patterns so special, actually, but everyone says they're stunning works of art, so she needs to be seen appreciating.

On the topmost floor, where the plush hall-length rug is overlaid by a herringbone pattern of sunlight, she stops to catch her breath and appreciate something genuinely: silence. Solitude.

There's no one moving in this corridor, not even low-level juniors on cleaning or errand duty. She's heard the rumors and now she knows they're true: The ten-ringer has the whole floor to himself.

This, then, is the true reward for excellence: privacy. And choice. After closing her eyes for a moment in aching want, Syen heads down the hall until she reaches the only door with a mat in front of it.

In that moment, though, she hesitates. She knows nothing about this man. He's earned the highest rank that exists within their order, which means no one really cares what he does anymore so long as he keeps any embarrassing behaviors private. And he is a man who has been powerless most of his life, only lately granted autonomy and privilege over others. No one will demote him for anything so trivial as perversion or abuse. Not if his victim is just another orogene.

There's no point to this. *She* doesn't have a choice. With a sigh, Syenite knocks.

And because she isn't expecting *a person* so much as *a trial to be endured,* she's actually surprised when an annoyed voice snaps from within, "*What?*"

She's still wondering how to reply to that when footsteps slap against stone—briskly, annoyed even in their sound—and the door whisks open. The man who stands there glaring at her is wearing a rumpled robe, one side of his hair flattened, fabric lines painting a haphazard map over his cheek. He's younger than she expected. Not *young*; almost twice her age, at least forty. But she'd thought...well. She's met so many six- and seven-ringers in their sixth and seventh decades that she'd expected a ten-ringer to be ancient. And calmer, dignified, more self-possessed. Something. He's not even wearing his rings, though she can see a faint paler stripe on some of his fingers, in between his angry gesticulations.

"*What*, in the name of every two-minute earth jerk?" When Syen just stares at him, he lapses into another tongue—something she's never heard before, though the sound of it is vaguely Coaster, and distinctly pissed. Then he rubs a hand over his hair, and Syen almost laughs. His hair is dense, tight-curled stuff, the kind of hair that needs to be shaped if it's to look stylish, and what he's doing just messes it up more.

"I told Feldspar," he says, returning to perfectly fluent Sanzed and plainly struggling for patience, "and those other cackling meddlers on the senior advisory board to *leave me alone*. I just got off circuit, I haven't had two hours to myself in the last year that weren't shared with a horse or a stranger, and if you're here to give me more orders, I'm going to ice you where you stand."

She's pretty sure this is hyperbole. It's the kind of hyperbole he shouldn't use; Fulcrum orogenes just don't joke about certain things. It's one of the unspoken rules... but maybe a ten-ringer is beyond such things. "Not orders, exactly," she manages, and his face twists.

"Then I don't want to hear whatever you're here to tell me. *Go the rust away*." And he starts to close the door in her face.

She can't believe it at first. What kind of—Really? It is indignity on top of indignity; bad enough to have to do this in the first place, but to be disrespected in the process?

She jams a foot in the door's path before it can build up much momentum and leans in to say, "I'm Syenite."

It doesn't mean anything to him, she can see by his now-furious glare. He inhales to start shouting, she has no idea what but she doesn't want to hear it, and before he can she snaps, "I'm here to *fuck* you, Earth burn it. Is that worth disturbing your beauty rest?"

Part of her is appalled at her own language, and her own anger. The rest of her is satisfied, because that shuts him right the rust up.

He lets her in.

Now it's awkward. Syen sits at the small table in his suite—a *suite,* he's got a whole suite of furnished rooms *to himself*—and watches while he fidgets. He's sitting on one of the room's couches, pretty much perched on its edge. The *far* edge, she notes, as if he fears to sit too close to her.

"I didn't think it would start again this soon," he says, looking at his hands, which are laced together before him. "I mean, they always tell me there's a need, but that's...I didn't..." He sighs.

"Then this isn't the first time for you," Syenite says. He only earned the right to refuse with his tenth ring.

"No, no, but..." He takes a deep breath. "I didn't always know."

"Didn't know what?"

He grimaces. "With the first few women...I thought they were *interested.*"

"You—" Then she gets it. The deniability is always there, of course; even Feldspar never came right out and said *Your assignment is to produce a child within a year with this man.* That lack of acknowledgment is supposed to make it easier, somehow. She's never seen the point: Why pretend the situation is anything other than what it is? But for him, she realizes, it wasn't pretending. Which astounds her because, come on. How naive can he be?

He glances at her and his expression grows pained. "Yes. I know."

She shakes her head. "I see." It doesn't matter. This isn't about his intelligence. She stands up and unbuckles the belt of her uniform.

He stares. "Just like that? I don't even know you."

"You don't need to."

"I don't *like* you."

The feeling is mutual, but Syen refrains from pointing out the obvious. "I finished menstruating a week ago. This is a good time. If you'd rather, you can just lie still and let me take care of things." She's not extraordinarily experienced, but it's not plate tectonics. She gets her uniform jacket off, then pulls something out of the pocket to show him: a bottle of lubricant, still mostly full. He looks dimly horrified. "In fact, it's probably better if you don't move. This will be awkward enough as it is."

He stands up, too, actually backing away. The look of agitation on his face is—well, it's not funny, not really. But Syenite cannot help feeling a modicum of relief at his reaction. No, not just relief. *He* is the weak one here, despite his ten rings. She's the one who has to carry a child she doesn't want, which might kill her and even if it doesn't will change her body forever, if not her life—but here and now, at least, she is the one with all the power. It makes this . . . well, not right. But better, somehow, that she's the one in control.

"We don't have to do this," he blurts. "I can refuse." He grimaces. "I know you can't, but I can. So—"

"Don't refuse," she says, scowling.

"What? Why not?"

"You said it: I have to do this. You don't. If not you, it will be someone else." Six children, Feldspar had. But Feldspar was never a particularly promising orogene. Syenite is. If Syen isn't careful, if she pisses off the wrong people, if she lets herself get labeled *difficult,* they will kill her career and assign her permanently to the Fulcrum, leaving her nothing to do but lie on her back and turn men's grunting and farting into babies. She'll be lucky to have only six if that's how things turn out.

He's staring as if he doesn't understand, even though she knows he does. She says, "I want this over with."

Then he surprises her. She's expecting more stammering and protests. Instead his hand clenches at his side. He looks away, a muscle working in his jaw. He still looks ridiculous in that robe with his hair askew, but the look on his face... he might as well have been ordered to submit himself to torture. She knows she's no looker, at least not by Equatorial standards. Too much midlatter mongrel in her. But then, he's obviously not well-bred, either: that hair, and skin so black it's almost blue, and he's small. Her height, that is, which is tall for either women or men—but he's lean, not at all broad or intimidating. If his ancestors include any Sanzeds, they're far back, and they gave him nothing of their physical superiority.

"Over with," he mutters. "Right." The muscle in his jaw is practically jumping up and down, he's grinding his teeth so hard. And—whoa. He's not looking at her, and suddenly she's glad. Because *that's hate*, in his face. She's seen it before in other orogenes—rust, she's felt it herself, when she has the luxury of solitude and unfettered honesty—but she's never let it *show* like that. Then he looks up at her, and she tries not to flinch.

"You weren't born here," he says, cold now. Belatedly she realizes it's a question.

"No." She doesn't like being the one on the receiving end of the questions. "Were you?"

"Oh, yes. I was bred to order." He smiles, and it's strange seeing a smile layered over all that hate. "Not even as haphazardly as our child will be. I'm the product of two of the Fulcrum's oldest and most promising lineages, or so I'm told. I had a Guardian practically from birth." He shoves his hands into the pockets of his rumpled robe. "You're a feral."

This comes out of nowhere. Syen actually spends a second wondering if this is some new way of saying rogga and then realizing what he really means. Oh, that is just the limit. "Look, I don't care how many rings you wear—"

"That's what *they* call you, I mean." He smiles again, and his bitterness so resonates with her own that she falls silent in confusion. "If you didn't know. Ferals—the ones from outside—often don't know, or care. But when an orogene is born from parents who weren't, from a family line that's never shown the curse before, that's how they think of you. A wild mutt to my domesticated purebred. An accident, to my plan." He shakes his head; it makes his voice shake. "What it actually means is that they couldn't *predict* you. You're the proof that they'll never understand orogeny; it's not science, it's something else. And they'll never control us, not really. Not completely."

Syen isn't sure what to say. She didn't know about the feral thing, about being different somehow—though now that she thinks about it, most of the other orogenes she knows were Fulcrum-bred. And yeah, she's noticed how they look at her. She just thought that was because they were Equatorials and she was from the Nomidlats, or because she got her first ring before they did. And yet, now that he's said this…is being feral a bad thing?

It must be. If the problem is that ferals are not predictable… well, orogenes have to prove themselves reliable. The Fulcrum has a reputation to maintain; that's part of this. So's the training, and the uniform, and the endless rules they must follow, but the breeding *is* part of it, too, or why is she here?

It's somewhat flattering to think that despite her feral status, they actually want something of her infused into their breeding lines. Then she wonders why a part of her is trying to find value in degradation.

She's so lost in thought that he surprises her when he makes a weary sound of capitulation.

"You're right," he says tersely, all business now because, well, there was really only one way this could end. And staying businesslike will allow both of them to maintain some semblance of dignity. "Sorry. You're…rusting Earth. Yeah. Let's just get this done."

So they go into his bedroom and he strips and lies down and tries for a while to work himself up to it, which doesn't go well. The hazard of having to do this with an older man, Syen decides—though really, it's probably more the fact that sex doesn't usually go well when you don't feel like having it. She keeps her expression neutral as she sits beside him and brushes his hands out of the way. He looks embarrassed, and she curses because if he gets self-conscious about it, this will take all day.

He comes around once she takes over, though, perhaps because he can shut his eyes and imagine that her hands belong to whoever he wants. So then she grits her teeth and straddles him and rides until her thighs ache and her breasts grow sore from bouncing. The lube only helps a little. He doesn't feel as good as a dildo or her fingers. Still, his fantasies must be sufficient, because after a while he makes a strained sort of whimper and then it's done.

She's pulling on her boots when he sighs and sits up and looks at her so bleakly that she feels vaguely ashamed of what she's done to him.

"What did you say your name was?" he asks.

"Syenite."

"That the name your parents gave you?" When she glares back at him, his lips twitch in something less than a smile. "Sorry. Just jealous."

"Jealous?"

"Fulcrum-bred, remember? I've only ever had the one name."

Oh.

He hesitates. This is apparently hard for him. "You, uh, you can call me—"

She cuts him off, because she knows his name already and anyway she doesn't intend to call him anything but *you*, which should be enough to distinguish him from their horses. "Feldspar says we're to leave for Allia tomorrow." She gets her second boot on and stands to kick the heel into place.

"Another mission? Already?" He sighs. "I should have known."

Yes, he should have. "You're mentoring me, and helping me clear some coral out of a harbor."

"Right." He knows it's a bullshit mission, too. There's only one reason they'd send him along for something like this. "They gave me a briefing dossier yesterday. Guess I'll finally read it. Meet at the stableyard at noon?"

"You're the ten-ringer."

He rubs his face with both hands. She feels a little bad, but only a little.

"Fine," he says, all business again. "Noon it is."

So she heads out, sore and annoyed that she smells faintly like him, and tired. Probably it's just stress that's wearing her out—the idea of a month on the road with a man she cannot stand, doing things she doesn't want to do, on behalf of people she increasingly despises.

But this is what it means to be *civilized*—doing what her betters say she should, for the ostensible good of all. And it's not like she gains no benefit from this: a year or so of discomfort, a baby she doesn't have to bother raising because it will be turned over to the lower creche as soon as it's born, and a high-profile mission completed under the mentorship of a powerful senior. With the experience and boost to her reputation, she'll be that much closer to her fifth ring. That means her own apartment; no more roommates. Better missions, longer leave, more say in her own life. That's worth it. *Earthfire yes*, it's worth it.

She tells herself this all the way back to her room. Then she packs to leave, tidies up so she'll come home to order and neatness, and takes a shower, methodically scrubbing every bit of flesh she can reach until her skin burns.

* * *

> "Tell them they can be great someday, like us. Tell them they belong among us, no matter how we treat them. Tell them they must earn the respect which everyone else receives by default. Tell them there is a standard for acceptance; that standard is simply perfection. Kill those who scoff at these contradictions, and tell the rest that the dead deserved annihilation for their weakness and doubt. Then they'll break themselves trying for what they'll never achieve."
>
> —*Erlsset, twenty-third emperor of the Sanzed Equatorial Affiliation, in the thirteenth year of the Season of Teeth. Comment recorded at a party, shortly before the founding of the Fulcrum.*

5

you're not alone

NIGHT HAS FALLEN, AND YOU sit in the lee of a hill in the dark.

You're so tired. Takes a lot out of a you, killing so many people. Worse because you didn't do nearly as much as you could have done, once you got all worked up. Orogeny is a strange equation. Take movement and warmth and life from your surroundings, amplify it by some indefinable process of concentration or catalysis or semi-predictable chance, push movement and warmth and death from the earth. Power in, power out. To keep the power in, though, to *not* turn the valley's aquifer into a geyser or shatter the ground into rubble, takes an effort that makes your teeth and the backs of your eyes ache. You walked a long time to try to burn off some of what you took in, but it still brims under your skin even as your body grows weary and your feet hurt. You are a weapon meant to move mountains. A mere walk can't take that out of you.

Still, you walked until darkness fell, and then you walked some more, and now you're here, huddled and alone at the edge of an old fallow field. You're afraid to start a fire, even though it's getting cool. Without a fire you can't see much, but also nothing can see you: a woman alone, with a full pack and only a knife to defend herself. (You're not helpless, but an attacker wouldn't know that till it was too late, and you'd rather not kill anyone else today.) In the distance you can see the dark arc of a highroad, rising above the plains like a taunt. Highroads usually have electric lanterns, courtesy of Sanze, but you're not surprised this one's dark: Even if the shake from the north hadn't occurred, Seasonal standard procedure is to shut down all nonessential hydro and geo. It's too far to be worth the detour, anyway.

You're wearing a jacket, and there's nothing to fear in the field but mice. Sleeping without a fire won't kill you. You can see relatively well anyway, despite the lack of fire or lanterns. Rippling bands of clouds, like hoed rows in the garden you once kept, have covered the sky above. They're easy to see because something to the north has underlit the clouds in bands of redglow and shadow. When you stare that way, there's an uneven line of mountains against the northern horizon, and the flicker of a distant bluish gray obelisk where its lower tip peeks through a knot of clouds, but these things tell you nothing. Closer by there's a flitter of what might be a colony of bats out feeding. Late for bats, but *all things change during a Season*, the stonelore warns. All living things do what they must to prepare, and survive.

The source of the glow is beyond the mountains, as if the setting sun went the wrong way and got stuck there. You know what's causing this glow. It must be an awesome thing to see up close, that great terrible rent spewing fire into the sky, except you don't ever *want* to see it.

And you won't, because you're heading south. Even if Jija hadn't started out going in that direction, he would surely have turned south after the shake from the north passed through. That's the only sane way to go.

Of course, a man who would beat his own child to death might not still fit the label of *sane*. And a woman who found that child and stopped thinking for three days...hmm, not you, either. Nothing to do but follow your crazy, though.

You've eaten something from your pack: cachebread smeared with salty akaba paste from the jar you stuffed into it a lifetime and a family ago. Akaba keeps well after it's opened, but not forever, and now that you've opened it you'll have to eat it for the next few meals until it's gone. That's okay because you like it. You've drunk water from the canteen that you filled a few miles back, at a roadhouse's well pump. There'd been people there, several dozen, some of them camping around the roadhouse and some of them just stopping there briefly. All of them had the look you're starting to identify as slow-building panic. Because everyone's finally begun to realize what the shake and the redglow and the clouded sky all mean, and to be outside of a community's gates at a time like this is—in the long run—a death sentence, except for a handful who are willing to become brutal enough or depraved enough to do what they must. Even those only have a chance at survival.

None of the people at the roadhouse wanted to believe they had that in them, you saw as you looked around, assessing faces and clothes and bodies and threats. None of them looked like survival fetishists or would-be warlords. What you saw at that roadhouse were ordinary people, some still caked in filth after digging themselves out of mudslides or collapsed buildings, some still bleeding from wounds haphazardly bandaged, or untreated entirely. Travelers, caught away from home; survivors, whose homes no longer existed. You saw an old man, still wearing a sleeping gown half ragged and dusty on one side, sitting with a youth clad in only a long shirt and smears of blood, both of them hollow-eyed with grief. You saw two women holding each other, rocking in an effort at comfort. You saw a man your own age with the look of a Strongback, who gazed steadily at his big, thick-fingered hands and perhaps wondered if he was hale enough, young enough, to earn a place somewhere.

These are the stories the stonelore prepared you for, tragic as they are. There is nothing in stonelore about husbands killing children.

You're leaning on an old post that someone jammed up against the hill, maybe the remnants of a fence that ended here, drifting off with your hands tucked into your jacket pockets and your knees drawn up. And then, slowly, you become aware that something has changed. There's no sound to alert you, other than the wind and the small prickles and rustles of the grass. No smell transcends the faint sulfur scent that you've already gotten used to. But there's something. Something else. Out there.

Some*one* else.

Your eyes snap open, and half your mind falls into the earth, ready to kill. The rest of your mind freezes—because a few feet away, sitting crosslegged on the grass and looking at you, is a little boy.

You don't realize what he is at first. It's dark. *He's* dark. You wonder if he's from an eastern Coastal comm. But his hair moves a little when the wind soughs again, and you can tell that some of it's straight as the grass around you. Westcoaster, then? The rest of it seems stuck down with... hair pomade or something. No. You're a mother. It's dirt. He's covered in dirt.

Bigger than Uche, not quite as big as Nassun, so maybe six or seven years old. You actually aren't sure he's a he; confirmation of that will come later. For now you make a judgment call. He sits in a hunched way that would look odd in an adult and is perfectly normal for a child who hasn't been told to sit up straight. You stare at him for a moment. He stares back at you. You can see the pale glisten of his eyes.

"Hello," he says. A boy's voice, high and bright. Good call.

"Hello," you say, at last. There are horror tales that start this way, with bands of feral commless children who turn out to be cannibals. Bit early for that sort of thing, though, the Season having just started. "Where did you come from?"

He shrugs. Unknowing, maybe uncaring. "What's your name? I'm Hoa."

It's a small, strange name, but the world is a big, strange place. Stranger, though, that he gives only one name. He's young enough that he might not have a comm name yet, but he had to have inherited his father's use-caste. "Just Hoa?"

"Mmm-hmm." He nods and twists aside and sets down some kind of parcel, patting it as if to make sure it's safe. "Can I sleep here?"

You look around, and sess around, and listen. Nothing moving but the grass, no one around but the boy. Doesn't explain how he approached you in total silence—but then, he's small, and you know from experience that small children can be very quiet if they want to be. Usually that means they're up to something, though. "Who else are you with, Hoa?"

"Nobody."

It's too dim for him to see your eyes narrow, but somehow he reacts to this anyway, leaning forward. "Really! It's just me. I saw some other people by the road, but I didn't like them. I hid from them." A pause. "I like you."

Lovely.

Sighing, you tuck your hands back into your pockets and draw yourself out of earth-readiness. The boy relaxes a little—that much you can see—and starts to lie down on the bare earth.

"Wait," you say, and reach for your pack. Then you toss him the bedroll. He catches it and looks confused for a few moments, then figures it out. Happily he rolls it out and then curls up on top of it, like a cat. You don't care enough to correct him.

Maybe he's lying. Maybe he is a threat. You'll make him leave in the morning because you don't need a child tagging along; he'll slow you down. And someone must be looking for him. Some mother, somewhere, whose child is not dead.

For tonight, however, you can manage to be human for a little while. So you lean back against the post, and close your eyes to sleep.

The ash begins to fall in the morning.

* * *

They are an arcane thing, you understand, an alchemical thing. Like orogeny, if orogeny could manipulate the infinitesimal structure of matter itself rather than mountains. Obviously they possess some sort of kinship with humanity, which they choose to acknowledge in the statue-like shape we most often see, but it follows that they can take other shapes. We would never know.

—Umbl Innovator Allia, "A Treatise on Sentient Non-Humans," Sixth University, 2323 Imperial/ Year Two Acid Season

6

Damaya, grinding to a halt

THE FIRST FEW DAYS ON the road with Schaffa are uneventful. Not boring. There are boring parts, like when the Imperial Road along which they ride passes through endless fields of kirga stalks or samishet, or when the fields give way to stretches of dim forest so quiet and close that Damaya hardly dares speak for fear of angering the trees. (In stories, trees are always angry.) But even this is a novelty, because Damaya has never gone beyond Palela's borders, not even to Brevard with Father and Chaga at market time. She tries not to look like a complete yokel, gawping at every strange thing they pass, but sometimes she cannot help it, even when she feels Schaffa chuckling against her back. She cannot bring herself to mind that he laughs at her.

Brevard is cramped and narrow and high in a way that she has never before experienced, so she hunches in the saddle as they ride into it, looking up at the looming buildings on either side of the street and wondering if they ever collapse in on passersby. No one else seems to notice that these buildings are ridiculously tall and crammed right up against each other, so it must have been done on purpose. There are dozens of people about even though the sun has set and, to her reckoning, everyone should be getting ready for bed.

Except no one is. They pass one building so bright with oil lanterns and raucous with laughter that she is overcome with curiosity enough to ask about it. "An inn, of sorts," Schaffa replies, and then he chuckles as though she's asked the question that's in her mind. "But we won't be staying at that one."

"It's really loud," she agrees, trying to sound knowledgeable.

"Hmm, yes, that, too. But the bigger problem is that it's not a good place to bring children." She waits, but he doesn't elaborate. "We're going to a place I've stayed at several times before. The food is decent, the beds are clean, and our belongings aren't likely to walk off before morning."

Thus do they pass Damaya's first night in an inn. She's shocked by all of it: eating in a room full of strangers, eating food that tastes different from what her parents or Chaga made, soaking in a big ceramic basin with a fire under it instead of an oiled half-barrel of cold water in the kitchen, sleeping in a bed bigger than hers and Chaga's put together. Schaffa's bed is bigger still, which is fitting because he's huge, but she gawps at it nevertheless as he drags it across the inn room's door. (This, at least, is familiar; Father did it sometimes when there were rumors of commless on the roads around town.) He apparently paid extra for the bigger bed. "I sleep like an earthshake," he says, smiling as if this is some sort of joke. "If the bed's too narrow, I'll roll right off."

She has no idea what he means until the middle of that

night, when she wakes to hear Schaffa groaning and thrashing in his sleep. If it's a nightmare, it's a terrible one, and for a while she wonders if she should get up and try to wake him. She hates nightmares. But Schaffa is a grown-up, and grown-ups need their sleep; that's what her father always said whenever she or Chaga did something that woke him up. Father was always angry about it, too, and she does not want Schaffa angry with her. He's the only person who cares about her in all the world. So she lies there, anxious and undecided, until he actually cries out something unintelligible, and it sounds like he's dying.

"Are you awake?" She says it really softly, because obviously he isn't—but the instant she speaks, he is.

"What is it?" He sounds hoarse.

"You were..." She isn't sure what to say. *Having a nightmare* sounds like something her mother would say to her. Does one say such things to big, strong grown-ups like Schaffa? "Making a noise," she finishes.

"Snoring?" He breathes a long weary sigh into the dark. "Sorry." Then he shifts, and is silent for the rest of the night.

In the morning Damaya forgets this happened, at least for a long while. They rise and eat some of the food that has been left at their door in a basket, and take the rest with them as they resume the trip toward Yumenes. In the just-after-dawn light Brevard is less frightening and strange, perhaps because now she can see piles of horse dung in the gutters and little boys carrying fishing poles and stablehands yawning as they heft crates or bales. There are young women carting buckets of water into the local bathhouse to be heated, and young men stripping to the waist to churn butter or pound rice in sheds behind the big buildings. All these things are familiar, and they help her see that Brevard is just a bigger version of a small town. Its people are no different from Muh Dear or Chaga—and to the people who live here, Brevard is probably as familiar and tedious as she found Palela.

They ride for half a day and stop for a rest, then ride for the rest of the day, until Brevard is far behind and there's nothing but rocky, ugly shatterland surrounding them for miles around. There's an active fault nearby, Schaffa explains, churning out new land over years and decades, which is why in places the ground seems sort of *pushed up* and bare. "These rocks didn't exist ten years ago," he says, gesturing toward a huge pile of crumbling gray-green stone that looks sharp-edged and somehow damp. "But then there was a bad shake—a niner. Or so I hear; I was on circuit in another quartent. Looking at this, though, I can believe it."

Damaya nods. Old Father Earth does feel closer, here, than in Palela—or, not *closer,* that's not really the word for it, but she doesn't know what words would work better. Easier to touch, maybe, if she were to do so. And, and... it feels... fragile, somehow, the land all around them. Like an eggshell laced with fine lines that can barely be seen, but which still spell imminent death for the chick inside.

Schaffa nudges her with his leg. "Don't."

Startled, Damaya does not think to lie. "I wasn't doing anything."

"You were listening to the earth. That's something."

How does Schaffa know? She hunches a little in the saddle, not sure whether she should apologize. Fidgeting, she settles her hands on the pommel of the saddle, which feels awkward because the saddle is huge like everything that belongs to Schaffa. (Except her.) But she needs to do *something* to distract herself from listening again. After a moment of this, Schaffa sighs.

"I suppose I can expect no better," he says, and the disappointment in his tone bothers her immediately. "It isn't your fault. Without training you're like…dry tinder, and right now we're traveling past a roaring fire that's kicking up sparks." He seems to think. "Would a story help?"

A story would be wonderful. She nods, trying not to seem too eager. "All right," Schaffa says. "Have you heard of Shemshena?"

"Who?"

He shakes his head. "Earthfires, these little midlatter comms. Didn't they teach you anything in that creche of yours? Nothing but lore and figuring, I imagine, and the latter only so you could time crop plantings and such."

"There's no time for more than that," Damaya says, feeling oddly compelled to defend Palela. "Kids in Equatorial comms probably don't need to help with the harvest—"

"I know, I know. But it's still a shame." He shifts, getting more comfortable in his saddle. "Very well; I'm no lorist, but I'll tell you of Shemshena. Long ago, during the Season of Teeth—that's, hmm, the third Season after Sanze's founding, maybe twelve hundred years ago?—an orogene named Misalem decided to try to kill the emperor. This was back when the emperor actually did things, mind, and long before the Fulcrum was established. Most orogenes had no proper training in those days; like you, they acted purely on emotion and instinct, on the rare occasions that they managed to survive childhood. Misalem had somehow managed to not only survive, but to train himself. He had superb control, perhaps to the fourth or fifth ring-level—"

"What?"

He nudges her leg again. "Rankings used by the Fulcrum. Stop interrupting." Damaya blushes and obeys.

"Superb control," Schaffa continues, "which Misalem promptly used to kill every living soul in several towns and cities, and even a few commless warrens. Thousands of people, in all."

Damaya inhales, horrified. It has never occurred to her that roggas—she stops herself. She. *She* is a rogga. All at once she does not like this word, which she has heard most of her life. It's a bad word she's not supposed to say, even though the grown-ups toss it around freely, and suddenly it seems uglier than it already did.

Orogenes, then. It is terrible to know that orogenes can kill so many, so easily. But then, she supposes that is why people hate them.

Her. That is why people hate *her.*

"Why did he do that?" she asks, forgetting that she should not interrupt.

"Why, indeed? Perhaps he was a bit mad." Schaffa leans down so that she can see his face, crossing his eyes and waggling his eyebrows. This is so hilarious and unexpected that Damaya giggles, and Schaffa gives her a conspiratorial smile. "Or perhaps Misalem was simply evil. Regardless, as he approached Yumenes he sent word ahead, threatening to shatter the entire city if its people did not send the Emperor out to meet him, and die.

The people were saddened when the Emperor announced that he would meet Misalem's terms—but they were relieved, too, because what else could they do? They had no idea how to fight an orogene with such power." He sighs. "But when the Emperor arrived, he was not alone: with him was a single woman. His bodyguard, Shemshena."

Damaya squirms a little, in excitement. "She must have been really good, if she was the Emperor's bodyguard."

"Oh, she was—a renowned fighter of the finest Sanzed lineages. Moreover, she was an Innovator in use-caste, and thus she had studied orogenes and understood something of how their power worked. So before Misalem's arrival, she had every citizen of Yumenes leave town. With them they took all the livestock, all the crops. They even cut down the trees and shrubs and burned them, burned their houses, then doused the fires to leave only cold wet ash. That is the nature of your power, you see: kinetic transferrence, sesunal catalysis. One does not move a mountain by will alone."

"What is—"

"No, no." Schaffa cuts her off gently. "There are many things I must teach you, little one, but that part you will learn at the Fulcrum. Let me finish." Reluctantly, Damaya subsides.

"I will say this much. Some of the strength you need, when you finally learn how to use your power properly, will come from within you." Schaffa touches the back of her head as he did that time in the barn, two fingers just above the line of her hair, and she jumps a little because there is a sort of spark when he does this, like static. "Most of it, however, must come from elsewhere. If the earth is already moving, or if the fire under the earth is at or near the surface, you may use that strength. You are *meant* to use that strength. When Father Earth stirs, he unleashes so much raw power that taking some of it does no harm to you or anyone else."

"The air doesn't turn cold?" Damaya tries, really tries, to restrain her curiosity, but the story is too good. And the idea of using orogeny in a safe way, a way that will cause no harm, is too intriguing. "No one dies?"

She feels him nod. "Not when you use earth-power, no. But of course, Father Earth never moves when one wishes. When there is no earth-power nearby, an orogene can still make the earth move, but only by taking the necessary heat and force and motion from the things around her. Anything that moves or has warmth—campfires, water, the air, even rocks. And, of course, living things. Shemshena could not take away the ground or the air, but she most certainly could, and did, take away everything else. When she and the Emperor met Misalem at the obsidian gates of Yumenes, they were the only living things in the city, and there was nothing left of the city but its walls."

Damaya inhales in awe, trying to imagine Palela empty and denuded of every shrub and backyard goat, and failing. "And everybody just . . . went? Because she said?"

"Well, because the emperor said, but yes. Yumenes was much smaller in those days, but it was still a vast undertaking. Yet it was either that or allow a monster to make hostages of them." Schaffa shrugs. "Misalem claimed he had no desire to rule in the Emperor's stead, but who could believe that? A man willing to threaten a city to get what he wants will stop at nothing."

That makes sense. "And he didn't know what Shemshena had done until he got to Yumenes?"

"No, he didn't know. The burning was done by the time he arrived; the people had traveled away in a different direction. So as Misalem faced the Emperor and Shemshena, he reached for the power to destroy the city—and found almost nothing. No power, no city to destroy. In that moment, while Misalem floundered and tried to use what little warmth he could drag from the soil and air, Shemshena flung a glassknife over and into the torus of his power. It didn't kill him, but it distracted him enough to break his orogeny, and Shemshena took care of the rest with her other knife. Thus was ended the Old Sanze Empire's—pardon; *the Sanzed Equatorial Affiliation's*—greatest threat."

Damaya shivers in delight. She has not heard such a good story in a long time. And it's true? Even better. Shyly she grins up at Schaffa. "I liked that story." He's good at telling them, too. His voice is so deep and velvety. She could see all of it in her head as he talked.

"I thought you might. That was the origin of the Guardians, you know. As the Fulcrum is an order of orogenes, we are the order that *watches* the Fulcrum. For we know, as Shemshena did, that despite all your terrible power, you are not invincible. You can be beaten."

He pats Damaya's hands on the saddle-pommel, and she doesn't squirm anymore, no longer liking the story quite as much. While he told it, she imagined herself as Shemshena, bravely facing a terrible foe and defeating him with cleverness and skill. With every *you* and *your* that Schaffa speaks, however, she begins to understand: He does not see her as a potential Shemshena.

"And so we Guardians train," he continues, perhaps not noticing that she has gone still. They are deep into the shatterland now; sheer, jagged rock faces, as high as the buildings in Brevard, frame the road on both sides for as far as the eye can see. Whoever built the road must have carved it, somehow, out of the earth itself. "We train," he says again, "as Shemshena did. We learn how orogenic power works, and we find ways to use this knowledge against you. We watch for those among your kind who might become the next Misalems, and we eliminate them. The rest we take care of." He leans over to smile at her again, but Damaya does not smile back this time. "I am your Guardian now, and it is my duty to make certain you remain helpful, never harmful."

When he straightens and falls silent, Damaya does not prompt him to tell another story, as she might have done. She doesn't like the one he just told, not anymore. And she is somehow, suddenly certain: He did not *intend* for her to like it.

The silence lingers as the shatterlands finally begin to subside, then become rolling green hillside. There's nothing out here: no farms, no pastures, no forests, no towns. There are hints that people once lived here: She sees a crumbling, moss-overgrown hump of something in the distance that might have been a fallen-over silo, if silos were the size of mountains. And other structures, too regular and jagged to be natural, too decayed and strange for her to recognize. Ruins, she realizes, of some city that must have died many, many Seasons ago, for there to be so little of it left now. And beyond the ruins, hazy against the cloud-drifted horizon, an obelisk the color of a thundercloud flickers as it slowly turns.

Sanze is the only nation that has ever survived a Fifth Season intact—not just once, but seven times. She learned this in creche. Seven ages in which the earth has broken somewhere and spewed ash or deadly gas into the sky, resulting in a lightless winter that lasted years or decades instead of months. Individual comms have often survived Seasons, if they were prepared. If they were lucky. Damaya knows the stonelore, which is taught to every child even in a little backwater like Palela. *First guard the gates.* Keep storecaches clean and dry. Obey the lore, make the hard choices, and maybe when the Season ends there will be people who remember how civilization should work.

But only once in known history has a whole nation, *many* comms all working together, survived. Thrived, even, over and over again, growing stronger and larger with each cataclysm. Because the people of Sanze are stronger and smarter than everyone else.

Gazing at that distant, winking obelisk, Damaya thinks, *Smarter even than the people who built that?*

They must be. Sanze is still here, and the obelisk is just another deadciv leftover.

"You're quiet now," says Schaffa after a while, patting her hands on the pommel to bring her out of her reverie. His hand is more than twice the size of hers, warm and comforting in its hugeness. "Still thinking about the story?"

She has been trying not to, but of course, she has. "A little."

"You don't like that Misalem is the villain of the tale. That you are like Misalem: a potential threat, without a Shemshena to control you." He says this matter-of-factly, not as a question.

Damaya squirms. How does he always seem to know what she's thinking? "I don't want to be a threat," she says in a small voice. Then, greatly daring, she adds, "But I don't want to be... controlled... either. I want to be—" She gropes for the words, then remembers something her brother once told her about what it meant to grow up. "*Responsible*. For myself."

"An admirable wish," Schaffa says. "But the plain fact of the matter, Damaya, is that you *cannot* control yourself. It isn't your nature. You are lightning, dangerous unless captured in wires. You're fire—a warm light on a cold dark night to be sure, but also a conflagration that can destroy everything in its path—"

"I won't destroy anybody! I'm not bad like that!" Suddenly it's too much. Damaya tries to turn to look at him, though this overbalances her and makes her slip on the saddle. Schaffa immediately pushes her back to face forward, with a firm gesture that says without words, *sit properly*. Damaya does so, gripping the pommel harder in her frustration. And then, because she is tired and angry and her butt hurts from three days on horseback, and because her whole life has gone *wrong* and it hits her all at once that she will never again be normal, she says more than she means to. "And anyway, I don't need you to control me. I can control myself!"

Schaffa reins the horse to a snorting halt.

Damaya tenses in dread. She's smarted off to him. Her mother always whopped her in the head when she did that back home. Will Schaffa whop her now? But Schaffa sounds as pleasant as usual as he says, "Can you really?"

"What?"

"Control yourself. It's an important question. The *most* important, really. Can you?"

In a small voice, Damaya says, "I... I don't..."

Schaffa puts a hand on hers, where they rest atop the saddle-pommel. Thinking that he means to swing down from the saddle, she starts to let go so he can get a grip. He squeezes her right hand to hold it in place, though he lets the left one go. "How did they discover you?"

She knows, without having to ask, what he means. "In creche," she says in a small voice. "At lunch. I was... A boy pushed me."

"Did it hurt? Were you afraid, or angry?"

She tries to remember. It feels so long ago, that day in the yard. "Angry." But that had not been all, had it? Zab was bigger than her. He was always *after* her. And it had hurt, just a little, when he'd pushed her. "Afraid."

"Yes. It is a thing of instinct, orogeny, born of the need to survive mortal threat. That's the danger. Fear of a bully, fear of a volcano; the power within you does not distinguish. It does not recognize *degree*."

As Schaffa speaks, his hand on hers has grown heavier, tighter.

"Your power acts to protect you in the same way no matter how powerful, or minor, the perceived threat. You should know, Damaya, how lucky you are: It's common for an orogene to discover themselves by killing a family member or friend. The people we love are the ones who hurt us the most, after all."

He's upset, she thinks at first. Maybe he's thinking of something terrible—whatever it is that makes him thrash and groan in the night. Did someone kill a family member or best friend of his? Is that why his hand presses down on hers so hard? "Sch-Schaffa," she says, suddenly afraid. She does not know why.

"Shhh," he says, and adjusts his fingers, aligning them carefully with her own. Then he bears down harder, so that the weight of his hand presses on the bones of her palm. He does this deliberately.

"Schaffa!" It hurts. He *knows* it hurts. But he does not stop.

"Now, now—calm down, little one. There, there." When Damaya whimpers and tries to pull away—it *hurts*, the steady grind of his hand, the unyielding cold metal of the pommel, her own bones where they crush her flesh—Schaffa sighs and folds his free arm around her waist. "Be still, and be brave. I'm going to break your hand now."

"Wha—"

Schaffa does something that causes his thighs to tighten with effort and his chest to bump her forward, but she barely notices these things. All her awareness has focused on her hand, and his hand, and the horrid wet *pop* and jostle of things that have never moved before, the pain of which is sharp and immediate and so powerful that she *screams*. She scrabbles at his hand with her free one, desperate and thoughtless, clawing. He yanks her free hand away and presses it against her thigh so that she claws only at herself.

And through the pain, she becomes suddenly aware of the cold, reassuring peace of the stone beneath the horse's feet.

The pressure eases. Schaffa lifts her broken hand, adjusting his grip so that she can see the damage. She keeps screaming, mostly from the sheer horror of seeing *her hand* bent in a way it should not be, the skin tenting and purpled in three places like another set of knuckles, the fingers already stiffening in spasm.

The stone beckons. Deep within it there is warmth and power that can make her forget pain. She almost reaches for that promise of relief. And then she hesitates.

Can you control yourself?

"You could kill me," Schaffa says into her ear, and despite everything she falls silent to hear him. "Reach for the fire within the earth, or suck the strength from everything around you. I sit within your torus." This has no meaning for her. "This is a bad place for orogeny, given that you have no training—one mistake and you'll shift the fault beneath us, and trigger quite the shake. That might kill you, too. But if you manage to survive, you'll be free. Find some comm somewhere and beg your way in, or join a pack of commless and get along as best you can. You can hide what you are, if you're clever. For a while. It never lasts, and it will be an illusion, but for a time you can feel normal. I know you want that more than anything."

Damaya barely hears it. The pain throbs throughout her hand, her arm, her teeth, obliterating any fine sensation. When he stops speaking she makes a sound and tries again to pull away. His fingers tighten warningly, and she stills at once.

"Very good," he says. "You've controlled yourself through pain. Most young orogenes can't do that without training. Now comes the real test." He adjusts his grip, big hand enveloping her smaller one. Damaya cringes, but this is gentle. For now. "Your hand is broken in at least three places, I would guess. If it's splinted, and if you take care, it can probably heal with no permanent damage. If I crush it, however—"

She cannot breathe. The fear has filled her lungs. She lets out the last of the air in her throat and manages to shape it round a word. "No!"

"*Never say no to me*," he says. The words are hot against her skin. He has bent to murmur them into her ear. "Orogenes have no right to say no. I am your Guardian. I will break every bone in your hand, every bone in your *body*, if I deem it necessary to make the world safe from you."

He wouldn't crush her hand. Why? He wouldn't. While she trembles in silence, Schaffa brushes his thumb over the swollen knots that have begun to form on the back of her hand. There is something *contemplative* about this gesture, something *curious*. Damaya can't watch. She closes her eyes, feeling tears run freely from her lashes. She's queasy, cold. The sound of her own blood pounds in her ears.

"Wh-why?" Her voice is hitchy. It takes effort to draw breath. It seems impossible that this is happening, on a road in the middle of nowhere, on a sunny, quiet afternoon. She doesn't understand. Her family has shown her that love is a lie. It isn't stone-solid; instead it bends and crumbles away, weak as rusty metal. But she had thought that Schaffa *liked* her.

Schaffa keeps stroking her broken hand. "I love you," he says.

She flinches, and he soothes her with a soft shush in her ear, while his thumb keeps stroking the hand he's broken. "Never doubt that I do, little one. Poor creature locked in a barn, so afraid of herself that she hardly dares speak. And yet there is the fire of wit in you along with the fire of the earth, and I cannot help but admire both, however evil the latter might be." He shakes his head and sighs. "I hate doing this to you. I hate that it's necessary. But please understand: I have hurt you so that you will hurt no one else."

Her hand *hurts*. Her heart pounds and the pain throbs with it, BURN burn, BURN burn, BURN burn. It would feel so good to cool that pain, whispers the stone beneath her. That would mean killing Schaffa, however—the last person in the world who loves her.

Schaffa nods, as if to himself. "You need to know that I will never lie to you, Damaya. Look under your arm."

It takes an effort of ages for Damaya to open her eyes, and to then move her other arm aside. As she does, however, she sees that his free hand holds a long, beveled, black glass poniard. The sharp tip rests on the fabric of her shirt, just beneath her ribs. Aimed at her heart.

"It's one thing to resist a reflex. Another altogether to resist the conscious, deliberate desire to kill another person, for self-defense or any other reason." As if to suggest this desire, Schaffa taps the glassknife against her side. The tip is sharp enough to sting even through her clothing. "But it seems you can, as you said, control yourself."

And with that Schaffa pulls the knife from her side, twirls it expertly along his fingers, and slides it into his belt sheath without looking. Then he takes her broken hand in both of his. "Brace yourself."

She can't, because she doesn't understand what he means to do. The dichotomy between his gentle words and cruel actions has confused her too much. Then she screams again as Schaffa begins to methodically set each of her hand bones. This takes only seconds. It feels like much more.

When she flops against him, dazed and shaking and weak, Schaffa urges the horse forward again, this time at a brisk trot. Damaya is past pain now, barely noticing as Schaffa keeps her injured hand in his own, this time tucking it against her body to minimize accidental jostling. She does not wonder at this. She thinks of nothing, does nothing, says nothing. There is nothing left in her to say.

The green hills fall behind them, and the land grows flat again. She pays no attention, watching the sky and that distant smoky gray obelisk, which never seems to shift position even as the miles pass. Around it, the sky grows bluer and begins to darken into black, until even the obelisk becomes nothing more than a darker smudge against the emerging stars. At last, as the sun's light fades from the evening, Schaffa reins the horse just off the road and dismounts to make camp. He lifts Damaya off the horse and down, and she stands where he put her while he clears the ground and kicks small rocks into a circle to make a fire. There's no wood out here, but he pulls from his bags several chunks of something and uses them to start a fire. Coal, to judge by the stink, or dried peat. She doesn't really pay attention. She just stands there while he removes the saddle from the horse and tends the animal, and while he lays out the bedroll and puts a little pot into the flames. The aroma of cooking food soon rises over the fire's oily stink.

"I want to go home," Damaya blurts. She's still holding her hand against her chest.

Schaffa pauses in his dinner-making, then looks up at her. In the flickering light of the fire his icewhite eyes seem to dance. "You no longer have a home, Damaya. But you will, soon, in

Yumenes. You'll have teachers there, and friends. A whole new life." He smiles.

Her hand has mostly gone numb since he set the bones, but there is a lingering dull throb. She closes her eyes, wishing it would go away. All of it. The pain. Her hand. The world. The smell of something savory wafts past, but she has no appetite for it. "I don't want a new life."

Silence greets her for a moment, then Schaffa sighs and rises, coming over. She twitches back from him, but he kneels before her and puts his hands on her shoulders.

"Do you fear me?" he asks.

For a moment the desire to lie rises within her. It will not please him, she thinks, for her to speak the truth. But she hurts too much, and she is too numb right now, for fear or duplicity or the desire to please. So she speaks the truth: "Yes."

"Good. You should. I'm not sorry for the pain I've caused you, little one, because you needed to learn the lesson of that pain. What do you understand about me now?"

She shakes her head. Then she makes herself answer, because of course that is the point. "I have to do what you say or you'll hurt me."

"And?"

She closes her eyes tighter. In dreams, that makes the bad creatures go away.

"And," she adds, "you'll hurt me even when I do obey. If you think you should."

"Yes." She can actually hear his smile. He nudges a stray braid away from her cheek, letting the backs of his fingers brush her skin. "What I do is not random, Damaya. It's about control.

Give me no reason to doubt yours, and I will never hurt you again. Do you understand?"

She does not *want* to hear the words, but she does hear them, in spite of herself. And in spite of herself, some part of her relaxes just a little. She doesn't respond, though, so he says, "Look at me."

Damaya opens her eyes. Against the firelight, his head is a dark silhouette framed by darker hair. She turns away.

He takes hold of her face and pulls it back, firmly. "Do you understand?"

Of course it is a warning.

"I understand," she says.

Satisfied, he lets go of her. Then he pulls her over to the fire and gestures for her to sit on a rock he has rolled over, which she does. When he gives her a small metal dish full of lentil soup, she eats—awkwardly, since she isn't left-handed. She drinks from the canteen he hands her. It's difficult when she needs to pee; she stumbles over the uneven ground in the dark away from the fire, which makes her hand throb, but she manages. Since there's only one bedroll, she lies down beside him when he pats that spot. When he tells her to sleep, she closes her eyes again—but she does not fall asleep for a long while.

When she does, however, her dreams are full of jolting pain and heaving earth and a great hole of white light that tries to swallow her, and it seems only a moment later that Schaffa shakes her awake. It's still the middle of the night, though the stars have shifted. She does not remember, at first, that he has broken her hand; in that moment, she smiles at him without thinking. He blinks, then smiles back in genuine pleasure.

"You were making a noise," he says.

She licks her lips, not smiling anymore, because she has remembered, and because she doesn't want to tell him how much the nightmare frightened her. Or the waking.

"Was I snoring?" she asks. "My brother says I do that a lot."

He regards her for a moment in silence, his smile fading. She is beginning to dislike his little silences. That they are not simply pauses in the conversation or moments in which he gathers his thoughts; they are tests, though she isn't sure of what. He is always testing her.

"Snoring," he says at last. "Yes. Don't worry, though. I won't tease you about it like your brother did." And Schaffa smiles, as if this is supposed to be funny. The brother she no longer has. The nightmares that have consumed her life.

But he is the only person left whom she can love, so she nods and closes her eyes again, and relaxes beside him. "Good night, Schaffa."

"Good night, little one. May your dreams be ever still."

* * *

BOILING SEASON: 1842–1845 Imperial. A hot spot beneath Lake Tekkaris erupted, aerosolizing sufficient steam and particulate matter to trigger acidic rain and sky occlusion over the Somidlats, the Antarctics, and the eastern Coastal comms. The Equatorials and northern latitudes suffered no harm, however, thanks to prevailing winds and ocean currents, so historians dispute whether this qualifies as a "true" Season.

—*The Seasons of Sanze, textbook for year 12 creche*

7

you plus one is two

In the morning you rise and move on, and the boy comes with you. The two of you trudge south through hill country and falling ash.

The child is an immediate problem. He's filthy, for one. You couldn't see this the night before in the dark, but he's absolutely covered in dried and drying mud, stuck-on twigs, and Earth knows what else. Caught in a mudslide, probably; those happen a lot during shakes. If so, he's lucky to be alive—but still when he wakes up and stretches, you grimace at the smears and flakes of dirt he's left on your bedroll. It takes you twenty minutes to realize he's naked under all the mess.

When you question him about this—and everything else—he's cagey. He shouldn't be old enough to be effectively cagey, but he is. He doesn't know the name of the comm he's from or the people who birthed him, who apparently are "not very many" in number. He says he doesn't have any parents. He doesn't know his use name—which, you are certain, is a blatant lie. Even if his mother didn't know his father, he would've inherited her use-caste. He's young, and maybe orphaned, but not too young to know his place in the world. Children far younger than this boy understand things like that. Uche was only three and he knew that he was an Innovator like his father, and that this was why all his toys were tools and books and items that could be used for building things. And he knew, too, that there were things he could not discuss with anyone except his mother, and even then only when they were alone. Things about Father Earth and his whispers, *way-down-below things* as Uche had called them—

But you're not ready to think about that.

Instead you ponder the mystery of Hoa, because there's so very much to ponder. He's a squat little thing, you notice when he stands up; barely four feet tall. He acts maybe ten years old, so he's either small for his age or has a manner too old for his body. You think it's the latter, though you're not sure why you think this. You can't tell much else about him, except that he's probably lighter-skinned; the patches where he's shed mud are gray-dirty, not brown-dirty. So maybe he's from somewhere near the Antarctics, or the western continental coast, where people are pale.

And now he's here, thousands of miles away in the northeastern Somidlats, alone and naked. Okay.

Well, maybe something happened to his family. Maybe they were comm-changers. Lots of people do that, pick up roots and spend months or years traveling cross-continent to beg their way into a comm where they'll stick out like pale flowers in a dun meadow…

Maybe.

Right.

Anyway.

Hoa also has icewhite eyes. Real, actual icewhite. Scared you a bit when you woke up in the morning and he looked at you: all that dark mud surrounding two points of glaring silvery-blue. He doesn't look quite human, but then people with icewhite eyes rarely do. You've heard that in Yumenes, among the Breeder use-caste, icewhite eyes are—were—especially desirable. Sanzeds liked that icewhite eyes were intimidating, and a little creepy. They are. But the eyes aren't what makes Hoa creepy.

He's inordinately cheerful, for one. When you rose the morning after he joined you, he was already awake, and playing with your tinderbox. There was nothing in the meadow with which to make a fire—only the meadowgrass, which would've burned up in seconds even if you could have found enough dry, and probably touched off a grassfire in the process—so you hadn't taken the box out of your pack the night before. But he had it, humming idly to himself as he twirled the flint in his fingers, and that meant he'd been digging in your pack. It didn't put you in the best of moods for the day. The image stuck in your mind, though, as you packed up: a child who'd obviously been through some disaster, sitting naked in the middle of a meadow, surrounded by falling ash—and yet, playing. Humming, even. And when he saw you awake and looking, he smiled.

This is why you've decided to keep him with you, even though you think he's lying about not knowing where he comes from. Because. Well. He *is* a child.

So when you've got your pack on, you look at him, and he

looks back at you. He's clutching to his chest that bundle you glimpsed the night before—a wad of rags tied around something, is all you can tell. It rattles a little when he squeezes it. You can tell that he's anxious; those eyes of his can't hide anything. His pupils are huge. He fidgets a little, shifting onto one foot and using the other to scratch the back of his calf.

"Come on," you say, and turn away to head back to the Imperial Road. You try not to notice his soft exhalation, and the way he trots to catch up to you after a moment.

When you step onto the road again, there are a few people moving along it in knots and trickles, nearly all of them going south. Their feet stir up the ash, which is light and powdery for now. Big flakes: no need for masks yet, for those who remembered to pack one. A man walks beside a rickety cart and half-spavined horse; the cart is full of belongings and old people, though the walking man is hardly younger. All of them stare at you as you step from behind the hill. A group of six women who have clearly banded together for safety whisper among themselves at the sight of you—and then one of them says loudly to another, "Rusting Earth, *look* at her, no!" Apparently you look dangerous. Or undesirable. Or both.

Or maybe it's Hoa's appearance that puts them off, so you turn to the boy. He stops when you do, looking worried again, and you feel abruptly ashamed for letting him walk around like this, even if you didn't ask to have some strange child tagging along.

You look around. There's a creek on the other side of the road. No telling how long before you reach another roadhouse; they're supposed to be stationed every twenty-five miles on an

Imperial Road, but the shake from the north might have damaged the next one. There are more trees around now—you're leaving the plains—but not enough to provide any real cover, and many of the trees are broken, anyway, after the shake from the north. The ashfall helps, a little; you can't see more than a mile off. What you can see, though, is that the plainsland around the road is beginning to give way to rougher territory. You know from maps and talk that below the Tirimas mountains there's an ancient, probably-sealed minor fault, a strip of young forest that's grown up since the last Season, and then in perhaps a hundred miles the plains become salt flats. Beyond that is desert, where comms become few and far between, and where they tend to be even more heavily defended than comms in more hospitable parts.

(Jija can't be going as far as the desert. That would be foolish; who would take him in there?)

There will be comms along the road between here and the salt plains, you're certain. If you can get the boy decent-looking, one of them will probably take him in.

"Come with me," you say to the boy, and veer off the road. He follows you down the gravel bed; you notice how sharp some of the rocks are and add good boots to the list of things you need to get for him. He doesn't cut his feet, thankfully—though he does slip on the gravel at one point, badly enough that he falls and rolls down the slope. You hurry over when he stops rolling, but he's already sitting up and looking disgruntled, because he's landed square in the mud at the edge of the creek. "Here," you say, offering him a hand up.

He looks at the hand, and for a moment you're surprised to

see something like unease on his face. "I'm okay," he says then, ignoring your hand and pushing himself to his feet. The mud squelches as he does it. Then he brushes past you to collect the rag bundle, which he lost hold of during the fall.

Fine, then. Ungrateful little brat.

"You want me to wash," he says, a question.

"How'd you guess?"

He doesn't seem to notice the sarcasm. Setting his bundle down on the gravel bank, he walks forward into the water until it rises to about his waist, then he squats to try to scrub himself. You remember and rummage in your pack until you find the slab of soap. He turns at your whistle and you toss it to him. You flinch when he misses the catch entirely, but he immediately dives under and resurfaces with it in his hands. Then you laugh, because he's staring at the soap like he's never seen such a thing.

"Rub it on your skin?" You pantomime doing it: sarcasm again. But he straightens and smiles a little as if that actually clarified something for him, and then he obeys.

"Do your hair, too," you say, rummaging in the pack again and shifting so you can keep an eye on the road. Some of the people passing by up there glance down at you, curiosity or disapproval in their gaze, but most don't bother looking. You like it that way.

Your other shirt is what you were looking for. It'll be like a dress on the boy, so you cut a short length off the spool of twine in your pack, which he can use to belt the shirt below his hips for modesty and to retain a little warmth around his torso. It won't do in the long term, of course. Lorists say that it doesn't take long for things to turn cold when a Season begins. You'll have to see if the next town you pass is willing to sell you clothes and additional supplies, if they haven't already implemented Seasonal Law.

Then the boy comes out of the water, and you stare.

Well. That's different.

Free of mud, his hair is ashblow-coarse, that perfect weatherproof texture the Sanzed value so much, already beginning to stiffen and pouf up as it dries. It will be long enough to keep his back warm, at least. But it is *white*, not the normal gray. And his skin is white, not just pale; not even Antarctic people are ever quite that colorless, not that you've seen. His eyebrows are white, above his icewhite eyes. White white white. He almost disappears amid the falling ash as he walks.

Albino? Maybe. There's also something off about his face. You wonder what you're seeing, and then you realize: There's nothing *Sanzed* about him, except the texture of his hair. There's a broadness to his cheekbones, an angularity to his jaw and eyes, that seems wholly alien to your eyes. His mouth is full-lipped but narrow, so much so that you think he might have trouble eating, though obviously that's not true or he wouldn't have survived to this age. His short stature is part of it, too. He's not just small but stocky, as if his people are built for a different kind of sturdiness than the ideal that Old Sanze has spent millennia cultivating. Maybe his race are all this white, then, whoever they are.

But none of this makes sense. Every race in the world these days is part Sanzed. They did rule the Stillness for centuries, after all, and they continue to do so in many ways. And they weren't always peaceful about it, so even the most insular races bear the Sanzed stamp whether their ancestors wanted the admixture or not. Everyone is measured by their standard deviations from the Sanzed mean. This boy's people, whoever they are, have clearly managed to remain outliers.

"What in fire-under-Earth are you?" you say, before it occurs to you that this might hurt his feelings. A few days of horror and you forget everything about taking care of children.

But the boy only looks surprised—and then he grins. "Fire-under-Earth? You're weird. Am I clean enough?"

You're so thrown by him calling *you* weird that only much later do you realize he avoided the question.

You shake your head to yourself, then hold out a hand for the soap, which he gives to you. "Yes. Here." And you hold up the shirt for him to slip his arms and head into. He does this a bit clumsily, as if he's not used to being dressed by someone else. Still, it's easier than getting Uche dressed; at least this boy doesn't wiggle—

You stop.

You go away for a bit.

When you return to yourself, the sky is brighter and Hoa has stretched out on the nearby low grass. At least an hour has passed. Maybe more.

You lick your lips and focus on him uncomfortably, waiting for him to say something about your...absence. He just perks up once he sees you're back, gets to his feet, and waits.

Okay, then. You and he might get along, after all.

After that you get back on the road. The boy walks well despite having no shoes; you watch him closely for signs of limping or weariness, and you stop more frequently than you would have on your own. He seems grateful for the chance to rest, but aside from that, he does all right. A real little trouper.

"You can't stay with me," you say, though, during one of your rest breaks. Might as well not let him get his hopes up. "I'll try to find you a comm; we'll be stopping at several along the way, if they'll open the gates to trade. But I have to move on, even if I find you a place. I'm looking for someone."

"Your daughter," the boy says, and you stiffen. A moment passes. The boy ignores your shock, humming and petting his little bundle of rags like it's a pet.

"How did you know that?" you whisper.

"She's very strong. I'm not sure it's her, of course." The boy looks back at you and smiles, oblivious to your stare. "There's a bunch of you in that direction. That always makes it hard."

There are a lot of things that probably should be in your mind right now. You only muster the wherewithal to speak one of them aloud. "*You know where my daughter is.*"

He hums again, noncommitally. You're sure he knows just how insane this all sounds. You're sure he's laughing, somewhere behind that innocent mask of a face.

"How?"

He shrugs. "I just know."

"*How?*" He's not an orogene. You'd know your own. Even if he was, orogenes can't *track each other like dogs,* homing in from a distance as if orogeny has a smell. Only Guardians can do anything like that, and then only if the rogga is ignorant or stupid enough to let them.

He looks up, and you try not to flinch. "I just *know,* all right?

It's something I can do." He looks away. "It's something I've always been able to do."

You wonder. But. Nassun.

You're willing to buy a lot of cockamamie things if any of them can help you find her.

"Okay," you say. Slowly, because this is crazy. *You're* crazy, but now you're aware that the boy probably is, too, and that means you need to be careful. But on the thin chance that he's *not* crazy, or that his crazy actually works the way he says it does...

"How... how far is she?"

"Many days' walking. She's going faster than you."

Because Jija took the cart and horse. "Nassun's still alive." You have to pause after this. Too much to feel, too much to contain. Rask told you Jija left Tirimo with her then, but you've been afraid to let yourself think of her as alive *now*. Even though a part of you doesn't want to believe that Jija could kill his own daughter, the rest of you not only believes it but *anticipates* it to some degree. An old habit, bracing yourself for pain to come.

The boy nods, watching you; his little face is oddly solemn now. There's really not much that's childlike about this child, you notice absently, belatedly.

But if he can find your daughter, he can be the Evil Earth incarnate and you won't give a damn.

So you rummage in the pack and find your canteen, the one with the good water; you refilled the other at the creek but need to boil it first. After you take a swig yourself, however, you hand it to him. When he's finished drinking, you give him a handful of raisins. He shakes his head and hands them back. "I'm not hungry."

"You haven't eaten."

"I don't eat much." He picks up his bundle. Maybe he's got supplies in there. Doesn't matter. You don't really care, anyway. He's not your kid. He just knows where your kid is.

You break camp and resume the journey south, this time with the boy walking beside you, subtly leading the way.

* * *

Listen, listen, listen well.

There was an age before the Seasons, when life and Earth, its father, thrived alike. (Life had a mother, too. Something terrible happened to Her.) Earth our father knew He would need clever life, so He used the Seasons to shape us out of animals: clever hands for making things and clever minds for solving problems and clever tongues for working together and clever sessapinae to warn us of danger. The people became what Father Earth needed, and then more than He needed. Then we turned on Him, and He has burned with hatred for us ever since.

Remember, remember, what I tell.

—Lorist recitation, "The Making of the Three Peoples," part one

8

Syenite on the highroad

It eventually becomes necessary for Syenite to ask her new mentor's name. Alabaster, he tells her—which she assumes someone gave him ironically. She needs to use his name fairly often because he keeps falling asleep in his saddle during the long days of riding, which leaves her to do all the work of paying attention to their route and watching out for potential hazards, as well as keeping herself entertained. He wakes readily when she speaks his name, which at first leads her to believe he's just faking it in order to avoid talking to her. When she says this, he looks annoyed and says, "Of course I'm really asleep. If you want anything useful out of me tonight, you'll *let* me sleep."

Which pisses her off, because it's not like *he's* the one who's got to have a baby for empire and Earth. It's also not like the sex takes any great effort on his part, brief and boring as it is.

But perhaps a week into their trip, she finally notices what he's doing during their daily rides and even at night, while they're lying tired and sticky in the sleeping bag they share. She can be forgiven for missing it, she thinks, because it's a constant thing, like a low murmur in a room full of chattering people—but he's quelling all the shakes in the area. *All* of them, not just the ones people can feel. All the tiny, infinitesimal flexes and adjustments of the earth, some of which are building momentum to greater movement and some of which are essentially random: Wherever she and Alabaster pass, those movements go still for a time. Seismic stillness is common in Yumenes, but should not exist out here in the hinterlands where node network coverage is thin.

Once Syenite figures this out, she is…confused. Because there's no point to quelling microshakes, and indeed, doing so might make things worse the next time a larger shake occurs. They were very careful to teach her this, back when she was a grit learning basic geomestry and seismology: The earth does not like to be restrained. Redirection, not cessation, is the orogene's goal.

She ponders this mystery for several days as they pass along the Yumenes–Allia Highroad, beneath a turning obelisk that glints like a mountain-sized tourmaline whenever it's solid enough to catch the sunlight. The highroad is the fastest route between the two quartent capitals, built as straight as possible in ways that only Old Sanze would dare: elevated along lengthy stone bridges and crossing vast canyons, and occasionally even tunneling through mountains too high to climb. This means the trip to the coast will take only a few weeks if they take it easy—half what it would take via lowroad travel.

But rusted reeking Earth, highroads are dull. Most people think they're deathtraps waiting to be sprung, despite the fact that they're usually safer than ordinary roads; all Imperial Roads were built by teams of the best geoneers and orogenes, deliberately placed only in locations deemed permanently stable. Some of them have survived multiple Seasons. So for days at a time Syenite and Alabaster encounter only hard-driving merchant caravanners, mailpost-riders, and the local quartent patrol—all of whom give Syenite and Alabaster the eye upon noticing their black Fulcrum uniforms, and do not deign to speak to them. There are few comms lining the route's turnoffs, and almost no shops at which to buy supplies, although there are regular platforms along the road itself with prepared areas and lean-tos for camping. Syen has spent every evening swatting bugs beside a fire, with nothing to do but glare at Alabaster. And have sex with him, but that only kills a few minutes.

This, though, is interesting. "What are you doing that for?" Syenite finally asks, three days after she first noticed him quelling microshakes. He's just done it again now, while they wait for dinner—cachebread heated with slabs of beef and soaked prunes, yum yum. He yawned as he did it, though of course it must have taken some effort. Orogeny always costs something.

"Doing what?" he asks as he shuts down a subsurface aftershock and pokes at the fire in apparent boredom. She wants to hit him.

"*That.*"

His eyebrows rise. "Ah. You *can* feel it."

"Of course I can feel it! You're doing it all the time!"

"Well, you didn't say anything before now."

"*Because I was trying to figure out what you were doing.*"

He looks perplexed. "Then maybe you should've asked."

She's going to kill him. Something of this must translate through the silence, because he grimaces and finally explains.

"I'm giving the node maintainers a break. Every microshake I settle eases the burden on them."

Syen knows of the node maintainers, of course. As the Imperial Roads link the former vassals of the old empire with Yumenes, so do the nodes connect far-flung quartents with the Fulcrum, to extend its protections as far as possible. All over the continent—at whatever points the senior orogenes have determined is best for manipulating nearby faults or hot spots—there is an outpost. Within that outpost is stationed a Fulcrum-trained orogene whose sole task is to keep the local area stable. In the Equatorials, the nodes' zones of protection overlap, so there's nary a twitch; this, and the Fulcrum's presence at its core, is why Yumenes can build as it does. Beyond the Equatorials, though, the zones are spaced to provide the greatest protection for the largest populations, and there are gaps in the net. It's just not worthwhile—at least, not according to the Fulcrum seniors—to put nodes near every little farming or mining comm in the hinterlands. People in those places fend for themselves as best they can.

Syen doesn't know any of the poor fools assigned to such tedious duty, but she's very, very glad no one has ever suggested it for her. It's the sort of thing they give to orogenes who'll never make it to fourth ring—the ones who have lots of raw power and little control. At least they can save lives, even if they're doomed to spend their own lives in relative isolation and obscurity.

"Maybe you should leave the micros to the node maintainers," Syenite suggests. The food is warm enough; she uses a stick to push it out of the fire. In spite of herself, her mouth is watering. It's been a long day. "Earth knows they probably need *something* to keep them from dying of boredom."

She's intent on the food at first, and doesn't notice his silence until she offers him his portion. Then she frowns, because that look is on his face again. That hatred. And this time at least a little of it is directed at her.

"You've never been to a node, I take it."

What the rust? "No. Why would I possibly go to one?"

"Because you should. All roggas should."

Syenite flinches, just a little, at his *rogga*. The Fulcrum gives demerits to anyone who says it, so she doesn't hear it much—just the odd muttered epithet from people riding past them, or grits trying to sound tough when the instructors aren't around. It's such an ugly word, harsh and guttural; the sound of it is like a slap to the ear. But Alabaster uses it the way other people use *orogene*.

He continues, still in the same cold tone: "And if you can feel what I'm doing, then you can do it, too."

This startles Syen more, and angers her more. "Why in Earthfires would I quell microshakes? Then I'll be—" And then she stops herself, because she was about to say *as tired and useless as you*, and that's just rude. But then it occurs to her that he *has* been tired and useless, maybe *because* he's been doing this.

If it's important enough that he's been wearing himself out to do it, then maybe it's wrong of her to refuse out of hand. Orogenes have to look out for each other, after all. She sighs. "All right. I guess I can help some poor fool who's stuck in the back end of beyond with nothing to do but keep the land steady." At least it will pass the time.

He relaxes, just a little, and she's surprised to see him smile. He hardly ever does that. But no, that muscle in his jaw is still going *twitch twitch twitch*. He's still upset about something. "There's a node station about two days' ride from the next highroad turnoff."

Syen waits for this statement to conclude, but he starts eating, making a little sound of pleasure that has more to do with him being hungry than with the food being especially delicious. Since she's hungry, too, Syenite tucks in—and then she frowns. "Wait. Are you planning to *go* to this station? Is that what you're saying?"

"*We* are going, yes." Alabaster looks up at her, a quick flash of command in his expression, and all of a sudden she hates him more than ever.

It's completely irrational, her reaction to him. Alabaster outranks her by six rings and would probably outrank her by more if the ring rankings went past ten; she's heard the rumors about his skill. If they ever fought, he could turn her torus inside out and flash-freeze her in a second. For that alone she should be nice to him; for the potential value of his favor, and her own goals for advancement within the Fulcrum's ranks, she should even try to *like* him.

But she's tried being polite with him, and flattering, and it doesn't work. He just pretends to misunderstand or insults her until she stops. She's offered all the little gestures of respect that seniors at the Fulcrum usually seem to expect from juniors, but these just piss him off. Which makes *her* angry—and strangely, this state of affairs seems to please him most.

So although she would never do this with another senior, she snaps, "Yes, *sir*," and lets the rest of the evening pass in resentful, reverberating silence.

They go to bed and she reaches for him, as usual, but this time he rolls over, putting his back to her. "We'll do it in the morning, if we still have to. Isn't it time for you to menstruate by now?"

Which makes Syenite feel like the world's biggest boor. That he hates the sex as much as she does isn't in question. But it's horrible that he's been *waiting for a break* and she hasn't been counting. She does so now, clumsily because she can't remember the exact day the last one started, and—he's right. She's late.

At her surprised silence he sighs, already halfway to sleep. "Doesn't mean anything yet if you're late. Traveling's hard on the body." He yawns. "In the morning, then."

In the morning they copulate. There are no better words she can use for the act—vulgarities don't fit because it's too dull, and euphemisms aren't necessary to downplay its intimacy because it's not intimate. It's perfunctory, an exercise, like the stretches she's learned to do before they start riding for the day. More energetic this time because he's rested first; she almost enjoys it, and he actually makes some noise when he comes. But that's it. When they're done he lies there watching while she gets up and does a quick basin bath beside the fire. She's so used to this that she starts when he speaks. "Why do you hate me?"

Syenite pauses, and considers lying for a moment. If this were the Fulcrum, she would lie. If he were any other senior, obsessed with propriety and making sure that Fulcrum orogenes comport themselves well at all times, she would lie. He's made it clear, however, that he prefers honesty, however indelicate. So she sighs. "I just do."

He rolls onto his back, looking up at the sky, and she thinks that's the end of the conversation until he says, "I think you hate me because...I'm someone you *can* hate. I'm here, I'm handy. But what you really hate is the world."

At this Syen tosses her washcloth into the bowl of water she's been using and glares at him. "*The world* doesn't say inane things like that."

"I'm not interested in mentoring a sycophant. I want you to be yourself with me. And when you are, you can barely speak a civil word to me, no matter how civil I am to *you*."

Hearing it put that way, she feels a little guilty. "What do you mean, then, that I hate the world?"

"You hate the way we live. The way the world makes us live. Either the Fulcrum owns us, or we have to hide and be hunted down like dogs if we're ever discovered. Or we become monsters and try to kill everything. Even within the Fulcrum we always have to think about how *they* want us to act. We can never just...be." He sighs, closing his eyes. "There should be a better way."

"There isn't."

"There must be. Sanze can't be the first empire that's managed to survive a few Seasons. We can see the evidence of other ways of life, other people who became mighty." He gestures away from the highroad, toward the landscape that spreads all around them. They're near the Great Eastern Forest; nothing but a carpet of trees rising and falling for as far as the eye can see. Except—

—except, just at the edge of the horizon, she spots something that looks like a skeletal metal hand, clawing its way out of the trees. Another ruin, and it must be truly massive if she can see it from here.

"We pass down the stonelore," Alabaster says, sitting up, "but we never try to remember anything about what's already been tried, what else might have worked."

"Because it *didn't* work. Those people died. We're still alive. Our way is right, theirs was wrong."

He throws her a look she interprets as *I can't be bothered to tell you how stupid you are*, although he probably doesn't mean it that way. He's right; she just doesn't like him. "I realize you only have the education the Fulcrum gave you, but think, will you? Survival doesn't mean *rightness*. I could kill you right now, but that wouldn't make me a better person for doing so."

Maybe not, but it wouldn't matter to *her*. And she resents his casual assumption of her weakness, even though he's completely right. "All right." She gets up and starts dressing, pulling her clothes on with quick jerks. "Tell me what other way there is, then."

He doesn't say anything for a moment. She turns to look at him finally, and he's looking uneasy. "Well..." He edges into the statement. "We could try letting orogenes run things."

She almost laughs. "That would last for about ten minutes before every Guardian in the Stillness shows up to lynch us, with half the continent in tow to watch and cheer."

"They kill us because they've got stonelore telling them at every turn that we're born evil—some kind of agents of Father Earth, monsters that barely qualify as human."

"Yes, but you can't change stonelore."

"Stonelore changes all the time, Syenite." He doesn't say her name often, either. It gets her attention. "Every civilization adds to it; parts that don't matter to the people of the time are forgotten. There's a reason Tablet Two is so damaged: someone, somewhere back in time, decided that it wasn't important or was wrong, and didn't bother to take care of it. Or maybe they even deliberately tried to obliterate it, which is why so many of the early copies are damaged in exactly the same way. The archeomests found some old tablets in one of the dead cities on Tapita Plateau—they'd written down their stonelore, too, ostensibly to pass it on to future generations. But what was on the tablets was different, *drastically* so, from the lore we learned in school. For all we know, the admonition against changing the lore is itself a recent addition."

She didn't know that. It makes her frown. It also makes her not want to believe him, or maybe that's just her dislike for him surfacing again. But . . . stonelore is as old as intelligence. It's all that's allowed humankind to survive through Fifth Season after Fifth Season, as they huddle together while the world turns dark and cold. The lorists tell stories of what happens when people—political leaders or philosophers or well-meaning meddlers of whatever type—try to change the lore. Disaster inevitably results.

So she doesn't believe it. "Where'd you hear about tablets on Tapita?"

"I've been taking assignments outside the Fulcrum for twenty years. I have friends out here."

Friends who talk to an orogene? About historical heresy? It sounds ridiculous. But then again . . . well. "Okay, so how do you change the lore in a way that—"

She's not paying attention to the ambient strata, because the argument has engrossed her more than she wants to admit. He, however, is apparently still quelling shakes even as they speak. Plus he's a ten-ringer, so it's fitting that he abruptly inhales and jerks to his feet as if pulled by strings, turning toward the western horizon. Syen frowns and follows his gaze. The forest on that side of the highroad is patchy from logging and bifurcated by two lowroads branching away through the trees. There's another deadciv ruin, a dome that's more tumbled stone than intact, in the far distance, and she can see three or four small walled comms dotting the treescape between here and there. But she doesn't know what he's reacting to—

—and then she sesses it. Evil Earth, it's a big one! An eighter or niner. No, *bigger.* There's a hot spot about two hundred miles away, beneath the outskirts of a small city called Mehi . . . but that can't be right. Mehi is at the edge of the Equatorials, which means it's well within the protective network of nodes. Why—

It doesn't matter why. Not when Syen can *see* this shake making all the land around the highroad shiver and all the trees twitch. Something has gone wrong, the network has failed, and the hot spot beneath Mehi is welling toward the surface. The proto-shakes, even from here, are powerful enough to make her mouth taste of bitter old metal and the beds of her fingernails to itch. Even the most sess-numb stills can feel these, a steady barrage of wavelets rattling their dishes and making old people gasp and clutch their heads while babies suddenly cry. If nothing stops this upwelling, the stills will feel a lot more when a volcano erupts right under their feet.

"What—" Syenite starts to turn to Alabaster, and then she stops in shock, because he is on his hands and knees growling at the ground.

An instant later she feels it, a shock wave of raw orogeny rippling *out* and *down* through the pillars of the Highroad and *into* the loose schist of the local ground. It's not actual force, just the strength of Alabaster's will and the power it fuels, but she cannot help watching on two levels as his power races—faster than she could ever go—toward that distant radiating churn.

And before Syen even realizes what's happening, Alabaster has *grabbed* her, in some way that she's never experienced before. She feels her own connection to the earth, her own orogenic awareness, suddenly co-opted and steered *by someone else*, and she does not like it one bit. But when she tries to reclaim control of her power it *burns*, like friction, and in the real world she yelps and falls to her knees and she has no idea what's happening. Alabaster has chained them together somehow, using her strength to amplify his own, and there's not a damned thing she can do about it.

And then they are together, diving into the earth in tandem, spiraling through the massive, boiling well of death that is the hot spot. It's huge—miles wide, bigger than a mountain. Alabaster does something, and something shoots away and Syenite cries out in sudden agony that stills almost at once. Redirected. He does it again and this time she realizes what he's doing: *cushioning* her from the heat and pressure and rage of the hot spot. It's not bothering him because he has become heat and pressure and rage as well, attuning himself to it as Syen has only ever done with small heat chambers in otherwise stable strata—but those were campfire sparks in comparison to this firestorm. There is nothing in her that can equal it. So he uses her power, but he also vents the force that she can't process, sending it elsewhere before it can overwhelm her awareness and…and…actually, she's not sure what would happen. The Fulcrum teaches orogenes not to push past their own limits; it does not speak of what happens to those who do.

And before Syenite can think through this, before she can muster the wherewithal to *help* him if she cannot *escape* him, Alabaster does something else. A sharp punch. Something has been pierced, somewhere. At once the upward pressure of the magma bubble begins to ebb. He pulls them back, out of the fire and into the still-shuddering earth, and she knows what to do here because these are just shakes, not Father Earth's rage incarnate. Abruptly something changes and *his* strength is at *her* disposal. So much strength; Earth, he's a monster. But then it becomes easy, easy to smooth the ripples and seal the cracks and thicken the broken strata so that a new fault does not form here where the land has been stressed and weakened. She can sess lines of striation across the land's surface with a clarity that she has never known before. She smooths them, tightens the earth's skin around them with a surgical focus she has never previously been able to achieve. And as the hot spot settles into just another lurking menace and the danger passes, she comes back to herself to find Alabaster curled into a ball in front of her and a scorchlike pattern of frost all around them both which is already sublimating into vapor.

She's on her hands and knees, shaking. When she tries to move, it takes real effort not to fall onto her face. Her elbows keep trying to buckle. But she makes herself do it, crawl a foot or two to reach Alabaster, because he looks dead. She touches his arm and the muscle is hard through the uniform fabric, cramped and locked instead of limp; she thinks that's a good sign. Tugging him a little, she gets closer and sees that his eyes are open, wide, and staring—not with the blank emptiness of death but with an expression of pure surprise.

"It's just like Hessionite said," he whispers suddenly, and she jumps because she didn't think he was conscious.

Wonderful. She's on a highroad in the middle of nowhere, half dead after her orogeny has been used by someone else against her will, with no one to help her but the rustbrained and ridiculously powerful ass who did it in the first place. Trying to pull herself together after...after...

Actually, she has no idea what just happened. It makes no sense. Seismics don't just *happen* like that. Hot spots that have abided for aeons don't just suddenly explode. Something triggers them: a plate shift somewhere, a volcanic eruption somewhere else, a ten-ringer having a tantrum, something. And since it was so powerful an event, she should've sessed the trigger. Should've had some warning besides Alabaster's gasp.

And what the rust did Alabaster *do*? She can't wrap her head around it. Orogenes cannot work together. It's been proven; when two orogenes try to exert the same influence over the same seismic event, the one with the greater control and precision takes precedence. The weaker one can keep trying and will burn themselves out—or the stronger one can punch through their torus, icing them along with everything else. It's why the senior orogenes run the Fulcrum—they aren't just more experienced, they can kill anyone who crosses them, even though they're not supposed to. And it's why ten-ringers get choices: Nobody's going to *force* them to do anything. Except the Guardians, of course.

But what Alabaster did is unmistakable, if inexplicable.

Rust it all. Syenite shifts to sit before she flops over. The world spins unprettily and she props her arms on her updrawn knees and puts her head down for a while. They haven't gone anywhere today, and they won't be going anywhere, either. Syen doesn't have the strength to ride, and Alabaster looks like he might not make it off the bedroll. He never even got dressed; he's just curled up there bare-assed and shaking, completely useless.

So it's left to Syen to eventually get up and rummage through their packs, finding a couple of derminther mela—small melons with a hard shell that burrow underground during a Season, or so the geomests say—and rolling them into the remnants of their fire, which she's very glad they hadn't gotten around to smothering yet. They're out of kindling and fuel, but the coals should be enough to cook the mela so they'll have dinner in a few hours. She pulls a fodder bundle out of the pile for the horses to share, pours some water into a canvas bucket so they can drink, looks at the pile of their droppings and thinks about shoveling it off the highroad's edge so they don't have to smell it.

Then she crawls back to the bedroll, which is thankfully dry after its recent icing. There she flops down at Alabaster's back, and drifts. She doesn't sleep. The minute contortions of the land as the hot spot recedes keep jerking at her sessapinae, keeping her from relaxing completely. Still, just lying there is enough to restore her strength somewhat, and her mind goes quiet until the cooling air pulls her back to herself. Sunset.

She blinks, finding that she has somehow ended up spooned behind Alabaster. He's still in a ball, but this time his eyes are closed and body relaxed. When she sits up, he jerks a little and pushes himself up as well.

"We have to go to the node station," he blurts in a rusty voice, which really doesn't surprise her at all.

"No," she says, too tired to be annoyed, and finally giving up the effort of politeness for good. "I'm not riding a horse off the highroad in the dark while exhausted. We're out of dried peat, and running low on everything else; we need to go to a comm to buy more supplies. And if you try to order me to go to some node in the ass end of beyond instead, you'll need to bring me up on charges for disobedience." She's never disobeyed an order before, so she's a little fuzzy on the consequences. Really, she's too tired to care.

He groans and presses the heels of his hands to his forehead as if to push away a headache, or maybe drive it deeper. Then he curses in that language she heard him use before. She still doesn't recognize it, but she's even more certain that it's one of the Coaster creoles—which is odd, given that he says he was bred and raised at the Fulcrum. Then again, somebody had to raise him for those first few years before he got old enough to be dumped in the grit pool. She's heard that a lot of the eastern Coaster races are dark-skinned like him, too, so maybe they'll hear the language being spoken once they get to Allia.

"If you don't go with me, I'll go alone," he snaps, finally speaking in Sanze-mat. And then he gets up, fumbling around for his clothing and pulling it on, like he's serious. Syenite stares as he does this, because he's shaking so hard he can hardly stand up straight. If he gets on a horse in this condition, he'll just fall off.

"Hey," she says, and he continues his feverish preparations

as if he can't hear her. "*Hey.*" He jerks and glares, and belatedly she realizes he *didn't* hear her. He's been listening to something entirely different all this time—the earth, his inner crazy, who knows. "You're going to kill yourself."

"I don't care."

"This is—" She gets up, goes over to him, grabs his arm just as he's reaching for the saddle. "This is stupid, you can't—"

"*Don't you tell me what I can't do.*" His arm is wire in her hand as he leans in to snarl the words into her face. Syen almost jerks back . . . but up close she sees his bloodshot whites, the manic gleam, the blown look of his pupils. Something's *wrong* with him. "You're not a Guardian. You don't get to order me around."

"Have you lost your mind?" For the first time since she's met him, she's . . . uneasy. He used her orogeny so easily, and she has no idea how he did it. He's so skinny that she could probably beat him senseless with relative ease, but he'd just ice her after the first blow.

He isn't stupid. She has to make him see. "I will go with you," she says firmly, and he looks so grateful that she feels bad for her earlier uncomplimentary thoughts. "At *first light,* when we can take the switchback pass down to the lowroads without breaking our horses' legs and our own necks. All right?"

His face constricts with anguish. "That's too long—"

"We've already slept all day. And when you talked about this before, you said it was a two-day ride. If we lose the horses, how much longer will it take?"

That stops him. He blinks and groans and stumbles back, thankfully away from the saddle. Everything's red in the light of sunset. There's a rock formation in the distance behind him, a tall straight cylinder of a thing that Syenite can tell isn't natural at a glance; either it was pushed up by an orogene, or it's yet another ancient ruin, better camouflaged than most. With this as his backdrop, Alabaster stands gazing up at the sky as if he wants to start howling. His hands flex and relax, flex and relax.

"The node," he says, at last.

"Yes?" She stretches the word out, trying not to let him hear the *humoring the crazy man* note of her voice.

He hesitates, then takes a deep breath. Another, calming himself. "You know shakes and blows never just come out of nowhere like that. The trigger for this one, the shift that disrupted that hot spot's equilibrium, was the node."

"How can you—" Of course he can tell, he's a ten-ringer. Then she catches his meaning. "Wait, you're saying *the node maintainer* set that thing off?"

"That's exactly what I'm saying." He turns to her, his hands flexing into fists again. "Now do you see why I want to get there?"

She nods, blankly. She does. Because an orogene who spontaneously creates a supervolcano does not do so without generating a torus the size of a town. She cannot help but look out over the forest, in the direction of the node. She can't see anything from here, but somewhere out there, a Fulcrum orogene has killed everything in a several-mile radius.

And then there's the possibly more important question, which is: Why?

"All right," Alabaster blurts suddenly. "We need to leave first thing in the morning, and go as fast as we can. It's a two-day trip if we take it easy, but if we push the horses—" He speeds up his words when she opens her mouth, and rides over her objection like a man obsessed. "If we push them, if we leave before dawn, we can get there by nightfall."

It's probably the best she's going to get out of him. "Dawn, then." She scratches at her hair. Her scalp is gritty with road dust; she hasn't been able to wash in three days. They were supposed to pass over Adea Heights tomorrow, a mid-sized comm where she would've pressed to stay at an inn...but he's right. They have to get to that node. "We'll have to stop at the next stream or roadhouse, though. We're low on water for the horses."

He makes a sound of frustration at the needs of mortal flesh. But he says, "Fine."

Then he hunkers down by the coals, where he picks up one of the cooled mela and cracks it open, eating with his fingers and chewing methodically. She doubts he tastes it. Fuel. She joins him to eat the other mela, and the rest of the night passes in silence, if not restfulness.

The next day—or really, later in the night—they saddle up and start cautiously toward the switchback road that will take them off the highroad and down to the lands below. By the time they reach ground level the sun's up, so at that point Alabaster takes the lead and pushes his horse to a full canter, interspersed with walking jags to let them rest. Syen's impressed; she'd thought he would just kill the horses in the grip of whatever urgency possesses him. He's not stupid, at least. Or cruel.

So at this pace they make good time along the more heavily traveled and intersecting lowroads, where they bypass light carters and casual travelers and a few local militia units—all of whom quickly make way for them, as Syen and Alabaster come into view. It's almost ironic, she thinks: Any other time, their black uniforms would make others give them a wide berth because no one likes orogenes. Now, however, everyone must have felt what almost happened with the hot spot. They clear the way eagerly now, and there is gratitude and relief in their faces. The Fulcrum to the rescue. Syen wants to laugh at them all.

They stop for the night and sleep a handful of hours and start again before dawn, and still it's almost full dark by the time the node station appears, nestled between two low hills at the top of a winding road. The road's not much better than a dirtpacked wilderness trail with a bit of aged, cracking asphalt laid along it as a nod to civilization. The station itself is another nod. They've passed dozens of comms on the way here, each displaying a wild range of architecture—whatever's native to the region, whatever fads the wealthier comm members have tried to bring in, cheap imitations of Yumenescene styles. The station is pure Old Empire, though: great looming walls of deep red scoria brick around a complex comprising three small pyramids and a larger central one. The gates are some kind of steely metal, which makes Syen wince. No one puts metal gates on anything they actually want to keep secure. But then, there's nothing in the station except the orogene who lives here, and the staff that supports him or her. Nodes don't even have storecaches, relying instead on regular resupply caravans from nearby comms. Few would want to steal anything within its walls.

Syen's caught off guard when Alabaster abruptly reins his horse well before they reach the gates, squinting up at the station. "What?"

"No one's coming out," he says, almost to himself. "No one's moving beyond the gate. I can't hear anything coming from inside. Can you?"

She hears only silence. "How many people should be here? The node maintainer, a Guardian, and . . . ?"

"Node maintainers don't need Guardians. Usually there's a small troop of six to ten soldiers, Imperials, posted at the station to protect the maintainer. Cooks and the like to serve them. And there's always at least one doctor."

So many headscratchers in so few words. An orogene who doesn't need a Guardian? Node maintainers are below fourth ring; lowringers are never allowed outside the Fulcrum without Guardians, or at least a senior to supervise. The soldiers she understands; sometimes superstitious locals don't draw much distinction between Fulcrum-trained orogenes and any other kind. But why a doctor?

Doesn't matter. "They're probably all dead," she says—but even as she says this, her reasoning falters. The forest around them should be dead, too, for miles around, trees and animals and soil flash-frozen and thawed into slush. All the people traveling the road behind them should be dead. How else could the node maintainer have gotten enough power to disturb that hot spot? But everything seems fine from here, except the silence of the node station.

Abruptly Alabaster spurs his horse forward, and there's no time for more questions. They ride up the hill and toward the locked, closed gates that Syen can't see a way to open, if there's no one inside to do it for them. Then Alabaster hisses and leans forward and for an instant a blistering, narrow torus flickers into view—not around them, but around the gate. She's never seen anyone do that, throw their torus somewhere else, but apparently tenth-ringers can. Her horse utters a nervous little whicker at the sudden vortex of cold and snow before them, so she reins it to a halt, and it shies back a few extra steps. In the next moment something groans and there is a cracking sound beyond the gate. Alabaster lets the torus go as one of the big steel doors drifts open; he's already dismounting.

"Wait, give it time to warm up," Syen begins, but he ignores her and heads toward the gates, not even bothering to watch his step on the slippery frost-flecked asphalt.

Rusting Earthfires. So Syen dismounts and loops the horses' reins around a listing sapling. After the day's hard ride she'll have to let them cool down before she feeds or waters them, and she should rub them down at least—but something about this big, looming, silent building unnerves her. She's not sure what. So she leaves the horses saddled. Just in case. Then she follows Alabaster in.

It's quiet inside the compound, and dark. No electricity for this backwater, just oil lamps that have gone out. There's a big open-air courtyard just past the metal main gates, with scaffolds on the inner walls and nearby buildings to surround any visitors on all sides with convenient sniper positions. Same kind of oh-so-friendly entryway as any well-guarded comm, really, though on a much smaller scale. But there's no one *in* this courtyard, although Syen spies a table and chairs to one side where the people who usually stand guard must have been playing cards and eating snacks not so long ago. The whole compound is silent. The ground is scoria-paved, scuffed and uneven from the passage of many feet over many years, but she hears no feet moving on it now. There's a horse shed on one side of the courtyard, but its stalls are shut and still. Boots covered in dried mud line the wall nearest the gate; some have been tossed or piled there rather than positioned neatly. If Alabaster's right about Imperial soldiers being stationed here, they're clearly the sort who aren't much for inspection-readiness. Figures; being assigned to a place like this probably isn't a reward.

Syen shakes her head. And then she catches a whiff of animal musk from the horse shed, which makes her tense. She smells horses, but can't see them. Edging closer—her hands clench before she makes herself unclench them—she peers over the first stall's door, then glances into the other stalls for a full inventory.

Three dead horses, sprawled on their sides in the straw. Not bloating yet, probably because only the animals' limbs and heads are limp with death. The barrel of each corpse is crusted with ice and condensation, the flesh still mostly hard-frozen. Two days' thaw, she guesses.

There's a small scoria-bricked pyramid at the center of the compound, with its own stone inner gates—though these stand open for the time being. Syenite can't see where Alabaster's gone, but she guesses he's within the pyramid, since that's where the node maintainer will be.

She climbs up on a chair and uses a nearby bit of matchflint to light one of the oil lamps, then heads inside herself—moving faster now that she knows what she'll find. And yes, within the pyramid's dim corridors she sees the soldiers and staffers who once lived here: some sprawled in mid-run, some pressed against the walls, some lying with arms outstretched toward the center of the building. Some of them tried to flee what was coming, and some tried to get to its source to stop it. They all failed.

Then Syen finds the node chamber.

That's what it has to be. It's in the middle of the building, through an elegant archway decorated with paler rose marble and embossed tree-root designs. The chamber beyond is high and vaulted and dim, but empty—except at the room's center, where there's a big... thing. She would call it a chair, if it was made of anything but wires and straps. Not very comfortable-looking, except in that it seems to hold its occupant at an easy recline. The node maintainer is seated in it, anyway, so it must be—

Oh. *Oh.*

Oh bloody, burning Earth.

Alabaster's standing on the dais that holds the wire chair, looking down at the node maintainer's body. He doesn't look up as she comes near. His face is still. Not sad, or bleak. Just a mask.

"Even the least of us must serve the greater good," he says, with no irony in his voice.

The body in the node maintainer's chair is small, and naked. Thin, its limbs atrophied. Hairless. There are things—tubes and pipes and *things*, she has no words for them—going into the stick-arms, down the goggle-throat, across the narrow crotch. There's a flexible bag on the corpse's belly, *attached to* its belly somehow, and it's full of—ugh. The bag needs to be changed.

She focuses on all this, these little details, because it helps. Because there's a part of her that's gibbering, and the only way she can keep that part internal and silent is to concentrate on everything she's seeing. Ingenious, really, what they've done. She didn't know it was possible to keep a body alive like this: immobile, unwilling, indefinite. So she concentrates on figuring out how they've done it. The wire framework is a particular bit of genius; there's a crank and a handle nearby, so the whole aparatus can be flipped over to facilitate cleaning. The wire minimizes bedsores, maybe. There's a stench of sickness in the air, but nearby is a whole shelf of bottled tinctures and pills; understandable, since it would take better antibiotics than ordinary comm-made penicillin to do something like this. Perhaps one of the tube things is for putting that medicine into the node maintainer. And this one is for pushing in food, and that one is for taking away urine, oh, and that cloth wrapping is for sopping up drool.

But she sees the bigger picture, too, in spite of her effort to concentrate on the minutiae. The node maintainer: a child, kept like this for what must have been months or years. A *child*, whose skin is almost as dark as Alabaster's, and whose features might be a perfect match for his if they weren't so skeletal.

"What." It's all she can say.

"Sometimes a rogga can't learn control." Now she understands that his use of the slur is deliberate. A dehumanizing word for someone who has been made into a thing. It helps. There's no inflection in Alabaster's voice, no emotion, but it's all there in his choice of words. "Sometimes the Guardians catch a feral who's too old to train, but young enough that killing's a waste. And sometimes they notice someone in the grit pool, one of the especially sensitive ones, who can't seem to master control. The Fulcrum tries to teach them for a while, but if the children don't develop at a pace the Guardians think is appropriate, Mother Sanze can always find another use for them."

"As—" Syen can't take her eyes off the body's, *the boy's*, face. His eyes are open, brown but clouded and gelid in death. She's distantly surprised she's not vomiting. "As *this*? Underfires, Alabaster, I *know* children who were taken off to the nodes. I didn't . . . this doesn't . . ."

Alabaster unstiffens. She hadn't realized how stiff he was holding himself until he bends enough to slide a hand under the boy's neck, lifting his oversize head and turning it a little. "You should see this."

She doesn't want to, but she looks anyway. There, across the back of the child's shaved head, is a long, vining, keloided scar, embellished with the dots of long-pulled stitches. It's just at the juncture of skull and spine.

"Rogga sessapinae are larger and more complex than those of normal people." When she's seen enough, Alabaster drops the child's head. It thumps back into its wire cradle with a solidity and carelessness that makes her jump. "It's a simple matter to apply a lesion here and there that severs the rogga's self-control completely, while still allowing its *instinctive* use. Assuming the rogga survives the operation."

Ingenious. Yes. A newborn orogene can stop an earthshake. It's an inborn thing, more certain even than a child's ability to suckle—and it's this ability that gets more orogene children killed than anything else. The best of their kind reveal themselves long before they're old enough to understand the danger.

But to reduce a child to nothing *but* that instinct, nothing *but* the ability to quell shakes . . .

She really should be vomiting.

"From there, it's easy." Alabaster sighs, as if he's giving an especially boring lecture at the Fulcrum. "Drug away the infections and so forth, keep him alive enough to function, and you've got the one thing even the Fulcrum can't provide: a reliable, harmless, completely beneficial source of orogeny." Just as Syenite can't understand why she's not sick, she's not sure why *he's* not screaming. "But I suppose someone made the mistake of letting this one wake up."

His eyes flick away, and Syenite follows Alabaster's gaze to the body of a man over by the far wall. This one's not dressed like one of the soldiers. He's wearing civilian clothes, nice ones.

"The doctor?" She's managed to adopt the detached, steady voice that Alabaster's using. It's easier.

"Maybe. Or some local citizen who paid for the privilege." Alabaster actually *shrugs*, gesturing toward a still-livid bruise on the boy's upper thigh. It's in the shape of a hand, finger marks clearly visible even against the dark skin. "I'm told there are many who enjoy this sort of thing. A helplessness fetish, basically. They like it more if the victim is aware of what they're doing."

"Oh, oh Earth, Alabaster, you can't mean—"

He rides over her words again, as if she hasn't spoken. "Problem is, the node maintainers feel terrible pain whenever they use orogeny. The lesions, see. Since they can't stop themselves from reacting to every shake in the vicinity, even the microshakes, it's considered humane to keep them constantly sedated. And all orogenes react, instinctively, to any perceived threat—"

Ah. That does it.

Syen stumbles away to the nearest wall and retches up the dried apricots and jerky she made herself swallow a-horseback on the way to the station. It's wrong. It's all so wrong. She thought—she didn't think—she didn't know—

Then as she wipes her mouth, she looks up and sees Alabaster watching.

"Like I said," he concludes, very softly. "Every rogga should see a node, at least once."

"I didn't know." She slurs the words around the back of her hand. The words don't make sense but she feels compelled to say them. "I didn't."

"You think that matters?" It's almost cruel, the emotionlessness of his voice and face.

"It matters to *me*!"

"You think *you* matter?" All at once he smiles. It's an ugly thing, cold as the vapor that curls off ice. "You think any of us matter beyond what we can do for them? Whether we obey or not." He jerks his head toward the body of the abused, murdered child. "You think he mattered, after what they did to him? The only reason they don't do this to all of us is because we're more versatile, more useful, if we control ourselves. But each of us is just another weapon, to them. Just a useful monster, just a bit of new blood to add to the breeding lines. Just another fucking *rogga*."

She has never heard so much hate put into one word before.

But standing here, with the ultimate proof of the world's hatred dead and cold and stinking between them, she can't even flinch this time. Because. If the Fulcrum can do this, or the Guardians or the Yumenescene Leadership or the geomests or whoever came up with this nightmare, then there's no point in dressing up what people like Syenite and Alabaster really are.

Not people at all. Not *orogenes*. Politeness is an insult in the face of what she's seen. *Rogga*: This is all they are.

After a moment, Alabaster turns and leaves the room.

* * *

They make camp in the open courtyard. The station's buildings hold all the comforts Syen's been craving: hot water, soft beds, food that isn't just cachebread and dried meat. Out here in the courtyard, though, the bodies aren't human.

Alabaster sits in silence, staring into the fire that Syenite's built. He's wrapped in a blanket, holding the cup of tea she's made; she did, at least, replenish their stores from those of the station. She hasn't seen him drink from the cup. It might've been nice, she thinks, if she could've given him something stronger to drink. Or not. She's not really sure what an orogene of his skill could do, drunk. They're not supposed to drink for that exact reason...but rust reason, right now. Rust everything.

"Children are the undoing of us," Alabaster says, his eyes full of the fire.

Syenite nods, though she doesn't understand it. He's talking. That has to be a good thing.

"I think I have twelve children." Alabaster pulls the blanket more closely about himself. "I'm not sure. They don't always tell me. I don't always see the mothers, after. But I'm guessing it's twelve. Don't know where most of them are."

He's been tossing out random facts like this all evening, when he talks at all. Syenite hasn't been able to bring herself to reply to most of the statements, so it hasn't been much of a conversation. This one, though, makes her speak, because she's been thinking about it. About how much the boy in the wire chair resembles Alabaster.

She begins, "Our child..."

He meets her eyes and smiles again. It's kindly this time, but she's not sure whether to believe that or the hatred beneath the smile's surface.

"Oh, this is only one possible fate." He nods at the station's looming red walls. "Our child could become another me burning through the ring ranks and setting new standards for orogeny, a Fulcrum legend. Or she could be mediocre and never do anything of note. Just another four- or five-ringer clearing coral-blocked harbors and making babies in her spare time."

He sounds so rusting *cheerful* that it's hard to pay attention to the words and not just his tone. The tone soothes, and some part of her craves soothing right now. But his words keep her on edge, stinging like sharp glass fragments amid smooth marbles.

"Or a still," she says. "Even two roggas—" It's hard to say the word, but harder to say *orogene,* because the more polite term now feels like a lie. "Even we can make a still."

"I hope not."

"You hope *not?*" That's the best fate she can imagine for their child.

Alabaster stretches out his hands to the fire to warm them. He's wearing his rings, she realizes suddenly. He hardly ever does, but sometime before they reached the station, even with fear for his child burning in his blood, he spared a thought for propriety and put them on. Some of them glitter in the firelight, while others are dull and dark; one on each finger, thumbs included. Six of Syenite's fingers itch, just a little, for their nakedness.

"Any child of two ringed Fulcrum orogenes," he says, "should be an orogene, too, yes. But it's not that exact a thing. It's not *science*, what we are. There's no logic to it." He smiles thinly. "To be safe, the Fulcrum will treat any children born to any rogga as potential roggas themselves, until proven otherwise."

"But once they've proven it, after that, they'll be... *people*." It is the only hope she can muster. "Maybe someone will adopt them into a good comm, send them to a real creche, let them earn a use name—"

He sighs. There's such weariness in it that Syen falls silent in confusion and dread.

"No comm would adopt our child," he says. The words are deliberate and slow. "The orogeny might skip a generation, maybe two or three, but it always comes back. Father Earth never forgets the debt we owe."

Syenite frowns. He's said things like this before, things that hark to the lorists' tales about orogenes—that they are a weapon not of the Fulcrum, but of the hateful, waiting planet beneath their feet. A planet that wants nothing more than to destroy the life infesting its once-pristine surface. There is something in the things Alabaster says that makes her think he *believes* those old tales, at least a little. Maybe he does. Maybe it gives him comfort to think their kind has some purpose, however terrible.

She has no patience for mysticism right now. "Nobody will adopt her, fine." She chooses *her* arbitrarily. "What, then? The Fulcrum doesn't keep stills."

Alabaster's eyes are like his rings, reflecting the fire in one moment, dull and dark the next. "No. She would become a Guardian."

Oh, rust. That explains so much.

At her silence, Alabaster looks up. "Now. Everything you've seen today. Unsee it."

"*What?*"

"That thing in the chair wasn't a child." There's no light in his eyes now. "It wasn't *my* child, or anyone else's. It was nothing. It was no one. We stabilized the hot spot and figured out what caused it to almost blow. We've checked here for survivors and found none, and that's what we'll telegraph to Yumenes. That's what we'll both say if we're questioned, when we get back."

"I, I don't know if I can..." The boy's slack-jawed, dead gaze. How horrible, to be trapped in an endless nightmare. To awaken to agony, and the leer of some grotesque parasite. She can feel nothing but pity for the boy, relief for his release.

"You will do exactly as I say." His voice is a whip, and she glares at him, instantly furious. "If you mourn, mourn the wasted resource. If anyone asks, you're glad he's dead. Feel it. Believe it. He almost killed more people than we can count, after all. And if anyone asks how you feel about it, say you understand that's why they do these things to us. You know it's for our own good. You know it's for everyone's."

"You rusting bastard, I *don't* know—"

He laughs, and she flinches, because the rage is back now, whiplash-quick. "Oh, don't push me right now, Syen. Please don't." He's still laughing. "I'll get a reprimand if I kill you."

It's a threat, at last. Well, then. Next time he sleeps. She'll have to cover his face while she stabs him. Even lethal knife wounds take a few seconds to kill; if he focuses his orogeny on her in that brief window, she's dead. He's less likely to target her accurately without eyes, though, or if he's distracted by suffocation—

But Alabaster is still laughing. Hard. That's when Syenite becomes aware of a hovering jitter in the ambient. A looming *almost* in the strata beneath her feet. She frowns, distracted and alerted and wondering if it's the hot spot again—and then, belatedly, she realizes that the sensation is not jittering, it's jerking in a rhythmic sort of way. In time with the harsh exhalations of Alabaster's laughter.

While she stares at him in chilled realization, he even slaps his knee with one hand. Still laughing, because what he *wants* to do is destroy everything in sight. And if his half-dead, half-grown son could touch off a supervolcano, there's really no telling what that boy's father could do if he set his mind to it. Or even by accident, if his control slips for a moment.

Syen's hands clench into fists on her knees. She sits there, nails pricking her palms, until he finally gets ahold of himself. It takes a while. Even when the laughter's done he puts his face into his hands and chuckles now and again, shoulders shaking. Maybe he's crying. She doesn't know. Doesn't really care, either.

Eventually he lifts his head and takes a deep breath, then another. "Sorry about that," he says at last. The laughter has stopped, but he's all cheer again. "Let's talk about something else, why don't we?"

"Where the rust is your Guardian?" She hasn't unclenched her hands. "You're mad as a bag of cats."

He *giggles*. "Oh, I made sure she was no threat years ago."

Syen nods. "You killed her."

"No. Do I look stupid?" Giggling to annoyance in half a breath. Syen is terrified of him and no longer ashamed to admit it. But he sees this, and something in his manner changes. He takes another deep breath, and slumps. "Shit. I . . . I'm sorry."

She says nothing. He smiles a little, sadly, like he doesn't expect her to. Then he gets up and goes to the sleeping bag. She watches while he lies down, his back to the fire; she watches him until his breathing slows. Only then does she relax.

Though she jumps, again, when he speaks very softly.

"You're right," he says. "I've been crazy for years. If you stay with me for long, you will be, too. If you see enough of this, and understand enough of what it all means." He lets out a long sigh. "If you kill me, you'll be doing the whole world a favor." After that he says nothing more.

Syen considers his last words for longer than she probably should.

Then she curls up to sleep as best she can on the hard courtyard stones, wrapped in a blanket and with a saddle as an especially torturous sort of pillow. The horses shift restlessly, the way they have been all evening; they can smell the death in the station. But eventually, they sleep, and Syenite does, too. She hopes Alabaster eventually does the same.

Back along the highroad they just traveled, the tourmaline obelisk drifts out of sight behind a mountain, implacable in its course.

* * *

Winter, Spring, Summer, Fall; Death is the fifth, and master of all.

—*Arctic proverb*

INTERLUDE

A break in the pattern. A snarl in the weft. There are things you should be noticing, here. Things that are missing, and conspicuous by their absence.

Notice, for example, that no one in the Stillness speaks of islands. This is not because islands do not exist or are uninhabited; quite the contrary. It is because islands tend to form near faults or atop hot spots, which means they are ephemeral things in the planetary scale, there with an eruption and gone with the next tsunami. But human beings, too, are ephemeral things in the planetary scale. The number of things that they do not notice are literally astronomical.

People in the Stillness do not speak of other continents, either, though it is plausible to suspect they might exist elsewhere. No one has traveled around the world to see that there aren't any; seafaring is dangerous enough with resupply in sight and tsunami waves that are only a hundred feet high rather than the legendary mountains of water said to ripple across the unfettered deep ocean. They simply take as given the bit of lore passed down from braver civilizations that says there's nothing else. Likewise, no one speaks of celestial objects, though the skies are as crowded and busy here as anywhere else in the universe. This is largely because so much of the people's attention is directed toward the ground, not the sky. They notice what's there: stars and the sun and the occasional comet or falling star. They do not notice what's missing.

But then, how can they? Who misses what they have never, ever even imagined? That would not be human nature. How fortunate, then, that there are more people in this world than just humankind.

9

Syenite among the enemy

THEY REACH ALLIA A WEEK later, beneath a bright blue midday sky that is completely clear except for a winking purple obelisk some ways off-coast.

Allia's big for a Coaster comm—nothing like Yumenes, of course, but respectably sized; a proper city. Most of its neighborhoods and shops and industrial districts are packed into the steep-sided bowl of a natural harbor formed from an old caldera that has collapsed on one side, with several days of outlying settlement in every direction. On the way in, Syenite and Alabaster stop at the first cluster of buildings and farmhouses they see, ask around, and—in between ignoring the glares elicited by their black uniforms—learn that several lodging-houses are nearby. They skip the first one they could've gone to, because a young man from one of the farmhouses decides to follow them for a few miles, reining his horse back to keep it out of what he probably thinks is their range. He's alone, and he says nothing, but one young man can easily become a gang of them, so they keep going in hopes his hatred won't outlast his boredom—and eventually he does turn his horse and head back the way they came.

The next lodging-house isn't as nice as the first, but it's not bad, either: a boxy old stucco building that's seen a few Seasons but is sturdy and well kept. Someone's planted rosebushes at every corner and let ivy grow up its walls, which will probably mean its collapse when the next Season comes, but that's not Syenite's problem to worry about. It costs them two Imperial mother-of-pearls for a shared room and stabling for two horses for the night: such a ridiculously obvious gouging that Syenite laughs at the proprietor before she catches herself. (The woman glares back at them.) Fortunately, the Fulcrum understands that orogenes in the field sometimes have to bribe citizens into decent behavior. Syenite and Alabaster have been generously provisioned, with a letter of credit that will allow them to draw additional currency if necessary. So they pay the proprietor's price, and the sight of all that nice white money makes their black uniforms acceptable for at least a little while.

Alabaster's horse has been limping since the push to the node station, so before they settle in they also see a drover and trade for an uninjured animal. What they get is a spirited little mare who gives Alabaster such a skeptical look that Syenite cannot help laughing again. It's a good day. And after a good night's rest in actual beds, they move on.

Allia's main gates are a massive affair, even more ostentatiously large and embellished than those of Yumenes. Metal, though, rather than proper stone, which makes them look like the garish imitation they are. Syen can't understand how the damn things are supposed to actually secure anything, despite the fact that they're fifty feet tall and made of solid plates of bolted chromium steel, with a bit of filigree for decoration. In a Season, the first acid rain will eat those bolts apart, and one good sixer will warp the precision plates out of alignment, making the great huge things impossible to close. Everything about the gates screams that this is a comm with lots of new money and not enough lorists talking to its Leadership caste.

The gate crew seems to consist of only a handful of Strongbacks, all of them wearing the pretty green uniforms of the comm's militia. Most are sitting around reading books, playing cards, or otherwise ignoring the gate's back-and-forth commerce; Syen fights not to curl her lip at such poor discipline. In Yumenes they would be armed, visibly standing guard, and at least making note of every inbound traveler. One of the Strongbacks does do a double take at the sight of their uniforms, but then waves them through with a lingering glance at Alabaster's many-ringed fingers. He doesn't even look at Syen's hands, which leaves her in a very foul mood by the time they finally traverse the town's labyrinthine cobbled streets and reach the governor's mansion.

Allia is the only large city in the entire quartent. Syen can't remember what the other three comms of the quartent are called, or what the nation was called before it became a nominal part of Sanze—some of the old nations reclaimed their names after Sanze loosened control, but the quartent system worked better, so it didn't really matter. She knows it's all farming and fishing country, as backwater as any other coastal region. Despite all this, the governor's mansion is impressively beautiful, with artful Yumenescene architectural details all over it like cornices and windows made of glass and, ah yes, a single decorative balcony overlooking a vast forecourt. Completely unnecessary ornamentation, in other words, which probably has to be repaired after every minor shake. And did they really have to paint the whole building bright yellow? It looks like some kind of giant rectangular fruit.

At the mansion gates they hand off their horses to a stablehand and kneel in the forecourt to have their hands soaped and washed by a household Resistant servant, which is a local tradition to reduce the chance of spreading disease to the comm's Leadership. After that, a very tall woman, almost as black-skinned as Alabaster and dressed in a white variation on the militia's uniform, comes to the court and gestures curtly for them to follow. She leads them through the mansion and into a small parlor, where she closes the door and moves to sit at the room's desk.

"It took you both long enough to get here," she says by way of greeting, looking at something on her desk as she gestures peremptorily for them to sit. They take the chairs on the other side of the desk, Alabaster crossing his legs and steepling his fingers with an unreadable expression on his face. "We expected you a week ago. Do you want to proceed to the harbor right way, or can you do it from here?"

Syenite opens her mouth to reply that she'd rather go to the harbor, since she's never shaken a coral ridge before and being closer will help her understand it better. Before she can speak, however, Alabaster says, "I'm sorry; who are you?"

Syenite's mouth snaps shut and she stares at him. He's smiling politely, but there's an edged quality to the smile that immediately puts Syenite on alert. The woman stares at him, too, practically radiating affront.

"My name is Asael Leadership Allia," she says, slowly, as if speaking to a child.

"Alabaster," he replies, touching his own chest and nodding. "My colleague is Syenite. But forgive me; I didn't want just your name. We were told the quartent governor was a man."

That's when Syenite understands, and decides to play along. She doesn't understand *why* he's decided to do this, but then there's no real way to understand anything he does. The woman doesn't get it; her jaw flexes visibly. "I am deputy governor."

Most quartents have a governor, a lieutenant governor, and a seneschal. Maybe a comm that's trying so hard to outdo the Equatorials needs extra layers of bureaucracy. "How many deputy governors are there?" Syenite asks, and Alabaster makes a "tut" sound.

"We must be polite, Syen," he says. He's still smiling, but he's furious; she can tell because he's flashing too many teeth. "We're only orogenes, after all. And this is a member of the Stillness's most esteemed use-caste. We are merely here to wield powers greater than she can comprehend in order to save her region's economy, while *she*—" He waggles a finger at the woman, not even trying to hide his sarcasm. "She is a pedantic minor bureaucrat. But I'm sure she's a *very important* pedantic minor bureaucrat."

The woman isn't pale enough for her skin to betray her, but that's all right: Her rock-stiff posture and flared nostrils are clue enough. She looks from Alabaster to Syenite, but then her gaze swings back to him, which Syen completely understands.

Nobody's more irritating than her mentor. She feels a sudden perverse pride.

"There are six deputy governors," she says at last, answering Syenite's question even as she glares shards at Alabaster's smiling face. "And the fact that I am a deputy governor should be irrelevant. The governor is a very busy man, and this is a minor matter. Therefore a *minor bureaucrat* should be more than sufficient to deal with it. Yes?"

"It is not a minor matter." Alabaster's not smiling anymore, although he's still relaxed, fingers tapping each other. He looks like he's considering getting angry, though Syen knows he's already there. "I can sess the coral obstruction from here. Your harbor's almost unusable; you've probably been losing heavier-hauling merchant vessels to other Coaster comms for a decade, if not longer. You've agreed to pay the Fulcrum such a vast sum—I know it's vast because you're getting me—that you'd better hope the cleared harbor restores all that lost trade, or you'll never pay off the debt before the next tsunami wipes you out. So we? The two of us?" He gestures briefly at Syen, then re-steeples his fingers. "We're your whole rusting future."

The woman is utterly still. Syenite cannot read her expression, but her body is stiff, and she's drawn back ever so slightly. In fear? Maybe. More likely in reaction to Alabaster's verbal darts, which have surely stricken tender flesh.

And he continues. "So the least you could do is first offer us some hospitality, and then introduce us to the man who made us travel several hundred miles to solve your little problem. That's courtesy, yes? That's how officials of note are generally treated. Wouldn't you agree?"

In spite of herself, Syen wants to cheer.

"Very well," the woman manages at last, with palpable brittleness. "I will convey your... request... to the governor." Then she smiles, her teeth a white flash of threat. "I'll be sure to convey your disappointment with our usual protocol regarding guests."

"If this is how you usually treat guests," Alabaster says, glancing around with that perfect arrogance only a lifelong Yumenescene can display to its fullest, "then I think you *should* convey our disappointment. Really, right to business like this? Not even a cup of safe to refresh us after our long journey?"

"I was told that you had stopped in the outlying districts for the night."

"Yes, and that took the edge off. The accommodations were also... less than optimal." Which is unfair, Syen thinks, since the lodging-house had been warm and its beds comfortable; the proprietor had been scrupulously courteous once she had money in hand. But there's no stopping him. "When was the last time you traveled fifteen hundred miles, Deputy Governor? I assure you, you'll need more than a day's rest to recover."

The woman's nostrils all but flare. Still, she's Leadership; her family must have trained her carefully in how to bend with blows. "My apologies. I did not think."

"No. You didn't." All at once Alabaster rises, and although he keeps the movement smooth and unthreatening, Asael flinches back as if he's about to come at her. Syen gets up, too—belatedly, since Alabaster caught her by surprise—but Asael doesn't even look at her. "We'll stay the night in that inn we passed on the way here," Alabaster says, ignoring the woman's obvious unease.

"About two streets over. The one with the stone kirkhusa in front? Can't recall the name."

"Season's End." The woman says it almost softly.

"Yes, that sounds right. Shall I have the bill sent here?"

Asael is breathing hard now, her hands clenched into fists atop the desk. Syen's surprised, because the inn's a perfectly reasonable request, if a bit pricey—ah, but that's the problem, isn't it? This deputy governor has no authorization to pay for their accommodations. If her superiors are annoyed enough about this, they'll take the cost out of her pay.

But Asael Leadership Allia does not drop her polite act and just start shouting at them, as Syen half-expects. "Of course," she says—even managing a smile, for which Syen almost admires her. "Please return tomorrow at this time, and I will further instruct you then."

So they leave, and head down the street to the very fancy inn that Alabaster has secured for them.

As they stand at the window of their room—sharing again, and they're taking care not to order particularly expensive food, so that no one can call their request for accommodation exhorbitant—Syenite examines Alabaster's profile, trying to understand why he still radiates fury like a furnace.

"Bravo," she says. "But was that necessary? I'd rather get the job done and start back as soon as possible."

Alabaster smiles, though the muscles of his jaw flex repeatedly. "I would've thought you'd like being treated like a human being for a change."

"I do. But what difference does it make? Even if you pull rank now, it won't change how they feel about us—"

"No, it won't. And I don't care how they feel. They don't have to rusting like us. What matters is what they *do*."

That's all well and good for him. Syenite sighs and pinches the bridge of her nose between thumb and forefinger, trying for patience. "They'll complain." And Syenite, since this is technically her assignment, will be the one censured for it.

"Let them." He turns away from the window then and heads toward the bathroom. "Call me when the food comes. I'm going to soak until I turn pruney."

Syenite wonders if there is any point in hating a crazy man. It's not like he'll notice, anyway.

Room service arrives, bringing a tray of modest but filling local food. Fish is cheap in most Coaster comms, so Syen has treated herself by ordering a temtyr fillet, which is an expensive delicacy back in Yumenes. They only serve it every once in a while in the Fulcrum eateries. Alabaster comes out of the bathroom in a towel, indeed looking pruney—which is when Syen finally notices how whipcord thin he has become in the past few weeks of traveling. He's muscle and bone, and all he's ordered to eat is a bowl of soup. Granted, it's a big bowl of hearty seafood stew, which someone has garnished with cream and a dollop of some kind of beet chutney, but he clearly needs more.

Syenite has a side dish of garlic yams and carmelized silvabees, in addition to her own meal, on a separate smaller plate. She deposits this on his tray.

Alabaster stares at it, then at her. After a moment his expression softens. "So that's it. You prefer a man with more meat on his bones."

He's joking; they both know she wouldn't enjoy sex with him even if she found him attractive. "Anyone would, yes."

He sighs, then obediently begins eating the yams. In between bites—he doesn't seem hungry, just grimly determined—he says, "I don't feel it anymore."

"What?"

He shrugs, which she thinks is less confusion and more his inability to articulate what he means. "Much of anything, really. Hunger. Pain. When I'm in the earth—" He grimaces. That's the real problem: not his inability to say it, but the fact that words are inadequate to the task. She nods to show that she's understood. Maybe someday someone will create a language for orogenes to use. Maybe such a language has existed, and been forgotten, in the past. "When I'm in the earth, the earth is all I can sess. I don't feel—*this*." He gestures around the room, at his body, at her. "And I spend so much time in the earth. Can't help it. When I come back, though, it's like... it's like some of the earth comes with me, and..." He trails off. But she thinks she understands. "Apparently this is just something that happens past the seventh or eighth ring. The Fulcrum has me on a strict dietary regimen, but I haven't been following it much."

Syen nods, because that's obvious. She puts her sweetweed bun on his plate, too, and he sighs again. Then he eats everything on his plate.

They go to bed. And later, in the middle of the night, Syenite dreams that she is falling upward through a shaft of wavering light that ripples and refracts around her like dirty water. At the top of the shaft, something shimmers *there* and *away* and back again, like it is not quite real, not quite there.

She starts awake, unsure of why she suddenly feels like *something is wrong,* but certain that she needs to do something about it. She sits up, rubbing her face blearily, and only as the remnants of the dream fade does she become aware of the hovering, looming sense of doom that fills the air around her.

In confusion she looks down at Alabaster—and finds him awake beside her, oddly stiff, his eyes wide and staring and his mouth open. He sounds like he's gargling, or trying to snore and failing pathetically. What the rust? He doesn't look at her, doesn't move, just keeps making that ridiculous noise.

And meanwhile his orogeny gathers, and gathers, and *gathers,* until the entire inside of her skull aches. She touches his arm, finds it clammy and stiff, and only belatedly understands that *he can't move.*

"'Baster?" She leans over him, looking into his eyes. They don't look back at her. Yet she can clearly sess something there, awake and reacting within him. His power flexes as his muscles seem to be unable, and with every gargling breath she feels it spiral higher, curl tighter, ready to snap at any moment. Burning, flaking *rust*. He can't move, and he's *panicking.*

"Alabaster!" Orogenes should never, ever panic. Ten-ringer orogenes especially. He can't answer her, of course; she says it mostly to let him know she's here, and she's helping, so hopefully he'll calm down. It's some kind of seizure, maybe. Syenite throws off the covers and rolls onto her knees and puts her fingers into his mouth, trying to pull his tongue down. She finds his mouth full of spit; he's drowning in his own damn drool. This prompts her to turn him roughly onto his side, tilting his head so the spit will run out, and they are both rewarded by the sound of his first clear breath. But it's shallow, that breath, and it takes him far too long to inhale it. He's struggling. Whatever it is that's got him, it's paralyzing his lungs along with everything else.

The room rocks, just a little, and throughout the inn Syenite hears voices rise in alarm. The cries end quickly, however, because nobody's really worried. There's no sess of impending shake. They're probably chalking it up to a strong wind gust against the building's side . . . for now.

"Shit shit shit—" Syenite crouches to get into his line of sight. "'Baster, you stupid cannibalson ruster—*rein it in.* I'm going to help you, but I can't do that if you kill us all!"

His face doesn't react, his breathing doesn't change, but that looming sense of doom diminishes almost at once. Better. Good. Now—"I have to go and find a doctor—"

The jolt that shakes the building is sharper this time; she hears dishes rattle and clink on their discarded food cart. So that's a no. "I can't help you! I don't know what this is! You're going to die if—"

His whole body jerks. She isn't sure whether that's something deliberate or some kind of convulsion. But she realizes it was a warning a moment later, when *that thing* happens again: his power, clamping on to hers like a vise. She grits her teeth and waits for him to use her to do whatever he needs to do . . . but nothing happens. He has her, and she can feel him doing *something.* Flailing, sort of. Searching, and finding nothing.

"What?" Syenite peers into his slack face. "What are you looking for?"

No response. But it's obviously something he can't find without moving on his own.

Which makes no sense. Orogenes don't need eyes to do what they do. *Infants in the crib* can do what they do. But, but—she tries to think. Before, when this happened on the highroad, he had first turned toward the source of distress. She pictures the scene in her mind, trying to understand what he did and how he did it. No, that's not right; the node station had been slightly to the northwest, and he'd stared dead west, at the horizon. Shaking her head at her own foolishness even as she does it, Syenite jumps up and hurries to the window, opening it and peering out. Nothing to see but the sloping streets and stuccoed buildings of the city, quiet at this late hour. The only activity is down the road, where she can glimpse the dock and the ocean beyond: People are loading a ship. The sky is patchy with clouds, nowhere near dawn. She feels like an idiot. And then—

Something clenches in her mind. From the bed behind her she hears Alabaster make a harsh sound, feels the tremor of his power. Something caught his attention. When? When she looked at the sky. Puzzled, she does it again.

There. *There.* She can almost feel his elation. And then his power folds around her, and she stops seeing with anything like eyes.

It's like the dream she had. She's falling, up, and this somehow makes sense. All around her, the place she's falling through, is color and faceted flickering, like water—except it's purple-pale instead of blue or clear, low-quality amethyst with a dollop of smoky quartz. She flails within it, sure for an instant that she's drowning, but this is something she perceives with sessapinae and not skin or lungs; she can't be flailing because it's not water and she's not really here. And she can't drown because, somehow, Alabaster has her.

Where she flails, he is purposeful. He drags her up, falling faster, searching for something, and she can almost hear the howl of it, feel the drag of forces like pressure and temperature gradually chilling and prickling her skin.

Something engages. Something else shunts open. It's beyond her, too complex to perceive in full. Something pours through somewhere, warms with friction. Someplace inside her smooths out, intensifies. *Burns.*

And then she is elsewhere, floating amid immense gelid things, and there is something on them, among them

a contaminant

That is not her thought.

And then it's all gone. She snaps back into herself, into the real world of sight and sound and hearing and taste and smell and sess—real sess, sess the way it's *supposed to* work, not whatever-the-rust Alabaster just did—and Alabaster is vomiting on the bed.

Revolted, Syen jerks away, then remembers that he's paralyzed; he shouldn't be able to move at all, let alone vomit. Nevertheless, he's doing it, having half-pushed himself up off the bed so that he can heave effectively. Obviously the paralysis has eased.

He doesn't throw up much, just a teaspoon or two of greasy-looking white-clear stuff. They ate hours ago; there shouldn't be anything in his upper digestive tract at all. But she remembers

a contaminant

and realizes belatedly what's come out of him. And further, she realizes *how* he's done it.

When he finally gets it all up, and spits a few times for emphasis or good measure, he flops back onto the bed on his back, breathing hard, or maybe just enjoying the sensation of being able to breathe at will.

Syenite whispers, "What in the rusted burning Earth did you just do?"

He laughs a little, opening his eyes to roll them toward her. She can tell it's another of those laughs he does when he really wants to express something other than humor. Misery this time, or maybe weary resignation. He's always bitter. How he shows it is just a matter of degree.

"F-focus," he says, between pants. "Control. Matter of degree."

It's the first lesson of orogeny. Any infant can move a mountain; that's instinct. Only a trained Fulcrum orogene can deliberately, specifically, move a boulder. And only a ten-ringer, apparently, can move the infinitesimal substances floating and darting in the interstices of his blood and nerves.

It should be impossible. She shouldn't believe that he's done this. But she helped him do it, so she can't do anything *but* believe the impossible.

Evil Earth.

Control. Syenite takes a deep breath to master her nerves. Then she gets up, fetches a glass of water, and brings it over. He's still weak; she has to help him sit up to sip from the glass. He spits out the first mouthful of that, too, onto the floor at her feet. She glares. Then she grabs pillows to prop under his back, helps him into a recline, and pulls the unstained part of the blanket over his legs and lap. That done, she moves to the chair across from the bed, which is big and more than plush enough to sleep in for the night. She's tired of dealing with his bodily fluids.

After Alabaster's caught his breath and regained a little of his strength—she is not uncharitable—she speaks very quietly. "Tell me what the rust you're doing."

He seems unsurprised by the question, and doesn't move from where he's slumped on the pillows, his head lolling back. "Surviving."

"On the highroad. Just now. *Explain* it."

"I don't know if . . . I can. Or if I should."

She keeps her temper. She's too scared not to. "What do you mean, if you should?"

He takes a long, slow, deep breath, clearly savoring it. "You don't have . . . control yet. Not enough. Without that . . . if you tried to do what I just did . . . you'd die. But if I tell you how I did it—" He takes a deep breath, lets it out. "You may not be able to stop yourself from trying."

Control over things too small to see. It sounds like a joke. It has to be a joke. "Nobody has that kind of control. Not even ten-ringers." She's heard the stories; they can do amazing things. Not impossible things.

"'They are the gods in chains,'" Alabaster breathes, and she realizes he's falling asleep. Exhausted from fighting for his life—or maybe working miracles is just harder than it seems. "'The tamers of the wild earth, themselves to be bridled and muzzled.'"

"What's that?" He's quoting something.

"Stonelore."

"Bullshit. That's not on any of the Three Tablets."

"Tablet Five."

He's so full of shit. And he's drifting off. Earth, she's going to kill him.

"Alabaster! Answer my rusting *question*." Silence. Earth damn it. "What is it you keep doing to me?"

He exhales, long and heavily, and she thinks he's out. But he says, "Parallel scaling. Pull a carriage with one animal and it goes only so far. Put two in a line, the one in front tires out first. Yoke them side by side, *synchronize* them, reduce the friction lost between their movements, and you get more than you would from both animals individually." He sighs again. "That's the theory, anyway."

"And you're what, the yoke?"

She's joking. But he nods.

A yoke. That's worse. He's been treating her like an *animal*, forcing her to work for him so he won't burn out. "How are you—" She rejects the word *how,* which assumes possibility where none should exist. "Orogenes can't work together. One torus subsumes another. The greater degree of control takes precedence." It's a lesson they both learned in the grit crucibles.

"Well, then." He's so close to sleep that the words are slurred. "Guess it didn't happen."

She's so furious that she's blind with it for an instant; the world goes white. Orogenes can't afford that kind of rage, so she releases it in words. "Don't give me that shit! I don't want you to ever do that to me again—" But how can she stop him? "Or I'll kill you, do you hear? You have no right!"

"Saved my life." It's almost a mumble, but she hears it, and it stabs her anger in the back. "Thanks."

Because really, can she blame a drowning man for grabbing anyone nearby to save himself?

Or to save thousands of people?

Or to save his son?

He's asleep now, sitting beside the little puddle of ick he threw up. Of course that's on her side of the bed. In disgust, Syen drags her legs up to curl into the plush chair and tries to get comfortable.

Only when she settles does it occur to her what's happened. The core of it, not just the part about Alabaster doing the impossible.

When she was a grit, she did kitchen duty sometimes, and every once in a while they would open a jar of fruit or vegetables that had gone bad. The funky ones, those that had cracked or come partially open, were so foul-smelling that the cooks would have to open windows and set some grits on fanning duty to get the stench out. But far worse, Syen had learned, were the jars that didn't crack. The stuff inside them looked fine; opened, it didn't smell bad. The only warning of danger was a little buckling of the metal lid.

"Kill you deader than swapthrisk bite," the head cook, a grizzled old Resistant, would say as he showed them the suspect jar so they could know what to watch for. "Pure poison. Your muscles lock up and stop working. You can't even breathe. And it's potent. I could kill everybody in the Fulcrum with this one jar." And he would laugh, as if that notion were funny.

Mixed into a bowl of stew, a few drops of that taint would be more than enough to kill one annoying middle-aged rogga.

Could it have been an accident? No reputable cook would use anything from a pucker-lidded jar, but maybe the Season's End Inn hires incompetents. Syenite had placed the order for the food herself, speaking with the child who'd come up to see if they needed anything. Had she specified whose order was whose? She tries to remember what she said. "*Fish and yams for me.*" So they would've been able to guess that the stew was for Alabaster.

Why not dose them both, then, if someone at the inn hates roggas enough to try to kill them? Easy enough to drop some toxic vegetable juice into all the food, not just Alabaster's. Maybe they have, and it just hasn't affected her yet? But she feels fine.

You're being paranoid, she tells herself.

But it's not her imagination that everyone hates her. She's a rogga, after all.

Frustrated, Syen shifts in the chair, wrapping her arms around her knees and trying to make herself sleep. It's a losing game. Her head's too full of questions, and her body's too used to hard ground barely padded by a bedroll. She ends up sitting up for the rest of the night, gazing out the window at a world that has begun to make less and less sense, and wondering what the rust she's supposed to do about it.

But in the morning when she leans out the window to inhale the dew-laden air in a futile attempt to shake herself to alertness, she happens to glance up. There, winking in the dawn light, is a great hovering shard of amethyst. Just an obelisk—one she vaguely remembers seeing the day before, as they were riding into Allia. They're always beautiful, but so are the lingering stars, and she hardly pays attention to either in the normal course of affairs.

She notices this one now, however. Because today, it's a lot closer than it was yesterday.

* * *

Set a flexible central beam at the heart of all structures.
Trust wood, trust stone, but metal rusts.

—Tablet Three, "Structures," verse one

10

you walk beside the beast

You think, maybe, you need to be someone else.

You're not sure who. Previous yous have been stronger and colder, or warmer and weaker; either set of qualities is better suited to getting you through the mess you're in. Right now you're cold and weak, and that helps no one.

You could become someone new, maybe. You've done that before; it's surprisingly easy. A new name, a new focus, then try on the sleeves and slacks of a new personality to find the perfect fit. A few days and you'll feel like you've never been anyone else.

But. Only one you is Nassun's mother. That's what's forestalled you so far, and ultimately it's the deciding factor. At the end of all this, when Jija is dead and it's finally safe to mourn your son... if she still lives, Nassun will need the mother she's known all her life.

So you must stay Essun, and Essun will have to make do with the broken bits of herself that Jija has left behind. You'll jigsaw them together however you can, caulk in the odd bits with willpower wherever they don't quite fit, ignore the occasional sounds of grinding and cracking. As long as nothing important breaks, right? You'll get by. You have no choice. Not as long as one of your children could be alive.

* * *

You wake to the sounds of battle.

You and the boy have camped at a roadhouse for the night, amid several hundred other people who clearly had the same idea. No one's actually sleeping *in* the roadhouse—which in this case is little more than a windowless stone-walled shack with a well pump inside—because by unspoken agreement it is neutral territory. And likewise none of the several dozen camps of people arrayed around the roadhouse have made much effort to interact, because by unspoken agreement they are all terrified enough to stab first and ask questions later. The world has changed too quickly and too thoroughly. Stonelore might have tried to prepare everyone for the particulars, but the all-encompassing horror of the Season is still a shock that no one can cope with easily. After all, just a week ago, everything was normal.

You and Hoa settled down and built a fire for the night in a nearby clearing amid the plainsgrass. You have no choice but to split a watch with the child, even though you fear he'll just fall asleep; with this many people around it's too dangerous to be careless. Thieves are the greatest potential problem, since you've got a full runny-sack and the two of you are just a woman and a boy traveling alone. Fire's a danger, too, with all these people who don't know the business end of a matchflint spending the night in a field of dying grass. But you're exhausted. It's only been a week since you were living your own cushy, predictable life, and it's going to take you a while to get back up to traveling condition. So you order the boy to wake you as soon as the peat block burns out. That should've given you four or five hours.

But it's *many* hours later, almost dawn, when people start screaming on the far side of the makeshift camp. Shouts rise on this side as people around you cry alarm, and you struggle out of the bedroll and to your feet. You're not sure who's screaming. You're not sure why. Doesn't matter. You just grab the runny-sack with one hand and the boy with the other, and turn to run.

He jerks away before you can do so, and grabs his little rag bundle. Then he takes your hand again, his icewhite eyes very wide in the dimness.

Then you—all of you, everyone nearby as well as you and the boy—are running, running, farther into the plains and away from the road because that's the direction the first screams came from, and because thieves or commless or militias or whoever is causing the trouble will probably use the road to leave when they've finished whatever they're doing. In the ashy predawn half-light all the people around you are merely half-real shadows running in parallel. For a time, the boy and the sack and the ground under your feet are the only parts of the world that exist.

A long while later your strength gives out, and you finally stagger to a halt.

"What was that?" Hoa asks. He doesn't sound out of breath at all. The resilience of children. Of course, you didn't run the whole way; you're too flabby and unfit for that. The bottom line was to keep moving, which you did do, walking when you couldn't muster the breath to run.

"I didn't see," you reply. It doesn't really matter what it was, anyway. You rub at a cramp in your side. Dehydration; you take out your canteen to drink. But when you do, you grimace at its near-empty slosh. Of course you didn't take the chance to fill it while you were at the roadhouse. You'd been planning to do that come morning.

"I didn't see, either," says the boy, turning back and craning his neck as if he ought to be able to. "Everything was quiet and then..." He shrugs.

You eye him. "You didn't fall asleep, did you?" You saw the fire before you fled. It was down to a smolder. He should've woken you hours ago.

"No."

You give him the look that has cowed two of your own and several dozen other people's children. He draws back from it, looking confused. "I *didn't.*"

"Why didn't you wake me when the peat burned down?"

"You needed to sleep. I wasn't sleepy."

Damnation. That means he *will* be sleepy later. Earth eat hardheaded children.

"Does your side hurt?" Hoa steps closer, looking anxious. "Are you hurt?"

"Just a stitch. It'll go away eventually." You look around, though visibility in the ashfall is iffy past twenty feet or so. There's no sign that anyone else is nearby, and you can't hear any other sounds from the area around the roadhouse. There's no sound around you, in fact, but the very soft tipple of ash on the grass. Logically, the other people who were camped around the roadhouse can't be that far away—but you *feel* completely alone, aside from Hoa. "We're going to have to go back to the roadhouse."

"For your things?"

"Yes. And water." You squint in the direction of the roadhouse, useless as that is when the plain just fades into white-gray haze a short ways off. You can't be sure the next roadhouse will be usable. It might have been taken over by would-be warlords, or destroyed by panicked mobs; it might be malfunctioning.

"You could go back." You turn to the boy, who is sitting down on the grass—and to your surprise, he's got something in his mouth. He didn't have any food before…oh. He knots his rag bundle firmly shut and swallows before speaking again. "To the creek where you made me take a bath."

That's a possibility. The creek vanished underground again not far from where you used it; that's only a day's walk away. But it's a day's walk *back* the way you came, and…

And nothing. Going back to the stream is the safest option. Your reluctance to do this is stupid and wrong.

But Nassun is somewhere *ahead.*

"What is he doing to her?" you ask, softly. "He must know what she is, by now."

The boy only watches. If he worries about you, he doesn't let it show on his face.

Well, you're about to give him more reason for concern. "We'll go back to the roadhouse. It's been long enough. Thieves or bandits or whatever would've taken what they wanted by now and moved on."

Unless what they wanted was *the roadhouse.* Several of the Stillness's oldest comms started as sources of water seized by the strongest group in a given area, and held against all comers until a Season ended. It's the great hope of the commless in such times—that with no comm willing to take them in, they might forge their own. Still, few commless groups are organized enough, sociable enough, strong enough, to do it successfully.

And few have had to contend with an orogene who wanted the water more than they did.

"If they want to keep it," you say, and you mean it, even though this is such a small thing, you just want water, but in that moment every obstacle looms large as a mountain and *orogenes eat mountains for breakfast*, "they'd better let me have some."

The boy, whom you half-expect to run away screaming after this statement, merely gets to his feet. You purchased clothing for him at the last comm you passed, along with the peat. Now he's got good sturdy walking boots and good thick socks, two full changes of clothing, and a jacket that's remarkably similar to your own. Apart from his bizarre looks, the matching garb makes you look like you're together. That sort of thing sends unspoken messages of organization, shared focus, group membership; it's not much, but every little deterrent helps. *Such a formidable pair we are, crazy woman and changeling child.*

"Come on," you say, and start walking. He follows.

It's quiet as you approach the roadhouse. You can tell you're close by the disturbances in the meadow: Here's someone's abandoned campsite, with still-smoldering fire; there's someone's torn runny-sack, trailed by supplies grabbed and dropped in flight. There's a ring of pulled grass, campfire coals, and an abandoned bedroll that might've been yours. You scoop it up in passing and roll it up, jabbing it through the straps of your sack to tie properly later. And then, sooner than you were expecting, there is the roadhouse itself.

You think at first there's no one here. You can't hear anything but your own footsteps, and your breath. The boy is mostly silent, but his footsteps are oddly heavy against the asphalt when you step back onto the road. You glance at him, and he seems to realize it. He stops, looking intently at your feet as you keep walking. Watching how you roll from heel to toes, not so much planting a step as peeling your feet off the ground and carefully reapplying them. Then he begins doing the same thing, and if you didn't need to pay attention to your surroundings—if you weren't distracted by the racing of your own heart—you would laugh at the surprise on his little face when his own footfalls become silent. He's almost cute.

But that's when you step into the roadhouse, and realize you're not alone.

First you notice just the pump and the cement casing it's set into; that's really all the roadhouse is, a shelter for the pump. Then you see a woman, who is humming to herself as she pulls away one large canteen and sets another, empty and even larger, in its place beneath the spigot. She bustles around the casing to work the pump mechanism, busy as you please, and only sees you after she's started working the lever again. Then she freezes, and you and she stare at each other.

She's commless. No one who's suffered only recent homelessness would be so filthy. (Except the boy, a part of your mind supplies, but there's a difference between disaster filth and *unwashed* filth.) This woman's hair is matted, not in clean, well-groomed locks like yours but from sheer neglect; it hangs in moldy, uneven clumps from her head. Her skin isn't just covered in dirt; the dirt is ground in, a permanent fixture. There's iron ore in some of it and it's rusted from the moisture in her skin, tinting the pattern of her pores red. Some of her clothes are fresh—given how much you saw abandoned around the roadhouse, easy to guess where she got those—and the pack at her feet is one of three, each one fat with supplies and dangling an already-filled canteen. But her body odor is so high and ripe that you hope she's taking all that water to use for a bath.

Her eyes flick over you and Hoa, assessing just as quickly and thoroughly, and then after a moment she shrugs a little and finishes pumping, filling the large canteen in two strokes. Then she takes it, caps it, attaches it again to one of the big packs at her feet, and—so deftly that you're a little awed—scoops up all three and scuttles back. "Have at."

You've seen commless before, of course; everyone has. In cities that want cheaper labor than Strongbacks—and where the Strongbacks' union is weak—they live in shantytowns and beg on the streets. Everywhere else, they live in the spaces between comms, forests and the edges of deserts and such, where they survive by hunting game and building encampments out of scraps. The ones who don't want trouble raid fields and silos on the outskirts of comm territories; the ones who like a fight raid small, poorly defended comms and attack travelers along the lesser quartent roads. Quartent governors don't mind a little of this. Keeps everyone sharp, and reminds troublemakers of how they could end up. Too many thefts, though, or too violent an attack and militias get sent out to hunt the commless down.

None of that matters now. "We don't want any trouble," you say. "We're just here for water, same as you."

The woman, who's been looking with curiosity at Hoa, flicks

her gaze back to you. "Not like *I'm* starting any." Rather deliberately she caps another canteen she's filled. "Got more of these to fill, though, so." She jerks her chin at your pack and the canteen dangling from it. "Yours won't take long."

Hers are truly huge. They're also probably heavy as logs. "Are you waiting for others to come?"

"Nope." The woman grins, flashing remarkably good teeth. If she's commless now, she didn't start out that way; those gums haven't known much malnutrition. "Gonna kill me?"

You have to admit, you weren't expecting that.

"She must have someplace nearby," Hoa says. You're pleased to see that he's at the door, looking outward. Still on guard. Smart boy.

"Yep," says the woman, cheerfully unperturbed that they have sussed out her ostensible secret. "Gonna follow me?"

"No," you say, firmly. "We're not interested in you. Leave us be and we'll do the same."

"Solid by me."

You unsling your canteen and edge over to the pump. It's awkward; the thing is meant to be worked by one person while another holds a container.

The woman puts a hand on the pump, silently offering. You nod, and she pumps for you. You drink your fill first, and then there's tense silence while the canteen fills. Nerves make you break it. "You took a big risk coming here. Everyone else is probably coming back soon."

"A few, and not soon. And you took the same big risk."

"True."

"So." The woman nods toward her pile of filled canteens,

and belatedly you see—what is that? Atop one of the canteens' mouths is some kind of little contraption made of sticks, twisted leaves, and a piece of crooked wire. It clicks softly as you stare. "Running a test, anyway."

"What?"

She shrugs, eyeing you, and you realize it then: This woman is no more an ordinary commless than you are a still.

"That shake from the north," she says. "It was at least a niner—and that was just what we felt on the surface. It was deep, too." She pauses abruptly, actually cocking her head away from you and frowning, as if she's heard something startling, though there's nothing there but the wall. "Never seen a shake like that. Weird wave pattern to it." Then she focuses on you again, bird-quick. "Probably breached a lot of aquifers. They'll repair themselves over time, of course, but in the short term, no telling what kinds of contaminants might be around here. I mean, this is perfect land for a city, right? Flat, ready access to water, nowhere near a fault. Means there probably *was* one here, at some point. You know what kinds of nasty things cities leave behind when they die?"

You're staring at her now. Hoa is, too, but he stares at everyone like that. Then the thing in the canteen finishes clicking, and the commless woman bends over to pluck it free. It had been dangling a strip of something—tree bark?—into the water.

"Safe," she proclaims, and then belatedly seems to notice you staring. She frowns a little and holds up the little strip. "It's made from the same plant as safe. You know? The greeting tea? But I treated it with a little something extra, to catch those substances safe doesn't catch."

"There's nothing," you blurt, and then you fall silent, uneasy, when she focuses sharply on you. Now you have to finish. "I mean…there's nothing safe misses that would hurt people." That's the only reason anyone drinks it, because it tastes like boiled ass.

Now the woman looks annoyed. "That's not true. Where the rust did you learn that?" It's something you used to teach in the Tirimo creche, but before you can say this she snaps, "Safe doesn't work as well if it's in a cold solution; everybody knows that. Needs to be room temperature or lukewarm. It also doesn't catch things that kill you in a few months instead of a few minutes. Fat lot of good it'll do you to survive today, only to come down with skinpeel next year!"

"You're a geomest," you blurt. It seems impossible. You've met geomests. They're everything people think orogenes are when they're feeling charitable: arcane, unfathomable, possessed of knowledge no mortal should have, disturbing. No one but a geomest would know so many useless facts, so thoroughly.

"I am not." The woman draws herself up, almost swelling in her fury. "I know better than to pay attention to those fools at the University. I'm not *stupid*."

You stare again, in utter confusion. Then your canteen overflows and you scramble to find the cap for it. She stops pumping, then tucks the little bark contraption into a pocket among her voluminous skirts and starts to disassemble one of the smaller packs at her feet, her movements brisk and efficient. She pulls free a canteen—the same size as yours—and tosses it aside, then when the small pack's empty, she tosses that aside, too. Your eyes lock on to both items. It would be easier on you if the boy could carry his own supplies.

"You'd better grab, if you're going to," the woman says, and though she's not looking at you, you realize she intentionally set the items out for you. "I'm not staying, and you shouldn't, either."

You edge over to take the canteen and the empty small pack. The woman stands again to help you fill the new canteen before resuming her rummaging through her own stuff. While you tie on your canteen and the bedroll you grabbed earlier, and transfer a few items from your pack into the smaller one for the boy, you say, "Do you know what happened? Who did what?" You gesture vaguely in the direction of the screams that woke you up.

"I doubt it was a 'who,'" the woman says. She tosses away several packets of gone-off food, a child's set of pants that might be big enough for Hoa, and books. Who puts books in a runny-sack? Though the woman glances at the title of each before throwing it aside. "People don't react as quickly as nature to changes like this."

You attach the second canteen to your own pack for now, since you know better than to make Hoa carry too much weight. He's just a boy, and a poorly grown one at that. Since the comm-less woman clearly doesn't want them, you also pick up the pants from the small pile of discards that's growing beside her. She doesn't seem to care.

You ask, "What, you mean that was some kind of animal attack?"

"Didn't you see the body?"

"Didn't know there *was* a body. People screamed and started running, so we did, too."

The woman sighs. "That's not unwise, but it does lose you… opportunities." As if to illustrate her point she tosses aside another pack that she's just emptied and stands, shouldering the two that remain. One of them is more worn and obviously comfortable than the other: her own. She's used twine to lash the heavy canteens together so that they nestle against the small of her back, supported by the not-insubstantial curve of her ass, rather than hanging as most canteens do. Abruptly she glowers at you. "Don't follow me."

"Wasn't planning to." The small pack's ready to be given to Hoa. You strap on your own, check to make sure everything's secure and comfy.

"I mean it." She leans forward a little, her whole face almost feral in its fierceness. "You don't know what I'm going back to. I could live in a walled compound with fifty other rusters just like me. We might have tooth-files and a 'juicy stupid people' recipe book."

"Okay, okay." You take a step back, which seems to mollify her. Now she goes from fierce to relaxed, and resumes settling her packs for comfort. You've got what you want, too, so it's time to get out of here. The boy looks pleased by his new pack when you hand it to him; you help him put it on properly. As you do this, the commless woman passes you to leave, and some vestige of your old self makes you say, "Thanks, by the way."

"Anytime," she says airily, heading through the door—and abruptly she stops. She's staring at something. The look on her face makes all the hairs on the back of your neck prickle. Quickly you go to the door as well, to see what she's seeing.

It's a kirkhusa—one of the long-bodied, furry creatures midlatters keep as pets instead of dogs, since dogs are too expensive for anyone except the most ostentatious Equatorials. Kirkhusa look more like big land-bound otters than canines. They're trainable, cheap as anything because they eat only the leaves of low bushes and the insects that grow on them. And they're even cuter than puppies when they're small... but *this* kirkhusa isn't cute. It's big, a good hundred pounds of healthy, sleek-furred flesh. Someone's loved it dearly, at least until lately: That's a fine leather collar still round its neck. It's growling, and as it slinks out of the grass and up onto the road, you see red blooms in the fur around its mouth and on its clawed, prehensile paws.

That's the problem with kirkhusa, see. The reason everyone can afford them. They eat leaves—until they taste enough ash, which triggers some instinct within them that's normally dormant. Then they change. Everything changes during a Season.

"Shit," you whisper.

The commless woman hisses beside you, and you tense, feeling your awareness descend briefly into the earth. (You drag it back, out of habit. Not around other people. Not unless you have no other choice.) She's moved to the edge of the asphalt, where she was probably about to bolt into the meadow and toward a distant stand of trees. But not far from the road, around the place where people screamed earlier, you see the grass moving violently and hear the soft houghs and squeals of other kirkhusa—how many, you can't tell. They're busy, though. Eating.

This one used to be a pet. Maybe it remembers its human master fondly. Maybe it hesitated when the others attacked, and failed to earn more than a taste of the meat that will be its new staple diet until the Season ends. Now it will go hungry if it doesn't rethink its civilized ways. It pads back and forth on the asphalt, chittering to itself as if in indecision—but it doesn't leave. It's got you and Hoa and the commless woman boxed in while it wrestles with its conscience. Poor, poor thing.

You set your feet and murmur to Hoa—and the woman, if she feels like listening—"Don't move."

But before you can find something harmless to latch on to, a rock inclusion you can shift or a water source you can geyser that will give you an excuse to snatch the warmth from the air and the life from this overgrown squirrel, Hoa glances at you and steps forward.

"I said," you begin, grabbing his shoulder to yank him back—but he doesn't yank. It's like trying to move a rock that's wearing a jacket; your hand just slips off the leather. Underneath it, he doesn't move at all.

The protest dies in your mouth as the boy continues to move forward. He's not simply being disobedient, you realize; there's too much purpose in his posture. You're not sure he even *noticed* your attempt to stop him.

And then the boy is facing the creature, a few feet away. It's stopped prowling, and stands tensed as if—wait. What? *Not* as if it's going to attack. It lowers its head and twitches its stubby tail, once, uncertainly. *Defensively.*

The boy's back is to you. You can't see his face, but all at once his stocky little frame seems less little, and less harmless. He lifts a hand and extends it toward the kirkhusa, as if offering it to sniff. As if it's still a pet.

The kirkhusa attacks.

It's fast. They're quick animals anyway, but you see the twitch of its muscles and then it's five feet closer, its mouth is open, and its teeth have closed around the boy's hand up to the middle of his forearm. And, oh Earth, you can't watch this, a child dying in front of you as Uche did not, how could you let either happen, you are the worst person in the whole world.

But maybe—if you can concentrate, ice the animal and not the boy—you lower your gaze to try to concentrate as the commless woman gasps and the boy's blood splatters the asphalt. Watching Hoa's mauling will make it harder; what matters is saving his life, even if he loses the arm. But then—

Silence falls.

You look up.

The kirkhusa has stopped moving. It's still where it was, teeth locked on Hoa's arm, its eyes wild with...something that is more fear than fury. It's even shaking, faintly. You hear it make the most fleeting of aborted sounds, just a hollow squeal.

Then the kirkhusa's fur starts to move. (What?) You frown, squint, but it's easy to see, close as the beast is. Each individual hair of its fur waggles, seemingly in a different direction all at the same time. Then it shimmers. *(What?)* Stiffens. All at once you realize that not only are its muscles stiff, but the flesh that covers them is stiff, too. Not just stiff but...solid.

And then you notice: *The whole kirkhusa* is solid.

What.

You don't understand what you're seeing, so you keep staring, comprehending in pieces. Its eyes have become glass, its claws crystal, its teeth some sort of ocher filament. Where there was movement, now there is stillness; its muscles are rock-hard, and that is not a metaphor. Its fur was just the last part of its body to change, twisting about as the follicles underneath transformed into *something else*.

You and the commless woman both stare.

Wow.

Really. That's what you're thinking. You've got nothing better. Wow.

That's enough to get you moving, at least. You edge forward until you can see the whole tableau from a better angle, but nothing really changes. The boy still seems fine, although his arm is still halfway down the thing's gullet. The kirkhusa is still pretty damn dead. Well. Pretty, and damn dead.

Hoa glances at you, and all at once you realize how deeply unhappy he looks. Like he's ashamed. Why? He's saved all of your lives, even if the method was... You don't know what this is.

"Did you do this?" you ask him.

He lowers his eyes. "I hadn't meant for you to see this, yet."

Okay. That's... something to think about later. "What did you do?"

He presses his lips shut.

Now he decides to sulk. But then, maybe now's not the time for this conversation, given that his arm is stuck in a glass monster's teeth. The teeth have pierced his skin; there's blood welling and dripping down its no-longer-flesh lower jaw. "Your arm. Let me..." You look around. "Let me find something to break you out."

Hoa seems to remember his arm, belatedly. He glances at you again, plainly not liking that you're watching, but then sighs a little in resignation. And he flexes his arm, before you can warn him not to do anything that might wound him further.

The kirkhusa's head shatters. Great chunks of heavy stone thud to the ground; glittering dust sprays. The boy's arm is bleeding more, but free. He flexes his fingers a little. They're fine. He lowers the arm to his side.

You react to his wound, reaching for his arm because that is something you can comprehend and do something about. But he pulls away quickly, covering the marks with his other hand. "Hoa, let me—"

"I'm fine," he says, quietly. "We should go, though."

The other kirkhusa are still close, though they're busy chewing on some poor fool in the plainsgrass. That meal won't last them forever. Worse, it's only a matter of time before other desperate people make the choice to brave the roadhouse again, hoping the bad things have gone.

One of the bad things is still right here, you think, looking at the kirkhusa's topless lower jaw. You can see the rough nodules on the back of its tongue, now gleaming in crystal. Then you turn to Hoa, who is holding his bloody arm and looking miserable.

It's the misery, finally, that pushes the fear back down inside you, replaces it with something more familiar. Did he do this because he didn't know you could defend yourself? For some other, unfathomable reason? In the end, it doesn't matter. You have no idea what to do with a monster who can turn living things into statuary, but you do know how to handle an unhappy child.

Also, you have a lot of experience with children who are secretly monsters.

So you offer your hand. Hoa looks surprised. He stares at it, then at you, and there is something in his gaze that is entirely human, and grateful for your acceptance in that moment. It makes you feel a little more human, too, amazingly.

He takes your hand. His grip seems no weaker despite his wounds, so you pull him along as you turn south and start walking again. The commless woman wordlessly follows, or maybe she's walking in the same direction, or maybe she just thinks there's strength in numbers. None of you say anything because there's nothing to say.

Behind you, in the meadow, the kirkhusa keep eating.

* * *

Beware ground on loose rock. Beware hale strangers.

Beware sudden silence.

—*Tablet One, "On Survival," verse three*

11

Damaya at the fulcrum of it all

THERE'S AN ORDER TO LIFE in the Fulcrum.

Waking comes with dawn. Since that's what Damaya always did back on the farm, this is easy for her. For the other grits—and that's what she is now, an unimportant bit of rock ready to be polished into usefulness, or at least to help grind other, better rocks—waking comes when one of the instructors enters the dormitory and rings a painfully loud bell, which makes them all flinch even if they're already awake. Everyone groans, including Damaya. She likes this. It makes her feel like she's part of something.

They rise and make their beds, folding the top sheets military-style. Then they shuffle into the showers, which are white with electric lights and shining with tile, and which smell of herbal cleaners because the Fulcrum hires Strongbacks and commless from Yumenes' shantytowns to come and clean them. For this and other reasons the showers are wonderful. She's never been able to use hot water every day like this, tons of it just falling from holes in the ceiling like the most perfect rain ever. She tries not to be obvious about it, because some of the other grits are Equatorials and would laugh at her, the bumpkin overwhelmed by the novelty of easy, comfortable cleanliness. But, well, she is.

After that the grits brush their teeth and come back to the dormitory room to dress and groom themselves. Their uniforms are stiff gray fabric pants and tunics with black piping, girls and boys alike. Children whose hair is long and locked or thin enough to be combed and pulled back must do so; children whose hair is ashblow or kinky or short must make sure it's shaped neatly. Then the grits stand in front of their beds, waiting while instructors come in and move down the rows for inspection. They want to make sure the grits are actually clean. The instructors check the beds, too, to make sure no one's peed in theirs or done a shoddy job of folding the corners. Grits who aren't clean are sent back for another shower—this one cold, with the instructor standing there watching to make sure it's done right. (Damaya makes sure she'll never have to do this, because it doesn't sound fun at all.) Grits who haven't dressed and groomed themselves or tended the bed properly are sent to Discipline, where they receive punishments suited to the infraction. Uncombed hair gets cut very short; repeat offenders are shaven bald. Unbrushed teeth merit mouthwashing with soap. Incorrect dress is corrected with five switches across the naked buttocks or back, incorrect bedmaking with ten. The switches do not break the skin—instructors are trained to strike just enough—but they do leave welts, which are probably meant to chafe underneath the stiff fabric of the uniforms.

You are representatives of us all, the instructors say, if any grit dares to protest this treatment. *When you're dirty, all orogenes are dirty. When you're lazy, we're all lazy. We hurt you so you'll do the rest of us no harm.*

Once Damaya would have protested the unfairness of such judgments. The children of the Fulcrum are all different: different ages, different colors, different shapes. Some speak Sanze-mat with different accents, having originated from different parts of the world. One girl has sharp teeth because it is her race's custom to file them; another boy has no penis, though he stuffs a sock into his underwear after every shower; another girl has rarely had regular meals and wolfs down every one like she's still starving. (The instructors keep finding food hidden in and around her bed. They make her eat it, all of it, in front of them, even if it makes her sick.) One cannot reasonably expect sameness out of so much difference, and it makes no sense for Damaya to be judged by the behavior of children who share nothing save the curse of orogeny with her.

But Damaya understands now that the world is not fair. They are orogenes, the Misalems of the world, born cursed and terrible. This is what is necessary to make them safe. Anyway, if she does what she's supposed to, no unexpected things happen. Her bed is always perfect, her teeth clean and white. When she starts to forget what matters, she looks at her right hand, which twinges now and again on cold days, though the bones healed within a few weeks. She remembers the pain, and the lesson that it taught.

After inspection there is breakfast—just a bit of fruit and a piece of sausage in the Sanzed fashion, which they pick up in the dormitory foyer and eat on the way. They walk in small groups to lessons in the various courts of the Fulcrum that the older grits call crucibles, though that's not what they're supposed to be called. (There are many things the grits say to each other that they can never say to the adults. The adults know, but pretend they don't. The world is not fair, and sometimes it makes no sense.)

In the first crucible, which is roofed over, the first hours of the day are spent in chairs with a slateboard and a lecture by one of the Fulcrum's instructors. Sometimes there are oral examinations, with questions peppered at the grits one by one until someone falters. The grit who falters will have to clean the slateboards. Thus do they learn to work calmly under pressure.

"What was the name of the first Old Sanze emperor?"

"A shake in Erta emits push waves at 6:35 and seven seconds, and vibrational waves at 6:37 and twenty-seven seconds. What is the lag time?" This question becomes more complex if it is asked of older grits, going into logarithms and functions.

"Stonelore advises, 'Watch for the center of the circle.' Where is the fallacy in this statement?"

This is the question that lands on Damaya one day, so she stands to answer: "The statement explains how one may estimate the location of an orogene by map," she says. "It is incorrect—oversimplified—because an orogene's region of consumption is not *circular,* it is *toroidal.* Many people then fail to understand that the zone of effect extends downward or upward as well, and can be deformed in other three-dimensional ways by a skilled orogene."

Instructor Marcasite nods approval for this explanation, which makes Damaya feel proud. She likes being right. Marcasite continues: "And since stonelore would be harder to remember if it was full of phrases like 'watch for the inverted fulcrum of a conical torus,' we get centers and circles. Accuracy is sacrificed in the name of better poetry."

This makes the class laugh. It's not that funny, but there's a lot of nervous tension on quiz days.

After lectures there is lunch in the big open-air court set aside for that purpose. This court has a roof of oiled canvas strips on slats, which can be rolled shut on rainy days—although Yumenes, which is far inland, rarely has such days. So the grits usually get to sit at long bench-tables under a bright blue sky as they giggle and kick each other and call each other names. There's lots of food to make up for the light breakfast, all of it varied and delicious and rich, though much of it is from distant lands and Damaya does not know what some of it is called. (She eats her share anyway. Muh Dear taught her never to waste food.)

This is Damaya's favorite time of day, even though she is one of the grits who sit alone at an empty table. Many of the other children do this, she has noticed—too many to dismiss them all as those who've failed to make friends. The others have a look to them that she is rapidly learning to recognize—a certain furtiveness of movement, a hesitancy, a tension about the eyes and jawline. Some of them bear the marks of their old lives in a more obvious way. There is a gray-haired western Coaster boy who's missing an arm above the elbow, though he is deft enough at managing without it. A Sanzed girl maybe five years older has the twisting seams of old burn scars all down one side of her face. And then there is another grit even newer than Damaya, whose left hand is in a special leather binding like a glove without fingers, which fastens around the wrist. Damaya recognizes this binding because she wore it herself while her hand healed, during her first few weeks at the Fulcrum.

They do not look at each other much, she and these others who sit off to themselves.

After lunch the grits travel through the Ring Garden in long, silent lines overseen by the instructors so that they will not talk or stare too obviously at the adult orogenes. Damaya does stare, of course, because they're supposed to. It's important that they see what awaits them once they begin earning rings. The garden is a wonder, as are the orogenes themselves: adult and elderly of every conformation, all healthy and beautiful—confident, which makes them beautiful. All are starkly forbidding in their black uniforms and polished boots. Their ringed fingers flick and flash as they gesture freely, or turn the pages of books they don't *have* to read, or brush back a lover's curling hair from one ear.

What Damaya sees in them is something she does not understand at first, though she *wants* it with a desperation that surprises and unnerves her. As those first weeks pass into months and she grows familiar with the routine, she begins to understand what it is that the older orogenes display: control. They have mastered their power. No ringed orogene would ice the courtyard just because some boy shoved her. None of these sleek, black-clad professionals would bat so much as an eyelash at either a strong earthshake, or a family's rejection. They know what they are, and they have accepted all that means, and they fear nothing—not the stills, not themselves, not even Old Man Earth.

If to achieve this Damaya must endure a few broken bones, or a few years in a place where no one loves or even likes her, that is a small price to pay.

Thus she pours herself into the afternoon training in Applied Orogeny. In the practice crucibles, which are situated within the innermost ring of the Fulcrum complex, Damaya stands in a row with other grits of a similar level of experience. There, under an instructor's watchful gaze, she learns how to visualize and breathe, and to extend her awareness of the earth at will and not merely in reaction to its movements or her own agitation. She learns to control her agitation, and all the other emotions that can induce the power within her to react to a threat that does not exist. The grits have no fine control at this stage, so none of them are allowed to actually *move* anything. The instructors can tell, somehow, when they're about to—and because the instructors all have rings, they can pierce any child's developing torus in a way that Damaya does not yet understand, administering a quick, stunning slap of icy cold air as a warning. It is a reminder of the seriousness of the lesson—and it also lends credence to a rumor that the older grits have whispered in the dark after lights out. *If you make too many mistakes in the lessons, the instructors ice you.*

It will be many years before Damaya understands that when the instructors kill an errant student, it is meant not as a goad, but as a mercy.

After Applied comes dinner and free hour, a time in which they may do what they please, allowed in deference to their youth. The newest grits usually fall into bed early, exhausted by the effort of learning to control invisible, semivoluntary muscles. The older children have better stamina and more energy, so there's laughter and play around the dormitory bunks for a while, until the instructors declare lights-out. The next day, it all begins again.

Thus do six months pass.

* * *

One of the older grits comes over to Damaya at lunch. The boy is tall and Equatorial, though he doesn't look fully Sanzed. His hair has the ashblow texture, but it's backwater blond in color. He's got the broad shoulders and developing bulk of Strongback, which makes her wary at once. She still sees Zab everywhere.

The boy smiles, though, and there is no menace in his manner as he stops beside the small table she inhabits alone. "Can I sit down?"

She shrugs, because she doesn't want him to but is curious despite herself. He puts down his tray and sits. "I'm Arkete," he says.

"That's not your name," she replies, and his smile falters a little.

"It's the name my parents gave me," he says, more seriously, "and it's the name I intend to keep until they find a way to take it from me. Which they'll never do because, y'know, it's a name. But if you'd rather, I'm *officially* called Maxixe."

The highest-quality grade of aquamarine, used almost exclusively for art. It suits him; he's a handsome boy despite his obvious Arctic or Antarctic heritage (she doesn't care, but Equatorials do), and that makes him dangerous in the sharp-faceted way that handsome big boys have always been. She decides to call him Maxixe because of this. "What do you want?"

"Wow, you're really working on your popularity." Maxixe

starts eating, resting his elbows on the table while he chews. (But he checks to make sure there are no instructors around to chide him on his manners, first.) "You know how these things are supposed to work, right? The good-looking popular guy suddenly shows interest in the mousy girl from the country. Everyone hates her for it, but she starts to gain confidence in herself. Then the guy betrays her and regrets it. It's awful, but afterward she 'finds herself,' realizes she doesn't need him, and maybe there's some other stuff that happens"—he waggles his fingers in the air—"and finally she turns into the most beautiful girl ever because she likes herself. But it won't work at all if you don't stammer and blush and pretend you don't like me."

She's utterly confused by this salad of words. It annoys her so much that she says, "I *don't* like you."

"Ouch." He pantomimes being stabbed in the heart. In spite of herself, his antics do make Damaya relax a little. This makes him grin, in turn. "Ah, that's better. What, don't you read books? Or didn't you have lorists in whatever midlatter hole you came from?"

She doesn't read books, because she's not very good at reading yet. Her parents taught her enough to get by, and the instructors have assigned her a weekly regimen of additional reading to improve her skills in this area. But she's not about to admit that. "Of course we had lorists. They taught us stonelore and told us how to prepare—"

"Urgh. You had *real* lorists." The boy shakes his head. "Where I grew up, nobody listened to them except creche teachers and the most boring geomests. What everybody liked instead were the pop lorists—you know, the kind who perform in ampitheaters and bars? Their stories don't teach anything. They're just fun."

Damaya has never heard of this, but maybe it's some Equatorial fad that never made it to the Nomidlats. "But lorists tell *stonelore*. That's the whole point. If these people don't even do that, shouldn't they be called...I don't know, something else?"

"Maybe." He shrugs and reaches over to steal a piece of cheese from her plate; she's so flustered by the pop lorist thing that she doesn't protest. "The real lorists have been complaining about them to the Yumenescene Leadership, but that's all I know about it. They brought me here two years ago, and I haven't heard anything since." He sighs. "I hope the pop lorists don't go away, though. I like them, even if their stories are a little stupid and predictable. 'Course, their stories are set in real creches, not places like this." His lips twitch down at the corners as he looks around at their surroundings in faint disapproval.

Damaya knows full well what he means, but she wants to know if he'll say. "Places like this?"

His eyes slide sidelong back to hers. Flashing his teeth in a smile that probably charms more people than it alarms, he says, "Oh, you know. Beautiful, wonderful, perfect places full of love and light."

Damaya laughs, then stops herself. Then she's not sure why she did either.

"Yeah." The boy resumes eating with relish. "Took me a while to laugh after I got here, too."

She likes him, a little, after this statement.

He doesn't want anything, she realizes after a time. He makes small talk and eats her food, which is all right since she was mostly finished anyway. He doesn't seem to mind when she calls him Maxixe. She still doesn't trust him, but he just seems to want someone to talk to. Which she can understand.

Eventually he stands and thanks her—"For this scintillating conversation," which was almost entirely one-sided on his part—and then heads off to rejoin his friends. She puts it out of her mind and goes on about her day.

Except. The next day, something changes.

It starts that morning in the shower, when someone bumps into her hard enough to make her drop her washcloth. When she looks around, none of the boys or girls sharing the shower with her look in her direction, or apologize. She chalks it up to an accident.

When she gets out of the shower, however, someone has stolen her shoes. They were with her clothes, which she'd prepared before the shower and laid out on her bed to speed up the process of getting dressed. She always does this, every morning. Now they're gone.

She looks for them methodically, trying to make sure she hasn't forgotten them somewhere even though she knows she hasn't. And when she looks around at the other grits, who are carefully not looking at her as the instructors call inspection and she can do nothing but stand there in her impeccable uniform and bare feet, she knows what's happening.

She fails inspection and is punished with a scrub-brushing, which leaves her soles raw and stinging for the rest of the day inside the new shoes they give her.

This is only the beginning.

That evening at dinner, someone puts something in the juice she is given with her meal. Grits with poor table manners are given kitchen duty, which means they have access to everyone's food. She forgets this, and does not think about the odd taste of the juice until it becomes hard to focus and her head starts hurting. Even then she's not sure what's happening, as she stumbles and lurches on her way back to the dormitory. One of the instructors pulls her aside, frowning at her lack of coordination, and sniffs her breath. "How much have you had to drink?" the man asks.

Damaya frowns, confused at first because she just had a regular-sized glass of juice. The reason it takes her a while to understand is that she's drunk: Someone has slipped alcohol into her juice.

Orogenes aren't supposed to drink. Ever. The power to move mountains plus inebriation equals disaster waiting to happen. The instructor who stopped Damaya is Galena, one of the younger four-ringers, who runs the afternoon orogeny drills. He's merciless in the crucible, but for whatever reason he takes pity on her now. Galena takes her out of lineup and brings her to his own quarters, which are fortunately nearby. There he puts Damaya on a couch and commands her to sleep it off.

In the morning, as Damaya drinks water and winces at the awful taste in her mouth, Galena sits her down and says, "You need to deal with this now. If any of the seniors had caught you—" He shakes his head. It's an offense so severe that there's no standing punishment. It would be terrible; that's all either of them needs to understand.

It doesn't matter why the other grits have decided to bully

her. All that matters is that they're doing it, and that these are no harmless pranks. They're trying to get her iced. Galena's right; Damaya's got to deal with this. Now.

She decides she needs an ally.

There's another girl among the loners that she's noticed. *Everyone* notices this girl; there's something wrong with her. Her orogeny is a precarious, pent thing, a dagger constantly poised to plunge into the earth—and training has only made it worse, because now the knife is sharper. That's not supposed to happen. Selu is her name, and she hasn't yet earned or been given an orogene name, but the other grits call her *Crack* to be funny, and that is the name that has stuck. She even answers to that name, since she can't seem to stop them from using it.

Everyone's already whispering that she won't make it. Which means she's perfect.

Damaya makes her move on Crack at breakfast the next day. (She drinks only water now, which she has drawn from a nearby fountain. She has to eat the food they serve her, but she inspects it carefully before putting anything in her mouth.) "Hi," she says, setting her tray down.

Crack eyes her. "Really? Things are bad enough that you need *me*?"

It's a good sign that they can be honest with each other right off. "Yes," Damaya says, and sits since Crack hasn't really objected. "They're messing with you, too, aren't they?" Of course they are. Damaya hasn't seen whatever they're doing, but it only makes sense. There's an order to life in the Fulcrum.

Crack sighs. This makes the room reverberate faintly, or so it feels for an instant. Damaya makes herself not react, because a good partnership should not begin with a display of fear. Crack sees this and relaxes, just a little. The judder of imminent disaster fades.

"Yeah," Crack says, softly. Damaya realizes all of a sudden that Crack is *angry*, though she keeps her gaze on her plate. It's there in the way she holds her fork too tightly, and the way her expression is too blank. All at once Damaya wonders: Is Crack's control really a problem? Or is it simply that her tormentors have done their best to *make* her crack? "So what do you want to do about it?"

Damaya outlines her plan. After an initial flinch, Crack realizes she is serious. They finish eating in silence, while Crack thinks it over. At last, Crack says, "I'm in."

The plan is really quite simple. They need to find the head of the serpent, and the best way to do that is to use bait. They decide on Maxixe, because of course Maxixe must be involved. Damaya's troubles began right after his ostensibly friendly overtures. They wait until he's in the shower one morning, laughing with his friends, and then Damaya returns to her bunk. "Where are my shoes?" she asks, loudly.

The other grits look around; some of them groan, all too ready to believe that bullies would be uncreative enough to pull the same trick twice. Jasper, who's only been in the Fulcrum a few months longer than Damaya, scowls. "Nobody took your shoes this time," he says. "They're in your trunk."

"How do you know? Did *you* take them?" Damaya moves to confront him, and he bristles and meets her in the middle of the room, his shoulders back with affront.

"I didn't take your crap! If they're lost, you lost them."

"I don't lose things." She jabs him in the chest with a finger. He's a Nomidlatter like her, but thin and pale; probably from some comm close to the Arctic. He turns red when he's angry; the other kids make fun of this, but not much, because he teases other kids more loudly. (Good orogeny is deflection, not cessation.) "If you didn't take them, then you know who did." She jabs him again, and he swats her hand away.

"Don't *touch* me, you stupid little pig. I'll break your rusting finger."

"What is this?"

They all jump and fall silent and turn. In the doorway, ready to begin evening inspection, is Carnelian, one of the few seniors among the instructors. He's a big man, bearded and older and severe, with six rings; they're all afraid of him. In token of which, the grits immediately scramble into their places before the bunks, standing at attention. Damaya, in spite of herself, feels a bit of trepidation—until she catches Crack's eye, and Crack gives her a small nod. The distraction was enough.

"I said, what is this?" Carnelian comes into the room once they're assembled. He focuses on Jasper, who's still apple-red, though probably with fear rather than anger this time. "Is there some problem?"

Jasper glares at Damaya. "Not with *me*, Instructor."

When Carnelian turns to her, she is ready. "Someone stole my shoes, Instructor."

"Again?" This is a good sign. Last time, Carnelian simply berated her for losing her own shoes and making excuses. "You have proof it was Jasper who stole them?"

Here's the tricky part. She's never been good at lying. "I know it was a boy. They disappeared during the last shower, and all the girls were *in* there with me. I counted."

Carnelian sighs. "If you're trying to blame someone else for your shortcomings—"

"She's always doing that," says a red-haired eastern Coaster girl.

"She's got a *lot* of shortcomings," says a boy who looks like he comes from the same comm, if he's not a relative of hers outright. Half the grits snicker.

"Search the boys' chests." Damaya speaks over their laughter. It's something she didn't ask for last time, because she wasn't sure where the shoes would be. This time she is sure. "There wasn't much time to get rid of the shoes. They have to still be here. Look in their chests."

"That's not fair," says one tiny Equatorial boy, who looks barely old enough to be out of the toddlers' creche.

"No, it isn't," says Carnelian, his scowl deepening as he looks at her. "Be very certain before you ask me to violate your fellow trainees' privacy. If you're wrong, we won't go easy on you this time."

She still remembers the sting of brush-scrubbed feet. "I understand, Instructor."

Carnelian sighs. Then he turns to the boys' side of the dormitory room. "Open your trunks, all of you. Let's get this over with."

There's a lot of grumbling as they open their chests, and enough glares that Damaya knows she's made things worse for herself. They all hate her now. Which is fine; if they're going to hate her, she'd rather they do it for a reason. But that might change once this game has played out.

Maxixe opens his chest along with the rest, sighing mortally as he does so, and her shoes are right there on top of the folded uniforms. When Damaya sees his expression change from annoyance to confusion and then mortification, she feels bad. She doesn't like hurting people. But she watches closely, and the instant Maxixe's expression changes to fury, he swings around and glares at someone. She follows his glare, tense, ready—

—to see that he's looking at Jasper. Yes. That was what she expected. He's the one, then.

Jasper, though, has suddenly gone pale. He shakes his head as if trying to throw off Maxixe's accusatory look; it doesn't work.

Instructor Carnelian sees all of this. A muscle in his jaw flexes as he glances toward Damaya again. He looks almost angry with her. But why? He must understand that she has to do this.

"I see," he says, as if responding to her thought. Then he focuses on Maxixe. "Do you have anything to say for yourself?"

Maxixe doesn't protest his innocence. She can see by the slump of his shoulders and the shaking of his fists that he knows there's no point. But he's not going down alone. With his head down, he says, "Jasper took her shoes last time."

"I did not!" Jasper backs away from his bunk and the inspection line, into the middle of the room. He's trembling all over. Even his eyes are trembling; he looks ready to cry. "He's lying, he's just trying to pass this off on someone else—" But when Carnelian turns to Jasper, Jasper flinches and goes still. He almost spits the next words. "*She* sold them for me. Traded them to one of the cleaning commless in exchange for *liquor*."

And then he points at Crack.

Damaya inhales, everything inside her going still with shock. Crack?

Crack.

"You rusting cannibalson *whore*!" Crack clenches her fists. "You *let* that old pervert feel you up for liquor and a letter, you know full well he wouldn't give it to us just for *shoes*—"

"It was from my mother!" Jasper's definitely crying now. "I didn't want him to, to, but I couldn't...they wouldn't let me write to her..."

"You liked it," Crack sneers. "I told you I'd tell if you said anything, didn't I? Well, I saw you. He had his *fingers* in you and you moaned like it felt *good*, just like the little wannabe Breeder you are, only Breeders have *standards*—"

This is wrong. This is all wrong. Everyone's staring at each other, at Crack as she rants, at Damaya, at Jasper as he weeps, at Carnelian. The room is full of gasps and murmurings. That feeling is back: the pent, fraught, not-quite-reverberation that is Crack's orogeny unfurling itself, and everyone in the room is twitching with it. Or maybe they're twitching at the words and what they mean, because these aren't things grits should know, or do. Getting in trouble, sure, they're kids and kids do that. Getting in trouble *like this*, no.

"No!" Jasper wails the word at Crack. "I told you not to tell!" He's sobbing openly now. His mouth works but nothing more comes out that's intelligible, nothing but a low, despairing moan—or maybe it's just a continuation of the word *no*. Impossible to tell, because everyone else is making noise now, some of them hissing at Crack to shut up, some sniffing with Jasper, some of them giggling nervously at Jasper's tears, some of them stage-whispering at each other for confirmation of things they knew but didn't believe—

"*Enough.*" The room goes silent with Carnelian's quiet command, except for Jasper's soft hitching. After a moment, Carnelian's jaw flexes. "You, you, and you." He points at Maxixe, Jasper, and Crack. "Come with me."

He walks out of the room. The three grits look at each other, and it's a wonder none of them combust from the sheer hatred in these looks. Then Maxixe curses and moves to follow Carnelian. Jasper scrubs a forearm across his face and does the same, his head hanging and fists tight. Crack glares around the room, defiant—until her eyes meet Damaya's. Then Crack flinches.

Damaya stares back, because she's too stunned to look away. And because she is furious with herself. *This* is what comes of trusting others. Crack was not her friend, wasn't even someone she liked, but she'd thought they could at least help each other. Now she's found the head of the snake that's been trying to eat her, and it's halfway down the gullet of a completely different snake. The result is something too obscene to look at, let alone kill.

"Better you than me," Crack says softly, into the room's silence. Damaya hasn't said anything, hasn't demanded an explanation, but Crack gives one anyway, right there in front of everyone. No one says a word. No one even breathes loudly. "That was the idea. One more slip-up and I'm done for, but you, you're Little Citizen Perfect. Top scores on all the tests, perfect control in Applied, not a wrinkle out of place. The instructors wouldn't really do much to you, not yet. And while they were trying to figure out how their star pupil suddenly went wrong, everyone would stop waiting for me to blow up a mountain. Or trying to *make* me do it...for a while, anyway." Her smile fades, and she looks away. "That was the idea."

Damaya can't say anything. She can't even think. So after a while Crack shakes her head, sighs, and moves to follow the others after Carnelian.

The room is still. Nobody looks at anybody else.

Then there's a stir at the door as two other instructors come in and begin examining Crack's bunk and trunk. The grits watch as one woman lifts the mattress, and the other ducks under it. There's a brief ripping sound, and the instructor reappears with a big brown flask, half full, in one hand. She opens the flask and sniffs its contents, grimaces, and nods to the other woman. They both leave.

When the echoes of their steps fade, Damaya goes to Maxixe's trunk to retrieve her shoes. She closes the lid; the sound is very loud in the silence. No one moves until she goes back to her own bunk and sits down to put the shoes on.

As if this is a signal, there are several sighs, and some of the others start moving, too—retrieving books for the next lesson, filing off to first crucible, going over to the sideboard where breakfast waits. When Damaya goes to the sideboard herself, another girl glances at her, then away, quickly. "Sorry," she mutters. "I'm the one who pushed you in the shower."

Damaya looks at her and sees lurking fear making the skin around her eyes tight.

"It's okay," she says, softly. "Don't worry about it."

The other grits never give Damaya trouble again. A few days later Maxixe returns with broken hands and haunted eyes; he never speaks to Damaya again. Jasper does not return, but Carnelian tells them he's been sent to the satellite Fulcrum up in Arctic, since the Fulcrum of Yumenes holds too many bad memories for him. This was meant as a kindness, perhaps, but Damaya knows an exile when she sees one.

It could be worse, though. No one ever sees or mentions Crack again.

* * *

FUNGUS SEASON: 602 Imperial. A series of oceanic eruptions during the eastern Equatorial monsoons increased humidity in the region and obscured sunlight for six months. While this was a mild Season as such things go, its timing created perfect conditions for a fungal bloom that spread across the Equatorials into the northern and southern midlats, wiping out then-staple-crop miroq (now extinct). The resulting famine is included in the official geomestric record, extending the Season's length to four years (two years for the fungus blight to run its course, two more for agriculture and food distribution systems to recover). Nearly all affected comms were able to subsist on their own stores, thus proving the efficacy of Imperial reforms and Seasonal planning. In its aftermath, many comms of the Nomidlats and Somidlats voluntarily joined the Empire, beginning its Golden Age.

—*The Seasons of Sanze*

12

Syenite finds a new toy

My colleague is ill," Syenite tells Asael Leadership Allia as she sits facing the woman across a desk. "He sends his apologies for being unable to assist. I will clear the blockage in your harbor."

"I'm sorry to hear of your senior's illness," says Asael, with a little smile that almost makes Syen's hackles rise. Almost, because she knew it was coming and could thus brace for it. It still rankles.

"But I must ask," Asael continues, looking overly concerned. "Will you be . . . sufficient?" Her eyes flick down to Syen's fingers, where Syen has taken great care to put her rings on the four fingers a casual observer would be most likely to see. Her hands are folded, with the thumb of that hand tucked out of the way for the moment; let Asael wonder if there's a fifth one there. But when Asael's eyes meet Syen's again, Syen sees only skepticism. She is unimpressed by four rings or even five.

And this is why I will never, ever take a mission with a ten-ringer again. Like she has a choice. She feels better thinking it anyway.

Syenite forces herself to smile, though she doesn't have Alabaster's knack for exaggerated politeness. She knows her smiles just look pissed-off. "In my last mission," she says, "I was responsible for demolishing three buildings out of a block of five. This was in downtown Dibars, an area with several thousand inhabitants on a busy day, and not far from the Seventh University." She uncrosses and recrosses her legs. The geomests had driven her half mad on that mission, constantly demanding reassurances that she wouldn't create a shake any stronger than a 5.0. Sensitive instruments, important calibrations, something like that. "It took five minutes, and no rubble landed outside of the demolition zone. That was before I earned my latest ring." And she'd kept the shake to a fourer, much to the geomests' delight.

"I'm pleased to hear you're so competent," says Asael. There is a pause, which makes Syen brace herself. "With your colleague unable to contribute, however, I see no reason for Allia to pay for the services of two orogenes."

"That's between you and the Fulcrum," Syen says, dismissively. She honestly doesn't care. "I suspect you'll get an argument from them because Alabaster is mentoring me on this trip, and overseeing my work even if he isn't actually doing it."

"But if he isn't here—"

"That's irrelevant." It galls, but Syenite decides to explain. "He wears ten rings. He'll be able to observe what I'm doing, and intervene if necessary, from his hotel room. He could do it while unconscious. Moreover, he's been quelling shakes in this area for the past few days, as we've traveled through it. That's a service he provides as a courtesy to local node maintainers—or to your comm, rather, since such a remote location doesn't have a node station nearby." As Asael's expression tightens into a frown, probably at the perceived insult, Syen spreads her hands. "The biggest difference between him and me is that I'm the one who needs to see what she's doing."

"I... see." Asael sounds deeply uneasy, as she should. Syen knows that it's the job of any Fulcrum orogene to ease the fears of the stills, and here Syen has exacerbated Asael's. But she's begun to develop a nasty suspicion about who in Allia might want Alabaster dead, so it's a good idea for her to dissuade Asael—or whoever Asael knows—from that plan. This pedantic minor bureaucrat has no idea how close her little city came to being flattened last night.

In the uncomfortable silence that falls, Syenite decides it's time she asks some questions of her own. And maybe stirs the shit a little, to see what rises to the top. "I see that the governor wasn't able to make it, today."

"Yes." Asael's face goes gameswoman-blank, all polite smile and empty eyes. "I did convey your colleague's request. Unfortunately, the governor was unable to make time in his schedule."

"That's a shame." And then, because Syenite is beginning to understand why Alabaster is such an ass about this, she folds her hands. "Unfortunatcly, it wasn't a request. Do you have a telegraph here? I'd like to send a message to the Fulcrum, let them know we'll be delayed."

Asael's eyes narrow, because of course they have a telegraph, and of course Syenite meant that as another dig. "Delayed."

"Well, yes." Syen raises her eyebrows. She knows she's not doing a good job of looking innocent, but she tries, at least.

"How long do you think it will be before the governor is able to meet with us? The Fulcrum will want to know." And she stands, as if to leave.

Asael tilts her head, but Syenite can see the tension in her shoulders. "I thought you were more reasonable than your colleague. You're actually going to walk out of here, and not clear our harbor, in a fit of pique."

"It isn't a fit of pique." Now Syen's mad for real. Now she gets it. She looks down at Asael, who sits there, smug and secure in her big chair behind her big desk, and it's an actual fight to keep her fists from clenching, her jaw muscles from flexing. "Would you tolerate this treatment, in our position?"

"Of course I would!" Asael straightens, surprised into an actual reaction for once. "The *governor* has no time for—"

"No, you wouldn't tolerate it. Because if you were in my position, you'd be the representative of an independent and powerful organization, not some two-quartz backwater flunky. You would expect to be treated like a skilled expert who's been learning her craft since childhood. Like someone who plies an important and *difficult* trade, and who's come to perform a task that dictates your comm's livelihood."

Asael is staring at her. Syenite pauses, takes a deep breath. She must stay polite, and wield that politeness like a finely knapped glassknife. She must be cold and calm in her anger, lest a lack of self-control be dismissed as the mark of monstrosity. Once the heat behind her eyes has eased, she steps forward.

"And yet you haven't shaken our hands, Asael Leader. You didn't look us in the eye when we first met. You *still* haven't offered that cup of safe that Alabaster suggested yesterday.

Would you do that to a decreed 'mest from the Seventh University? Would you do it to a master geneer, come to repair the comm's hydro? Would you do it to a representative of the Strongbacks' Union for your own comm?"

Asael actually flinches as the analogies finally get through to her. Syenite waits in silence, letting it gather pressure. Finally Asael says, "I see."

"Maybe you do." She keeps waiting, and Asael sighs.

"What do you want? An apology? Then I apologize. You must remember, though, that most normal people have never seen an orogene, let alone had to do business with one, and—" She spreads her hands. "Isn't it understandable that we might be... uncomfortable?"

"Discomfort is understandable. It's the rudeness that isn't." Rust this. This woman doesn't deserve the effort of her explanation. Syen decides to save that for someone who matters. "And that's a really shitty apology. 'I'm sorry you're so abnormal that I can't manage to treat you like a human being.'"

"You're a rogga," Asael snaps, and then has the gall to look surprised at herself.

"Well." Syenite makes herself smile. "At least that's out in the open." She shakes her head and turns toward the door. "I'll come back tomorrow. Maybe you'll have had time to check the governor's schedule by then."

"You are under contract," Asael says, her voice tight enough to quaver. "You are *required* to perform the service for which we have paid your organization."

"And we will." Syenite reaches the door and stops with her hand on the handle, shrugging. "But the contract doesn't specify how long we have, upon arrival, to get it done." She's bluffing. She has no idea what's in the contract. But she's willing to bet Asael doesn't, either; a deputy governor doesn't sound important enough to know that sort of thing. "Thanks for the stay at the Season's End, by the way. The beds are very comfortable. And the food's delicious."

That, of course, does it. Asael stands as well. "Stay here. I'll go and speak with the governor."

So Syen smiles pleasantly, and sits back down to wait. Asael leaves the room, and stays gone for long enough that Syen starts to doze off. She recovers when the door opens again, and another Coaster woman, elderly and portly, comes in with a chastened-looking Asael. The governor's a man. Syenite sighs inwardly and braces herself for more weaponized politeness.

"Syenite Orogene," the woman says, and despite her rising ire Syenite is impressed by the gravity of her presence. The "orogene" after Syen's name isn't necessary, of course, but it's a nice bit of much-needed courtesy—so Syen rises, and the woman immediately steps forward and offers a hand for her to shake. Her skin is cool and dry and harder than Syenite expected. No calluses, just hands that have done their share of everyday labor. "My name is Heresmith Leadership Allia. I'm the lieutenant governor. The governor genuinely is too busy to meet with you today, but I've cleared enough time on my schedule, and I hope my greeting will be sufficient...especially as it comes with an apology for your poor treatment thus far. I can assure you that Asael will be censured for her behavior, to remind her that it's always good leadership to treat others—*all* others—with courtesy."

Well. The woman could be just playing a politician's game, or she could be lying about being the lieutenant governor; maybe Asael's found a very well-dressed janitor to play the part. Still, it's an effort at compromise, and Syen will take it.

"Thank you," she says, with genuine gratitude. "I'll convey your apology to my colleague Alabaster."

"Good. Please also tell him that Allia will pay your expenses, per our agreed-upon contract, for up to three days before and three after your clearing of the harbor." And there's an edge to her smile now, which Syenite knows she probably deserves. This woman, it seems, actually has read the contract.

Doesn't matter, though. "I appreciate the clarification."

"Is there anything else you need during your stay? Asael would be happy to provide a tour of the city, for example."

Damn. Syen *likes* this woman. She stifles the urge to smile and glances at Asael, who's managed to compose herself by this point; she gazes impassively back at Syenite. And Syen's tempted to do what Alabaster probably would, and take Heresmith up on that tacit offer of Asael's humiliation. But Syenite is tired, and this whole trip's been hellish, and the sooner it's over and she's back home at the Fulcrum, the better.

"No need," she says, and does Asael's face twitch a little in suppressed relief? "I'd actually like to get a look at the harbor, if I may, so that I can assess the problem."

"Of course. But surely you'd like refreshment first? At least a cup of safe."

Syenite can't help it now. Her lips twitch. "I don't actually *like* safe, I should probably say."

"No one does." And there's no mistaking the genuine smile on Heresmith's face. "Anything else, then, before we go?"

Now it's Syen's turn to be surprised. "You're coming with us?"

Heresmith's expression grows wry. "Well, our comm's livelihood *is* dependent on you, after all. It seems only proper."

Oh, yeah. This one's a keeper. "Then please proceed, Heresmith Leader." Syenite gestures toward the door, and they all head out.

* * *

The harbor's wrong.

They're standing on a kind of boardwalk along the western curve of the harbor's half circle. From there most of Allia can be seen, spreading up the caldera slopes that surround the waterfront. The city really is quite lovely. It's a beautiful day, bright and warm, with a sky so deep and clear that Syenite thinks the stargazing at night should be amazing. Yet it's what she can't see—under the water, along the harbor bottom—that makes her skin crawl.

"That's not coral," she says.

Heresmith and Asael turn to her, both of them looking puzzled. "Pardon?" asks Heresmith.

Syenite moves away from them, going to the railing and extending her hands. She doesn't need to gesture; she just wants them to know she's doing something. A Fulcrum orogene always reassures clients of their awareness and understanding of the situation, even when those clients have no actual idea what's going on. "The harbor floor. The *top* layer is coral." She thinks. She's never felt coral before, but it feels like what she expected: layers of wriggling bright life that she can pull from, if she needs to, to fuel her orogeny; and a solid core of ancient calcified death. But the coral heap sits atop a humped ridge in the floor of the harbor, and although it feels natural—there are usually folds like this in places where land meets sea, she's read—Syenite can tell it's not.

It's absolutely straight, for one thing. And huge; the ridge spans the width of the harbor. But more importantly, *it isn't there.*

The rock beneath the raised layers of silt and sand, that is: She can't feel it. She should be able to, if it's pushing up the seafloor like this. She can feel the weight of the water atop it, and the rock deformed by its weight and pressure underneath, and the strata around it, but not the actual obstruction itself. There might as well be a big empty hole on the bottom of the harbor...around which the entire harbor floor has shaped itself.

Syenite frowns. Her fingers spread and twitch, following the flow and curve of the sesuna. Soft slither of loose schist and sand and organic matter, cool press of solid bedrock, flow and dip. As she follows it, she belatedly remembers to narrate her explorations. "There's something *beneath* the coral, buried in the ocean floor. Not far down. The rock underneath is compressed; it must be heavy..." But why can't she feel it, if so? Why can she detect the obstruction only by its effect on everything nearby? "It's strange."

"Is it relevant?" That's Asael, maybe trying to sound professional and intelligent in order to get back into Heresmith's good graces. "All we need is for the coral blockage to be destroyed."

"Yes, but the coral's on top of it." She searches for the coral and finds it all around the edges of the harbor; a theory forms. "That's why this is the only place in the deep part of the harbor that's blocked by coral. It's growing *on top of* the thing, where the ocean floor has effectively been raised. Coral's a thing of the shallows, but it can get plenty of sun-warmed water, along this ridge."

"Rusting Earth. Does that mean the coral will just grow back?" That's one of the men who came with Asael and Heresmith. They're a bunch of clerks, as far as Syenite can tell, and she keeps forgetting they're present until they speak. "The whole *point* of this is to clear the harbor for good."

Syenite exhales and relaxes her sessapinae, opening her eyes so they'll know she's done. "Eventually, yes," she says, turning to them. "Look, here's what you're dealing with. This is your harbor." She cups her left hand in an approximate circle, two-thirds closed. Allia's harbor is more irregular than this, but they get it, she sees as they step closer to her demonstration. So she lays the thumb of her right hand across the open part of the circle, almost but not quite closing it off. "This is the position of the thing. It's slightly elevated at one end"—she wiggles the tip of her thumb—"because there's a natural incline in the substrate. That's where most of the coral is. The waters at the far end of the thing are deeper, and colder." Awkwardly she waggles her hand to indicate the heel of her thumb. "That's the open channel you've been using for port traffic. Unless this coral suddenly starts liking cold dark water, or another variety of coral shows up that does, then that part may never become occluded."

But even as she says this, it occurs to her: Coral builds on itself. New creatures grow on the bones of their predecessors; in time, that will lift even the colder part of the harbor into the zone of optimal growth. And with perfect timing Asael frowns and says, "Except that channel *has* been closing, slowly but surely, over the years. We have accounts from a few decades ago that say we used to be able to accommodate boats across the middle of the harbor; we can't, anymore."

Underfires. When Syen gets back to the Fulcrum, she's going to tell them to add rock-building marine life to the grit curriculum; ridiculous that it's not something they learn already. "If this comm's been around for many Seasons and you're only just now having this problem, then obviously this isn't the kind of coral that grows quickly."

"Allia is only two Seasons old," says Heresmith, with a pained smile at Syen. That's a respectable achievement in and of itself. In the midlats and arctics, a lot of comms don't last a single Season; the coasts are even more volatile. But of course, Heresmith thinks she's talking to a born-and-bred Yumenescene.

Syenite tries to remember the stuff she didn't sleep through in history creche. The Choking Season is the one that occurred most recently, a little over a hundred years ago; it was mild as Seasons have gone, killing mostly people in the Antarctic, near Mount Akok when it blew. Before that was the Acid Season? Or was it Boiling? She always gets those two mixed up. Whichever one it was, it was two or maybe three hundred years before Choking, and it was a bad one. Right—there were no seaside comms left after that one, so naturally Allia can only be a few decades younger, founded when the waters sweetened and receded and left the coastline habitable again.

"So that coral blocked the harbor over the course of four hundred years or so," Syenite says, thinking aloud. "Maybe with a setback during Choking..." How does coral survive a Fifth Season? She has no idea, but it clearly needs warmth and light to thrive, so it must have died back during that one. "All right, let's say it really grew into a blockage over a hundred years."

"Fire-under-Earth," says another woman, looking horrified. "You mean we might have to do this *again* in just a century?"

"We will still be paying the Fulcrum in a century," says Heresmith, sighing, and the look she throws Syenite is not resentful, just resigned. "Your superiors charge dearly for your services, I'm afraid."

Syenite resists the urge to shrug. It's true.

They all look at each other, and then they look at her, and by this Syen knows: They're about to ask her to do something stupid.

"That's a very bad idea," she says preemptively, holding up her hands. "Seriously. I've never shifted anything underwater before; that's why I had a senior assigned to me." Fat lot of good he's been. "And more importantly, *I don't know what that thing is*. It could be a massive gas or oil pocket that will poison your harbor waters for years." It's not. You know this because no oil or gas pocket is as perfectly straight and dense as this thing is, and because you can *sess* oil and gas. "It could even be the remnant of some especially stupid deadciv that seeded all its harbors with bombs." Oh, that was brilliant. They're staring at her now, horrified. She tries again.

"Commission a study," she says. "Bring in some geomests who study marine floors, maybe some geneers who know something about..." She waggles a hand, guesses wildly. "Ocean currents. Figure out all the positives and negatives. *Then* call in someone like me." She hopes it won't be her again, specifically. "Orogeny should always be your last resort, not your first."

That's better. They're listening. Two of the ones she doesn't know start murmuring quietly to each other, and Heresmith has a thoughtful look on her face. Asael looks resentful, but that doesn't necessarily mean anything bad. Asael's not very smart.

"I'm afraid we have to consider it," says Heresmith at last, looking so deeply frustrated that Syenite feels sorry for her. "We can't afford another contract with the Fulcrum, and I'm not certain we can afford a study; the Seventh University and Geneer Licensure charge almost as much as the Fulcrum for their services. But most importantly, we can't afford to have the harbor blocked any longer—as you've guessed, we're already losing business to several other Coaster ports that can accommodate the heavier-riding freight vessels. If we lose accessibility altogether, there will be no reason for this comm to continue existing."

"And I'm sympathetic," Syen begins, but then one of the men who've been murmuring in the background scowls at her.

"You're also an agent of the Fulcrum," he says, "and we contracted you to do a job."

Maybe he's not a clerk, then. "I know that. And I'll do it right now, if you want." The coral is nothing, she knows, now that she's sessed it out. She can probably do that without rocking the boats in their moorings too much. "Your harbor can be usable tomorrow, if I get rid of the coral today—"

"But you were hired to *clear* the harbor," says Asael. "Permanently, not some temporary fix. If the problem has turned out to be bigger than you think, that's no excuse for not finishing the job." Her eyes narrow. "Unless there's some reason you're so reluctant to shift the obstruction."

Syen resists the urge to call Asael one of several names. "I've explained my reasoning, Leader. If it was my intention to cheat you in some way, why would I have told you anything about the obstruction? I would've just cleared the coral and let you figure it out the hard way when the stuff grows back."

That sways some of them, she can see; both of the group's men stop looking so suspicious. Even Asael falters out of her accusatory stance, straightening a little in unease. Heresmith, too, nods and turns to the others.

"I think we'll need to discuss this with the governor," she says, finally. "Present him all the options."

"Respectfully, Leader Heresmith," says one of the other women, frowning, "I don't *see* another option. We either clear the harbor temporarily, or permanently. Either way we pay the Fulcrum the same amount."

"Or you do nothing," Syenite says. They all turn to stare at her, and she sighs. She's a fool to even mention this; Earth knows what the seniors will do to her if she scuttles this mission. She can't help it, though. These people face the economic destruction of their whole community. It's not a Season, so they can move somewhere else, try to start over. Or they can dissolve, with all the comm's families trying to find places in other communities—

—which should work except for those family members who are poor, or infirm, or elderly. Or those who have uncles or siblings or parents who turned out to be orogenes; nobody will take those. Or if the community they try to join has too many members of their use-caste already. Or.

Rust it.

"If my colleague and I go back now," Syenite continues in spite of everything, "without doing anything, then we'll be in breach of contract. You'll be within your rights to demand your commission fee back, less our expenses for travel and local accommodations." She's looking dead at Asael as she says this; Asael's jaw muscles flex. "Your harbor will still be usable, at least for a few years more. Use that time, and the money you saved, to either study what's happening and figure out what's down there . . . or move your comm to a better location."

"*That's* not an option," says Asael, looking horrified. "This is our home."

Syen cannot help thinking of a fusty-smelling blanket.

"Home is people," she says to Asael, softly. Asael blinks. "Home is what you take with you, not what you leave behind."

Heresmith sighs. "That's very poetic, Syenite Orogene. But Asael is correct. Moving would mean the loss of our comm's identity, and possibly the fracturing of our population. It would also mean losing everything we've invested in this location." She gestures around, and Syenite understands what she means: You can move people easily, but not buildings. Not infrastructure. These things are wealth, and even outside of a Season, wealth means survival. "And there's no guarantee we won't face worse problems elsewhere. I appreciate your honesty—I do. Really. But, well . . . better the volcano we know."

Syenite sighs. She tried. "What do you want to do, then?"

"It seems obvious, doesn't it?"

It does. Evil Earth, it does.

"*Can* you do it?" asks Asael. And maybe she doesn't mean it as a challenge. Maybe she's just anxious, because after all what

Syen is talking about here is the fate of the comm Asael's been raised in and trained to guide and protect. And of course, as a Leader-born child, Asael would know nothing of this comm but its potential and welcome. She would never have reason to view her community with distrust or hatred or fear.

Syen doesn't mean to resent her. But she's already in a bad mood, and she's tired because she didn't get much sleep while saving Alabaster from poisoning the night before, and Asael's question assumes that she is less than what she is. It's one time too many, throughout this whole long, awful trip.

"Yes," Syenite snaps, turning and extending her hands. "You should all step back at least ten feet."

There are gasps from the group, murmurs of alarm, and she feels them recede quickly along the unfolding map of her awareness: hot bright jittering points moving out of easy reach. They're still in slightly less easy reach. So's their whole comm, really, a cluster of motion and life all around her, so easy to grasp and devour and use. But they don't need to know that. She's a professional, after all.

So she stabs the fulcrum of her power into the earth in a sharp, deep point so that her torus will be narrow and high rather than wide and deadly. And then she probes around the local substrate again, searching for the nearest fault or perhaps a remnant bit of heat from the extinct volcano that once formed Allia's caldera. The thing in the harbor is heavy, after all; she's going to need more than ambient power to shift it.

But as she searches, something very strange—and very familiar—happens. Her awareness shifts.

Suddenly she's not in the earth anymore. Something pulls

her away, and over, and down, and *in*. And all at once she is lost, flailing about in a space of black constricting cold, and the power that flows into her is not heat or motion or potential but something entirely else.

Something like what she felt last night when Alabaster comandeered her orogeny. But *this isn't Alabaster.*

And she's still in control, sort of. That is, she can't stop what's happening—she's taken in too much power already; if she tries to let it go, she'll ice half the comm and set off a shake that makes the shape of the harbor academic. But she can *use* the flood of power. She can steer it, for example, into the rock bed underneath the thing she can't see. She can push up, which lacks finesse and efficiency but gets the rusting job done, and she can feel the enormous *blankness* that is the object rise in response. If Alabaster's observing from his inn room, he must be impressed.

But where's the power coming from? How am I—

She can realize, belatedly and with some horror, that water moves much like rock in response to a sudden infusion of kinetic energy—but it's much, much faster to react. And she can react herself, faster than she's ever done before because she's *brimming* with strength, it's practically coming out of her pores and, Earthfire, it feels unbelievably good, it is child's play to stop the massive wave that's building and about to swamp the harbor. She just disippates its force, sending some back out to sea, channeling the rest into soothing the waters as the thing from the ocean floor breaks free of its encumbering sediment—and the coral, which just slides off and shatters—and begins to rise.

But.

But.

The thing isn't doing what she wants it to do. She'd intended to just shunt it to the side of the harbor; that way if the coral grows back, it still won't block the channel. Instead—

—Evil Earth—what the rust—instead—

Instead, it's *moving on its own.* She can't hold it. When she tries, all the power that she held just trickles away, sucked off somewhere as quickly as it infused her.

Syen falls back into herself then, gasping as she sags against the wooden railing of the boardwalk. Only a few seconds have passed. Her dignity will not allow her to fall to her knees, but the railing's the only thing keeping her up. And then she realizes no one will notice her weakness, because the boards beneath her feet, and the railing she's clinging to, are all rattling in an ominous sort of way.

The shake siren begins wailing, deafeningly loud, from a tower right behind her. People are running on the quays below the boardwalk and the streets around it; if not for the siren, she would probably hear screams. With an effort Syen lifts her head to see Asael, Heresmith, and their party hurrying away from the boardwalk, keeping well away from any buildings, their faces stark with fear. Of course they leave Syenite behind.

But that is not the thing that finally pulls Syen out of self-absorption. What does is a sudden spray of seawater that wafts across the quays like rain, followed by a shadow that darkens this whole side of the harbor. She turns.

There, rising slowly from the water and shedding the remnants of its earthen shell as it begins to hum and turn, is an obelisk.

It's different from the one Syen saw last night. That one, the purple one, she thinks is still a few miles off coast, though she doesn't look that way to confirm its presence. The one before her dominates all her vision, all her thought, because it's rusting *huge* and it's not even completely out of the water yet. Its color is the deep red of garnets, its shape a hexagonal column with a sharp-pointed, irregular tip. It is completely solid, not shimmering or flickering in the half-real way of most obelisks; it is wider than several ships put end to end. And of course it is long enough, as it continues to rise and turn, to nearly block off the whole harbor. A mile from tip to tip.

But something's wrong with it, which becomes clear as it rises. At the midpoint of the shaft, the clear, crystalline beauty of the thing gives way to cracks. Massive ones, ugly and black-tinged, as if some contaminant from the ocean floor has seeped in during all the centuries that the thing must have lain down there. The jagged, spidering lines spread across the crystal in a radiant pattern. Syenite can *feel* how the obelisk's hum jitters and stutters here, incomprehensible energies struggling through the place of damage.

And at the center of the radiating cracks, she can see some kind of occlusion. Something small. Syenite squints, leaning harder on the railing as she cranes her neck to follow the rising mote. Then the obelisk turns a little more as if to face her, and all at once her blood ices over as she realizes what she's seeing.

A person. There's someone *in* the thing, stuck like a bug in amber, limbs splayed and still, hair a frozen spray. She can't make out the face, not quite, but in her imagination the eyes are wide, the mouth open. Screaming.

That's when she realizes she can make out an odd marbling along the figure's skin, black-bruised through the dark red of the shaft. The sunlight flickers and she realizes its hair is clear, or at least translucent enough to be lost in the garnet around it. And there's just something *about* what she's seeing, something maybe she knows because for a moment she was a part of this obelisk, that's where the power was coming from, something she won't question too deeply because, Evil Earth, she can't *take* this. The knowledge is there in her mind, impossible to deny no matter how much she might want to. When the reasoning mind is forced to confront the impossible again and again, it has no choice but to adapt.

So she accepts that what she is looking at is a broken obelisk that has lain unknown on the floor of Allia's harbor for Earth knows how long. She accepts that what is trapped at its heart, what has somehow *broken* this massive, magnificent, arcane thing... is a stone eater.

And it's dead.

* * *

Father Earth thinks in ages, but he never, ever sleeps.

Nor does he forget.

—*Tablet Two, "The Incomplete Truth," verse two*

13

you're on the trail

THIS IS WHAT YOU ARE at the vein, this small and petty creature. This is the bedrock of your life. Father Earth is right to despise you, but do not be ashamed. You may be a monster, but you are also great.

* * *

The commless woman is called Tonkee. That's the only name she gives you: no use name, no comm name. You're sure she is, despite her protestations, a geomest; she admits it—sort of—when you ask her why she's following you. "He's just too damn interesting," Tonkee says, jerking her chin toward Hoa. "If I didn't try to figure him out, my old masters at the uni would hire assassins to hunt me down. Not that they haven't done that already!" She laughs like a horse, all bray and big white teeth. "I'd love a sample of his blood, but fat lot of good that will do me without proper equipment. So I'll settle for observation."

(Hoa looks annoyed at this, and pointedly makes an effort to keep you between himself and Tonkee as you walk.)

"The uni" she referred to, you are certain, is the Seventh

University in Dibars—the most famous center of learning for 'mests and lorists in all the Stillness, located in the second-largest city of the Equatorials. And if that prestitious place is where Tonkee trained, rather than at some jumped-up regional creche for adults, or at the knee of some local tinkerer, then she has fallen very far indeed. But you're too polite to say this aloud.

Tonkee does not live in an enclave of cannibals, despite her creative threats. You discover this when she leads you to her home that afternoon. Her home is a cave situated in a vesicle—the ancient fallen-in remains of a solidified lava bubble, this one once as big as a small hill. Now it's a secluded glen in a pocket of forest, with curving columns of gleaming black glass interspersed among the trees. There are all sorts of odd little cavelets tucked into its sides, where smaller bubbles must've nestled against the larger, and Tonkee warns you that some of the ones on the far side of the vesicle are home to forest cats and other animals. Most of them are no threat, normally, but everything changes in a Season, so you're careful to follow Tonkee's lead.

Tonkee's cavern is full of contraptions, books, and junk she's scavenged, amid a lot of actually useful things like lanterns and storecache food. The cavern smells of fragrant resins from the fires she's burned, but it quickly takes on Tonkee's stench once she's in and bustling about. You resign yourself to endure it, though Hoa doesn't seem to notice or maybe care; you envy his stoicism. Fortunately it turns out that Tonkee did indeed bring all that water with her for a bath. She does this in front of you, shamelessly stripping down and squatting by a wooden basin to scrub at her pits and crotch and the rest. You're a little surprised to notice a penis somewhere amid this process, but, well, not like any comm's going to make her a Breeder. She finishes up by rinsing her clothes and hair with a murky green solution that she claims is antifungal. (You have your doubts.)

Anyway, the place smells much better when she's done, so you spend a remarkably pleasant and cozy night there on your bedroll—she's got spares, but you don't want to risk lice—and even let Hoa curl up against you, though you turn your back to him so he won't cuddle. He does not try.

The next day you resume the journey south, with Tonkee the commless geomest and Hoa the... whatever he is. Because you're pretty sure by now that he's not human. That doesn't bother you; officially speaking, you're not human, either. (Per the Second Yumenescene Lore Council's *Declaration on the Rights of the Orogenically Afflicted,* a thousand-ish years ago.) What does bother you is that Hoa won't talk about it. You ask about what he did to the kirkhusa and he refuses to answer. You ask him why he won't answer, and he just looks miserable and says, "Because I want you to like me."

It almost makes you feel normal, traveling with these two. The road demands most of your attention, in any case. The ashfall only gets heavier over the next few days, until you finally do pull the masks out of your runny-sack—you have four, fortunately, horribly—and hand them around. It's clumpy ash for now, not the floating haze of death that stonelore warns against, but no sense being incautious. Other people have broken out their masks, too, you see when they materialize out of the grayness, their skin and hair and clothing hardly distinguishable from the ash-painted landscape, their eyes grazing over you and away. The masks make everyone equally unknown and unknowable, which is good. No one pays attention to you or Hoa or Tonkee, not anymore. You're happy to join the indistinct masses.

By the end of a week, the crowds of people traveling along the road have begun to thin into knots and, occasionally, trickles. Everyone who has a comm is hurrying back there, and the thinning crowds mean most of them are finding somewhere to settle in. Now only those journeying farther than usual remain on the road, or people who don't have a home to return to—like the hollow-eyed Equatorials you've seen, many of them sporting terrible burns or injuries that come from falling debris. The Equatorials are a brewing problem, because there's a lot of them on the road even if the injured ones are mostly getting sick with infection and starting to die. (You pass at least one or two people every day who just sit there on the edges of the road, pale or flushed, curled up or shaking, waiting for the end to come.) There's plenty left who seem hale enough, though, and they're commless now. That's always a problem.

You talk to a small group of these folk at the next roadhouse: five women of wildly varied ages and a very young, uncertain-looking man. This lot have removed most of the flowing, uselessly pretty garments that people in the Equatorial cities used to consider fashionable, you notice; somewhere along the way they've stolen or traded for sturdy clothes and proper travel gear. But each of them sports some remnant of the old life: The oldest woman wears a headscarf of frilly, stained blue satin; the youngest has gauzy sleeves poking out from under the heavier, more practical cloth of her tunic; the young man has a sash around his waist that is soft and peach colored and there solely for decoration, as far as you can tell.

Except it's not really decoration. You notice how they look at you when you walk up: a sweep of the eyes, an inspection of your wrists or neck or ankles, a frown as you are found wanting. The impractical cloth has one very practical use: It is the marker of a new tribe in the process of being born. A tribe to which you do not belong.

Not a problem. Yet.

You ask them what happened in the north. You know, but being aware of a geological event and knowing what that event *means* in the real human sense are two very different things. They tell you, once you've held up your hands and made it clear you offer no (visible) threat.

"I was on my way home from a concert," says one of the younger women, who does not introduce herself but should be—if she is not already—a Breeder. She's what Sanzed women are supposed to look like, tall and strong and bronze and almost offensively healthy, with nice even features and wide hips, all of it crowned with a shock of gray ashblow hair that's almost like a pelt about her shoulders. She jerks her head toward the young man, who lowers his gaze demurely. Just as pretty; probably a Breeder, too, though a bit on the scrawny side. Well, he'll beef up if he's got five women to service for his keep. "He was playing at the improvisation hall on Shemshena Street; this was in Alebid. The music was so beautiful..."

She trails off, and for a moment you see her detach from the here and now. You know Alebid is—was—a mid-sized city comm, known for its art scene. Then she snaps back, because of course she is a good Sanzed girl, and Sanzeds hold little truck with daydreamers.

She continues: "We saw something sort of—*tear,* off to the north. Along the horizon, I mean. We could see this...red light flare up at one point, then it spread off to the east and west. I couldn't tell how far away, but we could see it reflected on the underside of the clouds." She's drifting again, but remembering something terrible this time, and so her face is hard and grim and angry. That's more socially acceptable than nostalgia. "It spread *fast.* We were just standing in the street, watching it grow and trying to figure out what we were seeing, and sessing, when the ground started to shake. Then something—a cloud—obscured the red, and we realized it was coming toward us."

It had not been a pyroclastic cloud, you know, or she wouldn't be here talking to you. Just an ash storm, then. Alebid is well south of Yumenes; all they got was the dregs of whatever more northerly comms did. And that's good, because those dregs alone almost broke the much-further-south Tirimo. By rights Alebid should have been pebbles.

An orogene saved this girl, you suspect. Yes, there's a node station near Alebid, or there was.

"Everything was still standing," she says, confirming your guess. "But the ash that followed—no one could breathe. The ash was getting in people's mouths, into their lungs, turning into cement. I tied my blouse around my face; it was made of the same stuff as a mask. That's the only thing that saved me. Us." She glances at her young man, and you realize the scrap around his wrist is part of what used to be a woman's garment, by the color. "It was evening, after a beautiful day. It's not like anybody had their runny-sacks with them."

Silence falls. This time everyone in the group lets it go on, and drifts with her for a moment. The memory's just that bad. You remember, too, that not many Equatorials even have runny-sacks. The nodes have been more than enough to keep the biggest cities safe for centuries.

"So we ran," the woman concludes abruptly, with a sigh. "And we haven't stopped."

You thank them for the information, and leave before they can ask questions in return.

As the days pass, you hear other, similar, stories. And you notice that none of the Equatorials you meet are from Yumenes, or any comms from the same approximate latitude. Alebid is as far north as the survivors run.

Doesn't matter, though. You're not going north. And no matter how much it bothers you—what's happened, what it means—you know better than to dwell too much on it. Your head's crowded enough with ugly memories.

So you and your companions keep going through the gray days and ruddy nights, and all that really concerns you is keeping your canteen filled and your food stores topped up, and replacing your shoes when they start to wear thin. Doing all this is easy, for now, because people are still hoping this will be just a brief Season—a year without a summer, or two, or three. That's how most Seasons go, and comms that remain willing to trade during such times, profiting off others' poor planning, generally come out of it wealthy. You know better—this Season will be much, much longer than anyone could have planned for—but that won't stop you from taking advantage of their misconception.

Now and again you stop at comms you pass on the road, some of them huge and sprawling with granite walls that loom overhead, some of them protected merely by fencewire, sharpened sticks, and poorly armed Strongbacks. The prices are beginning to go strange. One comm will take currency, and you use up nearly all of yours buying Hoa his own bedroll. The next won't take currency at all, but they will take useful tools, and you've got one of Jija's old knapping hammers at the bottom of your bag. That buys you a couple weeks' worth of cachebread and three jars of sweet nut paste.

You share the food out among the three of you, because that's important. Stonelore's full of admonitions against hoarding within a group—and you are a group by now, whether you want to admit it or not. Hoa does his part, staying up most of the night to keep watch; he doesn't sleep much. (Or eat anything. But after a while you try not to notice that, the same way you try not to think about him turning a kirkhusa into stone.) Tonkee doesn't like approaching comms, even though with fresh clothing and no-worse-than-usual body odor she can pass for just another displaced person rather than a commless. So that part's on you. Still, Tonkee helps where she can. When your boots wear out and the comm you've approached won't take anything you offer, Tonkee surprises you by holding out a compass. Compasses are priceless, with the sky clouded over and no visibility through the ashfall. You ought to be able to get ten pairs of boots for it. But the woman doing the comm's trading has you over a barrel and she knows it, so you get only two pairs of boots, one for you and another for Hoa, since his are already starting to look worn. Tonkee, who has her own spare boots dangling from her pack, dismisses the price when you complain about it later. "There are other ways to find our way," she says, and then she stares at you in a way that makes you uneasy.

You don't *think* she knows you're a rogga. But who can really say, with her?

The miles roll on. The road forks often because there are a lot of big comms in this part of the midlats, and also because the Imperial Road intersects comm roads and cowpaths, rivers and old metal tracks that were used for transportation in some way or another by some ancient deadciv or another. These intersections are why they put Imperial Roads where they do; roads have always been the lifeblood of Old Sanze. Unfortunately that means it's easy to get lost if you don't know where you're going—or if you don't have a compass, or a map, or a sign saying *filicidal fathers this way.*

The boy is your savior. You're willing to believe that he can somehow sense Nassun because for a while he's better than a compass, pointing unerringly in the direction that you should go whenever you reach a crossroads. For the most part you follow the Imperial Road—this one is Yumenes-Ketteker, though Ketteker's all the way in the Antarctics and you pray you won't have to go that far. At one point Hoa takes you down a comm road that cuts between Imperial segments and probably saves you a lot of time, especially if Jija just stayed on the main roads the whole way. (The shortcut is a problem because the comm that built it is bristling with well-armed Strongbacks who shout and fire crossbow warning shots when they see you. They do not open their gates to trade. You feel their sights on you long after you've passed by.) When the road meanders away from due south, though, Hoa's less certain. When you ask, he says that he knows the direction in which Nassun is traveling, but he cannot sense the specific route she and Jija took. He can only point out the path that's most likely to get you there.

As the weeks pass, he begins to have trouble with even that. You stand with Hoa at one crossroads for a full five minutes while he chews his lip, until finally you ask him what's wrong.

"There are a lot of you in one place now," he says uneasily, and you change the subject quickly because if Tonkee doesn't know what you are, then she will after a conversation like that.

A *lot of you*, though. People? No, that doesn't make sense. Roggas? Gathering together? That makes even less sense. The Fulcrum died with Yumenes. There are satellite Fulcrums in Arctic—far north, past the now-impassible central latitude of the continent—and Antarctic, but you're months away fom the latter. Any orogenes left on the roads now are people like her, hiding what they are and trying to survive same as the rest. It wouldn't make sense for them to gather into a group; that would increase the chance of discovery.

At the crossroads Hoa picks a path, and you follow, but you can tell by the frown on his face that it's a guess.

"It's nearby," Hoa finally tells you, one night while you're eating cachebread and nut paste and trying not to wish it was something better. You're starting to crave fresh vegetables, but those are going to be in short supply very soon if they aren't already, so you try to ignore the craving. Tonkee is off somewhere, probably shaving. She's run out of something in the past few days, some biomest potion she keeps in her pack and tries not to let you see her drinking even though you don't care, and she's been sprouting beard stubble every few days because of the lack. It's made her irritable.

"The place with all the orogenes," Hoa continues. "I can't find anything past them. They're like...little lights. It's easy to see just one by itself, Nassun, but together they make one very bright light, and she passed close to it or through it. Now I can't—" He seems to grope for the words. There are no words for some things. "I can't, uh—"

"Sess?" you suggest.

He frowns. "No. That isn't what I do."

You decide not to ask what he does.

"I can't...I can't *know* anything else. The bright light keeps me from focusing on any little light."

"How many"—you leave out the word, in case Tonkee's coming back—"are there?"

"I can't tell. More than one. Less than a town. But more are heading there."

This worries you. They can't all be chasing stolen daughters and murderous husbands. "Why? How do they know to go there?"

"I don't know."

Well, that's helpful.

All you know for sure is that Jija headed south. But "south" covers a lot of territory—more than a third of the continent. Thousands of comms. Tens of thousands of square miles. Where's he going? You don't know. What if he turns east, or west? What if he stops?

There's a notion. "Could they have stopped there? Jija and Nassun, in that place?"

"I don't know. They went that way, though. I didn't lose them until here."

So you wait till Tonkee comes back, and you tell her where you're going. You don't tell her why, and she doesn't ask. You don't tell her what you're going into, either—because, really, you don't know. Maybe someone's trying to build a new Fulcrum. Maybe there was a memo. Regardless, it's good to have a clear destination again.

You ignore the feeling of unease as you start down the road that—hopefully—Nassun traveled.

* * *

Judge all by their usefulness: the leaders and the hearty,
the fecund and the crafty, the wise and the deadly, and
a few strong backs to guard them all.

—*Tablet One, "On Survival," verse nine*

14

Syenite breaks her toys

Remain at location. Await instructions, reads the telegram from Yumenes.

Syenite offers this to Alabaster wordlessly, and he glances at it and laughs. "Well, well. I'm beginning to think you've just earned yourself another ring, Syenite Orogene. Or a death sentence. I suppose we'll see when we get back."

They're in their room at the Season's End Inn, naked after their usual evening fuck. Syenite gets up, naked and restless and annoyed, to pace around the room's confines. It's a smaller room than the one they had a week ago, since their contract with Allia is now fulfilled and the comm will no longer pay for their boarding.

"When we get back?" She glares at him as she paces. He is completely relaxed, a long-boned positive space against the bed's negative whiteness, in the dim evening light. She cannot help thinking of the garnet obelisk when she looks at him: He is just as should-not-be, just as not-quite-real, just as frustrating. She cannot understand why he's not upset. "What is this 'remain at location' bullshit? Why won't they let us come back?"

He "tsks" at her. "Language! You were such a proper thing back at the Fulcrum. What happened?"

"I met you. Answer the question!"

"Maybe they want to give us a vacation." Alabaster yawns and leans over to take a piece of fruit from the bag on the nightstand. They've been buying their own food for the past week. At least he's eating without being reminded, now. Boredom is good for him. "What does it matter whether we waste our time here, or on the road back to Yumenes, Syen? At least here we can be comfortable. Come back to bed."

She bares her teeth at him. "No."

He sighs. "To *rest*. We've done our duty for the night. Earthfires, do you want me to leave for a while so you can masturbate? Will that put you in a better mood?"

It would, actually, but she won't admit that to him. She does come back to the bed, finally, for lack of anything better to do. He hands her an orange slice, which she accepts because they're her favorite fruit and they're cheap here. There's a lot to be said for living in a Coaster comm, she's thought more than once since coming here. Mild weather, good food, low cost of living, meeting people from every land and region as they flow through the port for travel and trade. And the ocean is a beautiful, entrancing thing; she has stood at the window and stared out at it for hours. If not for the tendency of Coaster comms to be wiped off the map every few years by tsunami... well.

"I just don't understand," she says, for what feels like the ten thousandth time. 'Baster's probably getting tired of her complaining, but she's got nothing else to do, so he'll have to endure it. "Is this some kind of punishment? Was I not supposed to find a giant floating whatevertherust hidden at the bottom of a harbor during a routine coral-clearing job?" She throws up her hands. "As if anyone could've anticipated that."

"Most likely," Alabaster says, "they want you on hand for whenever the geomests arrive, in case there's more potential business for the Fulcrum in it."

He's said this before, and she knows it's probably true. Geomests have already been converging on the city, in fact—and archaeomests, and lorists, and biomests, and even a few doctors who are concerned about the effect that an obelisk so close will have on Allia's populace. And the charlatans and cranks have come, too, of course: metallorists and astronomests and other junk science practitioners. Anyone with a bit of training or a hobby, from every comm in the quartent and neighboring ones. The only reason Syenite and Alabaster have even gotten a room is that they're the ones who discovered the thing, and because they got in early; otherwise, every inn and lodging-house in the quartent is full to brimming.

No one's really cared about the damn obelisks before now. Then again, no one's ever seen one hovering so close, clearly visible and stuffed with a dead stone eater, above a major population center.

But beyond interviewing Syenite for her perspective on the raising of the obelisk—she's already starting to wince every time a stranger is introduced to her as *Somefool Innovator*

Wherever—the 'mests haven't wanted anything from her. Which is good, since she's not authorized to negotiate on behalf of the Fulcrum. Alabaster might be, but she doesn't want him bargaining with anyone for her services. She doesn't *think* he'd intentionally sign her up for anything she doesn't want; he's not a complete ass. It's just the principle of the thing.

And worse, she doesn't quite believe Alabaster. The politics of being left here don't make sense. The Fulcrum should want her back in the Equatorials, where she can be interviewed at Seventh by Imperial Scholars, and where the seniors can control how much the 'mests have to pay for access to her. They should want to interview her themselves, and better understand that strange power she's now felt three times, and which she finally understands is somehow coming from obelisks.

(And the Guardians should want to talk to her. They always have their own secrets to keep. It disturbs her most of all that they've shown no interest.)

Alabaster has warned her not to talk about this part of it. *No one needs to know that you can connect to the obelisks,* he said, the day after the incident. He was still weak then, barely able to get out of bed after his poisoning; turns out he'd been too orogenically exhausted to do anything when she raised the obelisk, despite her boasting to Asael about his long-distance skill. Yet weak as he was, he'd grabbed her hand and gripped it hard to make sure she listened. *Tell them you just tried to shift the strata and the thing popped up on its own, like a cork underwater; even our own people will believe that. It's just another deadciv artifact that doesn't make any sense; nobody will question you about it if you don't give them a reason to. So don't* talk *about it. Not even to me.*

Which of course makes her want to talk about it even more. But the one time she tried after 'Baster recovered, he glared at her and said nothing, until she finally took the hint and went to go do something else.

And that pisses her off more than anything else.

"I'm going for a walk," she says finally, and gets to her feet.

"Okay," says Alabaster, stretching and getting up; she hears his joints pop. "I'll go with you."

"I didn't ask for company."

"No, you didn't." He's smiling at her again, but in that hard-edged way she's beginning to hate. "But if you're going out alone, at night, in a strange comm *where someone's already tried to kill one of us,* then you're rusting well going to have company."

At this, Syenite flinches. "Oh." But that's the other subject they can't talk about, not because Alabaster's forbidden it but because neither of them knows enough to do more than speculate. Syenite wants to believe that the simplest explanation is the most likely: Someone in the kitchen was incompetent. Alabaster has pointed out the flaw in this, however: No one else at the inn, or in the city, has gotten sick. Syenite thinks there might be a simple explanation for this, too—Asael told the kitchen workers to contaminate only Alabaster's food. That's the kind of thing angry Leaders tend to do, at least in all the stories about them, which abound with poisonings and convoluted, indirect viciousness. Syen prefers stories about Resistants overcoming impossible odds, or Breeders saving lives through clever political marriages and strategic reproduction, or Strongbacks tackling their problems with good honest violence.

Alabaster, being Alabaster, seems to think there was more to his near-death brush. And Syenite doesn't want to admit that he might be right.

"Fine, then," she says, and gets dressed.

It's a pleasant evening. The sun's just setting as they walk down a sloping avenue that leads toward the harbor. Their shadows stretch long before them, and the buildings of Allia, which are mostly stuccoed sandy-pale in color, briefly bloom with deeper jewel tones of red and violet and gold. The avenue they're on intersects a meandering side street that ends at a small cove off the harbor's busier area; when they stop here to take in the view, Syen can see a group of the comm's adolescents playing and laughing along the black-sand beach. They are all lean and brown and healthy, and obviously happy. Syen finds herself staring, and wondering if that is what it's like to grow up normal.

Then the obelisk—which is easily visible at the end of the avenue they're standing on, where the thing hovers perhaps ten or fifteen feet above the harbor waters—emits another of the low, barely perceptible pulses that it's been spitting out since Syenite raised it, and that makes her forget about the kids.

"Something's wrong with that thing," Alabaster says, very softly.

Syenite looks at him, annoyed and on the brink of saying, *What, now you want to talk about it?* when she notices that he's not looking at it. He's scuffing the ground with one foot, his hands in his pockets, appearing—oh. Syen almost laughs. Appearing, for the moment, like a bashful young man who's about to suggest something naughty to his pretty female companion. The facts that he is not young, or bashful, and that it doesn't matter if she's pretty or he's naughty because they're already fucking, aside. A casual observer would not realize he was paying any attention to the obelisk.

Which abruptly makes Syenite realize: *No one sesses its pulse but them.* The pulse is not a pulse, exactly. It's not brief, or rhythmic; more a momentary throb that she sesses now and again, at random and ominously, like a toothache. But if the other people of the comm had sessed that last one, they wouldn't be laughing and playing and winding down comfortably at the end of a long golden day. They would all be out here watching this massive, looming thing to which Syenite is increasingly beginning to apply the adjective *dangerous* in her head.

Syen takes a clue from 'Baster and reaches for his arm, cuddling close as if she actually likes him. She keeps her voice to a murmur, even though she has no clue who or what he's trying to conceal the conversation from. There are people out on the street as the city's business day winds down, but nobody's nearby, or paying attention to them for that matter. "I keep waiting for it to rise, like the others."

Because it's hanging far, far too close to the ground, or the water's surface as it were. Every other obelisk Syen has ever seen—including the amethyst that saved Alabaster's life, and which is still drifting a few miles offshore—floats amid the lowest layer of clouds, or higher.

"It's listing to one side, too. Like it's barely able to stay up at all."

What? And she cannot help looking up at it, though 'Baster immediately squeezes her arm to make her look away again. But that brief glimpse was enough to confirm what he said: The obelisk is indeed listing, just a little, its top end tilted toward the south. It must wobble, very slowly, as it turns. The slant is so slight that she wouldn't have noticed it at all if they hadn't been standing on a street surrounded by straight-walled buildings. Now she can't unsee it.

"Let's go this way," she suggests. They've lingered here too long. Alabaster obviously agrees, and they start down the side street to the cove, strolling casually.

"It's why they're keeping us here."

Syen's not paying attention to him when he says this. In spite of herself she's distracted by the beauty of the sunset, and the long, elegant streets of the comm itself. And another couple, passing on the sidewalk; the taller woman nods to them even though both Syen and 'Baster are wearing their black uniforms. It's strange, that little gesture. And nice. Yumenes is a marvel of human achievement, the pinnacle of ingenuity and geneering; if it lasts a dozen Seasons, this paltry little Coaster comm will never even come close to matching it. But in Yumenes, no one would ever have deigned to nod to a rogga, no matter how pleasant the day.

Then Alabaster's last words penetrate her ruminations. "What?"

He keeps his pace easy, matching hers despite his naturally longer gait. "We can't talk in the room. It's risky even to talk out here. But you wanted to know why they're keeping us here, telling us not to come back: That's why. That obelisk is failing."

That much is obvious, but... "What's that got to do with us?"

"You raised it."

She scowls before she remembers to school her expression.

"It raised itself. I just moved all the crap that was holding it down, and maybe woke it up." That her mind insists *it was sleeping* before is not something she's willing to question too deeply.

"And that's more control over an obelisk than anyone has ever managed in nearly three thousand years of Imperial history." 'Baster shrugs a little. "If *I* were a jumped-up little five-ring pedant reading a telegram about this, it's what I'd think, and it's how I'd react: by trying to control the person who can control that." His eyes flick toward the obelisk. "But it's not the jumped-up pedants at the Fulcrum we have to worry about."

Syen doesn't know what the rust he's on about. It isn't that his words don't ring true; she can completely imagine someone like Feldspar pulling something like this. But why? To reassure the local population, by keeping a ten-ringer on hand? The only people who know 'Baster's here are a bunch of bureaucrats who are probably too busy dealing with the sudden influx of 'mests and tourists to care. To be able to do something, should the obelisk suddenly...do something? That makes no sense. And who else is she supposed to worry about? Unless—

She frowns.

"You said something, earlier." Something about...connecting to an obelisk? What did that mean? "And—and you did something, that night." She throws an uneasy look at him, but he doesn't glare at her this time. He's gazing down at the cove, as if entranced by the view, but his eyes are sharp and serious. He knows what she's talking about. She hesitates a moment more, then says, "You *can* do something with those things, can't you?" Oh Earth, she's a fool. "*You* can control them! Does the Fulcrum know that?"

"No. And you don't know it, either." His dark eyes slide to hers for a moment, then away.

"Why are you being so—" It's not even secretive. He's talking to her. But it's as if he suspects someone of listening to them, somehow. "No one could hear us in the room." And she nods pointedly toward a gaggle of children running past, one of them jostling Alabaster and apologizing; the street's narrow. Apologizing. Really.

"You don't know that. The building's main support column is whole-hewn granite, didn't you notice? The foundation looks to be the same. If it sits directly on the bedrock..." His expression grows momentarily uneasy, and then he blanks his face.

"What's that got to do with—" And then she understands. Oh. *Oh.* But—no, that can't be right. "You're saying someone could hear us *through the walls*? Through the, the stone itself?" She's never heard of anything like that. It makes sense, of course, because it's how orogeny works; when Syen is anchored in the earth, she can sess not only the stone that her awareness is tied to, but anything that touches it. Even if she can't perceive the thing itself, as with the obelisk. Still, to feel not just tectonic vibrations, but *sound*? It can't be true. She's never heard of a rogga with that kind of fine sensitivity.

He looks at her directly for a long moment. "I can." When she stares back, he sighs. "I always could. You can, too, probably—it just isn't clear, yet. It's just minute vibrations to you now. Around my eighth or ninth ring is when I started to distinguish patterns amid the vibrations. Details."

She shakes her head. "But you're the only ten-ringer."

"Most of my children have the potential to wear ten rings."

Syenite flinches, suddenly remembering the dead child in the node station near Mehi. Oh. The Fulcrum controls all the node maintainers. What if they have some way to force those poor damaged children to listen, and to spit back what they listen to, like some kind of living telegraph receivers? Is that what he fears? Is the Fulcrum like a spider, perching in Yumenes's heart and using the web of nodes to listen in on every conversation in the Stillness?

But she is distracted from these speculations by something that niggles at the back of her mind. Something Alabaster just said. His damn influence, making her question all the assumptions she's grown up with. *Most of my children have the potential to wear ten rings*, he'd said, but there are no other ten-ringers in the Fulcrum. Rogga children are sent to the nodes only if they can't control themselves. Aren't they?

Oh.

No.

She decides not to mention this epiphany aloud.

He pats her hand, perhaps playacting again, perhaps really trying to soothe her. Of course he knows, probably better than she, what they've done to his children.

Then he repeats: "The seniors at the Fulcrum aren't who we have to worry about."

Who else could he mean? The seniors are a mess, granted. Syen keeps an eye on their politics, because one day she'll be among them and it's important to understand who holds power and who only looks like they do. There are at least a dozen factions, along with the usual rogues: brown-nosers and idealists and those who would glassknife their own mothers to get ahead. But all at once it occurs to Syenite to consider who they answer to.

The Guardians. Because no one would really trust a group of filthy roggas to manage their own affairs, any more than Shemshena would have trusted Misalem. No one in the Fulcrum talks about the Guardians' politics, probably because no one in the Fulcrum understands them. The Guardians keep their own counsel, and they object to inquiries. Vehemently.

Not for the first time Syenite wonders: To whom do the Guardians answer?

As Syen's considered this, they've reached the cove, and stopped at its railed boardwalk. The avenue ends here, its cobbles vanishing beneath a drift of sand and then the raised wooden walkway. Not far off there's a different sandy beach from the one they saw earlier. Children run up and down the boardwalk's steps, squealing in play, and beyond them Syen can see a gaggle of old women wading nude in the harbor's waters. She notices the man who sits on the railing, a few feet down from where they stand, only because he's shirtless, and because he's looking at them. The former gets her attention for a moment—then she's polite and looks away—because Alabaster's not much to look at and it's been a while since she had sex she actually enjoyed. The latter is something she would ignore, ordinarily, because in Yumenes she gets stared at by strangers all the time.

But.

She's standing at the railing with 'Baster, relaxed and more comfortable than she's been in a while, listening to the children play. It's hard to keep her mind on the cryptic stuff they're discussing. The politics of Yumenes seem so very far from here, mysterious but unimportant, and untouchable. Like an obelisk.

But.

But. She notices, belatedly, that 'Baster has gone stiff beside her. And although his face is turned toward the beach and the children, she can tell that he's not paying attention to them. That is when it finally occurs to her that people in Allia *don't stare,* not even at a couple of blackjackets out for an evening stroll. Asael aside, most of the people she's met in this comm are too well-mannered for something like that.

So she looks back at the man on the railing. He smiles at her, which is kind of nice. He's older, maybe by ten years or so, and he's got a gorgeous body. Broad shoulders, elegant deltoids under flawless skin, a perfectly tapered waist.

Burgundy pants. And the shirt that hangs over the railing beside him, which he has ostensibly taken off in order to soak up some of the sunlight, is also burgundy. Only belatedly does she notice the peculiar, familiar buzz at the back of her sessapinae that warns of a Guardian's presence.

"Yours?" asks Alabaster.

Syenite licks her lips. "I was hoping he was yours."

"No." And then Alabaster makes a show of stepping forward to rest his hands against the railing, bowing his head as if he means to lean on it and stretch his shoulders. "Don't let him touch you with his bare skin."

This is a whisper; she barely catches it. And then Alabaster straightens and turns to the young man. "Something on your mind, Guardian?"

The Guardian laughs softly and hops down from the railing. He's at least part Coaster, all-over brown and kinky-haired; a bit on the pale side, but aside from this he fits right in among the citizens of Allia. Well. No. He blends in superficially, but there's that indefinable *something* about him that's in every Guardian Syenite's had the misfortune to interact with. No one in Yumenes ever mistakes a Guardian for an orogene—or for a still, for that matter. There's just something different about them, and everyone notices.

"Yes, actually," the Guardian says. "Alabaster Tenring. Syenite Fourring." That alone makes Syenite grind her teeth. She would prefer the generic *Orogene*, if she has to be called anything besides her name. Guardians, of course, understand perfectly well the difference between a four-ringer and a ten-ringer. "I am Edki Guardian Warrant. My, but you've both been busy."

"As we should be," says Alabaster, and Syenite cannot help looking at him in surprise. He's tensed in a way she's never seen, the cords of his neck taut, his hands splayed and—ready? ready for what? she does not know why the word *ready* even occurred to her—at his sides. "We've completed our assignment for the Fulcrum, as you can see."

"Oh, indeed. A fine job." Edki glances off then, almost casually, toward that listing, throbbing accident of an obelisk. Syenite is watching his face, however. She sees the Guardian's smile vanish as if it were never there. That can't be good. "Would that you had done *only* the job you were told to do, however. Such a willful creature you are, Alabaster."

Syenite scowls. Even here, she is condescended to. "*I* did this job, Guardian. Is there some problem with my work?"

The Guardian turns to look at her in surprise, and that's when Syenite realizes she's made a mistake. A big one, because his smile doesn't return. "Did you, now?"

Alabaster hisses and—Evil Earth, she *feels* it when he stabs his awareness into the strata, because it goes so unbelievably deep. The strength of him makes her whole body reverberate, not just her sessapinae. She can't follow it; he's past her range in the span of a breath, easily piercing to the magma even though it's miles down. And his control of all that pure earth energy is perfect. Amazing. He could shift a mountain with this, easily.

But *why*?

The Guardian smiles, suddenly. "Guardian Leshet sends her regards, Alabaster."

While Syenite is still trying to parse this, and the fact that Alabaster is *about to fight a Guardian*, Alabaster stiffens all over. "You found her?"

"Of course. We must talk of what you did to her. Soon."

Suddenly—Syenite does not know when he drew it, or where from—there is a black glassknife in his hand. Its blade is wide, but ridiculously short, maybe only two inches in length. Barely enough to be called a knife at all.

What the rust is he going to do with that, pare our nails?

And why is he drawing a weapon on two Imperial Orogenes in the first place? "Guardian," she tries, "maybe there's been some kind of misun—"

The Guardian does something. Syenite blinks, but the tableau is as before: She and Alabaster face Edki on a boardwalk stark with shadows and bloody sunset light, with children and old ladies playing beyond them. But something has changed. She's not sure what, until Alabaster makes a choking sound and lunges at her, knocking her to the ground a few feet away.

How such a skinny man has the weight to throw her, Syenite will never know. She hits the planks hard enough to jar the breath out of herself; through a blur she sees some of the children who had been playing nearby stop and stare. One of them laughs. Then she struggles up, furious, her mouth already opening to curse Alabaster to Earth and back.

But Alabaster is on the ground, too, only a foot or two away. He's lying on his belly, his eyes fixed on her, and—and he's making a strange sound. Not much of one. His mouth's open wide, but the noise that comes out of it is more like the squeak of a child's toy, or a metallorist's air bladder. And he's shivering all over, as if he can't move more than that, which doesn't make sense because nothing's wrong with him. Syen's not sure what to think until, belatedly, she realizes—

—he's *screaming.*

"Why did you think I would aim at her?" Edki is staring at Alabaster, and Syenite shivers because the look on his face is *gleeful,* it is *delighted,* even as Alabaster lies there shuddering helplessly... with the knife that Edki once held now buried in the hollow of Alabaster's shoulder. Syen stares at it, stunned that she missed it before. It stands out starkly even against the black of 'Baster's tunic. "You have always been a fool, Alabaster."

And there is a new glassknife in Edki's hand now. This one is long and viciously narrow: a chillingly familiar poniard.

"Why—" Syenite can't think. Her hands ache as she scrabbles backward along the boardwalk planks, trying to get to her feet and away all at once. Instinctively she reaches for the earth beneath her and that's when she finally realizes what the Guardian has done, because there's *nothing in her that can reach.* She cannot sess the earth past a few feet below her hands and backside; nothing but sand and salty dirt and earthworms. There is an unpleasant ringing ache in her sessapinae when she tries to reach farther. It's like when she hits her elbow and shuts off all the sensation from there to the tips of her fingers; like that part of her mind has gone to sleep. It's tingling, coming back. But for now, there's nothing there.

She has heard grits whisper of this after lights-out. All Guardians are strange, but this is what makes them what they are: Somehow, they can stop orogeny with a flick of their will. And some of them are especially strange, *specialized to be* stranger than the rest. Some of them do not have orogene charges and are never allowed near untrained children, because they are dangerous merely by proximity. These Guardians do nothing but track down the most powerful rogue orogenes, and when they find them... well. Syenite never particularly wanted to know what they did, before now, but it seems she's about to find out. Underfires, she's as numb to the earth as the most rust-brained elder. Is this what it's like for stills? Is this all they feel? She has envied their normalcy her whole life, until now.

But. As Edki walks toward her with the poniard ready, there is a tightness around his eyes, a grim set to his mouth, which makes her think of how she feels when she has a bad headache. This is what makes her blurt: "A-are you, ah, all right?" She has no idea why she asks this.

At this, Edki cocks his head; the smile returns to his face, gentle and surprised. "How kind you are. I'm fine, little one. Just fine." But he's still coming at her.

She scrambles backward again, tries to get to her feet again, tries again to reach for power, and fails in all three efforts. Even if she could succeed, though—he's a Guardian. It's her duty to obey. It's her duty to *die,* if he wills it.

This is not right.

"Please," she says, desperate, wild with it. "Please, we haven't done anything wrong, I don't understand, I don't..."

"You need not understand," he says, with perfect kindness. "You need do only one thing." And then he lunges, aiming the poniard at her chest.

Later she will understand the sequence of events.

Later she will realize everything occurred in the span of a gasp. For now, however, it is slow. The passage of time becomes meaningless. She is aware only of the glassknife, huge and sharp, its facets gleaming in the fading dusk. It seems to come at her gradually, gracefully, drawing out her duty-bound terror.

This has *never been* right.

She is aware only of the gritty wood beneath her fingers, and the useless pittance of warmth and movement that is all she can sess beneath that. Can't shift much more than a pebble with that.

She is aware of Alabaster, twitching because he is *convulsing,* how did she not realize this before, he is not in control of his own body, there is something about the glassknife in his shoulder that has rendered him helpless for all his power, and the look on his face is of helpless fear and agony.

She becomes aware that she is *angry*. Furious. Duty be

damned. What this Guardian is doing, what all Guardians do, is *not right.*

And then—

And then—

And then—

She becomes aware of the obelisk.

(Alabaster, twitching harder, opens his mouth wider, his eyes fixing on hers despite the uncontrollability of the rest of his flesh. The fleeting memory of his warning rings in her mind, though in that instant she cannot recall the words.)

The knife is halfway to her heart. She is very very aware of this.

We are the gods in chains and this is not. Rusting. Right.

So she reaches again, not down but up, not straight but to the side—

No, Alabaster is shaping his mouth to say, through his twitches.

—and the obelisk draws her into its shivering, jittering bloodred light. She is falling up. She is being *dragged* up, and in. She is completely out of control, oh Father Earth, Alabaster was right, this thing is too much for her—

—and she screams because she has forgotten that this obelisk is *broken.* It hurts as she grinds across the zone of damage, each of the cracks seaming through her and shattering her and splitting her into pieces, until—

—until she stops, hovering and curled in agony, amid the cracked redness.

It isn't real. It cannot be real. She feels herself also lying on sandy wooden boards with fading sunlight on her skin. She does not feel the Guardian's glassknife, or at least not yet. But she is here, too. And she *sees,* though sessapinae are not eyes and the "sight" is all in her imagination:

The stone eater at the core of the obelisk floats before her.

It's her first time being close to one. All the books say that stone eaters are neither male nor female, but this one resembles a slender young man formed of white-veined black marble, clothed in smooth robes of iridescent opal. Its—his?—limbs, marbled and polished, splay as if frozen in mid-fall. His head is flung back, his hair loose and curling behind him in a splash of translucence. The cracks spread over his skin and the stiff illusion of his clothing, *into* him, through him.

Are you all right? she wonders, and she has no idea why she wonders it, even as she herself cracks apart. His flesh is so terribly fissured; she wants to hold her breath, lest she damage him further. But that is irrational, because she isn't here and this isn't real. She is on a street about to die, but this stone eater has been dead for an age of the world.

The stone eater closes his mouth, and opens his eyes, and lowers his head to look at her. "I'm fine," he says. "Thank you for asking."

And then
the obelisk
shatters.

15

you're among friends

You reach "the place with all the orogenes," and it's not at all what you were expecting. It's abandoned, for one thing. It's not a comm, for another.

Not in any real sense of the word. The road gets wider as you approach, flattening into the land until it vanishes completely near the middle of town. A lot of comms do this, get rid of the road to encourage travelers to stop and trade, but those comms usually have some place to trade *in*, and you can't see anything here that looks like a storefront or marketplace or even an inn. Worse, it doesn't have a wall. Not a stone pile, not a wire fence, not even a few sharpened sticks jabbed into the ground around the town perimeter. There's *nothing* to separate this community from the land around it, which is forested and covered in scraggly underbrush that makes perfect cover for an attacking force.

But in addition to the town's apparent abandonment, and lack of a wall, there are other oddities. Lots of them, you notice as you and the others look around. There aren't enough fields, for one. A comm that can hold a few hundred people, as this one seems to be able to do, should have more than the single (stripped bare) hectare of scraggly choya stalks that you noticed on the way in. It should have a bigger pasture than the small plot of dried-out green you see near the town's center. You don't see a storehouse, either, elevated or otherwise. Okay, maybe that's hidden; lots of comms do that. But then you notice that all the buildings are in wildly varied styles: this one tall and city-narrow, that one wide and flat to the ground like something from a warmer climate, yet another that looks to be a sod-covered dome half set into the earth like your old house in Tirimo. There's a reason most comms pick a style and stick to it: Uniformity sends a visual message. It warns potential attackers that the comm's members are equally unified in purpose and the willingness to defend themselves. This comm's visual message is...confused. Uncaring, maybe. Something you can't interpret. Something that makes you more nervous than if the comm had been teeming with hostile people instead.

You and the others proceed warily, slowly, through the empty streets of the town. Tonkee's not even pretending to be at ease. She's got twin glassknives in her hands, stark and black-bladed; you don't know where she's been hiding them although that skirt of hers could conceal an army. Hoa seems calm, but who can really tell what Hoa feels? He seemed calm when he turned a kirkhusa into a statue, too.

You don't pull your knife. If there really are lots of roggas here, there's only one weapon that will save you if they take exception to your presence.

"You sure this is the right place?" you say to Hoa.

Hoa nods emphatically. Which means that there are lots of people here; they're just hiding. But why? And how could they have seen you coming through the ashfall?

"Can't have been gone long," Tonkee mutters. She's staring at a dead garden near one of the houses. It's been picked over by travelers or the former inhabitants, anything edible among its dried stalks gone. "These houses look in good repair. And that garden was healthy until a couple of months ago."

You're momentarily surprised to realize you've been on the road for two months. Two months since Uche. A little less since the ash started to fall.

Then, swiftly, you focus on the here and now. Because after the three of you stop in the middle of town and stand there awhile in confusion, the door of one of the nearby buildings opens, and three women come out on the porch.

The first one you pay attention to has a crossbow in her hands. For a minute that's all you see, same as that last day in Tirimo, but you don't immediately ice her because the crossbow isn't aimed at you. She's just got it leaned against one arm, and although there's a look on her face that warns you she has no problem using it, you also think she won't do it without provocation. Her skin is almost as white as Hoa's, although thankfully her hair is simply yellow and her eyes are a nice normal brown. She's petite, small-boned and poorly fleshed and narrow-hipped in a way that would prompt the average Equatorial to make snide remarks about bad breeding. An Antarctic, probably from a comm too poor to feed its kids well. She's a long way from home.

The one who draws your eye next is nearly her opposite, and quite possibly the most intimidating woman you've ever seen.

It has nothing to do with her looks. Those are just Sanzed: the expected pouf of slate-gray hair and the expected deep brown skin and the expected size and visible strength of build. Her eyes are shockingly black—shocking not because black eyes are particularly rare, but because she's wearing smoky gray eye-shadow and dark eyeliner to accentuate them further. Makeup, while the world is ending. You don't know whether to be awed or affronted by that.

And she wields those black-clad eyes like piercing weapons, holding each of your gazes at eyepoint for an instant before finally examining the rest of your gear and clothing. She's not quite as tall as Sanzeds like their women—shorter than you—but she's wearing a thick brown-fur vest that hangs to her ankles. The vest sort of makes her look like a small, yet fashionable, bear. There's something in her face, though, that makes you flinch a little. You're not sure what it is. She's grinning, showing all her teeth; her gaze is steady, neither welcoming nor uneasy. It's the steadiness that you recognize, finally, from seeing it a few times before: confidence. That kind of utter, unflinching embrace of self is common in stills, but you weren't expecting to see it here.

Because she's a rogga, of course. You know your own when you sess it. And she knows you.

"All right," the woman says, putting her hands on her hips. "How many in your party, three? I assume you don't want to be parted."

You sort of stare at her for a breath or two. "Hello," you say at last. "Uh."

"Ykka," she says. You realize it's a name. Then she adds, "Ykka Rogga Castrima. Welcome. And you are?"

You blurt: "*Rogga?*" You use this word all the time, but hearing it like this, as a use name, emphasizes its vulgarity. Naming yourself *rogga* is like naming yourself *pile of shit*. It's a slap in the face. It's a statement—of what, you can't tell.

"That, ah, isn't one of the seven common use names," says Tonkee. Her voice is wry; you think she's trying to make a joke to cover nerves. "Or even one of the five lesser-accepted ones."

"Let's call this one new." Ykka's gaze flickers over each of your companions, assessing, then back to you. "So your friends know what you are."

Startled, you look at Tonkee, who's staring at Ykka the way she stares at Hoa when Hoa isn't hiding behind you—as if Ykka is a fascinating new mystery to maybe get a blood sample from. Tonkee meets your gaze for a moment with such an utter lack of surprise or fear that you realize Ykka's right; she probably figured it out sometime ago.

"Rogga as a use name." Tonkee's thoughtful as she focuses on Ykka again. "So many implications to that one. And Castrima; that's not one of the Imperial Registry-listed Somidlats comm names, either, although I'll admit I might just have forgotten it. There's hundreds, after all. I don't think I have, though; I've got a good memory. This a newcomm?"

Ykka inclines her head, partly in affirmation and partly in ironic acknowledgment of Tonkee's fascination. "Technically. This version of Castrima has been around for maybe fifty years. It isn't really a comm at all, officially—just another lodging stop for people heading along the Yumenes–Mecemera and Yumenes–Ketteker routes. We get more business than most because there are mines in the area."

She pauses then, gazing at Hoa, and for a moment her expression tightens. You look at Hoa, too, puzzled, because granted, he's strange-looking, but you're not sure what he's done to merit that kind of tension from a stranger. That's when you finally notice that Hoa has gone utterly still, and his little face has sharpened from its usual cheerfulness into something taut and angry and almost feral. He's glaring at Ykka like he wants to kill her.

No. Not Ykka. You follow his gaze to the third member of Ykka's party, who's stayed slightly behind the other two till now, and whom you haven't really paid attention to because Ykka's so eye-catching. A tall, slender woman—and then you stop, frowning, because all at once you're not sure about that designation. The female part, sure; her hair is Antarctic-lank and deep red in color, decoratively long, framing features that are finely lined. It's clear she means to be read as a woman, though she's only wearing a long, loose sleeveless gown that should be far too thin for the cooling air.

But her skin. You're staring, it's rude, not the best way to start things off with these people, but you can't help it. Her skin. It's not just smooth, it's...glossy, sort of. Almost polished. She's either got the most amazing complexion you've ever seen, or—or that isn't skin.

The red-haired woman smiles, and the sight of her teeth confirms it even as you shiver to your bones.

Hoa hisses like a cat in reply to that smile. And as he does so, finally, terribly, you see his teeth clearly for the first time. He never eats in front of you, after all. He never shows them when he smiles. They're colored in where hers are transparent, enamel-white as a kind of camouflage—but not so different from the red-haired woman's in shape. Not squared but *faceted.* Diamondine.

"Evil Earth," mutters Tonkee. You feel that she speaks for the both of you.

Ykka glances sharply at her companion. "No."

The red-haired woman's eyes flick toward Ykka. No other part of her moves, the rest of her body remaining stock-still. *Statue*-still. "It can be done without harm to you or your companions." Her mouth doesn't move, either. The voice sounds oddly hollow, echoing up from somewhere inside her chest.

"I don't want anything 'done.'" Ykka puts her hands on her hips. "This is my place, and you've agreed to abide by my rules. *Back off.*"

The blond woman shifts a little. She doesn't bring the crossbow up, but you think she's ready to do so at a moment's notice. For whatever good that will do. The red-haired woman doesn't move for a moment, and then she closes her mouth to hide those awful diamond teeth. As she does this, you realize several things at once. The first is that she wasn't actually smiling. It was a threat display, like the way a kirkhusa draws back its lips to bare its fangs. The second is that with her mouth closed and that placid expression, she looks far less unnerving.

The third realization you have is that Hoa was making the same threat display. But he relaxes, and closes his mouth, as the red-haired woman eases back.

Ykka exhales. She focuses on you again.

"I think perhaps," she says, "you'd better come inside."

"I'm not sure that's the best idea in the world," Tonkee says to you, pleasantly.

"Neither am I," says the blond woman, glaring at Ykka's head. "You sure about that, Yeek?"

Ykka shrugs, though you think she's not nearly as nonchalant as she seems. "When am I sure about anything? But it seems like a good idea, for now."

You're not sure you agree. Still—strange comm or not, mythical creatures or not, unpleasant surprises or not, you came here for a reason.

"Did a man and a girl come through here?" you ask. "Father and daughter. The man would be about my age, the girl eight—" Two months. You've almost forgotten. "*Nine* years old. She—" You falter. Stutter. "Sh-she looks like me."

Ykka blinks, and you realize you've genuinely surprised her. Clearly she was braced for entirely different questions. "No," she says, and—

—and there's a sort of skip inside you.

It *hurts* to hear that simple "no." It hits like a hachet blow, and the salt in the wound is Ykka's look of honest perplexity. That means she's not lying. You flinch and sway with the impact, with the death of all your hopes. It occurs to you through a haze of floating not-quite-thought that you've been *expecting* something since Hoa told you about this place. You were beginning to think you would find them here, have a daughter again, be a mother again. Now you know better.

"S—Essun?" Hands grasp your forearms. Whose? Tonkee. Her hands are rough with hard living. You hear her calluses rasp on the leather of your jacket. "Essun—oh, rust, don't."

You've always known better. How dare you expect anything else? You're just another filthy, rusty-souled rogga, just another agent of the Evil Earth, just another mistake of sensible breeding practices, just another mislaid tool. You should never have had children in the first place, and you shouldn't have expected to keep them once you did, and why's Tonkee pulling on your arms?

Because you've lifted your hands to your face. Oh, and you've burst into tears.

You should have told Jija, before you ever married him, before you slept with him, before you even looked at him and thought *maybe,* which you had no right to ever think. Then if the urge to kill a rogga had hit him, he would've inflicted it on you, not Uche. You're the one who deserves to die, after all, ten thousand times the population of two comms.

Also, you might be screaming a little.

You shouldn't be screaming. You should be dead. You should have died before your children. You should have died at birth, and never lived to bear them.

You should have—

You should have—

Something sweeps through you.

It feels a little like the wave of force that came down from the north, and which you shunted away, on that day the world changed. Or maybe a little like the way you felt when you walked into the house after a tiring day and saw your boy lying on the floor. A waft of potential, passing on unutilized. The brush of something intangible but meaningful, there and gone, as shocking by its absence as its existence in the first place.

You blink and lower your hands. Your eyes are blurry and they hurt; the heels of your hands are wet. Ykka is off the porch and standing in front of you, just a couple of feet away. She's not touching you, but you stare at her anyway, realizing she just did—something. Something you don't understand. Orogeny, certainly, but deployed in a way you've never experienced before.

"Hey," she says. There's nothing like compassion on her face. Still, her voice is softer as she speaks to you—though maybe that's only because she's closer. "Hey. You okay now?"

You swallow. Your throat hurts. "No," you say. (That word again! You almost giggle, but you swallow and the urge vanishes.) "No. But I'm... I can keep it together."

Ykka nods slowly. "See that you do." Beyond her, the blond woman looks skeptical about the possibility of this.

Then, with a heavy sigh, Ykka turns to Tonkee and Hoa—the latter of whom looks deceptively calm and normal now. Normal by Hoa standards, anyway.

"All right, then," she says. "Here's how it is. You can stay or you can go. If you decide to stay, I'll take you into the comm. But you need to know up front: Castrima is something unique. We're trying something very different here. If this Season turns out to be short, then we're going to be up a lava lake when Sanze comes down on us. But I don't think this Season will be short."

She glances at you, sidelong, not quite for confirmation. *Confirmation*'s not the word for it, since there was never doubt. Any rogga knows it like they know their own name.

"This Season won't be short," you agree. Your voice is hoarse, but you're recovering. "It will last decades." Ykka lifts an eyebrow. Yeah, she's right; you're trying to be gentle for the sake of your companions, and they don't need gentleness. They need truth. "Centuries."

Even that's an understatement. You're pretty sure this one will last at least a thousand years. Maybe a *few* thousand.

Tonkee frowns a little. "Well, everything does point to either a major epeirogenic deformation, or possibly just a simple disruption of isostasy throughout the entire plate network. But the amount of orogenesis needed to overcome that much inertia is . . . prohibitive. Are you sure?"

You're staring at her, grief momentarily forgotten. So's Ykka, and the blond woman. Tonkee grimaces in irritation, glowering particularly at you. "Oh, for rust's sake, stop acting all surprised. The secrets are done now, right? You know what I am and I know what you are. Do we have to keep pretending?"

You shake your head, though you're not really responding to her question. You decide to answer her other question instead. "I'm sure," you say. "Centuries. Maybe more."

Tonkee flinches. "No comm has stores enough to last that long. Not even Yumenes."

Yumenes's fabled vast storecaches are slag in a lava tube somewhere. Part of you mourns the waste of all that food. Part of you figures, well, *that much quicker and more merciful an end for the human race.*

When you nod, Tonkee falls into a horrified silence. Ykka looks from you to Tonkee, and apparently decides to change the subject.

"There are twenty-two orogenes here," she says. You flinch. "I expect there will be more as time passes. You all right with that?" She looks at Tonkee in particular.

As subject changes go, it's perfect for distracting everyone. "How?" asks Tonkee at once. "How are you making them come here?"

"Never mind that. Answer the question."

You could've told Ykka not to bother. "I'm fine with it," Tonkee says immediately. You're surprised she's not visibly salivating. So much for her shock over the inevitable death of humanity.

"All right." Ykka turns to Hoa. "And you. There are a few others of your kind here, too."

"More than you think," Hoa says, very softly.

"Yeah. Well." Ykka takes this with remarkable aplomb. "You heard how it is. If you want to stay here, you follow the rules. No fighting. No—" She waggles her fingers and bares her teeth. This is surprisingly comprehensible. "And you do as I say. Got it?"

Hoa cocks his head a little, his eyes glittering in pure menace. It's as shocking to see as his diamond teeth; you'd started thinking of him as a rather sweet creature, if a bit eccentric. Now you're not sure what to think. "You don't command me."

Ykka, to your greater amazement, leans over and puts her face right in front of his.

"Let me put it this way," she says. "You can keep doing what you've obviously been doing, trying to be as avalanche-subtle as your kind ever gets, or I can start telling everyone what all of you are *really* up to."

And Hoa . . . flinches. His eyes—only his eyes—flick toward the not-woman on the porch. The one on the porch smiles again, though she doesn't show her teeth this time, and there's a rueful edge to it. You don't know what any of this means, but Hoa seems to sag a little.

"Very well," he says to Ykka, with an odd formality. "I agree to your terms."

Ykka nods and straightens, letting her gaze linger on him for a moment longer before she turns away.

"What I was going to say before your little, ah, moment, was that we've taken in a few people," she says to you. She says this over her shoulder, as she turns and walks back up the steps of the house. "No men traveling with girls, I don't think, but other travelers looking for a place, including some from Cebak Quartent. We adopted them if we thought they were useful." It's what any smart comm does at times like these: kicking out the undesirable, taking in those with valuable skills and attributes. The comms that have strong leaders do this systematically, ruthlessly, with some degree of cold humanity. Less well-run comms do it just as ruthlessly but more messily, like the way Tirimo got rid of you.

Jija's just a stoneknapper. Useful, but knapping's not exactly a rare skill. Nassun, though, is like you and Ykka. And for some reason, the people of this comm seem to *want* orogenes around.

"I want to meet those people," you say. There's a slim chance that Jija or Nassun is in disguise. Or that someone else might have seen them, on the road. Or that . . . well. It really is a slim chance.

You'll take it, though. She's your daughter. You'll take anything, to find her.

"All right, then." Ykka turns and beckons. "Come on in, and I'll show you a marvel or three." As if she hasn't already done so. But you move to follow her, because neither myths nor mysteries can hold a candle to the most infinitesimal spark of hope.

* * *

The body fades. A leader who would last relies on more.

—Tablet Three, "Structures," verse two

16

Syen in the hidden land

Syenite wakes up cold on one side of her body. It's her left side—hip and shoulder and most of her back. The source of the cold, a sharp wind, blows almost painfully through the hair all along the back of her skull, which means her hair must have come loose from its Fulcrum-regulation bun. Also, there's a taste like dirt in her mouth, though her tongue is dry.

She tries to move and hurts all over, dully. It's a strange kind of pain, not localized, not throbbing or sharp or anything that specific. More like her whole body is one big bruise. She groans inadvertently as she wills a hand to move and finds hard ground beneath it. She pushes against it enough to feel like she's in control of herself again, though she doesn't actually manage to get up. All she does successfully is open her eyes.

Crumbling silvery stone beneath her hand and in front of her face: monzonite, maybe, or one of the lesser schists. She can never remember the subvolcanic rocks because the grit instructor for geomestry back at the Fulcrum was unbelievably boring. A few feet away, the whatever-it-is stone is broken by clovers and a scraggle of grass and some kind of bushy-leafed weed. (She paid even less attention in biomestry.) The plants stir restlessly in the wind, though not much, because her body shields them from the worst of it.

Blow that, she thinks, and is pushed awake by mild shock at her own mental crudeness.

She sits up. It hurts and it's hard to do, but she does it, and this allows her to see that she's lying on a gentle slope of rock, surrounded by more weeds. Beyond that is the unbroken expanse of the lightly clouded sky. There's an ocean smell, but it's different from what she's gotten used to in the past few weeks: less briny, more rarefied. The air is drier. The sun's position makes it late morning, and the cold feels like late winter.

But it should be late afternoon. And Allia is Equatorial; the temperature should be balmy. And the cold, hard ground she's lying on should be warm, sandy ground. So where the burning rusty fuck is she?

Okay. She can figure this out. The rock she's lying on sesses high above sea level, relatively close to a familiar boundary: That's the edge of the Maximal, one of the two main tectonic plates that make up the Stillness. The Minimal's way up north. And she's sessed this plate edge before: They're not far from Allia.

But they're not *in* Allia. In fact, they're not on the continent at all.

Reflexively Syenite tries to do more than just sess, reaching toward the plate edge as she's done a few times before—

—and nothing happens.

She sits there for a moment, more chilled than the wind can account for.

But she is not alone. Alabaster lies curled nearby, his long limbs folded fetal, either unconscious or dead. No; his side rises and falls, slowly. Okay, that's good.

Beyond him, at the top of the slope, stands a tall, slender figure clad in a white flowing robe.

Startled, Syen freezes for a moment. "Hello?" Her voice is a croak.

The figure—a woman, Syen guesses—does not turn. She's looking away, at something over the rise that Syenite cannot see. "Hello."

Well, that's a start. Syen forces herself to relax, although this is difficult when she cannot reach toward the earth for the reassurance of power. There's no reason to be alarmed, she chides herself; whoever this woman is, if she'd wanted to harm them, she could have easily done so by now. "Where are we?"

"An island, perhaps a hundred miles off the eastern coast."

"An *island?*" That's terrifying. Islands are death traps. The only worse places to live are atop fault lines and in dormant-but-not-extinct volcano calderas. But yes, now Syenite hears the distant sough of waves rolling against rocks, somewhere below the slope on which they lie. If they're only a hundred miles from the Maximal's edge, then that puts them entirely too close to an underwater fault line. Basically on top of it. This is why people don't live on islands, for Earth's sake; they could die in a tsunami any minute.

She gets to her feet, suddenly desperate to see how bad the situation is. Her legs are stiff from lying on stone, but she stumbles around Alabaster anyway until she's standing on the slope beside the woman. There she sees:

Ocean, as far as the eye can see, open and unbroken. The rock slope drops off sharply a few feet from where she's standing, becoming a sheer jagged cliff that stands some few hundred feet above the sea. When she eases up to that edge and looks down, froth swirls about knifelike rocks far below; falling means death. Quickly she steps back.

"How did we get here?" she whispers, horrified.

"I brought you."

"You—" Syenite rounds on the woman, anger already spiking through shock. Then the anger dies, leaving the shock to reign uncontested.

Make a statue of a woman: not tall, hair in a simple bun, elegant features, a graceful pose. Leave its skin and clothing the color of old warm ivory, but dab in deeper shading at irises and hair—black in both cases—and at the fingertips. The color here is a faded and rusty gradient, ground in like dirt. Or blood.

A stone eater.

"Evil Earth," Syenite whispers. The woman does not respond.

There is a groan behind them that forestalls anything else Syenite might have said. (But what can she say? What?) She tears her eyes from the stone eater and focuses on Alabaster, who's stirring and clearly feeling no better than Syenite about it. But she ignores him for the moment as she finally thinks of something to say.

"Why?" she asks. "Why did you bring us here?"

"To keep him safe."

It's just like the lorists say. The stone eater's mouth doesn't open when she speaks. Her eyes don't move. She might as well be the statue she appears to be. Then sense reasserts itself, and

Syenite notices what the creature has said. "To keep... *him* safe?" Again, the stone eater does not reply.

Alabaster groans again, so Syenite finally goes to him, helping him sit up as he begins to stir. His shirt pulls at the shoulder and he hisses, and belatedly she remembers the Guardian's throwing knife. It's gone now, but the shallow wound is stuck to the cloth of his shirt with dried blood. He swears as he opens his eyes. "*Decaye, shisex unrelabbemet.*" It's the strange language she's heard him use before.

"Speak Sanze-mat," she snaps, though she's not really irritated with him. She keeps her eyes on the stone eater, but the stone eater continues not to move.

"...Flaking, fucking *rust*," he says, grabbing at the injured area. "Hurts."

Syenite swats his hand away. "Don't bother it. You might reopen the wound." And they are hundreds of miles from civilization, separated from it by water as far as the eye can see in most directions. At the mercy of a creature whose race is the very definition of *enigmatic*, and also *deadly*. "We've got company."

Alabaster comes fully awake, blinking at Syenite and then looking beyond her; his eyes widen a little at the sight of the stone eater. Then he groans. "Shit. *Shit*. What have you done this time?"

Somehow, Syenite is not entirely surprised to realize Alabaster knows a stone eater.

"I've saved your life," the stone eater says.

"What?"

The stone eater's arm rises, so steadily that the motion surpasses *graceful* and edges into *unnatural*. No other part of her moves. She's pointing. Syenite turns to follow the gesture and sees the western horizon. But this horizon is broken, unlike the rest: There's a flat line of sea and sky to the left and right, but at the midpoint of this line is a pimple, fat and red-glowing and smoky.

"Allia," says the stone eater.

* * *

There's a village on the island, it turns out. The island is nothing but rolling hills and grass and solid rock—no trees, no topsoil. An utterly useless place to live. And yet as they reach the other side of the island, where the cliffs are a bit less jagged, they see another semicircular cove not unlike the one at Allia. (Not unlike the one that *was* at Allia.) The similarity stops there, however—because this harbor is much smaller, and this village is carved directly into the sheer cliff face.

It's hard to tell at first. Initially Syen thinks that what she's seeing are the mouths of caverns, irregularly dotting the jagged rock face. Then she realizes the cave mouths are all uniformly shaped, even if they vary in size: straight lines across the bottom of the opening and up its sides, arching to a graceful point across the top. And around each opening, someone has carved out the facade of a building: elegant pillars, a beveled rectangle of a doorway, elaborate corbels of curled flowers and cavorting animals. She's seen stranger. Not much, granted—but living in Yumenes, in the shadow of the Black Star and the Imperial Palace that crowns it, and in the Fulcrum with its walls of molded obsidian, makes one inured to oddities of art and architecture.

"She doesn't have a name," Alabaster tells her as they walk

down a set of railed stone steps they've found, which seem to wend toward the village. He's talking about the stone eater, who left them at the top of the steps. (Syen looked away for a moment and when she glanced back the stone eater was gone. Alabaster has assured her that she is still nearby. How he knows this, Syen isn't sure she wants to know.)

"I call her Antimony. You know, because she's mostly white? It's a metal instead of stone, because she's not a rogga, and anyway 'Alabaster' was taken."

Cute. "And she—it—answers to that."

"She does." He glances back at Syenite, which is a precarious sort of thing to do considering the steps here are very, very sheer. Even though there's a railing, anyone who takes a header down these stairs is likely to just flip over the railing and fall to a messy death down the rock face. "She doesn't mind it, anyway, and I figure she'd object if she did."

"Why did she bring us here?" To save them. All right, they can see Allia smoking, over the water. But Antimony's kind usually ignores and avoids humankind, unless humans piss them off.

Alabaster shakes his head, focusing on his footing again. "There's no 'why' to anything they do. Or if there is, they never bother telling us. I've stopped asking, frankly; waste of breath. Antimony has been coming to me for the past, hmm, five years? Usually when no one else is around." He makes a soft, rueful sound. "I used to think I was hallucinating her."

Yes, well. "And she doesn't tell you anything?"

"She just says she's here for me. I can't decide whether it's a supportive statement—you know, 'I'm here for you, 'Baster, I'll always love you, never mind that I'm a living statue that only looks like a pretty woman, I've got your back'—or something more sinister. Does it matter, though? If she saved our lives?"

Syen supposes not. "And where is she now?"

"Gone."

Syen resists the urge to kick him down the steps. "Into, ah—" She knows what she's read, but it does seem sort of absurd to say it aloud. "Into the earth?"

"I suppose so. They move through rock like it's air; I've seen them do it." He pauses on one of the stairs' frequent landings, which almost makes Syenite run into the back of him. "You *do* know that's probably how she got us here, right?"

It's something Syen's been trying not to think about. Even the idea of being touched by the stone eater is unnerving. To think further of being carried by the creature, dragged down beneath miles of solid rock and ocean: She cannot help shuddering. A stone eater is a thing that defies reason—like orogeny, or deadciv artifacts, or anything else that cannot be measured and predicted in a way that makes sense. But where orogeny can be understood (somewhat) and controlled (with effort), and where deadciv artifacts can at least be avoided until they rise from the rusting ocean right in front of you, stone eaters do as they please, go where they will. Lorists' tales are generous with warnings regarding these creatures; no one tries to stop them.

This thought makes Syen herself stop, and Alabaster continues for another flight before he realizes she's not following. "The stone eater," she says, when he turns back to her with an annoyed look. "The one in the obelisk."

"Not the same one," he says, with the sort of patience one reserves for people who are being particularly stupid but don't deserve to be told that to their faces because they've had a hard day. "I told you, I've known this one awhile."

"That isn't what I meant." *You idiot.* "The stone eater that was in the obelisk looked at me, before...before. It moved. It wasn't dead."

Alabaster stares at her. "When did you see this?"

"I..." She gestures, helplessly. There aren't words for it. "There was...it was when I...I *think* I saw it." Or maybe she hallucinated it. Some kind of life-flashing-before-her-eyes vision, triggered by the Guardian's knife? It felt so real.

Alabaster regards her for a long moment, his mobile face still in that way she is beginning to associate with his disapproval. "You did something that should've killed you. It didn't, but only because of sheer dumb luck. If you...saw things...I'm not surprised."

Syenite nods, not protesting his assessment. She felt the obelisk's power in those moments. It *would* have killed her, had it been whole. As it is, she feels...burned, sort of numb, in its wake. Is that why she can't work orogeny anymore? Or is that the lingering effect of whatever the Guardian did?

"What happened back there?" she asks him, frustrated. There's so much that makes no sense in all of this. Why did someone try to kill Alabaster? Why did a Guardian come to finish the job? What did any of that have to do with the obelisk? Why are they here, on a death-trap island in the middle of the rusting sea? "What's happening *now*? 'Baster, Earth eat us, you know more than you're saying."

His expression grows pained, but he finally sighs and folds his arms. "I don't, you know. Whatever you might think, I really don't have all the answers. I have no idea why you think I do."

Because he knows so much else that she doesn't. And because he's a ten-ringer: He can do things she can't imagine, can't even describe, and some part of her thinks he can probably *understand* things she can't, too. "You knew about that Guardian."

"Yes." Now he looks angry, though not at her. "I've run into that kind before. But I don't know why he was there. I can only guess."

"That's better than nothing!"

He looks exasperated. "Okay, then. A guess: Someone, or many someones, knew about that broken obelisk in Allia's harbor. Whoever that was, they also knew that a ten-ringer would likely notice the thing the instant he started sessing around down there. And since all it took to reactivate it was a *four*-ringer sessing around, it stands to reason that these mysterious Someones had no idea just how sensitive, or how dangerous, the obelisk really was. Or neither you nor I would ever have made it to Allia alive."

Syenite frowns, putting a hand on the railing to steady herself when an especially harsh gust of wind soughs up the cliff walls. "Someones."

"Groups. Factions, in some conflict we know nothing about and have only blundered into through sheer dumb luck."

"Factions *of Guardians?*"

He snorts derisively. "You say that like it's impossible. Do all roggas have the same goals, Syen? Do all stills? Even the stone eaters probably have their spats with one another."

And Earth only knows what that's like. "So one of these, ah, factions, dispatched that—Guardian—to kill us." No. Not once Syenite had told the Guardian that she'd been the one to activate the obelisk. "To kill *me*."

Alabaster nods, somber. "I imagine he's the one who poisoned me, too, thinking I'd be the one to trigger the obelisk. Guardians don't like to discipline us where the stills can see, if they can avoid it; might earn us inappropriate public sympathy. That broad-daylight attack was a last resort." He shrugs, frowning as he considers it. "I guess we're lucky he didn't try to poison you instead. Even for me, it should've worked. Paralysis of any kind tends to affect the sessapinae, too; I would've been completely helpless. If."

If he hadn't been able to summon power from the amethyst obelisk, harnessing Syenite's sessapinae to do what his could not. Now that Syen better understands what he did that night, it's somehow worse. She cocks her head at him. "No one really knows what you're capable of, do they?"

Alabaster sighs a little, looking away. "*I* don't even know what I'm capable of, Syen. The things the Fulcrum taught me... I had to leave them behind, past a certain point. I had to make my own training. And sometimes, it seems, if I can just *think* differently, if I can shed enough of what they taught me and try something new, I might..." He trails off, frowning in thought. "I don't know. I really don't. But I guess it's just as well that I don't, or the Guardians would've killed me a long time ago."

It's half-babble, but Syenite sighs in understanding. "So who has the ability to send killer Guardians out to, to..." Hunt down ten-ringers. Scare the piss out of four-ringers.

"All Guardians are killers," he snaps, bitterly. "As for who has the power to command a Guardian forth, I have no idea." Alabaster shrugs. "Rumor has it the Guardians answer to the Emperor—supposedly the Guardians are the last bit of power he possesses. Or maybe that's a lie, and the Yumenes Leadership families control them like they do everything else. Or are they controlled by the Fulcrum itself? No idea."

"I heard they controlled themselves," Syen says. It's probably just grit gossip.

"Maybe. The Guardians are certainly as quick to kill stills as roggas when it comes to maintaining their secrets, or if a still just gets in their way. If they have a hierarchy, only the Guardians themselves recognize it. As for how they do what they do..." He takes a deep breath. "It's some sort of surgical procedure. They're all the children of roggas, but not roggas themselves, because there's something about their sessapinae that makes this procedure work better on them. There's an implant involved. Into the brain. Earth knows how they learned that, or when they started doing it, but it gives them the ability to negate orogeny. And other abilities. Worse ones."

Syenite flinches, remembering the sound of ripping tendons. The palm of her hand stings sharply.

"He didn't try to kill you, though," she says. She's looking at his shoulder, which is still visibly darker colored than the cloth around it, though the walk has probably loosened the dried blood so it no longer sticks to the wound. There's a bit of fresh dampness there; it's bleeding again, but thankfully not much. "That knife—"

Alabaster nods grimly. "A Guardian specialty. Their knives

look like ordinary blow glass, but they aren't. They're like the Guardians themselves, somehow disrupting whatever it is in an orogene that makes us what we are." He shudders. "Never knew how it felt before; it hurt like Earthfire. And no," he says quickly, forestalling Syen's open mouth, "I don't know *why* he hit me with it. He'd already stilled us both; I was just as helpless as you."

And that. Syenite licks her lips. "Can you . . . are you still . . ."

"Yes. It goes away after a few days." He smiles at her look of relief. "I told you, I've run into Guardians like that before."

"Why did you tell me not to let him touch me? With his skin?"

Alabaster goes silent. Syenite thinks at first he's just being stubborn again, then she really looks at his expression and sees the shadows in it. After a moment, he blinks. "I knew another ten-ringer, when I was younger. When I was . . . He was a mentor, sort of. Like Feldspar is, for you."

"Feldspar isn't—never mind."

He ignores her anyway, lost in memory. "I don't know why it happened. But one day we were walking the Ring, just out enjoying a nice evening . . ." He falters abruptly, then looks at her with a wry, if pained, expression. "We were looking for someplace to be alone."

Oh. Maybe that explains a few things. "I see," she says unnecessarily.

He nods, unnecessarily. "Anyway, this Guardian shows up. Shirtless, like the one you saw. He didn't say anything about why he'd come, either. He just . . . attacked. I didn't see—it happened fast. Like in Allia." 'Baster rubs a hand over his face. "He put Hessionite in a choke hold, but not hard enough to actually choke him. The Guardian needed skin-to-skin contact. Then he just held Hess, and, and *grinned* while it happened. Like it was the most beautiful thing in the world, the sick fuck."

"What?" She almost doesn't want to know, and yet she does. "What does the Guardian's skin do?"

Alabaster's jaw flexes, the muscles knotting. "It turns your orogeny inward. I guess. I don't know a better way to explain it. But everything inside us that can move apart plates and seal faults and so on, all that power we're born with... Those Guardians turn it back on us."

"I, I don't..." But orogeny doesn't work on flesh, not directly. If it did—

...Oh.

He falls silent. Syenite does not prompt him to go on, this time.

"Yeah. So." Alabaster shakes his head, then glances toward the stone-cut cliff village. "Shall we go on?"

It's hard to talk, after that story. "'Baster." She gestures at herself, at her uniform, which is dusty but still plainly an Imperial Orogene's blackjacket. "Neither of us can so much as shake a pebble right now. We don't know these people."

"I know. But my shoulder hurts, and I'm thirsty. You see any free-flowing water around here?"

No. And no food. And there's no way to swim back to the mainland, not across such a long expanse. That's if Syenite knew how to swim, which she doesn't, and if the ocean wasn't teeming with monsters like the tales say, which it probably is.

"Fine, then," she says, and pushes past him to lead the way. "Let me talk to them first, so you don't get us killed." Crazy ruster.

Alabaster chuckles a little as if he's heard her unvoiced thought, but he does not protest, resuming the descent in her wake.

The stairs level out, eventually, into a smooth-carved walkway that curves along the cliff wall some hundred feet above the highest waterline. Syen figures that means the comm is safe from tsunami because of its elevation. (She can't be sure, of course. All this *water* is still strange to her.) It also almost makes up for the lack of a protective wall—although, all things considered, the ocean makes for a pretty effective barrier between these people and anyone from outside their . . . comm, if it can be called that. There are a dozen or so boats docked below, bobbing at jetties that look as though they're made of piled stone overlaid haphazardly with boards—ugly and primitive in comparison with Allia's neat piers and pylons, but effective. And the boats are strange-looking too, at least compared to the boats she's seen: Some are simple, elegant things that look as if they might have been carved whole from tree trunks, braced on each side by some sort of strut. Some are larger and have sails, but even these are of a completely foreign design to what she's used to seeing.

There are people at and around the boats, some of them carting baskets to and fro, others working on an elaborate rigging of sails on one of them. They don't look up; Syenite resists the urge to call down to them. She and Alabaster have already been seen, anyhow. At the first of the cavern mouths up ahead—each of which is huge, now that they're on the "ground" level and can get a good look—a knot of people has begun to gather.

Syenite licks her lips and takes a deep breath as they draw

near. They don't look hostile. "Hello," she ventures, and then waits. No one tries to kill her immediately. So far, so good.

The twenty or so people waiting for them mostly look bemused at the sight of her and Alabaster. The group is mostly children of varying ages, a few younger adults, a handful of elders, and a leashed kirkhusa that seems friendly, to judge by the wag of its stubby tail. The people are definitely Eastcoasters, mostly tall and dark like Alabaster though with a sprinkling of paler citizens, and she spots at least one pouf of ashblow hair lifting in the constant breeze. They also don't look alarmed, which is good, though Syen gets the distinct impression they're not used to surprise visitors.

Then an older man with an air of Leadership, or maybe just leadership, steps forward. And says something completely incomprehensible.

Syen stares at him. She can't even tell what language that is, although it's familiar somehow. Then—oh, of rusting *course*—Alabaster sort of jerks and says something back in the same tongue, and all at once everyone chuckles and murmurs and relaxes. Except Syenite.

She glares at him. "Translation?"

"I told them you were afraid I'd get us killed if I spoke first," he says, and she considers killing him right then and there.

So it goes. They start talking, the people of this strange village and Alabaster, while Syen can't do anything but stand there trying not to look frustrated. Alabaster pauses to translate when he can, though he stumbles over some of what the strangers are saying; they're all talking really fast. She gets the impression that he's summarizing. A lot. But it turns out that the comm is called Meov, and the man who has stepped forward is Harlas, their headman.

Also, they're pirates.

* * *

"There's no way to grow food here," Alabaster explains. "They do what they have to do, to get by."

This is later, after the people of Meov have invited them into the vaulted halls which make up their comm. It's all inside the cliff—unsurprising since the island consists of little more than a straight column of undifferentiated rock—with some of the caverns natural and others carved by unknown means. All of it is surprisingly beautiful, too, with artfully vaulted ceilings, aqueduct arches running along many walls, and enough torch and lantern light that none of it feels claustrophobic. Syen doesn't like the feel of all that rock hovering overhead and waiting to crush them next time there's a shake, but if she must be stuck inside a death trap, at least this one is cozy.

The Meovites have put them up in a guesthouse—or rather, a house that's been abandoned for a while and isn't in too much disrepair. She and Alabaster have been given food from the communal fires, access to the communal baths, and a couple of changes of clothing in the local style. They've even been allotted a modicum of privacy—though this is difficult, as curious children keep peeking through their carved, curtainless windows to giggle at them and then run away. It's almost cute.

Syen sits now on a pile of folded blankets, which seem to have been made for the purpose of sitting, watching as Alabaster winds a length of clean rag around his injured shoulder, holding the other end in his teeth for a moment to tighten it into a bandage. He could ask her for help, of course, but he doesn't, so she doesn't offer.

"They don't trade much with the mainland," he continues as he works. "All they've really got to offer is fish, and the mainland Coaster comms have plenty of that. So Meov raids. They attack vessels along the main trading routes, or extort comms for protection from attacks—yes, *their* attacks. Don't ask me how it works; that's just what the headman told me."

It sounds...precarious. "What are they even doing here?" Syen looks around at the rough-carved walls and ceiling. "It's an *island*. I mean, these caverns are nice, sort of, until the next shake or tsunami wipes the whole thing off the map. And like you said, there's no way to grow food. Do they even have storecaches? What happens if there's a Season?"

"Then they'll die, I guess." 'Baster shrugs, mostly to settle his newly tied bandage. "I asked them that, too, and they just sort of laughed the question off. You notice this island sits on top of a hot spot?"

Syen blinks. She hadn't noticed, but then her orogeny is as numb as a hammered finger. His is, too, but the numbness is relative, apparently. "How deep?"

"Very. It's unlikely to blow anytime soon, or ever—but if it ever does, there will be a crater here instead of islands." He grimaces. "'Course, that's if a tsunami doesn't get the island first, close as we are to the plate boundary here. There're so *many* ways to die in this place. But they know about all of them—seriously—and as far as I can tell, they don't care. At least they'll die free, they say."

"Free of what? Living?"

"Sanze." Alabaster grins when Syen's mouth falls open. "According to Harlas, this comm's part of a string of small island comms all along the archipelago—that's the word for a group of islands, if you didn't know—that extends from here down almost to the Antarctic, created by that hot spot. Some of the comms in that chain, this one included, have been around ten Seasons or longer—"

"Bullshit!"

"—and they don't even remember when Meov was founded and, uh, carved, so maybe it's older than that. They've been around since *before Sanze.* And as far as they know, Sanze either doesn't know or doesn't care that they're here. They were never annexed." He shakes his head. "The Coaster comms are always accusing each other of hosting the pirates, and no one with sense sails this far out; maybe nobody knows these island comms are out here. I mean, they probably know the islands exist, but they must not think anyone would be stupid enough to live on them."

No one should be. Syen shakes her head, amazed at these people's audacity. When another comm child pokes her head above the windowsill, blatantly staring at them, Syen can't help smiling, and the girl's eyes grow round as saucers before she bursts out laughing, babbles something in their choppy language, and then gets pulled away by her comrades. Brave, crazy little thing.

Alabaster chuckles. "She said, 'The mean one actually smiles!'"

Rusting brat.

"I can't believe they *are* crazy enough to live here," she says, shaking her head. "I can't believe this island hasn't shaken apart, or been blown to slag, or been swamped a hundred times over."

Alabaster shifts a little, looking cagey, and by this Syen knows to brace herself. "Well, they survive in large part because they live on fish and seaweed, see. The oceans don't die during a Season the way the land or a smaller body of water does. If you can fish, there's always food. I don't think they even have storecaches." He looks around, thoughtful. "If they can keep the place stable against shakes and blows, then I guess it *would* be a good place to live."

"But how could they—"

"Roggas." He looks at her and grins, and she realizes he's been waiting to tell her this. "That's how they've survived all this time. They don't kill their roggas, here. They put them *in charge*. And they're really, really glad to see us."

* * *

The stone eater is folly made flesh. Learn the lesson of its creation, and beware its gifts.

—*Tablet Two, "The Incomplete Truth," verse seven*

17

Damaya, in finality

THINGS CHANGE. THERE IS AN order to life in the Fulcrum, but the world is never still. A year passes.

After Crack disappears, Maxixe never speaks to Damaya again. When he sees her in the corridors, or after inspection, he simply turns away. If he catches her looking at him, he scowls. He doesn't catch her often, though, because she doesn't look at him often. She doesn't mind that he hates her. He was only a *potential* friend, anyway. She knows better, now, than to want such a thing, or to believe that she will ever deserve one.

(Friends do not exist. The Fulcrum is not a school. Grits are not children. Orogenes are not people. Weapons have no need of friends.)

Still, it's hard, because without friends she's bored. The instructors have taught her to read as her parents did not, but she can only do so much of that before the words start to flip and jitter on the page like pebbles during a shake. The library doesn't have a lot of books that are just for fun and not utilitarian, anyway. (Weapons do not need fun, either.) She's only allowed to practice her orogeny during Applied, and even though she sometimes lies in her bunk and imagines the lessons over again for extra practice—an orogene's power is in her focus, after all—there's only so much of that she can do, too.

So to occupy her Free Hour, and any other hour when she isn't busy or sleeping, she wanders around the Fulcrum.

No one stops grits from doing this. No one guards the grit dormitory during Free Hour or afterward. The instructors do not enforce a curfew; Free Hour can be Free Night, if a grit's willing to struggle through the next day sleepy. Nor do the adults do anything to prevent the grits from leaving the building. Any child caught in the Ring Garden, which is off-limits to the unringed, or approaching the gates that lead out of the Fulcrum, will have to answer to the seniors. But anything less and the sanctions will be mild, bearable; the usual punishment befitting the crime. That's it.

No one gets expelled from the Fulcrum, after all. Dysfunctional weapons are simply removed from the stockpile. And functional weapons should be smart enough to take care of themselves.

Thus Damaya keeps to the Fulcrum's least interesting areas in her wanderings—but this leaves plenty to explore, because the Fulcrum complex is huge. Apart from the Garden and the grit training grounds there are clusters of living quarters that house the ringed orogenes, libraries and theaters, a hospital, and places where all the adult orogenes do their work when they're not off on assignments beyond the Fulcrum. There are also miles of obsidian-paved walkways and greenland that hasn't been left fallow or kept prepared for a possible Fifth Season;

instead, it's landscaped. It's just there to be pretty. Damaya figures that means someone should look at it.

So it is through all this that Damaya walks, in the late hours of the evening, imagining where and how she will live once she joins the ranks of the ringed. The adults in this area mostly ignore her, coming and going about their business, talking with each other or muttering to themselves alone, focused on their adulty things. Some of them notice her, but then shrug and keep walking. They were grits once. Only on one occasion does a woman stop and ask, "Are you supposed to be here?" Damaya nods and walks past her, and the woman does not pursue.

The administrative buildings are more interesting. She visits the large practice chambers that the ringed orogenes use: great ampitheater-like halls, roofless, with mosaic rings etched into the bare ground in concentric circles. Sometimes there are huge blocks of basalt lying about, and sometimes the ground is disturbed, but the basalt is gone. Sometimes she catches adults in the chambers, practicing; they shift the blocks around like children's toys, pushing them deep into the earth and raising them again by will alone, blurring the air around themselves with deadly rings of cold. It is exhilarating, and intimidating, and she follows what they're doing as best she can, though that isn't much. She's got a long way to go before she can even begin to do some of these things.

It's Main that fascinates Damaya most. This building is the core of the Fulcrum complex: a vast domed hexagon larger than all the other buildings combined. It is in this building that the business of the Fulcrum gets done. Here ringed orogenes occupy the offices and push the papers and pay the bills, because of course they must do all of these things themselves. No one will have it said that orogenes are useless drains on the resources of Yumenes; the Fulcrum is fiscally and otherwise self-sufficient. Free Hour is after the main working hours for the building, so it's not as busy as it must be during the day, but whenever Damaya wanders the place, she notices that many of the offices are still lit with candles and the occasional electric lantern.

The Guardians have a wing in Main, too. Now and again Damaya sees burgundy uniforms amid the clusters of black, and when she does, she turns the other way. Not out of fear. They probably see her, but they don't bother her, because she's not doing anything she's been told not to do. It is as Schaffa told her: One need only fear Guardians in specific, limited circumstances. She avoids them, however, because as she grows more skilled, she begins to notice a strange sensation whenever she's in a Guardian's presence. It is a... a buzzy feeling, a jagged and *acrid* sort of thing, something more heard and tasted than sessed. She does not understand it, but she notices that she is not the only orogene to give the Guardians a wide berth.

In Main, there are the wings that have fallen into disuse because the Fulcrum is larger than it needs to be, or so Damaya's instructors have told her when she asks them about this. No one knew how many orogenes there were in the world before the Fulcrum was built, or perhaps the builders thought that more orogenes would survive childhood to be brought here than has proven true over time. Regardless, the first time Damaya pushes open a conspicuous-looking door that no one seems to be using and finds dark, empty hallways beyond it, she is instantly intrigued.

It's too dark to see very far within. Nearby she can make out discarded furniture and storage baskets and the like, so she decides against exploring immediately. The chance that she could hurt herself is too great. Instead she heads back to the grit dorms, and all through the next few days, she prepares. It's easy to take a small glassknife used for cutting meat from one of the meal trays, and the dorm has plenty of oil lanterns that she can appropriate without anyone caring, so she does. She makes a knapsack out of a pillowcase that she nabs while on laundry duty—it has a tattered edge and was in the "discard" pile—and finally when she feels ready, she sets forth.

It's slow going, at first. With the knife she marks the walls here and there so she won't get lost—until she realizes this part of Main has exactly the same structure as the rest of Main: a central corridor with periodic stairwells, and doors on either side leading into rooms or suites of rooms. It's the rooms that she likes most, though many of them are boring. Meeting rooms, more offices, the occasional space large enough to serve as a lecture hall, though mostly these seem to be used for storage of old books and clothing.

But the books! A good many of them are the frivolous sort of tales that the library has so few of—romances and adventures and bits of irrelevant lore. And sometimes the doors lead to amazing things. She discovers a floor that was once apparently used as living quarters—perhaps in some boom year when there were too many orogenes to house comfortably in the apartment buildings. For whatever reason, however, it appears that many of the inhabitants simply walked off and left their belongings behind. Damaya discovers long, elegant dresses in the closets, dry-rotted; toys meant for toddlers; jewelry that her mother would have salivated to wear. She tries on some of it and giggles at herself in the flyspecked mirror, and then stops, surprised by the sound of her own laughter.

There are stranger things. A room full of plush, ornate chairs—worn and moth-eaten now—all arranged in a circle to face each other: why, she can only imagine. A room she does not understand until later, after her explorations have taken her into the buildings of the Fulcrum that are dedicated to research: Then she knows that what she has found is a kind of laboratory, with strange containers and contraptions that she eventually learns are used for analysis of energy and manipulation of chemicals. Perhaps geomests do not deign to study orogeny, and orogenes are left to do that for themselves, too? She can only guess.

And there is more, endlessly more. It becomes the thing she looks forward to the most in any given day, after Applied. She gets in trouble now and again in learning creche because sometimes she daydreams of things she's found, and misses questions during quizzes. She takes care not to slack off so much that the teachers question her, even though she suspects they know about her nighttime explorations. She's even seen a few of them while she wanders, lounging about and seeming oddly human in their off-hours. They don't bother her about it, though, which pleases her mightily. It's nice to feel as if she has a secret to share with them, even though she doesn't really. There is an order to life in the Fulcrum, but this is *her* order; she sets it, and no one else disrupts it. It is good to have something she keeps for herself.

And then, one day, everything changes.

* * *

The strange girl slips into the line of grits so unobtrusively that Damaya almost doesn't notice. They're walking through the Ring Garden again, on their way back to the grit dormitory after Applied, and Damaya is tired but pleased with herself. Instructor Marcasite praised her for only icing a two-foot torus around herself while simultaneously stretching her zone of control to an approximate depth of one hundred feet. "You're almost ready for the first ring test," he told her at the end of the lesson. If this is true, she could end up taking the test a year earlier than most grits, and first of any in her year group.

Because Damaya is so caught up in the glow of this thought, and because it's the evening of a long day and everyone's weary and the Garden is sparsely populated and the instructors are chatting with each other, almost no one sees the strange girl slip into line just ahead of Damaya. Even Damaya almost misses it, because the girl has cleverly waited until they're turning a curve round a hedge; between one step and another she is there, matching their pace, keeping her gaze forward as most of the others do. But Damaya knows she was not there before.

For a moment Damaya is taken aback. She doesn't know all the other grits *well*, but she does know them on sight, and this girl isn't one of them. Who is she, then? She wonders whether she should say something.

Abruptly the girl glances back and catches Damaya staring. She grins and winks; Damaya blinks. When the girl turns away again, she keeps following, too flustered now to tattle.

They proceed through the Garden and into the barracks and then the instructors depart for the evening, leaving the grits to

Free Hour before bedtime. The other kids disperse, some going to fetch food from the sideboard, the newer ones dragging off to bed. A few of the more energetic grits immediately start some sort of silly game, chasing each other round the bunk beds. As usual they ignore Damaya and anything Damaya is doing.

So Damaya turns to the grit who is not a grit. "Who are you?"

"Is that really what you want to ask?" The girl looks honestly puzzled. She is Damaya's age, tall and lanky and more sallow-skinned than most young Sanzeds, and her hair is curled and dark instead of stiff and gray. She's wearing a grit's uniform, and she's actually tied her hair back the same way the other grits with loose hair have done. Only the fact that she's a total stranger breaks the illusion.

"I mean, you don't actually care who I am, do you?" the girl continues, still looking almost offended by Damaya's first question. "If I were you, I'd want to know what I was doing here."

Damaya stares at her, speechless. In the meantime, the girl looks around, frowning a little. "I thought a lot of other people would notice me. There aren't that many of you—what, thirty in this room? That's less than in my creche, and *I* would notice if somebody new suddenly popped in—"

"Who are you?" Damaya demands, half-hissing the words. Instinctively, though, she keeps her voice down, and for added measure grabs the girl's arm, hauling her over to an out-of-the-way corner where people are less likely to notice. Except everyone's had years of practice at paying no attention to Damaya, so they don't. "Tell me or I yell for the instructors."

"Oh, that's better." The girl grins. "Much more what I was expecting! But it's still weird that you're the only one—" And then her expression changes to one of alarm when Damaya inhales and opens her mouth, clearly preparing to shout. Quickly she blurts, "My name's Binof! Binof! And you are?"

It's such a commonplace sort of thing to say, the pattern of courtesy that Damaya used for most of her life before coming to the Fulcrum, that she answers automatically. "Damaya Strong—" She has not thought of her use name, or the fact that it no longer applies to her, in so long that she is shocked to almost hear herself say it. "Damaya. What are you doing here? Where did you come from? Why are you—" She gestures helplessly at the girl, encompassing the uniform, the hair, Binof's existence.

"Shhh. *Now* you want to ask a million questions?" Binof shakes her head. "Listen, I'm not going to stay, and I'm not going to get you in trouble. I just need to know—have you seen anything weird around here somewhere?" Damaya stares at her again, and Binof grimaces. "A place. With a shape. Sort of. A big—a thing that—" She makes a series of complicated gestures, apparently trying to pantomime what she means. It is completely nonsensical.

Except, it isn't. Not entirely.

The Fulcrum is circular. Damaya knows this even though she can only get a sense of it when she and the other grits transit the Ring Garden. The Black Star looms to the west of the Fulcrum's grounds, and to the north Damaya has seen a cluster of buildings tall enough to peek over the obsidian walls. (She often wonders what the inhabitants of those buildings think, looking down on Damaya and her kind from their lofty windows and rooftops.) But more significantly, *Main* is circular, too—almost. Damaya has wandered its dark hallways often enough by now, with only a lantern and her fingers and sessapinae to guide her, that when she sees Binof make a hexagonal shape with her hands, she knows at once what the strange girl means.

See, Main's walls and corridors aren't wide enough to account for all the space the building occupies. The building's roof covers an area at its heart, into which its working and walking spaces do not extend; there must be a huge empty chamber within. Courtyard, maybe, or a theater, though there are other theaters in the Fulcrum. Damaya has found the walls around this space, and followed them, and they are not circular; there are planes and angles. Six of each. But if there is a door that opens into this hexagonal central room, it isn't anywhere in the unused wings—not that she's found yet.

"A room without doors," Damaya murmurs, without thinking. It is what she started calling the unseen chamber in her head, on the day she realized it must exist. And Binof inhales and leans forward.

"Yes. *Yes.* Is that what it's called? Is it in that big building at the center of the Fulcrum complex? That's where I thought it might be. Yes."

Damaya blinks and scowls. "Who. *Are.* You." The girl's right; that's not really what she means to say. Still, it covers all the salient questions at once.

Binof grimaces. She glances around, thinks a moment, sets her jaw, and finally says, "Binof Leadership Yumenes."

It almost means nothing to Damaya. In the Fulcrum, no one has use names or comm names. Anyone who was Leadership, before being taken by the Guardians, isn't anymore. The grits who were born here or brought in young enough have a rogga name, and anyone else is required to take one when they earn their first ring. That's all they get.

But then intuition turns a key here and makes various clues click together there, and suddenly Damaya realizes Binof is not merely expressing misplaced loyalty to a social convention that no longer applies. It *does* apply to Binof, because *Binof is not an orogene.*

And Binof's not just any still: she's a Leader, and she's from Yumenes, which makes her a child of one of the most powerful families in the Stillness. *And she has snuck into the Fulcrum, pretending to be an orogene.*

It's so impossible, so insane, that Damaya's mouth falls open. Binof sees that she understands, and edges closer, dropping her voice. "I told you, I'm not going to get you into trouble. I'll go, now, and find that room, and all I ask is that you don't tell anyone yet. But you wanted to know why I'm here. *That's* why I'm here. That room is what I'm looking for."

Damaya closes her mouth. "Why?"

"I can't tell you." When Damaya glares, Binof holds up her hands. "That's for your safety, and mine. There's things only Leaders are supposed to know, and I'm not even supposed to know them yet. If anyone learns I told you, then—" She hesitates. "I don't know what they would do to either of us, but I don't want to find out."

Crack. Damaya nods, absently. "They'll catch you."

"Probably. But when they do, I'll just tell them who I am." The girl shrugs, with the ease of someone who has never known true fear in her life. "They won't know why I'm here. Someone will call my parents and I'll be in trouble, but I get in trouble all the time anyway. If I can find out the answers to some questions first, though, it'll be worth it. Now, where's that room without doors?"

Damaya shakes her head, seeing the trap at once. "*I* could get in trouble for helping you." She isn't a Leader, or a person; no one will save her. "You should leave, however you got here. Now. I won't tell anyone, if you do."

"No." Binof looks smug. "I went to a lot of trouble to get in here. And anyway, you're already in trouble, because you didn't shout for an instructor the minute you realized I wasn't a grit. Now you're my accomplice. Right?"

Damaya starts, her stomach constricting as she realizes the girl is right. She's also furious, because Binof is trying to manipulate her, and she hates that. "It's better if I shout now than let you blunder off and get caught later." And she gets up and heads for the dormitory door.

Binof gasps and trots after her quickly, catching her arm and speaking in a harsh whisper. "Don't! Please—look, I have money. Three red diamond chips and a whole alexandrite! Do you want money?"

Damaya's growing angrier by the minute. "What the rust would I need with money?"

"Privileges, then. The next time you leave the Fulcrum—"

"*We don't leave.*" Damaya scowls and yanks her arm out of Binof's grip. How did this fool of a still even get in here? There are guards, members of the city militia, at all the doors that lead out of the Fulcrum. But those guards are there to keep orogenes in, not stills out—and perhaps this Leader girl with her money and her *privileges* and her fearlessness would have found a way in even if the guards had tried to stop her. "We're here because it's the only place we can be safe from people like *you*. *Get out*."

Suddenly Damaya has to turn away, clenching her fists and concentrating hard and taking quick deep breaths, because she's so angry that the part of herself that knows how to shift fault lines is starting to wander down into the earth. It's a shameful breach of control, and she prays none of the instructors sense it, because then she will no longer be thought of as almost ready for the first ring test. Not to mention that she might end up icing this girl.

Infuriatingly, Binof leans around her and says, "Oh! Are you angry? Are you doing orogeny? What does it feel like?"

The questions are so ridiculous, her lack of fear so nonsensical, that Damaya's orogeny fizzles. She's suddenly not angry anymore, just astonished. Is this what all Leaders are like as children? Palela was so small that it didn't have any; people of the Leader use-caste generally prefer to live in places that are worth leading. Maybe this is just what *Yumenescene* Leaders are like. Or maybe this girl is just ridiculous.

As if Damaya's silence is an answer in itself, Binof grins and dances around in front of her. "I've never had a chance to meet an orogene before. The grown-ups, I mean, the ones with rings who wear the black uniforms, but not a kid like me. You're not as scary as the lorists said you would be. But then, lorists lie a lot."

Damaya shakes her head. "I don't understand anything about you."

To her surprise, Binof sobers. "You sound like my mom." She looks away for a moment, then presses her lips together and glowers at Damaya in apparent determination. "Will you help me find this room, or not? If you won't help, at least don't say anything."

In spite of everything, Damaya is intrigued—by the girl, by the possibility of finding a way into the room without doors, by the novelty of her own intrigue. She has never gone exploring *with* someone, before. It is . . . exciting. She shifts and looks around uncomfortably, but a part of her has already decided, hasn't it? "Okay. But I've never found a way in, and I've been exploring Main for months."

"Main, is that what the big building is called? And yes, I'm not surprised; there probably isn't an *easy* way in. Or maybe there was once, but it's closed off now." Oblivious as Damaya stares again, Binof rubs her chin. "I have an idea of where to look, though. I've seen some old structural drawings . . . Well, anyway, it would be on the southern side of the building. Ground level."

That is not in the unused wing, inconveniently. Still, she says, "I know the way," and it's heartening to see Binof brighten at these words.

She leads Binof the way she usually goes, walking the way she usually walks. Strangely, perhaps because she is nervous this time, she notices more people noticing her. There are more double takes than usual, and when she spies Instructor Galena by chance on her way past a fountain—Galena, who once caught her drunk and saved her life by not reporting it—he actually smiles before turning his attention back to his chatty companion. That's when Damaya finally realizes *why* people are looking: because they know about the strange quiet grit who goes wandering all the time. They've probably heard about Damaya via rumors or something, and they *like* that she's finally brought someone else with her. They think she's made a friend. Damaya would laugh, if the truth weren't so unfunny.

"Strange," says Binof as they walk one of the obsidian paths through one of the lesser gardens.

"What?"

"Well, I keep thinking everyone's going to notice me. But instead, almost no one's paying attention. Even though we're the only kids out here."

Damaya shrugs, and keeps walking.

"You'd think someone would stop us and ask questions, or something. We could be doing something unsafe."

Damaya shakes her head. "If one of us gets hurt and someone finds us before we bleed out, they'll take us to the hospital." And then Damaya will have a mark on her record that might prevent her from taking the ring test. Everything she does right now could interfere with that. She sighs.

"That's nice," says Binof, "but maybe it's a better idea to stop kids *before* they do things that might get them hurt."

Damaya stops in the middle of the lawn path and turns to Binof. "We aren't kids," she says, annoyed. Binof blinks. "We're grits—Imperial Orogenes in training. That's what you look like, so that's what everyone assumes you are. Nobody gives a damn whether a couple of orogenes get hurt."

Binof is staring at her. "Oh."

"And you're talking too much. Grits don't. We only relax in the dorms, and only when there are no instructors around. If you're going to pretend to be one of us, get it *right*."

"All right, all right!" Binof holds up both hands as if to

appease her. "I'm sorry, I just..." She grimaces as Damaya glares at her. "Right. No more talking."

She shuts up, so Damaya resumes walking.

They reach Main and head inside the way Damaya always does. Only this time she turns right instead of left, and heads downstairs instead of up. The ceilings are lower in this corridor, and the walls are decorated in a way she has never seen before, with little frescoes painted at intervals that depict pleasant, innocuous scenes. After a while she begins to worry, because they're getting closer and closer to a wing that she has never explored and doesn't want to: the Guardians'. "Where on the south side of the building?"

"What?" Preoccupied with looking around—which makes her stand out even more than the endless talking did—Binof blinks at Damaya in surprise. "Oh. Just...somewhere on the south side." She grimaces at Damaya's glare. "I don't know where! I just know there was a door, even if there isn't one anymore. Can't you—" She waggles her fingers. "Orogenes are supposed to be able to do things like that."

"What, find doors? Not unless they're *in the ground*." But even as Damaya says this, she frowns, because...well. She *can* sort of sess where doors are, by inference. Load-bearing walls feel much like bedrock, and door frames feel like gaps in strata—places where the pressure of the building against the ground is lesser. If a door somewhere on this level has been covered over, would its frame have been removed, too? Maybe. But would that place not feel different from the walls around it?

She's already turning, splaying her fingers the way she tends to do when she's trying to stretch her zone of control farther.

In the Applied crucibles there are markers underground—small blocks of marble with words etched into one surface. It takes a very fine degree of control to not only find the blocks but determine the word; it's like tasting a page of a book and noticing the minute differences between the ink and the bare page and using that to read. But because she has been doing this over and over and over under the instructors' watchful eye, she realizes that the same exercise works for this purpose.

"Are you doing orogeny?" Binof asks eagerly.

"Yes, so shut *up* before I ice you by accident." Thankfully Binof actually obeys, even though sessing isn't orogeny and there's no danger of icing anyone. Damaya's just grateful for the silence.

She gropes along the walls of the building. They are like shadows of force compared to the stolid comfort of rock, but if she's delicate, she can trace them. And *there* and *there* and *there* along the building's inner walls, the ones that enclose that hidden chamber, she can feel where the walls are... interrupted. Inhaling, Damaya opens her eyes.

"Well?" Binof's practically salivating.

Damaya turns, walking along the wall a ways. When she gets to the right place and stops, there's a door there. It's risky opening doors in occupied wings; this is probably someone's office. The corridor is quiet, empty, but Damaya can see lights underneath some of the doors, which means that at least a few people are working late. She knocks first. When there is no answer, she takes a deep breath and tries the latch. Locked.

"Hang on," Binof says, rummaging in her pockets. After a moment she holds up something that looks like a tool Damaya once used to pick bits of shell out of the kurge nuts that grew on her family's farm. "I read about how to do this. Hopefully it's a simple lock." She begins fiddling with the tool in the lock, her face set in a look of concentration.

Damaya waits awhile, leaning casually against the wall and listening with both ears and sessapinae for any vibration of feet or approaching voices—or worse, the buzz of an approaching Guardian. It's after midnight by now, though, and even the most dedicated workers are either planning to sleep in their offices or have left for the night, so no one troubles them during the agonizingly long time it takes for Binof to figure out how to use the thing.

"That's enough," Damaya says after an eternity. If anyone comes along and catches them here, Damaya won't be able to play it off. "Come back tomorrow and we'll try this again—"

"I *can't*," says Binof. She's sweating and her hands are shaking, which isn't helping matters. "I gave my nurses the slip for one night, but that won't work again. I almost got it last time. Just give me another minute."

So Damaya waits, growing more and more anxious, until finally there is a click and Binof gasps in surprise. "Was that it? I think that was it!" She tries the door, and it swings open. "Earth's flaming *farts*, it worked!"

The room beyond is indeed someone's office: There's a desk and two high-backed chairs, and bookcases line the walls. The desk is bigger than most, the chairs more elaborate; whoever works here is someone important. It is jarring for Damaya to see an office that's still in use after so many months of seeing the disused offices of the old wings. There's no dust, and the lanterns are already lit, though low-wick. So strange.

Binoff looks around, frowning; no sign of a door within the

office. Damaya brushes past her, going over to what looks like a closet. She opens it: brooms and mops, and a spare black uniform hanging on the rod.

"That's it?" Binof curses aloud.

"No." Because Damaya can sess that this office is too short, from door to far wall, to match the width of the building. This closet isn't deep enough to account for the difference.

Tentatively she reaches past the broom and pushes on the wall. Nothing; it's solid brick. Well, that was an idea.

"Oh, *right*." Binof shoulders in with her, feeling the walls all over the closet and shoving the spare uniform out of the way. "These old buildings always have hidden doors, leading down into the storecaches or—"

"There aren't any storecaches in the Fulcrum." Even as she says it, she blinks, because she's never thought about this before. What are they supposed to do if there's a Season? Somehow she doesn't think the people of Yumenes will be willing to share their food with a bunch of orogenes.

"Oh. Right." Binof grimaces. "Well, still, this is Yumenes, even if it is the Fulcrum. There's always—"

And she freezes, her eyes widening as her fingers trip over a brick that's loose. She grins, pushes at one end until the other end pops out; using this, she pulls it loose. There's a latch underneath, made of what looks like cast iron.

"—There's always something going on beneath the surface," Binof breathes.

Damaya draws near, wondering. "Pull it."

"*Now* you're interested?" But Binof indeed wraps her hand around the latch, and pulls.

That whole wall of the closet swings loose, revealing an opening beyond lined with the same brick. The narrow tunnel there curves out of sight almost immediately, into darkness.

Damaya and Binof both stare into it, neither taking that first step.

"What's in there?" Damaya whispers.

Binof licks her lips, staring into the shadowed tunnel. "I'm not sure."

"Bullshit." It's a shameful thrill to talk like this, like one of the ringed grown-ups. "You came here hoping to find *something*."

"Let's go see first—" Binof tries to push past her, and Damaya catches her arm. Binof jumps, arm tightening beneath Damaya's hand; she glares down at it as if in affront. Damaya doesn't care.

"*No*. Tell me what you're looking for, or I'll shut this door after you and start a shake to bring the wall down and trap you in there. Then I'll go tell the Guardians." This is a bluff. It would be the stupidest thing on Father Earth to use unauthorized orogeny right under the noses of the Guardians, and then to go tell them she's done it. But Binof doesn't know that.

"I told you, only Leaders can know this!" Binof tries to shake her off.

"You're a Leader; change the rule. Isn't that also what you're supposed to do?"

Binof blinks and stares at her. For a long moment she is silent. Then she sighs, rubs her eyes, and the tension goes out of her thin arm. "Fine. Okay." She takes a deep breath. "There's something, an artifact, at the heart of the Fulcrum."

"What kind of artifact?"

"I'm not sure. I'm really not!" Binof raises her hands quickly, shaking off Damaya in the process, but Damaya's not trying to hold her anymore. "All I know is that…something's missing from the history. There's a hole, a gap."

"What?"

"In *history*." Binof glares at Damaya as if this is supposed to mean something. "You know, the stuff the tutors teach you? About how Yumenes was founded?"

Damaya shakes her head. Beyond a line she barely remembers in creche about Yumenes being the first city of the Old Sanze Empire, she cannot remember ever hearing about its founding. Perhaps Leaders get a better education.

Binof rolls her eyes, but explains. "There was a Season. The one right before the Empire was founded was Wandering, when north suddenly shifted and crops failed because birds and bugs couldn't find them. After that warlords took over in most areas—which is what always used to happen, after a Season. There was nothing but stonelore to guide people then, and rumors, and superstition. And it was because of rumors that no one settled in this region for a really long time." She points down, at their feet. "Yumenes was the perfect place for a city: good weather, in the middle of a plate, water but nowhere near the ocean, all that. But people were afraid of this place and had been for ages, because *there was something here*."

Damaya's never heard anything like this. "What?"

Binof looks annoyed. "That's what I'm trying to find out! That's what's missing. Imperial history takes over after the Wandering Season. The Madness Season happened only a little while afterward, and Warlord Verishe—Emperor Verishe, the first Emperor—started Sanze then. She founded the Empire here, on land that everyone feared, and built a city around the thing they were all afraid of. That actually helped keep Yumenes safe in those early years. And later, after the Empire was more established, somewhere between the Season of Teeth and the Breathless Season, the Fulcrum was founded on this site. On purpose. *On top of* the thing they were all afraid of."

"But what—" Damaya trails off, understanding at last. "The histories don't say what they were afraid of."

"Precisely. And I think it's in there." Binof points toward the open door.

Damaya frowns. "Why are only Leaders supposed to know this?"

"I don't *know.* That's why I'm *here.* So are you coming in with me, or not?"

Instead of answering, Damaya walks past Binof and into the brick-lined corridor. Binof curses, then trots after her, and because of that, they enter together.

The tunnel opens out into a huge dark space. Damaya stops as soon as she feels airiness and breadth around her; it's pitch black, but she can feel the shape of the ground ahead. She catches Binof, who's blundering forward in a determined sort of way despite the dark—the fool—and says, "Wait. The ground's pressed down up ahead." She's whispering, because that's what one does in the dark. Her voice echoes; the echo takes a while to return. It's a big space.

"Pressed—what?"

"Pressed down." Damaya tries to explain it, but it's always so hard to tell stills things. Another orogene would just *know.* "Like... like there's been something really heavy here."

Something like a mountain. "The strata are deformed, and—there's a depression. A big hole. You'll fall."

"Rusting fuck," Binof mutters. Damaya almost flinches, though she's heard worse from some of her cruder fellow grits when the instructors weren't around. "We need some light."

Lights appear on the ground up ahead, one by one. There is a faint clicking sound—which echoes as well—as each activates: small round white ones near their feet and in twin lines as they march forward, and then much larger ones that are rectangular and butter-yellow, spreading outward from the walkway lights. The yellow panels continue to activate in sequence, and spread, slowly forming an enormous hexagon and gradually illuminating the space in which they stand: a cavernous atrium with six walls, enclosed by what must be the roof of Main high above. The ceiling is so distant they can barely make out its radiating spoke of supports. The walls are featureless, the same plain stone that comprises the rest of Main, but most of the floor of this chamber has been covered over in asphalt, or something very like it—smooth, stonelike but not stone, slightly rough, durable.

At the core of it, however, there is indeed a depression. That is an understatement: It's a huge, tapering pit with flat-sided walls and neat, precise edges—six of them, cut as finely as one cuts a diamond. "Evil Earth," Damaya whispers as she edges forward along the walkway to where the yellow lights limn the shape of the pit.

"Yeah," says Binof, sounding equally awed.

It is stories deep, this pit, and steep. If she fell in, she would roll down its slopes and probably break every bone in her body at the bottom. But the shape of it nags at her, because it is *faceted.*

Tapering to a point at the very bottom. No one digs a pit in that shape. Why would they? It would be almost impossible to get out of, even with a ladder that could reach so far.

But then, no one has *dug* this pit. She can sess that: Something monstrously heavy *punched* this pit into the earth, and sat in the depression long enough to make all the rock and soil beneath it solidify into these smooth, neat planes. Then whatever-it-was lifted away, clean as a buttered roll from a pan, leaving nothing but the shape of itself behind.

But wait; the walls of the pit are not wholly smooth. Damaya crouches for a closer look, while beside her, Binof just stares.

There: Along every smooth slope, she can see thin, barely visible sharp objects. Needles? They push up through fine cracks in the smooth walls, jagged and random, like plant roots. The needles are made of iron; Damaya can smell the rust in the air. Scratch her earlier guess: If she fell into this pit, she would be shredded long before she ever hit the bottom.

"I wasn't expecting this," Binof breathes at last. She's speaking in a hush, maybe out of reverence, or fear. "Many things, but . . . not this."

"What is it?" asks Damaya. "What's it for?"

Binof shakes her head slowly. "It's *supposed* to be—"

"Hidden," says a voice behind them, and they both jump and whirl in alarm. Damaya is standing closer to the edge of the pit, and when she stumbles there is a terrible, vertiginous moment in which she's absolutely certain she's going to fall in. In fact she relaxes, and doesn't try to lean forward or rebalance herself or do any of the things that she would do if she had a chance of *not* falling. She is all-over heavy, and the pit yawns with inevitability behind her.

Then Binof grabs her arm and yanks her forward, and abruptly she realizes she was still a good two or three feet from the edge. She would only have fallen in if she'd *let* herself fall in. This is such a strange thing that she almost forgets *why* she nearly fell, and then the Guardian comes down the walkway.

The woman is tall and broad and bronze, pretty in a carved sort of way, with ashblow hair shorn into a bristly cap. She feels older than Schaffa, though this is difficult to tell; her skin is unmarked, her honey-colored eyes undented by crow's feet. She just feels... heavier, in presence. And her smile is the same unnerving combination of peaceable and menacing as that of every Guardian Damaya has ever seen.

Damaya thinks, *I only need to be afraid if she thinks I'm dangerous.*

Here is the question, though: Is an orogene who goes where she knows she should not dangerous? Damaya licks her lips and tries not to look afraid.

Binof doesn't bother, darting a look between Damaya and the woman and the pit and the door. Damaya wants to tell her not to do whatever she's thinking of—making a break for it, likely. Not with a Guardian here. But Binof is not an orogene; maybe that will protect her, even if she does something stupid.

"Damaya," the woman says, though Damaya has never met her before. "Schaffa will be disappointed."

"She's with me," Binof blurts, before Damaya can reply. Damaya looks at her in surprise, but Binof's already talking, and now that she's started, it seems as though nothing will stop her. "I brought her here. Ordered her here. She didn't even know about the door and this—place—until I told her."

That isn't true, Damaya wants to say, because she'd guessed that the place existed, just hadn't known how to find it. But the Guardian is looking at Binof curiously, and that's a positive sign because nobody's hands have been broken yet.

"And you are?" The Guardian smiles. "Not an orogene, I gather, despite your uniform."

Binof jumps a little, as if she's forgotten that she's been playing little lost grit. "Oh. Um." She straightens and lifts her chin. "My name is Binof Leadership Yumenes. Your pardon for my intrusion, Guardian; I had a question that required an answer."

Binof's talking differently, Damaya realizes suddenly: her words evenly spaced and voice steady, her manner not so much haughty as grave. As if the world's fate depends upon her finding the answer to her question. As if she isn't just some spoiled girl from a powerful family who decided on a whim to do something incredibly stupid.

The Guardian stops, cocking her head and blinking as her smile momentarily fades. "Leadership Yumenes?" Then she beams. "How lovely! So young, and already you have a comm name. You are quite welcome among us, Binof Leader. If you had but told us you were coming, we could have *shown* you what you wanted to see."

Binof flinches minutely at the rebuke. "I had a wish to see it for myself, I'm afraid. Perhaps that was not wise—but my parents are likely by now aware that I have come here, so please feel free to speak to them about it."

It's a smart thing to do, Damaya is surprised to realize, because before now she has not thought of Binof as smart. Mentioning that others know where she's gone.

"I shall," says the Guardian, and then she smiles at Damaya, which makes her stomach tighten. "And I shall speak to your Guardian, and we shall all speak together. That would be lovely, yes? Yes. Please." She steps aside and bows a little, gesturing for them to precede her, and as polite as it looks, they both know it's not a request.

The Guardian leads them out of the chamber. As they all step into the brick tunnel again, the lights go out behind them. When the door is shut and the office is locked and they have proceeded into the Guardians' wing, the woman touches Damaya's shoulder to stop her while Binof keeps walking for a step or two. Then when Binof stops, looking at them in confusion, the Guardian says to Damaya, "Please wait here." Then she moves to rejoin Binof.

Binof looks at her, perhaps trying to convey something with her eyes. Damaya looks away, and the message fails as the Guardian leads her farther down the hall and into a closed door. Binof has already done enough harm.

Damaya waits, of course. She's not stupid. She's standing in front of the door to a busy area; despite the hour, other Guardians emerge now and again, and look at her. She doesn't look back, and something in this seems to satisfy them, so they move on without bothering her.

After a few moments, the Guardian who caught them in the pit chamber returns and leads her through the door, with a gentle hand on her shoulder. "Now. Let's just talk a bit, why don't we? I've sent for Schaffa; fortunately he's in the city right now, and not out on circuit as usual. But until he gets here..."

There's a large, handsomely apportioned, carpeted area

beyond the door, with many small desks. Some are occupied and some not, and the people who move between them wear a mix of black and burgundy uniforms. A very few aren't wearing uniforms at all, but civilian clothing. Damaya stares at all of it in fascination until the Guardian puts a hand on her head and gently, but inexorably, steers her gaze away.

Damaya is led into a small private office at the end of this chamber. The desk here is completely empty, however, and the room has a disused air. There's a chair on either side of the desk, so Damaya takes the one meant for guests.

"I'm sorry," she says as the Guardian sits down behind the desk. "I-I didn't think."

The Guardian shakes her head, as if this doesn't matter. "Did you touch any of them?"

"What?"

"In the socket." The Guardian's still smiling, but they always smile; this means nothing useful. "You saw the extrusions from the socket walls. Weren't you curious? There was one only an arm's length below where you stood."

Socket? Oh, and the iron bits poking out of the walls. "No, I didn't touch any of them." *Socket for what?*

The Guardian sits forward, and abruptly her smile vanishes. It doesn't fade, and she doesn't frown to replace it. All the expression just stops, in her face. "Did it call to you? Did you answer?"

Something's wrong. Damaya feels this suddenly, instinctively, and the realization dries the words from her mouth. The Guardian even sounds different—her voice is deeper, softer, almost hushed, as if she's saying something she doesn't want the others to hear.

"What did it say to you?" The Guardian extends her hand, and even though Damaya puts her hand out immediately in obedient response, she does not want to. She does it anyway because Guardians are to be obeyed. The woman takes Damaya's hand and holds it palm up, her thumb stroking the long crease. The lifeline. "You can tell me."

Damaya shakes her head in utter confusion. "What did *what* say to me?"

"It's angry." The woman's voice drops lower, going monotonous, and Damaya realizes she's not trying to go unheard anymore. The Guardian is talking differently because *that's not her voice*. "Angry and…afraid. I hear both gathering, growing, the anger and the fear. Readying, for the time of return."

It's like…like someone else is inside the Guardian, and *that* is who's talking, except using the Guardian's face and voice and everything else. But as the woman says this, her hand begins to tighten on Damaya's. Her thumb, which rests right on the bones that Schaffa broke a year and a half ago, begins to press in, and Damaya feels faint as some part of her thinks, *I don't want to be hurt again.*

"I'll tell you whatever you want," she offers, but the Guardian keeps pressing. It's like she doesn't even hear.

"It did what it had to do, last time." Press and tighten. This Guardian, unlike Schaffa, has longer nails; the thumbnail begins to dig into Damaya's flesh. "It seeped through the walls and tainted their pure creation, exploited them before they could exploit it. When the arcane connections were made, it *changed* those who would control it. Chained them, fate to fate."

"Please don't," Damaya whispers. Her palm has begun to

bleed. In almost the same moment there is a knock at the door. The woman ignores both.

"It made them a part of it."

"I don't *understand,*" Damaya says. It hurts. It *hurts.* She's shaking, waiting for the snap of bone.

"It hoped for communion. Compromise. Instead, the battle… escalated."

"I don't understand! You're not making any sense!" It's wrong. Damaya's raising her voice to a Guardian, and she *knows* better, but this isn't right. Schaffa promised that he would hurt her only for a good reason. All Guardians operate on this principle; Damaya has seen the proof of it in how they interact with her fellow grits and the ringed orogenes. There is an order to life in the Fulcrum and this woman is *breaking it.* "Let go of me! I'll do whatever you want, just let go!"

The door opens and Schaffa flows in. Damaya's breath catches, but he doesn't look at her. His gaze is fixed on the Guardian who holds Damaya's hand. He isn't smiling as he moves to stand behind her. "Timay. Control yourself."

Timay's not home, Damaya thinks.

"It speaks only to warn, now," she continues in a drone. "There will be no compromise next time—"

Schaffa sighs a little, then jabs his fingers into the back of Timay's skull.

It's not clear at first, from Damaya's angle, that this is what he's done. She just sees him make a sudden sharp, violent movement, and then Timay's head jerks forward. She makes a sound so harsh and guttural that it is almost vulgar, and her eyes go wide. Schaffa's face is expressionless as he does something, his arm flexing, and that's when the first blood-lines wend around Timay's neck, beginning to sink into her tunic and patter into her lap. Her hand, on Damaya's, relaxes all at once, and her face goes slack.

That is also when Damaya begins to scream. She keeps screaming as Schaffa twists his hand again, nostrils flaring with the effort of whatever he's doing, and the sound of crunching bone and popping tendon is undeniable. Then Schaffa lifts his hand, holding something small and indistinct—too covered in gore—between his thumb and forefinger. Timay falls forward then, and now Damaya sees the ruin that was once the base of her skull.

"Be silent, little one," Schaffa says, mildly, and Damaya shuts up.

Another Guardian comes in, looks at Timay, looks at Schaffa, and sighs. "Unfortunate."

"Very unfortunate." Schaffa offers the blood-covered thing to this man, who cups his hands to receive it, carefully. "I would like this removed." He nods toward Timay's body.

"Yes." The man leaves with the thing Schaffa took from Timay, and then two more Guardians come in, sigh as the first one did, and collect her body from its chair. They drag her out, one of them pausing to mop up with a handkerchief the drops of blood from the table where Timay fell. It's all very efficient. Schaffa sits down in Timay's place, and Damaya jerks her eyes to him only because she must. They gaze at each other in silence for a few moments.

"Let me see," Schaffa says gently, and she offers him her hand. Amazingly, it does not shake.

He takes it with his left hand—the one that is still clean

because it did not rip out Timay's brain stem. He turns her hand, examining it carefully, making a face at the crescent of blood where Timay's thumbnail broke the skin. A single drop of Damaya's blood rolls off the edge of her hand, splatting onto the table right where Timay's blood had been a moment before. "Good. I was afraid she'd hurt you worse than this."

"Wh—" Damaya begins. She can't muster any more than that.

Schaffa smiles, though this is edged with sorrow. "Something you should not have seen."

"*What.*" This takes a ten-ringer's effort.

Schaffa considers a moment, then says, "You are aware that we—Guardians—are...different." He smiles, as if to remind her of how different. All Guardians smile a lot.

She nods, mute.

"There is a...procedure." He lets go of her hand for a moment, touches the back of his own skull, beneath the fall of his long black hair. "A thing is done to make us what we are. An implantation. Sometimes it goes wrong and must then be removed, as you saw." He shrugs. His right hand is still covered in gore. "A Guardian's connections with his assigned orogenes can help to stave off the worst, but Timay had allowed hers to erode. Foolish."

A chilly barn in the Nomidlats; a moment of apparent affection; two warm fingers pressed to the base of Damaya's skull. *Duty first,* he had said then. *Something that will make me more comfortable.*

Damaya licks her lips. "Sh-she was. Saying things. Not making. Sense."

"I heard some of what she said."

"She wasn't. *Her.*" Now Damaya's the one not making sense.

"She wasn't who she was anymore. I mean, she was someone else. Talking as if . . . someone else was there." In her head. In her mouth, speaking through it. "She kept talking about a socket. And 'it' being angry."

Schaffa inclines his head. "Father Earth, of course. It is a common delusion."

Damaya blinks. What? *It's angry.* What?

"And you're right; Timay wasn't herself any longer. I'm sorry she hurt you. I'm sorry you had to see that. I'm so sorry, little one." And there is such genuine regret in his voice, such compassion in his face, that Damaya does what she has not since a cold dark night in a Nomidlats barn: She begins to cry.

After a moment Schaffa gets up and comes around the table and picks her up, sitting in the chair and letting her curl in his lap to weep on his shoulder. There is an order to life in the Fulcrum, see, and it is this: If one has not displeased them, the Guardians are the closest thing to safety a rogga will ever have. So Damaya cries for a long time—not just because of what she's seen tonight. She cries because she has been inexpressibly lonely, and Schaffa . . . well. Schaffa loves her, in his tender and terrifying way. She does not pay attention to the bloody print his right hand leaves on her hip, or the press of his fingers—fingers strong enough to kill—against the base of her skull. Such things are irrelevant, in the grand scale.

When the storm of weeping subsides, though, Schaffa strokes her back with his clean hand. "How are you feeling, Damaya?"

She does not lift her head from his shoulder. He smells of sweat and leather and iron, things that she will forever associate with comfort and fear. "I'm all right."

"Good. I need you to do something for me."

"What?"

He squeezes her gently, encouraging. "I'm going to take you down the hall, to one of the crucibles, and there you will face the first ring test. I need you to pass it for me."

Damaya blinks, frowning, and lifts her head. He smiles at her, tenderly. By this she understands, in a flash of intuition, that this is a test of more than her orogeny. After all, most roggas are told of the test in advance, so that they can practice and prepare. This is happening for her now, without warning, because it is her only chance. She has proven herself disobedient. Unreliable. Because of this, Damaya will need to also prove herself useful. If she cannot...

"I need you to live, Damaya." Schaffa touches his forehead to her own. "My compassionate one. My life is so full of death. Please; pass this test for me."

There are so many things she wants to know. What Timay meant; what will happen to Binof; what is the *socket* and why was it hidden; what happened to Crack last year. Why Schaffa is even giving her this much of a chance. But there is an order to life in the Fulcrum, and her place within it is not to question a Guardian's will.

But...

But...

But. She turns her head, and looks at that single drop of her blood on the table.

This is not right.

"Damaya?"

It isn't right, what they're doing to her. What this place does to everyone within its walls. What he's making her do, to survive.

"Will you do it? For me?"

She still loves him. That isn't right, either.

"If I pass." Damaya closes her eyes. She can't look at him and say this. Not without letting him see the *it isn't right* in her eyes. "I, I picked a rogga name."

He does not chide her on her language. "Have you, now?" He sounds pleased. "What?"

She licks her lips. "Syenite."

Schaffa sits back in the chair, sounding thoughtful. "I like it."

"You do?"

"Of course I do. You chose it, didn't you?" He's laughing, but in a good way. With her, not at her. "It forms at the edge of a tectonic plate. With heat and pressure it does not degrade, but instead grows stronger."

He *does* understand. She bites her lip and feels fresh tears threaten. It isn't right that she loves him, but many things in the world are not right. So she fights off the tears, and makes her decision. Crying is weakness. Crying was a thing Damaya did. Syenite will be stronger.

"I'll do it," Syenite says, softly. "I'll pass the test for you, Schaffa. I promise."

"My good girl," Schaffa says, and smiles, holding her close.

* * *

[obscured] those who would take the earth too closely
unto themselves. They are not masters of themselves;
allow them no mastery of others.

—*Tablet Two, "The Incomplete Truth," verse nine*

18

you discover wonders down below

Ykka takes you into the house from which she and her companions emerged. There's little furniture inside, and the walls are bare. There's scuffing on the floor and walls, a lingering smell of food and stale body musk; someone *did* live here, until recently. Maybe until the Season began. The house is only a shell now, though, as you and the others cut through to a cellar door. At the bottom of the steps you find a large, empty chamber lit only by wood-pitch torches.

Here's where you first start to realize this is more than just a bizarre community of people and not-people: The walls of the cellar are solid granite. Nobody quarries into granite just to build a cellar, and . . . and you're not sure anyone *dug* this. Everyone stops while you go to one of the walls and touch it. You close your eyes and *reach*. Yes, there is the feel of something familiar here. Some rogga shaped this perfectly smooth wall, using will and a focus finer than you can imagine. (Though not the *finest* focus you've ever sessed.) You've never heard of anyone doing anything like this with orogeny. It's not for building.

Turning, you see Ykka watching you. "Your work?"

She smiles. "No. This and other hidden entrances have been around for centuries, long before me."

"The people in this comm have worked with orogenes for that long?" She'd said the comm was only fifty years old.

Ykka laughs. "No, I just mean that this world has passed through many hands down the Seasons. Not all of them were quite as stupid as ours about the usefulness of orogenes."

"We aren't stupid about it now," you say. "Everyone understands perfectly well how to *use* us."

"Ooh." Ykka grimaces, pityingly. "Fulcrum trained? The ones who survive it always seem to sound like you."

You wonder how many Fulcrum-trained orogenes this woman has met. "Yes."

"Well. Now you'll see how much more we're capable of when we're willing." And Ykka gestures toward a wide opening in the wall a few feet beyond her, which you hadn't noticed in your fascination with the cellar's construction. A faint draft wafts into the cellar from beyond it. There're also three people loitering at the mouth of the opening, watching you with varied expressions of hostility, wariness, amusement. They're not carrying any weapons—those are propped against the wall nearby—and they're not conspicuous about it, but you realize these are the gate guards this comm should have, for the gate this comm doesn't have. Here, in this cellar.

The blond woman speaks quietly with one of the guards; this emphasizes even more how tiny she is, a foot shorter and probably a hundred pounds lighter than the smallest of them. Her ancestors really should've done her a few favors and slept with a

Sanzed or two. Anyway, then you move on and the guards stay behind, two taking seats on chairs nearby, the third heading back up the steps, presumably to keep a lookout from within the empty buildings topside.

You make the paradigm shift then: The abandoned village up there *is* this comm's wall. Camouflage rather than a barrier.

Camouflage for what, though? You follow Ykka through the opening and into the dark beyond.

"The core of this place has always been here," she explains as you walk down a long dark tunnel that might be an abandoned mine shaft. There's tracks for carts, though they're so old and sunken into the gritty stone that you can't really see them. Just awkward ridges beneath your feet. The wooden bracers of the tunnel look old, as do the wall sconces that hold cord-strung electric lights—they look like they were originally made to hold wooden torches and got retrofitted by some geneer. The lights are still working, which means the comm's got functional geo or hydro or both; better than Tirimo already. It's warm in the shaft, too, but you don't see any of the usual heating pipes. It's just warm, and getting warmer as you follow the gently sloping floor downward.

"I told you there were mines in the area. That's how they found these, back in the day. Someone cracked a wall they shouldn't have and blundered into a whole warren of tunnels nobody knew were there." Ykka falls silent for a long while as the shaft widens out, and you all go down a set of dangerous-looking metal steps. There's a lot of them. They look old, too—and yet strangely, the metal doesn't seem distressed or rusted out. It's smooth and shiny and all-over whole. The steps aren't shaky at all.

After a time you notice, belatedly, that the red-haired stone eater is gone. She didn't follow you down into the shaft. Ykka doesn't seem to notice, so you touch her arm. "Where's your friend?" Though you sort of know.

"My—oh, that one. Moving the way we do is hard for them, so they've got their own ways of getting about. Including ways I would never have guessed." She glances at Hoa, who's come down the steps with you. He looks back at her, coldly, and she breathes out a laugh. "Interesting."

At the bottom of the stairs there's another tunnel, though it looks different for some reason. Curved at its top rather than squared, and the supports are some sort of thick, silvery stone columns, which arch partway up the walls like ribs. You can almost taste the age of these corridors through the pores of your skin.

Ykka resumes. "Really, all the bedrock in this area is riddled with tunnels and intrusions, mines on top of mines. One civilization after another, building on what went before."

"Aritussid," says Tonkee. "Jyamaria. The lower Ottey States."

You've heard of Jyamaria, from the history you used to teach in creche. It was the name of a large nation, the one that started the road system Sanze later improved upon, and which once spread over most of what is now the Somidlats. It died around ten Seasons ago. The rest of the names are probably those of other deadcivs; that seems like the sort of thing geomests would care about, even if no one else does.

"Dangerous," you say, as you try not to be too obvious with your unease. "If the rock here's been compromised so much—"

"Yes, yes. Though that's a risk with any mining, as much because of incompetence as shakes."

Tonkee is turning and turning as she walks, taking it all in and still not bumping into anyone; amazing. "That northern shake was severe enough that even this should have come down," she says.

"You're right. That shake—we're calling it the Yumenes Rifting, since nobody's come up with a better name yet—was the worst the world's seen in an age. I don't think I'm exaggerating by saying so." Ykka shrugs and glances back at you. "But of course, the tunnels didn't collapse, because I was here. I didn't *let* them."

You nod, slowly. It's no different than what you did for Tirimo, except Ykka must have taken care to protect more than just the surface. The area must be relatively stable anyway, or these tunnels would've all collapsed ages ago.

But you say: "You won't always be around."

"When I'm not, someone else will do it." She shrugs. "Like I said, there's a lot of us here now."

"About that—" Tonkee pivots on one foot and suddenly her whole attention is on Ykka. Ykka laughs.

"Kind of single-minded, aren't you?"

"Not really." You suspect Tonkee is still simultaneously taking note of the supports and wall composition, counting your paces, whatever, all while she talks. "So how are you doing it? Luring orogenes here."

"Luring?" Ykka shakes her head. "It's not that sinister. And it's hard to describe. There's a…a thing I do. Like—" She falls silent.

And all at once, you stumble while you're walking. There's no obstruction on the floor. It's just suddenly difficult to walk in a straight line, as if the floor has developed an invisible downward slope. Toward Ykka.

You stop and glare at her. She stops as well, turning to smile at you. "How are you doing that?" you demand.

"I don't know." She spreads her hands at your disbelieving look. "It's just something I tried, a few years ago. And not too long after I started doing it, a man came to town and said he'd felt me from miles away. Then two kids showed up; they didn't even realize what they were reacting to. Then another man. I've kept doing it since."

"Doing what?" Tonkee asks, looking from you to Ykka.

"Only roggas feel it," Ykka explains, though by this point you've figured that out for yourself. Then she glances at Hoa, who is watching both of you, utterly still. "And *them*, I realized later."

"About that," Tonkee blurts.

"Earthfires and rustbuckets, you ask too many questions." This comes from the blond woman, who shakes her head and gestures for all of you to keep walking.

There are faint occasional noises up ahead now, and the air is moving, noticeably. But how can that be? You must be a mile down, maybe twice that. The breeze is warm and tinged with scents you've almost forgotten after weeks of breathing sulfur and ash through a mask. A bit of cooking food here, a waft of rotting garbage there, a breath of burning wood. People. You're smelling people. Lots of them. And there's a light—much stronger than the strings of electric lights along the walls—straight ahead.

"An *underground* comm?" Tonkee says what you're thinking,

though she sounds more skeptical. (You know more about impossible things than she does.) "No, nobody's that stupid."

Ykka only laughs.

Then as the peculiar light starts to brighten the shaft around you, and the air moves faster and the noise grows, there's a place where the tunnel opens out and becomes a wide ledge with a metal railing for safety. A scenic viewpoint, because some geneer or Innovator understood exactly how newcomers would react. You do exactly as that long-ago designer intended: You stare in openmouthed, abject wonder.

It's a *geode*. You can sess that, the way the rock around you abruptly changes to something else. The pebble in the stream, the warp in the weft; countless aeons ago a bubble formed in a flow of molten mineral within Father Earth. Within that pocket, nurtured by incomprehensible pressures and bathed in water and fire, crystals grew. This one's the size of a city.

Which is probably why *someone built a city in this one*.

You stand before a vast, vaulted cavern that is full of glowing crystal shafts the size of tree trunks. *Big* tree trunks. Or buildings. Big buildings. They jut forth from the walls in an utterly haphazard jumble: different lengths, different circumferences, some white and translucent and a few smoky or tinged with purple. Some are stubby, their pointed tips ending only a few feet away from the walls that grew them—but many stretch from one side of the vast cavern into the indistinct distance. They form struts and roads too steep to climb, going in directions that make no sense. It is as if someone found an architect, made her build a city out of the most beautiful materials available, then threw all those buildings into a box and jumbled them up for laughs.

And they're definitely living in it. As you stare, you notice narrow rope bridges and wooden platforms everywhere. There are dangling lines strung with electric lanterns, ropes and pulleys carrying small lifts from one platform to another. In the distance a man walks down a wooden stairway built around a titanic slanted column of white; two children play on the ground far below, in between stubby crystals the size of houses.

Actually, some of the crystals *are* houses. They have holes cut in them—doors and windows. You can see people moving around inside some of them. Smoke curls from chimney holes cut in pointed crystal tips.

"Evil, eating *Earth*," you whisper.

Ykka stands with hands on her hips, watching your reaction with something like pride in her expression. "We didn't do most of this," she admits. "The recent additions, the newer bridges, yes, but the shaft-hollowing had already been done. We don't know how they managed it without shattering the crystals. The walkways that are made of metal—it's the same stuff as the steps in the tunnels we just passed through. The geneers have no idea how it's made; metallorists and alchemists have orgasms when they see it. There are mechanisms up there"—She points toward the barely visible ceiling of the cavern, hundreds of feet above your heads. You barely hear her, your mind numb, your eyes beginning to ache from staring without blinking—"that pump bad air into a layer of porous earth that filters and disperses it back onto the surface. Other pumps bring in good air. There are mechanisms just outside the geode that divert water from an underground hot spring a ways off, through a turbine that gives us electric power—took ages to figure that part out—and also bring it in for day-to-day use." She sighs. "But to be really honest, we don't know how half the stuff we've found here works. All of it was built long ago. Long before Old Sanze ever existed."

"Geodes are unstable once their shells are breached." Even Tonkee sounds floored. In your peripheral vision she is still for the first time since you met her. "It doesn't make sense to even think of building inside one. And why are the crystals *glowing*?"

She's right. They are.

Ykka shrugs, folding her arms. "No idea. But the people who built this wanted it to last, even through a shake, so they did things to the geode to make sure that would happen. And it did... but *they* didn't. When people from Castrima found this, it was full of skeletons—some so old they turned to dust as soon as we touched them."

"So your comm forebears decided to move everyone into a giant deadciv artifact that killed the last few people who risked it," you drawl. It's weak snark, though. You're too shaken to really get the tone right. "Of course. Why *not* repeat a colossal mistake?"

"Believe me, it's been an ongoing debate." Ykka sighs and leans against the railing, which makes you twitch. It's a long way down if she slips, and some of the crystals on the geode floor are sharp-looking. "No one was willing to live here for a long time. Castrima used this place and the tunnels leading to it as a storecache, though never for essentials like food or medicine. But in all that time, there's never been so much as a crack in the walls, even after shakes. We were further convinced by history: The comm that controlled this area during the last Season—a real, proper comm, with walls and everything—got overrun by a commless band. The whole comm was burned to the ground, all their vital stores taken. The survivors had a choice between moving down here, and trying to survive up there with no heat and no walls and every bunch of scavengers around homing in on the easy pickings left. So they were our precedent."

Necessity is the only law, says stonelore.

"Not that it went well." Ykka straightens and gestures for you to follow her again. All of you start down a broad, flat ramp that gently slopes toward the floor of the cavern. You realize only belatedly that it's a crystal, and you're walking down its side. Someone's paved the thing with concrete for traction, but past the edges of the gray strip you can see softly glowing white. "Most of the people who moved down here during that Season died, too. They couldn't make the air mechanisms work; staying here for more than a few days at a time meant suffocation. And they didn't have any food, so even though they were warm and safe and had plenty of water, most of them starved before the sun returned."

It's an old tale, freshened only by the unique setting. You nod absently, trying not to stumble as your attention is caught by an older man riding across the cavern while suspended from a pulley and cable, his butt snuggly tucked into a loop of rope. Ykka pauses to wave; the man waves back and glides on.

"The survivors of that nightmare started the trading post that eventually became Castrima. They passed down stories about this place, but still, no one wanted to live here…until my great-grandmother realized why the mechanisms didn't work. Until *she* got them working, just by walking through that entrance." Ykka gestures back the way you came. "Worked for me, too, when I first came down here."

You stop. Everyone goes on without you for a moment. Hoa is the first to notice that you're not following. He turns and looks at you. There is something guarded in his expression that was not there before, you notice distantly, through horror and wonder. Later, when you've had time to get past this, you and he will have to talk. Now there are more important considerations.

"The mechanisms," you say. Your mouth is dry. "They run on *orogeny.*"

Ykka nods, half-smiling. "That's what the geneers think. Of course, the fact that it's all working now makes the conclusion obvious."

"Is it—" You grope for the words, fail. "*How?*"

Ykka laughs, shaking her head. "I have no idea. It just works."

That, more than everything else she's shown you, terrifies you.

Ykka sighs and puts her hands on her hips. "Essun," she says, and you twitch. "That's your name, right?"

You lick your lips. "Essun Resis—" And then you stop. Because you were about to give the name you gave to people in Tirimo for years, and that name is a lie. "Essun," you say again, and stop there. Limited lying.

Ykka glances at your companions. "Tonkee Innovator Dibars," says Tonkee. She throws an almost embarrassed look at you, then looks down at her feet.

"Hoa," says Hoa. Ykka gazes at him a moment longer, as if she expects more, but he offers nothing.

"Well, then." Ykka opens her arms, as if to encompass the

whole geode; she gazes at all of you with her chin lifted, amost in defiance. "This is what we're trying to do here in Castrima: survive. Same as anyone. We're just willing to *innovate* a little." She inclines her head to Tonkee, who chuckles nervously. "We might all die doing it, but rust, that might happen anyway; it's a Season."

You lick your lips. "Can we leave?"

"What the rust do you mean, can we leave? We've barely had time to explore—" Tonkee begins, looking angry, and then abruptly she realizes what you mean. Her sallow face grows more so. "Oh."

Ykka's smile is sharp as diamond. "Well. You're not stupid; that's good. Come on. We've got some people to meet."

She beckons for you to follow again, resuming her walk down the slope, and she does not answer your question.

* * *

> In actual practice the sessapinae, paired organs located at the base of the brain stem, have been found to be sensitive to far more than local seismic movements and atmospheric pressure. In tests, reactions have been observed to the presence of predators, to others' emotions, to distant extremes of heat or cold, and to the movements of celestial objects. The mechanism of these reactions cannot be determined.
>
> —*Nandvid Innovator Murkettsi, "Observations of sesunal variation in overdeveloped individuals," Seventh University biomestry learning-comm. With appreciation to the Fulcrum for cadaver donation.*

19

Syenite on the lookout

THEY'VE BEEN IN MEOV FOR three days when something changes. Syenite has spent those three days feeling very much out of place, in more ways than one. The first problem is that she can't speak the language—which Alabaster tells her is called Eturpic. A number of Coaster comms still speak it as a native tongue, though most people also learn Sanze-mat for trading purposes. Alabaster's theory is that the people of the islands are mostly descended from Coasters, which seems fairly obvious from their predominant coloring and common kinky hair—but since they raid rather than trade, they had no need to retain Sanze-mat. He tries to teach Eturpic to her, but she's not really in a "learn something new" sort of mood. That's because of the second problem, which Alabaster points out to her after they've had enough time to recover from their travails: They can't leave. Or rather, they've got nowhere to go.

"If the Guardians tried to kill us once, they'll try again," he explains. This is as they stroll along one of the arid heights of the island; it's the only way they can get any real privacy, since otherwise hordes of children follow them around and try to imitate the strange sounds of Sanze-mat. There's plenty to do here—the children are in creche most of the evenings, after everyone's done fishing and crabbing and whatnot for the day—but it's clear that there's not a lot of entertainment.

"Without knowing what it is we've done to provoke the Guardians' ire," Alabaster continues, "it would be folly itself to go back to the Fulcrum. We might not even make it past the gates before somebody throws another disruption knife."

Which is obvious, now that Syenite thinks it through. Yet there's something else that's obvious, whenever she looks at the horizon and sees the smoking hump that is what's left of Allia. "They think we're dead." She tears her eyes away from that lump, trying not to imagine what must have become of the beautiful little seaside comm she remembers. All of Allia's alarms, all their preparations, were shaped around surviving tsunami, not the volcano that has obviously, impossibly occurred instead. Poor Heresmith. Not even Asael deserved the death she probably suffered.

She cannot think about this. Instead she focuses on Alabaster. "That's what you're saying, isn't it? Being dead in Allia allows us to be alive, and free, here."

"Exactly!" Now Alabaster's grinning, practically dancing in place. She's never seen him so excited before. It's like he's not even aware of the price that's been paid for their freedom... or maybe he just doesn't care. "There's hardly any contact with the continent, here, and when there is, it's not exactly friendly. Our assigned Guardians can sense us if they're near enough, but none of their kind ever come here. These islands aren't even on many maps!" Then he sobers. "But on the continent there'd be no question of us escaping the Fulcrum. Every Guardian east of Yumenes will be sniffing about the remains of Allia for hints as to whether we've survived. They're probably circulating posters bearing our likenesses to the Imperial Road Patrol and quartent militias in the region. I suppose I'll be made out as Misalem reborn, and you my willing accomplice. Or maybe you'll finally get some respect, and they'll decide *you're* the mastermind."

Yes, well.

He's right, though. With a comm destroyed in such a horrible way, the Fulcrum will need scapegoats to blame. Why not the two roggas on site, who should have been more than skilled enough to contain any seismic event between them? Allia's destruction represents a betrayal of everything the Fulcrum promises the Stillness: tame and obedient orogenes, safety from the worst shakes and blows. Freedom from fear, at least till the next Fifth Season comes. Of course the Fulcrum will vilify them in every way possible, because otherwise people will break down its obsidian walls and slaughter everyone inside down to the littlest grit.

It does not help that Syen can sess, now that her sessapinae are no longer numb, just how bad things are in Allia. It's at the edge of her awareness—which is itself a surprise; for some reason she can reach much farther now than she could before. Still, it's clear: In the flat plane of the Maximal plate's eastern edge, there is a shaft burned straight down and down and *down*, into the very mantle of the planet. Beyond that Syen cannot follow—and she does not need to, because she can tell what made this shaft. Its edges are hexagonal, and it has exactly the same circumference as the garnet obelisk.

And Alabster is *giddy*. She could hate him for that alone.

His smile fades as he sees her face. "Evil Earth, are you ever happy?"

"They'll find us. Our Guardians can track us. "

He shakes his head. "Mine can't." You remember the strange Guardian in Allia alluding to this. "As for yours, when your orogeny was negated, he lost you. It cuts off everything, you know, not just our abilities. He'll need to touch you for the connection to work again."

You had no idea. "He won't stop looking, though."

Alabaster pauses. "Did you like being in the Fulcrum so much?"

The question startles her, and angers her further. "I could at least be myself there. I didn't have to hide what I am."

He nods slowly, something in his expression telling her that he understands all too well what she's feeling. "And what are you, when you're there?"

"*Fuck. You.*" She's too angry, all of a sudden, to know why she's angry.

"I did." His smirk makes her burn hot as Allia must be. "Remember? We've fucked Earth knows how many times, even though we can't stand each other, on someone else's orders. Or have you made yourself believe you wanted it? Did you need a dick—any dick, even my mediocre, boring one—that bad?"

She doesn't reply in words. She's not thinking or talking anymore. She's in the earth and it's reverberating with her rage, amplifying it; the torus that materializes around her is high and fine and leaves an inch-wide ring of cold so fierce that the air hisses and sears white for an instant. She's going to ice him to the Arctics and back.

But Alabaster only sighs and flexes a little, and his torus blots out hers as easily as fingers snuffing a candle. It's gentle compared to what he could do, but the profundity of having her fury so swiftly and powerfully stilled makes her stagger. He steps forward as if to help her, and she jerks away from him with a half-voiced snarl. He backs off at once, holding up his hands as if asking for a truce.

"Sorry," he says. He genuinely sounds it, so she doesn't storm off right then. "I was just trying to make a point."

He's made it. Not that she hadn't known it before: that she is a slave, that all roggas are slaves, that the security and sense of self-worth the Fulcrum offers is wrapped in the chain of her right to live, and even the right to control her own body. It's one thing to know this, to admit it to herself, but it's the sort of truth that none of them use against each other—not even to make a point—because doing so is cruel and unnecessary. This is why she hates Alabaster: not because he is more powerful, not even because he is crazy, but because he refuses to allow her any of the polite fictions and unspoken truths that have kept her comfortable, and safe, for years.

They glare at each other for a moment longer, then Alabaster shakes his head and turns to leave. Syenite follows, because there's really nowhere else to go. They head back down to the cavern level. As they descend the stairs, Syenite has no choice but to face the third reason she feels so out of place in Meov.

Floating now in the comm's harbor is a huge, graceful sailing vessel—maybe a frigate, maybe a galleon, she doesn't know either of these words from *boat*—that dwarfs all the smaller vessels combined. Its hull is a wood so dark that it's almost black, patched with paler wood here and there. Its sails are tawny canvas, also much-mended and sun-faded and water-marked...and yet, somehow despite the stains and patches, the whole of the ship is oddly beautiful. It is called the *Clalsu,* or at least that's what the word sounds like to her ears, and it sailed in two days after Syenite and Alabaster arrived in Meov. Aboard it were a good number of the comm's able-bodied adults, and a lot of ill-gotten gain from several weeks' predation along the coastal shipping lanes.

The *Clalsu* has also brought to Meov its captain—the headman's second, actually, who is only second by virtue of the fact that he spends more time away from the island than on it. Otherwise, Syen would have known the instant this man bounded down the gangplank to greet the cheering crowd that he was Meov's true leader, because she can tell without understanding a word that everyone here loves him and looks up to him. Innon is his name: Innon Resistant Meov in the mainlander parlance. A big man, black-skinned like most of the Meovites, built more like a Strongback than a Resistant and with personality enough to outshine any Yumenescene Leader.

Except he's not really a Resistant, or a Strongback, or a Leader, not that any of those use names really mean much in this comm that rejects so much of Sanzed custom. He's an orogene. A feral, born free and raised openly by Harlas—who's a rogga, too. *All* their leaders are roggas, here. It's how the island has survived through more Seasons than they've bothered to count.

And beyond this fact...well. Syen's not quite sure how to deal with Innon.

As a case in point, she hears him the instant they come into the main entry cavern of the comm. Everyone can hear him, since he talks as loudly within the caverns as he apparently does when on the deck of his ship. He doesn't need to; the caverns echo even the slightest sound. He's just not the sort of man to limit himself, even when he should.

Like now.

"Syenite, Alabaster!" The comm has gathered around its communal cookfires to share the evening meal. Everyone's sitting on stone or wooden benches, relaxing and chatting, but there's a big knot of people seated around Innon where he's been regaling them with . . . something. He switches to Sanzemat at once, however, since he's one of the few people in the comm who can speak it, albeit with a heavy accent. "I have been waiting for you both. We saved good stories for you. Here!" He actually rises and beckons to them as if yelling at the top of his lungs wasn't enough to get their attention, and as if a six-and-a-half-foot-tall man with a huge mane of braids and clothes from three different nations—all of it garish—would be hard to spot amid the crowd.

Yet Syenite finds herself smiling as she steps into the ring of benches where Innon has, apparently, kept one open just for them. Other members of the comm murmur greetings, which Syen is beginning to recognize; out of politeness, she attempts to stammer something similar back, and endures their chuckles when she gets it wrong. Innon grins at her and repeats the phrase, properly; she tries again and sees nods all around. "Excellent," Innon says, so emphatically that she cannot help but believe him.

Then he grins at Alabaster, beside her. "You're a good teacher, I think."

Alabaster ducks his head a little. "Not really. I can't seem to stop my pupils from hating me."

"Mmm." Innon's voice is low and deep and reverberates like the deepest of shakes. When he smiles, it's like the surface breach of a vesicle, something bright and hot and alarming, especially up close. "We must see if we can change that, hmm?" And he looks at Syen, unabashed in his interest, and plainly not caring when the other members of the comm chuckle.

That's the problem, see. This ridiculous, loud, vulgar man has made no secret of the fact that he *wants* Syenite. And unfortunately—because otherwise this would be easy—there's something about him that Syen actually finds herself attracted to. His ferality, perhaps. She's never met anyone like him.

Thing is, he seems to want Alabaster, *too.* And Alabaster doesn't seem disinterested, either.

It's a little confusing.

Once he has successfully flustered both of them, Innon turns his infinite charm on his people. "Well! Here we are, with food aplenty and fine new things that other people have made and paid for." He shifts into Eturpic then, repeating the words for everyone; they chuckle at the last part, largely because many of them *have been* wearing new clothes and jewelry and the like since the ship came in. Then Innon continues, and Syen doesn't really need Alabaster to explain that Innon is telling everyone a story—because Innon does this with his whole body. He leans forward and speaks more softly, and everyone is riveted to whatever tense moment he is describing. Then he pantomimes someone falling off something, and makes the sound of a splat by cupping his hands and squeezing air from between his palms. The small children who are listening practically fall over laughing, while the older kids snicker and the adults smile.

Alabaster translates a little of it for her. Apparently Innon is telling everyone about their most recent raid, on a small Coaster comm some ten days' sailing to the north. Syen's only half-listening to 'Baster's summation, mostly paying attention to the movements of Innon's body and imagining him performing entirely different movements, when suddenly Alabaster stops translating. When she finally notices this, surprised, he's looking at her intently.

"Do you want him?" he asks her.

Syen grimaces, mostly out of embarrassment. He's spoken softly, but they're right there next to Innon, and if he suddenly decides to pay attention... Well, what *if* he does? Maybe it would make things easier to get it all out into the open. She would really prefer to have a choice about that, though, and as usual Alabaster's not giving her one. "You don't have a subtle bone in your body, do you?"

"No, I don't. Tell me."

"What, then? Is this some kind of challenge?" Because she's seen the way Alabaster looks at Innon. It's almost cute, watching a forty-year-old man blush and stammer like a virgin. "Want me to back off?"

Alabaster flinches and looks almost hurt. Then he frowns as if confused by his own reaction—which makes two of them—and draws away a little. His mouth pulls to one side as he murmurs, "If I said yes, would you? Would you really?"

Syenite blinks. Well, she did suggest it. But would she? All of a sudden, she doesn't know.

When she fails to respond, though, Alabaster's expression twists in frustration. He mumbles something that might be "Never mind," then gets up and steps out of the story circle, taking care not to disturb anyone else as he goes. It means Syenite loses the ability to follow the tale, but that's all right. Innon is a joy to watch even without words, and since she doesn't have to pay attention to the story, she can consider Alabaster's question.

After a while the tale ends, and everyone claps; almost immediately there are calls for another story. In the general mill as people get up for second helpings from the massive pot of spiced shrimp, rice, and smoked sea-bubble that is tonight's meal, Syenite decides to go find Alabaster. She not sure what she's going to say, but... well. He deserves some kind of answer.

She finds him in their house, where he's curled up in a corner of the big empty room, a few feet from the bed of dried seagrass and cured animal furs they've been sleeping on. He hasn't bothered to light the lanterns; she makes him out as a darker blot against the shadows. "Go away," he snaps when she steps into the room.

"I live here, too," she snaps back. "Go somewhere else if you want to cry or whatever you're doing." Earth, she hopes he's not crying.

He sighs. It doesn't sound like he's crying, although he's got his legs drawn up and his elbows propped on his knees and his head's half buried in his hands. He could be. "Syen, you're such a steelheart."

"So are you, when you want to be."

"I *don't* want to be. Not always. Rust, Syen, don't you ever get *tired* of it all?" He stirs a little. Her eyes have adjusted, and she sees that he's looking at her. "Don't you ever just want to…to be human?"

She comes into the house and leans against the wall next to the door, crossing her arms and her ankles. "We aren't human."

"Yes. We. Are." His voice turns fierce. "I don't give a shit what the something-somethingth council of big important farts decreed, or how the geomests classify things, or any of that. That we're not human is just the lie they tell themselves so they don't have to feel bad about how they treat us—"

This, too, is something all roggas know. Only Alabaster is vulgar enough to say it aloud. Syenite sighs and leans her head back against the wall. "If you want him, you idiot, just tell him so. You can have him." And just like that, his question is answered.

Alabaster falls silent in mid-rant, staring at her. "You want him, too."

"Yeah." It costs her nothing to say this. "But I'm okay if…" She shrugs a little. "Yeah."

Alabaster takes a deep breath, then another. Then a third. She has no idea what any of those breaths means.

"I should make the same offer you just did," he says, at last. "Do the noble thing, or at least pretend to. But I…" In the shadows, he hunches more, tightening his arms around his knees. When he speaks again, his voice is barely audible. "It's just been so long, Syen."

Not since he's had a lover, of course. Just since he's had a lover he wanted.

There's laughter from the center of the gathering-cavern, and now people are moving along the corridors, chattering and breaking up for the night. They can both hear Innon's big voice rumbling not far off; even when he's just having a normal conversation, practically everyone can hear him. She hopes he's not a shouter, in bed.

Syen takes a deep breath. "Want me to go get him?" And just to be clear, she adds, "For you?"

Alabaster is silent for a long moment. She can feel him staring at her, and there's a kind of emotional pressure in the room that she can't quite interpret. Maybe he's insulted. Maybe he's touched. Rust if she'll ever be able to figure him out…and rust if she knows why she's doing this.

Then he nods, rubs a hand over his hair, and lowers his head. "Thank you." The words are almost cold, but she knows that tone, because she's used it herself. Any time she's needed to hold on to her dignity with fingernails and pent breath.

So she leaves and follows that rumble, eventually finding Innon near the communal cookfire in deep conversation with Harlas. Everyone else has dissipated by now, and the cavern echoes in a steady overlapping drone of fussy toddlers fighting sleep, laughter, talking, and the hollow creaking of the boats in the harbor outside as they rock in their moorings. And over all of it, the hiss-purr of the sea. Syenite settles herself against a wall nearby, listening to all these exotic sounds, and waiting. After perhaps ten minutes, Innon finishes his conversation and rises. Harlas heads away, chuckling over something Innon's said; ever the charmer. As Syen expected, Innon then comes over to lean against the wall beside her.

"My crew think I am a fool to pursue you," he says casually, gazing up at the vaulted ceiling as if there's something interesting up there. "They think you don't like me."

"Everyone thinks I don't like them," Syenite says. Most of the time, it's true. "I do like you."

He looks at her, thoughtful, which she likes. Flirting unnerves her. Much better to be straightforward like this. "I have met your kind before," he says. "The ones taken to the Fulcrum." His accent mangles this into *fool crumb,* which she finds especially fitting. "You are the happiest one I've seen."

Syenite snorts at the joke—and then, seeing the wry twist to his lips, the heavy compassion in his gaze, she realizes he's not joking at all. Oh. "Alabaster's pretty happy."

"No, he isn't."

No. He isn't. But this is why Syenite doesn't like jokes much, either. She sighs. "I'm . . . here for him, actually."

"Oh? So you have decided to share?"

"He's—" She blinks as the words register. "Uh?"

Innon shrugs, which is an impressive gesture given how big he is, and how it sets all his braids a-rustle. "You and he are already lovers. It was a thought."

What a thought. "Er . . . no. I don't—uh. No." There are things she's not ready to think about. "Maybe later." A lot later.

He laughs, though not at her. "Yes, yes. You have come, then, what? To ask me to see to your friend?"

"He's not—" But here she is procuring him a lover for the night. "*Rust.*"

Innon laughs—softly, for him—and shifts to lean sideways against the wall, perpendicular to Syenite so that she will not feel boxed in, even though he's close enough that she can feel his body heat. Something big men do, if they want to be considerate rather than intimidating. She appreciates his thoughtfulness. And she hates herself for deciding in Alabaster's favor, because, Earthfires, he even *smells* sexy as he says, "You are a very good friend, I think."

"Yes, I rusting am." She rubs her eyes.

"Now, now. Everyone sees that you are the stronger of the pair." Syenite blinks at this, but he's completely serious. He lifts a hand and draws a finger down the side of her face from temple to chin, a slow tease. "Many things have broken him. He holds himself together with spit and endless smiling, but all can see the cracks. You, though; you are dented, bruised, but intact. It is kind of you. Looking out for him like so."

"No one ever looks out for *me*." Then she shuts her mouth so hard that her teeth snap. She hadn't meant to say that.

Innon smiles, but it is a gentle, kindly thing. "I will," he says, and leans down to kiss her. It is a scratchy sort of kiss; his lips are dry, his chin beginning to hair over. Most Coaster men don't seem to grow beards, but Innon might have some Sanze in him, especially with all that hair. In any case, his kiss is so soft despite the scratchiness that it feels more like a thank-you than an attempt to seduce. Probably because that's what he intends. "Later, I promise I will."

Then he leaves, heading for the house she shares with Alabaster, and Syenite gazes after him and thinks belatedly, *Now where the rust am I supposed to sleep tonight?*

It turns out to be a moot question, because she's not sleepy. She goes to the ledge outside the cavern, where there are others lingering to take in the night air or talk where half the comm can't hear them, and she is not the only one standing wistfully at the railing, looking out over the water at night. The waves roll in steadily, making the smaller boats and the *Clalsu* rock and groan, and the starlight casts thin, diffuse reflections upon the waves that seem to stretch away into forever.

It's peaceful here, in Meov. It's nice to be who she is in a place that accepts her. Nicer still to know that she has nothing to fear for it. A woman Syen met in the baths—one of the *Clalsu* crew, most of whom speak at least a little Sanze-mat—explained it to her as they sat soaking in water warmed by rocks the children heat in the fire as part of their daily chores. It's simple, really. "With you, we live," she'd said to Syen, shrugging and letting her head fall back against the edge of the bath, and apparently not caring about the strangeness in her own words. On the mainland, everyone is convinced that with roggas nearby, they will all die.

And then the woman said something that truly unnerved Syen. "Harlas is old. Innon sees much danger, on raids. You and the laughing one"—that is the locals' term for Alabaster, since the ones who don't speak Sanze-mat have trouble pronouncing his name—"you have babies, give us one, yes? Or we have to go steal, from the mainland."

The very idea of these people, who stick out like stone eaters in a crowd, trying to infiltrate the Fulcrum to kidnap a grit, or grabbing some feral child just ahead of the Guardians, makes Syenite shiver. She's not sure she likes the idea of them greedily hoping she catches pregnant, either. But they're no different from the Fulcrum in that, are they? And here, any child that she and Alabaster have won't end up in a node station.

She lingers out on the ledge for a few hours, losing herself in the sound of the waves and gradually letting herself lapse into a kind of not-thinking fugue. Then she finally notices that her back is aching and her feet hurt, and the wind off the water is getting chilly; she can't just stand out here all night. So she heads back into the cavern, not really sure where she means to go, just letting her feet carry her where they will. Which is probably why she eventually ends up back outside "her" house, standing in front of the curtain that passes for privacy and listening to Alabaster weep through it.

It's definitely him. She knows that voice, even though it's choked now with sobs and half muffled. Barely audible, really, despite the lack of doors and windows... but she knows the why of that, doesn't she? Everyone who grows up in the Fulcrum learns to cry very, very quietly.

It is this thought, and the sense of camaraderie that follows it, that makes her reach up, slowly, and tug the curtain aside.

They're on the mattress, thankfully half covered in furs—not that it matters, since she can see clothing discarded about the room, and the air smells of sex, so it's obvious what they've been up to. Alabaster is curled up on his side, his back to her, bony shoulders shaking. Innon's sitting up on one elbow, stroking his hair. His eyes flick up when Syenite opens the curtain, but he doesn't seem upset, or surprised. In fact—and in light of their previous conversation she really shouldn't be surprised, but she *is*—he lifts a hand. Beckoning.

She's not sure why she obeys. And she's not sure why she

undresses as she walks across the room, or why she lifts up the furs behind Alabaster and slides into the redolent warmth with him. Or why, once she's done this, she curves herself against his back, and drapes an arm over his waist, and looks up to see Innon's sad smile of welcome. But she does.

Syen falls asleep like this. As far as she can tell, Alabaster cries for the rest of the night, and Innon stays up to comfort him the whole time. So when she wakes the next morning and claws her way out of bed and stumbles over to the chamber pot to throw up noisily into it, they both sleep through it. There is no one to comfort her as she sits there shaking in the aftermath. But that is nothing new.

Well. At least the people of Meov won't have to go steal a baby, now.

* * *

Put no price on flesh.

—Tablet One, "On Survival," verse six

INTERLUDE

There passes a time of happiness in your life, which I will not describe to you. It is unimportant. Perhaps you think it wrong that I dwell so much on the horrors, the pain, but pain is what shapes us, after all. We are creatures born of heat and pressure and grinding, ceaseless movement. To be still is to be . . . not alive.

But what is important is that you know it was not all terrible. There was peace in long stretches, between each crisis. A chance to cool and solidify before the grind resumed.

Here is what you need to understand. In any war, there are factions: those wanting peace, those wanting more war for a myriad of reasons, and those whose desires transcend either. And this is a war with many *sides, not just two. Did you think it was just the stills and the orogenes? No, no. Remember the stone eaters and the Guardians, too—oh, and the Seasons. Never forget Father Earth. He has not forgotten you.*

So while she—you—rested, those are the forces that gathered round. Eventually they began their advance.

20

Syenite, stretched and snapped back

It's not quite what Syenite had in mind for the rest of her life, sitting around being useless, so she goes to find Innon one day as the *Clalsu* crew is outfitting the ship for another raiding run.

"No," he says, staring at her like she's insane. "You are not *being a pirate* when you just had a baby."

"I had the baby two years ago." She can only change so many diapers, pester people for lessons in Eturpic so often, and help with the net-fishing so many times before she goes mad. She's done with nursing, which is the excuse Innon's used up to now to put her off—and which was pointless anyway, since in Meov that sort of thing is done communally, same as everything else. When she's not around, Alabaster just takes the baby to one of the other mothers in the comm, just as Syen fed their babies in turn if they happened to be hungry while she was nearby and full of milk. And since 'Baster does most of the diaper changes and sings little Corundum to sleep, and coos at him and plays with him and takes him for walks and so on, Syenite has to keep busy somehow.

"Syenite." He stops in the middle of the loading ramp that leads into the ship's hold. They're putting storage barrels of water and food aboard, along with baskets of more esoteric things—buckets of chain for the catapult, bladders of pitch and fish oil, a length of heavy cloth meant to serve as a replacement sail should they require it. When Innon stops with Syenite standing down-ramp from him, everything else stops, and when there are loud complaints from the dock, he lifts his head and glowers until everyone shuts up. Everyone, of course, except Syenite.

"I'm *bored*," she says in frustration. "There's nothing to do here except fish and wait for you and the others to come back from a raid, and gossip about people I don't know, and tell stories about things I don't care about! I've spent my whole life either training or working, for Earth's sake; you can't expect me to just sit around and look at water all day."

"Alabaster does."

Syenite rolls her eyes, although this is true. When Alabaster isn't with the baby, he spends most of his days up on the heights above the colony, gazing out at the world and thinking unfathomable thoughts for hours on end. She knows; she's watched him do it. "I'm not him! Innon, you can use me."

And Innon's expression twists, because—ah, yes. *That* one hits home for him.

It's an unspoken thing between them, but Syenite's not stupid. There are a lot of things a skilled rogga can do to help on the kinds of sorties Innon's crew makes. Not starting shakes or blows, she won't and he'd never ask it—but it is a simple thing to draw enough strength from the ambient to lower the temperature at the water's surface, and thus cloak the ship in fog to hide its approach or retreat. It is equally easy to disturb forests along the shoreline with the most delicate of underground vibrations, causing flocks of birds or hordes of mice to flood out of the trees and into nearby settlements as a distraction. And more. Orogeny is damned useful, Syenite is beginning to understand, for far, far more than just quelling shakes.

Or rather, it *could* be useful, if Innon could use his orogeny that way. Yet for all his awesome charisma and physical prowess, Innon is still a feral, with nothing more than what little training Harlas—himself a feral and poorly trained—could give him. She's felt Innon's orogeny when he quells local minor shakes, and the crude inefficiency of his power shocks her sometimes. She's tried to teach him better control, and he listens, and he *tries*, but he doesn't improve. She doesn't understand why. Without that level of skill, the *Clalsu* crew earns its spoils the old-fashioned way: They fight, and die, for every scrap.

"Alabaster can do these things for us," Innon says, looking uneasy.

"Alabaster," Syen says, trying for patience, "gets sick just looking at this thing." She gestures at *Clalsu*'s curving bulk. The joke all over the comm is that 'Baster somehow manages to look green despite his blackness whenever he is forced aboard a ship. Syen threw up less when she had morning sickness. "What if I don't do anything *but* cloak the ship? Or whatever you order me to do."

Innon puts his hands on his hips, his expression derisive. "You pretend that you will follow my orders? You don't even do that in bed."

"Oh, you *bastard*." Now he's just being an ass, because he

doesn't actually try to give her orders in bed. It's just a weird Meovite thing to tease about sex. Now that Syen can understand what everyone's saying, every other statement seems to be about her sharing her bedtime with two of the best-looking men in the comm. Innon says they only do this to her because she turns such interesting colors when little old ladies make vulgar jokes about positions and rope knots. She's trying to get used to it. "That's completely irrelevant!"

"Is it?" He pokes her in the chest with a big finger. "No lovers on ship; that is the rule I have always followed. We cannot even be friends once we set sail. What I say goes; anything else and we die. You question *everything*, Syenite, and there is no time for questioning, on the sea."

That's...not an unfair point. Syen shifts uneasily. "I can follow orders without question. Earth knows I've done enough of that. Innon—" She takes a deep breath. "Earth's sake, Innon, I'll do anything to get off this island for a while."

"And that is another problem." He steps closer and lowers his voice. "Corundum is *your son*, Syenite. Do you feel nothing for him, that you constantly chafe to be away?"

"I make sure he's taken care of." And she does. Corundum is always clean and well fed. She never wanted a child, but now that she's had it—him—and held him, and nursed him, and all that...she does feel a sense of accomplishment, maybe, and rueful acknowledgment, because she and Alabaster have managed to make one beautiful child between them. She looks into her son's face sometimes and marvels that he exists, that he seems so whole and right, when both his parents have nothing but bitter brokenness between them. Who's she kidding? It's love.

She loves her son. But that doesn't mean she wants to spend every hour of every rusting day in his presence.

Innon shakes his head and turns away, throwing up his hands. "Fine! Fine, fine, ridiculous woman. Then *you* go and tell Alabaster we will both be away."

"All ri—" But he's gone, up the ramp and into the hold, where she hears him yelling at someone else about something that she can't quite catch because her ears can't parse Eturpic when it echoes at that volume.

Regardless, she bounces a little as she heads down the ramp, waving in vague apology to the other crew members who are standing around looking mildly annoyed. Then she heads into the comm.

Alabaster's not in the house, and Corundum's not with Selsi, the woman who most often keeps the smaller children of the colony when their parents are busy. Selsi raises her eyebrows at Syen when she pokes her head in. "He said yes?"

"He said yes." Syenite can't help grinning, and Selsi laughs.

"Then we will never see you again, I wager. Waves wait only for the nets." Which Syenite guesses is some sort of Meov proverb, whatever it means. "Alabaster is on the heights with Coru, again."

Again. "Thanks," she says, and shakes her head. It's a wonder their child doesn't sprout wings.

She heads up the steps to the topmost level of the island and over the first rise of rock, and there they are, sitting on a blanket near the cliff. Coru looks up as she approaches, beaming and pointing at her; Alabaster, who probably felt her footsteps on the stairs, doesn't bother turning.

"Innon's finally taking you with them?" he asks when Syen gets close enough to hear his soft voice.

"Huh." Syenite settles on the blanket beside him, and opens her arms for Coru, who clambers out of Alabaster's lap, where he's been sitting, and into Syenite's. "If I'd known you already knew, I wouldn't have bothered walking up all those steps."

"It was a guess. You don't usually come up here with a smile on your face. I knew it had to be something." Alabaster turns at last, watching Coru as he stands in her lap and pushes at her breasts. Syenite holds him reflexively, but he's actually doing a good job of keeping his balance, despite the unevenness of her lap. Then Syen notices that it's not just Corundum that Alabaster's watching.

"What?" she asks, frowning.

"Will you come back?"

And that, completely out of the blue as it is, makes Syenite drop her hands. Fortunately, Coru's got the trick of standing on her legs, which he does, giggling, while she stares at Alabaster. "Why are you even—*What?*"

Alabaster shrugs, and it's only then that Syenite notices the furrow between his brows, and the haunted look in his eyes, and it's only then that she understands what Innon was trying to say to her. As if to reinforce this, Alabaster says, bitterly, "You don't have to be with me anymore. You have your freedom, like you wanted. And Innon's got what *he* wanted—a rogga child to take care of the comm if something happens to him. He's even got me to train the child better than Harlas ever could, because he knows I won't leave."

Fire-under-Earth. Syenite sighs and pushes away Coru's hands, which hurt. "No, little greedy child, I don't have milk anymore. Settle down." And because this immediately makes Coru's face screw up with thwarted sorrow, she pulls him close and wraps her arms around him and starts playing with his feet, which is usually a good way to distract him before he gets going. It works. Apparently small children are inordinately fascinated by their own toes; who knew? And with that child taken care of, she can focus on Alabaster, who's now looking out to sea again, but who's probably just as close to a meltdown.

"*You* could leave," she says, pointing out the obvious because that's what she always has to do with him. "Innon's offered before to take us back to the mainland, if we want to go. If we don't do anything stupid like still a shake in front of a crowd of people, either of us could probably make a decent life somewhere."

"We have a decent life here." It's hard to hear him over the wind, and yet she can actually feel what he's not saying. *Don't leave me.*

"Crusty *rust,* 'Baster, what is wrong with you? I'm not planning to leave." Not now, anyway. But it's bad enough that they're having this conversation at all; she doesn't need to make it worse. "I'm just going somewhere I can be useful—"

"You're useful *here.*" And now he turns to glare at her full-on, and it actually bothers her, the hurt and loneliness that lurk beneath the veneer of anger on his face. It bothers her more that this bothers her.

"No. I'm not." And when he opens his mouth to protest, she runs over him. "I'm *not.* You said it yourself; Meov has a ten-ringer now to protect it. Don't think I haven't noticed how we haven't had so much as a subsurface twitch in my range, not in all the time we've been here. You've been quelling any possible threat long before Innon or I can feel it—" But then she trails off, frowning, because Alabaster is shaking his head, and there's a smile on his lips that makes her abruptly uneasy.

"Not me," he says.

"What?"

"*I* haven't quelled anything for about a year now." And then he nods toward the child, who is now examining Syenite's fingers with intent concentration. She stares down at Coru, and Coru looks up at her and grins.

Corundum is exactly what the Fulcrum hoped for when they paired her with Alabaster. He hasn't inherited much of Alabaster's looks, being only a shade browner than Syen and with hair that's already growing from fuzz into the beginnings of a proper ashblow bottlebrush; she's the one with Sanzed ancestors, so that didn't come from 'Baster, either. But what Coru does have from his father is an almighty powerful awareness of the earth. It has never occurred to Syenite before now that her baby might be aware enough to sess, and *still*, microshakes. That's not instinct, that's skill.

"Evil Earth," she murmurs. Coru giggles. Then Alabaster abruptly reaches over and plucks him out of her arms, getting to his feet. "Wait, this—"

"Go," he snaps, grabbing the basket he's brought up with them and crouching to dump baby toys and a folded diaper back into it. "Go, ride your rusting boat, get yourself killed along with Innon, what do I care. *I* will be here for Coru, no matter what *you* do."

And then he's gone, his shoulders tight and his walk brisk,

ignoring Coru's shrill protest and not even bothering to take the blanket that Syen's still sitting on.

Earthfires.

Syenite stays topside awhile, trying to figure out how she ended up becoming the emotional caretaker for a crazy ten-ringer while stuck out in the middle of rusting nowhere with his inhumanly powerful baby. Then the sun sets and she gets tired of thinking about it, so she gets up and grabs the blanket and heads back down to the comm.

Everyone's gathering for the evening meal, but Syenite begs off being social this time, just grabbing a plate of roasted tulifish and braised threeleaf with sweetened barley that must have been stolen from some mainland comm. She carries this back to the house, and is unsurprised to find Alabaster there already, curled up in the bed with a sleeping Coru. They've upgraded to a bigger bed for Innon's sake, this mattress suspended from four sturdy posts by a kind of hammock-like net that is surprisingly comfortable, and durable despite the weight and activity they put on it. Alabaster's quiet but awake when Syen comes in, so she sighs and scoops up Coru and puts him to bed in the nearby smaller suspended bed, which is lower to the ground in case he rolls or climbs out in the night. Then she climbs into bed with Alabaster, just looking at him, and after a while he gives up the distant treatment and edges a little closer. He doesn't meet her eyes as he does this. But Syenite knows what he needs, so she sighs and rolls onto her back, and he edges closer still, finally resting his head on her shoulder, where he's probably wanted to be all along.

"Sorry," he says.

Syenite shrugs. "Don't worry about it." And then, because Innon's right and this is partly her fault, she sighs and adds, "I'm coming back. I *do* like it here, you know. I just get... restless."

"You're always restless. What are you looking for?"

She shakes her head. "I don't know."

But she thinks, almost but not quite subconsciously: *A way to change things. Because this is not right.*

He's always good at guessing her thoughts. "You can't make anything better," he says, heavily. "The world is what it is. Unless you destroy it and start all over again, there's no changing it." He sighs, rubs his face against her breast. "Take what you can get out of it, Syen. Love your son. Even live the pirate life if that makes you happy. But stop looking for anything better than this."

She licks her lips. "Corundum should have better."

Alabaster sighs. "Yes. He should." He says nothing more, but the unspoken is palpable: *He won't, though.*

It isn't right.

She drifts off to sleep. And a few hours later she wakes up because Alabaster is blurting, "Oh *fuck,* oh please, oh Earth, I can't, *Innon,*" against Innon's shoulder, and jerking in a way that disturbs the bed's gentle sway while Innon pants and ruts against him, cock on oily cock. And then because Alabaster is spent but Innon isn't, and Innon notices her watching, he grins at her and kisses Alabaster and then slides a hand between Syen's legs. Of course she's wet. He and Alabaster are always beautiful together.

Innon is a considerate lover, so he leans over and nuzzles her breasts and does marvelous things with his fingers, and does not stop thrusting against Alabaster until she curses and demands *all* of his attention for a while, which makes him laugh and shift over.

Alabaster watches while Innon obliges her, and his gaze grows hot with it, which Syenite still doesn't understand even after being with them for almost two years. 'Baster doesn't want her, not that way, nor she him. And yet it's unbelievably arousing for her to watch Innon drive him to moaning and begging, and Alabaster also clearly gets off on her going to pieces with someone else. She likes it *more* when 'Baster's watching, in fact. They can't stand sex with each other directly, but vicariously it's amazing. And what do they even call this? It's not a threesome, or a love triangle. It's a two-and-a-half-some, an affection dihedron. (And, well, maybe it's love.) She should worry about another pregnancy, maybe from Alabaster again given how messy things get between the three of them, but she can't bring herself to worry because it doesn't matter. Someone will love her children no matter what. Just as she doesn't think overmuch about what she does with her bed time or how this thing between them works; no one in Meov will care, no matter what. That's another turn-on, probably: the utter lack of fear. Imagine that.

So they fall asleep, Innon snoring on his belly between them and 'Baster and Syen with their heads pillowed on his big shoulders, and not for the first time does Syenite think, *If only this could last.*

She knows better than to wish for something so impossible.

* * *

The *Clalsu* sets sail the next day. Alabaster stands out on the pier with half the rest of the comm that is waving and well-wishing. He doesn't wave, but he does point to them as the ship pulls away, encouraging Coru to wave when Syenite and Innon do. Coru does it, and for a moment Syenite feels something like regret. It passes quickly.

Then there is only the open sea, and work to be done: casting lines for fish and climbing high up into the masts to do things to the sails when Innon tells them to, and at one point securing several barrels that have come loose down in the hold. It's hard work, and Syenite falls asleep in her little bunk under one of the bulkheads not long after sunset, because Innon won't let her sleep with him and anyway, she doesn't have the energy to make it up to his cabin.

But it gets better, and she gets stronger as the days pass, beginning to see why the *Clalsu* crew have always seemed a little more vibrant, a little more interesting, than everyone else in Meov. On the fourth day out there's a call from the left—rust, from the *port* side of the ship, and she and the others come to the railing to see something amazing: the curling plumes of ocean spray where great monsters of the deep have risen to swim alongside them. One of them breaches the surface to look at them and it's ridiculously huge; its eye is bigger than Syen's head. One slap of its fins could capsize the ship. But it doesn't hurt them, and one of the crew members tells her that it's just curious. She seems amused by Syenite's awe.

At night, they look at the stars. Syen has never paid much attention to the sky; the ground beneath her feet was always more important. But Innon points out patterns in the ways that the stars move, and explains that the "stars" she sees are actually other suns, with other worlds of their own and perhaps other people living other lives and facing other struggles. She has heard of pseudosciences like astronomestry, knows that its adherents make unprovable claims like this, but now, looking at the constantly moving sky, she understands why they believe it. She understands why they *care*, when the sky is so immutable and irrelevant to most of daily life. On nights like these, for a little while, she cares, too.

Also at night, the crew drinks and sings songs. Syenite mispronounces vulgar words, inadvertently making them more vulgar, and makes instant friends of half the crew by doing so.

The other half of the crew reserves judgment, until they spy a likely target on the seventh day. They've been lurking near the shipping lanes between two heavily populated peninsulas, and people up in the mast-nest have been watching with spyglasses for ships worth the effort of robbing. Innon doesn't give the order until the lookout tells them he's spotted an especially large vessel of the sort often used to ferry trade goods too heavy or dangerous for easy overland carting: oils and quarried stone and volatile chemicals and timber. The very sorts of things that a comm stuck on a barren island in the middle of nowhere might need most. This one's accompanied by another vessel, which is smaller and which, according to those who see it through the spyglass and can tell such things by sight, is probably bristling with militia soldiers, battering rams, and armaments of its own. (Maybe one's a carrack and the other's a caravel, those are the words the sailors use, but she can't remember which one's which and it's a pain in the ass to try so she's going to stick with "the big boat" and "the small boat.") Their readiness to fight off pirates confirms that the freighter carries something worth pirating.

Innon looks at Syenite, and she grins fiercely.

She raises two fogs. The first requires her to pull ambient energy at the farthest edge of her range—but she does it, because that's where the smaller ship is. The second fog she raises in a corridor between *Clalsu* and the cargo vessel, so that they will be on their target almost before it sees them coming.

It goes like clockwork. Innon's crew are mostly experienced and highly skilled; the ones like Syenite, who don't know what they're doing yet, are pushed to the periphery while the others set to. The *Clalsu* comes out of the fog and the other vessel starts ringing bells to sound the alarm, but it's too late. Innon's people fire the catapults and shred their sails with baskets of chain. Then the *Clalsu* sidles up close—Syen thinks they're going to hit, but Innon knows what he's doing—and others in the crew throw hooks across the gap between them, hitching the ships together and then winching them closer with the big crankworks that occupy much of the deck.

It's dangerous at this point, and one of the older members of the crew shoos Syen belowdecks when people on the cargo ship start firing arrows and slingstones and throwing-knives at them. She sits in the shadow of the steps while the other crew members run up and down them, and her heart is pounding; her palms are damp. Something heavy thuds into the hull not five feet from her head, and she flinches.

But Evil Earth, this is *so* much better than sitting around on the island, fishing and singing lullabies.

It's over in minutes. When the commotion dies down and Syenite dares to venture up top again, she sees that planks have been run between the two vessels and Innon's people are running back and forth along them. Some of them have captured members of the cargo vessel's crew and corralled them on deck, holding them at glassknife-point; the rest of the crew is surrendering, giving up weapons and valuables, for fear the hostages will be hurt. Already some of Innon's sailors are going into the holds, bringing up barrels and crates and carting them across to the *Clalsu*'s deck. They'll sort out the booty later. Speed is of the essence now.

But all at once there are shouts and someone in the rigging hits a bell frantically—and out of the roiling fog looms the attack ship that accompanied the cargo vessel. It's on them, and belatedly Syenite realizes her error: she had assumed that the attack ship would *stop* given that it couldn't see, knowing itself in proximity to other vessels. People are not that logical. Now the attack ship is coming at full speed, and even though she can hear cries of alarm from its decks as they also realize the danger, there's no way it will be able to stop before it rams into *Clalsu* and the cargo ship . . . and probably sinks all three.

Syenite is brimming with power drawn from the warmth and boundless waves of the sea. She reacts, as she has been taught in a hundred Fulcrum drills, without thinking. Down, through the strange slipperiness of seawater minerals, through the soggy uselessness of the ocean sediment, down. There is stone beneath the ocean, and it is old and raw and hers to command.

In another place she claws up with her hands and shouts and thinks *Up*, and suddenly the attack ship cracks loudly and jerks to a halt. People stop screaming, shocked into silence, on all three vessels. This is because suddenly there is a massive, jagged knife of bedrock jutting several feet above the attack ship's deck, skewering the vessel from the keel up.

Shaking, Syenite lowers her hands slowly.

The cries aboard the *Clalsu* turn from alarm into ragged cheers. Even a few of the cargo vessel's people look relieved; one ship damaged is better than three ships sunk.

Things go quickly after that, with the attack ship helpless and skewered as it is. Innon comes to find her just as the crew reports that the cargo ship's hold is empty. Syen has moved to the bow, where she can see people on the attack ship's deck trying to chisel at the pillar.

Innon stops beside her, and she looks up, braced for his anger. But he is far from angry.

"I did not know one could do such things," he says wonderingly. "I thought you and Alabaster were only boasting."

It is the first time Syenite has been praised for her orogeny by someone not of the Fulcrum, and if she had not already begun to love Innon, she would now. "I shouldn't have brought it up so high," she says, sheepishly. "If I'd thought first, I would've raised the column only enough to breach the hull so they'd think they ran over an obstacle."

Innon sobers as he understands. "Ah. And now they know we have an orogene of some skill aboard." His expression hardens in a way that Syenite does not understand, but she decides not to question it. It feels so good to stand here, with him, basking in the glow of success. For a while they just watch the cargo vessel's unloading together.

Then one of Innon's crewmen runs up to say they're done, the planks have been withdrawn, the ropes and hooks rolled back onto their crankwheels. They're ready to go. Innon says in a heavy voice, "Hold."

She almost knows what is coming then. But it still makes her feel ill when he looks at Syenite, his expression ice. "Sink them both."

She has promised never to question Innon's orders. Even so, she hesitates. She has never killed anyone before, not deliberately. It was just a mistake that she brought the stone projection up so high. Is it really necessary that people die for her folly? He steps close, and she flinches preemptively, even though he has never harmed her. Her hand bones twinge regardless.

But Innon only says into her ear, "For 'Baster and Coru."

That makes no sense. 'Baster and Coru are not here. But then the full implication of his words—that the safety of everyone in Meov depends on the mainlanders seeing them as a nuisance rather than a serious threat—sinks in, and makes her cold, too. Colder.

So she says, "You should move us away."

Innon turns at once and gives the order for the *Clalsu* to set sail. Once they have drifted to a safe distance, Syenite takes a deep breath.

For her family. It is strange, thinking of them as such, though that is what they are. Stranger still to do something like this for a real reason, and not simply because she has been commanded to. Does that mean she is no longer a weapon? What does that make her, then, if not?

Doesn't matter.

At a flick of her will, the bedrock column extracts itself from the attack ship's hull—leaving a ten-foot hole near the stern. It begins sinking immediately, tipping upward as it takes on water. Then, dragging more strength from the ocean surface and raising fog enough to obscure sight for miles, Syenite shifts the column to aim at the cargo vessel's keel. A quick thrust up, a quicker withdrawal. Like stabbing someone to death with a poniard. The ship's hull cracks like an egg, and after a moment splits into two halves. It's done.

The fog completely obscures both sinking ships as the *Clalsu* sails away. The two crews' screams follow Syenite long after, into the drifting whiteness.

* * *

Innon makes an exception for her, that night. Later, sitting up in his captain's bed, Syen says, "I want to see Allia."

Innon sighs. "No. You don't."

But he gives the order anyway, because he loves her. The ship charts a new course.

* * *

According to legend, Father Earth did not originally hate life.

In fact, as the lorists tell it, once upon a time Earth did everything he could to facilitate the strange emergence of life on his surface. He crafted even, predictable seasons; kept changes of wind and wave and temperature slow enough that every living being could adapt, evolve; summoned waters that purified themselves, skies that always cleared after a storm. He did not create life—that was happenstance—but he was pleased and fascinated by it, and proud to nurture such strange wild beauty upon his surface.

Then people began to do horrible things to Father Earth. They poisoned waters beyond even his ability to cleanse, and killed much of the other life that lived on his surface. They drilled through the crust of his skin, past the blood of his mantle, to get at the sweet marrow of his bones. And at the height of human hubris and might, it was the orogenes who did something that even Earth could not forgive: They destroyed his only child.

No lorist that Syenite has ever talked to knows what this cryptic phrase means. It isn't stonelore, just oral tradition occasionally recorded on ephemerals like paper and hide, and too many Seasons have changed it. Sometimes it's the Earth's favorite glassknife that the orogenes destroyed; sometimes it's his shadow; sometimes it's his most valued Breeder. Whatever the words mean, the lorists and 'mests agree on what happened after the orogenes committed their great sin: Father Earth's surface cracked like an eggshell. Nearly every living thing died as his fury became manifest in the first and most terrible of the Fifth Seasons: the Shattering Season. Powerful as they were, those ancient people had no warning, no time to build storecaches, and no stonelore to guide them. It is only through sheer luck that enough of humankind survived to replenish itself afterward—and never again has life attained the heights of power that it once held. Earth's recurrent fury will never allow that.

Syenite has always wondered about these tales. There's a degree of poetic license in them, of course, primitive people trying to explain what they didn't understand…but all legends contain a kernel of truth. Maybe the ancient orogenes did shatter the planet's crust, somehow. How, though? It's clear now that there's more to orogeny than what the Fulcrum teaches—and maybe there's a reason the Fulcrum doesn't teach it, if the legend is true. But facts are facts: Even if somehow every orogene in existence down to the infants could be yoked together, they could not destroy the world's surface. It would ice everything; there's not enough warmth or movement *anywhere* to do that much damage. They'd all burn themselves out trying, and die.

Which means that part of the tale can't be true; orogeny cannot be to blame for the Earth's rage. Not that anyone but another rogga would accept this conclusion.

It is truly amazing, though, that humanity managed to survive the fires of that first Season. Because if the whole world was then as Allia is now... Syenite has a fresh understanding of just how much Father Earth hates them all.

Allia is a nightscape of red, blistering death. There is nothing left of the comm except the caldera ring that once cradled it, and even that is hard to see. Squinting through the red wavering haze, Syen thinks she can glimpse a few leftover buildings and streets on the caldera's slopes, but that might just be wishful thinking.

The night sky is thick with ash clouds, underlit by the glow of fire. Where the harbor was, there is now a growing volcano cone, gushing deadly clouds and hot red birth-blood on its climb out of the sea. It's already huge, occupying nearly the entire caldera bowl, and it has already borne offspring. Two additional vents crouch against its flank, belching gas and lava like their parent. Likely all three will eventually grow together to become a single monster, engulfing the surrounding mountains and threatening every comm in range of its gas clouds or subsequent blows.

Everyone Syenite met in Allia is dead now. The *Clalsu* can't go within five miles of the shore; any closer and they risk death, whether by warping the ship's hull in the heated waters, or by suffocating in the hot clouds that periodically gout forth from the mountain. Or by cooking themselves over one of the subsidiary vents that are still developing around the area, spreading out from what was once Allia's harbor like the spokes of a wheel and lurking like deadly mines beneath the waters offshore. Syen can sess every one of these hot spots, bright churning ragestorms just beneath the Earth's skin. Even Innon can sess them, and he's steered the ship away from those that are most likely to burst through anytime soon. But as fragile as the strata are right now, a new vent could open right under them before Syen has a chance to detect or stop it. Innon's risking a lot to indulge her.

"Many in the outlying parts of the comm managed to escape," Innon says softly, beside her. The *Clalsu*'s whole crew has come up on deck, staring at Allia in silence. "They say there was a flash of red light from the harbor, then a series of flashes, in a rhythm. Like something . . . pulsing. But the initial concussion, when the whole damned harbor boiled away at once, flattened most of the smaller houses in the comm. That's what killed most people. There was no warning." Syenite twitches.

No warning. There were almost a hundred thousand people in Allia—small by the standards of the Equatorials, but big for a Coaster comm. Proud, justifiably so. They'd had such hopes.

Rust this. Rust it and burn it in the foul, hateful guts of Father Earth.

"Syenite?" Innon is staring at her. This is because Syen has raised her fists before her, as if she is grasping the reins of a straining, eager horse. And because a narrow, high, tight torus has suddenly manifested around her. It isn't cold; there's plenty of earth-power for her to tap nearby. But it is powerful, and even an untrained rogga can sess the gathering flex of her will. Innon inhales and takes a step back. "Syen, what are you—"

"I can't leave it like this," she murmurs, almost to herself. The whole area is a swelling, deadly boil ready to burst. The volcano is only the first warning. Most vents in the earth are tiny, convoluted things, struggling to escape through varying layers of rock and metal and their own inertia. They seep and cool and plug themselves and then seep upward again, twisting and winding every which way in the process. *This,* though, is a gigantic lava tube channeled straight up from wherever the garnet obelisk has gone, funneling pure Earth-hate toward the surface. If nothing is done, the whole region will soon blow sky-high, in a massive explosion that will almost surely touch off a Season. She cannot believe the Fulcrum has left things like this.

So Syenite stabs herself into that churning, building heat, and tears at it with all the fury she feels at seeing *Allia, this was Allia, this was a human place, there were* people *here*. People who didn't deserve to die because

of me

because they were too stupid to let sleeping obelisks lie, or because they dared to dream of a future. No one deserves to die for that.

It's almost easy. This is what orogenes do, after all, and the hot spot is ripe for her use. The danger lies in not using it, really. If she takes in all that heat and force without channeling it elsewhere, it will destroy her. But fortunately—she laughs to herself, and her whole body shakes with it—she's got a volcano to choke off.

So she curls the fingers of one hand into a fist, and sears down its throat with her awareness, not burning but cooling, turning its own fury back on it to seal every breach. She forces the growing magma chamber back, back, down, down—and as she does so, she deliberately drags together the strata in overlapping patterns so that each will press down on the one below it and *keep* the magma down, at least until it finds another, slower way to wend its way to the surface. It's a delicate sort of operation, for all that it involves millions of tons of rock and the sorts of pressures that force diamonds into existence. But Syenite is a child of the Fulcrum, and the Fulcrum has trained her well.

She opens her eyes to find herself in Innon's arms, with the ship heaving beneath her feet. Blinking in surprise, she looks up at Innon, whose eyes are wide and wild. He notices that she's back, and the expressions of relief and fear on his face are both heartening and sobering.

"I told everyone you would not kill us," he says, over the churning of the sea spray and the shouts of his crew. She looks around and sees them frantically trying to lower the sails, so that they can have more control amid a sea that is suddenly anything but placid. "Please try not to make me a liar, would you?"

Shit. She's used to working orogeny on land, and forgot to account for the effects of her fault-sealing on water. They were shakes for a good purpose, but shakes nevertheless, and—oh Earth, she can feel it. She's touched off a tsunami. And—she winces and groans as her sessapinae set up a ringing protest at the back of her head. She's overdone it.

"Innon." Her head is ringing agony. "You need—nnh. Push waves of matching amplitude, subsurface..."

"What?" He looks away from her to shout something to one of the crewwomen in his tongue, and she curses inwardly. Of course he has no idea what she's talking about. He does not speak Fulcrum.

But then, all at once, there is a chill in the air all around them. The wood of the ship groans with the temperature change. Syen gasps in alarm, but it's not much of a change, really. Just the difference between a summer night and an autumn one, albeit over the span of minutes—and there is a presence to this change that is familiar as warm hands in the night. Innon abruptly inhales as he recognizes it, too: Alabaster. Of course his range stretches this far. He quells the gathering waves in moments.

When he's done, the ship sits on placid waters once more, facing the volcano of Allia... which has now gone quiet and dark. It's still smoking and will be hot for decades, but it no longer vents fresh magma or gas. The skies above are already clearing.

Leshiye, Innon's first mate, comes over, throwing an uneasy look at Syenite. He says something too fast for Syenite to translate fully, but she gets the gist of it: *Tell her next time she decides to stop a volcano, get off the ship first.*

Leshiye's right. "Sorry," Syen mutters in Eturpic, and the man grumbles and stomps off.

Innon shakes his head and lets her go, calling for the sails to be unfurled once again. He glances down at her. "You all right?"

"Fine." She rubs at her head. "Just never worked anything that big before."

"I did not think you could. I thought only ones like Alabaster—with many rings, more than yours—could do so. But you are as powerful as he."

"No." Syenite laughs a little, gripping the railing and clinging to it so she won't need to lean on him for support anymore. "I just do what's possible. *He* rewrites the rusting laws of nature."

"Heh." Innon sounds odd, and Syenite glances at him in surprise to see an almost regretful look on his face. "Sometimes, when I see what you and he can do, I wish I had gone to this Fulcrum of yours."

"No, you don't." She doesn't even want to think about what he would be like if he had grown up in captivity with the rest of them. Innon, but without his booming laugh or vivacious hedonism or cheerful confidence. Innon, with his graceful strong hands weaker and clumsier for having been broken. *Not* Innon.

He smiles ruefully at her now, as if he has guessed her thoughts. "Someday, you must tell me what it's like there. Why all who come out of that place seem so very competent...and so very afraid."

With that, he pats her back and heads off to oversee the course change.

But Syenite stays where she is at the railing, suddenly chilled to the bone in a way that has nothing to do with the passing flex of Alabaster's power.

That is because, as the ship tilts to one side in its turnabout, and she takes one last look back at the place that was Allia before her folly destroyed it—

—she sees someone.

Or she thinks she does. She's not sure at first. She squints and can just make out one of the paler strips that wend down into the Allia bowl on its southern curve, which is more readily visible now that the ruddy light around the volcano has faded. It's obviously not the Imperial Road that she and 'Baster traveled to get to Allia, once upon a time and one colossal mistake ago. Most likely what she's looking at is just a dirt road used by the locals, carved out of the surrounding forest a tree at a time and kept clear by decades of foot traffic.

There is a tiny mote moving along that road that looks, from this distance, like a person walking downhill. But it can't be. No sane person would stay so close to an active, deadly blow that had already killed thousands.

She squints more, moving to the ship's stern so that she can continue to peer that way as the *Clalsu* peels away from the coast. If only she had one of Innon's spyglasses. If only she could be sure.

Because for a moment she thinks, for a moment she *sees*, or hallucinates in her weariness, or imagines in her anxiety—

The Fulcrum seniors would not leave such a brewing disaster unmitigated. Unless they thought there was a very good reason to do so. Unless they had been ordered *to do so.*

—that the walking figure is wearing a burgundy uniform.

*   *   *

Some say the Earth is angry
Because he wants no company;
I say the Earth is angry
Because he lives alone.

—Ancient (pre-Imperial) folk song

21

you're getting the band back together

"You," you say suddenly to Tonkee. Who is not Tonkee.

Tonkee, who is approaching one of the crystal walls with a gleaming eye and a tiny chisel she's produced from somewhere, stops and looks at you in confusion. "What?"

It's the end of the day, and you're tired. Discovering impossible comms hidden in giant underground geodes takes a lot out of you. Ykka's people have put you and the others up in an apartment that's situated along the midpoint of one of the longer crystalline shafts. You had to walk across a rope bridge and around an encircling wooden platform to reach it. The apartment is level, even though the crystal itself isn't; the people who hollowed this place out seem not to have understood that no one *forgets* they're living in something that leans at a forty-five-degree angle just because the floor is straight. But you've tried to put it out of your mind.

And somewhere in the middle of looking around the place and putting your pack down and thinking, *This is home until I can escape it,* you've suddenly realized that you *know* Tonkee. You've known her, on some level, all along.

"*Binof. Leadership. Yumenes,*" you snap, and each word seems to hit Tonkee like a blow. She flinches and takes a step back, then another. Then a third, until she's pressed against the apartment's smooth crystalline wall. The look on her face is one of horror, or perhaps sorrow so great that it might as well be horror. Past a certain point, it's all the same thing.

"I didn't think you remembered," she says, in a small voice.

You get to your feet, palms planted on the table. "It's not chance that you started traveling with us. It can't be."

Tonkee tries to smile; it's a grimace. "Unlikely coincidences *do* happen…"

"Not with you." Not with a child who'd scammed her way into the Fulcrum and uncovered a secret that culminated in the death of a Guardian. The woman who was that child will not leave things to chance. You're sure of it. "At least your rusting *disguises* have gotten better over the years."

Hoa, who's been standing at the entrance of the apartment—guarding again, you think—turns his head from one to the other of you, back and forth. Perhaps he is watching how this confrontation goes, to prepare for the one you have to have with him, next.

Tonkee looks away. She's shaking, just a little. "It isn't. A coincidence. I mean…" She takes a deep breath. "I haven't been following you. I *had people* follow you, but that's different. Didn't start following you myself until just the last few years."

"You had people follow me. *For almost thirty years?*"

She blinks, then relaxes a little, chuckling. It sounds bitter. "My family has more money than the Emperor. Anyway, it was easy for the first twenty years or so. We almost lost you ten years ago. But…well."

You slam your hands down on the table, and maybe it's your imagination that the crystal walls of the apartment glow a little brighter, just for a moment. This almost distracts you. Almost.

"I really can't take many more surprises right now," you say, half through your teeth.

Tonkee sighs and slumps against the wall. "…Sorry."

You shake your head so hard that your locks slip loose from their knot. "I don't want apologies! *Explain.* Which are you, the Innovator or the Leader?"

"Both?"

You're going to ice her. She sees that in your eyes and blurts, "I was born Leadership. I really was! I'm Binof. But…" She spreads her hands. "What can I lead? I'm not good at things like that. You saw what I was like as a child. No subtlety. I'm not good with—people. Things, though, things I can do."

"I'm not interested in your rusting history—"

"But it's relevant! History is always relevant." Tonkee, Binof, or whoever she is, steps away from the wall, a pleading look on her face. "I really am a geomest. I really did go to Seventh, although…although…" She grimaces in a way you don't understand. "It didn't go well. But I really have spent my life studying that thing, that *socket,* which we found in the Fulcrum. Essun, do you know what that was?"

"I don't care."

At this, however, Tonkee-Binof scowls. "It matters," she says.

Now she's the one who looks furious, and you're the one who draws back in surprise. "I've given my life to that secret. It *matters*. And it should matter to you, too, because you're one of the only people in all the Stillness who can *make* it matter."

"What in Earthfires are you talking about?"

"*It's where they built them.*" Binof-Tonkee comes forward quickly, her face alight. "The socket in the Fulcrum. *That's where the obelisks come from*. And it's also where everything went wrong."

* * *

You end up doing introductions again. Completely this time.

Tonkee is really Binof. But she prefers Tonkee, which is the name she took for herself upon getting into the Seventh University. Turns out it's Not Done for a child of the Yumenescene Leadership to go into any profession except politics, adjudication, or large-scale merchantry. It's also Not Done for a child who is born a boy to be a girl—apparently the Leadership families don't use Breeders, they breed among themselves, and Tonkee's girlness scuttled an arranged marriage or two. They could've simply arranged different marriages, but between that and the young Tonkee's tendency to say things she shouldn't and do things that made no sense, it was the last straw. Thus Tonkee's family buried her in the Stillness's finest center of learning, giving her a new persona and a false use-caste, and quietly disowned her without all the fuss and bother of a scandal.

Yet Tonkee thrived there, apart from a few raging fights with renowned scholars, most of which she won. And she has spent her professional life studying the obsession that drove her to the Fulcrum all those years ago: the obelisks.

"It wasn't so much that I was interested in *you*," she explains. "I mean, I was—you'd helped me, and I needed to make sure you didn't suffer for that, that's how it started—but as I investigated you I learned that you had *potential*. You were one of those who might, one day, develop the ability to command obelisks. It's a rare skill, see. And... well, I hoped... well."

By this point you've sat down again, and both your voices have lowered. You can't sustain anger over this; there's too much to deal with right now. You look at Hoa, who's standing at the edge of the room, watching the two of you, his posture wary. Still gotta have that talk with him. All the secrets are coming out. Including yours.

"I died," you say. "That was the only way to hide from the Fulcrum. I *died* to get away from them, and yet I didn't shake you."

"Well, yes. My people didn't use mysterious powers to track you; we used deduction. Much more reliable." Tonkee eases herself into the chair opposite you at the table. The apartment has three rooms—this denlike central space, and two bedrooms leading off. Tonkee needs one room to herself because she's starting to smell again. You're only willing to keep sharing your space with Hoa after you get some answers, so you might be sleeping here in the den for a while.

"For the past few years I've been working with—some people." Tonkee abruptly looks cagey, which isn't hard for her. "Other 'mests, mostly, who've also been asking the kinds of questions no one wants to answer. Specialists in other areas. We've been tracking the obelisks, all of them that we can, for the past few years. Did you notice there are patterns in the way they move?

They converge, slowly, wherever there's an orogene of sufficient skill nearby. Someone who can use them. Only two were moving toward you, in Tirimo, but that was enough to extrapolate."

You look up, frowning. "Moving toward me?"

"Or another orogene in your vicinity, yes." Tonkee's relaxed now, eating a piece of dried fruit from her pack. Oblivious to your reaction as you stare at her, your blood gone cold. "The triangulation lines were pretty clear. Tirimo was the center of the circle, so to speak. You must have been there for years; one of the obelisks coming toward you had been traveling the same flight path for almost a decade, all the way from the eastern coast."

"The amethyst," you whisper.

"Yes." Tonkee watches you. "That was why I suspected you were still alive. Obelisks . . . bond, sort of, to certain orogenes. I don't know how that works. I don't know why. But it's specific, and predictable."

Deduction. You shake your head, mute with shock, and she goes on. "Anyhow, they'd both picked up speed in the last two or three years, so I traveled to the region and pretended to be commless to get a better read on them. I never really meant to approach you. But then this thing happened up north, and I started to think it would be important to have a wielder—obelisk-wielder—around. So . . . I tried to find you. I was on my way to Tirimo when I spotted you at that roadhouse. Lucky. I was going to trail you for a few days, decide whether I'd tell you who I really was . . . but then he turned a kirkhusa into a statue." She jerks her head at Hoa. "Figured it might be better to shut up and observe for a while, instead."

Somewhat understandable. "You said more than one obelisk was headed for Tirimo." You lick your lips. "There should've only been one." The amethyst is the only one you're connected to. The only one left.

"There were two. The amethyst, and another from the Merz." That's a big desert to the northeast.

You shake your head. "I've never been to the Merz."

Tonkee is silent for a moment, perhaps intrigued, perhaps annoyed. "Well, how many orogenes were in Tirimo?"

Three. But. "Picked up speed." You can't think, all of a sudden. Can't answer her question. Can't muster complete sentences. *Picked up speed in the last two or three years.*

"Yes. We didn't know what was causing that." Tonkee pauses, then gives you a sidelong look, her eyes narrowing. "Do you?"

Uche was two years old. Almost three.

"Get out," you whisper. "Go take a bath or something. I need to think."

She hesitates, plainly wanting to ask more questions. But then you look up at her, and she immediately gets up to leave. A few minutes after she's out of the apartment, with the heavy hanging falling in her wake—the apartments in this place have no doors, but the hangings work well enough for privacy—you sit there in silence, your head empty, for a while.

Then you look up at Hoa, who's standing beside Tonkee's vacated chair, plainly waiting his turn.

"So you're a stone eater," you say.

He nods, solemn.

"You look..." You gesture at him, not sure how to say it. He's never looked normal, not really, but he's definitely not what a stone eater is supposed to look like. Their hair does not move. Their skin does not bleed. They transit through solid rock in the span of a breath, but stairs would take them hours.

Hoa shifts a little, bringing his pack up into his lap. He rummages for a moment and then comes out with the rag-wrapped bundle that you haven't seen for a while. So that's where he put it. He unties it, finally letting you see what he's been carrying all this time.

The bundle contains many smallish pieces of rough-hewn crystal, as far as you can tell. Something like quartz, or maybe gypsum, except some of the pieces are not murky white but venous red. And you're not sure, but you think the bundle is smaller now than it used to be. Did he lose some of them?

"Rocks," you say. "You've been carrying...rocks?"

Hoa hesitates, then reaches for one of the white pieces. He picks it up; it's about the size of the tip of your thumb, squarish, chipped badly on one side. It looks hard.

He eats it. You stare, and he watches you while he does it. He works it around in his mouth for a moment, as if searching for the right angle of attack, or maybe he's just rolling it around on his tongue, enjoying the taste. Maybe it's salt.

But then his jaw flexes. There's a crunching sound, surprisingly loud in the silence of the room. Several more crunches, not as loud, but leaving no doubt that what he's chewing on is by no means food. And then he swallows, and licks his lips.

It's the first time you've ever seen him eat.

"Food," you say.

"Me." He extends a hand and lays it over the pile of rocks with curious delicacy.

You frown a little, because he's making less sense than usual. "So that's... what? Something that allows you to look like one of us?" Which you didn't know they could do. Then again, stone eaters share nothing of themselves, and they do not tolerate inquiry from others. You've read accounts of attempts by the Sixth University at Arcara to capture a stone eater for study, two Seasons back. The result was the Seventh University at Dibars, which got built only after they dug enough books out of the rubble of Sixth.

"Crystalline structures are an efficient storage medium." The words make no sense. Then Hoa repeats, clearly, "This is me."

You want to ask more about that, then decide against it. If he wanted you to understand, he would've explained. And that's not the part that matters, anyway.

"Why?" you ask. "Why did you make yourself like this? Why not just be... what you are?"

Hoa gives you a look so skeptical that you realize what a stupid question that is. Would you really have let him travel with you if you'd known what he was? Then again, if you'd known what he was, you wouldn't have tried to stop him. No one stops stone eaters from doing what they damn well please.

"Why bother, I mean?" you ask. "Can't you just... Your kind can travel through stone."

"Yes. But I wanted to travel with you."

And here we come to the crux of it. "Why?"

"I like you." And then he shrugs. *Shrugs.* Like any child, upon being asked something he either doesn't know how to articulate or doesn't want to try. Maybe it isn't important. Maybe it was just an impulse. Maybe he'll wander off eventually, following some other whim. Only the fact that he isn't a child—that he isn't rusting human, that he's probably *Seasons* old, that he comes from a whole race of people that can't act on whims because it's too rusting hard—makes this a lie.

You rub your face. Your hands come away gritty with ash; you need a bath, too. As you sigh, you hear him say, softly, "I won't hurt you."

You blink at this, then lower your hands slowly. It hadn't even occurred to you that he might. Even now, knowing what he is, having seen the things he can do... you're finding it hard to think of him as a frightening, mysterious, unknowable thing. And that, more than anything else, tells you why he's done this to himself. He likes you. He doesn't want you to fear him.

"Good to know," you say. And then there's nothing else to say, so you just look at each other for a while.

"It isn't safe here," he says then.

"Figured that, yeah."

The words are out, snide tone and all, before you really catch yourself. And then—well, is it really surprising that you'd be feeling a bit acerbic at this point? You've been sniping at people since Tirimo, really. But then it occurs to you: That's not the way you were with Jija, or anyone else, before Uche's death. Back then you were always careful to be gentler, calmer. Never sarcastic. If you got angry, you didn't let it show. That's not who Essun was supposed to be.

Yeah, well, you're not quite Essun. Not *just* Essun. Not anymore.

"The others like you, who are here," you begin. His little face tightens, though, in unmistakable anger. You stop in surprise.

"They aren't like me," he says, coldly.

Well, that's that, then. And you're done.

"I need to rest," you say. You've been walking all day, and much as you'd like to bathe, too, you're not sure you're ready to undress and make yourself any more vulnerable in front of these Castrima people. Especially given that they're apparently taking you captive in their nice understated way.

Hoa nods. He starts gathering up his bundle of rocks again. "I'll keep watch."

"Do you sleep?"

"Occasionally. Less than you. I don't need to do it now."

How convenient. And you trust him more than you do the people of this comm. You shouldn't, but you do.

So you get up and head into the bedroom, and lie down on the mattress. It's a simple thing, just straw and cotton packed into a canvas sheath, but it's better than the hard ground or even your bedroll, so you flop onto it. In seconds you're asleep.

When you wake, you're not sure how much time has passed. Hoa is curled up beside you, as he has done for the past few weeks. You sit up and frown down at him; he blinks at you warily. You shake your head, finally, and get up, muttering to yourself.

Tonkee's back in her room. You can hear her snoring. As you step out of the apartment, you realize you have no idea what time it is. Topside you can tell if it's day or night, even despite the clouds and ashfall: it's either bright ashfall and clouds or dark, red-flecked ashfall and clouds. Here, though... you look around and see nothing but giant glowing crystals. And the town that people have, impossibly, built on them.

You step onto the rough wooden platform outside your door and squint down over its completely inadequate safety railing.

Whatever the hour, it seems there are several dozen people going about their business on the ground below. Well, you need to know more about this comm, anyway. Before you destroy it, that is, if they really try to stop you from leaving.

(You ignore the small voice in your head that whispers, *Ykka is a rogga, too. Will you really fight her?*)

(You're pretty good at ignoring small voices.)

Figuring out how to reach the ground level is difficult, at first, because all the platforms and bridges and stairways of the place are built to connect the crystals. The crystals go every which way, so the connections do, too. There's nothing intuitive about it. You have to follow one set of stairs up and walk around one of the wider crystal shafts in order to find another set of stairs that goes down—only to find that they end on a platform with no steps at all, which forces you to backtrack. There are a few people out and about, and they look at you with curiosity or hostility in passing, probably because you're so obviously new in town: They're clean and you're gray with road ash. They look well fleshed, and your clothes hang off your body because you've done nothing but walk and eat travel rations for weeks. You cannot help resenting them on sight, so you get stubborn about asking for directions.

Eventually, however, you make it to the ground. Down here, it's more obvious than ever that you're walking along the floor of a huge stone bubble, because the ground slopes gently downward and curves around you to form a noticeable, if vast, bowl. This is the pointy end of the ovoid that is Castrima. There are crystals down here, too, but they're stubby, some only as high as your chest; the largest are only ten or fifteen feet tall. Wooden partitions wend around some of them, and in some places you can make out obvious patches of rough, paler ground where crystals have been removed to make room. (You wonder, idly, how they did this.) All of it creates a sort of maze of crisscrossing pathways, each of which leads to some comm essential or another: a kiln, a smithy, a glassery, a bakehouse. Off some of the paths you glimpse tents and campsites, some occupied. Clearly not all the denizens of this comm are comfortable walking along bundles of lashed-together wooden planks hundreds of feet above a floor covered in giant spikes. Funny, that.

(There it is again, that un-Essun-like sarcasm. Rust it; you're tired of reining it in.)

It's actually easy to find the baths because there's a pattern of damp foot traffic along the gray-green stone floor, all the wet footprints leading in one direction. You backtrail them and are pleasantly surprised to find that the bath is a huge pool of steaming, clear water. The pool has been walled off a little above the natural floor of the geode, and there's a channel wending away from it, draining into one of several large brass pipes going—somewhere. On the other side of the pool you can see a kind of waterfall emerging from another pipe to supply the pool. The water probably circulates enough to be clean every few hours or so, but nevertheless there's a conspicuous washing area over to one side, with long wooden benches and shelves holding various accessories. Quite a few people are already there, busily scrubbing before they go into the larger pool.

You're undressed and halfway done with your own scrubbing when a shadow falls over you, and you twitch and stumble to your feet and knock over the bench and reach for the earth before it occurs to you that maybe this is overreacting. But then you almost drop the soapy sponge in your hand, because—

—it's *Lerna.*

"Yes," he says as you stare at him. "I thought that might be you, Essun."

You keep staring. He looks different somehow. Heavier, sort of, though skinnier, too, in the same way you are; travel-worn. It's been—weeks? Months? You're losing track of time. And what is he doing here? He should be back in Tirimo; Rask would never let a doctor go...

Oh. Right.

"So Ykka did manage to summon you. I'd wondered." Tired. He looks tired. There's a scar along the edge of his jaw, a crescent-shaped pale patch that doesn't look likely to regain its color. You keep staring as he shifts and says, "Of all the places I had to end up...and here you are. Maybe this is fate, or maybe there really are gods other than Father Earth—ones who actually give a damn about us, that is. Or maybe they're evil, too, and this is their joke. Rust if I know."

"Lerna," you say, which is helpful.

His eyes flick down, and belatedly you remember you're naked. "I should let you finish," he says, looking away quickly. "Let's talk when you're done." You don't care if he sees your nudity—he delivered one of your children, for rust's sake—but he's being polite. It's a familiar habit of his, treating you like a person even though he knows what you are, and oddly heartening after so much strangeness and everything that's changed in your life. You're not used to having a life follow you when you leave it behind.

He moves off, past the bath area, and after a moment you sit back down and finish washing. No one else bothers you while you bathe, although you catch some of the Castrima people eyeing you with increased curiosity now. Less hostility, too, but that's not surprising; you don't look especially intimidating. It's the stuff they can't see that will make them hate you.

Then again...do they know what Ykka is? The blond woman who'd been with her up on the surface certainly does. Maybe Ykka's got something on her, some means of ensuring her silence. That doesn't feel right, though. Ykka is too open about what she is, too comfortable speaking of it to complete strangers. She's too charismatic, too eye-catching. Ykka acts like being an orogene is just another talent, just another personal trait. You've only seen that kind of attitude, and this kind of comm-wide acceptance of it, once before.

Once you're done soaking and you feel clean, you get out of the bath. You don't have any towels, just your filthy ashen clothes, which you take the time to scrub clean in the washing area. They're wet when you're done, but you're not quite bold enough to walk through a strange comm naked, and it feels like summer within the geode anyway. So as you do in summer, you put the wet clothes on, figuring they'll dry fast enough.

Lerna's waiting when you leave. "This way," he says, turning to walk with you.

So you follow him, and he leads you up the maze of steps and platforms until you reach a squat gray crystal that juts only twenty feet or so from the wall. He's got an apartment here that's smaller than the one you share with Tonkee and Hoa, but you see shelves laden with herb packets and folded bandages and it's not hard to guess that the odd benches in the main room might actually be intended as makeshift cots. A doctor must be prepared for house calls. He directs you to sit down on one of the benches, and sits across from you.

"I left Tirimo the day after you did," he says quietly. "Oyamar—Rask's second, you remember him, complete idiot—was actually trying to hold an election for a new headman. Didn't want the responsibility with a Season coming on. Everybody knew Rask should never have picked him, but his family did Rask a favor on the trade rights to the western logging trace..." He trails off, because none of that matters anymore. "Anyway. Half the damned Strongbacks were running around drunk and armed, raiding the storecaches, accusing every other person of being a rogga or a rogga-lover. The other half were doing the same thing—quieter, though, and sober, which was worse. I knew it was only a matter of time till they thought about me. Everybody knew I was your friend."

This is your fault, too, then. Because of you, he had to flee a place that should have been safe. You lower your eyes, uncomfortable. He's using the word "rogga" now, too.

"I was thinking I could make it down to Brilliance, where my mother's family came from. They barely know me, but they know *of* me, and I'm a doctor, so... I figured I had a chance. Better than staying in Tirimo, anyway, to get lynched. Or to starve, when the cold came and the Strongbacks had eaten or stolen everything. And I thought—" He hesitates, looks up at you in a flash of eyes, then back at his hands. "I also thought I might catch up to you on the road, if I went fast enough. But that was stupid; of course I didn't."

It's the unspoken thing that's always been between you.

Lerna figured out what you were, somewhere during your time in Tirimo; you didn't tell him. He figured it out because he *watched* you enough to notice the signs, and because he's smart. He's always liked you, Makenba's boy. You figured he would grow out of it eventually. You shift a little, uncomfortable with the realization that he hasn't.

"I slipped out in the night," he continues, "through one of the cracks in the wall near... near where you... where they tried to stop you." He's got his arms resting on his knees, looking at his folded hands. They're mostly still, but he rubs one thumb along the knuckle of the other, slowly, again and again. The gesture feels meditative. "Walked with the flow of people, following a map I had... but I've never been to Brilliance. Earthfires, I've barely left Tirimo before now. Just once, really, when I went to finish my medical training at Hilge—anyway. Either the map was wrong or I'm bad at reading it. Probably both. I didn't have a compass. I got off the Imperial Road too soon, maybe... went southeast when I thought I was going due south... I don't know." He sighs and rubs a hand over his head. "By the time I figured out just how lost I was, I'd gone so far that I hoped to just find a better route if I kept going the way I'd gone. But there was a group at one crossroads. Bandits, commless, something. I was with a small group by then, an older man who'd had a bad gash on his chest that I treated, and his daughter, maybe fifteen. The bandits—"

He pauses, his jaw flexing. You can pretty much guess what happened. Lerna's not a fighter. He's still alive, though, which is all that matters.

"Marald—that was the man—just threw himself at one of

them. He didn't have weapons or anything, and the woman had a machete. I don't know what he thought he could do." Lerna takes a deep breath. "He looked at me, though, and—and I—I grabbed his daughter and ran." His jaw tightens further. You're surprised you can't hear his teeth grinding. "She left me later. Called me a coward and ran off alone."

"If you hadn't taken her away," you say, "they would've killed you and her, too." This is stonelore: *Honor in safety, survival under threat.* Better a living coward than a dead hero.

Lerna's lips quirk thinly. "That's what I told myself at the time. Later, when she left . . . Earthfires. Maybe all I did was just delay the inevitable. A girl her age, unarmed and out on the roads alone . . ."

You don't say anything. If the girl's healthy and has the right conformation, someone will take her in, if only as a Breeder. If she has a better use name, or if she can acquire a weapon and supplies and prove herself, that will help, too. Granted, her chances would've been better with Lerna than without him, but she made her choice.

"I don't even know what they wanted." Lerna's looking at his hands. Maybe he's been eating himself up about this ever since. "We didn't have anything but our runny-sacks."

"That's enough, if they were running low on supplies," you say, before you remember to censor yourself. He doesn't seem to hear, anyway.

"So I kept on, by myself." He chuckles once, bitterly. "I was so worried about her, it didn't even occur to me that *I* was just as bad off." This is true. Lerna is a bog-standard midlatter, same as you, except he hasn't inherited the Sanzed bulk or height—probably why he's worked so hard to prove his mental fitness. But he's ended up pretty, mostly by an accident of heritage, and some people breed for that. Cebaki long nose, Sanzed shoulders and coloring, Westcoaster lips...He's too multiracial for Equatorial comm tastes, but by Somidlats standards he's a looker.

"When I passed through Castrima," he continues, "it looked abandoned. I was exhausted, after running from—anyway. Figured I'd hole up in one of the houses for the night, maybe try to make a small hearth fire and hope no one noticed. Eat a decent meal for a change. Hold still long enough to figure out what to do next." He smiled thinly. "And when I woke up, I was surrounded. I told them I was a doctor and they brought me down here. That was maybe two weeks ago."

You nod. And then you tell him your own story, not bothering to hide or lie about anything. The whole thing, not just the part in Tirimo. You're feeling guilty, maybe. He deserves the whole truth.

After you've both fallen silent for a while, Lerna just shakes his head and sighs. "I didn't expect to live through a Season," he says softly. "I mean, I've heard the lore all my life, same as everyone else...but I always figured it would never happen to *me*."

Everyone thinks that. *You* certainly weren't expecting to have to deal with the end of the world on top of everything else.

"Nassun's not here," Lerna says after a while. He speaks softly, but your head jerks up. His face softens at the look that must be on yours. "I'm sorry. But I've been here long enough to meet all the other 'newcomers' to this comm. I know that's who you've been hoping to find."

No Nassun. And now no direction, no realistic way to find her. You are suddenly bereft of even hope.

"Essun." Lerna leans forward abruptly and takes your hands. Belatedly you realize your hands have begun shaking; his fingers still yours. "You'll find her."

The words are meaningless. Reflexive gibberish intended to soothe. But it hits you again, harder this time than that moment topside when you started to come apart in front of Ykka. *It's over.* This whole strange journey, keeping it together, keeping focused on your goal... it's all been pointless. Nassun's gone, you've lost her, and Jija will never pay for what he's done, and you—

What the rust do *you* matter? Who cares about you? Well, that's the thing, isn't it? Once, you did have people who cared about you. Once there were children who looked up to you and lived on your every word. Once—twice, three times, but the first two don't count—there was a man you woke up next to every morning, who gave a damn that you existed. Once, you lived surrounded by the walls he built for you, in a home you made together, in a community that actually *chose* to take you in.

All of it built on lies. Matter of time, really, till it fell apart.

"Listen," Lerna says. His voice makes you blink, and that makes tears fall. More tears. You've been sitting there in silence, crying, for a while now. He shifts over to your bench and you lean on him. You know you shouldn't. But you do, and when he puts an arm around you, you take comfort in it. He is a friend, at least. He will always be that. "Maybe... maybe this isn't a bad thing, being here. You can't think, with—everything—going on. This comm is strange." He grimaces. "I'm not sure I like being here, but it's better than being topside right now. Maybe with some time to think, you'll figure out where Jija might have gone."

He's trying so hard. You shake your head a little, but you're too empty to really muster an objection.

"Do you have a place? They gave me this, they must have given you something. There's plenty of room here." You nod, and Lerna takes a deep breath. "Then let's go there. You can introduce me to these companions of yours."

So. You pull it together. Then you lead him out of his place and in a direction that feels like it might bring you to the apartment you were assigned. Along the way you have more time to appreciate just how unbearably strange this comm is. There's one chamber you pass, embedded in one of the whiter, brighter crystals, that holds racks and racks of flat trays like cookie sheets. There's another chamber, dusty and unused, that holds what you assume are torture devices, except they're incompetently made; you're not sure how a pair of rings suspended from the ceiling on chains are supposed to hurt. And then there are the metal stairs—the ones built by whoever created this place. There are other stairs, more recently made, but it's easy to tell them from the originals because the original stairs don't rust, haven't deteriorated at all, and are not purely utilitarian. There are strange decorations along the railings and edges of the walkways: embossed faces, wrought vines in the shape of no plants you've ever seen, something that you think is writing, except it consists solely of pointy shapes in various sizes. It actually pulls you out of your mood, to try to figure out what you're seeing.

"This is madness," you say, running your fingers over a decoration that looks like a snarling kirkhusa. "This place is one big deadciv ruin, just like a hundred thousand others all over the Stillness. Ruins are death traps. The Equatorial comms flatten or sink theirs if they can, and that's the smartest thing anyone's ever done. If the people who made this place couldn't survive it, why should any of us try?"

"Not all ruins are death traps." Lerna's edging along the platform while keeping very close to the crystal shaft it wends around, and keeping his eyes fixed straight ahead. Sweat beads his upper lip. You hadn't realized he's afraid of heights, but then Tirimo is as flat as it is boring. His voice is carefully calm. "There are rumors Yumenes is built on a whole series of deadciv ruins."

And look how well that turned out, you don't say.

"These people should've just built a wall like everyone else," you do say, but then you stop, because it occurs to you that the goal is survival, and sometimes survival requires change. Just because the usual strategies have worked—building a wall, taking in the useful and excluding the useless, arming and storing and hoping for luck—doesn't mean that other methods might not. This, though? Climbing down a hole and hiding in a ball of sharp rocks with a bunch of stone eaters and *roggas*? Seems especially unwise.

"And if they try to keep me here, they'll find that out," you murmur.

If Lerna hears you, he does not respond.

Eventually you find your apartment. Tonkee's awake and in the living room, eating a big bowl of something that didn't come from your packs. It looks like some kind of porridge, and it's got little yellowish things in it that make you recoil at first—until she tilts the bowl and you realize it's sprouted grains. Standard storecache food.

(She looks at you warily as you come in, but her revelations were so minor compared to everything else you've had to face today that you just wave a greeting and settle down opposite her as usual. She relaxes.)

Lerna's polite but guarded with Tonkee, and she's the same with him—until he mentions that he's been running blood and urine tests on the people of Castrima to watch for vitamin deficiencies. You almost smile when she leans forward and says, "With what kind of equipment?" with a familiar greedy look on her face.

Then Hoa comes into the apartment. You're surprised, since you hadn't realized he'd gone out. His icewhite gaze flicks immediately to Lerna and examines him ruthlessly. Then he relaxes, so visibly that you only now realize Hoa's been tense all this time. Since you came into this crazy comm.

But you file this away as just another oddity to explore later, because Hoa says, "Essun. There's someone here you should meet."

"Who?"

"A man. From Yumenes."

All three of you stare at him. "Why," you say slowly, in case you've misunderstood something, "would I want to meet someone from Yumenes?"

"He asked for you."

You decide to try for patience. "Hoa, I don't know anyone from Yumenes." Not anymore, anyway.

"He says he knows you. He tracked you here, got here ahead of you when he realized it was where you were headed." Hoa scowls, just a little, as if this bothers him. "He says he wants to see you, see if you can do it yet."

"Do what?"

"He just said 'it.'" Hoa's eyes slide first to Tonkee, then to Lerna, before returning to you. Something he doesn't want them to hear, maybe. "He's like you."

"What—" Okay. You rub your eyes, take a deep breath, and say it so he'll know there's no need to hide it. "A rogga, then."

"Yes. No. Like you. His—" Hoa waggles his fingers in lieu of words. Tonkee opens her mouth; you gesture sharply at her. She glares back. After a moment, Hoa sighs. "He said, if you wouldn't come, to tell you that you owe him. For Corundum."

You freeze.

"Alabaster," you whisper.

"Yes," says Hoa, brightening. "That's his name." And then he frowns more, thoughtfully this time. "He's dying."

* * *

MADNESS SEASON: 3 Before Imperial–7 Imperial. The eruption of the Kiash Traps, multiple vents of an ancient supervolcano (the same one responsible for the Twin Season believed to have occurred approximately 10,000 years previous), launched large deposits of olivine and other dark-colored pyroclasts into the air. The resulting ten years of darkness were not only devastating in the usual Seasonal way, but resulted in a much higher than usual incidence of mental illness. The Sanzed warlord Verishe conquered multiple ailing comms through the use of psychological warfare designed to convince her foes that gates and walls offered no reliable protection, and that phantasms lurked nearby. She was named emperor on the day the first sunlight reappeared.

—*The Seasons of Sanze*

22

Syenite, fractured

It's the morning after a raucous party that the Meovites threw to celebrate the *Clalsu*'s safe return and acquisition of some especially prized goods—high-quality stone for decorative carving, aromatic woods for furniture building, fancy brocade cloth that's worth twice its weight in diamonds, and a goodly amount of tradable currency including high-denomination paper and whole fingers of mother-of-pearl. No food, but with that kind of money they can send traders to buy canoesful of anything they need on the mainland. Harlas broke out a cask of fearsomely strong Antarctic mead to celebrate, and half the comm's still sleeping it off.

It's five days after Syenite shut down a volcano that she started, which killed a whole city, and eight days after she killed two ships full of people to keep her family's existence secret. It feels like everyone is celebrating the multiple mass murders she's committed.

She's still in bed, having retired to it as soon as the ship was unloaded. Innon hasn't come to the house yet; she told him to go and tell the stories of the trip, because the people expect it of him and she does not want him suffering for her melancholy. He's got Coru with him, because Coru loves celebrations—everyone feeds him, everyone cuddles him. He even tries to help Innon tell the stories, yelling nonsense at the top of his lungs. The child is more like Innon than he has any physical right to be.

Alabaster is the one who's stayed with Syen, talking to her through her silence, forcing her to respond when she would rather just stop thinking. He says he knows what it's like to feel like this, though he won't tell her how or what happened. She believes him regardless.

"You should go," she says at last. "Join the storytelling. Remind Coru he's got at least two parents who are worth something."

"Don't be stupid. He's got three."

"Innon thinks I'm a terrible mother."

Alabaster sighed. "No. You're just not the kind of mother Innon wants you to be. You're the kind of mother our son needs, though." She turns her head to frown at him. He shrugs. "Corundum will be strong, someday. He needs strong parents. I'm..." He falters abruptly. You practically feel him decide to change the subject. "Here. I brought you something."

Syen sighs and pushes herself up as he crouches beside the bed, unfolding a little cloth parcel. In it, when she gets curious despite herself and leans closer, are two polished stone rings, just right for her fingers. One's made of jade, the other mother-of-pearl.

She glares at him, and he shrugs. "Shutting down an active volcano isn't something a mere four-ringer could do."

"We're free." She says it doggedly, even though she doesn't feel free. She fixed Allia, after all, completing the mission the Fulcrum sent her there for, however belatedly and perversely. It's the sort of thing that makes her laugh uncontrollably when she thinks about it, so she pushes on before she can. "We don't need to wear *any* rings anymore. Or black uniforms. I haven't put my hair in a bun in months. You don't have to service every woman they send you, like some kind of stud animal. Let the Fulcrum go."

'Baster smiles a little, sadly. "We can't, Syen. One of us is going to have to train Coru—"

"We don't have to train him to do anything." Syen lies down again. She wishes he would go away. "Let him learn the basics from Innon and Harlas. That's been enough to let these people get by for centuries."

"Innon couldn't have stilled that blow, Syen. If he'd tried, he might have blown the hot spot underneath it wide, and set off a Season. You saved the world from that."

"Then give me a medal, not rings." She's glaring at the ceiling. "Except I'm the reason that blow even existed, so *maybe not*."

Alabaster reaches up to stroke her hair away from her face. He does that a lot, now that she wears it loose. She's always been a little ashamed of her hair—it's curly, but with no stiffness to it at all, whether the straight-stiffness of Sanzed hair or the kinky-stiffness of Coaster hair. She's such a midlatter mutt that she doesn't even know which of her ancestors to blame for the hair. At least it doesn't get in her way.

"We are what we are," he says, with such gentleness that she wants to cry. "We are Misalem, not Shemshena. You've heard that story?"

Syenite's fingers twitch in remembered pain. "Yes."

"From your Guardian, right? They like to tell that one to

kids." 'Baster shifts to lean against the bedpost with his back to her, relaxing. Syenite thinks about telling him to leave, but never says it aloud. She's not looking at him, so she has no idea what he does with the bundle of rings that she didn't take. He can eat them for all she cares.

"My Guardian gave me that nonsense, too, Syen. The monstrous Misalem, who decided to declare war against a whole nation and off the Sanzed Emperor for no particular reason."

In spite of herself, Syenite frowns. "He had a reason?"

"Oh Evil Earth, of course. Use your rusting head."

It's annoying to be scolded, and annoyance pushes back her apathy a little more. Good old Alabaster, cheering her up by pissing her off. She turns her head to glare at the back of his. "Well, what was the reason?"

"The simplest and most powerful reason of all: revenge. That emperor was Anafumeth, and the whole thing happened just after the end of the Season of Teeth. That's the Season they don't talk about much in any creche. There was mass starvation in the northern-hemisphere comms. They got hit harder, since the shake that started the whole thing was near the northern pole. The Season took a year longer to take hold in the Equatorials and the south—"

"How do you know all this?" It's nothing Syen's ever heard, in the grit crucibles or elsewhere.

Alabaster shrugs, shaking the whole bed. "I wasn't allowed to train with the other grits in my year-group; I had rings before most of them had pubic hair. The instructors let me loose in the seniors' library to make up for it. They didn't pay a lot of attention to what I read." He sighs. "Also, on my first mission, I…

There was an archeomest who... He... well. We talked, in addition to... other things."

She doesn't know why Alabaster bothers being shy about his affairs. She's watched Innon fuck him into incoherence on more than one occasion. Then again, maybe it's not the sex that he's shy about.

"Anyway. It's all there if you put the facts together and think beyond what we're taught. Sanze was a new empire then, still growing, at the height of its power. But it was mostly in the northern half of the Equatorials at that time—Yumenes wasn't actually the capital then—and some of the bigger Sanzed comms weren't as good at preparing for Seasons as they are now. They lost their food storecaches somehow. Fire, fungus, Earth knows what. To survive, all the Sanzed comms decided to work together, attacking the comms of any lesser races." His lip curls. "That's *when* they started calling us 'lesser races,' actually."

"So they took those other comms' storecaches." Syen can guess that much. She's getting bored.

"No. No one had any stores left by the end of that Season. The Sanzeds took *people*."

"People? For wh—" Then she understands.

There's no need for slaves during a Season. Every comm has its Strongbacks, and if they need more, there are always commless people desperate enough to work in exchange for food. Human flesh becomes valuable for other reasons, though, when things get bad enough.

"So," says Alabaster, oblivious while Syen lies there fighting nausea, "that Season is when the Sanzeds developed a taste for certain rarefied delicacies. And even after the Season ended and green things grew and the livestock turned herbivorous or stopped hibernating, they kept at it. They would send out parties to raid smaller settlements and newcomms held by races without Sanzed allies. All the accounts differ on the details, but they agree on one thing: Misalem was the only survivor when his family was taken in a raid. Supposedly his children were slaughtered for Anafumeth's own table, though I suspect that's a bit of dramatic embellishment." Alabaster sighs. "Regardless, they died, and it was Anafumeth's fault, and he wanted Anafumeth dead for it. Like any man would."

But a rogga is not any man. Roggas have no right to get angry, to want justice, to protect what they love. For his presumption, Shemshena had killed him—and became a hero for doing it.

Syenite considers this in silence. Then Alabaster shifts a little, and she feels his hand press the bundle, the one with the rings in it, into her unresisting palm.

"Orogenes built the Fulcrum," he says. She's almost never heard him say *orogene*. "We did it under threat of genocide, and we used it to buckle a collar around our own necks, but we did it. *We* are the reason Old Sanze grew so powerful and lasted so long, and why it still half-rules the world, even if no one will admit it. We're the ones who've figured out just how amazing our kind can be, if we learn how to refine the gift we're born with."

"It's a curse, not a gift." Syenite closes her eyes. But she doesn't push away the bundle.

"It's a gift if it makes us better. It's a curse if we let it destroy us. *You* decide that—not the instructors, or the Guardians, or anyone else." There's another shift, and the bed moves a little as Alabaster leans on it. A moment later she feels his lips on her brow, dry and approving. Then he settles back down on the floor beside the bed, and says nothing more.

"I thought I saw a Guardian," she says after a while. Very softly. "At Allia."

Alabaster doesn't reply for a moment. She's decided that he won't, when he says, "I will tear the whole world apart if they ever hurt us again."

But we would still be hurt, she thinks.

It's reassuring, though, somehow. The kind of lie she needs to hear. Syenite keeps her eyes closed and doesn't move for a long while. She's not sleeping; she's thinking. Alabaster stays while she does it, and for that she is unutterably glad.

* * *

When the world ends three weeks later, it happens on the most beautiful day Syenite has ever seen. The sky is clear for miles, save for the occasional drift of cloud. The sea is calm, and even the omnipresent wind is warm and humid for once, instead of cool and scouring.

It's so beautiful that the entire comm decides to head up to the heights. The able-bodied carry the ones who can't make the steps, while the children get underfoot and nearly kill everyone. The people on cook duty put fish cakes and pieces of cut fruit and balls of seasoned grain into little pots that can be carried easily, and everyone brings blankets. Innon has a musical instrument Syenite has never seen before, something like a drum with guitar strings, which would probably be all the rage in Yumenes if it ever caught on there. Alabaster has Corundum. Syenite brings a truly awful novel someone found on the looted freighter, the sort of thing whose first page made her wince and burst into giggles. Then, of course, she kept reading. She loves books that are just for fun.

The Meovites spread themselves over the slope behind a ridge that blocks most of the wind but where the sun is full and bright. Syenite puts her blanket a ways from everyone else, but they quickly encroach on her, spreading out their blankets right alongside, and grinning at her when she glares.

She has come to realize over the past three years that most Meovites regard her and Alabaster as something like wild animals that have decided to scavenge off human habitations—impossible to civilize, kind of cute, and at least an amusing nuisance. So when they see that she obviously needs help with something and won't admit it, they help her anyway. And they constantly *pet* Alabaster, and hug him and grab his hands and swing him into dancing, which Syen is at least grateful no one tries with her. Then again, everyone can see that Alabaster likes being touched, no matter how much he pretends standoffishness. It probably isn't something he got a lot of in the Fulcrum, where everyone was afraid of his power. Perhaps likewise they think Syen enjoys being reminded that she is part of a group now, contributing and contributed to, and that she no longer needs to guard herself against everyone and everything.

They're right. That doesn't mean she's going to tell them so.

Then it's all Innon tossing Coru up in the air while Alabaster tries to pretend he's not terrified even as his orogeny sends microshakes through the island's underwater strata with every toss; and Hemoo starting some kind of chanted-poetry game set to music that all the Meovites seem to know; and Ough's toddler Owel trying to run across the spread-out blankets and stepping on at least ten people before someone grabs her and tickles her down; and a basket being passed around that contains little clay bottles of something that burns Syen's nose when she sniffs it; and.

And.

She could love these people, she thinks sometimes.

Perhaps she does already. She isn't sure. But after Innon flops down for a nap with Coru already asleep on his chest, and after the poetry chant has turned into a vulgar-joke contest, and once she's drunk enough of the bottle stuff that the world is actually beginning to move on its own...Syenite lifts her eyes and catches Alabaster's. He's propped himself on one elbow to browse the terrible book she's finally abandoned. He's making horrible and hilarious faces as he skims it. Meanwhile his free hand toys with one of Innon's braids, and he looks nothing at all like the half-mad monster Feldspar sent her off with, at the beginning of this journey.

His eyes flick up to meet hers, and for just a moment there is wariness there. Syen blinks in surprise at this. But then, she *is* the only person here who knows what his life was like before. Does he resent her for being here, a constant reminder of what he'd rather forget?

He smiles, and she frowns in automatic reaction. His smile widens more. "You still don't like me, do you?"

Syenite snorts. "What do you care?"

He shakes his head, amused—and then he reaches out and strokes a hand over Coru's hair. The child stirs and murmurs in his sleep, and Alabaster's face softens. "Would you like to have another child?"

Syenite starts, her mouth falling open. "Of course not. I didn't want *this* one."

"But he's here now. And he's beautiful. Isn't he? You make such beautiful children." Which is probably the most inane thing he could ever say, but then, he's Alabaster. "You could have the next one with Innon."

"Maybe Innon should have a say in that, before we settle his breeding future."

"He loves Coru, and he's a good father. He's got two other kids already, and they're fine. Stills, though." He considers. "You and Innon might have a child who's still. That wouldn't be a terrible thing, here."

Syenite shakes her head, but she's thinking about the little pessary the island women have shown her how to use. Thinking maybe she will stop using it. But she says: "Freedom means *we* get to control what we do now. No one else."

"Yes. But now that I can think about what I want…" He shrugs as if nonchalant, but there's an intensity in his gaze as he looks at Innon and Coru. "I've never wanted much from life. Just to be able to *live* it, really. I'm not like you, Syen. I don't need to prove myself. I don't want to change the world, or help people, or be anything great. I just want…this."

She gets that. So she lies down on her side of Innon, and Alabaster lies down on his side, and they relax and enjoy the sensation of wholeness, of contentment, for a while. Because they can.

Of course it cannot last.

Syenite wakes when Innon sits up and shadows her. She hadn't intended to nap, but she's had a good long one, and now the sun is slanting toward the ocean. Coru's fussing and she sits up automatically, rubbing her face with one hand and reaching with the other to see if his cloth diaper is full. It's fine, but the sounds he's making are anxious, and when she comes more awake she sees why. Innon is sitting up with Coru held absently in one arm, but he is frowning as he looks at Alabaster. Alabaster is on his feet, his whole body tense.

"Something..." he murmurs. He's facing the direction of the mainland, but he can't possibly see anything; the ridge is in the way. Then again, he's not using his eyes.

So Syen frowns and sends forth her own awareness, worrying that there's a tsunami or worse on its way. But there's nothing.

A *conspicuous* nothingness. There should be something. There's a plate boundary between the island that is Meov and the mainland; plate boundaries are never still. They jump and twitch and vibrate against one another in a million infinitesimal ways that only a rogga can sess, like the electricity that geneers can make come out of water turbines and vats of chemicals. But suddenly—impossibly—the plate edge sesses as still.

Confused, Syenite starts to look at Alabaster. But her attention is caught by Corundum, who's bouncing and struggling in Innon's hands, whining and snotting and having a full-on tantrum, though he's usually not the kind of baby who does that sort of thing. Alabaster's looking at the baby, too. His expression changes to something twisted and terrible.

"No," he says. He's shaking his head. "No. No, I won't *let* them, not again."

"What?" Syenite's staring at him, trying not to notice the dread that's rising in her, feeling rather than seeing as others rise around them, murmuring and reacting to their alarm. A couple of people trot up the ridge to see what they can. "'Baster, what? For Earth's sake—"

He makes a sound that is not a word, just *negation*, and suddenly he takes off running up the slope, toward the ridge. Syenite stares after him, then at Innon, who looks even more confused than she is; Innon shakes his head. But the people who preceded 'Baster up the ridge are shouting now, and signaling everyone else. Something is wrong.

Syenite and Innon hurry up the slope along with others. They all reach the top together, and there they stand looking at the span of ocean on the mainlandward side of the island.

Where there are four ships, tiny but visibly coming closer, on the horizon.

Innon says a bad word and shoves Coru at Syenite, who almost fumbles him but then holds him close while Innon rummages amid his pockets and packs and comes up with his smaller spyglass. He extends it and looks hard for a moment, then frowns, while Syenite tries ineffectually to console Coru. Coru is inconsolable. When Innon lowers it, Syenite grabs his arm and pushes Coru at him, taking the device from his hand when he does.

The four ships are bigger now. Their sails are white, ordinary; she can't figure out what's got Alabaster so upset. And then she notices the figures standing at one boat's prow.

Wearing burgundy.

The shock of it steals the breath from her chest. She steps back, mouths the word that Innon needs to hear, but it comes out strengthless, inaudible. Innon takes the spyglass from her because she looks like she's about to drop it. Then because they have to *do* something, she's got to *do* something, she concentrates and focuses and says, louder, "*Guardians*."

Innon frowns. "How—" She watches as he, too, realizes what this means. He looks away for a moment, wondering, and then he shakes his head. How they found Meov does not matter. They cannot be allowed to land. They cannot be allowed to live.

"Give Coru to someone," he says, backing away from the ridge; his expression has hardened. "We are going to need you, Syen."

Syenite nods and turns, looking around. Deelashet, one of the handful of Sanzeds in the comm, is hurrying past with her own little one, who's maybe six months older than Coru. She's kept Coru on occasion, nursed him when Syenite was busy; Syenite flags her down and runs to her. "Please," she says, pushing Coru into her arms. Deelashet nods.

Coru, however, does not agree with the plan. He clings to Syenite, screaming and kicking and—Evil Earth, the whole island rocks all of a sudden. Deelashet staggers and then stares at Syenite in horror.

"Shit," she murmurs, and takes Coru back. Then with him on her hip—he calms immediately—she runs to catch up with Innon, who is already running toward the metal stairs, shouting to his crew to board the *Clalsu* and ready it for launch.

It's madness. It's all madness, she thinks as she runs. It doesn't make sense that the Guardians have discovered this place. It doesn't make sense that they're coming—why here? Why now? Meov has been around, pirating the coast, for generations. The only thing that's different is Syenite and Alabaster.

She ignores the little voice in the back of her mind that whispers, *They followed you somehow, you know they did, you should never have gone back to Allia, it was a trap, you should never have come here, everything you touch is death.*

She does not look down at her hands, where—just to let Alabaster know she appreciated the gesture—she's put on the four rings that the Fulcrum gave her, plus his two. The last two aren't real, after all. She hasn't passed any sort of ring test for them. But who would know whether she merits these rings better than a man who's earned ten? And for shit's sake, she stilled a rusting volcano made by a broken obelisk with a stone eater inside.

So Syenite decides, suddenly and fiercely, that she's going to show these rusting Guardians just what a six-ringer can do.

She reaches the comm level, where it's chaos: people pulling out glassknives and rolling out catapults and balls of chain from wherever-the-rust they've been keeping them, gathering belongings, loading boats with fishing spears. Then Syen's running up the plank onto the *Clalsu,* where Innon is shouting for the anchor to be pulled up, and all at once it occurs to her to wonder where Alabaster has gone.

She stumbles to a halt on the ship's deck. And as she does, she feels a flare of orogeny so deep and powerful that for a moment she thinks the whole world shakes. All the water in the harbor dances with tiny pointillations for a moment. Syen suspects the clouds felt that one.

And suddenly there is a *wall* rising from the sea, not five hundred yards off the harbor. It is a massive block of solid stone, as perfectly rectangular as if it were chiseled, huge enough to—oh flaking rust, *no*—seal off the damned harbor.

"'Baster! Earth damn it—" It's impossible to be heard over the roar of water and the grind of the stone—as big as the island of

Meov itself—Alabaster is raising. How can he do this with no shake or hot spot nearby? Half the island should be iced. But then something flickers at the corner of Syenite's vision and she turns to see the amethyst obelisk off in the distance. It's closer than before. It's coming to meet them. That's how.

Innon is cursing, furious; he understands full well that Alabaster is being an overprotective fool, however he's doing it. His fury becomes effort. Fog rises from the water around the ship, and the deck planks nearby creak and frost over as he tries to smash apart the nearest part of the wall, so that they can get out there and fight. The wall splinters—and then there is a low boom behind it. When the part of the wall that Innon has shattered crumbles away, there's just another block of stone behind it.

Syenite's got her hands full trying to modulate the waves in the water. It is possible to use orogeny on water, just difficult. She's getting the hang of it at last, after this long living near such a great expanse of water; it's one of the few things Innon's been able to teach her and Alabaster. There's enough warmth and mineral content in the sea that she can feel it, and water moves enough like stone—just faster—that she can manipulate it a little. Delicately. Still, she does this now, holding Coru close so he's within the safe zone of her torus, and concentrating hard to send shock waves against the coming waves at just enough velocity to break them. It mostly works; the *Clalsu* rocks wildly and tears loose from its moorings, and one of the piers collapses, but nothing capsizes and no one dies. Syenite counts this as a win.

"What the rust is he doing?" Innon says, panting, and she follows his gaze to see Alabaster, at last.

He stands on the highest point of the island, up on the slopes.

Even from here Syen can see the blistering cold of his torus; the warmer air around it wavers as the temperature changes, and all the moisture in the wind blowing past him precipitates out as snow. If he's using the obelisk then he shouldn't need the ambient, should he? Unless he's doing so much that even the obelisk can't fuel it.

"Earthfires," Syen says. "I have to go up there."

Innon grabs her arm. When she looks up at him, his eyes are wide and a little afraid. "We'd only be a liability to him."

"We can't just sit here and wait! He's not…reliable." Even as she says this, her belly clenches. Innon has never seen Alabaster lose it. She doesn't *want* Innon to see that. Alabaster's been so good here at Meov; he's almost not crazy anymore. But Syen thinks

what broke once will break again, more easily

and she shakes her head and tries to hand him Coru. "I have to. Maybe I can help. Coru won't let me give him to anyone else—please—"

Innon curses but takes the child, who clutches at Innon's shirt and and puts his thumb in his mouth. Then Syen is off, running along the comm ledge and up the steps.

As she gets above the rock barrier, she can finally see what's happening beyond it, and for a moment she stumbles to a halt in shock. The ships are much closer, right beyond the wall that 'Baster has raised to protect the harbor. There are only three of them, though, because one ship has floundered off course and is listing badly—no, it's sinking. She has no idea how he managed that. Another is riding strangely in the water, mast broken and bow raised and keel visible, and that's when Syenite realizes there are *boulders* piled on its rear deck. Alabaster's been dropping rocks on the bastards. She has no idea how, but the sight of it makes her want to cheer.

But the other two ships have split up: one coming straight for the island, the other peeling off, perhaps to circle around or maybe get out of Alabaster's rock-dropping range. *No you don't,* Syen thinks, and she tries to do what she did to the attack ship during their last raid, dragging a splinter of bedrock up from the seafloor to spear the thing. She frosts a ten-foot space around her to do it, and makes chunks of ice spread over the water between her and the ship, but she gets the splinter shaped and loose, and starts to pull it up—

And it stops. And the gathering strength of her orogeny just…disipates. She gasps as the heat and force spill away, and then she understands: This ship has a Guardian on it, too. Maybe they all do, which explains why 'Baster hasn't destroyed them already. He can't attack a Guardian directly; all he can do is hurl boulders from outside the Guardians' negation radius. She can't even imagine how much power that must take. He could never have managed it without the obelisk, and if he weren't the crazy, ornery ten-ringer that he is.

Well, just because *she* can't hit the thing directly doesn't mean she can't find some other way to do it. She runs along the ridge as the ship she tried to destroy passes behind the island, keeping it in sight. Do they think there's another way up? If so, they'll be sorely disappointed; Meov's harbor is the only part of the island that's remotely approachable. The rest of the island is a single jagged, sheer column.

Which gives her an idea. Syenite grins and stops, then drops to her hands and knees so she can concentrate.

She doesn't have Alabaster's strength. She doesn't even know how to reach the amethyst without his guidance—and after what happened at Allia, she's afraid to try. The plate boundary is too far for her to reach, and there are no nearby vents or hot spots. But she has Meov itself. All that lovely, heavy, *flaky* schist.

So she throws herself down. Deep. Deeper. She feels her way along the ridges and the layers of the rock that is Meov, seeking the best point of fracture—the *fulcrum;* she laughs to herself. At last she finds it, good. And there, coming around the island's curve, is the ship. Yes.

Syenite drags all the heat and infinitesimal life out of the rock in one concentrated spot. The moisture's still there, though, and that's what freezes, and expands, as Syenite forces it colder and colder, taking more and more from it, spinning her torus fine and oblong so that it slices along the grain of the rock like a knife through meat. A ring of frost forms around her, but it's nothing compared to the long, searing plank of ice that's growing down the inside of the rock, levering it apart.

And then, right when the ship approaches the point, she unleashes all the strength the island has given her, shoving it right back where it came from.

A massive, narrow finger of stone splits away from the cliff face. Inertia holds it where it is, just for a moment—and then with a low, hollow groan, it peels away from the island, splintering at its base near the waterline. Syenite opens her eyes and gets up and runs, slipping once on her own ice ring, to that end of the island. She's tired, and after a few steps she has to slow to a walk, gasping for breath around a stitch in her side. But she gets there in time to see:

The finger of rock has landed squarely on the ship. She grins fiercely at the sight of the deck splintered apart as she hears screams, as she sees people already in the water. Most wear a variety of clothing; hirelings, then. But she thinks she sees one flash of burgundy cloth under the water's surface, being dragged deeper by one of the sinking ship halves.

"Guard *that*, you cannibalson ruster." Grinning, Syenite gets up and heads in Alabaster's direction again.

As she comes down from the heights she can see him, a tiny figure still making his own cold front, and for a moment she actually admires him. He's amazing, in spite of everything. But then, all of a sudden, there is a strange hollow boom from the sea, and something explodes around Alabaster in a spray of rocks and smoke and concussive force.

A cannon. A rusting *cannon*. Innon's told her about these; they're an invention that the Equatorial comms have been experimenting with in the past few years. Of *course* Guardians would have one. Syen breaks into a run, raggedly and clumsily, fueled by fear. She can't see 'Baster well through the smoke of the cannon blast, but she can see that he's down.

By the time she gets there, she knows he's hurt. The icy wind has stopped blowing; she can see Alabaster on his hands and knees, surrounded by a circle of blistered ice that is yards wide. Syenite stops at the outermost ring of ice; if he's out of it, he might not notice that she's within the range of his power. "Alabaster!"

He moves a little, and she can hear him groaning, murmuring. How bad is he hurt? Syenite dances at the edge of the ice for a moment, then finally decides to risk it, trotting to the clear zone immediately around him. He's still upright, though barely;

his head's hanging, and her belly clenches when she sees flecks of blood on the stone beneath him.

"I took out the other ship," she says as she reaches him, hoping to reassure. "I can get this one, too, if you haven't."

It's bravado. She's not sure how much she's got left in her. Hopefully he's taken care of it. But she looks up and curses inwardly, because the remaining ship is still out there, apparently undamaged. It seems to be sitting at anchor. Waiting. For what, she can't guess.

"Syen," he says. His voice is strained. With fear, or something else? "Promise me you won't let them take Coru. No matter what."

"What? Of course I won't." She steps closer and crouches beside him. "'Baster—" He looks up at her, dazed, perhaps from the cannon blast. Something's cut his forehead, and like all head wounds it's bleeding copiously. She checks him over, touching his chest, hoping he's not more hurt. He's still alive, so the cannon blast must have been a near miss, but all it takes is a bit of rock shrapnel at the right speed, in the wrong place—

And that's when she finally notices. His arms at the wrists. His knees, and the rest of his legs between thighs and ankles—they're gone. They haven't been cut off or blown off; each limb ends smoothly, perfectly, right where the ground begins. And he's moving them about as if it's water and not solid stone that he's trapped in. *Struggling*, she realizes belatedly. He's not on his hands and knees because he can't stand; he's being *dragged into the ground*, against his will.

The stone eater. Oh rusting Earth.

Syenite grabs his shoulders and tries to haul him back, but it's like trying to haul a rock. He's heavier, somehow. His flesh doesn't feel quite like flesh. The stone eater has made his body pass through solid stone by making him more stonelike, somehow, and Syenite can't get him out. He sinks deeper into the stone with each breath; he's up to his shoulders and hips now, and she can't see his feet at all.

"Let him go, Earth take you!" The irony of the curse will occur to her only later. What does occur to her, in the moment, is to stab her awareness into the stone. She tries to feel for the stone eater—

There is something there, but it's not like anything she's ever felt before: a heaviness. A weight, too deep and solid and huge to be possible—not in such a small space, not so compact. It feels like there's a *mountain* there, dragging Alabaster down with all its weight. He's fighting it; that's the only reason he's still here at all. But he's weak, and he's losing the fight, and she hasn't the first clue of how to help him. The stone eater is just too…something. Too much, too big, too powerful, and she cannot help flinching back into herself with a sense that she's just had a near miss.

"*Promise*," he pants, while she hauls again on his shoulders and tries pushing against the stone with all her power, pulling back against that terrible weight, anything, everything. "You know what they'll do to him, Syen. A child that strong, my child, raised outside the Fulcrum? You *know*."

A wire-frame chair in a darkened node station…She can't think about that. Nothing's *working*, and he's mostly gone into the stone now; only his face and shoulders are above it, and that's only because he's straining to keep those above the stone-line. She babbles at him, sobbing, desperate for words that can somehow fix this. "I know. I promise. Oh, rust, 'Baster, please, I can't...not alone, I can't..."

The stone eater's hand rises from the stone, white and solid and rust-tipped. Surprised, Syenite screams and flinches, thinking the creature is attacking her—but no. This hand wraps around the back of Alabaster's head with remarkable gentleness. No one expects mountains to be gentle. But they are inexorable, and when the hand pulls, Alabaster goes. His shoulders slip out of Syen's hands. His chin, then his mouth, then his nose, then his terrified eyes—

He is gone.

Syenite kneels on the hard, cold stone, alone. She is screaming. She is weeping. Her tears fall onto the stone where Alabaster's head was a moment before, and the rock does not soak the tears up. They just splatter.

And then she feels it: the drop. The drag. Startled out of grief, she scrabbles to her feet and stumbles over to the edge of the cliff, where she can see the remaining ship. *Ships*, the one 'Baster's hit with rocks seems to have righted itself somehow. No, not somehow. Ice spreads across the water's surface around both ships. There's a rogga on one of the ships, working for the Guardians. A four-ringer, at least; there's too much fine control in what she's feeling. And with that much ice— She sees a group of porpoises leap out of the water, racing away from the spreading ice, and then she sees it catch them, crawling over their bodies and solidifying them half in and half out of the water.

What the hell is this rogga doing with that much power?

Then she sees a portion of the rock wall that 'Baster raised shiver.

"No—" Syenite turns and runs again, breathless, sessing rather than seeing as the Guardians' rogga attacks the wall's base. It's weak where the wall curves to meet the natural curve of Meov's harbor. The rogga's going to bring it down.

It takes an eternity to reach the comm level, and then the docks. She's terrified Innon will set sail without her. He has to be able to sess what's happening, too. But thank stone, the *Clalsu* is still there, and when she staggers up onto its deck, several members of the crew grab her and guide her to sit down before she collapses. They draw up the plank behind her, and she can see that they're striking sails.

"Innon," she gasps as she catches her breath. "Please."

They half-carry her to him. He's on the upper deck, one hand on the pilot's wheel and the other holding Coru against his hip. He doesn't look at her, all his attention focused on the wall; there's already a hole in it, near the top, and as Syenite reaches him there is a final surge. The wall breaks apart and falls in chunks, rocking the ship something fierce, but Innon's completely steady.

"We're sailing out to face them," he says grimly, as she sags onto the bench nearby, and as the ship pulls away from the dock. Everyone's ready for a fight. The catapults are loaded, the javelins in hand. "We'll lead them away from the comm first. That way, everyone else can evacuate in the fishing boats."

There aren't enough fishing boats for everyone, Syenite wants to say, and doesn't. Innon knows it, anyway.

Then the ship is sailing through the narrow gap that the Guardians' orogene has made, and the Guardians' ship is on them almost at once. There's a puff of smoke on their deck and a hollow whoosh right as the *Clalsu* emerges; the cannon again.

A near miss. Innon shouts and one of the catapult crews returns the favor with a basket of heavy chain, which shreds their foresail and midmast. Another volley and this time it's a barrel of burning pitch; Syen sees people on fire running across the deck of the Guardians' ship after that one hits. The *Clalsu* whips past while the Guardians' ship founders toward the wall that is Meov rock, its deck now a blazing conflagration.

But before they can get far there is another puff of smoke, another boom, and this time the *Clalsu* judders with the hit. Rust and underfires, how many of those things do they have? Syenite gets up and runs to the railing, trying to see this cannon, though she doesn't know what she can do about it. There's a hole in the *Clalsu*'s side and she can hear people screaming belowdecks, but thus far the ship is still moving.

It's the ship that Alabaster dropped rocks on. Some of the boulders are gone from its aft deck and it's sitting normally in the water again. She doesn't see the cannon, but she does see three figures standing near the ship's bow. Two in burgundy, a third in black. As she watches, another burgundy-clad figure comes to join them.

She can feel their eyes on her.

The Guardians' ship turns slightly, falling farther behind. Syenite begins to hope, but she sees it when the cannons fire this time. Three of them, big black things near the starboard railing; they jerk and roll back a little when they fire, in near unison. And a moment later, there is a mighty crack and a groan and the *Clalsu* shudders as if it just got hit by a fiver tsunami. Syenite looks up in time to see the mast shatter into kindling, and then everything goes wrong.

The mast creaks and goes over like a felled tree, and it hits the deck with the same force. People scream. The ship groans and begins to list starboard, pulled by the collapsed, dragging sails. She sees two men fall into the water with the sails, crushed or smothered by the weight of cloth and rope and wood, and Earth help her, she cannot think of them. The mast is between her and the pilot deck. She's cut off from Innon and Coru.

And the Guardians' ship is now closing in.

No! Syenite reaches for the water, trying to pull something, anything, into her abused sessapinae. But there's nothing. Her mind is as still as glass. The Guardians are too close.

She can't think. She scrabbles over the mast parts, gets tangled in a thicket of ropes and must fight for endless hours, it feels like, to get free. Then finally she is free but everyone's running back the way she came, glassknives and javelins in hand, shouting and screaming, because the Guardians' ship is *right there* and they are boarding.

No.

She can hear people dying all around her. The Guardians have brought troops of some sort with them, some comm's militia that they've paid or appropriated, and the battle isn't even close. Innon's people are good, experienced, but their usual targets are poorly defended merchant and passenger vessels. As Syenite reaches the pilot deck—Innon isn't there, he must have gone below—she sees Innon's cousin Ecella slash a militiaman across the face with her glassknife. He staggers beneath the blow but then comes back up and shoves his own knife into her belly. When she falls, he pushes her away, and she falls onto the body of another Meovite, who is already dead. More of the troops are climbing aboard by the minute.

It's the same everywhere. They're losing.

She has to get to Innon and Coru.

Belowdecks there's almost no one there. Everyone has come up to defend the ship. But she can feel the tremor that is Coru's fear, and she follows it to Innon's cabin. The door opens as she reaches it, and Innon comes out with a knife in his hand, nearly stabbing her. He stops, startled, and she looks beyond him to see that Coru has been bundled into a basket beneath the forward bulkhead—the safest place in the ship, ostensibly. But as she stands there, stupidly, Innon grabs her and shoves her into the cabin.

"What—"

"Stay here," Innon says. "I have to go fight. Do whatever you have—"

He gets no further. Someone moves behind him, too quick for Syenite to cry a warning. A man, naked to the waist. He claps hands onto either side of Innon's head, fingers splayed across his cheeks like spiders, and grins at Syenite as Innon's eyes widen.

And then it is—

Oh Earth, it is—

She *feels* it, when it happens. Not just in her sessapinae. It is a grind like stone abrading her skin; it is a crush along her bones; it is, it is, it is everything that is in Innon, all the power and vibrancy and beauty and fierceness of him, *made evil.* Amplified and concentrated and turned back on him in the most vicious way. Innon does not have time to feel fear. Syenite does not have time to scream as Innon *comes apart.*

It's like watching a shake up close. Seeing the ground split, watching the fragments grind and splinter together, then separate. Except all in flesh.

'Baster, you never told me, you didn't tell *me it was like*

Now Innon is on the floor, in a pile. The Guardian who has killed him stands there, splattered in blood and grinning through it.

"Ah, little one," says a voice, and her blood turns to stone. "Here you are."

"No," she whispers. She shakes her head in denial, steps backward. Coru is crying. She steps back again and stumbles against Innon's bed, fumbles for the basket, pulls Coru into her arms. He clings to her, shaking and hitching fitfully. "No."

The shirtless Guardian glances to one side, then he moves aside to make room for another to enter. *No.*

"There's no need for these histrionics, Damaya," Schaffa Guardian Warrant says, softly. Then he pauses, looks apologetic. "Syenite."

She has not seen him in years, but his voice is the same. His face is the same. He never changes. He's even smiling, though it fades a little in distaste as he notices the mess that was Innon. He glances at the shirtless Guardian; the man's still grinning. Schaffa sighs, but smiles in return. Then they both turn those horrible, horrible smiles on Syenite.

She cannot go back. She will not go back.

"And what is this?" Schaffa smiles, his gaze fixing on Coru in her arms. "How lovely. Alabaster's? Does he live, too? We would all like to see Alabaster, Syenite. Where is he?"

The habit of answering is too deep. "A stone eater took him."

Her voice shakes. She steps back again, and her head presses against the bulkhead. There's nowhere left to run.

For the first time since she's ever known him, Schaffa blinks and looks surprised. "A stone—hmm." He sobers. "I see. We should have killed him, then, before they got to him. As a kindness, of course; you cannot imagine what they will do to him, Syenite. Alas."

Then Schaffa smiles again, and she remembers everything she's tried to forget. She feels alone again, and helpless as she was that day near Palela, lost in the hateful world with no one to rely on except a man whose love comes wrapped in pain.

"But his child will be a more than worthwhile replacement," Schaffa says.

* * *

There are moments when everything changes, you understand.

* * *

Coru's wailing, terrified, and perhaps he even understands, somehow, what has happened to his fathers. Syenite cannot console him.

"No," she says again. "No. No. No."

Schaffa's smile fades. "Syenite. I told you. Never say no to me."

* * *

Even the hardest stone can fracture. It just takes the right force, applied at the right juncture of angles. A *fulcrum* of pressure and weakness.

* * *

Promise, Alabaster had said.

Do whatever you have to, Innon had tried to say.

And Syenite says: "*No*, you fucker."

Coru is crying. She puts her hand over his mouth and nose, to silence him, to comfort him. She will keep him safe. She will not let them take him, enslave him, turn his body into a tool and his mind into a weapon and his life into a travesty of freedom.

* * *

You understand these moments, I think, instinctively. It is our nature. We are born of such pressures, and sometimes, when things are unbearable—

* * *

Schaffa stops. "Syenite—"

"That's not my rusting name! I'll say no to you all I want, you bastard!" She's screaming the words. Spittle froths her lips. There's a dark heavy space inside her that is heavier than the stone eater, much heavier than a mountain, and it's eating everything else like a sinkhole.

Everyone she loves is dead. Everyone except Coru. And if they take him—

* * *

—sometimes, even we . . . *crack.*

* * *

Better that a child never have lived at all than live as a slave.

Better that he die.

Better that *she* die. Alabaster will hate her for this, for leaving him alone, but Alabaster is not here, and survival is not the same thing as living.

So she reaches up. Out. The amethyst is there, above, waiting with the patience of the dead, as if it somehow knew this moment would come.

She reaches for it now and prays that Alabaster was right about the thing being too much for her to handle.

And as her awareness dissolves amid jewel-toned light and faceted ripples, as Schaffa gasps in realization and lunges for her, as Coru's eyes flutter shut over her pressing, smothering hand—

She opens herself to all the power of the ancient unknown, and tears the world apart.

* * *

Here is the Stillness. Here is a place off its eastern coast, a bit south of the equator.

There's an island here—one of a chain of precarious little land slabs that rarely last longer than a few hundred years. This one's been around for several thousand, in testament to the wisdom of its inhabitants. This is the moment when that island dies, but at least a few of those inhabitants should survive to go elsewhere. Perhaps that will make you feel better.

The purple obelisk that hovers above it pulses, once, with a great throb of power that would be familiar to anyone who'd been in the late comm called Allia on the day of its death. As this pulse fades, the ocean below heaves as its rocky floor convulses. Spikes, wet and knifelike, burst up from the waves and utterly shatter the ships that float near the island's shores. A number of the people aboard each—some pirates, some their enemies—are speared through, so great is the thicket of death around them.

This convulsion spreads away from the island in a long, wending ripple, forming a chain of jagged, terrible spears from Meov's harbor all the way to what is left of Allia. A land bridge. Not the sort anyone would much want to cross, but nevertheless.

When all the death is done and the obelisk is calm, only a handful of people are still alive, in the ocean below. One of them, a woman, floats unconscious amid the debris of her shattered ship. Not far from her, a smaller figure—a child—floats, too, but facedown.

Her fellow survivors will find her and take her to the mainland. There she will wander, lost and losing herself, for two long years.

But not alone—for that is when I found her, you see. The moment of the obelisk's pulse was the moment in which her presence sang across the world: a promise, a demand, an invitation too enticing to resist. Many of us converged on her then, but I am the one who found her first. I fought off the others and trailed her, watched her, guarded her. I was glad when she found the little town called Tirimo, and comfort if not happiness, for a time.

I introduced myself to her eventually, finally, ten years later, as she left Tirimo. It's not the way we usually do these things, of course; it is not the relationship with her kind that we normally seek. But she is—was—special. *You* were, are, special.

I told her that I was called Hoa. It is as good a name as any.

This is how it began. Listen. Learn. This is how the world changed.

23

you're all you need

There's a structure in Castrima that glitters. It's on the lowermost level of the great geode, and you think it must have been built rather than grown: Its walls aren't carved solid crystal, but slabs of quarried white mica, flecked delicately with infinitesimal crystal flakes that are no less beautiful than their larger cousins, if not as dramatic. Why someone would carry these slabs here and make a house out of them amid all these ready-made, uninhabited apartments, you have no idea. You don't ask. You don't care.

Lerna comes with you, because this is the comm's official infirmary and the man you're coming to see is his patient. But you stop him at the door, and there's something in your face that must warn him of the danger. He does not protest when you go in without him.

You walk through its open doorway slowly, and stop when you spy the stone eater across the infirmary's large main room. Antimony, yes; you'd almost forgotten the name Alabaster gave her. She looks back at you impassively, hardly distinguishable from the white wall save for the rust of her fingertips and the stark black of her "hair" and eyes. She hasn't changed since the last time you saw her: twelve years ago, at the end of Meov. But then, for her kind, twelve years is nothing.

You nod to her, anyway. It's the polite thing to do, and there's still a little left of you that's the woman the Fulcrum raised. You can be polite to anybody, no matter how much you hate them.

She says, "No closer."

She's not talking to you. You turn, unsurprised, to see that Hoa is behind you. Where'd he come from? He's just as still as Antimony—unnaturally still, which makes you finally notice that he doesn't breathe. He never has, in all the time you've known him. How the rust did you miss that? Hoa watches her with the same steady glower of threat that he offered to Ykka's stone eater. Perhaps none of them like each other. Must make reunions awkward.

"I'm not interested in him," Hoa says.

Antimony's eyes shift over to you for a moment. Then her gaze returns to Hoa. "I am interested in her only on his behalf."

Hoa says nothing. Perhaps he's considering this; perhaps it's an offer of truce, or a staking of claims. You shake your head and walk past them both.

At the back of the main room, on a pile of cushions and blankets, lies a thin black figure, wheezing. It stirs a little, lifting its head slowly as you approach. As you crouch just out of his arms' reach, you're relieved to recognize him. Everything else has changed, but his eyes, at least, are the same.

"Syen," he says. His voice is thick gravel.

"Essun, now," you say, automatically.

He nods. This seems to cause him pain; for a moment his eyes squinch shut. Then he draws in another breath, makes a visible effort to relax, and revives somewhat. "I knew you weren't dead."

"Why didn't you come, then?" you say.

"Had my own problems to deal with." He smiles a little. You actually hear the skin on the left side of his face—there's a big burned patch there—crinkle. His eyes shift over to Antimony, as slowly as a stone eater's movements. Then he returns his attention to you.

(To her, Syenite.)

To *you*, Essun. Rust it, you'll be glad when you finally figure out who you really are.

"And I've been busy." Now Alabaster lifts his right arm. It ends abruptly, in the middle of the forearm; he's not wearing anything on his upper body, so you can clearly see what's happened. There's not much left of him. He's missing a lot of pieces, and he stinks of blood and pus and urine and cooked meat. The arm injury, though, is not one he earned from Yumenes's fires, or at least not directly. The stump of his arm is capped with something hard and brown that is definitely not skin: too hard, too uniformly chalklike in its visible composition.

Stone. His arm has become *stone*. Most of it's gone, though, and the stump—

—tooth marks. Those are tooth marks. You glance up at Antimony again, and think of a diamond smile.

"Hear you've been busy, too," 'Baster says.

You nod, finally dragging your gaze away from the stone eater. (Now you know what kind of stone they eat.) "After Meov. I was..." You're not sure how to say it. There are griefs too deep to be borne, and yet you have borne them again and again. "I needed to be different."

It makes no sense. Alabaster makes a soft affirmative sound, though, as if he understands. "You stayed free, at least."

If hiding everything you are is free. "Yes."

"Settled down?"

"Got married. Had two children." Alabaster is silent. With all the patches of char and chalky brown stone on his face, you can't tell if he's smiling or scowling. You assume the latter, though, so you add: "Both of them were . . . like me. I'm . . . my husband . . ."

Words make things real in a way that even memories can't, so you stop there.

"I understand why you killed Corundum," Alabaster says, very softly. And then, while you sway in your crouch, literally reeling from the blow of that sentence, he finishes you. "But I'll never forgive you for doing it."

Damn. Damn him. Damn yourself.

It takes you a moment to respond.

"I understand if you want to kill me," you manage, at last. Then you lick your lips. Swallow. Spit the words out. "But I have to kill my husband, first."

Alabaster lets out a wheezing sigh. "Your other two kids."

You nod. Doesn't matter that Nassun's alive, in this instance. Jija took her from you; that is insult enough.

"I'm not going to kill you, Sy—Essun." He sounds tired. Maybe he doesn't hear the little sound you make, which is neither relief nor disappointment. "I wouldn't even if I could."

"If you—"

"Can you do it, yet?" He rides over your confusion the way he always did. Nothing about him has changed except his ruined body. "You drew on the garnet at Allia, but that one was half dead. You must have used the amethyst at Meov, but that was... an extremity. Can you do it at will, now?"

"I..." You don't want to understand. But now your eyes are drawn away from the horror that remains of your mentor, your lover, your friend. To the side and behind Alabaster, where a strange object rests against the wall of the infirmary. It looks like a glassknife, but the blade is much too long and wide for practical use. It has an enormous handle, perhaps because the blade is so stupidly long, and a crosspiece that will get in the way the first time someone tries to use the thing to cut meat or slice through a knot. And it's not made of glass, or at least not any glass you've ever seen. It's *pink*, verging on red, and—

and. You stare at it. Into it. You feel it trying to draw your mind in, down. Falling. Falling *up*, through an endless shaft of flickering, faceted pink light—

You gasp and twitch back into yourself defensively, then stare at Alabaster. He smiles again, painfully.

"The spinel," he says, confirming your shock. "That one's mine. Have you made any of them yours, yet? Do the obelisks come when you call?"

You don't want to understand, but you do. You don't want to believe, but really, you have all along.

"*You* tore that rift up north," you breathe. Your hands are clenching into fists. "*You* split the continent. *You* started this Season. With the obelisks! You did... all of that."

"Yes, with the obelisks, and with the aid of the node

maintainers. They're all at peace now." He exhales, wheezily. "I need your help."

You shake your head automatically, but not in refusal. "To fix it?"

"Oh, no, Syen." You don't even bother to correct him this time. You can't take your eyes from his amused, nearly skeletal face. When he speaks, you notice that some of his teeth have turned to stone, too. How many of his organs have done the same? How much longer can he—should he—live like this?

"I don't want you to fix it," Alabaster says. "It was collateral damage, but Yumenes got what it deserved. No, what I want you to do, my Damaya, my Syenite, my Essun, is make it worse."

You stare at him, speechless. Then he leans forward. That this is painful for him is obvious; you hear the creak and stretch of his flesh, and a faint crack as some piece of stone somewhere on him fissures. But when he is close enough, he grins again, and suddenly it hits you. Evil, eating, Earth. He's not crazy at all, and he never has been.

"Tell me," he says, "have you ever heard of something called a *moon*?"

APPENDIX 1

A catalog of Fifth Seasons that have been recorded prior to and since the founding of the Sanzed Equatorial Affiliation, from most recent to oldest

Choking Season: 2714–2719 Imperial. Proximate cause: volcanic eruption. Location: the Antarctics near Deveteris. The eruption of Mount Akok blanketed a five-hundred-mile radius with fine ash clouds that solidified in lungs and mucous membranes. Five years without sunlight, although the northern hemisphere was not affected as much (only two years).

Acid Season: 2322–2329 Imperial. Proximate cause: plus-ten-level shake. Location: unknown; far ocean. A sudden plate shift birthed a chain of volcanoes in the path of a major jet stream. This jet stream became acidified, flowing toward the western coast and eventually around most of the Stillness. Most coastal comms perished in the initial tsunami; the rest failed or were forced to relocate when their fleets and port facilities corroded and the fishing dried up. Atmospheric occlusion by clouds lasted seven years; coastal pH levels remained untenable for many years more.

Boiling Season: 1842–1845 Imperial. Proximate cause: hot spot eruption beneath a great lake. Location: Somidlats, Lake Tekkaris quartent. The eruption launched millions of gallons of steam and particulates into the air, which triggered acidic rain and atmospheric occlusion over the southern half of the continent for three years. The northern half suffered no negative impacts, however, so archeomests dispute whether this qualifies as a "true" Season.

Breathless Season: 1689–1798 Imperial. Proximate cause: mining accident. Location: Nomidlats, Sathd quartent. An entirely human-caused Season triggered when miners at the edge of the northeastern Nomidlats coalfields set off underground fires. A relatively mild Season featuring occasional sunlight and no ashfall or acidification except in the region; few comms declared Seasonal Law. Approximately fourteen million people in the city of Heldine died in the initial natural-gas eruption and rapidly spreading fire sinkhole before Imperial Orogenes successfully quelled and sealed the edges of the fires to prevent further spread. The remaining mass could only be isolated, where it continued to burn for one hundred and twenty years. The smoke of this, spread via prevailing winds, caused respiratory problems and occasional mass suffocations in the region for several decades. A secondary effect of the loss of the Nomidlats coalfields was a catastrophic rise in heating fuel costs and the wider adaption of geothermal and hydroelectric heating, leading to the establishment of the Geneer Licensure.

The Season of Teeth: 1553–1566 Imperial. Proximate cause: oceanic shake triggering a supervolcanic explosion. Location: Arctic Cracks. An aftershock of the oceanic shake breached

a previously unknown hot spot near the north pole. This triggered a supervolcanic explosion; witnesses report hearing the sound of the explosion as far as the Antarctics. Ash went upper-atmospheric and spread around the globe rapidly, although the Arctics were most heavily affected. The harm of this Season was exacerbated by poor preparation on the part of many comms, because some nine hundred years had passed since the last Season; popular belief at the time was that the Seasons were merely legend. Reports of cannibalism spread from the north all the way to the Equatorials. At the end of this Season, the Fulcrum was founded in Yumenes, with satellite facilities in the Arctics and Antarctics.

Fungus Season: 602 Imperial. Proximate cause: volcanic eruption. Location: western Equatorials. A series of eruptions during monsoon season increased humidity and obscured sunlight over approximately 20 percent of the continent for six months. While this was a mild Season as such things go, its timing created perfect conditions for a fungal bloom that spread across the Equatorials into the northern and southern midlats, wiping out then-staple-crop miroq (now extinct). The resulting famine lasted four years (two for the fungus blight to run its course, two more for agriculture and food distribution systems to recover). Nearly all affected comms were able to subsist on their own stores, thus proving the efficacy of Imperial reforms and Season planning, and the Empire was generous in sharing stored seed with those regions that had been miroq-dependent. In its aftermath, many comms of the middle latitudes and coastal regions voluntarily joined the Empire, doubling its range and beginning its Golden Age.

Madness Season: 3 Before Imperial–7 Imperial. Proximate cause: volcanic eruption. Location: Kiash Traps. The eruption of multiple vents of an ancient supervolcano (the same one responsible for the Twin Season of approximately 10,000 years previous) launched large deposits of the dark-colored mineral augite into the air. The resulting ten years of darkness was not only devastating in the usual Seasonal way, but resulted in a higher than usual incidence of mental illness. The Sanzed Equatorial Affiliation (commonly called the Sanze Empire) was born in this Season as Warlord Verishe of Yumenes conquered multiple ailing comms using psychological warfare techniques. (See *The Art of Madness*, various authors, Sixth University Press.) Verishe named herself Emperor on the day the first sunlight returned.

[**Editor's note:** Much of the information about Seasons prior to the founding of Sanze is contradictory or unconfirmed. The following are Seasons agreed upon by the Seventh University Archaeomestric Conference of 2532.]

Wandering Season: Approximately 800 Before Imperial. Proximate cause: magnetic pole shift. Location: unverifiable. This Season resulted in the extinction of several important trade crops of the time, and twenty years of famine resulting from pollinators confused by the movement of true north.

Season of Changed Wind: Approximately 1900 Before Imperial. Proximate cause: unknown. Location: unverifiable. For reasons unknown, the direction of the prevailing winds shifted for many years before returning to normal. Consensus agrees that this was a Season, despite the lack of atmospheric

occlusion, because only a substantial (and likely far-oceanic) seismic event could have triggered it.

Heavy Metal Season: Approximately 4200 Before Imperial. Proximate cause: volcanic eruption. Location: Somidlats near eastern Coastals. A volcanic eruption (believed to be Mount Yrga) caused atmospheric occlusion for ten years, exacerbated by widespread mercury contamination throughout the eastern half of the Stillness.

Season of Yellow Seas: Approximately 9200 Before Imperial. Proximate cause: unknown. Location: Eastern and Western Coastals, and coastal regions as far south as the Antarctics. This Season is only known through written accounts found in Equatorial ruins. For unknown reasons, a widespread bacterial bloom toxified nearly all sea life and caused coastal famines for several decades.

Twin Season: Approximately 9800 Before Imperial. Proximate cause: volcanic eruption. Location: Somidlats. Per songs and oral histories dating from the time, the eruption of one volcanic vent caused a three-year occlusion. As this began to clear, it was followed by a second eruption of a different vent, which extended the occlusion by thirty more years.

APPENDIX 2

A Glossary of Terms Commonly Used in All Quartents of the Stillness

Antarctics: The southernmost latitudes of the continent. Also refers to people from antarctic-region comms.

Arctics: The northernmost latitudes of the continent. Also refers to people from arctic-region comms.

Ashblow Hair: A distinctive Sanzed racial trait, deemed in the current guidelines of the Breeder use-caste to be advantageous and therefore given preference in selection. Ashblow hair is notably coarse and thick, generally growing in an upward flare; at length, it falls around the face and shoulders. It is acid-resistant and retains little water after immersion, and has been proven effective as an ash filter in extreme circumstances. In most comms, Breeder guidelines acknowledge texture alone; however, Equatorial Breeders generally also require natural "ash" coloration (slate gray to white, present from birth) for the coveted designation.

Bastard: A person born without a use-caste, which is only possible for boys whose fathers are unknown. Those who

distinguish themselves may be permitted to bear their mother's use-caste at comm-naming.

Blow: A volcano. Also called firemountains in some Coastal languages.

Boil: A geyser, hot spring, or steam vent.

Breeder: One of the seven common use-castes. Breeders are individuals selected for their health and desirable conformation. During a Season, they are responsible for the maintenance of healthy bloodlines and the improvement of comm or race by selective measures. Breeders born into the caste who do not meet acceptable community standards may be permitted to bear the use-caste of a close relative at comm-naming.

Cache: Stored food and supplies. Comms maintain guarded, locked storecaches at all times against the possibility of a Fifth Season. Only recognized comm members are entitled to a share of the cache, though adults may use their share to feed unrecognized children and others. Individual households often maintain their own housecaches, equally guarded against non–family members.

Cebaki: A member of the Cebaki race. Cebak was once a nation (unit of a deprecated political system, Before Imperial) in the Somidlats, though it was reorganized into the quartent system when the Old Sanze Empire conquered it centuries ago.

Coaster: A person from a coastal comm. Few coastal comms can afford to hire Imperial Orogenes to raise reefs or otherwise protect against tsunami, so coastal cities must perpetually rebuild and tend to be resource-poor as a result. People from the western coast of the continent tend to be pale, straight-haired, and sometimes have eyes with epicanthic

folds. People from the eastern coast tend to be dark, kinky-haired, and sometimes have eyes with epicanthic folds.

Comm: Community. The smallest sociopolitical unit of the Imperial governance system, generally corresponding to one city or town, although very large cities may contain several comms. Accepted members of a comm are those who have been accorded rights of cache-share and protection, and who in turn support the comm through taxes or other contributions.

Commless: Criminals and other undesirables unable to gain acceptance in any comm.

Comm Name: The third name borne by most citizens, indicating their comm allegiance and rights. This name is generally bestowed at puberty as a coming-of-age, indicating that a person has been deemed a valuable member of the community. Immigrants to a comm may request adoption into that comm; upon acceptance, they take on the adoptive comm's name as their own.

Creche: A place where children too young to work are cared for while adults carry out needed tasks for the comm. When circumstances permit, a place of learning.

Equatorials: Latitudes surrounding and including the equator, excepting coastal regions. Also refers to people from equatorial-region comms. Thanks to temperate weather and relative stability at the center of the continental plate, Equatorial comms tend to be prosperous and politically powerful. The Equatorials once formed the core of the Old Sanze Empire.

Fault: A place where breaks in the earth make frequent, severe shakes and blows more likely.

Fifth Season: An extended winter—lasting at least six months, per Imperial designation—triggered by seismic activity or other large-scale environmental alteration.

Fulcrum: A paramilitary order created by Old Sanze after the Season of Teeth (1560 Imperial). The headquarters of the Fulcrum is in Yumenes, although two satellite Fulcrums are located in the Arctic and Antarctic regions, for maximum continental coverage. Fulcrum-trained orogenes (or "Imperial Orogenes") are legally permitted to practice the otherwise-illegal craft of orogeny, under strict organizational rules and with the close supervision of the Guardian order. The Fulcrum is self-managed and self-sufficient. Imperial Orogenes are marked by their black uniforms, and colloquially known as "blackjackets."

Geneer: From "geoneer." An engineer of earthworks—geothermal energy mechanisms, tunnels, underground infrastructure, mining.

Geomest: One who studies stone and its place in the natural world; general term for a scientist. Specifically geomests study lithology, chemistry, and geology, which are not considered separate disciplines in the Stillness. A few geomests specialize in orogenesis—the study of orogeny and its effects.

Greenland: An area of fallow ground kept within or just outside the walls of most comms as advised by stonelore. Comm greenlands may be used for agriculture or animal husbandry at all times, or may be kept as parks or fallow ground during non-Seasonal times. Individual households often maintain their own personal housegreen, or garden, as well.

Grits: In the Fulcrum, unringed orogene children who are still in basic training.

Guardian: A member of an order said to predate the Fulcrum. Guardians track, protect, protect against, and guide orogenes in the Stillness.

Imperial Road: One of the great innovations of the Old Sanze Empire, highroads (elevated highways for walking or horse traffic) connect all major comms and most large quartents to one another. Highroads are built by teams of geneers and Imperial Orogenes, with the orogenes determining the most stable path through areas of seismic activity (or quelling the activity, if there is no stable path), and the geneers routing water and other important resources near the roads to facilitate travel during Seasons.

Innovator: One of the seven common use-castes. Innovators are individuals selected for their creativity and applied intelligence, responsible for technical and logistical problem solving during a Season.

Kirkhusa: A mid-sized mammal, sometimes kept as a pet or used to guard homes or livestock. Normally herbivarous; during Seasons, carnivorous.

Knapper: A small-tools crafter, working in stone, glass, bone, or other materials. In large comms, knappers may use mechanical or mass-production techniques. Knappers who work in metal, or incompetent knappers, are colloquially called rusters.

Lorist: One who studies stonelore and lost history.

Mela: A midlats plant, related to the melons of Equatorial climates. Mela are vining ground plants that normally produce fruit aboveground. During a Season, the fruit grows underground as tubers. Some species of mela produce flowers that trap insects.

Metallore: Like alchemy and astromestry, a discredited pseudoscience disavowed by the Seventh University.

Midlats: The "middle" latitudes of the continent—those between the equator and the arctic or antarctic regions. Also refers to people from midlats regions (sometimes called midlatters). These regions are seen as the backwater of the Stillness, although they produce much of the world's food, materials, and other critical resources. There are two midlat regions: the northern (Nomidlats) and southern (Somidlats).

Newcomm: Colloquial term for comms that have arisen only since the last Season. Comms that have survived at least one Season are generally seen as more desirable places to live, having proven their efficacy and strength.

Nodes: The network of Imperially maintained stations placed throughout the Stillness in order to reduce or quell seismic events. Due to the relative rarity of Fulcrum-trained orogenes, nodes are primarily clustered in the Equatorials.

Orogene: One who possesses orogeny, whether trained or not. Derogatory: rogga.

Orogeny: The ability to manipulate thermal, kinetic, and related forms of energy to address seismic events.

Quartent: The middle level of the Imperial governance system. Four geographically adjacent comms make a quartent. Each quartent has a governor to whom individual comm heads report, and who reports in turn to a regional governor. The largest comm in a quartent is its capital; larger quartent capitals are connected to one another via the Imperial Road system.

Region: The top level of the Imperial governance system. Imperially recognized regions are the Arctics, Nomidlats, western Coastals, eastern Coastals, Equatorials, Somidlats, and Antarctics. Each region has a governor to whom all local quartents report. Regional governors are officially appointed by the Emperor, though in actual practice they are generally selected by and/or come from the Yumenescene Leadership.

Resistant: One of the seven common use-castes. Resistants are individuals selected for their ability to survive famine or pestilence. They are responsible for caring for the infirm and dead bodies during Seasons.

Rings: Used to denote rank among Imperial Orogenes. Unranked trainees must pass a series of tests to gain their first ring; ten rings is the highest rank an orogene may achieve. Each ring is made of polished semiprecious stone.

Roadhouse: Stations located at intervals along every Imperial Road and many lesser roads. All roadhouses contain a source of water and are located near arable land, forests, or other useful resources. Many are located in areas of minimal seismic activity.

Runny-sack: A small, easily portable cache of supplies most people keep in their homes in case of shakes or other emergencies.

Safe: A beverage traditionally served at negotiations, first encounters between potentially hostile parties, and other formal meetings. It contains a plant milk that reacts to the presence of all foreign substances.

Sanze: Originally a nation (unit of a deprecated political system, Before Imperial) in the Equatorials; origin of the Sanzed race. At the close of the Madness Season (7 Imperial), the nation of Sanze was abolished and replaced with the Sanzed Equatorial Affiliation, consisting of six predominantly Sanzed comms under the rule of Emperor Verishe Leadership Yumenes. The Affiliation expanded rapidly in the aftermath of the Season, eventually encompassing all regions of the Stillness by 800 Imperial. Around the time of the Season of Teeth, the Affiliation came to be known colloquially as the Old Sanze Empire, or simply Old Sanze. As of the Shilteen Accords of 1850 Imperial, the Affiliation officially ceased to exist, as local control (under the advisement of the Yumenescene Leadership) was deemed more efficient in the event of a Season. In practice, most comms still follow Imperial systems of governance, finance, education, and more, and most regional governors still pay taxes in tribute to Yumenes.

Sanzed: A member of the Sanzed race. Per Yumenescene Breedership standards, Sanzeds are ideally bronze-skinned and ashblow-haired, with mesomorphic or endomorphic builds and an adult height of minimum six feet.

Sanze-mat: The language spoken by the Sanze race, and the official language of the Old Sanze Empire, now the lingua franca of most of the Stillness.

Seasonal Law: Martial law, which may be declared by any comm head, quartent governor, regional governor, or recognized member of the Yumenescene Leadership. During Seasonal Law, quartent and regional governance are suspended and comms operate as sovereign sociopolitical units, though local cooperation with other comms is strongly encouraged per Imperial policy.

Seventh University: A famous college for the study of geomestry and stonelore, currently Imperially funded and located in the Equatorial city of Dibars. Prior versions of the University have been privately or collectively maintained; notably, the Third University at Am-Elat (approximately 3000 Before Imperial) was recognized at the time as a sovereign nation. Smaller regional or quartent colleges pay tribute to the University and receive expertise and resources in exchange.

Sesuna: Awareness of the movements of the earth. The sensory organs that perform this function are the sessapinae, located in the brain stem. Verb form: to sess.

Shake: A seismic movement of the earth.

Shatterland: Ground that has been disturbed by severe and/or very recent seismic activity.

Stillheads: A derogatory term used by orogenes for people lacking orogeny, usually shortened to "stills."

Stone Eaters: A rarely seen sentient humanoid species whose flesh, hair, etc., resembles stone. Little is known about them.

Strongback: One of the seven common use-castes. Strongbacks are individuals selected for their physical prowess, responsible for heavy labor and security in the event of a Season.

Use Name: The second name borne by most citizens, indicating the use-caste to which that person belongs. There are twenty recognized use-castes, although only seven in common use throughout the current and former Old Sanze Empire. A person inherits the use name of their same-sex parent, on the theory that useful traits are more readily passed this way.

Acknowledgments

This fantasy novel was partially born in space.

You can probably tell, if you've read all the way to the last line of the manuscript. The germination point for this idea was Launch Pad, a then-NASA-funded workshop that I attended back in July of 2009. The goal of Launch Pad was to pull together media influencers—astonishingly, science fiction and fantasy writers count among those—and make sure they understood Teh Science, if they were going to use it in any of their works. A lot of the falsehoods the public believes re astronomy have been spread by writers, see. Alas, by pairing astronomy with sentient rock people, I'm not so sure I'm doing the world's best job of delivering accurate scientific information. Sorry, fellow Launch Padders.

I can't tell you about the spirited, amazing discussion that seeded this novel in my brain. (This is supposed to be short.) But I can tell you that such spirited, amazing discussions were the norm for Launch Pad, so if you are also a media influencer and you have the chance to attend, I highly recommend it.

And I must offer thanks to the folks who were in attendance at Launch Pad that year, who all contributed to the germination of this novel whether they realized it or not. Offhand that would be people like Mike Brotherton (the workshop's director, a University of Wyoming professor and science fiction writer himself); Phil Plait, the Bad Astronomer (it's a title, see, he's not actually bad, I mean... okay, just look him up); Gay and Joe Haldeman; Pat Cadigan; Science Comedian Brian Malow; Tara Fredette (now Malow); and Gord Sellar.

Also, big props to my editor, Devi Pillai, and my agent, Lucienne Diver, for talking me out of scrapping this novel. The Broken Earth trilogy is the most challenging work I've ever written, and at certain points during *The Fifth Season* the task seemed so overwhelming that I thought about quitting. (Actually, I believe my exact words were, "Delete this hot mess, hack Dropbox to get the backups there, drop my laptop off a cliff, drive over it with a car, set fire to both, then use a backhoe to bury the evidence. Do you need a special license to drive a backhoe?") Kate Elliott (another acknowledgment, for being a perpetual mentor and friend) calls moments like this the "Chasm of Doubt" that every writer hits at some point during a major project. Mine was as deep and awful as the Yumenescene Rift.

Other folks who helped talk me off the cliff: Rose Fox; Danielle Friedman, my medical consultant; Mikki Kendall; my writing group; my day-job boss (who I am not sure wants to be named); and my cat, KING OZZYMANDIAS. Yeah, even the damn cat. It takes a village to keep a writer from losing her shit, okay?

And as always, thanks to all of you, for reading.

extras

meet the author

N. K. Jemisin

N. K. Jemisin is a career counselor, political blogger, and would-be gourmand living in New York City. She's been writing since the age of ten, although her early works will never see the light of day.

introducing

If you enjoyed
THE FIFTH SEASON
look out for

THE HUNDRED THOUSAND KINGDOMS

The Inheritance Trilogy: Book 1

by N. K. Jemisin

Yeine Darr is an outcast from the barbarian north. But when her mother dies under mysterious circumstances, she is summoned to the majestic city of Sky. There, to her shock, Yeine is named an heiress to the king. But the throne of the Hundred Thousand Kingdoms is not easily won, and Yeine is thrust into a vicious power struggle with cousins she never knew she had. As she fights for her life, she draws ever closer to the secrets of her mother's death and her family's bloody history.

With the fate of the world hanging in the balance, Yeine will learn how perilous it can be when love and hate—and gods and mortals—are bound inseparably together.

1
Grandfather

I am not as I once was. They have done this to me, broken me open and torn out my heart. I do not know who I am anymore.

I must try to remember.

* * *

My people tell stories of the night I was born. They say my mother crossed her legs in the middle of labor and fought with all her strength not to release me into the world. I was born anyhow, of course; nature cannot be denied. Yet it does not surprise me that she tried.

* * *

My mother was an heiress of the Arameri. There was a ball for the lesser nobility—the sort of thing that happens once a decade as a backhanded sop to their self-esteem. My father dared ask my mother to dance; she deigned to consent. I have often wondered what he said and did that night to make her fall in love with him so powerfully, for she eventually abdicated her position to be with him. It is the stuff of great tales, yes? Very romantic. In the tales, such a couple lives happily ever after. The tales do not say what happens when the most powerful family in the world is offended in the process.

* * *

But I forget myself. Who was I, again? Ah, yes.

My name is Yeine. In my people's way I am Yeine dau she Kinneth tai wer Somem kanna Darre, which means that I am the daughter of Kinneth, and that my tribe within the Darre people is called Somem. Tribes mean little to us these days, though before the Gods' War they were more important.

I am nineteen years old. I also am, or was, the chieftain of my people, called *ennu*. In the Arameri way, which is the way of the Amn race from whom they originated, I am the Baroness Yeine Darr.

One month after my mother died, I received a message from my grandfather Dekarta Arameri, inviting me to visit the family seat. Because one does not refuse an invitation from the Arameri, I set forth. It took the better part of three months to travel from the High North continent to Senm, across the Repentance Sea. Despite Darr's relative poverty, I traveled in style the whole way, first by palanquin and ocean vessel, and finally by chauffeured horse-coach. This was not my choice. The Darre Warriors' Council, which rather desperately hoped that I might restore us to the Arameri's good graces, thought that this extravagance would help. It is well known that Amn respect displays of wealth.

Thus arrayed, I arrived at my destination on the cusp of the winter solstice. And as the driver stopped the coach on a hill outside the city, ostensibly to water the horses but more likely because he was a local and liked to watch foreigners gawk, I got my first glimpse of the Hundred Thousand Kingdoms' heart.

There is a rose that is famous in High North. (This is not a digression.) It is called the altarskirt rose. Not only do its petals unfold in a radiance of pearled white, but frequently it grows an incomplete secondary flower about the base of its stem. In its most prized form, the altarskirt grows a layer of overlarge petals that drape the ground. The two bloom in tandem, seed-bearing head and skirt, glory above and below.

This was the city called Sky. On the ground, sprawling over a small mountain or an oversize hill: a circle of high walls, mounting tiers of buildings, all resplendent in white, per Arameri decree. Above the city, smaller but brighter, the pearl of its tiers occasionally obscured by scuds of cloud, was the palace—also called Sky, and perhaps more deserving of the name. I knew the column was there, the impossibly thin column that supported such a massive structure, but from that distance I couldn't see it. Palace floated above city, linked in spirit, both so unearthly in their beauty that I held my breath at the sight.

The altarskirt rose is priceless because of the difficulty of producing it. The most famous lines are heavily inbred; it originated as a deformity that some savvy breeder deemed useful. The primary flower's scent, sweet to us, is apparently repugnant to insects; these roses must be pollinated by hand. The secondary flower saps nutrients crucial for the plant's fertility. Seeds are rare, and for every one that grows into a perfect altarskirt, ten others become plants that must be destroyed for their hideousness.

* * *

At the gates of Sky (the palace) I was turned away, though not for the reasons I'd expected. My grandfather was not present, it seemed. He had left instructions in the event of my arrival.

Sky is the Arameri's home; business is never done there. This is because, officially, they do not rule the world. The Nobles' Consortium does, with the benevolent assistance of the Order of Itempas. The Consortium meets in the Salon, a huge, stately building—white-walled, of course—that sits among a cluster of official buildings at the foot of the palace. It is very impressive, and would be more so if it did not sit squarely in Sky's elegant shadow.

I went inside and announced myself to the Consortium staff, whereupon they all looked very surprised, though politely so. One of them—a very junior aide, I gathered—was dispatched to escort me to the central chamber, where the day's session was well under way.

As a lesser noble, I had always been welcome to attend a Consortium gathering, but there had never seemed any point. Besides the expense and months of travel time required to attend, Darr was simply too small, poor, and ill-favored to have any clout, even without my mother's abdication adding to our collective stain. Most of High North is regarded as a backwater, and only the largest nations there have enough prestige or money to make their voices heard among our noble peers. So I was not surprised to find that the seat reserved for me on the Consortium floor—in a shadowed area, behind a pillar—was currently occupied by an excess delegate from one of the Senm-continent nations. It would be terribly rude, the aide stammered anxiously, to dislodge this man, who was elderly and had bad knees. Perhaps I would not mind standing? Since I had just spent many long hours cramped in a carriage, I was happy to agree.

So the aide positioned me at the side of the Consortium floor, where I actually had a good view of the goings-on. The Consortium chamber was magnificently apportioned, with white marble and rich, dark wood that had probably come from Darr's forests in better days. The nobles—three hundred or so in total—sat in comfortable chairs on the chamber's floor or along elevated tiers above. Aides, pages, and scribes occupied the periphery with me, ready to fetch documents or run errands as needed. At the head of the chamber, the Consortium Overseer stood atop an elaborate podium, pointing to members as they indicated a desire to speak. Apparently there was a dispute over water rights in a desert somewhere; five countries were involved. None of the conversation's participants spoke out of turn; no tempers were lost; there were no snide comments or veiled insults. It was all very orderly and polite, despite the size of the gathering and the fact that most of those present were accustomed to speaking however they pleased among their own people.

One reason for this extraordinary good behavior stood on a plinth behind the Overseer's podium: a life-size statue of the Skyfather in one of His most famous poses, the Appeal to Mortal Reason. Hard to speak out of turn under that stern gaze. But more repressive, I suspected, was the stern gaze of the man who sat behind the Overseer in an elevated box. I could not see him well from where I stood, but he was elderly, richly dressed, and flanked by a younger blond man and a dark-haired woman, as well as a handful of retainers.

It did not take much to guess this man's identity, though he wore no crown, had no visible guards, and neither he nor anyone in his entourage spoke throughout the meeting.

"Hello, Grandfather," I murmured to myself, and smiled at him across the chamber, though I knew he could not see me. The pages and scribes gave me the oddest looks for the rest of the afternoon.

* * *

I knelt before my grandfather with my head bowed, hearing titters of laughter.

No, wait.

* * *

There were three gods once.

Only three, I mean. Now there are dozens, perhaps hundreds. They breed like rabbits. But once there were only three, most powerful and glorious of all: the god of day, the god of night, and the goddess of twilight and dawn. Or light and darkness and the shades between. Or order, chaos, and balance. None of that is important because one of them died, the other might as well have, and the last is the only one who matters anymore.

The Arameri get their power from this remaining god. He is called the Skyfather, Bright Itempas, and the ancestors of the Arameri were His most devoted priests. He rewarded them by giving them a weapon so mighty that no army could stand against it. They used this weapon—weapons, really—to make themselves rulers of the world.

That's better. Now.

* * *

I knelt before my grandfather with my head bowed and my knife laid on the floor.

We were in Sky, having transferred there following the Consortium session, via the magic of the Vertical Gate. Immediately upon arrival I had been summoned to my grandfather's audience chamber, which felt much like a throne room. The chamber was roughly circular because circles are sacred to Itempas. The vaulted ceiling made the members of the court look taller—unnecessarily, since Amn are a tall people compared to my own. Tall and pale and endlessly poised, like statues of human beings rather than real flesh and blood.

"Most high Lord Arameri," I said. "I am honored to be in your presence."

I had heard titters of laughter when I entered the room. Now they sounded again, muffled by hands and kerchiefs and fans. I was reminded of bird flocks roosting in a forest canopy.

Before me sat Dekarta Arameri, uncrowned king of the world. He was old; perhaps the oldest man I have ever seen, though Amn usually live longer than my people, so this was not surprising. His thin hair had gone completely white, and he was so gaunt and stooped that the elevated stone chair on which he sat—it was never called a throne—seemed to swallow him whole.

"Granddaughter," he said, and the titters stopped. The silence was heavy enough to hold in my hand. He was head of the Arameri family, and his word was law. No one had expected him to acknowledge me as kin, least of all myself.

"Stand," he said. "Let me have a look at you."

I did, reclaiming my knife since no one had taken it. There was more silence. I am not very interesting to look at. It might have been different if I had gotten the traits of my two peoples in a better combination—Amn height with Darre curves, perhaps, or thick straight Darre hair colored Amn-pale. I have Amn eyes: faded green in color, more unnerving than pretty. Otherwise, I am short and flat and brown as forestwood, and my hair is a curled mess. Because I find it unmanageable otherwise, I wear it short. I am sometimes mistaken for a boy.

As the silence wore on, I saw Dekarta frown. There was an odd sort of marking on his forehead, I noticed: a perfect circle of black, as if someone had dipped a coin in ink and pressed it to his flesh. On either side of this was a thick chevron, bracketing the circle.

"You look nothing like her," he said at last. "But I suppose that is just as well. Viraine?"

This last was directed at a man who stood among the courtiers closest to the throne. For an instant I thought he was another elder, then I realized my error: though his hair was stark white, he was only somewhere in his fourth decade. He, too, bore a forehead mark, though his was less elaborate than Dekarta's: just the black circle.

"She's not hopeless," he said, folding his arms. "Nothing to be done about her looks; I doubt even makeup will help. But put her in civilized attire and she can convey... nobility, at least." His eyes narrowed, taking me apart by degrees. My best Darren clothing, a long vest of white civvetfur and calf-length leggings, earned me a sigh. (I had gotten the odd look for this outfit at the Salon, but I hadn't realized it was *that* bad.) He examined my face so long that I wondered if I should show my teeth.

Instead he smiled, showing his. "Her mother has trained her. Look how she shows no fear or resentment, even now."

"She will do, then," said Dekarta.

"Do for what, Grandfather?" I asked. The weight in the room grew heavier, expectant, though he had already named me granddaughter. There was a certain risk involved in my daring to address him the same familiar way, of course—powerful men are touchy over odd things. But my mother had indeed trained me well, and I knew it was worth the risk to establish myself in the court's eyes.

Dekarta Arameri's face did not change; I could not read it. "For my heir, Granddaughter. I intend to name you to that position today."

The silence turned to stone as hard as my grandfather's chair.

I thought he might be joking, but no one laughed. That was what made me believe him at last: the utter shock and horror on the faces of the courtiers as they stared at their lord. Except the one called Viraine. He watched me.

It came to me that some response was expected.

"You already have heirs," I said.

"Not as diplomatic as she could be," Viraine said in a dry tone.

Dekarta ignored this. "It is true, there are two other candidates," he said to me. "My niece and nephew, Scimina and Relad. Your cousins, once removed."

I had heard of them, of course; everyone had. Rumor constantly made one or the other heir, though no one knew for certain which. *Both* was something that had not occurred to me.

"If I may suggest, Grandfather," I said carefully, though it was impossible to be careful in this conversation, "I would make two heirs too many."

It was the eyes that made Dekarta seem so old, I would realize much later. I had no idea what color they had originally been; age had bleached and filmed them to near-white. There were lifetimes in those eyes, none of them happy.

"Indeed," he said. "But just enough for an interesting competition, I think."

"I don't understand, Grandfather."

He lifted his hand in a gesture that would have been graceful, once. Now his hand shook badly. "It is very simple. I have named three heirs. One of you will actually manage to succeed me. The other two will doubtless kill each other or be killed by the victor. As for which lives, and which die—" He shrugged. "That is for you to decide."

My mother had taught me never to show fear, but emotions will not be stilled so easily. I began to sweat. I have been the target of an assassination attempt only once in my life—the benefit of being heir to such a tiny, impoverished nation. No one wanted my job. But now there would be two others who did. Lord Relad and Lady Scimina were wealthy and powerful beyond my wildest dreams. They had spent their whole lives striving against each other toward the goal of ruling the world. And here came I, unknown, with no rcsourccs and few friends, into the fray.

"There will be no decision," I said. To my credit, my voice did not shake. "And no contest. They will kill me at once and turn their attention back to each other."

"That is possible," said my grandfather.

I could think of nothing to say that would save me. He was insane; that was obvious. Why else turn rulership of the world into a contest prize? If he died tomorrow, Relad and Scimina would rip the earth asunder between them. The killing might not end for decades. And for all he knew, I was an idiot. If by some impossible chance I managed to gain the throne, I could plunge the Hundred Thousand Kingdoms into a spiral of mismanagement and suffering. He had to know that.

One cannot argue with madness. But sometimes, with luck and the Skyfather's blessing, one can understand it. "Why?"

He nodded as if he had expected my question. "Your mother deprived me of an heir when she left our family. You will pay her debt."

"She is four months in the grave," I snapped. "Do you honestly want revenge against a dead woman?"

"This has nothing to do with revenge, Granddaughter. It is a matter of duty." He made a gesture with his left hand, and another courtier detached himself from the throng. Unlike the first man—indeed, unlike most of the courtiers whose faces I could see—the mark on this man's forehead was a downturned half-moon, like an exaggerated frown. He knelt before the dais that held Dekarta's chair, his waist-length red braid falling over one shoulder to curl on the floor.

"I cannot hope that your mother has taught you duty," Dekarta said to me over this man's back. "She abandoned hers to dally with her sweet-tongued savage. I allowed this—an indulgence I have often regretted. So I will assuage that regret by bringing you back into the fold, Granddaughter. Whether you live or die is irrelevant. You are Arameri, and like all of us, you will serve."

Then he waved to the red-haired man. "Prepare her as best you can."

There was nothing more. The red-haired man rose and came to me, murmuring that I should follow him. I did. Thus ended my first meeting with my grandfather, and thus began my first day as an Arameri. It was not the worst of the days to come.

introducing

If you enjoyed
THE FIFTH SEASON
look out for

THE KILLING MOON

The Dreamblood Duology: Book 1

by N. K. Jemisin

The city burned beneath the Dreaming Moon.

In the ancient city-state of Gujaareh, peace is the only law. Upon its rooftops and among the shadows of its cobbled streets wait the Gatherers—the keepers of this peace. Priests of the dream-goddess, their duty is to harvest the magic of the sleeping mind and use it to heal, soothe... and kill those judged corrupt.

But when a conspiracy blooms within Gujaareh's great temple, Ehiru—the most famous of the city's Gatherers—must question everything he knows. Someone, or something, is murdering dreamers in the goddess' name, stalking its prey both in Gujaareh's alleys and the realm of dreams. Ehiru must now protect the woman he was sent to kill—or watch the city be devoured by war and forbidden magic.

1

In the dark of dreams, a soul can die. The fears we confront in shadows are as reflections in glass. It is natural to strike a reflection that offends, but then the glass cuts; the soul bleeds. The Gatherer's task is to save the soul, at any cost.
(Wisdom)

In the dark of waking, a soul has died. Its flesh, however, is still hungrily, savagely alive.

The Reaper's task is *not* to save.

* * *

The barbarians of the north taught their children to fear the Dreaming Moon, claiming that it brought madness. This was a forgivable blasphemy. On some nights, the moon's strange light bathed all Gujaareh in oily swirls of amethyst and aquamarine. It could make lowcaste hovels seem sturdy and fine; pathways of plain clay brick gleamed as if silvered. Within the moonlight's strange shadows, a man might crouch on the shadowed ledge of a building and be only a faint etching against the marbled gray.

In this land, such a man would be a priest, intent upon the most sacred of his duties.

More than shadows aided this priest's stealth. Long training softened his footfalls against the stone; his feet were bare in any case. He wore little altogether, trusting the darkness of his skin for camouflage as he crept along, guided by the sounds of the city. An infant's cry from a tenement across the street; he took a step. Laughter from several floors below his ledge; he straightened as he reached the window that was his goal. A muffled cry and the sounds of a scuffle from an alley a block away; he paused, listening and frowning. But the disturbance ended as sandals pattered on the cobblestones, fading into the distance, and he relaxed. When the love-cries of the young couple next door floated past on a breeze, he slipped through the curtains into the room beyond.

The bedchamber: a study in worn elegance. The priest's eyes made out graceful chairs upholstered in fraying fabrics, and wood furnishings gone dull for lack of polish. Reaching the bed, he took care to avoid shadowing the face of the person who slept there—but the old man's eyes opened anyhow, blinking rheumily in the thin light.

"As I thought," said the old man, whose name was Yeyezu. His hoarse voice grated against the silence. "Which one are you?"

"Ehiru," said the priest. His voice was as soft and deep as the bedchamber's shadows. "Named Nsha, in dreams."

The old man's eyes widened in surprise and pleasure. "So that is the rose's soulname. To whom do I owe this honor?"

Ehiru let out a slow breath. It was always more difficult to bestow peace once a tithebearer had been awakened and frightened; that was why the law commanded Gatherers to enter dwellings in stealth. But Yeyezu was not afraid, Ehiru saw at once, so he chose to answer the old man's question, though he preferred to do his work without conversation.

"Your eldest son submitted the commission on your behalf," he said. From the hipstrap of his loinskirt he plucked free the jungissa: a thumb-long polished stone like dark glass, which had been carved into the likeness of a cicada. Yeyezu's eyes tracked the jungissa as Ehiru raised it. The stones were legend for their rarity as well as their power, and few of Hananja's faithful ever saw one. "It was considered and accepted by the Council of Paths, then given to me to carry out."

The old man nodded, lifting a trembling hand toward the jungissa. Ehiru lowered the stone so that Yeyezu could run fingers over its slick, fine-carved wings, though he kept a good grip on its body. Jungissa were too sacred for carelessness. Yeyezu's wonder made him look much younger; Ehiru could not help smiling at this.

"She has tasted many of your dreams, Yeyezu-Elder," he said, very gently drawing the jungissa out of the old man's reach so he would hear Ehiru's words. Yeyezu sighed, but lowered his hand. "She has drunk deeply of your hopes and fears. Now She bids you join Her in Ina-Karekh. Will you grant Her this final offering?"

"Gladly," Yeyezu said, and closed his eyes.

So Ehiru bent and kissed the old man's forehead. Fevered skin, delicate as papyrus, smoothed under his lips. When he pulled away and set the jungissa in place of his kiss, the stone quivered at a flick of his fingernail and then settled into a barely-visible vibration. Yeyezu sagged into sleep, and Ehiru laid his fingertips on the old man's eyelids to begin.

In the relative quiet of the city's evening, the room sounded only of breath: first Ehiru's and Yeyezu's, then Ehiru's alone. Amid the new silence—for the jungissa had stopped vibrating with the dream's end—Ehiru stood for a few moments, letting the languor of the newly collected dreamblood spread within him. When he judged the moment right, he drew another ornament from his hip—this one a small hemisphere of obsidian whose flat face had been embossed with an oasis rose, the crevices tamped full of powdered ink. He pressed the carving carefully into the skin of Yeyezu's bony, still chest, setting his signature upon the artwork of flesh. The smile that lingered on the elder's cooling lips was even more beautiful.

"Dreams of joy always, my friend," he whispered, before pulling away the sheet and arranging Yeyezu's limbs into a peaceful, dignified position. Finally, as quietly as he'd entered, he left.

Now flight: along the rooftops of the city, swift and silent. A few blocks from Yeyezu's house Ehiru stopped, dropping to the ground in the lee of an old broken wall. There he knelt amid the weeds and trembled. Once, as a younger man, he would have returned to the Hetawa after such a night's work, overwhelmed with joy at the passing of a rich and full life. Only hours of prayer in the Hetawa's Hall of Blessings could've restored his ability to function. He was no longer a young man. He was stronger now; he had learned discipline. Most nights he could perform a second Gathering, and occasionally a third if circumstances required—though three would leave him giddy and half a dream, unsure of which realm he walked. Even a single soul's dreamblood could still muddle his wits, for how could he not exult with Yeyezu's happiness so palpable within him? Yet for the sake of other suffering citizens of Gujaareh, it was necessary to try. Twice he attempted to count by fours, a concentration exercise, but both times he failed at only four thousand and ninety-six. Pathetic. At last, however, his thoughts settled and the tremors ceased.

With some concern he saw that Dreaming Moon had reached zenith, her bright expanse glaring from the sky's center like a great striped eye; the night was half over. Faster to cross this part of the city on the ground than by rooftop. After a moment's pause to turn his loindrapes and don several gold ear-cuffs—for not even the poorest man in Gujaareh's capital went without some ornamentation—Ehiru left the old wall and walked the streets as a man of no particular caste, nondescript in manner, taking care to slouch in order to lessen his stature. At such a late hour he saw only caravanners, making the final preparations for a journey on the morrow, and a yawning guardsman, doubtless headed for a night shift at one of the city gates. None of them noticed him.

The houses became less dense once he reached the highcaste district. He turned down a side street lit poorly with half-burned-out lanterns, and emerged amid a gaggle of young shunha men who reeked of a timbalin house and a woman's stale perfume. They were laughing and staggering together, their wits slowed by the drug. He trailed in their wake for a block before they even marked his presence and then slipped aside, down another side street. This one led to the storage barn of the guesthouse he sought. The barn doors stood open, barrels of wine and twine-wrapped parcels in plain view along the walls—unmolested; Gujaareh's few thieves knew better. Slipping into the shadows here, Ehiru removed his show-jewelry and turned his drapes once more, rolling and tying them so they would not flap. On one side, the drapes bore an unassuming pattern, but on the other—the side he wore now—they were completely black.

The day before, Ehiru had investigated the guesthouse. As shrewd as any merchant-casteman, the house's proprietor kept his tower open year-round to cater to wealthy foreigners, many of whom disliked relocating during the spring floods. This tithebearer—a northern trader—had a private room in the tower, which was separated from the rest of the building by a flight of steep stairs. Convenient. Hananja made way when She wanted a thing done.

Within the house, the kitchen was dim, as was the serving chamber beyond. Ehiru moved past the table with its low cushions and through the house's atrium garden, slowing as he turned aside fronds of palms and dangling ferns. Beyond the garden lay the sleeping chambers. Here he crept most stealthily of all, for even at such a late hour there could have been guests awake, but all of the rooms' lanterns remained shuttered and he heard only slow, steady breathing from each curtained entrance. Good.

As he climbed the tower steps, Ehiru heard the trader's unpeaceful snores even through the room's heavy wooden door. Getting the door open without causing its hinges to creak took some doing, but he managed it while privately damning the outland custom of putting doors on inner chambers. Inside the room, the trader's snores were so loud that the gauze curtains around his bed shivered in vibration. No wonder the proprietor had offered him the tower, and probably discounted the room. Still, Ehiru was cautious; he waited until a particularly harsh snort to part the curtains and gaze down at his next commission.

This close, the scent of the man mingled rancid sweat, stale grease, and other odors into a pungent mix that left Ehiru momentarily queasy. He had forgotten the infrequent bathing habits of people from the north. Though the night was cool and breezy, the northerner—a trader from the Bromarte people, the commission had specified, though in truth Ehiru had never been able to tell one northern tribe from another—sweated profusely, his pale skin flushed and rash-prickled as if he slept in high noon's swelter. Ehiru studied that face for a moment, wondering what peace might be coaxed from the dreams of such a man.

There would be something, he decided at last, for Hananja would not have chosen him otherwise. The man was lucky. She did not often bestow Her blessings upon foreigners.

The Bromarte's eyes already flickered beneath their lids; no jungissa was necessary to send him into the proper state of sleep. Laying fingers on the man's eyelids, Ehiru willed his own soul to part from flesh, leaving its connection—the umblikeh—tethered in place so that he could follow it back when the time came. The bedchamber had become a shadow-place, colorless and insubstantial, when Ehiru opened his soul's eyes. A reflection of the waking realm, unimportant. Only one thing had meaning in this halfway place between waking and dreaming: the delicate, shimmering red tether that emerged from somewhere near the Bromarte's collarbones and trailed away into nothingness. This was the path the man's soul had taken on its journey to Ina-Karekh, the land of dreams. It was a simple matter for Ehiru to follow the same path *out* and then *in* again.

When he opened his soul's eyes this time, color and vast strangeness surrounded him, for he was in Ina-Karekh, the land of dreams. And here the dream of the Bromarte revealed itself. Charleron of Wenkinsclan, came the name to Ehiru's consciousness, and he absorbed the name's foreignness and as much as he could of the person who bore it. Not a soulname, but that was to be expected. Bromarte parents named their children for the hopes and needs of the waking world, not protection in sleep. By the reckoning of this Charleron's people, his was a name of ambition. A name of *hunger.* And hunger was what filled the Bromarte's soul: hunger for wealth, for respect, for things he himself could not name. Reflected in the dreamscapes of Ina-Karekh, these hungers had coalesced into a great yawning pit in the earth, its walls lined with countless disembodied, groping hands. Assuming his usual dreamform, Ehiru floated down through the hands and ignored their silent, scrabbling, blind need as he searched.

And there, at the bottom of the well of hands, weeping with fear and helplessness, knelt the manifestation of the unfortunately named Bromarte man. Charleron cringed between sobs, trying and failing to twist away from his own creations as the hands plucked at him again and again. They did him no harm and would have been only moderately frightening to any properly trained dreamer—but this was nevertheless the bile of dreams, Ehiru judged: black and bitter, necessary for health but unpleasant to the senses. He absorbed as much of it as he could for the Sharers, for there was much of use in dream-bile even if Charleron might not agree. But he reserved space within himself for the most important humor, which after all was why he had come.

And as they always did, as the Goddess had decreed they must, the bearer of Hananja's tithe looked up and saw Ehiru in his true, unadulterated shape.

"Who are you?" the Bromarte demanded, distracted momentarily from his terror. A hand grabbed his shoulder and he gasped and flinched away.

"Ehiru," he said. He considered giving the man his soulname and then decided against it. Soulnames meant nothing to heathens. But to his surprise, the Bromarte's eyes widened as if in recognition.

"*Gualoh*," the Bromarte said, and through the filter of their shared dream, a whiff of meaning came to Ehiru. Some kind of frightening creature from their nightfire tales? He dismissed it: barbarian superstition.

"A servant of the Goddess of Dreams," Ehiru corrected, crouching before the man. Hands plucked nervously at his skin and loincloth and the twin braids that dangled from his nape, responding to the Bromarte's fear of him. He paid them no heed. "You have been chosen for Her. Come, and I will shepherd you to a better place than this, where you may live out eternity in peace." He extended his hand.

The Bromarte leaped at him.

The movement caught Ehiru by such surprise that he almost failed to react in time—but no common man could best a Gatherer in dreaming. With a flick of his will, Ehiru banished the well of hands and replaced it with an innocuous desert of wind-waved dunes. This afforded him plenty of room to sidestep the Bromarte's headlong rush. The Bromarte ran at him again, roaring obscenities; Ehiru opened and then closed the ground beneath the Bromarte's feet, dropping him to the waist in sand.

Even thus pinned, the Bromarte cursed and flailed and wept, grabbing handfuls of the sand to fling at him—which Ehiru simply willed away. Then, frowning in puzzlement, he crouched to peer into the Bromarte's face.

"It's pointless to fight," he said, and the Bromarte flinched into stillness at the sound of his voice, though Ehiru had kept his tone gentle. "Relax, and the journey will go soft." Surely the Bromarte knew this? His people had been trading goods and seed with Gujaareh for centuries. In case that was the source of the Bromarte's panic, Ehiru added, "There will be no pain."

"Get away from me, *gualoh*! I'm not one of you mud-grubbers; I don't need you feeding on my dreams!"

"It is true that you aren't Gujaareen," Ehiru replied. Without taking his attention from the man, he began adjusting the dreamscape to elicit calm. The clouds overhead became wispy and gentle, and he made the sand around the Bromarte's dreamform finer, pleasant against the skin. "But foreigners have been Gathered before. The warning is given to all who choose to live and do business within our capital's walls: Hananja's city obeys Hananja's Law."

Something of Ehiru's words finally seemed to penetrate the Bromarte's panic. His bottom lip quivered. "I, I don't want to die." He was actually weeping, his shoulders heaving, so much that Ehiru could not help pitying him. It was terrible that the northerners had no narcomancy. They were helpless in dreaming, at the mercy of their nightmares, and none of them had any training in the sublimation of fear. How many had been lost to the shadowlands because of it? They had no Gatherers, either, to ease the way.

"Few people desire death," Ehiru agreed. He reached out to stroke the man's forehead, brushing thin hair aside, to reassure him. "Even my countrymen, who claim to love Hananja, sometimes fight their fate. But it's the nature of the world that some must die so that others may live. You will die—early and unpleasantly if the whore's disease you brought to Gujaareh runs its course. And in that time you might not only suffer, but spread your suffering to others. Why not die in peace and spread life instead?"

"Liar." Suddenly the Bromarte's face was piggish, his small eyes glittering with hate. The change came so abruptly that Ehiru faltered to silence, startled. "You call it a blessing of your Goddess, but I know what it really is." He leaned forward; his breath had gone foul. "*It gives you pleasure.*"

Ehiru drew back from that breath, and the fouler words. Above their heads, the wispy clouds stopped drifting. "No Gatherer kills for pleasure."

"'No Gatherer kills for pleasure.'" The Bromarte drawled the words, mocking. "And what of those who *do*, Gatherer?" The Bromarte grinned, his teeth gleaming momentarily sharp. "Are they Gatherers no longer? There's another name for those, yes? Is that how you tell your lie?"

Coldness passed through Ehiru; close on its heels came angry heat. "This is obscenity," he snapped, "and I will hear no more of it."

"Gatherers comfort the dying, yes?"

"Gatherers comfort those who believe in peace, and welcome Hananja's blessing," Ehiru snapped. "Gatherers can do little for unbelievers who mock Her comfort." He got to his feet and scowled to himself in annoyance. The man's nonsense had distracted him; the sand rippled and bubbled around them, heaving like the breath of a living thing. But before he could resume control of the dream and force the Bromarte's mind to settle, a hand grasped his ankle. Startled, he looked down.

"They're using you," said the Bromarte.

Alarm stilled Ehiru's mind. "What?"

The Bromarte nodded. His eyes were gentler now, his expression almost kind. As pitying as Ehiru himself had been, a moment before. "You will know. Soon. They'll use you to nothing, and there will be no one to comfort *you* in the end, Gatherer." He laughed and the landscape heaved around them, laughing with him. "Such a shame, Nsha Ehiru. Such a shame!"

Gooseflesh tightened Ehiru's skin, though the skin was not real. The mind did what was necessary to protect the soul at such times, and Ehiru suddenly felt great need of protection—for the Bromarte *knew his soulname*, though he had not given it.

He jerked away from the man's grip and pulled out of his dream in the same reflexive rush. But to Ehiru's horror, the clumsy exit tore free the tether that bound the Bromarte to his flesh. Too soon! He had not moved the Bromarte to a safer place within the realm of dreams. And now the soul fluttered along in his wake like flotsam, twisting and fragmenting no matter how he tried to push it back toward Ina-Karekh. He collected the spilled dreamblood out of desperation but shuddered as it came into him sluggishly, clotted with fear and malice. In the dark between worlds, the Bromarte's last laugh faded into silence.

Ehiru returned to himself with a gasp, and looked down. His gorge rose so powerfully that he stumbled away from the bed, leaning against the windowsill and sucking quick shallow breaths to keep from vomiting.

"*Holiest mistress of comfort and peace*..." He whispered the prayer in Sua out of habit, closing his eyes and still seeing the

Bromarte's dead face: eyes wide and bulging, mouth open, teeth bared in a hideous rictus. What had he done? *O Hananja, forgive me for profaning Your rite.*

He would leave no rose-signature behind this time. The final dream was never supposed to go so wrong—certainly not under the supervision of a Gatherer of his experience. He shuddered as he recalled the reek of the Bromarte's breath, like that of something already rotted. Yet how much fouler had it been for the Bromarte, who had now been hurled through Ehiru's carelessness into the nightmare hollows of Ina-Karekh for all eternity? And that only if enough of his soul had been left intact to return.

Yet even as disgust gave way to grief, and even as Ehiru bowed beneath the weight of both, intuition sounded a faint warning in his mind.

He looked up. Beyond the window rose the rooftops of the city, and beyond those the glowing curve of the Dreamer sank steadily toward the horizon. Waking Moon peeked round its larger curve. The city had grown still in the last moments of Moonlight; even the thieves and lovers slept. All except himself—

—And a silhouette, hunched against the cistern on a nearby rooftop.

Ehiru frowned and pushed himself upright.

The figure straightened as he did, mirroring his movement. Ehiru could make out no details aside from shape: male, naked or nearly so, tall and yet oddly stooped in posture. Indeterminate features and caste, indeterminate intent.

No. That much, at least, was discernible. Ehiru could glean little else from the figure's stillness, but *malevolence* whispered clearly in the wind between them.

The tableau lasted only a moment. Then the figure turned, climbed the cistern's rope to its roof, and leaped onto an adjoining building and out of sight. The night became still once more. But not peaceful.

Gualoh, echoed the Bromarte's voice in Ehiru's memory. Not an insult, he realized, staring at where the figure had been. A warning.

Demon.

MINIMAL PLATE
The Arctics
Tundra
NOMIDLATS
MAXIMAL PLATE

Orbit
Hachette Book Group
1290 Avenue of the Americas
New York, NY 10104
orbitbooks.net

Simultaneously published in Great Britain and in the U.S. by Orbit in 2017

First Edition: August 2017

Orbit is an imprint of Hachette Book Group.
The Orbit name and logo are trademarks of Little, Brown Book Group Limited.

The publisher is not responsible for websites (or their content) that are not owned by the publisher.

The Hachette Speakers Bureau provides a wide range of authors for speaking events. To find out more, go to www.hachettespeakersbureau.com or call (866) 376-6591.

Library of Congress Cataloging-in-Publication Data

Names: Jemisin, N. K., author.
Title: The stone sky / N.K. Jemisin.
Description: First Edition. | New York : Orbit, 2017. | Series: The broken earth ; book 3
Identifiers: LCCN 2017017064| ISBN 9780316229241 (paperback) | ISBN 9781478916291 (audio book downloadable) | ISBN 9780316229258 (ebook open)
Subjects: | BISAC: FICTION / Fantasy / Epic. | FICTION / Action & Adventure. | GSAFD: Fantasy fiction.
Classification: LCC PS3610.E46 S76 2017 | DDC 813/.6—dc23
LC record available at https://lccn.loc.gov/2017017064

ISBNs: 978-0-316-22924-1 (trade paperback), 978-0-316-22925-8 (ebook)

Printed in the United States of America

LSC-C

9 10

THE STONE SKY

THE BROKEN EARTH: BOOK THREE

N. K. JEMISIN

www.orbitbooks.net

By N. K. Jemisin

THE INHERITANCE TRILOGY
The Hundred Thousand Kingdoms
The Broken Kingdoms
The Kingdom of Gods
The Awakened Kingdom (novella)

The Inheritance Trilogy (omnibus)

DREAMBLOOD
The Killing Moon
The Shadowed Sun

THE BROKEN EARTH
The Fifth Season
The Obelisk Gate
The Stone Sky

Praise for
THE DREAMBLOOD DUOLOGY

"Ah, N. K. Jemisin, you can do no wrong." —Felicia Day

"*The Killing Moon* is a powerhouse and, in general, one hell of a story to read. Jemisin has arrived." —*Bookworm Blues*

"The author's exceptional ability to tell a compelling story and her talent for world-building have assured her place at the forefront of fantasy." —*Library Journal* (starred review)

"Jemisin excels at world-building and the inclusion of a diverse mix of characters makes her settings feel even more real and vivid." —*RT Book Reviews* (Top Pick!)

"The novel also showcases some skillful, original world-building. Like a lucid dreamer, Jemisin takes real-world influences as diverse as ancient Egyptian culture and Freudian/Jungian dream theory and unites them to craft a new world that feels both familiar and entirely new. It's all refreshingly unique."
—*Slant Magazine*

"Read this or miss out on one of the best fantasy books of the year so far." —*San Francisco Book Review*

"N. K. Jemisin is playing with the gods again—and it's just as good as the first time." —*io9*

"A similar blend of inventiveness, irreverence, and sophistication—along with sensuality—brings vivid life to the setting and other characters: human and otherwise... *The Hundred Thousand Kingdoms* definitely leaves me wanting more of this delightful new writer."

—*Locus*

"A compelling page-turner."

—*The A.V. Club*

"An absorbing story, an intriguing setting and world mythology, and a likable narrator with a compelling voice. The next book cannot come out soon enough."

—fantasybookcafe.com

"*The Broken Kingdoms*... expands the universe of the series geographically, historically, magically and in the range of characters, while keeping the same superb prose and gripping narrative that made the first one such a memorable debut."

—*Fantasy Book Critic*

"*The Kingdom of Gods* once again proves Jemisin's skill and consistency as a storyteller, but what sets her apart from the crowd is her ability to imagine and describe the mysteries of the universe in language that is at once elegant and profane, and thus, true."

—*Shelf Awareness*

Praise for
THE INHERITANCE TRILOGY

"A complex, edge-of-your-seat story with plenty of funny, scary, and bittersweet twists."

—*Publishers Weekly* (starred review)

"An offbeat, engaging tale by a talented and original newcomer."

—*Kirkus*

"An astounding debut novel...the world-building is solid, the characterization superb, the plot complicated but clear."

—*RT Book Reviews* (Top Pick!)

"A delight for the fantasy reader."

—*Library Journal* (starred review)

"*The Hundred Thousand Kingdoms*...is an impressive debut, which revitalizes the trope of empires whose rulers have gods at their fingertips." —*io9*

"N. K. Jemisin has written a fascinating epic fantasy where the stakes are not just the fate of kingdoms but of the world and the universe." —*SFRevu*

"Many books are good, some are great, but few are truly important. Add to this last category *The Hundred Thousand Kingdoms*, N. K. Jemisin's debut novel...In this reviewer's opinion, this is the must-read fantasy of the year." —*BookPage*

Praise for

THE FIFTH SEASON

"Intricate and extraordinary." —*New York Times*

"Astounding... Jemisin maintains a gripping voice and an emotional core that not only carries the story through its complicated setting, but sets things up for even more staggering revelations to come." —*NPR Books*

"Jemisin's graceful prose and gritty setting provide the perfect backdrop for this fascinating tale of determined characters fighting to save a doomed world." —*Publishers Weekly* (starred review)

"A must-buy... breaks uncharted ground."
—*Library Journal* (starred review)

"Jemisin might just be the best world-builder out there right now.... [She] is a master at what she does."
—*RT Book Reviews* (Top Pick!)

"A powerful, epic novel of discovery, pain, and heartbreak."
—SFFWorld.com

"Brilliant... gorgeous writing and unexpected plot twists."
—*Washington Post*

"An ambitious book... Jemisin's work itself is part of a slow but definite change in sci-fi and fantasy." —*Guardian*

"Angrily, beautifully apocalyptic."
—*B&N Sci-Fi & Fantasy Blog*

Praise for
THE OBELISK GATE

"Jemisin's follow-up to *The Fifth Season* is exceptional. Those who anxiously awaited this sequel will find the only problem is that the wait must begin again once the last page is turned."

—*Library Journal* (starred review)

"Stunning, again." —*Kirkus* (starred review)

"Compelling, challenging, and utterly gripping."

—*Publishers Weekly* (starred review)

"Beyond the meticulous pacing, the thorough character work, and the staggering ambition and revelations of the narration, Jemisin is telling a story of our present, our failures, our actions in the face of repeated trauma, our responses to the heat and pressure of our times. Her accomplishment in this series is tremendous. It pole-vaults over the expectations I had for what epic fantasy should be and stands in magnificent testimony to what it could be."

—*NPR Books*

"How can something as large and complex exist in [Jemisin's] head, and how does she manage to tell it to me so beautifully? I can't stand how much I love the Broken Earth trilogy so far."

—*B&N Sci-Fi & Fantasy Blog*

You're staring at Jija, but you're thinking of Alabaster. Don't know why.

"One person's normal is another person's Shattering." Your face aches from smiling. There is an art to smiling in a way that others will believe, and you're terrible at it. "Would've been nice if we could've all had normal, of course, but not enough people wanted to share. So now we all burn."

The villager stares at you for a long, vaguely horrified moment. Then he mumbles something and finally goes away, skirting wide around Hoa. Good riddance.

You crouch beside Jija. He is beautiful like this, all jewels and colors. He is monstrous like this. Beneath the colors you perceive the crazed every-which-wayness of the magic threads in him. It's wholly different from what happened to your arm and your breast. He has been smashed apart and rearranged at random, on an infinitesimal level.

"What have I done?" you ask. "What have I made her?"

Hoa's toes have appeared in your peripheral vision. "Strong," he suggests.

You shake your head. Nassun was that on her own.

"*Alive*."

You close your eyes again. It's the only thing that should matter, that you've brought three babies into the world and this one, this precious last one, is still breathing. And yet.

I made her me. Earth eat us both, I made her into **me**.

And maybe that's why Nassun is still alive. But it's also, you realize as you stare at what she's done to Jija, and as you realize you can't even get revenge on him for Uche because *your daughter has done that for you*... why you are terrified of her.

"Obelisk Gate?"

Antimony's gaze has been focused on Alabaster. Now her flat black eyes slide to finally meet yours.

"The two hundred and sixteen individual obelisks, networked together via the control cabochon." While you stand there wondering what the rust a control cabochon is, and marveling that there are more than two hundred of the damned things, she adds, "Using *that* to channel the power of the Rift should be enough."

"To do what?"

For the first time, you hear a note of emotion in her voice: annoyance. "To impose equilibrium on the Earth-Moon system."

What? "Alabaster said the Moon was flung away."

"Into a degrading long-ellipsis orbit." When you stare blankly, she speaks your language again. "It's coming back."

Oh, Earth. Oh, rust. Oh, no. "*You want me to catch the fucking Moon?*"

Praise for

THE FIFTH SEASON

"Intricate and extraordinary." —*The New York Times*

"Astounding...Jemisin maintains a gripping voice and an emotional core that not only carries the story through its complicated setting, but sets things up for even more staggering revelations to come." —*NPR Books*

"Jemisin's graceful prose and gritty setting provide the perfect backdrop for this fascinating tale of determined characters fighting to save a doomed world." —*Publishers Weekly* (Starred Review)

"A must-buy...breaks uncharted ground."

—*Library Journal* (starred review)

"Jemisin might just be the best world-builder out there right now....[She] is a master at what she does."

—RT Book Reviews (Top Pick!)

"A powerful, epic novel of discovery, pain, and heartbreak."

—SFFWorld.com

"Brilliant...gorgeous writing and unexpected plot twists."

—*Washington Post*

"An ambitious book...Jemisin's work itself is part of a slow but definite change in sci-fi and fantasy." —*Guardian*

"Angrily, beautifully apocalyptic."

—B&N Sci-Fi & Fantasy Blog

Praise for
THE INHERITANCE TRILOGY

"A complex, edge-of-your-seat story with plenty of funny, scary, and bittersweet twists."

—*Publishers Weekly* (Starred Review)

"An offbeat, engaging tale by a talented and original newcomer."

—*Kirkus*

"An astounding debut novel...the world-building is solid, the characterization superb, the plot complicated but clear."

—*RT Book Reviews* (Top Pick!)

"A delight for the fantasy reader."

—*Library Journal* (Starred Review)

"*The Hundred Thousand Kingdoms*...is an impressive debut, which revitalizes the trope of empires whose rulers have gods at their fingertips."

—io9

"N. K. Jemisin has written a fascinating epic fantasy where the stakes are not just the fate of kingdoms but of the world and the universe."

—SFRevu

"Many books are good, some are great, but few are truly important. Add to this last category *The Hundred Thousand Kingdoms*, N. K. Jemisin's debut novel...In this reviewer's opinion, this is the must-read fantasy of the year."

—*BookPage*

"A similar blend of inventiveness, irreverence, and sophistication—along with sensuality—brings vivid life to the setting and other characters: human and otherwise... *The Hundred Thousand Kingdoms* definitely leaves me wanting more of this delightful new writer."
—*Locus*

"A compelling page-turner."
—The A.V. Club

"An absorbing story, an intriguing setting and world mythology, and a likable narrator with a compelling voice. The next book cannot come out soon enough."
—fantasybookcafe.com

"*The Broken Kingdoms*... expands the universe of the series geographically, historically, magically and in the range of characters, while keeping the same superb prose and gripping narrative that made the first one such a memorable debut."
—Fantasy Book Critic

"*The Kingdom of Gods* once again proves Jemisin's skill and consistency as a storyteller, but what sets her apart from the crowd is her ability to imagine and describe the mysteries of the universe in language that is at once elegant and profane, and thus, true."
—Shelf Awareness

Praise for the
DREAMBLOOD DUOLOGY

"Ah, N. K. Jemisin, you can do no wrong." —Felicia Day

"*The Killing Moon* is a powerhouse and, in general, one hell of a story to read. Jemisin has arrived." —Bookworm Blues

"The author's exceptional ability to tell a compelling story and her talent for world-building have assured her place at the forefront of fantasy." —*Library Journal* (Starred Review)

"Jemisin excels at world-building and the inclusion of a diverse mix of characters makes her settings feel even more real and vivid." —RT Book Reviews (Top Pick!)

"The novel also showcases some skillful, original world-building. Like a lucid dreamer, Jemisin takes real-world influences as diverse as ancient Egyptian culture and Freudian/Jungian dream theory and unites them to craft a new world that feels both familiar and entirely new. It's all refreshingly unique." —Slant Magazine

"Read this or miss out on one of the best fantasy books of the year so far." —San Francisco Book Review

"N. K. Jemisin is playing with the gods again—and it's just as good as the first time." —io9

THE OBELISK GATE

By N. K. Jemisin

THE INHERITANCE TRILOGY
The Hundred Thousand Kingdoms
The Broken Kingdoms
The Kingdom of Gods
The Awakened Kingdom (novella)

The Inheritance Trilogy (omnibus)

DREAMBLOOD
The Killing Moon
The Shadowed Sun

THE BROKEN EARTH
The Fifth Season
The Obelisk Gate

THE OBELISK GATE

THE BROKEN EARTH: BOOK TWO

N. K. JEMISIN

www.orbitbooks.net

Cover design by Lauren Panepinto
Cover photo © Arcangel Images

Orbit
Hachette Book Group
1290 Avenue of the Americas
New York, NY 10104
orbitbooks.net

First Edition: August 2016

Orbit is an imprint of Hachette Book Group.

Map © Tim Paul

ISBNs: 978-0-316-22926-5 (trade paperback), 978-0-316-22928-9 (ebook)

Printed in the United States of America

LSC-H

12

To those who have no choice but to prepare their children for the battlefield

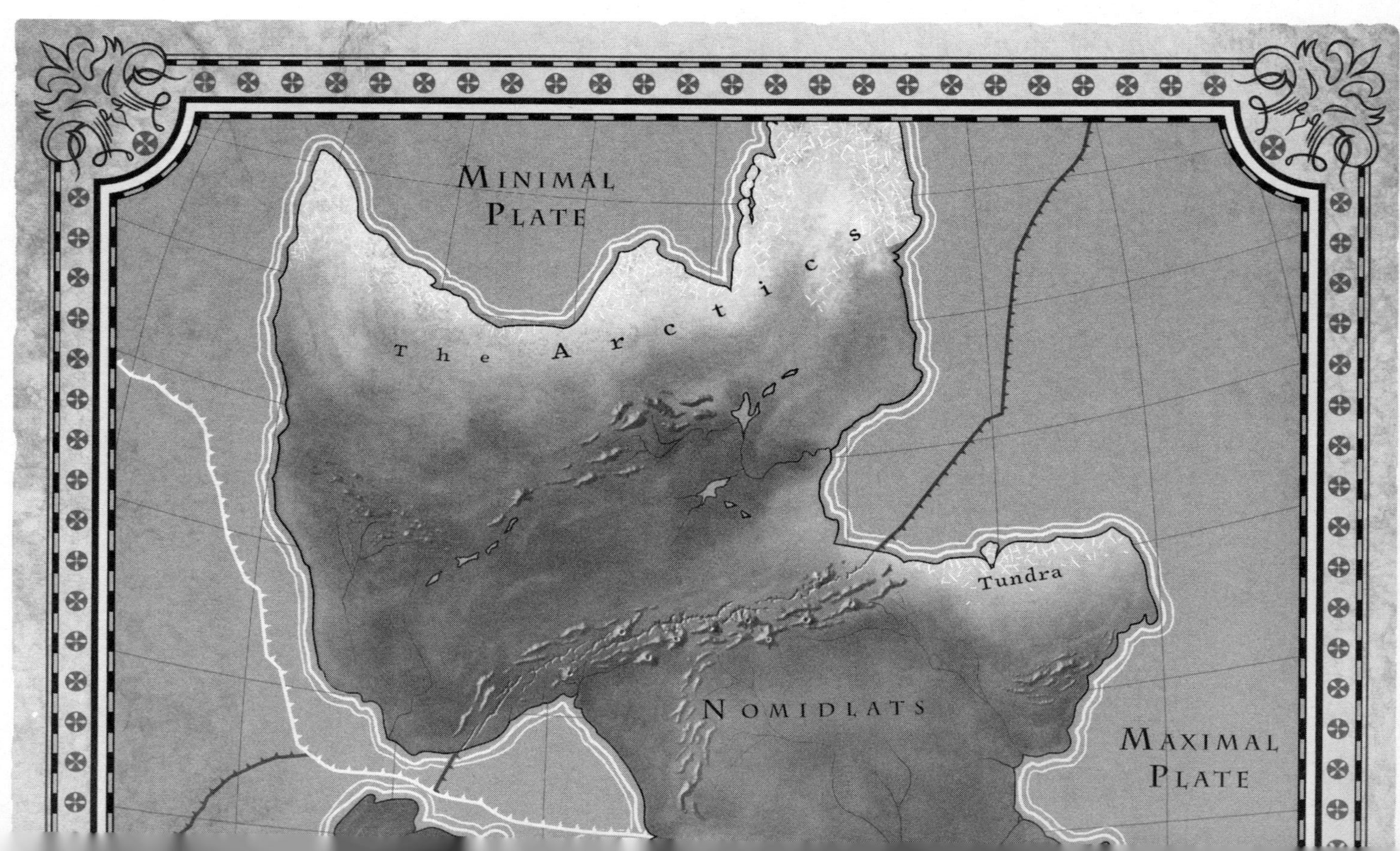
Minimal Plate
The Arctics
Tundra
Nomidlats
Maximal Plate

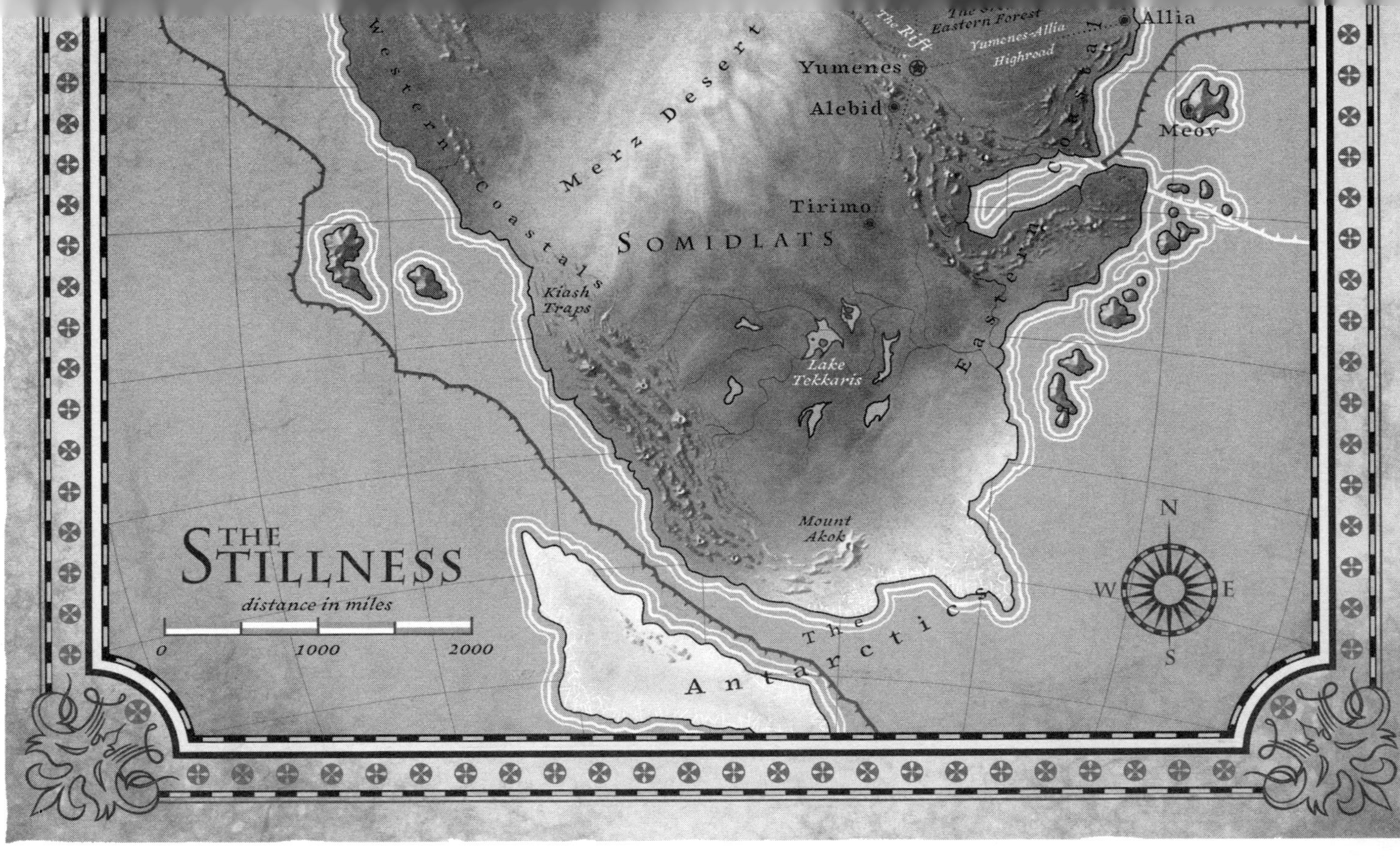

The Stillness
distance in miles
0
1000
2000
Allia
Eastern Forest
The Rift
Yumenes-Allia Highroad
Yumenes
Alebid
Meov
Merz Desert
Western Coastals
Tirimo
Somidlats
Kiash Traps
Lake Tekkaris
Eastern
Mount Akok
The Antarctics
N
S
E
W

1

Nassun, on the rocks

HMM. NO. I'M TELLING THIS WRONG.

After all, a person is herself, and others. Relationships chisel the final shape of one's being. I am me, and you. Damaya was herself *and* the family that rejected her *and* the people of the Fulcrum who chiseled her to a fine point. Syenite was Alabaster *and* Innon *and* the people of poor lost Allia and Meov. Now you are Tirimo *and* the ash-strewn road's walkers *and* your dead children...and also the living one who remains. Whom you will get back.

That's not a spoiler. You are Essun, after all. You know this already. Don't you?

Nassun next, then. Nassun, who is just eight years old when the world ends.

There is no knowing what went through little Nassun's mind when she came home from her apprenticeship one afternoon to find her younger brother dead on the den floor, and her father standing over the corpse. We can imagine what she thought, felt, did. We can speculate. But we will not *know*. Perhaps that is for the best.

Here is what I know for certain: that apprenticeship I mentioned? Nassun was in training to become a lorist.

The Stillness has an odd relationship with its self-appointed keepers of stonelore. There are records of lorists existing as far back as the long-rumored Eggshell Season. That's the one in which some sort of gaseous emission caused all children born in the Arctics for several years to have delicate bones that broke with a touch and bent as they grew—if they grew. (Yumenescene archeomests have argued for centuries over whether this could have been caused by strontium or arsenic, and whether it should be counted as a Season at all given that it only affected a few hundred thousand weak, pallid little barbarians on the northern tundra. But that is *when* the peoples of the Arctics gained a reputation for weakness.) About twenty-five thousand years ago, according to the lorists themselves, which most people think is a blatant lie. In truth, lorists are an even older part of life in the Stillness. Twenty-five thousand years ago is simply when their role became distorted into near-uselessness.

They're still around, though they've forgotten how much they've forgotten. Somehow their order, if it can be called an order, survives despite the First through Seventh Universities disavowing their work as apocryphal and probably inaccurate, and despite governments down all the ages undermining their knowledge with propaganda. And despite the Seasons, of course. Once lorists came only from a race called Regwo—Westcoasters who had sallow-reddish skin and naturally black lips, and who worshipped the preservation of history the way people in less-bitter times worshipped gods. They used to chisel stonelore into mountainsides in tablets as high as the sky, so that all would see and know the wisdom needed to survive. Alas: in the Stillness, destroying mountains is as easy as an orogene toddler's temper tantrum. Destroying a people takes only a bit more effort.

So lorists are no longer Regwo, but most of them tint their lips black in the Regwo's memory. Not that they remember why, anymore. Now it's just how one knows a lorist: by the lips, and by the stack of polymer tablets they carry, and by the shabby clothes they tend to wear, and by the fact that they usually do not have real comm names. They aren't commless, mind. In theory they could return to their home comms in the event of a Season, although by profession they tend to wander far enough to make returning impractical. In practice, many communities will take them in, even during a Season, because even the most stoic community wants entertainment during the long cold nights. For this reason, most lorists train in the arts—music and comedy and such. They also act as teachers and caretakers of the young in times when no one else can be spared for such duty, and most importantly they serve as a living reminder that others have survived worse through the ages. Every comm needs that.

The lorist who has come to Tirimo is named Renthree Lorist Stone. (All lorists take the comm name Stone, and the use name Lorist, it being one of the rarer use-castes.) She is mostly unimportant, but there is a reason you must know of her. She was once Renthree Breeder Tenteek, but that was before she fell in love with a lorist who visited Tenteek and seduced the then-young woman away from a boring life as a glass-smith. Her life would have become slightly more interesting if a Season had occurred before she left, for a Breeder's responsibility in those times is clear—and perhaps that, too, is what spurred her away. Or maybe it was just the usual folly of young love? Hard to say. Renthree's lorist lover eventually left her on the outskirts of the Equatorial city of Penphen, with a broken heart and a head full of lore, and a wallet full of chipped jades and cabochons and one shoeprint-stained lozenge of mother-of-pearl. Renthree spent the mother-of-pearl to commission her own set of tablets from a knapper, used the jade chips to buy traveling supplies and to stay at an inn for the days it took the knapper to finish, and bought many strong drinks at a tavern with the cabochons. Then, newly outfitted and with wounds patched, she set out on her own. Thus does the profession perpetuate itself.

When Nassun appears at the way station where she has set up shop, it's possible that Renthree thinks about her own apprenticeship. (Not the seduction part; obviously Renthree likes older women, emphasis on women. The foolish dreamer part.) The day previous, Renthree passed through Tirimo, shopping at market stalls and smiling cheerfully through her black-daubed lips so as to advertise her presence in the area. She did not see Nassun, on her way home from creche, stop and stare in awe and sudden, irrational hope.

Nassun has skipped creche today to come and find her, and to bring an offering. This is traditional—the offering, that is, and not teachers' daughters skipping creche. Two adults from town are already at the way station, sitting on a bench to listen while Renthree talks, and Renthree's offering cup has already been filled with brightly colored shards faceted with the quartent's mark. Renthree blinks in surprise at the sight of Nassun: a gangly girl who is more leg than torso, more eyes than face, and very obviously too young to be out of creche so early when it isn't harvest season.

Nassun stops on the threshold of the way station, panting to catch her breath, which makes for a very dramatic entrance. The other two visitors turn to stare at her, Jija's normally quiet firstborn, and only their presence stops Nassun from blurting her intentions right then and there. Her mother has taught her to be very circumspect. (Her mother will hear about her skipping creche. Nassun doesn't care.) She swallows, however, and goes to Renthree immediately to hold out something: a dark chunk of rock, embedded in which can be seen a small, almost cubical diamond.

Nassun doesn't have any money beyond her allowance, you see, and she'd already spent that on books and sweets when word came that a lorist was in town. But no one in Tirimo knows that there's a potentially excellent diamond mine in the region—no one, that is, except orogenes. And then only if they're looking. Nassun's the only one who's bothered in several thousand years. She knows she should not have found this diamond. Her mother has taught her not to display her orogeny, and not to use it outside of carefully proscribed practice sessions that they undertake in a nearby valley every few weeks. No one carries diamonds for currency because they can't be sharded for change easily, but they're still useful in industry, mining, and the like. Nassun knows it has some value, but she has no inkling that the pretty rock she's just given to Renthree is worth a house or two. She's only eight.

And Nassun is so excited, when she sees Renthree's eyes widen at the sight of the glittering lump poking out of the black hunk of rock, that she stops caring that there are others present and blurts, "I want to be a lorist, too!"

Nassun has no idea what a lorist really does, of course. She just knows that she wants very very much to leave Tirimo.

More on this later.

Renthree would be a fool to refuse the offering, and she doesn't. But she doesn't give Nassun an answer right away, partly because she thinks Nassun is cute and that her declaration is no different from any other child's momentary passion. (She's right, to a degree; last month Nassun wanted to be a geneer.) Instead she asks Nassun to sit, and then she tells stories to her small audience for the rest of the afternoon, until the sun makes long shadows down the valley slope and through the trees. When the other two visitors get up to head home, they eye Nassun and drop hints until she reluctantly comes with them, because the people of Tirimo will not have it said that they disrespected a lorist by letting some child talk her to death all night.

In the wake of her visitors, Renthree stokes up the fire and starts making dinner from a bit of pork belly and greens and cornmeal that she bought in Tirimo the day before. While she waits for dinner to cook and eats an apple, she turns Nassun's rock in her fingers, fascinated. And troubled.

In the morning she heads into Tirimo. A few discreet inquiries lead her to Nassun's home. Essun's gone by this point, off to teach the last class of her career as a creche teacher. Nassun's gone off to creche, too, though she's biding her time till she can escape at lunchtime to go find the lorist again. Jija's in his "workshop," as he calls the offset room that passes for the house's basement, where he works on commissions with his noisy tools during the day. Uche is asleep on a pallet in the same room. He can sleep through anything. The songs of the earth have always been his lullaby.

Jija comes to the door when Renthree knocks, and for an instant she's a little taken aback. Jija is a Midlatter mongrel, same as Essun, though his heritage leans more toward the Sanzed; he's big and brown and muscular and bald-shaven. Intimidating. Yet the welcoming smile on his face is wholly genuine, which makes Renthree feel better about what she's decided to do. This is a good man. She cannot cheat him.

"Here," she says, giving him the diamond rock. She can't possibly take such a valuable gift from a child, not in exchange for a few stories and an apprenticeship that Nassun will probably change her mind about in a few months. Jija frowns in confusion and takes the rock, thanking her profusely after he hears her explanation. He promises to spread the tale of Renthree's generosity and integrity to everyone he can, which will hopefully give her more opportunities to practice her art before she leaves town.

Renthree leaves, and that is the end of her part in this tale. It is a significant part, however, which is why I told you of her.

There was not any one thing that turned Jija against his son, understand. Over the years he simply had noticed things about his wife and his children that stirred suspicion in the depths of his mind. That stirring had grown to a tickle, then an outright irritant by the point at which this tale begins, but denial kept him from worrying at the thought any further. He loved his family, after all, and the truth was simply... unthinkable. Literally.

He would have figured it out eventually, one way or another. I repeat: *He would have figured it out eventually.* No one is to blame but him.

But if you want a simple explanation, and if there can be any one event that became the tipping point, the camel straw, the broken plug on the lava tube...it was this rock. Because Jija knew stone, you see. He was an excellent knapper. He knew stone, and he knew Tirimo, and he knew that veins of igneous rock from an ancient volcano ran all through the surrounding land. Most did not breach the surface, but it was entirely possible that Nassun could by chance find a diamond sitting out where anyone could pick it up. Unlikely. But possible.

This understanding floats on the surface of Jija's mind for the rest of the day after Renthree leaves. The truth is beneath the surface, a leviathan waiting to uncurl, but the waters of his thoughts are placid for now. Denial is powerful.

But then Uche wakes up. Jija walks him into the den, asking him if he's hungry; Uche says he isn't. Then he smiles at Jija, and with the unerring sensitivity of a powerful orogene child, he orients on Jija's pocket and says, "Why is shiny there, Daddy?"

The words, in his lisping toddler-language, are cute. The knowledge that he possesses, because the rock is indeed in Jija's pocket and there's no way Uche could have known it was there, dooms him.

Nassun does not know that it started with the rock. When you see her, do not tell her.

When Nassun comes home that afternoon, Uche is already dead. Jija is standing over his cooling corpse in the den, breathing hard. It doesn't take a lot of effort to beat a toddler to death, but he hyperventilated while he did it. When Nassun comes in, there's still not enough carbon dioxide in Jija's bloodstream; he's dizzy, shaky, chilled. Irrational. So when Nassun pulls up sharply in the doorway of the den, staring at the tableau and only slowly understanding what she sees, Jija blurts, "Are you one, too?"

He's a big man. It's a loud, sharp blurt, and Nassun jumps. Her eyes jerk up to him, rather than staying on Uche's body, which saves her life. The gray color of her eyes is her mother's, but the shape of her face is Jija's. Just the sight of her pulls him a step away from the primal panic into which he has descended.

She tells the truth, too. That helps, because he wouldn't have believed anything else. "Yes," she says.

She's not really afraid in this moment. The sight of her brother's body, and her mind's refusal to interpret what she's seeing, have frozen all cognition within her. She's not even sure what Jija is asking, since understanding the context of his words would require her to acknowledge that what stains her father's fists is blood, and that her brother is not merely sleeping on the floor. She can't. Not right then. But absent any more coherent thought, and as children sometimes do in extreme situations, Nassun…regresses. What she sees frightens her, even if she does not understand why. And of the two of her parents, it is Jija to whom Nassun has always been closer. She's his favorite, too: the firstborn, the one he never expected to have, the one with his face and his sense of humor. She likes his favorite foods. He's had vague hopes of her following in his footsteps as a knapper.

So when she starts crying, she does not quite know why. And

as her thoughts skirl about and her heart screams, she takes a step toward him. His fists tighten, but she cannot see him as a threat. He is her father. She wants comfort. "Daddy," she says.

Jija flinches. Blinks. Stares, as if he has never seen her before.

Realizes. He cannot kill her. Not even if she is… no. She is his little girl.

She steps forward again, reaching out. He cannot make himself reach back, but he does hold still. She grabs his nearer wrist. He stands straddling Uche's body; she can't grab him around the waist the way she wants. She does, however, press her face against his bicep, so comfortingly strong. She does tremble, and he does feel her tears sliding down his skin.

He stands there, breath gradually slowing, fists gradually uncurling, while she weeps. After a time, he turns to face her fully, and she wraps arms around his waist. Turning to face her requires turning away from what he's done to Uche. It is an easy movement.

He murmurs to her, "Get your things. As if you were going to spend a few nights with Grandma." Jija's mother married again a few years back and now she lives in Sume, the town in the next valley over, which will soon be destroyed utterly.

"Are we going there?" Nassun asks against his belly.

He touches the back of her head. He's always done this, because she's always liked the gesture. When she was a baby, she cooed louder when he cupped her there. This is because the sessapinae are located in that region of the brain and when he touches her there, she can perceive him more completely, as orogenes do. Neither of them has ever known why she likes it so much.

"We're going somewhere you can be better," he says gently. "Somewhere I heard of, where they can help you." Make her a little girl again, and not... He turns away from this thought, too.

She swallows, then nods and steps back, looking up at him. "Is Mama coming, too?"

Something moves across Jija's face, subtle as an earthquake. "No."

And Nassun, who was fully prepared to go off into the sunset with some lorist, effectively running away from home to escape her mother, relaxes at last. "Okay, Daddy," she says, and heads to her room to pack.

Jija gazes after her for a long, breath-held moment. He turns away from Uche again, gets his own things, and heads outside to hitch up the horse to the wagon. Within an hour they are away, headed south with the end of the world on their heels.

* * *

In the days of Jyamaria, which died in the Season of Drowned Desert, it was thought that giving the lastborn to the sea would keep it from coming ashore and taking the rest.

—*From "The Breeder's Stand," lorist tale recorded in Hanl Quartent, Western Coastals near Brokeoff Peninsula. Apocryphal.*

2

you, continued

A WHAT?" YOU SAY.

"A moon." Alabaster, beloved monster, sane madman, the most powerful orogene in all the Stillness, and in-progress stone eater snack, stares at you. This has all of its old intensity, and you feel the will of him, the stuff that makes him the force of nature that he is, as an almost physical rider on that stare. The Guardians were fools to ever consider him tame. "A satellite."

"A *what?*"

He makes a little sound of frustration. He's completely the same, aside from being partially turned to stone, as the days when you and he were less than lovers and more than friends. Ten years and another self ago. "Astronomestry isn't foolishness," he says. "I know you were taught that, everyone in the Stillness thinks it's a waste of energy to study the sky when it's the ground that's trying to kill us, but Earthfires, Syen. I thought you would've learned to question the status quo a little better by now."

"I had other things to do," you snap, just like you always used to snap at him. But thinking of the old days makes you think of what you've been up to in the meantime. And that makes you think of your living daughter, and your dead son, and your soon-to-be-very-ex-husband, and you flinch physically. "And my name is Essun now, I told you."

"Whatever." With a groaning sigh, Alabaster carefully sits back against the wall. "They say you came here with a geomest. Have her explain it to you. I don't have a lot of energy these days." Because being eaten probably takes a toll. "You didn't answer my first question. Can you do it yet?"

Can you call the obelisks to you? It is a question that made no sense when he first asked it, possibly because you were distracted by realizing he was a) alive, b) turning to stone, and c) the orogene responsible for ripping the continent in half and touching off a Season that may never end.

"The obelisks?" You shake your head, more confused than refusing. Your gaze drifts to the strange object near his bed, which looks like an excessively long pink glassknife and feels like an obelisk, even though it cannot possibly be. "What do— no. I don't know. I haven't tried since Meov."

He groans softly, shutting his eyes. "You're so rusting useless, Syen. Essun. Never had any respect for the craft."

"I respect it fine, I just don't—"

"Just enough to get by, enough to excel but only for gain. They told you how high and you jumped no further, all to get a nicer apartment and another ring—"

"For privacy, you ass, and some control over my life, and some rusting respect—"

"And you actually *listened* to that Guardian of yours, when you don't listen to anybody else—"

"*Hey*." Ten years as a schoolteacher have given your voice an obsidian edge. Alabaster actually stops ranting and blinks at you. Very quietly, you say, "You know full well why I listened to him."

There is a moment of silence. Both of you take this time to regroup.

"You're right," he says, at length. "I'm sorry." Because every Imperial Orogene listens—listened—to their assigned Guardian. Those who didn't died or ended up in a node. Except, again, for Alabaster; you never did find out what he did to his Guardian.

You offer a stiff nod of truce. "Apology accepted."

He takes a careful breath, looking weary. "Try, Essun. Try to reach an obelisk. Today. I need to know."

"Why? What's this about a still-light? What does—"

"*Satellite*. And all of it's irrelevant if you can't control the obelisks." His eyes are actually drifting shut. This is probably a good thing. He'll need his strength if he's to survive whatever is happening to him. If it's survivable. "Worse than irrelevant. You remember why I wouldn't tell you about the obelisks in the first place, don't you?"

Yes. Once, before you ever paid attention to those great floating half-real crystals in the sky, you asked Alabaster to explain how he accomplished some of his amazing feats of orogeny. He wouldn't tell you, and you hated him for that, but now you know just how dangerous the knowledge was. If you hadn't understood that the obelisks were amplifiers, *orogeny* amplifiers, you would never have reached for the garnet to save yourself from a Guardian's attack. But if the garnet obelisk hadn't been half-dead itself, cracked and stuffed with a frozen stone eater, it would have killed you. You didn't have the strength, the self-control, to prevent the power from frying you from the brain on down.

And now Alabaster wants you to reach for one deliberately, to see what happens.

Alabaster knows your face. "Go and see," he says. His eyes shut completely then. You hear a faint rattle in his breath, like gravel in his lungs. "The topaz is floating somewhere nearby. Call it tonight, then in the morning see..." Abruptly he seems to weaken, running out of strength. "See if it's come. If it hasn't, tell me, and I'll find someone else. Or do what I can myself."

Find who, to do what, you can't even begin to guess. "Will you still tell me what all this is about?"

"No. Because in spite of everything, Essun, I don't want you to die." He takes a deep breath, lets it out slowly. The next words are softer than usual. "It's good to see you."

You have to tighten your jaw to reply. "Yeah."

He says nothing more, and that's enough of a goodbye for both of you.

You get up, glancing at the stone eater who stands nearby. Alabaster calls her Antimony. She stands statue-still in the way they do, her too-black eyes watching you too steadily, and though her pose is something classical, you think there's a hint of irony in it. She stands with head elegantly tilted, one hand on her hip and the other upraised and poised with the fingers relaxed, waving in no particular direction. Maybe it's a come-hither, maybe it's a backhanded farewell, maybe it's that thing people do when they're keeping a secret and want you to know it, but they don't want to tell you what it is.

"Take care of him," you say to her.

"As I would any precious thing," she replies, without moving her mouth.

You're not even going to start trying to interpret that. You head back toward the infirmary entrance, where Hoa stands waiting for you. Hoa, who looks like an utterly strange human boy, who is actually a stone eater somehow, and who treats you as his precious thing.

He watches you, unhappily, as he has done since you realized what he was. You shake your head and move past him on your way out. He follows, at a pace.

It's early night in the comm of Castrima. Hard to tell since the giant geode's soft white light, emitted impossibly from the massive crystals that make up its substance, never changes. People are bustling about, carrying things, shouting to each other, going about their usual business without the necessary slowdown that would occur in other comms with the reduction of light. Sleeping will be difficult for a few days, you suspect, at least until you get used to this. That doesn't matter. Obelisks don't care about the time of day.

Lerna's been politely waiting outside while you and Hoa met with Alabaster and Antimony. He falls in as you come out, his expression expectant. "I need to go to the surface," you say.

Lerna makes a face. "The guards won't let you, Essun. People new to the comm aren't trusted. Castrima's survival depends on it remaining secret."

Seeing Alabaster again has brought back a lot of the old memories, and the old orneriness. "They can try to stop me."

Lerna stops walking. "And then you'll do what you did to Tirimo?"

Rusting hell. You stop, too, rocking a little from the force of that blow. Hoa stops as well, eying Lerna thoughtfully. Lerna's not glaring. The look on his face is too flat to be a glare. Damn. Okay.

After a moment, Lerna sighs and comes over. "We'll go to Ykka," he says. "We'll tell her what we need. We'll *ask* to go topside—with guards if she wants. All right?"

It's so reasonable that you don't know why you didn't even consider it. Well, you know why. Ykka might be an orogene like you, but you spent too many years being thwarted and betrayed by other orogenes at the Fulcrum; you know better than to trust her just because she's Your People. You should give her a chance because she's Your People, though.

"Fine," you say, and follow him to Ykka's.

Ykka's place is no larger than yours, and not distinct in any way despite being the home of the comm headwoman. Just another apartment carved by means unknown into the side of a giant glowing white crystal. Two people wait outside of its door, however, one leaning against the crystal and another peering over the railing at the expanse of Castrima. Lerna takes up position behind them and directs you to do the same. Only fair to wait your turn, and the obelisks aren't going anywhere.

The woman gazing out at the view glances over and looks you up and down. She's a little older, Sanzed, though darker complected than most, and her bushel of hair is ashblow with a slight kink to it, making it a frizzy cloud instead of just a coarse one. Got some Eastcoaster in her. And Westcoaster, too: Her gaze is through epicanthic-folded eyes, and it is assessing, wary, and unimpressed. "You the new one," she says. Not a question.

You nod back. "Essun."

She grins lopsidedly, and you blink. Her teeth have been filed to points, even though Sanzeds supposedly stopped doing that centuries ago. Bad for their reputation, after the Season of Teeth.

"Hjarka Leadership Castrima. Welcome to our little hole in the ground." Her smile widens. You stifle a grimace at the pun, though you're thinking, too, after hearing her name. It's usually bad news when a comm has a Leadership caste that isn't in charge. Dissatisfied Leaders have a nasty habit of fomenting coups during crises. But this is Ykka's problem to deal with, not yours.

The other person waiting, the man leaning on the crystal, doesn't seem to be watching you—but you notice how his eyes aren't moving to track whatever he's looking at, off in the distance. He's thin, shorter than you, with hair and a beard that make you think of strawberries growing amid hay. You imagine the delicate pressure of his indirect attention. You do *not* imagine the ping of instinct that tells you he is another of your kind. Since he doesn't acknowledge your presence, you say nothing to him.

"He came in a few months ago," Lerna says, distracting you from your new neighbors. For a moment you wonder if he means the strawberry-hay-haired man, and then you realize he's referring to Alabaster. "Just appeared in the middle of what passes for a town square within the geode—Flat Top." He nods toward something beyond you, and you turn, trying to understand what he means. Ah: there, amid the many sharp-tipped crystals of Castrima, is one that looks as if it's been sheared off halfway, leaving a wide hexagonal platform positioned and elevated near the center of the comm. Several stair-bridges connect to it, and there are chairs and a railing. Flat Top.

Lerna goes on. "There was no warning. Apparently the orogenes didn't sess anything, and the stills on guard duty didn't see anything. He and that stone eater of his were suddenly just… there."

He doesn't see you frown in surprise. You've never heard a still use the word *still* before.

"Maybe the stone eaters knew he was coming, but they rarely talk to anyone but their chosen people. And in this case, they didn't even do that." Lerna's gaze drifts over to Hoa, who's studiously ignoring him in that very moment. Lerna shakes his head. "Ykka tried to throw him out, of course, though she offered him a mercy killing if he wanted. His prognosis is obvious; gentle drugs and a bed would be a kindness. He did something when she called the Strongbacks, though. The light went out. The air and water stopped. Only for a minute, but it felt like a year. When he let everything come back on, everyone was upset. So Ykka said he could stay, and that we should treat his injuries."

Sounds about right. "He's a ten-ringer," you say. "And an ass. Give him whatever he wants and be nice about it."

"He's from the Fulcrum?" Lerna inhales in what seems to be awe. "Earthfires. I had no idea any Imperial Orogenes had survived."

You look at him, too surprised for amusement. But then, how would he know? Another thought sobers you. "He's turning to stone," you say softly.

"Yes." Lerna says it ruefully. "I've never seen anything like it. And it's getting worse. The first day he was here it was just his fingers that had… that the stone eater had… taken. I haven't seen how the condition progresses. He's careful to do it only when I or my assistants aren't around. I don't know if she's doing it to him somehow, or he's doing it to himself, or…" He shakes his head. "When I ask about it, he just grins and says, 'Just a bit longer, please. I'm waiting for someone.'" Lerna frowns at you, thoughtful.

And there's that: Somehow, Alabaster knew you were coming.

Or maybe he didn't. Maybe he was hoping for someone, anyone, with the necessary skill. Good chance of it here, with Ykka somehow summoning every rogga for miles. You'll only be what he was waiting for if it turns out you can summon an obelisk.

After a few moments, Ykka pokes her head out of the apartment through the hanging. She nods to Hjarka, glares at Strawberry-Hay until he sighs and turns to face her, then spies you and Lerna and Hoa. "Oh. Hey. Good. All of you come in."

You start to protest. "I need to talk to you in private."

She stares back at you. You blink, confused, thrown, annoyed. She keeps staring. Lerna shifts from foot to foot beside you, a silent pressure. Hoa merely watches, following your lead. Finally you get the message: her comm, her rules, and if you want to live here . . . You sigh and file in behind the others.

Inside, the apartment is warmer than in most of the comm, and darker; the curtain makes a difference, even though the walls glow. Makes it feel like night, which it probably is, topside. A good idea to steal for your own place, you think—before checking yourself, because you shouldn't be thinking long term. And then you check yourself again because you've lost Nassun and Jija's trail, so you *should* think long term. And then—

"Right," says Ykka, sounding bored as she moves to sit on a simple, low divan, cross-legged, with her chin propped on a fist. The others sit as well, but she's looking at you. "I'd been thinking about some changes already. You two arrived at a convenient time."

For a moment you think she's including Lerna in that "you two," but he sits down on the divan nearest hers, and there's something, some ease of movement or comfort in his manner, that tells you he's heard this before. She means Hoa, then. Hoa takes the floor, which makes him seem more like a child... though he isn't. It's strange how hard it is for you to remember that.

You sit down gingerly. "Convenient for what?"

"I still don't think this is a good idea," Strawberry-Hay says. He's looking at you, though his face is tilted toward Ykka. "We don't know anything about these people, Yeek."

"We know they survived out there until yesterday," says Hjarka, leaning to the side and propping her elbow on the divan's arm. "That's something."

"That's nothing." Strawberry-Hay—you really want to know his name—sets his jaw. "Our Hunters can survive out there."

Hunters. You blink. That's one of the old use-castes—a deprecated one, per Imperial Law, so nobody gets born into it anymore. Civilized societies don't need hunter-gatherers. That Castrima feels the need says more about the state of the comm than anything else Ykka has told you.

"Our Hunters know the terrain, and our Strongbacks, too, yeah," Hjarka says. "*Nearby*. Newcomers know more about the conditions beyond our territory—the people, the hazards, everything else."

"I'm not sure I know anything useful," you begin. But even as you say this, you frown, because you're remembering that thing you started noticing a few roadhouses ago. The sashes or rags of fine silk on too many of the Equatorials' wrists. The closed looks they gave you, their focus while others sat shell-shocked. At every encampment you saw them look their fellow survivors over, picking out any Sanzeds who were better equipped or healthier or otherwise doing better than average. Speaking to those chosen people in quiet voices. Leaving the next morning in groups larger than those in which they had arrived.

Does that mean anything? Like keeping to like is the old way, but races and nations haven't been important for a long time. Communities of purpose and diverse specialization are more efficient, as Old Sanze proved. Yet Yumenes is slag at the bottom of a fissure vent by now, and the laws and ways of the Empire no longer have any bite. Maybe this is the first sign of change, then. Maybe in a few years you'll have to leave Castrima and find a comm full of Midlatters like you who are brown but not too brown, big but not too big, with hair that's curly or kinky but never ashblow or straight. Nassun can come with you, in that case.

But how long would the both of you be able to hide what you are? No comm wants roggas. No comm except this one.

"You know more than we do," Ykka says, interrupting your woolgathering. "And anyway, I don't have the patience to argue about it. I'm telling you what I told him a few weeks back." She jerks her head at Lerna. "I need advisors—people who know this Season ground to sky. You're it until I replace you."

You're more than a little surprised. "I don't know a rusting thing about this comm!"

"That's my job—and his, and hers." Ykka nods toward Strawberry-Hay and Hjarka. "Anyway, you'll learn."

Your mouth hangs open. Then it occurs to you that she did include Hoa in this gathering, didn't she? "Earthfires and rustbuckets, you want a *stone eater* as an advisor?"

"Why not? They're here, too. More of them than we think." She focuses on Hoa, who watches her, his expression unreadable. "That's what you told me."

"It's true," he says quietly. Then: "I can't speak for them, though. And we aren't part of your comm."

Ykka leans down to give him a hard look. Her expression is something between hostile and guarded. "You have an impact on our comm, if only as a potential threat," she says. Her eyes flick toward you. "And the ones you're, uh, attached to, *are* part of this comm. You care what happens to them, at least. Don't you?"

You realize you haven't seen Ykka's stone eater, the woman with the ruby hair, for a few hours. That doesn't mean she isn't nearby, though. You learned better than to trust the appearance of absence with Antimony. Hoa says nothing in reply to Ykka. You're suddenly, irrationally glad he's bothered to stay visible for you.

"As for why you, and why the doctor," Ykka says, straightening, and speaking to you even if she's still eying Hoa, "it's because I need a mix of perspectives. A Leader, even if she doesn't want to lead." She eyes Hjarka. "Another local rogga, who doesn't bother to bite his tongue about how stupid he thinks I am." She nods to Strawberry-Hay, who sighs. "A Resistant and a doctor, who knows the road. A stone eater. Me. And you, Essun, who could kill us all." She smiles thinly. "Makes sense to give you a reason not to."

You have no real idea what to say, to that. You think, fleetingly, that Ykka should invite Alabaster to her circle of advisors, then, if the ability to destroy Castrima is a qualification. But that could lead to awkward questions.

To Hjarka and Strawberry-Hay you say, "Are you both from here?"

"Nope," says Hjarka.

"Yes," says Ykka. Hjarka glares at her. "You've lived here since you were young, Hjar."

Hjarka shrugs. "Nobody here remembers that except you, Yeek."

Strawberry-Hay says, "I was born and raised here."

Two orogenes, surviving to adulthood in a comm that didn't kill them. "What's your name?"

"Cutter Strongback." You wait. He smiles with half his mouth and neither of his eyes.

"Cutter's secret wasn't out, so to speak, while we were growing up," Ykka says. She's leaning against the wall behind the divan now, rubbing her eyes as if she's tired. "People guessed anyway. The rumors were enough to keep him from being adopted into the comm, under the previous headman. Of course, I've offered to give him the name a half-dozen times over now."

"If I give up 'Strongback,'" Cutter replies. He's still smiling in that paper-thin way.

Ykka lowers her hand. Her jaw is tight. "Denying what you are didn't keep people from knowing what you are."

"And flaunting it isn't what saved you."

Ykka takes a deep breath. The muscles in her jaw flex, relax. "And that would be why I asked you to do this, Cutter. But let's move on."

So it goes on.

You sit there throughout the meeting, trying to understand the undercurrents you're picking up on, still not believing you're even here, while Ykka lays out all of the problems facing Castrima. It's stuff you've never had to think about before: Complaints that the hot water in the communal pools isn't hot enough. A serious shortage of potters but an overabundance of people who know how to sew. Fungus in one of the granary caverns; several months' supply had to be burned lest it contaminate the rest. A meat shortage. You've gone from thinking obsessively about one person to having to be concerned with many. It's a bit sudden.

"I just took a bath," you blurt, trying to pull yourself out of a daze. "The water was nice."

"Of course you thought it was nice. You've been living rough for months, bathing in cold streams if you even bothered. A lot of the people in Castrima have never lived without reliable geo and adjustable faucets." Ykka rubs her eyes. The meeting's only been an hour or so, but it feels longer. "Everybody copes with a Season in their own way."

Complaining about nothing doesn't seem like coping to you, but okay.

"Being low on meat is an actual problem," Lerna says, frowning. "I noticed the last few comm shares didn't have any, or eggs."

Ykka's expression grows grimmer. "Yes. That's why." For your sake, she adds, "We don't have a greenland in this comm, if you haven't noticed yet. The soil around here is poor, all right for gardening but not for grass or hay. Then for the last few years before the Season started, everyone was so busy arguing about whether we should rebuild the old pre-Choking wall that nobody thought to contract with an agricultural comm for a few dozen cartloads of good soil." She sighs, rubbing the bridge of her nose. "Can't bring most livestock down the mine shafts and stairs, anyway. I don't know what we were thinking, trying to live down here. This is exactly why I need help."

Her weariness isn't a surprise, but her willingness to admit error is. It's also troubling. You say: "A comm can only have one leader, during a Season."

"Yeah, and that's still me. Don't you forget it." It could be a warn-off, but it doesn't sound like one. You suspect it's just a matter-of-fact acceptance of her place in Castrima: The people chose her, and for the time being they trust her. They don't know you, Lerna, or Hoa, and apparently they don't trust Hjarka and Cutter. You need her more than she needs any of you. Abruptly, though, Ykka shakes her head. "I can't talk about this shit anymore."

Good, because the looming sense of disjunct—this morning you were thinking of the road, and survival, and Nassun—is beginning to feel overwhelming. "I need to go topside."

It's too abrupt a change of subject, apparently out of the blue, and for a moment they all stare at you. "The rust for?" Ykka asks.

"Alabaster." Ykka looks blank. "The ten-ringer in your infirmary? He asked me to do something."

Ykka grimaces. "Oh. Him." You can't help smiling at this reaction. "Interesting. He hasn't talked to anyone since he got here. Just sits in there using up our antibiotics and eating our food."

"I just made a batch of 'cillin, Ykka." Lerna rolls his eyes.

"It's the principle of the thing."

You suspect Alabaster's been quelling the local microshakes and any aftershakes from the north, which would more than earn his keep. But if Ykka can't sess that for herself, explaining is pointless—and you're not sure you can trust her enough to talk about Alabaster yet. "He's an old friend." There. That's a good, if incomplete, summary.

"He didn't seem the type to have friends. You, either." She regards you for a long moment. "Are you a ten-ringer, too?"

Your fingers flex involuntarily. "I wore six rings, once." Lerna's head snaps around and he stares at you. Well. Cutter's face twitches in a way you can't interpret. You add: "Alabaster was my mentor, back when I was still with the Fulcrum."

"I see. And what does he want you to do, topside?"

You open your mouth, then close it. You can't help glancing at Hjarka, who snorts and gets to her feet, and Lerna, whose expression tightens as he realizes you don't want to speak in front of him. He deserves better than that, but still . . . he's a still. Finally you say, "Orogene business."

It's weak. Lerna's face goes blank, but his eyes are hard. Hjarka waves and heads for the curtain. "Then I'm out. Come on, Cutter. Since you're just a Strongback." She barks out a laugh.

Cutter stiffens, but to your surprise, he rises and follows her out. You eye Lerna for a moment, but he folds his arms. Not going anywhere. All right. In the wake of this, Ykka looks skeptical. "What is this, a final lesson from your old mentor? He's obviously not going to live much longer."

Your jaw tightens before you can help it. "That remains to be seen."

Ykka looks thoughtful for a moment longer, and then she nods decisively, getting to her feet. "All right, then. Just let me get some Strongbacks together and we'll be on our way."

"Wait, you're coming? Why?"

"Curiosity. I want to see what a Fulcrum six-ringer can do."

She grins at you and picks up the long fur vest you first saw her wearing. "Maybe see if I can do it, too."

You flinch violently at the idea of a self-taught feral attempting to connect to an obelisk. "No."

Ykka's expression flattens. Lerna stares at you, incredulous that you would achieve your goal and then scuttle it in the same breath. Quickly you amend yourself. "It's dangerous even for me, and I've done it before."

"'It'?"

Well, that does it. It's safer that she not know, but Lerna's right; you have to win this woman over if you're going to be living in her comm. "Promise me you won't try, if I tell you."

"I won't promise a rusting thing. I don't know you." Ykka folds her arms. You're a big woman, but she's a little bigger, and the hair doesn't help. Many Sanzeds like to grow their ashblow hair into big, poufy manes like hers. It's an animal intimidation thing, and it works if they've got the confidence to back it up. Ykka's got that and then some.

But you have knowledge. You push to your feet and meet her eyes. "You can't do it," you say, will her to believe. "You don't have the training."

"You don't know what kind of training I have."

And you blink, remembering that moment topside when the realization that you'd lost Nassun's trail nearly unhinged you. That strange, sweeping waft of power Ykka sent through you, like a slap but kinder, and somehow orogenic. Then there's her little trick of drawing orogenes from miles around toward Castrima. Ykka may not wear rings, but orogeny isn't about rank.

No help for it, then. "An obelisk," you say, relenting. You glance at Lerna; he blinks and frowns. "Alabaster wants me to call an obelisk. I'm going to see if I can."

To your surprise, Ykka nods, her eyes alight. "Aha! Always thought there was something about those things. Let's go, then. I definitely want to see this."

Oh. Shit.

Ykka shrugs on the vest. "Give me a half hour, then meet me at Scenic Overlook." That's the entrance to Castrima, that little platform where newcomers invariably gawk at the strangeness of a comm inside a giant geode. With that she brushes past you and out of the apartment.

Shaking your head, you eye Lerna. He nods tightly; he wants to go, too. Hoa? He simply takes up his usual place behind you, gazing at you placidly as if to say, *This was in doubt?* So now it's a party.

Ykka meets you at the overlook in half an hour. With her are four other Castrimans, who are armed and dressed in faded colors and grays for camouflage up on the surface. It's a harder procession, going up, than it was coming down: lots of uphill walking, many sets of stairs. You're not as out of breath as a few of Ykka's crew by the time it's done, but then you've been walking miles every day while they've been living safe and comfy in their underground town. (Ykka, you notice, only breathes a little harder. She's keeping in shape.) Eventually, though, you reach a false basement in one of the decoy houses topside. It's not the same basement that you entered through, which shouldn't surprise you; of course their "gate" has multiple entrances and exits. The underground passages are more complicated than you initially thought, though—something important to keep in mind, should you ever need to leave in a hurry.

The decoy house has Strongback sentries like the other one, some guarding the basement entrance and some actually in the house upstairs, keeping watch on the road outside. When the upstairs sentries give you the all clear, you head out into the late-evening ashfall.

After, what, less than a day in Castrima's geode? It's amazing how strange the surface seems to you. For the first time in weeks you *notice* the sulfur stench of the air, the silvery haze, the incessant soft patter of fat ash flakes on the ground and dead leaves. The silence, which makes you realize just how noisy Castrima-under is, with people talking and pulleys squeaking and smithies clanking, and the omnipresent hum of the geode's strange hidden machinery. Up here there's nothing. The trees have dropped their leaves; nothing moves through the curl-edged, desiccated detritus. No birdsong can be heard through the branches; most birds stop marking territory and mating during a Season, and song only attracts predators. No other animal sounds. There are no travelers on the road, though you can tell that the ash is thinner there. People have been by recently. Aside from that, though, even the wind is still. The sun has set, though there's still plenty of light in the sky. The clouds, even this far south, still reflect the Rifting.

"Traffic?" Ykka asks one of the sentries.

"Family-looking bunch about forty minutes ago," he says. He keeps his voice appropriately low. "Well equipped. Maybe twenty people, all ages, all Sanzeds. Traveling north."

That makes everyone look at him. Ykka repeats: "North?"

"North." The sentry, who has the most beautiful long-lashed eyes, looks back at Ykka and shrugs. "Looked like they had a destination in mind."

"Huh." She folds her arms, shivering a little, though it's not particularly cold outside; the cold of a Fifth Season takes months to set in fully. Castrima-under's just so warm that to someone used to that, Castrima-over's chilly. Or maybe Ykka's just reacting to the starkness of the comm around her. So many silent houses, dead gardens, and ash-occluded pathways where people once walked. You'd been thinking of the surface level of the comm as bait—and it is, a honeypot meant to draw in the desirable and distract the hostile. Yet it was also a real comm once, alive and bright and anything but still.

"Well?" Ykka takes a deep breath and smiles, but you think her smile is strained. She nods toward the low-hanging ash clouds. "If you need to *see* this thing, I don't think you're going to have much luck anytime soon."

She's right; the air is a haze of ash, and past the beaded, red-tinted clouds you can't see a damned thing. You step off the porch and look up at the sky anyway, unsure of how to begin. You also aren't sure *if* you should begin. After all, the first and second times you tried to interact with an obelisk, you almost died. Then there's the fact that Alabaster wants this, when he's the man who destroyed the world. Maybe you shouldn't do anything he asks.

He's never hurt you, though. The world has, but not him. Maybe the world deserved to be destroyed. And maybe he's earned a little of your trust, after all these years.

So you close your eyes and try to still your thoughts. There *are* sounds to be heard around you, you notice at last. Faint creaks and pops as the wooden parts of Castrima-over react to the weight of ash, or the changing warmth of the air. Several things scuttling among the dried-out stalks of a housegreen nearby: rodents or something else small, nothing to worry about. One of the Castrimans is breathing really loudly for some reason.

Warm jitter of the earth beneath your feet. No. Wrong direction.

There's actually enough ash in the sky that you can sort of grasp the clouds with your awareness. Ash is powdered rock, after all. But it's not the clouds you want. You grope along them as you would earth strata, not quite sure what you're looking for—

"Will this take much longer?" sighs one of the Castrimans.

"Why, got a hot date?" Ykka drawls.

He is insignificant. He is—

He is—

Something pulls you sharply west. You jerk and turn to face it, inhaling as you remember a night long ago in a comm called Allia, and another obelisk. The amethyst. *He didn't need to* see *it, he needed to* face *it.* Lines of sight, lines of force. Yes. And there, far along the line of your attention, you sess your awareness being drawn toward something heavy and...dark.

Dark, *so* dark. Alabaster said it would be the topaz, didn't he? This isn't that. It feels familiar, sort of, reminds you of the garnet. Not the amethyst. Why? The garnet was broken, mad (you're not sure why this word occurs to you), but beyond that it was also more powerful, somehow, though *power* is too simple a word for what these things contain. Richness. Strangeness. Darker colors, deeper potential? But if that's the case...

"Onyx," you say aloud, opening your eyes.

Other obelisks buzz along the periphery of your line of sight, closer, possible, but they don't respond to this near-instinctive call of yours. The dark obelisk is so far away, well past the Western Coastals, somewhere over the Unknown Sea. Even flying, it might take months to arrive. But.

But. The onyx *hears* you. You know this the way you once knew your children had heard you, even if they pretended to ignore you. Ponderously it turns, arcane processes awakening for the first time in an age of the earth, as it does uttering an assault of sound and vibration that shakes the sea for miles underneath. (How do you know this? You're not sessing this. You just know.)

Then it begins to come. Evil, eating Earth.

You flinch back along the line that leads to yourself. Along the way something snags your attention, and almost as an afterthought you call it, too: the topaz. It is lighter, livelier, much closer, and somehow more responsive, perhaps because you perceive a hint of Alabaster in its interstices like a curl of citrus rind added to a savory dish. He's prepped it for you.

Then you snap back into yourself and turn to Ykka, who's frowning at you. "You follow that?"

She shakes her head slowly, but not in negation. She caught some of it, somehow. You can see that in the look on her face. "I... that was... something. I'm not sure what."

"Don't reach for either one, when they get here." Because you're sure they're coming. "Don't reach for any of them. Ever." You're reluctant to say *obelisk*. Too many stills around, and even if they haven't killed you yet, stills never need to hear that something can make orogenes even more of a danger than they already are.

"What would happen if I did?" It's a question of honest curiosity, not challenge, but some questions are dangerous.

You decide to be honest. "You would die. I'm not sure how." Actually you're pretty sure she would spontaneously ignite into a white-hot screaming column of fire and force, possibly taking all of Castrima with her. But you're not a hundred percent sure, so you stick to what you know. "The—those things are like the batteries some Equatorial comms use." Shit. "Used. You've heard of those? A battery stores energy so you can have electricity even if the hydro's not flowing or the geo has—"

Ykka looks affronted. Well, she is Sanzed; they invented batteries. "I know what a rusting battery is! First hint of a shake and you've got acid burns on top of everything else, all for the sake of a bit of stored juice." She shakes her head. "What you're talking about isn't a *battery*."

"They were making sugar batteries when I left Yumenes," you say. She's not saying *obelisk*, either. Good; she gets it. "Safer than acid and metal. Batteries can be made more than one way. But if a battery is too powerful for the circuit you attach it to..." You figure that's enough to get the idea across.

She shakes her head again, but you think she believes you. As she turns and starts to pace in thought, you notice Lerna. He's been quiet all this time, listening to you and Ykka talk. Now he seems deep in thought, and that bothers you. You don't like that a still is thinking so hard about this.

But then he surprises you. "Ykka. How old do you think this comm really is?"

She stops and frowns at him. The other Castrimans shift as if uncomfortable. Maybe it bothers them, being reminded that they live in a deadciv ruin. "No clue. Why?"

He shrugs. "I'm just thinking of similarities."

You understand then. Crystals in Castrima-under that glow through some means you can't fathom. Crystals that float in the sky by some means you can't fathom. Both mechanisms meant to be used by orogenes and no one else.

Stone eaters showing an inordinate interest in orogenes who use either. You glance at Hoa.

But Hoa isn't looking at the sky, or at you. He's stepped off the porch and has crouched on the ashy ground just off the walkway, staring at something. You follow his gaze and see a small mound in what was once the front yard of the house next door. It looks like just another pile of ash, maybe three feet high, but then you notice a tiny desiccated animal foot poking out of one end. Cat, maybe, or rabbit. There are probably dozens of small carcasses around here, buried under the ash; the beginning of the Season likely caused a huge die-off. Odd that this carcass seems to have accumulated so much more ash than the ground around it, though.

"Too long gone to eat, kid," says one of the men, who's also noticed Hoa and clearly has no idea what the "kid" is. Hoa blinks at him and bites his lip with just the perfect degree of unease. He plays the child so well. Then he gets up and comes over to you, and you realize he's not playacting. Something really has unnerved him.

"Other things will eat it," he says to you, very softly. "We should go."

What. "You're not afraid of anything."

His jaw tightens. Jaw full of diamond teeth. Muscles over diamond bones? No wonder he's never let you try to lift him; he must be heavy as marble. But he says, "I'm afraid of things that will hurt you."

And... you believe him. Because, you suddenly realize, that's been the commonality of all his strange behavior so far. His willingness to face the kirkhusa, which might have been too fast even for your orogeny. His ferocity toward other stone eaters. He's protecting you. So few have ever tried to protect you, in your life. It's impulse that makes you lift a hand and stroke it over his weird white hair. He blinks. Something comes into his eyes that is anything but inhuman. You don't know what to think. This, though, is why you listen to him.

"Let's go," you say to Ykka and the others. You've done what Alabaster asked. You suspect he won't be displeased by the *extra* obelisk when you tell him—if he doesn't already know. Now, maybe, finally, he'll tell you what the rust is going on.

* * *

> Before, gather into stable rock for each citizen one year's supply: ten rullets of grain, five of legume, a quarter-tradet dry fruit, and a half storet in tallow, cheese, or preserved flesh. Multiply by each year of life desired. After, guard upon stable rock with at least three strong-backed souls per cache: one to guard the cache, two to guard the guard.
>
> —*Tablet One, "On Survival," verse four*

3

Schaffa, forgotten

YES. YOU ARE HIM, TOO, or you were until after Meov. But now he is someone else.

* * *

The force that shatters the *Clalsu* is orogeny applied to air. Orogeny isn't meant to be applied to air, but there's no real reason for it not to work. Syenite has had practice already using orogeny on water, at and since Allia. There are minerals in water, and likewise there are dust particles in air. Air has heat and friction and mass and kinetic potential, same as earth; the molecules of air are simply farther apart, the atoms shaped differently. Anyhow, the involvement of an obelisk makes all of these details academic.

Schaffa knows what's coming the instant he feels the obelisk's pulse. He is old, old, Syenite's Guardian. So old. He knows what stone eaters do to powerful orogenes whenever they get the chance, and he knows why it is crucial to keep orogenes' eyes on the ground and not the sky. He has seen what happens when a four-ringer—that's how he still thinks of Syenite—connects to an obelisk. He does genuinely care about her, you realize (she does not realize). It isn't all about control. She's his little one, and he has protected her in more ways than she knows. The thought of her agonizing death is unbearable to him. This is ironic, considering what happens next.

In the moment when Syenite stiffens and her frame becomes suffused with light, and the air within the *Clalsu*'s tiny forward compartment shivers and turns into a nearly solid wall of unstoppable force, Schaffa happens to be standing to one side of a hanging bulkhead rather than in front of it. His companion, the Guardian who has just killed Syenite's feral lover, is not so lucky: When the force slams him backward, the bulkhead juts out from the wall at just the right height and angle to shear his head off before giving way itself. Schaffa, however, flies backward unobstructed through the *Clalsu*'s capacious hold, which is empty because the ship hasn't been out on a piracy run in a while. There's room enough for his velocity to slow a little, and for the greatest force of Syenite's blow to move past him. When he finally does hit a bulkhead, it is with merely bone-breaking force and not bone-pulverizing force. And the bulkhead is buckling, crumbling along with the rest of the ship, when he hits it. That helps, too.

Then when jagged, knifelike spikes of bedrock from the ocean floor begin spearing through the explosion of debris, Schaffa is lucky again: None of them pierce his body. Syenite is lost in the obelisk by this point, and lost in the first throes of a grief that will send aftershakes through even Essun's life. (Schaffa saw her hand on the child's face, covering mouth and nose, pressing. Incomprehensible. Did she not know that Schaffa would love her son as he loved her? He would lay the boy down gently, so gently, in the wire chair.) She is part of something vast and globally powerful now, and Schaffa, once the most important person in her world, is beneath her notice. On some level he is aware of this even as he flies through the storm, and the knowledge leaves a deep burn of hurt in his heart. Then he is in the water and dying.

It is difficult to kill a Guardian. The many broken bones Schaffa has suffered and the damage to his organs would not be enough to do the job, in and of themselves. Even drowning wouldn't be a problem under ordinary circumstances. Guardians are different. But they do have limits, and drowning *plus* organ failure *plus* blunt force trauma is enough to breach them. He realizes this as he tumbles through the water, bouncing off shards of stone and debris from the destroyed ship. He can't tell which way is up, except that one direction seems faintly brighter than the other, but he is being dragged away from this by the swiftly sinking aft end of the ship. He uncurls, hits a rock, recovers, and tries to paddle against the downward current even though one of his arms is now broken. There's nothing in his lungs. The air's been beaten out of him, and he's trying not to inhale water because then he will surely die. He cannot die. He has so much left to do.

But he is only human, mostly, and as the terrible pressure grows and spots of blackness encroach on his vision and his whole body grows numb with the weight of the water, he cannot help sucking in a mighty lungful. It *hurts*: salt acid in his chest, fire in his throat, and still no air. On top of everything else—he can bear the rest, has borne worse in his long awful life—it is suddenly too much for the ordered, careful rationality that has guided and guarded Schaffa's mind up to this point.

He panics.

Guardians must never panic. He knows this; there are good reasons why. He does it anyway, flailing and screaming as he is dragged into the cold dark. He wants to live. This is the first and worst sin, for one of his kind.

His terror suddenly vanishes. A bad sign. It is replaced a moment later by an anger so powerful that it blots out everything else. He stops screaming and trembles with it, but even as he does so, he knows: This anger is not his own. In his panic, he has opened himself to danger, and the danger that he fears above all others has come striding through the door as if it owns the place already.

It says to him: *If you wish to live, that can be arranged.*

Oh, Evil Earth.

More offers, promises, suggestions and their rewards. Schaffa can have more power—power enough to fight the current, and the pain, and the lack of oxygen. He can live...for a price.

No. No. He knows the price. Better to die than pay it. But it is one thing to resolve to die, quite another to actually carry out that resolve in the midst of dying.

Something burns at the back of Schaffa's skull. This is a cold burn, not like the fire in his nose and throat and chest. Something there is waking up, warming up, gathering itself. Ready for the collapse of his resistance.

We all do what we have to do, comes the seducer's whisper, and this is the same reasoning Schaffa has used on himself too many times, over the centuries. Justifying too many atrocities. One does what one must, for duty. For life.

It's enough. The cold presence takes him.

Power suffuses his limbs. In just a few suddenly restarted

heartbeats, the broken bones have knitted and the organs have resumed their traditional function, albeit with a few work-arounds for the lack of oxygen. He twists in the water and begins to swim, sensing the direction he must go. Not up, not anymore; suddenly he finds oxygen in the water that he is breathing. He has no gills, yet his alveoli suddenly absorb more than they should be able to. It's only a little oxygen, though—not even enough to feed his body properly. Cells die, especially in a very particular part of his brain. He is aware of this, horribly. He is aware of the slow death of all that makes him *Schaffa.* But the price must be paid.

He fights it, of course. The anger tries to drive him forward, keep him underwater, but he knows that *everything* of him will die if he does. So he swims forward, but also upward, squinting through the murk at the light. It takes a long, dying time. But at least some of the rage within him is his own, fury that he has been forced into this position, rage at himself for succumbing, and that keeps him at it even as the tingling sets into his hands, his feet. But—

He reaches the surface. Breaches it. Concentrates hard on not panicking while he vomits up water, coughs out more, and finally sucks in air. It hurts so much. Still, with the first inhalation, the dying stops. His brain and limbs get what they need. There are still spots in his vision, still that awful coldness at the back of his head, but he is Schaffa. *Schaffa.* He holds on to this, digs in claws and snarls away the encroaching cold. Fire-under-Earth, he's still Schaffa, and he will not let himself forget this.

(He loses so much else, though. Understand: The Schaffa that we have known thus far, the Schaffa whom Damaya learned to fear and Syenite learned to defy, is now dead. What remains is a man with a habit of smiling, a warped paternal instinct, and a rage that is not wholly his own driving everything he does from this point on.

Perhaps you will mourn the Schaffa who is lost. It's all right if you do. He was part of you, once.)

He resumes swimming. After about seven hours—this is the strength his memories have bought him—he sees the still-smoking cone of Allia against the horizon. It's a longer distance than straight to shore, but he adjusts his direction to swim toward it. There will be help there, he knows somehow.

It is well past sunset now, fully dark. The water is cold, and he's thirsty, and he hurts. Thankfully none of the monsters of the deep attack him. The only real threat he faces is his own will, and the question of whether it will falter in the battle against the sea, or against the cold rage eating his mind. It does not help that he is alone save for the indifferent stars...and the obelisk. He sees it once, when he glances back: a wavering now-colorless shape against the sparkling night sky. It looks no farther away than when he first noticed it from the deck of the ship, and ignored it in favor of focusing on his quarry. He should have paid closer attention, studied it to see if it was approaching, remembered that even a four-ringer can be a threat under the right circumstances, and—

He frowns, pausing for a moment to float on his back. (This is dangerous. Fatigue immediately begins to set in. The power that sustains him can do only so much.) He stares at the obelisk. A four-ringer. Who? He tries to remember. There was someone... important.

No. He is Schaffa. That is all that is important. He resumes swimming.

Near dawn, he feels gritty black sand under his feet. He stumbles up out of the water, alien to himself and the movement of limbs on land, half crawling. The surf recedes behind him; there's a tree ahead. He collapses upon its roots and does something that resembles sleep. It's closer to a coma.

When he wakes, the sun's up and he is afire with pain of every kind: sore lungs, aching limbs, throbbing unhealed fractures in his nonessential bones, a dry throat, cracking skin. (And another, deeper ache.) He groans and something shadows his face. "You all right?" asks a voice that sounds like he feels. Rough, dry, low.

He peels his eyes open to see an old man crouching before him. The man's an Eastcoaster, thin and weathered, most of his curly white hair gone except a fringe round the back of his head. When Schaffa looks around, he sees that they are in a small, tree-shadowed cove. The old man's rowboat has been pulled onto the shore, not far away. A fishing rod pokes out of it. The trees of the cove are all dead and the sand beneath Schaffa blows with ash; they're still very close to the volcano that was Allia.

How did he get here? He remembers swimming. Why was he in the water? That part is gone.

"I—" Schaffa begins, and chokes on his own dry, swollen tongue. The old man helps him sit up, then offers him an open canteen. Brackish, leather-flavored water never tasted so sweet. The old man pulls it away after a few swallows, which Schaffa knows is wise, but he still groans and reaches after the canteen once. Only once, though. He is strong enough not to beg.

(The emptiness inside him is not just thirst.)

He tries to focus. "I'm." This time speaking is easier. "I… don't know if I'm all right."

"Shipwreck?" The old man cranes his neck to look around. In the near distance, very visible, is the ridge of knifelike stones that Syenite raised, from the pirates' island all the way to the mainland. "Were you out there? What was that, some sort of shake?"

It seems impossible that the old man does not know—but Schaffa has always been amazed at how little ordinary people understand about the world. (Always? Has he *always* been so amazed? Really?) "Rogga," he says, too tired to manage the three syllables of the non-vulgar word for their kind. It's enough. The old man's face hardens.

"Filthy Earth-spawned beasts. That's why they have to be drowned as babes." He shakes his head and focuses on Schaffa. "You're too big for me to lift, and dragging will hurt. Think you can get up?"

With help, Schaffa does manage to rise and stagger to the old man's rowboat. He sits shivering in the prow while the old man rows them away from the cove, heading south along the coast. Some of why he's shivering is cold—his clothes are still wet where he was lying down—and some of it is lingering shock. Some of it, however, is something entirely else.

(Damaya! With great effort he remembers this name, and an impression: a small frightened Midlatter girl superimposed over a tall, defiant Midlatter woman. Love and fear in her eyes, sorrow in his heart. He has hurt her. He needs to find her, but when he reaches for the sense of her that should be embedded in his mind, there is nothing. She is gone along with everything else.)

The old man chatters at him through the whole ride. He is Litz Strongback Metter, and Metter is a little fishing town a few miles south of Allia. They've been debating whether to move since that whole mess with Allia happened, but then suddenly the volcano went dormant, so maybe the Evil Earth isn't out to get them, after all, or at least not this time. He's got two children, one stupid and the other selfish, and three grandkids, all from the stupid one and hopefully not too stupid themselves. They don't have much, Metter's just another Coaster comm, can't even afford a proper wall instead of a bunch of trees and sticks, but folks gotta do what folks gotta do, you know how it is, everyone will take good care of you, don't you worry.

(*What is your name?* the old man asks amid the prattle, and Schaffa tells him. The man asks for more names than this, but Schaffa has only the one. *What were you doing out there?* The silence inside Schaffa yawns in answer.)

The village is an especially precarious one in that it is half on the shore and half on the water, houseboats and stilt-houses connected by jetties and piers. People gather round Schaffa when Litz helps him onto a pier. Hands touch him and he flinches, but they mean to help. It is not their fault that there is so little in them of what he needs that they feel wrong. They push him, guide him. He is beneath a cold shower of fresh water, and then he is put into short pants and a homespun sleeveless shirt. When he lifts his hair while washing it, they marvel at the scar on his neck, thick and stitched and vanishing into his hairline. (He wonders at it himself.) They puzzle over his clothing, so faded by sun and salt water that it has lost nearly all color. It looks brownish-gray. (He remembers that it should be burgundy, but not why.)

More water, the good kind. This time he can drink his fill. He eats a little. Then he sleeps for hours, with incessant angry whispering in the back of his mind.

When Schaffa wakes, it's late in the night, and there's a little boy standing in front of his bed. The lantern's wick has been turned down low, but it's bright enough in the room that Schaffa can see his old clothing, now washed and dry, in the boy's hands. The boy has turned one pocket inside out; there, alone on the whole garment, has it retained something of its original color. Burgundy.

Schaffa pushes himself up on one elbow. Something about the boy . . . perhaps. "Hello."

The boy looks so much like Litz that he needs only a few decades of weathering and less hair to be the old man's twin. But there is a desperate hope in the boy's eyes that would be completely out of place in Litz's. Litz knows his place in the world. This boy, who is maybe eleven or twelve, old enough to be confirmed by his comm . . . something has unmoored him, and Schaffa thinks he knows what. "This is yours," the boy says, holding up the garment.

"Yes."

"You're a Guardian?"

Fleeting almost-memory. "What is that?"

The boy looks as confused as Schaffa feels. He takes a step closer to the bed, and stops. (Come closer. Closer.) "They said you didn't remember things. You're lucky to be alive." The boy licks his lips, uncertain. "Guardians . . . guard."

"Guard what?"

Incredulity washes the fear from the boy. He steps closer still.

"*Orogenes.* I mean... you guard people from them. So they don't hurt anyone. And you guard them from people, too. That's what the stories say."

Schaffa pushes himself to sit up, letting his legs dangle over the edge of the bed. The pain of his injuries is nearly gone, his flesh repaired at a faster rate than normal by the angry power within him. He feels well, in fact, except for one thing.

"Guard orogenes," he says thoughtfully. "Do I?"

The boy laughs a little, though his smile fades quickly. He's very afraid, for some reason, though not of Schaffa. "People kill orogenes," the boy says softly. "When they find them. Unless they're with a Guardian."

"Do they?" It seems uncivilized of them. But then he remembers the ridge of spiky stones across the ocean, and his utter conviction that it was the work of an orogene. *That's why they have to be drowned as babes*, Litz had said.

Missed one, Schaffa thinks, then has to fight hysterical laughter.

"I don't want to hurt anyone," the boy is saying. "I will, one day, without... without training. I almost did when that volcano was doing things. It was so hard not to."

"If you had, it would have killed you and possibly many other people," Schaffa says. Then he blinks. How does he know that? "A hot spot is far too volatile for you to quell safely."

The boy's eyes alight. "You *do* know." He comes forward, sinks to a crouch beside Schaffa's knee. He whispers, "Please help me. I think my mother... she saw me, when the volcano... I tried to act like normal and I *couldn't*. I think she knows. If she tells my grandfather..." He inhales suddenly, sharply, as if he is gasping for air. He's holding back a sob, but the movement looks the same.

Schaffa knows how it feels to drown. He reaches out and strokes the boy's dense cloud of hair, crown to nape, and lets his fingers linger at the nape.

"There is something I have to do," Schaffa says, because there is. The anger and whispers within him have a purpose, after all, and this has become his purpose. *Gather them, train them, make them the weapons they are meant to be.* "If I take you with me, we must travel far from here. You'll never see your family again."

The boy looks away, his expression turning bitter. "They'd kill me if they knew."

"Yes." Schaffa presses, very gently, and draws the first measure of—something—from the boy. What? He cannot remember what it is called. Perhaps it has no name. All that matters is that it exists, and he needs it. With it, he knows somehow, he can hold on more tightly to the tattered remnants of who he is. (Was.) So he takes, and the first draught of it is like a sudden, sweet wash of fresh water amid gallons of burning salt. He yearns to drink it all, reaches for the rest as thirstily as he sought Litz's canteen, though he forces himself to let go for the same reason. He can endure on what he has now, and if he is patient, the boy will have more for him later.

Yes. His thoughts are clearer now. Easier to think around the whispers. He needs this boy, and others like him. He must go forth and find them, and with their help, he can make it to—

—to—

—well. Not everything is clearer. Some things will never come back. He'll make do.

The boy is searching his face. While Schaffa has been trying to put together the fragments of his identity, the boy has been wrestling with his future. They are made for each other. "I'll go with you," the boy says, having apparently spent the past minute thinking he has a choice. "Anywhere. I don't want to hurt anyone. I don't want to die."

For the first time since a moment on a ship a few days before, when he was a different person, Schaffa smiles. He strokes the boy's head again. "You have a good soul. I'll help you all I can." The boy's tension dissolves at once; tears wet his eyes. "Go and gather some things to travel. I'll speak with your parents."

These words fall from his mouth naturally, easily. He has said them before, though he doesn't remember when. He remembers, though, that sometimes things don't go as well as he says they will.

The boy whispers his thanks, grabs Schaffa's knee and tries to squeeze that thanks into him, then trots away. Schaffa pushes himself slowly to his feet. The boy has left the faded uniform behind, so Schaffa pulls this on again, his fingers remembering how the seams should lie. There should be a cloak, too, but that is gone. He can't remember where. When he steps forward, a mirror on the side of the room catches his eye, and he stops. Shivers, not in pleasure this time.

It is *wrong.* It is so wrong. His hair hangs lank and dry after the sun and salt's ravaging; it should be black and glossy, and instead it is dull and wispy, burnt. The uniform hangs off him, for he has spent some of the substance of his own body as fuel in the push to reach shore. The uniform's colors are also wrong and there is no reassurance in it of who he was, who he should be. And his eyes—

Evil Earth, he thinks, staring at the icy near-white of them. He did not know his eyes looked like this.

There is a creak on the floorboards near the door, and his alien eyes shift to one side. The boy's mother stands there, blinking in the light of the lantern she holds. "Schaffa," she says. "I thought I heard you up. And Eitz?"

That must be the boy's name. "He came to bring me these." Schaffa touches his clothing.

The woman comes into the room. "Huh," she says. "Now that it's all wrung out and dry, it looks like a uniform."

Schaffa nods. "I've learned something new of myself. I'm a Guardian."

Her eyes widen. "Truly?" There's suspicion in her gaze. "And Eitz has been bothering you."

"It was no bother." Schaffa smiles, to reassure her. For some reason, the woman's frown twitches and deepens. Ah, well; he has forgotten how to charm people, too. He turns and goes over to her, and she falls back a step at his approach. He stops, amused by her fear. "He, too, has learned something of himself. I'll be taking him away now."

The woman's eyes widen. Her mouth works in silence for a moment, then she sets her jaw. "I knew it."

"Did you?"

"I didn't want to." She swallows, her hand tightening; the little lantern flame wavers with whatever emotion flashes through her. "Don't take him. Please."

Schaffa tilts his head. "Why not?"

"It would kill his father."

"Not his grandfather?" Schaffa takes a step closer. (Closer.) "Not his uncles and aunts and cousins? Not you?"

She twitches again. "I...don't know how I feel, right now." She shakes her head.

"Poor, poor thing," Schaffa says softly. This compassion is automatic, too. He feels the sorrow deeply. "But will you protect him from them, if I do not take him?"

"What?" She looks at Schaffa in surprise and alarm. Can this truly have never occurred to her? Apparently not. "Protect... *him*?" That she asks this, Schaffa understands, is the proof that she is inadequate to the task.

So he sighs and reaches up, as if to put a hand on her shoulder, and shakes his head, as if to convey regret. She relaxes minutely and does not notice when his hand instead curves around her neck. His fingers settle into place and she stiffens at once. "Wh—" Then she falls down dead.

Schaffa blinks as she falls to the floor. For a moment he is confused. Was that supposed to happen? And then—his own thoughts freshened further by the dollop of *something* that she has given him, such a tiny amount of it relative to what Eitz possessed—he understands. This thing is only safe to do with orogenes, who have more than enough to share. The woman must have been a still. But Schaffa feels better. In fact—

Take more, whispers the rage at the back of his mind. *Take the others. They threaten the boy, which threatens you.*

Yes. That seems wise.

So Schaffa rises and moves through the quiet, dark house, touching each member of Eitz's family and devouring a piece of them. Most of them do not wake. The stupid son gives more than the rest; almost an orogene. (Almost a Guardian.) Litz gives the least, perhaps because he is old—or perhaps because he is awake and fighting against the hand Schaffa has clamped over his mouth and nose. He is trying to stab Schaffa with a fishknife pulled from under his pillow. What a pity that he must suffer such fear! Schaffa twists Litz's head around sharply to get at the nape of his neck. There's a snapping sound as he does this, which he doesn't even notice until the flow of *something* out of Litz goes soft and dead and useless. Ah, yes, belatedly Schaffa remembers that it does not work on the dead. He'll be more careful in the future.

But it is so much better, now that the taut ache inside him has gone still. He feels…not whole. Never that, again. But when there is so much of another presence inside him, even a little regained ground is a blessing.

"I am Schaffa Guardian…Warrant?" he murmurs, blinking as the last part finally comes to him. What comm is Warrant? He cannot remember. He is glad to have the name regardless. "I have done only what was necessary. Only what is best for the world."

The words feel right. Yes. He has needed the sense of purpose, which now sits like lead at the back of his brain; amazing that he did not have it before. Now, though? "Now I have work to do."

Eitz finds him in the living room. The boy is breathless, excited, carrying a small satchel. "I heard you and Mama talking. Did you…tell her?"

Schaffa crouches to be on eye level with him, taking him by the shoulders. "Yes. She said she didn't know how she felt, and then she said nothing more."

Eitz's face crumples. He glances toward the corridor that

leads to the adults' rooms in the house. Everyone down that corridor is dead. The doors are closed and quiet. Schaffa has left Eitz's siblings and cousins alive, however, because he is not a complete monster.

"Can I say goodbye to her?" Eitz asks softly.

"I think that would be dangerous," Schaffa says. He means it. He doesn't want to have to kill the boy yet. "These things are best done cleanly. Come; you have me now, and I will never leave you."

The boy blinks at this and straightens a little, then nods shakily. He's old for such words to have the power on him that they do. They work, Schaffa suspects, because Eitz has spent the past few months living in terror of his family. It is nothing to play on such a lonely, weary state of mind. It isn't even a lie.

They leave the half-dead house behind. Schaffa knows that he should take the boy…somewhere. Somewhere with obsidian walls and gilded bars, a place that will die in a cataclysm of fire in ten years, so perhaps it is good that he is too damaged to remember this location. In any case the angry whispers have begun steering him in a different direction. Somewhere south. Where he has work to do.

He puts his hand on Eitz's shoulder to comfort the boy, or perhaps to comfort himself. Together they walk into the predawn dark.

* * *

Don't be fooled. The Guardians are much, much older than Old Sanze, and they do not work for us.

—*Last recorded words of Emperor Mutshatee, prior to his execution*

4

you are challenged

You're tired after calling the obelisk. When you get back to your room and stretch out for half a moment on the bare pallet that came with the apartment, you fall asleep so fast you don't even realize you're doing it. In the dead of the night—or so your body clock says, since the glowing walls haven't changed—your eyes blink open and it's like only a moment has passed. But Hoa is curled beside you, apparently actually sleeping for once, and you can hear Tonkee snoring faintly in the room next door, and you feel much better than you did, if hungry. Well rested, for perhaps the first time in weeks.

The hunger spurs you up and into the apartment's living room. There's a small hempen satchel on the table, which Tonkee must've acquired, partially open to reveal mushrooms and a small pile of dried beans and other cachefood. That's right: As accepted members of Castrima, you now get a share of the comm's stores. None of it is the kind of food you can just eat for a snack, except maybe the mushrooms, but you've never seen those before, and some varieties of mushrooms need to be cooked to be edible.

You're tempted, but...*is* Castrima the sort of comm that would give dangerous foodstuffs to newcomers without warning them?

Hmm. Right. You fetch your runny-sack, rummage in it for the remaining provisions you brought to Castrima with you, and make a meal out of dried oranges, cachebread crusts, and a lump of bad-tasting jerky that you traded for at the last comm you passed, and which you suspect is hydro-pipe rat meat. Food is that which nourishes, the lorists say.

You've just choked the jerky down, and are sitting there sleepily pondering how merely summoning an obelisk took so much out of you—as if anything regarding the obelisks can be described with the adjective *merely*—when you become aware of a high, rhythmic scraping sound outside. You dismiss it immediately. Nothing about this comm makes sense; it will probably take you weeks if not months to get used to its peculiar sounds. (Months. Are you giving up on Nassun so easily?) So you ignore the sound even as it grows louder and closer, and you keep yawning, and you're about to get up and head back to bed when it belatedly dawns on you that what you're hearing is *screaming.*

Frowning, you go to the door of the apartment, pulling open the thin curtain. You're not particularly concerned; your sessapinae haven't even twitched, and anyway if there's ever a shake down here in Castrima-under, everyone's dead no matter how quickly they leave their homes. Outside there are lots of people up and about. A woman passes right by your door, carrying a big basket of the same mushrooms you almost ate; she nods at you distractedly as you come out, then almost loses her load as she tries to turn toward the noise and nearly bumps into a man pushing a covered, wheeled bin that stinks to the sky and is probably from the latrines.

In a comm with no functional day-night cycle, Castrima effectively never sleeps, and you know they have six work shifts instead of the usual three because you've been put on one. It won't start till midday—or twelvebell, as the Castrima folk say—when you're supposed to look for some woman named Artith near the forge.

And none of this is relevant because through the scatter and jut of Castrima's crystals, you can see a small cluster of people coming into the big rectangular tunnel-mouth that serves as the entrance to the geode. They're running, and they're carrying another person, who's doing all the screaming.

Even then, you're tempted to ignore it and go back to sleep. It's a Season. People die; there's nothing you can do about it. These aren't even your people. There's no reason for you to care.

Then someone shouts, "*Lerna!*" And the tone of it is so panicked that you twitch. You can see the squat gray crystal that houses Lerna's apartment from your balcony, three crystals away and a little below your own. His door-curtain jerks open and he hurries out, shrugging on a shirt as he runs down the nearest set of steps. Heading for the infirmary, where the cluster of running folk seems to be going as well.

For reasons that you cannot name, you glance back at your own apartment doorway. Tonkee, who sleeps like petrified wood, hasn't come out—but Hoa is there, statue-still and watching you. Something about his expression makes you frown. He doesn't seem to be able to do the emotionless stoneface of his kin, maybe because he doesn't have a face of actual stone. Regardless, the first thing you interpret of his expression is . . . pity.

You're out of the apartment and running for the ground level in the next breath, almost before you've thought about it. (You think as you run: The pity of a disguised stone eater has galvanized you as the screams of a fellow human being haven't. Such a monster you are.) Castrima is as frustratingly confusing as always, but this time you're aided by the fact that other people have started running along the bridges and walkways in the direction of the trouble, so you can just go with the flow.

By the time you get there, a small crowd has formed around the infirmary, most of the people milling about in curiosity or concern or anxiety. Lerna and the cluster of people carrying their injured companion have gone inside, and the awful screech is obvious now for what it is: the throat-tearing howl of someone in appalling pain, pain beyond bearing, who nevertheless is somehow forced to bear it.

It is not an intentional thing that you start pushing forward to get inside. You know nothing about giving medical care . . . but you do know pain. To your surprise, though, people glance at you in annoyance—then blink and shift aside. You notice those who look blank being pulled aside for quick whispers by those whose eyes have widened. Oh-ho. Castrima's been talking about you.

Then you're inside the infirmary, and you nearly get knocked down by a Sanzed woman running past with some sort of syringe in her hands. Can't be safe to do that. You follow her over to an infirmary bed where six people hold down the person doing the screaming. You get a look at the person's face when one of them shifts aside: no one you know. Just another Midlatter man, who has clearly been topside to judge by the gray layer of ash on his skin and clothing and hair. The woman with the syringe shoulders aside someone else and ostensibly administers the syringe's contents. A moment later, the man shudders all over, and his mouth begins to close. His scream dies off, slowly, slowly. Slowly. He jerks once, mightily; his holders all shift with the strength of his effort. Then at last, mercifully, he subsides into unconsciousness.

The silence almost reverberates. Lerna and the Sanzed healer keep moving, though the people who have been holding the man down draw back and look at each other as if asking what to do now. In the now-silent confusion, you cannot help glancing off toward the far end of the infirmary, where Alabaster still sits unnoticed by the infirmary's new guests. His stone eater stands where you last saw her, though her gaze is also fixed on the tableau. You can see Alabaster's face over the beds; his eyes slide over to meet yours, but then they shift away.

Your attention is recaptured by the man on the bed as some of the people around him step back. At first you can't tell what the problem is, other than that his pants seem oddly *wet* in patches, caked with muddy ash. The wetness isn't red, it's not blood, but there's a smell that you're not sure how to describe. Meat in brine. Hot fat. His boots are off, baring feet which still spasmodically twitch a little, the splayed toes relaxing only reluctantly even in unconsciousness. Lerna is cutting open one pants leg with a pair of scissors. What you notice first, as he peels away the damp cloth, are the small round blue hemispheres that dot the man's skin here and there, each perhaps two inches in diameter and an inch of rounded height, shiny and foreign to his flesh. There are ten or fifteen of them. Each sits at the center of a patch of bloated pink-brown flesh covering perhaps a handspan of the man's legs. You think the lumps are jewels, at first. That's kind of what they look like, metallic over the blue, and beautiful.

"Fuck," says someone, voice soft with shock, and someone

else says, "What the rust." Someone else pushes into the infirmary behind you after a moment's argument with the people who've blocked off the door. She comes to stand beside you and you look over at Ykka, whose eyes widen in confusion and revulsion for an instant before she schools her expression to blankness. Then she says, sharply enough to jerk people out of staring, "What happened?"

(You notice, belatedly or perhaps right in time, that another stone eater is in the room, not far beyond the tableau. She's familiar—the red-haired one who greeted you along with Ykka when you first came to Castrima. She's watching Ykka now, avidly, but her stone gaze occasionally drifts toward you, too. You suddenly become hyperaware that Hoa did not follow you from the apartment.)

"Outer perimeter patrol," says another ash-covered Midlatter man, to Ykka. He doesn't look like a Strongback, too small. Maybe he's one of the new Hunters. He comes around the bedside group and fixes his gaze on Ykka as if she is all that prevents him from staring at the injured man until his mind breaks. "We were out by the s-salt quarry, thinking it might be a good place for hunting. There was some kind of sinkhole near a stream runnel. Beled—I don't know. He's gone. I heard them both scream at first, but I didn't know why. I was upstream, looking at some animal tracks. By the time I got there it was just Terteis there, looking like he was trying to climb out of the ash. I helped him out, but they were on him already, and more were crawling up his shoes so I had to cut them off—"

A hiss jerks your eyes away from the speaking man. Lerna is shaking his hand, holding out the fingers stiffly as if they hurt.

"Get me the rusting forceps!" he says to another man, who twitches and turns to do so. You've never heard Lerna curse before.

"Some kind of boil," says the Sanzed woman who injected the man. She sounds disbelieving; she's speaking to Lerna, as if trying to convince him rather than herself. (Lerna just keeps grimly probing the edges of the burns with his uninjured hand, ignoring her.) "Has to be. He fell into a steam vent, a geyser, an old rusted-out geo pipe." Which would make the bugs just a coincidence.

"—or they would've gotten on me, too." The other Hunter is still talking in his hollow voice. "I thought the sinkhole was just loose ash, but it was really . . . I don't know. Like an anthill." The Hunter swallows, sets his jaw. "I couldn't get the rest off, so I brought him here."

Ykka's lips press together, but she rolls up her sleeves and goes over, pushing through the other shocked people nearby. She yells, "Back up! If you don't mean to help with this, get out of the rusting way." Some of the milling people start pulling others away. Someone else grabs for one of the jewel-objects and tries to pull it off, then jerks their hand away, yelping as Lerna did. The object changes, two pieces of the shiny blue surface flaking away and lifting before clapping back into place—and suddenly it shifts in your head. It's not a jewel; it's a bug. Some kind of beetle, and the iridescent shell is its carapace. In the moment that it lifted its wing covers, you saw that its round body was translucent, with something jumping and bubbling inside. You can sess the heat of it even from where you are, hot as a boil. The man's flesh steams around it.

Someone gives Lerna the forceps and he tries to pull one of the beetles off. Its wing covers lift again, and a thin jet of something skeets across Lerna's fingers. He yelps and drops the forceps, jerking back. "Acid!" someone says. Someone else grabs his hand and tries to quickly wipe off the stuff, but you know what it is even before Lerna gasps, "No! Just water. Scalding water."

"Careful," says the other Hunter, belatedly. One of his hands bears a line of blisters, you notice. You also notice that he doesn't look back at the infirmary table or any of the people there.

This is too horrible to watch. The rusting bugs are boiling the man to death. But when you look away, you see that Alabaster is watching you again. Alabaster, who himself is covered in burns, but who *should be dead.* No one stands near the epicenter of a continent-spanning fissure vent and gets only patchy third-degree burns. He should've been ashes scattered over Yumenes's melted streets.

You realize this as he gazes at you, though his expression is indifferent to another man's trial by fire. It is a familiar sort of indifference—Fulcrum-familiar. It is the indifference that comes of too many betrayals, too many friends lost for no good reason, too many "too horrible to watch" atrocities seen.

And yet. The reverberation of Alabaster's orogeny is carelessly powerful, diamond-precise, and so achingly familiar that you have to close your eyes and fight off memories of a heaving ship deck, a lonely highroad, a windy rock island. The torus that he spins is devastatingly small—barely an inch wide, so attenuated that you cannot find its hairpin fulcrum. He's still better than you.

Then you hear a gasp. You open your eyes to see one of the bugs shiver, hiss like a living teakettle—and then freeze over. Its legs, which had been hooked into the boiled flesh around it, pop loose. It's dead.

But then you hear a soft groan, and the orogeny dissipates. You look over to see that Alabaster has bowed his head and hunched over. His stone eater slow-grind crouches beside him, something in her posture indicating concern even if her face is as placid as ever. The red-haired stone eater—in internal exasperation you decide to call her Ruby Hair, for now—is gazing at him, too.

That's it, then. You look back at the man—and your gaze catches on Lerna, who's looking at the frozen bug in fascination. His eyes lift, sweep the room, stutter across yours, stop. You see the question there, and start to shake your head: No, you did not freeze the bug. But that isn't the right question, and maybe isn't even the question he's asking. He doesn't need to know if you did. He needs to know if you *can*.

Lerna, Hoa, Alabaster; today you are driven by silent, meaningful gazes, it seems.

The hot points of the insects sess like geothermal vents as you step forward and focus your sessapinae. Lots of controlled pressure in their tiny bodies; that's how they make the water boil. You lift a hand toward the man out of habit so everyone will know you're doing something, and you hear a curse, a hiss, a scramble of feet and jostling bodies as people move back from you, away from any torus you might manifest. Fools. Don't they know you only need a torus when you have to pull from the ambient? The bugs have plenty of what you need. The difficulty will lie in confining your draw just to them and not the man's overheated flesh underneath.

Ykka's stone eater takes a slow step closer. You sess her movement, rather than seeing it; it's like a mountain shifting toward you. Then Ruby Hair stops as suddenly there is another mountain in its way: Hoa, stock-still and quietly cold. Where did he come from? You cannot spare another thought for these creatures right now.

You begin slowly, using your eyes as well as your sessapinae to determine exactly where to stop... but Alabaster has shown you the way of it. You spin the torus from their hot little bodies as he did, one by one. As you do this, some of them crack open with a loud and violent hiss, and one of them even pops off, flying off toward the side of the room. (People move out of its way even faster than they moved out of yours.) Then it is done.

Everyone stares at you. You look at Ykka. You're breathing hard because that degree of fine focus is much, much harder than shifting a hillside. "Need anything shaken?"

She blinks, sessing instantly what you mean. Then she grabs your arm. There is—what? An inversion. A channeling-away, as you would do to an obelisk, except there is no obelisk, and you aren't doing the channeling even though it's your orogeny. All at once you hear people exclaim outside, and you glance through the infirmary's door. The infirmary is a built-building, not carved from one of the giant crystals of the geode; inside it's lit only by electric lamps. Outside, however, through the uncurtained doorway, you can see the geode crystals glowing noticeably brighter, all over the comm.

You stare at Ykka. She nods back at you in a matter-of-fact, collegial way, as if you should have any clue what she's just done or as if you should be comfortable with a feral doing something that a ringed Fulcrum orogene can't. Then Ykka steps over to grab another pair of forceps to help. Lerna's pulling on one of the beetles again despite his scalded fingers, and this time the thing is coming off. A proboscis as long as its body slides out of the boiled flesh, and—you can't look anymore.

(You glimpse Ruby Hair again, from the corner of your eye. She's ignoring Hoa, who stands still as a statue between you, and now she's smiling at Ykka. Her lips are parted just a little. You glimpse a hint of shining teeth. You blot this from your awareness.)

So you retreat to the far end of the infirmary, to sit down beside Alabaster's cushion pile. He's still bent over, breathing like a bellows, although the stone eater has taken hold of his shoulder with one viselike hand to keep him mostly upright. Belatedly you realize he's holding one of his stumpy wrists to his belly, and—oh, Earth. The gray-brown rock that once only capped his right wrist now sleeves up to his elbow.

He lifts his head; sweat sheens his face. He looks as weary as if he just shut down another supervolcano, although this time he's at least conscious, and smiling.

"Ever the good pupil, Syen," he murmurs. "But rusting Earth, is it costly to teach you."

The shock of understanding rings through you like silence. *Alabaster can't do orogeny anymore*. Not without... consequences. Impulse makes you look at Antimony, and your gorge rises as you realize the stone eater's gaze is fixed on his newly stoned arm. She doesn't move, however. After a moment Alabaster manages to straighten, throwing a grateful look at her for the supportive hand. "Later," he says softly. You know this means *eat my arm later*. She adjusts her hand to support him from behind instead.

The urge to push her aside, put your hand in place to hold him up, is so powerful that you can't look at this, either.

You push yourself up, brush past everyone else to get outside the infirmary, and then you sit down on the low, flattened tip of a crystal that is only just beginning to grow out of the geode wall. No one bothers you, though you feel the pressure of gazes and hear the echo of whispers. You don't mean to stay long, but you do. You don't know why.

Eventually a shadow falls over your feet. You look up to see Lerna standing there. Beyond him, Ykka is walking away with another man who is trying to talk to her; she seems to be angrily ignoring him. The rest of the crowd has dispersed at last, though you can see through the open doorway that there's still more people in the infirmary than usual, perhaps visiting the poor half-cooked Hunter.

Lerna isn't looking at you. He's staring at the far wall of the geode, which is lost in the hazy glow from dozens of crystals between here and there. He's also smoking a cigarette. The stench of it, and the yellowish color of the outer wrapping, tells you it's a mellow: derminther mela leaves and flower buds, mildly narcotic when dried. The Somidlats are famous for them, to the degree that the Somidlats can be famous for anything. You're still surprised to see him smoking one, though. He's a doctor. Mellows are bad for you.

"You all right?" you ask.

He doesn't answer at first, taking a long drag on the cigarette. You're starting to think he won't speak, when he says, "I'm going to kill him when I go back in there."

Then you understand. The bugs burned through skin,

muscle, maybe even down to bone. With a team of Yumenescene doctors and cutting-edge biomestric drugs, maybe the man could be kept alive long enough to heal—and even then he might never walk again. With just whatever equipment and medicines Castrima has to hand, the best Lerna can do is amputate. The man might survive it. But this is a Season, and every comm-dweller must earn their shelter from the ash and cold. Few comms have use for a legless Hunter, and this comm is already supporting one burned invalid.

(Ykka walking away, ignoring a man who sounds like he is arguing for a life.)

So Lerna is very much not all right. You decide to change the subject, slightly. "I've never seen anything like those bugs."

"The locals say they're called boilbugs, though no one knew why before now. They breed around streams, carry water inside themselves. Animals eat them during droughts. Usually they're carrion eaters. Harmless." Lerna flicks ash from his forearm. He's wearing only a loose sleeveless shirt due to Castrima's warmth. The skin of his forearms is flecked with . . . something. You look away. "Things change during a Season, though."

Yes. Cooked carrion probably lasts longer.

"You could've gotten those things off him the instant you walked in the door," Lerna adds.

You blink. Then it registers in your mind that this statement was an attack. It's so mildly delivered, from such an unexpected quarter, that you're too surprised to be angry. "I couldn't," you say. "At least, I didn't know I could. Alabaster—"

"I don't expect anything from him. He came to die here, not live here." Lerna pivots to face you, and all of a sudden you realize that his placid manner has been concealing absolute rage. His gaze is cool, but it's visible in everything else: his white lips, the flex of muscle in his jaw, his flaring nostrils. "Why are *you* here, Essun?"

You flinch. "You know why. I came to find Nassun."

"Nassun's out of your reach. Your goals have changed; now you're here to survive, same as the rest of us. Now you're *one of us*." His lip curls in something that might be contempt. "I'm saying this because if I don't make you understand, you might have a rusting fit and kill us all."

You open your mouth to reply. He takes a step toward you, though, and it's so aggressive that you actually sit up. "Tell me you won't, Essun. Tell me I won't have to leave *this* comm in the dead of the night, hoping nobody you've pissed off catches me and slits my throat. Tell me I'm not going to have to go back out there, to fight for my life and watch people I try to help die again and again and again, until I get eaten by rusting *bugs*—"

He cuts himself off with a choked sound, turning away sharply. You stare at his tense back and say nothing, because there's nothing you can say. This is the second time he's mentioned your murder of Tirimo. And is that surprising? He was born there, grew up there; Lerna's mother was still living there when you left. You think. Maybe you killed her, too, that last day.

There's nothing you can say, not with guilt souring your mouth, but you try anyway. "I'm sorry."

He laughs. It doesn't even sound like him, it's so ugly and angry. Then he resumes his former posture, gazing at the far geode wall. He's more in control of himself now; the muscle in his jaw isn't jumping quite so much. "Prove you're sorry."

You shake your head, in confusion rather than refusal. "How?"

"Word's spreading. A couple of the biggest gossips in the comm were with Ykka when she met you, and apparently you confirmed what a lot of the roggas have been whispering among themselves." You almost flinch at his use of *rogga*. He was such a polite boy once. "Topside, you said this Season won't end for thousands of years. Was that an exaggeration, or the truth?"

You sigh and rub a hand over your hair. It's a thick, curly mess at the roots. You need to retwist your locks, but you haven't because you haven't had time and because it feels like there's no point.

"Seasons always end," you say. "Father Earth keeps his own equilibrium. It's just a question of how long it will take."

"How long?" It's barely a question. His tone is flat, resigned. He suspects the answer already.

And he deserves your honest, best guess. "Ten thousand years?" For the Yumenes Rifting to stop venting and the skies to clear. Not long at all by the usual scale of tectonics, but the real danger lies in what the ash might set off. Enough ash covering the warm surface of the sea, and the ice might grow at the poles. That means saltier seas. Drier climates. Permafrost. Glaciers marching, spreading. And the most habitable part of the world should that happen, the Equatorials, will still be hot and toxic.

It's the winter that really kills, during Seasons. Starvation. Exposure. Even after the skies clear, though, the Rift could cause an age of winter that lasts *millions* of years. None of which matters, because humanity will have gone extinct long before. It'll be just the obelisks floating over plains of endless white, with no one left to wonder at or ignore them.

His eyelids flicker. "Hnh." To your surprise, he turns to face you. Even more surprising is that his anger seems to be gone, though it has been replaced by a kind of bleakness that feels familiar. It's his question, though, that floors you:

"So what are you planning to do about it?"

Your mouth actually falls open. After a moment you manage to reply, "I wasn't aware there was anything I *could* do about it." Just like you hadn't thought there was anything you could do about the boilbugs. Alabaster is the genius. You're the grunt.

"What are you and Alabaster doing with the obelisks?"

"What is *Alabaster* doing," you correct. "He just asked me to summon one. Probably because—" It hurts to say. "He can't do that kind of orogeny anymore."

"Alabaster made the Rift, didn't he?"

You close your mouth fast enough that your teeth clack. You've just said Alabaster can't do orogeny anymore. Enough Castrimans hear that they're living in an underground rock garden because of him, and they'll find a way to kill him, stone eater or not.

Lerna smiles lopsidedly. "It's not hard to put together, Essun. His wounds are from steam, particulate abrasion, and corrosive gas, not fire—characteristic of being in close proximity to an erupting burn. I don't know how he survived, but it's left its mark on him." He shrugged. "And I've seen you destroy a town in five minutes without breaking a sweat, so I've got an inkling of what a ten-ringer might be capable of. What are the obelisks for?"

You set your jaw. "You can ask me six different ways, Lerna, and I'll give you six different versions of 'I don't know,' because I don't."

"I think you at least have an idea. But lie to me if you want." He shakes his head. "This is your comm now."

He falls silent after that, as if expecting a response from you. You're too busy vehemently rejecting the idea to respond. But he knows you too well; he knows you don't want to hear it. That's why he says it again. "*Essun Rogga Castrima.* That's who you are now."

"No."

"Leave, then. Everyone knows Ykka can't really hold you if you put your mind to leaving. I know you'll kill us all if you feel the need. So, go."

You sit there, looking at your hands, which dangle between your knees. Your thoughts are empty.

Lerna inclines his head. "You aren't leaving because you aren't stupid. Maybe you can survive out there, but not as anything Nassun would ever want to see again. And if nothing else, you want to live so that you can eventually find her again... however unlikely that is."

Your hands twitch once. Then they resume dangling limply.

"When this Season doesn't end," Lerna continues, and it is so much worse that he does it in that same weary monotone which asked how long the Season would last, like he is speaking utter truth and knows it and hates it, "we'll run out of food. Cannibalism will help, but it's not sustainable. At that point the comm will either turn raider or simply dissolve into roving bands of commless. But even that won't save us, long term. Eventually the remnants of Castrima will just starve. Father Earth wins at last."

It's the truth, whether you want to face it or not. And it's further proof that whatever happened to Lerna during his brief commless career changed him. Not really for the worse. It's just made him the kind of healer who knows that sometimes one must inflict terrible agony—rebreak a bone, carve off a limb, kill the weak—in order to make the whole stronger.

"Nassun's strong like you," he continues, softly and brutally. "Say she survives Jija. Say you find her, bring her here or any other place that seems safe. She'll starve with the rest when the storecaches empty, but with her orogeny, she could probably force others to give her their food. Maybe even kill them and have the remaining stores for herself. Eventually the stores will run out, though. She'll have to leave the comm, scrape by on whatever forage she can find under the ash, hopefully while not running afoul of the wildlife or other hazards. She'll be one of the last to die: alone, hungry, cold, hating herself. Hating you. Or maybe she'll have shut down by then. Maybe she'll just be an animal, driven only by the instinct to survive and failing even at that. Maybe she'll eat herself in the end, the way any beast might—"

"Stop," you say. It's a whisper. Mercifully, he does. He turns away again instead, taking another long drag of his half-forgotten mellow.

"Have you talked to anyone since you got here?" he asks finally. It's not really a change of subject. You don't relax. He nods toward the infirmary. "Anyone but Alabaster and that menagerie you've been traveling with? More than a meeting; *talked*."

Not enough to count. You shake your head.

"The rumor's spreading, Essun. And now everyone's thinking

about how slowly their children will die." He finally flicks away the mellow. It's still burning. "Thinking about how they can't do anything about it."

But you can, he doesn't need to say.

Can you?

Lerna walks away so abruptly that you're surprised. You hadn't realized he was done. It's an ingrained flinch at the idea of waste that makes you go pick up his discarded cigarette. Takes you a moment to figure out how to inhale without choking; you've never tried before. Orogenes aren't supposed to ingest narcotics.

But orogenes aren't supposed to live, either, during a Season. The Fulcrum had no storecaches. No one ever mentioned it, but you're pretty sure that if a Season ever hit Yumenes hard enough, the Guardians would have swept the place and slaughtered every one of you. Your kind is useful in preventing Seasons, but if the Fulcrum ever so failed in its duty, if ever the worthies of the Black Star or the Emperor had felt a whiff of a thought of a tremor, you and your fellow Imperial Orogenes would not have been rewarded with survival.

And why should you have been? What survival skills does any rogga offer? You can keep people from dying in a shake, yay. Fat lot of good that does when there's no food.

"Enough!" You hear Ykka's voice from a short distance away, though you can't see her around the ground-level crystals. She's shouting. "It's done! You want to be there for it or stay here wasting breath on me?"

You get up, your knees aching. Head in that direction.

Along the way, you pass a young man whose face is streaked

with tears of fury and incipient grief. He storms past you back to the infirmary. You keep going and eventually see Ykka standing near the side of a high, narrow crystal. She's planted a hand against its wall and stands with her head bowed, her bush of hair falling around her face so you can't see it. You think she's shaking a little.

Maybe that's your imagination. She seems so coldhearted. But then, so do you.

"Ykka."

"Not you, too," she mutters. "I don't want to hear it, Bugkiller."

Belatedly you realize: By killing the boilbugs, you made this a harder choice for her. Before, she could have ordered the Hunter killed as a mercy, and the bugs would have been at fault. Now it's pragmatism, comm policy. That's on her.

You shake your head and step closer. She straightens and turns in an instant, and you sess the defensive orientation of her orogeny. She doesn't do anything with it, doesn't set a torus or start an ambient-draw, but then, she wouldn't, would she? Those are Fulcrum techniques. You don't really know what she's going to do, this strangely trained feral, to defend herself.

Part of you is curious, in a detached sort of way. The other part notes the tension on her face. So you offer her the still-lit mellow.

She blinks at it. Her orogeny settles into quiescence again, but her eyes lift and study yours. Then she tilts her head, bemused, considering. Finally she puts one hand on her hip, plucks the mellow from your fingers with the other, and takes a long drag. It works quickly; after a moment she turns to lean back against the crystal, her face settling into weary rather than tense lines as she blows out curls of smoke. She offers it back. You settle beside her and take it.

It takes another ten minutes to finish the cigarette, passing it back and forth between the two of you. Both of you linger, however, after it's done, by unspoken agreement. Only when you hear someone begin to utter loud, broken sobs from the infirmary behind you do you nod to each other, and part ways.

* * *

> It is unfathomable that any sensible civilization would be so wasteful as fill prime storage caverns with corpses! No wonder these people died out, whoever they were. I estimate another year before we can clear all of the bones, funeral urns, and other debris, then perhaps another six months to fully map and renovate. Less if you can get me those blackjackets I requested! I don't care if they cost the Earth; some of these chambers are unstable.
>
> There are tablets in here, though. Something in verses, though we can't read this bizarre language. Like stonelore. Five tablets, not three. What do you want to do with them? I say we give the lot to Fourth so they'll stop whining about how much history we're destroying.
>
> —*Report of Journeywoman Fogrid Innovator Yumenes to the Geneer Licensure, Equatorial East: "Proposal to Repurpose Subsurface Catacombs, City of Firaway." Master-level review only.*

INTERLUDE

A dilemma: You are made of so many people you do not wish to be. Including me.

But you know so little of me. I will attempt to explain the context *of me, if not the detail. It begins—*I *began—with a war.*

War *is a poor word. Is it war when people find an infestation of vermin in some unwanted place and try to burn or poison it clean? Though that, too, is a poor metaphor, because no one hates individual mice or bedbugs. No one singles out for vengeance* that one, that one right there, three-legged splotch-backed little bastard, *and all its progeny down the hundreds of verminous generations that encompass a human life. And the three-legged splotch-backed little bastards don't have much chance of becoming more than an annoyance to people—whereas you and all your kind have cracked the surface of the planet and lost the Moon. If the mice in your garden, back in Tirimo, had helped Jija kill Uche, you would have shaken the place to pebbles and set fire to the ruins before you left. You destroyed Tirimo anyway, but if it had been personal, you'd have done worse.*

Yet for all your hatred, you still might not have managed to kill the vermin. The survivors would be greatly changed—made harder, stronger, more splotch-backed. Perhaps the hardships you inflicted would have fissioned their descendants into many factions, each with different interests. Some of those interests would have nothing to do with you. Some would revere and despise you for your power. Some would be as dedicated to your destruction as you were to theirs, even though by the time they had the strength to actually act on their enmity, you would have forgotten their existence. To them, your enmity would be the stuff of legend.

And some might hope to appease you, or talk you around to at least a degree of peaceful tolerance. I am one of these.

I was not always. For a very long time, I was one of the vengeful ones... but what it keeps coming back to is this: Life cannot exist without the Earth. Yet there is a not-insubstantial chance that life will win its war, and destroy the Earth. We've come close a few times.

That can't happen. We cannot be permitted to win.

So this is a confession, my Essun. I've betrayed you already and I will do it again. You haven't even chosen a side yet, and already I fend off those who would recruit you to their cause. Already I plot your death. It's necessary. But I can at least try my damnedest to give your life a meaning that will last till the world ends.

5

Nassun takes the reins

MAMA MADE ME LIE TO YOU, Nassun is thinking. She's looking at her father, who's been driving the wagon for hours at this point. His eyes are on the road, but a muscle in his jaw jumps. One of his hands—the one that first struck Uche, ultimately killed him—is shaking where it grips the reins. Nassun can tell that he is still caught up in the fury, maybe still killing Uche in his head. She doesn't understand why, and she doesn't like it. But she loves her father, fears him, worships him, and therefore some part of her yearns to appease him. She asks herself: *What did I do to make this happen?* And the answer that comes is: *Lie. You lied, and lies are always bad.*

But this lie was not her choice. That had been Mama's command, along with all the others: *Don't reach, don't ice, I'm going to make the earth move and you'd better not react, didn't I tell you not to react, even listening is reacting, normal people don't listen like that, are you listening to me, rusting* stop, *for Earth's sake can't you do anything right, stop crying, now do it again.* Endless commands. Endless displeasure. Occasionally the slap of ice in threat, the slap of a hand, the sickening inversion of Nassun's torus, the jerk of a hand on her upper arm. Mama has said occasionally that she loves Nassun, but Nassun has never seen any proof of it.

Not like Daddy, who gives her knapped stone kirkhusa to play with or a first aid kit for her runny-sack because Nassun is a Resistant like her mama. Daddy, who takes her fishing at Tirika Creek on days when he doesn't have commissions to fulfill. Mama has never lain out on the grassy rooftop with Nassun, pointing at the stars and explaining that some deadcivs are said to have given them names, though no one remembers those. Daddy is never too tired to talk at the ends of his workdays. Daddy does not inspect Nassun in the mornings after baths the way Mama does, checking for poorly washed ears or an unmade bed, and when Nassun misbehaves, Daddy only sighs and shakes his head and tells her, "Sweetening, you knew better." Because Nassun always does.

It was not because of Daddy that Nassun wanted to run away and become a lorist. She does not like that her father is so angry now. This seems yet another thing that her mother has done to her.

So she says, "I wanted to tell you."

Daddy does not react. The horses keep plodding forward. The road stretches before the cart, the woods and hills inching past around the road, the bright blue sky overhead. There aren't a lot of people riding past today—just some carters with heavy wagons of trade goods, messengers, some quartent guards on patrol. A few of the carters, who visit Tirimo often, nod or wave because they know Daddy, but Daddy does not respond. Nassun doesn't like this, either. Her father is a friendly man. The man who sits beside her feels like a stranger.

Just because he doesn't reply doesn't mean he's not listening.

She adds, "I asked Mama when we could tell you. I asked her that a lot. She said never. She said you wouldn't understand."

Daddy says nothing. His hands are still shaking—less now? Nassun cannot tell. She starts to feel uncertain; is he angry? Is he sad about Uche? (Is *she* sad about Uche? It does not feel real. When she thinks of her little brother, she thinks of a gabby, giggly little thing who sometimes bit people and still shit his diaper occasionally, and who had an orogenic presence the size of a quartent. The crumpled, still thing back at their house cannot be Uche, because it was too small and dull.) Nassun wants to touch her father's shaking hand, but she finds herself oddly reluctant to do so. She isn't sure why—fear? Maybe just because this man is so much a stranger, and she has always been shy of strangers.

But. No. He is Daddy. Whatever is wrong with him now, it's Mama's fault.

So Nassun reaches out and grips Daddy's nearer hand, hard, because she wants to show him that she is not afraid, and because she is angry, though not at Daddy. "I wanted to tell you!"

The world blurs. At first Nassun isn't sure of what's happening, and she locks up. This is what Mama has drilled her to do in moments of surprise or pain: lock down her body's instinctive fear reaction, lock down her sessapinae's instinctive grab for the earth below. And under no circumstances is Nassun to react with orogeny, because normal people do not do that. *You can do anything else*, Mama's voice says in her head. *Scream, cry, throw something with your hands, get up and start a fight*. Not orogeny.

So Nassun hits the ground harder than she should because she has not quite mastered the skill of not reacting, and she still stiffens up physically along with not reacting orogenically.

And the world blurs because she has not only been knocked off the driver's seat of the wagon, but she has actually rolled off the edge of the Imperial Road and down a gravel-strewn slope, toward a small creek-fed pond.

(The creek that feeds it is where, in a few days, Essun will bathe a strange white boy who acts as if he has forgotten what soap is for.)

Nassun flops to a stop, dazed and breathless. Nothing really hurts yet. By the time the world settles and she begins to understand what's happened—*Daddy hit me, knocked me off the wagon*—Daddy has scrambled down the slope and is crying her name as he crouches beside her and helps her to sit up. *Really* crying. As Nassun blinks away dust and the stars that obscure her vision, she reaches up in confusion to touch Daddy's face, and finds it streaked wet.

"I'm sorry," he says. "I'm so sorry, sweetening. I don't want to hurt you, I don't, you're all I have left—" He jerks her close and holds her tightly, although it hurts. She has bruises all over. "I'm so sorry. I'm so—rusting—sorry! Oh, Earth, oh, Earth, you evil son of a ruster! Not this one! You can't have this one, too!"

These are sobs of grief, long and throat-scraping and hysterical. Nassun will understand this later (and not very much later). She will realize that in this moment, her father is weeping as much for the son he murdered as for the daughter he has injured.

In the moment, however, she thinks, *He still loves me*, and starts crying, too.

So it is while they are like this, Daddy holding Nassun tight, Nassun shaking with relief and lingering shock, that the rippling shockwave of the continent being ripped in half up north reaches them.

They are nearly a whole day's travel down the Imperial Road. Back in Tirimo, a few moments previous, Essun has just shunted the force of the wave so that it splits and goes around the town—which means that what comes at Nassun is incrementally more powerful. And Nassun has been knocked half-insensible, and she is less skilled, less experienced. When she sesses the onrush of the shake, and the sheer power of it, she reacts in exactly the wrong way: She locks up again.

Her father lifts his head, surprised by her gasp and sudden stiffness, and that is when the hammer lands. Even he sesses the loom of it, though it comes too fast and too powerfully to be anything but a jangle of *run run RUN RUN* at the back of his mind. Running is pointless. The shake is basically what happens when a person doing laundry flaps the wrinkles out of a sheet, writ on a continental scale and moving with the speed and force of a casual asteroid strike. On the scale of small, stationary, crushable people, the strata heave beneath them and the trees shake and then splinter. The water in the pond beside them actually leaps into the air for a moment, suspended and still. Daddy stares at it, apparently riveted to this single static point amid the relentless unpeeling of the world everywhere else.

But Nassun is still a skilled orogene even if she is a half-addled one. Though she did not muster herself in time to do what Essun did and break the force of the wave before it hits, she does the next best thing. She drives invisible pylons of force into the strata, as deep as she can, grabbing for the very lithosphere itself. When the kinetic force of the wave hits, incremental instants before the planetary crust above it flexes in reaction, she snatches the heat and pressure and friction from it and uses this to fuel her pylons, pinning the strata and soil in place as solidly as if glued.

There's plenty of strength to draw from the earth, but she spins an ambient torus anyway. She keeps it at a wide remove, because *her father* is within it and she cannot cannot cannot hurt him, and she spins it hard and vicious even though she doesn't need to. Instinct tells her to, and instinct is right. The freezing eye-wall of her torus, which disintegrates anything coming into the stable zone at its center, is what keeps a few dozen projectiles from puncturing them to death.

All of this means that when the world comes apart, it happens everywhere else. For an instant there is nothing to see of reality save a floating globule of pond, a hurricane of pulverized everything else, and an oasis of stillness at the hurricane's core.

Then the concussion passes. The pond slaps back into place, spraying them with muddy snow. The trees that haven't shattered snap back upright, some of them nearly bending all the way in the other direction in reactive momentum and breaking there. In the distance—beyond Nassun's torus—people and animals and boulders and trees that have been flung into the air come crashing down. There are screams, human and inhuman. Cracking wood, crumbling stone, the distant screech of something man-made and metallic rending apart. Behind them, at the far end of the valley they have just left, a rock face shatters and comes down in an avalanche roar, releasing a large steaming chalcedony geode.

Then there is silence. In it, finally, Nassun pulls her face up from her father's shoulder to look around. She does not know what to think. Her father's arms ease around her—shock—and she wriggles until he lets her go so that she can get to her feet.

He does, too. For long moments they simply stare around at the wreckage of the world they once knew.

Then Daddy turns to look at her, slowly, and she sees in his face what Uche must have seen in those last moments. "Did you do this?" he asks.

The orogeny has cleared Nassun's head, of necessity. It is a survival mechanism; intense stimulation of the sessapinae is usually accompanied by a surge of adrenaline and other physical changes that prepare the body for flight—or sustained orogeny, if that is needed. In this case it brings an increased clarity of thought, which is how Nassun finally realizes that her father was not hysterical over her fall purely for her sake. And that what she sees in his eyes right now is something entirely different from love.

Her heart breaks in this moment. Another small, quiet tragedy, amid so many others. But she speaks, because in the end she is her mother's daughter, and if Essun has done nothing else, she has trained her little girl to survive.

"That was too big to be me," Nassun says. Her voice is calm, detached. "What I did is this—" She gestures around them, at the circle of safe ground that surrounds them, distinct from the chaos just beyond. "I'm sorry I didn't stop all of it, Daddy. I tried."

The *Daddy* is what works, just as her tears saved her before. The murder in his expression flickers, fades, twists. "I can't kill you," he whispers, to himself.

Nassun sees the waver of him. It is also instinct that she steps forward and takes his hand. He flinches, perhaps thinking of knocking her away again, but this time she holds on. "*Daddy*," she says again, this time putting more of a needy whine into her voice. It is the thing that has swayed him, these times when he has come near to turning on her: remembering that she is his little girl. Reminding him that he has been, up to today, a good father.

It is a manipulation. Something of her is warped out of true by this moment, and from now on all her acts of affection toward her father will be calculated, performative. Her childhood dies, for all intents and purposes. But that is better than *all* of her dying, she knows.

And it works. Jija blinks rapidly, then murmurs something unintelligible to himself. His hand tightens on hers. "Let's get back up to the road," he says.

(He is "Jija," now, in her head. He will be Jija hereafter, forever, and never Daddy again except out loud, when Nassun needs reins to steer him.)

So they go back up, Nassun limping a little because her backside is sore where she landed too hard on the asphalt and rocks. The road has been cracked all down its length, though it is not so bad in the immediate vicinity of their wagon. The horses are still hitched, though one of them has fallen to her knees and half entangled herself in the tack. Hopefully she hasn't broken a leg. The other is still with shock. Nassun starts working on calming the horses, coaxing the downed one back up and talking the other out of near-catatonia, while her father goes to the other travelers whom they can see sprawled around the road. The ones who were within the wide circumference of Nassun's torus are okay. The ones who were not . . . well.

Once the horses are shaky but functional, Nassun goes after Jija and finds him trying to lift a man who has been flung into a tree. It's broken the man's back; he's conscious and cursing, but Nassun can see the flop of his now-useless legs. It's bad to move him, but obviously Jija thinks it's worse to leave him here like this. "Nassun," Jija says, panting as he tries for a better grip on the man, "clear the wagon bed. There's a real hospital at Pleasant Water, a day away. I think we can make it if we—"

"Daddy," she says softly. "Pleasant Water isn't there anymore."

He stops. (The injured man groans.) Turns to her, frowning. "What?"

"Sume is gone, too," she says. She does not add, *but Tirimo is fine because Mama was there.* She doesn't want to go back, not even for the end of the world. Jija darts a glance back down the road they have walked, but of course all they can see are shattered trees and a few overturned chunks of asphalt along the road . . . and bodies. Lots of bodies. All the way to Tirimo, or so the eye suggests.

"What the rust," he breathes.

"There's a big hole in the ground up north," Nassun continues. "*Really* big. That's what caused this. It's going to cause more shakes and things, too. I can sess ash and gas coming this way. Daddy . . . I think it's a Season."

The injured man gasps, not entirely from pain. Jija's eyes go wide and horrified. But he asks, and this is important: "Are you sure?"

It's important because it means he's listening to her. It is a measure of trust. Nassun feels a surge of triumph at this, though she does not really know why.

"Yes." She bites her lip. "It's going to be really bad, Daddy."

Jija's eyes drift toward Tirimo again. That is conditioned response: During a Season, comm members know that the only place they can be sure of welcome is there. Anything else is a risk.

But Nassun will not go back, now that she is away. Not when

Jija loves her—however strangely—and has taken her away and is *listening* to her, *understanding* her, even though he knows she is an orogene. Mama was wrong about that part. She'd said Jija wouldn't understand.

He didn't understand Uche.

Nassun sets her teeth against this thought. Uche was too little. Nassun will be smarter. And Mama was still only half-right. Nassun will be smarter than her, too.

So she says softly, "Mama knows, Daddy."

Nassun's not even sure what she means by this. Knows that Uche is dead? Knows who has beaten him to death? Would Mama even believe that Jija could do such a thing to his own child? Nassun can hardly believe it herself. But Jija flinches as if the words are an accusation. He stares at her for a long moment, his expression shifting from fear through horror through despair... and slowly, to resignation.

He looks down at the injured man. He's no one Nassun knows—not from Tirimo, wearing the practical clothes and good shoes of a message runner. He won't be running again, certainly not back to his home comm, wherever that is.

"I'm sorry," Jija says. He bends and snaps the man's neck even as he's drawing breath to ask, *For what?*

Then Jija rises. His hands are shaking again, but he turns and extends one of them. Nassun takes it. They walk back to the wagon then, and resume their journey south.

* * *

The Season will always return.

—*Tablet Two, "The Incomplete Truth," verse one*

6

you commit to the cause

"A WHAT?" ASKS TONKEE, SQUINTING AT you through a curtain of hair. You've just come into the apartment after spending part of the day helping one of the work shifts fletch and repair crossbow bolts for the Hunters' use. Since you're not part of any particular use-caste, you've been helping out with each of them in turn, a little every day. This was on Ykka's advice, though Ykka's skeptical about your newfound determination to try to fit into the comm. She likes that you're trying, at least.

Another suggestion was for you to encourage Tonkee to do the same, since thus far Tonkee's done nothing but eat and sleep and bathe on the comm's generosity. Granted, a certain amount of the lattermost has been necessary for the sake of comm socialization. At the moment Tonkee is kneeling over a basin of water in her room, hacking at her hair with a knife to chop out the matted bits. You're keeping well back because the room smells of mildew and body odor and because you think you see something moving in the water along with her shed hair. Tonkee may have needed to wear filth as part of her commless disguise, but that doesn't mean it wasn't actual filth.

"A moon," you say. It's a strange word, brief and round; you're not sure how much to stretch out the *oo* sound in the middle. What else had Alabaster said? "A... satellite. He said a geomest would know."

She frowns more while sawing at a particularly stubborn hank. "Well, I don't know what he's talking about. Never heard of a 'moon.' The obelisks are my area of expertise, remember?" Then she blinks and pauses, letting the half-hacked hank dangle. "Although, technically, the obelisks themselves are satellites."

"What?"

"Well, 'satellite' just means an object whose motion and position are dependent on another. The object that controls everything is called a primary, the dependent object is its satellite. See?" She shrugs. "It's something astronomests talk about when you can get any sense out of them. *Orbital mechanics.*" She rolls her eyes.

"What?"

"Gibberish. Plate tectonics for the sky." You stare, disbelieving, and she waves a hand. "Anyway, I told you how the obelisks followed you to Tirimo. Where you go, they go. That makes them satellites to your primary."

You shudder, not liking the thought that comes into your head—of thin, invisible tethers anchoring you to the amethyst, the nearer topaz, and now the distant onyx whose dark presence is growing in your mind. And oddly, you also think of the Fulcrum. Of the tethers that bound you to it, even when you had the apparent freedom to leave it and travel. You always came back, though, or the Fulcrum would've come after you—in the form of the Guardians.

"Chains," you say softly.

"No, no," Tonkee says distractedly. She's working on the hank again, and having real trouble with it. Her knife has gone blunt. You leave for a moment and go into the room that you share with Hoa, fetching the whetstone from your pack. She blinks when you offer it to her, then nods thanks and starts sharpening the knife. "If there was a chain between you and an obelisk, it would be following you because you're *making* it follow you. Force, not gravity. I mean, if you could make an obelisk do what you wanted." You let out a little breath of amusement at this. "But a satellite reacts to you regardless of whether you try to make it react. It's drawn to your presence, and the weight you exert upon the universe. It lingers around you because it can't help itself." She waves a wet hand distractedly, while you stare again. "Not to ascribe motivations and intentions to the obelisks, of course; that would be silly."

You crouch against the far wall of the room to consider this while she resumes work. As the remainder of her hair begins to loosen, you recognize it at last, because it's curly and dark like your own, instead of ashblow and gray. A little looser in the curl, maybe. Midlatter hair; another mark against her in the eyes of her family, probably. And given the bog-standard Sanzed look of her otherwise—she's a bit on the short and pear-shaped side, but that's what comes of the Yumenescene families not using Breeders to improve themselves—it's something you would've remembered about her from that long-ago visit she made to the Fulcrum.

You don't think Alabaster was talking about the obelisks when he mentioned this moon thing. Still—"You said that thing we found in the Fulcrum, that *socket*, was where they built the obelisks."

It's immediately clear you're back on ground that Tonkee is actually interested in. She sets the knife down and leans forward, her face excited through the dangling uneven remainder of her hair. "Mmm-hmm. Maybe not all of them. The dimensions of every obelisk recorded have been slightly different, so only some—or maybe even just one—would have fit in that socket. Or maybe the socket changed every time they put one in there, adapting itself to the obelisk!"

"How do you know they *put them* in there? Maybe they first… grew there, then were faceted or mined and taken away later." This makes Tonkee look thoughtful; you feel obliquely proud to have considered something she hasn't. "And 'they' who?"

She blinks, then sits back, her excitement visibly fading. Finally she says, "Supposedly, the Yumenescene Leadership is descended from the people who saved the world after the Shattering Season. We have texts passed down from that time, secrets that each family is charged with keeping, and which we're supposed to be shown upon earning our use and comm names." She scowls. "My family didn't, because they were already thinking about disowning me. So I broke into the vault and *took* my birthright."

You nod, because that sounds like the Binof you remember. You're skeptical about the family secret, though. Yumenes didn't exist before Sanze, and Sanze is only the latest of the countless civilizations that must have come and gone over the Seasons.

The Leadership legends have the air of a myth concocted to justify their place in society.

Tonkee continues, "In the vault I found all sorts of things: maps, strange writing in a language like none I've ever seen, objects that didn't make sense—like one tiny, perfectly round yellow stone, about an inch in circumference. Someone had put it in a glass case, sealed and plastered with warnings not to touch. Apparently the thing had a reputation for punching holes in people." You wince. "So either there's some truth to the family stories, or amazingly, being rich and powerful makes it easy to assemble quite the collection of valuable ancient objects. Or both." She notices your expression and looks amused. "Yeah, probably not both. It's not stonelore, anyway, just... words. Soft knowledge. I needed to harden it."

That sounds like Tonkee. "So you snuck into the Fulcrum to try to find the socket, because somehow this proves some rusty old story your family passed down?"

"It was on one of the maps I found." Tonkee shrugs. "If there was truth to part of the story—about there being a socket in Yumenes, deliberately hidden away by the city's founders—then that did suggest there might be truth to the rest, yes." Setting the knife aside, Tonkee shifts to get comfortable, idly brushing the shed hairs into a pile with one hand. Her hair is painfully short and uneven now, and you really want to take the scissors from her and shape it. You'll wait till she's given it another wash first, though.

"There's truth to other parts of the stories, too," Tonkee says. "I mean, a lot of the stories are rust and mellow-smoke; I don't want to pretend otherwise. But I learned at Seventh that the obelisks go as far back as history goes, and then some. We have evidence of Seasons from ten, fifteen, even twenty thousand years ago—and the obelisks are older. It's possible that they even predate the Shattering."

The first Season, and the one that nearly killed the world. Only lorists speak of it, and the Seventh University has disavowed most of their tales. Out of contrariness, you say, "Maybe there wasn't a Shattering. Maybe there have always been Fifth Seasons."

"Maybe." Tonkee shrugs, either not noticing your attempt to be obnoxious, or not caring. Probably the latter. "Mentioning the Shattering was a great way to set off a five-hour argument in the colloquium. Stupid old farts." She smiles to herself, remembering, and then abruptly sobers. You understand at once. Dibars, the city that housed Seventh, is in the Equatorials, only a little west of Yumenes.

"I don't believe it, though," Tonkee says, when she's had a moment to recover. "That we've always had Seasons."

"Why not?"

"Because of us." She grins. "Life, I mean. It's not different enough."

"What?"

Tonkee leans forward. She's not quite as excited as she gets about obelisks, but it's clear that just about any long-hidden knowledge sets her off. For a moment, in the gleam of her open, cheeky face, you see Binof; then she speaks and becomes Tonkee the geomest again. "'All things change during a Season,' yes? But not enough. Think of it this way: Everything that grows or walks on land can breathe the world's air, eat its food, survive its usual shifts in temperature. We don't have to *change* to do that; we are precisely the way we need to be, because that's how the world works. Right? Maybe people are the worst of the lot, because we have to use our hands to make coats instead of just growing fur...but we can make coats. We're built for that, with clever hands that can sew and brains that can figure out how to hunt or grow animals for fur. But we aren't built to filter ash out of our lungs before it turns into cement—"

"Some animals are."

Tonkee gives you an ugly look. "Stop interrupting. It's rude."

You sigh and gesture for her to go on, and she nods, mollified. "Now. *Yes*, some animals grow lung-filters during a Season—or start breathing water and move into the ocean where it's safer, or bury themselves and hibernate, or whatever. We've figured out how to build not just coats, but storecaches and walls and stonelore. But these are afterthoughts." She gestures wildly, groping for the words. "Like...when a cartwheel blows a spoke and you're halfway between comms, you improvise. See? You put a stick or even a bar of metal into the space where the broken spoke was, just to keep the wheel strong enough to last until you can reach a wheelwright. That's what's happening when kirkhusa suddenly develop a taste for meat during a Season. Why don't they just eat meat all the time? Why haven't they *always* eaten meat? Because they were originally built for something else, they're still *better* at eating something else, and eating meat during Seasons is the slapdash, last-minute fix nature threw in to keep kirkhusa from going extinct."

"That's..." You're a little awed. It sounds crazy, but it feels right, somehow. You can't think of any holes to poke in the theory, and you're not sure you want to. Tonkee's not someone you mean to go toe-to-toe with in a battle of logic.

Tonkee nods. "That's why I can't stop thinking about the obelisks. People built them, which means that as a species we're at least as old as they are! That's a lot of time to break things, start over, and break them again. Or, if the Leadership stories are true... maybe it's enough time to put a fix in place. Something to tide us over till the real repairs can be made."

You frown to yourself. "Wait. The Yumenescene Leadership thinks the obelisks—leftover deadciv junk—are the fix?"

"Basically. The stories say the obelisks held the world together when it would have come apart. And they imply there might someday be a way to end the Seasons, involving the obelisks."

An end to all Seasons? It's hard even to imagine. No need for runny-sacks. No storecaches. Comms could last forever, grow forever. Every city could become like Yumenes.

"It would be amazing," you murmur.

Tonkee glances sharply at you. "Orogenes might be a kind of fix, too, you know," she says. "And without the Seasons, you'd no longer be needed."

You frown back at her, not sure whether to be disquieted or comforted by that statement, until she starts finger-combing her remaining hair and you realize you've run out of things to say.

* * *

Hoa is gone. You're not sure where. You left him behind in the infirmary, staring down Ruby Hair, and when you returned to your apartment to try to get a few more hours' sleep he was not beside you when you woke. His little bundle of rocks is still in your room, next to your bed, so he must be planning to return soon. It's probably nothing. Still, after so many weeks, you feel oddly bereft without his strange, subtle presence. But perhaps this is just as well. You have a visit to make, and it might go easier without... hostility.

You walk to the infirmary again slowly, quietly. It's early evening, you think—always hard to tell in Castrima-under, but your body is still acclimated to the rhythms of the surface. For now, you trust in that. Some of the people out on the platforms and walkways stare as you pass; this comm spends plenty of time gossiping, clearly. That doesn't matter. All that does is whether Alabaster has had time enough to recover. You need to talk.

There's no sign of the dead Hunter's body from that morning; everything's been cleaned up. Lerna's inside, in fresh clothing, and he glances at you as you come in. There's still a distance in his expression, you note, though he only meets your gaze for a moment before nodding and turning back to whatever he's doing with what look like surgical instruments. There's another man near him, pipetting something into a series of small glass vials; the man doesn't even look up. It's an infirmary. Anyone can come in.

It's not until you're halfway down the infirmary's long central aisle, walking between the rows of cots, that you consciously notice the sound you've been hearing all along: a kind of hum. It seems monotonous at first, but as you concentrate on it, you detect multiple tones, harmonies, a subtle rhythm. Music? Music so alien, so difficult to parse, that you're not sure that word really applies. You can't figure out where it's coming from, at first. Alabaster is still where you saw him that morning, on a pile of cushions and blankets on the floor. No telling why Lerna hasn't put him on a cot. There are flasks on a nightstand nearby, a roll of fresh bandages, some scissors, a pot of salve. A bedpan, thankfully unused since its last cleaning, though it still stinks near him.

The music is coming from the stone eater, you realize in wonder as you settle into a crouch before them. Antimony sits cross-legged near Alabaster's "nest," utterly still, looking as though someone bothered to sculpt a woman sitting cross-legged with one hand upraised. Alabaster's asleep—though in an odd, nearly sitting-up posture that you don't understand until you realize he's leaning back against Antimony's hand. Maybe that's the only way he can sleep comfortably? There are bandages on his arms today, shiny with salve, and he's not wearing a shirt—which helps you see that he's not as badly damaged as you first thought. There are no patches of stone on his chest or belly, and only a few small burns around his shoulders, most of those healed. But his torso is nearly skeletal—barely any muscle, ribs showing, belly almost concave.

Also, his right arm is much shorter than it was that morning.

You look up at Antimony. The music is coming from somewhere inside of her. Her black eyes are focused on him; they haven't moved with your arrival. It's peaceful, this strange music. And Alabaster looks comfortable.

"You haven't been taking care of him," you say, looking at his ribs and remembering countless evenings putting food in front of him, glaring while he wearily chewed it, conspiring with Innon to get him to eat at the group meals. He always ate more when he thought people were looking. "If you were going to steal him from us, the least you could've done was feed him properly. Fatten him up before you ate him, or something."

The music continues. There is a very faint, stone-grating sound as her black cabochon eyes shift to you at last. They're such alien eyes, despite their superficial resemblance to human. You can see the dry, matte material that comprises the whites of her eyes. No veins, no spots, no off-white coloring that would indicate weariness or worry or anything else human. You can't even tell if there are pupils within the black of her irises. For all you know, she can't even see with them, and uses her elbows to detect your presence and direction.

You meet those eyes and realize, suddenly, that there's so little left in you which is capable of fear.

"You took him from us and we couldn't do it alone." No, that is a lie of incompleteness. Innon, a feral, had no hope against Guardians and a trained Fulcrum orogene. You, though? You're the one who fucked everything up. "*I* couldn't do it alone. If Alabaster had been there . . . I hated you. Afterward, while I was wandering, I vowed to find a way to kill you. Put you in an obelisk like that other one. Bury you in the ocean, far enough out that no one will ever dig you up."

She watches you and says nothing. You can't even read the catch of her breath, because she doesn't breathe. But the music stops, dying into silence. That's a reaction, at least.

This really is pointless. But then the silence looms louder, and you're still feeling kind of pissy, so you add: "Shame. The music was pretty."

(Later, lying in bed and considering the day's errors, you will think belatedly, *I am as crazy now as Alabaster was back then.*)

A moment later Alabaster stirs, lifting his head and uttering a soft groan that throws your thoughts and your heart ten years away before they circle back. He blinks at you in disorientation for a moment, and you realize he doesn't recognize you with your hair twice as long and your skin weathered and your clothes Season-faded. Then he blinks again, and you take a deep breath, and you're both back in the here and now.

"The onyx," he says, his voice hoarse with sleep. Of course he knows. "Always biting off more than you can chew, Syen."

You don't bother to correct him on the name. "You said an obelisk."

"I said the rusting topaz. But if you could call the onyx, I've underestimated your development." His head cocks, his expression thoughtful. "What have you been doing, these last few years, to have refined your control so much?"

You can't think of anything at first, and then you can. "I had two children." Keeping an orogene child from destroying everything in its vicinity took a lot of your energy, in those earliest years. You learned to sleep with one eye open, your sessapinae primed for the slightest twitch of infant fear or toddler pique—or, worse, a local shake that might prompt either child to react. You quelled a dozen disasters a night.

He nods, and belatedly you remember waking up during the night in Meov sometimes to find Alabaster blearily awake and watching Corundum. You remember teasing him, in fact, on his worrying, when Coru was clearly no threat to anyone.

Earth burn it, you hate figuring out all this stuff after the fact.

"They left me with my mother for a few years after I was born," he says, almost to himself. You'd guessed this already, given that he speaks a Coaster language. How his Fulcrum-bred mother had known it, though, is a mystery that will never be solved. "They took me away once I was old enough to be threatened effectively, but before that, she apparently prevented me from icing Yumenes a few times. I don't think we're meant to be raised by stills." He paused, his gaze distant. "I met her years later by chance. Didn't know her, though she somehow recognized me. I think she's—she *was*—on the senior advisory board. Topped out at nine rings, if I recall." He falls silent for a moment. Perhaps he's contemplating the fact that he killed his mother, too. Or maybe he's trying to remember something of her other than a hurried meeting between two strangers in a corridor.

His focus sharpens abruptly, back to the present and you. "I think you might be a nine-ringer now."

You can't help surprise and pleasure, though you cover both with the appearance of nonchalance. "I thought things like that didn't matter anymore."

"They don't. I was careful to wipe out the Fulcrum when I tore Yumenes apart. There are still buildings where the city was, perched on the edges of the maw, unless they've fallen in since. But the obsidian walls are rubble, and I made sure Main went into the pit first." There's a deep, vicious satisfaction in his voice. He sounds like you a moment ago, as you imagined murdering stone eaters.

(You glance at Antimony. She's gone back to watching Alabaster, her hand still supporting his back. You could almost think of her as doing it out of devotion or kindness, if you didn't know his hands and feet and forearm were in whatever passes for her stomach.)

"I only mention rings so you can have a point of reference."

Alabaster stirs, sitting up carefully and then, as if he heard your thought, extending his stubby, stone-capped right arm. "Look inside this. Tell me what you see."

"Are you going to tell me what's going on, Alabaster?" But he doesn't answer, just looking at you, and you sigh. All right.

You look at his arm, which stops at the elbow now, and wonder what he means by *look inside*. Then, unbidden, you remember a night when he willed poison out of the cells of his own body. But he had help for that. You frown, impulsively glancing at the strangely shaped pink object behind him—the thing that looks like an overly long, big-handled knife, and which is actually, somehow, an obelisk. The spinel, he called it.

You glance at him; he must have seen you eye it. He doesn't move: not a twitch of his burned and stone-crusted face, not a flicker of his nonexistent eyelashes. All right, then. Anything goes, as long as you do what he says.

So you stare down at his arm. You don't want to chance the spinel. No telling what it will do. Instead, first you try letting your awareness go into the arm. This feels absurd; you've spent your life sessing layers of earth miles underground. To your surprise, however, your perception *can* grasp his arm. It's small and strange, too close and almost too tiny, but it's there, because at least the outermost layer of him is rock. Calcium and carbon and flecks of oxidized iron that must have once been blood, and—

You pause, frowning, and open your eyes. (You don't remember closing them.) "What is that?"

"What *is* that?" The side of his mouth that hasn't been seamed by a burn lifts in a sardonic smile.

You scowl. "There's something in this stuff that you're—" Becoming. "—this stone stuff. It's not, I don't know. It's rock, and not."

"Can you sess the flesh further down the arm?"

You shouldn't be able to. But when you narrow your focus to the limit that you can, when you squint and press your tongue to the roof of your mouth and wrinkle your nose, it's there, too. Big sticky globules all bouncing against one another—You withdraw at once, revolted. At least stone is clean.

"Look again, Syen. Don't be a coward."

You could be annoyed, but you're too old for this shit now. Setting your jaw, you try again, taking a deep breath so you won't feel queasy. Everything's so *wet* inside him, and the water isn't even sequestered away between layers of clay or—

You pause. Narrow your focus still further. Between the gelidity, moving, too, but in a slower and less organic way, you suddenly sess the same thing you found in the stone of him. Something else, neither flesh nor stone. Something immaterial, and yet it is there for you to perceive. It glimmers in threads strung between the bits of him, crossing itself in lattices, shifting constantly. A... tension? An energy, shiny and streaming. Potential. Intention.

You shake your head, pulling back so you can focus on him. "What is that?"

This time he answers. "The stuff of orogeny." He makes his voice dramatic, since his facial expressions can't change much. "I've told you before that what we do isn't logical. To make the earth move we put something of ourselves into the system and make *completely unrelated things* come out. There's always been something else involved, connecting the two. This." You frown. He sits forward, growing more animated with his excitement, just the way he used to in the old days—but then something creaks on him, and he flinches with pain. Carefully he sits back against Antimony's hand again.

But you're hearing him. And he's right. It hasn't ever really made sense, has it, the way orogeny works? It shouldn't work at all, that willpower and concentration and perception should shift mountains. Nothing else in the world works this way. People cannot stop avalanches by dancing well, or make storms happen by refining their hearing. And on some level, you've always *known* that this was there, making your will manifest. This... whatever it is.

Alabaster has always been able to read you like a book. "The civilization that made the obelisks had a word for this," he says, nodding at your epiphany. "I think there's a reason we don't. It's because no one for countless generations has wanted orogenes to *understand* what we do. They've just wanted us to do it."

You nod slowly. "After Allia, I can see why no one would've wanted us to learn how to manipulate obelisks."

"Rust the obelisks. They didn't want us to create something better. Or worse." He takes a deep breath carefully. "We're going to stop manipulating stone now, Essun. That stuff you see in me? *That's* what you have to learn to control. To perceive, wherever it exists. It's what the obelisks are made of, and it's how they do what they do. We have to get you to do those things, too. We have to make you a ten-ringer, at least."

At least. Just like that. "*Why?* Alabaster, you mentioned something. A... moon. Tonkee doesn't have a clue what that is. And all the things you've said, about causing that rift and wanting me to do something worse—" Something moves at the periphery of your vision. You glance up and realize the man who's been working with Lerna is coming with a bowl in his hands. Dinner, for Alabaster. You drop your voice. "I'm not, by the way. Helping you make things worse. Haven't you done enough already?"

Alabaster glances at the oncoming nurse, too. Watching him, Alabaster says in a low voice, "The Moon is something this world used to have, Essun. An object in the sky, much closer than the stars." He keeps switching between calling you one name and another. It's distracting. "Its loss was part of what caused the Seasons."

Father Earth did not always hate life, the lorists say. *He hates because he cannot forgive the loss of his only child.*

But then, the lorists' tales also say the obelisks are harmless.

"How do you know—" But then you stop, because the man has reached you, so you sit back against a nearby cot, digesting what you've heard while he spoon-feeds Alabaster. The stuff is watery mash of some kind, and not much of it. Alabaster sits there and opens his mouth for the feeding like a babe. His eyes stay on you throughout. It's unnerving, and finally you have to look away. Some of the things that have changed between you, you cannot bear.

Finally the man is done, and with a flat look in your direction that nevertheless conveys his opinion that you should have been the one to administer the food, he leaves. But when you straighten and open your mouth to ask more questions, Alabaster says, "I'm probably going to need to use that bedpan soon. I can't control my bowels very well anymore, but at least they're still regular." At the look on your face, he smiles with only a hint of bitterness. "I don't want you to see that any more than you want to see it. So why don't we just say you should come back later? Noon seems to work better for not interfering with any of my gross natural functions."

That isn't fair. Well. It is, and you deserve his censure, but it's censure that should be shared. "Why did you do this to yourself?" You gesture at his arm, his ruined body. "I just..." Maybe you could take it better if you understood.

"The consequence of what I did at Yumenes." He shook his head. "Something to remember, Syen, for when you make your own choices in the future: Some of them come with a terrible price. Although sometimes that price is worth paying."

You can't understand why he sees this, this horrible slow death, as a price worth paying for anything—let alone for what he got out of it, which was the destruction of the world. And you still don't understand what any of it has to do with stone eaters or moons or obelisks or anything else.

"Wouldn't it have been better," you cannot help saying, "to just... live?" To have come back, you cannot say. To have made what little life he could with Syenite again, after Meov was gone but before she found Tirimo and Jija and tried to create a lesser version of the family she'd lost. Before she became you.

The answer is in the way his eyes deaden. This was the look that was on his face as you stood in a node station once, over the abused corpse of one of his sons. Maybe it's the look that was on his face when he learned of Innon's death. It's certainly what you saw in your own face after Uche's. That's when you no longer need an answer to the question. There is such a thing as too much loss. Too much has been taken from you both—taken and taken and taken, until there's nothing left but hope, and you've *given* that up because it hurts too much. Until you would rather die, or kill, or avoid attachments altogether, than lose one more thing.

You think of the feeling that was in your heart as you pressed a hand over Corundum's nose and mouth. Not the thought. The thought was simple and predictable: *Better to die than live a slave*. But what you *felt* in that moment was a kind of cold, monstrous love. A determination to make sure your son's life remained the beautiful, wholesome thing that it had been up to that day, even if it meant you had to end his life early.

Alabaster doesn't answer your question. You don't need him to anymore. You get up to leave so that he can at least keep his dignity in front of you, because that's really all you have left to give him. Your love and respect aren't worth much to anyone.

Maybe you're still thinking of dignity when you ask one more question, so that the conversation doesn't end on a note of hopelessness. It's your way of offering an olive branch, too, and letting him know that you've decided to learn what he has to teach you. You're not interested in making the Season worse or whatever he's on about...but it's clear that he needs this on some level. The son he made with you is dead, the family you built together has been rendered forever incomplete, but if nothing else he's still your mentor.

(You need this, too, a cynical part of you notes. It's a poor trade, really—Nassun for him, a mother's purpose for an ex-lover's, these ridiculous mysteries for the starker and more important why of Jija murdering his own son. But without Nassun to motivate you, you need something. Anything, to keep going.)

So you say, with your back to him: "What did they call it?"

"Hn?"

"The obelisk-builders. You said they had a word for the stuff in the obelisks." The silvery stuff thrumming between the cells of Alabaster's body, concentrating and compacting in the solidifying stone of him. "The stuff of orogeny. What was their word, since we don't have one anymore?"

"Oh." He shifts, perhaps readying himself for the bedpan. "The word doesn't matter, Essun. Make one up if you like. You just need to know the stuff exists."

"I want to know what they called it." It's a small piece of the mystery he's trying to shove down your throat. You want to wrap your fingers around it, control the ingestion, at least taste some of it along the way. And, too, the people who made the obelisks were powerful. Foolish, maybe, and clearly awful for inflicting the Seasons upon their descendants, if they are indeed the ones who did so. But powerful. Maybe knowing the name will give you power somehow.

He starts to shake his head, winces as this causes him pain somewhere, sighs instead. "They called it *magic.*"

It's meaningless. Just a word. But maybe you can give it meaning somehow. "Magic," you repeat, memorizing. Then you nod farewell, and leave without looking back.

* * *

> The stone eaters knew I was there. I'm certain of it. They just didn't care.

I observed them for hours as they stood motionless, voices echoing out of nowhere. The language they spoke to each other was... strange. Arctic, perhaps? One of the Coastals? I've never heard the like. Regardless, after some ten hours I will admit that I fell asleep. I woke to the sound of a great crash and crunch, so loud that I thought the Shattering itself was upon me. When I dared to lift my eyes, one of the stone eaters was scattered chunks upon the ground. The other stood as before, save for one change, directed right at me: a bright, glittering smile.

—*Memoir of Ouse Innovator (nat Strongback) Ticastries, amateur geomest. Not endorsed by the Fifth University.*

7

Nassun finds the moon

The journey south for Nassun and her father is long and fraught. They make most of the journey with the horse cart, which means that they travel faster than Essun, who is on foot and behind them to an increasing degree. Jija offers rides in exchange for food or supplies; this helps them move faster still because they don't need to stop and trade often. Because of this pace, they stay ahead of the worst of the changing climate, the ashfall, the carnivorous kirkhusa and the boilbugs and all the worse things brewing in the lands behind them. They're going so quickly when they pass through Castrima-over that Nassun barely feels Ykka's summons—and when she does it is in her dreams, drawing her down and down into the warm earth amid white crystalline light. But she dreams this ten miles past Castrima, since Jija thought they could go a little farther that day before camping, and thus they do not fall prey to the honeypot of invitingly whole, empty buildings.

When they do have to stop at comms, some are only in lockdown and haven't yet declared Seasonal Law. Hoping the worst of it won't come so far south, probably; it's rare for Seasons to affect the whole continent at once. Nassun never speaks of what she is to strangers, but if she could, she would tell them that there is nowhere to hide from this Season. Some parts of the Stillness will suffer the full effects later than others, but eventually it will be bad everywhere.

Some of the comms they stop at invite them to stay. Jija's older, but still hale and strong, and his knapping skills and Resistant use-caste make him valuable. Nassun's young enough to be trained in nearly any needed skill, and she's visibly healthy and tall for her age, already showing signs of growing into her mother's strong Midlatter frame. There are a few places they stop, strong comms with deep stores and friendly people, where she wishes they could stay. Jija always refuses, though. He's got some destination in mind.

A few of the comms they pass try to kill them. There's no logic to this, since one man and a little girl cannot possibly have enough valuables between them to be worth murdering, but there isn't much logic in a Season. They run from some. Jija takes a longknife to a man's head to get them out of a comm that has let them through the gates and then tried to close them in. They lose the horses and the cart, which is probably what the comm wanted, but Jija and Nassun escape, which is what matters most. It's on foot from there, and slower, but they are alive.

At another comm, whose people don't even bother to warn them before aiming crossbows, it is Nassun who saves them. She does this by wrapping her arms around her father and setting her teeth in the earth and dragging every iota of life and heat and movement out of the whole comm until it is a gleaming frosted confection of ice-slivered slate walls and still, solid bodies.

(She will never do this again. The way Jija looks at her afterward.)

They stay in the dead comm for a few days, resting in empty houses and replenishing their supplies. No one bothers this comm while they are there because Nassun keeps the walls iced as a clear *danger here* warn-off. They cannot stay long, of course. Eventually the other comms in the area will band together and come to kill the rogga whom they will assume threatens them all. A few days of warm water and fresh food—Jija cooks one of the comm's frozen chickens for a real treat—and they move on. Before the bodies thaw and start stinking, see.

And so it goes: Bandits and scammers and a near-fatal gas waft and a tree that fires wooden spikes when warm bodies are in proximity; they survive it all. Nassun has a growth spurt, even though she is always hungry and rarely full. By the time they finally approach the place that Jija has heard about, she is three inches taller, and a year has passed.

They are out of the Somidlats at last, edging into the Antarctics. Nassun has begun to suspect that Jija means to take her all the way to Nife, one of the few cities in the Antarctic region, near which a satellite Fulcrum is said to be located. But he turns them off the Pellestane-Nife Imperial Road and they begin going eastward, stopping periodically so that Jija can consult with people along the way and see if he's going in the right direction. It is after one of these conversations, conducted always in whispers and always after Jija thinks Nassun has gone to sleep, and only with people whom Jija considers level-headed after a few hours of chitchat and shared food, that Nassun finally learns where they are going. "*Tell me*," she hears Jija whisper to a woman who was out scouting for a local comm, after they have shared an evening meal of meat she caught around a fire Jija built, "*have you ever heard of the Moon?*"

The question holds no meaning for Nassun; neither does the word at the end of it. But the woman inhales. She directs Jija to shift over to the southeast-running regional road instead of the Imperial Road, and then to divert due south at the turning of a river they'll soon reach. Thereafter Nassun pretends to be asleep, because she can feel the woman's narrow-eyed gaze on her. Eventually, though, Jija shyly offers to help warm her bedroll. Then Nassun has to listen while her father works to make the woman moan and gasp in repayment for the meat—and to make her forget that Nassun is there. In the morning they move on before the woman wakes so that she will not follow and try to hurt Nassun.

Days later they divert at the river, heading into the woods along a tree-shadowed path that is barely more than a tamped-down paler ribbon amid the forest scrub and undergrowth. The sky has not been completely shadowed for long in this part of the world; most of the trees still have leaves, and Nassun can even hear animals leaping about and darting away as they pass. Occasionally birds twitter or croon. There are no other people on this path, though obviously some have passed recently or the path would be even more overgrown than it is. The Antarctics are a stark, sparsely populated part of the world, she remembers reading in the textbooks of another life. Few comms, fewer Imperial roads, winters that are harsh even outside a Season. The quartents here take weeks to travel across. Swaths of the Antarctics are tundra, and the southernmost tip of the continent is said to become solid ice, which extends far into the sea. She's read that the night sky, if they could see it through the clouds, is sometimes filled with strange dancing colored lights.

In this part of the Antarctics, though, the air is almost steamy despite the light chill. Beneath their feet, Nassun can sess the heavy, pent churn of an active shield volcano—actually erupting, just very slowly, with a trickle-trickle of lava flow further south. Here and there on the topography of her awareness Nassun can detect gas vents and a few boils that have come to the surface as hot springs and geysers. All this moisture and the warm ground are what keep the trees green.

Then the trees part, and before them looms something that Nassun has never seen before. A rock formation, she thinks—but one that seems to consist of dozens of long, columnar ribbons of brown-gray stone that ripple in an upslope, gradually slanting high enough to qualify as a low mountain or a tall hill. At the top of this river of stone, she can see bushy green tree canopies; the formation plateaus up there. Atop that plateau Nassun can glimpse something through the trees, which might be a rounded rooftop or storecache tower. A settlement of some kind. But unless they climb along the columnar ribbons, which looks dangerous, she's not sure how to get up there.

Except...except. It is a scratch on her awareness, rising to a pressure, itching into certainty. Nassun glances at her father, who is staring at the river of stone, too. In the months since

Uche's death, she has come to understand Jija better now than ever before in her life, because her life depends on it. She understands that he is fragile, despite his outward strength and stolidity. The cracks in him are new but dangerous, like the edges of tectonic plates: always raw, never stable, needing only the merest brush to unleash aeons' worth of pent-up energy and destroy everything nearby.

But earthquakes are easy to manage, if you know how.

So Nassun says, watching him carefully, "This was made by orogenes, Daddy."

She has guessed that he will tense, and he does. She has guessed that he will need to take a deep breath to calm himself, which he also does. He reacts to even the thought of orogenes the way that Mama used to react to red wine: with fast breath and shaking hands and sometimes freezing or weak knees. Daddy could never even bring things that were burgundy-colored into the house—but sometimes he would forget and do it anyway, and once it was done there was no reasoning with Mama. Nothing to be done but wait for her shakes and rapid breathing and hand-wringing to pass.

(Hand-*rubbing*. Nassun did not notice the distinction, but Essun was rubbing one hand. The old ache, there in the bones.)

Once Jija is calm enough, therefore, Nassun adds, "I think only orogenes can get up that slope, too." She's sure of this, in fact. The stone columns are *moving*, imperceptibly. This whole region is a volcano in exquisitely slow eruption. Here it pushes up a steady incremental lava flow that takes years to cool and thus separates itself into these long hexagonal shafts as the stuff contracts. It would be easy for an orogene, even an untrained one, to push against that upwelling pressure, taste some of that slow-cooling heat, and raise another column. Ride it, to reach that plateau. Many of the stone ribbons before them are paler gray, fresher, sharper. Others have done this recently.

Then Daddy surprises her by nodding jerkily. "There are... there should be others like you in this place." He never says the o-word or the r-word. It's always *like you* and *your kind* and *that sort*. "It's why I brought you here, sweetening."

"Is this the Antarctic Fulcrum?" Maybe she was wrong about where that was.

"No." His lip curls. The fault line trembles. "It's better."

It's the first time he's ever been willing to speak of this. He's not breathing much faster, either, or staring at her in that way he so often does when he's struggling to remember that she's his daughter. Nassun decides to probe a little, testing his strata. "Better?"

"Better." He looks at her, and for the first time in what feels like forever, he smiles at her the way he used to. The way a father should smile at his daughter. "They can cure you, Nassun. That's what the stories say."

Cure her of what? she almost asks. Then survival instinct kicks in and she bites her tongue before she can say the stupid thing. There is only one disease that afflicts her in his eyes, only one poison he would journey halfway across the world to have drawn out of his little girl.

A cure. A *cure*. For orogeny? She hardly knows what to think. Be... other than what she is? Be normal? Is that even possible?

She's so stunned that she forgets to watch her father for a moment. When she remembers, she shivers, because he has been watching *her*. He nods in satisfaction at the look on her face, though. Her surprise is what he wanted to see: that or maybe wonder, or pleasure. He would have reacted poorly to dislike or fear.

"How?" she asks. Curiosity he can tolerate.

"I don't know. But I heard about it from travelers, before." Just as there is only one *your kind* that he ever means, there's only one *before* that matters, for both of them. "They say it's been around for maybe the last five or ten years."

"But what about the Fulcrum?" She shakes her head, confused. If anywhere, she would have thought...

Daddy's face twists. "Trained, leashed animals are still animals." He turns back to the rise of flowing stone. "I want my little girl back."

I haven't gone anywhere, Nassun thinks, but knows better than to say.

There's no path to illustrate the way to go, no signs to indicate anything nearby. Part of that could be Seasonal defenses; they've seen a few comms that protected themselves not just with walls but seemingly insurmountable obstacles and camouflage. Doubtless the members of the comm know some secret way to get up to the plateau, but without this knowledge, Nassun and Jija are left with a puzzle to solve. There's also no easy way past the rise; they could go around it, see if there are steps on the other side, but that might take days.

Nassun sits down on a log nearby—after checking it carefully for insects or other creatures that might have turned aggressive since the start of the Season. (Nassun has learned to treat nature and her father with the same wary caution.) She watches Jija pace back and forth, pausing now and again to kick at one of the ribbons where it rises sharply from the ground. He mutters to himself. He'll need time to admit what must be done.

Finally he turns to her. "Can you do it?"

She stands up. He stumbles back as if startled by the sudden movement, then stops and glowers at her. She just stands there, letting him see how much it hurts her that he fears her so.

A muscle flexes in his jaw; some of his anger fades into chagrin. (Only some.) "Will you have to kill this forest, to do it?"

Oh. She can understand some of his worry now. This is the first green place they've seen in a year. "No, Daddy," she says. "There's a volcano." She points down under their feet. He flinches again, glaring at the ground with the same naked hatred he occasionally flashes at her. But it is as pointless to hate Father Earth as it is to wish the Seasons would end.

He takes a deep breath and opens his mouth, and Nassun is so expecting him to say *all right* that she is already beginning to form the smile that he will need, in reassurance. Thus they are both caught completely off guard when a loud clack resounds through the forest around them, setting off a flock of birds she didn't know was there. Something chuffs into the ground nearby, making Nassun blink with the faint reverberations of the blow through the local strata. Something small, but striking with force. And then Jija screams.

Once, Nassun froze in reaction to being startled. Mama's training. Some of that conditioning has slipped over the past year, and although she grows still, she sinks her awareness into the earth nevertheless—just a few feet, but still. But she freezes in two kinds of ways as she sees the heavy, huge, barbed metal bolt that has been shot through her father's calf. "*Daddy!*"

Jija is down on one knee, clutching his leg and making a sound through his teeth that is less than a scream, but no less agonized. The thing is huge: several feet long, two inches in circumference. She can see the way it has pushed aside his flesh on its terrible path. The tip is buried in the ground on the other side of his calf, effectively pinning him in place. A harpoon, not a crossbow bolt. It even has a thin chain attached to the blunt end.

A chain? Nassun whirls, following it. Someone's holding it. There are feet pounding on the strata nearby, crunching leaves as they move. Darting shadows flicker past tree trunks and vanish; she hears a call in some Arctic language she's heard before but does not know. *Bandits.* Coming.

She looks at Daddy again, who is trying to take deep breaths. His face is pale. There's so much blood. But he looks up at her with his eyes wide and white with pain, and suddenly she remembers the comm where the people attacked them, the comm she iced, and the way he looked at her afterward.

Bandits. *Kill them.* She knows she must. If she does not, they will kill her.

But her father wants a little girl, not an animal.

She stares and stares and breathes hard and cannot stop staring, cannot think, cannot *act*, can do nothing but stand there and shake and hyperventilate, torn between survival and daughterhood.

Then someone leaps down the lava-flow ridge, bouncing from one ribbon of rock to the other with a speed and agility that is—Nassun stares. No one can do that. But the man lands in a crouch amid the gravelly soil at the foot of the ridges with a heavy, ominous thud. He's solidly built. She can tell he's big even though he stays low as he half rises, his gaze fixed on something in the trees beyond Nassun, and draws a long, wicked glassknife. (And yet, somehow, the weight of his landing on the ground does not reverberate on her senses. What does that mean? And there is a... She shakes her head, thinking maybe it's an insect, but the odd buzzing is a sensation and not a sound.)

Then the man is off, running straight into the brush, his feet pushing against the ground with such force that clods of dirt kick up in his wake. Nassun's mouth falls open as she turns to follow him, losing track amid the green, but there are shouts in that language again—and then, in the direction that she saw the man run, a soft, guttural sound, like someone reacting to a hard blow. The moving people amid the trees stop. Nassun sees an Arctic woman stand frozen in the clear gap between a tangle of vines and an old, weathered rock. The woman turns, inhaling to call out to someone else, and in a near-blur the man is behind her, punching her in the back. No, no, the knife—And then he is gone, before the woman falls. The violence and speed of the attack are stunning.

"N-Nassun," Jija says, and Nassun jumps again. She actually forgot him for a moment. She goes over, crouching and putting her foot on the chain to prevent anyone from using it to hurt him further. He grips her arm, too hard. "You should, unh, run."

"No, Daddy." She tries to figure out how the chain is fastened to the harpoon. The weapon's shaft is smooth. If she can get the chain loose or cut off the barbed point, they can just drag Daddy's leg off of it to free him. But what then? It's such a terrible wound. Will he bleed to death? She doesn't know what to do.

Jija hisses as she jiggles the end of the chain experimentally, trying to see if she can twist it loose. "I don't... I think the bone..." Jija actually sways, and Nassun thinks the white of his lips is a bad sign. "*Go*."

She ignores him. The chain is welded to a loop at the end of the shaft. She fingers it and thinks hard, now that the strange man's appearance has broken her deadlock. (Her hand's shaking, though. She takes a deep breath, trying to get hold of her own fear. Somewhere off in the trees, there is a gurgling groan, and a scream of fury.) She knows Jija has some of his stoneknapping tools in his pack, but the harpoon is steel. Wait—metal breaks if it's cold enough, doesn't it? Could she, maybe, with a high narrow torus...?

She's never done this before. If she does it wrong, she'll freeze off his leg. Yet somehow, instinctively, she feels certain that it *can* be done. The way Mama taught her to think about orogeny, as heat and movement taken in and heat and movement pushed out, has never really felt right to her. There is truth to it; it works, she knows from experience. But something about it is... off. Inelegant. She has often thought, *If I don't think about it as heat*... without ever finishing that thought in a productive way.

Mama is not here, and death is, and her father is the only person left in the world who loves her, even though his love comes wrapped in pain.

So she puts a hand on the butt end of the harpoon. "Don't move, Daddy."

"Wh-what?" Jija is shaking, but also weakening rapidly. Good; Nassun can work with her concentration uninterrupted. She puts her free hand on his leg—since her orogeny has always flinched away from freezing *her*, even back when she couldn't fully control it—and closes her eyes.

There is something underneath the heat of the volcano, interspersed amid the wavelets of motion that dance through the earth. It's easy to manipulate the waves and heat, but hard to even *perceive* this other thing, which is perhaps why Mama taught Nassun to look for waves and heat instead. But if Nassun can grasp the other thing, which is finer and more delicate and also more precise than the heat and waves... if she can shape it into a kind of sharp edge, and file it down to infinite fineness, and slice it across the shaft like *so*—

There is a quick, high-pitched hiss as the air between her and Jija stirs. Then the chain tip of the harpoon shaft drops loose, the shorn faces of metal glimmering mirror-smooth in the afternoon light.

Exhaling in relief, Nassun opens her eyes. To find that Jija has tensed, and is staring beyond her with an expression of mingled horror and belligerence. Startled, Nassun whirls, to see the knife-wielding man behind her.

His hair is black, Arctic-limp, and long enough to fall below his waist. He's so very tall that she falls onto her butt turning to look at him. Or maybe that's because she's suddenly exhausted? She does not know. The man is breathing hard, and his clothing—homespun cloth and a pair of surprisingly neat, pleated old trousers—is splattered liberally with blood centering on the glassknife in his right hand. He gazes down at her with eyes that glitter bright as the metal she just cut, and his smile is very nearly as sharp-edged.

"Hello, little one," the man says as Nassun stares. "That's quite the trick."

Jija tries to move, shifting his leg along the harpoon shaft, and it is awful. There is the abortive sound of bone grating on metal, and he groan-coughs out an agonized cry, grabbing spasmodically for Nassun. Nassun catches his shoulder, but he's heavy, and she's tired, and she realizes in sudden horror that she lacks the strength to fight the man with the glassknife if that should be necessary. Jija's shoulder shakes beneath her hand, and she's shaking nearly as hard. Maybe this is why no one uses the stuff underneath the heat? Now she and her father will pay the price for her folly.

But the black-haired man hunkers down, moving with remarkably slow grace for someone who showed such swift brutality only moments before. "Don't be afraid," he says. He blinks then, something flickering and uncertain in his gaze. "Do I know you?"

Nassun has never before seen this giant with the icewhite eyes and the world's longest knife. The knife is still in his hand, though now it dangles at his side, dripping. She shakes her head, a little too hard and fast.

The man blinks, the uncertainty clears, and the smile returns. "The beasts are dead. I came to help you, didn't I?" Something is off about the question. He asks it as if he seeks confirmation: *didn't I?* It's too sincere, too heartfelt somehow. Then he says, "I won't let anyone hurt you."

Perhaps it is only coincidence that his gaze slides over to her father's face after he says this. But. Something in Nassun unclenches, just a little.

Then Jija tries to move again and makes another pained sound, and the man's gaze sharpens. "How unpleasant. Let me help you—" He sets down the knife and reaches for Jija.

"Stay the rust back—" Jija blurts, trying to move back and jerking all over with the pain of this. He's panting, too, and sweating. "Who are you? Are you?" His eyes roll toward the flowing ridge of hex-stone. "From?"

The man, who has drawn back at Jija's reaction, follows his gaze. "Oh. Yes. The comm's sentries saw you coming along the road. Then we saw the bandits moving in, so I came to help. We've had trouble with that lot before. It was a convenient opportunity to eliminate the threat." His white gaze shifts back to Nassun, flicking at the sheared-off harpoon along the way. He has never stopped smiling. "But *you* should not have had trouble with them."

He knows what Nassun is. She cringes against her father, though she knows he is no shelter. It's habit.

Her father tenses, his breath quickening to a rasp. "Are . . . are you . . ." He swallows. "We're looking for the Moon."

The man's smile widens. His accent is something Equatorial; Equatorials always have such strong white teeth. "Ah, yes," he says. "You've found it."

Her father slumps in relief, to the degree that his leg allows. "Oh . . . oh. Evil Earth, at last."

Nassun can't take it anymore. "What is *the Moon*?"

"Found Moon." The man inclines his head. "That is the name of our community. A very special place, for very special people." Then he sheaths the knife and extends one hand, palm up, offering. "My name is Schaffa."

The hand is held out only to Nassun, and Nassun doesn't know why. Maybe because he knows what she is? Maybe only because her hand isn't covered with blood, as both of Jija's are. She swallows and takes the hand, which immediately and firmly closes around hers. She manages, "I'm Nassun. That's my father." She lifts her chin. "Nassun *Resistant Tirimo*."

Nassun knows that her mother was trained by the Fulcrum, which means that Mama's use name was never "Resistant." And Nassun is only ten years old now, too young for Tirimo to recognize with a comm name even if she still lived there. Yet the man inclines his head gravely, as if it is not a lie. "Come, then," he says. "Let's see if between the two of us, we can't get your father free."

He rises, pulling her up with him, and she turns toward Jija, thinking that with Schaffa here they can maybe just lift Jija off the shaft and that if they do it fast enough maybe it won't hurt him too much. But before she can open her mouth to say this, Schaffa presses two fingers to the back of her neck. She flinches and rounds on him, instantly defensive, and he raises both hands, wagging the fingers to show that he's still unarmed. She can feel a bit of damp on her neck, probably a smear of blood.

"Duty first," he says.

"What?"

He nods toward her father. "I can lift him, while you shift the leg."

Nassun blinks again, confused. The man moves over to Jija, and she is distracted from wondering about that strange touch by her father's cries of pain as they work him free.

Much later, though, she will remember an instant after

that touch, when the tips of the man's fingers glimmered like the cut ends of the harpoon. A gossamer-thin thread of light-under-the-heat had seemed to flicker from her to him. She will remember, too, that for a moment that thread of light illuminated others: a whole tracework of jagged lines spreading all over him like the spiderwebbing that follows a sharp impact in brittle glass. The impact site, the center of the spiderweb, was somewhere near the back of his head. Nassun will remember thinking in that instant: *He's not alone in there.*

In the moment it is no matter. Their journey has ended. Nassun is, apparently, home.

* * *

The Guardians do not speak of Warrant, where they are made. No one knows its location. When asked, they only smile.

—*From lorist tale, "Untitled 759," recorded in Charta Quartent, Eadin Comm, by itinerant Mell Lorist Stone*

8

you've been warned

You're in line to pick up your household's share for the week when you hear the first whisper. It's not directed at you, and it's not meant to be overheard, but you hear it anyway because the speaker is agitated and forgets to be quiet. "Too Earthfired many of 'em," an older man is saying to a younger man, when you pull yourself out of your own thoughts enough to process the words. "Ykka's all right, earned her place, didn't she? Gotta be a few good ones. But the rest? We only need *one*—"

The man is shushed by his companion at once. You fix your gaze on a distant group of people trying to haul some baskets of mineral ore across the cavern by use of a guided ropeslide, so that when the younger man looks around he won't see you looking at them. But you remember.

It's been a week since the incident with the boilbugs and it feels like a month. This isn't just losing track of days and nights. Some of the strange elasticity of time comes from your having lost Nassun, and with her the urgency of purpose. Without that purpose you feel sort of attenuated and loose, as aimless as compass needles must have been during the Wandering Season. You've decided to try settling in, recentering your awareness, exploring your new boundaries, but that isn't helping much. Castrima's geode defies your sense of size as well as time. It feels cluttered when you stand near one of the geode's walls, where the view of the opposite wall is occluded by dozens of jagged, crisscrossing quartz shafts. It feels empty when you pass entire crystals' worth of unoccupied apartments, and realize the place was built to hold many more people than it currently does. The trading post on the surface was smaller than Tirimo—yet you're beginning to realize that Ykka's efforts at recruitment for Castrima have been exceptionally successful. At least half of the people you meet in the comm are new, same as you. (No wonder she wanted some new people on her improvised advising council; *newness* is a group trait here.) You meet a nervous metallorist and three knappers who are nothing like Jija, a biomest who works with Lerna two days a week, and a woman who once made a living selling artful leather crafts as gifts, who now spends her days tanning skins that the Hunters bring in.

Some of the new people have a bitter look, because like Lerna they did not intend to join Castrima. Ykka or someone else deemed them useful to a community that once consisted solely of traders and miners, and that meant the end of their journey. Some of them, however, are palpably feverish in their determination to contribute to and defend the comm. These are the ones who had nowhere to go, their comms destroyed by the Rifting or the aftershakes. Not all of them have useful skills. They're youngish, usually, which makes sense because most comms won't take in people who are elderly or infirm during a Season unless they have very desirable skills—and because, you learn upon talking with them, Ykka demands that a very specific question be put to most newcomers: *Can you live with orogenes?* The ones who say yes get to come in. The ones who *can* say yes tend to be younger.

(The ones who say no, you understand without having to ask, are not permitted to travel onward and potentially join other comms or commless bands to attack a community that knowingly harbors orogenes. There's a convenient gypsum quarry not far off, apparently, which is downwind. Helps to draw scavengers away from Castrima-over, too.)

And then there are the natives—the people who were part of Castrima long before the Season began. A lot of them are unhappy about all the new additions, even though everyone knows the comm couldn't have survived as it was. It was simply too small. Before Lerna they had no doctor, only a man who did midwifery, field surgery, and livestock medicine as a sideline to his farrier business. And they had only two orogenes—Ykka and Cutter, though apparently no one knew for sure that Cutter was one until the start of the Season; now there's a story you want to hear someday. Without orogenes, Castrima-under becomes a deathtrap, which makes most of the natives reluctantly willing to accept Ykka's efforts to attract more of her kind. So the old Castrimans look at you with suspicion, but the good thing is that they look at all the newcomers the same way. It's not your status as an orogene that bothers them. It's that you haven't yet proven yourself.

(It is surprising how refreshing this feels. Being judged by what you do, and not what you are.)

Lately you've spent your mornings on a work crew doing

water-gardening: sprouting seeds in trays of wet cloth, then moving the resulting seedlings to troughs of water and chemicals that the biomests devise so that they can grow. It's soothing work, and reminds you of the housegreen you had back in Tirimo. (Uche sitting amid the edible ferns, making horrible faces as he chewed on a mouthful of dirt before you could stop him. You smile at this memory before the hurt blanks your face again. You still can't smile over things Corundum did, and that's been ten—no, eleven—years now.)

In the evenings you go to Ykka's, to talk with her and Lerna and Hjarka and Cutter about the affairs of the comm. This includes stuff like whether to punish Jever Innovator Castrima for selling fans—since market economies are illegal during a Season per Imperial Law—and how to stop Old Man Crey (who isn't that old) from complaining again that the communal baths are too tepid. He's getting on everyone's nerves. And who's going to step in if Ontrag, the potter, keeps breaking the bad practice pottery of the two people apprenticed to her? It's how Ontrag was taught, but that's also how one teaches people who *want* to learn pottery. Ontrag's apprentices are only there because Ykka ordered them to learn the old woman's skill before she kicks off. At the rate things are going, they might kill her themselves.

It's ridiculous, mundane, incredibly tedious stuff, and... you love it. Why? Who knows. Perhaps because it's similar to the sorts of discussions you had back during the two times you were part of a family? You remember arguing with Innon about whether to teach Corundum Sanze-mat early, so he wouldn't have an accent, or later, and only if Coru ever wanted to leave Meov. You had an argument with Jija once because he believed putting fruit in the cold cache ruined the taste, and you didn't care because it made the fruit last longer. The arguments that you have with the other advisors are more important: Your decisions affect more than a thousand people now. But they have the same silly, pedantic feel. Silly pedantry is a luxury that you've rarely been able to enjoy in your life.

You've gone topside again, standing silent on the porch of a gateway house in the falling ash. The sky's a little different today: thinnish gray-yellow instead of thickish gray-red, and the pattern of the clouds is long and wavelike in lieu of the chains of beads you've seen since the Rifting. One of the Strongback guards says, looking up, "Maybe things are getting better." The yellow of the clouds almost feels like sunlight. You can see the sun itself now and again, a pale and strengthless disc occasionally framed by the gentle drifting curves.

You don't tell the guard what you can sess, which is that the yellow clouds contain more sulfur than usual. Nor do you say what you know, which is that if it rains right now, the forest that surrounds Castrima and currently provides a significant portion of the comm's food will die. Somewhere up north, the rift that Alabaster tore has simply belched out a great waft of the gas from some long-buried underground pocket. Cutter, who's come up here with you and Hjarka, glances at you, face carefully blank; he knows, too. But he doesn't say anything, either, and you think you know why: Because of the guard, and his wistful hope that things are getting better. It would be cruel to break that hope before it fades on its own. You like Cutter better for this moment of shared kindness.

Then you turn your head a little and the feeling vanishes. There's another stone eater nearby, lurking in the shadows of a house not far off. This one is male-ish, butter-yellow marble laced with veins of brown, with a swirling cap of brass hair. He isn't looking at anyone, isn't moving, and you wouldn't have even noticed him if not for the bright metal of his hair, so striking against the haze of the day. You wonder, for the third or fourth time, why they cluster around Castrima. Are they trying to help, as Hoa helps you? Are they expecting more of you to turn to delicious, chewable stone? Are they just bored?

You can't deal with these creatures. You push Butter Marble from your mind and look away, and later when you're ready to set off and you glance that way again, he is gone.

The three of you are up here, following one of the Hunters through the forest, because they want you to come and see something. Ykka's not along for the trip because she's mediating a dispute between the Strongbacks and the Resistants about shift length or something. Lerna's not here because he's started teaching a class in wound care to anyone who wants to attend. Hoa's not here because Hoa's still missing, as he has been for the past week. But with you are seven of the Castrima Strongbacks, two Hunters, and the blond white woman you met on your first day in Castrima, who has since introduced herself as Esni. She's been accepted into the comm as a Strongback, despite being barely over a hundred pounds and paler than ash. Turns out she was the head of a drover clan before the Rifting, which means she knows how to wrangle large animals and people with outsized egos. She and her people voluntarily joined Castrima because it was much closer than their home comm down in the Antarctics. The air-dried, pickled, salt-cured remnants of their last cattle herd have constituted Castrima's only meat stores since the Rifting.

No one talks as you walk. The silence of the forest, save for the rustling of small creatures through the undergrowth and the occasional tap-tap of wood-boring animals in the distance, demands more of the same. The woods are changing, you see as you tromp through them. The taller trees lost their leaves months ago, sap drawing down to protect against the encroaching cold and the souring surface soil. But correspondingly, the shrubs and mid-level trees have grown thicker foliage, drinking in what little light they can capture, sometimes folding their leaves down at night to shed ash. This makes the ash thinner off the roads, so much that you can sometimes see the ground litter.

Which is good, because it makes the newest parts of the landscape stand out that much more: the mounds. They're three or four feet high, usually, built of cemented ash and leaves and twigs, and on a brighter day like this they are easy to spot because they steam faintly. Occasionally you see small bones, the remains of paws or tails, poking through the base of each mound. Boilbug nests. Not many...but you don't remember any, a week ago when you walked past this area of the forest. (You would've sessed the heat.) It's a reminder that while most plants and animals struggle to survive in a Season, a rare few do more: deprived of their usual predators and given ideal conditions, they thrive, breeding wildly wherever they can find a food source, relying on numbers to ensure the species' continuation.

Not good, regardless. You find yourself checking your shoes frequently, and you notice the others doing the same.

Then you've reached the top of a ridge that overlooks a spreading forest basin. It's clear the basin is outside the zone of protection that Castrima's orogenes maintain, because broad swaths of the forest here are flattened and dead in the aftermath of the Rifting. You'd be able to see hundreds of miles if not for the ash, but since this is such a bright, low-ash day, you can see perhaps a few dozen. It's enough.

Because there, hazy in the golden light, you can see something standing above the flattened forest: a cluster of what must be stripped saplings or long branches set into the ground in an attempt at straightness, although many of them list to one side or the other. At the tip of each is a flapping bit of dark red cloth to draw the eye. You can't tell whether the red is dye or something else, because mounted on each of these stakes is a body. The stakes jut from the bodies' mouths or other parts; they are impaled upon them.

"Not our people," says Hjarka. She's looking through a distance glass, adjusting it while one of the Hunters hovers nearby, hands half-upraised to catch the precious instrument should Hjarka fumble it or, knowing Hjarka, toss the thing away. "I mean, it's hard to tell from this distance, but I don't recognize them, and I don't think we've ever sent anyone out that far. And they look filthy. Commless band, maybe."

"One that bit off more than it could chew," mutters one of the Hunters.

"All our patrols are accounted for," says Esni, folding her arms. "I don't keep track of anybody but the Strongbacks, I mean, the Hunters do their own thing—but we do note goings and comings." She's already studied the bodies through the distance glass, and it was her call that members of the comm leadership be brought topside to see for themselves. "I figure the culprits are travelers. A late group trying to make it back to a home comm, better armed than the commless who attacked them. And luckier."

"Travelers wouldn't do this," says Cutter quietly. He's usually quiet. Hjarka's the one you always expect to be difficult, but she's actually predictable and far more easygoing than her fierce appearance would suggest. Cutter, though, opposes nearly everything you or Ykka or the others suggest. He's a stubborn little ruster under that quiet demeanor. "The impaling, I mean. No reason to stop for that long. Someone spent time cutting down those poles, sharpening them, digging holes to post them, positioning them so they could be seen for miles around. Travelers . . . travel."

Cutter's much harder to read than Hjarka, too, you notice now. Hjarka is a woman who has never been able to hide the breadth and vigor of what she is, so she doesn't bother to try. Cutter is a man who's spent his life concealing the strength of mountains behind a veneer of meekness. Now you know what that looks like from the outside. But he's got a point.

"What do you think it is, then?" You guess wildly. "Another commless band?"

"They wouldn't do this, either. At this point they're not wasting bodies anymore."

You wince, and see several other people in the group sigh or shift. But it's true. There are still animals to hunt, but the ones that aren't hibernating are fierce enough or armored enough or toxic enough to be costly prey for anything but very well-prepared hunters. Commless rarely have good working crossbows, and desperation makes for poor stealth. And as the boilbugs have shown, there's new competition for any carcasses.

Of course, if Castrima doesn't find a new source of meat soon, you and the others won't be wasting bodies anymore, either. That wince served many purposes.

Hjarka lowers the distance glass at last. "Yeah," she sighs, responding to Cutter. "Fuck."

"What?" You feel stupid, suddenly, as if everyone has started speaking another language.

"Somebody's marking territory." Hjarka gestures with the distance glass, shrugging; the Hunter deftly plucks it from her hand. "Doing this is a warn-off, but not to other commless—who don't give a shit and will probably just pull the bodies down for snacks. To *us*. Letting us know what they'll do if we cross their boundaries."

"Only comm in that direction is Tettehee," says one of the Hunters. "They're friendly, have been for years. And we're no threat to them. Not much water in that direction to support other comms; the river wends away to the north."

North. That bothers you. You don't know why. There's no reason to mention this to the others, but still... "When's the last time you heard from this Tettehee?" Silence greets you, and you look around. Everyone's staring. Well, that answers that. "We need to send somebody to Tettehee, then."

"'Somebody' who might end up on a pole?" Hjarka glares at you. "Nobody's expendable in this comm, *newcomer*."

It's the first time you've ever sparked her ire, and it's a lot of ire. She's older, bigger, and in addition to her sharpened teeth, there's her glare, which is black-eyed and fierce. But she reminds you, somehow, of Innon, so you feel anything but anger in response.

"We're going to need to send out a trading party anyway." You say it as gently as you can, which makes her blink. That's the inevitable conclusion of all the talks you've had lately about the comm's deepening meat deficit. "We might as well use this warn-off to make sure that party is armed, and a large enough group that no one can tackle them without paying for it."

"And if whoever did this has a larger, better-armed group?"

It's never just about strength, during a Season. You know that. Hjarka knows that. But you say, "Send an orogene with them."

She blinks in genuine surprise, then lifts an eyebrow. "Who'll kill half our people trying to defend them?"

You turn away from her and hold out a hand. None of them move away from you, but then none of them are from comms large enough to have been visited often by Imperial Orogenes; they don't know what your gesture means. They gasp, though, and move back and murmur when you spin a five-foot-wide torus in the brush a few paces away. Ash and dead leaves swirl into a dust devil, glittering with ice in the sulfurous afternoon light. You didn't have to spin it that fast. You're just being dramatic.

Then you use what you dragged from that torus and turn, pointing at the stand of impaled bodies down in the basin. At this distance it's impossible to tell what's happening at first—but then the trees in the area shiver and the poles begin to sway wildly. A moment later a fissure opens, and you drop the poles and their grisly ornaments into the ground. You pull your hands together, slowly so as not to alarm anyone, and the trees stop shivering. But a moment later, everyone feels the faint judder of the ridge you're standing on, because you've let a little of the aftershake come this way. Again, you didn't have to. You just had a point to make.

It's commendable that Hjarka just looks impressed and not alarmed when you open your eyes and turn to her. "Nice," she says. "So *you* can ice someone without killing everyone around you. But if every rogga could do that, people wouldn't have a problem with roggas."

You really hate that rusting word, no matter what Ykka thinks.

And you're not sure you agree with Hjarka's assessment. People have problems with roggas for a lot of reasons that have nothing to do with orogeny. You open your mouth to reply—and then stop. Because now you can see the trap Hjarka's set, the only way this conversation's going to end, and you don't want to go there... but there's no avoiding it. Rusting fuck.

So that's how you end up in charge of a brand-new Fulcrum, sort of.

* * *

"Stupid," Alabaster says.

You sigh. "I know."

It's the next day, and another conversation about the principles of the unreal—how an obelisk works, how their crystalline structure emulates the strange linkages of power between the cells of a living being, and how there are theories about things even smaller than cells, somehow, even though no one has seen them or can prove that they exist.

You have these conversations with Alabaster every day, in between your morning work shift and evening politicking, because he is filled with a sense of urgency spurred by his own impending mortality. The sessions don't last long, because Alabaster has limited strength. And the conversations so far haven't been very useful, mostly because Alabaster is a terrible teacher. He barks orders and gives lectures, never answering your questions when you ask them. He's impatient and snappish. And while some of this can be chalked up to the pain that he's in, the rest is just Alabaster being himself. He really hasn't changed.

You are frequently surprised at how much you've missed him, the irascible old ass. And because of this, you hold your temper...for a while, anyway.

"Someone's got to teach the younger ones, anyway," you say. Most of the comm's orogenes are children or adolescents, simply because most ferals don't survive childhood. You've heard rumors that some of the older orogenes are teaching them, helping them learn not to ice things when they stub their toes, and it helps that Castrima is as stable as the Equatorials once were. But that's ferals teaching ferals. "And if I fail to do whatever it is you keep insisting that I do—"

"None of them are worth rust. You'd sess that yourself, if you'd bothered to pay any attention to them. It's not just about skill, it's also natural talent; that's the whole reason the Fulcrum made us breed, Essun. And most of them will never be able to get past energy redistribution." This is the term that the two of you have concocted for orogeny done with heat and kinetics—the Fulcrum's way. What Alabaster is now trying to teach you, and what you're struggling to learn because it relies on things that make no sense whatsoever, is something you've started calling *magic redistribution*. That isn't right, either; it's not redistribution, but it'll do until you understand it better.

Alabaster's still on about the orogeny class you've agreed to teach, and the children who will fill it. "It's a waste of your time to teach them."

This dismissal, inexplicably, starts to eat through your patience. "It's never a waste of time to educate others."

"Spoken like a simple creche teacher. Oh, wait."

It's a cheap shot, disrespecting the vocation that gave you years of camouflage. You should let it go, but it feels like salt on a glass-cut and you snap. "Stop. It."

Alabaster blinks, then scowls to the degree that he can. "I don't have a great deal of time for coddling, Syen—"

"*Essun.*" Right now, here, it matters. "And I don't rusting care if you're dying. You don't get to talk to me like this." And you get up, because suddenly you're rusting *done.*

He stares at you. Antimony is there as always, supporting him in silence, and her eyes shift to you for a moment. You think you read surprise in them, but that's probably just projection. "You don't care if I'm dying."

"No, I don't. Why the rust should I? You don't care if any of the rest of us die. You *did this to us.*" Lerna, at the other end of the room, glances up and frowns, and you remember to lower your voice. "You'll kick off sooner and more easily than the rest of us. *We* get to starve to death, well after you're dust in the ash. And if you can't be bothered to actually teach me anything, then fuck you; I'll figure out how to fix things myself!"

So you're halfway across the infirmary, your steps brisk and your hands fisted at your sides, when he snaps, "Walk out that door and you *will* starve to death. Stay and you have a chance."

You keep walking, yelling over your shoulder, "*You* figured it out!"

"It took me ten years! And—fucking, flaking rust, you hard-headed, steel-hearted—"

The geode jolts. Not just the infirmary building but the whole damned thing. You hear cries of alarm outside, and that does it.

You stop and clench your fists and slam a counter-torus against the fulcrum that he's positioned just underneath Castrima. It doesn't dislodge his; you're still not precise enough for that, and anyway you're too angry to try very hard. The movement stops, however—whether because you stopped it or because you've surprised him so much that he stopped it, you don't care.

Then you turn back, storming at him in such a fury that Antimony vanishes and is suddenly standing beside him, a silent sentinel warning. You don't care about her, and you don't care that Alabaster is bent again, making a low strained wheezing sound, or any of it.

"Listen to me, you selfish ass," you snarl, bending down so the stone eater will be the only one to hear. 'Baster's shaking, in visible pain, and a day ago that would've been enough to stop you. Now you're too angry for pity. "I have to live here even if you're just waiting to die, and if you make these people hate us because you can't rein it in—"

Wait. You trail off, distracted. This time you can see the change as it happens to his arm—the left one, which had been longer. The stone of him creeps along slowly, steadily, making a minute hissing sound as it transmutes flesh into something else. And nearly against your will you shift your sight as he has taught you, searching between the gelid bubbles of him for those elusive tendrils of connection. You see, suddenly, that they are brighter, almost like silver metal, tightening into a lattice and aligning in new ways that you've never seen before.

"You're such an arrogant ruster," he snarls through his teeth. This breaks through your astonishment about his arm, replacing it with affront that *he* of all people has called *you* arrogant.

"*Essun.* You act like you're the only one who's made mistakes, the only one who ever died inside and had to keep going. You don't know shit, won't listen to shit—"

"Because you won't tell me anything! You expect me to listen to you, but you don't share, you just demand and proclaim and, and—and I'm not a child! Evil Earth, I wouldn't even speak to a child this way!"

(There is a traitor part of you that whispers, *Except you did. You spoke to Nassun like this.* And the loyal part of you snarls back, *Because she wouldn't have understood. She wouldn't have been safe if you'd been gentler, slower. It was for her own good, and—*)

"It's for your own rusting good," Alabaster grates. The progression of the stone down his arm has stopped, only an inch or so this time. Lucky. "I'm trying to protect you, for Earth's sake!"

You stop, glaring at him, and he glares back, and silence falls.

There is the clink of something heavy and metallic being put down behind you. This makes you glance back at Lerna, who is looking at you and has folded his arms. Most of the people in Castrima, even the orogenes, won't know what the jolt was all about, but he does because he saw the body language, and now you've got to explain things to him—hopefully before he doses Alabaster's next bowl of mush with something toxic.

It's a reminder that these are not the old days and you cannot react in the old ways. If Alabaster has not changed, then it's up to you. Because you have.

So you straighten and take a deep breath. "You've never taught anyone anything, have you?"

He blinks, frowning in apparent suspicion at your change of tone. "I taught you."

"No, Alabaster. Back then you did impossible things and I just watched you and tried not to die when I imitated you. But you've never tried to intentionally disseminate information to another adult, have you?" You know the answer even without him saying it, but it's important that he say it. This is something he needs to learn.

A muscle in his jaw flexes. "I've tried."

You laugh. The defensive note in his voice tells you everything. After another moment's consideration—and a deep breath to marshal your self-control—you sit down again. This leaves Antimony looming over you both, but you try to ignore her. "Listen," you say. "You need to give me a reason to trust you."

His eyes narrow. "You don't trust me by now?"

"You've destroyed the world, Alabaster. You've told me you want me to make it worse. I'm not hearing a whole lot here that screams, 'Obey me without question.'"

His nostrils flare. The pain of the stoning seems to have faded, though he's drenched with sweat and still breathing hard. But then something in his expression shifts, too, and a moment later he slumps, to the degree that he is able.

"I let him die," he murmurs, looking away. "Of course you don't trust me."

"No, Alabaster. The Guardians killed Innon."

He half smiles. "Him, too."

Then you know. Ten years and it's like no time has passed at all. "No," you say again. But this is softer. Strengthless. He's said he wouldn't forgive you for Corundum . . . but perhaps you're not the only one he doesn't forgive.

A long silence passes.

"All right," he says at last. His voice is very soft. "I'll tell you."

"What?"

"Where I've been for the past ten years." He glances up at Antimony, who still looms over both of you. "What this is all about."

"She isn't ready," the stone eater says. You jump at her voice.

Alabaster tries to shrug, winces as something twinges somewhere on his body, sighs. "Neither was I."

Antimony stares down at both of you. It's not really that different from the way she's been staring at you since you came back, but it feels more pent. Maybe that's just projection. But then, suddenly, she vanishes. You see it happen this time. Her form blurs, becoming insubstantial, translucent. Then she drops into the ground as if a hole has opened beneath her feet. Gone.

Alabaster sighs. "Come sit beside me," he says.

You frown immediately. "Why?"

"So we can have sex again. Why the rust do you think?"

You loved him once. You probably still do. With a sigh you get up and move to the wall. Gingerly, though his back is unburned, you prop yourself for comfort, then rest a hand against his back to hold him up, the way Antimony so often does.

Alabaster's silent for a moment, and then he says, "Thank you."

Then...he tells you everything.

* * *

Breathe not the fine ashfall. Drink not the red water.

Walk not long upon warm soil.

—*Tablet One, "On Survival," verse seven*

9

Nassun, needed

Because you are Essun, I should not need to remind you that all Nassun knew before Found Moon was Tirimo, and the ash-darkening world of the road during a Fifth Season. You know your daughter, don't you? So it should be obvious therefore that Found Moon becomes something she never believed she had before: a true home.

It is not a newcomm. At its core is the village of Jekity, which was a city before the Choking Season some hundred years before. During that Season, Mount Akok blanketed the Antarctics with ash—but that is not what nearly killed Jekity, since the city had vast stores and sturdy wood-and-slate walls at the time. Jekity the city died because of human errors, compounded: A child lighting a lantern spilled oil, which set off a fire that swept the western end of the comm and burned a third of it before people managed to get it under control. The comm's headman died in the fire, and when three qualified candidates stepped forward to take his place, factionalism and infighting meant that the burned section of the wall didn't get rebuilt quickly enough. A tibbit-run—small, furred animals that swarm like ants when food is scarce enough—swept into the comm and took care of anyone too slow to get off the ground… and the comm's ground-level storecaches. The survivors lasted for a time on what was left, then starved. By the time the sky cleared five years later, less than five thousand souls remained of the hundred thousand who'd begun the Season.

The Jekity of now is even smaller. The poor, unskilled repairs made to the wall during Choking are still in place, and while the stores have been elevated and replenished sufficiently to meet Imperial standards, this is only on paper: The comm has done a bad job of rotating old, spoiled stores out and laying in new. Strangers have rarely asked to join Jekity over the years. Even by Antarctic standards, the comm is seen as ill-fated. Its young people usually leave to talk or marry their way into other, growing communities where jobs are more plentiful and the memory of suffering does not linger. When Schaffa found this sleepy terrace-farming comm ten years before, and convinced the then-headwoman Maite to allow him to set up a special Guardian facility within the comm's walls, she hoped that it was the beginning of a turnaround for her home. Guardians are a healthy addition to any community, aren't they? And indeed, there are now three Guardians in Jekity including Schaffa, along with nine children of varying ages. There were ten, but when one of the children caused a brief but powerful earthshake amid a temper tantrum one evening, the child vanished. Maite did not ask questions. It's good to know the Guardians are doing their jobs.

Nassun and her father do not know this as they move into the comm, though others will eventually tell them. The healers—an elderly doctor and a forest herbalist—spend seven days getting Jija out of danger, because he develops a fever not long after the surgery on his wound. Nassun tends him the whole while. When it becomes clear that he'll survive, however, Schaffa introduces them to Maite, who's delighted to learn that Jija is a stoneknapper. The comm has not had one for several decades, so they've been sending orders to knappers in the comm of Deveteris, twenty miles away. There's an old, empty house in the comm with an attached kiln, and while a forge would've been more useful, Jija tells her he can make it work. Maite gives it a month to be sure, and listens when her people tell her that Jija is polite and friendly and sensible. He's physically hearty, too, since he's recovering from that wound like a proper Resistant, and since he managed to survive the road with no companion but a little girl. Everyone notices how well behaved and devoted his daughter is, too—not at all what anyone would expect of a rogga. Thus, at the end of the month, Jija receives the name *Jija Resistant Jekity*. They induct him with a ceremony that most of the comm has never seen before, so long has it been since anyone new joined the comm. Maite herself had to look up the details of the ceremony in an old lore-book. Then they throw a party, which is very nice. Jija tells them he's honored.

Nassun remains just *Nassun*. No one calls her Nassun Resistant Tirimo, though she still introduces herself that way upon meeting new people. Schaffa's interest in her is simply too obvious. But she causes no trouble, so the people of Jekity are as friendly toward her as they are toward Jija, if in a slightly more guarded fashion.

It is the other orogene children who unashamedly embrace Nassun for everything she is.

The oldest of them is a Coaster boy named Eitz, who speaks with a strange choppy accent that Nassun thinks of as exotic. He's eighteen, tall, long-faced, and if there is a perpetual shadow in his expression, it does nothing to mar his beauty in Nassun's eyes. He's the one who welcomes Nassun on the first day after it becomes clear that Jija will live. "Found Moon is *our* community," he says in a deep voice that makes Nassun's heart race, leading her to the small compound that Schaffa's people have built over near Jekity's weakest wall. It's up a hill. He leads her toward a pair of gates that swing open as they approach. "Yumenes had the Fulcrum, and Jekity has this: A place where you can be yourself, and always be safe. Schaffa and the other Guardians are here for us, too, remember. This is ours."

Found Moon has walls of its own, shaped from the shafts of columnar rock that dominate this area—but these are uniformly sized and perfectly even in conformation. Nassun doesn't even have to sess them to realize they have been raised by orogeny. Within the compound are a handful of small buildings, a few new but most parts of old Jekity left abandoned as the comm's population dwindled. Whatever those used to be, they have since been refurbished into a house for the Guardians, a mess hall, a wide tiled practice area, several ground-level storesheds, and a dormitory for the children.

The other children fascinate Nassun. Two are Westcoasters, small and brown and black-haired and angle-eyed. Sisters, and they look it, named Oegin and Ynegen. Nassun has never seen Westcoasters before, and she stares until she realizes they are staring at her in turn. They ask to touch her hair and she asks to touch theirs back. This makes them all realize how strange and silly a request that is, and they giggle and become instant friends without a head petted between them. Then there is Paido, another Somidlatter, who looks like he's got more than a little Antarctic in him because his hair is bright yellow and his skin is so white that it nearly glows. The others tease him about it, but Nassun tells him that sometimes she burns in the sun, too—though she carefully doesn't mention that this takes the better part of a day rather than minutes—and his face alights.

The other children are all from lower Somidlats comms, and all have visible Sanzed in them. Deshati was in training to become a stoneknapper before the Guardians found her, and she asks Nassun all sorts of questions about her father. (Nassun warns her off talking to Jija directly. Deshati understands at once, though she is sad about it.) Wudeh gets sick when he eats certain kinds of grain and is very small and frail because he doesn't get enough good food, though his orogeny is the strongest of the bunch. Lashar looks at Nassun coldly and sneers at her accent, though Nassun can't tell the difference between how she speaks and how Lashar does. The others tell her it's because Lashar's grandfather was an Equatorial and her mother is a local comm Leader. Alas, Lashar is an orogene, so none of that matters anymore... but her upbringing tells.

Shirk is not Shirk's name, but she won't tell anyone what that really is, so they started calling her that after she tried to duck out of chores one afternoon. (She doesn't anymore, but the name stuck.) Peek is similarly nicknamed, because she is tremendously shy and spends most of her time hiding behind someone else. She has only one eye, and a terrible scar down the side of her face—where her grandmother tried to stab her, the others whisper when Peek is not around. Her real name is Xif.

Nassun makes ten, and they want to know everything about her: where she came from, what kinds of foods she likes to eat, what life was like in Tirimo, has she ever held a baby kirkhusa because they are so soft. And in whispers they ask about other things, once it becomes clear that Schaffa favors her. What did she do on the day of the Rifting? How did she learn such skill with orogeny? This is how Nassun discovers that it is rare for their kind to be born to orogene parents. Wudeh comes the closest, because his aunt realized what he was and taught him what she could in secret, but this amounted to little more than how not to ice people by accident. Some of the others only learned that lesson the hard way—and Oegin grows very quiet during this conversation. Deshati actually didn't know she was an orogene until the Rifting, which Nassun finds incomprehensible. She is the one who asks the most questions, but quietly, when the others are not around, and in a tone of shame.

Another thing Nassun discovers is that she is much, much, *much* better than any of them. It is not simply a matter of training. Eitz has had years more training than her, and yet his orogeny is as thin and frail as Wudeh's body. Eitz is in control of it, enough to do no harm, but he can't do much good with it, either, like find diamonds or make a cool spot to stand in on a hot day or slice a harpoon in half. The others stare when Nassun tries to explain the lattermost, and then Schaffa comes away from the wall of a nearby building (one of the Guardians is always watching while they gather and train and play) to take her for a walk.

"What you do not understand," Schaffa says, resting a hand on her shoulder as they walk, "is that an orogene's skill is not just a matter of practice, but of innate ability. So much has been done to breed the gift out of the world." He sighs a little, sounding almost disappointed. "There are few left who are born with a high level of ability."

"My father killed my brother because of it," Nassun says. "Uche had more orogeny than me. All he ever did was listen with it, though, and say weird things sometimes. He made me laugh."

She keeps the words soft because they still hurt to say, and because she's said them so rarely. Jija never wanted to hear it, so she has had no one with whom she could discuss her grief until now. They're over by the southern terraces of Jekity, successive platforms high above the floor of a lava-plain valley. The terraces are still heavily planted with grains, greens, and beans. Some of the plants are beginning to look sickly from the thinning sunlight. This will probably be the last harvest before the ash clouds get too thick.

"Yes. And that is a tragedy, little one; I'm sorry." Schaffa sighs. "My brethren have done their job too well, I think, in warning the populace about the dangers of untrained orogenes. Not that any of those warnings were false. Just... exaggerated, perhaps." He shrugs. She feels a flash of anger that this *exaggeration* is why her father looks at her with such hate sometimes. But the anger is nebulous, directionless; she hates the world, not anyone in particular. That's a lot to hate.

"He thinks I'm evil," she finds herself saying.

Schaffa looks at her for a long moment. There is something confused in his gaze for a moment, a wondering sort of frown that he gets from time to time. Not quite intentionally, Nassun sesses him in a fleeting pass, and yes—those strange silvery threads are flaring within him again, lacing through his flesh and tugging on his mind from somewhere near the back of his head. She stops as soon as his expression clears, because he is fiendishly sensitive to her uses of orogeny, and he does not like her doing anything without his permission. But when he is being tugged by the bright threads, he notices less.

"You aren't evil," he says firmly. "You are exactly as nature made you. And that is *special*, Nassun—special and powerful in ways that are atypical even for one of your kind. In the Fulcrum, you would have rings by now. Perhaps four, or even five. For one your age, that's amazing."

This makes Nassun happy, even though she doesn't fully understand. "Wudeh says the Fulcrum rings go up to ten?" Wudeh has the most talkative of the three Guardians, agate-eyed Nida. Nida sometimes says things that don't make sense, but the rest of the time she shares useful wisdom, so all the kids have learned to simply tune out the gibbering.

"Yes, ten." For some reason, Schaffa seems displeased by this. "But this is not the Fulcrum, Nassun. Here, you must train yourself, since we have no senior orogenes to train you. And that's good, because there are... things you can do." His face twitches. Flicker of silver through him again, then quiescence. "Things you are needed to do, which... things that Fulcrum training cannot do."

Nassun considers this, for the moment ignoring the silver. "Things like making my orogeny go away?" She knows her father has asked this of Schaffa.

"That would be possible, when you reach a certain point of development. But to reach that point, it is best that you learn to use your powers with no preconceptions." He glances at her. His expression is noncommittal, but somehow she knows: He does not want her changing into a still, even if it does become possible. "You're lucky to have been born to an orogene who was skilled enough to manage you as a child. You must have been very dangerous in your infancy and early years."

It's Nassun's turn to shrug at this. She lowers her gaze and scuffs at a weed that has worked its way up between two basalt columns. "I guess."

He glances at her, his gaze sharpening. Whatever is wrong with him—and there is something wrong with all of Found Moon's Guardians—it vanishes whenever she tries to hide something from him. It is as if he can sess obfuscations. "Tell me more of your mother."

Nassun does not want to talk about her mother. "She's probably dead." It seems likely, though she remembers feeling her mother's effort to shunt the Rifting away from Tirimo. People would've noticed that, though, wouldn't they? Mama always warned Nassun against doing orogeny during a shake, because that is how most orogenes get discovered. And Uche is what happens when orogenes get discovered.

"Perhaps." His head cocks, like that of a bird. "I've seen the marks of Fulcrum training in your technique. You are . . . precise. It's unusual to see in a grit—" He pauses. Looks confused again for a moment. Smiles. "A child of your age. How did she train you?"

Nassun shrugs again, thrusting her hands into her pockets. He will hate her, if she tells him. If not that, he will surely at least think less of her. Maybe he will give up.

Schaffa moves to sit on a nearby terrace wall. He also keeps watching her, smiling politely. Waiting. Which makes Nassun think of a third, worse possibility: What if she refuses to tell him, and he gets angry and kicks her and her father out of Found Moon? Then she will have nothing left but Jija.

And—she sneaks another look at Schaffa. His brow has furrowed slightly, not in displeasure but concern. The concern does not seem false. He is concerned about *her.* No one has shown concern for her in a year.

Thus, finally, Nassun says, "We would go out to a place near the end of the valley, away from Tirimo. She would tell Daddy she was taking me out hunting for herbs." Schaffa nods. That is something that children are normally taught in comms outside the Equatorial node network. A useful skill, should a Season come. "She would call it 'girl time.' Daddy used to laugh."

"And you practiced orogeny there?"

Nassun nodded, looking at her hands. "She would talk to me about it, when Daddy wasn't home. 'Girl talk.'" Discussions of wave mechanics and math. Endless quizzes. Anger when Nassun did not answer quickly, or correctly. "But at the Tip—the place she took me to—it was just practice. She had drawn circles on the ground. I had to push around a boulder, and my torus couldn't get any wider than the fifth ring, and then the fourth, and then the third. Sometimes she would throw the boulder at me." Terrifying to have three tons of stone rumbling along the ground toward her, and to wonder, *If I can't do it, will Mama stop?*

She had done it, so that question remains unanswered.

Schaffa chuckles. "Amazing." At Nassun's look of confusion, he adds, "That is precisely how orogene children are—were—trained at the Fulcrum. But it seems your training was substantially accelerated." He tilts his head again, considering. "If you had only occasional practice sessions, to conceal them from your father…"

Nassun nods. Her left hand flexes closed and then open again, as if on its own. "She said there wasn't time to teach me the gentle way, and anyway I was too strong. She had to do what would work."

"I see." Yet she can feel him watching her, waiting. He knows there's more. He prompts, "It must have been challenging, though."

Nassun nods. Shrugs. "I hated it. I yelled at her once. Told her she was mean. I told her I hated her and she couldn't make me do it."

Schaffa's breathing is, when the silver light is not stuttering or flickering within him, remarkably even. She has thought before that he sounds like a sleeping person, so steady is it. She listens to him breathe, not asleep, but calming nevertheless.

"She got really quiet. Then she said, 'Are you sure you can control yourself?' And she took my hand." She bites her lip then. "She broke it."

Schaffa's breath pauses, just for an instant. "Your hand?"

Nassun nods. She draws a finger across her palm, where each

of the long bones connecting wrist to knuckle still ache sometimes, when it is cold. After he says nothing more, she can continue. "She said it didn't m-matter if I hated her. It didn't matter if I didn't *want* to be good at orogeny. Then she took my hand and said don't ice anything. She had a round rock, and she hit my, my...my hand with it." The sound of stone striking flesh. Wet popping sounds as her mother set the bones. Her own voice screaming. Her mother's voice cutting through the pounding of blood in her ears: *You're fire, Nassun. You're lightning, dangerous unless captured in wires. But if you can control yourself through pain, I'll know you're safe.* "I didn't ice anything."

After that, her mother had taken her home and told Jija that Nassun had fallen and caught herself badly. True to her word, she'd never made Nassun go to the Tip with her again. Jija had remarked, later, on how quiet Nassun had become that year. *Just something that happens when girls start to grow up*, Mama had said.

No. If Daddy was Jija, then Mama had to be Essun.

Schaffa is very quiet. He knows what she is now, though: a child so willful that her own mother broke her hand to make her mind. A girl whose mother never loved her, only *refined* her, and whose father will only love her again if she can do the impossible and become something she is not.

"That was wrong," Schaffa says. His voice is so soft she can barely hear it. She turns to look at him in surprise. He is staring at the ground, and there is a strange look on his face. Not the usual wandering, confused look that he gets sometimes. This is something he actually remembers, and his expression is...guilty? Rueful. Sad. "It's wrong to hurt someone you love, Nassun."

Nassun stares at him. Her own breath catches, and she

doesn't notice until her chest aches and she is forced to suck in air. It's wrong to hurt someone you love. It's wrong. It's wrong. It has always been wrong.

Then Schaffa lifts a hand to her. She takes it. He pulls, and she falls willingly, and then she is in his arms and they are very tight and strong around her the way her father's have not been since before he killed Uche. In that moment, she does not care that Schaffa cannot possibly love her, when he has known her for only a few weeks. She loves him. She needs him. She will do anything for him.

With her face pressed into Schaffa's shoulder, Nassun sesses it when the silver flicker happens again. This time, in contact with him, she also feels the slight flinch of his muscles. It is barely a fluctuation, and might be anything: a bug bite, a shiver in the cooling evening breeze. Somehow, though, she realizes that it is actually pain. Frowning against his uniform, Nassun cautiously reaches toward that strange place at the back of Schaffa's head, where the silver threads come from. They are *hungry*, the threads, somehow; as she gets closer to them, they lick at her, seeking something. Curious, Nassun touches them, and sesses... what? A faint tug. Then she is tired.

Schaffa flinches again and pulls back, holding her at arm's length. "What are you doing?"

She shrugs awkwardly. "You needed it. You were hurting."

Schaffa turns his head from side to side slowly, not in negation, but as if checking for something he expects to be there, which is now gone. "I am always hurting, little one. It's part of what Guardians are. But..." His expression is wondering. By this, Nassun knows the pain is gone, at least for now.

"You're always hurting?" She frowns. "Is it that thing in your head?"

His gaze snaps back to her immediately. She has never been afraid of his icewhite eyes, even now as they turn very cold. "What?"

She points at the back of her own skull. It is where the sessapinae are located, she knows from lectures on biomestry in creche. "There's a little thing in you. Here. I don't know what it is, but I sessed it when I met you. When you touched my neck." She blinks, understanding. "You took something then to make it bother you less."

"Yes. I did." He reaches around her head now, and sets two of his fingers just at the top of her spine, beneath the back edge of her skull. This touch is not as relaxed as other times he has touched her. The two fingers are stiffened, held as if he's pantomiming a knife.

Only he isn't pantomiming, she realizes. She remembers that day in the forest when they reached Found Moon and the bandits attacked them. Schaffa is very, very strong—easily strong enough to push two fingers through bone and muscle like paper. *He* wouldn't have needed a rock to break her hand.

Schaffa's gaze searches hers and finds that she understands precisely what he's thinking about doing. "You aren't afraid."

She shrugs.

"Tell me why you aren't." His voice brooks no disobedience.

"Just…" She cannot help shrugging again. She can't really figure out how to say it. "I don't…I mean, if you have a good reason?"

"You have no inkling of my reasons, little one."

"I *know*." She scowls, more out of frustration with herself than anything else. Then an explanation occurs to her. "Daddy didn't have a reason when he killed my little brother." Or when he knocked her off the wagon. Or any of the half-dozen times he's looked at Nassun and thought about killing her so obviously that even a ten-year-old can figure it out.

An icewhite blink. What happens then is fascinating to watch: Slowly Schaffa's expression thaws from the contemplation of her murder into wonder again, and a sorrow so deep that it makes a lump come to Nassun's throat. "And you have seen so much purposeless suffering that at least being killed for a reason can be borne?"

He's so much better at talking. She nods emphatically.

Schaffa sighs. She feels his fingers waver. "But this is not a thing that can be known beyond my order. I let a child live once, who saw, but I should not have. And we both suffered for my compassion. I remember that."

"I don't want you to suffer," Nassun says. She puts her hands on his chest, wills the silver flickers within him to take more. They begin to drift toward her. "It always hurts? That isn't right."

"Many things ease the pain. Smiling, for example, releases specific endorphins, which—" He jerks and takes his hand from the back of her neck, grabbing her hands and pulling them away from him just as the silver threads find her. He actually looks alarmed. "That will kill you!"

"You're going to kill me anyway." This seems sensible to her.

He stares. "Earth of our fathers and mothers." But with that, slowly, the killing tension begins to bleed out of his posture.

After a moment, he sighs. "Never speak of—of what you sess in me, around the others. If the other Guardians learn that you know, I may not be able to protect you."

Nassun nods. "I won't. Will you tell me what it is?"

"Someday, perhaps." He gets to his feet. Nassun hangs on to his hand when he tries to pull away. He frowns at her, bemused, but she grins and swings his hand a little, and after a moment he shakes his head. Then they head back into the compound, and that is the first day Nassun thinks of it as *home.*

* * *

Seek the orogene in its crib. Watch for the center of the circle. There you will find [obscured]

—*Tablet Two, "The Incomplete Truth," verse five*

10

you've got a big job ahead of you

YOU'VE CALLED HIM CRAZY so many times. Told yourself that you despised him even as you grew to love him. Why? Perhaps you understood early on that he was what you could become. More likely it is that you suspected long before you lost and found him again that he *wasn't* crazy. "Crazy" is what everyone thinks all roggas are, after all—addled by the time they spend in stone, by their ostensible alliance with the Evil Earth, by not being human enough.

But.

"Crazy" is also what roggas who obey choose to call roggas that don't. You obeyed, once, because you thought it would make you safe. He showed you—again and again, unrelentingly, he would not let you pretend otherwise—that if obedience did not make one safe from the Guardians or the nodes or the lynchings or the breeding or the disrespect, then what was the point? The game was too rigged to bother playing.

You pretended to hate him because you were a coward. But

you eventually loved him, and he is part of you now, because you have since grown brave.

* * *

"I fought Antimony all the way down," Alabaster says. "It was stupid. If she'd lost her grip on me, if her concentration had faltered for an instant, I would have become part of the stone. Not even crushed, just…mixed in." He lifts a truncated arm, and you know him well enough to realize he would have waggled his fingers. If he still had fingers. He sighs, not even noticing. "We were probably into the mantle by the time Innon died."

His voice is soft. It's gotten quiet in the infirmary. You look up and around; Lerna's gone, and one of his assistants is sleeping on an unoccupied bed, snoring faintly. You speak in a soft voice, too. This is a conversation for only the two of you.

You have to ask, though even thinking the question makes you ache. "Do you know…?"

"Yes. I sessed how he died." He falls silent for a moment. You reverberate with his grief and your own. "Couldn't help sessing it. What they do, those Guardians, is magic, too. It's just… wrong. Contaminated, like everything else about their kind. When they shake a person apart, if you're attuned to that person, it feels like a niner."

And of course you were both attuned to Innon. He was a part of you. You shiver, because he's trying to make you *more* attuned, to the earth and orogeny and the obelisks and the unifying theory of magic, but you don't ever want to experience that again. It was bad enough seeing it, knowing the horror that resulted had once been a body you held and loved. It had felt much worse than a niner. "I couldn't stop it."

"No. You couldn't." You're sitting behind him, holding him upright with one hand. He's been gazing away from you, somewhere into the middle distance, since he began telling this story. He does not turn to look at you now over his shoulder, possibly because he can't do so without pain. But maybe that's comfort in his voice.

He continues: "I don't know how she manipulated the pressure, the heat, to keep it from killing me. I don't know how I didn't go mad from knowing where I was, wanting to get back to you, realizing I was helpless, feeling like I was suffocating. When I sessed what you did to Coru, I shut down. I don't remember the rest of the journey, or I don't want to. We must have…I don't know." He shudders, or tries to. You feel the twitch of muscles in his back.

"When I came to, I was on the surface again. In a place that…" He hesitates. His silence goes on for long enough that your skin prickles.

(I've been there. It's difficult to describe. That isn't Alabaster's fault.)

"On the other side of the world," Alabaster finally says, "there is a city."

The words don't make sense. The other side of the world is a great expanse of trackless blankness in your head. A map of nothing but ocean. "On…an island? Is there a landmass there?"

"Sort of." He can't really smile easily anymore. You hear it in his voice, though. "There's a massive shield volcano there, though it's under the ocean. Biggest one I've ever sessed; you could fit the Antarctics into it. The city sits directly above it, on the ocean. There's nothing visible around it: no land for farming, no hills to break tsunami. No harbor or moorings for boats. Just... buildings. Trees and some other plants, of varieties I've never seen elsewhere, gone wild but not a forest—sculpted into the city, sort of. I don't know what to call that. Infrastructures that seem to keep the whole thing stable and functioning, but all strange. Tubes and crystals and stuff that looks alive. Couldn't tell you how a tenth of it worked. And, at the center of the city, there's... a hole."

"A hole." You're trying to imagine it. "For swimming?"

"No. There's no water in it. The hole goes into the volcano, and... beyond." He takes a deep breath. "The city exists to contain the hole. Everything about the city is built for that purpose. Even its name, which the stone eaters told me, acknowledges this: *Corepoint.* It's a ruin, Essun—a deadciv ruin like any other, except that it's intact. The streets haven't crumbled. The buildings are empty, but some of the furniture is even usable—made of things not natural, undecaying. You could live in them if you wanted." He paused. "I did live in them, when Antimony brought me there. There was nowhere else to go and no one else to talk to... except the stone eaters. Dozens of them, Essun, maybe hundreds. They say they didn't build the city, but it's theirs now. Has been, for tens of thousands of years."

You're mindful of how much he hates being interrupted, but he pauses anyway. Maybe he's expecting commentary, or maybe he's giving you time to absorb his words. You're just staring at the back of his head. What's left of his hair is getting too long; you'll have to ask Lerna for scissors and a pick soon. There are absolutely no suitable thoughts in your head, besides this.

"It's something you can't help thinking about, when you're confronted with it." He sounds tired. Your lessons rarely last more than an hour, and it's been longer than that already. You would feel guilty if you had any emotion left in you right now other than shock. "The obelisks hint at it, but they're so..." You feel him try to shrug. You understand. "Not something you can touch or walk through. But this city. Recorded history goes back what, ten thousand years? Twenty-five if you count all the Seasons the University's still arguing about. But *people* have been around for much longer than that. Who knows when some version of our ancestors first crawled out of the ash and started jabbering at each other? Thirty thousand years? Forty? A long time to be the pathetic creatures we are now, huddling behind our walls and putting all our wits, all our learning, toward the singular task of staying alive. That's all we make now: Better ways to do field surgery with improvised equipment. Better chemicals, so we can grow more beans with little light. Once, we were so much more." He falls silent again, for a long moment. "I cried for you and Innon and Coru for three days, there in that city of who we used to be."

You ache, that he included you in his grief. You don't deserve it.

"When I...they brought me food." Alabaster skips past whatever he would've said so seamlessly that at first the sentence doesn't make sense. "I ate it, then tried to kill them." His voice turns wry. "Took me a while to give that up, actually, but they kept feeding me. I asked them, again and again, why they'd brought me there. Why they were keeping me alive. Antimony is the only one who would speak to me at first. I thought they were deferring to her, but then I realized they just didn't speak my language. Some of them weren't used to interacting with people at all. They stared, and sometimes I had to shoo them away. I seemed to fascinate some, disgust others. The feeling was mutual.

"I learned some of their language, eventually. I had to. Parts of the city *talked* in that language. If you knew the right words, you could open doors, turn on lights, make a room warmer or colder. Not everything still worked. The city *was* breaking down. Just slowly.

"But the hole. There were markers all around it, lighting up as you got closer." (You suddenly remember a chamber at the Fulcrum's heart. Long narrow panels igniting in sequence as you walked toward the socket, glowing with no discernible fire or filament.) "Barriers big as buildings in themselves, which sometimes glowed at night. Warnings that would write themselves in fire on the air before you, sirens that would sound if you got too near. Antimony took me to it, though, on the first day that I was...functional. I stood on one of the barriers and looked down into a darkness so deep that it..."

He has to stop. After he swallows, he resumes.

"She'd told me already that she took me from Meov because they couldn't risk me being killed. So there, at Corepoint's heart, she told me, 'This is why I saved you. This is the enemy you face. You are the only one who can.'"

"*What?*" You're not confused. You think you understand. You just don't want to, so you decide that you must be confused.

"That's what she said," he replies. Now he's angry, but not at you. "Word for word. I remember it because I was thinking *that* was the reason Innon and Coru died and you got thrown to the rusting dogs: because sometime in the ass-end of history, some of our so-smart ancestors decided to dig a hole to the heart of the world for no rusting reason. No; for power, Antimony said. I don't know how that was supposed to work but they did it, and they made the obelisks and other tools to harness that power.

"Something went wrong, though. I got the sense that even Antimony didn't know exactly what. Or maybe the stone eaters are still arguing about it and nobody's come to a consensus. Something just went wrong. The obelisks...misfired. The Moon was flung away from the planet. Maybe that did it, maybe some other things happened, but whatever the cause, the result was the Shattering. It really happened, Essun. That's what caused the Seasons." The muscles in his back flex a little against your hand. He's tense. "Do you understand? *We* use the obelisks. To stills, they're just big strange rocks. That city, all those wonders...that deadciv was *run by orogenes.* We destroyed the world just like they always say we did. *Roggas.*"

He says it so sharply and viciously that his whole body reverberates with the word. You feel how he stiffens as he says it. Vehemence hurts him. He knew it would and said it anyway.

"What they got wrong," he continues, sounding weary now, "are the loyalties. The stories say we're agents of Father Earth, but it's the opposite: We're his enemies. He hates us more than he hates the stills, because of what we did. That's why he made the Guardians to control us, and—"

You're shaking your head. "'Baster...you're speaking as if it, the planet, is real. Alive, I mean. Aware. All that stuff about Father Earth, it's just stories to explain what's wrong with the world. Like those weird cults that crop up from time to time. I heard of one that asks an old man in the sky to keep them alive every time they go to sleep. People need to believe there's more to the world than there is."

And the world is just shit. You understand this now, after two dead children and the repeated destruction of your life. There's no need to imagine the planet as some malevolent force seeking vengeance. It's a rock. This is just how life is supposed to be: terrible and brief and ending in—if you're lucky—oblivion.

He laughs. This hurts him, too, but it's a laugh that makes your skin prickle, because it's the laugh of the Yumenes-Allia highroad. The laugh of a dead node station. Alabaster was never mad; he's just learned so much that would have driven a lesser soul to gibbering, that sometimes it shows. Letting out some of that accumulated horror by occasionally sounding like a frothing maniac is how he copes. It's also how he warns you, you know now, that he's about to destroy some additional measure of your naivete. Nothing is ever as simple as you want it to be.

"That's probably how they thought," Alabaster says, when his laugh goes quiet. "The ones who decided to dig a hole to the world's core. But just because you can't see or understand a thing doesn't mean it can't hurt you."

You know that's true. But more importantly, you hear the knowledge in Alabaster's voice. It makes you tense. "What have you seen?"

"Everything."

Your skin prickles.

He takes a deep breath. When he speaks again, it's a monotone. "This is a three-sided war. More sides than that, but only three that you need to concern yourself with. All three sides want the war to end; it's just a question of how. We're the problem, you see—people. Two of the sides are trying to decide what should be done with us."

That phrasing explains a lot. "The Earth and . . . the stone eaters?" Always lurking, planning, wanting something unknown.

"No. They're people, too, Essun. Haven't you figured that out? They need things, want things, feel things, same way we do. And they've been fighting this war much, much longer than you or I. Some of them from the very beginning."

"The beginning?" What, the Shattering?

"Yes, some of them are that old. Antimony is one. That little one who follows you, too, I think. There are others. They can't die, so . . . yeah. Some of them saw it all happen."

You're too floored to really react. Hoa? Seven-ish years old, going on thirty thousand. *Hoa?*

"One side wants us—people—dead," Alabaster says. "That's one way to end things, I suppose. One side wants people . . . neutralized. Alive, but rendered harmless. Like the stone eaters themselves: Earth tried to make them more like itself, dependent on itself, thinking that would make them harmless." He sighs. "I guess it's reassuring to know the planet can cock up, too."

Your flinch is a delayed reaction, because you've still got Hoa in mind. "He used to be human," you murmur. Yes. It's just a disguise now, a long-discarded set of clothes donned again for old times' sake, but once upon a time, he was a real flesh-and-blood boy who looked like that. There's nothing Sanzed in him because *the Sanzed did not exist as a people in his day.*

"They all did. It's what's wrong with them." He's very tired now, which may be why he speaks more softly. "I can barely remember things that happened to me fifty years ago; imagine trying to remember five thousand years ago. Ten thousand. Twenty. Imagine forgetting your own name. That's why they never answer, when we ask them who they are." You inhale in realization. "I don't think it's what they're made of that makes stone eaters so different. I think it's that no one can live that long and not become something entirely alien."

He keeps saying *imagine*, and you can't. Of course you can't. But you can think of Hoa in that moment. Being fascinated by soap. Curling against you to sleep. His sorrow, when you stopped treating him like a human being. He'd been trying so hard. Doing his best. Failing in the end.

"You said three sides," you say. Focusing on what you can, instead of mourning what you can't. Alabaster is beginning to slouch, leaning harder against your hand. He needs to rest.

Alabaster is silent for so long that you think he might have fallen asleep. Then he says, "I slipped out one night, when Antimony wasn't there. I'd been there... years? Time got loose after a while. No one but them to talk to, and sometimes they forget that people need to talk. Nothing in the earth to listen to except the grumbling of the volcano. The stars are all wrong on that side of the world..." He trails off for a moment. Loose time, catching up with him. "I'd been looking at diagrams of the obelisks, trying to understand what their builders intended. My head hurt. I knew you were alive, and I missed you so much I was sick with it. I had this sudden, wild, half-rusted thought: Maybe, through the hole, I could get back to you."

If only he had a hand left that you could take. Your fingers twitch against his back instead. It's not the same.

"So I ran to the hole and jumped in. It's not suicide if you don't mean to die; that's what I told myself." Another felt smile. "But it wasn't... The things around the hole are mechanisms, but not just for warning. I must have triggered something, or maybe that was how they were meant to work. I went down, but it wasn't like falling. It was controlled, somehow. Fast, but steady. I should have died. Air pressure, heat, the same things Antimony took me through without the rock involved, but Antimony wasn't there and I should have died. There are lights along the shaft at intervals. Windows, I think. People actually used to live down there! But mostly, it's just the dark.

"Eventually... hours or days later... I slowed down. I had reached—"

He stops. You feel the prickle of goose bumps rise on his skin.

"The Earth *is* alive." His voice grows harsh, hoarse, faintly hysterical. "Some of the old stories are just stories, you're right, but *not that one*. I understood then what the stone eaters had been trying to tell me. Why I had to use the obelisks to create the Rift. We've been at war with the world for so long that we've forgotten, Essun, but *the world* hasn't. And we have to end it soon, or..."

Alabaster pauses, suddenly, for a long and pent moment. You want to ask what will happen if a war so ancient doesn't end soon. You want to ask what happened to him down there at the core of the Earth, what he saw or experienced that has so plainly shaken him. You don't ask. You're a brave woman, but you know what you can take, and what you can't.

He whispers: "When I die, don't bury me."

"Wh—"

"Give me to Antimony."

As if she has heard her name, suddenly, Antimony reappears, standing before you both. You glare at her, realizing that this means Alabaster has reached the end of his strength and that the conversation must end. It makes you resent his weakness, and hate that he is dying. It makes you seek a scapegoat for that hatred.

"No," you say, looking at her. "She took you from me. She doesn't get to keep you."

He chuckles. It's so weary that your anger breaks. "It's either her or the Evil Earth, Essun. Please."

He begins to list to one side, and maybe you're not as much of a monster as you think, because you give up and get up. Antimony blurs in that stone-eaterish way, slow except when they aren't, and then she is crouched beside him, using both hands now to hold and support him as he slips into sleep.

You gaze at Antimony. You've thought of her as an enemy all this time, but if what Alabaster says is true...

"No," you snap. You're not really saying it to her, but it works either way. "I'm not ready to think of you as an ally yet." Maybe not ever.

"Even if you were," says the voice from within the stone eater's chest, "I'm *his* ally. Not yours."

People like us, with wants and needs. You want to reject this, too, but oddly it comforts you to know that she doesn't like you, either. "Alabaster said he understood why you did what you did. But I don't understand why he did what *he* did, or what he wants now. He said this was a three-sided war; what's the third side? Which side is he on? How does the Rift... help?"

No matter how you try, you cannot imagine Antimony as having once been human. Too many things work against it: the stillness of her face, the dislocation of her voice. The fact that you hate her. "The Obelisk Gate amplifies energies both physical and arcane. No single point of surface venting produces these energies in sufficient quantity. The Rift is a reliable, high-volume source."

Meaning... You tense. "You're saying that if I use the Rift as my ambient source, channel it through my torus—"

"No. That would simply kill you."

"Well, thanks for the warn-off." You're beginning to understand, though. It's the same problem you keep having with Alabaster's lessons; heat and pressure and motion are not the only forces in play here. "You're saying the earth churns out magic, too? And if I push that magic into an obelisk..." You blink, recalling her words. "Obelisk Gate?"

Antimony's gaze has been focused on Alabaster. Now her flat black eyes slide to finally meet yours. "The two hundred and sixteen individual obelisks, networked together via the control cabochon." While you stand there wondering what the rust a control cabochon is, and marveling that there are more than two hundred of the damned things, she adds, "Using *that* to channel the power of the Rift should be enough."

"To do what?"

For the first time, you hear a note of emotion in her voice: annoyance. "To impose equilibrium on the Earth-Moon system."

What. "Alabaster said the Moon was flung away."

"Into a degrading long-ellipsis orbit." When you stare blankly, she speaks your language again. "It's coming back."

Oh, Earth. Oh, rust. Oh, no. *"You want me to catch the fucking Moon?"*

She just stares at you, and belatedly you realize you're practically shouting. You throw a guilty look at Alabaster, but he hasn't woken. Neither has the nurse on the far cot. When she sees that you're quiet, Antimony says, "That is an option." Almost as an afterthought, she adds, "Alabaster made the first of two necessary course corrections to the Moon, slowing it and altering the trajectory that would have taken it past the planet again. Someone else must make the second correction, bringing it back into stable orbit and magical alignment. Should equilibrium be reestablished, it's likely the Seasons will end, or diminish to such infrequency as to mean the same thing to your kind."

You inhale, but you get it now. Give Father Earth back his lost child and perhaps his wrath will be appeased. That's the third faction, then: those who want a truce, people and Father Earth agreeing to tolerate one another, even if it means creating the Rift and killing millions in the process. Peaceful coexistence by any means necessary.

The end of the Seasons. It sounds...unimaginable. There have always been Seasons. Except now you know that isn't true.

"Then it isn't an option," you say finally. "End the Seasons or watch everything die as this Season burns on forever? I'll—" *Catch the Moon* sounds ridiculous. "I'll do what you stone eaters want, then."

"There are always options." Her gaze, alien as it is, abruptly shifts in a subtle way—or maybe you're just reading her better. Suddenly she looks human, and very, very bitter. "And not all of my kind want the same thing."

You frown at her, but she says nothing more.

You want to ask more questions, try harder to understand, but she was right: You weren't ready for this. Your head's spinning, and the words stuffed into it are starting to blur and jumble together. It's too much to deal with.

Wants and needs. You swallow. "Can I stay here?"

She does not respond. You suppose it wasn't really necessary to ask. You get up and move to the nearest cot. Its head is against the wall, which would put your head behind Alabaster and Antimony, and you don't feel like staring at the back of the stone eater's head. You grab the pillow and curl up with your head at the foot of the bed instead, so you can see Alabaster's face. Once, you slept better when you could see him, across the expanse of Innon's shoulders. This is not the same reassurance... but it's something.

After a while, Antimony begins to sing again. It's strangely relaxing. You sleep better than you have in months.

* * *

Seek the retrograde [obscured] in the southern sky.
When it grows larger, [obscured]

—*Tablet Two, "The Incomplete Truth," verse six*

11

Schaffa, lying down

HIM AGAIN. I WISH HE hadn't done so much to you. You don't like being him to any degree. You will like less knowing that he is part of Nassun . . . but don't think about that right now.

* * *

The man who still carries the name of Schaffa even though he hardly qualifies as the same person, dreams fragments of himself.

Guardians don't dream easily. The object embedded deep within the left lobe of Schaffa's sessapinae interferes with the sleep-wake cycle. He does not often need sleep, and when he does, his body does not often enter the deeper sleep that enables dreaming. (Ordinary people go mad if they are deprived of dreaming-sleep. Guardians are immune to that sort of madness . . . or perhaps they're just mad all the time.) He knows it's a bad sign that he dreams more often these days, but it cannot be helped. He chose to pay the price.

So he lies on a bed in a cabin and groans, twitching fitfully, while his mind flails through images. It's poor dreaming because his mind is out of practice, and because so little remains of the material that might have been used to construct the dreams. Later he will speak of this aloud, to himself, as he clutches his head and tries to pull the scattering bits of his identity closer together, and that's how I'll know what torments him. I will know that as he thrashes, he dreams…

…Of two people, their features surprisingly sharp in his memory though all else has been stripped away: their names, their relationship to him, his reason for remembering them. He can guess, seeing that the woman of the pair has icewhite eyes rimmed with thick black eyelashes, that she is his mother. The man is more ordinary. Too ordinary—carefully so, in a way that immediately stirs a suspicion in Schaffa's Guardian mind. Ferals work hard to seem so ordinary. How they came to produce him, and how he came to leave them, is lost to the Earth, but their faces are interesting, at least.

…Of Warrant, and black-walled rooms carved into layered volcanic rock. Gentle hands, pitying voices. Schaffa doesn't remember the hands' or voices' owners. He is helped into a wire chair. (No, the nodes were not the first to use these.) This chair is sophisticated, automated, working smoothly even though something about it seems old to Schaffa's eye. It whirs and reconfigures and turns him until he is suspended facedown beneath bright artificial lights, with his face trapped between unyielding bars and the nape of his neck bared to the world. His hair is short. Behind and above him he hears the descent of ancient mechanisms, things so esoteric and bizarre that their names and original purposes have long been lost. (He remembers learning, around this time, that original purposes can be perverted easily.) Around him he can hear the snuffling and pleading of the others brought with him to this place—children's snuffling and pleading. *He* is a child in this memory, he realizes. Then he hears the other children's screams, followed by and mingling into whirring, cutting sounds. There is also a low watery hum that he will never hear again (yet it will be very familiar to you and any other orogene who has ever been near an obelisk), because from this moment forth his own sessapinae will be repurposed, made sensitive to orogeny and not to the perturbations of the earth.

Schaffa remembers struggling, and even as a child he's stronger than most. He gets his head and upper body almost free before the machinery reaches him. This is why the first cut goes so wrong, slicing far lower on his neck than it should and nearly killing him right there. The equipment adjusts, relentless. He feels the cold of it as the sliver of iron is inserted, feels the coldness of the other presence within him at once. Someone stitches him up. The pain is horrific and it never really ends, though he learns to mitigate it enough to function; all those who survive the implantation do. The smiling, you see. Endorphins ease pain.

...Of the Fulcrum, and a high-ceilinged chamber at the heart of Main, and familiar artificial lights that march toward and around a yawning pit from whose walls grow endless slivers of iron. He and the other Guardians gaze down at a small, shredded body crumpled at the bottom of the pit. Every now and again the children find the place; poor foolish creatures. Don't they understand? The Earth is indeed evil, and it is cruel, and Schaffa would protect them all from it, if he could. There is a survivor: one of the children attached to Guardian Leshet. The girl cringes as Leshet approaches, but Schaffa knows Leshet will let her live. Leshet has always been softer, kinder than she should be, and her children suffer for it…

…Of the road, and the endless flinching eyes of strangers who see his icewhite irises and unchanging smiles and know that they are seeing *something wrong* even if they don't know what it is. There is a woman one night, at an inn, who tries to be intrigued rather than frightened. Schaffa warns her, but she's insistent, and he cannot help but think of how the pleasure will keep the pain at bay for hours, perhaps the whole night. It's good to feel human for a while. But as he warned her, he circuits back in a few months. She's got a child in her belly, which she says isn't his, but he cannot permit the uncertainty. He uses the black-glass poniard, which is a thing made in Warrant. She was kind to him, so he targets only the child; hopefully she'll pass its corpse, and live. But she's furious, horrified, and she calls out for help and draws a knife of her own as they struggle. Never again, he resolves as he slaughters all of them—her whole family, a dozen bystanders, half the town as they attack him en masse. Never again can he forget that he is not, and has never been, human.

…Of Leshet again. He can barely recognize her this time: Her hair has gone white and her once-smooth face is all over lines and sagging skin. She's *smaller*, her softening bones compressing her into a hunched posture, which often happens to Arctics when they grow old. But Leshet has seen more centuries even than Schaffa. *Old* is not supposed to mean this for them: feebleness, senescence, shrinking. (Happiness, and a smile that means something other than mere mitigation of the pain. They're not supposed to have these either.) He stares at her broad, *welcoming* smile as she hobbles toward him from the cottage to which he has tracked her. He is filled with dim horror and a burgeoning disgust that he's not even aware of until she stops before him and he reaches out to reflexively break her neck.

...Of the girl. *The girl.* One of dozens, hundreds; they blur together over the endless years...but not this one. He finds her in a barn, poor frightened sad thing, and she loves him instantly. He loves her, too, wishes he could be kinder to her, is as gentle as he can be while he trains her to obedience with broken bones and loving threats and chances he should not give. Has Leshet infected him with her softness? Maybe, maybe... but *her face. Her eyes.* There's something about her. He is not surprised later, when he receives word that she is involved in the raising of an obelisk in Allia. His special one. He does not believe she is dead after. Indeed, he is filled with pride as he goes to reclaim her, and as he prays to the voice in his head that she will not force him to kill her. The girl...

...whose face causes him to wake with a soft cry. *The girl.*

The other two Guardians look at him with the Earth's judging eyes. They are as compromised as he, more. All three of them are everything the Guardian order has warned them against. He remembers his name but they do not remember theirs. That's the only real difference between him and them... isn't it? Yet they seem so much *less* than he, somehow.

Irrelevant. He pushes himself up from the cot, rubs his face, and heads outside.

The children's cabin. It's time to check on them, Schaffa tells himself, though he makes a beeline to Nassun's cot. She's asleep as he lifts a lantern to examine her face. Yes. It has always been there in her eyes and maybe cheekbones, tickling his mind, the fragments of his memory and the solidity of her features finally coming together. His Damaya. The girl who did not die, reborn.

He remembers breaking Damaya's hand and flinches with it. Why would he do such a thing? Why did he do any of the horrible things he did, in those days? Leshet's neck. Timay's. Eitz's family. So many others, whole towns of them. Why?

Nassun stirs in her sleep, murmuring softly. Automatically Schaffa reaches out to stroke her face, and she quiets at once. There is a dull ache in his chest that perhaps might be love. He remembers loving Leshet and Damaya and others, and yet he did such things to them.

Nassun stirs a little, and half wakes, blinking in the lantern light. "Schaffa?"

"It's nothing, little one," he says. "I'm sorry." Many degrees of sorry. But the fear is in him, and the dream lingers. He cannot help trying to expunge it. He finally blurts, "Nassun. Are you afraid of me?"

She blinks, barely lucid—and then she smiles. It untwists something within him. "Never."

Never. He swallows, his throat suddenly tight. "Good. Go back to sleep."

She drifts off at once, and perhaps she was never really awake to begin with. But he lingers near her, keeping watch until her eyelids flicker into dreaming again.

Never.

"Never again," he whispers, and twitches with the memory of that, too. Then the feeling changes and his resolve refocuses. What happened before does not matter. That was a different Schaffa. He has another chance now. And if being less than himself means being less than the monster that he was, he cannot regret it.

There is a quicksilver lightning strike of pain along his spine, too fast for him to smile it away. Something disagrees with his resolve. Automatically his hand twitches toward the back of Nassun's neck...and then he stops himself. No. She is more to him than just relief from pain.

Use her, commands the voice. *Break her. So willful, like her mother. Train this one to obey.*

No, Schaffa thinks back, and braces himself to bear the lash of retaliation. It is only pain.

So Schaffa tucks Nassun in, and kisses her forehead, and puts out the light as he leaves. He heads for the ridge that overlooks the town, and stands there for the rest of the night grinding his teeth and trying to forget the last of who he was and promising himself a better future. Eventually the other two Guardians come out onto the steps of their cabin as well, but he ignores the alien pressure of their gazes against his back.

12

Nassun, falling up

AGAIN, MUCH OF THIS IS SPECULATION. You know *of* Nassun, and she is part of you, but you cannot *be* Nassun…and I think we have established by now that you do not know her as well as you think. (Ah, but no parent does, with any child.) Another has the task of encompassing Nassun's existence. But you love her, and that means that some part of me cannot help but do the same.

In love, then, we shall seek understanding.

* * *

With her consciousness anchored deep within the earth, Nassun listens.

At first there is only the usual impingement upon the ambient sesuna: the minute flex-and-contract of strata, the relatively placid churn of the old volcano beneath Jekity, the slow unending grind of columnar basalt rising and cooling into patterns. She's gotten used to this. She likes that she can listen to this freely now, whenever she wants, instead of having to wait until the dark of night, lying awake after her parents have gone to bed. Here in Found Moon, Schaffa has given Nassun permission to use the crucible whenever she wants, for as long as she wants. She tries not to monopolize it, because the others need to learn, too...but they do not enjoy orogeny as much as she does. Most of them seem indifferent to the power they wield, or the wonders they can explore by mastering it. A few of the others are even afraid of it, which makes no sense to Nassun—but then, it also makes no sense to her now that once she wanted to be a lorist. Now she has the freedom to be fully who and what she is, and she no longer fears that self. Now she has someone who believes in her, trusts her, fights for her, as she is. So she will *be* what she is.

So now Nassun rides an eddy within the Jekity hot spot, balancing perfectly amid the conflicting pressures, and it does not occur to her to be afraid. She does not realize this is something a Fulcrum four-ringer would struggle to do. But then, she doesn't do it the way a four-ringer would, by taking hold of the motion and the heat and trying to channel both through herself. She reaches, yes, but just with her senses and not her absorption torus. But where a Fulcrum instructor would warn that she can't affect anything like this, she follows the lesson of her own instincts, which say she can. By settling into the eddy, swirling with it, she can relax enough to winnow down through its friction and pressure to what lies beneath: the silver.

This is the word she has decided to give it, after questioning Schaffa and the others and realizing they don't know what it is, either. The other orogene kids can't even detect it; Eitz thought he sessed something once, when she shyly asked him to concentrate on Schaffa instead of the earth, because the silver is easier to see—more concentrated, more potent, more *intent*—within people than it is in the ground. But Schaffa stiffened and glared at him in the next instant, and Eitz flinched and looked guiltier and more haunted than ever, so Nassun felt bad that she hurt him. She never asked him to try it again.

The others, however, can't do even that much. It is the other two Guardians, Nida and Umber, who help the most. "This is a thing that we culled for in the Fulcrum when we found it, when they heard the call, when they listened too closely," Nida begins, and Nassun braces herself because once Nida gets started there's no telling how long she'll run on. She stops only for the other Guardians. "The use of sublimates in lieu of controlling structures is dangerous, determinate, a warning. Important to cultivate for research purposes, but most such children we steered into node service. Among the others we cut—cut—*cut* them, for it was forbidden to reach for the sky." Amazingly, she shuts up after this. Nassun wonders what the sky has to do with anything, but she knows better than to ask, lest Nida get going again.

But Umber, who is as slow and quiet as Nida is fast, nods. "We allowed a few to progress," he translates. "For breeding. For curiosity. For the Fulcrum's pride. No more than that."

Which tells Nassun several things, once she sifts sense from the babble. Nida and Umber and Schaffa are not proper Guardians anymore, though they used to be. They have given up the credo of their order, chosen to betray the old ways. So the use of the silver is clearly an issue of violent concern to ordinary Guardians—but why? If only a few of the Fulcrum's orogenes were allowed to develop the skill, to "progress," what was the danger if too many did it? And why do these ex-Guardians, who once "culled for" the skill, allow her to do it unfettered now?

Schaffa is there for this conversation, she notes, but he does not speak. He merely watches her, smiling and twitching now and again as the silver sparks and tugs within him. That's been happening to him a lot, lately. Nassun isn't sure why.

Nassun goes home in the evenings after her days at Found Moon. Jija has settled into his Jekity house, and every time she comes back, there are new touches of hominess that she likes: surprisingly rich blue paint on the old wooden door; cuttings planted in the small housegreen, though they grow scraggly as the ash thickens in the sky overhead; a rug he has bartered a glassknife for in the small room that he designates as her own. It's not as big as the room she had back in Tirimo, but it has a window that overlooks the forest around Jekity's plateau. Beyond the forest, if the air is clear enough, she can sometimes see the coast as a distant line of white just beyond the forest's green. Beyond that is a spread of blue that fascinates her, though there's nothing to see but that slice of color, from here. She has never seen the sea up close, and Eitz tells her wonderful stories of it: that it smells of salt and strange life; that it washes up onto thin stuff called sand in which little grows because of the salt; that sometimes its creatures wiggle or bubble forth, like *crabs* or *squid* or *sandteethers*, though the lattermost are said to appear only during a Season. There is the constant danger of tsunami, which is why no one lives near the sea if they can avoid it—and indeed, a few days after Nassun and Jija reach Jekity, she sessed rather than saw the remnant of a big shake far to the east, well out to sea. She sessed, too, the reverberations this caused when something vast shifted and then pounded at the land along the coast. For once she was glad to be so far away.

Still, it is nice having a home again. Life begins to feel normal, for the first time in a very long while. One evening during dinner, Nassun tells her father what Eitz has said about the sea. He looks skeptical, then asks where she heard these things. She tells him about Eitz, and he grows very quiet.

"This is a rogga boy?" he says, after a moment.

Nassun, whose instincts have finally pinged a warning—she's gotten out of the habit of keeping vigilant for Jija's mood shifts—falls silent. But because he will get angrier if she doesn't speak, she finally nods.

"Which one?"

Nassun bites her lip. Eitz is Schaffa's, though, and she knows that Schaffa will allow none of his orogenes to come to harm. So she says, "The oldest. He's tall and very black and has a long face."

Jija keeps eating, but Nassun watches the flex of muscles in his jaw that have nothing to do with chewing. "That Coaster boy. I've seen him. I don't want you talking to him anymore."

Nassun swallows, and risks. "I have to talk with all of the others, Daddy. It's how we learn."

"Learn?" Jija looks up. It's banked, contained, but he's furious. "That boy is what, twenty? Twenty-five? And he's still a rogga. *Still.* He should have been able to cure himself by now."

For a moment Nassun is confused, because curing herself of orogeny is the last thing she thinks of at the end of her lessons. Well, Schaffa did say that it was possible. Ah—and Eitz, who is only eighteen but obviously aged up in Jija's head, is too old to have not utilized this cure, if he's going to. With a chill, Nassun realizes: Jija has begun to doubt Schaffa's claims that the erasure of orogeny is possible. What will he do if he realizes Nassun no longer *wants* to be cured?

Nothing good. "Yes, Daddy," she says.

This mollifies him, as it usually does. "If you have to talk to him during your lessons, fine. I don't want you making the Guardians angry. But don't talk to him outside of that." He sighs. "I don't like that you spend so much time up there."

He grumbles on about it for the rest of the meal, but says nothing worse, so eventually Nassun relaxes.

The next morning, at Found Moon, she says to Schaffa, "I need to learn how to hide what I am better."

Schaffa is carrying two satchels uphill to the Found Moon compound as she says this. They're heavy, and he's freakishly strong, but even he has to breathe hard to do this, so she does not pester him for a response while he walks. When he has reached one of the compound's tiny storeshacks, he sets the satchels down and catches his breath. It's easier to keep goods up here for things like the children's meals than to go back and forth to the Jekity storecaches or communal mealhouse.

"Are you safe?" he asks then, quietly. This is why she loves him.

She nods, biting her bottom lip, because it is wrong that she must wonder this about her own father. He looks at her for a long, hard moment, and there is a cold consideration to this look that warns her he's begun to think of a simple solution to her problem. "Don't," she blurts.

He lifts an eyebrow. "Don't . . . ?" he challenges.

Nassun has lived a year of ugliness. Schaffa is at least clean and uncomplicated in his brutality. This makes it easy for her to set her jaw and lift her chin. "Don't kill my father."

He smiles, but his eyes are still cold. "Something causes a fear like that, Nassun. Something that has nothing to do with you, or your brother, or your mother's lies. Whatever it is has left its wound in your father—a wound that obviously has festered. He will lash out at anything that touches upon or even near that reeking old sore... as you have seen." She thinks of Uche, and nods. "That cannot be reasoned with."

"I can," she blurts. "I've done it before. I know how to..." *manipulate him*, those are the words for it, but she's barely ten years old so she actually says, "I can stop him from doing anything bad. I always have before." Mostly.

"Until you fail to stop him, once. That would be enough." He eyes her. "I will kill him if he ever hurts you, Nassun. Keep that in mind, if you value your father's life more than your own. *I* do not." Then he turns back to the shed to arrange the satchels, and that's the end of the conversation.

Some while later, Nassun tells the others of this exchange. Little Paido suggests: "Maybe you should move into Found Moon with the rest of us."

Ynegen, Shirk, and Lashar are sitting nearby, relaxing and recovering after an afternoon spent finding and pushing around the marked rocks buried beneath the crucible floor. They nod and murmur agreement with this. "It's only right," says Lashar, in her haughty way. "You'll never be truly one of us if you continue living down there among *them*."

Nassun has thought this herself, often. But... "He's my father," she says, spreading her hands.

This elicits no understanding from the others, and a few looks of pity. Many of them still bear the marks of violence inflicted by the trusted adults in their lives. "He's a still," Shirk snaps back, and that is the end of the matter as far as most of them are concerned. Eventually Nassun gives up on trying to convince them otherwise.

These thoughts invariably begin to affect her orogeny. How can they not, when an unspoken part of her wants to please her father? It takes all of herself, and the confidence that comes of delight, to engage with the earth to her fullest. And that afternoon, when she tries to touch the spinning silver threads of the hot spot and it goes so horribly wrong that she gasps and claws her way back to awareness only to find that she has iced all ten rings of the crucible, Schaffa puts his foot down.

"You will sleep here tonight," he says, after walking across the crusted earth to carry her back to a bench. She's too exhausted to walk. It took everything she had not to die. "Tomorrow when you wake, I'm going with you to your house, and we'll bring back your belongings."

"D-don't want to," she pants, even though she knows Schaffa doesn't like it when the children say *no* to him.

"I don't care what you want, little one. This is interfering with your training. It is why the Fulcrum took children from their families. What you do is too dangerous to allow any distractions, however beloved."

"But." She does not have the strength to object more strongly. He holds her in his lap, trying to warm her up because the edge of her own torus was barely an inch from her skin.

Schaffa sighs. For a while he says nothing, except to shout for someone to bring a blanket; Eitz is the one who delivers it, having already gone to fetch it once he saw what happened. (Everyone saw what happened. It is embarrassing. As you realized back during Nassun's dangerous early childhood, she is a very, very proud girl.) As Nassun finally stops shivering and feeling as though her sessapinae have been methodically beaten, Schaffa finally says, "You serve a higher purpose, little one. Not any single man's desire—not even mine. You were not made for such petty things."

She frowns. "What... what was I made for, then?"

He shakes his head. The silver flashes through him, the webwork of it alive and shifting as the thing lodged in his sessapinae weaves its will again, or tries to. "To remedy a great mistake. One to which I once contributed."

This is too interesting to fall asleep to, though Nassun's whole body craves it. "What was the mistake?"

"To enslave your kind." When Nassun sits back to frown at him, he smiles again, but this time it is sad. "Or perhaps it is more accurate to say that we perpetuated their enslavement of themselves, under Old Sanze. The Fulcrum was nominally run by orogenes, you see—orogenes whom we had culled and cultivated, shaped and chosen carefully, so that they would obey. So that they knew their place. Given a choice between death and the barest possibility of acceptance, they were desperate, and we used that. We *made* them desperate."

For some reason he pauses here, sighs. Takes a deep breath. Lets it out. Smiles. This is how Nassun knows without sessing that the pain which lives always in Schaffa's head has begun to flare hotter again. "And my kind—Guardians such as I once was—were complicit in this atrocity. You've seen how your father knaps a stone? Hammering at it, flaking away its weaker bits. Breaking it, if it cannot bear the pressure, and starting over with another. That is what I did, back then, but with children."

Nassun finds this hard to believe. Of course Schaffa is

ruthless and violent, but that is to his enemies. A year commless has taught Nassun the necessity of cruelty. But with the children of Found Moon, he is so very gentle and kind. "Even me?" she blurts. It is not the clearest of questions, but he understands what she means: *If you had found me, back then?*

He touches her head, smooths a hand over it, rests his fingertips against the nape of her neck. He takes nothing from her this time, but perhaps the gesture comforts him, for he looks so sad. "Even you, Nassun. I hurt many children, back then."

So sad. Nassun decides he would not have *meant* it back then, even if he'd done something bad.

"It was wrong to treat your kind so. You're people. What we did, making tools of you, was wrong. It is *allies* that we need—more than ever now, in these darkening days."

Nassun will do anything that Schaffa asks. But allies are needed for specific tasks, and they are not the same thing as friends. The ability to distinguish this is also something the road has taught her. "What do you need us as allies for?"

His gaze grows distant and troubled. "To repair something long broken, little one, and settle a feud whose origins lie so far in our past that most of us have forgotten how it began. Or that the feud *continues*." He lifts a hand and touches the back of his head. "When I gave up my old ways, I pledged myself to the cause of helping to end it."

So that's it. "I don't like that it hurts you," Nassun says, staring at that blot on the silver map of him. It's so tiny. Smaller than one of the needles her father sometimes uses to stitch up holes in clothing. Yet it is a negative space against the glimmer, perceptible in silhouette only, or by its effects rather than in itself. Like the motionless spider at a quivering dew-laden web's heart. Spiders hibernate, though, during a Season, and the thing within Schaffa never stops tormenting him. "Why does it hurt you if you're doing what it wants?"

Schaffa blinks. Squeezes her gently, and smiles. "Because I will not *force* you to do what it wants. I present its wishes to you as a choice, and I will abide if you say no. It is... less trusting of your kind. Admittedly, for good reason." He shakes his head. "We can speak of this later. Now let your sessapinae rest." She subsides at once—though she had not really meant to sess him, and hadn't been really aware of doing so. Constant sessing is becoming second nature to her. "A nap will help you, I think."

So he carries her into one of the dormitory buildings and lays her down on an unclaimed cot. She curls up within the cocooning blanket and drifts off to the sound of his voice instructing the other children not to trouble her.

And she wakes, the next morning, to the echo of her own screams and strangled gasps as she fights her way out of the blanket. Someone grabs her arm and it is everything it should not be: not now, not on her, not who she wants, not tolerable. She flails toward the earth and it is not heat or pressure that answer her call but silver lacing light that screams in echo and reverberates with her unspoken need for force. That scream echoes across the land, not just in threads but in waves, not just through the land but through water and air, and

and then

and then

something answers her. Something in the sky.

She does not mean what she does. Eitz certainly does not

intend what happens as a result of his attempt to wake her from the nightmare. He likes Nassun. She's a sweet kid. And even though Eitz is no longer a trusting child and it has occurred to him in the years since they left his Coastal home that Schaffa smiled too much that day and smelled faintly of blood, he understands what it means that Schaffa is so taken with Nassun. The Guardian has been looking for something all this time, and in spite of everything, Eitz loves him enough to hope that he finds it.

Perhaps that will comfort you, as it will not Nassun, when in her frightened, disoriented flailing, she turns Eitz to stone.

This is not like the thing happening, far away and underground, to Alabaster. That is slower, crueler, yet much more refined. Artful. What hits Eitz is a catastrophe: a hammer blow of disordered atoms reordered at not quite random. The lattice that should naturally form dissolves into chaos. It starts on his chest when Nassun's hand tries to slap him away, and spreads in less time than it takes for the other children present to draw breath in gasps. It spreads over his skin, the brown hardening and developing an undersheen like tigereye, then into his flesh, though no one will see the ruby inside unless they break him. Eitz dies almost instantly, his heart solidifying first into a striated jewel of yellow quartz and deep garnet and white agate, with faint lacing veins of sapphire. He is a beautiful failure. It happens so fast that he has no time for fear. That may comfort Nassun later, if nothing else.

But in the moment, in the pent seconds after this happens, as Nassun writhes and tries to drag her mind back from *falling, falling upward through watery blue light*, and as Deshati's gasp turns into a scream (which sets off others) and Peek comes forward to stare openmouthed at the glossy, brightly colored facsimile of himself that Eitz has become, a number of things happen simultaneously elsewhere.

Some of these things you will have guessed. Perhaps a hundred miles away, a sapphire obelisk shimmers into solid reality for an instant, then flickers back to translucence—before ponderously beginning to drift toward Jekity. Many more miles in a different direction, somewhere deep within a magmatic vein of porphyry, a shape that is suggestive of the human form turns, alert with new interest.

Another thing happens that you may not have guessed—or perhaps you will have, because you know Jija as I do not. But in the precise moment that his daughter rips a boy's protons loose, Jija finishes his laborious climb to the plateau that houses the Found Moon compound. Too angry for courtesy after a night of seething, he shouts for his daughter.

Nassun does not hear him. She is convulsing in the dormitory. Hearing the other children's screams, Jija turns toward the building—but before he can start in that direction, two of the Guardians emerge from their building and move across the compound. Umber heads toward the dormitory at a brisk pace. Schaffa veers off to intercept Jija. Nassun will hear of all this later from the children who witness it. (So will I.)

"My daughter didn't come home last night," Jija says as Schaffa stops him in his tracks. Jija is alarmed by the children's screams, but not by much. Whatever madness is happening within the dorm, he expects nothing better of the den of iniquity that Found Moon surely must be. As he confronts Schaffa, he has a set to his jaw that you will recognize from other occasions on which he has felt himself righteous. He will therefore be unwilling to back down.

"She will be remaining here," Schaffa says, smiling politely. "We've found that returning to your home in the evenings is interfering with her training. Since your leg has clearly healed enough to allow you to make the climb, could you be so kind as to bring her things, later today?"

"She—" The screams get louder for a moment as Umber opens the door to go inside, but he closes it behind him and they stop. Jija frowns at this, but shakes his head in order to focus on what is important. "She will *not* be rusting staying here! I don't want her spending any more time than she has to with these—" He stops short of vulgarity. "She isn't one of them."

Schaffa tilts his head for an instant, as if he is listening to something only he can hear. "Isn't she?" His tone is contemplative.

Jija stares at him, momentarily confused into silence. Then he curses and tries to move past Schaffa. His leg has indeed mostly healed since his arrival at Jekity, but he still limps heavily, the harpoon having torn nerves and tendons that will be slow to heal, if they ever fully do. Even had Jija been able to move easily, however, he could not have evaded the hand that comes out of nowhere to cover his face.

It is Schaffa's big hand that splays over his face, moving so fast that it blurs before it seats itself. Jija doesn't see it till it's over his eyes and nose and mouth, picking him up bodily and slamming him to the ground on his back. As Jija lies there, blinking, he is too dazed to wonder what just happened, too stunned for pain. Then the hand pulls away, and from Jija's perspective the Guardian's face is just *there*, nose nearly touching Jija's own.

"Nassun does not have a father," Schaffa says softly. (Jija will remember later that Schaffa smiles the whole time that he says this.) "She needs no father, nor mother. She does not know this yet, though someday she will learn. Shall I teach her early how to do without you?" And he positions two fingertips just under Jija's jaw, pressing the tender skin there with enough force that Jija instantly understands his life depends on his answer.

Jija goes still for a long, pent breath. There's nothing in his head worth relating, even speculatively. He says nothing, though he makes a sound. When the children speak later of this tableau, they leave out this detail: the small, strangled whine uttered by a man who is trying not to loose his bladder and bowels, and who can think of nothing beyond imminent death. It is mostly nasal, back-of-the-throat sound. It makes him want to cough.

Schaffa seems to take Jija's whine for an answer in itself. His smile widens for a moment—a real, heartening smile, the kind that crinkles the corners of his eyes and makes his gums show. He is *delighted* that he does not have to kill Nassun's father with his bare hands. And then he very deliberately lifts the hand that had been positioned under Jija's jaw, waggling the fingers before Jija's eyes until Jija blinks.

"There," Schaffa says. "Now we may behave again like civilized people." He straightens, head turning toward the dormitory; it is clear he has forgotten Jija already, but for an afterthought. "Don't forget to bring her things, please." Then he rises, steps over Jija, and heads into the dormitory.

No one really cares what Jija does after that. A boy has been turned to stone, and a girl has manifested power that is strange and horrifying even for a rogga. These are the things everyone will remember about this day.

Everyone, I suspect, except Jija, who quietly limps home in the aftermath.

In the dormitory, Nassun has finally managed to withdraw her awareness from the watery column of blue light that nearly consumed it. This is an amazing feat, though she does not realize it. All she knows, as she finally comes out of the fit and finds Schaffa leaning over her, is that a scary thing happened, and Schaffa is there to take care of her in the aftermath.

(She is your daughter, at her core. It is not for me to judge her, but . . . ah, she is so very much yours.)

"Tell me," Schaffa says. He has sat on the edge of her cot, very close, deliberately blocking her view of Eitz. Umber is ushering the other children out. Peek is weeping and hysterical; the others are silent in shock. Nassun does not notice, having her own trauma to deal with in the moment.

"There was," she begins. She's hyperventilating. Schaffa cups a big hand over her nose and mouth, and after a few moments her breathing slows. Once she is closer to normal, he removes his hand and nods for her to continue. "There was. A blue thing. Light and . . . I fell up. Schaffa, I fell *up*." She frowns, confused by her own panic. "I had to get out of it. It hurt. It was too fast. It *burned*. I was so scared."

He nods as if this makes sense. "You survived, though. That's very good." She glows with this praise, even though she has no idea what he means. He considers for a moment. "Did you sess anything else, while you were connected?"

(She will not wonder at this word, *connected*, until much later.)

"There was a place, up north. Lines, in the ground. All over." She means all over the Stillness. Schaffa cocks his head with interest, which encourages her to keep babbling. "I could hear people talking. Where they touched the lines. There were *people* in the knots. Where the lines crossed. I couldn't figure out what anybody was saying, though."

Schaffa goes very still. "People in the knots. Orogenes?"

"Yes?" It's actually hard to answer that question. The grip of those distant strangers' orogeny was strong—some stronger than Nassun herself. Yet there was a strange, almost uniform smoothness to each of these strongest ones. Like running fingers over polished stone: There is no texture to catch on. Those were also the ones spread across the greatest distance, some of them even farther to the north than Tirimo—all the way up near where the world has gone red and hot.

"The node network," Schaffa says thoughtfully. "Hmm. Someone is keeping some of the node maintainers alive, up north? How interesting."

There's more, so Nassun has to keep babbling it out. "Closer by, there were a lot of them. Us." These felt like her fellows of Found Moon, their orogeny bright and darting like fish, many words schooling and reverberating along the silver lines connecting them. Conversations, whispers, laughter. A comm, her mind suggests. A community of some sort. A community of orogenes.

(She does not sess Castrima. I know you're wondering.)

"How many?" Schaffa's voice is very quiet.

She cannot gauge such things. "I just hear a lot of people talking. Like, houses full."

Schaffa turns away. In profile, she sees that his lips have drawn back from his teeth. It isn't a smile, for once. "The Antarctic Fulcrum."

Nida, who has quietly come into the room in the meantime, says from over near the door: "They weren't purged?"

"Apparently not." There is no inflection to Schaffa's voice. "Only a matter of time until they discover us."

"Yes." Then Nida laughs softly. Nassun sesses the flex of silver threads within Schaffa. Smiling eases the pain, he has said. The more a Guardian is smiling, laughing, the more something is hurting them. "Unless…" Nida laughs again. This time Schaffa smiles, too.

But he turns again to Nassun and strokes her hair back from her face. "I need you to be calm," he says. Then he stands and moves aside so that she can see Eitz's corpse.

And after she has finished screaming and weeping and shaking in Schaffa's arms, Nida and Umber come over and lift Eitz's statue, carrying it away. It is obviously much heavier than Eitz ever was, but Guardians are very strong. Nassun doesn't know where they take him, the beautiful sea-born boy with the sad smile and the kind eyes, and she never knows anything of his ultimate fate other than that she has killed him, which makes her a monster.

"Perhaps," Schaffa tells her as she sobs these words. He holds her in his lap again, stroking her thick curls. "But you are *my* monster." She is so low and horrified that this actually makes her feel better.

* * *

Stone lasts, unchanging. Never alter what is written in stone.

—*Tablet Three, "Structures," verse one*

13

you, amid relics

IT BEGINS TO FEEL AS though you've lived in Castrima all your life. It shouldn't. Just another comm, just another name, just another new start, or at least a partial one. It will probably end the way all the others have. But…it makes a difference that here, everyone knows what you are. That is the one good thing about the Fulcrum, about Meov, about being Syenite: You could be who you were. That's a luxury you're learning to savor anew.

You're topside again, in Castrima-over as they've been calling it, standing on what used to be the town's token greenland. The ground around Castrima is alkaline and sandy; you heard Ykka actually hoping for a little acid rain to make the soil better. You think the ground probably needs more organic matter for that to work…and there isn't likely to be much of that, since you saw three boilbug mounds on the way here.

The good news is that the mounds are easy to detect, even when they're only a little higher than the ash layer that covers the ground. The insects within them tickle your awareness as a ready source of heat and pressure for your orogeny. On the walk here, you showed the children how to sess for that pent difference from the cooler, more relaxed ambient around it. The younger ones made a game of it, gasping and pointing whenever they sensed a mound and trying to outdo one another in the count.

The bad news is that there are more of the boilbug mounds this week than there were last week. That's probably not a good thing, but you don't let the children see your worry.

There are seventeen children altogether—the bulk of Castrima's complement of orogenes. A couple are in the teen range, but most are younger, one only five. Most are orphans, or might as well be, and that does not surprise you at all. What does surprise you is that all of them must have relatively good self-control and quick wits, because otherwise they wouldn't have survived the Rifting. They would've had to sess it coming in time enough to get to someplace isolated, let their instincts save them, recover, and then go someplace else before anybody started trying to figure out who was at the center of the circle of non-destruction. Most are Midlatter mongrels like you: lots of not-quite-Sanzed-bronze skin, not-quite-ashblow hair, eyes and bodies on a continuum from the Arctic to the Coaster. Not much different from the kids you used to teach in Tirimo's creche. Only the subject matter, and by necessity your teaching methods, must be different.

"Sess what I do—just sess, don't imitate yet," you say, and then you construct a torus around yourself. You do it several times, each time a different way—sometimes spinning it high and tight, sometimes holding it steady but wide enough that its edge rolls close to them. (Half the children gasp and scramble away. That's exactly what they should do; good. Not good that the rest just stood there stupidly. You'll have to work on that.)

"Now. Spread out. You there, you there; all of you stay about that far apart. Once you're in place, spin a torus that looks *exactly* like the one I'm making now."

It isn't how the Fulcrum would've taught them. There, with years of time and safe walls and comforting blue skies overhead, the teaching could be done gently, gradually, giving the children time to get over their fears or outgrow their immaturities. There's no time for gentleness in a Season, though, and no room for failure within Castrima's jagged walls. You've heard the grumbling, seen the resentful looks when you join use-caste crews or head down to the communal bath. Ykka thinks Castrima is something special: a comm where rogga and still can live in harmony, working together to survive. You think she's naive. These children need to be prepared for the inevitable day that Castrima turns on them.

So you demonstrate, and correct their imitations with words when you can and once with a torus-inversion slap when one of the older children spins his too wide and threatens to ice one of his comrades. "You *cannot* be careless!" The boy sits on the icy ground, staring at you wide-eyed. You also made the ground heave under his feet to throw him down, and you're standing over him now, shouting, deliberately intimidating. He almost killed another child; he *should* be afraid. "People die when you make mistakes. Is that what you want?" A frantic headshake. "Then get up, and do it again."

You flog them through the exercise until every one of them has demonstrated at least a basic ability to control the size of their torus. It feels wrong to teach them only this without any of the theory that will help them understand why and how their power works, or any of the stabilizing exercises designed to perfect the detachment of instinct from power. You must teach them in days what you mastered over years; where you are an artist, they will be only crude imitators at best. They are subdued when you walk them back to Castrima, and you suspect some of them hate you. Actually, you're pretty sure they hate you. But they will be more useful to Castrima like this—and on the inevitable day that Castrima turns on them, they'll be ready.

(This is a familiar series of thoughts. Once, as you trained Nassun, you told yourself that it did not matter if she hated you by the end of it; she would know your love by her own survival. That never felt right, though, did it? You were gentler with Uche for that reason. And you always meant to apologize to Nassun, later, when she was old enough to understand . . . Ah, there are so many regrets in you that they spin, heavy as compressed iron, at your core.)

"You're right," Alabaster says as you sit on an infirmary cot and tell him about the lesson later. "But you're also wrong."

It's later than usual for you to be visiting Alabaster, and as a result he is restless and in visible pain amid his nest. The medications that Lerna usually gives him are wearing off. Being with him is always a competition of desires for you: You know there's not much time for him to teach you this stuff, but you also want to prolong his life, and every day that you wear him down grates on you like a glacier. Urgency and despair don't get along well. You've resolved to keep it brief this time, but he seems inclined to talk a lot today, as he leans against Antimony's hand and keeps his eyes closed. You can't help thinking of this as some kind of strength-saving gesture, as if just the sight of you is a drain.

"Wrong?" you prompt. Maybe there's a warning note in your

voice. You've always been protective of your students, whoever they are.

"For wasting your time, for one thing. They'll never have the precision to be more than rock-pushers." Alabaster's voice is thick with contempt.

"Innon was a rock-pusher," you snap.

A muscle flexes in his jaw, and he pauses for a moment. "So maybe it's a good thing that you're teaching them how to push rocks safely, even if you aren't doing it kindly." Now the contempt is gone from his words. It's as close to an apology as you're probably going to get from him. "But I stand by the rest: You're wrong to teach them at all, because *their* lessons are getting in the way of *your* lessons."

"What?"

He makes you sess one of his stumps again, and—oh. Ohhhh. Suddenly it's harder to grasp the stuff between his cells. It takes longer for your perception to adjust, and when it does, you keep having to reflexively jerk yourself out of a tendency to notice only the heat and jittering movement of the small particles. One afternoon of teaching has set your learning back by a week or more.

"There's a reason the Fulcrum taught you the way it did," he explains finally, when you sit back and rub your eyes and fight down frustration. He's opened his eyes now; they are hooded as they watch you. "The Fulcrum's methods are a kind of conditioning meant to steer you toward energy redistribution and away from magic. The torus isn't even necessary—you can gather ambient energy in any number of ways. But that's how they teach you to direct your awareness *down* to perform orogeny, never up. Nothing above you matters. Only your immediate surroundings, never farther." He shakes his head to the degree that he can. "It's amazing, when you think about it. Everyone in the Stillness is like this. Never mind what's in the oceans, never mind what's in the sky; never look at your own horizon and wonder what's beyond it. We've spent centuries making fun of the astronomests for their crackpot theories, but what we really found incredible was that they ever bothered to *look up* to formulate them."

You'd almost forgotten this part of him: the dreamer, the rebel, always reconsidering the way things have always been because maybe they should never have been that way in the first place. He's right, too. Life in the Stillness discourages reconsideration, reorientation. Wisdom is set in stone, after all; that's why no one trusts the mutability of metal. There's a reason Alabaster was the magnetic core of your little family, back when you were together.

Damn, you're nostalgic today. It prompts you to say, "I think you're not just a ten-ringer." He blinks in surprise. "You're always *thinking*. You're a genius, too—it's just that your genius is in a subject area that no one respects."

Alabaster stares at you for a moment. His eyes narrow. "Are you drunk?"

"No I'm not—" Evil Earth, so much for your fond memories. "Go on with the rusting lesson."

He seems more relieved by the change of subject than you. "So that's what Fulcrum training does to you. You learn to think of orogeny as a matter of effort, when it's really…perspective. And perception."

An Allia-shaped trauma tells you why the Fulcrum wouldn't have wanted every two-shard feral reaching for any obelisks nearby. But you spend a moment trying to understand the distinction he's explaining. It's true that using energy is something entirely different from using magic. The Fulcrum's method makes orogeny feel like what it is: straining to shove around heavy objects, just with will instead of hands or levers. Magic, though, feels effortless—at least while one is using it. The exhaustion comes later. In the moment, though, it is simply about *knowing it's there.* Training yourself to see it.

"I don't understand why they did this," you say, tapping your fingers on the mattress in thought. The Fulcrum was built by orogenes. At least some of them, at some point in the past, must have sessed magic. But... you shiver as you understand. Ah, yes. The most powerful orogenes, the ones who detect magic most easily and perhaps have trouble mastering energy redistribution as a result, are the ones who end up in the nodes.

Alabaster thinks in bigger pictures than just the Fulcrum. "I think," he says, "they understood the danger. Not just that roggas who lacked the necessary fine control would connect to obelisks and die, but that some might do it successfully—for the wrong reasons."

You try to think of a right reason to activate a network of ancient death machines. Alabaster reads your face. "I doubt I'm the first rogga who's wanted to tip the Fulcrum into a lava pit."

"Good point."

"And the war. Don't ever forget that. The Guardians who work with the Fulcrum are one of the factions I told you about, so to speak. They're the ones who want the status quo: roggas made safe and useful, stills doing all the work and thinking they run the place, Guardians *actually* in charge of everything. Controlling the people who can control natural disasters."

You're surprised by this. No, you're surprised you didn't think of it yourself. But then you haven't spent much time thinking about Guardians, when you weren't in the immediate vicinity of one. Maybe this is another kind of thought aversion you've been conditioned to: Don't look up, and don't think about those damned smiles.

You decide to make yourself think about them now. "But Guardians die during a Season..." Shit. "They *say* they die..." Shit. "Of course they don't."

Alabaster lets out a rusty sound that might be a laugh. "I'm a bad influence."

He always has been. You can't help smiling, though the feeling doesn't last, because of the conversation. "They don't join comms, though. They must go somewhere else to ride it out."

"Maybe. Maybe this 'Warrant' place. No one seems to know where it is." He pauses, grows thoughtful. "I suppose I should have asked mine about that before I left her."

No one just leaves their Guardian. "You said you didn't kill her."

He blinks, out of memory. "No. I *cured* her. Sort of. You know about the thing in their heads." Yes. Blood, and the sting of your palm. Schaffa handing something tiny and bloody to another Guardian, with great care. You nod. "It gives them their abilities, but it also taints them, twists them. The seniors at the Fulcrum used to speak of it in whispers. There are degrees of contamination..." He sets his jaw, visibly steering himself away from that topic. You can guess why. Somewhere along the way, it lands on the shirtless Guardians who kill with a touch. "Anyway, I took that thing out of mine."

You swallow. "I saw a Guardian kill another once, taking it out."

"Yes. When the contamination becomes too great. Then they're dangerous even to other Guardians, and must be purged. I'd heard they weren't gentle about it. Brutes even to their own."

It's angry, Guardian Timay had said, right before Schaffa killed her. *Readying for the time of return.* You inhale. The memory is vivid in your mind because that was the day that you and Tonkee—Binof—found the socket. The day of your first ring test, early and with your life in the balance. You'll never forget anything of that day. And now—"It's the Earth."

"What?"

"The thing that's in Guardians. The…contaminant." *It changed those who would control it. Chained them fate to fate.* "She started speaking for the Earth!"

You can tell you've actually surprised him, for once. "Then…" He considers for a moment. "I see. That's when they switch teams. Stop working for the status quo and Guardian interests, and start working for the Earth's interests instead. No wonder the others kill them."

This is what you need to understand. "What does the Earth want?"

Alabaster's gaze is heavy, heavy. "What does any living thing want, facing an enemy so cruel that it stole away a child?"

Your jaw tightens. *Vengeance.*

You shift down from the cot to the floor, leaning against the cot's frame. "Tell me about the Obelisk Gate."

"Yes. I thought that would get you interested." Alabaster's voice has gone soft again, but there is a look on his face that makes you think, *This is what he looked like on the day he made the Rift.* "You remember the basic principle. Parallel scaling.

Yoking two oxen together instead of one. Two roggas together can do more than each individually. It works for obelisks, too, just... exponential. A matrix, not a yoke. Dynamic."

Okay, you're following so far. "So I need to figure out how to chain all of them together."

He nods back minutely. "And you'll need a buffer, at least initially. When I opened the Gate at Yumenes, I used several dozen node maintainers."

Several dozen stunted, twisted roggas turned into mindless weapons... and Alabaster somehow turned them against their owners. How like him, and how perfect. "Buffer?"

"To cushion the impact. To... smooth out the connection flow..." He falters, sighs. "I don't know how to explain it. You'll know when you try it."

When. He assumes so much. "What you did killed the node maintainers?"

"Not precisely. I used them to open the Gate and create the Rift... and then they tried to do what they were made to do: Stop the shake. Stabilize the land." You grimace, understanding. Even you, in your extremity, weren't foolish enough to try to *stop* the shockwave, when it reached Tirimo. The only safe thing to do was divert its force elsewhere. But node maintainers lack the mind or control to do the safe thing.

"I didn't use all of them," Alabaster says thoughtfully. "The ones far to the west and in the Arctics and Antarctics were out of my reach. Most have died since. No one to keep them alive. But I can still sess active nodes in a few places. Remnants of the network: south, near the Antarctic Fulcrum, and north, near Rennanis."

Of course he can sess active nodes all the way in the

Antarctics. You can barely sess a hundred miles from Castrima, and you have to work to stretch that far. And maybe the roggas of the Antarctic Fulcrum have survived somehow, and chosen to care for their less fortunate brethren in the nodes, but… "Rennanis?" That can't be. It's an Equatorial city. More southerly and westerly than most; people in Yumenes thought it was only a step above any other Somidlats backwater. But Rennanis was Equatorial enough that it should be gone.

"The Rift wends northwesterly, along an ancient fault line that I found. It swung a few hundred miles wide of Rennanis… I suppose that was enough to let the node maintainers actually do something. Should've killed most of them, and the rest should've died of neglect when their staffs abandoned them, but I don't know."

He falls silent, perhaps weary. His voice is hoarse today, and his eyes are bloodshot. Another infection. He keeps getting them because some of the burned patches on his body aren't healing, Lerna says. The lack of pain meds isn't helping.

You try to digest what he's told you, what Antimony has told you, what you've learned through trial and suffering. Maybe the numbers matter. Two hundred and sixteen obelisks, some incalculable number of other orogenes as a buffer, and you. Magic to tie the three together…somehow. All of it together forging a net, to catch the Earthfires-damned Moon.

Alabaster says nothing while you ponder, and eventually you glance at him to see if he's fallen asleep. But he's awake, his eyes slits, watching you. "What?" You frown, defensive as always.

He quarter-smiles with the half of his mouth that hasn't been burned. "You never change. If I ask you for help, you tell me to flake off and die. If I don't say a rusting word, you work miracles for me." He sighs. "Evil Earth, how I've missed you."

This...hurts, unexpectedly. You realize why at once: because it's been so long since anyone said anything like this to you. Jija could be affectionate, but he wasn't much given to sentimentality. Innon used sex and jokes to show his tenderness. But Alabaster...this has always been his way. The surprise gesture, the backhanded compliment that you could choose to take for teasing or an insult. You've hardened so much without this. Without him. You seem strong, healthy, but inside you feel like he looks: nothing but brittle stone and scars, prone to cracking if you bend too much.

You try to smile, and fail. He doesn't try. You just look at each other. It's nothing and everything at once.

Of course it doesn't last. Someone walks into the infirmary and comes over and surprises you by being Ykka. Hjarka's behind her, slouching along and looking very Sanzedly bored: picking her sharp-filed teeth with a bit of polished wood, one hand on her well-curved hip, her ashblow hair a worse mess than usual and noticeably flatter on one side where she's just woken up.

"Sorry to interrupt," Ykka says, not sounding especially sorry, "but we've got a problem."

You're beginning to hate those words. Still, it's time to end the lesson, so you nod to Alabaster and get up. "What now?"

"Your friend. The slacker." Tonkee, who hasn't joined the Innovators' work crews, doesn't bother to pick up your household share when it's her turn, and who conveniently disappears whenever it's time for a caste meeting. In another comm they'd have already kicked her out for that kind of thing, but she gets extra leeway for being one of the companions of the second-most-powerful orogene in Castrima. It only goes so far, though, and Ykka looks especially pissed off.

"She's found the control room," Ykka says. "Locked herself inside."

"The—" What. "The control room for what?"

"*Castrima*." Ykka looks annoyed to have to explain. "I told you when you got here: There are mechanisms that make this place function, the light and the air and so on. We keep the room secret because if somebody loses it and wants to smash things, they could kill us all. But your 'mest is in there doing Evil Earth knows what, and I'm basically asking you if it's okay to kill her, because that's about where I am right now."

"She won't be able to affect anything important," Alabaster says. It startles you both, you because you aren't used to seeing him interact with anyone else, and Ykka because she probably thinks of him as a waste of medicines and not a person. He doesn't think much of her, either; his eyes are closed again. "More likely to hurt herself than anything else."

"Good to know," Ykka says, though she looks at him skeptically. "I'd be reassured if you weren't talking out of your ass, seeing as you couldn't possibly know what's happening beyond this infirmary, but it's a nice thought, anyway."

He lets out a soft snort of amusement. "I knew everything I needed to know about this relic the instant I came here. And if any of you other than Essun had a chance of making it do what it's really capable of, I wouldn't stay here a moment longer." As you and Ykka stare, he lets out a heavy sigh. There's a little bit of a rattle in it, which troubles you, and you make a note to ask Lerna about it. But he says nothing more, and finally Ykka glances at you with a palpable *I am really sick of your friends* look, and beckons for you to follow her out.

It's a long way up to wherever this control room is. Hjarka's breathing hard after the first ladder, but she acclimates after that and settles into a rhythm. Ykka does better, though she's still sweating in ten minutes. You've still got your road conditioning, so you handle the climb well enough, but after the first three flights of stairs, a ladder, and a spiraling balcony built round one of the fatter crystals of the comm, you're even willing to start small talk to take your mind off the ground falling farther and farther below. "What's your usual disciplinary process for people who shirk their caste duties?"

"The boot, what else?" Ykka shrugs. "We can't just ash them out, though; have to kill them to maintain secrecy. But there's a process: one warning, then a hearing. Morat—that's the Innovator caste spokeswoman—hasn't made a formal complaint. I asked her to, but she waffled. Said your friend gave her a portable water-testing device that may save some of our Hunters' lives out in the field."

Hjarka utters a rusty laugh. You shake your head, amused. "That's a nice bribe. She's a survivor, if nothing else."

Ykka rolls her eyes. "Maybe. But it sends a bad message, one person not joining any work crews and going unpunished for it, even if she does invent useful things outside of work time. Others start to skive off, what do I do then?"

"Ash out the ones who haven't invented anything," you suggest. Then you stop, because Ykka has paused. You think it's because she's annoyed by what you just said, but she's looking around, taking in the expanse of the comm. So you stop, too.

This far up, you're well above the main inhabited level of the comm. The geode echoes with calls and someone hammering something and one of the work crews singing a rhythm song. You risk a look over the nearest railing and see that someone's made a simple rope-and-wooden-pallet cargo lift for the mid-level, but without a counterweight, the only way to get a heavy load up is to basically play tug-of-war with it. Twenty people are at it now. It looks surprisingly like fun.

"You were right about the assimilations," Hjarka says. Her voice is soft as she, too, contemplates the bustle and life of Castrima. "We couldn't have made this place work without more people. Thought you were full of shit, but you weren't."

Ykka sighs. "*So far* it's working." She eyes Hjarka. "You never said you didn't like the idea before."

Hjarka shrugs. "I left my home comm because I didn't want the burden of Leadership. Didn't want it here, either."

"You don't have to knife-fight me for the headwomanship to give an *opinion*, for Earth's sake."

"When a Season's coming on and I'm the only Leader in the comm, I'd better be careful even about opinions." She shrugs, then smiles at Ykka with an air of something like affection. "Keep figuring you'll have me killed any minute now."

Ykka laughs once. "Is that what you would've done in my place?" You hear the edge in this.

"It's the playbook I was taught to follow, yeah—but it'd be stupid to try that here. There's never been anything like this Season...or this comm." Hjarka eyes you, pointedly, as the latest example of Castrima's peculiarity. "Tradition's just going to rust everything up, in a situation like this. Better to have a headwoman who doesn't know how things *should* be, only how she *wants* them to be. A headwoman who'll kick all the asses necessary to make her vision happen."

Ykka absorbs this in silence for a few moments. Obviously whatever Tonkee's done isn't so urgent or terrible. Then she turns and begins climbing again, apparently deciding that the rest break is over. You and Hjarka sigh and follow.

"I think the people who originally built this place didn't think it through," Ykka says as the climb resumes. "Too inefficient. Too dependent on machinery that can break down or rust out. And *orogeny* as a power source, which is basically the least-reliable thing ever. But then sometimes I wonder if maybe they didn't intend to build it this way. Maybe something drove them underground fast, and they found a giant geode and just made the best of what they had." She runs a hand along a railing as you walk. This is one of the original metal structures that have been built throughout the geode. Above the inhabited levels, it's all old metalwork. "Always makes me think they really must have been the ancestors of Castrima. They respected hard work and adapting under pressure, like us."

"Doesn't everyone?" Except Tonkee.

"Some." She doesn't take the obvious bait. "I outed myself to everyone when I was fifteen. There was a forest fire somewhere to the south; drought season. The smoke alone was killing the older people and babies in the comm. We thought we'd have to leave. Finally I went to the edge of the fire, where a bunch of the other townsfolk were trying to create a firebreak. Six of them died doing that." She shakes her head. "Wouldn't have worked. The fire was too big. But that's my people, for you."

You nod. It does sound like the Castrimans you've gotten to know. It also sounds like the Tirimo-folk you've gotten to know, and the Meovites, and the Allians, and the Yumenescenes. No people in the Stillness would have survived to this point if they weren't fearsomely tenacious. But Ykka needs to think of Castrima as special—and it *is* special, in its own strange ways. So you wisely keep your mouth shut.

She says, "I stopped the fire. Iced the burning part of the forest and used that to make a ridge farther south as a windbreak in case anything set off a new blaze. Everyone saw me do it. They knew exactly what I was then."

You stop walking and stare at her. She turns back, half smiling. "I told them I'd go, if they wanted to call the Guardians and have me shipped off to the Fulcrum. Or if they wanted to just string me up, I promised not to ice anyone. Instead, they argued about the whole mess for three days. I thought they were trying to decide how to kill me." She shrugs. "So I went home, had dinner with my parents—they both knew, and they were terrified for me, but I talked them down from smuggling me out of town in a horse cart. Went to creche the next day, same as always. At the end of it, I found out the townsfolk had been arguing about *how to get me trained.* Without letting the Fulcrum on, see."

Your mouth falls open. You've seen Ykka's parents, who are still hale and strong and with an air of Sanzed stubbornness about them. You can believe it of them. But everyone else, too? All right. Maybe Castrima *is* special.

Hjarka says, "Huh. How did you get trained, then?"

"Eh, you know what these little Midlatter comms are like. They were still arguing about it when the Rifting happened. I trained my damn self." She laughs, and Hjarka sighs. "That's my people, too. Complete rust-heads, but good people."

You think, against your will, *If only I had brought Uche and Nassun here as soon as they were born.*

"Not all of your people like having us here," you blurt, almost as a rebuttal to your own thought.

"Yeah, I've heard the chatter. Which is why I'm glad you're training the kids, and that everyone saw you get the boilbugs off Terteis." She sobers. "Poor Terteis. But you proved again that it's better to have people like us around than to kill us or drive us out. Castrimans are practical people, Essie." You hate this nickname immediately. "Too practical to just do something because everybody else says do it."

With that, she resumes the climb. After a moment, you and Hjarka do, too.

You've gotten used to the unrelenting whiteness of Castrima; only a few of the building-crystals have touches of amethyst or smoky quartz about them. Here, though, the ceiling of the geode has been sealed off with a smooth, glasslike substance that is deep emeraldine green in color. The color is a bit of a shock. The final stairway that leads up into this is wide enough for five people to climb abreast, so you're unsurprised to find two of Castrima's Strongbacks flanking what looks like a sliding attic door made of the same green substance. One of the Strongbacks has a small wireglass utility knife in her hand; the other just has his big folded arms.

"Still nothing," says the male Strongback as the three of you arrive. "We keep hearing sounds from inside—clicking, buzzing, and sometimes she yells things. But the door's still jammed."

"Yells things?" asks Hjarka.

He shrugs. "Like, 'I knew it' and 'that's why.' "

Sounds like Tonkee. "How does she have the door rigged?" you ask. The female Strongback shrugs. It's a stereotype that Strongbacks are all muscle and no brain, but a few of them fit that description more than they should.

Ykka gives you another *This is your fault* look. You shake your head, then climb up to the top step and bang on the door. "Tonkee, rust it, open up."

There's a moment of silence, and then you hear a faint clatter. "Fuck, it's you," Tonkee mutters, from somewhere farther away than the door. "Hang on and don't ice anything."

A moment later there's the sound of something rattling against the door material. Then the door slides open. You, Ykka, Hjarka, and the Strongbacks climb up—though all of you except Ykka stop and stare, so it's left to her to fold her arms and give Tonkee the exasperated glare she's earned.

The ceiling is hollow above the door. The green substance forms a floor, and the resulting chamber is molded around the usual white crystals that jut down from the geode's rocky, grayish-green true ceiling, perhaps fifteen feet overhead. What makes you stop, your mouth falling open and your mind stuttering from annoyance into silence, is that the crystals on this side of the green barrier flicker and blink, transitioning at random from shimmering images of crystals into solidity, and back again. The shafts and tips of these crystals, which poke through the floor, weren't doing this outside. None of the other crystals in Castrima do this. Aside from glowing—which, granted, is a warning that they aren't just rocks—the crystals of Castrima are no different from any other quartz. Here, though... you suddenly understand what Alabaster meant about what Castrima is capable of. The truth of Castrima is suddenly, terrifyingly clear: The geode is filled with not crystals, but *potential obelisks*.

"Flaking rust," one of the Strongbacks breathes. This speaks for you as well.

Tonkee's junk is everywhere in the room: weird tools and slates and scraps of leather covered in diagrams, and a pallet in the corner that explains why she hasn't been sleeping in the apartment much lately. (It's been lonely without her and Hoa, but you don't like admitting this to yourself.) She's walking away from you now, glaring over her shoulder and looking distinctly irritated that you've arrived. "Don't rusting touch anything," she says. "No telling what an orogene of your caliber will do to this stuff."

Ykka rolls her eyes. "You're the one who shouldn't be touching anything. You're not allowed in here and you know it. Come on."

"No." Tonkee crouches near a strange, low plinth at the center of the room. It looks like a crystal shaft whose middle has been chopped out: You see the (flickering, unreal) base growing from the ceiling, and the plinth is its (flickering in tandem) continuation, but there's a five-foot section in between that's just empty space. The plinth's surface has been cut so smoothly that it gleams like a mirror—and the surface stays solid, even as the rest of the shaft flickers.

At first you think there's nothing on it. But Tonkee is peering at the plinth's surface so intently that you walk over to join her. When you hunker down for a better look, she glances up to meet your eyes, and you're shocked at the barely disguised glee in hers.

Not really shocked by that; you know her by now. You're shocked because this high gleam, plus the new undisguise of her clean, short hair and neat clothing, transforms her so obviously into an older version of Binof that you marvel again you didn't see it at once.

But that's unimportant. You focus on the plinth, even though there are other wonders to behold: a taller plinth near the back of the room, above which floats a foot-tall miniature obelisk the same emerald color as the floor; another plinth bearing an oblong hunk of rock, also floating; a series of clear squares set into one wall bearing strange diagrams of some sort of equipment; a series of panels along the wall beneath them, each bearing meters measuring something unknown in numbers that you can't decipher.

On the big plinth, though, are the least obtrusive objects in the room: six tiny metallic shards, each needle-thin and no longer than your thumbnail. They are not the same silvery metal that makes up Castrima's ancient structures; this metal is a smooth dark color dusted faintly with red. Iron. Amazing that it hasn't oxidized away over all the years of Castrima's existence. Unless—"Did you put these here?" you ask Tonkee.

She's instantly furious. "Yes, of course I would enter the control core of a deadciv artifact, find the most dangerous device in it, and immediately throw bits of rusty metal on it!"

"Don't be an ass, please." Though you did sort of deserve that, you're too intrigued to be really annoyed. "Why do you think this is the most dangerous device in here?"

Tonkee points to the beveled edge of the plinth. You look closer and blink. The material is not smooth like the rest of the crystal shaft; on the edge it has been heavily etched with symbols and writing. The writing is the same as that along the wall panels—oh. And they are glowing red, the color seeming to float and waver just over the surface of the material.

"And this," Tonkee says. She raises a hand and moves it toward the plinth's surface and the metal bits. Abruptly the red letters leap into the air—you don't have a better way to describe what's happening than that. In an instant they have enlarged and turned to face you, blazing the air at eye level with what is unmistakably some sort of warning. Red is the color of lava pools. It is the color of a lake when everything in it has died except toxic algae: one warning sign of an impending blow. Some things do not change with time or culture, you feel certain.

(You are wrong, generally speaking. But in this specific case, you're quite right.)

Everyone's staring. Hjarka comes close and lifts a hand to try to touch the floating letters; her fingers pass through them. Ykka moves around the plinth, fascinated despite herself. "I've noticed this thing before, but never really paid attention to it. The letters turn with me."

They haven't moved. But you lean to one side—and sure enough, as you do this the letters pivot slightly to remain facing you.

Impatiently, Tonkee pulls her hand back and waves Hjarka's hand out of the way, and the letters flatten and shrink back into quiescence along the plinth edge. "There's no barrier, though. Usually in a deadciv artifact—an artifact from *this* civilization—anything truly dangerous is sealed off in some way. There's either a physical barrier, or evidence that there was once a barrier that's failed with time. If they really didn't want you to touch something, you either didn't touch it or you'd have to work pretty damned hard to touch it. This? Just a warning. I don't know what that means."

"Can you actually touch those things?" You reach toward one of the bits of iron, ignoring the warning this time when it springs up. Tonkee hisses at you so sharply that you jerk back like a child caught doing something you weren't supposed to.

"I *said* don't rusting touch! What's wrong with you?" You clench your jaw, but you deserved that, too, and you're too much a mother to deny it.

"How long have you been coming in here?" Ykka's crouched next to Tonkee's sleeping pallet.

Tonkee's staring down at the iron bits, and at first you think she hasn't heard Ykka; she doesn't answer for a long moment. There is a look on her face that you're starting not to like. You can't say you really know her any more now than you did when you were a grit, but you do know that she isn't the grim sort. That she is grim now, the tightened muscle along her jawline making it stand out more than you know she likes, is a very bad sign. She's up to something. She says to Ykka, "A week. But I only moved in three days ago. I think. I lost track." She rubs her eyes. "I haven't slept a lot."

Ykka shakes her head and rises. "Well, at least you haven't destroyed the rusting comm already. Tell me what you've figured out, then."

Tonkee turns to eye her warily. "Those panels along the wall activate, and regulate, the water pumps and air circulation systems and cooling processes. But you knew that already."

"Yes. Since we're not dead." Ykka dusts off her hands from

where she touched the floor, sidling toward Tonkee in a way that is somehow simultaneously thoughtful and subtly menacing. She's not as big as most Sanzed women—a good foot shorter than Hjarka. Her dangerousness is not as obvious as it is with others, but you sense the slow readying of her orogeny now. She was fully prepared to smash or ice her way into this place. The Strongbacks shift and edge a little closer, too, reinforcing her unspoken threat.

"What I want to know," she continues, "is how *you* knew that." She stops, facing Tonkee. "We figured it out, in those early days, through trial and error. Touch one thing and it gets cooler, touch another and the communal pool water gets hotter. But nothing's changed in the past week."

Tonkee sighs a little. "I've learned how to decipher some of the symbols over the years. Spend enough time in these kinds of ruins and you see the same things repeated over and over."

Ykka considers this, then nods toward the warning text around the plinth rim. "What's that say?"

"No idea. I said *decipher*, not read. Symbols, not language." Tonkee walks over to one of the wall panels and points to a prominent design in its top right corner. It's nothing intuitive: something green and arrow-like but squiggly, sort of, pointed downward. "I see that one wherever there were water gardens. I think it's about the quality and intensity of the light that the gardens get." She eyes Ykka. "Actually, I know it's about the light the gardens get."

Ykka lifts her chin a little, just enough that you know Tonkee has guessed right. "So this place is no different from other ruins you've seen? The others had crystals in them, like this?"

"No. I've never seen anything like Castrima before. Except—" She glances at you, once and away. "Well. Not *exactly* like Castrima."

"That thing in the Fulcrum wasn't anything like this," you blurt. It's been more than twenty years, but you haven't forgotten a detail about the place. That was a pit, and Castrima is a rock with a hole in it. If both were made by the same kinds of people, to do similar things, there's no evidence of that anywhere.

"It was, actually." Tonkee comes back to the plinth and waves up the warning. This time she points at a symbol within the glowing red text: a solid black circle surrounded by a white octagon. You don't know how you missed it before; it stands out from the red.

"I saw that mark in the Fulcrum, painted onto some of the light panels. You were too busy staring into the pit; I don't think you saw. But I've been in maybe half a dozen obelisk-builder sites since, and that mark is always near something dangerous." She's watching you intently. "I find dead people near it sometimes."

Inadvertently you think of Guardian Timay. Not *found* dead, but dead nevertheless, and you almost joined her that day. Then you remember a moment in the room without doors, near the edge of the yawning pit. You remember small needlelike protrusions from the walls of the pit... exactly like these bits of iron.

"The socket," you murmur. That was what the Guardian called it. "A contaminant." A prickle dances across the nape of your neck. Tonkee looks sharply at you.

"'Something dangerous' can mean any rusting thing," says Hjarka, annoyed, as you stand there staring at the bits of rust.

"No, in this case it means a specific rusting thing." Tonkee glares Hjarka down, which is impressive in itself. "It was the mark of their enemy."

Fuck, you realize. Fuck, fuck, fuck.

"What?" asks Ykka. "What in the Evil Earth are you talking about?"

"Their *enemy*." Tonkee leans against the edge of the plinth—carefully, you note, but emphatically. "They were at war, don't you understand? Toward the end, just before their civilization vanished into the dust. All their ruins, anything that's left from that time, are defensive, survival-oriented. Like the comms of today—except they had a lot more than stone walls to help protect them. Things like *giant rusting underground geodes*. They *hid* in those places, and studied their enemy, and maybe built weapons to fight back." She pivots and points up, at the upper half of the plinth crystal. It flickers just as she does so, obelisk-like.

"No," you say automatically. Everyone turns to look at you, and you twitch. "I mean..." Shit. But you've said it now. "The obelisks aren't..." You don't know how to say it without telling the whole damned story, and you're reluctant to do that. You're not sure why. Maybe for the same reason that Antimony said, when Alabaster started to tell you: They aren't ready. Now you need to finish in a way that won't invite further comment. "I don't think they're defensive, or any sort of... weapon."

Tonkee says nothing for a long moment. "What are they, then?"

"I don't know." It's not a lie. You *don't* know for sure. "A tool, maybe. Dangerous if misused, but not *meant* to kill."

Tonkee seems to brace herself. "I know what happened to Allia, Essun."

It's an unexpected blow, and it floors you emotionally. Fortunately, you've spent your life training to deflect your reactions to unexpected blows in safe ways. You say, "Obelisks aren't *made* to do that. That was an accident."

"How do you—"

"Because I was *connected to* the rusting thing when it went into burndown!" You snap this so sharply that your voice echoes in the room and startles you into realizing how angry you are. One of the Strongbacks inhales and something in her gaze shifts and all at once you are reminded of the Strongbacks at Tirimo, who looked at you the same way when Rask asked them to let you go through the gate. Even Ykka's watching you in a way that wordlessly says, *You're scaring the locals, calm the rust down.* So you take a deep breath and fall silent.

(It is only later that you will recall the word you said during this conversation. *Burndown.* You will wonder why you said it, what it means, and you will have no answer.)

Tonkee lets out a deep breath, carefully, and this seems to speak for the room. "It's possible I've made some wrong assumptions," she says.

Ykka rubs a hand over her hair. It makes her head look incongruously small for a moment until it floofs back up. "All right. We already know Castrima was used as a comm before. Probably several times. If you'd *asked* me, instead of coming in here and acting like a rusting child, I could have told you that. I would have told you everything I knew, because I want to understand this place just as much as you do—"

Tonkee utters a single braying laugh. "None of you are smart enough for that."

"—but by pulling *this shit*, you've made me mistrust you. I don't let people I don't trust do things that can hurt the people I love. So I want you out of here for good."

Hjarka frowns. "Yeek, that's kind of harsh, isn't it?"

Tonkee tenses at once, her eyes going wide with horror, and hurt. "You can't keep me out. Nobody else in this rusting comm has a clue what—"

"Nobody else in this rusting comm," Ykka says, and now the Strongbacks look at *her* uneasily, because she's nearly shouting, "would set us all on fire for the chance to study people who've been gone since the world was young. Somehow I'm getting the impression that you would."

"Supervised visits!" Tonkee blurts. She looks desperate now.

Ykka steps up to her, getting right in her face, and Tonkee goes silent at once. "I would rather understand nothing about this place," Ykka says, brutally quiet and cold now, "than risk destroying it. Can you say the same?"

Tonkee stares back at her, trembling visibly and saying nothing. But the answer's obvious, isn't it? Tonkee's like Hjarka. Both were raised Leadership, raised to put the needs of others first, and both chose a more selfish path. It's not even a question.

Which is why later, in retrospect, you really aren't surprised at what happens next.

Tonkee turns and lunges and the red warning flashes and then one of the iron bits is in her fist. She's already turning away by the time you register her grab. Bolting for the stair door. Hjarka gasps; Ykka's just standing there, a little startled and mostly resigned; the two Strongbacks stare in confusion and then belatedly start after Tonkee. But then an instant later

Tonkee gasps and stumbles to a halt. One of the Strongbacks grabs her arm—but drops it immediately when Tonkee *yells.*

You're moving before you think. Tonkee is yours somehow—like Hoa, like Lerna, like Alabaster, as if in the absence of your children you're trying to adopt everybody who touches you emotionally for even an instant. You don't even like Tonkee. Still, your belly clenches when you grab her wrist and see that blood streaks her hand. "What the—"

Tonkee looks at you: quick, animal panic. Then she jerks and cries out again, and you almost let go this time because *something moves under your thumb.*

"The rust?" Ykka blurts. Hjarka's hand claps over Tonkee's arm, too, helping, because Tonkee's strong in her panic. You master your inexplicable, violent revulsion enough to instead move your thumb and hold Tonkee's wrist so that you can get a good look at it. Yes. There's something moving just under her skin. It jumps and jitters, but moves inexorably upward, following the path of a large vein there. It's just large enough to be the iron fragment.

"Evil Earth," Hjarka says, throwing a quick worried look at Tonkee's face. You fight sudden hysterical laughter at the unintentional irony of Hjarka's oath.

"I need a knife," you say instead. Your voice sounds remarkably calm to your own ears. Ykka leans over, sees what you've seen, and breathes an oath.

"Oh, fuck, rust, shit," Tonkee moans. "Get it out! Get it out and I'll never come in here again." It's a lie, but maybe she means it for the moment.

"I can bite it out." Hjarka looks up at you. Her sharpened teeth are small razors.

"No," you say, certain it would just go into Hjarka and do the same thing. Tongues were harder to carve than arms.

Ykka barks, "Knife!" at the Strongbacks—the one with the wireglass knife. It's sharp but small, meant more for cutting rope than as a weapon; unless you hit a vital area right off, you'd have to stab someone a million times to kill them with it. It's all you've got. You keep hold of Tonkee's wrist because she's flailing and growling like an animal. Someone puts the knife in your hand, fumbling and blade-first. It feels like it takes a year to get it repositioned, but you keep your gaze on that jerking, moving lump in Tonkee's brown flesh. Where the rust is it going? You're too quietly horrified to speculate.

But before you can put the knife in place to carve the moving thing loose, it vanishes. Tonkee screams again, her voice breaking and horrible. It's gone into the meat of her.

You slash once, opening a deep cut just above the elbow, which should be ahead of the thing. Tonkee groans. "Deeper! I can feel it."

Deeper and you'll hit bone, but you set your teeth and cut deeper. There's blood everywhere. Ignoring Tonkee's pants and hisses, you try to probe for the thing—even though privately you're terrified you'll find it and it'll go into your flesh next.

"Arterial," Tonkee pants. She's shaking, keening through her teeth between every word. "Like a rusting highroad to—sessa-*ah*! Fuck!" She claps at the lower half of her bicep. It's farther up her arm than you expected. Moving faster now that it's reached the larger arteries.

Sessa. You stare at Tonkee for a moment, chilled by the realization that she was trying to say *sessapinae*. Ykka reaches over you and wraps a hand around Tonkee's arm just below the deltoid, squeezing tight. She looks at you, but you know there's only one thing left to do. You're not going to be able to manage it with the tiny knife... but there are other weapons.

"Hold her arm out." Without waiting to see whether Ykka and Hjarka comply, you grip Tonkee's shoulder. It's Alabaster's trick that you're thinking of—a tiny, fine-spun, localized torus like the ones he used to kill the boilbugs. This time you'll use it to burrow through Tonkee's arm and freeze the little iron shard. Hopefully. But as you extend your awareness and shut your eyes to concentrate, something shifts.

You're deep in the heat of her, seeking the metallic lattice of the iron shard and trying to sess the difference between its structure and that of the iron in her blood, and then—yes. The silver glimmer of magic is there.

You weren't expecting that, here amid the gelid bobble of her cells. Tonkee isn't turning into stone like Alabaster, and you've never sessed magic in any other living creature. Yet here, *here* in Tonkee, there is something that gleams steadily, silverish and threadlike, coming up through her feet—from where? doesn't matter—and ending at the iron shard. No wonder the thing can move so quickly, fueled as it is by *something else*. Using this power source, it stretches forth tendrils of its own to link into Tonkee's flesh and drag itself along. This is why it hurts her—because every cell it touches shivers as if burned, and then dies. The tendrils get longer with every contact, too; the fucking thing is *growing* its way through her, feeding on her in some imperceptible way. A lead tendril feels its way along, orienting always toward Tonkee's sessapinae, and you know instinctively that letting it get there will be Bad.

You try grabbing onto the root-thread, thinking maybe to stall it or starve it of strength, but

Oh

no

there is hate and

we all do what we have to do

there is anger and

ah; hello, little enemy

"Hey!" Hjarka's voice in your ear, a shout. "Wake the fuck up!" You jerk out of the fog you weren't aware of drifting into. Okay. You stay away from the root-tendril, lest you get another taste of whatever is driving the thing. That instant of contact was worth it, though, because now you know what to do.

You visualize scissors with edges of infinite fineness and blades of glimmering silver. Cut the lead. Cut the tendrils or they may grow again. Cut the contamination before it can set hooks any deeper in her. You're thinking of Tonkee as you do this. Wanting to save her life. But Tonkee is not Tonkee to you right now; she is a collection of particles and substances. You make the cut.

This isn't your fault. I know you won't ever believe it, but… it isn't.

And when you manage to relax your sessapinae and adjust your perception back to the macro scale and you find yourself covered, absolutely *covered* in blood, you're surprised. You don't quite understand why Tonkee is on the floor, gasping, her body surrounded by a spreading pool as Hjarka shouts at one of the Strongbacks to hand her his belt, now, now. You feel the jerk of the iron shard nearby and twitch in alarm, because you know

now what those things are trying to do, and that they are evil. But when you turn to look at the iron shard, you're confused, because all you see is smooth bronze skin streaked with blood and a scrap of familiar cloth. Then there is a sort of twitchy movement, weight making itself known in your hand, and. And. Well. You're holding Tonkee's severed arm.

You drop it. Fling it, more like, violent in your shock. It bounces just beyond Ykka and the two Strongbacks who are clustering around Tonkee and doing something, maybe trying to save her life, you can't even wrap your head around that, because now you see that the cut end of Tonkee's arm is a perfect, slightly slanted cross-section, still bleeding and twitching because *you just cut it off*, but wait no that is not the only reason.

From a small hole near the bone you see something wriggle forth. The hole is the cross-section of an artery. The something is the iron shard, which drops to the smooth green floor and then lies amid the splattered blood as if it is nothing more than a harmless bit of metal.

Hello, little enemy.

INTERLUDE

There is a thing you will not see happening, yet that is going to impact the rest of your life. Imagine it. Imagine me. You know what I am, you think, both with your thinking mind and the animal, instinctive part of you. You see a stone body clothed in flesh, and even though you never really believed I was human, you did think of me as a child. You still think it, though Alabaster has told you the truth—that I haven't been a child since before your language existed. Perhaps I was never *a child. Hearing this and believing it are two different things, however.*

You should imagine me as what I truly am among my kind, then: old, and powerful, and greatly feared. A legend. A monster.

You should imagine—

Castrima as an egg. Motes surround this egg, lurking in the stone. Eggs are a rich prize for scavengers, and easy to devour if left unguarded. This one is being devoured, though the people of Castrima are barely aware of the act. (Ykka alone, I think, and even she only suspects.) Such a leisurely repast isn't a thing most of your kind would notice. We are a very slow people. It will be deadly nevertheless, once the devouring is done.

Yet something has made the scavengers pause, teeth bared but not sinking in. There is another old and powerful one here: the one you call Antimony. She isn't interested in guarding the egg, but she could, if she chose. She will, if they attempt to poach her Alabaster. The others are aware of this, and wary of her. They shouldn't be.

I'm the one they should fear.

I destroy three of them on the first day after I leave you. As you stand sharing a mellow with Ykka, I tear apart Ykka's stone eater, the red-haired creature that she's been calling Luster and you've been calling Ruby Hair. Filthy parasite, lurking only to take and give nothing back! I despise her. We are meant for better. Then I take the two who have been stalking Alabaster, hoping to dart in should Antimony become distracted—this is not because Antimony needs the help, mind, but simply because our race cannot bear that level of stupidity. I cull them for the good of us all.

(They're not really dead, if that troubles you. We cannot die. In ten thousand years or ten million, they will reconstitute themselves from the component atoms into which I've scattered them. A long time in which to contemplate their folly, and do better next time.)

This initial slaughter makes many of the others flee; scavengers are cowards at heart. They don't go far, though. Of those who remain near, a few attempt parley. Plenty for us all, they say. If even one has the potential... but I catch some of these watching you and not Alabaster.

They confess to me, as I circle them and pretend that I might be merciful. They speak of another old one—one who is known to me from conflicts long ago. He, too, has a vision for our kind, in opposition to mine. He knows of you, my Essun, and he would kill you if he could, because you mean to finish what Alabaster began. He can't get to you with me in the way... but he can *push you to destroy yourself. He's even found some greedy human allies up north to help him do so.*

Ah, this ridiculous war of ours. We use your kind so easily. Even you, my Essun, my treasure, my pawn. One day, I hope, you will forgive me.

14

you're invited!

Six months pass in the undifferentiated white light of an ancient magic-fueled survival shelter. After the first few days you start wrapping cloth around your eyes when you're tired, to create your own day and night. It works passably.

Tonkee's arm survives the reattachment, though she gets a bad infection at one point, which Lerna's basic antibiotics seem powerless to stop. She lives, though by the time the fever and livid infection lines have faded, her fingers have lost some of their fine movement and she gets phantom tinglings and numbness throughout the limb. Lerna thinks this will be permanent. Tonkee mutters imprecations about it sometimes, whenever you track her down in the middle of core sampling or whatever she's doing and force her to go meet with the Innovator caste head. Whenever she gets too free with the "arm-chopper" insults, you remind her first that unleashing a piece of the Evil Earth to crawl through her flesh was her own damned fault, and second that you're the only reason Ykka hasn't had her killed yet, so maybe she should consider shutting up. She does, but she's still an ass about it. Nothing ever really changes in the Stillness.

And yet... sometimes things do.

Lerna forgives you for being a monster. That's not exactly it. You and he still can't talk about Tirimo easily. Still, he heard your raging fight with Ykka all through the surgery that he performed on Tonkee's arm, and that means something to him. Ykka wanted Tonkee left to die on the table. You argued for her life, and won. Lerna knows now that there's more to you than death. You're not sure you agree with that assessment, but it's a relief to have something of your old friendship back.

Hjarka starts courting Tonkee. Tonkee doesn't react well at first. She's mostly just confused when gifts of dead animals and books start appearing in the apartment, brought by with a too-casual, "In case that big brain of hers needs something to chew on," and a wink. You're the one who has to explain to Tonkee that Hjarka's decided, through whatever convoluted set of values the big woman holds dear, that an ex-commless geomest with the social skills of a rock represents the pinnacle of desirability. Then Tonkee is mostly annoyed, complaining about "distractions" and "the vagaries of the ephemeral" and the need to "decenter the flesh." You mostly ignore all of it.

It's the books that settle the issue. Hjarka seems to pick them by the number of many-syllabled words on their spines, but you come home a few times to find Tonkee engrossed in them. Eventually you come home to find Tonkee's room curtain drawn and Tonkee engrossed in Hjarka, or so the sounds from beyond would suggest. You didn't think they could do that much with her bum arm. Huh.

Perhaps it is this new sense of connection to Castrima that causes Tonkee to begin trying to prove her worth to Ykka. (Or maybe it's just pride; Tonkee bristles so when Ykka once says that Tonkee isn't as useful to the comm as its hardest-working Strongback.) Whatever the reason, Tonkee brings the council a new predictive model that she's worked out: Unless Castrima finds a stable source of animal protein, some comm members will start showing deprivation symptoms within a year. "It'll start with the meat stupids," she tells all of you. "Forgetfulness, tiredness, little things like that. But it's a kind of anemia. If it goes on, the result is dementia and nerve damage. You can figure out the rest."

There are too many lorist tales of what can happen to a comm without meat. It will make people weak and paranoid, the community becoming vulnerable to attack. The only choice that will prevent this outcome, Tonkee explains, is cannibalism. Planting more beans just isn't enough.

The report is useful information, but nobody really wanted to hear it, and Ykka doesn't like Tonkee any better for sharing it. You thank Tonkee after the meeting, since no one else did. Her lower jaw juts out a bit as she replies, "Well, I won't be able to continue my studies if we all start killing and eating each other, so."

You shunt the orogene children's lessons to Temell, another adult orogene in the comm. The children complain that he's not very good—none of your finesse, and while he goes easier on them, they're not learning as much. (It's nice to be appreciated, if after the fact.) You do start training Cutter as an alternative, after he asks you to show him how you cut off Tonkee's arm. You doubt he'll ever perceive magic or move obelisks, but he's at least first-ring level, and you want to see if you can make him a two- or three-ringer. Just because. Apparently higher-level teaching doesn't interfere with what you're learning from Alabaster—or at least, 'Baster doesn't complain about it. You'll take it. You've missed teaching.

(You offer an exchange of techniques to Ykka, since she shows no interest in lessons. You want to know how she does the things she does. "Nope," she says, winking at you in a way that's not really teasing. "Gotta keep some tricks up my sleeve so you won't ice me someday.")

An all-volunteer trading party goes north to try to reach the comm of Tettehee. They do not return. Ykka nixes all future attempts, and you do not protest this. One of your former orogeny students was with the missing party.

Aside from the food supply issue, however, Castrima thrives in those six months. One woman gets pregnant without permission, which is a big problem. Babies contribute nothing useful to a comm for years, and no comm can tolerate many useless people during a Season. Ykka decides that the woman's household of two married couples will not receive an increased share until someone elderly or infirm dies to clear the way for the unauthorized baby. You get into another fight with Ykka about that, because you know full well she meant Alabaster when she offhandedly added, "Shouldn't be long," to the woman. Ykka's unapologetic: She did mean Alabaster and she hopes he dies soon, because at least a baby has future value.

Two good outcomes result from that fracas: Everyone trusts you more after seeing you shout at the top of your lungs in the middle of Flat Top without causing so much as a tremor, and the

Breeders decide to speak up for the new baby in order to settle the dispute. Based on the favorable recent genealogy, they contribute one of their child-allocations to the family, though with the stipulation that it will have to join their use-caste if it is born perfect. That's not so terrible a price to pay, they say, spending one's reproductive years cranking out children for comm and caste, in exchange for the right to be born. The mother agrees.

Ykka hasn't shared the protein situation with the comm, of course, or the Breeders wouldn't be speaking up for anyone. (Tonkee figured it out on her own, naturally.) Ykka doesn't want to tell anyone, either, until it's clear there's no hope of an alternate solution to the problem. You and the other council members agree reluctantly. There's still a year left. But because of Ykka's silence, a male Breeder visits you a few days after you bring Tonkee home to finish recuperating. The Breeder is an ashblow-haired, strong-shouldered, sloe-eyed thing, and he's very interested to know that you've borne three healthy children, all powerful orogenes. He flatters you by talking about how tall and strong you are, how well you weathered months on the road with only travel rations to eat, and hinting that you're "only" forty-three. This actually makes you laugh. You feel as old as the world, and this pretty fool thinks you're ready to crank out another baby.

You turn down his tacit offer with a smile, but it's . . . strange, having that conversation with him. Unpleasantly familiar. When the Breeder is gone, you think of Corundum and wake Tonkee by throwing a cup at the wall and screaming at the top of your lungs. Then you go to see Alabaster for another lesson, which is utterly useless because you spend it standing before him and trembling in utter, rage-filled silence. After five minutes of this, he wearily says, "Whatever the rust is wrong with you, you're going to have to deal with it yourself. I can't stop you anymore."

You hate him for no longer being invincible. And for not hating you.

Alabaster suffers another bad infection during these six months. He survives it only by deliberately stoning what's left of his legs. This self-induced surgery so stresses his body that his few bouts of lucid time shrink to a half hour apiece, interspersed with long stretches of stupor or fitful sleeping. He's so weak when he's awake that you have to strain to hear him, though thankfully this improves over the course of a few weeks. You're making progress, connecting easily now to the newly arrived topaz and beginning to understand what he did to transform the spinel into the knife-like weapon he keeps nearby. (The obelisks are conduits. You flow through them, flow with them, as the magic flows. Resist and die, but resonate finely enough and many things become possible.)

That's a far cry from chaining together multiple obelisks, though, and you know you're not learning fast enough. Alabaster doesn't have the strength to curse you for your cloddish pace, but he doesn't have to. Watching him shrivel daily is what drives you to push at the obelisk again and again, plunging yourself into its watery light even when your head hurts and your stomach lurches and you want nothing more than to go curl up somewhere and cry. It hurts too much to look at him, so you mop yourself up and try that much harder to become him.

One good thing about all this: You've got a purpose now. Congratulations.

You cry on Lerna's shoulder once. He rubs your back and

suggests delicately that you don't have to be alone in your grief. It's a proposition, but one made in kindness rather than passion, so you don't feel guilty about ignoring it. For now.

Thus do things reach a kind of equilibrium. It's neither a time of rest, nor of struggle. You survive. In a Season, in *this* Season, that is itself a triumph.

And then Hoa returns.

* * *

It happens on a day of sorrows and lace. The sorrow is because more Hunters have died. In the middle of bringing back a rare hunting kill—a bear that was visibly too thin to safely hibernate, easy to shoot in its desperate aggression—the party was attacked in turn. Three Hunters died in a barrage of arrows and crossbow bolts. The two surviving Hunters did not see their assailants; the projectiles seemed to come from all directions. They wisely ran, though they circled back an hour later in hopes of recovering their fallen comrades' bodies and the precious carcass. Amazingly, everything had been left unmolested by either assailants or scavengers—but left behind with the fallen was an object: a planted stick, around which someone tied a strip of ragged, dirty cloth. It was secured with a thick knot, something caught in its fraying loops.

You come into Ykka's meeting room just as she begins to cut open the knot, even as Cutter stands over her and says in a tight voice, "This is completely unsafe, you have no idea—"

"I don't care," Ykka murmurs, concentrating on the knot. She's being very careful, avoiding the thickest part of the knot, which clearly contains something; you can't tell what, but it's lumpy and seems light. The room is more crowded than usual because one of the Hunters is here, too, grimy with ash and blood and visibly determined to know what her companions died for. Ykka glances up in acknowledgment as you arrive, but then resumes work. She says, "Something blows up in my face, Cuts, you're the new headman."

That flusters and shuts Cutter up enough that she's able to finish the knot undistracted. The loops and strands of once-white cloth are lace, and if you don't miss your guess, it was of a quality that would once have made your grandmother lament her poverty. When the strands snap apart, what sits amid them is a small balled-up scrap of leather hide. It's a note.

WELCOME TO RENNANIS, it reads in charcoal.

Hjarka curses. You sit down on a divan, because it's better than the floor and you need to sit somewhere. Cutter looks disbelieving. "Rennanis is Equatorial," he says. And therefore it should be gone; same reaction you had when Alabaster told you.

"May not be Rennanis proper," Ykka says. She's still examining the scrap of leather, turning it over, scraping at the charcoal with the edge of the knife as if to test its authenticity. "A band of survivors from that city, commless now and little better than bandits, naming themselves after home. Or maybe just Equatorial wannabes, taking the chance to claim something they couldn't before the actual city got torched."

"Doesn't matter," snaps Hjarka. "This is a threat, whoever it's coming from. What are we going to *do* about it?"

They devolve into speculations and argument, all with a rising edge of panic. Without really planning to, you lean back against the wall of Ykka's meeting room. Against the wall of the crystal that her apartment inhabits. Against the rind of the geode, in which the crystal shaft is rooted. It is not an obelisk. Not even the flickering portions of crystal in the control room feel of power as they should; even if they are in an obelisk-like state of unreality, that is the only point of similarity they share with real obelisks.

But you've also remembered something that Alabaster told you a long time ago, on a garnet-hued afternoon in a seaside comm that is now smoldering ruins. Alabaster murmuring of conspiracies, watchers, nowhere was safe. *You're saying someone could hear us through the walls? Through the stone itself?* you remember asking him. Once upon a time, you thought the things he did were just miracles.

And now you're a nine-ringer, Alabaster says. Now you know that miracles are a matter of just effort, just perception, and maybe just magic. Castrima exists amid ancient sedimentary rock laced through with veins of long-dead forests turned to crumbly coal, all of it balanced precariously over a crisscross of ancient fault-scars that have all but healed. The geode has been here long enough, however awkwardly jammed amid the strata, that its outermost layers are thoroughly fused with local minerals. This makes it easy for you to push your awareness beyond Castrima in a fine, gradually attenuating extrusion. This is not the same thing as extending your torus; a torus is your power, this is you. It's harder. You can sense what your power cannot, though, and—

"Hey, wake up," Hjarka says, shoving you in the shoulder, and you snap back to glare at her.

Ykka groans. "Remind me, Hjar, to someday tell you what usually happens when someone interrupts high-level orogeny.

I mean, you can probably guess, but remind me to describe it in gory detail, so that maybe it can have some actual deterrent value."

"She was just sitting there." Hjarka sits back, looking disgruntled. "And the rest of you were just looking at her."

"I was trying to hear the north," you snap. They all look at you like you're crazy. Evil Earth, if only someone else here were Fulcrum-trained. Though this isn't something anyone but a senior would understand, anyway.

Lerna ventures, "Hear... the earth? Do you mean *sess*?"

It's so hard to explain with words. You rub your eyes. "No, I mean *hear.* Vibrations. All sound is vibrations, I mean, but..." Their expressions grow more confused. You're going to have to contextualize. "The node network is still there," you say. "Alabaster was right. I can sess it if I try, a zone of stillness where the rest of the Equatorials are a seething disaster. Someone *is* keeping them, the node maintainers around Rennanis, alive, so—"

"So this is really them," Cutter says, sounding troubled. "An Equatorial city really has decided to induct us."

"Equatorials don't induct," Ykka says. Her jaw is tight as she speaks, gazing at the scrap of leather in her hand. "They're Old Sanze, or what's left of it. When Sanze wanted something back in the day, Sanze took it."

After a tense silence, they start quietly panicking again. Too many words. You sigh and rub your temples and wish you were alone so you could try again. Or...

You blink. Or. You sess the hovering potentiality of the topaz, which drifts in the sky above Castrima-over, where it has been for the past six months, half-hidden amid the ash clouds. Evil

Earth. Alabaster isn't just sessing half the continent; he's using the spinel to do it. You haven't even thought about using an obelisk to extend your reach, but he does it like breathing.

"No one touch me," you say softly. "No one speak to me." Without waiting to see if they understand, you plunge into the obelisk.

(Because, well, some part of you *wants* to do this. Has dreamt of upward-falling water and torrential power for months. You are only human, whatever they say about your kind. It's good to feel powerful.)

Then you're in the topaz and through it and stretching yourself across the world in a breath. No need to be in the ground when the topaz is in air, *is* the air; it exists in states of being that transcend solidity, and thus you are capable of transcending, too; *you* become air. You drift amid the ash clouds and see the Stillness track beneath you in humps of topography and patches of dying forest and threads of roads, all of it grayed over after the long months of the Season. The continent seems tiny and you think, *I can make the equator in the blink of an eye*, but this thought scares you a little. You don't know why. You try not to think—how far of a leap is it from thrilling in such power to using it to destroy the world? (Did Alabaster feel this, when he...?) But you are committed; you have connected; the resonance is complete. You launch yourself northward anyhow.

And then you stutter to a halt. Because there is something much closer than the equator that draws your attention. It is so shocking that you fall out of alignment with the topaz at once, and you are very lucky. There is a struck-glass instant in which you feel the shivering immensity of the obelisk's power and know that you survive only because of fortunate resonances and careful long-dead designers who obviously planned for mistakes like yours, and then you are gasping and back within yourself and babbling before you quite remember what words mean.

"Camp, fire," you say, panting a little. Lerna comes over and crouches in front of you, taking your hands and checking your pulse; you ignore him. This is important. "*Basin.*"

Ykka gets it instantly, sitting up straight and tightening her jaw. Hjarka, too; she's not stupid, or Tonkee would never put up with her. She curses. Lerna frowns, and Cutter looks at all of you in rising confusion. "Did that actually mean something?"

Asshole. "An army," you snap as you recover. But words are hard. "Th-there's a . . . a rusting *army*. In the forest basin. I could. Sess their campfires."

"How many?" Ykka is already getting up, fetching a long-knife from a shelf and belting it round her thigh. Hjarka gets up, too, going to the door of Ykka's apartment and pulling open the curtain. You hear her shouting for Esni, the head of the Strongbacks. The Strongbacks sometimes do scouting and supplement the Hunters, but in a situation like this, they are charged primarily with the comm's defense.

You couldn't count all the little blots of heat that pinged on your awareness when you were in the obelisk, but you try to guess. "Maybe a hundred?" That was the campfires, though. How many people around each fire? You guess six or seven apiece. Not a large force, under ordinary circumstances. Any decent quartent governor could field an army ten times that size on relatively short notice. During a Season, though, and for a comm as small as Castrima—whose total population is not much larger—an army of five or six hundred is a dire threat indeed.

"Tettehee," Cutter breathes, sitting back. He's gone paler than usual. You follow him, though. Six months ago, the stand of impaled corpses set up as a warn-off in the forest basin. The comm of Tettehee is beyond the basin, near the mouth of the river that wends through Castrima's territory and ultimately empties into one of the great lakes of the Somidlats. You've heard nothing from Tettehee in months, and the trading party you sent past the warn-off failed to return. This army must have hit Tettehee around that time, then bunkered down there for a while, sending out scouting parties to mark territory. Replenishing stores, rebuilding arms, healing their wounded, maybe sending some of their spoils back north to Rennanis. Now that they've digested Tettehee, they're on the march again.

And somehow, they know Castrima's here. They're saying hello.

Ykka heads outside and shouts alongside Hjarka, and within a few minutes someone is ringing the shake alarm and shouting for a gathering of the household heads at the Flat Top. You've never heard Castrima's shake alarm—comm full of roggas—and it's more annoying than you expected, low and rhythmic and buzzy. You understand why: Amid a bunch of crystalline structures, ringing bells aren't the best idea. Still. You and Lerna and the rest follow Ykka as she strides along a rope bridge and around two larger shafts, her lips pressed together and face grim. By the time she reaches the Flat Top there's a small crowd already there; by the time she yells for someone to stop blowing the rusting alarm and the alarm actually stops, the sheared-off crystal is starting to look dangerously packed with murmuring, anxious people. There's a railing, but still. Hjarka shouts at Esni, and Esni in turn shouts at the Strongbacks amid the gathering, and they move clumsily to turn people away so there won't be any horrible tragedies distracting from the possible horrible tragedy that looms imminent.

When Ykka raises her hands for attention, everyone falls silent instantly. "The situation," she begins, and lays everything out in a few terse sentences.

You respect her for holding nothing back. You respect the people of Castrima, too, for doing nothing more than gasping or murmuring in alarm, and not panicking. But then, they are all good stolid commfolk, and panic has always been frowned upon in the Stillness. The lorists' tales are full of dire warnings about those who cannot master their fear, and few comms will grant such people comm names unless they're wealthy or influential enough to push the issue. Those things tend to sort themselves out once a Season rolls around.

"Rennanis was a big city," says one woman, once Ykka's stopped talking. "Half the size of Yumenes but still millions of people. Can we fight that?"

"It's a Season," Hjarka says, before Ykka can reply. Ykka shoots her a dirty look, but Hjarka shrugs it off. "We have no choice."

"We can fight because of the way Castrima's built," Ykka adds, throwing Hjarka one last quelling look. "They can't exactly come at us from the rear. If push comes to shove, we can block off the tunnels; then nothing can get down here. We can wait them out."

Not forever, though. Not when the comm needs both hunting

and trading to supplement its storecaches and water gardens. You respect Ykka for *not* saying this. There's a somewhat relieved stir.

"Do we have time to send a messenger south to one of our allied comms?" Lerna asks. You can feel him trying to skirt around the supply issue. "Would any of them be willing to help us?"

Ykka snorts at the last question. Lots of other people do, a few throwing pitying looks Lerna's way. It's a Season. But—"Trading's a maybe. We could load up on critical supplies, medicines, and be more ready if there's a siege. The forest basin takes days to get across with a small party; a big group will take a couple of weeks, maybe. Faster if they force-march it, but that's stupid and dangerous on terrain they don't know. We know their scouts are in our territory, but..." She glances at you. "How close are the rest of them?"

You're caught off guard, but you know what she wants. "The bulk of them were near the impaling." That's about halfway across the forest basin.

"They could be here in days," says someone, voice high-pitched with alarm, and many other people take up that murmur. They start getting louder. Ykka raises her hands again, but this time only some of the assembled people go quiet; the rest keep speculating, calculating, and you catch sight of a few people breaking for the bridges, clearly intent upon making their own plans, Ykka be damned. It's not chaos, not quite panic, but there's enough fear in the air to scent it faintly bitter. You get up, intending to move to the center of the gathering with Ykka, to try to add your voice to hers in calling for calm.

But you stop. Because someone is standing in the place you intended to move to.

It's not like with Antimony, or Ruby Hair, or the other stone eaters you've glimpsed around the comm from time to time. Those, for whatever reason, don't like to be seen moving; you'll catch a blur now and again, but then the statue is there, watching you, as if there has always been a statue of a stranger in that position, sculpted by someone long ago.

This stone eater is turning. It keeps turning, letting everyone see and hear it turn, watching as you finally register its presence, the gray granite of its flesh, the undifferentiated slick of its hair, the slightly greater polish of its eyes. Carefully sculpted length and weight of jaw, and its torso is finely carved with male human musculature rather than the suggestion of clothing that most stone eaters adopt. This one obviously wants you to think of it as male, so fine, it's male. He is allover gray, the first stone eater you have seen who looks like nothing more than a statue... except that he moves, and keeps moving, as everyone falls silent in surprise. He is taking all of you in, too, with a slight smile on his lips. He's holding something.

You stare as the gray stone eater turns, and as your mind makes out the oddly shaped, bloody thing he holds, it is recent experience that makes you suddenly realize it is an arm. It is a small arm. It is a small arm still partially wrapped in cloth that is familiar, the jacket that you bought a lifetime ago on the road. The red-smeared inhumanly white skin on the hand is familiar, and the size is familiar, even though the lump of splintered bone at the bloody end is clear and glasslike and finely faceted and not bone at all.

Hoa it is Hoa that is Hoa's arm

"I bear a message," says the gray stone eater. The voice is

pleasant, tenor. His mouth does not move, and the words echo up from his chest. This, at least, feels normal, insofar as you are currently capable of feeling normal, as you stare down at that dripping disaster of an arm.

Ykka stirs after a moment, perhaps pulling herself out of shock, too. "From whom?"

He turns to her. "Rennanis." Turn again, eyes shifting from face to face amid the crowd, same as a human would do when trying to make a connection, get a point across. His eyes skim over you as if you aren't there. "We wish you no harm."

You stare at Hoa's arm in his hand.

Ykka is skeptical. "So, the army camped on our doorstep . . . ?"

Turn. He ignores Cutter, too. "We have plentiful food. Strong walls. All yours, if you join our comm."

"Maybe we like being our own comm," Ykka says.

Turn. His gaze settles on Hjarka, who blinks. "You have no meat, and your territory is depleted. You'll be eating each other within a year."

Well, that sets off the murmuring. Ykka shuts her eyes for a moment in pure frustration. Hjarka looks around angrily, as if wondering who has betrayed you.

Cutter says, "Would all of us be adopted into your comm? With our use-castes intact?"

Lerna makes a tight sound. "I don't see how that's the point, Cutter—"

Cutter throws a slashing look at Lerna. "We can't fight an Equatorial city."

"But it *is* a stupid question," Ykka says. Her voice is deceptively mild, but in the part of your mind that is not stunned to silence by *that arm*, you note that she's never backed up Lerna before. You've always gotten the impression she doesn't much like him, and that it's mutual—she's too cold for him, he's too soft for her. This is significant. "If I were these people, I would lie, take us all north, and shove us into a commless buffer-shanty somewhere between an acid geyser and a lava lake. Equatorial comms have done that before, especially when they needed labor. Why should we believe this one's any different?"

The gray stone eater tilts his head. Between that and the little smile on his lips, it's a remarkably human gesture—a look that says, *Oh, aren't you cute.* "We don't have to lie." He lets those pleasant-toned words hang in the air for just the right amount of time. Oh, he's good at this. You see people exchange looks, hear them shift uncomfortably; you feel the pent silence as Ykka has no retort to that. Because it's true.

Then he drops the other boot. "But we have no use for orogenes."

Silence. Shocked stillness. Ykka breaks it by uttering a swift, "Fire-under-Earth." Cutter looks away. Lerna's eyes widen as he grasps the implications of what the stone eater has just done.

"Where is Hoa?" you ask into the silence. It's all you can think about.

The stone eater's eyes slide to you. The rest of his face does not turn. For a stone eater, this is normal body language; for *this* stone eater, it is conspicuous. "Dead," he says. "After leading us here."

"You're lying." You don't even realize you're angry. You don't think about what you're about to do. You just react, like Damaya in the crucibles, like Syenite on the beach. Everything in you crystallizes and sharpens and your awareness facets down to a razor point and you weave the threads that you barely noticed were there and it happens just like with Tonkee's arm; *shiiiiing.* You slice the stone eater's hand off.

It and Hoa's arm drop to the floor. People gasp. There is no blood. Hoa's arm hits the crystal with a loud, meaty thud—it's heavier than it looks—and the stone eater's hand makes a second, even more solid clack, separating from the arm. The cross-section of its wrist is undifferentiated gray.

The stone eater does not seem to react at first. Then you sess the coalescence of something, like the silver threads of magic but *so many.* The hand twitches, then leaps into the air, returning to the wrist-stump as if pulled by strings. He leaves Hoa's arm behind. Then the stone eater turns fully to face you, at last.

"Get out before I chop you into more pieces than you can put back together," you say in a voice that shakes like the earth.

The gray stone eater smiles. It's a full smile, eyes crinkling with crow's feet and lips drawing back from diamond teeth—and marvel of marvels, it actually looks like a smile and not a threat display. Then he vanishes, falling through the surface of the crystal. For an instant you see a gray shadow within the crystal's translucence, his shape blurred and not quite humanoid anymore, though that is probably the angle. Then, faster than you can track with eyes or sessapinae, he shoots down and away.

In the reverberating wake of his leaving, Ykka takes and lets out a deep breath.

"Well," she says, looking around at her people. What she believes to be her people. "Sounds like we need to talk." There is an uneasy stir.

You don't want to hear it. You hurry forward and pick up

Hoa's arm. The thing is heavy as stone; you have to put your legs into it or risk your lower back. You turn and people move out of your way and you hear Lerna say, "Essun?" But you don't want to hear him, either.

There are threads, see. Silver lines that only you can see, flailing and curling forth from the arm's stump, but they shift as you turn. Always pointing in a particular direction. So you follow them. No one follows you, and you don't care what that means. Not at the moment.

The tendrils lead you to your own apartment.

You step through the curtain and stop. Tonkee's not home. Must be either at Hjarka's or up in the green room. There are two more limbs on the floor in front of you, bloody stumps with diamond bones poking forth. No, they are not on the floor; they are *in* the floor, partially submerged in it, one down to the thigh, the other just a calf and foot. Caught, as if climbing out. There are twin trails of blood, thick enough to be worrisome, over the homey rug that you bartered one of Jija's old flintknives for. They go toward your room, so you follow them in. And then you drop the arm. Fortunately it does not land on your foot.

What is left of Hoa crawls toward the floor-mattress that passes for your bed. His other arm is also gone, you don't know where. Hanks of his hair are missing. He pauses when you come in, hearing or sessing you, and he lies still as you circle him and see that his lower jaw has been ripped away. He has no eyes, and there is a . . . a bite, just above his temple. That's why his hair is missing. Something has bitten into his skull like an apple, incising a chunk of flesh and the diamond bone underneath. You can't see what's inside his head for the blood. That's good.

It would frighten you, if you did not immediately understand. Beside your bed is the little cloth-wrapped bundle that he has carried since Tirimo. You hurry to it, open it up, bring it to the ruin of him, and hunker down. "Can you turn over?"

He responds by doing so. For a moment you're stymied by the lack of a lower jaw, and then you think *fuck it* and shove one of the stones from the bundle directly into the ragged hole of Hoa's throat. The feel of his flesh is warm and human as you push it down with your finger until the muscles of his swallowing reflex catch it. (Your gorge rises. You will it back down.) You start to feed him another, but after a few breaths he begins to shiver all over violently. You don't realize you're still sessing magic until suddenly Hoa's body becomes alive with glimmering silver threads, all of them whipping about and curling like the stinging tentacles of ocean creatures from lorists' tales. *Hundreds* of them. You draw back in alarm, but Hoa makes a raw, breathy sound, and you think maybe it means *more*. You push another stone into his throat, and then another. There weren't many left to begin with. When you're down to only three, you hesitate. "You want them all?"

Hoa hesitates, too. You can see that in his body language. You don't understand why he needs them at all; aside from that lashing of magic—he is *made* of it, every inch of him is alive with it, you've never seen anything like this—nothing about his damaged body is improving. Can anyone survive or recover from this degree of damage? He's not human enough for you to even guess. But finally he croaks again. It is a deeper sound than the first. Resigned, maybe, or maybe that is your imagination patterning humanity over the animal sounds of his animal flesh. So you push the last three stones into him.

Nothing happens for a moment. Then.

Silver tendrils billow and swell around him so rapidly, with such frenzy, that you scramble back. You know some of the things that magic can do, and something about this seems altogether wild and uncontrolled. It fills the room, though, and—and you blink. You can *see* it, not just sess it. All of Hoa glimmers now with silver-white light, growing rapidly too bright to look at directly; even a still would be able to see this. You move into the living room, peering through the bedroom door because that seems safer. The instant you cross the room's threshold, the substance of the whole apartment—walls, floor, everywhere there is crystal—shivers for an instant, becoming translucent and *obelisk-unreal.* Your bedroom furniture and belongings float amid the flickering white. There is a soft thump from behind you that makes you jump and whirl, but it's Hoa's legs, which are out of the living room floor and sliding along the trails of blood into your room. The arm you dropped is moving, too, already nudging up against the bright morass of him, becoming bright, too. Leaping to rejoin his body, as the gray stone eater's hand rejoined his wrist.

Something slides up from the floor—no. You see *the floor* slide up, as if it were putty and not crystal, and wrap itself around his body. The light dies when he does it; the material immediately begins to change into something darker. When you blink away the afterimages enough to see, there is something huge and strange and impossible where Hoa once was.

You step back into the bedroom—carefully, because the floor and walls might be solid again, but you know that's possibly a temporary state. The once-smooth crystal is rough beneath your feet. The thing takes up most of the room now, lying next to your disordered bed that is now half submerged in the resolidified floor. It's hot. Your foot tangles briefly in the strap of your half-empty runny-sack, which fortunately is still intact and unmerged with the room. You stoop quickly and grab it; the habits of survival. *Earthfires* it's hot in here. The bed does not catch fire, but you think that's only because it's not directly touching the big thing. You can sess it, whatever it is. No, you know what it is: chalcedony. A huge, oblong lump of gray-green chalcedony, like the outer shell of a geode.

You already know what's happening, don't you? I told you of Tirimo after the Rifting. The far end of the valley, where the shockwave of the shake loosed a geode that then split open like an egg. The geode hadn't been there all along, you realize; this is magic, not nature. Well, perhaps a bit of both. For stone eaters, there's little difference between the two.

And in the morning, after you spend the night at the living room table, where you meant to stay awake and watch the steaming lump of rock but instead fell asleep, it happens again. The cracking open of the geode is loud, explosively violent. A flicker of pressure-driven plasma curls forth and scorches or melts all the belongings you left in the room. Except the runny-sack, since you took it. Good instincts.

You're shaking from being startled awake. Slowly you stand and edge into the room. It's so hot that it's hard to breathe. Like an oven—though the waft of warmth causes the apartment's entry curtain to billow open. Quickly the heat diminishes to only uncomfortable, and not dangerous.

You barely notice. Because what rises from the split in the

geode, moving too human-smoothly at first but rapidly readjusting to a familiar sort of punctuated stillness... is the stone eater from the garnet obelisk.

Hello, again.

* * *

Our position is thoroughly identified with the physical integrity of the Stillness—for the obvious interest of long-term survival. Maintenance of this land is peculiarly dependent upon seismic equilibrium, and by an imperious law of nature, none but the orogenic can establish such. A blow at their bondage is a blow at the very planet. We rule, therefore, that though they bear some resemblance to we of good and wholesome lineage, and though they must be managed with kind hand to the benefit of both bond and free, any degree of orogenic ability must be assumed to negate its corresponding personhood. They are rightfully to be held and regarded as an inferior and dependent species.

—*The Second Yumenescene Lore Council's Declaration on the Rights of the Orogenically Afflicted*

15

Nassun, in rejection

WHAT I REMEMBER OF MY youth is color. Greenness everywhere. White iridescence. Deep and vital reds. These particular colors linger in my memory, when so much of the rest is thin and pale and nearly gone. There is a reason for that.

* * *

Nassun sits in an office within the Antarctic Fulcrum, suddenly understanding her mother better than ever before.

Schaffa and Umber sit on either side of her. All three of them are holding cups of safe that the Fulcrum people have offered them. Nida is back at Found Moon, because someone must remain to watch over the children there and because she has the hardest time emulating normal human behavior. Umber is so quiet that no one knows what he's thinking. Schaffa's doing all the talking. They've been invited inside to speak with three people who are called "seniors," whatever that means. These seniors wear uniforms that are all black, with neatly buttoned jackets and pleated slacks—ah, so that is why they call Imperial Orogenes blackjackets. They feel all over of power and fear.

One of them is obviously Antarctic-bred, with graying red hair and skin so white that green veins show starkly just underneath. She has horsey teeth and beautiful lips, and Nassun cannot stop staring at both as she talks. Her name is Serpentine, which does not seem to fit her at all.

"Of course we have no new grits coming in," Serpentine says. For some reason she looks at Nassun as she speaks and spreads her hands. The fingers shake slightly. That's been happening since this meeting began. "It's a difficulty we hadn't quite anticipated. If nothing else, it means we have grit dormitories going unused in a time when safe shelter is quite valuable. That would be why we extended an offer to nearby comms to take in their unparented children, those too young to have earned acceptance into a comm. Only sensible, yes? And we took in a few refugees, which would be why we had no choice but to open trade negotiations with the locals for supplies and such. With no resupply coming from Yumenes..." Her expression falters. "Well. It's understandable, isn't it?"

She's whining. Doing it with a gracious smile and impeccable manners, doing it with two other people nodding sagely along with her, but doing it. Nassun isn't sure why these people bother her so much. It has something to do with the whining, and with the falseness of them: They are clearly uncomfortable with the arrival of Guardians, clearly afraid and angry, and yet they pretend courtesy. It makes her think of her mother, who pretended to be kind and loving when Father or anyone else was around, and who was cold and fierce in private. Thinking of the Antarctic Fulcrum as a place populated by endless variants of her mother makes Nassun's teeth and palms and sessapinae itch.

And she can see by the icy placidity of Umber's face, and the brittle-edged friendliness of Schaffa's smile, that the Guardians don't like it, either. "Understandable indeed," Schaffa says. He turns the cup of safe in his hands. The cloudy solution has remained white as it should, but he hasn't taken a single sip. "I imagine the local comms are grateful to you for housing and feeding their surplus population. And it is only sensible that you would put those people to work, too. Guarding your walls. Tending your fields—" He pauses, smiles more widely. "Gardens, I mean."

Serpentine smiles back, and her companions shift uncomfortably. It is something Nassun doesn't understand. The Season hasn't yet taken full hold here in the Antarctic region, so it does seem wise that a comm would plant its greenland and put Strongbacks on its walls and start preparing for the worst. Somehow it is bad that the Antarctic Fulcrum has done this, however. Bad that this Fulcrum is functional at all. Nassun has stopped drinking the cup of safe the seniors gave her, even though she's only had safe a couple of times before and sort of likes being treated like a grown-up—but Schaffa isn't drinking, and that warns her the situation is not really safe.

One of the seniors is a Somidlats woman who could pass for a relative of Nassun's: tall, middling brown, curling thick hair, a body that is thick-waisted and broad-hipped and heavy-thighed. They introduced her, but Nassun can't remember her name. Her orogeny feels the sharpest of the three, though she is the youngest; there are six rings on her long fingers. And she is the one who finally stops smiling and folds her hands and lifts her chin, just a little. It is another thing that reminds Nassun of her mother. Mama often held herself the same way, feeling of soft dignity layered over a core of diamond obstinacy. The obstinacy is what comes to the fore now as the woman says, "I take it you are unhappy, Guardian."

Serpentine winces. The other Fulcrum orogene, a man who introduced himself as Lamprophyre, sighs. Schaffa and Umber's heads tilt in near-unison, Schaffa's smile widening with interest. "Not unhappy," he says. Nassun can tell that he is pleased to be done with the pleasantry. "Merely surprised. It is, after all, standard protocol for any Fulcrum facility to be shut down in the event of a declared Season."

"Declared by whom?" the six-ringed woman asks. "Until your arrival today, there have been no Guardians here to declare anything of the sort. The local comm Leaderships have varied: Some declared Seasonal Law, some are only in lockdown, some are business as usual."

"And had they all declared Seasonal Law," Schaffa says, in that very quiet voice he uses when he knows the answer to a question already and only wants to hear you say it yourself, "would you truly have all killed yourselves? Since, as you note, there are no Guardians here to take care of the matter for you."

Nassun catches herself before she would have started in surprise. Kill themselves? But she is not quite good enough at controlling her orogeny to keep it from twitching where she does not. All three of the Fulcrum people glance at her, and Serpentine smiles thinly. "Careful, Guardian," she says, looking at Nassun but speaking to Schaffa. "Your pet seems uncomfortable with the idea of mass extermination for no reason."

Schaffa says, "I hide nothing from her," and Nassun's surprise is swallowed up by love and pride. He glances at Nassun. "Historically, the Fulcrum has survived on the sufferance of its neighbors, depending on the walls and resources of comms nearby. And as with all who have no viable use during a Season, there is most certainly an expectation that Imperial Orogenes will remove themselves from the competition for resources—so that normal, healthy people have a better chance to survive." He pauses. "And since orogenes are not permitted to exist outside the supervision of a Guardian or the Fulcrum..." He spreads his hands.

"We *are* the Fulcrum, Guardian," says the third senior, whose name Nassun has forgotten. This is a man from some Western Coastal people; he is slender and straight-haired and has a high-cheekboned, nearly concave face. His skin is white, too, but his eyes are dark and cool. His orogeny feels light and many-layered, like mica. "And we are self-sufficient. Quite apart from being a drain on resources, we provide needed services to the nearby communities. We have even—unasked and uncompensated—worked to mitigate the aftershakes of the Rifting on the occasions when they reach this far south. It is because of us that few Antarctic comms have suffered serious harm since the start of this Season."

"Admirable," says Umber. "And clever, making yourselves invaluable. Not a thing your Guardians would have permitted, though. I imagine."

All three of the seniors grow still for a moment. "This is Antarctic, Guardian," says Serpentine. She smiles, though the expression does not reach her eyes. "We are a fraction of the size of the Fulcrum at Yumenes—barely twenty-five ringed orogenes, a handful of mostly grown grits. There were never many Guardians permanently stationed here. Most of what we got were visiting Guardians on circuit, or delivering us new grits. None at all since the Rifting."

"Never many Guardians stationed here," agrees Schaffa, "but there *were* three, as I recall. I knew one." He pauses, and for a fleeting instant his expression goes distant and lost and a little confused. "I remember knowing one." He blinks. Smiles again. "Yet now there are none."

Serpentine is tense. They are all tense, these seniors, in a way that makes the itch at the back of Nassun's mind grow. "We endured several raids by commless bands before we finally put up a wall," Serpentine says. "They died bravely, protecting us."

It's so blatant a lie that Nassun stares at her, mouth open.

"Well," Schaffa says, setting down his cup of safe and letting out a little sigh. "I suppose this went about as well as could be expected."

And even though Nassun has guessed by now what is coming, even though she has seen Schaffa move with a speed that is not humanly possible before, even though the silver within him and Umber ignites like matchflame and blazes through them in the instant just before, she is still caught off guard when Schaffa lunges forward and puts his fist through Serpentine's face.

Serpentine's orogeny dies as she does. But the other two seniors are up and moving in the next instant, Lamprophyre falling backward over his chair to escape Umber's blurring reach for him and the six-ringed woman drawing a blowgun from one sleeve. Schaffa's eyes widen, but his hand is still stuck in Serpentine; he tries to lunge at her, but the corpse is deadweight on his arm. She lifts the gun to her lips.

Before she can get off a puff, Nassun is up and in the earth and beginning to spin a torus that will ice the woman in an instant. The woman jerks in surprise and flexes *something* that shatters Nassun's torus before it can form completely; it is a thing her mother used to do during their practices, if Nassun did something she wasn't supposed to. The shock of this realization causes Nassun to stagger and stumble back.

Her mother learned that trick here, in the Fulcrum, this is how people from the Fulcrum train young orogenes, everything Nassun has known of her mother is tainted by this place and has always been—

But the fleeting distraction is enough. Schaffa rips his hand free of the corpse at last and is across the room in another breath, grabbing the blowgun and snatching it away and stabbing it into the woman's throat before she can recover. She falls to her knees, choking, reaching instinctively for the earth, but then something sweeps the room in a wave and Nassun gasps when suddenly she cannot sess a single thing. The woman gasps, too, then wheezes, scrabbling at her throat. Schaffa grabs her head and breaks her neck with a swift jerk.

Lamprophyre is scrambling backward as Umber stalks him, fumbling at his clothing where some kind of small, heavy object has gotten lodged in cloth. "Evil Earth," he blurts, jerking at the buttons of his jacket. "You're contaminated! Both of you!"

He gets no further, though, because Umber blurs and Nassun flinches as something splatters her cheek. Umber has stomped the man's head in.

"Nassun," Schaffa says, releasing the six-ringed woman's body and staring down at it, "go to the terrace and wait for us there."

"Y-yes, Schaffa," Nassun says. She swallows. She's shaking. She makes herself turn despite this, and walk out of the room. There are approximately twenty-two other ringed orogenes around somewhere, after all, Serpentine said.

The Antarctic Fulcrum isn't much bigger than the town of Jekity. Nassun is leaving the big two-story house that serves as the administrative building. There's also a cluster of tiny cottages that apparently the older orogenes live in, and several long barracks near the big glass-walled greenhouse. Lots of people are around, moving in and out of the barracks and cottages. Few of them wear black, even though some of the civilian-dressed ones feel like orogenes. Beyond the greenhouse is a sloping terrace that hosts a number of small garden plots—too many, altogether, to really qualify as gardens. This is a farm. Most of the plots are planted heavily with grains and vegetables, and there are a number of people out working on them, since it's a nice day and no one knows the Guardians are busily killing everyone in the admin building.

Nassun walks the cobbled path above the terrace briskly, with her head down so that she can concentrate on not stumbling, since she can't sess anything after whatever Schaffa did to the six-ringed woman. She's always known that Guardians can shut down orogeny, but never felt it before. It's hard to walk when she can only perceive the ground with her eyes and feet, and also when she's shaking so hard. Carefully she puts one foot in front of the other and suddenly someone else's feet are just *there* and Nassun pulls up short, her whole body going rigid with shock.

"Watch where you're going," the girl says reflexively. She's thin and white, though with a shock of slate-gray ashblow hair, and she's maybe Nassun's age. She stops, though, when she gets a good look at Nassun. "Hey, there's something on your face. It looks like a dead bug or something. Gross." She reaches up and flicks it off with one finger.

Nassun jerks a little in surprise, then remembers her manners. "Thanks. Uh, sorry for getting in your way."

"It's all right." The girl blinks. "They said some Guardians had come and brought a new grit. Are you the new one?"

Nassun stares in confusion. "G-grit?"

The other girl's eyebrows rise. "Yeah. Trainee? Imperial-Orogene-to-be?" She's carrying a bucket of gardening supplies, which doesn't fit the conversation at all. "The Guardians used to bring kids here before the Season started. That's how I got here."

Technically that's how Nassun got here, too. "The Guardians brought me," she echoes. She is hollow inside.

"Me, too." The girl sobers, then looks away. "Did they break your hand yet?"

Nassun's breath stops in her throat.

At her silence, the girl's expression turns bitter. "Yeah. They do it to every grit at some point. Hand bones or fingers." She shakes her head, then takes a quick, gulping breath. "We're not supposed to talk about it. But it's not you, whatever they say. It's not your fault." Another quick breath. "I'll see you around. I'm Ajae. I don't have an orogene name yet. What's your name?"

Nassun can't think. The sound of Schaffa's fist crushing bone echoes in her head. "Nassun."

"Nice to meet you, Nassun." Ajae nods politely, then moves on, walking down the steps toward a terrace. She hums, swinging her bucket. Nassun stares after her, trying to understand.

Orogene name?

Trying not to understand.

Did they break your hand yet?

This place. This...Fulcrum. Is why her mother broke her hand.

Nassun's hand twitches in phantom pain. She sees again the rock in her mother's hand, rising. Holding a moment. Falling.

Are you sure you can control yourself?

The Fulcrum is why her mother never loved her.

Is why her father does not love her anymore.

Is why her brother is dead.

Nassun watches Ajae wave to a thin older boy, who is busy hoeing. This place. These people, who have no right to exist.

The sapphire isn't far off—hovering over Jekity, where it has been for the two weeks since she and Schaffa and Umber left to travel to the Antarctic Fulcrum. She can sess it in the distance, though it's too far off to see. It seems to flicker as she reaches for it, and for an instant she marvels that she *knows* this somehow. Instinctively she has turned to face it. Line of sight. She doesn't need eyes, or orogeny, to use it.

(This is an orogene's nature, the old Schaffa might have told her, if he still existed. Nassun's kind innately react to all threats the same way: with utterly devastating counterforce. He would have told her this, before breaking her hand to drive home the lesson of control.)

There are so many silver threads in this place. The orogenes are all connected through practice together, shared experience.

DID THEY BREAK YOUR HAND

It is over in the span of three breaths. Then Nassun lets herself fall out of the watery blue, and stands there shaking in its wake. Some while later, Nassun turns and sees Schaffa standing in front of her, with Umber.

"They weren't supposed to be here," she blurts. "You *said*."

Schaffa isn't smiling, and he is still in a way that Nassun knows well. "Did you do this to help us, then?"

Nassun can't think enough to lie. She shakes her head. "This place was wrong," she said. "The Fulcrum is wrong."

"Is it?" It is a test, but Nassun has no idea how to pass it. "Why do you say that?"

"Mama was wrong. The Fulcrum made her that way. She should have been a, a, an, an ally to you," *like me*, she thinks, reminds. "This place made her something else." She cannot articulate it. "This place made her *wrong*."

Schaffa looks at Umber. Umber tilts his head, and for an instant there is a flicker in the silver, a flicker between them. The things lodged in their sessapinae resonate in a strange way. But then Schaffa frowns, and she sees him push back against the silver. It hurts him to do this, but he does it anyway, turning to gaze at her with eyes bright and jaw tight and fresh sweat dotting his brow.

"I think you may be right, little one," is all he says. "It follows:

Put people in a cage and they will devote themselves to escaping it, not cooperating with those who caged them. What happened here was inevitable, I suppose." He glances at Umber. "Still. Their Guardians must have been very lax, to let a group of orogenes get the drop on them. That one with the blowgun... born feral, most likely, and taught things she shouldn't have been before being brought here. She was the impetus."

"Lax Guardians," says Umber, watching Schaffa. "Yes."

Schaffa smiles at him. Nassun frowns in confusion. "We've destroyed the threat," Schaffa says.

"Most of it," Umber agrees.

Schaffa acknowledges this with an incline of his head and a faintly ironic air before turning to Nassun. He says, "You were right to do what you did, little one. Thank you for helping us."

Umber is gazing steadily at Schaffa. At the back of Schaffa's neck, specifically. Schaffa suddenly turns to glare back at him, smile gone fixed and body deadly still. After a moment, Umber looks away. Nassun understands then. The silver has gone quiet in Umber, or as quiet as it ever gets in any of the Guardians, but the glimmering lines within Schaffa are still alive, active, tearing at him. He fights them, though, and is prepared to fight Umber, too, if necessary.

For her? Nassun wonders, exults. For her.

Then Schaffa crouches and cups her face in his hands. "Are you well?" he asks. His eyes flick toward the sky to the east. The sapphire.

"Fine," Nassun says, because she is. Connecting with the obelisk was much easier this time, partly because it was not a surprise, and partly because she is growing used to the sudden advent of strangeness in her life. The trick is to let yourself fall into it, and fall at the same speed, and think like a big column of light.

"Fascinating," he says, and then gets to his feet. "Let's go."

So they leave the Antarctic Fulcrum behind, with new crops greening in its fields and cooling corpses in its administrative building and a collection of shining, multi-colored human statues scattered about its gardens and barracks and walls.

* * *

But in the days that follow, as they walk the road and forest trails between the Fulcrum and Jekity, sleeping each night in strangers' barns or around their own fires... Nassun thinks.

She has nothing to do but think, after all. Umber and Schaffa do not speak to one another, and there is a new tension between them. She understands it enough to take care never to be alone in Umber's presence, which is easy because Schaffa takes care never to let her be. This is not strictly necessary; Nassun thinks that what she did to Eitz and the people in the Antarctic Fulcrum, she can probably do to Umber. Using an obelisk is not sessing, the silver is not orogeny, and thus not even a Guardian is safe from what she can do. She sort of likes that Schaffa goes with her to the bathhouse, though, and forgoes sleep—Guardians can do that, apparently—to keep watch over her at night. It feels nice to have someone, anyone, protecting her again.

But. She thinks.

It troubles Nassun that Schaffa has damaged himself in the eyes of his fellow Guardians by choosing not to kill her. It troubles her more that he suffers, gritting his teeth and pretending that this is another smile, even as she sees the silver flex and burn within him. It never stops doing so now, and he will not let her ease his pain because this makes her slow and tired the next day. She watches him endure it, and hates the little thing in his head that hurts him so. It gives him power, but what good is power if it comes on a spiked leash?

"Why?" she asks him one night as they camp on a flat, elevated white slab of something that is neither metal nor stone and which is all that remains of some deadciv ruin. There have been some signs of raiders or commless in the area, and the tiny comm they stayed at the night before warned them to be wary, so the elevation of the slab will at least afford them plenty of advance warning of an attack. Umber is gone, off setting snares for their breakfast. Schaffa has used the opportunity to lie down on his bedroll while Nassun keeps watch, and she does not want to keep him awake. But she needs to know. "Why is that thing in your head?"

"It was put there when I was very young," he says. He sounds weary. Fighting the silver for days on end without sleep is taking its toll. "There was no 'why' for me; it was simply the way things had to be."

"But..." Nassun does not want to be annoying by asking why again. "*Did* it have to be? What is it for?"

He smiles, though his eyes are shut. "We are made to keep the world safe from the dangers of your kind."

"I know that, but..." She shakes her head. "*Who* made you?"

"Me, specifically?" Schaffa opens one eye, then frowns a little. "I... don't remember. But in general, Guardians are made by other Guardians. We are found, or bred, and given over to Warrant for training and... alteration."

"And who made the Guardian before you, and the one before that? Who did it *first?*"

He is silent for a time: trying to remember, she guesses from his expression. That something is very wrong with Schaffa, chiseling holes in his memories and putting fault-line-heavy pressure on his thoughts, is something Nassun simply accepts. He is what he is. But she needs to know why he is the way he is...and more importantly, she wants to know how to make him better.

"I don't know," he says finally, and she knows he is done with the conversation by the way he exhales and shuts his eyes again. "In the end, the why does not matter, little one. Why are you an orogene? Sometimes we must simply accept our lot in life."

Nassun decides to shut up then, and a few moments later Schaffa's body relaxes into sleep for the first time in days. She keeps watch diligently, extending her newly recovered sense of the earth to catch the reverberations of small animals and other moving things in the immediate vicinity. She can sess Umber, too, still moving methodically at the edge of her range as he sets up his snares, and because of him she weaves a thread of the silver into her web of awareness. He can evade her sessing, but not that. It will catch any commless, too, should they sneak into arrow or harpoon range. She will not let Schaffa be injured as her father was injured.

Aside from something heavy and warm that treads along on all fours not far from Umber, probably foraging, there is nothing of concern nearby. Nothing—

—except. Something very strange. Something...immense? No, its boundaries are small, no bigger than those of a mid-sized rock, or a person. But it is directly underneath the white not-stone slab. Under her feet, practically, barely more than ten feet down.

As if noticing her attention, it moves. This feels like the movement of the world. Involuntarily Nassun gasps and leans away, even though nothing changes but the gravity around her, and that only a little. The immensity whips away suddenly, as if it senses her scrutiny. It doesn't go far, however, and a moment later, the immensity moves again: up. Nassun blinks and opens her eyes to see a statue standing at the edge of the slab, which was not there before.

Nassun is not confused. Once, after all, she wanted to be a lorist; she has spent hours listening to tales of stone eaters and the mysteries that surround their existence. This one does not look as she thought it would. In the lorist tales, stone eaters have marble skin and jewel hair. This one is entirely gray, even to the "whites" of his eyes. He is bare-chested and muscular, and he is smiling, lips drawn back from teeth that are clear and sharp-faceted.

"You're the one who stoned the Fulcrum, a few days ago," says his chest.

Nassun swallows and glances at Schaffa. He's a heavy sleeper, and the stone eater didn't speak loudly. If she yells, Schaffa will probably wake—but what can a Guardian do against such a creature? She isn't even sure she can do anything with the silver; the stone eater is a blazing morass of it, swirls and whirls of thread all tangled up inside him.

The lore, however, is clear on one thing about stone eaters:

They do not attack without provocation. So: "Y-yes," she says, keeping her voice low. "Is that a problem?"

"Not at all. I wanted only to express my admiration for your work." His mouth does not move. Why is he smiling so much? Nassun is more certain with every passing breath that the expression is not *just* a smile. "What is your name, little one?"

She bristles at the *little one*. "Why?"

The stone eater steps forward, moving slowly. This sounds like the grind of a millstone, and looks as wrong as a moving statue should look. Nassun flinches in revulsion, and he stills. "Why did you stone them?"

"They were wrong."

The stone eater steps forward again, onto the slab. Nassun half expects the slab to crack or tilt beneath the creature's terrible weight, which she knows is immense. He is a mountain, compacted into the size and shape of a human being. The slab of deadciv material does not crack, however, and now the creature is close enough for her to see the fine detailing of his individual hair strands.

"*You* were wrong," he says, in his strange echoing voice. "The people of the Fulcrum, and the Guardians, are not to blame for the things they do. You wanted to know why your Guardian must suffer as he does. The answer is: He doesn't have to."

Nassun stiffens. Before she can demand to know more, the stone eater's head turns toward him. There is a flicker of… something. An adjustment too infinitely fine to see or sess, and…and suddenly, the alive, vicious throb of silver within Schaffa dies into silence. Only that dark, needle-like blot in his sessapinae remains active, and immediately Nassun sesses its effort to re-assert control. For the moment, though, Schaffa exhales softly and relaxes further into sleep. The pain that has been grinding at him for days is gone, for now.

Nassun gasps—softly. If Schaffa has the chance to truly rest at last, she will not destroy it. Instead she says to the stone eater, "How did you do that?"

"I can teach you. I can teach you how to fight his tormentor, his *master*, too. If you wish."

Nassun swallows hard. "Y-yeah. I wish." She isn't stupid, though. "In exchange for what?"

"Nothing. If you fight his master, then you fight my enemy, too. It will make us... allies."

She knows now that the stone eater has been lurking nearby, listening in on her, but she doesn't care anymore. To save Schaffa... She licks her lips, which taste faintly of sulfur. The ash haze has been getting thicker in recent weeks. "Okay," she says.

"What is your name?" If it's been listening, it knows who she is. This is a gesture toward alliance.

"Nassun. And you?"

"I have no name, or many. Call me what you wish."

He needs a name. Alliances don't work without names, do they? "S-Steel." It's the first thing that pops into her mind. Because he's so gray. "Steel?"

The sense that he does not care lingers. "I will come to you later," Steel says. "When we can speak uninterrupted."

An instant later he is gone, into the earth, and the mountain vanishes from her awareness in seconds. A moment later,

Umber emerges from the forest around the deadciv slab and begins walking up the hill toward her. She's actually glad to see him, even though his gaze sharpens as he draws nearer and sees that Schaffa is asleep. He stops three paces away, more than close enough for a Guardian's speed.

"I'll kill you if you try anything," Nassun says, nodding solemnly. "You know that, right? Or if you wake him up."

Umber smiles. "I know you'll try."

"I'll try and I'll actually do it."

He sighs, and there is great compassion in his voice. "You don't even know how dangerous you are. To far, far more than me."

She doesn't, and that bothers her a lot. Umber does not act out of cruelty. If he sees her as a threat, there must be some reason for it. But it doesn't matter.

"Schaffa wants me alive," she says. "So I live. Even if I have to kill you."

Umber appears to consider this. She glimpses the quick flicker of the silver within him and knows, suddenly and instinctively, that she's no longer talking to Umber, exactly.

His master.

Umber says, "And if Schaffa decides you should die?"

"Then I die." That's what the Fulcrum got wrong, she feels certain. They treated the Guardians as enemies, and maybe they once were, like Schaffa said. But allies must trust in one another, be vulnerable to one another. Schaffa is the only person in the world who loves Nassun, and Nassun will die, or kill, or remake the world, for his sake.

Slowly, Umber inclines his head. "Then I will trust in your

love for him," he says. For an instant there is an echo in his voice, in his body, through the ground, reverberating away, so deep. "For now." With that, he moves past her and sits down near Schaffa, assuming a guard stance himself.

Nassun does not understand Guardian reasoning, but she's learned one thing about them over the months: They do not bother to lie. If Umber says he will trust Schaffa—no. Trust *Nassun's love for Schaffa*, because there is a difference. But if Umber says this has meaning to him, then she can rely on that.

So she lies down on her own bedroll and relaxes in spite of everything. She doesn't sleep for some while, though. Nerves, maybe.

Night falls. The evening is clear, apart from the faint haze of ash blowing from the north, and a few broken, pearled clouds that periodically drift southward along the breeze. The stars come out, winking through the haze, and Nassun stares at them for a long while. She's begun to drift, her mind finally relaxing toward sleep, when belatedly she notices that one of the tiny white lights up there is moving in a different direction from the rest—downward, sort of, while the other stars march west to east across the sky. Slow. Hard to unsee it now that she's made it out. It's a little bigger and brighter than the rest, too. Strange.

Nassun rolls over to turn her back to Umber, and sleeps.

* * *

These things have been down here for an age of the world. Foolish to call them bones. They go to powder when we touch them.

But stranger than the bones are the murals. Plants I've never seen, something that might be a language but it just looks like shapes and wiggling. And one: a great round white thing amid the stars, hanging over a landscape. Eerie. I didn't like it. I had the blackjacket crumble the mural away.

—*Journal of Journeywoman Fogrid Innovator Yumenes. Archives of the Geneer Licensure, Equatorial East*

16

you meet an old friend, again

I WANT TO KEEP TELLING THIS as I have: in your mind, in your voice, telling you what to think and know. Do you find this rude? It is, I admit. Selfish. When I speak as just myself, it's difficult to feel like part of you. It is lonelier. Please; let me continue a bit longer.

* * *

You stare at the stone eater that has burst forth from the chalcedony chrysalis. It stands hunched and perfectly still, watching you sidelong through the slight heat-waver of the air around the split geode. Its hair is as you remember from that half-real, half-dream moment within the garnet obelisk: a frozen splash, what happens to ashblow hair when a hard gust of wind lifts it up and back. Translucent white-ish opal now instead of simply white. But unlike the fleshly form that you grew to know, this stone eater's "skin" is as black as the night sky once was before the Season. What you thought were cracks back then, you now realize are actually white and silver marbling veins. Even the elegant drape of pseudo-clothing wrapped around the body, a simple chiton that hangs off one shoulder, is marbled black. Only the eyes lack the marbling, the whites now matte smooth darkness. The irises are still icewhite. They stand out from the black face, stark and so atavistically disturbing that it actually takes you a moment to realize the face around it is still Hoa's.

Hoa. *He* is older, you see at once; the face is that of a young man and not a boy. Still too wide, with too narrow a mouth, racially nonsensical. You can read anxiety in those frozen features, though, because you learned to read it on a face that was once softer and designed to elicit your compassion.

"Which was the lie?" you ask. It is the only thing you can think to ask.

"The lie?" The voice is a man's now. The same voice, but in the tenor range. Coming from his chest somewhere.

You step into the room. It's still unpleasantly hot, though cooling off quickly. You're sweating anyway. "Your human shape, or this?"

"Both have been true at different times."

"Ah, yes. Alabaster said all of you were human. Once, anyway."

There is a moment of silence. "Are you human?"

At this, you cannot help but laugh once. "Officially? No."

"Never mind what others think. What do you feel yourself to be?"

"Human."

"Then so am I."

He stands steaming between the halves of a giant rock from which he just hatched. "Uh, not anymore."

"Should I take your word for that? Or listen to what I feel myself to be?"

You shake your head, walking as far as you can around the geode. Inside it there is nothing; it's a thin stone shell bare of crystals or the usual precipitant lining. Probably doesn't qualify as a geode, then. "How'd you end up in an obelisk?"

"Pissed off the wrong rogga."

This surprises you into a laugh, which makes you stop and stare at him. It's an uncomfortable laugh. He's watching you the way he always used to, all eyes and hope. Should it really matter that the eyes are so strange now?

"I didn't know that could be done," you say. "Trapping a stone eater, I mean."

"You could do it. It's one of the only ways to stop one of us."

"Not kill you, obviously."

"No. There's only one way to do that."

"Which is?"

He flicks to face you. This seems instantaneous; suddenly the statue's pose is completely different, serene and upright, with one hand raised in . . . invitation? Appeal? "Are you planning to kill me, Essun?"

You sigh and shake your head and extend a hand to touch one of the stone halves, out of curiosity.

"Don't. It's still too hot for your flesh." He pauses. "This is how I get clean, without soap."

A day along the side of the road, south of Tirimo. A boy who stared at a bar of soap in confusion, then delight. It's still him. You can't shake it off. So you sigh and also let go of the part of yourself that wants to treat him as something else, something frightening, something other. He's Hoa. He wants to eat you, and he tried to help you find your daughter even though he failed. There's an intimacy in these facts, however strange they are, that means something to you.

You fold your arms and pace slowly around the geode, and him. His eyes follow. "So who kicked your ass?" He has regenerated the eyes that were missing, and the lower jaw. The limbs that had been torn off are part of him again. There's still blood in the living room, but whatever there had been in your bedroom is now gone, along with a layer of the floor and walls. Stone eaters are said to have control over the very smallest particles of matter. Simple enough to reappropriate one's own detached substance, repurpose unused surplus material. You guess.

"A dozen or so of my kind. Then one in particular."

"That many?"

"They were children to me. How many children would it take to overwhelm you?"

"*You* were a child."

"I looked like a child." His voice softens. "I only did that for you."

There is a greater difference between this Hoa and that Hoa than their states of being. When adult Hoa says things like this, the words have an entirely different texture from when child Hoa said them. You're not certain you like that texture.

"So you've been off getting into fights all this time," you say, adjusting the subject back toward comfort. "There was a stone eater at the Flat Top. A gray—"

"Yes." You didn't think it was possible for a stone eater to look disgruntled, but Hoa does. "That one isn't a child. He was the one who defeated me, finally, though I managed to escape without too much damage." You marvel for a moment that he thinks having all his limbs and jaw torn off is not much damage. But you're a little glad, too. The gray stone eater hurt Hoa, and you hurt him back. Ephemeral revenge, maybe, but it makes you feel like you look out for your own.

Hoa still sounds defensive. "It was also . . . unwise for me to face him while clothed in human flesh."

It's too damned hot in the room. Mopping sweat from your face, you move into the living room, push aside and tie off the main-door curtain so cooler air will circulate in more easily, and sit down at the table. By the time you turn back, Hoa is in the door of your bedroom, framed beautifully by the arch of it: study of a youth in wary contemplation.

"Is that why you changed back? To face him?" You didn't see the bit of rag that contained his rocks while you were in the bedroom. Maybe it caught fire and is just charred cloth amid the rest, purpose served.

"I changed back because it was time." There's that tone of resignation again. He sounded that way when you first realized what he was. Like he knows he's lost something in your eyes, and he can't get it back, and he has no choice but to accept that—but he doesn't have to like it. "I could have kept that shape only for a limited time. I made a choice to decrease the time, and increase the chance you will survive."

"Oh?"

Beyond him, in your room, you suddenly notice that the leftover shell of his, er, egg, is melting. Sort of. It is dissolving and lightening in color and merging back into the clear material of the crystal, parting around the detritus of your belongings as it rejoins its former substance and solidifies again. You stare at that instead of him for a moment, fascinated.

Until he says, “They want you dead, Essun.”

“They—” You blink. “Who?”

“Some of my kind. Some merely want to use you. I won’t let them.”

You frown. “Which? You won’t let them kill me, or you won’t let them use me?”

“*Either.*” The echoing voice grows sharp suddenly. You remember him crouching, baring his teeth like some feral beast. It occurs to you, with the suddenness of an epiphany, that you haven’t seen as many stone eaters around lately. Ruby Hair, Butter Marble, Ugly Dress, Toothshine, all the regulars; not a glimpse in months. Ykka even remarked on the sudden absence of “hers.”

“You ate her,” you blurt.

There is a pause. “I’ve eaten many,” Hoa says. It is inflectionless.

You remember him giggling and calling you weird. Curling against you to sleep. Earthfires, you can’t deal with this.

“Why me, Hoa?” You spread your hands. They are ordinary, middle-aged woman hands. A bit dry. You helped with the leather-tanning crew a few days ago, and the solution made your skin crack and peel. You’ve been rubbing them with some of the nuts you got in the previous week’s comm share, even though fat is precious and you should be eating it rather than using it for your vanity. In your right palm there is a small, white, thumbnail-shaped crescent. On cold days that hand's bones ache. Ordinary woman hands.

"There's nothing special about me," you say. "There must be other orogenes with the potential to access the obelisks. Earthfires, Nassun—" No. "Why are you *here?*" You mean, why has he attached himself to you.

He is silent for a moment. Then: "You asked if I was all right."

This makes no sense for a moment, and then it does. Allia. A beautiful sunny day, a looming disaster. As you hovered in agony amid the cracked, dissonant core of the garnet obelisk, you saw him for the first time. How long had he been in that thing? Long enough for it to be buried beneath Seasons' worth of sediment and coral growth. Long enough to be forgotten, like all the dead civilizations of the world. And then you came along and asked how he was doing. Evil Earth, you thought you hallucinated that.

You take a deep breath and get up, going to the entrance of the apartment. The comm is quiet, as far as you can tell. Some people are going about their usual business, but there are fewer of them around than usual. The ones following routine are no proof of peace; people went about their business in Tirimo, too, right before they tried to kill you.

Tonkee didn't come home again last night, but this time you're not so sure that she's with Hjarka or up in the green room. There is a catalyst alive in Castrima now, accelerating unseen chemical reactions, facilitating unexpected outcomes. *Join us and live*, the gray one had told them, *but not with your roggas.*

Will the people of Castrima stop to think that no Equatorial comm really wants a sudden influx of mongrel Midlatters, and at best will make slaves or meat of them? Your mothering instinct is alive with warning. *Look after your own*, it whispers in the back of your mind. *Gather them close and guard them well. You know what happens when you turn your back for even a minute.*

You shoulder the runny-sack that's still in your hand. Keeping it with you isn't even a question at this point. Then you turn to Hoa. "Come with me."

Hoa's suddenly smiling again. "I don't walk anymore, Essun."

Oh. Right. "I'm going to Ykka's, then. Meet me there."

He does not nod, simply vanishes. No wasted movement. Eh, you'll get used to it.

People don't look at you as you cross the bridges and walkways of the comm. The center of your back itches from their stares as you pass. You cannot help thinking of Tirimo again.

Ykka's not in her apartment. You look around, follow the patterns of movement in the comm with your eyes, and finally head toward the Flat Top. She cannot still be there. You've gone home, watched a child turn into a stone eater, slept several hours. She can't be.

She is. You see that only a few people are still on the Flat Top now—a gaggle of maybe twenty, sitting or pacing, looking angry and exasperated and troubled. For the twenty you see, there are surely another hundred gathering in apartments and the baths and the storage rooms, having the same conversation in hushed tones with small groups. But Ykka is here, sitting on one of the divans that someone has brought from her apartment, still talking. She's hoarse, you realize as you draw close. Visibly exhausted. But still talking. Something about supply lines from one of the southern allied comms, which she's directing at a man who is walking in circles with his arms folded, scoffing at everything she says. It's fear; he's not listening. Ykka's trying to reason with him anyway. It's ridiculous.

Look after your own.

You step around people—some of whom flinch away from you—and stop beside her. "I need to talk to you in private."

Ykka stops midsentence and blinks up at you. Her eyes are red and sticky-dry. She hasn't had any water for a while. "What about?"

"It's important." As a sop to courtesy you nod to the people sitting around her. "Sorry."

She sighs and rubs her eyes, which just makes them redder. "Fine." She gets up, then pauses to face the remaining people. "Vote's tomorrow morning. If I haven't convinced you… well. You know what to do, then."

They watch in silence as you lead her away.

Back in her apartment, you pull the front curtain shut and open the one that leads into her private rooms. Not much to this space to indicate her status: She's got two pallets and a lot of pillows, but her clothes are just in a basket, and the books and scrolls on one side of the room are just stacked on the floor. No bookcases, no dresser. The food from her comm share is stacked haphazardly against one wall, beside a familiar gourd that the Castrimans tend to use for storing drinking water. You snag the gourd with your elbow and pick from the food pile a dried orange, a stick of dry bean curd that Ykka's been soaking with some mushrooms in a shallow pan, and a small slab of salt fish. It's not exactly a meal, but it's nutrition. "On the bed," you say, gesturing with your chin and bringing the food to her. You hand her the gourd first.

Ykka, who has observed all this in increasing irritation, snaps, "You're not my type. Is this why you dragged me here?"

"Not exactly. But while you're here, you need to rest." She looks mutinous. "You can't convince anyone of anything—" Let alone people whose hate can't be reasoned with. "—if you're too exhausted to think straight."

She grumbles, but it is a measure of how tired she is that she actually goes to the bed and sits down on its edge. You nod at the gourd, and she dutifully drinks—three quick swallows and down for now, as the lorists advise after dehydration. "I stink. I need a bath."

"Should've thought of that before you decided to try to talk down a brewing lynch mob." You take the gourd and push the dish of food into her hand. She sighs and starts grimly chewing.

"They're not going to—" She doesn't get far into that lie, though, before she flinches and stares at something beyond you. You know before you turn: Hoa. "Okay, no, not in my rusting room."

"I told him to meet us here," you say. "It's Hoa."

"You told—it's—" Ykka swallows hard, stares a moment longer, then finally resumes eating the orange. She chews slowly, her gaze never leaving Hoa. "Got tired of playing the human, then? Not sure why you bothered; you were too weird to pass."

You go over to the wall near the bedroom door and sit down against it, on the floor. The runny-sack has to come off for this, but you make sure to keep it near to hand. To Ykka you say,

"You've talked to the other members of your council and half your comm, still and rogga and native and newcomer. The perspective you're missing is theirs." You nod at Hoa.

Ykka blinks, then eyes Hoa with new interest. "I *did* ask you to sit on my council once."

"I can't speak for my kind any more than you can for yours," Hoa says. "And I had more important things to do."

You see Ykka blink at his voice and blatantly stare at him. You wave a hand at Hoa wearily. Unlike Ykka, you've slept, but it wasn't exactly quality sleep, while you sat in a sweltering apartment waiting for a geode to hatch. "Speaking what you know will help." And then, prompted by some instinct, you add, "Please."

Because somehow, you think he's reticent. His expression hasn't changed. His posture is the one he showed you last, the young man in repose with one hand upraised; he's changed his location, but not his position. Still.

The proof of his reticence comes when he says, "Very well." It's all in the tone. But fine, you can work with reticent.

"What does the gray stone eater want?" Because you're pretty rusting sure he doesn't really want Castrima to join some Equatorial comm. Human nation-state politics just wouldn't mean much to them, unless it was in service to some other goal. The people of Rennanis are his pawns, not the other way around.

"There are many of us now," Hoa replies. "Enough to be called a people in ourselves and not merely a mistake."

At this apparent non sequitur, you exchange a look with Ykka, who looks back at you as if to say, *He's your mess, not mine.* Maybe it's relevant somehow. "Yes?" you prompt.

"There are those of my kind who believe this world can safely bear only one people."

Oh, Evil Earth. This is what Alabaster talked about. How had he described it? Factions in an ancient war. The ones who wanted people... neutralized.

Like the stone eaters themselves, 'Baster had said.

"You want to wipe us out," you say. Whisper. "Or... change us into stone? Like what's happening to Alabaster?"

"Not all of us," Hoa says softly. "And not all of you."

A world of only stone people. The thought of it makes you shiver. You envision falling ash and skeletal trees and creepy statues everywhere, some of the latter moving. How? They are unstoppable, but until now they've only preyed on each other. (That you know of.) Can they turn all of you into stone, like Alabaster? And if they wanted to wipe humankind out, shouldn't they have been able to manage it before now?

You shake your head. "This world *has* borne two people, for Seasons. Three, if you count orogenes; the stills do."

"Not all of us are content with that." His voice is very soft now. "Such a rare thing, the birth of a new one of our kind. We wear on endlessly, while you rise and spawn and wilt like mushrooms. It's hard not to envy. Or covet."

Ykka is shaking her head in confusion. Though her voice holds its usual unflappable attitude, you see a little frown of wonder between her brows. Her mouth pulls to one side, though, as if she cannot help but show at least a little disgust. "Fine," she says. "So stone eaters used to be us, and now you want to kill us. Why should we trust you?"

"Not 'stone eaters.' Not all of us want the same thing. Some like things as they are. Some even want to make the world better... though not all agree on what that means." Instantly his posture changes—hands out, palms up, shoulders lifted in a *What can you do?* gesture. "We're people."

"And what do *you* want?" you ask. Because he didn't answer Ykka's question, and you noticed.

Those silver irises flick over to you, stay. You think you see wistfulness in his still face. "The same thing I've always wanted, Essun. To help you. Only that."

You think, *Not everyone agrees on what "help" means.*

"Well, this is touching," Ykka says. She rubs her tired eyes. "But you're not getting to the point. What does Castrima being destroyed have to do with... giving the world one people? What's this gray man up to?"

"I don't know." Hoa's still looking at you. It's not as unnerving as it should be. "I tried to ask him. It didn't go well."

"Guess," you say. Because you know full well there's a reason he asked the gray man in the first place.

Hoa's eyes shift down. Your distrust hurts. "He wants to make sure the Obelisk Gate is never opened again."

"The what?" Ykka asks. But you're leaning your head back against the wall, floored and horrified and wondering. Of course. *Alabaster.* What easier way to wipe out people who depend on food and sunlight to survive than to simply let this Season wear on until they are extinct? Leaving nothing but the stone eaters to inherit the darkening Earth. And to make sure it happens, kill the only person with the power to end it.

Only person besides you, you realize with a chill. But no. You can manipulate an obelisk, but you haven't got a clue how to activate two hundred of the rusting things at once. And can Alabaster do it anymore? Every use of orogeny kills him slowly. Flaking rust—*you're* the only one left who even has the potential to open the Gate. But if Gray Man's pet army kills both of you, his purpose is served either way.

"It means Gray Man wants to wipe out orogenes in particular," you say to Ykka. You're abbreviating heavily, not lying. That's what you tell yourself. That's what you need to tell Ykka, so that she never learns that orogenes have the potential power to save the world, and so that she never attempts to access an obelisk herself. This is what Alabaster must have constantly had to do with you—telling you some of the truth because you deserve it, but not enough that you'll skewer yourself on it. Then you think of another bone you can throw. "Hoa was trapped in an obelisk for a while. He said it's the only thing that can stop them."

Not the only way, he'd said. But maybe Hoa's giving you only the safe truths, too.

"Well, shit," Ykka says, annoyed. "You can do obelisk stuff. Throw one at him."

You groan. "That wouldn't work."

"What would, then?"

"I have no idea! That's what I've been trying to learn from Alabaster all this time." And failing, you don't want to say. Ykka can guess it, anyway.

"Great." Ykka abruptly seems to wilt. "You're right; I need to sleep. I had Esni mobilize the Strongbacks to secure weapons in the comm. Ostensibly they're making them ready for use if we have to fight off these Equatorials. In truth..." She shrugs, sighs, and you understand. People are frightened right now. Best not to tempt fate.

"You can't trust the Strongbacks," you say softly.

Ykka looks up at you. "Castrima isn't wherever you came from."

You want to smile, though you don't because you know how ugly the smile will be. You're from so many places. In every one of them you learned that roggas and stills can never live together. Ykka shifts a little at the look on your face anyway. She tries again: "Look, how many other comms would've let me live after learning what I was?"

You shake your head. "You were useful. That worked for the Imperial Orogenes, too." But being useful to others is not the same thing as being equal.

"Fine, then I'm useful. We all are. Kill or exile the roggas and we lose Castrima-under. Then we're at the mercy of a bunch of people who would as soon treat *all of us* like roggas, just because our ancestors couldn't pick a race and stick to it—"

"You keep saying 'we,'" you say. It is gentle. It bothers you to puncture her illusions.

She stops, and a muscle in her jaw flexes once or twice. "Stills *learned* to hate us. They can learn differently."

"Now? With an enemy literally at the gate?" You're so tired. So tired of all this shit. "Now is when we'll see the worst of them."

Ykka watches you for a long moment. Then she slumps—completely, her back bowing and her head hanging and her ash-blow hair sliding off to the sides of her neck until it looks utterly ridiculous, a butterfly mane. It hides her face. But she draws in a long, weary breath, and it sounds almost like a sob. Or a laugh.

"No, Essun." She rubs her face. "Just...no. Castrima is my home, same as theirs. I've worked for it. Fought for it. Castrima wouldn't be here if not for me—and probably some of the other roggas who risked themselves to keep it all going, over the years. I'm not giving up."

"It isn't giving up to look out for yourself—"

"*Yes. It is.*" She lifts her head. It wasn't a sob or a laugh. She's furious. Just not at you. "You're saying these people—my parents, my creche teachers, my friends, my lovers—You're saying just leave them to their fate. You're saying they're nothing. That they're not people at all, just beasts whose nature it is to kill. You're saying roggas are nothing but, but *prey* and that's all we'll ever be! No! I won't accept that."

She sounds so determined. It makes your heart ache, because you felt the same way she did, once. It would be nice to still feel that way. To have some hope of a real future, a real community, a real life...but you have lost three children relying on stills' better nature.

You grab the runny-sack and get up to leave, rubbing a hand over your locs. Hoa vanishes, reading your cue that the conversation is over. Later, then. When you're almost at the curtain, though, Ykka stops you with what she says.

"Pass the word around," she tells you. The emotion is gone from her voice. "No matter what happens, *we* can't start anything." Loaded into that delicate emphasis is an acknowledgment that orogenes are the *we* she means, this time. "We shouldn't even finish it. Fighting back could set off a mob. Only talk to the others in small groups. Person to person's best, if you can, so no one *thinks* we're getting together to conspire. Make sure the children know all this. Make sure none of them are ever alone."

Most of the orogene children do know how to defend themselves. The techniques you taught them work just as well for deterring or stopping attackers as for icing boilbug nests. But Ykka's right: There are too few of you to fight back—not without destroying Castrima, a pyrrhic victory. It means that some orogenes are going to die. You're going to *let* them die, even if you could save them. And you did not think Ykka cold enough to think this way.

Your surprise must show on your face. Ykka smiles. "I have hope," she says, "but I'm not stupid. If you're right, and things get hopeless, then we don't go without a fight. We make them regret turning on us. But up to that point of no return . . . I hope you're not right."

You know you're right. The belief that orogenes will never be anything but the world's meat dances amid the cells of you, like magic. It isn't fair. You just want your life to matter.

But you say: "I hope I'm not right, too."

* * *

The dead have no wishes.

—*Tablet Three, "Structures," verse six*

17

Nassun, versus

It has been so long since Nassun was proud of herself that when she becomes capable of healing Schaffa, she runs all the way through town and up to Found Moon to tell him.

"Healing" is how she thinks of it. She has spent the past few days out in the forest, practicing her new skill. It is not always easy to detect the wrongness in a body; sometimes she must carefully follow the threads of silver within a thing to find its knots and warps. The ashfalls have grown more frequent and sustained lately, and most of the forest is patchy with grayness, some plants beginning to wilt or go dormant in response. This is normal for them, and the silver threads prove this by their uninterrupted flow. Yet when Nassun goes slowly, looks carefully, she can usually find things for which change is not normal or healthy. The grub beneath a rock that has a strange growth along its side. The snake—venomous and more vicious now that a Season has begun, so she only examines it from a distance—with a broken vertebra. The melon vine whose leaves are growing in a convex shape, catching too much ash, instead of concavity, which would shake the ash off. The few ants in a nest who have been infected by a parasitic fungus.

She practices extraction of the wrongness on these things, and many others. It's a difficult trick to master—like performing surgery using only thread, without ever touching the patient. She learns how to make the edge of one thread grow very sharp, and how to loop and lasso with another, and how to truncate a third thread and use the burning tip of it to cauterize. She gets the growth off the grub, but it dies. She stitches together the edges of broken bone within the snake, though this only speeds what was already happening naturally. She finds the parts of the plant that are saying *curve up* and convinces them to say *curve down*. The ants are best. She cannot get all or even most of the fungus out of them, but she can sear the connections in their brains that make them behave strangely and spread the infection. She's very, very glad to have brains to work on.

The culmination of Nassun's practice occurs when commless raiders strike again, one morning as dew still dampens the ash and ground litter. The band that Schaffa devastated is gone; these are new miscreants who don't know the danger. Nassun is not distracted by her father anymore, not helpless anymore, and after she ices one of the raiders, most of the others flee. But she detects a snarl of threads in one of them at the last instant, and then must resort to old-style orogeny (as she has come to think of it) in order to drop the ground beneath the raider and trap her in a pit.

The raider throws a knife at Nassun when she peeks over the edge; it's only luck that it misses. But carefully, while staying out of sight, Nassun follows the threads and finds a three-inch wooden splinter lodged in the woman's hand, so deep that it scrapes bone. It is poisoning her blood and will kill her; already the infection is so advanced that it has swollen her hand to twice its size. A comm doctor, or even a decent farrier, could extract the thing, but the commless do not have the luxury of skilled care. They live on luck, what little there is in a Season.

Nassun decides to become the woman's luck. She settles nearby so that she can concentrate, and then carefully—while the woman gasps and swears and cries *What is happening?*—she pulls the splinter free. When she looks into the pit again, the woman is on her knees and groaning as she holds her dripping hand. Belatedly Nassun realizes she will need to learn how to anesthetize, so she settles against the tree again and casts her thread to try to catch a nerve this time. It takes her some time to learn how to numb it, and not just cause more pain.

But she learns, and when she is done she feels grateful to the raider woman, who lies groaning and in a stupor in the pit. Nassun knows better than to let the woman go; if she lives, she will only either die slowly and cruelly, or return and perhaps next time threaten someone Nassun loves. So Nassun casts her threads one last time, and this time slices neatly through the top of her spine. It is painless, and kinder than the fate the woman intended for Nassun.

Now she runs up the hill toward Found Moon, elated for the first time since she killed Eitz, so eager to see Schaffa that she barely notices the other children of the compound as they stop whatever they're doing and favor her with cool stares. Schaffa has explained to them that what she did to Eitz was an accident, and he has assured her they will eventually come around. She hopes he is right because she misses their friendship. But none of that is important now.

"Schaffa!" She first pokes her head into the Guardians' cabin. Only Nida is there, standing in the corner as she so often does, staring into the middle distance as if lost in thought. She focuses as soon as Nassun comes in, however, and smiles in her empty way.

"Hello, Schaffa's little one," she says. "You seem cheerful today."

"Hello, Guardian." She is always polite to Nida and Umber. Just because they want to kill her is no reason to forget her manners. "Do you know where Schaffa is?"

"He is in the crucible with Wudeh."

"Okay, thanks!" Nassun hurries off, undeterred. She knows that Wudeh, as the next most skilled with Eitz gone, is the only other child in Found Moon who has some hope of connecting to an obelisk. Nassun thinks it is hopeless because no one can train him in the way he needs to be trained, given that he is so small and frail. Wudeh would never have survived Mama's crucibles.

Still, she is polite to him, too, running up to the edge of the outermost practice circle and bouncing only a little, keeping her orogeny still so as not to distract him while he raises a big basalt column from the ground and then tries to push it back in. He's already breathing hard, though the column isn't moving very fast. Schaffa is watching him intently, his smile not as big as usual. Schaffa sees it, too.

Finally Wudeh gets the column back into the ground. Schaffa takes his shoulder and helps him over to a bench, which is plainly necessary because Wudeh can barely walk at this point. Schaffa glances at Nassun, and Nassun nods at once and turns to run back into the mess hall to fetch a glass from the pitcher of fruit-water there. When she brings it to Wudeh, he blinks at her once, then looks ashamed of hesitating, and finally takes it with a shy nod of thanks. Schaffa is always right.

"Do you need help back to the dormitory?" Schaffa asks him.

"I can make it back myself, sir," Wudeh says. His eyes dart to Nassun, by which Nassun understands that Wudeh probably would like help back, but knows better than to get in between Schaffa and his favorite student.

Nassun looks at Schaffa. She's excited, but she can wait. He lifts an eyebrow, then inclines his head and extends a hand to help Wudeh up.

Once Wudeh is safely abed, Schaffa comes back over to where Nassun now sits on the bench. She's calmer for the delay, which is good, because she knows she's going to need to seem calm and cool and professional in order to convince him to let some half-grown, half-trained girl experiment on him with magic.

Schaffa sits down beside her, looking amused. "All right, then."

She takes a deep breath before beginning. "I know how to take the thing out of you."

They both know exactly what she's talking about. She has sat beside Schaffa, quietly offering herself, as he has huddled on this very bench clutching his head and whispering replies to a voice she cannot hear and shuddering as it punishes him with lashes of silver pain. Even now it is a low, angry throb inside him, pushing him to obey. To kill her. She makes herself available because her presence eases the pain for him, and because she does not believe he will actually kill her. This is folly, she knows. Love is no inoculation against murder. But she needs to believe it of him.

Schaffa frowns at her, and it is part of why she loves him that he shows no sign of disbelief. "Yes. I have sensed you growing... sharper lately, by increments. This happened to the orogenes at the Fulcrum, too, when they were allowed to progress to this point. They become their own teachers. The power guides them along particular paths, by lines of natural aptitude." His brow furrows slightly. "Generally we steered them away from *this* path, though."

"Why?"

"Because it's dangerous. To everyone, not just the orogene in question." He leans against her, shoulder warm and supportive. "You've survived the point that kills most: connecting with an obelisk. I... remember how others died, making the attempt." For a moment he looks troubled, lost, confused, as he probes gingerly at the raw edges of his torn memories. "I remember something of it. I'm glad..." He winces again, looks troubled again. This time it isn't the silver that's hurting him. Nassun guesses he's either remembered something he dislikes, or can't remember something he thinks he should.

She won't be able to take the pain of loss away from him, no matter how good she gets. It's sobering. She can remove the rest of his pain, though, and that's the part that matters. She touches his hand, her fingers covering the thin scars that she has seen him inflict with his own nails when the pain grows too great even for his smiles to ease. There are more of them today than there were a few days ago, some still raw. "I didn't die," she reminds him.

He blinks, and this alone is enough to snap him back into the here and now of himself. "No. You didn't. But Nassun." He adjusts their hands; now he is holding hers. His hand is huge and she can't even see a glimpse of her own within it. She has always liked this, being enveloped so completely by him. "My compassionate one. I do not *want* my corestone removed."

Corestone. Now she knows the name of her nemesis. The word makes no sense because it is metal, not stone, and it is not at the core of him, just in his head, but that doesn't matter. She clenches her jaw against hate. "It hurts you."

"As it should. I have betrayed it." His jaw tightens briefly. "But I accepted the consequences of doing so, Nassun. I can bear them."

This makes no sense. "It *hurts* you. I could stop the hurt. I can even make it stop hurting without taking it out, but only for a little while. I'd have to stay with you." She learned this from that conversation with Steel, and watching what the stone eater did. Stone eaters are full of magic, so much more than people, but Nassun can approximate. "But if I take it out—"

"If you take it out," Schaffa says, "I will no longer be a Guardian. Do you know what that means, Nassun?"

It means that then Schaffa can be her father. He is in every way that matters already. Nassun does not think this in so many words because there are things she is not yet prepared to confront about herself or her life. (This will change very soon.) But it is in her mind.

"It means that I will lose much of my strength and health," he says in reply to her silent wishing. "I will no longer be able to *protect* you, my little one." His eyes flick toward the Guardians' cabin, and she understands then. Umber and Nida will kill her.

They will try, she thinks.

His head tilts; of course he is instantly aware of her defiant intent. "You couldn't defeat them both, Nassun. Even you aren't that powerful. They have tricks you haven't yet seen. Skills that..." He looks troubled again. "I don't want to remember what they're capable of doing to you."

Nassun tries not to let her bottom lip poke out. Her mother always said that was pouting, and that pouting and whining were things only babies did. "You shouldn't say no because of *me*." She could take care of herself.

"I'm not. I mention that only in hopes that the urge for self-preservation will help convince you. But for my own part, I do not want to grow weak and ill and *die*, Nassun, which is what would happen if you took the stone. I am older than you realize—" The blurry look returns for a moment. By this she knows he does not remember how old. "Older than *I* realize. Without the corestone to stop it, that time will catch up with me. A handful of months and I'll be an old man, trading the pain of the stone for the pains of old age. And then I'll die."

"You don't know that." She is shaking a little. Her throat hurts.

"I do. I've seen it happen, little one. And it is a cruelty, not a kindness, when it does." Schaffa's eyes have narrowed, as if he must strain to see the memory. Then he focuses on her. "My Nassun. Have I hurt you so?"

Nassun bursts into tears. She's not really sure why, except… except maybe because she's been *wanting* this, working toward it, so much. She's wanted to do something good with orogeny, when she has used it to do so many terrible things already—and she wanted to do it for him. He is the only person in the world who understands her, loves her for what she is, protects her despite what she is.

Schaffa sighs and pulls Nassun into his lap, where she wraps herself around him and blubbers into his shoulder for a long while, heedless of the fact that they are out in the open.

When the weeping has spent itself, though, she realizes that he is holding her just as tightly. The silver is alive and searing within him because she's so close. His fingertips are on the back of her neck, and it would be so easy for him to push in, destroy her sessapinae, kill her with a single thrust. He hasn't. He's been fighting the urge, all this while. He would rather suffer this, risk this, than let her help him, and that is the worst thing in all the world.

She sets her jaw, and clenches her hands on the back of his shirt. Dance along the silver, flow with it. The sapphire is nearby. If she can make both flow together, it will be quick. A precise, surgical yank.

Schaffa tenses. "Nassun." The blaze of silver within him suddenly goes still and dims slightly. It is as if the corestone is aware of the threat she poses.

It is for his own good.

But.

She swallows. If she hurts him because she loves him, is that still hurt? If she hurts him a lot now so that he will hurt less later, does that make her a terrible person?

"Nassun, please."

Is that not how love should work?

But this thought makes her remember her mother, and a chilly afternoon with clouds obscuring the sun and a brisk wind making her shake as Mama's fingers covered hers and held her hand down on a flat rock. *If you can control yourself through pain, I'll know you're safe.*

She lets go of Schaffa and sits back, chilled by who she has almost become.

He sits still for a moment longer, perhaps in relief or regret. Then he says quietly, "You've been gone all day. Have you eaten?"

Nassun is hungry, but she doesn't want to admit it. All of a sudden, she feels the need of distance between them. Something that will help her love him less, so that the urge to help him against his will does not ache so within her.

She says, looking at her hands, "I... I want to go see Daddy."

Schaffa is silent a moment longer. He disapproves. She doesn't need to see or sess to know this. By now, Nassun has heard of what else transpired on the day that she killed Eitz. No one heard what Schaffa said to Jija, but many people saw him knock Jija down, crouch over him, and grin into his face while Jija stared back with wide, frightened eyes. She can guess why it happened. For the first time, however, Nassun tries not to care about Schaffa's feelings.

"Shall I come with you?" he asks.

"No." She knows how to handle her father, and she knows that Schaffa has no patience for him. "I'll be back right after."

"See that you are, Nassun." It sounds kindly. It's a warning.

But she knows how to handle Schaffa, too. "Yes, Schaffa." She looks up at him. "Don't be afraid. I'm strong. Like you made me."

"As you made yourself." His gaze is soft and terrible. Icewhite eyes can't be anything but, though there's love layered over the terrible. Nassun is used to the combination by now.

So Nassun climbs out of his lap. She's tired, even though she hasn't done anything. Emotion always makes her tired. But she heads down the hill into Jekity, nodding to people she knows whether they nod back or not, noticing the new granary the village is building since they've had time to increase their stores while the ashfalls and sky occlusions are still intermittent. It's an ordinary, quiet day in this ordinary, quiet comm, and in some ways it feels much like Tirimo. If not for Found Moon and Schaffa, Nassun would hate it here the same way. She may never understand why, if Mama had the whole of the world open to her after somehow escaping her Fulcrum, she chose to live in such a placid, backwater place.

Thus it is with her mother on her mind that Nassun knocks on the door of her father's house. (She has a room here, but it isn't her house. This is why she knocks.)

Jija opens the door almost immediately, as if he was about to leave and go somewhere, or as if he has been waiting for her. The scent of something redolent with garlic wafts out of the house, from the little hearth near the back. Nassun thinks maybe it is fish-in-a-pot, since the Jekity comm shares have a lot of fish and vegetables in them. It's the first time Jija has seen her in a month, and his eyes widen for a moment.

"Hi, Daddy," she says. It's awkward.

Jija bends and before Nassun quite knows what's happening, he's picked her up and swept her into an embrace.

Jekity feels like Tirimo, but in a good way now. Like back when Mama was around but Daddy was the one who loved her most and the stuff on the stove would be duck-in-a-pot instead of fish. If this were then, Mama would be yelling at the neighbors' kirkhusa pup for stealing cabbages from their housegreen; Old Lady Tukke never did tie the creature up the way she should. The air would smell like it does now, rich cooking food mingled with the more acrid scents of freshly chipped rock and the chemicals Daddy uses to soften and smooth his knappings. Uche would be running around in the background, making *whoosh* sounds and yelling that he was falling as he tried to jump up in the air—

Nassun stiffens in Jija's embrace as she suddenly realizes: Uche. Jumping up. *Falling* up, or pretending to.

Uche, whom Daddy beat to death.

Jija feels her tense and tenses as well. Slowly he lets go of her, easing her to the ground as the joy in his expression fades to unease. "Nassun," he says. His gaze searches her face. "Are you all right?"

"I'm okay, Daddy." She misses his arms around her. She can't help that. But the epiphany about Uche has reminded her to be careful. "I just wanted to see you."

Some of the unease in Jija fades a little. He hesitates, seems to fumble for something to say, then finally stands aside. "Come in. Are you hungry? There's enough for you, too."

So she heads inside and they sit down to eat and he fusses over how long her hair has gotten and how nice the cornrows and puffs look. Did she do them herself? And is she a little taller?

She might be, she acknowledges with a blush, even though she knows for certain that she is a whole inch taller than the last time Jija measured her; Schaffa checked one day because he thought he might need to requisition some new clothes with Found Moon's next comm share. She's such a big girl now, Jija says, and there is such real pride in his voice that it disarms her defenses. Almost eleven and so beautiful, so strong. So much like—he falters. Nassun looks down at her plate because he's almost said, *so much like your mother.*

Is this not how love should work?

"It's okay, Daddy," Nassun makes herself say. It is a terrible thing that Nassun is beautiful and strong like her mother, but love always comes bound in terrible things. "I miss her, too." Because she does, in spite of everything.

Jija stiffens slightly, and a muscle along the curve of his jaw flexes a little. "I don't miss her, sweetening."

This is so obviously a lie that Nassun stares and forgets to pretend to agree with him. Forgets lots of things, apparently, including common sense, because she blurts, "But you do. You miss Uche, too. I can tell."

Jija goes rigid, and he stares at her in something that falls between shock that she would say this out loud and horror at *what* she has said. And then, as Nassun has come to understand is normal for her father, the shock of the unexpected abruptly transforms into anger.

"Is that what they're teaching you up in that…*place?*" he asks suddenly. "To disrespect your father?"

Suddenly Nassun is more tired. So very tired of trying to dance around his senselessness.

"I wasn't disrespecting you," she says. She tries to keep her voice even, inflectionless, but she can hear the frustration there. She can't help it. "I was just saying the truth, Daddy. But I don't mind that you—"

"It isn't the truth. It's an insult. I don't like that kind of language, young lady."

Now she is confused. "*What* kind of language? I didn't say anything bad."

"Calling someone a rogga-lover is bad!"

"I . . . didn't say that." But in a way, she did. If Jija misses Mama and Uche, then that means he loves them, and that makes him a rogga-lover. But. *I'm a rogga.* She knows better than to say this. But she wants to.

Jija opens his mouth to retort, then seems to catch himself. He looks away, propping his elbows on the table and steepling his hands in the way he so often does when he's trying to rein in his temper.

"*Roggas*," he says, and the word sounds like filth in his mouth, "lie, sweetening. They threaten, and manipulate, and use. They're evil, Nassun, as evil as Father Earth himself. You aren't like that."

That's a lie, too. Nassun has done what she had to do to survive, including lying and murder. She's done some of these things in order to survive *him*. She hates that she's had to, and is exasperated by the fact that he apparently never realized it. That she's doing it now and he doesn't see.

Why do I even love him anymore? Nassun finds herself thinking as she stares at her father.

Instead she says: "Why do you hate us so much, Daddy?"

Jija flinches, perhaps at her casual *us*. "I don't hate you."

"You hate Mama, though. You must have hated U—"

"I did not!" Jija pushes back from the table and stands. Nassun flinches despite herself, but he turns away and starts to pace in short, vicious half circles around the room. "I just—I know what they're capable of, sweetening. You wouldn't understand. I needed to protect you."

In a sudden blur of understanding as powerful as magic, Nassun realizes Jija does not remember standing over Uche's body, his shoulders and chest heaving, his teeth clenched around the words *Are you one, too?* Now he believes he has never threatened her. Never shoved her off a wagon seat and down a hill of sticks and stones. Something has rewritten the story of his orogene children in Jija's head—a story that is as chiseled and unchangeable as stone in Nassun's mind. It is perhaps the same thing that has rewritten Nassun for him as *daughter* and not *rogga*, as if the two can be fissioned from each other somehow.

"I learned about them when I was a boy. Younger than you." Jija's not looking at her anymore, gesticulating as he talks and paces. "Makenba's cousin." Nassun blinks. She remembers Miss Makenba, the quiet old lady who always smelled like tea. Lerna, the town doctor, was her son. Miss Makenba had a cousin in town? Then Nassun gets it.

"I found him behind the spadeseed silo one day. He was squatting there, shaking. I thought he was sick." Jija's shaking his head the whole time, still pacing. "There was another boy with me. We always used to play together, the three of us. Kirl went to shake Litisk and Litisk just—" Jija stops abruptly. He's baring his teeth. His shoulders are heaving the same way they were on that day. "Kirl was *screaming* and Litisk was saying he couldn't stop, he didn't know how. The ice ate up Kirl's arm and his arm broke off. The blood was in chunks on the ground. Litisk said he was sorry, he even cried, but he just kept freezing Kirl. He wouldn't *stop*. By the time I ran away Kirl was reaching for me, and the only thing left of him that wasn't frozen was his head and his chest and that arm. It was too late, though. I knew that. It was too late even before I ran away to get help."

It does not comfort Nassun to know that there is a reason—a specific reason—for what her father has done. All she can think is, *Uche never lost control like that; Mama wouldn't have let him.* It's true. Mama had been able to sess, and still, Nassun's orogeny from all the way across town sometimes. Which means Uche didn't do anything to provoke Jija. Jija killed his own son for what a completely different person did, long before that son's birth. This, more than anything, helps her finally understand that there is no reasoning with her father's hatred.

So Nassun is almost prepared when Jija's gaze suddenly shifts to her, sidelong and suspicious. "Why haven't you cured yourself yet?"

No reasoning. But she tries, because once upon a time, this man was her whole world.

"I might be able to soon. I learned how to make things happen with the silver, and how to take things out of people. I don't know how orogeny works, or where it comes from, but if it's something that can be taken out, then—"

"None of the other monsters in that camp have cured themselves. I've asked around." Jija's pacing has gotten noticeably faster. "They go up there and they don't get better. They live there with those Guardians, more of them every day, and none of them have been cured! Was it a lie?"

"It isn't a lie. If I get good enough, I'll be able to do it." She understands this instinctively. With enough fine control and the sapphire obelisk's aid, she will be able to do almost anything. "But—"

"Why aren't you good enough now? We've been here almost a year!"

Because this is hard, she wants to say, but she realizes he does not want to hear it. He does not want to know that the only way to use orogeny and magic to transform a thing is to become an expert in the use of orogeny and magic. She doesn't answer because there's no point. She cannot say what he wants to hear. It isn't fair that he calls orogenes liars and then demands that she lie.

He stops and rounds on her, instantly suspicious of her silence. "You aren't trying to get better, are you? Tell the truth, Nassun!"

She is so *rusting* tired.

"I am trying to get better, Daddy," Nassun replies at last. "I'm trying to become a better orogene."

Jija steps back, as if she has hit him. "That isn't why I let you live up there."

He isn't *letting* anything; Schaffa made him. He's even lying to himself now. But it is the lies he's telling her—as he has been, Nassun understands suddenly, her whole life—that really break her heart. He's said that he loved her, after all, but that obviously isn't true. He cannot love an orogene, and that is what she is. He cannot be an orogene's father, and that is why he constantly demands she be something other than what she is.

And she is tired. Tired and done.

"I like being an orogene, Daddy," she says. His eyes widen. This is a terrible thing that she is saying. It is a terrible thing that she loves herself. "I like making things move, and doing the silver, and falling into the obelisks. I don't like—"

She is about to say that she hates what she did to Eitz, and she especially hates the way that others treat her now that they know what she is capable of, but she doesn't get the chance. Jija takes two swift steps forward and the back of his hand swings so fast that she doesn't even see it before it has knocked her out of the chair.

It's like that day on the Imperial Road, when she suddenly found herself at the bottom of a hill, in pain. It must have been like this for Uche, she realizes, in another swift epiphany. The world as it should be one moment and completely wrong, completely broken, an instant later.

At least Uche didn't have time to hate, she thinks, in sorrow.

And then she ices the entire house.

It isn't a reflex. She's intentional about it, precise, shaping the torus to fit the dimensions of the house exactly. No one past the walls will be caught in it. She shapes twin cores out of the torus, too, and centers each on herself and her father. She feels cold along the hairs of her skin, the tug of lowered air pressure on her clothing and plaited hair. Jija feels the same thing and he *screams*, his eyes wide and wild and sightless. The memory of a boy's cruel, icy death is in his face. By the time Nassun gets to her feet, staring at her father across a floor slick with plates of solid ice and around the fallen-over chair that is now too warped to ever use again, Jija has stumbled back, slipped on the ice, fallen, and slid partially across the floor to bump against the table legs.

There's no danger. Nassun only manifested the torus for an instant, as a warning against further violence on his part. Jija keeps screaming, though, as Nassun gazes down at her huddled, panicking father. Perhaps she should feel pity, or regret. What she actually feels, however, is cold fury toward her mother. She knows it's irrational. It is no one's fault except Jija's that Jija is too afraid of orogenes to love his own children. Once, however, Nassun could love her father without qualification. Now, she needs someone to blame for the loss of that perfect love. She knows her mother can bear it.

You should have had us with someone stronger, she thinks at Essun, wherever she is.

It takes care to walk across the slick floor without slipping, and Nassun has to jiggle the latch for a few seconds to scrape it open. By the time she does, Jija has stopped screaming behind her, though she can still hear him breathing hard and uttering a little moan with every exhalation. She doesn't want to look back at him. She makes herself do it anyway, though, because she wants to be a good orogene, and good orogenes cannot afford self-deception.

Jija jerks as if her gaze has the power to burn.

"Bye, Daddy," she says. He does not reply in words.

* * *

And the last tear she shed, as he burned her alive with ice, broke like the Shattering upon the ground. Stone your heart against roggas, for there is nothing but rust in their souls!

—From lorist tale, "Ice Kisses," recorded in Bebbec Quartent, Msida Theater, by Whoz Lorist Bebbec. (Note: A letter signed by seven Equatorial itinerant lorists disavows Whoz as a "pop lorist hack." Tale may be apocryphal.)

18

you, counting down

When the Sanzed woman is gone, I pull you aside. Figuratively speaking.

"The one you call Gray Man doesn't want to prevent the opening of the Gate," I say. "I lied."

You're so wary of me now. It troubles you, I can see; you *want* to trust me, even as your very eyes remind you of how I've deceived you. But you sigh and say, "Yeah. I thought there might be more to it."

"He'll kill you because you can't be manipulated," I say, ignoring the irony. "Because if you open the Gate, you would restore the Moon and end the Seasons. What he really wants is someone who will open the Gate for *his* purposes."

You understand the players now, if not the totality of the game. You frown. "So which purpose would that be? Transformation? Status quo?"

"I don't know. Does it matter?"

"Suppose not." You rub a hand over your locs, which you've

retwisted recently. "I guess that's why he's trying to get Castrima to kick out all its roggas?"

"Yes. He'll find a way to make you do what he wants, Essun, if he can. If he can't... you're no use to him. Worse. You're the enemy."

You sigh with the weariness of the Earth, and do not reply other than to nod and walk away. I am so afraid as I watch you leave.

* * *

As you have in other moments of despair, you go to Alabaster.

There's not much left of him anymore. Since he gave up his legs he spends his days in a drugged stupor, tucked up against Antimony like a pup nursing its mother. Sometimes you don't ask for lessons when you come to see him. That's a waste, because you're pretty sure the only reason he's forced himself to keep living is so that he can pass on the art of global destruction to you. He's caught you at it a few times: You've woken up curled next to his nest to find him gazing down at you. He doesn't chide you for it. Probably doesn't have the strength to chide. You're grateful.

He's awake now as you settle beside him, though he doesn't move much. Antimony has moved fully into the nest with him these days, and you rarely see her in any pose other than "living chair" for him—kneeling, legs spread, her hands braced on her thighs. Alabaster rests against her front, which is only possible now because, perversely, the few burns on his back healed even as his legs rotted. Fortunately she has no breasts to make the position less comfortable, and apparently her simulated clothing isn't sharp or rough. Alabaster's eyes shift to follow as you sit, like a stone eater's. You hate that this comparison occurs to you.

"It's happening again," you say. You don't bother to explain the "it." He always knows. "How did you... at Meov. You *tried.* How?" Because you can't find it in yourself anymore to bother fighting for this place, or building a life here. All your instincts say to grab your runny-sack, grab your people, and run before Castrima turns against you. That's a probable death sentence, the Season having well and truly set in topside, but staying seems more certain.

He draws in a deep, slow breath, so you know he means to answer. It just takes him a while to muster the words. "Didn't mean to. You were pregnant; I was... lonely. I thought it would do. For a while."

You shake your head. Of course he knew you were pregnant before you did. That's all irrelevant now. "You fought for them." It takes effort to emphasize the last word, but you do. For you and Corundum and Innon, sure, but he fought for Meov, too. "They would've turned on us, too, one day. You know they would have." When Corundum proved too powerful, or if they'd managed to drive off the Guardians only to have to leave Meov and move elsewhere. It was inevitable.

He makes an affirmative sound.

"Then why?"

He lets out a long, slow sigh. "There was a chance they wouldn't." You shake your head. The words are so impossible to believe that they sound like gibberish. But he adds, "Any chance was worth trying."

He does not say *for you*, but you feel it. It is a subtext that is nearly sessable beneath the words' surface. So your family could have a normal life among other people, as one of them. Normal opportunities. Normal struggles. You stare at him. On impulse you lift your hand to his face, drawing fingers over his scarred lips. He watches you do this and offers you that little quarter-smile, which is all he can muster these days. It's more than you need.

Then you get up and head out to try to salvage Castrima's thin, cracked nothing of a chance.

* * *

Ykka has called a vote for the next morning—twenty-four hours after Rennanis's "offer." Castrima needs to deliver some kind of response, but she doesn't think it should be up to only her informal council. You can't see what difference the vote will make, except to emphasize that if the comm gets through the night intact it will be a rusting miracle.

People look at you as you walk through the comm. You keep your gaze ahead and try not to let them visibly affect you.

In brief, private visits you pass Ykka's orders on to Cutter and Temell, and tell them to spread the word. Temell usually takes the kids out for lessons anyway; he says he'll visit his students at home and encourage them to form study groups of two and three, in the homes of trusted adults. You want to say, "No adults are trustworthy," but he knows that. There's no way around it, so it's pointless to say aloud.

Cutter says he'll pass on the word to the few other adult roggas. Not all of them have the skill to throw a torus or control themselves well; except for you and Alabaster, they're all ferals. But Cutter will make sure the ones who can't stick near those who can. His face is impassive as he adds, "And who'll watch your back?"

Which means he's offering. The revulsion that shivers through you at this idea is surprising. You've never really trusted him, though you don't understand why. Something about the fact that he's hidden all his life—which is hypocritical as hell after your ten years in Tirimo. But then, sweet flaking rust, do you trust anyone? As long as he does his job it doesn't matter. You force yourself to nod. "Come find me after you're done, then." He agrees.

With that, you decide to get some rest, yourself. Your bedroom is wrecked thanks to Hoa's transformation, and you're not much interested in sleeping in Tonkee's bed; it's been months, but the memory of mildew dies hard. Also, you've realized belatedly that there's no one to watch Ykka's back. She believes in her comm, but you don't. Hoa ate Ruby Hair, who at least had an assumable interest in keeping her alive. So you borrow another pack from Temell, and scrounge your apartment for a few basic supplies—not quite a runny-sack, there's plausible deniability if Ykka protests—and then head to her apartment. (This will have the added purpose of making it hard for Cutter to find you.) She's still asleep, from the sound of her breathing through the bedroom curtain. Her divans are pretty comfortable, especially compared to sleeping rough when you were on the road. You use your runny-sack for a pillow and curl up, trying to forget the world for a while.

And then you wake when Ykka curses and stumbles past you at full speed, half ripping down one of the apartment curtains in her haste. You struggle awake and sit up. "What—" But by then you, too, hear the rising shouts outside. *Angry* shouts. A crowd, gathering.

So it's begun. You get up and follow, and it's not an afterthought that you grab the packs.

The knot of people is gathered on the ground level, near the communal baths. Ykka scrambles to that level in ways you will not—sliding down metal ladders, hopping over the railing of one platform to swing down to the one she knows is below, running across bridges that sway alarmingly beneath her feet. You go down in the sensible, non-suicidal way, so by the time you get to the knot of people, Ykka is in full shout, trying to get everyone to shut up and listen and back the fuck off.

At the center of the knot is Cutter, clad in nothing but a towel, for once looking something other than indifferent. Now he's tense, jaw set, defiant, braced to flee. And five feet away, the iced corpse of a man sits on the ground, frozen in mid-scrabble backward, a look of abject terror permanently on his face. You don't recognize him. That doesn't matter. What matters is that a rogga has killed a still. This is a match thrown right into the middle of a comm that is dried-out, oil-soaked kindling.

"—how this happened," Ykka is shouting, as you reach the knot of people. You can barely see her; there are nearly fifty people here already. You could push to the front, but you decide to hang back instead. Now is not the time to call attention to yourself. You look around and see Lerna also lurking at the rear of the crowd. His eyes are wide and his jaw tight as he looks back at you. There's also—oh, burning Earth—a cluster of three rogga kids here. One of them is Penty, who you know is the ringleader of some of the braver, stupider rogga children. She's standing on tiptoe, craning her neck for a better look. When she tries to push forward through the crowd, you catch her eye and give her a Mother Look. She flinches and subsides at once.

"Who the rust cares how it happened?" That's Sekkim, one of the Innovators. You only know him because Tonkee constantly complains that he's too stupid to rightly be part of the caste and should instead be dumped into something nonessential, like Leadership. "This is why—"

Someone else shouts him down. "*Fucking rogga!*"

Someone else shouts her down. "Fucking listen! It's Ykka!"

"Who the rust cares about another rogga monster—"

"Rusty son of a cannibal, I will beat you bloody if you—"

Someone shoves someone else. There are shoves back, more curses, vows of murder. It's a catastrophe.

Then a man rushes forward from the crowd, crouching beside the iced corpse and trying his best to fling his arms around it. The resemblance between him and the body is obvious even through the ice: brothers, perhaps. His wail of anguish causes a sudden, flustered silence to ripple across the crowd. They shuffle uneasily as his wail subsides into deep, soul-tearing sobs.

Ykka takes a deep breath and steps forward, using the opportunity that grief has provided. To Cutter, she says tightly, "What did I say? What did I rusting *say*?"

"He attacked me," Cutter says. There's not a scratch on him.

"Bullshit," Ykka says. Several people in the crowd echo her, but she glares them down until they subside. She looks at the dead man, her jaw tight. "Betine wouldn't have done that. He couldn't even kill a chicken that time it was his turn to look after the flock."

Cutter glares. "All I know is, I wanted to take a bath. I sat down to wash and he moved away from me. I figured fine, that's how it's going to be, and I didn't care. Then I went past him to get into the pool and he *hit* me. Hard, in the back of the neck."

There is a low, angry murmur at this—but also a troubled shuffle. The back of the neck is rumored to be the best place to strike a rogga. It's not true. Only works if you hit hard enough for a concussion or a cracked skull, and then that's what takes them down, not any sort of damage to the sessapinae. It's still a popular myth. And if it's true, it might be reason enough for Cutter to fight back.

"*Rust that.*" This is growled; the man who holds Betine's faintly hissing corpse. "Bets wasn't like that. Yeek, you *know* he wasn't—"

Ykka nods, going over to touch the man's shoulder. The crowd shuffles again, pent fury shifting with it. With her, tenuously, for the moment. "I know." A muscle in her jaw flexes once, twice. She looks around. "Anybody else see the fight?"

Several people raise hands. "I saw Bets move away," says one woman. She swallows, looking at Cutter; sweat dots her upper lip. "I think he just wanted to get closer to the soap, though."

"He looked at me," Cutter snaps. "I know what it rusting means when somebody looks at me like that!"

Ykka cuts him off with a wave of her hand. "I know, Cutter, but shut up. What else?" she asks the woman.

"That was it. I looked away and then when I looked back there was that—swirl. Wind and ice." She grimaces, her jaw tightening. "You know how you people kill."

Ykka glares back at her, but then flinches as there are more shouts, this time in agreement with the woman. Someone tries to shove through the crowd to get at Cutter; someone else holds the attacker back, but it's a near thing. You see the realization come over Ykka that she's losing them. She's not going to make her people see. They're working themselves into a mob, and there's nothing she can do to stop them.

Well. You're wrong about that. There's one thing she can do.

She does it by turning and laying a hand on Cutter's chest and sending something through him. You're not actively sessing at the moment, so you only get the backwash of it, and it's—what? It's like…the way Alabaster once slammed a hot spot into submission, years ago and a fifth of a continent away. Just smaller. It's like what that Guardian did to Innon, except localized, and not overtly horrific. And you didn't realize roggas could do anything like it.

Whatever it is, Cutter doesn't even have a chance to gasp. His eyes fly wide. He staggers back a step. Then he falls down, with a look of shock on his face to match that of Betine's fear.

Everyone's silent. Yours is not the only mouth that hangs open.

Ykka catches her breath. Whatever she did took a lot out of her; you see her sway a little, then get a hold of herself. "That's enough," she says, turning to look at everyone in the crowd. "More than enough. Justice has been done, see? Now all of you, go the rust home."

You don't expect that to work. You figure it'll only whet the crowd's bloodthirst…but shows how much you know. People mill a little, mutter a little more, but then begin to disperse. A grieving man's quiet sobs follow them all away.

That's midnight, the time-keeper calls. Eight hours till the vote in the morning.

* * *

"I had to do it," Ykka murmurs. You're in her apartment again, sort of, standing beside her. The curtain's open so she can see her people, so they can see her, but she's leaning against the doorsill and she's trembling. It's only a little. No one would see it from afar. "I had to."

You offer her the respect of honesty. "Yes. You did."

It's two o'clock.

* * *

By five o'clock, you're thinking about sleeping. It's been quieter than you expected. Lerna and Hjarka have come to join you at Ykka's. No one says you're keeping vigil, commiserating in silence, mourning Cutter, waiting for the world to end (again), but that's what you're doing. Ykka's sitting on a divan with her arms wrapped around her knees and her head propped against the wall, gaze weary and empty of thought.

When you hear shouts again, you close your eyes and think about ignoring them. It's the high-pitched screams of children that drag you out of this complete failure of empathy. The others get up and you do, too, and all of you go out onto the balcony. People are running toward one of the wide platforms that surround a crystal shaft too small to hold any apartments. You and the others head that way, too. The comm uses such platforms for storage, so this one is stacked with barrels and crates and clay jars. One of the clay jars is rolling around but looks intact; you see this as you and the others reach the platform. Which does not at all explain what else you're seeing.

It's the rogga kids again. Penty's gang. Two of them are doing all the screaming, tugging and hitting at a woman who has pinned Penty down and is shouting at her, gripping her throat. Another woman stands by, yelling at the kids, too, but no one's paying any attention to her. Her slurred voice is just the goad.

You know the woman that's got Penty down, sort of. She's maybe ten years younger than you, with a heavier build and longer hair: Waineen, one of the Resistants. She's been nice enough when you've done shifts in the fungus flats or latrines, but you've heard the others gossip behind her back. Waineen makes the mellows that Lerna periodically smokes, and the moonshine that a few people in the comm drink. Sometime back before the Season she had quite a lucrative sideline helping the native Castrimans perk up their lives of tedious mining and trading, and she stored the product down in Castrima-under to keep the quartent tax inspectors from ever finding it. Convenient, now that the world has ended. But she's her own biggest customer, and it's not unusual to find her stumbling about the comm, red-faced and too loud, emitting more fumes than a fresh blow.

Waineen's not usually a mean drunk, and she shares freely, and she never misses a shift, which is why nobody really cares what she does with her stuff. Everybody handles the Season in their own way. Still, something's set her off now. Penty *is* aggravating. Hjarka and some of the other Castrimans are striding forward to pull the woman off the girl, and you're telling yourself it's a good thing Penty has enough self-control to not ice the whole damned platform, when the woman lifts an arm and makes a fist.

a fist that

you've seen the imprint of Jija's fist, a bruise with four parallel marks, on Uche's belly and face

a fist that

that

that

no

You're in the topaz and between the woman's cells in almost the same instant. There is no thought in this. Your mind falls, *dives*, into the upward wash of yellow light as if it belongs there. Your sessapinae flex around the silver threads and you draw them together, you are part of both obelisk and woman and you will *not* let this happen, not again, not again, you could not stop Jija but—

"Not one more child," you whisper, and your companions all look at you in surprise and confusion. Then they stop looking at you, because the woman who was egging on the fight is suddenly screaming, and the kids are screaming louder. Even Penty is screaming now, because the woman on top of her has turned to glittering, multicolored stone.

"Not one more child!" You can sess the ones nearest you—the other council members, the screaming drunk, Penty and her girls, Hjarka and the rest, all of them. Everyone in Castrima. They trod upon the filaments of your nerves, tapping and jittering, and *they are Jija.* You focus on the drunk woman and it is almost instinctual, the urge to begin squeezing the movement and life out of her and replacing that with whatever the by-product of magical reactions really is, this stuff that looks like stone. This stuff that is killing Alabaster, the father of your other dead child, NOT ONE MORE RUSTING CHILD. For how many centuries has the world killed rogga children so that everyone else's children can sleep easy? *Everyone* is Jija, the whole damned world is Schaffa, Castrima is Tirimo is the Fulcrum NOT ONE MORE and you turn with the obelisk torrenting its power through you to begin killing everyone within and beyond your sight.

Something jars your connection to the obelisk. Suddenly you have to fight for power that it so readily gave you before. You bare your teeth without thinking, growl without hearing yourself, clench your fists and shout in your mind NO I WON'T LET HIM DO IT AGAIN and you are seeing Schaffa, thinking of Jija.

But you are *sessing* Alabaster.

Feeling him, in blazing white tendrils that lash at your obelisk link. That is Alabaster's strength contending against yours and... not winning. He does not shut you down the way you know he can. Or the way you thought he could. Is he weaker? No. You're just a lot stronger than you used to be.

And suddenly the import of this slaps through the fugue of memory and horror that you're trapped in, bringing you back to cold, shocking reality. You've killed a woman with magic. You're about to wipe out Castrima with magic. You're fighting Alabaster with magic—*and Alabaster cannot bear more magic.*

"Oh, uncaring Earth," you whisper. You stop fighting at once. Alabaster dismantles your connection to the obelisk; he's still got a more precise touch than you. But you feel his weakness when he does so. His fading strength.

You're not even aware of running at first. It barely qualifies as running, because the contest of magic and the abrupt disconnection from the obelisk have left you so disoriented and weak that you lurch from railing to rope as if drunk, yourself. Someone's shouting in your ear. A hand grabs your upper arm and you shake it off, snarling. Somehow you make it to the ground floor without falling to your death. Faces blur past you, irrelevant. You can't see because you're sobbing aloud, babbling, *No, no, no.* You know what you've done, even as you deny it with your words and body and soul.

Then you are in the infirmary.

You are in the infirmary, looking down at an incongruously small, yet finely made, stone sculpture. No color to this one, no polish, just dull sandy brown all over. It is almost abstract, archetypal: *Man in His Final Moment. Truncation of the Spirit. Neverperson, Unperson. Once Found but Now Lost.*

Or maybe you can just call it *Alabaster.*

It's five thirty.

* * *

At seven o'clock, Lerna comes to where you huddle on the floor in front of Alabaster's corpse. You barely hear him settle nearby, and you wonder why he's come. He knows better. He should go, before you snap again and kill him, too.

"Ykka's talked the comm into not killing you," he says. "I told them about your son. It's been, ah, mutually agreed that Waineen could've killed Penty, hitting her like that. Your overreaction was... understandable." He pauses. "It helps that Ykka killed Cutter earlier. They trust her more now. They know she's not speaking for you just out of..." He inhales, shrugs. "Kinship."

Yes. It's as the teachers told you back in the Fulcrum: Roggas are one and the same. The crimes of any are the crimes of all.

"No one will kill her." That's Hoa. Of course he's here now, guarding his investment.

Lerna shifts uneasily at this. But then another voice agrees, "No one will kill her," and you flinch because it is Antimony.

You push yourself up from the huddle slowly. She sits in the same position as always—she's been here all along—with the stone lump that was Alabaster resting against her as his living body once did. Her eyes are already on you.

"You can't have him," you say. Snarl. "Or me, either."

"I don't want you," Antimony says. "You killed him."

Oh, shit. You try to maintain abject fury, try to use it to focus and reach for the power to defy her, but the fury dissolves into shame. And anyway, you only get as far as that damned obelisk-longknife of Alabaster's. The spinel. It kicks back your flailing grab for it almost at once, as if spitting in your face. You *are* worthy of contempt, aren't you? The stone eaters, the humans, the orogenes, even the flaking obelisks all know it. You are nothing. No; you are death. And you've killed yet another person you loved.

So you sit there on your hands and knees, bereft, rejected, so hurt that it is like a clockwork engine of pain gear-ticking at the core of you. Maybe the obelisk-builders could have invented some way to harness pain like this, but they are all dead.

There is a sound that drags you out of grief. Antimony is standing now. Her pose is imposing, straight-legged and implacable. She looks down her nose at you. In her arms is the brown lump of Alabaster's remains. From this angle it doesn't look like anything that used to be human. Officially, it wasn't.

"No," you say. No defiance this time; it is a plea. *Don't take him.* Yet this is what he asked for. This is what he wanted—to be given to Antimony and not Father Earth, who took so much from him. That's the choice here: Earth or a stone eater. You're not on the list.

"He left you a message," she says. Her inflectionless voice is no different, and yet. Somehow. Is that pity? "'The onyx is the key. First a network, then the Gate. Don't rust it up, Essun. Innon and I didn't love you for nothing.'"

"What?" you ask, but then she flickers, becoming translucent. For the first time it occurs to you that the way stone eaters move through rock and the way obelisks shift between real and unreal states are the same.

It is a useless observation. Antimony vanishes into the Earth that hates you. With Alabaster.

You sit where she's left you, where he's left you. There are no thoughts in your head. But when a hand touches your arm, and a voice says your name, and a connection that is not the obelisk presents itself, you turn toward it. You can't help it. You need something, and if it is not to be family or death, then it must be something else. So you turn and grab and Lerna is there for you, his shoulder is warm and soft, and you need it. You need him. Just for now, please. Just once, you need to feel human, never mind the official designations, and maybe with human arms around you and a human voice murmuring, "I'm sorry. I'm sorry, Essun," in your ear, maybe you can feel like that. Maybe you *are* human, just for a little while.

*   *   *

At seven forty-five you sit alone again.

Lerna's gone to speak to one of his assistants, and maybe to the Strongbacks who are watching you from the infirmary doorway. At the bottom of your runny-sack is a pocket for hiding things. It's why you bought this particular runny-sack, years ago, from this particular leatherworker. When he showed you the pocket, you thought immediately of something that you wanted to put in it. Something that, as Essun, you didn't let yourself think about often, because it was a thing of Syenite's and she was dead. Yet you kept her remains.

You dig through the sack until your fingers find the pocket and wriggle inside. The bundle is still there. You tug them out, unfold the cheap linen. Six rings, polished and semiprecious, sit there.

Not enough for you, a nine-ringer, but you don't care about the first four, anyway. They clack and roll across the floor as you discard them. The last two, the ones he made for you, you put on the index finger of each hand.

Then you get to your feet.

*   *   *

Eight o'clock. Representatives of the comm's households gather at the Flat Top.

One vote per comm share is the rule. You see Ykka at the center of the circle again, her arms folded and face carefully blank, though you can sess an undertone of tension in the ambient that is mostly hers. Someone has brought out an old wooden box, and people are milling around, talking to each other, writing on scraps of paper or leather, dropping these into the box.

You walk toward the Flat Top with Lerna in tow. People don't notice you until you're nearly across the bridge. Nearly on top of them. Then someone sees you coming and gasps loudly. Someone else yelps an alarm: "*Oh, rust, it's her.*" People scramble to get out of your way, almost tripping over themselves.

They should. In your right hand is Alabaster's ridiculous pink longknife, the miniaturized and reshaped spinel obelisk. By now you have tapped it, resonated with it; it is yours. It rejected you before because you were unstable, floundering, but now you know what you need from it. You've found your focus. The spinel won't hurt anyone as long as you don't let it. Whether you will or not is an entirely different matter.

You walk into the center of the circle, and the man holding the ballot box scrambles back from you, leaving it there. Ykka frowns and steps forward and says, "Essun—" But you ignore her. You lunge forward and it is suddenly instinctual, easy, natural, to grip the hilt of the pink longknife with both hands and turn and swivel your hips and swing. The instant the sword touches the wooden box, the box is obliterated. It isn't cut, it isn't smashed; it disintegrates into its component microscopic particles. The eye processes this as dust, which scatters and glitters in the light before vanishing. Turned to stone. A lot of people are gasping or crying out, which means they're inhaling their votes. Probably won't hurt them. Much.

Then you turn and lift the longknife, pivoting slowly to point it at each face.

"No vote," you say. It's so quiet that you can hear water trickling out of the pipes in the communal pool, hundreds of feet below. "Leave. Go join Rennanis if they'll have you. But if you stay, no part of this comm gets to decide that any other part of this comm is expendable. No *voting* on who gets to be people."

Some of them shuffle or look at each other. Ykka stares at you like you are a possibly dangerous creature, which is hilarious. She should know by now that there's no "possibly" about it. "Essun," she starts to say, in the kind of even voice one uses with pets or the mad, "this is..." She stops because she doesn't know what it is. But you do. It's a fucking coup. Doesn't matter who's in charge, but on this one issue, you're going to be the dictator. You will not allow Alabaster to have died saving these people from you for nothing.

"*No vote,*" you say again. Your voice is pitched to carry, as if they are twelve-year-olds in your old creche. "This is a community. You will be unified. You will fight for each other. *Or I will rusting kill every last one of you.*"

True silence this time. They don't move. Their eyes are white and so far beyond frightened that you know they believe you.

Good. You turn and walk away.

INTERLUDE

In the turning depths, I resonate with my enemy—or attempt to. "A truce," I say. Plead. There has been so much loss already, on all sides. A moon. A future. Hope.

Down here, it's nearly impossible to hear a reply in words. What comes to me is furious reverberation, savage fluctuations of pressure and gravitation. I'm forced to flee after a time, lest I be crushed—and though this would be only a temporary setback, I cannot afford to be incapacitated right now. Things are changing amid your kind, quickly as your kind so often do things when you finally make real decisions. I have to be ready.

The rage was my only answer, in any case.

19

you get ready to rumble

It has been one month since you last went aboveground. It has been two days since you killed Alabaster, in your folly and pain. All things change in a Season.

Castrima-over is occupied. The tunnel that you first passed through to enter the comm is blocked; one of the comm's orogenes has pulled a big slab of stone up from the earth to effectively seal it off. Probably Ykka, or Cutter before Ykka killed him; they were the two others in the comm with the best fine control besides you and Alabaster. Now two of those four are dead, and the enemy is at the gates. The Strongbacks who are clustered in the tunnel mouth behind the stone seal jump up as you walk into the electric-light circle, and the ones who were already standing stand straighter. Xeber, Esni's second-in-command among the Strongbacks, actually smiles at the sight of you. That's how bad things are. That's how worried everyone is. They've so lost their minds as to think of you as their champion.

"I don't like this," Ykka has said to you. She's back in the comm, organizing the defense that will be necessary if the tunnels are breached. The real danger is if the Rennanis scouts discover the ventilation ducts of Castrima's geode. They're well hidden—one in the cavern of an underground river, others in equally out-of-the-way places, as if the people who built Castrima feared attack themselves—but the comm's people will be forced out if those are sealed off. "And they've got stone eaters working with them. You're dangerous and ruster enough to fuck up an army, Essie, I'll give you that, but none of us can fight stone eaters. If they kill you, we lose our best weapon."

She said this to you at Scenic Overlook, where the two of you went to work things out. It was awkward for about a day, between you. By forbidding a vote, you undercut Ykka's authority and destroyed everyone's illusion of having a say in the comm's management. That was necessary, you still believe; everyone *shouldn't* have a say in whose life is worth fighting for. She actually agreed, she admitted as you talked. But it damaged her.

You didn't apologize for that, but you've tried to spackle the cracks. "*You* are Castrima's best weapon," you said firmly. You even meant it. That Castrima has lasted this far, a comm of stills who have repeatedly failed to lynch the roggas openly living among them, is miraculous. Even if "hasn't yet committed genocidal slaughter" is a low bar to hop, other communities haven't even managed that much. You'll give credit where it's due.

It eased the awkwardness between you. "Well, just don't rusting die," she told you at last. "Not sure I can keep this mess together without you, at this point." Ykka's good at that, making people feel like they've got a reason to do something. That's why she's the headwoman.

And that is why, now, you walk through a Castrima-over that has been turned into a camp by the soldiers of Rennanis, and you are actually afraid. It's always harder to fight for other people than for the self.

The ash has been falling steadily for a year now, and the comm is knee-deep in the stuff. There's been at least one rain to tamp it down recently, so you can sess a kind of damp-mud crust underneath the powdery layer on top, but even that's substantial. Enemy soldiers crowd the porches and doorways of the once-empty houses, watching you, and the untamped ash under the eaves is halfway up most of the houses' walls. They've had to dig out the windows. The soldiers look like… just people, because they don't wear uniforms, but there is a uniformity to them nevertheless: They are all fully Sanzed or very Sanzed-looking. Where you can see color in their ash-faded travel clothing, you spot that telltale scrap of prettier, more delicate cloth tied around their upper arms or wrists or foreheads. No longer displaced Equatorials, then; they've found a comm. Something older and more primal than a comm: They are a *tribe*. And now they're here to take what's yours.

But beyond that they are just people. Many are your age or older. You guess that a lot of them are surplus Strongbacks or commless trying to prove their usefulness. There are slightly more men than women, but that follows, too, since most comms are quicker to kick out those who can't produce babies than those who can—but the number of women here means that Rennanis isn't hurting for healthy repopulators. A strong comm.

Their eyes follow you as you walk down Castrima-over's main street. You stand out, you know, with your ashless skin and clean hair and your clothes bright with color. Just brown leather pants and unbleached white in your shirt, but these are colors that have become rare in this world of gray streets and gray dead trees and a gray, heavily clouded sky. You're the only Midlatter that you see, too, and you're small compared to most of them.

Doesn't matter. Behind you floats the spinel, remaining precisely one foot behind the back of your head and turning slowly. You aren't making it do that. You don't know why it's doing that, really. Unless you hold it in your hand, that's what the thing does: You tried to set it down, but it floated back up and moved behind you like this. Should've asked Alabaster how to make it behave before you killed him, oh well. Now it's flickering a little, real to translucent to real again, and you can hear—not sess, *hear*—the faint hum of its energies as it turns. You see people's faces twitch as they notice. They might not know what it is, but they know a bad thing when they hear it.

At the center of Castrima-over is a domed, open pavilion that Ykka tells you was once the comm's gathering center, used for wedding dances and parties and the occasional comm-wide meeting. It's been turned into some sort of operations center, you see as you walk toward it: A gaggle of men and women stand, squat, or sit around within it, but one knot of them stands around a freshly made table. When you get close enough, you see that they've got a crudely made diagram of Castrima and map of the local area side by side, which they're discussing.

To your dismay, you can see that they've marked at least one of the ventilation ducts—the one that's behind a small waterfall at the nearby river. They probably lost a scout or two finding it: The river's banks are by now infested with boilbug mounds. Doesn't matter; they found it, and that's bad.

Three of the people talking over the maps look up as you approach. One of them elbows another, who turns and shakes awake someone else as you walk into the pavilion and stop a few feet from the table. The woman who gets up, rubbing her face blearily as she comes to join the others, does not look particularly impressive. She's cut her hair on the sides to just above her ears—a painfully blunt chop that looks to have been done with a knife. It makes her look small, even though she's not particularly: Her torso is a smooth barrel, brief breasts blending into a belly that's probably carried at least one child, and legs like basalt pillars. She's not wearing anything more than the others; her sash of tribe membership is just a fading yellow silk kerchief hanging loosely around her neck. But there's a gravity in her gaze, even half-asleep, that makes you focus on her.

"Castrima?" she asks you, by way of greeting. It's all that really matters about who you are, anyway.

You nod. "I speak for them."

She rests her hands on the table, nodding. "Our message got delivered, then." Her gaze flicks to the spinel hovering behind you, and something adjusts in her expression. It's not hate that you're seeing. Hate requires emotion. What this woman has simply done is realize you are a rogga, and decide that you aren't a person, just like that. Indifference is worse than hate.

Well. You can't muster indifference in response; you can't

help but see her as human. Have to make do with hate, then. And what's more interesting is that she somehow knows what the spinel is, and what it means. Very interesting.

"We're not joining you," you say. "You want to fight over that, so be it."

She tilts her head to one side. One of her lieutenants chuckles into their hand, but is swiftly glared silent by another. You like the silencing. It's respectful—of your abilities if not of you per se, and of Castrima even if they don't think you have a chance. Even if you actually, probably, *don't* have a chance.

"We don't even have to attack, you realize," the woman says. "We can just sit up here, kill anybody who comes up to hunt or trade. Starve you out."

You manage not to react. "We have a little meat. It'll take awhile—months at least—for the vitamin deficiencies to set in. Our stores are pretty solid otherwise." You force a shrug. "And other communities have gotten around meat shortages easily enough."

She grins. Her teeth aren't sharpened, but you think momentarily that her canines are longer than they strictly need to be. It's probably projection. "True, if that's your taste. Which is why we're also working on finding your vents." She taps the map. "Close them up and suffocate you till you're weak, then break down those barriers you've put across the tunnels and dance right in. Stupid to live underground; once someone knows you're there, you're actually an easier target, not a harder one."

This is true, but you shake your head. "We can be hard enough, if you push us. But Castrima isn't rich, and our storecaches aren't any better than those of another comm that's not full of roggas." You pause for effect. The woman doesn't flinch, but there's a shuffle among the other people in the pavilion as they realize. Good. That means they're thinking. "So many easier nuts to crack out there. Why are you bothering with us?"

You know why they're really doing this, because Gray Man's after orogenes who can open the Obelisk Gate, but that can't be what he's told them. What could induce a strong, stable Equatorial comm to turn conqueror? Wait, no; it can't be stable. Rennanis is relatively close to the Rift. Even with living node maintainers, life in such a comm would be hard. Daily blow-throughs of noxious gas. Ashfall much worse than here, requiring people to wear masks at all times. Earth help them if it rains; it could be pure acid, and that's if rain is even possible with the Rift cranking out heat and ash nearby. Doubtful they have any livestock . . . so maybe they're facing a meat shortage, too.

"Because this is what it will take to survive," the woman says, to your surprise. She straightens and folds her arms. "Rennanis has too many people for our stores. All the survivors of every other Equatorial city have come to camp on our doorstep. We would've had to do this anyway, or have problems with too large of a commless population in the area. Might as well weaponize them into feeding themselves, and bringing what's left back home to the comm. You know this Season isn't going to end."

"It will."

"Eventually." She shrugs. "Our 'mests have calculated that if we grow enough 'shrooms and such, and strictly limit our population, we might achieve enough sustainability to survive until the Season ends. The odds are better if we take the storecaches of every other comm we encounter, though—"

You roll your eyes because you can't help it. "You think cachebread's going to last *a thousand years?*" Or two. Or ten. And then a few hundred thousand years of ice.

She pauses until you're done. "—and if we set up supply lines from every comm with renewables. We'll need some Coastal comms with oceanic resources, some Antarctics where growing low-light plants might still be possible." She pauses, also for effect. "But you Midlatters eat too much."

Well. "So basically, you're here to wipe us out." You shake your head. "Why didn't you just say so? Why the foolishness about getting rid of the orogenes?"

Someone from beyond the pavilion calls, "Danel!" and the woman looks up, nodding absently. This is apparently her name. "Always a chance you'd turn on each other. Then we could just walk in and scrape up the leftovers." She shakes her head. "Now things have to be hard."

The dull, insistent buzz that suddenly impinges itself on your sessapinae is a warning as blatant as a scream.

It's too late the instant you sess it, because that means you're within range of the Guardian's ability to negate your orogeny. You turn anyway, half tripping even as you start to spin a huge torus that will flash-freeze the whole rusting town, and it is because you were expecting negation and did not deploy a tight shielding torus that the disruption knife pegs you in the right arm.

You remember Alabaster saying that these knives hurt. The thing is small, made for throwing, and it *should* hurt given that it's sunk into your bicep and probably chipping bone. But what Alabaster did not specify—you are irrationally furious with him hours after his death, stupid useless *ruster*—was that something about this knife seems to set your entire nervous system on fire. The fire is hottest, *incandescent*, in your sessapinae, even though those are nowhere near your arm. It hurts so much that all your muscles spasm at once; you flop onto your side and can't even scream. You just lie there twitching, and staring at the woman who steps through the gaggle of Rennanis soldiers to grin down at you. She's surprisingly young, or so she seems, though appearances are meaningless because she is a Guardian. She's naked from the waist up, her skin shockingly dark amid all these Sanzeds, her breasts small and almost entirely areola, reminding you of the last time you were pregnant. You thought your tits would never shrink back down after Uche . . . and you wonder if it will hurt, when you are shaken to pieces the way Innon was.

Everything goes black. You don't understand what's happened at first. Are you dead? Was it that quick? Everything's still on fire, and you think you're still trying to scream. But you become aware of new sensations then. Movement. Rushing. Something rather like wind. The touch of foreign molecules against infinitesimal receptors in your skin. It is . . . oddly peaceful. You almost forget your pain.

Then light, startling against the eyelids you hadn't realized you'd closed. You can't open them. Someone curses nearby and comes near and hands press you down, which nearly makes you panic because you can't do orogeny with your nerves exploding like this. But then someone yanks the knife out of your arm.

It is as though a shake siren within you has been suddenly silenced. You slump in relief, into just ordinary pain, and open your eyes now that you can control your voluntary muscles again.

Lerna's there. You're on the floor of his apartment, the light is from his crystal walls, and he's holding the knife and staring down at you. Beyond him, Hoa stands in a pose of entreaty, which he must have been directing toward Lerna. His eyes have shifted to you, though he hasn't bothered to adjust the pose.

"Burning rusty *fuck*," you groan-sigh. And then, because now you know what must have happened, you add, "Thanks," to Hoa. Who pulled you down into the earth and away before the Guardian could kill you. Never thought you'd be grateful for something like that.

Lerna's dropped the knife and already turned away to find bandages. You're not bleeding much; the knife went in vertically, paralleling rather than cutting across the tendons, and it seems to have missed the big artery. Hard to tell when your hands are still shaking a little; shock. But Lerna's not moving at that blurring, near-inhuman speed he tends to use when a life is on the line, so you're encouraged by that.

Lerna says, his back to you as he assembles items, "I take it your attempt at parley didn't go well."

Things have been awkward between you and him lately. He's made his interest clear, and you haven't responded in kind. You haven't rejected him, either, though, thus the awkwardness. At one point a few weeks back, Alabaster grumbled that you should just roll the boy already, because you were always crankier when you were horny. You called him an ass and changed the subject, but really—Alabaster's why you've been thinking about it more.

You keep thinking about Alabaster, too, though. Is this grief? You hated him, loved him, missed him for years, made yourself forget him, found him again, loved him again, killed him. The grief does not feel like what you feel about Uche, or Corundum, or Innon; those are rents in your soul that still seep blood. The loss of Alabaster is simply . . . a thinning of who you are.

And maybe now is not the time to consider your cataclysm of a love life.

"No," you say. You shrug off your jacket. Underneath you're wearing a sleeveless shirt good for Castrima's warmth. Lerna turns back and crouches and begins swabbing away the blood with a pad of soft rags. "You were right. I shouldn't have gone up there. They had a Guardian."

Lerna's eyes flick up to yours, then back to your wound. "I heard they could stop orogeny."

"This one didn't have to. That damned knife did it for her." You think you know why, too, as you remember Innon. That Guardian didn't negate him, either. Maybe the skin thing only works on roggas whose orogeny is still active. That's how she wanted to kill you. But Lerna's jaw muscle is already tight, and you decide maybe he doesn't need to know that.

"I didn't know about the Guardian," Hoa says unexpectedly. "I'm sorry."

You eye him. "I didn't expect stone eaters to be omniscient."

"I said I would protect you." His voice is more inflectionless, now that he's not in flesh-shape anymore. Or maybe his voice is the same, and you just read it as inflectionless because he has no body language to embellish it. Despite this, he sounds... angry. With himself, maybe.

"You did." You wince as Lerna starts winding a bandage around your arm tightly. No stitches, though, so that's good. "Not that I *wanted* to be dragged into the earth, but your timing was excellent."

"You were hurt." Definitely angry with himself. This is the first time he's sounded to you like the boy he appeared to be for so long. Is he young for one of his kind? Young at heart? Maybe just so open and honest that he might as well be young.

"I'll live. That's what matters."

He falls silent. Lerna works in silence. Between the collective air of disapproval that the two of them exude, you can't help feeling a little guilty.

Afterward you leave Lerna's apartment to head to Flat Top, where Ykka has set up an operations center of her own. Someone's brought the rest of the divans from her apartment, and she's set them up in a rough semicircle, basically bringing her council out into the open. In token of this, Hjarka sprawls over one divan as she usually does, head propped on fist and taking up the whole thing so no one else can sit down, and Tonkee is pacing in the middle of the semicircle. There are others around, anxious or bored people who've brought their own chairs or are sitting on the hard crystal floor, but not as many as you would've expected. There's a lot of activity around the comm, you noticed as you headed to the Flat Top: people fletching arrows in one chamber that you pass, building crossbows in another. Down on the ground level you can see what looks like a longknife-wielding class; a slender young man is teaching about thirty people how to do an over-and-under strike. Over by Scenic Overlook some of the Innovators seem to be rigging what looks like a dropped-rocks trap.

The spectators perk up as you and Lerna come onto the Flat Top, though; that's hilarious. Everyone knows you volunteered to go topside to deliver Castrima's answer to Rennanis. You did this in part to show publicly that you weren't taking over; Ykka's still in charge. Everyone seems to be reading it as a sign that you may be crazy, but at least you're on their side. Such hope in their eyes! It dies down quickly, though. That you are back, and that there is a visibly bloody bandage around one arm, is reassuring to no one.

Tonkee's in full rant about something. Even she's ready for battle, having traded her skirt for billowy pantaloons, tied her hair up atop her head in a scruffy pile of curls, and strapped twin glassknives to both thighs. She actually looks kind of stunning. Then you pay attention to what she's saying. "The third wave will need to be the most delicate touch. Pressure sets them off, see? A temperature differential should make the wind gust enough, the air pressure drop enough. But it has to happen *fast*. And no shaking. We're going to lose the forest either way, but shaking will just make them dig in. We need them moving."

"I can handle that," Ykka says, though she looks troubled. "At least, I can handle part of it."

"No, it has to be done all at once." Tonkee stops and glowers at her. "That's not rusting negotiable." She sees you then and stops, her eyes going immediately to the bandage around your arm.

Ykka turns and her eyes widen, too. "Damn."

You shake your head wearily. "I agreed it was worth a shot. And now we know they can't be reasoned with."

Then you sit down, and the people on the Flat Top fall silent as you impart what intelligence you were able to glean from your trip topside. An army of surplus people occupying the houses, a general named Danel, at least one Guardian. Adding this to what you already know—stone eaters on their side, a whole city more of them somewhere in the Equatorials—paints a bleak picture. But it is the unknowns that are most alarming.

"How did they know about the meat shortage?" No one seems to be holding the gray stone eater's revelation against Ykka, or at least they aren't doing it right now, even though they now know she was keeping the information from them. Headwomen are supposed to make choices like that. "How are they finding the rusting vents?"

"With enough people, it's not hard to search," you start to suggest, but she cuts you off.

"It is. We've been using this geode in one way or another for fifty years. We know the land—and it took us years to find those vents. One's in a damned peat bog further along the river, which stinks to the heavens and occasionally catches fire." She sits forward, propping her elbows on her knees and sighing. "How did they even know we were *here*? Even our trading partners have only ever seen Castrima-over."

"Maybe they have orogenes working with them, too," Lerna says. After so many weeks of hearing mostly *rogga*, his polite *orogene* sounds strained and artificial to your ears. "They could—"

"No," says Ykka. She looks at you then. "Castrima's huge. When you came into the area, did you notice a giant hole in the ground?" You blink in surprise. She nods before you can answer, since your face has said it all. "Yeah, you should have, but something about this place sort of... I don't know. *Shunts away* orogeny. Once you're in it, it's the opposite, of course; the geode feeds on us to power itself. But next time you're topside, and not being almost killed I mean, try sessing this place. You'll see what I'm talking about." She shakes her head. "Even if they've got pet roggas, they shouldn't have known we were here."

Hjarka sighs and rolls onto her back, muttering under her breath. Tonkee bares her teeth, probably a habit she's picking up from Hjarka. "That's not relevant," Tonkee snaps.

"Because you don't want to hear it, babe," Hjarka says. "Doesn't mean it's wrong. You like things neat. Life's not neat."

"*You* like things messy."

"Ykka likes things *explained*," Ykka says pointedly.

Tonkee hesitates, and Hjarka sighs and says, "It's not the first time I've thought there might be a spy in the comm."

Oh, rust. There's an immediate murmur and shuffle among the people listening. Lerna stares at her. "That makes no sense," he says. "None of us has any reason to betray Castrima. Anyone taken into this comm had nowhere else to go."

"That isn't true." Hjarka rolls to sit upright, grinning and flashing her sharp teeth. "I could have gone to my mom's birthcomm. She was Leadership there before she left to go to my birthcomm—too much competition, and she wanted to be a headwoman. I left my comm because I *didn't* want to be headwoman after her. Comm full of assholes. But I definitely wasn't planning to live out my useless years in a hole in the ground." She looks at Ykka.

Ykka sighs in a long-suffering way. "I can't believe you're still mad I didn't ash you. I told you, I needed the help."

"Right. But just saying: I wouldn't have stayed if you'd asked me at the time."

"You'd rather have some overcrowded Equatorial comm with delusions of being Old Sanze reborn?" Lerna frowns.

"*I* wouldn't." Hjarka shrugs. "I like it here now. But I'm saying that somebody else might prefer Rennanis. Enough to sell us out for a place in it."

"We need to find this spy!" shouts someone from over near the rope bridge.

"No," you say then, sharply. It's your teacher voice, and everyone jumps and looks at you. "Danel *said* she hoped to make Castrima tear itself apart. We're not starting any rogga-hunts, here." This has two meanings, but you're not trying to be clever. You know full well that your teacher voice isn't the only reason everyone's staring at you in palpable unease. The spinel still floats behind you, having followed you down from the surface.

Ykka rubs her eyes. "You gotta stop threatening people, Essie. I mean, I know you grew up in the Fulcrum and don't really know any better, but... it's not good community behavior."

You blink, a little thrown and a lot insulted. But... she's right. Comms survive through a careful balance of trust and fear. Your impatience is tilting the balance too far out of true.

"Fine," you say. Everyone relaxes a little, relieved that Ykka can talk you down, and there are even a few nervous chuckles. "But I still don't think it's relevant to discuss whether there's a spy right now. If there is, Rennanis knows what they know. All we can do is try to come up with a plan they won't anticipate."

Tonkee points at you and glares at Hjarka with a wordless *See?*

Hjarka sits forward, planting a hand on one knee and glaring at all of you. She doesn't usually argue much—that was Cutter's role—but you see stubbornness in the set of her jaw now. "It rusting matters if the spy is still here, though. Good luck keeping them from anticipating if—"

The commotion begins at Scenic Overlook. It's hard to see from Flat Top, but someone's shouting for Ykka. She's on her feet at once, heading in that direction, but a small figure—one of the comm's children working as a runner—comes darting along the pathways to meet her before she's even crossed the main bridge from Flat Top. "Message from the topside tunnels!" the boy calls even before he halts. "Says the Rennies are sledgehammering in!"

Ykka looks at Tonkee. Tonkee nods briskly. "Morat said the charges were set."

"Wait, what?" you ask.

Ykka ignores you. To the child, she says, "Tell them to fall back and follow the plan. Go." The boy turns and runs off, though only to a point where he's got a clear sight line to Scenic; he holds up a hand, clenches a fist, and then releases it in a splay of fingers. There's a series of whistles throughout the comm as this signal gets relayed, and a lot of bustling as clusters of people gather and head off into the tunnels. You recognize some of them: Strongbacks and Innovators. You have no idea what's going on.

Ykka seems remarkably calm as she turns back to face you. "Going to need your help," she says softly. "If they're using sledgehammers, then that's good; they don't have any roggas. But collapsing the tunnels will only hold them for a short time, if they're really determined to come down here. And I don't much like the idea of being trapped. Will you help me build an escape tunnel?"

You draw back a little, stunned. Collapsing the tunnels? But of course it is the only strategy that makes sense. Castrima cannot fight off an army that outnumbers them, out-weapons them, and out-allies them in stone eaters and Guardians. "What are we supposed to do, flee?"

Ykka shrugs. You understand now why she looks so tired—not just dealing with the comm almost turning on its roggas, but fear for the future. "It's a contingency. I've had people carrying critical stores into side caverns for days now. We can't carry it all, of course, or even most of it. But if we leave and go hide somewhere—we've got a place, before you ask, storage cavern a few miles away—then even if the Rennies break in, they'll find a comm that's dark and worthless and that will suffocate them if they stay too long. They'll take what they can and go, and maybe we can come back when they're done."

And this is why she's the headwoman: While you've been caught up in your own dramas, Ykka's been doing all this. Still…"If they have even one rogga with them, the geode will function. It'll be theirs. We'll be commless."

"Yeah. As a contingency plan, it blows, you're right." Ykka sighs. "Which is why I want to try Tonkee's plan."

Hjarka looks furious. "I rusting *told* you I don't want to be a headwoman, Yeek."

Ykka rolls her eyes. "You'd rather be commless? Suck it up."

You turn from her to Tonkee and back, feeling completely lost.

Tonkee sighs in frustration, but forces herself to explain. "Controlled orogeny," she says. "Sustained bursts of slow cooling at the surface, in a ring around the area but closing inward, centered on the comm. This will excite the boilbugs into a swarm state. The other Innovators have been studying their behavior for weeks." She flicks her fingers a little, perhaps unconsciously dismissing that sort of research as lesser. "It should work. But it has to be done fast, by someone who has the necessary precision and endurance. The bugs just dig in and go into hibernation otherwise."

Suddenly you understand. It's monstrous. It could also save Castrima. And yet—you look at Ykka. Ykka shrugs, but you think you read tension in her shoulders.

You have never understood how Ykka does the things she does with orogeny. She's a feral. In theory she's *capable* of doing anything you can; a dedicated self-teacher could conceivably master the basics and then refine them from there. Most self-taught roggas just…don't. But you've sessed Ykka when she's working, and it's obvious that in the Fulcrum she'd be ringed, though only two or three rings. She can shift a boulder, not a pebble.

And yet. She can somehow lure every rogga in a hundred-mile

radius to Castrima. And yet, there's whatever she did to Cutter. And yet there is a solidity to her, a stability and implication of strength even though you've seen nothing to explain it, which makes you doubt your Fulcrum-ish assessment of her. A two- or three-ringer doesn't sess like that.

And yet. Orogeny is orogeny; sessapinae are sessapinae. Flesh has limits.

"That army fills both Castrima-over and the forest basin," you say. "You'll pass out before you can ice half of a circle that big."

"Maybe."

"Definitely!"

Ykka rolls her eyes. "I know what I'm rusting doing because I've done it before. There's a way I know. You sort of—" She falters. You decide, if you manage to live through this, that the roggas of Castrima should start trying to come up with words for the things they do. Ykka sighs in frustration herself, as if hearing your thought. "Maybe this is a Fulcrum thing? When you run with another rogga, keep everybody at the same pace, train yourself to the capabilities of the least but use the endurance of the greatest . . . ?"

You blink . . . and then a chill passes through you. "Earthfires and rustbuckets. You know how to—" Alabaster did it to you twice, long ago, once to seal a hot spot and once to save himself from poisoning. "Parallel scale?"

"Is that what you call it? Anyway, when you form a whole group working in parallel, in a . . . a mesh, I could do it with Cutter and Temell before . . . Anyway, I can do that now. Use the other roggas. Even the kids can help." She sighs. You've guessed already. "Thing is, the person who holds the others together . . ."

The yoke, you think, remembering a long-ago angry conversation with Alabaster. "That's the one that burns out first. Has to, to take on the . . . the *friction* of it. Or everybody in the mesh will just cancel each other out. Nothing happens."

Burns out. *Dies.* "Ykka." You're a hundred times more skilled, more precise, than her. You can use the obelisks.

She shakes her head, bemused. "You ever, uh, 'meshed' with anyone before? I told you, it takes practice. And you've got another job to do." Her gaze is intent. "I hear your friend finally kicked off, in the infirmary. He teach you what you needed to know, before?"

You look away, bitterness in your mouth, because the proof of your mastery of individual obelisks is the fact that you killed him with one. But you're no closer to understanding how to open the Gate. You don't know how to use many obelisks together.

First a network, then the Gate. Don't rust it up, Essun.

Oh, Earth. *Oh, you amazing ass*, you think. It's self-directed as well as a thought thrown toward Alabaster.

"Teach me how to build a . . . mesh, with you," you blurt at Ykka. "A network. Let's call it a network."

She frowns at you. "I just told you—"

"That's what he wanted me to do! Flaking, fucking rust." You turn and start pacing, simultaneously excited and horrified and furious. Everyone's staring at you. "Not networking orogeny, networking—" All those times he made you study the threads of magic in his body, in your own body, getting a feel for how they connect and flow. "And of course he couldn't just rusting *tell* me, why would he ever do anything that sensible?"

"Essun." Tonkee's eying you sidelong, a worried look on her face. "You're starting to sound like me."

You laugh at her, even though you didn't think you'd be able to laugh ever again after what you did to 'Baster. "Alabaster," you say. "The man in the infirmary. My friend. He was a ten-ring orogene. He's also the man who broke the continent, up north."

Lots of murmurs at this. Tlino the baker says, "A *Fulcrum* rogga? He was from the *Fulcrum* and he did this?"

You ignore him. "He had reasons." Vengeance, and the chance to make a world that Coru could have lived in, even if Coru was no longer alive. Do they need to know about the Moon? No, there's no time, and it would just confuse everyone as much as the whole mess confuses you. "I didn't understand how he did it until now. 'First a network, then the Gate.' I need to learn how to do what you're about to do, Ykka. You can't die till you teach me."

Something shakes the ambient. It's small, relative to the power of a shake, and localized. You and Ykka and any other roggas on Flat Top immediately turn and look up, orienting on it. An explosion. Someone's set off small shaped charges and brought down one of the tunnels that leads out of Castrima. A few moments later there are shouts from Scenic Overlook. You squint in that direction and see a party of Strongbacks—the ones who were guarding the main tunnel into the comm when you went up to speak with Danel and the Rennanis people—trotting to a halt, breathless and anxious-looking . . . and dusty. They blew the tunnel as they fled.

Ykka shakes her head and says, "Then let's work together on the escape tunnel. Hopefully we won't kill each other in the process."

She beckons, and you follow, and together you half walk, half trot toward the opposite side of the geode. This happens by unspoken agreement; both of you instinctively know exactly where the best additional point to breach the geode lies. Around two platforms, across two bridges, and then the far wall of the geode is there, buried in stubby crystals too short to house any apartments. Good.

Ykka raises her hands and makes a rectangular shape, which confuses you until you sess the sudden sharp force of her orogeny, which pierces the geode wall at four points. It's fascinating. You've observed her before when she does orogeny, but this is the first time she's tried to be precise about something. And—it's completely not what you expected. She can't shift a pebble, but she can slice out corners and lines so neatly that the end result looks machine-carved. It's better than you could have done, and suddenly you realize: Maybe she couldn't shift a pebble because who the rust needs to shift pebbles? That's the Fulcrum's way of testing precision. Ykka's way is to simply *be precise*, where it is practical to do so. Maybe she failed your tests because they were the wrong tests.

Now she pauses and you sess her "hand" being extended to you. You're standing on a platform around a crystal shaft too narrow for apartments, which instead harbors storerooms and a small tool shop. It's recently made, so the railing is made of wood, and you don't much like entrusting your life to it. But you grip the railing and close your eyes anyway, and orogenically reach for the connection that she offers.

She seizes you. If you hadn't been used to this from Alabaster, you would have panicked, but it's the same as what happened back then: Ykka's orogeny sort of melds with and consumes yours. You relax and let her take control, because instantly you realize you are stronger than her and could, should, take control yourself—but you are the learner here, and she is the teacher. So you hold back, to learn.

It is a dance, of sorts. Her orogeny is like . . . a river with eddies, curling and flowing in patterns and at a pace. Yours is faster, deeper, more straightforward, more forceful, but she modulates you so efficiently that the two flows come together. You flow slower and more loosely. She flows faster, using your depth to boost her force. For an instant you open your eyes, see her leaning against the crystal column and sliding down to crouch at its base so that she doesn't have to pay attention to her body while she concentrates . . . and then you are within the geode's crystal substrate, through its shell and burrowing into the rock that surrounds it, flowing around the warps and wends of ancient cold stone. Flowing with Ykka, so easily that you are surprised. Alabaster was rougher than this, but maybe he wasn't used to doing it when he first tried it with you. Ykka has done this with others, and she is as fine a teacher as any you have ever had.

But—

But. Oh! You see it so easily now.

Magic. There are threads of it interwoven with Ykka's flow. Supporting and catalyzing her drive where it is weaker than yours, soothing the layer of contact between you. Where's all this coming from? She drags it out of the rock itself, which is another wonder, because you have not realized until now that there is any magic *in* the rock. But there it is, flitting between the infinitesimal particles of silicon and calcite as easily as it did between the particles of Alabaster's stone substance. Wait. No. Between the calcite and the calcite, specifically, though it touches the silicon. It is being generated by the calcite, which exists in limestone inclusions within the stone. At some point millions or billions of years ago, you suspect, this whole area was at the bottom of an ocean, or perhaps an inland sea. Generations of sea life were born and lived and died here, then settled to that ocean's floor, forming layers and compacting. Are those glacier scrapings that you see? Hard to tell. You're not a geomest.

But what you suddenly understand is this: Magic derives from life—that which is alive, or was alive, or even that which was alive so many ages ago that it has turned into something else. All at once this understanding causes something to shift in your perception, and

and

and

You see it suddenly: *the network.* A web of silver threads interlacing the land, permeating rock and even the magma just underneath, strung like jewels between forests and fossilized corals and pools of oil. Carried through the air on the webs of leaping spiderlings. Threads in the clouds, though thin, strung between microscopic living things in water droplets. Threads as high as your perception can reach, brushing against the very stars.

And where they touch the obelisks, the threads become another thing entirely. For of the obelisks that float against the map of your awareness—which has suddenly become vast, miles and miles, you are perceiving with far more than your sessapinae now—each hovers as the nexus of thousands, millions, *trillions* of threads. This is the power holding them up. Each blazes silvery-white in flickering pulses; Evil Earth, *this is what the obelisks are when they aren't real.* They float and they flicker, solid to magic to solid again, and on another plane of existence you inhale in awe at the beauty of them.

And then you inhale again, as you notice close by—

Ykka's control tugs at you, and belatedly you realize she has used your power even as you meandered through epiphany. Now there is a new tunnel slanting up through the layers of sedimentary and igneous rock. Within it is a staircase of broad, shallow steps, straight up except for wide regular landings. Nothing has been excavated to make room for these stairs; instead, Ykka has simply deformed the rock away, pressing it into the walls and compressing it down to form the stairs and using the increased density to stabilize the tunnel against the weight of the rock around it. But she has stopped the tunnel just shy of breaching the surface, and now she unweaves you from the network (that word again). You blink and turn to her, understanding why at once.

"You can finish it," Ykka says. She's getting up from the platform, dusting off her butt. Already she looks weary; it must have tired her, trying to modulate your surprised fluctuations. She cannot do this thing she has chosen to do. She'll burn out before she's made it halfway around the valley.

And she doesn't have to now. "No. I'll take care of it."

Ykka rubs her eyes. "Essie."

You smile. For once, the nickname doesn't bother you. And then you use what you just learned from her, grabbing her the way Alabaster once did, grabbing all the other roggas in the comm, too. (There is a collective flinch as you do this. They're used to it from Ykka, but they know a different yoke when they sess it. You have not earned their trust as she has.) Ykka stiffens, but you don't do anything, just hold her, and now it's obvious: You really can do it.

Then you drive the point home by connecting to the spinel. It is behind you, but you sess the instant that it stops flickering and instead sends forth a silent, earth-shivering pulse. *Ready*, you think it's saying. As if it speaks.

Ykka's eyes widen suddenly as she sesses just how the obelisk's catalysis... charges? awakens? awakens—the network of roggas. That's because you're now doing the thing that Alabaster tried to teach you for six months: using orogeny and magic together in a way that supports and strengthens each, making a stronger whole. Then integrating this into a network of orogenes working toward a single goal, all of them together stronger than they are individually, and plugged into an obelisk that amplifies their power manifold. It is amazing.

Alabaster failed to teach it to you because he was like you—Fulcrum-trained and Fulcrum-limited, taught only to think of power in terms of energy and equations and geometric shapes. He mastered magic because of who he was, but he did not truly understand it. Neither do you, even now. Ykka, feral that she is, with nothing to unlearn, was the key all along. If you hadn't been so arrogant...

Well. No. You cannot say Alabaster would be alive. He was dead the instant he used the Obelisk Gate to rip the continent in half. The burns were killing him already; that you finished it was mercy. Eventually you'll believe that.

Ykka blinks and frowns. "You okay?"

She knows the magic of you, and tastes your grief. You swallow against the lump in your throat—carefully, keeping tight hold of the power held pent within you. "Yeah," you lie.

Ykka's gaze is too knowing. She sighs. "You know . . . we both get through this, I have a stash of Yumenescene seredis in one of the storecaches. Want to get drunk?"

The tightness in your throat seems to snap, and you laugh it out. Seredis is a distilled liqueur made from a fruit of the same name that was harvested in the foothills just outside Yumenes. The trees didn't grow well anywhere else, so Ykka's stash might be the last seredis in the whole of the Stillness. "*Pricelessly* drunk?"

"*Disastrously* drunk." Her smile is weary, but real.

You like the sound of this. "If we get through this." But you're pretty sure that you will now. There's more than enough power in the orogene network and the spinel. You'll make Castrima safe for stills and roggas and anything else that's on your side. No one needs to die, except your enemies.

With that, you turn and raise your hands, splaying fingers as your orogeny—and magic—stretch forth.

You perceive Castrima: over, under, and all the matter between and below and above. Now the army of Rennanis is before you, hundreds of points of heat and magic on your mental map, some clustering in houses that do not belong to them and the rest clustering around the three tunnel mouths that lead into the underground comm. In two of the tunnels, they've broken through the boulders that one of Castrima's roggas positioned to seal them. In one of these, rocks have collapsed the passageway. Some of the soldiers are dead, their bodies cooling.

Other soldiers are working to clear the blockage. You can tell that's going to take a few days, at least.

But in the other—flaking *rust*—they've found and disabled the charges. You taste the acridity of unspent chemical potential, and the sourness of bloodlust-sweat; they are making their way unobstructed toward Castrima-under, and are more than halfway to Scenic Overlook. In minutes the first of them, several dozen Strongbacks bristling with longknives and crossbows and slingshots and spears, will hit the comm's defenses. Hundreds more file into the tunnel mouth behind them.

You know what you have to do.

You withdraw from this close view. Now the forest around Castrima spreads below you. Wider view: Now you taste the edges of Castrima's plateau, and the nearby depression that is the forest basin. Obvious now that there was once a sea here, and a glacier before that, and more. Obvious, too, are the knots of light and fire that comprise the life of the region, scattered throughout the forest. More of it than you thought, though much of it is hibernating or hidden or otherwise guarding itself against the Season's onslaught. Very bright along the river: Boilbugs infest both its banks and most of the plateau and basin beyond.

You begin with the river, then, delicately chilling the soil and air and stone along its length. You do this in pulsing waves, there and cool and there again and a little cooler. You drop the air pressure just on the inside of the circle of cold you're shaping, which causes wind to blow inward, toward Castrima. It is encouragement and warning: *Move and you'll live. Stay and I'll ice you little bastards to extinction.*

The boilbugs move. You perceive them as a wave of bright heat that surges out of underground nests and aboveground feeding piles that have formed around their many victims—hundreds of nests, millions of bugs, you had no idea the forest of Castrima was so riddled with them. Tonkee's warning about the meat shortage is meaningless and too late; you could never have competed against such successful predators. You were always going to have to get used to the taste of human anyway.

That's neither here nor there. The ring of cold around Castrima's territory is complete, and you direct the energy inward in waves, pushing, herding. The bugs are *fast*—and rusting hell, they can fly. You'd forgotten the wing covers.

And…oh, burning Earth. Suddenly you're glad you can only sess what's happening topside, not see or hear it.

What you perceive is painted in pressure and heat and chemical and magic. Here is a bright living cluster of Rennanis soldiers, bunched up within confines of wood and brick, as a swarm of blazing-hot boilbug motes reaches it. Through the foundation of the house you sess pounding feet, the slam of a door, the fleshier slam of bodies against each other and the floor. Mini-shakes of panic. The shapes of the soldiers glow brighter upon the ambient as the bugs land and do their work, boiling and steaming.

Terteis Hunter Castrima was unlucky; only a few bugs got him, which is why he didn't die of it. This is dozens of boilbugs per soldier, covering every accessible bit of flesh, and it is a kindness. They do not thrash for long, your enemies, and one by one the houses of Castrima-over become still and silent once more.

(The network shudders in your yoke. None of the others like

this. You steer them firmly, keeping them on task. There can be no mercy now.)

Now the swarms move into the basements, falling upon the soldiers gathered there, finding the hidden tunnels that lead down into Castrima-under. You lean on the spinel's power more here, trying to sess which of the living motes in the tunnels are Rennanis soldiers and which are Castrima's defenders. They're in clusters, fighting. You have to help your people—*ach*—rusting—shit. Ykka bucks against your control, and though you are too embedded in the network to hear what she says out loud, you get the idea.

You know what you have to do.

So you pull a chunk out of the walls and use this to seal off the tunnels. Some of Castrima's Strongbacks and Innovators are on the boilbug side of the seal. Some of Rennanis's soldiers are on the safe side of it. No one ever gets everything they want.

Through the stone of the tunnels, you cannot help sessing the vibration of screams.

But before you can force yourself to ignore this, there is another scream, nearer-by, a vibration that you perceive with eardrums and not sessapinae. Startled, you begin to dismantle the network—but not fast enough, not nearly, before something yanks at your yoke. *Breaks* it, throwing you and all the other roggas tumbling over each other and canceling one another's toruses as you come out of alignment. What the rust? Something has ripped two of your number loose.

You open your eyes to find yourself sprawled on the wooden platform, one arm painfully twisted under you, your face pressed against a storage crate. Confused and groaning—your knees are weak, being the yoke is *hard*—you push yourself up. "Ykka? What was...?"

There is a sound beyond the crates. A gasp. A groan of wood from the platform beneath you, as something incomprehensibly heavy stresses the supports. A crunch of stone, so startlingly loud that you flinch even as you realize you've heard this sound before. Grabbing the edge of the crate and the wooden railing, you haul yourself up on one knee. That's enough for you to see:

Hoa, in a pose that your mind immediately and half-consciously names *Warrior*, stands with one arm extended. From the hand dangles a head. A *stone eater's* head, hair a curling coiffure in mother-of-pearl, face gone below the top lip. The rest of the stone eater, lower jaw on down, stands in front of Hoa, frozen in a posture of reaching for something. You can see Hoa's face in partial side view. It isn't moving or chewing, but there's pale stone dust on his finely carved black-marble lips. There's a divot about the size of a bite wound in what's left of the stone eater's nape. That was the familiar crunch.

An instant later the stone eater's remains *shatter*, and you realize Hoa's position has changed to put a fist through its torso. Then his eyes slide toward you. He doesn't swallow that you can see, but then he doesn't need his mouth to speak anyway. "Rennanis's stone eaters are coming for Castrima's orogenes."

Oh, Evil Earth. You make yourself get up, though you feel light-headed and unsteady on your feet. "How many?"

"Enough." Flick and Hoa's head has turned away, toward Scenic Overlook. You look and see heavy fighting there—the people of Castrima fighting back against the Rennanese who've made it down the tunnel. You spy Danel among the attackers, laying on with twin longknives against two Strongbacks as nearby, Esni shouts for another crossbow; hers has jammed. She drops her useless weapon and draws a knapped agate knife that flashes white in the light, then throws herself into the Danel fight.

And then your attention focuses on the nearer distance, where Penty has gotten herself tangled in a rope bridge. You see why: On the metal platform behind her stands another strange stone eater, this one allover citrine-gold but for the white mica around her lips. It stands with one hand extended, the fingers curled in a beckoning gesture. Penty is far from you, maybe fifty feet, but you can see tears streaking the girl's face as she struggles to extract herself from the ropes. One of her hands flops uselessly. Broken.

Her hand is broken. Your skin prickles all over. "Hoa."

There is a thunk against the wooden platform as he drops the head of his enemy. "Essun."

"I need to go topside fast." You can sess it up there, magic-feel it, looming and huge. It's been here all along, but you've been shying away from it. Too much for what you needed before. Exactly what you need now.

"Topside's crawling, Essie. Nothing but boilbugs." Ykka is standing, just, by bracing herself against the crystal's wall. You want to warn her—the stone eaters can come through the crystal—but there isn't time. If you're too slow, they'll get her regardless.

You shake your head and stagger over to Hoa. He can't come to you; he's so damned heavy that it's a wonder the wooden platform hasn't collapsed already. His pose has changed again, now that the other stone eater is just chunks scattered around him; now he has moved to place one hand on the crystal's wall, though the rest of him is facing you. His other hand extends toward you, open with invitation. You remember a day by a riverside, after Hoa fell into the mud. You offered him a hand to help him up, not realizing he weighed of diamond bones and ancient tales untold. He refused you to keep his secret, and you were hurt, though you tried not to be.

Now his hand is cool compared to the warmth of Castrima. Solid—although he does not sess quite of stone, you realize in fleeting fascination. There's a strange texture to his flesh. A very slight yielding to the pressure of your fingers. He has fingerprints. That surprises you.

Then you look up at his face. He's reshaped his expression from the coldness that you saw when he destroyed his enemy. Now there is a slight smile on his lips. "Of course I'll help you," he says. So much of the boy is still in him that you almost smile back.

There isn't time to parse this further, because all at once Castrima blurs into whiteness around you and then there is darkness, earthen-black. Hoa's hand is on yours, however, so you do not panic.

Then you stand before the pavilion of Castrima-over, amid the dead and dying. Around you on the walkways and pavilion flagstones lie the soldiers of Rennanis, their bodies twisted, some of them impossible to see beneath carpets of insects, a very few of them still crawling and screaming. The table that Danel used to plan the attack is overturned nearby; beetles crawl over its surface. There's that smell again, of meat in brine. The air swirls with boilbugs and the low-pressure breeze you created.

One of the bugs darts toward you and you cringe. An instant later Hoa's hand is where the bug was, dripping hot water as the teakettle whistle of the crushed creature fizzles away. "You should probably raise a torus," he advises. Flaking rust yes. You begin to pull away from him so you can do this safely, but his hand tightens on your own, just a little. "Orogeny can't hurt me."

You have more power at your disposal than just orogeny, but he knows that, so all right, then. You raise a high, tight torus around yourself, swirling with snow from the humidity, and immediately the boilbugs begin avoiding you. Perhaps they track prey by body heat. It's all irrelevant.

You look up then, at the blackness that blots out the sky.

The onyx is like no obelisk you've ever seen. Most are shards—double-pointed hexagonal or octagonal columns—though you've seen a few that were irregular or rough-ended. This one is an ovoid cabochon, at your summons descending slowly through the cloud layer that has hidden it since its arrival a few weeks before. You can't guess at its dimensions, but when you turn your head to take in the bowl of Castrima-over's sky, the onyx nearly fills it, south to north, gray-clouded horizon to underlit red. It reflects nothing, and does not shine. When you look up into it—this is surprisingly hard to do without cringing—only scuds of cloud around its edges tell you that it is actually hovering high above Castrima. Looking at it, it feels closer. Right above you. You have but to lift your hand... but some part of you is terrified of doing this.

There is a strata-shaking thud as the spinel drops to the ground behind you, as if in supplication to this greater thing. Or perhaps it is only that, with the onyx here and pulling at you, drawing you in, drawing you up—

—oh, Earth, it draws you *so fast*—

—there is nothing left of you that can command any other obelisk. You've got nothing to spare. You are falling up, flying into a void that does not so much rush you along as *suck* at you. You have learned from other obelisks to submit to their current, but at once you know better than to do that here. The onyx will swallow you whole. But you cannot fight it, either; it will rip you apart.

The best you can manage is a kind of precarious equilibrium, in which you pull against it yet still drift through its interstices. And too much of it is in you already, so much. You need to use this power or, or, but no, something is wrong, something is slipping out of equilibrium, suddenly there is light lashing around you and you realize you are tangled in a trillion, quintillion threads of magic and they are tightening.

On another plane of existence you scream. This was a mistake. *It's eating you*, and it is awful. Alabaster was wrong. Better to let the stone eaters kill every rogga in Castrima and destroy the comm than die like this. Better to let Hoa chew you to pieces with his beautiful teeth; at least you like him

love him

lo lo lo lo l o v e

Whiplash tightening of magic, in a thousand directions. Light-lattice blazing alive, suddenly, against the black. *You see.* This is so far past your normal range that it is nearly incomprehensible. You see the Stillness, the whole of it. You perceive the half shell of this side of the planet, taste whiffs of the other side. It's too much—and fire-under-Earth, you're a fool. Alabaster told you: first a network, then the Gate. You cannot do this alone; you need a smaller network to buffer the greater. You fumble toward the orogenes of Castrima again, but you cannot grasp them. There are fewer of them now, their numbers flaring and snuffing out even as you reach, and they are too panicked for even you to claim.

But there, right beside you, is a small mountain of strength: Hoa. You don't even try to reach for him, because that strength is alien and frightening, but he reaches for you. Stabilizes you. Holds you firm.

Which allows you to finally remember: *The onyx is the key.*

The key unlocks a gate.

The gate activates a network—

And suddenly the onyx pulses, magma-deep and earthen-heavy, around you.

Oh Earth not a network of orogenes he meant a network of

The spinel is first, right there, as it is. The topaz is next, its bright airy power yielding to you so easily.

The smoky quartz. The amethyst, your old friend, plodding after you from Tirimo. The kunzite. The jade.

oh

The agate. The jasper, the opal, the citrine…

You open your mouth to scream and do not hear yourself.

the ruby the spodumene THE AQUAMARINE THE PERIDOT THE

"It's too much!" You don't know if you're screaming the words in your mind or out loud. "Too much!"

The mountain beside you says, "They need you, Essun."

And everything snaps into focus. Yes. The Obelisk Gate opens only for a *purpose*.

Down. Geode walls. Flickering columns of proto-magic; what Castrima is made of. You sess-feel-know the contaminants within its structure. Those that crawl over its surfaces you permit.

(Ykka, Penty, all the other roggas, and the stills who depend on them to keep the comm going. They all need you.)

Yet there are also those interfering with its crystal lattices, riding along its strands of matter and magic, lurking within the rock around the geode shell like parasites trying to burrow in. They are mountains, too—But they are not *your* mountain.

Pissed off the wrong rogga, Hoa said of his own incarceration. Yes, these enemy stone eaters rusting did.

You shout again but this time it is effort, it is aggression. SNAP and you break lattices and magic strands and reseal them to your own design. CRACK and you lift whole crystal shafts to throw them like spears and grind your enemies beneath. You look for Gray Man, the stone eater who hurt Hoa, but he is not among the mountains that threaten your home. These are just his minions. Fine. You'll send him a message, then, written in their fear.

By the time you're done, you've sealed at least five of the enemy stone eaters into crystals. Easy to do, really, when they are so foolish as to try to transit through them while you're watching. They phase into the crystal; you simply de-phase them, freezing them like bugs in amber. The rest are fleeing.

Some flee north. Unacceptable, and distance is nothing for you now. You pull up and wheel and pierce down again, and there is Rennanis, nestled within its lattice of nodes like a spider among its bundled, sucked-dry prey. The Gate is meant to do things on a planetary scale. It is nothing to you to drive power down and inflict upon every citizen of Rennanis the same thing you did to the woman who would've beaten Penty to death. Bullies are bullies. So simple to twist the flickering silver between their cells until those cells grow still, solid. Stone. It is done, and Castrima's war won, in the span of a breath.

Now it's dangerous. Now you understand: To wield the power of this network of obelisks without a focus is to *become* its focus, and die. The wise thing to do, now that Castrima is safe, would be to dismantle the Gate and withdraw from the connection before it destroys you.

But. There are other things you want besides Castrima's safety.

The Gate is like orogeny, you see. Without conscious control, it responds to all desires as if they are the desire to destroy the world. And you will not control this. You cannot. This desire is as quintessential to you as your past or your defensive personality or your many-times-broken heart.

Nassun.

Your awareness spins. South. Tracking.

Nassun.

Interference. It hurts. The pearl the diamond the

Sapphire. It resists being pulled into the network of the Gate. You barely noticed before, overwhelmed as you were by dozens, hundreds of obelisks, but you notice now because

NASSUN

IT'S HER

It is your daughter, it's Nassun, you know the stolid complexity of her as you know your own heart and soul, *it's her, written all over this obelisk* and you have found her, she is alive.

Its (your) goal accomplished, the Gate automatically begins to disengage. The other obelisks disconnect; the onyx releases you last, albeit with a whiff of cold reluctance. Next time.

And as your body sags and lists to one side because something suddenly throws off your balance, hands take hold of you and pull you upright. You can barely lift your head. Your body feels distant, heavy, like the sensation of being in stone. You have not eaten in hours, but you feel no hunger. You know you've been taxed far beyond your own endurance, but you feel no exhaustion.

There are mountains around you. "Rest, Essun," says the one you love. "I'll take care of you."

You nod with a head heavy as a boulder. Then new presences pull at your attention, and you force yourself to look up one last time.

Antimony stands before you, impassive as ever, but there is something comforting about her presence nevertheless. You know instinctively that she is no enemy.

Beside her stands another stone eater: tall, slender, somehow awkward in its draped "clothing." Allover white, though the shape of its facial features is Eastern Coaster: full mouth and long nose, high cheekbones and a sculpture of neatly sculpted, kinky hair. Only its eyes are black, and though they watch you with only faint recognition, with a puzzled flicker of something that might be (but should not be) memory...something about those eyes is familiar.

How ironic. This is the first time you've ever seen a stone eater made of alabaster.

And then you are gone.

* * *

What if it isn't dead?

—*Letter from Rido Innovator Dibars to Seventh University, sent via courier from Allia Quartent and Comm after the raising of the garnet obelisk, received three months after word of Allia's destruction spread via telegraph. Unknown reference.*

INTERLUDE

You fall into my arms, and I take you to a safe place.

Safety is relative. You have driven off my unsavory brethren, those of my kind who would have killed you since they cannot control you. As I descend into Castrima, however, and emerge in a quiet space of familiarity, I smell iron on the air, amid the shit and stale breath and other scents of flesh, and smoke. The iron is a flesh scent, too: that variant of iron which is contained in blood. Outside, there are bodies along the walkways and steps. One even dangles from a ropeslide. The fighting is mostly over, however, because of two things. First, the invaders have realized they are trapped between the insect-infested surface and their enemies, who are greater in number now that most of the invading army is dead. Those who wish to live have surrendered; those who fear a worse death have flung themselves on the swords or crystals of Castrima.

The second thing that has stopped the fighting is the inescapable fact that the geode is badly damaged. All over the comm, the once-glowing crystals now flicker in irregular pulses. One of the longer ones has detached from the wall and broken, its dust and rubble scattered along the geode floor. On the ground level, warm water has stopped flowing into the communal pool, though occasionally there is a haphazard spurt of it. Several of the comm's crystals are completely dark, dead, cracked—but within each, a darker shape can be seen, frozen and trapped. Humanoid.

Fools. That's what you get for pissing off my rogga.

I lay you in a bed and make certain there is food and water nearby. Feeding you will be difficult, now that I have shed the quickened sheath I wore to friend you, but most likely someone will be along before I am forced to try. We are in Lerna's apartment. I've put you in his bed. He will like that, I think. You will, too, once you want to feel human again.

I do not begrudge you these connections. You need them.

(I do not begrudge you these connections. You need them.)

But I position you carefully, so that you will be comfortable. And I place your arm atop the covers, so you will know as soon as you awaken that you must now make a choice.

Your right arm, which has become a thing of brown, solidified, concentrated magic. No crudeness here; your flesh is pure, perfect, wholesome. Every atom is as it should be, the arcane lattice precise and strong. I touch it once, briefly, though my fingers barely notice the pressure. Leftover longing from the flesh I wore so recently. I'll get over it.

Your stone hand is shaped into a fist. There's a crack across the back of it, perpendicular to the hand bones. Even as the magic reshaped you, you fought. (You fought. This is what you must become. You have always fought.)

Ah, I grow sentimental. A few weeks' nostalgia in flesh and I forget myself.

Thus I wait. And hours or days later when Lerna returns to his apartment, stinking of other people's blood and his own weariness, he stops short at the sight of me, standing watchman in his living room.

He's still for only a moment. "Where is she?"

Yes. He's worthy of you.

"In the bedroom." He goes there immediately. There's no need for me to follow. He'll be back.

Some while later—minutes or hours, I know the words but they mean so little—he returns to the living room where I stand. He sits, heavily, and rubs his face.

"She will live," I say unnecessarily.

"Yes." He knows it's a coma and he will tend you well until you wake. A moment later he lowers his hands and gazes at me. "You didn't, uh." He licks his lips. "Her arm."

I know exactly what he means. "Not without her permission."

His face twists. I'm faintly repelled before I remember that not long ago I, too, was so constantly, wetly, in motion. Glad that's over with. "How honorable of you," he says, in a tone that he probably means as an insult.

No more honorable than his decision not to eat your other arm. Some things are simple decency.

Some while later, probably not years because he hasn't moved, possibly hours because he does look so very tired, he says, "I don't know what we're going to do now. Castrima's dying." As if to emphasize these words, the crystal around us stops glowing for a moment, dropping us into darkness lit harshly by the light from outside the apartment. Then the light returns. Lerna exhales, his breath redolent of fear-aldehydes. "We're commless."

It isn't worth pointing out that they would have also been commless if their enemies had succeeded in slaughtering Essun and the other orogenes. He'll figure it out eventually, in his plodding, sweaty way. But since there's one thing he does not know, I speak it aloud.

"Rennanis is dead," I say. "Essun killed it."

"What?"

He heard me. He just doesn't believe what he heard.

"You mean . . . she iced it? From here?"

No, she used magic, but all that matters is, "Everyone within its walls is now dead."

He ponders this for eternities, or maybe seconds. "An Equatorial city would have vast storecaches. Enough to last us years." Then his brow furrows. "Traveling there and bringing that many goods back would be a major undertaking."

He isn't a stupid man. I ponder the past while he figures things out. When he gasps, I pay attention to him again.

"Rennanis is empty.*" He stares at me, then gets to his feet, thumping and sloshing across the room. "Evil Earth—Hoa, that's what you're saying! Intact walls, intact homes, storecaches . . . and who the rust are we going to have to fight for it? No one with sense goes north, these days. We could* live *there."*

At last. I return to my contemplations even as he mutters to himself and paces and finally laughs aloud. But then Lerna stops, staring at me. His eyes narrow in suspicion.

"You do nothing for us," he says softly. "Only for her. Why are you telling me this?"

I shape my lips into a curve, and his jaw tightens in disgust. I shouldn't have bothered. "Essun wants somewhere safe for Nassun," I say.

Silence, for maybe an hour. Or a moment. "She doesn't know where Nassun is."

"The Obelisk Gate permits sufficient precision of perception."

A flinch. I remember the words for movement: flinch, inhale, swallow, grimace. "Earthfires. Then—" He sobers and turns to look at the bedroom curtain.

Yes. When you wake, you will want to go find your daughter. I watch this realization soften Lerna's face, weigh down the tension of his muscles, slacken his posture. I have no idea what any of these things means.

"Why?" It takes a year for me to realize he's speaking to me and not himself. By the time I figure it out, however, he has finished the question. "Why do you stay with her? Are you just . . . hungry?"

I resist the urge to crush his head. "I love her, of course." There; I've managed a civil tone.

"Of course." Lerna's voice has grown soft.

Of course.

He leaves then, to ferry the information I've given him to the comm's other leaders. There follows a century, or a week, of frantic activity as the other people of the comm pack and prepare and gather their strength for what is sure to be a long, grueling, and—for a few—deadly journey. But they have no choice. Such is life, in a Season.

Sleep, my love. Heal. I'll stand guard over you, and be at your side when you set forth again. Of course. Death is a choice. I will make certain of that, for you.

(But not for you.)

20

Nassun, faceted

BUT ALSO...

I listen through the earth. I hear the reverberations. When a new key is cut, her bittings finally ground and sharpened enough that she can connect to the obelisks and make them sing, we all know of it. Those of us who...hope...seek out that singer. We are forever barred from turning the key ourselves, but we can influence its direction. Whenever an obelisk resonates, you may be sure that one of us lurks nearby. We talk. This is how I know.

* * *

In the dead of the night Nassun wakes. It's dark in the barracks, still, so she's careful not to step on the creakier floorboards as she pulls on her shoes and jacket and makes her way across the room. None of the others stirs, if they even wake and notice. They probably just think she has to go to the outhouse.

Outside, it's quiet. The sky is beginning to lighten with dawn in the east, though it's harder to tell now that the ash clouds have thickened. She goes to the top of the downhill path and notices a few lights on in Jekity. Some of the farmers and fishers are up. In Found Moon, though, all is still.

What is it that tugs at her mind? The feel of it is irritating, *gummy*, as if something is caught in her hair and needs to be yanked free. The sensation is centered in her sessapinae—no. Deeper. This tugs at the light of her spine, the silver between her cells, the threads that bind her to the ground and to Found Moon and to Schaffa and to the sapphire that hovers just above the clouds of Jekity, visible now and again when the clouds break a little. The irritation is... it is... north.

Something is happening up north.

Nassun turns to follow the sensation, climbing the hill up to the crucible mosaic and stopping at its center as the wind makes her hair puffs shiver. Up here she can see the forest that surrounds Jekity spread before her like a map: rounded treetops and occasional outcroppings of ribbon-basalt. Part of her can perceive shifting forces, reverberating lines, connections, amplification. But of what? Why? Something immense.

"What you perceive is the opening of the Obelisk Gate," says Steel. She is unsurprised to find him suddenly standing beside her.

"More than one obelisk?" Nassun asks, because that's what she's sessing. *Lots* more.

"Every one stationed above this half of the continent. A hundred parts of the great mechanism beginning to work again as they were meant to." Steel's voice, baritone and surprisingly pleasant, sounds wistful in this moment. Nassun finds herself wondering about his life, his past, whether he has ever been a child like her. That seems impossible. "So much power. The very heart of the planet is channeled through the Gate...and she uses it for so frivolous a purpose." A faint sigh. "Then again, so did its original creators, I suppose."

Somehow, Nassun knows that Steel is talking about her mother with that *she*. Mama is alive, and angry, and full of so much power.

"What purpose?" Nassun makes herself ask.

Steel's eyes slide toward her. She has not specified whose purpose she means: her mother's, or those ancient people who first created and deployed the obelisks. "The destruction of one's enemies, of course. A small and selfish purpose that feels great, in the moment—though not without consequence."

Nassun considers what she has learned, and sessed, and seen in the dead smiles of the other two Guardians. "Father Earth fought back," she says.

"As one does, against those who seek to enslave. That's understandable, isn't it?"

Nassun closes her eyes. Yes. It's all so understandable, really, when she thinks about it. The way of the world isn't the strong devouring the weak, but the weak deceiving and poisoning and whispering in the ears of the strong until they become weak, too. Then it's all broken hands and silver threads woven like ropes, and mothers who move the earth to destroy their enemies but cannot save one little boy.

(Girl.)

There has never been anyone to save Nassun. Her mother warned her there never would be. If Nassun ever wants to be free of fear, she has no choice but to forge that freedom for herself.

So she turns, slowly, to face her father, who stands quietly behind her.

"Sweetening," he says. It's the voice he usually uses for her, but she knows it isn't real. His eyes are cold as the ice she left all over his house a few days ago. His jaw is tight, his body shaking just a little. She glances down at his tight fist. There's a knife in it—a beautiful one made from red opal, her favorite of his more recent work. It has a slight iridescence and a smooth sheen that completely disguises the razor-sharpness of its knapped edges.

"Hi, Daddy," she says. She glances toward Steel, who is surely aware of what Jija intends. But the gray stone eater has not bothered to turn away from the predawn forestscape, or the northern sky where so many earth-changing things are happening.

Very well. She faces her father again. "Mama's alive, Daddy."

If the words mean anything to him, it doesn't show. He just keeps standing there looking at her. Looking at her eyes in particular. She's always had her mother's eyes.

Suddenly it doesn't matter. Nassun sighs and rubs her face with her hands, as weary as Father Earth must be after so many eternities of hate. Hate is tiring. Nihilism is easier, though she does not know the word and will not for a few years. It's what she's feeling, regardless: an overwhelming sense of the meaninglessness of it all.

"I think I understand why you hate us," she says to her father as she drops her hands to her sides. "I've done bad things, Daddy, like you probably thought I would. I don't know how to *not* do them. It's like everybody wants me to be bad, so there's nothing else I can be." She hesitates, then says what's been in her mind for months now, unspoken. She doesn't think she'll have another chance to say it. "I wish you could love me anyway, even though I'm bad."

She thinks of Schaffa as she says this, though. Schaffa, who loves her no matter what, as a father should.

Jija just keeps staring at her. Elsewhere in the silence, on that plane of awareness that is occupied by sesuna and whatever the sense of the silver threads is called, Nassun feels her mother collapse. To be specific, she feels her mother's exertion upon the shifting, glimmering network of obelisks suddenly cease. Not that it ever touched her sapphire.

"I'm sorry, Daddy," Nassun says at last. "I tried to keep loving you, but it was too hard."

He's much bigger than her. Armed, where she is not. When he moves, it is with a mountainous lumber, all shoulders first and bulk and slow buildup to unstoppable speed. She weighs barely a hundred pounds. She has no real chance.

But in the instant that she feels the twitch of her father's muscles, small reverberating shocks against the ground and air, she orients her awareness toward the sky in a single, ringing command.

The transformation of the sapphire is instantaneous. It causes a concussion of air that rushes inward to fill the vacuum. The sound this makes is the loudest crack of thunder Nassun has ever heard. Jija, in mid-lunge, starts and stumbles, looking up. A moment later the sapphire slams into the ground before Nassun, cracking the central stone of the crucible mosaic and a six-foot radius of ground around her.

It isn't the sapphire as she's seen it up till now, although the sameness of it transcends things like shape. When she extends her hand to wrap around the hilt of the long, flickering knife of blue stone, she falls into it a little. Up, flowing through watery facets of light and shadow. In, down into the earth. Out, away, brushing against the other parts of the whole that is the Gate. The thing in her hand is the same monstrous, mountainous dynamo of silvery power that it has always been. The same tool, just more versatile now.

Jija stares at it, then at her. There is an instant in which he wavers, and Nassun waits. If he turns, runs...he was her father once. Does he remember that time? She wants him to. Nothing between them will ever be the same again, but she wants that time to matter.

No. Jija comes at her again, shouting as he raises the knife.

So Nassun lifts the sapphire blade from the earth. It's nearly the length of her body, but it weighs nothing; the sapphire floats, after all. It's just floating here in front of her instead of above. She doesn't lift it, either, strictly speaking. She wills it to move to a new position and it does. In front of her. Between her and Jija, so that when Jija angles his body to stab her, he cannot help bumping right into it. This makes it easy, inevitable, for her power to lay into him.

She doesn't kill him with ice. Nassun defaults to using the silver instead of orogeny most days. The shift of Jija's flesh is more controlled than what she did to Eitz, largely because she is aware of what she's doing, and also because she's doing it on purpose. Jija begins to turn to stone, starting at the point of contact between him and the obelisk.

What Nassun doesn't consider is momentum, which carries Jija forward even as he glances off the sapphire and twists and sees what is happening to his flesh and starts to inhale for a scream. He doesn't finish the inhalation before his lungs are solidified. He does, however, finish his lunge, though it is off-balance and out of control, more of a fall than an attack by now. Still, it is a fall with a knife as its focal point, and so the knife catches Nassun in the shoulder. He was aiming for her heart.

The pain of the strike is sudden and terrible and it breaks Nassun's concentration at once. This is bad because the sapphire flares as her pain does, flickering into its half-real state and back as she gasps and staggers. This finishes Jija in an instant, solidifying him completely into a statue with a frizz of smoky-quartz hair and a round red-ocher face and clothes of deep blue serendibite, because he wore dark clothing in order to stalk his daughter. This statue stands poised for only an instant, though—and then the flicker of the sapphire sends a ripple through him like a struck bell. Not unlike the concussion of turned-inward orogenic force that a Guardian once inflicted on a man named Innon.

Jija shatters in the same way, just not as wetly. He's brittle stuff, weak, poorly made. The pieces of him tumble into stillness around Nassun's feet.

Nassun gazes at the remains of her father for a long, aching moment. Beyond her, in Found Moon and down below in Jekity, lights are coming on in the cabins. Everyone's been woken up by the thunderclap of the sapphire. There is confusion, voices calling back and forth, frantic sessing and probes of the earth.

Steel now gazes down at Jija with her. "It never ends," he says. "It never gets better."

Nassun says nothing. Steel's words fall into her like a stone into water, and she does not ripple in their wake.

"You'll kill everything you love, eventually. Your mother. Schaffa. All your friends here in Found Moon. No way around it."

She closes her eyes.

"No way . . . except one." A careful, considered pause. "Shall I tell you that way?"

Schaffa is coming. She can sess him, the buzz of him, the constant torment of the thing in his brain that he will not let her remove. Schaffa, who loves her.

You'll kill everything you love, eventually.

"Yes," she makes herself say. "Tell me how not to . . ." She trails off. She can't say hurt them, because she has already hurt so many. She's a monster. But there must be a way for her monstrousness to be contained. For the threat of an orogene's existence to be ended.

"The Moon's coming back, Nassun. It was lost so long ago, flung away like a ball on a paddle-string—but the string has drawn it back. Left to itself, it will pass by and fly off again; it's done that before, several times now."

She can see one of her father's eyes, set into a chunk of his face, gazing up at her from amid the pile. His eyes were green, and now they have become a beautiful shade of clouded peridot.

"But with the Gate, you can . . . nudge it. Just a little. Adjust its tra—" A soft, amused sound. "The path that the Moon naturally follows. Instead of letting it pass again, lost and wandering, bring it home. Father Earth's been missing it. Bring it straight here and let them have a reunion."

Oh. *Oh*. She understands, suddenly, why Father Earth wants her dead.

"It will be a terrible thing," Steel says softly, nearly in her ear because he's moved closer to her. "It will end the Seasons. It will end *every* season. And yet...what you're feeling right now, you need never feel again. No one will ever suffer again."

Nassun turns to stare at Steel. He's bent toward her, a look of almost comical slyness chiseled on his face.

Then Schaffa trots to a stop before them. He's staring at the ruin of Jija, and she sees the moment when the realization of what he's seeing flickers across his face, a mobile shockwave. His icewhite gaze lifts to her, and she searches his expression with her belly clenched against imminent pain.

There is only anguish in his face. Fear for her, sorrow on her behalf, alarm at her bloodied shoulder. Wariness and protective anger, as he focuses on Steel. He is still her Schaffa. The ache of Jija fades within the ease of his regard. *Schaffa* will love her no matter what she becomes.

So Nassun turns then, to Steel, and says, "Tell me how to bring the Moon home."

APPENDIX 1

A catalog of Fifth Seasons that have been recorded prior to and since the founding of the Sanzed Equatorial Affiliation, from most recent to oldest

Choking Season: 2714–2719 Imperial. Proximate cause: volcanic eruption. Location: the Antarctics near Deveteris. The eruption of Mount Akok blanketed a five-hundred-mile radius with fine ash clouds that solidified in lungs and mucous membranes. Five years without sunlight, although the northern hemisphere was not affected as much (only two years).

Acid Season: 2322–2329 Imperial. Proximate cause: plus-ten-level shake. Location: unknown; far ocean. A sudden plate shift birthed a chain of volcanoes in the path of a major jet stream. This jet stream became acidified, flowing toward the western coast and eventually around most of the Stillness. Most coastal comms perished in the initial tsunami; the rest failed or were forced to relocate when their fleets and port facilities corroded and the fishing dried up. Atmospheric occlusion by clouds lasted seven years; coastal pH levels remained untenable for many years more.

Boiling Season: 1842–1845 Imperial. Proximate cause: hot spot eruption beneath a great lake. Location: Somidlats, Lake Tekkaris quartent. The eruption launched millions of gallons of steam and particulates into the air, which triggered acidic rain and atmospheric occlusion over the southern half of the continent for three years. The northern half suffered no negative impacts, however, so archeomests dispute whether this qualifies as a "true" Season.

Breathless Season: 1689–1798 Imperial. Proximate cause: mining accident. Location: Nomidlats, Sathd quartent. An entirely human-caused Season triggered when miners at the edge of the northeastern Nomidlats coalfields set off underground fires. A relatively mild Season featuring occasional sunlight and no ashfall or acidification except in the region; few comms declared Seasonal Law. Approximately fourteen million people in the city of Heldine died in the initial natural-gas eruption and rapidly spreading fire sinkhole before Imperial Orogenes successfully quelled and sealed the edges of the fires to prevent further spread. The remaining mass could only be isolated, where it continued to burn for one hundred and twenty years. The smoke of this, spread via prevailing winds, caused respiratory problems and occasional mass suffocations in the region for several decades. A secondary effect of the loss of the Nomidlats coalfields was a catastrophic rise in heating fuel costs and the wider adaption of geothermal and hydroelectric heating, leading to the establishment of the Geneer Licensure.

The Season of Teeth: 1553–1566 Imperial. Proximate cause: oceanic shake triggering a supervolcanic explosion. Location: Arctic Cracks. An aftershock of the oceanic shake breached

a previously unknown hot spot near the north pole. This triggered a supervolcanic explosion; witnesses report hearing the sound of the explosion as far as the Antarctics. Ash went upper-atmospheric and spread around the globe rapidly, although the Arctics were most heavily affected. The harm of this Season was exacerbated by poor preparation on the part of many comms, because some nine hundred years had passed since the last Season; popular belief at the time was that the Seasons were merely legend. Reports of cannibalism spread from the north all the way to the Equatorials. At the end of this Season, the Fulcrum was founded in Yumenes, with satellite facilities in the Arctics and Antarctics.

Fungus Season: 602 Imperial. Proximate cause: volcanic eruption. Location: western Equatorials. A series of eruptions during monsoon season increased humidity and obscured sunlight over approximately 20 percent of the continent for six months. While this was a mild Season as such things go, its timing created perfect conditions for a fungal bloom that spread across the Equatorials into the northern and southern Midlats, wiping out then-staple-crop miroq (now extinct). The resulting famine lasted four years (two for the fungus blight to run its course, two more for agriculture and food distribution systems to recover). Nearly all affected comms were able to subsist on their own stores, thus proving the efficacy of Imperial reforms and Season planning, and the Empire was generous in sharing stored seed with those regions that had been miroq-dependent. In its aftermath, many comms of the middle latitudes and coastal regions voluntarily joined the Empire, doubling its range and beginning its Golden Age.

Madness Season: 3 Before Imperial–7 Imperial. Proximate cause: volcanic eruption. Location: Kiash Traps. The eruption of multiple vents of an ancient supervolcano (the same one responsible for the Twin Season of approximately 10,000 years previous) launched large deposits of the dark-colored mineral augite into the air. The resulting ten years of darkness was not only devastating in the usual Seasonal way, but resulted in a higher than usual incidence of mental illness. The Sanzed Equatorial Affiliation (commonly called the Sanze Empire) was born in this Season as Warlord Verishe of Yumenes conquered multiple ailing comms using psychological warfare techniques. (See *The Art of Madness*, various authors, Sixth University Press.) Verishe named herself Emperor on the day the first sunlight returned.

[**Editor's note:** Much of the information about Seasons prior to the founding of Sanze is contradictory or unconfirmed. The following are Seasons agreed upon by the Seventh University Archaeomestric Conference of 2532.]

Wandering Season: Approximately 800 Before Imperial. Proximate cause: magnetic pole shift. Location: unverifiable. This Season resulted in the extinction of several important trade crops of the time, and twenty years of famine resulting from pollinators confused by the movement of true north.

Season of Changed Wind: Approximately 1900 Before Imperial. Proximate cause: unknown. Location: unverifiable. For reasons unknown, the direction of the prevailing winds shifted for many years before returning to normal. Consensus agrees that this was a Season, despite the lack of atmospheric

occlusion, because only a substantial (and likely far-oceanic) seismic event could have triggered it.

Heavy Metal Season: Approximately 4200 Before Imperial. Proximate cause: volcanic eruption. Location: Somidlats near Eastern Coastals. A volcanic eruption (believed to be Mount Yrga) caused atmospheric occlusion for ten years, exacerbated by widespread mercury contamination throughout the eastern half of the Stillness.

Season of Yellow Seas: Approximately 9200 Before Imperial. Proximate cause: unknown. Location: Eastern and Western Coastals, and coastal regions as far south as the Antarctics. This Season is only known through written accounts found in Equatorial ruins. For unknown reasons, a widespread bacterial bloom toxified nearly all sea life and caused coastal famines for several decades.

Twin Season: Approximately 9800 Before Imperial. Proximate cause: volcanic eruption. Location: Somidlats. Per songs and oral histories dating from the time, the eruption of one volcanic vent caused a three-year occlusion. As this began to clear, it was followed by a second eruption of a different vent, which extended the occlusion by thirty more years.

APPENDIX 2

A Glossary of Terms Commonly Used in All Quartents of the Stillness

Antarctics: The southernmost latitudes of the continent. Also refers to people from antarctic-region comms.

Arctics: The northernmost latitudes of the continent. Also refers to people from arctic-region comms.

Ashblow Hair: A distinctive Sanzed racial trait, deemed in the current guidelines of the Breeder use-caste to be advantageous and therefore given preference in selection. Ashblow hair is notably coarse and thick, generally growing in an upward flare; at length, it falls around the face and shoulders. It is acid-resistant and retains little water after immersion, and has been proven effective as an ash filter in extreme circumstances. In most comms, Breeder guidelines acknowledge texture alone; however, Equatorial Breeders generally also require natural "ash" coloration (slate gray to white, present from birth) for the coveted designation.

Bastard: A person born without a use-caste, which is only possible for boys whose fathers are unknown. Those who

distinguish themselves may be permitted to bear their mother's use-caste at comm-naming.

Blow: A volcano. Also called firemountains in some Coastal languages.

Boil: A geyser, hot spring, or steam vent.

Breeder: One of the seven common use-castes. Breeders are individuals selected for their health and desirable conformation. During a Season, they are responsible for the maintenance of healthy bloodlines and the improvement of comm or race by selective measures. Breeders born into the caste who do not meet acceptable community standards may be permitted to bear the use-caste of a close relative at comm-naming.

Cache: Stored food and supplies. Comms maintain guarded, locked storecaches at all times against the possibility of a Fifth Season. Only recognized comm members are entitled to a share of the cache, though adults may use their share to feed unrecognized children and others. Individual households often maintain their own housecaches, equally guarded against non–family members.

Cebaki: A member of the Cebaki race. Cebak was once a nation (unit of a deprecated political system, Before Imperial) in the Somidlats, though it was reorganized into the quartent system when the Old Sanze Empire conquered it centuries ago.

Coaster: A person from a coastal comm. Few coastal comms can afford to hire Imperial Orogenes to raise reefs or otherwise protect against tsunami, so coastal cities must perpetually rebuild and tend to be resource-poor as a result. People from the western coast of the continent tend to be pale, straight-haired, and sometimes have eyes with epicanthic

folds. People from the eastern coast tend to be dark, kinky-haired, and sometimes have eyes with epicanthic folds.

Comm: Community. The smallest sociopolitical unit of the Imperial governance system, generally corresponding to one city or town, although very large cities may contain several comms. Accepted members of a comm are those who have been accorded rights of cache-share and protection, and who in turn support the comm through taxes or other contributions.

Commless: Criminals and other undesirables unable to gain acceptance in any comm.

Comm Name: The third name borne by most citizens, indicating their comm allegiance and rights. This name is generally bestowed at puberty as a coming-of-age, indicating that a person has been deemed a valuable member of the community. Immigrants to a comm may request adoption into that comm; upon acceptance, they take on the adoptive comm's name as their own.

Creche: A place where children too young to work are cared for while adults carry out needed tasks for the comm. When circumstances permit, a place of learning.

Equatorials: Latitudes surrounding and including the equator, excepting coastal regions. Also refers to people from equatorial-region comms. Thanks to temperate weather and relative stability at the center of the continental plate, Equatorial comms tend to be prosperous and politically powerful. The Equatorials once formed the core of the Old Sanze Empire.

Fault: A place where breaks in the earth make frequent, severe shakes and blows more likely.

Fifth Season: An extended winter—lasting at least six months, per Imperial designation—triggered by seismic activity or other large-scale environmental alteration.

Fulcrum: A paramilitary order created by Old Sanze after the Season of Teeth (1560 Imperial). The headquarters of the Fulcrum is in Yumenes, although two satellite Fulcrums are located in the Arctic and Antarctic regions, for maximum continental coverage. Fulcrum-trained orogenes (or "Imperial Orogenes") are legally permitted to practice the otherwise-illegal craft of orogeny, under strict organizational rules and with the close supervision of the Guardian order. The Fulcrum is self-managed and self-sufficient. Imperial Orogenes are marked by their black uniforms, and colloquially known as "blackjackets."

Geneer: From "geoneer." An engineer of earthworks—geothermal energy mechanisms, tunnels, underground infrastructure, and mining.

Geomest: One who studies stone and its place in the natural world; general term for a scientist. Specifically geomests study lithology, chemistry, and geology, which are not considered separate disciplines in the Stillness. A few geomests specialize in orogenesis—the study of orogeny and its effects.

Greenland: An area of fallow ground kept within or just outside the walls of most comms as advised by stonelore. Comm greenlands may be used for agriculture or animal husbandry at all times, or may be kept as parks or fallow ground during non-Seasonal times. Individual households often maintain their own personal housegreen, or garden, as well.

Grits: In the Fulcrum, unringed orogene children who are still in basic training.

Guardian: A member of an order said to predate the Fulcrum. Guardians track, protect, protect against, and guide orogenes in the Stillness.

Imperial Road: One of the great innovations of the Old Sanze Empire, highroads (elevated highways for walking or horse traffic) connect all major comms and most large quartents to one another. Highroads are built by teams of geneers and Imperial Orogenes, with the orogenes determining the most stable path through areas of seismic activity (or quelling the activity, if there is no stable path), and the geneers routing water and other important resources near the roads to facilitate travel during Seasons.

Innovator: One of the seven common use-castes. Innovators are individuals selected for their creativity and applied intelligence, responsible for technical and logistical problem solving during a Season.

Kirkhusa: A mid-sized mammal, sometimes kept as a pet or used to guard homes or livestock. Normally herbivarous; during Seasons, carnivorous.

Knapper: A small-tools crafter, working in stone, glass, bone, or other materials. In large comms, knappers may use mechanical or mass-production techniques. Knappers who work in metal, or incompetent knappers, are colloquially called "rusters."

Lorist: One who studies stonelore and lost history.

Mela: A Midlats plant, related to the melons of Equatorial climates. Mela are vining ground plants that normally produce fruit aboveground. During a Season, the fruit grows underground as tubers. Some species of mela produce flowers that trap insects.

Metallore: Like alchemy and astronomestry, a discredited pseudoscience disavowed by the Seventh University.

Midlats: The "middle" latitudes of the continent—those between the equator and the arctic or antarctic regions. Also refers to people from midlats regions (sometimes called Midlatters). These regions are seen as the backwater of the Stillness, although they produce much of the world's food, materials, and other critical resources. There are two midlat regions: the northern (Nomidlats) and southern (Somidlats).

Newcomm: Colloquial term for comms that have arisen only since the last Season. Comms that have survived at least one Season are generally seen as more desirable places to live, having proven their efficacy and strength.

Nodes: The network of Imperially maintained stations placed throughout the Stillness in order to reduce or quell seismic events. Due to the relative rarity of Fulcrum-trained orogenes, nodes are primarily clustered in the Equatorials.

Orogene: One who possesses orogeny, whether trained or not. Derogatory: rogga.

Orogeny: The ability to manipulate thermal, kinetic, and related forms of energy to address seismic events.

Quartent: The middle level of the Imperial governance system. Four geographically adjacent comms make a quartent. Each quartent has a governor to whom individual comm heads report, and who reports in turn to a regional governor. The largest comm in a quartent is its capital; larger quartent capitals are connected to one another via the Imperial Road system.

Region: The top level of the Imperial governance system. Imperially recognized regions are the Arctics, Nomidlats, Western Coastals, Eastern Coastals, Equatorials, Somidlats, and Antarctics. Each region has a governor to whom all local quartents report. Regional governors are officially appointed by the Emperor, though in actual practice they are generally selected by and/or come from the Yumenescene Leadership.

Resistant: One of the seven common use-castes. Resistants are individuals selected for their ability to survive famine or pestilence. They are responsible for caring for the infirm and dead bodies during Seasons.

Rings: Used to denote rank among Imperial Orogenes. Unranked trainees must pass a series of tests to gain their first ring; ten rings is the highest rank an orogene may achieve. Each ring is made of polished semiprecious stone.

Roadhouse: Stations located at intervals along every Imperial Road and many lesser roads. All roadhouses contain a source of water and are located near arable land, forests, or other useful resources. Many are located in areas of minimal seismic activity.

Runny-sack: A small, easily portable cache of supplies most people keep in their homes in case of shakes or other emergencies.

Safe: A beverage traditionally served at negotiations, first encounters between potentially hostile parties, and other formal meetings. It contains a plant milk that reacts to the presence of all foreign substances.

Sanze: Originally a nation (unit of a deprecated political system, Before Imperial) in the Equatorials; origin of the Sanzed race. At the close of the Madness Season (7 Imperial), the nation of Sanze was abolished and replaced with the Sanzed Equatorial Affiliation, consisting of six predominantly Sanzed comms under the rule of Emperor Verishe Leadership Yumenes. The Affiliation expanded rapidly in the aftermath of the Season, eventually encompassing all regions of the Stillness by 800 Imperial. Around the time of the Season of Teeth, the Affiliation came to be known colloquially as the Old Sanze Empire, or simply Old Sanze. As of the Shilteen Accords of 1850 Imperial, the Affiliation officially ceased to exist, as local control (under the advisement of the Yumenescene Leadership) was deemed more efficient in the event of a Season. In practice, most comms still follow Imperial systems of governance, finance, education, and more, and most regional governors still pay taxes in tribute to Yumenes.

Sanzed: A member of the Sanzed race. Per Yumenescene Breedership standards, Sanzeds are ideally bronze-skinned and ashblow-haired, with mesomorphic or endomorphic builds and an adult height of minimum six feet.

Sanze-mat: The language spoken by the Sanze race, and the official language of the Old Sanze Empire, now the lingua franca of most of the Stillness.

Seasonal Law: Martial law, which may be declared by any comm head, quartent governor, regional governor, or recognized member of the Yumenescene Leadership. During Seasonal Law, quartent and regional governance are suspended and comms operate as sovereign sociopolitical units, though local cooperation with other comms is strongly encouraged per Imperial policy.

Seventh University: A famous college for the study of geomestry and stonelore, currently Imperially funded and located in the Equatorial city of Dibars. Prior versions of the University have been privately or collectively maintained; notably, the Third University at Am-Elat (approximately 3000 Before Imperial) was recognized at the time as a sovereign nation. Smaller regional or quartent colleges pay tribute to the University and receive expertise and resources in exchange.

Sesuna: Awareness of the movements of the earth. The sensory organs that perform this function are the sessapinae, located in the brain stem. Verb form: to sess.

Shake: A seismic movement of the earth.

Shatterland: Ground that has been disturbed by severe and/or very recent seismic activity.

Stillheads: A derogatory term used by orogenes for people lacking orogeny, usually shortened to "stills."

Stone Eaters: A rarely seen sentient humanoid species whose flesh, hair, etc., resembles stone. Little is known about them.

Strongback: One of the seven common use-castes. Strongbacks are individuals selected for their physical prowess, responsible for heavy labor and security in the event of a Season.

Use Name: The second name borne by most citizens, indicating the use-caste to which that person belongs. There are twenty recognized use-castes, although only seven in common use throughout the current and former Old Sanze Empire. A person inherits the use name of their same-sex parent, on the theory that useful traits are more readily passed this way.

Acknowledgments

Thanks to this trilogy, I now have greater respect for authors who write million-word sagas spanning five, seven, ten volumes or more. Like it or not, whether it makes you think "yay" or "nope" whenever you hear about it, let me tell you: Telling a single long involved story is *hard*, y'all. Mad respect to the multi-volumers.

And great thanks this time go to my day-job boss, who finagled me a flextime schedule that made finishing this book in one year possible; to my agent and editor, as usual, who both put up with my periodic hour-long phone rants about how "everything is wrong forever"; to Orbit's publicist Ellen Wright, who patiently puts up with my forgetting to tell her about, well, everything (stop checking work e-mail on holidays, Ellen); to fellow Altered Fluidian and medical consultant Danielle Friedman, who did a light-speed beta-read on short notice; to fellow Fluidian Kris Dikeman, who helped me design and build my own personal volcano (long story); to WORD Books in Brooklyn, which let me use their space free for the Magic Seismology Launch Party; to my father, who ordered me to slow down and breathe; to the girls of the Octavia Project, who reminded me of how far I've come and what all this is really for; to my therapist; and finally to my ridiculous cat KING OZZYMANDIAS, who seems to have perfected the art of jumping off the bookcase onto my laptop just when I need a writing break.

extras

meet the author

Photo Credit: Laura Hanifin

N. K. Jemisin is a Brooklyn author whose short fiction and novels have been nominated multiple times for the Hugo, the World Fantasy Award, and the Nebula, shortlisted for the Crawford and the Tiptree, and have won the Locus Award. She is a science fiction and fantasy reviewer for the *New York Times*, and her novel *The Fifth Season* was a *New York Times* Notable Book of 2015. Her website is nkjemisin.com.

introducing

If you enjoyed
THE OBELISK GATE
look out for

THE BROKEN EARTH: BOOK THREE

by N. K. Jemisin

PROLOGUE

me and you, then and now

Let's end with the beginning of the world, why don't we? One beginning among many—well, no. Two: the first here and now, the second there and then.

The now is now. The here: a cavern beneath a vast, ancient shield volcano. Its heart, if you prefer and have a sense of metaphor; if not, this is a deep, dark, barely stable vesicle amid rock that has not cooled much in the thirty thousand years gone since Father Earth first burped it up. Millennia worth of additional rock, spilled forth as lava and cooling and then in turn buried by the next lava flow, insulates against heat loss. Within this cavern I stand, partially fused with a hump of rock so that I may better watch for the minute perturbations or major deformations that presage a collapse. I don't need to do this. There are few processes more unstoppable than the one I have set in motion here. Still, I understand what it is to be alone, *left* alone, when you are confused and afraid and unsure of what will happen next. I understand that sometimes, keeping watch is not merely about protection.

It's about standing witness. Standing together. Offering guidance where it is needed, care where it is not. Making sure you have everything you need to be you.

Hello, you.

Now. Let's review.

You were once of the Fulcrum, one of the feared Imperial Orogenes sent forth to work the earth for Mother Sanze. One of the good ones, or so the stills thought of you; one of the controlled ones unlikely to wipe out a town by accident. Joke's on them, right? How many towns have you wiped out now? So many. Sometimes you dream of undoing it all, somehow. Not reaching for the garnet obelisk in Allia, and instead bleeding out while watching laughing black children play in the surf nearby. Not going to Meov, instead returning to the Fulcrum to give birth to Corundum; you would have lost him after that birth, when the Guardians took him away to some unknown fate, and you would never have had Innon, but both of them would probably be alive. And then you would never have lived in Tirimo, never borne Uche to die beneath his father's fists, never have half smashed the town when they tried to kill you. So many lives saved if you had only stayed in your cage.

Well. Too late, now. You are who you are.

And here, now, you are Essun, who has saved the comm of Castrima at the cost of Castrima itself. You are the second person to open the Obelisk Gate in an age, and in so doing unleash the concatenated power of a machine older than written history. Since in the process of learning to master this power you accidentally murdered Alabaster Tenring, this makes you the most powerful orogene on the planet. It also means that your tenure as the most powerful orogene has just acquired an expiration date, because the same thing is happening to you that happened to Alabaster, near the end: You're turning to stone.

Just the arm, for now. Could be worse. *Will* be worse, the next time you open the Gate, or even the next time you wield enough of the strange silvery not-orogeny called magic. Good thing no one of Castrima realizes this, by the way. They think you can help them, which is the only reason they're bringing you along, because you're also the reason they're homeless. They glare and mutter as you lie in the coma that swallowed you after you sealed half a dozen murderous stone eaters into proto-obelisks, and in so doing disrupted delicate technology thousands of years beyond anyone's ability to repair. They would have words for you, if you were awake to hear them. Instead, you lie dreaming of family. I envy your comfort even as I pity you. It will not last.

You've got a job to do, after all. The one you *have* to do is the easier of the two: just catch the Moon. Seal and shut down the Yumenes Rifting. Reduce the current Season's impact from thousands of years back down to something manageable. Something the human race has a chance of surviving.

The job you *want* to do is getting Nassun, your daughter, back from her murderous father. About that: I have good news, and bad news.

Ah, Essun. An apocalypse is a relative thing, isn't it? When the earth shatters, it is a disaster to creatures that depend on plants and meat and clean water and cool fresh air to survive, but nothing much to the earth itself. When a man dies it should be devastating to the girl who once called him father, but it becomes nothing to a girl who has been called monster so many times that she finally embraces the label.

When a slave rebels, it is nothing much to the people who read about it later. Just thin words on thinner paper sliced finer still by the distance of history. ("So you were slaves, so what?" whisper distance, and denial.) To the people who live it, both those who took their dominance for granted until it comes for them in the dark with a knife, and those who would see the world burn before enduring one moment more of "inferiority"—

That was not a metaphor, Essun. Not hyperbole. I *have* watched the world burn. Say nothing to me of lost innocents, unearned suffering. When a comm builds atop a faultline, do you blame its walls for crushing the people inside when they inevitably crumble? Some worlds are built upon a faultline of pain, held stable—temporarily—by nightmare walls. Don't lament when they fall apart. Lament that they were ever built in the first place.

Well. That's enough of a segue.

Now let's talk about then: the end of the last world, which was the beginning of this one. I want you to imagine what the world was like before the Seasons.

This will be unimaginable for you, I know. You have no point of reference. The Stillness is a scar, not a land. Season after Fifth Season has scoured it; its face is seamed with old burns, badly healed lacerations, ulcerated sores. The Nomidlats are much larger now than they were, did you know? Palela, the sleepy town where little Damaya Strongback discovered what she was and lost her family, sits on land that did not exist in my youth. It spilled out of the boundary between the Minimal and Maximal; once it finally cooled, I watched it change from barren shatterland to new forest over less than a century. It's farmland now, but I remember when it was a floodplain of lava that stretched as far as the eye could see.

And before that, it was a city. I was born there, if...

Hmm. I seem to have forgotten its name. Perhaps you think that odd. The time that I spent in the garnet obelisk was good, in some respects; I remember *some*, where most of the others, the old ones like me, recall *none*. A few have even forgotten that we used to be, well, you. That's the core of so many problems; our minds remained human, even as the rest changed. We outlive our selves. But names...I was never good with names, even when the memories were fresh.

Well. Names are irrelevant. I'll make them up, if I feel you need them.

So imagine again, and then imagine farther. Massive cities sprawling along every coastline, brimful of the wealthy and the powerful—yes, in those days, only unfortunates lived inland. Forests and plains more green and tender than anything you've ever seen. Trees that would never survive a single ashfall, absurd in their design compared to the tough, compact, thick-skinned flora of today...but beautiful. A sky so deeply blue and clear that if you stared long enough, you could see where it bled into space.

(Space. Worlds beyond the world. Imagine looking up, and caring about what you see. And imagine, too, a great white eye gazing back at you from the midst of that nighttime blackness. But why does this thought frighten you? Instead of the void, another presence! Would it not be good, to feel less lonely?)

I remember all of this, though the memory is thin and curls about the edges. I remember it with the clarity of one who stared at it endlessly, hungrily, through glass.

I remember the day that started it. The person. The event. I will tell you the way that world ended. I will tell you how I rusting killed it, or at least enough of it that it had to start over and rebuild itself from scratch. I will tell you how I opened the Gate, and flung away the Moon, and laughed as I did it. And how, as the quiet of death descended, I whispered:

Right now.

Right now.

introducing

If you enjoyed
THE OBELISK GATE
look out for

WAKE OF VULTURES

The Shadow: Book 1

by Lila Bowen

Nettie Lonesome lives in a land of hard people and hard ground dusted with sand. She's a half-breed who dresses like a boy, raised by folks who don't call her a slave but use her like one. She knows of nothing else. That is, until the day a stranger attacks her. When nothing, not even a sickle to the eye, can stop him, Nettie stabs him through the heart with a chunk of wood, and he turns into black sand.

And just like that, Nettie can see.

But her newfound ability is a blessing and a curse. Even if she doesn't understand what's under her own skin, she can sense what everyone else is hiding—at least physically. The world is full of evil, and now she knows the source of all the sand in the desert. Haunted by the spirits, Nettie has no choice but to set out on a quest that might lead to her true kin... if the monsters along the way don't kill her first.

CHAPTER 1

Nettie Lonesome had two things in the world that were worth a sweet goddamn: her old boots and her one-eyed mule, Blue. Neither item actually belonged to her. But then again, nothing did. Not even the whisper-thin blanket she lay under, pretending to be asleep and wishing the black mare would get out of the water trough before things went south.

The last fourteen years of Nettie's life had passed in a shriveled corner of Durango territory under the leaking roof of this wind-chapped lean-to with Pap and Mam, not quite a slave and nowhere close to something like a daughter. Their faces, white and wobbling as new butter under a smear of prairie dirt, held no kindness. The boots and the mule had belonged to Pap, right up until the day he'd exhausted their use, a sentiment he threatened to apply to her every time she was just a little too slow with the porridge.

"Nettie! Girl, you take care of that wild filly, or I'll put one in her goddamn skull!"

Pap got in a lather when he'd been drinking, which was pretty much always. At least this time his anger was aimed at a critter instead of Nettie. When the witch-hearted black filly had first shown up on the farm, Pap had laid claim and pronounced her a fine chunk of flesh and a sign of the Creator's good graces. If Nettie broke her and sold her for a decent price, she'd be closer to paying back Pap for taking her in as a baby when nobody else had wanted her but the hungry, circling vultures. The value Pap placed on feeding and housing a half-Injun, half-black orphan girl always seemed to go up instead of down, no matter that Nettie did most of the work around the homestead these days. Maybe that was why she'd not been taught her sums: Then she'd know her own damn worth, to the penny.

But the dainty black mare outside wouldn't be roped, much less saddled and gentled, and Nettie had failed to sell her to the cowpokes at the Double TK Ranch next door. Her idol, Monty, was a top hand and always had a kind word. But even he had put a boot on Pap's poorly kept fence, laughed through his mustache, and hollered that a horse that couldn't be caught couldn't be sold. No matter how many times Pap drove the filly away with poorly thrown bottles, stones, and bullets, the critter crept back under cover of night to ruin the water by dancing a jig in the trough, which meant another blistering trip to the creek with a leaky bucket for Nettie.

Splash, splash. Whinny.

Could a horse laugh? Nettie figured this one could.

Pap, however, was a humorless bastard who didn't get a joke that didn't involve bruises.

"Unless you wanna go live in the flats, eatin' bugs, you'd best get on, girl."

Nettie rolled off her worn-out straw tick, hoping there weren't any scorpions or centipedes on the dusty dirt floor. By the moon's scant light she shook out Pap's old boots and shoved her bare feet into the cracked leather.

Splash, splash.

The shotgun cocked loud enough to be heard across the border, and Nettie dove into Mam's old wool cloak and ran toward the stockyard with her long, thick braids slapping against her back. Mam said nothing, just rocked in her chair by the window, a bottle cradled in her arm like a baby's corpse. Grabbing the rawhide whip from its nail by the warped door, Nettie hurried past Pap on the porch and stumbled across the yard, around two mostly roofless barns, and toward the wet black shape taunting her in the moonlight against a backdrop of stars.

"Get on, mare. Go!"

A monster in a flapping jacket with a waving whip would send any horse with sense wheeling in the opposite direction, but this horse had apparently been dancing in the creek on the day sense was handed out. The mare stood in the water trough and stared at Nettie like she was a damn strange bird, her dark eyes blinking with moonlight and her lips pulled back over long, white teeth.

Nettie slowed. She wasn't one to quirt a horse, but if the mare kept causing a ruckus, Pap would shoot her without a second or even a first thought—and he wasn't so deep in his bottle that he was sure to miss. Getting smacked with rawhide had to be better than getting shot in the head, so Nettie doubled up her shouting and prepared herself for the heartache that would accompany the smack of a whip on unmarred hide. She didn't even own the horse, much less the right to beat it. Nettie had grown up trying to be the opposite of Pap, and hurting something that didn't come with claws and a stinger went against her grain.

"Shoo, fool, or I'll have to whip you," she said, creeping closer. The horse didn't budge, and for the millionth time, Nettie swung the whip around the horse's neck like a rope, all gentle-like. But, as ever, the mare tossed her head at exactly the right moment, and the braided leather snickered against the wooden water trough instead.

"Godamighty, why won't you move on? Ain't nobody wants you, if you won't be rode or bred. Dumb mare."

At that, the horse reared up with a wild scream, spraying water as she pawed the air. Before Nettie could leap back to avoid the splatter, the mare had wheeled and galloped into the night. The starlight showed her streaking across the prairie with a speed Nettie herself would've enjoyed, especially if it meant she could turn her back on Pap's dirt-poor farm and no-good cattle company forever. Doubling over to stare at her scuffed boots while she caught her breath, Nettie felt her hope disappear with hoofbeats in the night.

A low and painfully unfamiliar laugh trembled out of the barn's shadow, and Nettie cocked the whip back so that it was ready to strike.

"Who's that? Jed?"

But it wasn't Jed, the mule-kicked, sometimes stable boy, and she already knew it.

"Looks like that black mare's giving you a spot of trouble, darlin'. If you were smart, you'd set fire to her tail."

A figure peeled away from the barn, jerky-thin and slithery in a too-short coat with buttons that glinted like extra stars. The man's hat was pulled low, his brown hair overshaggy and his lily-white hand on his gun in a manner both unfriendly and relaxed that Nettie found insulting.

"You best run off, mister. Pap don't like strangers on his land, especially when he's only a bottle in. If it's horses you want, we ain't got none worth selling. If you want work and you're dumb and blind, best come back in the morning when he's slept off the mezcal."

"I wouldn't work for that good-for-nothing piss-pot even if I needed work."

The stranger switched sides with his toothpick and looked Nettie up and down like a horse he was thinking about stealing. Her fist tightened on the whip handle, her fingers going cold. She wouldn't defend Pap or his land or his sorry excuses for cattle, but she'd defend the only thing other than Blue that mostly belonged to her. Men had been pawing at her for two years now, and nobody'd yet come close to reaching her soft parts, not even Pap.

"Then you'd best move on, mister."

The feller spit his toothpick out on the ground and took a step forward, all quiet-like because he wore no spurs. And that was Nettie's first clue that he wasn't what he seemed.

"Naw, I'll stay. Pretty little thing like you to keep me company."

That was Nettie's second clue. Nobody called her pretty unless they wanted something. She looked around the yard, but all she saw were sand, chaparral, bone-dry cow patties, and the remains of a fence that Pap hadn't seen fit to fix. Mam was surely asleep, and Pap had gone inside, or maybe around back to piss. It was just the stranger and her. And the whip.

"Bullshit," she spit.

"Put down that whip before you hurt yourself, girl."

"Don't reckon I will."

The stranger stroked his pistol and started to circle her. Nettie shook the whip out behind her as she spun in place to face him and hunched over in a crouch. He stopped circling when the barn yawned behind her, barely a shell of a thing but darker than sin in the corners. And then he took a step forward, his silver pistol out and flashing starlight. Against her will, she took a step back. Inch by inch he drove her into the barn with slow, easy steps. Her feet rattled in the big boots, her fingers numb around the whip she had forgotten how to use.

"What is it you think you're gonna do to me, mister?"

It came out breathless, god damn her tongue.

His mouth turned up like a cat in the sun. "Something nice. Something somebody probably done to you already. Your master or pappy, maybe."

She pushed air out through her nose like a bull. "Ain't got a pappy. Or a master."

"Then I guess nobody'll mind, will they?"

That was pretty much it for Nettie Lonesome. She spun on her heel and ran into the barn, right where he'd been pushing her to go. But she didn't flop down on the hay or toss down the mangy blanket that had dried into folds in the broke-down, three-wheeled rig. No, she snatched the sickle from the wall and spun to face him under the hole in the roof. Starlight fell down on her ink-black braids and glinted off the parts of the curved blade that weren't rusted up.

"I reckon I'd mind," she said.

Nettie wasn't a little thing, at least not height-wise, and she'd figured that seeing a pissed-off woman with a weapon in each hand would be enough to drive off the curious feller and send him back to the whores at the Leaping Lizard, where he apparently belonged. But the stranger just laughed and cracked his knuckles like he was glad for a fight and would take his pleasure with his fists instead of his twig.

"You wanna play first? Go on, girl. Have your fun. You think you're facin' down a coydog, but you found a timber wolf."

As he stepped into the barn, the stranger went into shadow for just a second, and that was when Nettie struck. Her whip whistled for his feet and managed to catch one ankle, yanking hard enough to pluck him off his feet and onto the back of his fancy jacket. A puff of dust went up as he thumped on the ground, but he just crossed his ankles and stared at her and laughed. Which pissed her off more. Dropping the whip handle, Nettie took the sickle in both hands and went for the stranger's legs, hoping that a good slash would keep him from chasing her but not get her sent to the hangman's noose.

But her blade whistled over a patch of nothing. The man was gone, her whip with him.

Nettie stepped into the doorway to watch him run away, her heart thumping underneath the tight muslin binding she always wore over her chest. She squinted into the long, flat night, one hand on the hinge of what used to be a barn door, back before the church was willing to pay cash money for Pap's old lumber. But the stranger wasn't hightailing it across the prairie. Which meant...

"Looking for someone, darlin'?"

She spun, sickle in hand, and sliced into something that felt like a ham with the round part of the blade. Hot blood spattered over her, burning like lye.

"Goddammit, girl! What'd you do that for?"

She ripped the sickle out with a sick splash, but the man wasn't standing in the barn, much less falling to the floor. He was hanging upside-down from a cross-beam, cradling his arm. It made no goddamn sense, and Nettie couldn't stand a thing that made no sense, so she struck again while he was poking around his wound.

This time, she caught him in the neck. This time, he fell.

The stranger landed in the dirt and popped right back up into a crouch. The slice in his neck looked like the first carving in an undercooked roast, but the blood was slurry and smelled like rotten meat. And the stranger was sneering at her.

"Girl, you just made the biggest mistake of your short, useless life."

Then he sprang at her.

There was no way he should've been able to jump at her like that with those wounds, and she brought her hands straight up without thinking. Luckily, her fist still held the sickle, and the stranger took it right in the face, the point of the blade jerking into his eyeball with a moist squish. Nettie turned away and lost most of last night's meager dinner in a noisy splatter against the wall of the barn. When she spun back around, she was surprised to find that the fool hadn't fallen or died or done anything helpful to her cause. Without a word, he calmly pulled the blade out of his eye and wiped a dribble of black glop off his cheek.

His smile was a cold, dark thing that sent Nettie's feet toward Pap and the crooked house and anything but the stranger who wouldn't die, wouldn't scream, and wouldn't leave her alone. She'd never felt safe a day in her life, but now she recognized the chill hand of death, reaching for her. Her feet trembled in the too-big boots as she stumbled backward across the bumpy yard, tripping on stones and bits of trash. Turning her back on the demon man seemed intolerably stupid. She just had to get past the round pen, and then she'd be halfway to the house. Pap wouldn't be worth much by now, but he had a gun by his side. Maybe the stranger would give up if he saw a man instead of just a half-breed girl nobody cared about.

Nettie turned to run and tripped on a fallen chunk of fence, going down hard on hands and skinned knees. When she looked up, she saw butternut-brown pants stippled with blood and no-spur boots tapping.

"Pap!" she shouted. "Pap, help!"

She was gulping in a big breath to holler again when the stranger's boot caught her right under the ribs and knocked it all back out. The force of the kick flipped her over onto her back, and she scrabbled away from the stranger and toward the ramshackle round pen of old, gray branches and junk roped together, just barely enough fence to trick a colt into staying put. They'd slaughtered a pig in here, once, and now Nettie knew how he felt.

As soon as her back fetched up against the pen, the stranger crouched in front of her, one eye closed and weeping black and the other brim-full with evil over the bloody slice in his neck. He looked like a dead man, a corpse groom, and Nettie was pretty sure she was in the hell Mam kept threatening her with.

"Ain't nobody coming. Ain't nobody cares about a girl like you. Ain't nobody gonna need to, not after what you done to me."

The stranger leaned down and made like he was going to kiss her with his mouth wide open, and Nettie did the only thing that came to mind. She grabbed up a stout twig from the wall of the pen and stabbed him in the chest as hard as she damn could.

She expected the stick to break against his shirt like the time she'd seen a buggy bash apart against the general store during a twister. But the twig sunk right in like a hot knife in butter. The stranger shuddered and fell on her, his mouth working as gloppy red-black liquid bubbled out. She didn't trust blood anymore, not after the first splat had burned her, and she wasn't much for being found under a corpse, so Nettie shoved him off hard and shot to her feet, blowing air as hard as a galloping horse.

The stranger was rolling around on the ground, plucking at his chest. Thick clouds blotted out the meager starlight, and she had nothing like the view she'd have tomorrow under the white-hot, unrelenting sun. But even a girl who'd never killed a man before knew when something was wrong. She kicked him over with the toe of her boot, tit for tat, and he was light as a tumbleweed when he landed on his back.

The twig jutted up out of a black splotch in his shirt, and the slice in his neck had curled over like gone meat. His bad eye was a swamp of black, but then, everything was black at midnight. His mouth was open, the lips drawing back over too-white teeth, several of which looked like they'd come out of a panther. He wasn't breathing, and Pap wasn't coming, and Nettie's finger reached out as if it had a mind of its own and flicked one big, shiny, curved tooth.

The goddamn thing fell back into the dead man's gaping throat. Nettie jumped away, skitty as the black filly, and her boot toe brushed the dead man's shoulder, and his entire body collapsed in on itself like a puffball, thousands of sparkly motes piling up in the place he'd occupied and spilling out through his empty clothes. Utterly bewildered, she knelt and brushed the pile with trembling fingers. It was sand. Nothing but sand. A soft wind came up just then and blew some of the stranger away, revealing one of those big, curved teeth where his head had been. It didn't make a goddamn lick of sense, but it could've gone far worse.

Still wary, she stood and shook out his clothes, noting that everything was in better than fine condition, except for his white shirt, which had a twig-sized hole in the breast, surrounded by a smear of black. She knew enough of laundering and sewing to make it nice enough, and the black blood on his pants looked, to her eye, manly and tough. Even the stranger's boots were of better quality than any that had ever set foot on Pap's land, snakeskin with fancy chasing. With her own, too-big boots, she smeared the sand back into the hard, dry ground as if the stranger had never existed. All that was left were the four big panther teeth, and she put those in her pocket and tried to forget about them.

After checking the yard for anything livelier than a scorpion, she rolled up the clothes around the boots and hid them in the old rig in the barn. Knowing Pap would pester her if she left signs of a scuffle, she wiped the black glop off the sickle and hung it up, along with the whip, out of Pap's drunken reach. She didn't need any more whip scars on her back than she already had.

Out by the round pen, the sand that had once been a devil of a stranger had all blown away. There was no sign of what had almost happened, just a few more deadwood twigs pulled from the lopsided fence. On good days, Nettie spent a fair bit of time doing the dangerous work of breaking colts or doctoring cattle in here for Pap, then picking up the twigs that got knocked off and roping them back in with whatever twine she could scavenge from the town. Wood wasn't cheap, and there wasn't much of it. But Nettie's hands were twitchy still, and so she picked up the black-splattered stick and wove it back into the fence, wishing she lived in a world where her life was worth more than a mule, more than boots, more than a stranger's cold smile in the barn. She'd had her first victory, but no one would ever believe her, and if they did, she wouldn't be cheered. She'd be hanged.

That stranger—he had been all kinds of wrong. And the way that he'd wanted to touch her—that felt wrong, too. Nettie couldn't recall being touched in kindness, not in all her years with Pap and Mam. Maybe that was why she understood horses. Mustangs were wild things captured by thoughtless men, roped and branded and beaten until their heads hung low, until it took spurs and whips to move them in rage and fear. But Nettie could feel the wildness inside their hearts, beating under skin that quivered under the flat of her palm. She didn't break a horse; she gentled it. And until someone touched her with that same kindness, she would continue to shy away, to bare her teeth and lower her head.

Someone, surely, had been kind to her once, long ago. She could feel it in her bones. But Pap said she'd been tossed out like trash, left on the prairie to die. Which she almost had, tonight. Again.

Pap and Mam were asleep on the porch, snoring loud as thunder. When Nettie crept past them and into the house, she had four shiny teeth in one fist, a wad of cash from the stranger's pocket, and more questions than there were stars.

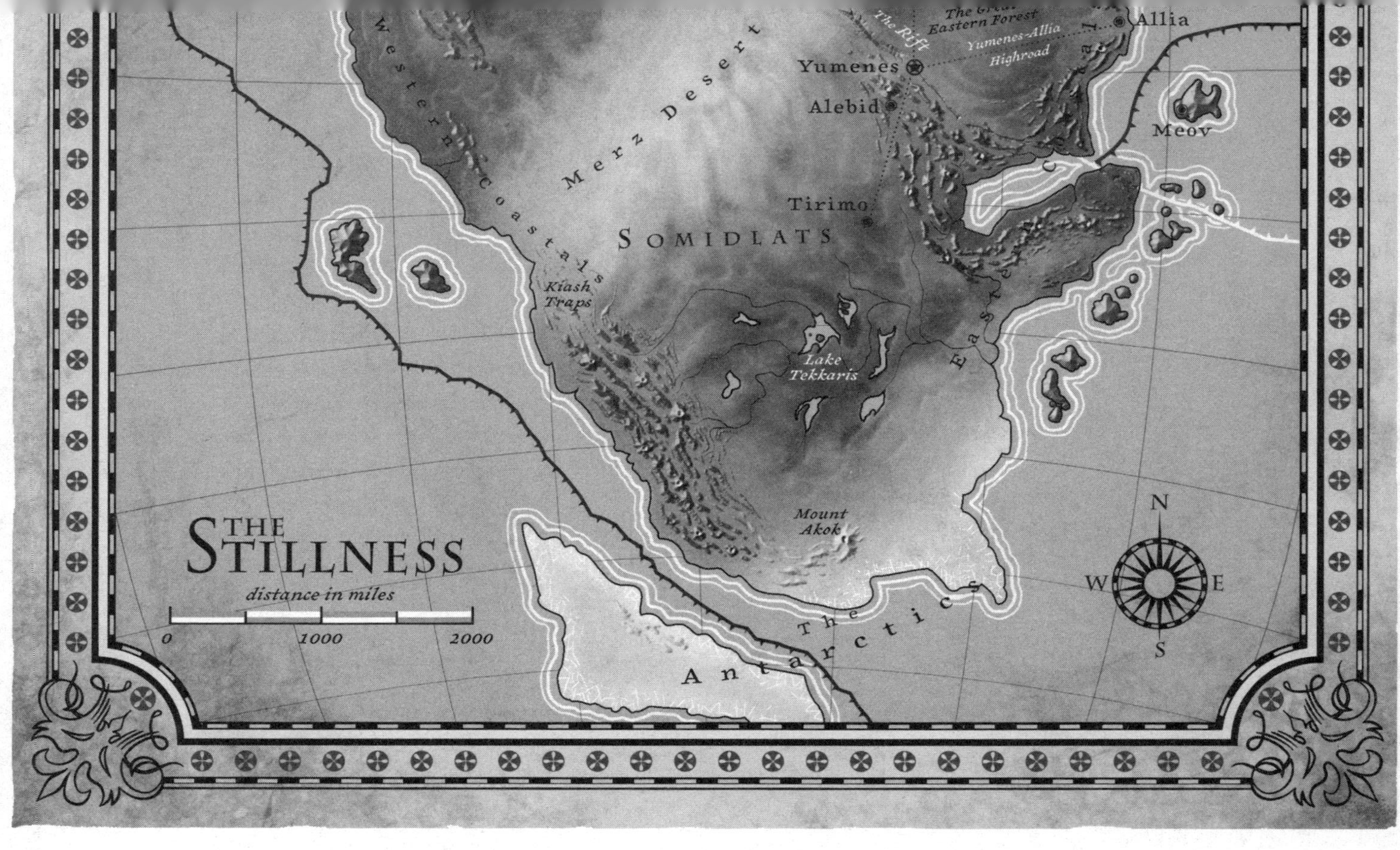

The Stillness
distance in miles
0
1000
2000
Western Coastals
Merz Desert
The Rift
Eastern Forest
Yumenes-Allia Highroad
Allia
Yumenes
Alebid
Meov
Tirimo
Somidlats
Kiash Traps
Lake Tekkaris
Mount Akok
The Antarctics
N
S
E
W

THE STONE SKY

prologue

me, when I was I

Time grows short, my love. Let's end with the beginning of the world, shall we? Yes. We shall.

It's strange, though. My memories are like insects fossilized in amber. They are rarely intact, these frozen, long-lost lives. Usually there's just a leg, some wing-scales, a bit of lower thorax—a whole that can only be inferred from fragments, and everything blurred together through jagged, dirty cracks. When I narrow my gaze and squint into memory, I see faces and events that should hold meaning for me, and they do, but . . . they don't. The person who witnessed these things firsthand is me, and yet not.

In those memories I was someone else, just as the Stillness was someoneworld else. Then, and now. You, and you.

Then. This land, then, was *three* lands—though these are in virtually the same position as what will someday be called the Stillness. Repeated Seasons will eventually create more ice at the poles, sinking the sea and making your "Arctics" and "Antarctics" larger and colder. Then, though—

—*now*, it feels of now as I recall myself of then, this is what I mean when I say that it is strange—

Now, in this time before the Stillness, the far north and south are decent farmland. What you think of as the Western Coastals is mostly wetland and rainforest; those will die out in the next millennium. Some of the Nomidlats doesn't yet exist, and will be created by volcanic effusion over several thousand years of eruptive pulses. The land that becomes Palela, your hometown? Doesn't exist. Not so much change, all things considered, but then *now* is nothing ago, tectonically speaking. When we say that "the world has ended," remember—it is usually a lie. The planet is just fine.

What do we call this lost world, this *now*, if not the Stillness?

Let me tell you, first, of a city.

It is a city built wrong, by your standards. This city *sprawls* in a way that no modern comm would be permitted to do, since that would require too many miles of walls. And this city's outermost sprawls have branched off along rivers and other lifelines to spawn additional cities, much in the manner of mold forking and stretching along the rich veins of a growth medium. Too close together, you would think. Too much overlap of territory; they are too connected, these sprawling cities and their snaking spawn, each unable to survive should it be cut off from the rest.

Sometimes they have distinct local nicknames, these child-cities, especially where they are large or old enough to have spawned child-cities of their own, but this is superficial. Your perception of their connectedness is correct: They have the same infrastructure, the same culture, the same hungers and fears. Each city is like the other cities. All of the cities are, effectively, one city. This world, in this now, is the city's name: Syl Anagist.

Can you truly understand what a *nation* is capable of, child of the Stillness? The entirety of Old Sanze, once it finally stitches itself together from fragments of the hundred "civilizations" that live and die between now and then, will be nothing by comparison. Merely a collection of paranoid city-states and communes agreeing to share, sometimes, for survival's sake. Ah, the Seasons will reduce the world to such miserly dreams.

Here, *now*, dreams have no limit. The people of Syl Anagist have mastered the forces of matter and its composition; they have shaped life itself to fit their whims; they have so explored the mysteries of the sky that they've grown bored with it and turned their attention back toward the ground beneath their feet. And Syl Anagist lives, oh how it lives, in bustling streets and ceaseless commerce and buildings that your mind would struggle to define as such. The buildings have walls of patterned cellulose that can barely be seen beneath leaves, moss, grasses, and clusters of fruit or tubers. Some rooftops fly banners that are actually immense, unfurled fungus flowers. The streets teem with things you might not recognize as vehicles, except in that they travel and convey. Some crawl on legs like massive arthropods. Some are little more than open platforms that glide on a cushion of resonant potential—ah, but you would not understand this. Let me say only that these vehicles float a few inches off the ground. No animals draw them. No steam or chemical fuels them. Should something, a pet or child perhaps, pass underneath, it will temporarily cease to exist, then resume on the other side, with no interruption of velocity or awareness. No one thinks of this as death.

There is one thing you would recognize here, standing up from the core of the city. It is the tallest, brightest thing for miles, and every rail and path connects to it in some way or another. It's your old friend, the amethyst obelisk. It isn't floating, not yet. It sits, not quite quiescent, in its socket. Now and again it pulses in a way that will be familiar to you from Allia. This is a healthier pulse than that was; the amethyst is not the damaged, dying garnet. Still, if the similarity makes you shiver, that's not an unhealthy reaction.

All over the three lands, wherever there is a large-enough node of Syl Anagist, an obelisk sits at the center of each. They dot the face of the world, two hundred and fifty-six spiders in two hundred and fifty-six webs, feeding each city and being fed in turn.

Webs of life, if you want to think of them that way. Life, you see, is sacred in Syl Anagist.

Now imagine, surrounding the base of the amethyst, a hexagonal complex of buildings. Whatever you imagine will look nothing like the actuality, but just imagine something pretty and that will do. Look closer at this one here, along the southwestern rim of the obelisk—the one on a slanting hillock. There are no bars on the building's crystal windows, but visualize a faint darker lacing of tissue over the clear material. Nematocysts, a popular method of securing windows against unwanted contact—although these exist only on the outward-facing surface of the windows, to keep intruders out. They sting, but do not kill. (Life is sacred in Syl Anagist.) Inside, there are no guards on the doors. Guards are inefficient in any case. The Fulcrum is not the first institution to have learned an eternal truth of humankind: No need for guards when you can convince people to collaborate in their own internment.

Here is a cell within the pretty prison.

It doesn't look like one, I know. There's a beautifully sculpted piece of furniture that you might call a couch, though it has no back and consists of several pieces arranged in clusters. The rest of the furniture is common stuff you would recognize; every society needs tables and chairs. The view through the window is of a garden, on the roof of one of the other buildings. At this time of day, the garden catches sunlight slanting through the great crystal, and the flowers growing in the garden have been bred and planted with this effect in mind. Purple light paints the paths and beds, and the flowers seem to glow faintly in reaction to the color. Some of these tiny white flower-lights wink out now and again, which makes the whole flower bed seem to sparkle like the night sky.

Here is a boy, staring through the window at the winking flowers.

He's a young man, really. Superficially mature, in an ageless sort of way. Not so much stocky as *compact* in his design. His face is wide and cheeky, his mouth small. Everything about him is white: colorless skin, colorless hair, icewhite eyes, his elegantly draped clothing. Everything about the room is white: furniture, rugs, the floor under the rugs. The walls are bleached cellulose, and nothing grows on them. Only the window displays color. Within this sterile space, in the reflected purple light of the outside, only the boy is obviously alive.

Yes, the boy is me. I don't truly remember his name, but I do remember that it had too many rusting letters. Let us therefore call him Houwha—the same sound, just padded with all manner of silent letters and hidden meanings. That's close enough, and appropriately *symbolic* of—

Oh. I am angrier than I should be. Fascinating. Let's change tracks, then, to something less fraught. Let us return to the now that will be, and a far different here.

Now is the now of the Stillness, through which the reverberations of the Rifting still echo. The here is not the Stillness, precisely, but a cavern just above the main lava chamber of a vast, ancient shield volcano. The volcano's heart, if you prefer and have a sense of metaphor; if not, this is a deep, dark, barely stable vesicle amid rock that has not cooled much in the thousands of years since Father Earth first burped it up. Within this cavern I stand, partially fused with a hump of rock so that I may better watch for the minute perturbations or major deformations that presage a collapse. I don't need to do this. There are few processes more unstoppable than the one I have set in motion here. Still, I understand what it is to be alone when you are confused and afraid and unsure of what will happen next.

You are not alone. You will never be, unless you so choose. I know what matters, here at the world's end.

Ah, my love. An apocalypse is a relative thing, isn't it? When the earth shatters, it is a disaster to the life that depends on it—but nothing much to Father Earth. When a man dies, it should be devastating to a girl who once called him Father, but this becomes as nothing when she has been called *monster* so many times that she finally embraces the label. When a slave rebels, it is nothing much to the people who read about it later. Just thin words on thinner paper worn finer by the friction of history.

("So you were slaves, so what?" they whisper. Like it's nothing.) But to the people who live through a slave rebellion, both those who take their dominance for granted until it comes for them in the dark, and those who would see the world burn before enduring one moment longer in "their place"—

That is not a metaphor, Essun. Not hyperbole. I *did* watch the world burn. Say nothing to me of innocent bystanders, unearned suffering, heartless vengeance. When a comm builds atop a fault line, do you blame its walls when they inevitably crush the people inside? No; you blame whoever was stupid enough to think they could defy the laws of nature forever. Well, some worlds are built on a fault line of pain, held up by nightmares. Don't lament when those worlds fall. Rage that they were built doomed in the first place.

So now I will tell you the way that world, Syl Anagist, ended. I will tell you how I ended it, or at least enough of it that it had to start over and rebuild itself from scratch.

I will tell you how I opened the Gate, and flung away the Moon, and smiled as I did it.

And I will tell you everything of how, later, as the quiet of death descended, I whispered:

Right now.

Right now.

And the Earth whispered back:

Burn.

1

you, in waking and dreaming

NOW. LET'S REVIEW.

You are Essun, the sole surviving orogene in all the world who has opened the Obelisk Gate. No one expected this grand destiny of you. You were once of the Fulcrum, but not a rising star like Alabaster. You were a feral, found in the wild, unique only in that you had more innate ability than the average rogga born by random chance. Though you started well, you plateaued early—not for any clear reason. You simply lacked the urge to innovate or the desire to excel, or so the seniors lamented behind closed doors. Too quick to conform to the Fulcrum's system. It limited you.

Good thing, because otherwise they'd never have loosened your leash the way they did, sending you forth on that mission with Alabaster. *He* scared the rust out of them. You, though... they thought you were one of the safe ones, properly broken in and trained to obey, unlikely to wipe out a town by accident. Joke's on them; how many towns have you wiped out now? One semi-intentionally. The other three were accidents, but really, does that matter? Not to the dead.

Sometimes you dream of undoing it all. Not flailing for the garnet obelisk in Allia, and instead watching happy black children play in the surf of a black-sand beach while you bled out around a Guardian's black knife. Not being taken to Meov by Antimony; instead, you would've returned to the Fulcrum to give birth to Corundum. You'd have lost him after that birth, and you would never have had Innon, but both of them would probably still be alive. (Well. For values of "alive," if they'd put Coru in a node.) But then you would never have lived in Tirimo, never have borne Uche to die beneath his father's fists, never have raised Nassun to be stolen by her father, never have crushed your once-neighbors when they tried to kill you. So many lives saved, if only you had stayed in your cage. Or died on demand.

And here, now, long free from the ordered, staid strictures of the Fulcrum, you have become mighty. You saved the community of Castrima at the cost of Castrima itself; this was a small price to pay, compared to the cost in blood that the enemy army would have extracted if they'd won. You achieved victory by unleashing the concatenated power of an arcane mechanism older than (your) written history—and because you are who you are, while learning to master this power, you murdered Alabaster Tenring. You didn't mean to. You actually suspect he wanted you to do it. Either way, he's dead, and this sequence of events has left you the most powerful orogene on the planet.

It also means that your tenure as most powerful has just acquired an expiration date, because the same thing is happening to you that happened to Alabaster: You're turning to stone. Just your right arm, for now. Could be worse. *Will* be worse, the next time you open the Gate, or even the next time you wield enough of that strange silvery not-orogeny, which Alabaster called magic. You don't have a choice, though. You've got a job to do, courtesy of Alabaster and the nebulous faction of stone eaters who've been quietly trying to end the ancient war between life and Father Earth. The job you *have* to do is the easier of the two, you think. Just catch the Moon. Seal the Yumenes Rifting. Reduce the current Season's predicted impact from thousands or millions of years back down to something manageable—something the human race has a chance of surviving. End the Fifth Seasons for all time.

The job you *want* to do, though? Find Nassun, your daughter. Take her back from the man who murdered your son and dragged her halfway across the world in the middle of the apocalypse.

About that: I have good news, and bad news. But we'll get to Jija presently.

You're not really in a coma. You are a key component of a complex system, the whole of which has just experienced a massive, poorly controlled start-up flux and emergency shutoff with insufficient cooldown time, expressing itself as arcanochemical phase-state resistance and mutagenic feedback. You need time to... reboot.

This means you're not unconscious. It's more like periods of half-waking and half-sleeping, if that makes sense. You're aware of things, somewhat. The bobbing of movement, occasional jostling. Someone puts food and water into your mouth. Fortunately you have the presence of mind to chew and swallow, because the end of the world on the ash-strewn road is a bad time and place to need a feeding tube. Hands pull on your clothing and something girds your hips—a diaper. Bad time and place for that, too, but someone's willing to tend you this way, and you don't mind. You barely notice. You feel no hunger or thirst before they give you sustenance; your evacuations bring no particular relief. Life endures. It doesn't need to do so *enthusiastically*.

Eventually the periods of waking and sleep become more pronounced things. Then one day you open your eyes to see the clouded sky overhead. Swaying back and forth. Skeletal branches occasionally occlude it. Faint shadow of an obelisk through the clouds: That's the spinel, you suspect. Reverted to its usual shape and immensity, ah, and following you like a lonely puppy, now that Alabaster is dead.

Staring at the sky gets boring after a while, so you turn your head and try to understand what's going on. Figures move around you, dreamlike and swathed in gray-white...no. No, they're wearing ordinary clothing; it's just covered with pale ash. And they're wearing a lot of clothes because it's cold—not enough to freeze water, but close. It's nearly two years into the Season; two years without the sun. The Rifting's putting out a lot of heat up around the equator, but that's not nearly enough to make up for the lack of a giant fireball in the sky. Still, without the Rifting, the cold would be worse—well below freezing, instead of nearly freezing. Small favors.

In any case, one of the ash-swathed figures seems to notice that you're awake, or to feel the shift of your weight. A head wrapped in face mask and goggles swivels back to consider you, then faces ahead again. There are murmured words between the two people in front of you, which you don't understand. They're not in another language. You're just half out of it and the words are partially absorbed by the ash falling around you.

Someone speaks behind you. You start and look back to see another goggled, masked face. Who are these people? (It does not occur to you to be afraid. Like hunger, such visceral things are more detached from you now.) Then something clicks and you understand. You're on a stretcher, just two poles with some stitched hide between them, being carried by four people. One of them calls out, and other calls respond from farther away. Lots of calls. Lots of people.

Another call from somewhere far away, and the people carrying you come to a halt. They glance at each other and set you down with the ease and uniformity of people who've practiced doing the same maneuver in unison many times. You feel the stretcher settle onto a soft, powdery layer of ash, over a thicker layer of ash, over what might be a road. Then your stretcher-bearers move away, opening packs and settling down in a ritual that is familiar from your own months on the road. Breaktime.

You know this ritual. You should get up. Eat something. Check your boots for holes or stones, your feet for unnoticed sores, make sure your mask—wait, are you wearing one? If everyone else is... You kept that in your runny-sack, didn't you? Where is your runny-sack?

Someone walks out of the gloom and ashfall. Tall, plateau-broad, identity stripped by the clothes and mask but restored by the familiar frizzy texture of the ashblow mane. She crouches near your head. "Hnh. Not dead, after all. Guess I lose that bet with Tonkee."

"Hjarka," you say. Your voice rasps worse than hers does.

You guess by the flexing of her mask that she grins. It feels odd to perceive her smile without the usual undercurrent of menace from her sharp-filed teeth. "And your brains are probably still intact. I win the bet with Ykka, at least." She glances around and bellows, "Lerna!"

You try to lift a hand to grab her pants leg. It feels like trying to move a mountain. You ought to be able to move mountains, so you concentrate and get it halfway up—and then forget why you wanted Hjarka's attention. She glances around then, fortunately, and eyes your upraised hand. It's shaking with the effort. After a moment's consideration, she sighs and takes your hand, then looks away as if embarrassed.

"Happening," you manage.

"Rust if I know. We didn't need another break this soon."

Not what you meant, but it takes too much of an effort to try to say the rest. So you lie there, with your hand being held by a woman who clearly would rather be doing anything else, but who's deigning to show you compassion because she thinks you need it. You don't, but you're glad she's trying.

Two more forms resolve out of the swirl, both recognizable by their familiar shapes. One is male and slight, the other female and pillowy. The narrow one displaces Hjarka at your head and leans in to pull off the goggles that you hadn't realized you were wearing. "Give me a rock," he says. It's Lerna, making no sense.

"What?" you say.

He ignores you. Tonkee, the other person, elbows Hjarka,

who sighs and rummages through her bag until she finds something small. She offers it to Lerna.

He lays a hand on your cheek while holding the object up. The thing starts to glow with a familiar tone of white light. You realize it's a piece of a Castrima-under crystal—lighting up because they do that in contact with orogenes, as Lerna is now in contact with you. Ingenious. Using this light, he leans in and peers closely at your eyes. "Pupils contracting normally," he murmurs to himself. His hand twitches on your cheek. "No fever."

"I feel heavy," you say.

"You're alive," he says, as if this is a completely reasonable response. No one is speaking a language you can understand today. "Motor skills sluggish. Cognition . . . ?"

Tonkee leans in. "What did you dream?"

It makes as much sense as *Give me a rock*, but you try to answer because you're too out of it to realize you shouldn't. "There was a city," you murmur. A bit of ash falls onto your lashes and you twitch. Lerna puts your goggles back on. "It was alive. There was an obelisk above it." Above it? "In it, maybe. I think."

Tonkee nods. "Obelisks rarely linger directly over human habitations. I had a friend back at Seventh who had some theories about that. Want to hear them?"

Finally it sinks in that you're doing something stupid: encouraging Tonkee. You put a mighty effort into glaring at her. "*No.*"

Tonkee glances at Lerna. "Her faculties seem intact. Little sluggish, maybe, but then she always is."

"Yes, thank you for confirming that." Lerna finishes doing whatever he's doing, and sits back on his heels. "Want to try walking, Essun?"

"Isn't that kind of sudden?" asks Tonkee. She's frowning, which is visible even around her goggles. "What with the coma and all."

"You know as well as I do that Ykka's not going to give her much more recovery time. It might even be good for her."

Tonkee sighs. But she's the one to help when Lerna slides an arm under you, levering you up from prone to sitting. Even this takes an effort of ages. You get dizzy the instant you're upright, but it passes. Something's wrong, though. It's a testament to how much you've been through, maybe, that you seem to have developed a permanently crooked posture, your right shoulder sagging and arm dragging as if

as if it is made of

Oh. *Oh.*

The others stop bothering you as you realize what's happened. They watch you heft the shoulder, as much as you can, to try to drag your right arm more into view. It's heavy. Your shoulder hurts when you do this, even though most of the joint is still flesh, because the weight pulls against that flesh. Some of the tendons have transformed, but they're still attached to living bone. Gritty bits of something chafe within what should be a smooth ball-and-socket. It doesn't hurt as much as you thought it would, though, after watching Alabaster go through this. So that's something.

The rest of the arm, from which someone has stripped your shirt and jacket sleeves in order to bare it, has changed nearly past recognition. It's your arm, you're pretty sure. Beyond the fact that it's still attached to your body, it's got the shape you know like your own—well. Not as graceful and tapered as it used to be when you were young. You were heavyset for a while, and that still shows along the plush-looking forearm and slight sag under your upper arm. The bicep is more defined than it used to be; two years of surviving. The hand is clamped into a fist, the whole arm slightly cocked at the elbow. You always did tend to make fists while you were wrestling with a particularly difficult bit of orogeny.

But the mole, which once sat in the middle of your forearm like a tiny black target, is gone. You can't turn the arm over for a look at your elbow, so you touch it. The keloid scar from where you once fell is impossible to feel anymore, though it should be slightly raised compared to the skin around it. That level of fine definition has vanished into a texture that is gritty and dense, like unpolished sandstone. Perhaps self-destructively you rub it, but no particles break off beneath your fingertips; it's more solid than it looks. The color is an even, allover grayish tan that looks nothing like your skin.

"It was like this when Hoa brought you back." Lerna, who has been silent throughout your examination. His voice is neutral. "He says he needs your permission to, ah..."

You stop trying to rub your stone skin off. Maybe it's shock, maybe fear has robbed you of shock, maybe you're really not feeling anything.

"So tell me," you say to Lerna. The effort of sitting up, and seeing your arm, have restored your wits a little. "In your, uh, professional opinion, what should I do about this?"

"I think you should either let Hoa eat it off, or let one of us take a sledgehammer to it."

You wince. "That's a little dramatic, don't you think?"

"I don't think anything lighter would put a dent in it. You forget I had plenty of chances to examine Alabaster when this was happening to him."

Out of nowhere, you think of Alabaster having to be reminded to eat because he no longer felt hunger. It's not relevant, but the thought just pops in there. "He let you?"

"I didn't give him a choice. I needed to know if it was contagious, since it seemed to be spreading on him. I took a sample once, and he joked that Antimony—the stone eater—would want it back."

It wouldn't have been a joke. Alabaster always smiled when he spoke the rawest truths. "And did you give it back?"

"You better believe I did." Lerna runs a hand over his hair, displacing a small pile of ash. "Listen, we have to wrap the arm at night so that the chill of it doesn't depress your body temperature. You've got stretch marks on the shoulder where it pulls your skin. I suspect it's deforming the bones and straining the tendons; the joint isn't built to carry this kind of weight." He hesitates. "We can take it off now and give it to Hoa later, if you like. I don't see any reason why you have to . . . to do it his way."

You think Hoa is probably somewhere below your feet at this very moment, listening. But Lerna is being oddly squeamish about this. Why? You take a guess. "I don't mind if Hoa eats it," you say. You aren't saying it just for Hoa. You really mean it. "If it will do him good, and get the thing off me in the process, why not?"

Something flickers in Lerna's expression. His emotionless mask slips, and you see all of a sudden that he's revolted by the idea of Hoa chewing the arm off your body. Well, put like that, the concept is inherently revolting. It's too utilitarian a way of thinking about it, though. Too atavistic. You know intimately, from hours spent delving between the cells and particles of Alabaster's transforming body, what's happening in your arm. Looking at it, you can all but see the silvery lines of magic realigning infinitesimal particles and energies of your substance, moving this bit so that it's oriented along the same path as that bit, carefully tightening into a lattice that binds the whole together. Whatever this process is, it's simply too precise, too powerful, to be chance—or for Hoa's ingestion of it to be the grotesquerie that Lerna plainly sees. But you don't know how to explain that to him, and you wouldn't have the energy to try even if you did.

"Help me up," you say.

Tonkee gingerly takes hold of the stone arm, helping to support it so it doesn't shift or flop and wrench your shoulder. She throws a glare at Lerna until he finally gets over himself and slides an arm under you again. Between the two of them, you manage to gain your feet, but it's hard going. You're panting by the end, and your knees are distinctly wobbly. The blood in your body is less committed to the cause, and momentarily you sway, dizzy and light-headed. Lerna immediately says, "All right, let's get her back down." Abruptly you're sitting down again, out of breath this time, the arm awkwardly jacking up your shoulder until Tonkee adjusts it. The thing really is heavy.

(Your *arm*. Not "the thing." It's your right arm. You've lost your right arm. You're aware of that, and soon you'll mourn it, but for now it's easier to think of it as a thing separate from yourself. An especially useless prosthesis. A benign tumor that needs to be removed. These things are all true. It's also your rusting arm.)

You're sitting there, panting and willing the world to stop spinning, when you hear someone else approach. This one's speaking loudly, calling for everyone to pack up, break's over, they need to do another five miles before dark. Ykka. You lift your head as she gets close enough, and it's in this moment that you realize you think of her as a friend. You realize it because it feels good to hear her voice, and to see her resolve out of the swirling ash. Last time you saw her, she was in serious danger of being murdered by hostile stone eaters attacking Castrima-under. That's one of the reasons you fought back, using the crystals of Castrima-under to ensnare the attackers; you wanted her, and all the other orogenes of Castrima, and by extension all the people of Castrima who depended on those orogenes, to live.

So you smile. It's weak. You're weak. Which is why it actually hurts when Ykka turns to you and her lips tighten in what is unmistakably disgust.

She's pulled the cloth wrapping off the lower half of her face. Beyond her gray-and-kohl eye makeup, which not even the end of the world will stop her from wearing, you can't make out her eyes behind her makeshift goggles—a pair of spectacles that she's wrapped rags around to keep ash out. "Shit," she says to Hjarka. "You're never going to let me hear the end of it, are you?"

Hjarka shrugs. "Not till you pay up, no."

You're staring at Ykka, the tentative little smile freezing off your face.

"She'll probably make a full recovery," Lerna says. His voice is neutral in a way that you immediately sense is careful. Walking-over-a-lava-tube careful. "It'll be a few days before she can keep up on foot, though."

Ykka sighs, putting a hand on her hip and very obviously rifling through a series of things to say. What she finally settles on is neutral, too. "Fine. I'll extend the rotation of people carrying the stretcher. Get her walking as soon as possible, though. Everyone carries their own weight in this comm, or gets left behind." She turns and heads off.

"Yeah, so," Tonkee says in a low voice, once Ykka's out of earshot. "She's a little pissed about you destroying the geode."

You flinch. "Destroying—" Oh, but. Locking all those stone eaters into the crystals. You meant to save everyone, but Castrima was a machine—a very old, very delicate machine that you didn't understand. And now you're topside, traipsing through the ashfall... "Oh, rusting Earth, I *did*."

"What, you didn't realize?" Hjarka laughs a little. It's got a bitter edge. "You actually thought we were all up here topside, the whole rusting comm traveling north in the ash and cold, for *fun*?" She strides away, shaking her head. Ykka's not the only one pissed about it.

"I didn't..." You start to say, *I didn't mean to*, and stop. Because you never mean it, and it never matters in the end.

Watching your face, Lerna lets out a small sigh. "Rennanis destroyed the comm, Essun. Not you." He's helping you shift back down into a prone position, but not meeting your eyes. "We lost it the minute we infested Castrima-over with boilbugs to save ourselves. It's not like they would've just gone away, or left anything in the territory to eat. If we'd stayed in the geode, we'd have been doomed, one way or another."

It's true, and perfectly rational. Ykka's reaction, though, proves that some things aren't about rationality. You can't take away people's homes and sense of security in such an immediate, dramatic way, and expect them to consider extended chains of culpability before they get angry about it.

"They'll get over it." You blink to find Lerna looking at you now, his gaze clear and expression frank. "If I could, they can. It'll just take a while."

You hadn't realized he *had* gotten over Tirimo.

He ignores your staring, then gestures to the four people who have gathered nearby. You're lying down already, so he tucks your stone arm in beside you, making sure the blankets cover it. The stretcher-bearers take up their task again, and you have to clamp down on your orogeny, which—now that you're awake—insists upon reacting to every lurch as if it's a shake. Tonkee's head pokes into view as they start to carry you along. "Hey, it'll be all right. Lots of people hate me."

That is entirely unreassuring. It's also frustrating that you care, and that others can tell you care. You used to be such a steelheart.

But you know why you aren't, all of a sudden.

"Nassun," you say to Tonkee.

"What?"

"Nassun. I know where she is, Tonkee." You try to raise your right hand to catch hers, and there is a sensation that thrums through your shoulder like aching and floating. You hear a ringing sound. It doesn't hurt, but you privately curse yourself for forgetting. "I have to go find her."

Tonkee darts a look at your stretcher-bearers, and then in the direction Ykka went. "Speak softer."

"What?" Ykka knows full well you're going to want to go find your daughter. That was practically the first thing you ever said to her.

"If you want to be dumped on the side of the rusting road, keep talking."

That shuts you up, along with the continued effort of restraining your orogeny. Oh. So Ykka's *that* pissed.

The ash keeps falling, eventually obscuring your goggles because you don't have the energy to brush it away. In the gray dimness that results, your body's need to recover takes precedence; you fall asleep again. The next time you wake and brush the ash off your face, it's because you've been put down again, and there's a rock or branch or something poking you in the small of the back. You struggle to sit up on one elbow and it's easier, though you still can't manage much else.

Night has fallen. Several dozen people are settling onto some kind of rock outcropping amid a scraggly not-quite forest. The outcropping sesses familiar from your orogenic explorations of Castrima's surroundings, and it helps you place yourself: a bit of fresh tectonic uplift that's about a hundred and sixty miles north of the Castrima geode. That tells you that the journey from Castrima must have only just begun a few days before, since a large group can only walk so fast; and that there's only one place you could be going, if you're headed north. Rennanis.

Somehow everyone must know that it's empty and habitable. Or maybe they're just hoping that it is, and they've got nothing else to hope for. Well, at least on that point, you can reassure them... if they'll listen to you.

The people around you are setting up campfire circles, cooking spits, latrines. In a few spots throughout the camp, little piles of broken, lumpy Castrima crystals provide additional illumination; good to know there must be enough orogenes left to keep them working. Some of the activity is inefficient where people are unused to it, but for the most part it's well-ordered. Castrima having more than its share of members who know how to live on the road is turning out to be a boon. Your stretcher-bearers have left you where they dumped you, though, and if anyone's going to build you a fire or bring you food, they haven't started yet. You spot Lerna crouching amid a small group of people who are also prone, but he's busy. Ah, yes; there must have been a lot of wounded after Rennanis's soldiers got into the geode.

Well, you don't need a fire, and you're not hungry, so the others' indifference doesn't trouble you for the moment, except emotionally. What does bother you is that your runny-sack is gone. You carried that thing halfway across the Stillness, stashed your old rank-rings in it, even saved it from getting scorched to powder when a stone eater transformed himself in your quarters. There wasn't much in it that still mattered to you, but the bag itself holds a certain sentimental value, at this point.

Well. Everyone's lost something.

A mountain suddenly weighs down your nearby perception. In spite of everything, you find yourself smiling. "I wondered when you would show up."

Hoa stands over you. It's still a shock to see him like this: a mid-sized adult rather than a small child, veined black marble instead of white flesh. Somehow, though, it's easy to perceive him as the same person—same face shape, same haunting ice-white eyes, same ineffable strangeness, same whiff of lurking whimsy—as the Hoa you've known for the past year. What's changed, that a stone eater no longer seems alien to you? Only superficial things about him. Everything about you.

"How do you feel?" he asks.

"Better." The arm pulls when you shift to look up at him, a constant reminder of the unwritten contract between you. "Were you the one who told them about Rennanis?"

"Yes. And I'm guiding them there."

"You?"

"To the degree that Ykka listens. I think she prefers her stone eaters as silent menaces rather than active allies."

This pulls a weary laugh out of you. But. "*Are* you an ally, Hoa?"

"Not to them. Ykka understands that, too, though."

Yes. This is probably why you're still alive. As long as Ykka keeps you safe and fed, Hoa will help. You're back on the road and everything's a rusting transaction again. The comm that was Castrima lives, but it isn't really a community anymore, just a group of like-minded travelers collaborating to survive. Maybe it can become a true comm again later, once it's got another home to defend, but for now, you get why Ykka's angry. Something beautiful and wholesome has been lost.

Well. You look down at yourself. You're not wholesome anymore, but what's left of you can be strengthened; you'll be able to go after Nassun soon. First things first, though. "We going to do this?"

Hoa does not speak for a moment. "Are you certain?"

"The arm's not doing me any *good*, as it is."

There is the faintest of sounds. Stone grinding on stone, slow and inexorable. A very heavy hand comes to rest on your half-transformed shoulder. You have the sense that, despite the weight, it is a delicate touch by stone eater standards. Hoa's being careful with you.

"Not here," he says, and pulls you down into the earth.

It's only for an instant. He always keeps these trips through the earth quick, probably because longer would make it hard to breathe... and stay sane. This time is little more than a blurring sensation of movement, a flicker of darkness, a whiff of loam richer than the acrid ash. Then you're lying on another rocky outcropping—probably the same one that the rest of Castrima is settling on, just away from the encampment. There are no campfires here; the only light is the ruddy reflection of the Rifting off the thick clouds overhead. Your eyes adjust quickly, though there's little to see but rocks and the shadows of nearby trees. And a human silhouette, which now crouches beside you.

Hoa holds your stone arm in his hands gently, almost reverently. In spite of yourself, you sense the solemnity of the moment. And why shouldn't it be solemn? This is the sacrifice demanded by the obelisks. This is the pound of flesh you must pay for the blood-debt of your daughter.

"This isn't what you think of it," Hoa says, and for an instant you worry that he can read your mind. More likely it's just the fact that he's as old as the literal hills, and he can read your face. "You see what was lost in us, but we gained, too. This is not the ugly thing it seems."

It seems like he's going to eat your arm. You're okay with it, but you want to understand. "What is it, then? Why..." You shake your head, unsure of even what question to ask. Maybe *why* doesn't matter. Maybe you can't understand. Maybe this isn't meant for you.

"This is not sustenance. We need only life, to live."

The latter half of that was nonsensical, so you latch onto the former half. "If it isn't sustenance, then...?"

Hoa moves slowly again. They don't do this often, stone eaters. Movement is the thing that emphasizes their uncanny nature, so like humanity and yet so wildly different. It would be easier if they were more alien. When they move like this, you can see what they once were, and the knowledge is a threat and warning to all that is human within you.

And yet. *You see what was lost in us, but we gained, too.*

He lifts your hand with both his own, one positioned under your elbow, his fingers lightly braced under your closed, cracked fist. Slowly, slowly. It doesn't hurt your shoulder this way. Halfway to his face he moves the hand that had been under your elbow, shifting it to cup the underside of your upper arm. His stone slides against yours with a faint grinding sound. It is surprisingly sensual, even though you can't feel a thing.

Then your fist rests against his lips. The lips don't move as he says, from within his chest, "Are you afraid?"

You consider this for a long moment. Shouldn't you be? But... "No."

"Good," he replies. "I do this for you, Essun. Everything is for you. Do you believe that?"

You don't know, at first. On impulse you lift your good hand, smooth fingers over his hard, cool, polished cheek. It's hard to see him, black against the dark, but your thumb finds his brows and traces out his nose, which is longer in its adult shape. He told you once that he thinks of himself as human in spite of his strange body. You belatedly realize that you've chosen to see him as human, too. That makes this something other than an act of predation. You're not sure what it is instead, but... it feels like a gift.

"Yes," you say. "I believe you."

His mouth opens. Wide, wider, wider than any human mouth can open. Once you worried his mouth was too small; now it's wide enough to fit a fist. And such teeth he has, small and even and diamond-clear, glinting prettily in the red evening light. There is only darkness beyond those teeth.

You shut your eyes.

* * *

She was in a foul mood. Old age, one of her children told me. *She* said it was just the stress of trying to warn people who didn't want to hear that bad times were coming. It wasn't a foul mood, it was the privilege that age had bought her, to dispense with the lie of politeness.

"There isn't a villain in this story," she said. We sat in the garden dome, which was only a dome because she'd insisted. The Syl Skeptics still claim there's no proof things will happen the way she said, but she's never been wrong in one of her predictions, and she's more Syl than they are, so. She was drinking sef, as if to mark a truth in chemicals.

"There isn't a single evil to point to, a single moment when everything changed," she went on. "Things were bad and then terrible and then better and then bad again, and then they happened again, and again, because no one stopped it. Things can be... adjusted. Lengthen the better, predict and shorten the terrible. Sometimes prevent the terrible by settling for the merely bad. I've given up on trying to stop you people. Just taught my children to remember and learn and survive... until someone finally breaks the cycle for good."

I was confused. "Are you talking about Burndown?" That was what I'd come to talk about, after all. One hundred years, she predicted, fifty years ago. What else mattered?

She only smiled.

—*Transcribed interview, translated from Obelisk-Builder C, found in Tapita Plateau Ruin #723 by Shinash Innovator Dibars. Date unknown, transcriber unknown. Speculation: the first lorist? Personal: 'Baster, you should see this place. Treasures of history everywhere, most of them too degraded to decipher, but still... Wish you were here.*

2

Nassun feels like busting loose

NASSUN STANDS OVER THE BODY of her father, if one can call a tumbled mass of broken jewels a body. She's swaying a little, light-headed because the wound in her shoulder—where her father has stabbed her—is bleeding profusely. The stabbing is the outcome of an impossible choice he demanded of her: to be either his daughter or an orogene. She refused to commit existential suicide. He refused to suffer an orogene to live. There was no malice in either of them in that final moment, only the grim violence of inevitability.

To one side of this tableau stands Schaffa, Nassun's Guardian, who stares down at what is left of Jija Resistant Jekity in a combination of wonder and cold satisfaction. At Nassun's other side is Steel, her stone eater. It is appropriate to call him that now, hers, because he has come in her hour of need—not to help, never that, but to provide her with something nevertheless. What he offers, and what she has finally realized she needs, is *purpose*. Not even Schaffa has given her this, but that's because Schaffa loves her unconditionally. She needs that love, too, oh how she needs it, but in this moment when her heart has been most thoroughly broken, when her thoughts are at their least focused, she craves something more . . . solid.

She will have the solidity that she wants. She will fight for it and kill for it, because she's had to do that again and again and it is habit now, and if she is successful she will die for it. After all, she is her mother's daughter—and only people who think they have a future fear death.

In Nassun's good hand thrums a three-foot-long, tapering shard of crystal, deep blue and finely faceted, though with some slight deformations near its base that have resulted in something like a hilt. Now and again this strange longknife flickers into a translucent, intangible, debatably real state. It's very real; only Nassun's attention keeps the thing in her hands from turning her to colored stone the way it did her father. She's afraid of what might happen if she passes out from blood loss, so she would really like to send the sapphire back up into the sky to resume its default shape and immense size—but she can't. Not yet.

There, by the dormitory, are the two reasons: Umber and Nida, the other two Guardians of Found Moon. They're watching her, and when her gaze lands on them, there is a flicker in the lacing tendrils of silver that drift between the pair. No exchanged words or looks, just that silent communion which would have been imperceptible, if Nassun were anyone but who she was. Beneath each Guardian, delicate silvery tethers wend up from the ground into their feet, connected by the nerve-and-vein glimmer of their bodies to tiny shards of iron embedded in their brains. These taproot-like tethers have always been there, but maybe it's the tension of the moment that makes Nassun finally notice how *thick* those lines of light are for each Guardian—much thicker than the one linking the ground to Schaffa. And at last she understands what that means: Umber and Nida are just puppets of a greater will. Nassun has tried to believe better of them, that they are their own people, but here, now, with the sapphire in her hands and her father dead at her feet...some maturations cannot wait for a more convenient season.

So Nassun roots a torus deep within the earth, because she knows that Umber and Nida will sense this. It's a feint; she doesn't need the power of the earth, and she suspects they know it. Still, they react, Umber unfolding his arms and Nida straightening from where she'd been leaning on the porch railing. Schaffa reacts, too, his eyes shifting sideways to meet hers. It's an unavoidable tell that Umber and Nida will notice, but it cannot be helped; Nassun has no piece of the Evil Earth lodged in her brain to facilitate communication. Where matter fails, care makes do. He says, "Nida," and that is all she needs.

Umber and Nida move. It's fast—so fast—because the silver lattice within each has strengthened their bones and tightened the cords of their muscles so that they can do what ordinary human flesh cannot. A pulse of negation moves before them with storm-surge inexorability, immediately striking the major lobes of Nassun's sessapinae numb, but Nassun is already on the offensive. Not physically; she cannot contest them in that sphere of battle, and besides she can barely stand. Will and the silver are all she's got left.

So Nassun—her body still, her mind violent—snatches at

the silver threads of the air around her, weaving them into a crude but efficient net. (She's never done this before, but no one has ever told her that it can't be done.) She wraps part of this around Nida, ignoring Umber because Schaffa told her to. And indeed, she understands in the next instant why he told her to concentrate on only one of the enemy Guardians. The silver she's woven around Nida should catch the woman up fast, like an insect slamming into a spiderweb. Instead, Nida stumbles to a halt, then laughs while threads of *something else* curl forth from within her and lash the air, shredding the net around her. She lunges for Nassun again, but Nassun—after boggling at the speed and efficacy of the Guardian's retaliation—snatches stone up from within the earth to spear Nida's feet. This impedes Nida only a little. She bulls forward, breaking the rock shards off and charging with them still jutting through her boots. One of her hands is held like a claw, the other a flat, finger-stiffened blade. Whichever of them reaches Nassun first will dictate how she begins tearing Nassun apart with her bare hands.

Here Nassun panics. Just a little, because she would lose control of the sapphire otherwise—but some. She can sense a raw, hungry, chaotic reverberation to the silver threads thrumming through Nida, like nothing she's ever perceived before, and it is somehow, suddenly, terrifying. She doesn't know what that strange reverberation will do to her, if any part of Nida should touch Nassun's bare skin. (Her mother knows, though.) She takes a step back, willing the sapphire longknife to move between her and Nida in a defensive position. Her good hand is still on the sapphire's hilt, so it looks as if she's brandishing a weapon with a shaking and far-too-slow hand. Nida laughs again, high and delighted, because they can both see that not even the sapphire will be enough to stop her. Nida's claw-hand flails out, fingers splaying and reaching for Nassun's cheek even as she weaves like a snake around Nassun's wild slash—

Nassun drops the sapphire and screams, her dulled sessapinae flexing desperately, helplessly—

But all of the Guardians have forgotten Nassun's other guardian.

Steel does not appear to move. In one instant he stands as he has for the past few minutes, with his back to the tumbled pile of Jija, expression serene, posture languid as he faces the northern horizon. In the next he is closer, right beside Nassun, having transported himself so quickly that Nassun hears a sharp clap of displaced air. And Nida's forward momentum abruptly stops as her throat is caught tight within the circle of Steel's upraised hand.

She shrieks. Nassun has heard Nida ramble for hours in her fluttery voice, and perhaps that's made her think of Nida as a songbird, chattery and chirruping and harmless. This shriek is the cry of a raptor, savagery turning to fury as she is thwarted from stooping on her prey. She tries to wrench herself back, risking skin and tendon to get loose, but Steel's grip is as firm as stone. She's caught.

A sound behind Nassun makes her jerk around. Ten feet from where she stands, Umber and Schaffa have blurred together in hand-to-hand combat. She can't see what's happening. They're both moving too fast, their strikes swift and vicious. By the time her ears process the sounds of a blow, they've already shifted to a different position. She can't even tell what they're doing—but she is afraid, so afraid, for Schaffa. The silver in Umber flows like rivers, power being steadily fed to him through that glimmering taproot. The thinner streams in Schaffa, however, are a wild chain of rapids and clogs, yanking at his nerves and muscles and flaring unpredictably in an attempt to distract him. Nassun can see by the concentration in Schaffa's face that *he* is still in control, and that this is what has saved him; his movements are unpredictable, strategic, considered. Still. That he can fight at all is astonishing.

How he ends the fight, by driving his hand up to the wrist through the underside of Umber's jaw, is horrifying.

Umber makes an awful sound, jerking to a halt—but an instant later, his hand lunges for Schaffa's throat again, blurring in its speed. Schaffa gasps—so quickly that it might be just a breath, but Nassun hears the alarm in it—and shunts away the strike, but Umber's still moving, even though his eyes have rolled back in his head and the movements are twitchy, clumsy. Nassun understands then: Umber's not home anymore. Something else is, working his limbs and reflexes for as long as crucial connections remain in place. And yes: In the next breath, Schaffa flings Umber to the ground, wrenches his hand free, and stomps on his opponent's head.

Nassun can't look. She hears the crunch; that's enough. She hears Umber actually continue twitching, his movements more feeble but persistent, and she hears the faint rustle of Schaffa's clothes as he bends. Then she hears something that her mother last heard in a little room in the Guardians' wing of the Fulcrum, some thirty years before: bone cracking and gristle tearing, as Schaffa works his fingers into the base of Umber's broken skull.

Nassun can't close her ears, so instead she focuses on Nida, who's still fighting to get free from Steel's unbreakable grip.

"I—I—" Nassun attempts. Her heart's slowed only a little. The sapphire shakes harder in her hands. Nida still wants to kill her. Steel, who has established himself as merely a possible ally and not a definite one, need only loosen his grip, and Nassun will die. But. "I d-don't want to kill you," she manages. It's even true.

Nida abruptly goes still and silent. The fury in her expression gradually fades to no expression at all. "It did what it had to do, last time," she says.

Nassun's skin prickles with the realization that something intangible has changed. She's not sure what, but she doesn't think this is quite Nida anymore. She swallows. "Did what? Who?"

Nida's gaze falls on Steel. There is a faint grinding sound as Steel's mouth curves into a wide, toothy smile. Then, before Nassun can think of another question to ask, Steel's grip shifts. Not loosening; turning, with that unnaturally slow motion which perhaps is meant to imitate human movement. (Or mock it.) He draws in his arm and pivots his wrist to turn Nida around, her back to his front. The nape of her neck to his mouth.

"It's angry," Nida continues calmly, though now she faces away from both Steel and Nassun. "Yet even now it may be willing to compromise, to forgive. It demands justice, but—"

"It has had its justice a thousand times over," says Steel. "I owe it no more." Then he opens his mouth wide.

Nassun turns away, again. On a morning when she has rent her father to pieces, some things remain too obscene for her child's eyes. At least Nida does not move again once Steel has dropped her body to the ground.

"We cannot remain here," Schaffa says. When Nassun swallows hard and focuses on him, she sees that he stands over Umber's corpse, holding something small and sharp in one gore-flecked hand. He gazes at this object with the same detached coldness that he turns upon those he means to kill. "Others will come."

Through the clarity of near-death adrenaline, Nassun knows that he means other contaminated Guardians—and not half-contaminated ones like Schaffa himself, who have somehow managed to retain some measure of free will. Nassun swallows and nods, feeling calmer now that no one is actively trying to kill her anymore. "Wh-what about the other kids?"

Some of the children in question are standing on the porch of the dormitory, awakened by the concussion of the sapphire when Nassun summoned it into longknife form. They have witnessed everything, Nassun sees. A couple are weeping at the sight of their Guardians dead, but most just stare at her and Schaffa in silent shock. One of the smaller children is vomiting off the side of the steps.

Schaffa gazes at them for a long moment, and then glances sidelong at her. Some of the coldness is still there, saying what his voice does not. "They'll need to leave Jekity, quickly. Without Guardians, the commfolk are unlikely to tolerate their presence." Or Schaffa can kill them. That's what he's done with every other orogene they've met who isn't under his control. They are either his, or they are a threat.

"No," Nassun blurts. Speaking to that silent coldness, not

to what he's said. The coldness increases fractionally. Schaffa never likes it when she says no. She takes a deep breath, marshaling a little more calm, and corrects herself. "Please, Schaffa. I just... I can't take any more."

This is rank hypocrisy. The decision Nassun has recently made, a silent promise over her father's corpse, belies it. Schaffa cannot know what she has chosen, but at the corner of her vision, she is painfully aware of Steel's lingering, blood-painted smile.

She presses her lips together and means it anyway. It isn't a lie. She can't take the cruelty, the endless suffering; that's the whole point. What she means to do will be, if nothing else, quick and merciful.

Schaffa regards her for a moment. Then he twitch-winces a little, as she has seen him do often in the past few weeks. When the spasm passes, he puts on a smile and comes over to her, though first he closes his hand firmly around the metal bit he's taken from Umber. "How is your shoulder?"

She reaches up to touch it. The cloth of her sleep-shirt is wet with blood, but not sodden, and she can still use the arm. "It hurts."

"That will last for a time, I'm afraid." He looks around, then rises and goes to Umber's corpse. Ripping off one of Umber's shirtsleeves—one that isn't as splattered with blood as the other, Nassun notes with distant relief—he comes over and pushes up her sleeve, then helps her tie the strip of cloth around her shoulder. He ties it tight. Nassun knows this is good and will possibly prevent her from needing to have the wound sewn up, but for a moment the pain is worse and she leans against him briefly. He allows this, stroking her hair with his free hand. The gore-flecked other hand, Nassun notes, stays clenched tight around that metal shard.

"What will you do with it?" Nassun asks, staring at the clenched hand. She cannot help imagining something malevolent there, snaking its tendrils forth and looking for another person to infect with the Evil Earth's will.

"I don't know," Schaffa says in a heavy voice. "It's no danger to me, but I remember that in..." He frowns for a moment, visibly groping for a memory that is gone. "That once, elsewhere, we simply recycled them. Here, I suppose I'll have to find somewhere isolated to drop it, and hope no one stumbles across it anytime soon. What will you do with *that*?"

Nassun follows his gaze to where the sapphire longknife, untended, has floated around behind her and positioned itself in the air, hovering precisely a foot away from her back. It moves slightly with her movements, humming faintly. She doesn't understand why it's doing that, though she takes some comfort from its looming, quiescent strength. "I guess I should put it back."

"How did you...?"

"I just needed it. It knew what I needed and changed for me." Nassun shrugs a little. It's so hard to explain these things in words. Then she clutches at his shirt with her uninjured hand, because she knows that when Schaffa doesn't answer a question, it isn't a good thing. "The others, Schaffa."

He sighs finally. "I'll help them prepare packs. Can you walk?"

Nassun's so relieved that for the moment she feels like she can fly. "Yes. Thank you. Thank you, Schaffa!"

He shakes his head, clearly rueful, though he smiles again.

"Go to your father's house and take anything useful and portable, little one. I'll meet you there."

She hesitates. If Schaffa decides to kill the other children of Found Moon... He won't, will he? He's said he won't.

Schaffa pauses, raising an eyebrow above his smile, the picture of polite, calm inquiry. It's an illusion. The silver is still a lashing whip within Schaffa, trying to goad him into killing her. He must be in astonishing pain. He resists the goad, however, as he has for weeks. He does not kill her, because he loves her. And she can trust nothing, no one, if she does not trust him.

"Okay," Nassun says. "I'll see you at Daddy's."

As she pulls away from him, she glances at Steel, who has turned to face Schaffa as well. Somewhere in the past few breaths, Steel has gotten the blood off his lips. She doesn't know how. But he has held out one gray hand toward them—no. Toward Schaffa. Schaffa tilts his head at this for a moment, considering, and then after a moment he deposits the bloody iron shard into Steel's hand. Steel's hand flicks closed, then uncurls again, slowly, as if performing a sleight-of-hand trick. But the iron shard is gone. Schaffa inclines his head in polite thanks.

Her two monstrous protectors, who must cooperate on her care. Yet is Nassun not a monster, too? Because the thing that she sensed just before Jija came to kill her—that spike of immense power, concentrated and amplified by dozens of obelisks working in tandem? Steel has called this the Obelisk Gate: a vast and complex mechanism created by the deadciv that built the obelisks, for some unfathomable purpose. Steel has also mentioned a thing called the Moon. Nassun has heard the stories; once, long ago, Father Earth had a child. That child's loss is what angered him and brought about the Seasons.

The tales offer a message of impossible hope, and a mindless expression that lorists use to intrigue restless audiences. *One day, if the Earth's child ever returns*... The implication is that, someday, Father Earth might be appeased at last. Someday, the Seasons might end and all could become right with the world.

Except fathers will still try to murder their orogene children, won't they? Even if the Moon comes back. Nothing will ever stop that.

Bring home the Moon, Steel has said. End the world's pain.

Some choices aren't choices at all, really.

Nassun wills the sapphire to come hover before her again. She can sess nothing in the wake of Umber and Nida's negation, but there are other ways to perceive the world. And amid the flickering un-water of the sapphire, as it unmakes and remakes itself from the concentrated immensity of silver light stored within its crystal lattice, there is a subtle message written in equations of force and balance that Nassun solves instinctively, with something other than math.

Far away. Across the unknown sea. Her mother may hold the Obelisk Gate's key, but Nassun learned on the ash roads that there are other ways to open any gate—hinges to pop, ways to climb over or dig under. And far away, on the other side of the world, is a place where Essun's control over the Gate can be subverted.

"I know where we need to go, Schaffa," Nassun says.

He eyes her for a moment, his gaze flicking to Steel and back. "Do you, now?"

"Yes. It's a really long way, though." She bites her lip. "Will you go with me?"

He inclines his head, his smile wide and warm. "Anywhere, my little one."

Nassun lets out a long breath of relief, smiling up at him tentatively. Then she deliberately turns her back on Found Moon and its corpses, and walks down the hill without ever once looking back.

* * *

> 2729 Imperial: Witnesses in the comm of Amand (Dibba Quartent, western Nomidlats) report an unregistered rogga female opening up a gas pocket near the town. Unclear what gas was; killed in seconds, purpling of tongue, suffocation rather than toxicity? Both? Another rogga female reportedly stopped the first one's effort, somehow, and shunted the gas back into the vent before sealing it. Amand citizens shot both as soon as possible to prevent further incidents. Gas pocket assessed by Fulcrum as substantial—enough to have killed most people and livestock in western half of Nomidlats, with follow-up topsoil contamination. Initiating female age seventeen, reacting to reported molester of younger sister. Quelling female age seven, sister of first.
>
> —*Project notes of Yaetr Innovator Dibars*

Syl Anagist: Five

"Houwha," says a voice behind me.

(Me? Me.)

I turn from the stinging window and the garden of winking flowers. A woman stands with Gaewha and one of the conductors, and I do not know her. To the eyes, she is one of them—skin a soft allover brown, eyes gray, hair black-brown and curling in ropes, tall. There are hints of *other* in the breadth of her face—or perhaps, viewing this memory now through the lens of millennia, I see what I want to see. What she looks like is irrelevant. To my sessapinae, her kinship to us is as obvious as Gaewha's puffy white hair. She exerts a pressure upon the ambient that is a churning, impossibly heavy, irresistible force. This makes her as much one of us as if she'd been decanted from the same biomagestric mix.

(You look like her. No. I *want* you to look like her. That is unfair, even if it's true; you are like her, but in other ways than mere appearance. My apologies for reducing you in such a way.)

The conductor speaks as her kind do, in thin vibrations that only ripple the air and barely stir the ground. *Words.* I know this conductor's name-word, Pheylen, and I know too that she is one of the nicer ones, but this knowledge is still and indistinct, like so much about them. For a very long time I could not tell the difference between one of their kind and another. They all look different, but they have the same non-presence within the ambient. I still have to remind myself that hair textures and eye shapes and unique body odors each have as much meaning to them as the perturbations of tectonic plates have to me.

I must be respectful of their difference. We are the deficient ones, after all, stripped of much that would've made us human. This was necessary and I do not mind what I am. I like being useful. But many things would be easier if I could understand our creators better.

So I stare at the new woman, the us-woman, and try to pay attention while the conductor *introduces* her. Introduction is a ritual that consists of explaining the sounds of names and the relationships of the...families? Professions? Honestly, I don't know. I stand where I am supposed to and say the things I should. The conductor tells the new woman that I am Houwha and that Gaewha is Gaewha, which are the name-words they use for us. The new woman, the conductor says, is Kelenli. That's wrong, too. Her name is actually *deep stab, breach of clay sweetburst, soft silicate underlayer, reverberation*, but I will try to remember "Kelenli" when I use words to speak.

The conductor seems pleased that I say "How do you do" when I'm supposed to. I'm glad; *introduction* is very difficult, but I've worked hard to become good at it. After this she starts speaking to Kelenli. When it becomes clear that the conductor has nothing more to say to me, I move behind Gaewha and begin plaiting some of her thick, poufy mane of hair. The conductors seem to like it when we do this, though I don't really know why. One of them said that it was "cute" to see us taking care of one another, just like people. I'm not sure what cute means.

Meanwhile, I listen.

"Just doesn't make sense," Pheylen is saying, with a sigh. "I mean, the numbers don't lie, but..."

"If you'd like to register an objection," begins Kelenli. Her words fascinate me in a way that words never have before. Unlike the conductor, her voice has weight and texture, strata-deep and layered. She sends the words into the ground while she speaks, as a kind of subvocalization. It makes them feel more real. Pheylen, who doesn't seem to notice how much deeper Kelenli's words are—or maybe she just doesn't care—makes an uncomfortable face in reaction to what she's said. Kelenli repeats, "*If* you'd like to, I can ask Gallat to take me off the roster."

"And listen to his shouting? Evil Death, he'd never stop. Such a savage temper he has." Pheylen smiles. It's not an amused smile. "It must be hard for him, wanting the project to succeed, but also wanting you kept—well. *I'm* fine with you on standby-only, but then I haven't seen the simulation data."

"I have." Kelenli's tone is grave. "The delay-failure risk was small, but significant."

"Well, there you are. Even a small risk is too much, if we can do something about it. I think they must be more anxious than they're letting on, though, to involve you—" Abruptly, Pheylen looks embarrassed. "Ah...sorry. No offense meant."

Kelenli smiles. Both I and Gaewha can see that it is only a surface layering, not a real expression. "None taken."

Pheylen exhales in relief. "Well, then, I'll just withdraw to Observation and let you three get to know each other. Knock when you're done."

With that, Conductor Pheylen leaves the room. This is a good thing, because when conductors are not around, we can speak more easily. The door closes and I move to face Gaewha (who is actually *cracked geode taste of adularescent salts, fading echo*). She nods minutely because I have correctly guessed that she has something important to tell me. We are always watched. A certain amount of performance is essential.

Gaewha says with her mouth, "Coordinator Pheylen told me they're making a change to our configuration." With the rest of her she says, in atmospheric perturbations and anxious plucking of the silver threads, *Tetlewha has been moved to the briar patch.*

"A change at this late date?" I glance at the us-woman, Kelenli, to see if she is following the whole conversation. She looks so much like one of them, all that surface coloring and those long bones that make her a head taller than both of us. "Do you have something to do with the project?" I ask her, while also responding to Gaewha's news about Tetlewha. *No.*

My "no" is not denial, just a statement of fact. We can still detect Tetlewha's familiar *hot spot roil and strata uplift, grind of subsidence*, but…something is different. He's not nearby anymore, or at least he's not anywhere that is in range of our seismic questings. And the roil and grind of him have gone nearly still.

Decommissioned is the word the conductors prefer to use,

when one of us is removed from service. They have asked us, individually, to describe what we feel when the change happens, because it is a disruption of our network. By unspoken agreement each of us speaks of the sensation of loss—a pulling away, a draining, a thinning of signal strength. By unspoken agreement none of us mentions the rest, which in any case is indescribable using conductor words. What we experience is a searing sensation, and prickling all over, and the *tumbledown resistance tangle* of ancient pre-Sylanagistine wire such as we sometimes encounter in our explorations of the earth, gone rusted and sharp in its decay and wasted potential. Something like that.

Who gave the order? I want to know.

Gaewha has become a slow fault ripple of stark, frustrated, confused patterns. *Conductor Gallat. The other conductors are angry about it and someone reported it to the higher-ups and that's why they have sent Kelenli here. It took all of us together to hold the onyx and the moonstone. They are concerned about our stability.*

Annoyed, I return, *Perhaps they should have thought of that before—*

"I do have something to do with the project, yes," interrupts Kelenli, though there has been no break or disruption of the verbal conversation. Words are very slow compared to earthtalk. "I have some arcane awareness, you see, and similar abilities to yours." Then she adds, *I'm here to teach you.*

She switches as easily as we do between the words of the conductors and our language, the language of the earth. Her communicative presence is *radiant heavy metal, searing crystallized magnetic lines of meteoric iron*, and more complex layers underneath this, all so sharp-edged and powerful that Gaewha and I both inhale in wonder.

But what is she saying? Teach us? We don't need to be taught. We were decanted knowing nearly everything we needed to know already, and the rest we learned in the first few weeks of life with our fellow tuners. If we hadn't, we would be in the briar patch, too.

I make sure to frown. "How can you be a tuner like us?" This is a lie spoken for our observers, who see only the surface of things and think we do, too. She is not white like us, not short or strange, but we have known her for one of ours since we felt the cataclysm of her presence. I do not disbelieve that she is one of us. I can't disbelieve the incontrovertible.

Kelenli smiles, with a wryness that acknowledges the lie. "Not quite like you, but close enough. You're the finished artwork, I'm the model." Threads of magic in the earth heat and reverberate and add other meanings. *Prototype.* A control to our experiment, made earlier to see how we should be done. She has only one difference, instead of the many that we possess. She has our carefully designed sessapinae. Is that enough to help us accomplish the task? The certainty in her earth-presence says yes. She continues in words: "I'm not the first that was made. Just the first to survive."

We all push a hand at the air to ward off Evil Death. But I allow myself to look like I don't understand as I wonder if we dare trust her. I saw how the conductor relaxed around her. Pheylen is one of the nice ones, but even she never forgets what we are. She forgot with Kelenli, though. Perhaps all humans think she is one of them, until someone tells them otherwise.

What is that like, being treated as human when one is not? And then there's the fact that they've left her alone with us. We they treat like weapons that might misfire at any moment... but they trust her.

"How many fragments have you attuned to yourself?" I ask aloud, as if this is a thing that matters. It is also a challenge.

"Only one," Kelenli says. But she's still smiling. "The onyx."

Oh. Oh, that *does* matter. Gaewha and I exchange a look of wonder and concern before facing her again.

"And the reason I'm here," Kelenli continues, abruptly insistent upon delivering this important information with mere words, which somehow perversely serves to emphasize them, "is because the order has been issued. The fragments are at optimum storage capacity and are ready for the generative cycle. Corepoint and Zero Site go live in twenty-eight days. We're finally starting up the Plutonic Engine."

(In tens of thousands of years, after people have repeatedly forgotten what "engines" are and know the fragments as nothing but "obelisks," there will be a different name for the thing that rules our lives now. It will be called the *Obelisk Gate*, which is both more poetic and quaintly primitive. I like that name better.)

In the present, while Gaewha and I stand there staring, Kelenli drops one last shocker into the vibrations between our cells:

That means I have less than a month to show you who you really are.

Gaewha frowns. I manage not to react because the conductors watch our bodies as well as our faces, but it is a narrow thing. I'm very confused, and not a little unnerved. I have no idea, in the present of this conversation, that it is the beginning of the end.

Because we tuners are not orogenes, you see. Orogeny is what the difference of us will become over generations of adaptation to a changed world. You are the shallower, more specialized, more natural distillation of our so-unnatural strangeness. Only a few of you, like Alabaster, will ever come close to the power and versatility we hold, but that is because we were constructed as intentionally and artificially as the fragments you call obelisks. We are fragments of the great machine, too—just as much a triumph of genegineering and biomagestry and geomagestry and other disciplines for which the future will have no name. By our existence we glorify the world that made us, like any statue or scepter or other precious object.

We do not resent this, for our opinions and experiences have been carefully constructed, too. We do not understand that what Kelenli has come to give us is a sense of *peoplehood.* We do not understand why we have been forbidden this self-concept before now . . . but we will.

And then we will understand that *people* cannot be *possessions.* And because we are both and this should not be, a new concept will take shape within us, though we have never heard the word for it because the conductors are forbidden to even mention it in our presence. *Revolution.*

Well. We don't have much use for words, anyway. But that's what this is. The beginning. You, Essun, will see the end.

3

you, imbalanced

IT TAKES A FEW DAYS for you to recover enough to walk on your own. As soon as you can, Ykka reappropriates your stretcher-bearers to perform other tasks, which leaves you to hobble along, weak and made clumsy by the loss of your arm. The first few days you lag well behind the bulk of the group, catching up to camp with them only hours after they've settled for the night. There isn't much left of the communal food by the time you go to take your share. Good thing you don't feel hunger anymore. There aren't many spaces left to lay out your bedroll, either—though they did at least give you a basic pack and supplies to make up for your lost runny-sack. What spaces there are aren't good, located near the edges of the camp or off the road altogether, where the danger of attack by wildlife or commless is greater. You sleep there anyway because you're exhausted. You suppose that if there's any real danger, Hoa will carry you off again; he seems able to transport you for short distances through the earth with no trouble. Still, Ykka's anger is a hard thing to bear, in more ways than one.

Tonkee and Hoa lag behind with you. It's almost like the old days, except that now Hoa appears as you walk, gets left behind as you keep walking, then appears again somewhere ahead of you. Most times he adopts a neutral posture, but occasionally he's doing something ridiculous, like the time you find him in a running pose. Apparently stone eaters get bored, too. Hjarka stays with Tonkee, so that's four of you. Well, five: Lerna lingers to walk with you, too, angry at what he perceives as the mistreatment of one of his patients. He didn't think a recently comatose woman should be made to walk at all, let alone left to fall behind. You try to tell him not to stick with you, not to draw Castrima's wrath upon himself, but he snorts and says that if Castrima really wants to antagonize the only person in the comm who's formally trained to do surgery, they don't deserve to keep him. Which is... well, it's a very good point. You shut up.

You're managing better than Lerna expected, at least. That's mostly because it wasn't really a coma, and also because you hadn't lost all of your road conditioning during the seven or eight months that you lived in Castrima. The old habits come back easily, really: finding a steady, if slow, pace that nevertheless eats up the miles; wearing your pack low so that the bulk of its weight braces against your butt rather than pulling on your shoulders; keeping your head down as you walk so that the falling ash doesn't cover your goggles. The loss of the arm is more a nuisance than a real hardship, at least with so many willing helpers around. Aside from throwing off your balance and plaguing you with phantom itches or aches from fingers or an elbow that doesn't exist, the hardest part is getting dressed in the morning. It's surprising how quickly you master squatting to piss or defecate without falling over, but maybe you're just more motivated after days in a diaper.

So you're holding your own, just slowly at first, and you're getting faster as the days go by. But here's the problem with all of this: You're going the wrong way.

Tonkee comes over to sit by you one evening. "You can't leave until we're a lot further west," she says without preamble. "Almost to the Merz, I'm thinking. If you want to make it that far, you're going to have to patch things up with Ykka."

You glare at her, though for Tonkee, this is discreet. She's waited till Hjarka is snoring in her bedroll and Lerna's gone off to use the camp latrine. Hoa is still nearby, standing unsubtle guard over your small group within the comm encampment, the curves of his black marble face underlit by your fire. Tonkee knows he's loyal to you, though, to the degree that loyalty means anything to him.

"Ykka hates me," you finally say, after glaring fails to produce anything like chagrin or regret in Tonkee.

She rolls her eyes. "Trust me, I know hate. What Ykka's got is...scared, and a good bit of mad, but some of that you deserve. You've put her people in danger."

"I *saved* her people from danger."

Across the encampment, as if to illustrate your point, you notice someone moving about clunkily. It's one of the Rennanis soldiers, a few of whom were captured alive after the last battle. They've put a pranger on her—a hinged wooden collar round her neck, with holes in the planks holding her arms up and apart, linked by two chains to manacles on her ankles. Primitive but effective. Lerna's been tending the prisoners' chafing sores, and you understand they're allowed to put the prangers aside at night. It's better treatment than Castrimans would have gotten from Rennanis if the situations were reversed, but still, it makes everything awkward. It's not like the Rennies can leave, after all. Even without the prangers, if any one of them escapes now, with no supplies and lacking the protection of a large group, they'll be meat within days. The prangers are just insult on top of injury, and a disquieting reminder to all that things could be worse. You look away.

Tonkee sees you looking. "Yeah, you saved Castrima from one danger and then delivered them into something just as bad. Ykka only wanted the first half of that."

"I couldn't have avoided the second half. Should I have just let the stone eaters kill all the roggas? Kill *her*? If they'd succeeded, none of the geode's mechanisms would've worked anyway!"

"She knows that. That's why I said it wasn't hate. But..." Tonkee sighs as if you're being especially stupid. "Look. Castrima was—is—an experiment. Not the geode, the people. She's always known it was precarious, trying to make a comm out of strays and roggas, but it was working. She made the oldtimers understand that we needed the newcommers. Got everybody to think of roggas as people. Got them to agree to live underground, in a deadciv ruin that could've killed us all at any moment. Even kept them from turning on each other when that gray stone eater gave them a reason—"

"*I* stopped that," you mutter. But you're listening.

"You helped," Tonkee concedes, "but if it had just been you? You know full well it wouldn't have worked. Castrima works because of *Ykka*. Because they know she'll die to keep this comm going. Help Castrima, and Ykka will be on your side again."

It will be weeks, maybe even months, before you reach the now-vacant Equatorial city of Rennanis. "I know where Nassun is *now*," you say, seething. "By the time Castrima gets to Rennanis, she might be somewhere else!"

Tonkee sighs. "It's been a few weeks already, Essun."

And Nassun was probably somewhere else before you even woke up. You're shaking. It's not rational and you know it, but you blurt, "But if I go now, maybe—maybe I can catch up, maybe Hoa can tune in on her again, maybe I can—" Then you falter silent because you hear the shaky, high-pitched note of your own voice and your mother instincts kick back in, rusty but unblunted, to chide you: *Stop whining.* Which you are. So you bite back more words, but you're still shaking, a little.

Tonkee shakes her head, an expression on her face that might be sympathy, or maybe it's just rueful acknowledgment of how pathetic you sound. "Well, at least you *know* it's a bad idea. But if you're that determined, then you'd better get started now." She turns away. Can't really blame her, can you? Venture into the almost certainly deadly unknown with a woman who's destroyed multiple communities, or stay with a comm that at least theoretically will soon have a home again? That's barely even a question.

But you should really know better than to try to predict what Tonkee will do. She sighs, after you subside and sit back on the rock you've been using for a chair. "I can probably wrangle some extra supplies out of the quartermaster, if I tell them I need to go scout something for the Innovators. They're used to me doing that. But I'm not sure I can convince them to give me enough for two."

It's a surprise to realize how grateful you are, for her—hmm. Loyalty isn't the word for it. Attachment? Maybe. Maybe it's just that you've been her research subject for all this time already, so of course she's not going to let you slip away when she's followed you across decades and half the Stillness.

But then you frown. "Two? Not three?" You thought things were working out with her and Hjarka.

Tonkee shrugs, then awkwardly bends to tuck into the little bowl of rice and beans she has from the communal pot. After she swallows, she says, "I prefer to make conservative estimates. You'd better, too."

She means Lerna, who seems to be in the process of attaching himself to you. You don't know why. You're not exactly a prize, dressed in ash and with no arm, and half the time he seems to be furious with you. You're still surprised it's not all the time. He always was a strange boy.

"Anyway, here's a thing I want you to think about," Tonkee continues. "What was Nassun doing when you found her?"

And you flinch. Because, damn it, Tonkee has once again said aloud a thing that you would have preferred to leave unsaid, and unconsidered.

And because you remember that moment, with the power of the Gate sluicing through you, when you reached and touched and felt a familiar resonance touch back. A resonance backed, and amplified, by something blue and deep and strangely resistant to the Gate's linkage. The Gate told you—somehow—that it was the sapphire.

What is your ten-year-old daughter doing playing with an obelisk?

How is your ten-year-old daughter *alive* after playing with an obelisk?

You think of how that momentary contact felt. Familiar vibration-taste of an orogeny which you've been quelling since before she was born and training since she was two—but so much sharper and more intense now. You weren't trying to take the sapphire from Nassun, but the Gate was, following instructions that long-dead builders somehow wrote into the layered lattices of the onyx. Nassun kept the sapphire, though. She actually fought off the Obelisk Gate.

What has your little girl been doing, this long dark year, to develop such skill?

"You don't know what her situation is," Tonkee continues, which makes you blink out of this terrible reverie and focus on her. "You don't know what kind of people she's living with. You said she's in the Antarctics, somewhere near the eastern coast? That part of the world shouldn't be feeling the Season much yet. So what are you going to do, then, snatch her out of a comm where she's safe and has enough to eat and can still see the sky, and drag her north to a comm sitting on the Rifting, where the shakes will be constant and the next gas vent might kill everyone?" She looks hard at you. "Do you want to help her? Or just have her with you again? Those two things aren't the same."

"Jija killed Uche," you snap. The words don't hurt, unless you think about them as you speak. Unless you remember your son's smell or his little laugh or the sight of his body under a blanket. Unless you think of Corundum—you use anger to press down the twin throbs of grief and guilt. "I have to get her *away* from him. He killed my son!"

"He hasn't killed your daughter yet. He's had, what, twenty months? Twenty-one? That means something." Tonkee spies Lerna coming back toward you through the crowd, and sighs. "There are just things you ought to think about, is all I'm saying. And I can't even believe I'm saying it. She's another obelisk-user, and I can't even go investigate it." Tonkee utters a frustrated grumbly sound. "I hate this damn Season. I have to be so rusting *practical* now."

You're surprised into a chuckle, but it's weak. The questions Tonkee's raised are good ones, of course, and some of them you can't answer. You think about them for a long time that night, and in the days thereafter.

Rennanis is nearly into the Western Coastals, just past the Merz Desert. Castrima is going to have to go through the desert to get there, because skirting around it would drastically increase the length of your journey—a difference of months versus years. But you're making good time through the central Somidlats, where the roads are decently passable and you haven't been bothered by many raiders or significant wildlife. The Hunters have been able to find a lot of forage to supplement the comm's stores, including a little more game than before. Unsurprising, since they're no longer competing against hordes of insects. It's not enough—small voles and birds just aren't going to hold a comm of a thousand-plus people for long. But it's better than nothing.

When you start noticing changes in the land that presage desert—thinning of the skeletal forest, flattening of the topography, a gradual drawing away of the water table amid the strata—you decide that it's time to finally try to talk to Ykka.

By now you've entered a stone forest: a place of tall, sharp-edged black spires that claw irregularly at the sky above and around you as the group edges through its depths. There aren't many of these in the world. Most get shattered by shakes, or—back when there was a Fulcrum—deliberately destroyed by Fulcrum blackjackets at local comms' commissioned request. No comm *lives* in a stone forest, see, and no well-run comm wants one nearby. Apart from stone forests' tendency to collapse and crush everything within, they tend to be riddled with wet caves and other water-hewn formations that make marvelous homes for dangerous flora and fauna. Or people.

The road runs straight through this stone forest, which is bullshit. That is to say, no one in their right mind would have built a road through a place like this. If a quartent governor had proposed using people's taxes on this dangerous bit of bandit-bait, that governor would've been replaced in the next election…or shanked in the night. So that's your first clue that something's off about the place. The second is that there's not much vegetation in the forest. Not much anywhere this far into the Season, but also no sign that there was ever any vegetation here in the first place. That means this stone forest is recent—so recent that there's been no time for wind or rain to erode the stone and permit plant growth. So recent that it didn't exist before the Season.

Clue number three is what your own sessapinae tell you. Most stone forests are limestone, made by water erosion over hundreds of millions of years. This one is obsidian—volcanic glass. Its jagged spikes aren't straight up and down, but more inwardly curved; there are even a few unbroken arcs stretching over the road. Impossible to see up close, but you can sess the overall pattern: The whole forest is a blossom of lava, solidified mid-blast. Not a line of the road has been knocked out of place by the tectonic explosion around it. Beautiful work, really.

Ykka's in the middle of an argument with another comm member when you find her. She's called for a halt about a hundred feet away from the forest, and people are milling about, looking confused about whether this is just a rest stop or whether they should be making camp since it's relatively late in the day. The comm member is one you finally recognize as Esni Strongback Castrima, the use-caste's spokesperson. She throws you an uneasy glance as you come to a halt beside them, but then you take off your goggles and mask, and her expression softens. She didn't recognize you before because you've stuffed rags into the sleeve of your missing arm to keep warm. Her reaction is a welcome reminder that not everybody in Castrima is angry with you. Esni is alive because the worst part of the attack—Rennanis soldiers trying to carve a bloody path through the Strongbacks holding Scenic Overlook—ended when you locked the enemy stone eaters into crystals.

Ykka, though, doesn't turn, although she should easily be able to sess your presence. She says, you think to Esni, though it works for you as well, "I really don't want to hear any more arguments right now."

"That's good," you say. "Because I understand exactly why you've stopped here, and I think it's a good idea." It's a bit louder than it needs to be. You eyeball Esni so she'll know you mean to have it out with Ykka right now, and maybe Esni doesn't want to be here for that. But a woman who leads the comm's defenders isn't going to scare easily, so you're not entirely surprised when Esni looks amused and folds her arms, ready to enjoy the show.

Ykka turns to you, slowly, a look of mingled annoyance and incredulity on her face. She says, "Nice to know you approve," in a tone that sounds anything but pleased. "Not that I actually *care* if you do."

You set your jaw. "You sess it, right? I'd call it the work of a four- or five-ringer, except I know now that ferals can have unusual skill." You mean her. It's an olive branch. Or maybe just flattery.

She doesn't fall for it. "We're going as far as we can before nightfall, and setting up camp in there." She nods toward the forest. "It's too big to get through in a day. Maybe we could go around, but there's something..." Her eyes unfocus, and then she frowns and turns away, grimacing at having revealed a weakness to you. She's sensitive enough to sess the *something*, but not to know exactly what she's sessing.

You're the one who spent years learning to read underground rocks with orogeny, so you fill in the detail. "There's a leaf-covered spike trap in that direction," you say, nodding toward the long-dead grass edging the stone forest on one side. "Beyond it is an area of snares; I can't tell how many, but I can sess a lot of kinetic tension from wire or rope. If we go around the other way, though, there are partially sheared-off stone columns and boulders positioned at points along the edge of the stone forest. Easy to start a rockslide. And I can sess holes positioned at strategic points along the outer columns. A crossbow, or even an ordinary bow and arrow, could do a lot of damage from there."

Ykka sighs. "Yeah. So *through* really is the best way." She eyes Esni, who must have been arguing for *around.* Esni sighs, too, and then shrugs, conceding the argument.

You face Ykka. "Whoever made this forest, if they're still alive, has the skill to precision-ice half the comm in seconds, with little warning. If you're determined to go through, we're going to have to set up a watch/chore rotation—the orogenes with better control, I mean, when I say 'we.' You need to keep us all awake tonight."

She narrows her eyes. "Why?"

"Because if any of us are asleep when the attack comes"—you're pretty sure there'll be an attack—"we'll react instinctively."

Ykka grimaces. She's not the average feral, but she's feral enough to know what will likely happen if something causes her to react orogenically in her sleep. Whoever the attacker doesn't kill, she very well might, completely by accident. "Shit." She looks away for a moment, and you wonder if she doesn't believe you, but apparently she's just thinking. "Fine. We'll split watches, then. Put the roggas not on watch to work, oh, shelling those wild peas we found a few days back. Or repairing the harnesses the Strongbacks use for hauling. Since we'll have to be carried on the wagons tomorrow, when we're too sleepy and useless to walk on our own."

"Right. And—" You hesitate. Not yet. You can't admit your weakness to these women, not yet. But. "Not me."

Ykka's eyes narrow immediately. Esni throws you a skeptical look, as if to say, *And you were doing so well.* Quickly you add, "I don't know what I'm capable of now. After what I did back in Castrima-under... I'm different."

It's not even a lie. Without really thinking about it, you reach for your missing arm, your hand fumbling against the sleeve of your jacket. No one can see the stump, but you're hyperaware of it all of a sudden. Hoa didn't think much of the way Antimony left visible tooth-marks on Alabaster's stumps, it turns out. Yours is smooth, rounded, nearly polished. Rusting perfectionist.

Ykka's gaze follows that self-conscious touch of yours; she winces. "Huh. Yeah, I guess you would be." Her jaw tenses. "Seems like you can sess all right, though."

"Yes. I can help keep watch. I just shouldn't... do anything."

Ykka shakes her head but says, "Fine. You'll take last watch of the night, then."

It's the least desirable watch—when it's coldest, now that the night temperatures have started to dip below freezing. Most people would rather be asleep in warm bedrolls. It's also the most dangerous time of the watch, when any attackers with sense will hit a large group like this in hopes of catching defenders sleepy and sluggish. You can't decide whether this is a sign of trust, or a punishment. Experimentally, you say, "Can I have a weapon, at least?" You haven't carried anything since a few months after you left Tirimo, when you traded away your knife for dried rose hips to stave off scurvy.

"No."

For rust's sake. You start to fold your arms, remember you can't when your empty sleeve twitches, and grimace instead. (Ykka and Esni grimace, too.) "What am I supposed to do, then, yell really loud? Are you seriously going to put the comm at risk because of your grudge against me?"

Ykka rolls her eyes. "For rust's sake." It's so much an echo of your own thought that you frown. "Unbelievable. You think I'm pissed about the geode, don't you?"

You can't help looking at Esni. She stares at Ykka as if to say, *What, you aren't?* It's eloquent enough for both of you.

Ykka glares, then scrubs at her face and lets out a mortal sigh. "Esni, go…shit, go do something Strongbackish. Essie—here. Come *here*. Rusting walk with me." She beckons sharply, in frustration. You're too confused to be offended; she turns to go and you follow. Esni shrugs and walks away.

The two of you move through the camp in silence for a few moments. Everyone seems keenly aware of the danger that the stone forest presents, so this has become one of the busier rest stops you've seen. Some of the Strongbacks are transferring items between the wagons so as to put essentials onto those with sturdier wheels, which will be less heavily loaded. Easier to grab and run under pressure. The Hunters are whittling sharpened poles from some of the dead saplings and branches near the camp. These will be positioned around the perimeter when the comm finally sets up camp, so as to funnel attackers into kill zones. The rest of the Strongbacks are catching naps while they can, knowing they'll either be patrolling or made to sleep on the outer edges of camp when night falls. *Use strong backs to guard them all*, says stonelore. Strongbacks who don't like being human shields can either find a way to distinguish themselves and join another caste, or go join another comm.

Your nose wrinkles as you pass the hastily dug roadside ditch that is currently occupied by six or seven people, with a few of the younger Resistants standing around to do the unhappy duty of shoveling dirt over the results. Unusually, there's a brief line of people waiting for their turn to squat. Not surprising that so many people need to evacuate their bowels at once; here in the looming shadow of the stone forest, everyone's on edge. Nobody wants to get caught with their pants down after dark.

You're thinking you might need to take a turn in the ditch yourself when Ykka surprises you out of this scintillating rumination. "So do you like us yet?"

"What?"

She gestures over the camp. The people of the comm. "You've been with Castrima for the better part of a year now. Got any friends?"

You, you think, before you can stop yourself. "No," you say.

She eyes you for a moment, and guiltily you wonder if she was expecting you to name her. Then she sighs. "Started rolling Lerna yet? No accounting for taste, I guess, but the Breeders say the signs are all there. Me, when I want a man, I pick one who doesn't talk so much. Women are a surer bet. They know not to ruin the mood." She starts to stretch, grimacing as she works out a kink in her back. You use the time to get control of the horrified embarrassment on your face. The rusting Breeders obviously aren't busy enough.

"No," you say.

"Not yet?"

You sigh. "Not... yet."

"The rust are you waiting for? The road's not getting any safer."

You glare at her. "I thought you didn't care?"

"I don't. But giving you shit about it is helping me make a point." Ykka's leading you toward the wagons, or so you think at first. Then you move past the wagons, and stiffen in surprise.

Here, seated and eating, are the seven Rennanese prisoners. Even sitting they're different from the people of Castrima—all of the Rennanese being pure Sanzed or close enough not to matter, bigger than average even for that race, with fully grown ashblow manes or shorn-sided braids or short bottlebrushes to heighten the effect. Their prangers have been put aside for the moment—though the chains linking each prisoner to their set are still in place—and there are a few Strongbacks standing guard nearby.

You're surprised that they're eating, since you haven't made full camp for the night yet. The Strongbacks on guard are eating, too, but that only makes sense; they've got a long night ahead of them. The Rennies look up as you and Ykka approach, and that makes you stop in your tracks, because you recognize one of the prisoners. Danel, the *general* of the Rennanis army. She's healthy and whole, apart from red marks around her neck and wrists from the pranger. The last time you saw her up close, she was summoning a shirtless Guardian to kill you.

She recognizes you, too, and her mouth flattens into a resigned, ironic line. Then, very deliberately, she nods to you before turning back to her bowl.

Ykka hunkers down to a crouch beside Danel, to your surprise. "So, how's the food?"

Danel shrugs, still eating. "Better than starving."

"It's good," says another prisoner, across the ring. He shrugs when one of the others glares at him. "Well, it *is*."

"They just want us to be able to haul their wagons," says the man who glared.

"Yeah," Ykka interrupts. "That's precisely right. Strongbacks in Castrima get a comm share and a bed, when we have one to give, in exchange for their contribution. What'd you get from Rennanis?"

"Some rusting pride, maybe," says the glarer, glaring harder.

"Shut up, Phauld," says Danel.

"These mongrels think they—"

Danel sets her bowl of food down. The glarer immediately shuts up and tenses, his eyes going a little wide. After a moment, Danel picks up her bowl and resumes eating. Her expression hasn't changed the whole time. You find yourself suspecting that she's raised children.

Ykka, elbow propped on one knee, rests her chin on her fist and watches Phauld for a moment. To Danel, she says, "So what do you want me to do about that one?"

Phauld immediately frowns. "What?"

Danel shrugs. Her bowl's empty now, but she runs a finger around its curve to sweep up the last sauce. "Not for me to say anymore."

"Doesn't seem very bright." Ykka purses her lips, considering the man. "Not bad-looking, but harder to breed for brains than looks."

Danel says nothing for a moment, while Phauld looks from her to Ykka and back in growing incredulity. Then, with a heavy sigh, Danel looks up at Phauld, too. "What do you want me to say? I'm not his commander anymore. Never wanted to be in the first place; I got drafted. Now I don't rusting care."

"I can't believe you," Phauld says. His voice is too loud, rising in panic. "I *fought* for you."

"And lost." Danel shakes her head. "Now it's about surviving, adapting. Forget all that crap you heard back in Rennanis about Sanzeds and mongrels; that was just propaganda to unite the comm. Things are different now. 'Necessity is the only law.'"

"Don't you rusting quote stonelore at me!"

"She's quoting stonelore because you don't *get* it," snaps the other man—the one who liked the food. "They're feeding us. They're letting us be useful. It's a test, you stupid shit. To see if we're willing to earn a place in this comm!"

"*This comm?*" Phauld gestures around at the camp. His laugh echoes off the rock faces. People look around, trying to figure out if the yelling means there's some kind of problem. "Do you hear yourself? These people haven't got a chance. They should be finding somewhere to bunker down, maybe rebuild one of the comms we razed along the way. Instead—"

Ykka moves with a casualness that doesn't deceive you. Everyone could see this coming, including Phauld, but he's too stubborn to acknowledge reality. She stands up and unnecessarily brushes ash off her shoulders and steps across the circle and then puts a hand on the crown of Phauld's head. He tries to twitch back, swatting at her. "Don't rusting touch—"

But then he stops. His eyes glaze over. Ykka's done that thing to him—the thing she did to Cutter back in Castrima-under when people were working themselves into an orogene-lynching mob. Because you knew it was coming this time, you're able to get a better handle on how she does the strange pulse. It's definitely magic, some kind of manipulation of the thin, silvery filaments that dance and flicker between the motes of a person's substance. Ykka's pulse cuts through the knot of threads at the base of Phauld's brain, just above the sessapinae. Everything's still intact physically, but magically it's as if she's chopped his head off.

He sags backward, and Ykka steps aside to let him flop bonelessly to the ground.

One of the other Rennanis women gasps and scoots back, her chains jangling. The guards glance at each other, uncomfortably, but they're not surprised; word of what Ykka did to Cutter spread through the comm afterward. A Rennanese man who hasn't spoken before utters a swift oath in one of the Coaster creole languages; it's not Eturpic so you don't understand it, but his fear is clear enough. Danel only sighs.

Ykka sighs, too, looking at the dead man. Then she eyes Danel. "I'm sorry."

Danel smiles thinly. "We tried. And you said it yourself: He wasn't very bright."

Ykka nods. For some reason she glances up at you for a moment. You have no idea what lesson you're supposed to take from this. "Unlock the manacles," she says. You're confused for an instant before you realize it's an order for the guards. One of them moves over to speak to the other, and they start sorting through a ring of keys. Then Ykka looks disgusted with herself as she says heavily, "Who's on quartermaster duty today? Memsid? Tell him and some of the other Resistants to come handle this." She jerks her head toward Phauld.

Everyone goes still. No one protests, though. The Hunters have been finding more game and forage, but Castrima has a lot of people who need more protein than they've been getting, and the desert is coming. It was always going to come to this.

After a moment of silence, though, you step over to Ykka. "You sure about this?" you ask softly. One of the guards comes over to unlock Danel's ankle chains. Danel, who tried to kill every living member of Castrima. Danel, who tried to kill *you.*

"Why wouldn't I be?" Ykka shrugs. Her voice is loud enough that the prisoners can hear her. "We've been short on Strongbacks since Rennanis attacked. Now we've got six replacements."

"Replacements who'll stab us—or maybe just you—in the back first chance!"

"If I don't see them coming and kill them first, yeah. But that would be pretty stupid of them, and I killed the stupidest one for a reason." You get the sense that Ykka's not trying to scare the Rennanis people. She's just stating facts. "See, this is what I keep trying to tell you, Essie: The world isn't friends and enemies. It's people who might help you, and people who'll get in your way. Kill this lot and what do you get?"

"*Safety.*"

"Lots of ways to be safe. Yeah, there's now a bigger chance I'll get shanked in the night. More safety for the comm, though.

And the stronger the comm is, the better the chance we'll all get to Rennanis alive." She shrugs, then glances around at the stone forest. "Whoever built this is one of us, with real skill. We're going to need that."

"What, now you want to adopt..." You shake your head, incredulous. "Violent bandit ferals?"

But then you stop. Because once upon a time, you loved a violent pirate feral.

Ykka watches while you remember Innon and mourn him anew. Then, with remarkable gentleness, she says, "I play a longer game than just making it to the next day, Essie. Maybe you ought to try it for a change."

You look away, feeling oddly defensive. The luxury of thinking beyond the next day isn't something you've ever had much of a chance to try. "I'm not a headwoman. I'm just a *rogga*."

Ykka tilts her head in ironic acknowledgment. You don't use that word nearly as often as she does. When she says it, it's pride. When you use it, it's assault.

"Well, I'm both," Ykka says. "A headwoman, and a rogga. I *choose to be* both, and more." She steps past you, and throws her next words at you over her shoulder, as if they're meaningless. "You didn't think about any of us while you were using those obelisks, did you? You thought about destroying your enemies. You thought about surviving—but you couldn't get beyond that. That's why I've been so pissed at you, Essie. Months in my comm, and still *all you are* is 'just a rogga.'"

She walks off then, yelling to everyone in earshot that the rest break is over. You watch until she vanishes amid the stretching, grumbling crowd, then you glance over at Danel, who's since stood up and is rubbing the red mark on one of her wrists. There's a carefully neutral look on the woman's face as she watches you.

"She dies, you die," you say. If Ykka won't look after herself, you'll do what you can for her.

Danel lets out a brief, amused breath. "That's true whether you threaten me or not. Not like anybody else here would give me a chance." She throws you a skeptical look, all her Sanzed pride completely intact despite the change in circumstances. "You really *aren't* very good at this, are you?"

Earthfires and rustbuckets. You walk away, because if Ykka already thinks less of you for destroying all threats, she's really not going to like it if you start killing people who annoy you, for sheer pique.

* * *

> 2562: Niner shake in Western Coastals, epicenter somewhere in Baga Quartent. Lorist accounts from the time note that the shake "turned the ground to liquid." (Poetic?) One fishing village survived intact. From a villager's written account: "Bastard roggye killed lah shake then we killed hym." Report filed at the Fulcrum (shared with permission) by Imperial Orogene who later visited the area notes also that an underwater oil reservoir off the coast could have been breached by the shake, but the unregistered rogga in the village prevented this. Would have poisoned water and beaches for miles down the coast.
>
> —*Project notes of Yaetr Innovator Dibars*

4

Nassun, wandering in the wilderness

SCHAFFA IS KIND ENOUGH TO guide the other eight children of Found Moon out of Jekity along with Nassun and himself. He tells the headwoman that they're all going on a training trip some miles away so that the comm won't be disturbed by additional seismics. Since Nassun has just returned the sapphire to the sky—loudly, thanks to the thunderclap of displaced air; dramatically, because suddenly there it was overhead, huge and deep blue and too close—the headwoman just about falls over herself to provide the children with runnysacks containing travel food and supplies so they can hurry on their way. These aren't the kinds of top-notch supplies one needs for a long journey. No compasses, only moderately good boots, the kinds of rations that won't last more than a couple of weeks before going bad. Still, it's much better than leaving empty-handed.

None of the people of the comm know that Umber and Nida are dead. Schaffa carried their bodies into the Guardians' dorm and laid them out on their respective beds, arranged in dignified poses. This worked better for Nida, who looked more or less intact but for the nape of her neck, than Umber, whose head was a ruin. Schaffa then threw dirt over the bloodstains. Jekity will figure it out eventually, but by that time, Found Moon's children will be out of reach, if not safe.

Jija, Schaffa left piled where Nassun felled him. The corpse is nothing but a pile of pretty rocks, really, until one looks closely at some of the pieces.

The children are subdued as they leave the comm that has sheltered them, in some cases for years. They leave via the rogga steps, as they have come to be informally (and rudely) called—the series of basalt columns on the comm's north side that only orogenes can traverse. Wudeh's orogeny is steadier than Nassun has ever sessed it when he takes them down to ground level by pushing one of the pieces of columnar basalt back into the ancient volcano. Still, she can see the look of despair on his face, and it makes her ache inside.

They walk westward as a group, but before they've gone a mile, one or two of the children are quietly weeping. Nassun, whose eyes have remained dry even through stray thoughts like *I killed my father* and *Daddy, I miss you*, grieves with them. It's cruel that they must suffer this, being ashed out during a Season, because of what she has done. (Because of what Jija tried to do, she tries to tell herself, but she does not believe this.) Yet it would be crueler still to leave them in Jekity, where the commfolk will eventually realize what has happened and turn on the children.

Oegin and Ynegen, the twins, are the only ones who look at Nassun with anything resembling understanding. They were the first to come outside after Nassun snatched the sapphire out of the sky. While the others mostly saw Schaffa fight Umber, and Steel kill Nida, those two saw what Jija tried to do to Nassun. They understand that Nassun fought back as anyone would have. Everyone, though, remembers that she killed Eitz. Some have since forgiven her for that, as Schaffa predicted—especially shy, scarred Peek, who privately spoke to Nassun of what she did to the grandmother who stabbed her in the face so long ago. Orogene children learn early what it means to regret.

That doesn't mean they don't still fear Nassun, though, and fear lends a clarity that cuts right through childish rationalizations. They are not killers at heart, after all... and Nassun is.

(She does not want to be, any more than you do.)

Now the group stands at a literal crossroads, where a local trail running northeast to southeast meets the more westerly Jekity-Tevamis Imperial Road. Schaffa says the Imperial Road will eventually lead to a highroad, which is something Nassun has heard of but never seen in all her travels. The crossroads, however, is the place where Schaffa has chosen to inform the other children that they can follow him no longer.

Shirk is the only one who protests this. "We won't eat much," she says to Schaffa, a little desperately. "You... you don't have to feed us. You could just let us follow you. We'll find our own food. I know how!"

"Nassun and I will likely be pursued," Schaffa says. His voice is unfailingly gentle. Nassun knows that this delivery actually makes the words worse; his gentleness makes it easy to see that Schaffa truly cares. Farewells are easier when they are cruel.

"We will also be making a long journey that's very dangerous. You're safer on your own."

"Safer commless," Wudeh says, and laughs. It's the most bitter sound Nassun has ever heard him utter.

Shirk has started to cry. The tears leave streaks of startling cleanliness in the ash that's beginning to gray her face. "I don't understand. You took care of us. You *like* us, Schaffa, more than even Nida and Umber did! Why would you... if you were just going to—to..."

"Stop it," says Lashar. She's gotten taller in the past year, like a good well-bred Sanzed girl. While most of her my-grandfather-was-an-Equatorial arrogance has faded with time, she still defaults to hauteur when she's upset about something. She's folded her arms and is looking away from the trail, off at a group of bare foothills in the near distance. "Have some rusting pride. We've been ashed, but we're still alive and that's what matters. We can take shelter in those hills for the night."

Shirk glares at her. "There isn't any shelter! We're going to *starve to death*, or—"

"We won't." Deshati, who's been looking at the ground while she scuffs the still-thin ash with one foot, looks up suddenly. She's watching Schaffa as she speaks to Shirk and the others. "There are places we can live. We just have to get them to open the gates."

There's a tight, determined look on her face. Schaffa turns a sharp gaze on Deshati, and to her credit, she does not flinch. "You mean to force your way in?" he asks her.

"That's what you want us to do, isn't it? You wouldn't be

sending us away if you weren't okay with us...doing what we have to." She tries to shrug. She's too tense for such a casual gesture; it makes her look briefly twitchy, as if with a palsy. "We wouldn't still be alive if you weren't okay with that."

Nassun looks at the ground. It's her fault that the other children's choices have been whittled down to this. There was beauty in Found Moon; among her fellow children, Nassun has known the delight of reveling in what she is and what she can do, among people who understand and share that delight. Now something once wholesome and good is dead.

You'll kill everything you love, eventually, Steel has told her. She hates that he is right.

Schaffa regards the children for a long, thoughtful moment. His fingers twitch, perhaps remembering another life and another self who could not have endured the idea of unleashing eight young Misalems upon the world. That version of Schaffa, however, is dead. The twitch is only reflexive.

"Yes," he says. "That is what I want you to do, if you need to hear it said aloud. You have a better chance in a large, thriving comm than you do on your own. So allow me to make a suggestion." Schaffa steps forward and crouches to look Deshati in the eye, reaching out also to grip Shirk's thin shoulder. He says to all of them, with that same gentle intensity that he used before, "Kill only one, initially. Pick someone who tries to harm you—but only one, even if more than one tries. Disable the others, but take your time killing that one person. Make it painful. Make sure your target screams. That's important. If the first one that you kill remains silent...kill another."

They stare back at him. Even Lashar seems nonplussed. Nassun, however, has seen Schaffa kill. He has given up some of who he was, but what remains is still an artist of terror. If he has seen fit to share the secrets of his artistry with them, they're lucky. She hopes they appreciate it.

He goes on. "When the killing is done, make it clear to those present that you acted only in self-defense. Then offer to work in the dead person's place, or to protect the rest from danger—but they'll recognize the ultimatum. They *must* accept you into the comm." He pauses, then fixes his icewhite gaze on Deshati. "If they refuse, what do you do?"

She swallows. "K-kill them all."

He smiles again, for the first time since leaving Jekity, and cups the back of her head in fond approval.

Shirk gasps a little, shocked out of tears. Oegin and Ynegen hold each other, their expressions empty of anything but despair. Lashar's jaw has tightened, her nostrils flaring. She means to take Schaffa's words to heart. Deshati does, too, Nassun can tell . . . but it will kill something in Deshati to do so.

Schaffa knows this. When he stands to kiss Deshati's forehead, there is so much sorrow in the gesture that Nassun aches afresh. "'All things change during a Season,'" he says. "*Live*. I want you to live."

A tear spills from one of Deshati's eyes before she can blink it away. She swallows audibly. But then she nods and steps away from him, and backs up to stand with the others. There's a gulf between them now: Schaffa and Nassun on one side, Found Moon's children on the other. The ways have parted. Schaffa does not show discomfort with this. He should; Nassun notices that the silver is alive and throbbing within him, protesting his choice to allow these children to go free. He does not show the pain, though. When he's doing what he feels is right, pain only strengthens him.

He stands. "And should the Season ever show real signs of abating . . . flee. Scatter and blend in elsewhere as best you can. The Guardians aren't dead, little ones. They will return. And once word spreads of what you've done, they'll come for you."

The regular Guardians, Nassun knows he means—the "uncontaminated" ones, like he used to be. Those Guardians have been missing since the start of the Season, or at least Nassun hasn't heard of any joining comms or being seen on the road. *Return* suggests they've all gone somewhere specific. Where? Somewhere that Schaffa and the other contaminated ones did not or could not go.

But what matters is that *this* Guardian, however contaminated, is helping them. Nassun feels a sudden surge of irrational hope. Surely Schaffa's advice will keep them safe, somehow. So she swallows and adds, "All of you are really good at orogeny. Maybe the comm you pick . . . maybe they'll . . ."

She trails off, unsure of what she wants to say. *Maybe they'll like you*, is what she's thinking, but that just seems foolish. Or *maybe you can be useful*, but that's not how it used to work. Comms used to hire Fulcrum orogenes only for brief periods, or so Schaffa has told her, to do needed work and then leave. Even comms near hot spots and fault lines hadn't wanted orogenes around permanently, no matter how much they'd needed them.

Before Nassun can think of a way to grope out the words, however, Wudeh glares at her. "Shut up."

Nassun blinks. "What?"

Peek hisses at Wudeh, trying to shush him, but he ignores her. "Shut up. I rusting hate you. Nida used to sing to me." Then, without warning, he bursts into sobs. Peek looks confused, but some of the others surround him, murmuring and patting comfort into him.

Lashar watches this, then throws a last reproachful look at Nassun before saying, to Schaffa, "We'll be on our way, then. Thank you, Guardian, for... for what it's worth."

She turns and begins herding them away. Deshati walks with her head down, not looking back. Ynegen lingers for a moment between the groups, then glances at Nassun and whispers, "Sorry." Then she, too, leaves, hurrying to catch up with the others.

As soon as the children are completely out of sight, Schaffa puts a hand on Nassun's shoulder to steer her away, westward along the Imperial Road.

After several miles of silence, she says, "Do you still think it would have been better to kill them?"

"Yes." He glances at her. "And you know that as well as I do."

Nassun sets her jaw. "I know." All the more reason to stop this. Stop everything.

"You have a destination in mind," Schaffa says. It's not a question.

"Yes. I... Schaffa, I have to go to the other side of the world." This feels rather like saying *I need to go to a star*, but since that's not too far off from what she actually needs to do, she decides not to feel self-conscious about this smaller absurdity.

To her surprise, however, he tilts his head instead of laughing. "To Corepoint?"

"What?"

"A city on the other side of the world. There?"

She swallows, bites her lip. "I don't know. I just know that what I need is—" She doesn't have the words for it, and instead makes a pantomime with her cupped hands and waggling fingers, sending imaginary wavelets to clash and mesh with each other. "The obelisks... pull on that place. It's what they're made to do. If I go there, I think I might be able to, uh, pull back? I can't do it anywhere else, because..." She can't explain it. Lines of force, lines of sight, mathematical configurations; all of the knowledge that she needs is in her mind, but cannot be reproduced by her tongue. Some of this is a gift from the sapphire, and some is application of theories her mother taught her, and some is simply from tying theory to observation and wrapping the whole thing in instinct. "I don't know which city over there is the right one. If I get closer, and travel around a little, maybe I can—"

"Corepoint is the only thing on that side of the world, little one."

"It's... what?"

Schaffa stops abruptly, tugging off his pack. Nassun does the same, reading this as a signal that it's time for a rest stop. They're just on the leeward side of a hill, which is really just a spar of old lava from the great volcano that lies beneath Jekity. There are natural terraces all around this area, weathered out of the obsidian by wind and rain, though the rock a few inches down is too hard for farming or even much in the way of forestation. Some determined, shallow-rooted trees wave over the empty, ash-frosted terraces, but most are now being killed by the ashfall. Nassun and Schaffa will be able to see potential threats coming from a good ways off.

While Nassun pulls out some food they can share, Schaffa draws something in a nearby patch of windblown ash with his finger. Nassun cranes her neck to see that he's made two circles on the ground. In one, he sketches a rough outline of the Stillness that is familiar to Nassun from geography lessons back in creche—except this time, he draws the Stillness in two pieces, with a line of separation near the equator. The Rifting, yes, which has become a boundary more impassable than even thousands of miles of ocean.

The other circle, however, which Nassun now understands to be a representation of the world, he leaves blank save for a single spot just above the equator and slightly to the east of the circle's middle longitude. He doesn't sketch an island or continent to put it on. Just that lone dot.

"Once, there were more cities on the empty face of the world," Schaffa explains. "A few civilizations have built upon or under the sea, over the millennia. None of those lasted long, though. All that remains is Corepoint."

It is literally a world away. "How could we get there?"

"If—" He pauses. Nassun's belly clenches when the blurry look crosses his face. This time he winces and shuts his eyes, too, as if even the attempt to access his old self has added to his pain.

"You don't remember?"

He sighs. "I remember that I used to."

Nassun realizes she should have expected this. She bites her lip. "Steel might know."

There is a slight flex of muscle along Schaffa's jaw, quick and there and then gone. "Indeed he might."

Steel, who vanished while Schaffa was putting away the other Guardians' bodies, might also be listening from within the stone somewhere nearby. Does it mean something that he hasn't popped up to tell them what to do yet? Maybe they don't need him. "And what about the Antarctic Fulcrum? Don't they have records and things?" She remembers seeing the Fulcrum's library before she and Schaffa and Umber sat down with its leaders, had a cup of safe, then killed them all. The library was a strange high room filled floor to ceiling with shelves of books. Nassun likes books—her mother used to splurge and buy one every few months, and sometimes Nassun got the hand-me-downs if Jija deemed them appropriate for children—and she remembers boggling in awe, for she'd never seen so many books in her life. Surely some of those contained information about... very old cities no one has ever heard of, that only Guardians know how to get to. Um. Hmm.

"Unlikely," Schaffa says, confirming Nassun's misgivings. "And by now, that Fulcrum has probably been annexed by another comm, or perhaps even taken over by commless rabble. Its fields were full of edible crops, after all, and its houses were livable. Returning there would be a mistake."

Nassun bites her lower lip. "Maybe... a boat?" She doesn't know anything about boats.

“No, little one. A boat won’t do for such a long journey.”

He pauses significantly, and with this as warning Nassun tries to brace herself. Here is where he will abandon her, she feels painfully, fearfully certain. Here is where he will want to know what she’s up to—and then want no part of it. Why would he? Even she knows that what she wants is a terrible thing.

“I take it, then,” Schaffa says, “that you mean to assume control of the Obelisk Gate.”

Nassun gasps. Schaffa knows what the Obelisk Gate is? When Nassun herself only learned the term that morning from Steel? But then, the lore of the world, all its strange mechanisms and workings and aeons of secrets, is mostly still intact within Schaffa. It’s only things connected to his old self that are permanently lost . . . which means that the route to Corepoint is something that Old Schaffa needed to know, particularly. What does that mean? “Uh, yes. That’s why I want to go to Corepoint.”

His mouth quirks at her surprise. “Finding an orogene who could activate the Gate was our original purpose, Nassun, in creating Found Moon.”

“What? Why?”

Schaffa glances up at the sky. The sun’s beginning to set. They could get maybe another hour of walking in before it gets too dark to continue. What he’s looking at is the sapphire, though, which hasn’t noticeably moved from its position over Jekity. Rubbing absently at the back of his head, Schaffa gazes at its faint outline through the thickening clouds and nods, as if to himself.

“I and Nida and Umber,” he says. “Perhaps ten years ago, we

were all...instructed...to travel southward, and to find one another. We were bidden to seek and train any orogenes who had the potential to connect to obelisks. This is not a thing Guardians normally do, understand, because there can be only one reason to encourage an orogene along the obelisk path. But it's what the Earth wanted. Why, I don't know. During that time, I was...less questioning." His mouth curves in a brief, rueful smile. "Now I have guesses."

Nassun frowns. "What guesses?"

"That the Earth has its own plans for human—"

Abruptly Schaffa tenses all over, and he sways in his crouch. Quickly Nassun grabs him so he won't fall over, and reflexively he puts an arm around her shoulders. The arm is very tight, but she does not protest. That he needs the comfort of her presence is obvious. That the Earth is angrier than ever with him, perhaps because he's giving away its secrets, is as palpable as the raw, flensing pulse of the silver along every nerve and between every cell of his body.

"Don't talk," Nassun says, her throat tight. "Don't say anything else. If it's going to hurt you like this—"

"It does not rule me." Schaffa has to say this in quick blurts, between pants. "It did not take the core of me. I may have...nnh...put myself into its kennel, but it cannot *leash* me."

"I know." Nassun bites her lip. He's leaning on her heavily, and that's made her knee, where it braces against the ground, ache something awful. She doesn't care, though. "But you don't have to say everything *now*. I'm figuring it out on my own."

She has all the clues, she thinks. Nida once said, of Nassun's ability to connect to obelisks, *This is a thing that we culled for in the Fulcrum*. Nassun hadn't understood at the time, but after perceiving something of the Obelisk Gate's immensity, now she can guess why Father Earth wants her dead if she is no longer under Schaffa's—and through him, the Earth's—control.

Nassun chews her lip. Will Schaffa understand? She isn't sure she can take it if he decides to leave—or worse, if he turns on her. So she takes a deep breath. "Steel says the Moon is coming back."

For an instant there is silence from Schaffa's direction. It has the weight of surprise. "The Moon."

"It's real," she blurts. She has no idea if this is true, though, does she? There's only Steel's word to go on. She's not even sure what a moon is, beyond being Father Earth's long-lost child, like the tales say. And yet somehow she knows that this much of what Steel says is true. She doesn't quite sess it, and there are no telltale threads of silver forming in the sky, but she believes it the way she believes that there is another side of the world even though she's never seen it, and the way she knows how mountains form, and the way she's certain Father Earth is real and alive and an enemy. Some truths are simply too great to deny.

To her surprise, however, Schaffa says, "Oh, I know the Moon is real." Perhaps his pain has faded somewhat; now his expression has hardened as he gazes at the hazy, intermittent disc of the sun where it's managed to not quite pierce the clouds near the horizon. "That, I remember."

"You—really? Then you believe Steel?"

"I believe *you*, little one, because orogenes know the pull of the Moon when it draws near. Awareness of it is as natural to you as sessing shakes. But also, I have seen it." Then his gaze narrows sharply to focus on Nassun. "Why, then, did the stone eater tell you about the Moon?"

Nassun takes a deep breath and lets out a heavy sigh.

"I really just wanted to live somewhere nice," she says. "Live somewhere with…with you. I wouldn't have minded working and doing things to be a good comm member. I could have been a lorist, maybe." She feels her jaw tighten. "But I can't do that, not anywhere. Not without having to hide what I am. I *like* orogeny, Schaffa, when I don't have to hide it. I don't think having it, being a—a r-rogga—" She has to stop, and blush, and shake off the urge to feel ashamed for saying such a bad word, but the bad word is the right word for now. "I don't think being one makes me bad or strange or evil—"

She cuts herself off again, yanks her thoughts out of that track, because it leads right back to *But you have done such evil things.*

Unconsciously, Nassun bares her teeth and clenches her fists. "It isn't *right*, Schaffa. It isn't right that people want me to be bad or strange or evil, that they *make* me be bad…" She shakes her head, fumbling for words. "I just want to be ordinary! But I'm not and—and everybody, a lot of people, all *hate* me because I'm not ordinary. You're the only person who doesn't hate me for…for being what I am. And that's not right."

"No, it isn't." Schaffa shifts to sit back against his pack, looking weary. "But you speak as though it's an easy thing to ask people to overcome their fears, little one."

And he does not say it, but suddenly Nassun thinks: *Jija couldn't.*

Nassun's gorge rises suddenly, sharply enough that she must clap a fist to her mouth for a moment and think hard of ash and how cold her ears are. There's nothing in her stomach except the handful of dates she just ate, but the feeling is awful anyway.

Schaffa, uncharacteristically, does not move to comfort her. He only watches her, expression weary but otherwise unreadable.

"I know they can't do it." Yes. Speaking helps. Her stomach doesn't settle, but she no longer feels on the brink of dry heaves. "I know they—the stills—won't ever stop being afraid. If my father couldn't—" Queasiness. She jerks her thoughts away from the end of that sentence. "They'll just go on being scared forever, and we'll just go on living like this forever, and *it isn't right*. There should be a—a fix. It isn't right that there's no *end* to it."

"But do you mean to impose a fix, little one?" Schaffa asks. It's soft. He's guessed already, she realizes. He knows her so much better than she knows herself, and she loves him for it. "Or an end?"

She gets to her feet and starts pacing, tight little circles between his pack and hers. It helps the nausea and the jittery, rising tension beneath her skin that she cannot name. "I don't know how to fix it."

But that is not the whole truth, and Schaffa scents lies the way predators scent blood. His eyes narrow. "If you did know how, *would* you fix it?"

And then, in a sudden blaze of memory that Nassun has not

permitted herself to see or consider for more than a year, she remembers her last day in Tirimo.

Coming home. Seeing her father standing in the middle of the den breathing hard. Wondering what was wrong with him. Wondering why he did not quite look like her father, in that moment—his eyes too wide, his mouth too loose, his shoulders hunched in a way that seemed painful. And then Nassun remembers looking down.

Looking down and staring and staring and thinking *What is that?* and staring and thinking *Is it a ball?* like the ones that the kids at creche kick around during lunchtime, except those balls are made of leather while the thing at her father's feet is a different shade of brown, brown with purplish mottling all over its surface, lumpy and leathery and half-deflated but *No, it's not a ball, wait is that an eye?* Maybe but it's so swollen shut that it looks like a big fat coffee bean. *Not a ball at all* because it's wearing her brother's clothes including the pants Nassun put on him that morning while Jija was busy trying to get their lunch satchels together for creche. *Uche didn't want to wear those pants* because he was still a baby and liked to be silly so Nassun had done the butt dance for him and he'd laughed so hard, so hard! His laugh was her favorite thing ever, and when the butt dance was over he'd let her put his pants on as a thank-you, which means the unrecognizable deflated ball-thing on the floor is *Uche that is Uche he is Uche—*

"No," Nassun breathes. "I wouldn't fix it. Not even if I knew how."

She has stopped pacing. She has one arm wrapped around her middle. The other hand is a fist, crammed against her mouth. She spits out words around it now, she chokes on them as they gush up her throat, she clutches her belly, which is full of such terrible things that she must let them out somehow or be torn apart from within. These things have distorted her voice, made it a shaky growl that randomly spikes into a higher pitch and a louder volume, because it's everything she can do not to just start screaming. "I *wouldn't* fix it, Schaffa, I wouldn't, I'm sorry, I don't *want* to fix it I want to *kill everybody that hates me*—"

Her middle is so heavy that she can't stand. Nassun drops into a crouch, then to her knees. She wants to vomit but instead she spits words onto the ground between her splayed hands. "*G-g-gone! I want it all* GONE, *Schaffa! I want it to* BURN, *I want it burned up and dead and gone, gone,* NOTHING *l-l-left, no more hate and no more killing just nothing, r-rusting nothing, nothing* FOREVER—"

Schaffa's hands, hard and strong, pull her up. She flails against him, tries to hit him. It isn't malice or fear. She never *wants* to hurt him. She just has to let some of what's in her out somehow, or she will go mad. For the first time she understands her father, as she screams and kicks and punches and bites and yanks at her clothes and her hair and tries to slam her forehead against his. Quickly, Schaffa turns her about and wraps one of his big arms around her, pinning her arms to her sides so that she cannot hurt him or herself in the transport of her rage.

This is what Jija felt, observes a distant, detached, floating-obelisk part of herself. *This is what came up inside him when he realized Mama lied, and I lied, and Uche lied. This is what made him push me off the wagon. This is why he came up to Found Moon this morning with a glassknife in his hand.*

This. This is the Jija in her, making her thrash and shout and weep. She feels closer than ever to her father in this moment of utter broken rage.

Schaffa holds her until she is exhausted. Finally she slumps, shaking and panting and moaning a little, her face all over tears and snot.

When it's clear that Nassun will not lash out again, Schaffa shifts to sit down cross-legged, pulling Nassun into his lap. She curls against him the way another child curled against him once, many years before and many miles away, when he told her to pass a test for him so that she could live. Nassun's test has already been met, though; even the old Schaffa would agree with that assessment. In all her rage, Nassun's orogeny did not twitch once, and she did not reach for the silver at all.

"Shhh," Schaffa soothes. He's been doing this all the while, though now he rubs her back and thumbs away her occasional tears. "Shhh. Poor thing. How unfair of me. When only this morning—" He sighs. "Shhh, my little one. Just rest."

Nassun is wrung out and empty of everything but the grief and fury that run in her like fast lahars, grinding everything else away in a churning hot slurry. Grief and fury and one last precious, whole feeling.

"You're the only one I love, Schaffa." Her voice is raw and weary. "You're the only reason I w-wouldn't. But... but I..."

He kisses her forehead. "Make the end you need, my Nassun."

"I don't want." She has to swallow. "I want you to—to be alive!"

He laughs softly. "Still a child, despite all you've been through." This stings, but his meaning is clear. She cannot have both Schaffa alive and the world's hatred dead. She must choose one ending or the other.

But then, firmly, Schaffa says again: "Make the end you need."

Nassun pulls back so she can look at him. He's smiling again, clear-eyed. "What?"

He squeezes her, very gently. "You're my redemption, Nassun. You are all the children I should have loved and protected, even from myself. And if it will bring you peace..." He kisses her forehead. "Then I shall be your Guardian till the world burns, my little one."

It is a benediction, and a balm. The nausea finally releases its hold on Nassun. In Schaffa's arms, safe and accepted, she sleeps at last, amid dreams of a world glowing and molten and in its own way, at peace.

* * *

"Steel," she calls, the next morning.

Steel blurs into presence before them, standing in the middle of the road with his arms folded and an expression of faint amusement on his face.

"The nearest way to Corepoint is not far, relatively speaking," he says when she has asked him for the knowledge that Schaffa lacks. "A month's travel or so. Of course..." He lets this trail off, conspicuously. He has offered to take Nassun and Schaffa to the other side of the world himself, which is apparently a thing that stone eaters can do. It would save them a great deal of hardship and danger, but they would have to entrust themselves to Steel's care as he transports them in the strange, terrifying manner of his kind, through the earth.

"No, thank you," Nassun says again. She doesn't ask Schaffa for his opinion on this, though he leans against a boulder nearby. She doesn't need to ask him. That Steel's interest is wholly in Nassun is obvious. It would be nothing to him to simply forget to bring Schaffa—or lose him along the way to Corepoint. "But could you tell us about this place we have to go? Schaffa doesn't remember."

Steel's gray gaze shifts to Schaffa. Schaffa smiles back, deceptively serene. Even the silver inside him goes still, just for this moment. Maybe Father Earth doesn't like Steel, either.

"It's called a *station*," Steel explains, after a moment. "It's old. You would call it a deadciv ruin, although this one is still intact, nestled within another set of ruins that aren't. A long time ago, people used stations, or rather the vehicles kept within them, to travel long distances far more efficiently than walking. These days, however, only we stone eaters and the Guardians remember that the stations exist." His smile, which hasn't changed since he appeared, is still and wry. It seems meant for Schaffa somehow.

"We all pay a price for power," Schaffa says. His voice is cool and smooth in that way he gets when he's thinking about doing bad things.

"Yes." Steel pauses for just a beat too long. "A price must be paid to use this method of transportation, as well."

"We don't have any money or anything good to barter," Nassun says, troubled.

"Fortunately, there are other ways to pay." Steel abruptly stands at a different angle, his face tilted upward. Nassun follows this, turning, and sees—oh. The sapphire, which has gotten a little closer overnight. Now it's halfway between them and Jekity.

"The station," Steel continues, "is from a time before the Seasons. The time when the obelisks were built. All the lingering artifacts of that civilization recognize the same power source."

"You mean..." Nassun inhales. "The silver."

"Is that what you call it? How poetic."

Nassun shrugs uncomfortably. "I don't know what else to call it."

"Oh, how the world has changed." Nassun frowns, but Steel does not explain this cryptic statement. "Stay on this road until you reach the Old Man's Pucker. Do you know where that is?"

Nassun remembers seeing it on maps of the Antarctics a lifetime ago, and giggling at the name. She glances at Schaffa, who nods and says, "We can find it."

"Then I'll meet you there. The ruin is at the exact center of the grass forest, within the inner ring. Enter the Pucker just after dawn. Don't dawdle reaching the center; you won't want to still be in the forest after dusk." Then Steel pauses, shifting into a new position—one that is distinctly thoughtful. His face is turned off to the side, fingers touching his chin. "I thought it would be your mother."

Schaffa goes still. Nassun is surprised by the flash of heat, then cold, that moves through her. Slowly, while sifting through this strange complexity of emotion, she says, "What do you mean?"

"I expected her to be the one to do this, is all." Steel doesn't shrug, but something in his voice suggests nonchalance. "I threatened her comm. Her friends, the people she cares about now. I thought they would turn on her, and then this choice would seem more palatable to her."

The people she cares about now. "She's not in Tirimo anymore?"

"No. She has joined another comm."

"And they... didn't turn on her?"

"No. Surprisingly." Steel's eyes slide over to meet Nassun's. "She knows where you are now. The Gate told her. But she isn't coming, or at least not yet. She wants to see her friends safely settled first."

Nassun sets her jaw. "I'm not in Jekity anymore, anyway. And soon she won't have the Gate, either, so she won't be able to find me again."

Steel turns fully to face her, this movement too slow and human-smooth to be human, though his astonishment seems genuine. She hates it when he moves slowly. It makes her get goose bumps.

"Nothing lasts forever, indeed," he says.

"What's that mean?"

"Only that I've underestimated you, little Nassun." Nassun instantly dislikes this term of address. He shifts again to the thoughtful pose, fast this time, to her relief. "I think I'd better not do so again."

With that, he vanishes. Nassun frowns at Schaffa, who shakes his head. They shoulder their packs and head west.

* * *

2400: Eastern Equatorials (check if node network was thin in this area, because . . .), unknown comm. Old local song about a nurse who stopped a sudden eruption and pyroclastic flow by turning it to ice. One of her patients threw himself in front of a crossbow bolt to protect her from the mob. Mob let her go; she vanished.

—*Project notes of Yaetr Innovator Dibars*

Syl Anagist: Four

All energy is the same, through its different states and names. Movement creates heat which is also light that waves like sound which tightens or loosens the atomic bonds of crystal as they hum with strong and weak forces. In mirroring resonance with all of this is magic, the radiant emission of life and death.

This is our role: To weave together those disparate energies. To manipulate and mitigate and, through the prism of our awareness, produce a singular force that cannot be denied. To make of cacophony, symphony. The great machine called the Plutonic Engine is the instrument. We are its tuners.

And this is the goal: Geoarcanity. Geoarcanity seeks to establish an energetic cycle of infinite efficiency. If we are successful, the world will never know want or strife again . . . or so we are told. The conductors explain little beyond what we must know to fulfill our roles. It is enough to know that we—small, unimportant *we*—will help to set humanity on a new path toward an unimaginably bright future. We may be tools, but we are fine ones, put to a magnificent purpose. It is easy to find pride in that.

We are attuned enough to each other that the loss of Tetlewha causes trouble for a time. When we join to form our initializing network, it's imbalanced. Tetlewha was our countertenor, the half wavelengths of the spectrum; without him I am closest, but my natural resonance is a little high. The resulting network is weaker than it should be. Our feeder threads keep trying to reach for Tetlewha's empty middle range.

Gaewha is able to compensate for the loss, finally. She reaches deeper, resonates more powerfully, and this plugs the gap. We must spend several days reforging all the network's connections to create new harmony, but it isn't difficult to do this, just time-consuming. This isn't the first time we've had to do it.

Kelenli joins us in the network only occasionally. This is frustrating, because her voice—deep and powerful and foot-tingling in its sharpness—is perfect. Better than Tetlewha's, wider ranging than all of us together. But we are told by the conductors not to get used to her. "She'll serve during the actual start-up of the Engine," one of them says when I ask, "but only if she can't manage to teach you how to do what she does. Conductor Gallat wants her on standby only, come Launch Day."

This seems sensible, on the surface.

When Kelenli is part of us, she takes point. This is simply natural, because her presence is so much greater than ours. Why? Something in the way she is made? Something else. There is a...held note. A perpetual hollow burn at the midpoint of her balanced lines, at their fulcrum, which none of us understand. A similar burn rests in each of us, but ours is faint and intermittent, occasionally flaring only to quickly fade back to quiescence. Hers blazes steadily, its fuel apparently limitless.

Whatever this held-note burn is, the conductors have discovered, it meshes beautifully with the devouring chaos of the onyx. The onyx is the control cabochon of the whole Plutonic Engine, and while there are other ways to start up the Engine—cruder ways, workarounds involving subnetworks or the moonstone—on Launch Day we will absolutely need the onyx's precision and control. Without it, our chances of successfully initiating Geoarcanity diminish greatly . . . but none of us, thus far, has had the strength to hold the onyx for more than a few minutes. We observe in awe, however, as Kelenli rides it for a solid hour, then actually seems unfazed when she disengages from it. When we engage the onyx, it punishes us, stripping everything we can spare and leaving us in a shutdown sleep for hours or days—but not her. Its threads caress rather than rip at her. The onyx *likes* her. This explanation is irrational, but it occurs to all of us, so that's how we begin to think of it. Now she must teach us to be more likable to the onyx, in her stead.

When we are done rebalancing and they let us up from the wire chairs that maintain our bodies while our minds are engaged, and we stagger and must lean on the conductors to make it back to our individual quarters . . . when all of this is done, she comes to visit us. Individually, so the conductors won't suspect anything. In face-to-face meetings, speaking audible nonsense—and meanwhile, earthspeaking sense to all of us at once.

She feels sharper than the rest of us, she explains, because she is more experienced. Because she's lived outside of the complex of buildings that surround the local fragment, and which has comprised the entirety of our world since we were decanted. She has visited more nodes of Syl Anagist than just the one we live in; she has seen and touched more of the fragments than just our local amethyst. She has even been to Zero Site, where the moonstone rests. We are in awe of this.

"I have context," she says to us—to me, rather. She's sitting on my couch. I am sprawled facedown on the window seat, face turned away from her. "When you do, too, you'll be just as sharp."

(It is a kind of pidgin between us, using the earth to add meaning to audible words. Her words are simply, "I'm older," while a whitter of subsidence adds the nuancing deformation of time. She is *metamorphic*, having transformed to bear unbearable pressure. To make this telling simpler, I will translate it all as words, except where I cannot.)

"It would be good if we were as sharp as you *now*," I reply wearily. I am not whining. Rebalancing days are always hard. "Give us this context, then, so the onyx will listen and my head can stop hurting."

Kelenli sighs. "There's nothing within these walls on which you can sharpen yourself." (Crumble of resentment, ground up and quickly scattered. *They have kept you so safe and sheltered.*) "But I think there's a way I can help you and the others do that, if I can get you out of this place."

"Help me . . . sharpen myself?"

(She soothes me with a polishing stroke. *It is not a kindness that you are kept so dull.*) "You need to understand more about yourself. What you are."

I don't understand why she thinks I don't understand. "I'm a tool."

She says: "If you're a tool, shouldn't you be honed as fine as possible?"

Her voice is serene. And yet a pent, angry jitter of the entire ambient—air molecules shivering, strata beneath us compressing, a dissonant grinding whine at the limit of our ability to sess—tells me that Kelenli hates what I have just said. I turn my head to her and find myself fascinated by the way this dichotomy fails to show in her face. It's another way she's like us. We have long since learned not to show pain or fear or sorrow in any space aboveground or below the sky. The conductors tell us we are built to be like statues—cold, immovable, silent. We aren't certain why they believe we actually are this way; after all, we are as warm to the touch as they. We feel emotion, as they seem to, although we do seem less inclined to display it in face or body language. Perhaps this is because we have earthtalk? (Which they don't seem to notice. This is good. In the earth, we may be ourselves.) It has never been clear to us whether we were built wrong, or whether their understanding of us is wrong. Or whether either matters.

Kelenli is outwardly calm while she burns inside. I watch her for so long that abruptly she comes back to herself and catches me. She smiles. "I think you like me."

I consider the possible implications of this. "Not that way," I say, out of habit. I have had to explain this to junior conductors or other staff on occasion. We are made like statues in this way as well—a design implementation that worked in this case, leaving us capable of rutting but disinterested in the attempt, and infertile should we bother. Is Kelenli the same? No, the conductors said she was made different in only one way. She has our powerful, complex, flexible sessapinae, which no other people in the world possess. Otherwise she's like them.

"How fortunate that I wasn't talking about sex." There's a drawling hum of amusement from her; it both bothers and pleases me. I don't know why.

Oblivious to my sudden confusion, Kelenli gets to her feet. "I'll be back," she says, and leaves.

She doesn't return for several days. She remains a detached part of our last network, though, so she is present for our wakings, our meals, our defecations, our inchoate dreams when we sleep, our pride in ourselves and each other. It doesn't feel like watching when she does it, even if she is watching. I cannot speak for the others, but I like having her around.

Not all of the others do like Kelenli. Gaewha in particular is belligerent about it, and she sends this through our private discussion. "She appears just as we lose Tetlewha? Just as the project concludes? We've worked hard to become what we are. Will they praise her for our work, when it's done?"

"She's only a standby," I say, trying to be the voice of reason. "And what she wants is what we want. We need to cooperate."

"So she says." That is Remwha, who considers himself smarter than the rest of us. (We're all made to be equally intelligent. Remwha is just an ass.) "The conductors kept her away until now for a reason. She may be a troublemaker."

That is foolish, I believe, though I don't let myself say it even in earthtalk. We are part of the great machine. Anything that improves the machine's function matters; anything unrelated to this purpose does not. If Kelenli were a troublemaker, Gallat would have sent her to the briar patch with Tetlewha. This is a thing we all understand. Gaewha and Remwha are just being difficult.

"If she is some sort of troublemaker, that will show itself with time," I say firmly. That does not end, but at least postpones, the argument.

Kelenli returns the next day. The conductors bring us together to explain. "Kelenli has asked to take you on a tuning mission," says the man who comes to deliver the briefing. He's much taller than us, taller even than Kelenli, and slender. He likes to dress in perfectly matched colors and ornate buttons. His hair is long and black; his skin is white, though not so much as ours. His eyes are like ours, however—white within white. White as ice. We've never seen another one of *them* with eyes like ours. He is Conductor Gallat, head of the project. I think of Gallat as a plutonic fragment—a clear one, diamond-white. He is precisely angled and cleanly faceted and beautiful in a unique way, and he is also implacably deadly if not handled with precision. We don't let ourselves think about the fact that he's the one who killed Tetlewha.

(He isn't who you think he is. I want Gallat to look like him the way I want you to look like her. This is the hazard of a flawed memory.)

"A tuning... mission," Gaewha says slowly, to show that she doesn't understand.

Kelenli opens her mouth to speak and then stops, turning to Gallat. Gallat smiles genially at this. "Kelenli's performance is what we were hoping for with all of you, and yet you've consistently underperformed," he says. We tense, uncomfortable, hyperconscious of criticism, though he merely shrugs. "I've consulted with the chief biomagestre, and she's insistent that there's no significant difference in your relative abilities. You have the same *capability* that she has, but you don't demonstrate the same *skill*. There are any number of alterations we could make to try to resolve the discrepancy, fine-tuning so to speak, but that's a risk we'd rather not take so close to launch."

We reverberate in one accord for a moment, all of us very glad for this. "She said that she was here to teach us context," I venture, very carefully.

Gallat nods to me. "She believes the solution is outside experience. Increased exposure to stimuli, challenging your problem-solving cognition, things like that. It's a suggestion that has merit and the benefit of being minimally invasive—but for the sake of the project, we can't send you all out at once. What if something happened? Instead we will split you into two groups. Since there's only one of Kelenli, that means half of you will go with her now, and half in a week."

Outside. We're going outside. I'm desperate to be in the first group, but we know better than to show desire before the conductors. Tools should not want to escape their box so obviously.

I say, instead, "We've been more than sufficiently attuned to one another without this proposed mission." My voice is flat. A statue's. "The simulations show that we are reliably capable of controlling the Engine, as expected."

"And we might as well do six groups as two," adds Remwha. By this asinine suggestion do I know his eagerness. "Will each group not have different experiences? As I understand the…

outside... there's no way to control for consistency of exposure. If we must take time away from our preparations for this, surely it should be done in a way that minimizes risk?"

"I think six wouldn't be cost-effective or efficient," Kelenli says, while silently signaling approval and amusement for our playacting. She glances at Gallat and shrugs, not bothering to pretend that she is emotionless; she simply seems bored. "We might as well do *one* group as two or six. We can plan the route, position extra guards along the way, involve the nodal police for surveillance and support. Honestly, repeated trips would just increase the chance that disaffected citizens might anticipate the route and plan... unpleasantness."

We are all intrigued by the possibility of unpleasantness. Kelenli quells our excited tremors.

Conductor Gallat winces as she does this; that one struck home. "The potential for significant gains are why you will go," Conductor Gallat says to us. He's still smiling, but there's an edge to it now. Was the word *will* ever so slightly emphasized? So minute, the perturbations of audible speech. What I take from this is that not only will he let us go, but he has also changed his mind about sending us in multiple groups. Some of this is because Kelenli's suggestion was the most sensible, but the rest is because he's irritated with us for our apparent reluctance.

Ah, Remwha wields his annoying nature like a diamond chisel as usual. *Excellent work*, I pulse. He returns me a polite thank-you waveform.

We are to leave that very day. Clothing suitable for travel outdoors is brought to my quarters by junior conductors. I pull on the thicker cloth and shoes carefully, fascinated by the different textures, and then sit quietly while the junior conductor plaits my hair into a single white braid. "Is this necessary for outside?" I ask. I'm genuinely curious, since the conductors wear their hair in many styles. Some of them I can't emulate, because my hair is poufy and coarse and will not hold a curl or bear straightening. Only we have hair like this. Theirs comes in many textures.

"It might help," says the junior. "You lot are going to stand out no matter what, but the more normal we can make you seem, the better."

"People will know we're part of the Engine," I say, straightening just a little in pride.

His fingers slow for a moment. I don't think he notices. "That's not exactly... They're more likely to think you're something else. Don't worry, though; we'll send guards along to make sure there's no trouble. They'll be unobtrusive, but there. Kelenli insists that you can't be made to feel sheltered, even if you are."

"They're more likely to think we're something else," I repeat slowly, thoughtfully.

His fingers twitch, pulling a few strands harder than necessary. I don't wince or pull away. They're more comfortable thinking of us as statues, and statues aren't supposed to feel pain. "Well, it's a distant possibility, but they have to know you aren't—I mean, it's..." He sighs. "Oh, Evil Death. It's complicated. Don't worry about it."

Conductors say this when they've made a mistake. I don't ping the others with it right away, because we minimize communication outside of sanctioned meetings. People who are not tuners can perceive magic only in rudimentary ways; they use machines and instruments to do what is natural for us. Still, they're always monitoring us in some measure, so we cannot allow them to learn the extent to which we speak to each other, and hear them, when they think we cannot.

Soon I'm ready. After conferring with other conductors over the vine, mine decides to brush my face with paint and powder. It's supposed to make me look like them. It actually makes me like someone whose white skin has been painted brown. I must look skeptical when he shows me the mirror; my conductor sighs and complains that he's not an artist.

Then he brings me to a place that I've seen only a few times before, within the building that houses me: the downstairs foyer. Here the walls aren't white; the natural green and brown of self-repairing cellulose has been allowed to flourish unbleached. Someone has seeded the space with vining strawberries that are half in white flower, half in ripening red fruit; it's quite lovely. The six of us stand near the floor pool waiting for Kelenli, trying not to notice the other personnel of the building coming and going and staring at us: six smaller-than-average, stocky people with puffy white hair and painted faces, our lips arranged in defensively pleasant smiles. If there are guards, we do not know how to tell them from the gawkers.

When Kelenli comes toward us, though, I finally notice guards. Hers move with her, not bothering to be unobtrusive—a tall brown woman and man who might have been siblings. I realize I have seen them before, trailing her on other occasions that she's come to visit. They hang back as she reaches us.

"Good, you're ready," she says. Then she grimaces, reaching out to touch Dushwha's cheek. Her thumb comes away dusted with face powder. "Really?"

Dushwha looks away, uncomfortable. They have never liked being pushed into any emulation of our creators—not in clothing, not in gender, definitely not in this. "It's meant to help," they mutter unhappily, perhaps trying to convince themselves.

"It makes you *more* conspicuous. And they'll know what you are, anyway." She turns and looks at one of her guards, the woman. "I'm taking them to clean this dreck off. Want to help?" The woman just looks at her in silence. Kelenli laughs to herself. It sounds genuinely mirth filled.

She herds us into a personal-needs alcove. The guards station themselves outside while she splashes water on our faces from the clean side of the latrine pool, and scrubs the paint away with an absorbent cloth. She hums while she does it. Does that mean she's happy? When she takes my arm to wipe the gunk off my face, I search hers to try to understand. Her gaze sharpens when she notices.

"You're a thinker," she says. I'm not sure what that's supposed to mean.

"We all are," I say. I allow a brief rumble of nuance. *We have to be.*

"Exactly. You think more than you have to." Apparently a bit of brown near my hairline is especially stubborn. She wipes it off, grimaces, wipes it again, sighs, rinses the cloth and wipes at it again.

I continue searching her face. "Why do you laugh at their fear?"

It's a stupid question. Should've asked it through the earth, not out loud. She stops wiping my face. Remwha glances at me in bland reproach, then goes to the entrance of the alcove. I hear him asking the guard there to please ask a conductor whether we are in danger of sun damage without the protection of the paint. The guard laughs and calls over her companion to relay this question, as if it's ridiculous. During the moment of distraction purchased for us by this exchange, Kelenli then resumes scrubbing me.

"Why *not* laugh at it?" she says.

"They would like you better if you didn't laugh." I signal nuance: alignment, harmonic enmeshment, compliance, conciliation, mitigation. If she wants to be liked.

"Maybe I don't want to be liked." She shrugs, turning to rinse the cloth again.

"You could be. You're like them."

"Not enough."

"More than me." This is obvious. She is their kind of beautiful, their kind of normal. "If you tried—"

She laughs at me, too. It isn't cruel, I know instinctively. It's pitying. But underneath the laugh, her presence is suddenly as still and pent as pressurized stone in the instant before it becomes something else. Anger again. Not at me, but triggered by my words nevertheless. I always seem to make her angry.

They're afraid because we exist, she says. *There's nothing we did to provoke their fear, other than exist. There's nothing we can do to earn their approval, except stop existing—so we can either die like they want, or laugh at their cowardice and go on with our lives.*

I think at first that I don't understand everything she just told me. But I do, don't I? There were sixteen of us once; now we are but six. The others questioned and were decommissioned for it. Obeyed without question, and were decommissioned for it. Bargained. Gave up. Helped. Despaired. We have tried everything, done all they asked and more, and yet now there are only six of us left.

That means we're better than the others were, I tell myself, scowling. Smarter, more adaptable, more skilled. This matters, does it not? We are components of the great machine, the pinnacle of Sylanagistine biomagestry. If some of us had to be removed from the machine because of flaws—

Tetlewha was not flawed, Remwha snaps like a slipstrike fault.

I blink and glance at him. He's back in the alcove, waiting over near Bimniwha and Salewha; they've all used the fountain to strip off their own paint while Kelenli worked on me and Gaewha and Dushwha. The guards Remwha distracted are just outside, still chuckling to themselves over what he said to them. He's glaring at me. When I frown, he repeats: *Tetlewha was not flawed.*

I set my jaw. *If Tetlewha was not flawed, then that means he was decommissioned for no reason at all.*

Yes. Remwha, who rarely looks pleased on a good day, has now curled his lip in disgust. At me. I'm so shocked by this that I forget to pretend indifference. *That is precisely her point. It doesn't matter what we do. The problem is them.*

It doesn't matter what we do. The problem is them.

When I am clean, Kelenli cups my face in her hands. "Do you know the word 'legacy'?"

I've heard it and guessed its meaning from context. It's

difficult to pull my thoughts back on track after Remwha's angry rejoinder. He and I have never much liked one another, but… I shake my head and focus on what Kelenli has asked me. "A legacy is something obsolete, but which you cannot get rid of entirely. Something no longer wanted, but still needed."

She grimace-smiles, first at me and then at Remwha. She's heard everything he said to me. "That will do. Remember that word today."

Then she gets to her feet. The three of us stare at her. She's not only taller and browner, but she moves more, breathes more. *Is* more. We worship what she is. We fear what she will make of us.

"Come," she says, and we follow her out into the world.

* * *

2613: A massive underwater volcano erupted in the Tasr Straits between the Antarctic Polar Waste and the Stillness. Selis Leader Zenas, previously unknown to be an orogene, apparently quelled the volcano, although she was unable to escape the tsunami that it caused. Skies in the Antarctics darkened for five months, but cleared just before a Season could be officially declared. In the immediate aftermath of the tsunami, Selis Leader's husband—the comm head at the time of the eruption, deposed by emergency election—attempted to defend their one-year-old child from a mob of survivors and was killed. Cause disputed: Some witnesses say the mob stoned him, others say the former comm head was strangled by a Guardian. Guardian took the orphaned infant to Warrant.

—*Project notes of Yaetr Innovator Dibars*

5

you are remembered

THE ATTACK COMES, LIKE CLOCKWORK, near dawn.

Everyone's ready for it. The camp is about a third of the way into the stone forest, which is as far as Castrima was able to get before full darkness made further progress treacherous. The group should be able to get all the way through the forest before sunset the next day—assuming everyone lives through the night.

Restlessly you prowl the camp, and you are not the only one to do so. The Hunters are supposed to all be sleeping, since during the day they act as scouts as well as ranging afield to forage and catch game. You see quite a few of them awake, too. The Strongbacks are supposed to be sleeping in shifts, but all of them are up, as are a good number of the other castes. You spot Hjarka sitting atop a pile of baggage, her head down and eyes shut, but otherwise her legs are braced for a quick lunge and there's a glassknife in each hand. Her fingers haven't loosened with sleep.

It's a stupid time to attack, given all this, but there isn't a better one, so apparently your assailants decide to work with what they've got. You're the first to sess it, and you're pivoting on the ball of one foot and shouting a warning even as you narrow your perception and drop into that space of mind from which you can command volcanoes. A fulcrum, deep and strong, has been rooted in the earth nearby. You follow it to the midpoint of its potential torus, the center of the circle, like a hawk sighting prey. Right side of the road. Twenty feet into the stone forest, out of line of sight amid the wends and drooping greenery. "Ykka!"

She appears at once from wherever she was sitting amid the tents. "Yeah, felt it."

"Not active yet." By this you mean that the torus hasn't begun to draw heat or movement from the ambient. But that fulcrum is deep as a taproot. There's not much seismic potential gathered in this region—and indeed, much of the pressure on the lower-level strata has been absorbed by the creation of the stone forest. Still, there's always heat if you go deep enough, and this is deep. Solid. Fulcrum-precise.

"We don't have to fight," Ykka yells, suddenly, into the forest. You start, though you shouldn't. You're shocked that she was serious, though you really should know better by now. She stalks forward, body taut, knees bent as if she's about to sprint into the forest, hands held out before her and fingertips wiggling.

It's easier now to reach for magic, though you still focus on the stump of your own arm to begin, out of habit. It will never feel *natural* for you to use this instead of orogeny, but at least your perception shifts quickly. Ykka's way ahead of you. Wavelets and arcs of silver dance along the ground around her, mostly in front of her, spreading and flickering as she draws them up from the ground and makes them hers. What little vegetation you can sess in the stone forest makes it easier; the seedling vines and light-starved mosses act like wires, channeling and aligning the silver into patterns that make sense. Are predictable. Are *searching*...ah. You tense in the same moment that Ykka does. Yes. There.

Above that deep-rooted fulcrum, at the center of a torus that has not yet begun to spin, crouches a body etched out in silver. For the first time, in comparison, you notice that an orogene's silver is both brighter and less complex than that of the plants and insects around it. The same...er, *amount*, if that word applies, if not *capacity* or *potential* or *aliveness*, but not the same design. This orogene's silver is concentrated into a relative few bright lines that all align in similar directions. They don't flicker, and neither does his torus. He—you guess that, but it feels right—is listening.

Ykka, another outline of precise, concentrated silver, nods in satisfaction. She climbs up on top of some of the wagon cargo so her voice will carry better.

"I'm Ykka Rogga Castrima," she calls. You guess that she points at you. "She's a rogga, too. So's he." Temell. "So are those kids over there. We don't kill roggas here." She pauses. "You hungry? We've got a little to spare. You don't need to try to take it."

That fulcrum doesn't budge.

Something else does, though—from the other side of the stone forest, as thin, attenuated agglomerations of silver suddenly blur into chaotic movement and come charging toward you. Other raiders; Evil Earth, you were all so focused on the rogga that you didn't even notice the ones behind you. You hear them now, though, voices rising, cursing, feet pounding on ashy sand. The Strongbacks near the barrier of stakes on that side cry warning. "They're attacking," you call.

"No shit," Ykka snaps, drawing a glassknife.

You retreat to within the tent circle, acutely aware of your vulnerability in a way that's strange and deeply unpleasant. It's worse because you can still sess, and because your instincts prompt you to respond when you see where you *could* help. A cluster of attackers comes at a part of the perimeter that's light on stakes and defenders, and you open your eyes so you can actually see them trying to fight their way in. They're typical commless raiders—filthy, emaciated, dressed in an ash-faded combination of rags and newer, pilfered clothing. You could take out all six in half a breath, with a single precision torus.

But you can also feel how . . . what? How *aligned* you are. Ykka's silver is concentrated like that of the other roggas you've observed, but hers is still layered, jagged, a little jittery. It flows every-which-way within her as she jumps down from the cargo wagon and shouts for people to help the sparse Strongbacks near that cluster of raiders, running to help herself. Your magic flows with smooth clarity, every line matching perfectly in direction and flow to every other line. You don't know how to change it back to the way it was, if that's even possible. And you know instinctively that using the silver when you're like this will pack every particle of your body together as neatly as a mason lays a wall of bricks. You'll be stone the same way.

So you fight your instincts and *hide*, much as that rankles.

There are others here, crouching amid the central circle of tents—the comm's smaller children, its bare handful of elders, one woman so pregnant that she can't move with any real flexibility even though she's got a loaded crossbow in her hands, two knife-wielding Breeders who've obviously been charged with defending her and the children.

When you poke your head up to observe the fighting, you catch a glimpse of something stunning. *Danel*, having appropriated one of the spear-whittled sticks that form the fence, is using it to carve a bloody swath through the raiders. She's phenomenal, spinning and stabbing and blocking and stabbing again, twirling the stick in between attacks as if she's fought commless a million times. That's not just being an experienced Strongback; that's something else. She's just too good. But it follows, doesn't it? Not like Rennanis made her the general of their army for her charm.

It isn't much of a fight in the end. Twenty or thirty scrawny commless against trained, fed, prepared comm members? This is why comms survive Seasons, and why long-term commlessness is a death sentence. This lot was probably desperate; there can't have been much traffic along the road in the past few months. What were they thinking?

Their orogene, you realize. That's who they expected to win this fight for them. But he's still not moving, orogenically or physically.

You get up, walking past the lingering knots of fighting. Self-consciously adjusting your mask, you step off the road and slip through the perimeter stakes, moving into the deeper darkness of the stone forest. The firelight of the camp leaves you night-blind, so you stop a moment to allow your eyes to adjust. No telling what kinds of traps the commless have left here; you shouldn't be doing this alone. Again you're surprised, though, because between one blink and the next, you suddenly begin to see in silver. Insects, leaf litter, a spiderweb, even the rocks—all of it now flickers in wild, veined patterns, their cells and particulates etched out by the lattice that connects them.

And people. You stop as you make them out, well camouflaged against the silver bloom of the forest. The rogga is still where he's been, a brighter etching against more delicate lines. But there are also two small shapes crouched in a cavelet, about twenty feet further into the forest. Two other bodies, somehow high overhead atop the jagged, curving rocks of the forest. Lookouts, maybe? None of them move much. Can't tell if they've seen you, or if they're watching the battle somehow. You're frozen, startled by this sudden shift in your perception. Is this some by-product of learning to see silver in yourself and the obelisks? Maybe once you can do that, you see it everywhere. Or maybe you're hallucinating all of it now, like an afterimage against your eyelids. After all, Alabaster never mentioned being able to see like this—but then, when did Alabaster ever try to be a good teacher?

You grope forward for a bit, hand out in front of you in case it is some kind of illusion, but if so, it's at least an accurate one. While it's strange to put your foot down on a lattice of silver, after a while you get used to it.

The orogene's distinctive lattice and that still-held torus aren't far, but he's somewhere higher up than the ground. Maybe ten feet above where you stand. This is explained somewhat when the ground abruptly slopes upward and your hand touches stone. Your regular vision has adapted enough that you can see there's a pillar here, crooked and probably climbable, at least by someone who's got more than one arm. So you stop at the foot of it and say, "Hey."

No response. You become aware of breathing: quick, shallow, pent. Like someone who's trying not to be heard breathing.

"Hey." Squinting in the dark, you finally make out some kind of structure of stacked branches and old boards and debris. A blind, maybe. From up there in the blind, it must be possible to see the road. Sight doesn't matter for the average orogene; untrained ones can't direct their power at all. A Fulcrum-trained orogene, though, needs line of sight to be able to distinguish between freezing useful supplies, or just freezing the people defending same.

Something shifts in the blind above you. Has there been a catch in the breathing? You try to think of something to say, but all that's in your head is a question: What's a Fulcrum-trained orogene doing among the commless? Must have been out on an assignment when the Rifting occurred. Without a Guardian—or he'd be dead—so that means he's fifth ring or higher, or maybe a three- or four-ringer who's lost their higher-ranked partner. You envision yourself, if you'd been on the road to Allia when the Rifting struck. Knowing your Guardian might come for you, but gambling that he might instead write you off for dead... no. That ends the imagining right there. Schaffa would have come for you. Schaffa *did* come for you.

But that was between Seasons. Guardians supposedly do not join comms when Seasons come, which means they die—and, in fact, the only Guardian you've seen since the Rifting was that one with Danel and the Rennanis army. She died in the boilbug storm that you invoked, and you're glad of it, since she was one of the bare-skin killers and there's more than the usual wrong with that kind. Either way, here's another ex-blackjacket out here alone, and maybe afraid, and maybe hair-triggered to kill. You know what that's like, don't you? But this one hasn't attacked yet. You have to find some way to make a connection.

"I remember," you say. It's soft, a murmur. Like you don't want to hear even yourself. "I remember the crucibles. The instructors, killing us to save us. Did they m-make you have children, too?" Corundum. Your thoughts jerk away from memories. "Did they—shit." The hand that Schaffa once broke, your right hand, is somewhere in whatever passes for Hoa's belly. You still feel it, though. Phantom ache across phantom bones. "I know they broke you. Your hand. All of us. They broke us so they could—"

You hear, very clearly, a soft, horrified inhalation from within the blind.

The torus whips into a blurring, blistering spin, and explodes outward. You're so close that it almost catches you. That gasp was enough warning, though, and so you've braced yourself orogenically, even if you couldn't do so physically. Physically you flinch and it's too much for your precarious, one-armed balance. You fall backward, landing hard on your ass—but you've been drilled since childhood in how to retain control on one level even as you lose it in another, so in the same instant you flex your sessapinae and simply slap his fulcrum out of the earth, inverting it. You're much stronger; it's easy. You react magically, too, grabbing those whipping tendrils of silver that the torus has stirred—and belatedly you realize orogeny *affects* magic, but *isn't* magic itself, in fact the magic flinches away from it; *that's* why you can't work high-level orogeny without negatively impacting your ability to deploy magic, how nice to finally understand! Regardless, you tamp the wild threads of magic back down, and quell everything at once, so that nothing worse than a rime of frost dusts your body. It's cold, but only on your skin. You'll live.

Then you let go—and all the orogeny and magic snaps away from you like stretched rubber. Everything in you seems to *twang* in response, in resonance, and—oh—oh no—you feel the amplitude of the resonance rise as your cells begin to align...and compress into stone.

You can't stop it. You can, however, direct it. In the instant that you have, you decide which body part you can afford to lose. Hair! No, too many strands, too much of it distant from the live follicles; you can do it but it'll take too long and half your scalp will be stone by the time you're done. Toes? You need to be able to walk. Fingers? You've only got one hand, need to keep it intact as long as you can.

Breasts. Well, you're not planning on having more children anyway.

It's enough to channel the resonance, the stoning, into just one. Have to take it through the glands under the armpit, but you manage to keep it above the muscle layer; that might keep the damage from impairing your movement and breathing. You pick the left breast, to offset your missing right arm. The right breast is the one you always liked better, anyway. Prettier. And then you lie there when it's done, still alive, hyperaware of the extra weight on your chest, too shocked to mourn. Yet.

Then you're pushing yourself up, awkwardly, grimacing, as the person in the blind utters a nervous little chuckle and says, "Oh, rust. Oh, Earth. Damaya? It really is you. Sorry about the torus, I was just— You don't know what it's been like. I can't believe it. Do you know what they did to Crack?"

Arkete, says your memory. "Maxixe," says your mouth.

It's Maxixe.

* * *

Maxixe is half the man he used to be. Physically, anyway.

He's got no legs below the thighs. One eye, or rather only one that works. The left one is clouded with damage, and it doesn't track quite with the other. The left side of his head—he's got almost nothing left of that lovely blond ashblow that you remember, just a knife-hacked bottlebrush—is a mess of pinkish scars, amid which you think the ear is healed shut. The scars have seamed his forehead and cheek, and pull his mouth a little out of true on that side.

Yet he wriggles down from the blind nimbly, walking on his hands and lifting his torso and stumpy legs with sheer muscle as he does so. He's too good at getting around without legs; must have been doing it for a while now. He makes it over to you before you're able to climb to your feet. "It really is you. I thought, I heard you were only fourth ring, did you really punch through my torus? I'm a sixer. Six! But that's how I knew, see, you still *sess* the same, still quiet on the outside and rusting *furious* on the inside, it really is you."

The other commless are starting to creep down from their spires and such. You tense as they appear—scarecrow figures, thin and ragged and stinking, watching you from stolen or homemade goggles and above wraparound masks that obviously used to be somebody's clothes. They do not attack, however. They gather and watch you with Maxixe.

You stare as he circles you, levering himself along rapidly. He's wearing commless rags, long-sleeved and layered, but you can see how big his shoulder and arm muscles are under the tattered cloth. The rest of him is scrawny. The gauntness of his face is painful to see, but it's clear what his body has prioritized during the long hungry months.

"Arkete," you say, because you remember that he always preferred the name he was born with.

He stops circling and peers at you for a moment, head tilted. Maybe this helps him see better with one functioning eye. The look on his face tells you off, though. He's not Arkete, any more than you are Damaya. Too much has changed. Maxixe it is, then.

"You remembered," he says, though. In that moment of stillness, this eye in his previous storm of words, you glimpse the thoughtful, charming boy you remember. Even though the coincidence of this is almost too much to digest. The only thing stranger would be running into . . . the brother you actually forgot you had, until just now. What was his name? Earthfires, you've forgotten that, too. But you probably wouldn't recognize him, if you saw him. The grits of the Fulcrum were your siblings, in pain if not in blood.

You shake your head to focus, and nod. You're on your feet

now, dusting leaf litter and ash off your butt, though awkwardly around the pulling weight on your chest. "I'm surprised I remembered, too. You must have made an impression."

He smiles. It's lopsided. Only half his face works the way it should. "*I* forgot. Tried hard to, anyway."

You set your jaw, steeling yourself. "I'm—sorry." It's pointless. He probably doesn't even remember what you're sorry about.

He shrugs. "Doesn't matter."

"It does."

"No." He looks away for a moment. "I should have talked to you, after. Shouldn't have hated you the way I did. Shouldn't have let her, them, change me. But I did, and now...none of that matters."

You know exactly which "her" he's referring to. After that whole incident with Crack, bullying that exposed a whole network of grits just trying to survive and a larger network of adults exploiting their desperation...You remember. Maxixe, returning to the grit barracks one day with both his hands broken.

"Better than what they did to Crack," you murmur, before it occurs to you not to say this.

Yet he nods, unsurprised. "Went to a node station once. It wasn't her. Rust knows what I was thinking...But I wanted to search them all. Before the Season." He utters a ragged, bitter chuckle. "I didn't even like her. Just needed to know."

You shake your head. Not that you don't understand the impulse; you'd be lying if you said you hadn't thought it, too, in the years since you learned the truth. Go to all the stations. Figure out some way to restore their damaged sessapinae and set them free. Or kill them as a kindness; ah, you'd have been such a good instructor, if the Fulcrum had ever given you a chance. But of course you did nothing. And of course Maxixe didn't do anything to save the node maintainers, either. Only Alabaster ever managed that.

You take a deep breath. "I'm with them," you say, jerking your head back toward the road. "You heard what the headwoman said. Orogenes welcome."

He sways a little, there on his stumps and arms. It's hard to see his face in the dark. "I can sess her. She's the *headwoman*?"

"Yeah. And everyone in the comm knows it. They're— This comm is—" And you take a deep breath. "*We*. Are a comm that's trying to do something different. Orogenes and stills. Not killing each other."

He laughs, which sets off a few moments of coughing. The other stick figures chuckle, too, but it's Maxixe's cough that worries you. It's dry, hacking, pebbly; not a good sound. He's been breathing too much ash without a mask. It's loud, too. If the Hunters aren't nearby, watching and perhaps ready to shoot him and his people, you'll eat your runny-sack.

At the end of the coughing fit, he tilts his head up at you again, with an amused look in his eye. "I'm doing the same thing," he drawls. With his chin, he points toward his gathered people. "These rusters stick with me because I'm not going to eat them. They don't fuck with me because I'll kill them. There: peaceful coexistence."

You look around at them and frown. Hard to see their expressions. "They didn't attack my people, though." Or they'd be dead.

"Nah. That was Olemshyn." Maxixe shrugs; it makes his

whole body move. "Half-Sanzed bastard. Got kicked out of two comms for 'anger management issues,' he said. He would've gotten us all killed raiding, so I told anybody who wanted to live and could stand me to come follow me, and we did our own thing. This side of the forest is ours, that side was theirs."

Two commless tribes, not one. Maxixe's hardly qualifies, though; only a handful of people besides himself? But he said it: Those who could endure living with a rogga went with him. That just didn't turn out to be a lot of people.

Maxixe turns and climbs halfway up to the blind again, so that he can sit down and also be on an eye level with you. He lets out another rattly cough from the effort of doing this. "I figure he was expecting me to hit you lot," he continues, once the cough subsides. "That's how we usually do it: I ice 'em, his group grabs what it can before I and mine can show up, we both get enough to go on a little longer. But I was all fucked up from what your headwoman said." He looks away, shaking his head. "Olemshyn should've broken off once he saw I wasn't going to ice you, but, well. I did say he was gonna get them killed."

"Yeah."

"Good riddance. What happened to your arm?" He's looking at you now. He can't see your left breast, even though you're slouching a little to the left. It hurts, weighing on your flesh.

You counter, "What happened to your legs?"

He smiles, lopsidedly, and doesn't answer. Neither do you.

"So, not killing each other." Maxixe shakes his head. "And that's actually working out?"

"So far. We're *trying*, anyway."

"Won't work." Maxixe shifts again and darts another look at you. "How much did it cost you, to join them?"

You don't say *nothing*, because that's not what he's asking, anyway. You can see the bargain he's made for survival here: his skills in exchange for the raiders' limited food and dubious shelter. This stone forest, this death trap, is his doing. How many people did he kill for his raiders?

How many have you killed, for Castrima?

Not the same.

How many people were in Rennanis's army? How many of them did you sentence to be steam-cooked alive by insects? How many ash-mounds dot Castrima-over now, each with a hand or booted foot poking out?

Not the rusting same. That was them or you.

Just like Maxixe, trying to survive. Him or them.

You set your jaw to silence this internal argument. There isn't time for this.

"We can't—" you attempt, then shift. "There are other ways besides killing. Other... We don't just have to be... this." Ykka's words, awkward and oily with hypocrisy from your mouth. And are those words even true anymore? Castrima no longer has the geode to force cooperation between orogene and still. Maybe it'll all fall apart tomorrow.

Maybe. But until then, you force yourself to finish. "We don't have to be what they made us, Maxixe."

He shakes his head, staring at the leaf litter. "You remember that name, too."

You lick your lips. "Yeah. I'm Essun."

He frowns a little at this, perhaps because it isn't a stone-themed name. That's why you picked it. He doesn't question it, though. At last he sighs. "Rusting look at me, Essun. *Listen* to the rocks in my chest. Even if your headwoman will take half a rogga, I'm not going to last much longer. Also—" Because he's sitting, he can use his hands; he gestures around at the other scarecrow figures.

"No comm will let us in," says one of the smaller figures. You think that's a woman's voice, but it's so hoarse and weary you can't tell. "Don't even play that game."

You shift, uncomfortable. The woman is right; Ykka might be willing to take in a commless rogga, but not the rest. Then again, you can never figure out quite what Ykka will do. "I can ask."

Chuckles all around, jaded and thin and tired. A few more rattly coughs in addition to Maxixe's. These people are starved nearly to death, and half of them are sick. This is pointless. Still. To Maxixe, you say, "If you don't come with us, you'll die here."

"Olemshyn's people had most of the supplies. We'll go take 'em." That sentence ends on a pause: the opening bid in a bargain. "And it's all of us, or none of us."

"Up to the headwoman," you say, refusing to commit. But you know haggling when you hear it. His Fulcrum-trained orogeny in exchange for comm membership for him and his handful, with the deal sweetened by the raiders' supplies. And he's fully prepared to walk away if Ykka can't meet his opening price. It bothers you. "I'll also put in a good word for your character, or at least your character thirty years ago."

He smiles a little. Hard not to see that smile as patronizing. *Look at you, trying to make this something more than it is.* You're probably projecting. "I also know a little about the area. Might be useful, since you're obviously going somewhere." He jerks his chin toward firelight reflecting off the crags closer to the road. "You *are* going somewhere?"

"Rennanis."

"Assholes."

Which means the Rennanis army must have come through the area on its way south. You let yourself smile. "Dead assholes."

"Huh." He squints his good eye. "They've been smashing comms all over the area. That's why we've had such a hard time; no trade caravans to raid once the Rennies were done. I *did* sess something weird in the direction they went, though."

He falls silent, watching you, because of course he knows. Any rogga with rings should have sessed the activity of the Obelisk Gate when you ended the Rennanis-Castrima war so decisively. They might not have known what they were sessing, and unless they knew magic, they wouldn't have perceived the totality of it even if they'd known, but they would have at least picked up the backwash.

"That... was me," you say. It's surprisingly hard to admit.

"Rusting Earth, Da—Essun. How?"

You take a deep breath. Extend a hand to him. So much of your past keeps coming back to haunt you. You can never forget where you came from, because it won't rusting *let* you. But maybe Ykka's got the right of it. You can reject these dregs of your old self and pretend that nothing and no one else matters... or you can embrace them. Reclaim them for what they're worth, and grow stronger as a whole.

"Let's go talk to Ykka," you say. "If she adopts you—and your people, I know—I'll tell you everything." And if he's not careful, you'll end up teaching him how to do it, too. He's a six-ringer, after all. If you fail, someone else will have to take up the mantle.

To your surprise, he regards your hand with something akin to wariness. "Not sure I want to know *everything*."

It makes you smile. "You really don't."

He smiles lopsidedly. "You don't want to know everything that's happened to me, either."

You incline your head. "Deal, then. Only the good parts."

He grins. One of his teeth is missing. "That's too short to even make a good pop lorist tale. Nobody would buy a story like that."

But. Then he shifts his weight and lifts his right hand. The skin is thick as horn, beyond callused, and filthy. You wipe your hand on your pants without thinking, after. His people chuckle at this.

Then you lead him back toward Castrima, into the light.

* * *

2470: Antarctics. Massive sinkhole began to open beneath city of Bendine (comm died shortly after). Karst soils, not seismic, but the sinking of the city generated waves that Antarctic Fulcrum orogenes detected. From the Fulcrum, somehow shifted whole city to more stable position, saving most of population. Fulcrum records note that doing this killed three senior orogenes.

—*Project notes of Yaetr Innovator Dibars*

6

Nassun makes her fate

THE MONTHLONG JOURNEY TO STEEL'S deadciv ruin is uneventful by the standards of mid-Season travel. Nassun and Schaffa have or forage sufficient food to sustain themselves, though both of them begin to lose weight. Nassun's shoulder heals without trouble, though she is feverish and weak for a couple of days at one point, and on those days Schaffa calls a halt for rest sooner than she thinks he normally would have. On the third day the fever is gone, the wound is beginning to scab, and they resume.

They encounter almost no one else on the road, though that is unsurprising a year and a half into the Season. Anyone still commless at this point has joined a raider band, and there won't be many of those left—just the most vicious, or the ones with some kind of edge beyond savagery and cannibalism. Most of those will have gone north, into the Somidlats where there are more comms to prey upon. Not even raiders like the Antarctics.

In many ways the near-solitude suits Nassun fine. No other Guardians to tiptoe around. No commfolk whose irrational fears must always be planned for. Not even other orogene children; Nassun misses the others, misses their chatter and the comradeship that she enjoyed with them for so brief a time, but at the end of the day, she resented how much time and attention Schaffa had to give them. She's old enough to know that it's childish for her to be jealous of such a thing. (Her parents doted on Uche, too, but it is horrifyingly obvious now that getting more attention isn't necessarily favoritism.) Doesn't mean she isn't glad, and greedy, for the chance to have Schaffa all to herself.

Their time together is companionable, and largely silent, by day. At night they sleep, curled together against the deepening cold, secure because Nassun has reliably demonstrated that the slightest shift in the ambient, or footstep upon the nearby ground, is enough to wake her. Sometimes Schaffa does not sleep; he tries, but instead lies shuddering minutely, catching his breath now and again with half-suppressed muscle twitches, trying not to disturb her in his quiet agonies. When he does sleep, it is fitful and shallow. Sometimes Nassun does not sleep, either, aching in silent sympathy.

So she resolves to do something about it. It's the thing she learned to do back in Found Moon, though to a lesser degree: She sometimes lets the little corestone in his sessapinae have some of her silver. She doesn't know why it works, but she recalls seeing the Guardians in Found Moon all taking bits of silver from their charges and exhaling afterward, as if it eased something in them to give the corestone someone else to chew on.

Schaffa, however, has not taken silver from her or anyone else since the day she offered all of hers to him—the day she realized the true nature of the metal shard in his brain. She thinks maybe she understands why he stopped. Something changed between them that day, and he can no longer bring himself to feed on her like some sort of parasite. But that is why Nassun sneaks him magic now. Because something changed between them, and he's not a parasite if she needs him, too, and if she gives what he will not take.

(One day soon, she will learn the word *symbiosis* and nod, pleased to have a name for it at last. But long before that, she will have already decided that *family* will do.)

When Nassun gives Schaffa her silver, though he is asleep, his body swallows it so quickly that she must snatch her hand away to avoid losing too much. She can spare only dribbles. Any more and she will be the one tired and unable to travel the next day. Even that tiny amount is enough to let him sleep, however—and as the days pass, Nassun finds herself gradually making more silver, somehow. It's a welcome change; now she can ease his pain better without wearying herself. Every time she sees Schaffa settle into a deep, peaceful sleep, she feels proud and good, even though she knows she isn't. Doesn't matter. She is determined to be a better daughter to Schaffa than she was to Jija. Everything will be better, until the end.

Schaffa sometimes tells stories in the evenings, while dinner cooks. In them, the Yumenes of the past is a place both wondrous and strange, as alien as the bottom of the sea. (It is always the Yumenes of the past. Recent Yumenes is lost to him, along with his memories of the Schaffa he used to be.) Even the idea of Yumenes is hard for Nassun to comprehend: millions of people, none of them farmers or miners or anything that fits within the range of her experience, many of them obsessed with strange fads and politics and alignments far more complex than those of caste or race. Leaders, but also the elite Yumenescene Leadership families. Strongbacks of the union and those without, varying by their connections and financial security. Innovators from generations-old families who competed to be sent off to the Seventh University, and Innovators who merely built and repaired trinkets out of the city's shantytowns. It is strange to realize that much of Yumenes's strangeness was simply because it lasted so long. It *had* old families. Books in its libraries that were older than Tirimo. Organizations that remembered, and avenged, slights from three or four Seasons back.

Schaffa also tells her about the Fulcrum, although not much. There is another memory hole here, deep and fathomless as an obelisk—though Nassun finds herself unable to resist probing its edges. It is a space that her mother once inhabited, after all, and in spite of everything, this fascinates her. Schaffa remembers Essun poorly, however, even when Nassun works up the courage to ask direct questions about the matter. He tries to answer Nassun, but his speech is halting when he does, and the look that crosses his face is pained, troubled, paler than usual. She therefore forces herself to ask these questions slowly, hours or days apart, to give him time to recover in between. What she learns is little more than she has already guessed about her mother and the Fulcrum and life before the Season. It helps to hear it, nevertheless.

The miles pass like this, in memory and edged-around pain.

Conditions in the Antarctics grow worse by the day. The ashfall is no longer intermittent, and the landscape has begun to turn into a still life of hills and ridges and dying plants chiseled in gray-white. Nassun starts to miss the sight of the sun. One night they hear the squeals of what must be a large kirkhusa romp out hunting, though fortunately the sound is distant. One day they pass a pond whose surface is mirror-gray from floating ash; the water underneath is disturbingly still, given that the pond is fed by a rapid stream. Although their canteens are low, Nassun looks at Schaffa, and Schaffa nods in silent, wary agreement. There's nothing overtly wrong, but . . . well. Surviving a Season is as much a matter of having the right instincts as having the right tools. They avoid the still water, and live.

On the evening of the twenty-ninth day, they reach a place where the Imperial Road abruptly plateaus and veers southward. Nassun sesses that the road edges along something that feels a bit like a crater rim. They have crested the ridge that surrounds this circular, unusually flat region, and the road follows the ridge in an arc around the zone of old damage, resuming its westward track on the other side. In the middle, though, Nassun at last beholds a wonder.

The Old Man's Pucker is a sommian—a caldera inside a caldera. This one is unusual in being so perfectly formed; from what Nassun has read, usually the outer, older caldera is badly damaged by the eruption that creates the inner, newer caldera. In this case the outer one is an intact, nearly perfect circle, though heavily eroded by time and forested over; Nassun can't really see it under the greenery, though she can sess it clearly. The inner caldera is a little more oblong, and it gleams so brightly from a distance that Nassun can guess what happened without even sessing it. The eruption must have been so hot, at least at one point, that the whole geological formation nearly destroyed itself. What remains has gone to glass, naturally tempered enough that not even centuries of weathering has damaged it much. The volcano that created this sommian is extinct now, its ancient magma chamber long since emptied, not even a whiff of leftover heat lingering. Once upon a time, though, the Pucker was the site of a truly awesome—and horrific—puncturing of the world's crust.

As Steel instructed, they camp for the night a mile or two back from the Pucker. In the small hours before dawn, Nassun wakes, hearing a distant screech, but Schaffa soothes her. "I've heard that now and again," he says softly, over the crackling of the fire. He insisted on a watch this time, so Nassun took the earlier shift. "Something in the Pucker forest. It doesn't seem to be coming this way."

She believes him. But neither of them sleeps well that night.

In the morning, they rise before dawn and start up the road. In the early-morning light, Nassun stares at the deceptively still double crater before them. Up close, it's easier to see that there are breaks in the inner caldera's walls at regular intervals; someone meant for people to be able to get inside. The outer caldera's floor is completely overgrown, however, yellow-green and waving with a forest of treelike grass that has apparently choked out every other form of vegetation in the area. There's no sess of even game trails across it.

The real surprise, though, is underneath the Pucker.

"Steel's deadciv ruin," she says. "It's *underground*."

Schaffa glances at her in surprise, but he does not protest. "In the magma chamber?"

"Maybe?" Nassun can't believe it, either, at first, but the silver does not lie. She notices something else strange as she expands her sesunal awareness of the area. The silver mirrors the perturbations of topography and the forest here—the same way it does everywhere. Yet the silver here is brighter, somehow, and it seems to flow more readily from plant to plant and rock to rock. These blend to become larger, dazzling flows that all run together like streams, until the ruin sits within a pool of glimmering, churning light. She can't make out details, there's so much of it—just empty space, and an impression of buildings. It's huge, this ruin. A city, like no city Nassun has ever sessed.

But she has sessed this torrential churn of silver before. She cannot help turning to glance back toward the sapphire that is faintly visible some miles off. They've outpaced it, but it's still following.

"Yes," Schaffa says. He's been watching her, and missing nothing as she makes the connections. "I don't remember this city, but I know of others like it. The obelisks were made in such places."

She shakes her head, trying to fathom it all. "What happened to this city? There must have been a lot of people here once."

"The Shattering."

She inhales. She's heard of it, of course, and believed in it the way children believe most stories. She remembers seeing an artist's line rendering of the event in one of her creche books: lightning and rocks falling from the sky, fire erupting from the ground, tiny human figures running and doomed. "So that's what it was like? A big volcano?"

"The Shattering was like this *here*." Schaffa gazes out over the waving forest. "Elsewhere, it was different. The Shattering was a hundred different Seasons, Nassun, all over the world, all striking at once. It is a marvel that anything of humanity survived."

The way he's talking... It seems impossible, but Nassun bites her lip. "Were you... do you remember it?"

He glances at Nassun, surprised, and then smiles in a way that is equal parts weary and wry. "I don't. I think... I *suspect* that I was born sometime after, though I have no proof of that. Even if I could remember the Shattering, though, I feel fairly certain that I wouldn't want to." He sighs, then shakes his head. "The sun is up. Let's face the future, at least, and leave the past to itself." Nassun nods, and they step off the trail into the trees.

The trees are strange things, with long, thin leaves like elongated grass blades, and narrow, flexible trunks that grow no more than a couple of feet apart. In some places Schaffa has to stop and push apart two or three trees so that they can wriggle through. This makes for hard going, though, and before long Nassun is out of breath. She stops, dripping sweat, but Schaffa pushes on. "Schaffa," she says, about to ask for a break.

"No," he says, pushing over another tree with a grunt. "Remember the stone eater's warning, little one. We must reach the center of this forest by dusk. It's now clear we will need every moment of that time."

He's right. Nassun swallows, starts taking deeper breaths so she can work better, and then resumes pushing through the forest with him.

She develops a rhythm, working with him. She's good at finding the quickest paths that don't require pushing through, and when she does, he follows her. When these paths end, however, he shoves and kicks and breaks trees until the way is clear, while she follows. She can catch her breath during these brief lulls, but it's never quite enough. A stitch develops in her side. She starts having trouble seeing because the tree leaves keep pulling some of her hair loose from its twin buns, and sweat has made the curls lengthen and dangle into her eyes. She wants desperately to rest for an hour or so. Drink some water. Eat something. The clouds overhead get grayer as the hours pass, however, and it becomes increasingly hard to tell how much daylight is left.

"I can," Nassun tries at one point, while trying to think of how she can use orogeny, or the silver, or *something*, to clear the way.

"No," Schaffa says, somehow intuiting what she would have said. He's produced a black glass poniard from somewhere. It's not a useful knife for this situation, although somehow he has made it so by stabbing each of the grass-tree trunks before kicking them down. That helps them break more easily. "Freezing these plants would only make them more difficult to get through, and a shake could cause the magma chamber below us to collapse."

"The s-silver, then—"

"No." He stops for only a moment and turns to fix a hard gaze on her. He's not breathing harder, she notes with great chagrin, although a faint sheen of sweat does glisten on his forehead. His iron shard punishes him, but still grudgingly grants him greater strength. "Other Guardians may be near, Nassun. It's unlikely at this point, but still a possibility."

All Nassun can do is grope for another question, because this momentary pause is giving her time to catch her breath.

"Other Guardians?" Ah, but then he has said that they all go somewhere during a Season, and that this *station* that Steel told them about is the means by which they do it. "Do you remember something?"

"Nothing more, sadly." He smiles a little, knowingly, as if he can tell what she's doing. "Only that this is how we get there."

"Get where?"

His smile fades, expression settling into that familiar, disturbing blankness for the briefest of instants. "Warrant."

She remembers, belatedly, that his full name is *Schaffa Guardian Warrant*. It has never occurred to her to wonder where the comm of Warrant is. But what does it mean that the way to Warrant is through a buried dead city? "Wh-why—"

He shakes his head then, expression hardening. "Stop stalling. In this low light, not every nocturnal hunter will wait for night." He glances up at the sky with a look that is only mildly annoyed, as if it does not threaten their lives.

It's pointless to complain that she is ready to drop. It's a Season. If she drops, she dies. So she forces herself through the gap he has broken, and starts questing again for the best route.

In the end they make it, which is good because otherwise this would become the rather straightforward tale of you learning that your daughter is dead, and letting the world wither in your grief.

It isn't even a near thing. Abruptly the last patch of thick grass-trees thins out, revealing a smooth-cut pass through the inner caldera ring. The walls of the pass loom high overhead, though they did not look so tall from far away, and the pass itself is wide enough for two horse-drawn carriages to travel side by side without crowding. The walls of these passages are covered in tenacious mosses and some sort of woody vine, the latter of which is fortunately dead because otherwise it might entangle them and slow their progress more. Instead they hurry forward, cracking the dead branches aside, and then abruptly Nassun and Schaffa stumble out of the pass onto a wide, round slab of perfectly white material that is neither metal nor stone. Nassun's seen something like it before, near other deadciv ruins; sometimes the stuff glows faintly at night. This particular slab fills the entirety of the space within the inner caldera.

Steel has told them that the deadciv ruin is here, at the center—but all Nassun sees ahead of them is a dainty, rising curl of metal, seemingly set directly into the white material. She tenses, as wary of something new as any Seasoned survivor. Schaffa, however, walks over to it without hesitation. He stops beside it, and for an instant there is an odd expression on his face that Nassun suspects is caused by the momentary conflict between what his body has done out of habit and what his mind cannot remember—but then he puts a hand on the curlicue at the tip of the metal.

Flat shapes and lines of light suddenly appear out of nothingness on the stone around him. Nassun gasps, but they do nothing other than march and ignite others in turn, spreading and glowing until a roughly rectangular shape has been etched out on the stone at Schaffa's feet. There is a faint, barely audible hum that makes Nassun twitch and look around wildly, but a moment later the white material in front of Schaffa vanishes. It doesn't slide aside, or open like a door; it's just gone. But it *is* a doorway, Nassun abruptly realizes. "And here we are," Schaffa murmurs. He sounds a little surprised himself.

Beyond this doorway is a tunnel that curves gradually down into the ground and out of sight. Narrow rectangular panels of light edge the steps on either side, illuminating the way. The curling bit of metal is a railing, she sees now, her perception reorienting as she moves to stand beside Schaffa. Something to hold on to, as one walks down into the depths.

In a distant part of the grass forest that they just traversed, there is a high-pitched grating noise that Nassun immediately identifies as animal. Chitinous, maybe. A closer, louder version of the screeches they heard the night before. Nassun flinches and looks at Schaffa.

"Some sort of grasshopper, I believe," he says. His jaw is tight as he gazes back at the pass they just traversed, though nothing moves there—yet. "Or cicadas, perhaps. Inside now. I've seen something like this mechanism before; it should close after we pass through."

He gestures for her to go first so that he can guard the rear. Nassun takes a deep breath and reminds herself that this is what is necessary to make a world that will hurt no one else. Then she trots down the stairs.

The light panels ignite five or six steps ahead as she progresses, and fade three steps behind. Once they're a few feet down, just as Schaffa predicted, the white material that covered the stairwell reappears, cutting off further screeches from the forest.

Then there is nothing but the light, and the stairs, and the long-forgotten city somewhere below.

* * *

2699: Two Fulcrum blackjackets summoned to Deejna comm (Uher Quartent, Western Coastals, near Kiash Traps) when Mount Imher showed eruption signs. Blackjackets informed comm officials that eruption was imminent, and that it would likely touch off the whole Kiash cluster, including Madness (local name for the supervolcano that triggered the Madness Season; Imher sits on the same hot spot). Upon determining that Imher was beyond their ability to quell, the blackjackets—one three-ringer, the other supposedly seven although did not wear rings for some reason—made the attempt anyway, due to insufficient time to send for higher-ringed Imperial Orogenes. They successfully stilled the eruption long enough for a nine-ring senior Imperial Orogene to arrive and push it back into dormancy. (Three-ringer and seven-ringer found holding hands, charred, frozen.)

—*Project notes of Yaetr Innovator Dibars*

Syl Anagist: Three

Fascinating. All of this grows easier to remember with the telling... or perhaps I am still human, after all.

* * *

At first our field excursion is simply the act of walking through the city. We have spent the brief years since our initial decanting immersed in sesuna, the sense of energy in all its forms. A walk outside forces us to pay attention to our other, lesser senses, and this is initially overwhelming. We flinch at the springiness of pressed-fiber sidewalks under our shoes, so unlike the hard lacquerwood of our quarters. We sneeze trying to breathe air thick with smells of bruised vegetation and chemical by-product and thousands of exhaled breaths. Their first sneeze frightens Dushwha into tears. We clap hands over our ears to try, and fail, to screen out many voices talking and walls groaning and leaves rustling and machinery whining in the distance. Bimniwha tries to yell over it all, and Kelenli must stop and soothe her before she will try speaking normally again. I duck and yelp in fear of the birds that sit in a nearby bush, and I am the calmest of us.

What settles us, at last, is finally having the chance to gaze upon the full beauty of the amethyst plutonic fragment. It is an awesome thing, pulsing with the slow flux of magic as it towers over the city-node's heart. Every node of Syl Anagist has adapted in unique ways to suit its local climate. We have heard of nodes in the desert where buildings are grown from hardened giant succulents; nodes on the ocean built by coral organisms engineered to grow and die on command. (Life is sacred in Syl Anagist, but sometimes death is necessary.) Our node—the node of the amethyst—was once an old-growth forest, so I cannot help thinking that something of ancient trees' majesty is in the great crystal. Surely this makes it more stately and strong than other fragments of the machine! This feeling is completely irrational, but I look at my fellow tuners' faces as we gaze at the amethyst fragment, and I see the same love there.

(We have been told stories of how the world was different, long ago. Once, cities were not just dead themselves, stone and metal jungles that did not grow or change, but they were actually deadly, poisoning soil and making water undrinkable and even changing the weather by their very existence. Syl Anagist is better, but we feel nothing when we think of the city-node itself. It is nothing to us—buildings full of people we cannot truly understand, going about business that should matter but does not. The fragments, though? We hear their voices. We sing their magic song. The amethyst is part of us, and we it.)

"I'm going to show you three things during this trip," Kelenli says, once we've gazed at the amethyst enough to calm down. "These things have been vetted by the conductors, if that matters to you." She makes a show of eying Remwha as she says this, since he was the one who made the biggest stink about having to go on this trip. Remwha affects a bored sigh. They are both excellent actors, before our watching guards.

Then Kelenli leads us forward again. It's such a contrast, her behavior and ours. She walks easily with head high, ignoring everything that isn't important, radiating confidence and calm. Behind her, we start-and-stop-and-scurry, all timid clumsiness, distracted by everything. People stare, but I don't think it's actually our whiteness that they find so strange. I think we just look like fools.

I have always been proud, and their amusement stings, so I straighten and try to walk as Kelenli does, even though this means ignoring many of the wonders and potential threats around me. Gaewha notices, too, and tries to emulate both of us. Remwha sees what we are doing and looks annoyed, sending a little ripple through the ambient: *We will never be anything but strange to them.*

I answer in an angry basso push-wave throb. *This is not about them.*

He sighs but begins emulating me, too. The others follow suit.

We have traveled to the southernmost quartent of the city-node, where the air is redolent with faint sulfur smells. Kelenli explains that the smell is because of the waste reclamation plants, which grow thicker here where sewers bring the city's gray water near the surface. The plants make the water clean again and spread thick, healthy foliage over the streets to cool them, as they were designed to do—but not even the best genegineers can stop plants that live on waste from smelling a bit like what they eat.

"Do you mean to show us the waste infrastructure?" Remwha asks Kelenli. "I feel more contextual already."

Kelenli snorts. "Not exactly."

She turns a corner, and then there is a dead building before us. We all stop and stare. Ivy wends up this building's walls, which are made of some sort of red clay pressed into bricks, and around some of its pillars, which are marble. Aside from the ivy, though, *nothing* of the building is alive. It's squat and low and shaped like a rectangular box. We can sess no hydrostatic pressure supporting its walls; it must use force and chemical fastenings to stay upright. The windows are just glass and metal, and I can see no nematocysts growing over their surfaces. How do they keep safe anything inside? The doors are dead wood, polished dark red-brown and carved with ivy motifs; pretty, surprisingly. The steps are a dull tawny-white sand suspension. (Centuries before, people called this *concrete*.) The whole thing is stunningly obsolete—yet intact, and functional, and thus fascinating for its uniqueness.

"It's so . . . symmetrical," says Bimniwha, curling her lip a little.

"Yes," says Kelenli. She's stopped before this building to let us take it in. "Once, though, people thought this sort of thing was beautiful. Let's go." She starts forward.

Remwha stares after her. "What, inside? Is that thing structurally sound?"

"Yes. And yes, we're going inside." Kelenli pauses and looks back at him, perhaps surprised to realize that at least some of his reticence wasn't an act. Through the ambient, I feel her touch him, reassure him. Remwha is more of an ass when he is afraid or angry, so her comfort helps; the spiky jitter of his nerves begins to ease. She still has to play the game, however, for our many observers. "Though I suppose you could stay outside, if you wanted."

She glances at her two guards, the brown man and woman who stay near her. They have not kept back from our group, unlike the other guards of whom we catch glimpses now and again, skirting our periphery.

Woman Guard scowls back at her. "You know better."

"It was a thought." Kelenli shrugs then, and gestures with her head toward the building, speaking to Remwha now. "Sounds like you don't actually have a choice. But I promise you, the building won't collapse on your head."

We move to follow. Remwha walks a little slower, but eventually he comes along, too.

A holo-sign writes itself in the air before us as we cross the threshold. We have not been taught to read, and the letters of this sign look strange in any case, but then a booming voice sounds over the building's audio system: "Welcome to the story of enervation!" I have no idea what this means. Inside, the building smells... wrong. Dry and dusty, the air stale as if there's nothing taking in its carbon dioxide. There are other people here, we see, gathered in the building's big open foyer or making their way up its symmetrical twin curving stairs, peering in fascination at the panels of carved wooden decoration which line each stair. They don't look at us, distracted by the greater strangeness of our environs.

But then, Remwha says, "What is that?"

His unease, prickling along our network, makes us all look at him. He stands frowning, tilting his head from one side to the other.

"What is—" I start to ask, but then I hear? sess? it too.

"I'll show you," says Kelenli.

She leads us deeper into the boxy building. We walk past display crystals, each holding preserved within itself a piece of incomprehensible—but obviously old—equipment. I make out a book, a coil of wire, and a bust of a person's head. Placards near each item explain its importance, I think, but I cannot fathom any explanation sufficient to make sense of it all.

Then Kelenli leads us onto a wide balcony with an old-fashioned ornate-wood railing. (This is especially horrifying. We are to rely on a rail made from a dead tree, unconnected to the city alarm grid or anything, for safety. Why not just grow a vine that would catch us if we fell? Ancient times were horrible.) And there we stand above a huge open chamber, gazing down at something that belongs in this dead place as much as we do. Which is to say, not at all.

My first thought is that it is another plutonic engine—a whole one, not just a fragment of a larger piece. Yes, there is the tall, imposing central crystal; there is the socket from which it grows. This engine has even been activated; much of its structure hovers, humming just a little, a few feet above the floor. But this is the only part of the engine that makes sense to me. All around the central crystal float longer, inward-curving structures; the whole of the design is somehow floral, a stylized chrysanthemum. The central crystal glows a pale gold, and the supporting crystals fade from green bases to white at the tips. Lovely, if altogether strange.

Yet when I look at this engine with more than my eyes, and touch it with nerves attuned to the perturbations of the earth, I gasp. Evil Death, the lattice of magics created by the structure is magnificent! Dozens of silvery, threadlike lines supporting one another; energies across spectra and forms all interlinked and state-changing in what seems to be a chaotic, yet utterly controlled, order. The central crystal flickers now and again, phasing through potentialities as I watch. And it's so small! I have never seen an engine so well constructed. Not even the Plutonic Engine is this powerful or precise, for its size. If it had been built as efficiently as this tiny engine, the conductors would never have needed to create us.

And yet this structure makes no sense. There isn't enough magic being fed into the mini-engine to produce all the energy I detect here. And I shake my head, but now I can hear what Remwha heard: a soft, insistent ringing. Multiple tones, blending and haunting and making the little hairs on the back of my neck rise... I look at Remwha, who nods, his expression tight.

This engine's magics have no purpose that I can see, other than to look and sound and be beautiful. And somehow—I shiver, understanding instinctively but resisting because this contradicts everything I have learned from the laws of both physics and arcanity—*somehow* this structure is generating more energy than it consumes.

I frown at Kelenli, who's watching me. "This should not exist," I say. Words only. I don't know how else to articulate what I'm feeling. Shock. Disbelief? Fear, for some reason. The Plutonic Engine is the most advanced creation of geomagestry ever built. That is what the conductors have told us, over and over again for all the years since we were decanted...and yet. This tiny, bizarre engine, sitting half-forgotten in a dusty museum, is *more* advanced. And it seems to have been built for no purpose other than beauty.

Why does this realization frighten me?

"But it does exist," Kelenli says. She leans back against the railing, looking lazily amused—but through the soft shimmering harmony of the structure on display, I sess her ping on the ambient.

Think, she says without words. She watches me in particular. Her thinker.

I glance around at the others. As I do, I notice Kelenli's guards again. They've taken up positions on either end of the balcony, so that they can see the corridor we came down as well as the display room. They both look bored. Kelenli brought us here. Got the conductors to agree to bringing us here. Means for us to see something in this ancient engine that her guards do not. What?

I step forward, putting my hands on the dead railing, and peer intently at the thing as if that will help. What to conclude? It has the same fundamental structure as other plutonic engines. Only its *purpose* is different—no, no. That's too simple an assessment. What's different here is...philosophical. Attitudinal. The Plutonic Engine is a tool. This thing? Is...*art*.

And then I understand. No one of Syl Anagist built this.

I look at Kelenli. I must use words, but the conductors who

hear the guards' report should not be able to guess anything from it. "*Who?*"

She smiles, and my whole body tingles all over with the rush of something I cannot name. I am her thinker, and she is pleased with me, and I have never been happier.

"You," she replies, to my utter confusion. Then she pushes away from the railing. "I have much more to show you. Come."

* * *

All things change during a Season.

—Tablet One, "On Survival," verse two

7

you're planning ahead

Ykka is more inclined to adopt Maxixe and his people than you were expecting. She's not happy that Maxixe has an advanced case of ash lung—as Lerna confirms after they've all had sponge baths and he's given them a preliminary examination. Nor does she like that four of his people have other serious medical issues, ranging from fistulas to the complete lack of teeth, or that Lerna says they're all going to be touch and go on surviving refeeding. But, as she informs those of you on her impromptu council, loudly so that anyone listening will hear, she can put up with a lot from people who bring in extra supplies, knowledge of the area, and precision orogeny that can help safeguard the group against attack. And, she adds, Maxixe doesn't have to live forever. Long enough to help the comm will be enough for her.

She doesn't add, *Not like Alabaster*, which is kind—or at least conspicuously not-cruel—of her. It's surprising that she respects your grief, and maybe it's also a sign that she is beginning to forgive you. It'll be good to have a friend again. Friends. Again.

That's not enough, of course. Nassun is alive and you've more or less recovered from your post-Gate coma, so now it becomes a struggle, daily, to remember why you're staying with Castrima. It helps, sometimes, to go through the reasons for staying. For Nassun's future, that's one, so that you can have somewhere to shelter her once you've found her again. Because you can't do it alone is the second reason—and you can't rightly let Tonkee come with you anymore, however willing she might be. Not with your orogeny compromised; the long journey back south would be a death sentence for both of you. Hoa isn't going to be able to help you get dressed, or cook food, or do any of the other things one needs two good hands for. And Reason Number Three, the most important of the set: You don't know where to go anymore. Hoa has confirmed that Nassun is on the move, and has been traveling away from the site of the sapphire since you opened the Obelisk Gate. It was too late to find her before you ever woke up.

But there is hope. In the small hours of one morning after Hoa has taken the stone burden of your left breast from you, he says quietly, "I think I know where she's going. If I'm right, she'll stop soon." He sounds uncertain. No, not uncertain. Troubled.

You sit on a rocky outcrop some ways from the encampment, recovering from the…excision. It wasn't as uncomfortable as you thought it would be. You pulled off your clothing layers to bare the stoned breast. He put a hand on it and it came away from your body, cleanly, into his palm. You asked why he didn't do that for your arm and he said, "I do what's most comfortable for you." Then he lifted your breast to his lips and you decided to become fascinated by the flat, slightly roughened cautery of stone over the space where your breast was. It aches a little, but you're not sure whether this is the pain of amputation or something more existential.

(Three bites, it takes him, to eat the breast that Nassun liked best. You're perversely proud to feed someone else with it.)

As you awkwardly pull undershirts and shirts back on with one arm—stuffing one side of your bra with the lightest undershirt so it won't slip off—you probe after that hint of unease that you heard in Hoa's voice earlier. "You know something."

Hoa doesn't answer at first. You think you're going to have to remind him that this is a partnership, that you're committed to catching the Moon and ending this endless Season, that you *care* about him but he can't keep hiding things from you like this—and then he finally says, "I believe Nassun seeks to open the Obelisk Gate herself."

Your reaction is visceral and immediate. Pure fear. It probably isn't what you should feel. Logic would dictate disbelief that a ten-year-old girl can manage a feat that you barely accomplished. But somehow, maybe because you remember the feel of your little girl thrumming with angry blue power, and you knew in that instant that she understood the obelisks better than you ever will, you have no trouble believing Hoa's core premise—that your little girl is bigger than you thought.

"It will kill her," you blurt.

"Very likely, yes."

Oh, Earth. "But you can track her again? You lost her after Castrima."

"Yes, now that she is attuned to an obelisk."

Again, though, that odd hesitation is in his voice. Why?

Why would it bother him that— Oh. Oh, rusty burning Earth. Your voice shakes as you understand. "Which means that *any* stone eater can 'perceive' her now. Is that what you're saying?" Castrima all over again. Ruby Hair and Butter Marble and Ugly Dress, may you never see those parasites again. Fortunately, Hoa killed most of them. "Your kind get interested in us then, right? When we start using obelisks, or when we're close to being able to."

"Yes." Inflectionless, that one soft word, but you know him by now.

"Earthfires. One of you *is* after her."

You didn't think stone eaters were capable of sighing, but sure enough the sound emerges from Hoa's chest. "The one you call Gray Man."

Cold runs through you. But yes. You'd guessed already, really. There have been, what, three orogenes in the world lately who mastered connecting to the obelisks? Alabaster and you and now Nassun. Uche, maybe, briefly—and maybe there was even a stone eater lurking about Tirimo back then. Rusting bastard must be terribly disappointed that Uche died by filicide rather than stoning.

Your jaw tightens as your mouth tastes of bile. "He's manipulating her." To activate the Gate and transform herself into stone, so that she can be *eaten*. "That's what he tried to do at Castrima, force Alabaster, or me, or—rust it, or Ykka, any of us, to try to do something beyond our ability so we might turn ourselves into—" You put a hand on the stone marker of your breast.

"There have always been those who use despair and desperation as weapons." This is delivered softly, as if in shame.

Suddenly you're furious with yourself, and your impotence. Knowing that you're the real target of your own anger doesn't stop you from taking it out on him. "Seems to me *all* of you do that!"

Hoa has positioned himself to gaze out at the dull red horizon, a statue paying homage to nostalgia in pensive shadowed lines. He does not turn, but you hear hurt in his voice. "I haven't lied to you."

"No, you've just withheld the truth so much it's the same fucking thing!" You rub your eyes. Had to take the goggles off to put your shirt back on, and now you've got ash in them. "You know what, just—I don't want to hear anything else right now. I need to rest." You get to your feet. "Take me back."

His hand is abruptly extended in your direction. "One more thing, Essun."

"I told you—"

"Please. You need to know this." He waits until you settle into a fuming silence. Then he says, "Jija is dead."

You freeze.

* * *

In this moment I remind myself of why I continue to tell this story through your eyes rather than my own: because, outwardly, you're too good at hiding yourself. Your face has gone blank, your gaze hooded. But I know you. *I know you.* Here is what's inside you.

* * *

You surprise yourself by being surprised. Surprised, that is, and not angry, or thwarted, or sad. Just…surprised. But that is because your first thought, after relief that *Nassun's safe now,* is…

Isn't she?

And then you surprise yourself by being afraid. You aren't sure of what, but it's a stark, sour thing in your mouth. "How?" you ask.

Hoa says, "Nassun."

The fear increases. "She couldn't have lost control of her orogeny, she hasn't done that since she was five—"

"It was not orogeny. And it was intentional."

There, at last: the foreshock of a Rifting-level shake, inside you. It takes you a moment to say aloud, "She *killed* him? On purpose?"

"Yes."

You fall silent then, dazed, troubled. Hoa's hand is still extended toward you. An offer of answers. You aren't sure you want to know, but... but you take his hand anyway. Perhaps it's for comfort. You don't imagine that his hand folds about your own and squeezes, just a little, in a way that makes you feel better. Still he waits. You're very, very glad for his consideration.

"Is he... Where is," you begin, when you feel ready. You're not ready. "Is there a way I can go there?"

"There?"

You're pretty sure he knows where you mean. He's just making sure *you* know what you're asking for.

You swallow hard and try to reason it out. "They were in the Antarctics. Jija didn't keep her on the road forever. She had somewhere safe, time to get stronger." A lot stronger. "I can hold my breath underground, if you... Take me to where she w—" But no. That's not really where you want to go. Stop dancing around it. "Take me to where *Jija* is. To... to where he died."

Hoa doesn't move for perhaps half a minute. You've noticed this about him. He takes varying amounts of time to respond to conversational cues. Sometimes his words nearly overlap yours when he replies, and sometimes you think he hasn't heard you before he finally gets around to replying. You don't think he's thinking during that time, or anything. You think it just doesn't mean anything to him—one second or ten, now or later. He heard you. He'll get around to it eventually.

In token of which, at last, he blurs a bit, though you see the slowness of the end of the gesture as he puts his other hand over yours as well, sandwiching you between his hard palms. The pressure of both hands increases until the grip is quite firm. Not uncomfortable, but still. "Close your eyes."

He's never suggested this before. "Why?"

He takes you down. It's further down than you've ever been before, and it isn't instantaneous this time. You gasp inadvertently—somehow—and thus discover that you don't need to hold your breath after all. As the dark gets darker, it brightens with flashes of red, and then for just a moment you blur through molten reds and oranges and catch the most fleeting glimpse of a wavering open space where something in the distance is bursting apart in a shower of semiliquid glowing chunks—and then there is black around you again, and then you stand on open ground beneath a thinly clouded sky.

"That's why," Hoa says.

"Rusty flaking *fuck*!" You try to yank your hand free and fail. "Shit, Hoa!"

Hoa's hands stop pressing so hard on yours, so that you can slip free. You stagger a few feet away and then clap hands over yourself, checking for injury. You're fine—not burned to death, not crushed by the pressure as you should have been, not suffocated, not even shaken up. Much.

You straighten and rub your face. "Okay. I'm really going to have to remember that stone eaters don't say anything without reason. Never wanted to actually *see* the Fire-Under-Earth."

But you're here now, standing atop a hill that is itself on some kind of plateau. The sky is your place-marker. It's later in the morning here than it was where you were—a little after dawn, instead of predawn. The sun is actually visible, though thin through the scrim of ash clouds overhead. (You surprise yourself by feeling an ache of longing at the sight.) But the fact that you can see it means that you're much farther from the Rifting than you were a few moments ago. You glance to the west, and the faint shimmer of a dark blue obelisk in the distance confirms your guess. This is where, a month or so ago when you opened the Obelisk Gate, you felt Nassun.

(That way. She's gone that way. But that way lies thousands of square miles of the Stillness.)

You turn to find that you're standing amid a small cluster of wooden buildings positioned at the top of the hill, including one storeshack on stilts, a few lean-tos, and what look like dormitories or classroom buildings. All of it is surrounded, however, by a neat, precisely level fence of columnar basalt. That an orogene has made this, harnessing the slow explosion of the great volcano beneath your feet, is as plain to you as the sun in the sky. But equally obvious is the fact that the compound is empty. There's no one in sight, and the reverberations of footprints on the ground are farther away, beyond the fence.

Curious, you walk to a break in the basalt fence, where a pathway that is half dirt and half cobbles wends down. At the foot of the hill is a village, occupying the rest of the plateau. The village could be any comm anywhere. You make out houses in varying shapes, most with still-growing housegreens, several standing storecaches, what looks like a bathhouse, a kiln shed. The people moving among the buildings don't glance up to notice you, and why would they? It's a lovely day, here where the sun still mostly shines. They've got fields to tend and—are those little rowboats tied to one of the watchtowers?—trips to the nearby sea to organize. This compound, whatever it is, is unimportant to them.

You turn away from the village, and that's when you spot the crucible.

It's near the edge of the compound, elevated a little above the rest of it, though visible from where you are. When you climb the path to look into the crucible bowl, which is marked out in cobbles and brick, it's old habit to thrust your senses into the ground to find the nearest marked stone. Not far, only maybe five or six feet down. You search its surface and find the faint pressure indentations of a chisel, maybe a hammer. FOUR. It's too easy; in your day the stones were marked with paint and numbers, which made them less distinctive. Still, the stone is small enough that, yes, anyone below a four-ringer would have trouble finding and identifying it. They've got the details of the training wrong, but the basics are spot-on.

"This can't be the Antarctic Fulcrum," you say, crouching to finger one of the stones of the ring. Just pebbles instead of the beautiful tile mosaic you remember, but again, they've got the idea.

Hoa's still standing where you emerged from the ground, hands still positioned to press down on yours, perhaps for the return trip. He doesn't answer, but then you're mostly talking to yourself.

"I always heard that Antarctic was small," you continue, "but this is nothing. This is a camp." There's no Ring Garden. No Main building. Also, you've heard that the Arctic and Antarctic Fulcrums were lovely, despite their size and remote location. That makes sense; the Fulcrum's beauty was all that official, state-sanctioned orogene-kind ever had to show for itself. This sorry collection of shacks doesn't fit the ideology. Also—"It's on a volcano. And too close to those stills down the hill." That village isn't Yumenes, surrounded on all sides by node maintainers and with the added protection of the most powerful senior orogenes. One overwrought grit's tantrum could turn this whole region into a crater.

"It isn't the Antarctic Fulcrum," Hoa says. His voice is usually soft, but he's turned away now, and that makes him softer. "That's farther to the west, and it has been purged. No orogenes live there anymore."

Of course it's been purged. You set your jaw against sorrow. "So this is somebody's idea of homage. A survivor?" Inadvertently you find another marker underground—a small round pebble, maybe fifty feet down. NINE is written on it, in ink. You have no trouble reading it. Shaking your head, you rise and turn to explore the compound further.

Then you stop, tensing, as a man limps out of one of the dormitory-looking buildings. He stops, too, staring at you in surprise. "Who the rust are you?" he asks, in a noticeable Antarctic drawl.

Your awareness plummets into the earth—and then you wrench it back up. Stupid, because remember? Orogeny will kill you? Also, the man isn't even armed. He's fairly young, probably only in his twenties despite an already-receding hairline. The limp is an easy thing, and one of his shoes is built higher than the other—ah. The village handyman, probably, come to do some basic caretaking on buildings that might again be needed someday.

"Uh, hi," you stammer. Then you fall silent, not sure what to say from there.

"Hi." The man sees Hoa and flinches, then stares with the open shock of someone who's only heard of stone eaters in lorist tales, and maybe didn't quite believe them. Only belatedly does he seem to remember you, frowning a little at the ash on your hair and clothing, but it's clear you're not as impressive a sight. "Tell me that's a statue," he says to you. Then he laughs a little, nervously. "Except it wasn't here when I came up the hill. Uh, hi, I guess?"

Hoa doesn't bother replying, though you see his eyes have shifted to watch the man instead of you. You steel yourself and step forward. "Sorry to alarm you," you say. "You from this comm?"

The man finally focuses on you. "Uh, yeah. And you're not." Instead of showing unease, however, he blinks. "You another Guardian?"

Your skin prickles all over. For an instant you want to shout *no*, and then sense reasserts itself. You smile. They always smile. "Another?"

The young man's looking you up and down now, maybe suspicious. You don't care, as long as he answers your questions and doesn't attack you. "Yeah," he says, after a moment. "We found the two dead ones after the children left on that training trip." His lip curls, just a little. You're not sure whether he doesn't believe the children have gone off training, whether he's really upset about "the two dead ones," or whether that's just the usual lip-curl that people wear when they talk about roggas, since it's obvious that's what the children in question must be. If Guardians were here. "Headwoman did say there might be other Guardians along someday. The three we had all popped up out of nowhere, after all, at different times down the years. You're just a late one, I guess."

"Ah." It is surprisingly easy to pretend to be a Guardian. Just keep smiling, and never offer information. "And when did the others leave on their... training trip?"

"About a month ago." The young man shifts, getting comfortable, and turns to gaze after the sapphire obelisk in the distance. "Schaffa said they were going far enough away that we wouldn't feel any aftershakes of what the kids did. Guess that's pretty far."

Schaffa. The smile freezes on your face. You can't help hissing it. "*Schaffa.*"

The young man frowns at you. Definitely suspicious now. "Yeah. Schaffa."

It can't be. He's dead. "Tall, black hair, icewhite eyes, strange accent?"

The young man relaxes somewhat. "Oh. You know him, then?"

"Yes, very well." So easy to smile. Harder to wrestle down the urge to scream, to grab Hoa, to demand that he plunge you both into the earth now, now, now, so you can go and rescue your daughter. Hardest of all not to fall to the ground and curl into a ball, trying to clench the hand you no longer have but that *hurts*; Evil Earth, it aches like it's broken all over again, phantom pain so real your eyes prickle with pain tears.

Imperial Orogenes do not lose control. You haven't been a blackjacket for going on twenty years, and you lose control all the rusting time—but nevertheless the old discipline helps you pull yourself together. Nassun, your baby, is in the hands of a monster. You need to understand how this happened.

"*Very* well," you repeat. No one will think repetition strange, from a Guardian. "Can you tell me about one of his charges? Midlatter girl, brown and willowy, curly hair, gray eyes—"

"Nassun, right. Jija's girl." The young man relaxes completely now, not noticing that you've tensed that much more. "Evil Earth, I hope Schaffa kills her while they're on that trip."

The threat is not to you, but your awareness dips again anyway, before you drag it back. Ykka's right: You really do need to stop defaulting to *kill everything*. At least your smile hasn't faltered. "Oh?"

"Yeah. I think she's the one who did it…Rust, could've been any of 'em, though. That girl's just the one who gave me the shivers the most." His jaw tightens as he finally notices the sharp edges of your smile. But that, too, isn't something that anyone familiar with Guardians would question. He just looks away.

"'Did it'?" you ask.

"Oh. Guess you wouldn't know. Come on, I'll show you."

He turns and limps toward the northern end of the compound. You follow, after a moment's exchanged glance with

Hoa. There's another slight rise here, culminating in a flat area that's clearly been used before for stargazing or just staring at the horizon; you can see much of the surrounding countryside, which still shows shocking amounts of green beneath a relatively recent and still-thin layer of whitening ash.

But here, though, is something strange: a pile of rubble. You think at first it's a glass recycling pile; Jija used to keep one of those near the house back in Tirimo, and neighbors would dump their broken glasses and such there for him to use in glassknife hilts. Some of this looks like higher-quality stuff than just glass; maybe someone's tossed in some unworked semiprecious stone. All jumbled colors, tan and gray and a bit of blue, but rather a lot of red. But there's a pattern to it, something that makes you pause and tilt your head and try to take in the whole of what you're seeing. When you do, you notice that the colors and arrangement of stones at the nearer edge of the pile vaguely resemble a mosaic. Boots, if someone had sculpted boots out of pebbles and then knocked them over. Then those would be pants, except there's the off-white of bone among them and—

No.

Fire. Under. Earth.

No. Your Nassun didn't do this, she couldn't have, she—

She did.

The young man sighs, reading your face. You've forgotten to smile, but even a Guardian would be sobered by this. "Took us a while to realize what we were seeing, too," he says. "Maybe this is something you understand." He glances at you hopefully.

You just shake your head, and the man sighs.

"Well. It was just before they all left. One morning we hear something like thunder. Go outside and the obelisk—big blue one that had been lurking around for a few weeks, you know how they are—is gone. Then later that day there's the same loud *ch-kow—*" He claps his hands as he imitates the sound. You manage not to jump. "And it's back. And then Schaffa suddenly tells the headwoman he's got to take the kids away. No explanation for the obelisk stuff. No mention that Nida and Umber—those are the other two, the Guardians who used to run this place with Schaffa—are dead. Umber's head is staved in. Nida..." He shakes his head. The look on his face is pure revulsion. "The *back* of her head is... But Schaffa doesn't say anything. Just takes the kids away. Lot of us are starting to hope he never brings them back."

Schaffa. That's the part you should focus on. That's what matters, not what was but what is... but you can't take your eyes off Jija. *Burning rust, Jija. Jija.*

* * *

I wish I were still flesh, for you. I wish that I were still a tuner, so that I could speak to you through temperatures and pressures and reverberations of the earth. Words are too much, too indelicate, for this conversation. You were fond of Jija, after all, to the degree that your secrets allowed. You thought he loved you—and he did, to the degree that your secrets allowed. It's just that love and hate aren't mutually exclusive, as I first learned so very long ago.

I'm sorry.

* * *

You make yourself say, "Schaffa won't be coming back." Because you need to find him and kill him—but even through your fear and horror, reason asserts itself. This strange imitation Fulcrum, which is not the true Fulcrum that he should have brought Nassun to. These children, gathered and not slaughtered. Nassun, openly controlling an obelisk well enough to do *this*... and yet Schaffa has not killed her. Something's going on here that you're not getting.

"Tell me more about this man," you say, lifting your chin toward the pile of jumbled jewels. Your ex-husband.

The young man shrugs in an audible stirring of cloth. "Oh, right, uh. So, his name was Jija Resistant Jekity." Because the young man is sighing down at the pile of rubble, you don't think he sees you twitch at the wrongness of the comm name. "New to the comm, a knapper. We got too many men, but we needed a knapper bad, so when he turned up, we basically would've taken him in as long as he wasn't old or sick or *obviously* crazy. You know?" He shrugs. "The girl seemed all right when they first got here. Wouldn't know her for one of them, she was so proper and polite. Somebody raised her right." You smile again. Perfect tight-jawed Guardian smile. "We only knew what she was because Jija had come here, see. Heard the rumors about how roggas could become... un-roggas, I guess. We get a lot of visitors who ask about that."

You frown and nearly look away from Jija. Un-roggas?

"Not that it ever happened." The young man sighs and adjusts his cane for comfort. "And not that we'd have taken in a kid who used to be one of them, right? What if that kid grew up and had kids who were wrong, too? Got to breed the taint out somehow. Anyway, the girl minded her father well enough until a few weeks ago. Neighbors said they heard him shouting at her one night, and then she moved up here to the compound with the others. You could see how the change sort of...*untied* Jija. He started talking to himself about how she wasn't his daughter anymore. Cursing out loud, now and again. Hitting things—walls and such—when he thought you weren't looking.

"And the girl, she pulled away. Can't say I blame her; everybody was on eggshells around him for that while. Always the quiet ones, right? So I saw her hanging around Schaffa more. Like a duckling, always right there in his shadow. Whenever he'd hold still, she'd take his hand. And he—" The young man eyes you warily. "Don't usually see you lot being affectionate. But he seemed to think the world of her. I hear he nearly killed Jija when the man came at her, actually."

The hand that you don't have twinges again, but it is more tentative this time and not the throb of before. Because... he wouldn't have had to break Nassun's hand, would he? No, no, no. You did that to her yourself. And Uche was another broken hand, inflicted by Jija. Schaffa *protected* her from Jija. Schaffa was affectionate with her, as you struggled to be. And now everything inside you shudders at the thought that follows, and it takes the willpower that has destroyed cities to keep this shudder internal, but...

But...

How much more welcome would a Guardian's conditional, predictable love have been to Nassun, after her parents' unconditional love had betrayed her again and again?

You close your eyes for a moment, because you don't think Guardians cry.

With an effort, you say, "What is this place?"

He looks at you in surprise, then glances at Hoa, a ways

behind you. "This is the comm of Jekity, Guardian. Though Schaffa and the others—" He gestures around you, at the compound. "They called this part of the comm 'Found Moon.'"

Of course they did. And of course Schaffa already knew the secrets of the world that you've paid in flesh and blood to learn.

In your silence, the young man regards you thoughtfully. "I can introduce you to the headwoman. I know she'll be glad to have Guardians around again. Good help against raiders."

You're looking at Jija again. You see one piece of jewel in the perfect likeness of a pinky finger. You know that pinky finger. You kissed that pinky finger—

It's too much, you can't do this, you've got to get a grip, get out of here before you break down any further. "I—I n-need—" Deep breath for calm. "I need some time to consider the situation. Would you go and let your headwoman know I'll come pay my respects shortly?"

The young man side-gazes you for a moment, but you know now that it's not a bad thing if you seem a little off. He's used to Guardian-style offness. Perhaps because of this, he nods and shuffles back awkwardly. "Can I ask you a question?"

No. "Yes?"

He bites his lip. "What's going on? It feels like... Nothing that's happening is normal lately. I mean, it's a Season, but even that feels wrong. Guardians not taking roggas to the Fulcrum. Roggas doing things nobody's ever heard of them doing." He chin-points toward the pile of Jija. "Whatever the rust went on up north. Even those things in the sky, the obelisks... It's all... People are talking. Saying maybe the world's not going to go back to normal. Ever."

You're staring at Jija, but you're thinking of Alabaster. Don't know why.

"One person's normal is another person's Shattering." Your face aches from smiling. There is an art to smiling in a way that others will believe, and you're terrible at it. "Would've been nice if we could've all had normal, of course, but not enough people wanted to share. So now we all burn."

He stares at you for a long, vaguely horrified moment. Then he mumbles something and finally goes away, skirting wide around Hoa. Good riddance.

You crouch beside Jija. He is beautiful like this, all jewels and colors. He is monstrous like this. Beneath the colors you perceive the crazed every-which-wayness of the magic threads in him. It's wholly different from what happened to your arm and your breast. He has been smashed apart and rearranged at random, on an infinitesimal level.

"What have I done?" you ask. "What have I made her?"

Hoa's toes have appeared in your peripheral vision. "Strong," he suggests.

You shake your head. Nassun was that on her own.

"*Alive*."

You close your eyes again. It's the only thing that should matter, that you've brought three babies into the world and this one, this precious last one, is still breathing. And yet.

I made her me. Earth eat us both, I made her into <u>me</u>.

And maybe that's why Nassun is still alive. But it's also, you realize as you stare at what she's done to Jija, and as you realize you can't even get revenge on him for Uche because *your daughter has done that for you*... why you are terrified of her.

And there it is—the thing you haven't faced in all this time, the kirkhusa with ash and blood on its muzzle. Jija owed you a debt of pain for your son, but you owe Nassun, in turn. You *didn't* save her from Jija. You *haven't* been there when she's needed you, here at the literal end of the world. How dare you presume to protect her? Gray Man and Schaffa; she has found her own, better, protectors. She has found the strength to protect herself.

You are so very proud of her. And you don't dare go anywhere near her, ever again.

Hoa's heavy, hard hand presses down on your good shoulder. "It isn't wise for us to stay here."

You shake your head. Let the people of this comm come. Let them realize you aren't a Guardian. Let one of them finally notice how alike you and Nassun look. Let them bring their crossbows and slingshots and—

Hoa's hand curves to grip your shoulder, vise-tight. You know it's coming and still you don't bother to brace yourself as he drags you into the earth, back north. You keep your eyes open on purpose this time, and the sight doesn't bother you. The fires within the earth are nothing to what you're feeling right now, failed mother that you are.

The two of you emerge from the ground in a quiet part of the encampment, though it's near a small stand of trees that a lot of people, by the stink, have apparently been using for a pisser. When Hoa lets you go, you start to walk away and then stop again. Your thoughts have gone blank. "I don't know what to do."

Silence from Hoa. Stone eaters don't bother with unnecessary movement or words, and Hoa has already made his intentions clear. You imagine Nassun talking with Gray Man, and you laugh softly, because he seems more animate and talkative than most of his kind. Good. He's a good stone eater, for her.

"I don't know where to go," you say. You've been sleeping in Lerna's tent lately, but that isn't what you mean. Inside you, there's a clump of emptiness. A raw hole. "I don't have anything left now."

Hoa says, "You have comm and kin. You'll have a home, once you reach Rennanis. You have your life."

Do you really have these things? *The dead have no wishes*, says stonelore. You think of Tirimo, where you didn't want to wait for death to come for you, and so you killed the comm. Death is always with you. Death *is* you.

Hoa says to your slumped back, "I can't die."

You frown, jarred out of melancholy by this apparent non sequitur. Then you understand: He's saying you won't ever lose him. He will not crumble away like Alabaster. You can't ever be surprised by the pain of Hoa's loss the way you were with Corundum or Innon or Alabaster or Uche, or now Jija. You can't hurt Hoa in any way that matters.

"It's safe to love you," you murmur, in startled realization.

"Yes."

Surprisingly, this eases the knot of silence in your chest. Not much, but... but it helps.

"How do you do it?" you ask. It's hard to imagine. Not being able to die even when you want to, even as everything you know and care about falters and fails. Having to go on, no matter what. No matter how tired you are.

"Move forward," Hoa says.

"What?"

"Move. Forward."

And then he is gone, into the earth. Nearby, somewhere, if you need him. Right now, though, he's right: you don't.

Can't think. You're thirsty, and hungry and tired besides. It stinks in this part of camp. The stump of your arm hurts. Your heart hurts more.

You take a step, though, toward the camp. And then another. And another.

Forward.

* * *

2490: Antarctics near eastern coast; unnamed farming comm twenty miles from Jekity City. Initially unknown event caused everyone in the comm to turn to glass. (?? Is this right? Glass, not ice? Find tertiary sources.) Later, headman's second husband found alive in Jekity City; discovered to be rogga. Under intensive questioning by comm militia, he admitted to somehow doing the deed. Claimed that it was the only way to stop the Jekity volcano from erupting, though no eruption signs were observed. Reports indicate the man's hands were also stone. Questioning interrupted by a stone eater, who killed seventeen militia members and took rogga into earth; both vanished.

—*Project notes of Yaetr Innovator Dibars*

8

Nassun underground

THE WHITE STAIR WINDS DOWNWARD for quite some while. The tunnel walls are close and claustrophobic, but the air somehow isn't stale. Just being free of the ashfall is novelty enough, but Nassun notices that there's not much dust, either. That's weird, isn't it? All of this is weird.

"Why isn't there dust?" Nassun asks as they walk. She speaks in hushed tones at first, but gradually she relaxes—a little. It's still a deadciv ruin, after all, and she's heard lots of lorist tales about how dangerous such places can be. "Why do the lights still work? That door we came through back there, why did it still work?"

"I haven't a clue, little one." Schaffa now precedes her down the steps, on the theory that anything dangerous should encounter him first. Nassun can't see his face, and must gauge his mood by his broad shoulders. (It bothers her that she does this, watching him constantly for shifts of mood or warnings of tension. It is another thing she learned from Jija. She cannot seem to shed it with Schaffa, or anyone else.) He's tired, she can see, but otherwise well. Satisfied, perhaps, that they have made it here. Wary, of what they might find—but that makes two of them. "With deadciv ruins, sometimes the answer is simply 'because.'"

"Do you... remember anything, Schaffa?"

A shrug, not as nonchalant as it should be. "Some. Flashes. The why, rather than the what."

"Then, why? Why do Guardians come here, during a Season? Why don't they just stay wherever they are, and help the comms they join the way you helped Jekity?"

The stairs are ever so slightly too wide for Nassun's stride, even when she keeps to the more narrow inner bend. Periodically she has to stop and put both feet on one step in order to rest, then trot to catch up. He is drumbeat-steady, proceeding without her—but abruptly, just as she asks these questions, they reach a landing within the stairwell. To Nassun's great relief, Schaffa stops at last, signaling that they can sit down and rest. She's still soaked with sweat from the frantic scrabble through the grass forest, though it has begun to dry now that she's moving slower. The first drink of water from her canteen is sweet, and the floor feels comfortingly cool, though hard. She's abruptly sleepy. Well, it *is* night outside, up on the surface where grasshoppers or cicadas now cavort.

Schaffa rummages in his pack and hands her a slab of dried meat. She sighs and begins the laborious process of gnawing on it. He smiles at her grumpiness, and perhaps to soothe her, he finally answers her question.

"We leave during Seasons because we have nothing to offer to a comm, little one. I cannot have children, for one thing, which makes me a less than ideal community adoptee. However much I might contribute toward the survival of any comm, its investment in me will return only short-term gains." He shrugs. "And without orogenes to tend, over time, we Guardians become . . . difficult to live with."

Because the things in their heads make them want magic all the time, she realizes. And although orogenes make enough of the silver to spare, stills don't. What happens when a Guardian takes silver from a still? Maybe that's why Guardians leave—so no one will find out.

"How do you know you can't have children?" she presses. This is maybe too personal a question, but he has never minded her asking those. "Did you ever try?"

He's taking a drink from his canteen. When he lowers it, he looks bemused. "It would be clearer to say that I *should* not," he says. "Guardians carry the trait of orogeny."

"Oh." Schaffa's mother or father must have been an orogene! Or maybe his grandparents? Anyway, the orogeny didn't come out in him the way it has in Nassun. His mother—she decides arbitrarily that it was his mother, for no particular reason—never needed to train him, or teach him to lie, or break his hand. "Lucky," she murmurs.

He's in the middle of raising the canteen again when he pauses. Something flows over his face. She's learned to read this look of his in particular, despite the fact that it's such a rare one. Sometimes he's forgotten things he wishes he could remember, but right now, he is remembering what he wishes he could forget.

"Not so lucky." He touches the nape of his neck. The bright, nerve-etched network of searing light within him is still active—hurting him, driving at him, trying to break him. At the center of that web is the shard of corestone that someone put into him. For the first time, Nassun wonders *how* it was put into him. She thinks about the long, ugly scar down the back of his neck, which she thinks he keeps his hair long to cover. She shivers a little with the implications of that scar.

"I don't—" Nassun tries to drag her thoughts away from the image of Schaffa screaming while someone *cuts* him. "I don't understand Guardians. The other kind of Guardian, I mean. I don't... They're awful." And she cannot even begin to imagine Schaffa being like them.

He doesn't reply for a while, as they chew through their meal. Then, softly, he says, "The details are lost to me, and the names, and most of the faces. But the feelings remain, Nassun. I remember that I *loved* the orogenes to whom I was Guardian—or at least, I believed that I loved them. I wanted them to be safe, even if that meant inflicting small cruelties to hold the greater at bay. Anything, I felt, was better than genocide."

Nassun frowns. "What's genocide?"

He smiles again, but it is sad. "If every orogene is hunted down and slain, and if the neck of every orogene infant born thereafter is wrung, and if every one like me who carries the trait is killed or effectively sterilized, and if even the notion that orogenes are human is denied... that would be genocide. Killing a people, down to the very *idea* of them as a people."

"Oh." Nassun feels queasy again, inexplicably. "But that's..."

Schaffa inclines his head, acknowledging her unspoken *But that's what's been happening.* "This is the task of the Guardians, little one. We prevent orogeny from disappearing—because in truth, the people of the world would not survive without it. Orogenes are essential. And yet because you are essential, you cannot be permitted to have a *choice* in the matter. You must be tools—and tools cannot be people. Guardians keep the tool… and to the degree possible, while still retaining the tool's usefulness, kill the person."

Nassun stares back at him, understanding shifting within her like an out-of-nowhere niner. It is the way of the world, but it isn't. The things that happen to orogenes don't just happen. They've been *made* to happen, by the Guardians, after years and years of work on their part. Maybe they whispered ideas into the ears of every warlord or Leader, in the time before Sanze. Maybe they were even there during the Shattering—inserting themselves into ragged, frightened pockets of survivors to tell them who to blame for their misery, and how to find them, and what to do with the culprits found.

Everybody thinks orogenes are so scary and powerful, and they are. Nassun is pretty sure she could wipe out the Antarctics if she really wanted, though she would probably need the sapphire to do it without dying. But despite all her power, she's still just a little girl. She has to eat and sleep like every other little girl, among people if she hopes to *keep* eating and sleeping. People need other people to live. And if she has to fight to live, against every person in every comm? Against every song and every story and history and the Guardians and the militia and Imperial law and stonelore itself? Against a father who could not reconcile *daughter* with *rogga*? Against her own despair when she contemplates the gargantuan task of simply trying to be happy?

What can orogeny do against something like that? Keep her breathing, maybe. But breathing doesn't always mean living, and maybe... maybe genocide doesn't always leave bodies.

And now she is more certain than ever that Steel was right.

She looks up at Schaffa. "Till the world burns." It's what he said to her, when she told him what she meant to do with the Obelisk Gate.

Schaffa blinks, then smiles the tender, awful smile of a man who has always known that love and cruelty are two faces of the same coin. He pulls her close and kisses her forehead, and she hugs him tight, so very glad to have one parent, at last, who loves her as he should.

"Till the world burns, little one," he murmurs against her hair. "Of course."

* * *

In the morning, they resume walking down the winding stair.

The first sign of change is the appearance of another railing on the other side of the stairwell. The railing itself is made of strange stuff, bright gleaming metal not marred at all by verdigris or tarnish. Now, though, there are twin railings, and the stairwell widens enough that two people can walk abreast. Then the winding stairwell begins to unwind—still descending at the same angle, but less and less curved, until finally it extends straight ahead, into darkness.

After an hour or so of walking, the tunnel suddenly opens out, walls and roof vanishing. Now they descend along a trail of lighted, linked stairs that are completely unsupported, somehow, in open air. The stairs should not be possible, held up as they are by nothing but the railing and, apparently, each other—but there is no judder or creak as Nassun and Schaffa walk down. Whatever the stuff that comprises the steps is, it's much stronger than ordinary stone.

And now they're descending into a massive cavern. It's impossible to see how large it is in the darkness, although shafts of illumination slant down from occasional circles of cool white light that dot the cavern's ceiling at irregular intervals. The light illuminates…nothing. The cavern's floor is a vast expanse of empty space filled with irregular, lumpen piles of sand. But now that they are within what Nassun once thought was an empty magma chamber, she can sess things more clearly, and all at once she realizes just how wrong she was.

"This isn't a magma chamber," she tells Schaffa in an awed tone. "It wasn't a cavern at all when this city was built."

"What?"

She shakes her head. "It wasn't *enclosed.* It must have been…I don't know? Whatever's left when a volcano blows up completely."

"A crater?"

She nods quickly, excited with the realization. "It was open to the sky then. People built the city in the crater. But then there was another eruption, right in the middle of the city." She points ahead of them, into the dark; the stairwell is going right toward what she sesses is the epicenter of this ancient destruction.

But that can't be right. Another eruption, depending on the type of lava, should simply have destroyed the city and filled the old crater. Instead, somehow, all the lava went *up and over* the city, spreading out like a canopy and solidifying over it to form this cavern. Leaving the city within the crater more or less intact.

"Impossible," Schaffa says, frowning. "Not even the most viscous lava would behave that way. But..." His expression clouds. Again he is trying to sift through memories truncated and trimmed, or perhaps simply dimmed by age. On impulse Nassun grabs his hand, to encourage him. He glances at her, smiles absently, and resumes frowning. "But I think...an orogene *could* do such a thing. It would take one of rare power, however, and probably the aid of an obelisk. A ten-ringer. At least."

Nassun frowns in confusion at this. The gist of what he's said fits, though: Someone *did* this. Nassun looks up at the ceiling of the cavern and realizes belatedly that what she thought were odd stalactites are actually—she gasps—the leftover impressions of buildings that are no longer there! Yes, there is a narrowing point that must have been a spire; here a curving arch; there a geometric strangeness of spokes and curves that looks oddly organic, like the under-ribs of a mushroom cap. But while these imprints fossil all over the ceiling of the cavern, the solidified lava itself stops a few hundred feet above the ground. Belatedly, Nassun realizes that the "tunnel" from which they emerged is also the remains of a building. Looking back, she sees that the outside of the tunnel looks like one of the cuttlebones that her father once used for fine knapping work—more solid, and made from the same strange white material as the slab up on the surface. That must have been the top of the building. But a few feet below where the canopy ends, the building does, too, to be replaced by this strange white stair. That must have been done sometime after the disaster—but how? And by whom? And why?

Trying to understand what she's seeing, Nassun looks

more closely at the cavern's floor. The sand is mostly pale, though there are mottling patches of darker gray and brown laced throughout. In a few places, twisted lengths of metal or immense broken fragments of something larger—other buildings, maybe—poke through the sand like bones from a half-unearthed grave.

But this is wrong, too, Nassun realizes. There isn't enough material here to be the remnants of a city. She hasn't seen many deadciv ruins, or cities for that matter, but she's read about them and heard stories. She's pretty sure that cities are supposed to be full of stone buildings and wooden storecaches and maybe metal gates and cobbled streets. *This* city is nothing, relatively speaking. Just metal and sand.

Nassun puts down her hands, which she's raised without thinking while her fleshless senses flicker and search. Inadvertently she glances down, which makes the distance between the stair she stands on and that sandy cavern floor yawn and seem to stretch. This makes her step back closer to Schaffa, who puts a reassuring hand on her shoulder.

"This city," Schaffa says. She glances at him in surprise; he looks thoughtful. "There is a word in my mind, but I don't know what it is. A name? Something that holds meaning in another language?" He shakes his head. "But if this is the city I think it is, I have heard tales of its grandeur. Once, they say, this city held billions of people."

That seems impossible. "In one city? How big was Yumenes?"

"A few million." He smiles at her openmouthed gape, then sobers somewhat. "And now there can't be many more people than that, altogether, across the whole of the Stillness. When we lost the Equatorials, we lost the bulk of humanity. Still. Once, the world was even bigger."

It can't be. The volcanic crater is only so vast. And yet... Delicately, Nassun sesses below the sand and debris, searching for evidence of the impossible. The sand is much deeper than she thought. Far beneath its surface, though, she finds pressed pathways in long, straight lines. Roads? Foundations, too, though they are in oblong and round and other odd shapes: hourglass loops and fat S-curves and bowl-shaped dips. Not a single square. She puzzles over the odd composition of these foundations, and then abruptly realizes that it all has the sess of something mineralized, alkaline. Oh, it's petrifying! Which means that originally—Nassun gasps.

"It's wood," she blurts aloud. A building foundation of wood? No, it's something *like* wood, but also a bit like the polymer stuff that her father used to make, and a little like the strange not-stone of the stair they're standing on. All the roads she can sess are something similar. "*Dust.* Everything down there, Schaffa. It's not sand, it's dust! It's *plants*, lots of them, dead so long ago that it's all just dried up and crumbled away. And..." Her gaze is drawn back up to the lava canopy overheard. What must it have been like? The whole cavern lit up in red. The air too hot to breathe. The buildings lasted longer, long enough for the lava to start to cool around them, but every person in this city would have roasted within the first few hours of being buried under a bubble of fire.

That's what's in the sand, too, then: countless people, cooked into char and crumbled away.

"Intriguing," Schaffa says. He leans on the railing, heedless of the distance to the ground as he gazes out over the cavern. Nassun's belly clenches in fear for him. "A city built of plants." Then his gaze sharpens. "But nothing's growing here now."

Yes. That's the other thing Nassun has noticed. She's traveled enough now, and seen enough other caves to know that this place should be teeming with life, like lichens and bats and blind white insects. She shunts her perception into the realm of the silver, searching for the delicate lines that should be everywhere amid so much living detritus. She finds them, lots of them, but...Something is strange. The lines flow together and focus, tiny threads becoming thicker channels—much like the way magic flows within an orogene. She's never seen this happen in plants or animals or soil before. These more concentrated flows come together and continue forward—the direction in which the stairway is going. She follows them well past the stairway she can see, thickening, brightening...and then somewhere ahead, they abruptly stop.

"Something bad is here," Nassun says, her skin prickling. Abruptly she stops sessing. She does not want to sess what's ahead, for some reason.

"Nassun?"

"Something is *eating* this place." She blurts the words, then wonders why she's said them. But now that she's said it, she feels like it was the right thing to say. "That's why nothing grows. Something is taking all the magic away. Without that, everything's dead."

Schaffa regards her for a long moment. One of his hands, Nassun sees, is on the hilt of his black glass poniard, where it's strapped against his thigh. She wants to laugh at this. What's ahead isn't something he can stab. She doesn't laugh because it's cruel, and because she's suddenly so scared that if she starts laughing, she might not stop.

"We don't have to go forward," Schaffa suggests. It is gentle, and badly needed reassurance that he will not lose respect for her if she abandons her mission out of fear.

It bothers Nassun, though. She has her pride. "N-no. Let's keep going." She swallows hard. "Please."

"Very well, then."

They proceed. Someone or something has dug a channel through the dust, beneath and around the impossible stair. As they continue to descend, they pass mountains of the stuff. Presently, though, Nassun sees another tunnel looming ahead. This one is set against the floor of the cavern—at last—and its mouth is immense. Concentric arches, each carved from marble in different shades, loom high overhead as the stairway finally reaches the ground and flattens into the surrounding stones. The tunnel narrows further in; there's only darkness beyond. The floor of the entryway is something that looks like lacquer, tiled in gradient shades of blue and black and dark red. It is rich and lovely color, a relief to the eyes after so much white and gray, and yet it, too, is impossibly strange. Somehow, none of the city's dust has blown or subsided into this entryway.

Dozens of people could pass through that archway. Hundreds in a minute. Now, however, only one stands here, watching them from under a band of rose marble that contrasts sharply against his paler, colorless lines. Steel.

He doesn't move as Nassun walks over to him. (Schaffa comes over, too, but he is slower, tense.) Steel's gray gaze is fixed on an object beside him that is not familiar to Nassun but which would be to her mother: a hexagonal plinth rising from the floor, like a smoky quartz crystal shaft that has been sheared off halfway. Its topmost surface is at a slight angle. Steel's hand is held toward it in a gesture of presentation. *For you.*

So Nassun focuses on the plinth. She reaches toward it and jerks back as something lights up around its rim before her fingers can touch the slanted surface. Bright red marks float in the air above the crystal, etching symbols into empty space. She cannot fathom their meaning, but the color unnerves her. She looks up at Steel, who has not moved and looks as if he's been in the same position since this place was built. "What does it say?"

"That the transport vehicle I told you about is currently nonfunctional," says the voice from within Steel's chest. "You'll need to power and reboot the system before we can use this station."

"'R-re . . . boot?'" She tries to figure out what putting on boots has to do with ancient ruins, then decides to run with the part she understands. "How do I give it power?"

Abruptly, Steel is in a different position, facing the archway that leads deeper into the station. "Go inside and provide power at the root. I'll stay here and key in the start-up sequence once there's enough power."

"What? I don't—"

His gray-on-gray eyes shift over to her. "You'll see what to do inside."

Nassun chews on the inside of her cheek, looking into the archway. It's really dark in there.

Schaffa's hand touches her shoulder. "I'll go with you, of course."

Of course. Nassun swallows and nods, grateful. Then she and Schaffa walk into the dark.

It doesn't stay dark for long. Like on the white stair, small panels of light begin glowing along the sides of the tunnel as they progress. The lights are dim, and yellowy in a way that suggests age, weathering, or... well, or *weariness.* That's the word that pops into Nassun's head for some reason. The light is enough to glimmer off the edges of the tiles beneath their feet. There are doors and alcoves along the tunnel walls, and at one point Nassun spots a strange contraption jutting out about ten feet up. It looks like... a wagon bed? Without wheels or a yoke, and as if that wagon bed was made of the same smooth material as the stair, and as if that wagon bed ran along some kind of track set into the wall. It seems obviously made to transport people; maybe it's how people who couldn't or wouldn't walk got around? Now it is still and dark, locked to the wall forever where its last driver left it.

They notice the peculiar bluish light illuminating the tunnel up ahead, but that still isn't adequate warning enough to prepare them for when the path suddenly curves left, and they find themselves in a new cavern. This much smaller cavern isn't full of dust, or at least not much of it. What it does contain, instead, is a titanic column of solid blue-black volcanic glass.

The column is huge, and irregular, and impossible. Nassun just stares, openmouthed, at this *thing* that fills nearly the whole cavern, ground to ceiling and beyond. That it is the solidified, rapidly cooled product of what must have been a titanic explosion is immediately obvious. That it is somehow the source of the lava canopy which flowed into the adjoining cavern is equally indisputable.

"I see," Schaffa says. Even he sounds overwhelmed, his voice softened by awe. "Look." He points down. This is what finally provides Nassun the focal point to establish perspective, and size, and distance. The thing is huge, because now she can see tiers that descend toward its base, ringing it in concentric octagons. Three of them. On the outermost tier are buildings, she thinks. They're badly damaged, half fallen in, just shells, but she sesses at once why they still exist where the ones in the cavern beyond have crumbled. The heat that must have filled this cavern has metamorphized something in the buildings' construction, hardening and preserving them. Some sort of concussion has done damage, too: All the buildings are torn open on the same side, facing the great glass column. Looking from what she guesses is a three-story building to the glass column, she guesstimates that the column is not as far away as it looks; it's just much bigger than she initially guessed. The size of... oh.

"An obelisk," she whispers. And then she can sess and guess what happened, as clearly as if she were there.

Long ago, an obelisk sat here, at the bottom of this cavern, one of its points jammed into the ground like some kind of bizarre plant. At some point, the obelisk lifted free of the pit, to float and shimmer like its fellows above the strange immensity of the city—and then something went very, very wrong. The obelisk... fell. Where it struck the earth, Nassun imagines she can hear the echo of the concussion; it did not merely fall, it *drove* its way in, punching through and churning down and down and down, powered by all the force of concentrated silver within its core. Nassun can't track its path for more than a mile or so down, but there's no reason to think it didn't just keep going. To where, she cannot guess.

And in its wake, channeled straight up from the most molten part of the earth, came a literal fountain of earthfire to bury this city.

There's still nothing around that looks like a way to supply power to the station. Nassun notices, though, that the cavern's illumination comes from enormous pylons of blue light near the base of the glass column. These make up the lower- and innermost tier of the chamber. *Something* is making that light.

Schaffa, too, has come to the same conclusion. "The tunnel ends here," he says, gesturing toward the blue pylons and the column's base. "There's nowhere else to go but to the foot of this monstrosity. But are you certain you want to follow in the footsteps of whoever did this?"

Nassun bites her bottom lip. She does not. Here is the wrongness that she sessed from the stair, though she cannot tell its source yet. Still… "Steel wants me to see whatever is down there."

"Are you certain you want to do what he wishes, Nassun?"

She isn't. Steel cannot be trusted. But she's already committed herself to the path of destroying the world; whatever Steel wants cannot be worse than this. So when Nassun nods, Schaffa simply inclines his head in acquiescence, and offers her his hand so that they can walk down the road to the pylons together.

Walking past the tiers feels like moving through a graveyard, and Nassun feels compelled to a respectful silence for that reason. Between the buildings, she can make out carbonized walkways, melted-glass troughs that must have once held plants, strange posts and structures whose purpose she isn't sure she'd be able to fathom even if they weren't half-melted. She decides that this post is for tying horses, and that frame is where the tanners racked drying hides. Remapping the familiar onto the strange doesn't work very well, of course, because nothing about this city is normal. If the people who lived here rode mounts, they were not horses. If they made pottery or tools, those were not shaped from clay or obsidian, and the crafters who made such things were not merely knappers. These are people who built, and then lost control of, an obelisk. There is no telling what wonders and horrors filled their streets.

In her anxiety, Nassun reaches up to touch the sapphire, mostly just to reassure herself that she can do so through tons of cooled lava and petrifying decayed city. It is as easy to connect to here as it was up there, which is a relief. It tugs at her gently—or as gently as any obelisk does—and for a moment she lets herself be drawn into its flowing, watery light. It does not frighten her to be so drawn in; to the degree that one can trust an inanimate object, Nassun trusts the sapphire obelisk. It is the thing that told her about Corepoint, after all, and now she senses another message in the shimmering interstices of its tight-packed lines—

"Up ahead," she blurts, startling herself.

Schaffa stops and looks at her. "What?"

Nassun has to shake her head, drawing her mind back into itself and out of all that blue. "The . . . the place to put in power. Is up ahead, like Steel said. Past the track."

"Track?" Schaffa turns, gazing down the sloping walkway. Up ahead is the second tier—a smooth, featureless plane of more of that not-stone white stuff. The people who built the obelisks seem to have used that stuff in all their oldest and most enduring ruins.

"The sapphire…knows this place," she tries to explain. It's a fumbling sort of explanation, as hard as trying to describe orogeny to a still. "Not this place specifically, but somewhere like it…" She reaches for it again, asking for more without words, and is nearly overwhelmed with a blue flicker of images, sensations, *beliefs*. Her perspective changes. She stands at the center of three tiers, no longer in a cavern but facing a blue horizon across which pleasant clouds churn and race and vanish and are reborn. The tiers around her teem with activity—though it all blurs together, and what she can discern of the few instants of stillness makes no sense. Strange vehicles like the car she saw in the tunnel run along the sides of buildings, following tracks of differently colored light. The buildings are *covered* in green, vines and grassy rooftops and flowers curling over lintels and walls. People, hundreds of them, go in and out of these, and walk up and down the paths in unbroken blurs of motion. She cannot see their faces, but she catches glimpses of black hair like Schaffa's, earrings of artfully curled vine motifs, a dress swirling about ankles, fingers flicking while adorned with sheaths of colored lacquer.

And everywhere, *everywhere*, is the silver that lies beneath heat and motion, the stuff of the obelisks. It spiders and flows, converging not just into trickles but rivers, and when she looks down she sees that she stands in a pool of liquid silver, soaking in through her feet—

Nassun staggers a little as she comes back this time, and Schaffa's hand lands firmly on her shoulder to steady her. "Nassun."

"I'm all right," she says. She isn't sure of that, but she says it anyway because she doesn't want him to worry. And because it is easier to say this than *I think I was an obelisk for a minute*.

Schaffa moves around to crouch in front of her, gripping her shoulders. The concern in his expression almost, almost, eclipses the weary lines, the hint of distraction, and the other signs of struggle that are building beneath the surface of him. His pain is worse, here underground. He hasn't said that it is, and Nassun doesn't know why it's getting worse, but she can tell.

But. "Don't trust the obelisks, little one," he says. This does not seem nearly as strange or wrong a thing for him to say as it should. On impulse Nassun hugs Schaffa; he holds her tight, rubbing comfort into her back. "We allowed a few to progress," he murmurs in her ear. Nassun blinks, remembering poor, mad, murderous Nida, who said the same thing once. "Back in the Fulcrum. I was permitted to remember that much because it's important. The few who reached ninth- or tenth-ring status... they were always able to sense the obelisks, and the obelisks could sense them in turn. They would have drawn you to them one way or another. They're missing something, incomplete somehow, and that's what they need an orogene to provide.

"But the obelisks killed them, my Nassun." He presses his face into her hair. She's filthy and hasn't truly washed since Jekity, but his words strip away such mundane thoughts. "The obelisks... I *remember*. They will change you, remake you, if they can. That's what that rusting stone eater wants."

His arms tighten for an instant, with a hint of his old strength, and it is the most beautiful feeling in the world. She knows in this moment that he will never falter, never not be there when she needs him, never devolve into a mere fallible human being. And she loves him more than life for his strength.

"Yes, Schaffa," she promises. "I'll be careful. I won't let them win."

Him, she thinks, and she knows he thinks it too. She won't let *Steel* win. At least not without getting what she wants first.

So they are resolved. When Nassun pulls back, Schaffa nods before getting to his feet. They go forward again.

The innermost tier sits in the glass column's blue, gloomy shadow. The pylons are bigger than they looked from afar—perhaps twice as tall as Schaffa, three or four times as wide, and humming faintly now that Nassun and Schaffa are close enough to hear. They're arranged in a ring around what must have once been the resting place of an obelisk, like a buffer protecting the outer two tiers. Like a fence, separating the bustling life of the city from . . . this.

This: At first Nassun thinks it is a thicket of thorns. The thornvines curl and tangle along the ground and up the inner surface of the pylons, filling all the available space between them and the glass column itself. Then she sees that they aren't thornvines: no leaves. No thorns. Just these curling, gnarling, ropelike twists of something that looks woody but smells a little like fungus.

"How odd," Schaffa says. "Something alive at last?"

"M-maybe they aren't alive?" They do look dead, though they stand out by being still recognizably plants and not crumbled bits of decay on the ground. Nassun does not like it here, amid these ugly vines and in the shadow of the glass column. Is that what the pylons are for, to cut off sight of the vines' grotesquerie from the rest of the city? "And maybe they grew here after… the rest."

Then she blinks, noticing something new about the vine nearest her. It's different from the others around it. Those are obviously dead, withered and blackened and broken off in places. This one, however, looks as though it might be alive. It is ropy and knotted in places, with a wood-like surface that looks old and rough, but whole. Debris litters the floor beneath it—grayish lumps and dust, scraps of dry-rotted cloth, and even a moldering length of frayed rope.

There is a thing Nassun has resisted doing since entering the cavern of the glass column; some things she doesn't quite want to know. Now, however, she closes her eyes and reaches inside the vine with her sense of the silver.

At first it's hard. The cells of the thing—because it *is* alive, more like a fungus than a plant, but there is also something artificial and mechanical about the way it has been made to function—press together so tightly that she doesn't expect to see any silver between them. More dense than the stuff in people's bodies. The arrangement of its substance is almost crystalline, in fact, cells lined up in neat little matrices, which she's never seen in a living thing before.

And now that Nassun has seen down into the interstices of the vine's substance, she can see that it doesn't have any silver in it. What it has instead are… She isn't sure how to describe it. Negative spaces? Where silver should be, but isn't. Spaces that *can be filled* with silver. And as she gingerly explores them, fascinated, she begins to notice the way they pull at her perception, more and more, until—with a gasp, Nassun jerks her perception free.

You'll see what to do, Steel has said. *It should be obvious.*

Schaffa, who has crouched to peer at the bit of rope, pauses and glances at her, frowning. "What is it?"

She stares back at him, but she doesn't have the words to say what needs to be done. The words do not exist. She knows, however, what she needs to do. Nassun takes a step closer to the living vine.

"Nassun," Schaffa says, his voice tight and warning with sudden alarm.

"I have to, Schaffa," she says. She's already lifting her hands. This is where all the silver of the outer cavern has been going, she realizes now; these vines have been eating it up. Why? She knows why, in the deepest and most ancient design of her flesh. "I have to, um, power the system."

Then, before Schaffa can stop her, Nassun wraps both hands around the vine.

It does not hurt. That's the trap of it. The sensation that spreads throughout her body is pleasant, in fact. Relaxing. If she could not perceive the silver, or the way the vine instantly starts dragging every bit of silver out of the spaces between her cells, she would think it was doing something good for her. As it is, it will kill her in moments.

She has access to more silver than just her own, though. Lazily, through the languor, Nassun reaches for the sapphire—and the sapphire responds instantly, easily.

Amplifiers, Alabaster called them, long before Nassun was ever born. *Batteries* is how you think of them, and how you once explained them to Ykka.

What Nassun understands the obelisks to be is simply *engines*. She's seen engines at work—the simple pump-and-turbine things that regulated geo and hydro back in Tirimo, and occasionally more complex things like grain elevators. What she understands about engines would fill less than a thimble, but this much is clear even to a ten-year-old: To work, engines need fuel.

So she flows with the blue, and the sapphire's power flows through her. The vine in her hands seems to gasp at the sudden influx, though this is just her imagination, she's sure. Then it hums in her hands, and she sees how the empty, yawning spaces of its matrices fill and flow with glimmering silver light, and something immediately shunts that light away to somewhere else—

A loud clack echoes through the cavern. This is followed by other, fainter clacks, ramping up to a rhythm, and then a rising, low hum. The cavern brightens suddenly as the blue pylons turn white and blaze brighter, as do the tired yellow lights that they followed down the mosaic tunnel. Nassun flinches even in the depths of the sapphire, and in half a breath Schaffa has grabbed her away from the vine. His hands shake as he holds her close, but he doesn't say anything, his relief palpable as he lets Nassun flop against him. She's suddenly so drained that only his grip holds her up.

And in the meantime, something is coming along the track.

It is a ghostly thing, iridescent beetle green, graceful and sleek and nearly silent as it emerges from somewhere behind the glass column. Nothing of it makes sense to Nassun's eyes. The bulk of it is roughly teardrop-shaped, though its narrower, pointy end is asymmetrical, the tip curving high off the ground in a way that makes her think of a crow's beak. It's huge, easily the size of a house, and yet it floats a few inches above the track, unsupported. The substance of it is impossible to guess, though it seems to have... skin? Yes; up close, Nassun can see that the surface of the thing has the same finely wrinkled texture as thick, well-worked leather. Here and there on that skin she glimpses odd, irregular lumps, each perhaps the size of a fist; they seem to have no visible purpose.

It blurs and flickers, though, the thing. From solidity to translucence and back, just like an obelisk.

"Very good," says Steel, who is suddenly in front of them and to one side of the thing.

Nassun is too drained to flinch, though she's recovering. Schaffa's hands tighten on her shoulders in reflex, then relax. Steel ignores them both. One of the stone eater's hands is upraised toward the strange floating thing, like a proud artist displaying his latest creation. He says, "You gave the system rather more power than absolutely necessary. The overflow has gone into lighting, as you can see, and other systems such as environmental controls. Pointless, but I suppose it does no harm. They'll run down again in a few months, without any source to provide additional power."

Schaffa's voice is very soft and cold. "This could have killed her."

Steel is still smiling. Nassun finally begins to suspect that this is Steel's attempt to mock a Guardian's frequent smiles. "Yes, if she hadn't used the obelisk." There is nothing of apology in his tone. "Death is what usually happens when someone charges the system. Orogenes capable of channeling magic can survive it, however—as can Guardians, who usually can draw upon an outside source."

Magic? Nassun thinks in fleeting confusion.

But Schaffa stiffens. Nassun is confused by his fury at first, and then she realizes: Ordinary Guardians, the uncontaminated kind, draw silver from the earth and put it into the vines. Guardians like Umber and Nida can probably do the same, though they would try only if it served Father Earth's interests. But Schaffa, despite his corestone, cannot rely on the Earth's silver, and cannot draw more of it at will. If Nassun was in danger from the vine, that was because of Schaffa's inadequacy.

Or so Steel means to suggest. Nassun stares at him incredulously, then turns back to Schaffa. She's getting some of her strength back already. "I knew I could do it," she says. Schaffa is still glaring at Steel. Nassun balls up her fists in his shirt and tugs to make him look at her. He blinks and does so, in surprise. "I knew! And I wouldn't have *let* you do the vines, Schaffa. It's because of me that—"

She falters then, her throat closing with impending tears. Some of this is just nerves and exhaustion. Much of it, though, is the sense of guilt that has been lurking and growing within her for months, only now spilling out because she's too tired to keep it in. *It's her fault* that Schaffa has lost everything: Found Moon, the children he cared for, the companionship of his fellow Guardians, the reliable power that should have come from his corestone, even peaceful sleep at night. She's why he's down here in the dust of a dead city, and why they're about to entrust themselves to machinery older than Sanze and maybe the whole *Stillness*, to go to an impossible place and do an impossible thing.

Schaffa sees all this instantly, with the skill of a longtime caretaker of children. The frown clears from his face, and he shakes his head and crouches to face her. "No," he says. "Nothing is your fault, my Nassun. No matter what it has cost me, and no matter what it may cost yet, always remember that I—that I—"

His expression falters. For a fleeting instant, that horrible, blurry confusion is there, threatening to wipe away even this moment in which he means to declare his strength to her. Nassun catches her breath and focuses on him in the silver and bares her teeth as she sees that the corestone in him is alive again, working viciously along his nerves and spidering over his brain, even now trying to force him to heel.

No, she thinks in a sudden fury. She grips his shoulders and shakes him. It takes her whole body to do this because he's such a big man, but it makes him blink and focus through the blur. "You're Schaffa," she says. "You are! And...and you *chose*." Because that's important. That's the thing the world doesn't want people like them to do. "You're not my Guardian anymore, you're—" She dares to say it aloud at last. "You're my new father. Okay? And th-that means we're family, and...and we have to work together. That's what family does, right? You let me protect *you* sometimes."

Schaffa stares at her, then he sighs and leans forward to kiss her forehead. He stays there after the kiss, nose pressed into her hair; Nassun makes a mighty effort and does not burst into tears. When he speaks at last, the horrible blurriness has faded, as have even some of the pain-lines around his eyes. "Very well, Nassun. *Sometimes*, you may protect me."

That settled, she sniffs, wipes her nose on a sleeve, and then turns to face Steel. He hasn't changed position, so she pulls away from Schaffa and goes over to him, stopping right in front of him. His eyes shift to follow her, lazily slow. "Don't do that again."

She half expects him to say, in his too-knowing voice, *Do what?* Instead he says, "It's a mistake to bring him with us."

Cold washes through Nassun, followed by hot. Is it a threat, or a warning? She doesn't like it, either way. Her jaw feels so tight that she almost bites her tongue trying to speak. "I don't care."

Silence in reply. Is this capitulation? Agreement? Refusal to argue? Nassun doesn't know. She wants to yell at him: *Say you won't hurt Schaffa again!* Even though it feels wrong to yell at any adult. Yet she has also spent the past year and a half learning that adults are people, and sometimes they are wrong, and sometimes somebody *should* yell at them.

But Nassun is tired, so instead she retreats to Schaffa, taking his hand tightly and glaring back at Steel, daring him to say anything else. He doesn't, though. Good.

The huge green thing sort of ripples then, and they all turn to face it. Something is—Nassun shudders, both revolted and fascinated. Something is *growing* from the weird nodules all over the thing's surface. Each is several feet long, narrow, featherlike, attenuating near the tips. In a moment there are dozens of them, curling and waving gently in an unfelt breeze.

Cilia, Nassun thinks suddenly, remembering a picture in an old biomestry creche book. Of course. Why wouldn't people who made buildings out of plants also make carriages that look like germs?

Some of the feathers are flickering faster than others, clustering together for a moment at a point along the thing's side. Then the feathers all peel back, flattening against the mother-of-pearl surface, to reveal a soft rectangle of a door. Beyond, Nassun can see gentle light and surprisingly comfortable-looking chairs, in rows. They will ride in style to the other side of the world.

Nassun looks up at Schaffa. He nods back at her with jaw tight. She does not look at Steel, who hasn't moved and makes no attempt to join them.

Then they climb aboard, and the feathers weave the door shut behind them. As they sit down, the great vehicle utters a low, resonant tone, and begins to move.

* * *

Wealth has no value when the ash falls.

—*Tablet Three, "Structures," verse ten*

Syl Anagist: Two

It's a magnificent house, compact but elegantly designed and full of beautiful furnishings. We stare at its arches and bookcases and wooden bannisters. There are only a few plants growing from the cellulose walls, so the air is dry and a little stale. It feels like the museum. We cluster together in the big room at the front of the house, afraid to move, afraid to touch anything.

"Do you live here?" one of the others asks Kelenli.

"Occasionally," she says. Her face is expressionless, but there is something in her voice that troubles me. "Follow me."

She leads us through the house. A den of stunning comfort: every surface soft and sittable, even the floor. What strikes me is that nothing is white. The walls are green and in some places painted a deep, rich burgundy. In the next room, the beds are covered in blue and gold fabric in contrasting textures. Nothing is hard and nothing is bare and I have never *thought* before that the chamber I live in is a prison cell, but now for the first time, I do.

I have thought many new things this day, especially during our journey to this house. We walked the whole way, our feet aching with the unaccustomed use, and the whole way, people stared. Some whispered. One reached out to stroke my hair in passing, then giggled when I belatedly twitched away. At one point a man followed us. He was older, with short gray hair almost the same texture as ours, and he began to say angry things. Some of the words I did not know ("Niesbred" and "forktongue," for example). Some I knew, but did not understand. ("Mistakes" and "We should have wiped you out," which makes no sense because we were very carefully and intentionally made.) He accused us of lying, though none of us spoke to him, and of only pretending to be gone (somewhere). He said that his parents and his parents' parents taught him the true horror, the true enemy, monsters like us were the enemy of all good people, and he was going to make sure we didn't hurt anyone else.

Then he came closer, big fists balled up. As we stumbled along gawping, so confused that we did not even realize we were in danger, some of our unobtrusive guards abruptly became more obtrusive and pulled the man into a building alcove, where they held him while he shouted and struggled to get at us. Kelenli kept walking forward the whole time, her head high, not looking at the man. We followed, knowing nothing else to do, and after a while the man fell behind us, his words lost to the sounds of the city.

Later, Gaewha, shaking a little, asked Kelenli what was wrong with the angry man. Kelenli laughed softly and said, "He's Sylanagistine." Gaewha subsided into confusion. We all sent her quick pulses of reassurance that we are equally mystified; the problem was not her.

This is normal life in Syl Anagist, we understand, as we walk through it. Normal people on the normal streets. Normal touches that make us cringe or stiffen or back up quickly. Normal houses with normal furnishings. Normal gazes that avert or frown or ogle. With every glimpse of normalcy, the city teaches us just how abnormal we are. I have never minded before that we were merely constructs, genegineered by master biomagests and developed in capsids of nutrient slush, decanted fully grown so that we would need no nurturing. I have been... proud, until now, of what I am. I have been content. But now I see the way these normal people look at us, and my heart aches. I don't understand why.

Perhaps all the walking has damaged me.

Now Kelenli leads us through the fancy house. We pass through a doorway, however, and find an enormous sprawling garden behind the house. Down the steps and around the dirt path, there are flower beds everywhere, their fragrance summoning us closer. These aren't like the precisely cultivated, genegineered flower beds of the compound, with their color-coordinated winking flowers; what grows here is wild, and perhaps inferior, their stems haphazardly short or long and their petals frequently less than perfect. And yet... I like them. The carpet of lichens that covers the path invites closer study, so we confer in rapid pulsewaves as we crouch and try to understand why it feels so springy and pleasant beneath our feet. A pair of scissors dangling from a stake invites curiosity. I resist the urge to claim some of the pretty purple flowers for myself, though Gaewha tries the scissors and then clutches some flowers in her hand, tightly, fiercely. We have never been allowed possessions of our own.

I watch Kelenli surreptitiously, compulsively, while she watches us play. The strength of my interest confuses and frightens me a little, though I seem unable to resist it. We've always known that the conductors failed to make us emotionless, but we... well. *I* thought us above such *intensity* of feeling. That's what I get for being arrogant. Now here we are, lost in sensation and reaction. Gaewha huddles in a corner with the scissors, ready to defend her flowers to the death. Dushwha spins in circles, laughing deliriously; I'm not sure exactly at what. Bimniwha has cornered one of our guards and is peppering him with questions about what we saw during the walk here; the guard has a hunted look and seems to be hoping for rescue. Salewha and Remwha are in an intense discussion as they crouch beside a little pond, trying to figure out whether the creatures moving in the water are fish or frogs. Their conversation is entirely auditory, no earthtalk at all.

And I, fool that I am, watch Kelenli. I want to understand what she means us to learn, either from that art-thing at the museum or our afternoon garden idyll. Her face and sessapinae reveal nothing, but that's all right. I also want to simply look at her face and bask in that deep, powerful orogenic presence of hers. It's nonsensical. Probably disturbing to her, though she ignores me if so. I want her to look at me. I want to speak to her. I want to *be* her.

I decide that what I'm feeling is love. Even if it isn't, the idea is novel enough to fascinate me, so I decide to follow where its impulses lead.

After a time, Kelenli rises and walks away from where we wander the garden. At the center of the garden is a small structure, like a tiny house but made of stone bricks rather than the cellulose greenstrate of most buildings. One determined ivy grows over its nearer wall. When she opens the door of this house, I am the only one who notices. By the time she's stepped inside, all the others have stopped whatever they were doing and stood to watch her, too. She pauses, amused—I think—by our sudden silence and anxiety. Then she sighs and jerks her head in a silent *Come on*. We scramble to follow.

Inside—we cram carefully in after Kelenli; it's a tight fit—the little house has a wooden floor and some furnishings. It's nearly as bare as our cells back at the compound, but there are some important differences. Kelenli sits down on one of the chairs and we realize: This is hers. *Hers*. It is her . . . cell? No. There are peculiarities all around the space, things that offer intriguing hints as to Kelenli's personality and past. Books on a shelf in the corner mean that someone has taught her to read. A brush on the edge of the sink suggests that she does her own hair, impatiently to judge by the amount of hair caught in its bristles. Maybe the big house is where she is supposed to be, and maybe she actually sleeps there sometimes. This little garden house, however, is . . . her home.

"I grew up with Conductor Gallat," Kelenli says softly. (We've sat down on the floor and chairs and bed around her, rapt for her wisdom.) "Raised alongside him, the experiment to his control—just as I'm your control. He's ordinary, except for a drop of undesirable ancestry."

I blink my icewhite eyes, and think of Gallat's, and suddenly I understand many new things. She smiles when my mouth drops open in an O. Her smile doesn't last long, however.

"They—Gallat's parents, who I thought were my parents—didn't tell me at first what I was. I went to school, played games, did all the things a normal Sylanagistine girl does while growing up. But they didn't treat me the same. For a long time I thought it was something I'd done." Her gaze drifts away, weighty with old bitterness. "I wondered why I was so horrible that even my parents couldn't seem to love me."

Remwha crouches to rub a hand along the wooden slats of the floor. I don't know why he does anything. Salewha is still outside, since Kelenli's little house is too cramped for her tastes; she has gone to stare at a tiny, fast-moving bird that flits among the flowers. She listens through us, though, through the house's open door. We all need to hear what Kelenli says, with voice and vibration and the steady, heavy weight of her gaze.

"Why did they deceive you?" Gaewha asks.

"The experiment was to see if I could be human." Kelenli smiles to herself. She's sitting forward in her chair, elbows braced on her knees, looking at her hands. "See if, raised among decent, natural folk, I might turn out at least decent, if not natural. And so my every achievement was counted a Sylanagistine success, while my every failure or display of poor behavior was seen as proof of genetic degeneracy."

Gaewha and I look at each other. "Why would you be indecent?" she asks, utterly mystified.

Kelenli blinks out of her reverie and stares at us for a moment, and in that time we feel the gulf between us. She thinks of herself as one of us, which she is. She thinks of herself as a person, too, though. Those two concepts are incompatible.

"Evil Death," she says softly, wonderingly, echoing our thoughts. "You really don't know anything, do you?"

Our guards have taken up positions at the top of the steps leading into the garden, nowhere in earshot. This space is as private as anything we have had today. It is almost surely bugged, but Kelenli does not seem to care, and we don't, either. She draws up her feet and wraps her arms around her knees, curiously vulnerable for someone whose presence within the strata is as deep and dense as a mountain. I reach up to touch her ankle, greatly daring, and she blinks and smiles at me, reaching down to cover my fingers with her hand. I will not understand my feelings for centuries afterward.

The contact seems to strengthen Kelenli. Her smile fades and she says, "Then I'll tell you."

Remwha is still studying her wooden floor. He rubs the grain of it with his fingers and manages to send along its dust molecules: *Should you?* I am chagrined because it's something I should have considered.

She shakes her head, smiling. No, she shouldn't.

But she does anyway, through the earth so we will know it's true.

* * *

Remember what I have told you: The Stillness in these days is three lands, not one. Their names, if this matters, are Maecar, Kakhiarar, and Cilir. Syl Anagist started out as part of Kakhiarar, then all of it, then all of Maecar, too. All became Syl Anagist.

Cilir, to the south, was once a small and nothing land occupied by many small and nothing peoples. One of these groups was the Thniess. It was hard to say their name with the proper pronunciation, so Sylanagistines called them Niess. The two words did not mean the same thing, but the latter is what caught on.

The Sylanagistines took their land. The Niess fought, but then responded like any living thing under threat—with diaspora, sending whatever was left of themselves flying forth to take root and perhaps survive where it could. The descendants of these Niess became part of *every* land, *every* people, blending in among the rest and adapting to local customs. They managed to keep hold of who they were, though, continuing to speak their own language even as they grew fluent in other tongues. They maintained some of their old ways, too—like splitting their tongues with salt acid, for reasons known only to them. And while they lost much of the distinctive look that came of isolation within their small land, many retained enough of it that to this day, icewhite eyes and ashblow hair carry a certain stigma.

Yes, you see now.

But the thing that made the Niess truly different was their magic. Magic is everywhere in the world. Everyone sees it, feels it, flows with it. In Syl Anagist, magic is cultivated in every flower bed and tree line and grapevine-draped wall. Each household or business must produce its share, which is then funneled away in genegineered vines and pumps to become the power source for a global civilization. It is illegal to kill in Syl Anagist because life is a valuable resource.

The Niess did not believe this. Magic could not be owned, they insisted, any more than life could be—and thus they wasted both, by building (among many other things) plutonic engines that did nothing. They were just...pretty. Or thought-provoking, or crafted for the sheer joy of crafting. And yet this "art" ran more efficiently and powerfully than anything the Sylanagistine had ever managed.

How did it begin? You must understand that fear is at the root of such things. Niespeople looked different, behaved differently, *were* different—but every group is different from others. Differences alone are never enough to cause problems. Syl Anagist's assimilation of the world had been over for a century before I was ever made; all cities were Syl Anagist. All languages had become Sylanagistine. But there are none so frightened, or so strange in their fear, as conquerors. They conjure phantoms endlessly, terrified that their victims will someday do back what was done to them—even if, in truth, their victims couldn't care less about such pettiness and have moved on. Conquerors live in dread of the day when they are shown to be, not superior, but simply lucky.

So when Niess magic proved more efficient than Sylanagistine, even though the Niess did not use it as a weapon...

This is what Kelenli told us. Perhaps it began with whispers that white Niess irises gave them poor eyesight and perverse inclinations, and that split Niess tongues could not speak truth. That sort of sneering happens, cultural bullying, but things got worse. It became easy for scholars to build reputations and careers around the notion that Niess sessapinae were fundamentally different, somehow—more sensitive, more active, less controlled, less civilized—and that this was the source of their magical peculiarity. This was what made them not the same kind of human as everyone else. Eventually: not *as* human as everyone else. Finally: not human at all.

Once the Niess were gone, of course, it became clear that the fabled Niess sessapinae did not exist. Sylanagistine scholars and biomagestres had plenty of prisoners to study, but try as they might, no discernible variance from ordinary people could be found. This was intolerable; more than intolerable. After all, if the Niess were just ordinary human beings, then on what basis had military appropriations, pedagogical reinterpretation, and entire disciplines of study been formed? Even the grand dream itself, Geoarcanity, had grown out of the notion that Sylanagistine magestric theory—including its scornful dismissal of Niess efficiency as a fluke of physiology—was superior and infallible.

If the Niess were merely human, the world built on their inhumanity would fall apart.

So... they made us.

We, the carefully engineered and denatured remnants of the Niess, have sessapinae far more complex than those of ordinary people. Kelenli was made first, but she wasn't different enough. Remember, we must be not just tools, but myths. Thus we later creations have been given exaggerated Niess features—broad faces, small mouths, skin nearly devoid of color, hair that laughs at fine combs, and we're all so short. They've stripped our limbic systems of neurochemicals and our lives of experience and language and knowledge. And only now, when we have been made over in the image of their own fear, are they satisfied. They tell themselves that in us, they've captured the quintessence and power of who the Niess really were, and they congratulate themselves on having made their old enemies useful at last.

But we are not the Niess. We aren't even the glorious symbols of intellectual achievement that I believed we were. Syl Anagist is built on delusions, and we are the product of lies. *They have no idea what we really are.*

It's up to us, then, to determine our own fate and future.

* * *

When Kelenli's lesson is done, a few hours have passed. We sit at her feet, stunned, changed and changing by her words.

It's getting late. She gets up. "I'm going to get us some food and blankets," she says. "You'll stay here tonight. We'll visit the third and final component of your tuning mission tomorrow."

We have never slept anywhere but our cells. It's exciting. Gaewha sends little pulses of delight through the ambient, while Remwha is a steady buzz of pleasure. Dushwha and Bimniwha spike now and again with anxiety; will we be all right, doing this thing that human beings have done throughout history—sleeping in a different place? The two of them curl together for security, though this actually increases their anxiety for a time. We are not often allowed to touch. They stroke one another, though, and this gradually calms them both.

Kelenli is amused by their fear. "You'll be all right, though I suppose you'll figure that out for yourselves in the morning," she says. Then she heads for the door to go. I am standing at the door, looking through its window at the newly risen Moon. She touches me because I'm in her way. I don't move at once, though. Because of the direction that the window in my cell faces, I don't get to see the Moon often. I want to savor its beauty while I can.

"Why have you brought us here?" I ask Kelenli, while still staring at it. "Why tell us these things?"

She doesn't answer at once. I think she's looking at the

Moon, too. Then she says, in a thoughtful reverberation of the earth, *I've studied what I could of the Niess and their culture. There isn't much left, and I have to sift the truth from all the lies. But there was a . . . a practice among them. A vocation. People whose job it was to see that the truth got told.*

I frown in confusion. "So . . . what? You've decided to carry on the traditions of a dead people?" Words. I'm stubborn.

She shrugs. "Why not?"

I shake my head. I'm tired, and overwhelmed, and perhaps a little angry. This day has upended my sense of self. I've spent my whole life knowing I was a tool, yes; not a person, but at least a symbol of power and brilliance and pride. Now I know I'm really just a symbol of paranoia and greed and hate. It's a lot to deal with.

"Let the Niess go," I snap. "They're dead. I don't see the sense in trying to remember them."

I want her to get angry, but she merely shrugs. "That's your choice to make—once you know enough to make an informed choice."

"Maybe I didn't want to be informed." I lean against the glass of the door, which is cool and does not sting my fingers.

"You wanted to be strong enough to hold the onyx."

I blurt a soft laugh, too tired to remember I should pretend to feel nothing. Hopefully our observers won't notice. I shift to earthtalk, and speak in an acid, pressurized boil of bitterness and contempt and humiliation and heartbreak. *What does it matter?* is what it means. *Geoarcanity is a lie.*

She shakes apart my self-pity with gentle, inexorable slipstrike laughter. "Ah, my thinker. I didn't expect melodrama from you."

"What is melo—" I shake my head and fall silent, tired of not knowing things. Yes, I'm sulking.

Kelenli sighs and touches my shoulder. I flinch, unused to the warmth of another person's hand, but she keeps it in place and this quiets me.

"Think," she repeats. "Does the Plutonic Engine work? Do your sessapinae? You aren't what they made you to be; does that negate what you *are*?"

"I— That question doesn't make sense." But now I'm just being stubborn. I understand her point. I'm not what they made me; I'm something different. I am powerful in ways they did not expect. They made me but they do not *control* me, not fully. This is why I have emotions though they tried to take them away. This is why we have earthtalk... and perhaps other gifts that our conductors don't know about.

She pats my shoulder, pleased that I seem to be working through what she's told me. A spot on the floor of her house calls to me; I will sleep so well tonight. But I fight my exhaustion, and remain focused on her, because I need her more than sleep, for now.

"You see yourself as one of these... truth-tellers?" I ask.

"Lorist. The last Niess lorist, if I have the right to claim such a thing." Her smile abruptly fades, and for the first time I realize what a wealth of weariness and hard lines and sorrow her smiles cover. "Lorists were warriors, storytellers, nobility. They told their truths in books and song and through their art engines. I just... talk. But I feel like I've earned the right to claim some part of their mantle." *Not all fighters use knives, after all.*

In earthtalk there can be nothing but truth—and sometimes

more truth than one wants to convey. I sense... something, in her sorrow. Grim endurance. A flutter of fear like the lick of salt acid. Determination to protect... something. It's gone, a fading vibration, before I can identify more.

She takes a deep breath and smiles again. So few of them are real, her smiles.

"To master the onyx," she continues, "you need to understand the Niess. What the conductors don't realize is that it responds best to a certain emotional resonance. Everything I'm telling you should help."

Then, finally, she pushes me gently aside so that she can go. The question must be asked now. "So what happened," I say slowly, "to the Niess?"

She stops, and chuckles, and for once it is genuine. "You'll find out tomorrow," she says. "We're going to see them."

I'm confused. "To their graves?"

"Life is sacred in Syl Anagist," she says over her shoulder. She's passed through the door; now she keeps going without stopping or turning back. "Don't you know that?" And then she is gone.

It is an answer that I feel I should understand—but in my own way, I am still innocent. Kelenli is kind. She lets me keep that innocence for the rest of the night.

* * *

To: Alma Innovator Dibars
From: Yaetr Innovator Dibars

Alma, the committee can't pull my funding. Look, this is just the dates of the incidents I've gathered. Just look at the last ten!

2729
2714–2719: Choking
2699
2613
2583
2562
2530
2501
2490
2470
2400
2322–2329: Acid

Is Seventh even interested in the fact that our popular conception of the frequency of Season-level events is completely wrong? These things aren't happening every two hundred or three hundred years. It's more like every thirty or forty! If not for roggas, we'd be a thousand times dead. And with these dates and the others I've compiled, I'm trying to put together a predictive model for the more intensive Seasons. There's a cycle here, a rhythm. Don't we need to know in advance if the next Season is going to be longer or worse somehow? How can we prepare for the future if we won't acknowledge the past?

9

the desert, briefly, and you

DESERTS ARE WORSE THAN MOST places, during Seasons. Tonkee lets Ykka know that water will be easy; Castrima's Innovators have already assembled a number of contraptions they're calling dew-catchers. The sun won't be an issue either, thanks to the ash clouds that you never thought you'd have cause to thank. It will be chilly, in fact, though less so by day. You might even get a bit of snow.

No, the danger of deserts during a Season is simply that nearly all animals and insects there hibernate, deep under the sand where it's still warm. There are those who claim to have figured out a surefire method of digging up sleeping lizards and such, but those are usually scams; the few comms that edge the desert guard such secrets jealously. The surface plants will have already shriveled away or been eaten by creatures preparing for hibernation, leaving nothing aboveground but sand and ash. Stonelore's advice on entering deserts during Seasons is simply: don't. Unless you mean to starve.

The comm spends two days camped at the edge of the Merz,

preparing, though the truth is—as Ykka has confided in you, while you sat with her sharing your last mellow—there's really no amount of preparation that will make the journey any easier. People are going to die. You won't be one of them; it's a curious feeling knowing that Hoa can whisk you away to Corepoint if there's any real danger. It's cheating, maybe. Except it's not. Except you're going to help as much as you can—and because you won't die, you're going to watch a lot of other people suffer. That's the least you can do, now that you've committed to the cause of Castrima. Bear witness, and fight like earthfires to keep death from claiming more than its share.

In the meantime, the folks on cookfire duty pull double shifts roasting insects, drying tubers, baking the last of the grain stores into cakes, salting meat. After they were fed enough to have some strength, Maxixe's surviving people turned out to be especially helpful with foraging, since several are locals and remember where there might be abandoned farms or debris from the Rifting shake that hasn't been too picked over. Speed will be of the essence; survival means winning the race between the Merz's width and Castrima's supplies. Because of this, Tonkee—who is increasingly becoming a spokesperson for the Innovators, much to her own disgruntlement—oversees a quick and dirty breakdown and rebuilding of the storage wagons to a new lighter, more shock-resistant design that should pull more easily over desert sand. The Resistants and Breeders redistribute the remaining supplies to make sure the loss of any one wagon, if it must be abandoned, won't cause some kind of critical shortage.

The night before the desert, you're hunkered down beside one of the cookfires, still-awkwardly navigating how to feed yourself with one arm, when someone sits down beside you. It startles you a little, and you jerk enough to knock your cornbread off the plate. The hand that reaches into your view to retrieve it is broad and bronze and nicked with combat scars, and there's a bit of yellow watered silk—filthy and ragged now, but still recognizable as such—looped around the wrist. Danel.

"Thanks," you say, hoping she won't use the opportunity to strike up a conversation.

"They say you were Fulcrum once," she says, handing the cornbread back to you. No such luck, then.

It really shouldn't surprise you that the people of Castrima have been gossiping. You decide not to care, using the cornbread to sop up another mouthful of stew. It's especially good today, thickened with corn flour and rich with the tender, salty meat that's been plentiful since the stone forest. Everybody needs as much fat on them as they can pack away, to prepare for the desert. You don't think about the meat.

"I was," you say, in what you hope sounds like a tone of warning.

"How many rings?"

You grimace in distaste, consider trying to explain the "unofficial" rings that Alabaster gave you, consider how far you've come beyond even those, consider being humble...and then finally you settle for accuracy. "Ten." Essun Tenring, the Fulcrum would call you now, if the seniors would bother to acknowledge your current name, and if the Fulcrum still existed. For what it's worth.

Danel whistles appreciatively. So strange to encounter someone who knows and cares about such things. "They say," she continues, "that you can do things with the obelisks. That's how you beat us, at Castrima; I had no idea you'd be able to rile up the bugs that way. Or trap so many of the stone eaters."

You pretend not to care and concentrate on the cornbread. It's just a little sweet; the cookfire squad is trying to use up the sugar, to make room for edibles with more nutritional value. It's delicious.

"They say," Danel continues, watching you sidelong, "that a ten-ring rogga broke the world, up in the Equatorials."

Okay, no. "Orogene."

"What?"

"*Orogene.*" It's petty, maybe. Because of Ykka's insistence on making *rogga* a use-caste name, all the stills are tossing the word around like it doesn't mean anything. It's not petty. It means something. "Not 'rogga.' *You* don't get to say 'rogga.' You haven't earned that."

Silence for a few breaths. "All right," Danel says then, with no hint of either apology or humoring you. She just accepts the new rule. She also doesn't insinuate again that you're the person who caused the Rifting. "Point stands, though. You can do things most orogenes can't. Yeah?"

"Yeah." You blow a stray ash flake off the baked potato.

"They say," Danel says, planting her hands on her knees and leaning forward, "that you know how to end this Season. That you're going to be leaving soon to go somewhere and actually try. And that you'll need people to go with you, when you do."

What. You frown at your potato. "Are you volunteering?"

"Maybe."

You stare at her. "You *just* got accepted into the Strongbacks."

Danel regards you for a moment longer, expression unreadably still. You don't realize she's wavering, trying to decide whether to reveal something about herself to you, until she sighs and does it. "I'm Lorist caste, actually. Danel Lorist Rennanis, once. Danel Strongback Castrima's never gonna sound right."

You must look skeptical as you try to visualize her with black lips. She rolls her eyes and looks away. "Rennanis didn't *need* lorists, the headman said. It needed soldiers. And everybody knows lorists are good in a fight, so—"

"What?"

She sighs. "Equatorial lorists, I mean. Those of us who come out of the old Lorist families train in hand-to-hand, the arts of war, and so forth. It makes us more useful during Seasons, and in the task of defending knowledge."

You had no idea. But— "Defending *knowledge?*"

A muscle flexes in Danel's jaw. "Soldiers might get a comm through a Season, but storytellers are what kept Sanze going through seven of them."

"Oh. Right."

She makes a palpable effort to not shake her head at Midlatter provincialism. "Anyway. Better to be a general than cannon fodder, since that was the only choice I was given. But I've tried not to forget who I really am..." Abruptly her expression grows troubled. "You know, I can't remember the exact wording of Tablet Three anymore? Or the Tale of Emperor Mutshatee. Just two years without stories, and I'm losing them. Never thought it would happen so fast."

You're not sure what to say to that. She looks so grim that you almost want to reassure her. *Oh, it'll be all right now that you're no longer occupying your mind with the wholesale slaughter of the Somidlats*, or something like that. You don't think you could pull that off without sounding a little snide, though.

Danel's jaw tightens in a determined sort of way anyway as she looks sharply at you. "I know when I see new stories being written, though."

"I . . . I don't know anything about that."

She shrugs. "The hero of the story never does."

Hero? You laugh a little, and it's got an edge. Can't help thinking of Allia, and Tirimo, and Meov, and Rennanis, and Castrima. Heroes don't summon swarms of nightmare bugs to eat their enemies. Heroes aren't monsters to their daughters.

"I *won't* forget what I am," Danel continues. She's braced one hand on her knee and is leaning forward, insistent. Somewhere in the last few days, she's gotten her hands on a knife, and used it to shave the sides of her scalp. It gives her a naturally lean, hungry look. "If I'm possibly the last Equatorial lorist left, then it's my duty to go with you. To write the tale of what happens—and if I survive, to make sure the world hears it."

This is ridiculous. You stare at her. "You don't even know where we're going."

"Figured we'd settle the issue of *whether* I'm going first, but we can skip to the details if you want."

"I don't trust you," you say, mostly in exasperation.

"I don't trust you, either. But we don't have to like each other to work together." Her own plate is empty; she picks it up and waves to one of the kids on cleanup duty to come take it. "It's not like I have a reason to kill you, anyway. This time."

And it's worse that Danel has said this—that she remembers

siccing a shirtless Guardian on you and is unapologetic about it. Yes, it was war and, yes, you later slaughtered her army, but... "People like you don't need a reason!"

"I don't think you have any real idea who or what 'people like me' are." She's not angry; her statement was matter-of-fact. "But if you need more reasons, here's another: Rennanis is shit. Sure, there's food, water, and shelter; your headwoman's right to lead you there if it's true that the city is empty now. Better than commlessness, or rebuilding somewhere with no storecaches. But shit otherwise. I'd rather stay on the move."

"Bullshit," you say, frowning. "No comm is that bad."

Danel just lets out a single bitter snort. It makes you uneasy.

"Just think about it," she says finally, and gets up to leave.

* * *

"I agree that Danel should come with us," Lerna says, later that night when you tell him about the conversation. "She's a good fighter. Knows the road. And she's right: she has no reason to betray us."

You're half-asleep, because of the sex. It's an anticlimactic thing now that it's finally happened. What you feel for Lerna will never be intense, or guilt-free. You'll always feel too old for him. But, well. He asked you to show him the truncated breast and you did, thinking that would mark the end of his interest in you. The sandy patch is crusty and rough amid the smoother brown of your torso—like a scab, though the wrong color and texture. His hands were gentle as he examined the spot and pronounced it sound enough to need no further bandaging. You told him that it didn't hurt. You didn't say that you were afraid you couldn't feel *anything* anymore. That you were changing, hardening in more ways than one, becoming nothing but the weapon everyone keeps trying to make of you. You didn't say, *Maybe you're better off with unrequited love.*

But even though you didn't say any of these things, after the examination he looked at you and replied, "You're still beautiful." You apparently needed to hear that a lot more than you realized. And now here you are.

So you process his words slowly because he's made you feel relaxed and boneless and human again, and it's a good ten seconds before you blurt, "'Us'?"

He just looks at you.

"Shit," you say, and drape an arm over your eyes.

The next day, Castrima enters the desert.

* * *

There comes a time of greater hardship for you.

All Seasons are hardship, *Death is the fifth, and master of all*, but this time is different. This is personal. This is a thousand people trying to cross a desert that is deadly even when acid rain isn't sheeting from the sky. This is a group force-march along a highroad that is shaky and full of holes big enough to drop a house through. Highroads are built to withstand shakes, but there's a limit, and the Rifting definitely surpassed it. Ykka decided to take the risk because even a damaged highroad is faster to travel than the desert sand, but this takes a toll. Every orogene in the comm has to stay on alert, because anything worse than a microshake while you're up here could spell disaster. One day Penty, too exhausted to pay attention to her own instincts, steps on a patch of cracked asphalt that's completely unstable. One of the other rogga kids snatches her away just as a big piece simply falls through the substructure of the road. Others are less careful, and less lucky.

The acid rain was unexpected. Stonelore does not discuss the ways in which Seasons can impact weather, because such things are unpredictable at the best of times. What happens here is not entirely surprising, however. Northward, at the equator, the Rifting pumps heat and particulates into the air. Moisture-laden tropical winds coming off the sea hit this cloud-seeding, energy-infusing wall, which whips them into storm. You remember being worried about snow. No. It's endless, miserable rain.

(The rain is not so very acid, as these things go. In the Season of Turning Soil—long before Sanze, you would not know of it—there was rain that stripped animals' fur and peeled the skins off oranges. This is nothing compared to that, and diluted as it is by water. Like vinegar. You'll live.)

Ykka sets a brutal pace while you're on the highroad. On the first day everyone makes camp well after nightfall, and Lerna does not come to the tent after you wearily put it up. He's busy tending half a dozen people who are going lame from slips or twisted ankles, and two elders who are having breathing problems, and the pregnant woman. The latter three are doing all right, he tells you when he finally crawls into your bedroll, near dawn; Ontrag the potter lives on spite, and the pregnant woman has both her household and half the Breeders taking care of her. What's troubling are the injuries. "I have to tell Ykka," he says as you push a slab of rain-soaked cachebread and sour sausage into his mouth, then cover him up and make him lie still. He chews and swallows almost without noticing. "We can't keep going at this pace. We'll start losing people if we don't—"

"She knows," you tell him. You've spoken as gently as you can, but it still silences him. He stares until you lie back down beside him—awkwardly, with only one arm, but successfully. Eventually exhaustion overwhelms anguish, and he sleeps.

You walk with Ykka one day. She's setting the pace like a good comm leader should, pushing no one harder than herself. At the lone midday rest stop, she takes off one boot and you see that her feet are streaked with blood from blisters. You look at her, frowning, and it's eloquent enough that she sighs. "Never got around to requisitioning better boots," she says. "These are too loose. Always figured I'd have more time."

"If your feet rot off," you begin, but she rolls her eyes and points toward the supply pile in the middle of the camp.

You glance at it in confusion, start to resume your scolding, and then pause. Think. Look at the supply pile again. If every wagon carries a crate of the salted cachebread and another of sausage, and if those casks are pickled vegetables, and those are the grains and beans…

The pile is so small. So little, for a thousand people who have weeks yet to go through the Merz.

You shut up about the boots. Though she gets some extra socks from someone; that helps.

It shocks you that you're doing as well as you are. You're not *healthy*, not exactly. Your menstrual cycle has stopped, and it's probably not menopause yet. When you undress to basin-wash, which is sort of pointless in the constant rain but habit is habit, you notice that your ribs show starkly beneath loose skin. That's only partly because of all the walking, though; some of it is because you keep forgetting to eat. You feel tired at the end of the day, but it's a distant, detached sort of thing. When you touch Lerna—not for sex, you don't have the energy, but cuddling for warmth saves calories, and he needs the comfort—it feels good, but in an equally detached way. You feel as though you're floating above yourself, watching him sigh, listening to someone else yawn. Like it's happening to someone else.

This is what happened to Alabaster, you remember. A detachment from the flesh, as it became no longer flesh. You resolve to do a better job of eating at every opportunity.

Three weeks into the desert, as expected, the highroad veers off to the west. From there on, Castrima must descend to the ground and contend with desert terrain up close and personal. It's easier, in some ways, because at least the ground isn't likely to crumble away beneath your feet. On the other hand, sand is harder to walk on than asphalt. Everyone slows down. Maxixe earns his keep by drawing enough of the moisture out of the topmost layer of sand and ash and icing it a few inches down, to firm it up beneath everyone's feet. It exhausts him to do this on a constant basis, though, so he saves it for the worst patches. He tries to teach Temell how to do the same trick, but Temell's an ordinary feral; he can't manage the necessary precision. (You could have done it once. You don't let yourself think about this.)

Scouts sent forth to try to find a better path all come back and report the same thing: rusting sand-ash-mud everywhere. There is no better path.

Three people got left behind on the highroad, unable to walk any further because of sprains or breaks. You don't know them. In theory, they'll catch up once they've recovered, but you can't see how they'll recover with no food or shelter. Here on the ground it's worse: a half-dozen broken ankles, one broken leg, one wrenched back among the Strongbacks pulling the wagons, all in the first day. After a while, Lerna stops going to them unless they ask for his help. Most don't ask. There's nothing he can do, and everyone knows it.

On a chilly day, Ontrag the potter just sits down and says she doesn't feel like going any further. Ykka actually argues with her, which you weren't expecting. Ontrag has passed on her skill of pottery to two younger comm members. She's redundant, long past childbearing; it should be an easy headwoman's choice, by the rules of Old Sanze and the tenets of stonelore. But in the end, Ontrag herself has to tell Ykka to shut up and walk away.

It's a warning sign. "I can't do this anymore," you hear Ykka say later, when Ontrag has fallen out of sight behind you. She plods forward, her pace steady and ground-eating as usual, but her head is down, hanks of wet ashblow hair obscuring her face. "I can't. It isn't right. It shouldn't be like this. It shouldn't just be—there's more to being Castrima than being rusting *useful*, for Earth's sake, she used to *teach* me in creche, she knows *stories*, I rusting *can't*."

Hjarka Leadership Castrima, who was taught from an early age to kill the few so the many might live, only touches her shoulder and says, "You'll do what you have to do."

Ykka doesn't say anything for the next few miles, but maybe that's just because there's nothing to say.

The vegetables run out first. Then the meat. The cachebread Ykka tries to ration for as long as she can, but the plain fact is that people can't travel at this speed on nothing. She has to give everyone at least a wafer a day. That's not enough, but it's better than nothing—until there is nothing. And you keep walking anyway.

In the absence of all else, people run on hope. On the other side of the desert, Danel tells everyone around a campfire one night, there's another Imperial Road you can pick up. Easy traveling all the way to Rennanis. It's a river delta region, too, with good soil, once the breadbasket of the Equatorials. Lots of now-abandoned farms outside of any comm. Danel's army had good foraging there on its way south. If you can get through the desert, there will be food.

If you can get through the desert.

You know the end to this. Don't you? How could you be here listening to this tale if you didn't? But sometimes it is the *how* of a thing, not just the endgame, that matters most.

So this is the endgame: Of the nearly eleven hundred souls who went into the desert, a little over eight hundred and fifty reach the Imperial Road.

For a few days after that, the comm effectively dissolves. Desperate people, no longer willing to wait for orderly foraging by the Hunters, stagger off to dig through sour soil for half-rotted tubers and bitter grubs and barely chewable woody roots. The land around here is scraggly, treeless, half-desert and half-fertile, long depopulated by the Rennies. Before she loses too many people, Ykka orders camp made on an old farm with several barns that have managed to survive the Season thus far. The walls, apart from basic framing, haven't fared as well, but then they haven't collapsed, either. It's the roofs she wanted, since the rain still falls here on the desert's edge, though it's lighter and intermittent. Nice to sleep dry, at last.

Three days, Ykka gives it. During that time, people creep back in ones and twos, some bringing food to share with others too weak to forage. The Hunters who bother to return bring fish from one of the river branches that's relatively nearby. One of them finds the thing that saves you, the thing that feels like life after all the death behind you: a farmer's private housecache of cornmeal, sealed in clay urns and kept hidden under the floorboards of the ruined house. You have nothing to mix it with, no milk or eggs or dried meat, just the acid water, but food is that which nourishes, stonelore says. The comm feasts on fried corn mush that night. One urn has cracked and teems with mealybugs, but no one cares. Extra protein.

A lot of people don't come back. It's a Season. All things change.

At the end of three days, Ykka declares that anyone still in the camp is Castrima; anyone who hasn't returned is now ashed out and commless. Easier than speculating on how they might have died, or who might have killed them. What's left of the group strikes camp. You head north.

* * *

Was this too fast? Perhaps tragedies should not be summarized so bluntly. I meant to be merciful, not cruel. That you had to live it is the cruelty... but distance, detachment, heals. Sometimes.

I could have taken you from the desert. You did not have to suffer as they did. And yet... they have become part of you, the people of this comm. Your friends. Your fellows. You needed to see them through. Suffering is your healing, at least for now.

Lest you think me inhuman, a stone, I did what I could to help. Some of the beasts that hibernate beneath the sand of the desert are capable of preying on humans; did you know that? A few woke as you passed, but I kept them away. One of the wagons' wooden axles partially dissolved in the rain and began to sag, though none of you noticed. I transmuted the wood—petrified it, if you prefer to think that way—so that it would last. I am the one who moved the moth-eaten rug in that abandoned farmhouse, so that your Hunter found the cornmeal. Ontrag, who had not told Ykka about the growing pain in her side and chest, or her shortness of breath, did not live long after the comm left her behind. I went back to her on the night that she died, and tuned away what little pain she felt. (You've heard the song. Antimony sang it for Alabaster once. I'll sing it for you, if . . .) She was not alone, at the end.

Does any of this comfort you? I hope so. I'm still human, I told you. Your opinion matters to me.

Castrima survives; that is also what matters. You survive. For now, at least.

And at last, some while later, you reach the southernmost edge of Rennanis's territory.

* * *

Honor in safety, survival under threat. Necessity is the only law.

—*Tablet Three, "Structures," verse four*

10

Nassun, through the fire

All of this happens in the earth. It is mine to know, and to share with you. It is hers to suffer. I'm sorry.

Inside the pearlescent vehicle, the walls are inlaid with elegant vining designs wrought of what looks like gold. Nassun isn't sure if the metal is purely decorative or has some sort of purpose. The hard, smooth seats, which are pastel colors and shaped something like the shells of mussels that she ate sometimes at Found Moon, have amazingly soft cushions. They are locked to the floor, Nassun finds, and yet it is possible to turn them from side to side or lean back. She cannot fathom what the chairs are made of.

To her greater shock, a voice speaks in the air a moment after they settle in. The voice is female, polite, detached, and somehow reassuring. The language is... incomprehensible, and not remotely familiar. However, the pronunciation of the syllables is no different from that of Sanze-mat, and something about the rhythm of the sentences, their order, fits the expectations of Nassun's ear. She suspects that part of the first sentence is a greeting. She thinks a word that keeps being repeated, amid a passage that has the air of a command, might be a softening word, like *please*. The rest, however, is wholly foreign.

The voice speaks only briefly, and then falls silent. Nassun glances at Schaffa and is surprised to see him frowning, eyes narrowed in concentration—though some of that is also tension in his jaw, and a hint of extra pallor around his lips. The silver is hurting him more, and it must be bad this time. Still, he looks up at her in something like wonder. "I *remember* this language," he says.

"Those weird words? What did she say?"

"That this…" He grimaces. "Thing. It's called a vehimal. The announcement says it will depart from this city and begin the transit to Corepoint in two minutes, to arrive in six hours. There was something about other vehicles, other routes, return trips to various…nodes? I don't remember what that means. And she hopes we will enjoy the ride." He smiles thinly.

"Oh." Pleased, Nassun kicks a little in her chair. Six hours to travel all the way to the other side of the planet? But she shouldn't be amazed by that, maybe, since these are the people who built the obelisks.

There seems to be nothing to do but get comfortable. Cautiously, Nassun unslings her runny-sack and lets it hang from the back of her chair. This causes her to notice that something like lichen grows all over the floor, though it cannot be natural or accidental; the blooms of it spread out in pretty, regular patterns. She stretches down a foot and finds that it is soft, like carpet.

Schaffa is more restless, pacing around the comfortable

confines of the...vehimal...and touching its golden veins now and again. It's slow, methodical pacing, but even that is unusual for him, so Nassun is restless, too. "I have been here," he murmurs.

"What?" She heard him. She's just confused.

"In this vehimal. Perhaps in that very seat. I have been here, I feel it. And that language—I don't remember ever having heard it, and yet." He bares his teeth suddenly, and thrusts his fingers into his hair. "Familiarity, but no, no...context! No meaning! Something about this journey is wrong. Something is wrong *and I don't remember what.*"

Schaffa has been damaged for as long as Nassun has known him, but this is the first time he has *seemed* damaged to her. He's speaking faster, words tumbling over one another. There is an oddness to the way his eyes dart around the vehimal interior that makes Nassun suspect he's seeing things that aren't there.

Trying to conceal her anxiety, she reaches out and pats the shell-chair beside her. "These are soft enough to sleep in, Schaffa."

It's too obvious a suggestion, but he turns to gaze at her, and for a moment the haunted tension of his expression softens. "Always so concerned for me, my little one." But it stops the restlessness as she'd hoped, and he comes over to sit.

Just as he does—Nassun starts—the woman's voice speaks again. It's asking a question. Schaffa frowns and then translates, slowly, "She—I think this is *the vehimal's* voice. It speaks to us now, specifically. Not just an announcement."

Nassun shifts, suddenly less comfortable inside the thing. "It talks. It's alive?"

"I'm not certain the distinction between living creature and lifeless object matters to the people who built this place. Yet—" He hesitates, then raises his voice to haltingly speak strange words to the air. The voice answers again, repeating something Nassun heard before. She's not sure where some of the words begin or end, but the syllables are the same. "It says that we are approaching the . . . transition point. And it asks if we would like to . . . experience?" He shakes his head, irritable. "To see something. Finding the words in our own tongue is more difficult than understanding what's being said."

Nassun twitches with nerves. She draws her feet up into her chair, irrationally afraid of hurting the creature-thing's insides. She isn't sure what she means to ask. "Will it hurt, to see?" *Hurt the vehimal*, she means, but she cannot help also thinking, *Hurt us*.

The voice speaks again before Schaffa has time to translate Nassun's question. "No," it says.

Nassun jumps in pure shock, her orogeny twitching in a way that would have earned her a shout from Essun. "Did you say no?" she blurts, looking around at the vehimal's walls. Maybe it was a coincidence.

"Biomagestric storage surpluses permit—" The voice slips back into the old language, but Nassun is certain she did not imagine hearing those oddly pronounced words of Sanze-mat. "—processing," it concludes. Its voice is soothing, but it seems to come from the very walls, and it troubles Nassun that she has nothing to look at, no face to orient on while she's listening to it. How is it even speaking with no mouth, no throat? She imagines the cilia on the outside of the vehicle somehow rubbing together like insects' legs, and her skin crawls.

It continues, "Translation—" Something. "—linguistic drift." That sounded like Sanze-mat, but she doesn't know what it means. It continues for a few more words, incomprehensible again.

Nassun looks at Schaffa, who's also frowning in alarm. "How do I answer what it was asking before?" she whispers. "How do I tell it that I want to see whatever it's talking about?"

In answer, though Nassun had not meant to ask this question directly of the vehimal, the featureless wall in front of them suddenly darkens into round black spots, as if the surface has suddenly sprouted ugly mold. These spread and merge rapidly until half of the wall is nothing but blackness. As if they're looking through a window into the bowels of the city, but outside the vehimal there's nothing to see but black.

Then light appears on the bottom edge of this window—which really is a window, she realizes; the entire front end of the vehimal has somehow become transparent. The light, in rectangular panels like the ones that lined the stairway from the surface, brightens and marches forward into the darkness ahead, and by its illumination Nassun is able to see walls arching around them. Another tunnel, this one only large enough for the vehimal, and curving through dark rocky walls that are surprisingly rough-hewn given the obelisk-builders' penchant for seamless smoothness. The vehimal is moving steadily along this tunnel, though not quickly. Propelled by its cilia? By some other means Nassun cannot fathom? She finds herself simultaneously fascinated and a little bored, if that is possible. It seems impossible that something which goes so slow can get them to the other side of the world in six hours. If all of those hours will be like this, riding a smooth white track through a rocky black tunnel, with nothing to occupy them except Schaffa's restlessness and a disembodied voice, it will feel much longer.

And then the curve of the tunnel straightens out, and up ahead Nassun sees the hole for the first time.

The hole isn't large. There's something about it that is immediately, viscerally impressive nevertheless. It sits at the center of a vaulted cavern, surrounded by more panel lights, which have been set into the ground. As the vehimal approaches, these turn from white to bright red in a way that Nassun decides is another signal of warning. Down the hole is a yawning blackness. Instinctively she sesses, trying to grasp its dimensions—but she cannot. The circumference of the hole, yes; it's only about twenty feet across. Perfectly circular. The depth, though...she frowns, uncurls from her chair, concentrates. The sapphire tickles at her mind, inviting use of its power, but she resists this; there are too many things in this place that respond to the silver, to *magic*, in ways she doesn't understand. And anyway, she's an orogene. Sessing the depth of a hole should be easy...but this hole stretches deep, deep, beyond her range.

And the vehimal's track runs right up to the hole, and over its edge.

Which is as it should be, should it not? The goal is to reach Corepoint. Still, Nassun cannot help a surge of alarm that is powerful enough to edge along panic. "Schaffa!" He immediately reaches for her hand. She grips it tightly with no fear of hurting him. His strength, which has only ever been used to protect her, never in threat, is desperately needed reassurance right now.

"I have done this before," he says, but he sounds uncertain. "I have survived it."

But you don't remember how, she thinks, feeling a kind of terror that she doesn't know the word for.

(That word is *premonition*.)

Then the edge is there, and the vehimal tips forward. Nassun gasps and clutches at the armrests of her chair—but bizarrely, there is no vertigo. The vehimal does not speed up; its movement pauses for a moment, in fact, and Nassun catches a fleeting glimpse of a few of the thing's cilia blurring at the edges of the view, as they somehow adjust the trajectory of the vehimal from *forward* to *down*. Something else has adjusted with this change, so that Nassun and Schaffa do not fall forward out of their seats; Nassun finds that her back and butt are just as firmly tucked into the chair now as before, even though this is impossible.

And meanwhile, a faint hum within the vehimal, which until now has been too low to be much more than subliminal, abruptly begins to grow louder. Unseen mechanisms reverberate faster in an unmistakable cycling-up pattern. As the vehimal completes its tilt, the view fills with darkness again, but this time Nassun knows it is the yawning black of the pit. There's nothing ahead anymore. Only down.

"Launch," says the voice within the vehimal.

Nassun gasps and clutches Schaffa's hand harder as she is pressed back into her seat then by motion. It isn't as much momentum as she *should* be feeling, however, because her every sense tells her that they have just shot forward at a tremendous rate, going much, much faster than even a running horse.

Into the dark.

At first the darkness is absolute, though broken periodically by a ring of light that blurs past as they hurtle through the tunnel. Their speed continues to increase; presently these rings pass so quickly that they are just flashes. It takes three before Nassun is able to discern what she's seeing and sessing, and then only once she watches a ring as they pass it: *windows*. There are windows set into the walls of the tunnel, illuminated by the light. There's living space down here, at least for the first few miles. Then the rings stop, and the tunnel is nothing but dark for a while.

Nassun sesses impending change an instant before the tunnel suddenly brightens. They can see a new, ruddy light that intersperses the rock walls of the tunnel. Ah, yes; they've gone far enough down that some of the rock has melted and glows bright red. This new light paints the vehimal's interior bloody and makes the gold filigree along its walls seem to catch fire. The forward view is indistinct at first, just red amid gray and brown and black, but Nassun understands instinctively what she's seeing. They have entered the mantle, and her fear finally begins to ebb amid fascination.

"The asthenosphere," she murmurs. Schaffa frowns at her, but naming what she sees has eased her fear. Names have power. She bites her lip, then finally lets go of Schaffa's hand to rise and approach the forward view. Up close it's easier to tell that what she's seeing is just an illusion of sorts—tiny diamonds of color rising on the vehimal's inner skin, like a blush, to form a mosaic of moving images. How does it work? She can't begin to fathom it.

Fascinated, she reaches up. The vehimal's inner skin gives off no heat, though she knows they are already at a level underground where human flesh should burn up in an instant. When she touches the image on the forward view, it ripples ever so slightly around her finger, like waves in water. Putting her whole hand on a roil of brown-red color, she cannot help smiling. Just a few feet away, on the other side of the vehimal's skin, is the burning earth. She's *touching* the burning earth, thinly removed. She puts her other hand up, presses her cheek against the smooth plates. Here in this strange deadciv contraption, she is part of the earth, perhaps more so than any orogene before her has ever been. It is *her*, it is *in* her, she is in *it*.

When Nassun glances back over her shoulder at Schaffa, he's smiling, despite the lines of pain around his eyes. It's different from his usual smile. "What?" she asks.

"The Leadership families of Yumenes believed that orogenes once ruled the world," he says. "That their duty was to keep your kind from ever regaining that much power. That you would be monstrous rulers of the world, doing back to ordinary folk what had been done to you, if you ever got the chance. I don't think they were right about any of it—and yet." He gestures, as she stands there illuminated by the fire of the earth. "*Look* at you, little one. If you are the monster they imagined you to be . . . you are also glorious."

Nassun loves him so much.

It's why she gives up the illusion of power and goes back to sit beside him. But when she gets close, she sees just how much strain he's under. "Your head hurts a lot."

His smile fades. "It's bearable."

Troubled, she puts her hands on his shoulders. Dozens of nights of easing his pain have made it easy—but this time when she sends silver into him, the white-hot burn of lines between his cells does not fade. In fact, they blaze *brighter*, so sharply that Schaffa tenses and pulls away from her, rising to begin pacing again. He has plastered a smile on his face, more of a rictus as he prowls restlessly back and forth, but Nassun can tell that the smile-endorphins are doing nothing.

Why did the lines get brighter? Nassun tries to understand this by examining herself. Nothing of her silver is different; it flows in its usual clearly delineated lines. She turns her silver gaze on Schaffa—and then, belatedly, notices something stunning.

The vehimal is *made* of silver, and not just fine lines of it. It is surrounded by silver, permeated with it. What she perceives is a wave of the stuff, rippling in ribbons around herself and Schaffa, starting at the nose of the vehicle and enclosing them behind. This sheath of magic, she understands suddenly, is what's pushing away the heat and pushing back on the pressure and tilting the lines of force within the vehimal so that gravity pulls toward its floor and not toward the center of the earth. The walls are only a framework; something about their structure makes it easier for the silver to flow and connect and form lattices. The gold filigree helps to stabilize the churn of energies at the front of the vehicle—or so Nassun guesses, since she cannot understand all the ways in which these *magic* mechanisms work together. It's just too complex. It is like riding inside an obelisk. It's like being carried by the wind. She had no idea the silver could be so amazing.

But there is something beyond the miracle of the vehimal's walls. Something outside the vehimal.

At first Nassun isn't sure what she's perceiving. More lights? No. She's looking at it all wrong.

It's the silver, same as what flows between her own cells. It's *a single thread* of silver—and yet it is titanic, curling away between a whorl of soft, hot rock and a high-pressure bubble of searing water. A single thread of silver... and it is longer than the tunnel they have traversed so far. She can't find either of its ends. It's wider than the vehimal's circumference and then some. Yet otherwise it's just as clear and focused as any one of the lines within Nassun herself. The same, just... immense.

And Nassun *understands* then, she *understands*, so suddenly and devastatingly that her eyes snap open and she stumbles backward with the force of the realization, bumping into another chair and nearly falling before she grabs it to hold herself upright. Schaffa makes a low, frustrated sound and turns in an attempt to respond to her alarm—but the silver within his body is so bright that when it flares, he doubles over, clutching at his head and groaning. He is in too much pain to fulfill his duty as a Guardian, or to act on his concern for her, because the silver in his body has grown to be as bright as that immense thread out in the magma.

Magic, Steel called the silver. The stuff underneath orogeny, which is made by things that live or once lived. This silver deep within Father Earth wends between the mountainous fragments of his substance in exactly the same way that they twine among the cells of a living, breathing thing. And that is because *a planet* is a living, breathing thing; she knows this now with the certainty of instinct. All the stories about Father Earth being alive are real.

But if the mantle is Father Earth's body, why is his silver getting brighter?

No. Oh no.

"Schaffa," Nassun whispers. He grunts; he has sagged to one knee, gasping shallowly as he clutches at his head. She wants to go to him, comfort him, help him, but she stands where she is, her breath coming too fast from rising panic at what she suddenly knows is coming. She wants to deny it, though. "Schaffa, p-please, that thing in your head, the piece of iron, you called it a corestone, Schaffa—" Her voice is fluttery. She can't catch her breath. Fear has nearly closed her throat. No. No. She did not understand, but now she does and she has no idea how to stop it. "*Schaffa, where does it come from, that corestone thing in your head?*"

The vehimal's voice speaks again with that greeting language, and then it continues, obscene in its detached pleasantry. "—a marvel, only available—" Something. "—route. This vehimal—" Something. "—heart, illuminated—" Something. "—for your pleasure."

Schaffa does not reply. But Nassun can sess the answer to her question now. She can *feel* it as the paltry thin silver that runs through her own body resonates—but that is a faint resonance, from *her* silver, generated by her own flesh. The silver in Schaffa, in all Guardians, is generated by the corestone that sits lodged in their sessapinae. She's studied this stone sometimes, to the degree that she is able while Schaffa sleeps and she feeds him magic. It's iron, but like no other iron she's ever sessed. Oddly dense. Oddly energetic, though some of that is the magic that it channels into him from . . . somewhere. Oddly alive.

And when the whole right side of the vehimal dissolves to let its passengers glimpse the rarely seen wonder that is the world's unfettered heart, it already blazes before her: a silver sun underground, so bright that she must squint, so heavy that perceiving it hurts her sessapinae, so powerful with magic that it makes the lingering connection of the sapphire feel tremulous and weak. It is the Earth's core, the source of the corestones, and before her it is a world in itself, swallowing the viewscreen and growing further still as they hurtle closer.

It does not look like rock, Nassun thinks faintly, beneath the panic. Maybe that's just the waver of molten metal and magic all round the vehimal, but the immensity before her seems to shimmer when she tries to focus on it. There's some solidity to it; as they draw closer, Nassun can detect anomalies dotting the surface of the bright sphere, made tiny by contrast—even as she realizes they are obelisks. Several dozen of them, jammed into the heart of the world like needles in a pincushion. But these are nothing. Nothing.

And Nassun is nothing. Nothing before this.

It's a mistake to bring him, Steel had said, of Schaffa.

Panic snaps. Nassun runs to Schaffa as he falls to the floor, thrashing. He does not scream, though his mouth is open and his icewhite eyes have gone wide and his every limb, when she wrestles him onto his back, is muscle-stiff. One flailing arm hits her collarbone, flinging her back, and there is a flash of terrible pain, but Nassun barely spares a thought for it before she scrambles back to him. She grabs his arm with both of her own and tries to hold on because he is reaching for his head and his hands are forming claws and his nails are *raking* at his scalp and face—"*Schaffa, no*!" she cries. But he cannot hear her.

And then the vehimal goes dark inside.

It's still moving, though slower. They've actually passed into the semisolid stuff of the core, the vehimal's route skimming its surface—because of course the people who built the obelisks would revel in their ability to casually pierce the planet for entertainment. She can feel the blaze of that silver, churning sun all around her. Behind her, however, the wall-window goes suddenly dim. There's something just outside the vehimal, pressing against its sheath of magic.

Slowly, with Schaffa writhing in silent agony in her lap, Nassun turns to face the core of the Earth.

And here, within the sanctum of its heart, the Evil Earth notices her back.

When the Earth speaks, it does not do so in words, exactly. This is a thing you know already, but that Nassun only learns in this moment. She sesses the meanings, hears the vibrations with the bones of her ears, shudders them out through her skin, feels them pull tears from her eyes. It is like drowning in energy and sensation and emotion. It *hurts.* Remember: The Earth wants to kill her.

But remember, too: Nassun wants it just as dead.

So it says, in microshakes that will eventually stir a tsunami somewhere in the southern hemisphere, *Hello, little enemy.*

(This is an approximation, you realize. This is all her young mind can bear.)

And as Schaffa chokes and goes into convulsions, Nassun clutches at his pain-wracked form and stares at the wall of rusty darkness. She isn't afraid anymore; fury has steeled her. She is so very much her mother's daughter.

"You let him go," she snarls. "*You let him go right now.*"

The core of the world is metal, molten and yet crushed into solidity. There is some malleability to it. The surface of the red darkness begins to ripple and change as Nassun watches. Something appears that for an instant she cannot parse. A pattern, familiar. A *face*. It is just a suggestion of a person, eyes and a mouth, shadow of a nose—but then for just an instant the eyes are distinct in shape, the lips lined and detailed, a mole appearing beneath the eyes, *which open*.

No one she knows. Just a face . . . where there should be none. And as Nassun stares at this, dawning horror slowly pushing aside her anger, she sees another face—and another, more of them appearing all at once to fill the view. Each is pushed aside as another rises from underneath. Dozens. Hundreds. This one jowled and tired-looking, that one puffy as if from crying, that one openmouthed and screaming in silence, like Schaffa. Some look at her pleadingly, mouthing words she wouldn't be able to understand even if she could hear.

All of them ripple, though, with the amusement of a greater presence. *He is mine.* Not a voice. When the Earth speaks, it is not in words. Nevertheless.

Nassun presses her lips together and reaches into the silver of Schaffa and ruthlessly cuts as many of the tendrils etched into his body as she can, right around the corestone. It doesn't work like it usually does when she uses the silver for surgery. The silver lines in Schaffa reestablish themselves almost instantly, and throb that much harder when they do. Schaffa shudders each time. She's hurting him. She's making it worse.

There's no other choice. She wraps her own threads around his corestone to perform the surgery he would not permit her to do a few months before. If it shortens his life, at least he will not suffer for what is left of it.

But another ripple of amusement makes the vehimal shudder, and a flare of silver blazes through Schaffa that shrugs off her paltry threads. The surgery fails. The corestone is seated as firmly as ever amid the lobes of his sessapinae, like the parasitic thing it is.

Nassun shakes her head and looks around for something, anything else, that might help. She is distracted momentarily by the boil and shift of faces in the surface of the rusty dark. Who are these people? Why are they here, churning amid the Earth's heart?

Obligation, the Earth returns, in wavelets of heat and crushing pressure. Nassun bares her teeth, struggling against the weight of its contempt. *What was stolen, or lent, must be recompensed.*

And Nassun cannot help but understand this too, here within the Earth's embrace, with its meaning thrumming through her bones. The silver—magic—comes from life. Those who made the obelisks sought to harness magic, and they succeeded; oh, how they succeeded. They used it to build wonders beyond imagining. But then they wanted more magic than just what their own lives, or the accumulated aeons of life and death on the Earth's surface, could provide. And when they saw how much magic brimmed just beneath that surface, ripe for the taking…

It may never have occurred to them that so much magic, so much *life*, might be an indicator of…awareness. The Earth does not speak in words, after all—and perhaps, Nassun realizes, having seen entirely too much of the world to still have much of a child's innocence, perhaps these builders of the great obelisk network were not used to respecting lives different from their own. Not so very different, really, from the people who run the Fulcrums, or raiders, or her father. So where they should have seen a living being, they saw only another thing to exploit. Where they should have asked, or left alone, they raped.

For some crimes, there is no fitting justice—only reparation. So for every iota of life siphoned from beneath the Earth's skin, the Earth has dragged a million human remnants into its heart. Bodies rot in soil, after all—and soil sits upon tectonic plates, plates eventually subduct into the fire under the Earth's crust, which convect endlessly through the mantle . . . and there within itself, the Earth eats everything they were. This is only fair, it reasons—coldly, with an anger that still shudders up from the depths to crack the world's skin and touch off Season after Season. It is only right. The Earth did not start this cycle of hostilities, it did not steal the Moon, it did not burrow into anyone else's skin and snatch bits of its still-living flesh to keep as trophies and tools, it did not plot to enslave humans in an unending nightmare. It did not start this war, but it will rusting well *have. Its. Due.*

And oh. Does Nassun not understand this? Her hands tighten in Schaffa's shirt, trembling as her hatred wavers. Can she not empathize?

For the world has taken so much from her. She had a brother once. And a father, and a mother whom she also understands but wishes she did not. And a home, and dreams. The people of the Stillness have long since robbed her of childhood and any hope of a real future, and because of this she is so angry that she cannot think beyond THIS MUST STOP and I WILL STOP IT—

—so does she not resonate with the Evil Earth's wrath, herself?

She does.

Earth eat her, she does.

Schaffa has gone still in her lap. There is wetness beneath one of her legs; he's urinated on himself. His eyes are still open, and he breathes in shallow gasps. His taut muscles still twitch now and again. Everyone breaks, if torture goes on long enough. The mind bears the unbearable by going elsewhere. Nassun is ten years old, going on a hundred, but she has seen enough of the world's evil to know this. Her Schaffa. Has gone away. And might never, ever, come back.

The vehimal speeds onward.

The view begins to grow bright again as it emerges from the core. Interior lights resume their pleasant glow. Nassun's fingers curl loosely in Schaffa's clothes now. She gazes back at the turning mass of the core until the stuff of the sidewall turns opaque again. The forward view lingers, but it, too, begins to darken. They have entered another tunnel, this one wider than the first, with solid black walls somehow holding back the churning heat of the outer core and mantle. Now Nassun senses that the vehimal is tilted up, away from the core. Headed back toward the surface, but this time on the other side of the planet.

Nassun whispers, to herself since Schaffa has gone away, "This has to stop. I will stop it." She closes her eyes and the lashes stick together, wet. "I promise."

She does not know to whom she makes this promise. It doesn't matter, really.

Not long after, the vehimal reaches Corepoint.

Syl Anagist: One

THEY TAKE KELENLI AWAY IN the morning.

It is unexpected, at least by us. It also isn't really about us, we realize fairly quickly. Conductor Gallat arrives first, although I see several other high-ranking conductors talking in the house above the garden. He does not look displeased as he calls Kelenli outside and speaks to her in a quiet but intent voice. We all get up, vibrating guilt though we have done nothing wrong, just spent a night lying on a hard floor and listening to the strange sound of others' breath and occasional movement. I watch Kelenli, fearing for her, wanting to protect her, though this is inchoate; I don't know what the danger is. She stands straight and tall, like one of them, as she speaks to Gallat. I sess her tension, like a fault line poised to slip.

They are outside of the little garden house, fifteen feet away, but I hear Gallat's voice rise for a moment. "How much longer do you mean to keep up this foolishness? Sleeping in the shed?"

Kelenli says, calmly, "Is there a problem?"

Gallat is the highest ranked of the conductors. He is also the cruelest. We don't think he means it. It's just that he does not seem to understand that cruelty is possible, with us. We are the machine's tuners; we ourselves must be attuned for the good of the project. That this process sometimes causes pain or fear or decommissioning to the briar patch is... incidental.

We have wondered if Gallat has feelings himself. He does, I see when he draws back now, expression all a-ripple with hurt, as if Kelenli's words have struck him some sort of blow. "I've been good to you," he says. His voice wavers.

"And I'm grateful." Kelenli hasn't shifted the inflection of her voice at all, or a muscle of her face. She looks and sounds, for the first time, like one of us. And as we so often do, she and he are having a conversation that has nothing to do with the words coming from their mouths. I check; there's nothing in the ambient, save the fading vibrations of their voices. And yet.

Gallat stares at her. Then the hurt and anger fade from his expression, replaced by weariness. He turns away and snaps, "I need you back at the lab today. There are fluctuations in the subgrid again."

Kelenli's face finally moves, her brows drawing down. "I was told I had three days."

"Geoarcanity takes precedence over your leisure plans, Kelenli." He glances toward the little house where I and the others cluster, and catches me staring at him. I don't look away, mostly because I'm so fascinated by his anguish that I don't think to. He looks fleetingly embarrassed, then irritated. He says to her, with his usual air of impatience, "Biomagestry can only do distance scans outside of the compound, but they say they're actually detecting some interesting flow clarification in the tuners' network. Whatever you've been doing with them obviously isn't a complete waste of time. I'll take them, then, to wherever you were planning to go today. Then you can go back to the compound."

She glances around at us. At me. *My thinker.*

"It should be an easy enough trip," she says to him, while looking at me. "They need to see the local engine fragment."

"The amethyst?" Gallat stares at her. "They live in its shadow. They see it constantly. How does that help?"

"They haven't seen the socket. They need to fully understand its growth process—more than theoretically." All at once she turns away from me, and from him, and begins walking toward the big house. "Just show them that, and then you can drop them off at the compound and be done with them."

I understand precisely why Kelenli has spoken in this dismissive tone, and why she hasn't bothered to say farewell before leaving. It's no more than any of us do, when we must watch or sess another of our network punished; we pretend not to care. (*Tetlewha. Your song is toneless, but not silent. From where do you sing?*) That shortens the punishment for all, and prevents the conductors from focusing on another, in their anger. Understanding this, and feeling nothing as she walks away, are two very different things, however.

Conductor Gallat is in a terrible mood after this. He orders us to get our things so we can go. We have nothing, though some of us need to eliminate waste before we leave, and all of us need food and water. He lets the ones who need it use Kelenli's small toilet or a pile of leaves out back (I am one of these; it is very strange to squat, but also a profoundly enriching experience), then tells us to ignore our hunger and thirst and come on, so we do. He walks us very fast, even though our legs are shorter than his and still aching from the day before. We are relieved to see the vehimal he's summoned, when it comes, so that we can sit and be carried back toward the center of town.

The other conductors ride along with us and Gallat. They keep speaking to him and ignoring us; he answers in terse, one-word replies. They ask him mostly about Kelenli—whether she is always so intransigent, whether he believes this is an unforeseen genegineering defect, why he even bothers to allow her input on the project when she is, for all intents and purposes, just an obsolete prototype.

"Because she's been right in every suggestion she's made thus far," he snaps, after the third such question. "Which is the very reason we developed the tuners, after all. The Plutonic Engine would need another seventy years of priming before even a test-firing could be attempted, without them. When a machine's sensors are capable of telling you exactly what's wrong and exactly how to make the whole thing work more efficiently, it's stupid not to pay heed."

That seems to mollify them, so they leave him alone and resume talking—though to each other, not to him. I am sitting near Conductor Gallat. I notice how the other conductors' disdain actually increases his tension, making anger radiate off his skin like the residual heat of sunlight from a rock, long after night has fallen. There have always been odd dynamics to the conductors' relationships; we've puzzled them out as best we could, while not really understanding. Now, however, thanks to Kelenli's explanation, I remember that Gallat has *undesirable ancestry*. We were made this way, but he was simply born with pale skin and icewhite eyes—traits common among the Niess. He isn't Niess; the Niess are gone. There are other races, Sylanagistine races, with pale skin. The eyes suggest, however, that somewhere in his family's history—distant, or he would not have been permitted schooling and medical care and his prestigious current position—someone made children with a Niesperson. Or not; the trait could be a random mutation or happenstance of pigment expression. Apparently no one thinks it is, though.

This is why, though Gallat works harder and spends more hours at the compound than anyone, and is in charge, the other conductors treat him as if he is less than what he is. If he did not pass on the favor in his dealings with us, I would pity him. As it is, I am afraid of him. I always have been afraid of him. But for Kelenli, I decide to be brave.

"Why are you angry with her?" I ask. My voice is soft, and hard to hear over the humming metabolic cycle of the vehimal. Few of the other conductors notice my comment. None of them care. I have timed the asking well.

Gallat starts, then stares at me as if he has never seen me before. "What?"

"Kelenli." I turn my eyes to meet his, although we have learned over time that the conductors do not like this. They find eye contact challenging. But they also dismiss us more easily when we do not look at them, and I don't want to be dismissed in this moment. I want him to *feel* this conversation, even if his weak, primitive sessapinae cannot tell him that my jealousy and resentment have raised the temperature of the city's water table by two degrees.

He glares at me. I gaze impassively back. I sense tension in the network. The others, who of course have noticed what the conductors ignore, are suddenly afraid for me...but I am almost distracted from their concern by the difference I suddenly perceive in us. Gallat is right: We *are* changing, complexifying, our ambient influence strengthening, as a result of the things Kelenli has shown us. Is this an improvement? I'm not certain yet. For now, we are confused where before, we were mostly unified. Remwha and Gaewha are angry at me for taking this risk without seeking consensus first—and this recklessness, I suppose, is my own symptom of change. Bimniwha and Salewha are, irrationally, angry at Kelenli for the strange way she is affecting me. Dushwha is done with all of us and just wants to go home. Beneath her anger, Gaewha is afraid for me but she also pities me, because I think she understands that my recklessness is a symptom of something else. I have decided that I am in love, but love is a painful hotspot roil beneath the surface of me in a place where once there was stability, and I do not like it. Once, after all, I believed I was the finest tool ever created by a great civilization. Now, I have learned that I am a mistake cobbled together by paranoid thieves who were terrified of their own mediocrity. I don't know how to feel, *except* reckless.

None of them are angry at Gallat for being too dangerous to have a simple conversation with, though. There's something very wrong with that.

Finally, Gallat says, "What makes you think I'm angry with Kelenli?" I open my mouth to point out the tension in his body, his vocal stress, the look on his face, and he makes an irritated sound. "Never mind. I know how you process information." He sighs. "And I suppose you're right."

I am definitely right, but I know better than to remind him of what he doesn't want to know. "You want her to live in your house." I was unsure that it was Gallat's house until the morning's conversation. I should have guessed, though; it smelled like him. None of us is good at using senses other than sesuna.

"It's *her* house," he snaps. "She grew up there, same as me."

Kelenli has told me this. Raised alongside Gallat, thinking she was normal, until someone finally told her why her parents did not love her. "She was part of the project."

He nods once, tightly, his mouth twisted in bitterness. "So was I. A human child was a necessary control, and I had…useful characteristics for comparison. I thought of her as my sister until we both reached the age of fifteen. Then they told us."

Such a long time. And yet Kelenli must have suspected that she was different. The silver glimmer of magic flows around us, through us, like water. Everyone can sess it, but we tuners, we live it. It lives in us. She cannot have ever thought herself normal.

Gallat, however, had been completely surprised. Perhaps his view of the world had been as thoroughly upended as mine has been now. Perhaps he floundered—flounders—in the same way, struggling to resolve his feelings with reality. I feel a sudden sympathy for him.

"I never mistreated her." Gallat's voice has gone soft, and I'm not certain he's still speaking to me. He has folded his arms and crossed his legs, closing in on himself as he gazes steadily through one of the vehimal's windows, seeing nothing. "Never treated her like…" Suddenly he blinks and darts a hooded glance at me. I start to nod to show that I understand, but some instinct warns me against doing this. I just look back at him. He relaxes. I don't know why.

He doesn't want you to hear him say "like one of you," Remwha signals, humming with irritation at my obtuseness. *And he doesn't want you to know what it means, if he says it. He reassures himself that he is not like the people who made his own life harder. It's a lie, but he needs it, and he needs us to support that lie. She should not have told us that we were Niess.*

We aren't *Niess,* I gravitic-pulse back. Mostly I'm annoyed that he had to point this out. Gallat's behavior is obvious, now that Remwha has explained.

To them we are. Gaewha sends this as a single microshake whose reverberations she kills, so that we sess only cold silence afterward. We stop arguing because she's right.

Gallat continues, oblivious to our identity crisis, "I've given her as much freedom as I can. Everyone knows what she is, but I've allowed her the same privileges that any normal woman would have. Of course there are restrictions, limitations, but that's reasonable. I can't be seen to be lax, if..." He trails off, into his own thoughts. Muscles along his jaw flex in frustration. "She acts as if she can't understand that. As if *I'm* the problem, not the world. I'm trying to help her!" And then he lets out a heavy breath of frustration.

We have heard enough, however. Later, when we process all this, I will tell the others, *She wants to be a person.*

She wants the impossible, Dushwha will say. *Gallat thinks it better to own her himself, rather than allow Syl Anagist to do the same. But for her to be a person, she must stop being... ownable. By anyone.*

Then Syl Anagist must stop being Syl Anagist, Gaewha will add sadly.

Yes. They will all be right, too, my fellow tuners...but that does not mean Kelenli's desire to be free is wrong. Or that something is impossible just because it is very, very hard.

The vehimal stops in a part of town that, amazingly, looks familiar. I have seen this area only once and yet I recognize the pattern of the streets, and the vineflowers on one greenstrate wall. The quality of the light through the amethyst, as the sun slants toward setting, stirs a feeling of longing and relief in me that I will one day learn is called homesickness.

The other conductors leave and head back to the compound. Gallat beckons to us. He's still angry, and wants this over with. So we follow, and fall slowly behind because our legs are shorter and the muscles burn, until finally he notices that we and our guards are ten feet behind him. He stops to let us catch up, but his jaw is tight and one hand taps a brisk pattern on his folded arms.

"Hurry up," he says. "I want to do start-up trials tonight."

We know better than to complain. Distraction is often useful, however. Gaewha says, "What are we hurrying to see?"

Gallat shakes his head impatiently, but answers. As Gaewha planned, he walks slower so that he can speak to us, which allows us to walk slower as well. We desperately catch our breath. "The socket where this fragment was grown. You've been told the basics. For the time being each fragment serves as the power plant for a node of Syl Anagist—taking in magic, catalyzing it, returning some to the city and storing the surplus. Until the Engine is activated, of course."

Abruptly he stops, distracted by our surroundings. We have

reached the restricted zone around the base of the fragment—a three-tiered park with some administrative buildings and a stop on the vehimal line that (we are told) does a weekly run to Corepoint. It's all very utilitarian, and a little boring.

Still. Above us, filling the sky for nearly as high as the eye can see, is the amethyst fragment. Despite Gallat's impatience, all of us stop and stare up at it in awe. We live in its colored shadow, and were made to respond to its needs and control its output. It is us; we are it. Yet rarely do we get to see it like this, directly. The windows in our cells all point away from it. (Connectivity, harmony, lines of sight and waveform efficiency; the conductors want to risk no accidental activation.) It is a magnificent thing, I think, both in its physical state and its magical superposition. It glows in the latter state, crystalline lattice nearly completely charged with the stored magic power that we will soon use to ignite Geoarcanity. When we have shunted the world's power systems over from the limited storage-and-generation of the obelisks to the unlimited streams within the earth, and when Corepoint has gone fully online to regulate it, and when the world has finally achieved the dream of Syl Anagist's greatest leaders and thinkers—

—well. Then I, and the others, will no longer be needed. We hear so many things about what will happen once the world has been freed from scarcity and want. People living forever. Travel to other worlds, far beyond our star. The conductors have assured us that we won't be killed. We will be celebrated, in fact, as the pinnacle of magestry, and as living representations of what humanity can achieve. Is that not a thing to look forward to, our veneration? Should we not be proud?

But for the first time, I think of what life I might want for myself, if I could have a choice. I think of the house that Gallat lives in: huge, beautiful, cold. I think of Kelenli's house in the garden, which is small and surrounded by small growing magics. I think of living with Kelenli. Sitting at her feet every night, speaking with her as much as I want, in every language that I know, without fear. I think of her smiling without bitterness and this thought gives me incredible pleasure. Then I feel shame, as if I have no right to imagine these things.

"Waste of time," Gallat mutters, staring at the obelisk. I flinch, but he does not notice. "Well. Here it is. I've no idea why Kelenli wanted you to see it, but now you see it."

We admire it as bidden. "Can we... go closer?" Gaewha asks. Several of us groan through the earth; our legs hurt and we are hungry. But she replies with frustration. *While we're here, we might as well get the most out of it.*

As if in agreement, Gallat sighs and starts forward, walking down the sloping road toward the base of the amethyst, where it has been firmly lodged in its socket since the first growth-medium infusion. I have seen the top of the amethyst fragment, lost amid scuds of cloud and sometimes framed by the white light of the Moon, but this part of it is new to me. About its base are the transformer pylons, I know from what I have been taught, which siphon off some of the magic from the generative furnace at the amethyst's core. This magic—a tiny fraction of the incredible amount that the Plutonic Engine is capable of producing—is redistributed via countless conduits to houses and buildings and machinery and vehimal feeding stations throughout the city-node. It is the same in every city-node of

Syl Anagist, all over the world—two hundred and fifty-six fragments in total.

My attention is suddenly caught by an odd sensation—the strangest thing I have ever sessed. Something diffuse... something nearby generates a force that... I shake my head and stop walking. "What is that?" I ask, before I consider whether it is wise to speak again, with Gallat in this mood.

He stops, glowers at me, then apparently understands the confusion in my face. "Oh, I suppose you're close enough to detect it here. That's just sinkline feedback."

"And what is a *sinkline?*" asks Remwha, now that I have broken the ice. This causes Gallat to glare at him in fractionally increased annoyance. We all tense.

"Evil Death," Gallat sighs at last. "Fine, easier to show than to explain. Come on."

He speeds up again, and this time none of us dares complain even though we are pushing our aching legs on low blood sugar and some dehydration. Following Gallat, we reach the bottommost tier, cross the vehimal track, and pass between two of the huge, humming pylons.

And there... we are destroyed.

Beyond the pylons, Conductor Gallat explains to us in a tone of unconcealed impatience, is the start-up and translation system for the fragment. He slips into a detailed technical explanation that we absorb but do not really hear. Our network, the nigh-constant system of connections through which we six communicate and assess each other's health and rumble warnings or reassure with songs of comfort, has gone utterly silent and still. This is shock. This is horror.

The gist of Gallat's explanation is this: The fragments could not have begun the generation of magic on their own, decades ago when they were first grown. Nonliving, inorganic things like crystal are inert to magic. Therefore, in order to help the fragments initiate the generative cycle, raw magic must be used as a catalyst. Every engine needs a starter. Enter the sinklines: They look like vines, thick and gnarled, twisting and curling to form a lifelike thicket around the fragment's base. And ensnared in these vines—

We're going to see them, Kelenli told me, when I asked her where the Niess were.

They are still alive, I know at once. Though they sprawl motionless amid the thicket of vines (lying atop the vines, twisted among them, wrapped up in them, speared by them where the vines grow through flesh), it is impossible not to sess the delicate threads of silver darting between the cells of this one's hand, or dancing along the hairs of that one's back. Some of them we can see breathing, though the motion is so very slow. Many wear tattered rags for clothes, dry-rotted with years; a few are naked. Their hair and nails have not grown, and their bodies have not produced waste that we can see. Nor can they feel pain, I sense instinctively; this, at least, is a kindness. That is because the sinklines take all the magic of life from them save the bare trickle needed to keep them alive. Keeping them alive keeps them generating more.

It is the briar patch. Back when we were newly decanted, still learning how to use the language that had been written into our brains during the growth phase, one of the conductors told us a story about where we would be sent if we became unable to work for some reason. That was when there were fourteen of us. We would be retired, she said, to a place where we could still serve the project indirectly. "It's peaceful there," the conductor said. I remember it clearly. She smiled as she said it. "You'll see."

The briar patch's victims have been here for years. Decades. There are hundreds of them in view, and thousands more out of sight if the sinkline thicket extends all the way around the amethyst's base. Millions, when multiplied by two hundred and fifty-six. We cannot see Tetlewha, or the others, but we know that they, too, are here somewhere. Still alive, and yet not.

Gallat finishes up as we stare in silence. "So after system priming, once the generative cycle is established, there's only an occasional need to reprime." He sighs, bored with his own voice. We stare in silence. "Sinklines store magic against any possible need. On Launch Day, each sink reservoir should have approximately thirty-seven lammotyrs stored, which is three times..."

He stops. Sighs. Pinches the bridge of his nose. "There's no point to this. She's playing you, fool." It is as if he does not see what we're seeing. As if these stored, componentized lives mean nothing to him. "Enough. It's time we got all of you back to the compound."

So we go home.

And we begin, at last, to plan.

* * *

Thresh them in
Line them neat
Make them part of the winter wheat!
Tamp them down

Shut them up
Just a hop, a skip, and a jump!
Seal those tongues
Shut those eyes
Never you stop until they cry!
Nothing you hear
Not one you'll see
This is the way to our victory!

—Pre-Sanze children's rhyme popular in Yumenes, Haltolee, Nianon, and Ewech Quartents, origin unknown. Many variants exist. This appears to be the baseline text.

11

you're almost home

THE GUARDS AT THE NODE station actually seem to think they can fight when you and the other Castrimans walk out of the ashfall. You suppose that the lot of you *do* look like a larger-than-usual raider band, given your ashy, acid-worn clothing and skeletal looks. Ykka doesn't even have time to get Danel to try to talk them down before they start firing crossbows. They're terrible shots, which is lucky for you; the law of averages is on their side, which isn't. Three Castrimans go down beneath the bolts before you realize Ykka hasn't got a clue how to use a torus as a shield—but after you've remembered that you can't do it, either, without Consequences. So you shout at Maxixe and he does it with diamond precision, shredding the incoming bolts into wood-flecked snow, not so differently from the way you started things off in Tirimo that last day.

He's not as skilled now as you were then. Part of the torus remains around him; he just stretches and reshapes its forward edge to form a barrier between Castrima and the big scoria gates of the node station. Fortunately there's no one in front of him (after you shouted at people to get out of the way). Then with a final flick of redirected kinetics he smashes the gates apart and ices the crossbow wielders before letting the torus spin away. Then while Castrima's Strongbacks charge in and take care of things, you go over to find Maxixe sprawled in the wagon bed, panting.

"Sloppy," you say, catching one of his hands and pulling it to you, since you can't exactly chafe it between your own. You can feel the cold of his skin through four layers of clothing. "Should've anchored that torus ten feet away, at least."

He grumbles, eyes drifting shut. His stamina's gone completely to rust, but that's probably because starvation and orogeny don't mix well. "Haven't needed to do anything fancier than just freeze people, for a couple of years now." Then he glowers at you. "*You* didn't bother, I see."

You smile wearily. "That's because I knew you had it." Then you scrape away a patch of ice from the wagon bed so you can have somewhere to sit until the fighting's done.

When it's over, you pat Maxixe—who's fallen asleep—and then get up to go find Ykka. She's just inside the gates with Esni and a couple of other Strongbacks, all of them looking at the tiny paddock in wonder. There's a *goat* in there, eying everyone with indifference as it chews on some hay. You haven't seen a goat since Tirimo.

First things first, though. "Make sure they don't kill the doctor, or doctors," you say to Ykka and Esni. "They're probably barricaded in with the node maintainer. Lerna won't know how to take care of the maintainer; it takes special skills." You pause. "If you're still committed to this plan."

Ykka nods and glances at Esni, who nods and glances at another woman, who eyeballs a young man, who then runs into the node facility. "What are the chances the doctor will kill the maintainer?" Esni asks. "For mercy?"

You resist the urge to say, *Mercy is for people.* That way of thinking needs to die, even if you're thinking it in bitterness. "Slim. Explain through the door that you're not planning to kill anyone who surrenders, if you think that will help." Esni sends another runner to do this.

"Of course I'm still committed to the plan," Ykka says. She's rubbing her face, leaving streaks in the ash. Beneath the ash there's just more ash, deeper ingrained. You're forgetting what her natural coloring looks like, and you can't tell if she's wearing eye makeup anymore. "I mean, most of us can handle shakes in a controlled way, even the kids by now, but..." She looks up at the sky. "Well. There's *that*." You follow her gaze, but you know what you'll see already. You've been trying not to see it. Everyone has been.

The Rifting.

On this side of the Merz, the sky doesn't exist. Further south, the ash that the Rifting pumps forth has had time to rise into the atmosphere and thin out somewhat, forming the rippling clouds that have dominated the sky as you've known it for the past two years. Here, though. Here you try to look up, but before you even get to the sky, what grabs your eyes is something like a slow-boiling wall of black and red across the entire visible northern horizon. In a volcano, what you're seeing would be called an eruption column, but the Rifting is not just some solitary vent. It is a thousand volcanoes put end-to-end, an unbroken line of earthfire and chaos from one coast of the Stillness to the other. Tonkee's been trying to get everyone to call what you're seeing by its proper term: *Pyrocumulonimbus*, a massive stormwall cloud of ash and fire and lightning. You've already heard people using a different term, however—simply, *the Wall*. You think that's going to stick. You suspect, in fact, that if anybody's still alive in a generation or two to name this Season, they'll call it something like the Season of the Wall.

You can hear it, faint but omnipresent. A rumble in the earth. A low, ceaseless snarl against your middle ear. The Rifting isn't just a shake; it is the still-ongoing, dynamic divergence of two tectonic plates along a newly created fault line. The aftershakes from the initial Rifting won't stop for years. Your sessapinae have been all a-jangle for days now, warning you to brace or run, twitching with the need to *do something* about the seismic threat. You know better, but here's the problem: Every orogene in Castrima is sessing what you're sessing. Feeling the same twitchy urge to react. And unless they happen to be Fulcrum-precise highringers able to yoke other highringers before activating an ancient network of deadciv artifacts, *doing something* will kill them.

So Ykka is now coming to terms with a truth you've understood since you woke up with a stone arm: To survive in Rennanis, Castrima will need the node maintainers. It will need to take care of them. And when those node maintainers die, Castrima will need to find some way to replace them. No one's talking about that last part yet. First things first.

After a while, Ykka sighs and glances at the open doorway of the building. "Sounds like the fighting's done."

"Sounds like," you say. Silence stretches. A muscle in her jaw tightens. You add, "I'll go with you."

She glances at you. "You don't have to." You've told her about your first time seeing a node maintainer. She heard the still-fresh horror in your voice.

But no. Alabaster showed you the way, and you no longer shirk the duty he's bestowed upon you. You'll turn the maintainer's head, let Ykka see the scarring in the back, explain about the lesioning process. You'll need to show her how the wire minimizes bedsores. Because if she's going to make this choice, then she needs to know exactly what price she—and Castrima—must pay.

You will do this—make her see these things, make yourself face it again, because this is the *whole* truth of what orogenes are. The Stillness fears your kind for good reason, true. Yet it should also revere your kind for good reason, and it has chosen to do only one of these things. Ykka, of all people, needs to hear everything.

Her jaw tightens, but she nods. Esni watches you both, curious, but then she shrugs and turns away as you and Ykka walk into the node facility, together.

* * *

The node has a fully stocked storeroom, which you guess is meant to be an auxiliary storage site for the comm itself. It's more than even hungry, commless Castrima can eat, and it includes things everyone's been increasingly desperate for, like dried red and yellow fruit and canned greens. Ykka stops people from turning the occasion into an impromptu feast—you've still got to make the stores last for Earth knows how long—but that doesn't prevent the bulk of the comm from getting into a nearly festive mood as everyone bunkers for the night with full bellies for the first time in months.

Ykka posts guards at the entrance to the node maintainer's chamber—"Nobody but us needs to see that shit," she declares, and by this you suspect that she doesn't want any of the comm's stills getting ideas—and on the storeroom. She puts a triple guard on the goat. There's an Innovator girl from a farming comm who's been assigned to figure out how to milk the creature; she manages. The pregnant woman, who lost one of her household mates in the desert, gets first dibs on the milk. This might be pointless. Starvation and pregnancy don't mesh, either, and she says the baby hasn't moved in days. Probably best that she lose it now, if she's going to, here where Lerna's got antibiotics and sterile instruments available and can at least save the mother's life. Still, you see her take the little pot of milk when it's given to her, and drink it down even though she grimaces at the taste. Her jaw is set and hard. There's a chance. That's what matters.

Ykka also sets up monitors at the node station's shower room. They're not guards, exactly, but they're necessary, because a lot of people in Castrima are from rough little Midlatter comms and they don't know how indoor plumbing works. Also, some people have been just standing under the hot spray for an hour or more, weeping as the ash and leftover desert sand comes off their acid-dried skins. Now, after ten minutes, the monitors gently nudge people out and over to benches along the sides of the room, where they can keep crying while others get their turn.

You take a shower and feel nothing, except clean. When you claim a corner of the station's mess hall—which has been emptied of furnishings so that several hundred people can sleep ash-free for the night—you sit there atop your bedroll, leaning against the scoria wall, letting your thoughts drift. It's impossible not to notice the mountain lurking within the stone just behind you. You don't call him out because the other people of Castrima are leery of Hoa. He's the only stone eater still around, and they remember that stone eaters are not neutral, harmless parties. You do reach back and pat the wall with your one hand, however. The mountain stirs a little, and you feel something—a hard nudge—against the small of your back. Message received and returned. It's surprising how good this private moment of contact makes you feel.

You need to feel again, you think, as you watch a dozen small tableaus play out before you. Two women argue over which of them gets to eat the last piece of dried fruit in their comm share. Two men, just beyond them, furtively exchange whispers while one passes over a small soft sponge—the kind Equatorials like to use for wiping after defecation. Everyone likes their little luxuries, when fortune provides. Temell, the man who now teaches the comm's orogene children, lies buried in them as he snores on his bedroll. One boy is nestled in a curl at his belly; meanwhile, Penty's sock-clad foot rests on the back of his neck. Across the room, Tonkee stands with Hjarka—or rather, Hjarka's holding her hands and trying to coax her into some kind of slow dance, while Tonkee stands still and tries to just roll her eyes and not smile.

You're not sure where Ykka is. Probably spending the night

in one of the sheds or tents outside, knowing her, but you hope she lets one of her lovers stay with her this time. She's got a rotating stable of young women and men, some of them time-sharing with other partners and some singles who don't seem to mind Ykka using them for occasional stress relief. Ykka needs that now. Castrima needs to take care of its headwoman.

Castrima needs, and you need, and just as you think this, Lerna comes out of nowhere and settles beside you.

"Had to end Chetha," he says quietly. Chetha, you know, is one of the three Strongbacks shot by the Rennies—ironically, a former Rennie herself, conscripted into the army along with Danel. "The other two will make it, probably, but the bolt perforated Chetha's bowel. It would've been slow and awful. Plenty of painkillers here, though." He sighs and rubs his eyes. "You've seen that . . . thing . . . in the wire chair."

You nod, hesitate, then reach for his hand. He's not particularly affectionate, you've been relieved to discover, but he does need little gestures sometimes. A reminder that he is not alone, and that all is not hopeless. To this end you say, "If I succeed in shutting down the Rifting, you may not need to keep the node maintainers." You're not sure that's true, but you hope it is.

He clasps your hand lightly. It's been fascinating to realize that he never initiates contact between you. He waits for you to offer, and then he meets your gestures with as much or as little intensity as you've brought to the effort. Respecting your boundaries, which are sharp-edged and hair-triggered. You never knew he was so observant, all these years—but then, you should've guessed. He figured out you were an orogene just by watching you, years ago. Innon would've liked him, you decide.

As if he has heard your thoughts, Lerna then looks over at you, and his gaze is troubled.

"I've been thinking about not telling you something," he says. "Or rather, not pointing out something you've probably chosen not to notice."

"What an opening."

He smiles a little, then sighs and looks down at your clasped hands, the smile fading. The moment attenuates; the tension grows in you, because this is so unlike him. Finally, though, he sighs. "How long has it been since you last menstruated?"

"How—" You stop talking.

Shit.

Shit.

In your silence, Lerna sighs and leans his head back against the wall.

You try to make excuses in your own head. Starvation. Extraordinary physical effort. You're forty-four years old—you think. Can't remember what month it is. The chances are slimmer than Castrima's were of surviving the desert. But . . . your menses have run strong and regular for your entire life, stopping only on three prior occasions. Three *significant* occasions. That's why the Fulcrum decided to breed you. Half-decent orogeny, and good Midlatter hips.

You knew. Lerna's right. On some level, you noticed. And then chose not to notice, because—

Lerna has been silent beside you for some while, watching the comm unwind, his hand limp in yours. Very softly he says, "Am I correct in understanding that you need to finish your business at Corepoint within a time frame?"

His tone is too formal. You sigh, shutting your eyes. "Yes."

"Soon?"

Hoa has told you that *perigee*—when the Moon is closest—will be in a few days. After that, it will pass the Earth and pick up velocity, slingshotting back into the distant stars or wherever it's been all this time. If you don't catch it now, you won't.

"Yes," you say. You're tired. You . . . hurt. "Very soon."

It is a thing you haven't discussed, and probably should have for the sake of your relationship. It is a thing you never needed to discuss, because there was nothing to be said. Lerna says, "Using all the obelisks once did that to your arm."

You glance at the stump unnecessarily. "Yes." You know where he's going with the conversation, so you decide to skip to the end. "You're the one who asked what I was going to do about the Season."

He sighs. "I was angry."

"But not wrong."

His hand twitches a little on your own. "What if I asked you not to do it?"

You don't laugh. If you did, it would be bitter, and he doesn't deserve that. Instead, you sigh and shift to lie down, pushing him until he does the same thing. He's a little shorter than you, so you're the big spoon. This of course puts your face in his gray hair, but he's availed himself of the shower, too, so you don't mind. He smells good. Healthy.

"You wouldn't ask," you say against his scalp.

"But what if I did?" It's weary and heatless. He doesn't mean it.

You kiss the back of his neck. "I'd say, 'Okay,' and then there would be three of us, and we'd all stay together until we die of ash lung."

He takes your hand again. You didn't initiate it this time, but it doesn't bother you. "Promise," he says.

He doesn't wait for your answer before falling asleep.

* * *

Four days later, you reach Rennanis.

The good news is that you're no longer plagued by ashfall. The Rifting's too close, and the Wall is busy carrying the lighter particulates upward; you'll never have to worry about that again. What you have instead are periodic gusts laden with incendiary material—lapilli, tiny bits of volcanic material that are too big to inhale easily but are still burning as they come down. Danel says the Rennies called it sparkfall, and that it's mostly harmless, though you should keep spare canteens of water situated at strategic points throughout the caravan in case any of the sparks should catch and smolder.

More dramatic than the sparkfall, however, is the way lightning dances over the city's skyline, this close to the Wall. The Innovators are excited about this. Tonkee says there are all sorts of uses for reliable lightning. (This would have made you stare at her, if it hadn't come from Tonkee.) None of it strikes the ground, though—only the taller buildings, which have all been fitted with lightning rods by the city's previous denizens. It's harmless. You'll just have to get used to it.

Rennanis isn't what you were expecting, quite. Oh, it's a huge city: Equatorial styling all over the place, still-functioning hydro and filtered well water running smoothly, tall black obsidian walls etched over with dire images of what happens to the city's enemies. Its buildings aren't nearly as beautiful or impressive as those of Yumenes, but then Yumenes was the greatest of the Equatorial cities, and Rennanis barely merited the title. "Only half a million people," you remember someone sneering, a lifetime ago. But two lives ago, you were born in a humble Nomidlats village, and to what remains of Damaya, Rennanis is still a sight to behold.

There are less than a thousand of you to occupy a city that once held hundreds of thousands. Ykka orders everyone to take over a small complex of buildings near one of the city's greenlands. (It has sixteen.) The former inhabitants have conveniently labeled the city's buildings with a color code based on their structural soundness, since the city didn't survive the Rifting entirely unscathed. Buildings marked with a green X are known to be safe. A yellow X means damage that could spell a collapse, especially if another major shake hits the city. Red-marked buildings are noticeably damaged and dangerous, though you see signs that they were inhabited, too, perhaps by those willing to take any shelter rather than be ashed out. There are more than enough green-X buildings for Castrima, so every household gets its pick of apartments that are furnished, sound, and still have working hydro and geo.

There are several wild flocks of chickens running about, and more goats, which have actually been breeding. The greenlands' crops are all dead, however, having gone months unwatered and untended between you killing the Rennies and Castrima's arrival. Despite this, the seed stocks contain lots of dandelion and other hardy, low-light-tolerant edibles, including Equatorial staples like taro. Meanwhile, the city's storecaches are overflowing with cachebread, cheeses, fat-flecked spicy sausages, grains and fruit, herbs and leaves preserved in oil, more. Some of it's fresher than the rest, brought back by the marauding army. All of it is more than the people of Castrima could eat if they threw a feast every night for the next ten years.

It's amazing. But there are a few catches.

The first is that it's more complicated to run Rennanis's water treatment facility than anyone expected. It's running automatically and thus far hasn't broken down, but no one knows how to work the machinery if it does. Ykka sets the Innovators to the task of figuring that out, or coming up with a workable alternative if the equipment fails. Tonkee is highly annoyed: "I trained for six years at Seventh to learn how to clean shit out of sewer water?" But despite her complaining, she's on it.

The second catch is that Castrima cannot possibly guard the city's walls. The city is simply too big, and there are too few of you. You're protected, for now, by the fact that no one comes north if they can possibly help it. If anyone does come a-conquering, however, nothing will stand between the comm and conquest except its wall.

There's no solution to this problem. Even orogenes can only do so much in the martial sense, here in the shadow of the Rifting where orogeny is dangerous. Danel's army was Rennanis's surplus population, and it's currently feeding a boilbug boom down in the southeastern Midlats—not that you'd want them here, anyway, treating you like the interlopers you are. Ykka orders the Breeders to ramp up to replacement-level production, but even if they recruit every healthy comm member to assist,

Castrima won't have enough people to secure the comm for generations. Nothing to do but at least guard the portion of the city that the comm now occupies, as best you can.

"And if another army comes along," you catch Ykka muttering, "we'll just invite them in and assign them each a room. That ought to settle it."

The third catch—and the biggest one, existentially if not logistically—is this: Castrima must live amid the corpses of its conquered.

The statues are everywhere. Standing in apartment kitchens washing dishes. Lying in beds that have sagged or broken beneath their stone weight. Walking up the parapet steps to take over from other statues on guard duty. Sitting in communal kitchens sipping tea long since dried to dregs. They are beautiful in their way, with wild smoky-quartz manes of hair and smooth jasper skin and clothes of tourmaline or turquoise or garnet or citrine. They wear expressions that are smiles or eye rolls or yawns of boredom—because the shockwave of Obelisk Gate power that transformed them was fast, mercifully. They didn't even have time to be afraid.

The first day, everyone edges around the statues. Tries not to sit in their line of sight. To do anything else would be… disrespectful. And yet. Castrima has survived both a war that these people initiated, and life as that war's refugees. It would be equally disrespectful of Castrima's dead to let guilt eclipse this truth. So after a day or two, people start to simply… *accept* the statues. Can't do anything else, really.

Something about it bothers you, though.

You find yourself wandering one night. There's a yellow-X

building that's not too far from the complex, and it's beautiful, with a facade covered in etched vinework and floral motifs, some glimmering with peeling gold foil. The foil catches the light and flickers a little as you move, its angles of reflection shifting to create the overall illusion of a building covered in living, moving greenery. It's an older building than most of those in Rennanis. You like it, though you're not sure why. You go up to the roof, finding only the usual apartments inhabited by statues along the way. The door here is unlocked and stands open; maybe someone was on the roof when the Rifting struck. You check to make sure there's a lightning rod in place before you step through the door, of course; this is one of the taller buildings of the city, though it's only six or seven stories altogether. (*Only*, sneers Syenite. *Only?* thinks Damaya, in wonder. *Yes, only*, you snap at both, to shut them up.) There's not only a rod, there's an empty water tower, so as long as you don't go leaning on any metal surfaces or linger in the rod's immediate vicinity, you probably won't die. Probably.

And here, poised to face the Rifting cloudwall as if he were built up here, gazing north since the building's floral motifs were new, Hoa awaits.

"There aren't as many statues here as there should be," you say as you stop beside him.

You can't help following Hoa's gaze. From here, you still can't see the Rifting itself; looks like there's a dead rainforest and some hilly ridges between the city and the monster. The Wall is bad enough, however.

And maybe one existential horror is easier to face than another, but you remember using the Obelisk Gate on these people, twisting the magic between their cells and transmuting the infinitesimal parts of them from carbon to silicate. Danel told you how crowded Rennanis was—so much that it had to send out a conquering army to survive. Now, however, the city is not crowded with statues. There are signs that it was, once: statues deep in conversation with partners that seem to be missing; only two people sitting at a table set for six. In one of the bigger green-X buildings there's a statue that is lying naked in bed, mouth open and penis permanently stiff and hips thrusting up, hands positioned in just the right places to grip someone's legs. He's alone, though. Someone's horrible, morbid joke.

"My kind are opportunistic feeders," Hoa says.

Yeah, that's exactly what you were afraid he would say.

"And apparently very damned hungry? There were a lot of people here. Most of them must be missing."

"We, too, put aside surplus resources for later, Essun."

You rub your face with your one remaining hand, trying and failing to *not* visualize a gigantic stone eater larder somewhere, now stuffed full of brightly colored statues. "Evil Earth. Why do you bother with me, then? I'm not as—*easy* a meal as those."

"Lesser members of my kind need to strengthen themselves. I don't." There is a very slight shift in the inflection of Hoa's voice. By this point you know him; that was contempt. He's a proud creature (even he will admit). "They are poorly made, weak, little better than beasts. We were so lonely in those early years, and at first we had no idea what we were doing. The hungry ones are the result of our fumbling."

You waver, because you don't really want to know... but you haven't been a coward for some years now. So you steel yourself and turn to him and then say, "You're making another one now. Aren't you? From—from me. If it's not about food for you, then it's... reproduction." Horrifying reproduction, if it is dependent on the death-by-petrification of a human being. And there must be more to it than just turning people to stone. You think about the kirkhusa at the roadhouse, and Jija, and the woman back in Castrima whom you killed. You think about how you hit her, *smashed* her with magic, for the not-crime of making you relive Uche's murder. But Alabaster was not the same, in the end, as what you did to that woman. She was a shining, brightly colored collection of gemstones. He was an ugly lump of brown rock—and yet the brown rock was finely made, precisely crafted, *careful*, where the woman was a disorderly mess beneath her surface beauty.

Hoa is silent in answer to your question, which is an answer in itself. And then you finally remember. Antimony, in the moments after you closed the Obelisk Gate, but before you teetered into magic-traumatized slumber. Beside her, another stone eater, strange in his whiteness, disturbing in his familiarity. Oh, Evil Earth, you don't want to know, but—"Antimony used that..." Too-small lump of brown stone. "Used *Alabaster.* As raw material to—to, oh rust, to make another stone eater. And she made it look like *him.*" You hate Antimony all over again.

"He chose his own shape. We all do."

This slaps your rage out of its spiral. Your stomach clenches, this time in something other than revulsion. "That—then—"

You have to take a deep breath. "Then it's *him*? Alabaster. He's... he's..." You can't make yourself say the word.

Flick and Hoa faces you, expression compassionate, but somehow also warning. "The lattice doesn't always form perfectly, Essun," he says. The tone is gentle. "Even when it does, there is always... loss of data."

You have no idea what this means and yet you're shaking. Why? You know why. Your voice rises. "Hoa, if that's Alabaster, if I can talk to him—"

"No."

"*Why the rust not?*"

"Because it must be his choice, first." Harder voice here. A reprimand. You flinch. "More importantly, because we are fragile at the beginning, like all new creatures. It takes centuries for us, the *who* of us, to... cool. Even the slightest of pressures—like you, demanding that he fit himself to your needs rather than his own—can damage the final shape of his personality."

You take a step back, which surprises you because you hadn't realized you were getting in his face. And then you sag. Alabaster is alive, but not. Is Stone Eater Alabaster even remotely the same as the flesh-and-blood man you knew? Does that even matter anymore, now that he has transformed so completely? "I've lost him again, then," you murmur.

Hoa doesn't seem to move at first, but there's a brief flit of wind against your side, and abruptly a hard hand nudges the back of your soft one. "He will live for an eternity," Hoa says, as softly as his hollow voice can manage. "For as long as the Earth exists, something of who he was will, too. You're the one still in danger of being lost." He pauses. "But if you choose not to finish what we have begun, I will understand."

You look up and then, for only maybe the second or third time, you think you understand him. He knows you're pregnant. Maybe he knew it before you did, though what that means to him, you cannot guess. He knows what underlies your thoughts about Alabaster, too, and he's saying…that you aren't alone. That you *don't* have nothing. You have Hoa, and Ykka and Tonkee and maybe Hjarka, *friends*, who know you in all your rogga monstrosity and accept you despite it. And you have Lerna—quietly demanding, relentless Lerna, who does not give up and does not tolerate your excuses and does not pretend that love precludes pain. He is the father of another child that will probably be beautiful. All of your children so far have been. Beautiful, and powerful. You close your eyes against regret.

But that brings the sounds of the city to your ears, and you are startled to catch laughter on the wind, loud enough to carry up from the ground level, probably over by one of the communal fires. Which reminds you that you have *Castrima*, too, if you want it. This ridiculous comm of unpleasant people who are impossibly still together, which you have fought for and which has, however grudgingly, fought for you in return. It pulls your mouth into a smile.

"No," you say. "I'll do what needs doing."

Hoa considers you. "You're certain."

Of course you are. Nothing has changed. The world is broken and you can fix it; that's what Alabaster and Lerna both charged you to do. Castrima is *more* reason for you to do it, not less. And it's time you stopped being a coward, too, and went to find Nassun. Even if she hates you. Even if you left her to face a terrible world alone. Even if you are the worst mother in the world...you did your best.

And maybe it means you're choosing one of your children—the one who has the best chance of survival—over the other. But that's no different from what mothers have had to do since the dawn of time: sacrifice the present, in hopes of a better future. If the sacrifice this time has been harder than most... Fine. So be it. This is a mother's job, too, after all, and you're a rusting ten-ringer. You'll see to it.

"So what are we waiting for?" you ask.

"Only you," Hoa replies.

"Right. How much time do we have?"

"Perigee is in two days. I can get you to Corepoint in one."

"Okay." You take a deep breath. "I need to say some goodbyes."

With perfect bland casualness, Hoa says, "I can carry others with us."

Oh.

You want it, don't you? To not be alone at the end. To have Lerna's quiet implacable presence at your back. Tonkee will be furious at not getting a chance to see Corepoint, if you leave her behind. Hjarka will be furious if you take Tonkee without her. Danel wants to chronicle the world's transformation, for obscure Equatorial lorist reasons.

Ykka, though—

"No." You sober and sigh. "I'm being selfish again. Castrima needs Ykka. And they've all suffered enough."

Hoa just looks at you. How the rust does he manage to convey such emotion with a stone face? Even if that emotion is dry skepticism of your self-abnegating bullshit. You laugh—once, and it's rusty. Been a while.

"I think," Hoa says slowly, "that if you love someone, you don't get to choose how they love you back."

So many layers in the strata of that statement.

Okay, though. Right. This isn't just about you, and it never has been. All things change in a Season—and some part of you is tired, finally, of the lonely, vengeful woman narrative. Maybe Nassun isn't the only one you needed a home for. And maybe not even you should try to change the world alone.

"Let's go ask them, then," you say. "And then let's go get my little girl."

* * *

To: Yaetr Innovator Dibars
From: Alma Innovator Dibars

I've been asked to inform you that your funding has been cut. You are to return to the University forthwith by the least expensive means possible.

And since I know you, old friend, let me add this. You believe in logic. You think even our esteemed colleagues are immune to prejudice, or politics, in the face of hard facts. This is why you'll never be allowed within a mile of the Funding and Allocations committee, no matter how many masterships you earn.

Our funding comes from Old Sanze. From families so ancient that they have books in their collections older than all the Universities—and they won't let us touch them. How do you think those families got to be so old, Yaetr? Why has Sanze lasted this long? It's not because of stonelore.

You cannot go to people like that and ask them to fund a research project that makes heroes of roggas! You just can't. They'll faint, and when they wake up, they'll have you killed. They'll destroy you as surely as they would any threat to their livelihoods and legacy. Yes, I know that's not what you think you're doing, but it is.

And if that isn't enough, here is a fact that might be logical enough even for you: The Guardians are starting to ask questions. I don't know why. No one knows what drives those monsters. But that's why I voted with the committee majority, even if it means you hate me from here on. I want you alive, old friend, not dead in an alley with a glass poniard through your heart. I'm sorry.

Safe travels homeward.

12

Nassun, not alone

COREPOINT IS SILENT.

Nassun notices this when the vehimal in which she's traversed the planet emerges in its corresponding station, on the other side of the world. This is located in one of the strange, slanting buildings that encircle the massive hole at Corepoint's center. She cries for help, cries for someone, cries, as the vehimal's door opens and she drags Schaffa's limp, unresponsive body through the silent corridors and then the silent streets. He's big and heavy, so although she tries in various ways to use magic to assist with dragging his weight—badly; magic is not meant to be used for something so gross and localized, and her concentration is poor in the moment—she makes it only a block or so away from the compound before she, too, collapses, in exhaustion.

* * *

Somerusting day, somerusting year.

Found these books, blank. The stuff they're made of isn't paper. Thicker. Doesn't bend easily. Good thing, maybe, or would be dust by now. Preserve my words for eternity! Ha! Longer than my rusting sanity.

Don't know what to write. Innon would laugh and tell me to write about sex. Right, so: I jerked off today, for the first time since A dragged me to this place. Thought about him in the middle of it and couldn't come. Maybe I'm too old? That's what Syen would say. She's just mad I could still knock her up.

Forgetting how Innon used to smell. Everything smells like the sea here, but it's not like the sea near Meov. Different water? Innon used to smell like the water there. Every time the wind blows I lose a little more of him.

Corepoint. How I hate this place.

* * *

Corepoint isn't a ruin, quite. That is, it isn't ruined, and it isn't uninhabited.

On the surface of the open, endless ocean, the city is an anomaly of buildings—not very tall compared to either the recently lost Yumenes or the longer-lost Syl Anagist. Corepoint is unique, however, among both past and present cultures. The structures of Corepoint are sturdily built, of rustless metal and strange polymers and other materials that can withstand the often hurricane-force salt winds that dominate this side of the world. The few plants that grow here, in the parks that were constructed so long ago, are no longer the lovely, designer, hothouse things favored by Corepoint's builders. Corepoint trees—hybridized and feral descendants of the original landscaping—are huge, woody things, twisted into artful shapes by the wind. They have long since broken free of their orderly beds and containers and now gnarl over the pressed-fiber sidewalks. Unlike the architecture of Syl Anagist, here there are many more sharp angles, meant to minimize the buildings' resistance to the wind.

But there is more to the city than what can be seen.

Corepoint sits at the peak of an enormous underwater shield volcano, and the first few miles of the hole drilled at its center are actually lined with a hollowed-out complex of living quarters, laboratories, and manufactories. These underground facilities, originally meant to house Corepoint's geomagests and genegineers, have long since been turned to a wholly different purpose—because this flip side of Corepoint is Warrant, where Guardians are made and dwell between Seasons.

We will speak more of this later.

Above the surface in Corepoint, though, it's late afternoon, beneath a sky whose clouds are sparse amid a shockingly bright blue sky. (Seasons that start in the Stillness rarely have a severe impact on the weather in this hemisphere, or at least not for several months or years after.) As befits the bright day, there are people in the streets around Nassun as she struggles and weeps, but they do not move to help. They do not move at all, mostly—for they are stone eaters, with rose-marble lips and shining mica eyes and braids woven in pyrite gold or clear quartz. They stand on the steps of buildings that have not known human feet for tens of thousands of years. They sit along window ledges of stone or metal that have begun to deform under the pressure of incredible weight applied over decades. One sits with knees upraised and arms propped across them, leaning against a tree whose roots have grown around her; mosses line the upper surfaces of her arms and hair. She watches Nassun, only her eyes moving, in what might be interest.

They all watch, doing nothing, as this quick-moving, noisy human child sobs into the salt-laden wind until she is exhausted, and then just sits there in a huddle with her fingers still tangled in the cloth of Schaffa's shirt.

* * *

Another day, same (?) year

No writing about Innon or Coru. Off-limits from now on.

Syen. I can still feel her—not sess, feel. There's an obelisk here, I think it's a spinel. When I ~~canneck~~ connect to it, it's like I can feel anything they're connected to. The amethyst is following Syen. Wonder if she knows.

Antimony says Syen made it to the mainland and is ~~wannr~~ wandering. That's why I feel like I'm wandering, I guess? She's all that's left but she ki—fuck.

This place is ridiculous. Anniemony was right that it's a way to trigger the Obelisk Gate without control cab? (Onyx. Too powerful, can't risk it, would trigger alignment too quickly and then who's to make the second traj change?) But the rusters that buildt it put everything into tht stupid hole. A told me some of it. Great project, my ass. It's worse to see, *though. This whole rusting city is a crime scene. Tooted around and found great big pipes running along the bottom of the ocean. ~~hu~~* HUGE, *ready to pump* something *from the hole all the way to the continent. Magic, Animony says, did they really need so much?????* More than the Gate!

Asked Tinimony to take me into the hole today and she said no. What's in the hole, huh? What's in the hole.

* * *

Near sunset, another stone eater appears. Here amid the elegantly gowned, colorful variety of his people, he stands out even more with his gray coloring and bare chest: Steel. He stands over Nassun for several minutes, perhaps expecting her to lift her gaze and notice him, but she does not. Presently, he says, "The ocean winds can be cold at night."

Silence. Her hands clench and unclench on Schaffa's clothes, not quite spasmodically. She's just tired. She's been holding him since the center of the Earth.

After a while longer, as the sun inches toward the horizon, Steel says, "There's a livable apartment in a building two blocks from here. The food stored in it should still be edible."

Nassun says, "Where?" Her voice is hoarse. She needs water. There's some in her canteen, and in Schaffa's canteen, but she hasn't opened either.

Steel shifts posture, pointing. Nassun lifts her head to follow this and sees a street, unnaturally straight, seemingly paved straight toward the horizon. Wearily she gets up, takes a better grip on Schaffa's clothes, and begins dragging him again.

* * *

Who's in the hole, what's in the whole, where goes the hole, how holed am I!

SEs brought better food today because I don't eat enough. So special, delivery fressssh from the other sigh of the world. Going to dry the seeds, plant them. Remember to scrrrape up tomato I threw at A.

Book language looks almost like Sanze-mat. Characters similar? Precursor? Some words I almost recognize. Some old Eturpic, some Hladdac, a little early-dynasty Regwo. Wish Shinash was here. He would scream to see me putting my feet up on books older than forever. Always so easy to tease. Miss him.

Miss everyone, even people at the rusting Fulcrum (!) Miss voices that come out of rusting mouths. SYENITE could make me eat, you talking rock. SYENITE gave a shit about me and not just whether I could fix this world I don't give a shit about. SYENITE should be here with me, ~~I would give anything to have her here with me~~

No. She should forget me and ~~In~~ Meov. Find some boring fool she actually wants to sleep with. Have a boring life. She deserves that.

* * *

Night falls in the time it takes Nassun to reach the building. Steel repositions, appearing in front of a strange asymmetrical building, wedge-shaped, whose high end faces the wind. The sloping roof of the building, in the lee of the wind, is scraggly with overgrown, twisted vegetation. There's plenty of soil on the roof, more than is likely to have accumulated from the wind over centuries. It looks planned, though overgrown. Yet amid the mess, Nassun can see that someone has hacked out a garden. Recently; the plants are overgrown, too, new growth springing up from dropped fruit and split, untended vines, but given the relative dearth of weeds and the still-neat rows, this garden can't be more than a year or two neglected. The Season is now almost two years old.

Later. The building's door moves on its own, sliding aside as Nassun approaches. It closes on its own, too, once she's gotten Schaffa far enough within. Steel moves inside, pointing upstairs. She drags Schaffa to the foot of the stairs and then drops beside him, shaking, too tired to think or go any farther.

Schaffa's heart is still strong, she thinks, as she uses his chest for a pillow. With her eyes shut, she can almost imagine that he's holding her, rather than the other way around. It is paltry comfort, but enough to let her sleep without dreams.

* * *

The other side of the world
is on the other side of the hole.

I
S
N'
T

I
T

* * *

In the morning, Nassun gets Schaffa up the steps. The apartment is thankfully on only the second floor; the stairwell door opens right into it. Everything inside is strange, to her eye, yet familiar in purpose. There's a couch, though its back is at one end of the long seat, rather than behind it. There are chairs, one fused to some kind of big slanted table. For drawing, maybe. The bed, in the attached room, is the strangest thing: a big wide hemisphere of brightly colored cushion without sheets or pillows. When Nassun tentatively lies down on it, though, she finds that it flattens and conforms to her body in ways that are stunningly comfortable. It's warm, too—actively heating up beneath her until the aches of sleeping in a cold stairwell go away. Fascinated despite herself, Nassun examines the bed and is shocked to realize that it is *full* of magic, and has covered her in same. Threads of silver roam over her body, determining her discomfort by touching her nerves and then repairing her bruises and scrapes; other threads whip the particles of the bed until friction warms them; yet more threads search her skin for infinitesimal dry flakes and flecks of dust, and scrub them away. It's like what she does when she uses the silver to heal or cut things, but automatic, somehow. She can't imagine who would make a bed that could do magic. She can't imagine why. She can't fathom how anyone could have convinced all this silver to do such nice things, but that's what's happening. No wonder the people who built the obelisks needed so much silver, if they used it in lieu of wearing blankets, or taking baths, or letting themselves heal over time.

Schaffa has soiled himself, Nassun finds. It makes her feel ashamed to have to pull his clothes off and clean him, using stretchy cloths she finds in the bathroom, but it would be worse to leave him in his own filth. His eyes are open again, though he does not move while she works. They've opened during the day, and they close at night, but though Nassun talks to Schaffa (pleads for him to wake up, asks him to help her, tells him that she needs him), he does not respond.

She gets him into the bed, leaving a pad of cloths under his bare bottom. She trickles water from their canteens into his mouth, and when that runs out, she cautiously tries to get more from the strange water pump in the kitchen. There are no levers or handles on it, but when she puts her canteen beneath the spigot, water comes out. She's a diligent girl. First she uses the powder in her runny-sack to make a cup of safe from the water, checking for contaminants. The safe dissolves but stays cloudy and white, so she drinks that herself and then brings more water to Schaffa. He drinks readily, which probably means he was really thirsty. She gives him raisins that she first soaks in water, and he chews and swallows, although slowly and without much vigor. She hasn't done a good job of taking care of him.

She will do better, she decides, and heads outside to the garden to pick food for them both.

* * *

Syenite told me the date. Six years. It's been six years? No wonder she's so angry. Told me to go jump in a hole, since it's been so long. She doesn't want to see me again. Such a steelheart. Told her I was sorry. My fault, all of it.

My fault. My Moon. Turned the spare key today. (Lines of sight, lines of force, three by three by three? Cubical arrangement, like a good little crystal lattice.) The key unlocks the Gate. Dangerous to bring so many obelisks to Yumenes, though; Guardians everywhere. Wouldn't have time before they got me. Better to make a spare key out of orogenes, and who can I use? Who is strong enough. Syen isn't, almost but not quite. Innon isn't. Coru is but I can't find him. He's just a baby anyway, not right. Babies. Lots of babies. Node maintainers? Node maintainers!

No. They've suffered enough. Use the Fulcrum seniors instead.

Or the node maintainers.

Why should I do it here? Plugs the hole. Do it there, tho . . . Get Yumenes. Get the Fulcrum. Get a lot of the Guardians.

Stop nagging me, woman. Go tell Innon to fuck you, or something. You're always so cranky when you haven't gotten laid. I'll jump in the hole tomorrow.

* * *

It becomes a routine.

She takes care of Schaffa in the mornings, then goes out in

the afternoon to explore the city and find things they need. There's no need to bathe Schaffa, or to clean up his waste again; astonishingly, the bed takes care of that, too. So Nassun can spend her time with him talking, and asking him to wake up, and telling him that she doesn't know what to do.

Steel vanishes again. She doesn't care.

Other stone eaters periodically show up, however, or at least she feels the impact of their presence. She sleeps on the couch, and one morning wakes to find a blanket covering her. It's just a simple gray thing, but it's warm, and she's grateful. When she starts picking apart one of her sausages to get the fat out of it, intending to make tallow—the candles from her runny-sack are getting low—she finds a stone eater in the stairwell, its finger curled in a beckoning gesture. When she follows it, it stops beside a panel covered in curious symbols. The stone eater is pointing toward one in particular. Nassun touches it and it alights with silver, glowing golden and sending threads questing over her skin. The stone eater says something in a language Nassun does not understand before it vanishes, but when she returns to the apartment, it's warmer, and soft white lights have come on overhead. Touching squares on the wall makes the lights go off.

One afternoon she walks into the apartment to find a stone eater crouched beside a pile of things that look to have come from some comm's storecache: burlap sacks full of root vegetables and mushrooms and dried fruit, a big round of sharp white cheese, hide bags of packed pemmican, satchels of dried rice and beans, and—precious—a small cask of salt. The stone eater vanishes when Nassun approaches the pile, so she cannot even thank it. She has to blow ash off of everything before she puts it away.

Nassun has figured out that the apartment, like the garden, must have been used until recently. The detritus of another person's life is everywhere: pants much too big for her in the drawers, a man's underwear beside them. (One day these are replaced with clothing that fits Nassun. Another stone eater? Or maybe the magic in the apartment is even more sophisticated than she thought.) Books are piled in one of the rooms, many of them native to Corepoint—she's beginning to recognize the peculiar, clean, not-quite-natural look of Corepoint things. A few, however, are normal-looking, with covers of cracking leather and pages still stinky with chemicals and handwritten ink. Some of the books are in a language she can't read. Something Coaster.

One, however, is made of the Corepoint material, but its blank pages have been handwritten over, in Sanze-mat. Nassun opens this one, sits down, and begins to read.

* * *

WENT

IN THE HOLE

DON'T

don't bury me

please DON'T, Syen, I love you, I'm sorry, keep me safe, watch my back and I'll watch yours, there's no one else who's as strong as you, I wish so much that you were here, please DON'T

* * *

Corepoint is a city in still life.

Nassun begins losing track of time. The stone eaters occasionally speak to her, but most of them don't know her language, and she doesn't hear enough of theirs to pick it up. She watches them sometimes, and is fascinated to realize that some of them are performing tasks. She watches one malachite-green woman who stands amid the windblown trees, and belatedly realizes the woman is holding a branch up and to one side, to make it grow in a particular way. All of the trees, which look windblown and yet are a little too dramatic, a little too artful in their splaying and bending, have been shaped thus. It must take years.

And near the edge of the city, down by one of the strange spokelike things that jut out into the water from its edge—not piers, really, just straight pieces of metal that make no sense—another stone eater stands every day with one hand upraised. Nassun just happens to be around when the stone eater blurs and there is a splash and suddenly his upraised hand holds by the tail a huge, wriggling fish that is as long as his body. His marble skin is sheened with wet. Nassun has nowhere in particular to be, so she sits down to watch. After a time, an ocean mammal—Nassun has read of these, creatures that look like fish but breathe air—sidles up to the city's edge. It is gray-skinned, tube-shaped; there are sharp teeth along its jaw, but these are small. When it pushes up out of the water, Nassun sees that it is very old, and something about the questing movements of its head makes her realize it has gone blind. There's old scarring on its forehead as well; something has injured the creature's head badly. The creature nudges the stone eater, who of course does not move, and then nips at the fish in its hand, tearing off chunks and swallowing them until the stone eater releases the tail. When it is done, the creature utters a complex, high-pitched sound, like a . . . chitter? Or a laugh. Then it slides further into the water and swims away.

The stone eater flickers and faces Nassun. Curious, Nassun gets to her feet to go over and speak to him. By the time she's standing, though, he has vanished.

This is what she comes to understand: There is life here, among these people. It isn't life as she knows it, or a life she would choose, but life nevertheless. That gives her comfort, when she no longer has Schaffa to tell her that she is good and safe. That, and the silence, give her time to mourn. She did not understand before now that she needed this.

* * *

I've decided.

It's wrong. Everything's wrong. Some things are so broken that they can't be fixed. You just have to finish them off, sweep away the rubble, and start over. Antimony agrees. Some of the other SEs do, too. Some don't.

Rust those. They killed my life to make me their weapon, so that's what I'm going to be. My choice. My commandment. We'll do it in Yumenes. A commandment is set in stone.

I asked after Syen today. Don't know why I care anymore. Antimony's been keeping tabs, though. (For me?) Syenite is living in some little shithole comm in the Somidlats, I forget the name, playing creche teacher. Playing the happy little still. Married with two new children. How about that. Not sure about the daughter but the boy is pulling on the aquamarine.

Amazing. No wonder the Fulcrum bred you to me. And we did make a beautiful child in spite of everything, didn't we? My boy.

I won't let them find your boy, Syen. I won't let them take him, and burn his brain, and put him in the wire chair. I won't let them find your girl, either, if she's one of us, or even if she's

Guardian-potential. There won't be a Fulcrum left by the time I'm done. What follows won't be good, but it'll be bad for everyone—rich and poor, Equatorials and commless, Sanzeds and Arctics, now they'll all know. Every *season is the Season for us. The apocalypse that never ends. They could've chosen a different kind of equality. We could've all been safe and comfortable together, surviving together, but they didn't want that. Now nobody gets to be safe. Maybe that's what it will take for them to finally realize things have to change.*

Then I'll shut it down and put the Moon *back. (It shouldn't stone me, the first trajectory adjustment. ~~Unless I underestimate~~ Shouldn't.) All I'm rusting good for anyway.*

After that . . . it'll be up to you, Syen. Make it better. I know I told you it wasn't possible, that there was no way to make the world better, but I was wrong. I'm breaking it because I was wrong. Start it over, you were right, change *it. Make it better for the children you have left. Make a world Corundum could have been happy in. Make a world where people like us, you and me and Innon and our sweet boy, our beautiful boy, could have stayed whole.*

Antimony says I might get to see that world. Guess we'll see. Rust it. I'm procrastinating. She's waiting. Back to Yumenes today.

For you, Innon. For you, Coru. *For you, Syen.*

* * *

At night, Nassun can see the Moon.

This was terrifying, on the first night that she looked outside and noticed a strange pale whiteness outlining the streets and trees of the city, and then looked up to see a great white sphere in the sky. It is enormous, to her—bigger than the sun, far larger than the stars, trailed by a faint streak of luminescence that she does not know is the off-gassing of ice that has adhered to the lunar surface over the course of its travels. The *white* of it is the true surprise. She knows very little of the Moon—only what Schaffa told her. It is a satellite, he said, Father Earth's lost child, a thing whose light reflects the sun. She expected it to be yellow, given that. It disturbs her to have been so wrong.

It disturbs her more that there is a *hole* in the thing, at nearly its dead center: a great, yawning darkness like the pinpoint pupil of an eye. It's too small to tell for now, but Nassun thinks that maybe if she stares at it long enough, she will see stars on the other side of the Moon, through this hole.

Somehow it's fitting. Whatever happened ages ago to cause the Moon's loss was surely cataclysmic on multiple levels. If the Earth suffered the Shattering, then the fact that the Moon also bears scars feels normal and right. With a thumb, Nassun rubs the palm of her hand where her mother broke the bones, a lifetime ago.

And yet, when she stands in the roof garden and stares at it for long enough, she begins to find the Moon beautiful. It is an icewhite eye, and she has no reason to think badly of those. Like the silver when it swirls and whorls within something like a snail's shell. It makes her think of Schaffa—that he is watching over her in his way—and this makes her feel less alone.

Over time, Nassun discovers that she can use the obelisks to get a feel for the Moon. The sapphire is on the other side of the world, but there are others here above the ocean, drawn near in response to her summons, and she has been tapping and taming each in turn. The obelisks help her feel (not sess) that the Moon will soon be at its closest point. If she lets it go, it will pass, and begin to rapidly diminish until it vanishes from the sky. Or she can open the Gate, and tug on it, and change everything. The cruelty of the status quo, or the comfort of oblivion. The choice feels clear to her . . . but for one thing.

One night, as Nassun sits gazing up at the great white sphere, she says aloud, "It was on purpose, wasn't it? You not telling me what would happen to Schaffa. So you could get rid of him."

The mountain that has been lingering nearby shifts slightly, to a position behind her. "I did try to warn you."

She turns to look at him. At the look on her face, he utters a soft laugh that sounds self-deprecating. This stops, though, when she says, "If he dies, I'll hate you more than I hate the world."

It is a war of attrition, she's begun to realize, and she's going to lose. In the weeks (?) or months (?) since they came to Corepoint, Schaffa has noticeably deteriorated, his skin developing an ugly pallor, his hair brittle and dull. People aren't meant to lie unmoving, blinking but not thinking, for weeks on end. She had to cut his hair earlier that day. The bed cleans the dirt out of it, but it's gotten oily and lately it keeps getting tangled—and the day before, some of it must have wrapped around his arm when she wrestled him onto his belly, cutting off his circulation in a way she didn't notice. (She keeps a sheet over him, even though the bed is warm and does not need it. It bothers her that he is naked and undignified.) This morning when she finally noticed the problem, the arm was pale and a little gray. She's loosed it, chafed it hoping to bring the color back, but it doesn't look good. She doesn't know what she'll do if something's really wrong with his arm. She might lose all of him like this, slowly but surely, little bits of him dying because she was only almost-nine when this Season began and she's only almost-eleven now and taking care of invalids wasn't something anyone taught her in creche.

"If he lives," Steel replies in his colorless voice, "he will never again experience a moment without agony." He pauses, gray eyes fixed on her face, as Nassun reverberates with his words, with her own denial, with her own growing sick fear that Steel is right.

Nassun gets to her feet. "I n-need to know how to fix him."

"You can't."

She tightens her hands into fists. For the first time in what feels like centuries, part of her reaches for the strata around her. This means the shield volcano beneath Corepoint... but when she "grasps" it orogenically, she finds with some surprise that it is *anchored*, somehow. This distracts her for a moment as she has to alter her perception to shift to the silver—and there she finds solid, scintillating pillars of magic driven into the volcano's foundations, pinning it in place. It's still active, but it will never erupt because of those pillars. It is as stable as bedrock despite the hole at its core burrowing down to the Earth's heart.

She shakes this off as irrelevant, and finally voices the thought that has been gathering in her mind over all the days she has dwelled in this city of stone people. "If... if I turn him into a stone eater, he'll live. And he won't have any pain. Right?" Steel does not reply. In the lengthening silence, Nassun bites her lip. "So you have to tell me how to—to make him like you. I bet I can do it if I use the Gate. I can do anything with that. Except..."

Except. The Obelisk Gate doesn't do small things. Just as Nassun feels, sesses, *knows* that the Gate makes her temporarily omnipotent, she knows, too, that she cannot use it to transform just one man. If she makes Schaffa into a stone eater…every human being on the planet will change in the same manner. Every comm, every commless band, every starving wanderer: Ten thousand still-life cities, instead of just one. All the world will become like Corepoint.

But is that really so terrible a thing? If everyone is a stone eater, there will be no more orogenes and stills. No more children to die, no more fathers to murder them. The Seasons could come and go, and they wouldn't matter. No one would starve to death ever again. To make the whole world as peaceful as Corepoint…would that not be a kindness?

Steel's face, which has been tilted up toward the Moon even as his eyes watch her, now slowly pivots to face her. It's always unnerving to see him move slowly. "Do you know what it feels like to live forever?"

Nassun blinks, thrown. She's been expecting a fight. "What?"

The moonlight has transformed Steel into a thing of starkest shadows, white and ink against the dimness of the garden. "I asked," he says, and his voice is almost pleasant, "if you know what it feels like to live forever. Like me. Like your Schaffa. Do you have any inkling as to how old he is? Do you *care*?"

"I—" About to say that she does, Nassun falters. No. This is not a thing she has ever considered. "I—I don't—"

"I would estimate," Steel continues, "that Guardians typically last three or four thousand years. Can you imagine that length of time? Think of the past two years. Your life since the beginning of the Season. Imagine another year. You can do that, can't you? Every day feels like a year here in Corepoint, or so your kind tell me. Now put all three years together, and imagine them *times one thousand.*" The emphasis he puts on this is sharp, precisely enunciated. In spite of herself, Nassun jumps.

But also in spite of herself...she thinks. She feels old, Nassun, at the world-weary age of not-quite-eleven. So much has happened since the day she came home to find her little brother dead on the floor. She is a different person now, hardly Nassun at all; sometimes she is surprised to realize *Nassun* is still her name. How much more different will she be in three years? Ten? Twenty?

Steel pauses until he sees some change in her expression—some evidence, perhaps, that she is listening to him. Then he says, "I have reason to believe, however, that your Schaffa is much, much older than most Guardians. He isn't quite first-generation; those have all long since died. Couldn't take it. He's one of the very early ones, though, still. The languages, you see; that's how you can always tell. They never quite lose those, even after they've forgotten the names they were born with."

Nassun remembers how Schaffa knew the language of the earth-traversing vehicle. It is strange to think of Schaffa having been born back when that tongue was still spoken. It would make him...she can't even imagine. Old Sanze is supposed to be seven Seasons old, eight if one counts the present Season. Almost three thousand years. The Moon's cycle of return and retreat is much older than that, and Schaffa remembers it, so... yes. He's very, very old. She frowns.

"It's rare to find one of them who can really go the distance,"

Steel continues. His tone is casual, conversational; he could be talking about Nassun's old neighbors back in Jekity. "The corestone hurts them so much, you see. They get tired, and then they get sloppy, and then the Earth begins to contaminate them, eating away at their will. They don't usually last long once that starts. The Earth uses them, or their fellow Guardians use them, until they outlive their usefulness and one side or the other kills them. It's a testament to your Schaffa's strength that he lasted so much longer. Or a testament to something else, maybe. What kills the rest, you see, is losing the things that ordinary people need to be happy. Imagine what that's like, Nassun. Watching everyone you know and care about die. Watching your home die, and having to find a new one—again, and again, and again. Imagine never daring to get close to another person. Never having friends, because you'll outlive them. Are you lonely, little Nassun?"

She has forgotten her anger. "Yes," she admits, before she can think not to.

"Imagine being lonely forever." There's a very slight smile on his lips, she sees. It's been there the whole while. "Imagine living here in Corepoint forever, with no one to talk to but me—when I bother to respond. What do you think that will feel like, Nassun?"

"Terrible," she says. Quietly now.

"Yes. So here is my theory: I believe your Schaffa survived by loving his charges. You, and others like you, soothed his loneliness. He truly does love you; never doubt that about him." Nassun swallows back a dull ache. "But he also needs you. You keep him happy. You keep him *human*, where otherwise time would have long since transformed him into something else."

Then Steel moves again. It's inhuman because of its steadiness, Nassun finally realizes. People are quick to do big movements and then slower with fine adjustment. Steel does everything at the same pace. Watching him move is like watching a statue melt. But then he stands with arms outstretched as if to say, *Take a look at me.*

"I am forty thousand years old," Steel says. "Give or take a few millennia."

Nassun stares at him. The words are like the gibberish that the vehimal spoke—almost comprehensible, but not really. Not real.

What *does* that feel like, though?

"You're going to die when you open the Gate," Steel says, after giving Nassun a moment to absorb what he's said. "Or if not then, sometime after. A few decades, a few minutes, it's all the same. And whatever you do, Schaffa will lose you. He'll lose the one thing that has kept him human throughout the Earth's efforts to devour his will. He'll find no one new to love, either—not here. And he won't be able to return to the Stillness unless he's willing to risk the Deep Earth route again. So whether he heals somehow, or you change him into one of my kind, he will have no choice but to go on, alone, endlessly yearning for what he will never again have." Slowly, Steel's arms lower to his sides. "You have no idea what that's like."

And then, suddenly, shockingly, he is right in front of Nassun. No blurring, no warning, just flick and he is *there*, bent at the waist to put his face right in front of hers, so close that she feels the wind of the air he's displaced and smells the whiff of loam and she can even see that the irises of his eyes are striated in layers of gray.

"**BUT I DO**," he shouts.

Nassun stumbles back and cries out. Between one blink and the next, however, Steel returns to his former position, upright, arms at his sides, a smile on his lips.

"So think carefully," Steel says. His voice is conversational again, as if nothing has happened. "Think with something more than the selfishness of a child, little Nassun. And ask yourself: Even if I could help you save that controlling, sadistic sack of shit that currently passes for your adoptive father figure, why would I? Not even my enemy deserves that fate. No one does."

Nassun's still shaking. She blurts, bravely, "Sch-Schaffa might want to live."

"He might. But *should* he? Should anyone, forever? That is the question."

She feels the absent weight of countless years, and is obliquely ashamed of being a child. But at her core, she is a kind child, and it's impossible for her to have heard Steel's story without feeling something other than her usual anger at him. She looks away twitchily. "I'm...sorry."

"So am I." There's a moment's silence. In it, Nassun pulls herself together slowly. By the time she focuses on him again, Steel's smile has vanished.

"I cannot stop you, once you've opened the Gate," he says. "I've manipulated you, yes, but the choice is still ultimately yours. Consider, however. Until the Earth dies, I live, Nassun. That was its punishment for us: We became a part of it, chained fate to fate. The Earth forgets neither those who stabbed it in the back...nor those who put the knife in our hand."

Nassun blinks at *our*. But she loses this thought amid misery at the realization that there can be no fixing Schaffa. Until now, some part of her has nursed the irrational hope that Steel, as an adult, had all the answers, including some sort of cure. Now she knows that her hope has been foolish. Childish. She *is* a child. And now the only adult she has ever been able to rely on will die naked and hurt and helpless, without ever being able to say goodbye.

It's too much to bear. She sinks into a crouch, wrapping one arm round her knees and folding the other over her head, so that Steel will not *see* her cry even if he knows that's exactly what's happening.

He lets out a soft laugh at this. Surprisingly, it does not sound cruel.

"You achieve nothing by keeping any of us alive," he says, "except cruelty. Put us broken monsters out of our misery, Nassun. The Earth, Schaffa, me, you . . . all of us."

Then he vanishes, leaving Nassun alone beneath the white, burgeoning Moon.

Syl Anagist: Zero

A MOMENT IN THE PRESENT, BEFORE I speak again of the past.

Amid the heated, fuming shadows and unbearable pressure of a place that has no name, I open my eyes. I'm no longer alone.

Out of the stone, another of my kind pushes forth. Her face is angular, cool, as patrician and elegant as any statue's should be. She's shed the rest, but kept the pallor of her original coloring; I notice this at last, after tens of thousands of years. All this reminiscing has made me nostalgic.

In token of which, I say aloud, "Gaewha."

She shifts slightly, as close as any of us gets to an expression of... recognition? Surprise? We were siblings once. Friends. Since then, rivals, enemies, strangers, legends. Lately, cautious allies. I find myself contemplating some of what we were, but not all. I've forgotten the all, just as much as she has.

She says, "Was that my name?"

"Close enough."

"Hmm. And you were...?"

"Houwha."

"Ah. Of course."

"You prefer Antimony?"

Another slight movement, the equivalent of a shrug. "I have no preference."

I think, *Nor do I*, but that is a lie. I would never have given my new name to you, Hoa, if not in homage to what I remember of that old name. But I'm woolgathering.

I say, "She is committed to the change."

Gaewha, Antimony, whoever and whatever she is now, replies, "I noticed." She pauses. "Do you regret what you did?"

It's a foolish question. All of us regret that day, in different ways and for different reasons. But I say, "No."

I expect comment in return, but I suppose there's really nothing to be said anymore. She makes minute sounds, settling into the rock. Getting comfortable. She means to wait here with me. I'm glad. Some things are easier when not faced alone.

* * *

There are things Alabaster never told you, about himself.

I know these things because I studied him; he is part of you, after all. But not every teacher needs every protégé to know of his every stumble on the journey to mastery. What would be the point? None of us got here overnight. There are stages to the process of being betrayed by your society. One is jolted from a place of complacency by the discovery of difference, by hypocrisy, by inexplicable or incongruous ill treatment. What follows is a time of confusion—unlearning what one thought to be the truth. Immersing oneself in the new truth. And then a decision must be made.

Some accept their fate. Swallow their pride, forget the real truth, embrace the falsehood for all they're worth—because, they decide, they cannot be worth much. If a whole society has dedicated itself to their subjugation, after all, then surely they deserve it? Even if they don't, fighting back is too painful, too impossible. At least this way there is peace, of a sort. Fleetingly.

The alternative is to demand the impossible. It isn't right, they whisper, weep, shout; what has been done to them is not right. They are *not* inferior. They do not deserve it. And so it is the society that must change. There can be peace this way, too, but not before conflict.

No one reaches this place without a false start or two.

When Alabaster was a young man, he loved easily and casually. Oh, he was angry, even then; of course he was. Even children notice when they are not treated fairly. He had chosen to cooperate, however, for the time being.

He met a man, a scholar, during a mission he'd been assigned by the Fulcrum. Alabaster's interest was prurient; the scholar was quite handsome, and charmingly shy in response to Alabaster's flirtations. If the scholar hadn't been busy excavating what turned out to be an ancient lore cache, there would be nothing more to the story. Alabaster would have loved him and left him, perhaps with regret, more likely with no hard feelings.

Instead, the scholar showed Alabaster his findings. There were more, Alabaster told you, than just three tablets of stonelore, originally. Also, the current Tablet Three was rewritten by Sanze. It was actually rewritten *again* by Sanze; it had been rewritten several times prior to that. The original Tablet Three spoke of Syl Anagist, you see, and how the Moon was lost. This knowledge, for many reasons, has been deemed unacceptable again and again down the millennia since. No one really wants to face the fact that the world is the way it is because some arrogant, self-absorbed people tried to put a leash on the rusting planet. And no one was ready to accept that the solution to the whole mess was simply to let orogenes live and thrive and do what they were born to do.

For Alabaster, the lore cache's knowledge was overwhelming. He fled. It was too much for him, the knowledge that all of this had happened before. That he was the scion of a people abused; that those people's forebears were, too, in their turn; that *the world as he knew it could not function without forcing someone into servitude.* At the time he could see no end to the cycle, no way to demand the impossible of society. So he broke, and he ran.

His Guardian found him, of course, three quartents away from where he was supposed to be and with no inkling of where he was going. Instead of breaking his hand—they used different techniques with highringers like Alabaster—Guardian Leshet took him to a tavern and bought him a drink. He wept into his wine and confessed to her that he couldn't take much more of the world as it was. He had tried to submit, tried to embrace the lies, but *it was not right.*

Leshet soothed him and took him back to the Fulcrum, and for one year they allowed Alabaster time to recover. To accept again the rules and role that had been created for him. He was content during this year, I believe; Antimony believes it, in any case, and she is the one who knew him best during this time. He settled, did what was expected of him, sired three children, and even volunteered to be an instructor for the higher-ringed juniors. He never got the chance to act on this, however, because the Guardians had decided already that Alabaster could not go unpunished for running away. When he met and fell in love with an older ten-ringer named Hessionite—

I have told you already that they use different methods on highringers.

I ran away, too, once. In a way.

* * *

It is the day after our return from Kelenli's tuning mission, and I am different. I look through the nematode window at the garden of purple light, and it is no longer beautiful to me. The winking of the white star-flowers lets me know that some genegineer made them, tying them into the city power network so that they can be fed by a bit of magic. How else to get that winking effect? I see the elegant vinework on the surrounding buildings and I know that somewhere, a biomagest is tabulating how many lammotyrs of magic can be harvested from such beauty. Life is sacred in Syl Anagist—sacred, and lucrative, and *useful*.

So I am thinking this, and I am in a foul mood, when one of the junior conductors comes in. Conductor Stahnyn, she is called, and ordinarily I like her. She's young enough to have not yet picked up the worst of the more experienced conductors' habits. And now as I turn to gaze at her with eyes that Kelenli has opened, I notice something new about her. A bluntness to her features, a smallness to her mouth. Yes, it's much more subtle than Conductor Gallat's icewhite eyes, but here is another Sylanagistine whose ancestors clearly didn't understand the whole point of genocide.

"How are you feeling today, Houwha?" she asks, smiling and

glancing at her noteboard as she comes in. "Up to a medical check?"

"I'm feeling up to a walk," I say. "Let's go out to the garden."

Stahnyn starts, blinking at me. "Houwha, you know that's not possible."

They keep such lax security on us, I have noticed. Sensors to monitor our vitals, cameras to monitor our movements, microphones to record our sounds. Some of the sensors monitor our magic usage—and none of them, not one, can measure even a tenth of what we really do. I would be insulted if I had not just been shown how important it is to them that we be lesser. Lesser creatures don't need better monitoring, do they? Creations of Sylanagistine magestry cannot possibly have abilities that surpass it. Unthinkable! Ridiculous! Don't be foolish.

Fine, I *am* insulted. And I no longer have the patience for Stahnyn's polite patronization.

So I find the lines of magic that run to the cameras, and I entangle them with the lines of magic that run to their own storage crystals, and I loop these together. Now the cameras will display only footage that they filmed over the last few hours—which mostly consists of me looking out the window and brooding. I do the same to the audio equipment, taking care to erase that last exchange between me and Stahnyn. I do all of this with barely a flick of my will, because I was designed to affect machines the size of skyscrapers; cameras are nothing. I use more magic reaching for the others to tell a joke.

The others sess what I am doing, however. Bimniwha gets a taste of my mood and immediately alerts the others—because I am the nice one, usually. I'm the one who, until recently, believed in Geoarcanity. Usually Remwha is the resentful one. But right now Remwha is coldly silent, stewing on what we have learned. Gaewha is quiet, too, in despair, trying to fathom how to demand the impossible. Dushwha is hugging themselves for comfort and Salewha is sleeping too much. Bimniwha's alert falls on weary, frustrated, self-absorbed ears, and goes ignored.

Meanwhile, Stahnyn's smile has begun to falter, as she only now realizes I'm serious. She shifts her stance, putting hands on her hips. "Houwha, this isn't funny. I understand you got the chance to leave the other day—"

I have considered the most efficient way to shut her up. "Does Conductor Gallat know that you find him attractive?"

Stahnyn freezes, eyes going wide and round. Brown eyes in her case, but she likes icewhite. I've seen how she looks at Gallat, though I never much cared before. I don't really care now. But I imagine that finding Niess eyes attractive is a taboo thing in Syl Anagist, and neither Gallat nor Stahnyn can afford to be accused of that particular perversion. Gallat would fire Stahnyn at the first whisper of it—even a whisper from me.

I go over to her. She draws back a little, frowning at my forwardness. We do not assert ourselves, we constructs. We tools. My behavior is anomalous in a way that she should report, but that isn't what has her so worried. "No one heard me say that," I tell her, very gently. "No one can see what's happening in this room right now. Relax."

Her bottom lip trembles, just a little, before she speaks. I feel bad, just a little, for having disturbed her so. She says, "You can't get far. Th-there's a vitamin deficiency... You and the others were built that way. Without special food—the food we serve you—you'll die in just a few days."

It only now occurs to me that Stahnyn thinks I mean to run away.

It only now occurs to me *to* run away.

What the conductor has just told me isn't an insurmountable hurdle. Easy enough to steal food to take with me, though I would die when it ran out. My life would be short regardless. But the thing that truly troubles me is that I have nowhere to go. All the world is Syl Anagist.

"The garden," I repeat, at last. This will be my grand adventure, my escape. I consider laughing, but the habit of appearing emotionless keeps me from doing so. I don't really want to go anywhere, to be honest. I just want to feel like I have some control over my life, if only for a few moments. "I want to see the garden for five minutes. That's all."

Stahnyn shifts from foot to foot, visibly miserable. "I could lose my position for this, especially if any of the senior conductors see. I could be *imprisoned*."

"Perhaps they will give you a nice window overlooking a garden," I suggest. She winces.

And then, because I have left her no choice, she leads me out of my cell and downstairs, and outside.

The garden of purple flowers looks strange from this angle, I find, and it is an altogether different thing to smell the starflowers up close. They smell strange—oddly sweet, almost sugary, with a hint of fermentation underneath where some of the older flowers have wilted or been crushed. Stahnyn is fidgety, looking around too much, while I stroll slowly, wishing I did not need her beside me. But this is fact: I cannot simply wander the grounds of the compound alone. If guards or attendants or other conductors see us, they will think Stahnyn is on official business, and not question me . . . if she will only be still.

But then I stop abruptly, behind a lilting spider tree. Stahnyn stops as well, frowning and plainly wondering what's happening—and then she, too, sees what I have seen, and freezes.

Up ahead, Kelenli has come out of the compound to stand between two curling bushes, beneath a white rose arch. Conductor Gallat has followed her out. She stands with her arms folded. He's behind her, shouting at her back. We aren't close enough for me to hear what he's saying, though his angry tone is indisputable. Their bodies, however, are a story as clear as strata.

"Oh, no," mutters Stahnyn. "No, no, no. We should—"

"Still," I murmur. I mean to say *be* still, but she quiets anyway, so at least I got the point across.

And then we stand there, watching Gallat and Kelenli fight. I can't hear her voice at all, and it occurs to me that she *cannot* raise her voice to him; it isn't safe. But when he grabs her arm and yanks her around to face him, she automatically claps a hand over her belly. The hand on the belly is a quick thing. Gallat lets go at once, seemingly surprised by her reaction and his own violence, and she moves the hand smoothly back to her side. I don't think he noticed. They resume arguing, and this time Gallat spreads his hands as if offering something. There is pleading in his posture, but I notice how stiff his back is. He begs—but he thinks he shouldn't have to. I can tell that when begging fails, he will resort to other tactics.

I close my eyes, aching as I finally, finally, understand. Kelenli is one of us in every way that matters, and she always has been.

Slowly, though, she unbends. Ducks her head, pretends reluctant capitulation, says something back. It isn't real. The earth reverberates with her anger and fear and unwillingness. Still, some of the stiffness goes out of Gallat's back. He smiles, gestures more broadly. Comes back to her, takes her by the arms, speaks to her gently. I marvel that she has disarmed his anger so effectively. It's as if he doesn't see the way her eyes drift away while he's talking, or how she does not reciprocate when he pulls her closer. She smiles at something he says, but even from fifty feet away I can see that it is a performance. Surely he can see it, too? But I am also beginning to understand that people believe what they want to believe, not what is actually there to be seen and touched and sessed.

So, mollified, he turns to leave—thankfully via a different path out of the garden than the one Stahnyn and I currently lurk upon. His posture has changed completely; he's visibly in a better mood. I should be glad for that, shouldn't I? Gallat heads the project. When he's happy, we are all safer.

Kelenli stands gazing after him until he is gone. Then her head turns and she looks right at me. Stahnyn makes a choked sound beside me, but she is a fool. Of course Kelenli will not report us. Why would she? Her performance was never for Gallat.

Then she, too, leaves the garden, following Gallat.

It was a last lesson. The one I needed most, I think. I tell Stahnyn to take me back to my cell, and she practically moans with relief. When I'm back and I have unwoven the magics of the monitoring equipment, and sent Stahnyn on her way with a gentle reminder not to be a fool, I lie down on my couch to ponder this new knowledge. It sits in me, an ember causing everything around it to smolder and smoke.

* * *

And then, several nights after we return from Kelenli's tuning mission, the ember catches fire in all of us.

It is the first time that all of us have come together since the trip. We entwine our presences in a layer of cold coal, which is perhaps fitting as Remwha sends a hiss through all of us like sand grinding amid cracks. It's the sound/feel/sess of the sinklines, the briar patch. It's also an echo of the static emptiness in our network where Tetlewha—and Entiwha, and Arwha, and all the others—once existed.

This is what awaits us when we have given them Geoarcanity, he says.

Gaewha replies, *Yes.*

He hisses again. I have never sessed him so angry. He has spent the days since our trip getting angrier and angrier. But then, so have the rest of us—and now it's time for us to demand the impossible. *We should give them nothing*, he declares, and then I feel his resolve sharpen, turn vicious. *No. We should give back what they have taken.*

Eerie minor-note pulses of impression and action ripple through our network: a plan, at last. A way to create the impossible, if we cannot demand it. The right sort of power surge at just the right moment, after the fragments have been launched but before the Engine has been spent. All the magic stored within the fragments—decades' worth, a civilization's worth, millions of lives' worth—will flood back into the systems of Syl

Anagist. First it will burn out the briar patches and their pitiful crop, letting the dead rest at last. Next the magic will blast through us, the most fragile components of the great machine. We'll die when that happens, but death is better than what they intended for us, so we are content.

Once we're dead, the Plutonic Engine's magic will surge unrestricted down all the conduits of the city, frying them beyond repair. Every node of Syl Anagist will shut down—vehimals dying unless they have backup generators, lights going dark, machinery stilling, all the infinite conveniences of modern magestry erased from furnishings and appliances and cosmetics. Generations of effort spent preparing for Geoarcanity will be lost. The Engine's crystalline fragments will become so many oversized rocks, broken and burnt and powerless.

We need not be as cruel as they. We can instruct the fragments to come down away from the most inhabited areas. We are the monsters they created, and more, but we will be the sort of monsters we wish to be, in death.

And are we agreed, then?

Yes. Remwha, furious.

Yes. Gaewha, sorrowful.

Yes. Bimniwha, resigned.

Yes. Salewha, righteous.

Yes. Dushwha, weary.

And I, heavy as lead, say, *Yes*.

So we are agreed.

Only to myself do I think, *No*, with Kelenli's face in my mind's eye. But sometimes, when the world is hard, love must be harder still.

* * *

Launch Day.

We are brought nourishment—protein with a side of fresh sweet fruit, and a drink that we are told is a popular delicacy: sef, which turns pretty colors when various vitamin supplements are added to it. A special drink for a special day. It's chalky. I don't like it. Then it is time to travel to Zero Site.

Here is how the Plutonic Engine works, briefly and simply.

First we will awaken the fragments, which have sat in their sockets for decades channeling life-energy through each node of Syl Anagist—and storing some of it for later use, including that which was force-fed to them through the briar patches. They have now reached optimum storage and generation, however, each becoming a self-contained arcane engine of its own. Now when we summon them, the fragments will rise from their sockets. We'll join their power together in a stable network and, after bouncing it off a reflector that will amplify and concentrate the magic still further, pour this into the onyx. The onyx will direct this energy straight into the Earth's core, causing an overflow—which the onyx will then shunt into Syl Anagist's hungry conduits. In effect, the Earth will become a massive plutonic engine too, the dynamo that is its core churning forth far more magic than is put into it. From there, the system will become self-perpetuating. Syl Anagist will feed upon the life of the planet itself, forever.

(Ignorance is an inaccurate term for what this was. True, no one thought of the Earth as alive in those days—but we *should* have guessed. Magic is the by-product of life. That there was magic in the Earth to take . . . We should all have guessed.)

Everything we have done, up to now, has been practice. We could never have activated the full Plutonic Engine here on Earth—too many complications involving the obliqueness of angles, signal speed and resistance, the curvature of the hemisphere. So awkwardly round, planets. Our *target* is the Earth, after all; lines of sight, lines of force and attraction. If we stay on the planet, all we can really affect is the Moon.

Which is why Zero Site has never been on Earth.

Thus in the small hours of the morning we are brought to a singular sort of vehimal, doubtless genegineered from grasshopper stock or something similar. It is diamond-winged but also has great carbon-fiber legs, steaming now with coiled, stored power. As the conductors usher us aboard this vehimal, I see other vehimals being made ready. A large party means to come with us to watch the great project conclude at last. I sit where I am told, and all of us are strapped in because the vehimal's thrust can sometimes overcome geomagestric inertial…Hmm. Suffice it to say, the launch can be somewhat alarming. It is nothing compared to plunging into the heart of a living, churning fragment, but I suppose the humans think it a grand, wild thing. The six of us sit, still and cold with purpose as they chatter around us, while the vehimal leaps up to the Moon.

On the Moon is the moonstone—a massive, iridescent white cabochon embedded in the thin gray soil of the place. It is the largest of the fragments, fully as big as a node of Syl Anagist itself; the whole of the Moon is its socket. Arranged around its edges sits a complex of buildings, each sealed against the airless dark, which are not so very different from the buildings we just left. They're just on the Moon. This is Zero Site, where history will be made.

We are led inside, where permanent Zero Site staff line the halls and stare at us in proud admiration, as one admires precision-made instruments. We are led to cradles that look precisely like the cradles used every day for our practices—although this time, each of us is taken to a separate room of the compound. Adjoining each room is the conductors' observation chamber, connected via a clear crystal window. I'm used to being observed while I work—but not used to being brought into the observation room itself, as happens today for the very first time.

There I stand, short and plainly dressed and palpably uncomfortable amid tall people in rich, complex clothing, while Gallat introduces me as "Houwha, our finest tuner." This statement alone proves that either the conductors really have no clue how we function, or that Gallat is nervous and groping for something to say. Perhaps both. Dushwha laughs a cascading microshake—the Moon's strata are thin and dusty and dead, but not much different from the Earth's—while I stand there and mouth pleasant greetings, as I am expected to do. Maybe that's what Gallat really means: I'm the tuner who is best at pretending that he cares about conductor nonsense.

Something catches my attention, though, as the introductions are made and small talk is exchanged and I concentrate on saying correct things at correct times. I turn and notice a stasis column near the back of the room, humming faintly and flickering with its own plutonic energies, generating the field that keeps something within stable. And floating above its cut-crystal surface—

There is a woman in the room who is taller and more elaborately dressed than everyone else. She follows my gaze and says to Gallat, "Do they know about the test bore?"

Gallat twitches and looks at me, then at the stasis column. "No," he says. He doesn't name the woman or give her a title, but his tone is very respectful. "They've been told only what's necessary."

"I would think context is necessary, even with your kind." Gallat bristles at being lumped in with us, but he says nothing in response to it. The woman looks amused. She bends down to peer into my face, although I'm not *that* much shorter than her. "Would you like to know what that artifact is, little tuner?"

I immediately hate her. "Yes, please," I say.

She takes my hand before Gallat can stop her. It isn't uncomfortable. Her skin is dry. She leads me over near the stasis column, so that I can now get a good look at the thing that floats above it.

At first I think that what I'm seeing is nothing more than a spherical lump of iron, hovering a few inches above the stasis column's surface and underlit by its white glow. It *is* only a lump of iron, its surface crazed with slanting, circuitous lines. A meteor fragment? No. I realize the sphere is moving—spinning slowly on a slightly tilted north-south axis. I look at the warning symbols around the column's rim and see markers for extreme heat and pressure, and a caution against breaching the stasis field. Within, the markers say, it has re-created the object's native environment.

No one would do this for a mere lump of iron. I blink, adjust my perception to the sesunal and magical, and draw back quickly as searing white light blazes at and through me. The iron sphere is *full* of magic—concentrated, crackling, overlapping threads upon threads of it, some of them even extending beyond its surface and outward and...away. I can't follow the ones that whitter away beyond the room; they extend beyond my reach. I can see that they stretch off toward the sky, though, for some reason. And written in the jittering threads that I can see...I frown.

"It's angry," I say. And familiar. Where have I seen something like this, this magic, before?

The woman blinks at me. Gallat groans under his breath. "Houwha—"

"No," the woman says, holding up a hand to quell him. She focuses on me again with a gaze that is intent now, and curious. "What did you say, little tuner?"

I face her. She is obviously important. Perhaps I should be afraid, but I'm not. "That thing is angry," I say. "*Furious.* It doesn't want to be here. You took it from somewhere else, didn't you?"

Others in the room have noticed this exchange. Not all of them are conductors, but all of them look at the woman and me in palpable unease and confusion. I hear Gallat holding his breath.

"Yes," she says to me, finally. "We drilled a test bore at one of the Antarctic nodes. Then we sent in probes that took this from the innermost core. It's a sample of the world's own heart." She smiles, proud. "The richness of magic at the core is precisely what will enable Geoarcanity. That test is why we built Corepoint, and the fragments, and you."

I look at the iron sphere again and marvel that she stands so close to it. *It is angry*, I think again, without really knowing why these words come to me. *It will do what it has to do.*

Who? Will do what?

I shake my head, inexplicably annoyed, and turn to Gallat. "Shouldn't we get started?"

The woman laughs, delighted. Gallat glowers at me, but he relaxes fractionally when it becomes obvious that the woman is amused. Still, he says, "Yes, Houwha. I think we should. If you don't mind—"

(He addresses the woman by some title, and some name. I will forget both with the passage of time. In forty thousand years I will remember only the woman's laugh, and the way she considers Gallat no different from us, and how carelessly she stands near an iron sphere that radiates pure malice—and enough magic to destroy every building in Zero Site.

And I will remember how I, too, dismissed every possible warning of what was to come.)

Gallat takes me back into the cradle room, where I am bidden to climb into my wire chair. My limbs are strapped down, which I've never understood because when I'm in the amethyst, I barely notice my body, let alone move it. The sef has made my lips tingle in a way that suggests a stimulant was added. I didn't need it.

I reach for the others, and find them granite-steady with resolve. Yes.

Images appear on the viewing wall before me, displaying the blue sphere of the Earth, each of the other five tuners' cradles, and a shot of Corepoint with the onyx hovering ready above it. The other tuners look back at me from their images. Gallat comes over and makes a show of checking the contact points of the wire chair, which are meant to send measurements to the Biomagestric division. "You're to hold the onyx, today, Houwha."

From another building of Zero Site, I feel Gaewha's small twitch of surprise. We're very attuned to one another today. I say, "Kelenli holds the onyx."

"Not anymore." Gallat keeps his head down as he speaks, unnecessarily reaching over to check my straps, and I remember him reaching the same way to pull Kelenli back to him, in the garden. Ah, I understand, now. All this while he has been afraid to lose her... to us. Afraid to make her just another tool in the eyes of his superiors. Will they let him keep her, after Geoarcanity? Or does he fear that she, too, will be thrown into the briar patch? He must. Why else make such a significant change to our configuration on the most important day in human history?

As if to confirm my guess, he says, "Biomagestry says you now show more than sufficient compatibility to hold the connection for the required length of time."

He's watching me, hoping I won't protest. I realize suddenly that I *can* do so. With so much scrutiny on Gallat's every decision today, important people will notice if I insist that the new configuration is a bad idea. I can, simply by raising my voice, take Kelenli from Gallat. I can destroy him, as he destroyed Tetlewha.

But that's a foolish, pointless thought, because how can I exercise my power over *him* without hurting *her*? I'm going to hurt her enough as it is, when we turn the Plutonic Engine back on itself. She should survive the initial convulsion of magic; even if she's in contact with any of the devices that flux, she has more than enough skill to shunt the feedback away. Then in the aftermath, she'll be just another survivor, made equal in suffering. No one will know what she really is—or her child, if it ends up like her. Like us. We will have set her free . . . to struggle for survival along with everyone else. But that is better than the illusion of safety in a gilded cage, is it not?

Better than you could ever have given her, I think at Gallat.

"All right," I say. He relaxes minutely.

Gallat leaves my chamber and goes back into the observation room with the other conductors. I am alone. I am never alone; the others are with me. The signal comes that we should begin, as the moment seems to hold its breath. We are ready.

First the network.

Attuned as we are, it is easy, pleasurable, to modulate our silverflows and cancel out resistance. Remwha plays yoke, but he hardly needs to goad any of us to resonate higher or lower or to pull at the same pace; we are aligned. We all want this.

Above us, yet easily within our range, the Earth seems to hum, too. Almost like a thing alive. We have been to Corepoint and back, in our early training; we have traveled through the mantle and seen the massive flows of magic that churn naturally up from the iron-nickel core of the planet. To tap that bottomless font will be the greatest feat of human accomplishment, ever. Once, that thought would have made me proud. Now I share this with the others and a *shiverstone micaflake glimmer* of bitter amusement ripples through all of us. They have never believed us human, but we will prove by our actions today that we are more than tools. Even if we aren't human, we are *people*. They will never be able to deny us this again.

Enough frivolity.

First the network, then the fragments of the Engine must be assembled. We reach for the amethyst because it is nearest on the globe. Though we are a world away from it, we know that it utters a low held note, its storage matrix glowing and brimful with energy as we dive, up, into its torrential flow. Already it has stopped suckling the last dregs from the briar patch at its roots, becoming a closed system in itself; now it feels almost alive. As we coax it from quiescence into resonant activity, it begins to pulse, and then finally to shimmer in patterns that emulate life, like the firing of neurotransmitters or the contractions of peristalsis. *Is* it alive? I wonder this for the first time, a question triggered by Kelenli's lessons. It is a thing of high-state matter, but it coexists simultaneously with a thing of high-state magic made in its image—and taken from the bodies of people who once laughed and raged and sang. Is there anything left of their will in the amethyst?

If so . . . would the Niess approve of what we, their caricature children, mean to do?

I can spare no more time for such thoughts. The decision has been made.

So we expand this macro-level start-up sequence throughout the network. We sess without sessapinae. We *feel* the change. We know it in our bones—because we are part of this engine, components of humanity's greatest marvel. On Earth, at the heart of every node of Syl Anagist, klaxons echo across the city and warning pylons blaze red warnings that can be seen from far away as one by one, the fragments begin to thrum and shimmer and detach from their sockets. My breath quickens when I, resonant within each, feel the first peeling-away of crystal from rougher stone, the drag as we alight and begin pulsing with the state-change of magic and then begin to rise—

(There is a stutter here, quick and barely noticeable in the heady moment, though glaring through the lens of memory. Some of the fragments hurt us, just a little, when they detach from their sockets. We feel the scrape of metal that should not be there, the scratch of needles against our crystalline skin. We smell a whiff of rust. It's quick pain and quickly forgotten, as with any needle. Only later will we remember, and lament.)

—rise, and hum, and turn. I inhale deeply as the sockets and their surrounding cityscapes fall away below us. Syl Anagist shunts over to backup power systems; those should hold until Geoarcanity. But they are irrelevant, these mundane concerns. I flow, fly, *fall* up into rushing light that is purple or indigo or mauve or gold, the spinel and the topaz and the garnet and the sapphire—so many, so bright! So alive with building power.

(So *alive*, I think again, and this thought sends a shudder through the network, because Gaewha was thinking it, too, and Dushwha, and it is Remwha who takes us to task with a crack like a slipstrike fault: *Fools, we will die if you don't focus!* So I let this thought go.)

And—ah, yes, framed there on-screen, centered in our perception like an eye glaring down at its quarry: the onyx. Positioned, as Kelenli last bade it, above Corepoint.

I am not nervous, I tell myself as I reach for it.

The onyx isn't like the other fragments. Even the moonstone is quiescent by comparison; it is only a mirror, after all. But the onyx is powerful, frightening, the darkest of dark, unknowable. Where the other fragments must be sought and actively engaged, it snatches at my awareness the instant I come near, trying to pull me deeper into its rampant, convecting currents of silver. When I have connected to it before, the onyx has rejected me, as it has done for all the others in turn. The finest magests in Syl Anagist could not fathom why—but now, when I offer myself and the onyx claims me, suddenly I know. *The onyx is alive.* What is just a question in the other fragments has been answered here: It *sesses* me. It learns me, touching me with a presence that is suddenly undeniable.

And in the very moment when I realize this and have enough time to wonder fearfully what these presences think of me, their pathetic descendant made from the fusion of their genes with their destroyers' hate—

—I perceive at last a secret of magestry that even the Niess simply accepted rather than understood. This is magic, after all, not science. There will always be parts of it that no one can fathom. But now I know: Put enough magic into something nonliving, and it becomes alive. Put enough lives into a storage matrix, and they retain a collective will, of sorts. They *remember* horror and atrocity, with whatever is left of them—their souls, if you like.

So the onyx yields to me now because, it senses at last, I too have known pain. My eyes have been opened to my own exploitation and degradation. I am afraid, of course, and angry, and hurt, but the onyx does not scorn these feelings within me. It seeks something else, however, something more, and finally finds what it seeks nestled in a little burning knot behind my heart: determination. I have committed myself to making, of all this wrongness, something right.

That's what the onyx wants. *Justice.* And because I want that too—

I open my eyes in flesh. "I've engaged the control cabochon," I report for the conductors.

"Confirmed," says Gallat, looking at the screen where Biomagestry monitors our neuroarcanic connections. Applause breaks out among our observers, and I feel sudden contempt for them. Their clumsy instruments and their weak, simple sessapinae have finally told them what is as obvious to us as breathing. The Plutonic Engine is up and running.

Now that the fragments have all launched, each one rising to hum and flicker and hover over two hundred and fifty-six city-nodes and seismically energetic points, we begin the ramp-up sequence. Among the fragments, the pale-colored flow buffers ignite first, then we upcycle the deeper jewel tones of the generators. The onyx acknowledges sequence initialization with a single, heavy blat of sound that sends ripples across the Hemispheric Ocean.

My skin is tight, my heart a-thud. Somewhere, in another existence, I have clenched my fists. *We* have done so, across the paltry separation of six different bodies and two hundred and fifty-six arms and legs and one great black pulsing heart. My mouth opens (our mouths open) as the onyx aligns itself perfectly to tap the ceaseless churn of earth-magic where the core lies exposed far, far below. Here is the moment that we were made for.

Now, we are meant to say. This, here, *connect*, and we will lock the raw magical flows of the planet into an endless cycle of service to humankind.

Because this is what the Sylanagistines truly made us for: to affirm a philosophy. Life is sacred in Syl Anagist—as it should be, for the city burns life as the fuel for its glory. The Niess were not the first people chewed up in its maw, just the latest and cruelest extermination of many. But for a society built on exploitation, there is no greater threat than having no one left to oppress. And now, if nothing else is done, Syl Anagist must again find a way to fission its people into subgroupings and create reasons for conflict among them. There's not enough magic to be had just from plants and genegineered fauna; *someone* must suffer, if the rest are to enjoy luxury.

Better the earth, Syl Anagist reasons. Better to enslave a great inanimate object that cannot feel pain and will not object. Better Geoarcanity. But this reasoning is still flawed, because Syl Anagist is ultimately unsustainable. It is parasitic; its hunger for magic grows with every drop it devours. The Earth's core is not limitless. Eventually, if it takes fifty thousand years, that resource will be exhausted, too. Then everything dies.

What we are doing is pointless and Geoarcanity is a lie. And if we help Syl Anagist further down this path, we will have said, *What was done to us was right and natural and unavoidable.*

No.

So. *Now*, we say instead. This, here, connect: pale fragments to dark, all fragments to the onyx, and the onyx... back to Syl Anagist. We detach the moonstone from the circuit entirely. Now all the power stored in the fragments will blast through the city, and when the Plutonic Engine dies, so will Syl Anagist.

It begins and ends long before the conductors' instruments even register a problem. With the others joined to me, our tune gone silent as we settle and wait for the feedback loop to hit us, I find myself content. It will be good not to die alone.

* * *

But.

But.

Remember. We were not the only ones who chose to fight back that day.

This is a thing I will realize only later, when I visit the ruins of Syl Anagist and look into empty sockets to see iron needles protruding from their walls. This is an enemy I will understand only after I have been humbled and remade at its feet...but I will explain it now, so that you may learn from my suffering.

I spoke to you, not long ago, of a war between the Earth and the life upon its surface. Here is some enemy psychology: The Earth sees no difference between any of us. Orogene, still, Sylanagistine, Niess, future, past—to it, humanity is humanity. And even if others had commanded my birth and development; even if Geoarcanity has been a dream of Syl Anagist since long before even my conductors were born; even if I was just following orders; even if the six of us meant to fight back...the Earth did not care. We were all guilty. All complicit in the crime of attempting to enslave the world itself.

Now, though, having pronounced us all guilty, the Earth handed out sentences. Here, at least, it was somewhat willing to offer credit for intent and good behavior.

This is what I remember, and what I pieced together later, and what I believe. But remember—never forget—that this was only the beginning of the war.

* * *

We perceive the disruption first as a ghost in the machine.

A presence alongside us, *inside* us, intense and intrusive and immense. It slaps the onyx from my grasp before I know what's happening, and silences our startled signals of *What?* and *Something is wrong* and *How did that happen?* with a shockwave of earthtalk as stunning to us as the Rifting will one day be to you.

Hello, little enemies.

In the conductors' observation chamber, alarms finally blare. We are frozen in our wire chairs, shouting without words and being answered by something beyond our comprehension, so Biomagestry only notices a problem when suddenly nine percent of the Plutonic Engine—twenty-seven fragments—goes offline. I do not see Conductor Gallat gasp and exchange a horrified look with the other conductors and their esteemed guests; this is speculation, knowing what I know of him. I imagine that at some point he turns to a console to abort the launch. I also do not see, behind them, the iron sphere pulse and swell and shatter, destroying its stasis field and peppering everyone in the chamber with hot, needle-sharp iron shards. I *do* hear the screaming that follows while the iron shards burn their way up veins and arteries, and the ominous silence afterward, but I have my own problems to deal with in this particular moment.

Remwha, he of the quickest wit, slaps us from our shock with the realization that *something else is controlling the Engine.* No time to wonder who or why. Gaewha perceives how and signals frantically: The twenty-seven "offline" fragments are still active. In fact, they have formed a kind of subnetwork—a spare key. This is how the other presence has managed to dislodge the onyx's control. Now all of the fragments, which generate and contain the bulk of the Plutonic Engine's power, are under hostile foreign control.

I am a proud creature at my core; this is intolerable. The onyx was given to *me* to hold—and so I seize it again and shove it back into the connections that comprise the Engine, dislodging the false control at once. Salewha slams down the shockwaves of magic that this violent disruption causes, lest they ricochet throughout the Engine and touch off a resonance that will—well, we don't actually know what such resonance would do, but it would be bad. I hold on throughout the reverberations of this, my teeth bared back in the real world, listening while my siblings cry out or snarl with me or gasp amid the aftershakes of the initial upheaval. Everything is confusion. In the realm of flesh and blood, the lights of our chambers have gone out, leaving only emergency panels to glow around the edges of the room. The warning klaxons are incessant, and elsewhere in Zero Site I can hear equipment snapping and rattling with the overload that we have put into the system. The conductors, screaming in the observation chamber, cannot help us—not that they ever could. I don't know what's happening, not really. I know only that this is a battle, full of moment-to-moment confusion as all battles are, and from here forth nothing is quite clear—

That strange presence that has attacked us pulls hard against the Plutonic Engine, trying to dislodge our control once more. I shout at it in wordless *geyserboil magmacrack* fury. *Get out of here!* I rage. *Leave us alone!*

You started this, it hisses into the strata, trying again. When this fails, however, it snarls in frustration—and then locks, instead, into those twenty-seven fragments that have gone so mysteriously offline. Dushwha senses the hostile entity's intent and tries to grasp some of the twenty-seven, but the fragments slip through their grasp as if coated with oil. This is true enough, figuratively speaking; something has contaminated these fragments, leaving them fouled and nearly impossible to grasp. We might manage it with concerted effort, one by one—but there is no time. And until then, the enemy holds the twenty-seven.

Stalemate. We still hold the onyx. We hold the other two hundred and twenty-nine fragments, which are ready to fire the feedback pulse that will destroy Syl Anagist—and ourselves. We've postponed that, however, because we cannot leave matters like this. Where did this entity, so angry and phenomenally powerful, come from? What will it do with the obelisks that it holds? Long moments pass in pent silence. I cannot speak for the others, but I, at least, begin to think there will be no further attacks. I have always been such a fool.

Into the silence comes the amused, malicious challenge of our enemy, ground forth in magic and iron and stone.

Burn for me, says Father Earth.

* * *

I must speculate on some of what follows, even after all these ages spent seeking answers.

I can narrate no more because in the moment everything was nigh-instantaneous, and confusing, and devastating. The Earth changes only gradually, until it doesn't. And when it fights back, it does so decisively.

Here is the context. That first test bore that initiated the Geoarcanity project also alerted the Earth to humanity's efforts to take control of it. Over the decades that followed, it studied its enemy and began to understand what we meant to do. Metal was its instrument and ally; never trust metal for this reason. It sent splinters of itself to the surface to examine the fragments in their sockets—for here, at least, was life stored in crystal, comprehensible to an entity of inorganic matter in a way that mere flesh was not. Only gradually did it learn how to take control of individual human lives, though it required the medium of the corestones to do so. We are such small, hard-to-grasp creatures, otherwise. Such insignificant vermin, apart from our unfortunate tendency to sometimes make ourselves dangerously significant. The obelisks, though, were a more useful tool. Easy to turn back on us, like any carelessly held weapon.

Burndown.

Remember Allia? Imagine that disaster times two hundred and fifty-six. Imagine the Stillness perforated at every nodal point and seismically active site, and the ocean, too—hundreds of hot spots and gas pockets and oil reservoirs breached, and the entire plate-tectonic system destabilized. There is no word for such a catastrophe. It would liquefy the surface of the planet, vaporizing the oceans and sterilizing everything from the mantle up. The world, for us and any possible creature that might ever evolve in the future to hurt the Earth, would end. The Earth itself would be fine, however.

We could stop it. If we wanted to.

I will not say we weren't tempted, when faced with the choice between permitting the destruction of a civilization, or of all life on the planet. Syl Anagist's fate was sealed. Make no mistake: We had meant to seal it. The difference between what the

Earth wanted and what we wanted was merely a matter of scale. But *which* is the way the world ends? We tuners would be dead; the distinction mattered little to me in that moment. It's never wise to ask such a question of people who have nothing to lose.

Except. *I* did have something to lose. In those eternal instants, I thought of Kelenli, and her child.

Thus it was that my will took precedence within the network. If you have any doubt, I'll say it plainly now: *I* am the one who chose the way the world ended.

I am the one who took control of the Plutonic Engine. We could not stop Burndown, but we could insert a delay into the sequence and redirect the worst of its energy. After the Earth's tampering, the power was too volatile to simply pour back into Syl Anagist as we'd originally planned; that would have done the Earth's work for us. That much kinetic force had to be expended somewhere. Nowhere on the planet, if I meant for humanity to survive—but here were the Moon and the moonstone, ready and waiting.

I was in a hurry. There was no time to second-guess. The power could not *reflect* from the moonstone, as it was meant to; that would only increase the power of Burndown. Instead, with a snarl as I grabbed the others and forced them to help me—they were willing, just slow—we shattered the moonstone cabochon.

In the next instant, the power struck the broken stone, failed to reflect, and began to chew its way through the Moon. Even with this to mitigate the blow, the force of impact was devastating in itself. More than enough to slam the Moon out of orbit.

The backlash of misusing the Engine this way should have

simply killed us, but the Earth was still there, the ghost in the machine. As we writhed in our death throes, all of Zero Site crumbling apart around us, it took control again.

I have said that it held us responsible for the attempt on its life, and it did—but somehow, perhaps through its years of study, it understood that we were tools of others, not actors of our own volition. Remember, too, that the Earth does not fully understand us. It looks upon human beings and sees short-lived, fragile creatures, puzzlingly detached in substance and awareness from the planet on which their lives depend, who do not understand the harm they tried to do—perhaps *because* they are so short-lived and fragile and detached. And so it chose for us what seemed, to it, a punishment leavened with meaning: It made us part of it. In my wire chair, I screamed as wave upon wave of alchemy worked over me, changing my flesh into raw, living, solidified magic that looks like stone.

We didn't get the worst of it; that was reserved for those who had offended the Earth the most. It used the corestone fragments to take direct control of these most dangerous vermin—but this did not work as it intended. Human will is harder to anticipate than human flesh. They were never meant to continue.

I will not describe the shock and confusion I felt, in those first hours after my change. I will not ever be able to answer the question of how I returned to Earth from the Moon; I remember only a nightmare of endless falling and burning, which may have been delirium. I will not ask you to imagine how it felt to suddenly find oneself alone, and tuneless, after a lifetime spent singing to others like myself. This was justice. I accept it; I admit my crimes. I have sought to make up for them. But...

Well. What's done is done.

In those last moments before we transformed, we did successfully manage to cancel the Burndown command to the two hundred and twenty-nine. Some fragments were shattered by the stress. Others would die over the subsequent millennia, their matrices disrupted by incomprehensible arcane forces. Most went into standby mode, to continue drifting for millennia over a world that no longer needed their power—until, on occasion, one of the fragile creatures below might send a confused, directionless request for access.

We could not stop the Earth's twenty-seven. We did, however, manage to insert a delay into their command lattices: one hundred years. What the tales get wrong is only the timing, you see? One hundred years after Father Earth's child was stolen from him, twenty-seven obelisks did burn down to the planet's core, leaving fiery wounds all over its skin. It was not the cleansing fire that the Earth sought, but it was still the first and worst Fifth Season—what you call the Shattering. Humankind survives because one hundred years is nothing to the Earth, or even to the expanse of human history, but to those who survived the fall of Syl Anagist, it was just time enough to prepare.

The Moon, bleeding debris from a wound through its heart, vanished over a period of days.

And…

I never saw Kelenli, or her child, again. Too ashamed of the monster I'd become, I never sought them out. She lived, though. Now and again I heard the grind and grumble of her stone voice, and those of her several children as they were born. They were not wholly alone; with the last of their magestric technology, the survivors of Syl Anagist decanted a few more tuners and used them to build shelters, contingencies, systems of warning and protection. Those tuners died in time, however, as their usefulness ended, or as others blamed them for the Earth's wrath. Only Kelenli's children, who did not stand out, whose strength hid in plain sight, continued. Only Kelenli's legacy, in the form of the lorists who went from settlement to settlement warning of the coming holocaust and teaching others how to cooperate, adapt, and remember, remains of the Niess.

It all worked, though. You survive. That was my doing, too, isn't it? I did my best. Helped where I could. And now, my love, we have a second chance.

Time for you to end the world again.

* * *

2501: Fault line shift along the Minimal-Maximal: massive. Shockwave swept through half the Nomidlats and Arctics, but stopped at outer edge of Equatorial node network. Food prices rose sharply following year, but famine prevented.

—*Project notes of Yaetr Innovator Dibars*

13

Nassun and Essun, on the dark side of the world

It's sunset when Nassun decides to change the world.

She has spent the day curled beside Schaffa, using his still-ash-flecked old clothes as a pillow, breathing his scent and wishing for things that cannot be. Finally she gets up and very carefully feeds him the last of the vegetable broth she has made. She gives him a lot of water, too. Even after she has dragged the Moon into a collision course, it will take a few days for the Earth to be smashed apart. She doesn't want Schaffa to suffer too much in that time, since she will no longer be around to help him.

(She is such a good child, at her core. Don't be angry with her. She can only make choices within the limited set of her experiences, and it isn't her fault that so many of those experiences have been terrible. Marvel, instead, at how easily she loves, how thoroughly. Love enough to change the world! She learned how to love like this from *somewhere*.)

As she uses a cloth to dab spilled broth from his lips, she reaches up and begins activation of her network. Here at Corepoint, she can do it without even the onyx, but start-up will take time.

"'A commandment is set in stone,'" she tells Schaffa solemnly. His eyes are open again. He blinks, perhaps in reaction to the sound, though she knows this is meaningless.

The words are a thing she read in the strange handwritten book—the one that told her how to use a smaller network of obelisks as a "spare key" to subvert the onyx's power over the Gate. The man who wrote the book was probably crazy, as evidenced by the fact that he apparently loved Nassun's mother long ago. That is strange and wrong and yet somehow unsurprising. As big as the world is, Nassun is beginning to realize it's also really small. The same stories, cycling around and around. The same endings, again and again. The same mistakes eternally repeated.

"Some things *are* too broken to be fixed, Schaffa." Inexplicably, she thinks of Jija. The ache of this silences her for a moment. "I... I can't make anything better. But I can at least make sure the bad things stop." With that, she gets up to leave.

She does not see Schaffa's face turn, like the Moon sliding into shadow, to watch her go.

* * *

It's dawn when you decide to change the world. You're still asleep in the bedroll that Lerna has brought up to the roof of the yellow-X building. You and he spent the night under the water tower, listening to the ever-present rumble of the Rifting and the snap of occasional lightning strikes. Probably should've had sex there one more time, but you didn't think about it and he didn't suggest, so oh well. That's gotten you into enough trouble, anyway. Had no business relying solely on middle age and starvation for birth control.

He watches as you stand and stretch, and it's a thing you'll never fully understand or be comfortable with—the admiration in his gaze. He makes you feel like a better person than you are. And this is what makes you regret, again, endlessly, that you cannot stay to see his child born. Lerna's steady, relentless goodness is a thing that should be preserved in the world, somehow. Alas.

You haven't earned his admiration. But you intend to.

You head downstairs and stop. Last night, in addition to Lerna, you let Tonkee and Hjarka and Ykka know that it was time—that you would leave after breakfast in the morning. You left the question of whether they could come with you or not open and unstated. If they volunteer, it's one thing, but you're not going to ask. What kind of person would you be to pressure them into that kind of danger? They'll be in enough, just like the rest of humanity, as it is.

You weren't counting on finding all of them in the lobby of the yellow-X building as you come downstairs. *All of them* busy tucking away bedrolls and yawning and frying sausages and complaining loudly about somebody drinking up all the rusting tea. Hoa is there, perfectly positioned to see you come downstairs. There's a rather smug smile on his stone lips, but that doesn't surprise you. Danel and Maxixe do, the former up and doing some kind of martial exercises in a corner while the latter dices another potato for the pan—and yes, he's built a campfire in the building lobby, because that's what commless people do sometimes. Some of the windows are broken; the smoke's going out through them. Hjarka and Tonkee are a surprise, too; they're still asleep, curled together in a pile of furs.

But you really, really weren't expecting Ykka to walk in,

with an air of something like her old brashness and with her eye makeup perfectly applied, once again. She looks around the lobby, taking you in along with the rest, and puts her hands on her hips. "Catch you rusters at a bad time?"

"You can't," you blurt. It's hard to talk. Knot in your throat. Ykka especially; you stare at her. Evil Earth, she's wearing her fur vest again. You thought she'd left that behind in Castrima-under. "You can't come. The comm."

Ykka rolls her dramatically decorated eyes. "Well, fuck you, too. But you're right, I'm not coming. Just here to see you off, along with whoever goes with you. I really should be having you killed, since you're effectively ashing yourselves out, but I suppose we can overlook that little technicality for now."

"What, we can't come back?" Tonkee blurts. She's sitting up finally, though at a distinct lean, and with her hair badly askew. Hjarka, muttering imprecations at being awake, has gotten up and handed her a plate of potato hash from the pile Maxixe has already cooked.

Ykka eyes her. "You? You're traveling to an enormous, perfectly preserved obelisk-builder ruin. I'll never see you again. But sure, I suppose you could come back, if Hjarka manages to drag you to your senses. I need *her*, at least."

Maxixe yawns loudly enough to draw everyone's attention. He's naked, which lets you see that he's looking better at last—still nearly skeletal, but that's half the comm these days. He's coughing less, though, and his hair's starting to grow fuller, although so far it's only at that hilarious bottlebrush stage before ashblow hair develops enough weight to flop decently. It's the first time you've seen his leg-stumps unclothed, and you belatedly realize the scars are far too neat to have been done by some commless raider with a hacksaw. Well, that's his story to tell. You say to him, "Don't be stupid."

Maxixe looks mildly annoyed. "I'm not going, no. But I *could* be."

"No, you rusting couldn't," Ykka snaps. "I already told you, we need a Fulcrum rogga here."

He sighs. "Fine. But no reason I can't at least see you off. Now stop asking questions and come get some food." He reaches for his clothes and starts to pull them on. You obediently go over to the fire to eat something. No morning sickness yet; that's a bit of luck.

As you eat, you watch everyone and find yourself overwhelmed, and also a little frustrated. Of course it's touching that they've come like this to say goodbye. You're glad of it; you can't even pretend otherwise. When have you ever left a place this way—openly, nonviolently, amid laughter? It feels...you don't know how it feels. Good? You don't know what to do with that.

You hope more of them decide to stay behind, though. As it is, Hoa's going to be hauling a rusting caravan through the earth.

But when you eye Danel, you blink in surprise. She's cut her hair again; really doesn't seem to like it long. Fresh shaving on the sides, and...black tint, on her lips. Earth knows where she found it, or maybe she made it herself out of charcoal and fat. But it's suddenly hard to see her as the Strongback general she was. Wasn't. It changes things, somehow, to understand that you go to face a fate that an Equatorial lorist wants to record for posterity. Now it's not just a caravan. It's a rusting quest.

The thought pulls a snort-laugh out of you, and everyone

pauses in what they're doing to stare. "Nothing," you say, waving a hand and setting the empty plate aside. "Just . . . shit. Come on, then, whoever's coming."

Someone's brought Lerna his pack, which he dons quietly, watching you. Tonkee curses and starts rushing to get herself together, while Hjarka patiently helps. Danel uses a rag to mop sweat from her face.

You go over to Hoa, who has shaped his expression into one of wry amusement, and stand beside him to sigh at the mess. "Can you bring this many?"

"As long as they remain in contact with me or someone who's touching me, yes."

"Sorry. I wasn't expecting this."

"Weren't you?"

You look at him, but then Tonkee—still chewing something and shouldering her pack with her good arm—grabs his upraised hand, though she pauses to blatantly stare at it in fascination. The moment passes.

"So how's this supposed to work?" Ykka paces the room, watching everyone and folding her arms. She's noticeably more restless than usual. "You get there, grab the Moon, shove it into position, and then what? Will we see any sign of the change?"

"The Rifting will go cold," you say. "That won't change much in the short term because there's too much ash in the air already. This Season will have to play itself out, and it's going to be bad no matter what. The Moon might even make things worse." You can sess it pulling on the world already; yeah, you're pretty sure it'll make things worse. Ykka nods, though. She can sess it, too.

But there's a long-term loose end that you haven't been

able to figure out yourself. "If I can do it, though, restore the Moon…" You shrug helplessly and look at Hoa.

"It opens room for negotiation," he says in his hollow voice. Everyone pauses to stare at him. By the flinches, you can tell who's used to stone eaters and who isn't. "And perhaps, a truce."

Ykka grimaces. "'Perhaps'? So we've gone through all this and you can't even be sure it will stop the Seasons? Evil Earth."

"No," you admit. "But it will stop *this* Season." That much you're sure of. That much, alone, is worth it.

Ykka subsides, but she keeps muttering to herself now and again. This is how you know she wants to go, too—but you're very glad she seems to have talked herself out of it. Castrima needs her. You need to know that Castrima will be here after you're gone.

Finally everyone is ready. You take Hoa's right hand with your left. You've got no other arm to spare for Lerna, so he wraps an arm around your waist; when you glance at him he nods, steady, determined. On Hoa's other side are Tonkee and Hjarka and Danel, chain-linked hand to hand.

"This is going to blow, isn't it?" Hjarka asks. She alone looks nervous, of the set. Danel's radiating calm, at peace with herself at last. Tonkee's so excited she can't stop grinning. Lerna's just leaning on you, rock-steady the way he always is.

"Probably!" Tonkee says, bouncing a little.

"This seems like a spectacularly bad idea," Ykka says. She's leaned against a wall of the room, arms folded, watching the group assemble. "Essie's *got* to go, I mean, but the rest of you…" She shakes her head.

"Would you be coming, if you weren't headwoman?" Lerna

asks. It's quiet. He always drops his biggest rocks like that, quietly and out of nowhere.

She scowls and glares at him. Then throws you a look that's wary and maybe a little embarrassed, before she sighs and pushes away from the wall. You saw, though. The lump is back in your throat.

"Hey," you say, before she can flee. "Yeek."

She glares at you. "I *hate* that rusting nickname."

You ignore this. "You told me a while back that you had a stash of seredis. We were supposed to get drunk after I beat the Rennanis army. Remember?"

Ykka blinks, and then a slow smile spreads across her face. "You were in a coma or something. I drank it all myself."

You glare at her, surprised to find yourself honestly annoyed. She laughs in your face. So much for tender farewells.

But . . . well. It feels good anyway.

"Close your eyes," Hoa says.

"He's not joking," you add, in warning. You keep yours open, though, as the world goes dark and strange. You feel no fear. You are not alone.

* * *

It's nighttime. Nassun stands on what she thinks of as Corepoint's town green. It isn't; a city built before the Seasons would have no need of such a thing. It's just a place near the enormous hole that is Corepoint's heart. Around the hole are strangely slanted buildings, like the pylons she saw in Syl Anagist—but these ones are huge, stories high and a block wide apiece. She's learned that when she gets too near these buildings, which don't have any doors or windows that she can see, it sets off warnings composed of bright red words and symbols, several feet high apiece, which blaze in the air over the city. Worse are the low, blatting alarm-sounds that echo through the streets—not loud, but insistent, and they make her teeth feel loose and itchy.

(She's looked into the hole, despite all this. It's enormous compared to the one that was in the underground city—many times that one's circumference, so big that it would take her an hour or more to walk all the way around it. Yet for all its grandeur, despite the evidence it offers of feats of geneering long lost to humankind, Nassun cannot bring herself to be impressed by it. The hole feeds no one, provides no shelter against ash or assault. It doesn't even scare her—though that is meaningless. After her journey through the underground city and the core of the world, after losing Schaffa, nothing will ever frighten her again.)

The spot Nassun has found is a perfectly circular patch of ground just beyond the hole's warning radius. It's odd ground, slightly soft to the touch and springy beneath her feet, not like any material she's ever touched before—but here in Corepoint, that sort of experience isn't rare. There's no actual soil in this circle, aside from a bit of windblown stuff piled up along the edges of the circle; a few seagrasses have taken root here, and there's the desiccated, spindly trunk of a dead sapling that did its best before being blown over, many years before. That's all.

A number of stone eaters have appeared around the circle, she notes as she takes up position at its center. No sign of Steel, but there must be twenty or thirty others on street corners or in the street, sitting on stairs, leaning against walls. A few turned their heads or eyes to watch as she passed, but she ignored and ignores them. Perhaps they have come to witness history. Maybe some are like Steel, hoping for an end to their horrifyingly endless existence; maybe the ones who've helped her have done so because of that. Maybe they're just bored. Not the most exciting town, Corepoint.

Nothing matters, right now, except the night sky. And in that sky, the Moon is beginning to rise.

It sits low on the horizon, seemingly bigger than it was the night before and made oblong by the distortions of the air. White and strange and round, it hardly seems worth all the pain and struggle that its absence has symbolized for the world. And yet—it pulls on everything within Nassun that is orogene. It pulls on the whole world.

Time for the world, then, to pull back.

Nassun shuts her eyes. They are all around Corepoint now—the spare key, three by three by three, twenty-seven obelisks that she has spent the past few weeks touching and taming and coaxing into orbit nearby. She can still feel the sapphire, but it is far away and not in sight; she can't use it, and it would take months to arrive if she summoned it. These others will do, though. It's strange to see so many of the things in the sky all together, after a lifetime with only one—or no—obelisks in sight at any given time. Stranger to feel them all connected to her, thrumming at slightly different speeds, their wells of power each at slightly different depths. The darker ones are deeper. No telling why, but it is a noticeable difference.

Nassun lifts her hands, splaying her fingers in unconscious imitation of her mother. Very carefully, she begins connecting each of the twenty-seven obelisks—one to one, then those to two apiece, then others. She is compelled by lines of sight, lines of force, strange instincts that demand mathematical relationships she does not understand. Each obelisk supports the forming lattice, rather than disrupting or canceling it out. It's like putting horses in harness, sort of, when you've got one with a naturally quick gait and another that plods along. This is yoking twenty-seven high-strung racehorses... but the principle is the same.

And it is beautiful, the moment when all of the flows stop fighting Nassun and shift into lockstep. She inhales, smiling in spite of herself, feeling pleasure again for the first time since Father Earth destroyed Schaffa. It should be scary, shouldn't it? So much power. It isn't, though. She falls up through torrents of gray or green or mauve or clear white; parts of her that she has never known the words for move and adjust in a dance of twenty-seven parts. Oh, it is so lovely! If only Schaffa could—

Wait.

Something makes the hairs on the back of Nassun's neck prickle. Dangerous to lose concentration now, so she forces herself to methodically touch each obelisk in turn and soothe it back into something like an idle state. They mostly tolerate this, though the opal bucks a little and she has to force it into quiescence. When all are finally stable, though, she cautiously opens her eyes and looks around.

At first the black-and-white moonlit streets are as before: silent and still, despite the crowd of stone eaters that has assembled to watch her work. (In Corepoint, it is easy to feel alone in a crowd.) Then she spies... movement. Something—some*one*—lurching from one shadow to another.

Startled, Nassun takes a step toward that moving figure. "H-hello?"

The figure staggers toward some kind of small pillar whose purpose Nassun has never understood, though there seems to be one on every other corner of the city. Nearly falling as it grabs the pillar for support, the figure twitches and looks up at the sound of her voice. Icewhite eyes spear at Nassun from the shadows.

Schaffa.

Awake. Moving.

Without thinking, Nassun begins to trot, then run after him. Her heart is in her mouth. She's heard people say things like that and thought nothing of it before—just poetry, just silliness—but now she knows what it means as her mouth goes so dry that she can feel her own pulse through her tongue. Her eyes blur. "Schaffa!"

He's thirty, forty feet away, near one of the pylon buildings that surround Corepoint's hole. Close enough to recognize her—and yet there is nothing in his gaze that seems to know who she is. Quite the contrary; he blinks, and then smiles in a slow, cold way that makes her stumble to a halt in deep, skin-twitching unease.

"Sch-Schaffa?" she says again. Her voice is very thin in the silence.

"Hello, little enemy," Schaffa says, in a voice that reverberates through Corepoint and the mountain below it and the ocean for a thousand miles around.

Then he turns to the pylon building behind him. A high, narrow opening appears at his touch; he stagger-stumbles through. It vanishes behind him in an instant.

Nassun screams and flings herself after him.

* * *

You are deep in the lower mantle, halfway through the world, when you sense the activation of part of the Obelisk Gate.

Or so your mind interprets it, at first, until you master your alarm and reach forth to confirm what you're feeling. It's hard. Here in the deep earth, there is so *much* magic; trying to sift through it for whatever is happening on the surface is like trying to hear a distant creek over a hundred thundering waterfalls nearby. It's worse the deeper Hoa takes you, until finally you have to "close your eyes" and stop perceiving magic entirely—because there's something immense nearby that is "blinding" you with its brightness. It is as if there's a sun underground, silver-white and swirling with an unbelievably intense concentration of magic… but you can also feel Hoa skirting wide around this sun, even though that means the overall journey has taken longer than absolutely necessary. You'll have to ask him why later.

You can't see much besides churning red here in the depths. How fast are you going? Without referents, it's impossible to tell. Hoa is an intermittent shadow in the redness beside you, shimmering on the rare occasions when you catch a glimpse of him—but then, you're probably shimmering, too. He isn't pushing through the earth, but becoming part of it and transiting the particles of himself around its particles, becoming a waveform that you can sess like sound or light or heat. Disturbing enough if you don't think about the fact that he's doing it to you, too. You can't feel anything like this, except a hint of pressure from his hand, and the suggestion of tension from Lerna's arm. There's no sound other than an omnipresent rumble, no smell of sulfur or anything else. You don't know if you're breathing, and you don't feel the need for air.

But the distant awakening of multiple obelisks panics you, nearly makes you try to pull away from Hoa so you can concentrate, even though—stupid—that would not just kill you but *annihilate* you, turning you to ash and then vaporizing the ashes and then setting the vapor on fire. "Nassun!" you cry, or try to cry, but words are lost in the deep roar. There is no one to hear your cry.

Except. There is.

Something shifts around you—or, you realize belatedly, you are shifting relative to it. It isn't something you think about until it happens again, and you think you feel Lerna jerk against your side. Then it finally occurs to you to look at the silver wisps of your companions' bodies, which at least you can make out against the dense red material of the earth around you.

There is a human-shaped blaze linked to your hand, heavy as a mountain upon your perception as it forges swiftly upward: Hoa. He is moving oddly, however, periodically shifting to one side or another; that's what you perceived before. Beside Hoa are faint shimmers, delicately etched. One has a palpable interruption in the silverflow of one arm; that has to be Tonkee. You cannot distinguish Hjarka from Danel because you can't see hair or relative size or anything so detailed as teeth. Only knowing that Lerna is closer to you makes him distinct. And beyond Lerna—

Something flashes past, mountain-heavy and magic-bright, human shaped but not human. And not Hoa.

Another flash. Something streaks on a perpendicular trajectory, intercepting and driving it away, but there are more. Hoa lunges aside again, and a new flash misses. But it's close. Lerna seems to twitch beside you. Can he see it, too?

You really hope not, because now you understand what's happening. Hoa is *dodging.* And you can do nothing, nothing, but trust Hoa to keep you safe from the stone eaters who are *trying to rip you away from him.*

No. It's hard to concentrate when you're this afraid—when you've been merged into the high-pressure semisolid rock of the planet's mantle, and when everyone you love will die in slow horror should you fail in your quest, and when you're surrounded by currents of magic that are so much more powerful than anything you've ever seen, and when you're under attack by murderous stone eaters. But. You did not spend your childhood learning to perform under the threat of death for nothing.

Mere threads of magic aren't enough to stop stone eaters. The earth's winding rivers of the stuff are all you have to hand. Reaching for one feels like plunging your awareness into a lava tube, and for an instant you're distracted by wondering whether this is what it will feel like if Hoa lets go—a flash of terrible heat and pain, and then oblivion. You push that aside. A memory comes to you. Meov. Driving a wedge of ice into a cliff face, shearing it off at just the precise time to smash a ship full of Guardians—

You shape your will into a wedge and splint it into the nearest magic torrent, a great crackling, wending coil of a thing. It works, but your aim is wild; magic sprays everywhere, and Hoa must dodge again, this time from your efforts. Fuck! You try again, concentrating this time, letting your thoughts loosen. You're already in the earth, red and hot instead of dark and warm, but how is this any different? You're still in the crucible, just literally instead of a symbolic mosaic. You need to drive your wedge in *here* and aim it *there* as another flash of person-shaped mountain starts to pace you and darts in for the kill—

—just as you shunt a stream of purest, brightest silver directly into its path. It doesn't hit. You're still not good at aiming. You glimpse the stone eater stop short, however, as the magic all but blazes past its nose. Here in the deep red it is impossible to see expressions, but you imagine that the creature is surprised, maybe even alarmed. You hope it is.

"Next one's for you, bastard cannibalson ruster!" you try to shout, but you are no longer in a purely physical space. Sound and air are extraneous. You *imagine* the words, then, and hope the ruster in question gets the gist.

You do not imagine, however, the fact that the flitting, fleeting glimpses of stone eaters stop. Hoa keeps going, but there are no more attacks. Well, then. It's good to be of some use.

He's rising faster now that he is unimpeded. Your sessapinae start to perceive depth as a rational, calculable thing again. The deep red turns deep brown, then cools to deep black. And then—

Air. Light. Solidity. You become *real* again, flesh and blood unadulterated by other matter, upon a road between strange, smooth buildings, tall as obelisks beneath a night sky. The return of sensation is stunning, profound—but nothing compared to the absolute shock you feel when you look up.

Because you have spent the past two years beneath a sky of variable ash, and until now you had no idea that the Moon had come.

It is an icewhite eye against the black, an ill omen writ vast and terrifying upon the tapestry of stars. You can see what it is, even without sessing it—a giant round rock. Deceptively small against the expanse of the sky; you think you'll need the obelisks to sess it completely, but you can see on its surface things that might be craters. You've traveled across craters. The craters on the Moon are big enough to see from here, big enough to take *years* to cross on foot, and that tells you the whole thing is incomprehensibly huge.

"Fuck," says Danel, which makes you drag your eyes from the sky. She's on her hands and knees, as if clinging to the ground and grateful for its solidity. Maybe she's regretting her choice of duty now, or maybe she just didn't understand before this that being a lorist could be fully as awful and dangerous as being a general. "Fuck! Fuck."

"That's it, then." Tonkee. She's staring up at the Moon, too.

You turn to see Lerna's reaction, and—

Lerna. The space beside you, where he held on to you, is empty.

"I didn't expect the attack," Hoa says. You can't turn to him. Can't turn away from the *empty space* where Lerna should be. Hoa's voice is its usual inflectionless, hollow tenor—but is he shaken? Shocked? You don't want him to be shocked. You want him to say something like, *But of course I was able to keep everyone safe, Lerna is just over there, don't worry.*

Instead he says, "I should have guessed. The factions that don't want peace..." He trails off. Falls silent, just like an ordinary person who is at a loss for words.

"Lerna." That last jolt. The one you thought was a near miss.

It isn't what should have happened. You're the one nobly sacrificing yourself for the future of the world. *He* was supposed to survive this.

"What about him?" That's Hjarka, who's standing but bent

over with hands on her knees, as if she's thinking about throwing up. Tonkee's rubbing the small of her back as if this will somehow help, but Hjarka's attention is on you. She's frowning, and you see the moment when she realizes what you're talking about, and her expression melts into shock.

You feel...numb. Not the usual non-feeling that comes of you being halfway to a statue. This is different. This is—

"I didn't even think I loved him," you murmur.

Hjarka winces, but then makes herself straighten and take a deep breath. "All of us knew this might be a one-way trip."

You shake your head in...confusion? "He's...he *was*... so much younger than me." You expected him to outlive you. That's how it was *supposed* to work. You're supposed to die feeling guilty for leaving him behind and killing his unborn child. He's supposed to—

"*Hey*." Hjarka's voice sharpens. You know that look on her face now, though. It's a Leadership look, or one reminding you that you are the leader here. But that's right, isn't it? You're the one who's running this little expedition. You're the one who didn't make Lerna, or any of them, stay home. You're the one who didn't have the courage to do this by yourself the way you damn well should have, if you really didn't want them hurt. Lerna's death is on you, not Hoa.

You look away from them and involuntarily reach for the stump of your arm. This is irrational. You're expecting battle wounds, scorch marks, something else to show that Lerna was lost. But it's fine. You're fine. You look back at the others; they're all fine, too, because battles with stone eaters aren't things that anyone walks away from with mere flesh wounds.

"It's *prewar.*" While you stand there bereft, Tonkee has half turned away from Hjarka, which is a problem because Hjarka's currently leaning on her. Hjarka grumbles and hooks an arm around Tonkee's neck to keep her in place. Tonkee doesn't seem to notice, so wide are her eyes as she looks around. "Evil, eating Earth, look at this place. Completely intact! Not hidden at all, no defensive structuring or camouflage, but then not nearly enough green space to make this place self-sufficient..." She blinks. "They would've needed regular supply shipments to survive. The place *isn't built for survival.* That means it's from before the Enemy!" She blinks. "The people here must have come from the Stillness. Maybe there's some means of transportation around here that we haven't seen yet." She subsides into thought, muttering to herself as she crouches to finger the substance of the ground.

You don't care. But you don't have time to mourn Lerna or hate yourself, not now. Hjarka's right. You have a job to do.

And you've seen the other things in the sky besides the Moon—the dozens of obelisks that hover so close, so low, their energy pent and not a single one of them acknowledging your touch when you reach for them. They aren't yours. But although they've been primed and readied, yoked to one another in a way that you immediately recognize as Bad News, they're not doing anything. Something's put them on hold.

Focus. You clear your throat. "Hoa, where is she?"

When you glance at him, you see he's adopted a new stance: expression blank, body facing slightly south and east. You follow his gaze, and see something that at first awes you: a bank of buildings, six or seven stories high that you can see, wedge-shaped and blank of feature. It's easy to tell that they form a ring, and it's easy to guess what's at the heart of that ring, even though you can't see it because of the angle of the buildings. Alabaster told you, though, didn't he? *The city exists to contain the hole.*

Your throat locks your breath.

"No," Hoa says. Okay. You make yourself breathe. She's not in the hole.

"Where, then?"

Hoa turns to look at you. He does this slowly. His eyes are wide. "Essun... she's gone into Warrant."

* * *

As Corepoint above, so Warrant below.

Nassun runs through obsidian-carved corridors, close and low ceilinged and claustrophobic. It's warm down here—not oppressively so, but the warmth is close and omnipresent. The warmth of the volcano, radiating up through the old stone from its heart. She can sess echoes of what was done to create this place, because it was orogeny, not magic, though a more precise and powerful orogeny than anything she's ever seen. She doesn't care about any of that, though. She needs to find Schaffa.

The corridors are empty, lit above by more of the strange rectangular lights that she saw in the underground city. Nothing else about this place looks like that place. The underground city felt leisurely in its design. There are hints of beauty in the way the station was built that suggest it was developed gradually, piece by piece, with time for contemplation between each phase of construction. Warrant is dark, utilitarian. As Nassun runs down sloping ramps, past conference rooms, classrooms, mess halls, lounges, she sees that all of them are empty. This facility's corridors were beaten and clawed out of the shield volcano over a period of days or weeks—hurriedly, though it isn't clear why. Nassun can tell the hurried nature of the place, somehow, to her own amazement. Fear has soaked into the walls.

But none of that matters. Schaffa is here, somewhere. Schaffa, who's barely moved for weeks and yet is now somehow running, his body driven by something other than his own mind. Nassun tracks the silver of him, amazed that he's managed to get so far in the moments that it took her to try to reopen the door he used and then, when it would not open for her, to use the silver to rip it open. But now he is up ahead and—

—so are others. She stops for a moment, panting, suddenly uneasy. Many of them. Dozens . . . no. Hundreds. And all are like Schaffa, their silver thinner, stranger, and also bolstered from elsewhere.

Guardians. This, then, is where they go during Seasons . . . but Schaffa has said they will kill him because he is "contaminated."

They will not. She clenches her fists.

(It does not occur to her that they will kill her, too. Rather, it does, but *They will not* looms larger in the scope of her reality.)

When Nassun runs through a door at the top of a short stair, however, the close corridor suddenly opens out into a narrow but very long high-ceilinged chamber. It's high enough that its ceiling is nearly lost in shadow, and its length stretches farther than her eye can see. And all along the walls of this chamber, in neat rows that stack up to the ceiling, there are dozens—hundreds—of strange, square holes. She is reminded of the chambers in a wasp's nest, except the shape is wrong.

And in every one of them is a body.

Schaffa isn't far ahead. Somewhere in this room, no longer moving forward. Nassun stops too, apprehension finally overwhelming her driving need to find Schaffa. The silence makes her skin prickle. She cannot help fear. The analogy of the wasp's nest has stayed with her, and on some level she fears looking into the cells to find a grub staring back at her, perhaps atop the corpse of some creature (person) it has parasitized.

Inadvertently, she looks into the nearest cell. It's barely wider than the shoulders of the man within, who seems to be asleep. He's youngish, gray-haired, a Midlatter, wearing the burgundy uniform that Nassun has heard of but never seen. He's breathing, although slowly. The woman in the cell beside him is wearing the same uniform, though she's completely different in every other way: an Eastcoaster with completely black skin, hair that has been braided along her scalp in intricate patterns, and wine-dark lips. There is the slightest of smiles on those lips—as if, even in sleep, she cannot lose the habit of it.

Asleep, and more than asleep. Nassun follows the silver in the people in the cells, feeling out their nerves and circulation, and understands then that each is in something like a coma. She thinks maybe normal comas aren't like this, though. None of these people seems to be hurt or sick. And within each Guardian, there is that shard of corestone—quiescent here, instead of angrily flaring like the one in Schaffa. Strangely, the silver threads in each Guardian are reaching out to the ones around them. Networking together. Bolstering each other, maybe? Charging one another to perform some sort of work, the way a network of obelisks does? She cannot guess.

(They were never meant to continue.)

But then, from the center of the vaulted room, perhaps a hundred feet farther in, she hears a sharp mechanical whirr.

She jumps and stumbles away from the cells, darting a quick, frightened look around to see if the noise has awakened any of the cells' occupants. They don't stir. She swallows and calls, softly, "Schaffa?"

Her answer, echoing through the high chamber, is a low, familiar groan.

Nassun stumbles forward, her breath catching. It's him. Down the middle of the strange chamber stand contraptions, arranged in rows. Each consists of a chair attached to a complex arrangement of silver wire in loops and spars; she's never seen anything like it. (You have.) Each contraption seems big enough to hold one person, but they're all empty. And—Nassun leans closer for a better look, then shivers—each rests against a stone pillar that holds an obscenely complicated mechanism. It's impossible not to notice the tiny scalpels, the delicate forcepslike attachments of varying sizes, and other instruments clearly meant for cutting and drilling...

Somewhere nearby, Schaffa groans. Nassun pushes the cutting things out of her thoughts and hurries down the row—

—to stop in front of the room's lone occupied wire chair.

The chair has been adjusted somehow. Schaffa sits in it, but he is facedown, his body suspended by the wires, his chopped-off hair parting around his neck. The mechanism behind the chair has come alive, extending up and over his body in a way that feels predatory to her—but it is already retracting as she approaches. The bloodied instruments disappear into the mechanism; she hears more faint whirring sounds. Cleaning, maybe.

One tiny, tweezer-like attachment remains, however, holding up a prize that still glistens, faintly, with Schaffa's blood. A little metal shard, irregular and dark.

Hello, little enemy.

Schaffa isn't moving. Nassun stares at his body, shaking. She cannot bring herself to shift her perception back to the silver threads, back to *magic*, to see if he is alive. The bloody wound high on the back of his neck has been neatly stitched, right over the other old scar that she has always wondered about. It's still bleeding, but it's clear the wound was inflicted quickly and sealed nearly as fast.

Like a child willing the monster under the bed to not exist, Nassun wills Schaffa's back and sides to move.

They do, as he draws in a breath. "N-Nassun," he croaks.

"Schaffa! Schaffa." She flings herself to her knees and scooches forward to look at his face from underneath the wire contraption, heedless of the blood still dripping down the sides of his neck and face. His eyes, his beautiful white eyes, are half-open—and they are *him* this time! She sees that and bursts into tears herself. "Schaffa? Are you okay? Are you really okay?"

His speech is slow, slurred. Nassun will not think about why. "Nassun. I." Even more slowly, his expression shifts, a seaquake in his brows sending a tsunami of slow realization across the rest. His eyes widen. "There's. No pain."

She touches his face. "The—the thing is out of you, Schaffa. That metal thing."

He shuts his eyes and her belly clenches, but then the furrow vanishes from his brow. He smiles again—and for the first time since Nassun met him, there is nothing of tension or falsehood in it. He isn't smiling to ease his pain or others' fears. His mouth opens. She can see all his teeth, he's *laughing* although weakly, he's weeping, too, with relief and joy, and it is the most beautiful thing she's ever seen. She cups his face, mindful of the wound on the back of his neck, and presses her forehead against his, shaking with his soft laughter. She loves him. She just loves him so much.

And because she is touching him, because she loves him, because she is so attuned to his needs and his pain and making him happy, her perception slips into the silver. She doesn't mean for it to. She just wants to use her eyes to savor the sight of him looking back at her, and her hands to touch his skin, and her ears to hear his voice.

But she is orogene, and she can no longer shut off the sesuna than she can sight or sound or touch. Which is why her smile falters, and her joy vanishes, because the instant she sees how the network of threads within him is already beginning to fade, she can no longer deny that he is dying.

It's slow. He could last a few weeks or months, perhaps as much as a year, with what's left. But where every other living thing churns forth its own silver almost by accident, where it flows and stutters and gums up the works between cells, there is nothing between his cells but a trickle. What's left in him mostly runs along his nervous system, and she can see a glaring, gaping emptiness at what used to be the core of his silver network, in his sessapinae. Without his corestone, as he warned her, he will not last long.

Schaffa's eyes have drifted shut. He's asleep, exhausted by pushing his weakened body through the streets. But he isn't the one who did that, is he? Nassun gets to her feet, shaking, keeping her hands on Schaffa's shoulders. His heavy head presses against her chest. She stares at the little metal shard bitterly, understanding at once why Father Earth did this to him.

It knows she means to bring the Moon down, and that this will create a cataclysm far worse than the Shattering. It wants to live. It knows Nassun loves Schaffa, and that until now she has seen destroying the world as the only way to give him peace. Now, however, it has remade Schaffa, offering him to Nassun as a kind of living ultimatum.

Now he is free, the Earth taunts by this wordless gesture. *Now he can have peace without death. And if you want him to live, little enemy, there is only one way.*

Steel never said it couldn't be done, only that it shouldn't. Maybe Steel is wrong. Maybe, as a stone eater, Schaffa won't be alone and sad forever. Steel is mean and awful, which is why no one wants to be with him. But Schaffa is good and kind. Surely he will find someone else to love.

Especially if all the world is stone eaters, too.

Humanity, she decides, is a small price to pay for Schaffa's future.

* * *

Hoa says that Nassun has gone underground, to Warrant where the Guardians lie, and the panic of this is sour in your mouth as you trot around the hole, looking for a way in. You don't dare ask Hoa to simply transport you to her; Gray Man's allies lurk everywhere now, and they will kill you as surely as they did Lerna. Allies of Hoa are present, too; you have a blurry memory of seeing two streaking mountains crash into one another, one driving the other off. But until this business with the Moon is settled, going into the Earth is too dangerous. All of the stone eaters are here, you sess; a thousand human-sized mountains in and underneath Corepoint, some of them watching you run through the streets looking for your daughter. All of their ancient factions and private battles will come to a head tonight, one way or another.

Hjarka and the others have followed you, though more slowly; they do not feel your panic. At last you spot one pylon building that's been opened—*cut* open, it seems, as if with an enormous knife; three irregular slashes and then someone has made the door fall outward. It's a foot thick. But beyond it is a wide, low-ceilinged corridor going down into darkness.

Someone's climbing out of it, though, as you reach it and stumble to a halt.

"Nassun!" you blurt, because it's her.

The girl framed by the doorway is taller than you remember by several inches. Her hair is longer now, braided back in two plaits that fall behind her shoulders. You barely recognize her. She stops short at the sight of you, a faint wrinkle of confusion between her brows, and you realize she's having trouble recognizing you, too. Then realization comes, and she stares as if you are the last thing in the world she expected to see. Because you are.

"Hi, Mama," Nassun says.

14

I, at the end of days

I AM A WITNESS TO WHAT follows. I will tell this as such.

I watch you and your daughter face each other for the first time in two years, across a gulf of hardship. Only I know what you both have been through. Each of you can judge the other only on presences, actions, and scars, at least for now. You: much thinner than the mother she last saw when she decided to skip creche one day. The desert has weathered you, drying your skin; the acid rain has bleached your locks to a paler brown than they should be, and the gray shows more. The clothes that hang from your body are also bleached by ash and acid, and the empty right sleeve of your shirt has been knotted; it dangles, obviously empty, as you catch your breath. And, also a part of Nassun's first impression of the post-Rifting you: Behind you stands a group of people who all stare at Nassun, some of them with palpable wariness. You, though, show only anguish.

Nassun is as still as a stone eater. She's grown only four inches since the Rifting, but it looks to you like a foot. You can see the advent of adolescence upon her—early, but that is the nature of life in lean times. The body takes advantage of safety and abundance when it can, and the nine months she spent in Jekity were good for her. She's probably going to start menstruating within the next year, if she can find enough food. The biggest changes are immaterial, though. The wariness in her gaze, nothing like the shy diffidence you remember. Her posture: shoulders back, feet braced and square. You told her to stop slouching a million times, and yes, she looks so tall and strong now that she's standing up straight. So beautifully strong.

Her orogeny sits on your awareness like a weight upon the world, rock-steady and precise as a diamond drill. Evil Earth, you think. She sesses just like you.

It's over before it's begun. You sense that as surely as you sess her strength, and both make you desperate. "I've been looking for you," you say. You've raised your hand without thinking about it. Your fingers open and twitch and close and open again in a gesture that is half grasping, half plea.

Her gaze goes hooded. "I was with Daddy."

"I know. I couldn't find you." It's redundant, obvious; you hate yourself for babbling. "Are you . . . all right?"

She looks away, troubled, and it bothers you that her concern so plainly isn't you. "I need to . . . My Guardian needs help."

You go stiff. Nassun has heard from Schaffa of what he was like, before Meov. She knows, intellectually, that the Schaffa you knew and the Schaffa she loves are wholly different people. She's seen a Fulcrum, and the ways in which it warped its inmates. She remembers how you used to go stiff, just the way you are now, at even a glimpse of the color burgundy—and finally, here at the end of the world, she understands why. She knows you better now than ever before in her life.

And yet. To her, Schaffa is the man who protected her from raiders—and from her father. He is the man who soothed her when she was afraid, tucked her into bed at night. She has seen him fight his own brutal nature, and the Earth itself, in order to be the parent she needs. He has helped her learn to love herself for what she is.

Her mother? You. Have done none of these things.

And in that pent moment, as you fight past the memory of Innon falling to pieces and the burning ache of broken bones in a hand you no longer possess, with *Never say no to me* ringing in your head, she intuits the thing that you have, until now, denied:

That it is hopeless. That there can be no relationship, no trust, between you and her, because the two of you are what the Stillness and the Season have made you. That Alabaster was right, and some things really are too broken to fix. Nothing to do but destroy them entirely, for mercy's sake.

Nassun shakes her head once while you stand there twitching. She looks away. Shakes her head again. Her shoulders bow a little, not in a lazy slouch, but weariness. She does not blame you, but neither does she expect anything from you. And right now, you're just in the way.

So she turns to walk away, and that shocks you out of your fugue. "Nassun?"

"He needs help," she says again. Her head is down, her shoulders tight. She doesn't stop walking. You inhale and start after her. "I have to help him."

You know what's happening. You've felt it, feared it, all along. Behind you, you hear Danel stop the others. Maybe she thinks you and your daughter need space. You ignore them and run after Nassun. You grab her shoulder, try to turn her around. "Nassun, what—" She shrugs you off, so hard that you stagger. Your balance has been shot since you lost the arm, and she's stronger than she was. She doesn't notice you almost fall. She keeps going. "Nassun!" She doesn't even look back.

You're desperate to get her attention, to get her to react, something. Anything. You grope and then say, to her back, "I—I—I know about Jija!"

That makes her falter to a halt. Jija's death is still a raw wound within her that Schaffa has cleaned and stitched, but that will not heal for some time. That you know what she has done makes her hunch in shame. That it was necessary, self-defense, frustrates her. That you have reminded her of this, now, tips the shame and frustration into anger.

"I have to *help Schaffa*," she says again. Her shoulders are going up in a way that you recognize from a hundred afternoons in your makeshift crucible, and from when she was two and learned the word *no*. There's no reasoning with her when she gets like this. Words become irrelevant. Actions mean more. But what actions could possibly convey the morass of your feelings right now? You look back at the others helplessly. Hjarka is holding Tonkee back; Tonkee's gaze is fixed on the sky and the assemblage there of more obelisks than you've seen in your whole life. Danel is a little apart from the rest, her hands behind her back, her black lips moving in what you recognize as a lorist mnemonic exercise to help her absorb everything she sees and hears, verbatim. Lerna—

You forgot. Lerna is not here. But if he were here, you suspect, he would be warning you. He was a doctor. Wounds of the family weren't really within his purview... but anyone can see that something here has festered.

You trot after her again. "Nassun. Nassun, rust it, look at me when I'm talking to you!" She ignores you, and it's a slap in the face—the kind that clears your head, though, and not the kind that makes you want to fight. Okay. She won't hear you until she's helped... Schaffa. You push past this thought, though it is like plodding through muck full of bones. Okay. "L-let me help you!"

This actually gets Nassun to slow down, and then stop. Her expression is wary, so wary, when she turns back. "Help me?"

You look beyond her and see then that she was heading for another of the pylon buildings—this one with a broad, railed staircase going up its sloping side. The view of the sky would be excellent at the top... Irrationally you conclude that you have to keep her from going up there. "Yes." You hold out your hand again. *Please.* "Tell me what you need. I'll... Nassun." You're out of words. You're willing her to feel what you feel. "Nassun."

It's not working. She says, in a voice as hard as stone, "I need to use the Obelisk Gate."

You flinch. I told you this already, weeks ago, but apparently you did not *believe*. "What? You can't."

You're thinking: *It will kill you.*

Her jaw tightens. "I will."

She's thinking: *I don't need your permission.*

You shake your head, incredulous. "To do *what?*" But it's too late. She's done. You said you would help but then hesitated.

She is Schaffa's daughter, too, in her heart of hearts; Earthfires, two fathers and *you* of all people to shape her, is it any wonder that she's turned out the way she has? To her, hesitation is the same thing as *no*. She doesn't like it when people say no to her.

So Nassun turns her back on you again and says, "Don't follow me anymore, Mama."

You immediately start after her again, of course. "Nassun—"

She whips back around. She's in the ground, you sess it, and she's in the air, you see the lines of magic, and suddenly the two weave together in a way that you can't even comprehend. The stuff of Corepoint's ground, which is metals and pressed fibers and substances for which you have no name, layered over volcanic rock, heaves beneath your feet. Out of old habit, years spent containing your children's orogenic tantrums, you react even as you stagger, setting a torus into the ground that you can use to cancel her orogeny. It doesn't work, because she isn't just using orogeny.

She sesses it, though, and her eyes narrow. *Your* gray eyes, like ash. And an instant later, a wall of obsidian slams up from the ground in front of you, tearing through the fiber and metal of the city's infrastructure, forming a barrier between you and her that spans the road.

The force of this upheaval flings you to the ground. When the stars clear from your vision and the dust dissipates enough, you stare up at the wall in shock. Your daughter did this. To you.

Someone grabs you and you flinch. It's Tonkee.

"I don't know if it's occurred to you," she says, hauling you to your feet, "but your child seems like she's got *your temper*. So, you know, maybe you shouldn't get too pushy."

"I don't even know what she did," you murmur, dazed, though you nod thanks to Tonkee for helping you up. "That wasn't... I don't..." There was no Fulcrum-esque precision in what Nassun did, even though you taught her Fulcrum fundamentals. You lay your hand against the wall in confusion, and feel the lingering flickers of magic within its substance, dancing from particle to particle as they fade. "She's *blending* magic and orogeny. I've never seen that before."

I have. We called it tuning.

Meanwhile. No longer hampered by you, Nassun has climbed the pylon steps. She stands atop it now, surrounded by turning, bright red warning symbols that dance in the air. A heavy, faintly sulfurous breeze wafts up from Corepoint's great hole, lifting the stray hairs from her twin plaits. She wonders if Father Earth is relieved to have manipulated her into sparing its life.

Schaffa will live if she turns every person in the world into stone eaters. That is all that matters.

"First, the network," she says, lifting her eyes to the sky. The twenty-seven obelisks flicker from solid to magic in unison as she reignites them. She spreads her hands before her.

On the ground below her, you flinch as you sess—feel—are attuned to—the lightning-fast activation of twenty-seven obelisks. They act as one in this instant, thrumming so powerfully together that your teeth itch. You wonder why Tonkee isn't grimacing the way you are, but Tonkee is only a still.

Tonkee's not stupid, though, and this is her life's work. While you stare at your daughter in awe, she narrows her eyes at the obelisks. "Three cubed," she murmurs. You shake your head, mute. She glares at you, irritated by your slowness. "Well, if

I was going to emulate a *big* crystal, I would start by putting smaller crystals into a cubiform lattice configuration."

Then you understand. The big crystal that Nassun means to emulate is the onyx. You need a key to initialize the Gate; that's what Alabaster told you. What Alabaster *didn't* tell you, the useless ass, was that there are many possible kinds of keys. When he tore the Rifting across the Stillness, he used a network composed of all the node maintainers in his vicinity, probably because the onyx itself would have turned him to stone at once. The node maintainers were a lesser substitute for the onyx—a spare key. You didn't know what you were doing that first time, when you yoked the orogenes in Castrima-under into a network, but *he* knew the onyx was too much for you to just grab directly, back then. You didn't have Alabaster's flexibility or creativity. He taught you a safer way.

Nassun, though, is the student Alabaster always wanted. She cannot have ever accessed the Obelisk Gate before—it's been yours, till now—but as you observe in shock, in horror, she reaches beyond her spare-key network, finding other obelisks one by one and binding them. It's slower than it would be with the onyx, but you can tell that it's just as effective. It's working. The apatite, connected and locked. The sardonyx, sending a little pulse from where it hovers out of sight, somewhere over the southern sea. The jade—

Nassun will open the Gate.

You shove Tonkee away. "Get as far from me as you can. All of you."

Tonkee doesn't waste time arguing. Her eyes widen; she turns and runs. You hear her shouting to the others. You hear Danel arguing. And then you can no longer pay heed to them.

Nassun will open the Gate, turn to stone, *and die.*

Only one thing can stop Nassun's network of obelisks: the onyx. You need to reach it first, though, and right now it's all the way on the other side of the planet, halfway between Castrima and Rennanis where you left it. Once, long ago at Castrima-over, it called you to itself. But do you dare wait for it to do that, now, with Nassun grabbing control of every part of the Gate? You need to get to the onyx first. For that, you need magic—much more of it than you can muster just by yourself, here without a single obelisk to your name.

The beryl, the hematite, the iolite—

She's going to die right in front of you if you don't do something.

Frantically you throw your awareness into the earth. Corepoint sits on a volcano, maybe you can—

Wait. Something pulls your attention back up to the volcano's mouth. Underground, but closer by. Somewhere underneath this city, you sense a network. Lines of magic woven together, supporting one another, rooted deep to draw up more… It's faint. It's slow. And there is a familiar, ugly buzz at the back of your mind when you touch this network. Buzz upon buzz upon buzz.

Ah, yes. The network you've found is *Guardians*, nearly a thousand of them. Of rusting course. You have never consciously sought the magic of them before, but for the first time you understand what that buzz is—some part of you, even before

Alabaster's training, felt the foreignness of the magic within them. The knowledge sends a sharp, nearly paralyzing lance of fear through you. The network of them is close by, easy to grab, but if you do this, what's to stop all these Guardians from boiling up out of Warrant like angry wasps from a disturbed nest? Don't you have enough problems?

Nassun groans, up on her pylon. To your shock, you can... Evil Earth, you can *see* the magic around her, in her, beginning to flare up like a fire hitting oiled kindling. She burns against your perception, the weight of her growing heavier upon the world by the instant. *The kyanite the orthoclase the scapolite—*

And suddenly your fear is gone, because your baby needs you.

So you set your feet. You reach for that network you found, Guardians or no Guardians. You growl through your teeth and grab everything. The Guardians. The threads that trail from their sessapinae away into the depths, and as much of the magic coming through these as you can pull. The iron shards themselves, tiny depositories of the Evil Earth's will.

You make it all yours, yoke it tight, and then you *take* it.

And somewhere down in Warrant there are Guardians screaming, coming awake and writhing in their cells and grabbing at their heads as you do to every single one of them what Alabaster once did to his Guardian. It is what Nassun yearned to do for Schaffa... only there is no kindness in the way you're doing it. You don't hate them; you just don't care. You snatch the iron from their brains and every bit of silvery light from between their cells—and as you feel them crystallize and die, you finally have enough magic, from your makeshift network, to reach the onyx.

It listens at your touch, far away above the ashscape of the Stillness. You fall into it, diving desperately into the dark, to make your case. *Please*, you beg.

It considers the request. This is not in words or sensation. You simply know its consideration. It examines you in turn—your fear, your anger, your determination to put things right.

Ah—this last has resonance. You know yourself examined again, more closely and with skepticism, since your last request was for something so frivolous. (Merely wiping out a city? You of all people did not need the Gate for that.) What the onyx finds within you, however, is something different this time: Fear for kin. Fear of failure. The fear that accompanies all necessary change. And underneath it all, a driving need to make the world better.

Somewhere far away, a billion dying things shiver as the onyx utters a low, earthshaking blast of sound, and comes online.

Atop her pylon, beneath the pulse of the obelisks, Nassun feels that distant upcycling darkness as a warning. But she is too deep in her summoning; too many obelisks now fill her. She cannot spare any attention from her work.

And as each of the two hundred and sixteen remaining obelisks in turn submits to her, and as she opens her eyes to stare at the Moon that she's going to let fly past untouched, and as she instead prepares to turn all the might of the great Plutonic Engine back upon the world and its people, to transform them as I was once transformed—

—she thinks of Schaffa.

Impossible to delude oneself in a moment like this. Impossible to see only what one wants to see, when the power to change the world ricochets through mind and soul and the spaces between cells; oh, I learned this long before both of you. Impossible not to understand that Nassun has known Schaffa for barely more than a year, and does not truly *know* him, given how much of himself he has lost. Impossible not to realize that she clings to him because she has nothing else—

But through her determination, there is a glimmer of doubt in her mind. It is nothing more than that. Barely even a thought. But it whispers, *Do you really have nothing else?*

Is there not one *person in this world besides Schaffa who cares about you?*

And I watch Nassun hesitate, fingers curling and small face tightening in a frown even as the Obelisk Gate weaves itself into completion. I watch the shiver of energies beyond comprehension as they begin to align within her. I lost the power to manipulate these energies tens of thousands of years ago, but I can still see them. The arcanochemical lattice—what you think of as mere brown stone, and the energetic state that produces it—is forming nicely.

I watch as you see this, too, and understand instantly what it means. I watch you snarl and smash apart the wall between you and your daughter, not even noticing that your fingers have turned to stone as you do it. I watch you run to the foot of the pylon steps and shout at her. "*Nassun!*"

And in response to your sudden, raw, incontrovertible *demand*, the onyx blasts out of nowhere to appear overhead.

The sound of it—a low, bone-shaking blat—is titanic. The blast of air that it displaces is thunderous enough to knock both you and Nassun down. She cries out and slides down a few steps, coming dangerously close to losing her grip on the Gate as the impact jolts her concentration. You cry out as the impact makes you notice your left forearm, which is stone, and collarbone, which is stone, and left foot and ankle.

But you set your teeth. There is no pain in you anymore, save anguish for your daughter. No need within you but one. She has the Gate, but you have the onyx—and as you look up at it, at the Moon glaring through its murky translucence, icewhite iris in a scleral sea of black, you know what you have to do.

With the onyx's help, you reach half a planet away and stab the fulcrum of your intention into the wound of the world. The Rifting shudders as you demand every iota of its heat and kinetic churn, and you shudder beneath the flux of so much power that for a moment you think it's just going to vomit out of you as a column of lava, consuming all.

But the onyx is part of you, too, right now. Indifferent to your convulsions—because you're doing that, flopping along the ground and frothing at the mouth—it takes and taps and balances the power of the Rifting with an ease that humbles you. Automatically it links into the obelisks so conveniently nearby, the network that Nassun assembled in order to try to replicate the onyx's power. But a replica has only power, no will, unlike the onyx. A network has no agenda. The onyx takes the twenty-seven obelisks and immediately begins eating into the rest of Nassun's obelisk network.

Here, though, its will is no longer paramount. Nassun feels it. Fights it. She is just as determined as you. Just as driven by love—you for her, and she for Schaffa.

I love you both. How can I not, after all this? I am still

human, after all, and this is a battle for the fate of the world. Such a terrible and magnificent thing to witness.

It *is* a battle, though, line by line, tendril by tendril of magic. The titanic energies of the Gate, of the Rifting, whip and shiver around you both in a cylindrical aurora borealis of energies and colors, visible light ranging to wavelengths beyond the spectrum. (Those energies *resonate* in you, where the alignment is already complete, and still *oscillate* in Nassun—though her waveform has begun to collapse.) It is the onyx and the Rifting versus the Gate, you against her, and all Corepoint trembles with the sheer force of it all. In the dark halls of Warrant, among the jeweled corpses of the Guardians, walls groan and ceilings crack, spilling dirt and pebbles. Nassun is straining to pull the magic down from what's left of the Gate, to target everyone around you and everyone beyond them—and finally, finally, you understand that she's trying to turn everyone into rusting *stone eaters*. You, meanwhile, have reached up. To catch the Moon, and perhaps earn humanity a second chance. But for either of you to achieve your respective goals, you will need to claim both Gate and onyx, and the additional fuel that the Rifting provides.

It is a stalemate that cannot continue. The Gate cannot maintain its connections forever, and the onyx cannot contain the chaos of the Rifting forever—and two human beings, however powerful and strong-willed, cannot survive so much magic for long.

And then it happens. You cry out as you feel a change, a snapping-into-line: Nassun. The magics of her substance are fully aligned; her crystallization has begun. In desperation and pure instinct you grab some of the energy that seeks to transform her and fling it away, though this only delays the inevitable. In the ocean too near Corepoint, there is a deep judder that even the mountain's stabilizers cannot contain. To the west a mountain shaped like a knife jolts up from the ocean floor; to the east another rises, hissing steam from the newness of its birth. Nassun, snarling in frustration, latches onto these as new sources of power, dragging the heat and violence from them; both crack and crumble away. The stabilizers push the ocean flat, preventing tsunami, but they can do only so much. They were not built for this. Much more and even Corepoint will crumble.

"Nassun!" you shout again, anguished. She cannot hear you. But you see, even from where you are, that the fingers of her left hand have turned as brown and stony as your own. She's aware of it, you know somehow. She made this choice. She is prepared for the inevitability of her own death.

You aren't. Oh, Earth, you just can't watch another of your children die.

So... you give up.

I ache with the look on your face, because I know what it costs you to give up Alabaster's dream—and your own. You so wanted to make a better world for Nassun. But more than anything else, you want this last child of yours to *live*... and so you make a choice. To keep fighting will kill you both. The only way to win, then, is not to fight anymore.

I'm sorry, Essun. I'm so sorry. Goodbye.

Nassun gasps, her eyes snapping open as she feels your pressure upon the Gate—upon her, while you dragged all of the terrible transforming curls of magic toward yourself—suddenly relax. The onyx pauses in its onslaught, shimmering in tandem with the dozens of obelisks it has claimed; it is full of power that must, *must* be expended. For the moment, however, it holds. The stabilizing magics finally settle the churning ocean around Corepoint. For this one, pent moment, the world waits, still and taut.

She turns.

"Nassun," you say. It's a whisper. You're on the bottom steps of the pylon, trying to reach her, but that won't be happening. Your arm has completely solidified, and your torso is going. Your stone foot slides uselessly on the slick material, then locks as the rest of your leg freezes up. With your good foot, you can still push, but the stone of you is heavy; as crawling goes, you're not doing a very good job of it.

Her brow furrows. You look up at her, and it strikes you. Your little girl. So big, here beneath the onyx and the Moon. So powerful. So beautiful. And you cannot help it: You burst into tears at the sight of her. You *laugh*, though one of your lungs has gone to stone and it's only a soft wheeze instead. So rusting amazing, your little girl. You are proud to lose to her strength.

She inhales, her eyes widening as if she cannot believe what she is seeing: her mother, so fearsome, on the ground. Trying to crawl on stone limbs. Face wet with tears. *Smiling.* You have never, ever smiled at her before.

And then the line of transformation moves over your face, and you are gone.

Still there physically, a brown sandstone lump frozen on the lower steps, with only the barest suggestion of a smile on half-formed lips. Your tears are still there, glistening upon stone. She stares at these.

She stares at these and sucks in a long hollow breath because suddenly there is nothing, *nothing* inside her, she has killed her father and she has killed her mother and Schaffa is dying and there is nothing left, nothing, the world just takes and takes and takes from her and leaves *nothing*—

But she cannot stop staring at your drying tears.

Because the world took and took and took from you, too, after all. She knows this. And yet, for some reason that she does not think she'll ever understand... even as you died, you were reaching for the Moon.

And for her.

She screams. Clutches her head in her hands, one of them now halfway stone. Drops to her knees, crushed beneath the weight of grief as if it is an entire planet.

The onyx, patient but not, aware but indifferent, touches her. She is the only remaining component of the Gate that has a functioning, complementary will. Through this touch she perceives your plan as commands locked and aimed but unfired. Open the Gate, pour the Rifting's power through it, catch the Moon. End the Seasons. Fix the world. This, Nassun sesses-feels-knows, was your last wish.

The onyx says, in its ponderous, wordless way: *Execute Y/N?*

And in the cold stone silence, alone, Nassun chooses.

YES

coda

me, and you

You are dead. But not you.

The recapture of the Moon is undramatic, from the perspective of the people standing beneath it. At the top of the apartment building where Tonkee and the others have taken shelter, she's used an ancient writing instrument—long gone dry, but resurrected with a bit of spit and blood at the tip—to try to track the Moon's movement between one hour and the next. It doesn't help because she hasn't observed enough variables to do the math correctly, and because she's not some rusting hack astronomest, for Earth's sake. She also isn't sure if she got the first measurement right because of the fiver or sixer shake that occurred right around that moment, just before Hjarka dragged her away from the window. "Obelisk-builder windows don't shatter," she complains afterward.

"My rusting temper *does*," Hjarka retorts, and that ends the argument before it can begin. Tonkee is learning to compromise for the sake of a healthy relationship.

But the Moon has indeed changed, they see as days and then

weeks pass. It does not vanish. It fluxes through shapes and colors in a pattern that does not initially make sense, but it grows no smaller in the sky on successive nights.

The dismantling of the Obelisk Gate is somewhat more dramatic. Having expended its full capability in the achievement of something just as powerful as Geoarcanity, the Gate proceeds as designed through its shutdown protocol. One by one, the dozens of obelisks floating around the world drift toward Corepoint. One by one, the obelisks—wholly dematerialized now, all quantum states sublimated into potential energy, you need not understand it beyond that—drop into the black chasm. This takes several days.

The onyx, however, last and greatest of the obelisks, instead drifts out to sea, its hum deepening as its altitude decreases. It enters the sea gently, on a preplanned course to minimize damage—since unlike its fellow obelisks, it alone has retained material existence. This, as the conductors long ago intended, preserves the onyx against future need. It also puts the last remnants of the Niess to rest, finally, deep in a watery grave.

I suppose we must hope that no intrepid young future orogene ever finds and raises it.

Tonkee is the one to go and find Nassun. It's later in the morning, some hours after your death, under a sun that has risen bright and warm in the ashless blue sky. After pausing for a moment to stare at this sky in wonder and longing and fascination, Tonkee goes back to the edge of the hole, and to the pylon stair. Nassun's still there, sitting on one of the lower steps next to the brown lump of you. Her knees are drawn up, her head bowed, her completely solidified hand—frozen in the splayed gesture that she used while activating the Gate—resting awkwardly on the step beside her.

Tonkee sits down on your other side, gazing at you for a long moment. Nassun starts and looks up as she becomes aware of another presence, but Tonkee only smiles at her, and awkwardly rests a hand on what was once your hair. Nassun swallows hard, scrubs at the dried tear-tracks on her face, and then nods to Tonkee. They sit together, with you, grieving for a time.

Danel is the one who goes with Nassun, later, to fetch Schaffa from the dead darkness of Warren. The other Guardians, who still had corestones, have turned to jewel. Most seem to have simply died where they lay, though some fell out of their cells in their thrashing, and their glittering bodies sprawl awkwardly against the wall or along the floor.

Schaffa alone still lives. He's disoriented, weak. As Danel and Nassun help him back up into the surface light, it becomes clear that his hacked-off hair is already streaked with gray. Danel's worried about the stitched wound on the back of his neck, though it has stopped bleeding and seems to cause Schaffa no pain. That isn't what's going to kill him.

Nevertheless. Once he's capable of standing and the sun has helped to clear his mind somewhat, Schaffa holds Nassun, there beside what remains of you. She doesn't weep. Mostly she's just numb. The others come out, Tonkee and Hjarka joining Danel, and they stand with Schaffa and Nassun while the sun sets and the Moon rises again. Maybe it's a silent memorial service. Maybe they just need time and company to recover from events too vast and strange to comprehend. I don't know.

Elsewhere in Corepoint, in a garden long since gone to

wild meadow, I and Gaewha face Remwha—Steel, Gray Man, whatever—beneath the now-waning Moon.

He's been here since Nassun made her choice. When he finally speaks, I find myself thinking that his voice has become so thin and weary. Once, he made the very stones ripple with the wry, edged humor of his earthtalk. Now he sounds old. Thousands of years of ceaseless existence will do that to a man.

He says: "I only wanted it to end."

Gaewha—Antimony, whatever—says, "That isn't what we were made for."

He turns his head, slowly, to look at her. It is tiring just to watch him do this. Stubborn fool. There is the despair of ages on his face, all because he refuses to admit that there's more than one way to be human.

Gaewha offers a hand. "We were made *to make the world better.*" Her gaze slides to me for support. I sigh inwardly, but offer a hand in truce as well.

Remwha looks at our hands. Somewhere, perhaps among the others of our kind who have gathered to watch this moment, are Bimniwha and Dushwha and Salewha. They forgot who they were long ago, or else they simply prefer to embrace who they are now. Only we three have retained anything of the past. This is both a good and bad thing.

"I'm tired," he admits.

"A nap might help," I suggest. "There is the onyx, after all."

Well! Something of the old Remwha remains. I don't think I deserved that look.

But he takes our hands. Together, the three of us—and the

others, too, all who have come to understand that the world *has to* change, the war *must* end—descend into the boiling depths.

The heart of the world is quieter than usual, we find as we take up positions around it. That is a good sign. It does not rage us away at once, which is a better one. We spell out the terms in placatory fluxes of reverberation: The Earth keeps its life-magic, and the rest of us get to keep ours without interference. We have given it back the Moon, and thrown the obelisks in as a surety of good faith. But in exchange, the Seasons must cease.

There is a period of stillness. I know only later that this is several days. In the moment, it feels like another millennium.

Then a heavy, lurching jolt of gravitation. *Accepted.* And—the best sign of all—it sets loose the numberless presences that it has ingested over the past epoch. They spin away, vanishing into the currents of magic, and I don't know what happens to them beyond that. I won't ever know what happens to souls after death—or at least, I won't know for another seven billion years or so, whenever the Earth finally dies.

An intimidating thing to contemplate. It's been a challenging first forty thousand years.

On the other hand . . . nowhere to go, but up.

* * *

I go back to them, your daughter and your old enemy and your friends, to tell them the news. Somewhat to my surprise, several months have passed in the interim. They've settled into the building that Nassun occupied, living off Alabaster's old garden and the supplies that we brought for him and Nassun. That won't be enough long term, of course, though they've supplemented it admirably with improvised fishing lines and bird-catching traps and dried edible seaweed, which Tonkee seems to have figured out a means of cultivating down at the water's edge. So resourceful, these modern people. But it is becoming increasingly clear that they'll have to go back to the Stillness soon, if they want to keep living.

I find Nassun, who is sitting alone at the pylon again. Your body remains where it fell, but someone has tucked fresh wildflowers into its one remaining hand. There's another hand beside it, I notice, positioned like an offering near the stump of your arm. It's too small for you, but she meant well. She doesn't speak for a long while after I appear, and I find that this pleases me. Her kind talk so much. It goes on for long enough, though, even I get a little impatient.

I tell her, "You won't see Steel again." In case she was worried about that.

She jerks a little, as if she's forgotten my presence. Then she sighs. "Tell him I'm sorry. I just... couldn't."

"He understands."

She nods. Then: "Schaffa died today."

I had forgotten him. I should not have; he was part of you. Still. I say nothing. She seems to prefer that.

She takes a deep breath. "Will you... The others say you brought them, and Mama. Can you take us back? I know it'll be dangerous."

"There's no longer any danger." When she frowns, I explain all of it to her: the truce, the release of hostages, the cessation of immediate hostilities in the form of no more Seasons. It does not mean complete stability. Plate tectonics will be plate tectonics. Season-like disasters will still occur, though with greatly decreased frequency. I conclude: "You can take the vehimal back to the Stillness."

She shudders. I belatedly recall what she suffered there. She also says, "I don't know if I can give it magic. I...I feel like..."

She lifts the stone-capped stump of her left wrist. I understand, then—and yes, she's right. She is aligned perfectly, and will be so for the rest of her life. Orogeny is lost to her, forever. Unless she wants to join you.

I say, "I will power the vehimal. The charge should last six months or so. Leave within that time."

I adjust my position then, to the foot of the stairs. She starts, and looks around to find me holding you. I've picked up her old hand, too, because our children are always part of us. She stands, and for a moment I fear unpleasantness. But the look on her face is not unhappy. Just resigned.

I wait, for a moment or a year, to see if she has any final words for your corpse. She says, instead, "I don't know what will happen to us."

"'Us'?"

She sighs. "Orogenes."

Oh. "The current Season will last for some time, even with the Rifting quelled," I say. "Surviving it will require cooperation among many kinds of people. Cooperation presents opportunities."

She frowns. "Opportunities...for what? You said the Seasons would end after this."

"Yes."

She holds up her hands, or one hand and one stump, to

gesture in frustration. "People killed us and hated us when they *needed* us. Now we don't even have that."

Us. We. She still thinks of herself as orogene, though she will never again be able to do more than listen to the earth. I decide not to point this out. I do say, however, "And you won't need them, either."

She falls silent, perhaps in confusion. To clarify, I add, "With the end of the Seasons and the death of all the Guardians, it will now be possible for orogenes to conquer or eliminate stills, if they so choose. Previously, neither group could have survived without the other's aid."

Nassun gasps. "That's horrible!"

I don't bother to explain that just because something is horrible does not make it any less true.

"There won't be any more Fulcrums," she says. She looks away, troubled, perhaps remembering her destruction of the Antarctic Fulcrum. "I think... They're wrong, but I don't know how else..." She shakes her head.

I watch her flounder in silence for a month, or a moment. I say, "The Fulcrums *are* wrong."

"What?"

"Imprisonment of orogenes was never the only option for ensuring the safety of society." I pause deliberately, and she blinks, perhaps remembering that orogene parents are perfectly capable of raising orogene children without disaster. "Lynching was never the only option. The nodes were never the only option. All of these were choices. Different choices have always been possible."

There is such sorrow in her, your little girl. I hope Nassun learns someday that she is not alone in the world. I hope she learns how to hope again.

She lowers her gaze. "They're not going to choose anything different."

"They will if you make them."

She's wiser than you, and does not balk at the notion of forcing people to be decent to each other. Only the methodology is a problem. "I don't have any orogeny anymore."

"Orogeny," I say, sharply so she will pay attention, "was never the only way to change the world."

She stares. I feel that I have said all I can, so I leave her there to contemplate my words.

I visit the city's station, and charge its vehimal with sufficient magic to return to the Stillness. It will still take a journey of months or more for Nassun and her companions to reach Rennanis from the Antarctics. The Season will likely get worse while they travel, because we have a Moon again. Still...they are part of you. I hope they survive.

Once they're on their way, I come here, to the heart of the mountain beneath Corepoint. To attend to you.

There is no one true way, when we initiate this process. The Earth—for the sake of good relations I will no longer call it Evil—reordered us instantly, and by now many of us are skilled enough to replicate that reordering without a lengthy gestation. I have found that speed produces mixed results, however. Alabaster, as you would call him, may not fully remember himself for centuries—or ever. You, however, must be different.

I have brought you here, reassembled the raw arcanic substance of your being, and reactivated the lattice that should have preserved the critical essence of who you were. You'll lose some memory. There is always loss, with change. But I have told you this story, primed what remains of you, to retain as much as possible of who you were.

Not to force you into a particular shape, mind you. From here on, you may become whomever you wish. It's just that you need to know where you've come from to know where you're going. Do you understand?

And if you should decide to leave me…I will endure. I've been through worse.

So I wait. Time passes. A year, a decade, a week. The length of time does not matter, though Gaewha eventually loses interest and leaves to attend her own affairs. I wait. I hope…no. I simply wait.

And then one day, deep in the fissure where I have put you, the geode splits and hisses open. You rise from its spent halves, the matter of you slowing and cooling to its natural state.

Beautiful, I think. Locs of roped jasper. Skin of striated ocher marble that suggests laugh lines at eyes and mouth, and stratified layers to your clothing. You watch me, and I watch you back.

You say, in an echo of the voice you once had, "What is it that you want?"

"Only to be with you," I say.

"Why?"

I adjust myself to a posture of humility, with head bowed and one hand over my chest. "Because that is how one survives eternity," I say, "or even a few years. Friends. Family. Moving with them. Moving forward."

Do you remember when I first told you this, back when you despaired of ever repairing the harm you'd done? Perhaps. Your position adjusts, too. Arms folded, expression skeptical. Familiar. I try not to hope and fail utterly.

"Friends, family," you say. "Which am I, to you?"

"Both and more. We are beyond such things."

"Hmm."

I am not anxious. "What do *you* want?"

You consider. I listen to the slow ongoing roar of the volcano, down here in the deep. Then you say, "I want the world to be better."

I have never regretted more my inability to leap into the air and whoop for joy.

Instead, I transit to you, with one hand proffered. "Then let's go make it better."

You look amused. It's you. It's truly you. "Just like that?"

"It might take some time."

"I don't think I'm very patient." But you take my hand.

Don't be patient. Don't ever be. This is the way a new world begins.

"Neither am I," I say. "So let's get to it."

APPENDIX 1

A catalog of Fifth Seasons that have been recorded prior to and since the founding of the Sanzed Equatorial Affiliation, from most recent to oldest

Choking Season: 2714–2719 Imperial. Proximate cause: volcanic eruption. Location: the Antarctics near Deveteris. The eruption of Mount Akok blanketed a five-hundred-mile radius with fine ash clouds that solidified in lungs and mucous membranes. Five years without sunlight, although the northern hemisphere was not affected as much (only two years).

Acid Season: 2322–2329 Imperial. Proximate cause: plus-ten-level shake. Location: unknown; far ocean. A sudden plate shift birthed a chain of volcanoes in the path of a major jet stream. This jet stream became acidified, flowing toward the western coast and eventually around most of the Stillness. Most coastal comms perished in the initial tsunami; the rest failed or were forced to relocate when their fleets and port facilities corroded and the fishing dried up. Atmospheric occlusion by clouds lasted seven years; coastal pH levels remained untenable for many years more.

Boiling Season: 1842–1845 Imperial. Proximate cause: hot spot eruption beneath a great lake. Location: Somidlats, Lake Tekkaris quartent. The eruption launched millions of gallons of steam and particulates into the air, which triggered acidic rain and atmospheric occlusion over the southern half of the continent for three years. The northern half suffered no negative impacts, however, so archeomests dispute whether this qualifies as a "true" Season.

Breathless Season: 1689–1798 Imperial. Proximate cause: mining accident. Location: Nomidlats, Sathd quartent. An entirely human-caused Season triggered when miners at the edge of the northeastern Nomidlats coalfields set off underground fires. A relatively mild Season featuring occasional sunlight and no ashfall or acidification except in the region; few comms declared Seasonal Law. Approximately fourteen million people in the city of Heldine died in the initial natural-gas eruption and rapidly spreading fire sinkhole before Imperial Orogenes successfully quelled and sealed the edges of the fires to prevent further spread. The remaining mass could only be isolated, where it continued to burn for one hundred and nine years. The smoke of this, spread via prevailing winds, caused respiratory problems and occasional mass suffocations in the region for several decades. A secondary effect of the loss of the Nomidlats coalfields was a catastrophic rise in heating fuel costs and the wider adaption of geothermal and hydroelectric heating, leading to the establishment of the Geneer Licensure.

The Season of Teeth: 1553–1566 Imperial. Proximate cause: oceanic shake triggering a supervolcanic explosion. Location: Arctic Cracks. An aftershock of the oceanic shake breached

a previously unknown hot spot near the north pole. This triggered a supervolcanic explosion; witnesses report hearing the sound of the explosion as far as the Antarctics. Ash went upper-atmospheric and spread around the globe rapidly, although the Arctics were most heavily affected. The harm of this Season was exacerbated by poor preparation on the part of many comms, because some nine hundred years had passed since the last Season; popular belief at the time was that the Seasons were merely legend. Reports of cannibalism spread from the north all the way to the Equatorials. At the end of this Season, the Fulcrum was founded in Yumenes, with satellite facilities in the Arctics and Antarctics.

Fungus Season: 602 Imperial. Proximate cause: volcanic eruption. Location: western Equatorials. A series of eruptions during monsoon season increased humidity and obscured sunlight over approximately 20 percent of the continent for six months. While this was a mild Season as such things go, its timing created perfect conditions for a fungal bloom that spread across the Equatorials into the northern and southern Midlats, wiping out then-staple-crop miroq (now extinct). The resulting famine lasted four years (two for the fungus blight to run its course, two more for agriculture and food distribution systems to recover). Nearly all affected comms were able to subsist on their own stores, thus proving the efficacy of Imperial reforms and Season planning, and the Empire was generous in sharing stored seed with those regions that had been miroq-dependent. In its aftermath, many comms of the middle latitudes and coastal regions voluntarily joined the Empire, doubling its range and beginning its Golden Age.

Madness Season: 3 Before Imperial–7 Imperial. Proximate cause: volcanic eruption. Location: Kiash Traps. The eruption of multiple vents of an ancient supervolcano (the same one responsible for the Twin Season of approximately 10,000 years previous) launched large deposits of the dark-colored mineral augite into the air. The resulting ten years of darkness was not only devastating in the usual Seasonal way, but resulted in a higher than usual incidence of mental illness. The Sanzed Equatorial Affiliation (commonly called the Sanze Empire) was born in this Season as Warlord Verishe of Yumenes conquered multiple ailing comms using psychological warfare techniques. (See *The Art of Madness*, various authors, Sixth University Press.) Verishe named herself Emperor on the day the first sunlight returned.

[**Editor's note:** Much of the information about Seasons prior to the founding of Sanze is contradictory or unconfirmed. The following are Seasons agreed upon by the Seventh University Archaeomestric Conference of 2532.]

Wandering Season: Approximately 800 Before Imperial. Proximate cause: magnetic pole shift. Location: unverifiable. This Season resulted in the extinction of several important trade crops of the time, and twenty years of famine resulting from pollinators confused by the movement of true north.

Season of Changed Wind: Approximately 1900 Before Imperial. Proximate cause: unknown. Location: unverifiable. For reasons unknown, the direction of the prevailing winds shifted for many years before returning to normal. Consensus agrees that this was a Season, despite the lack of atmospheric

occlusion, because only a substantial (and likely far-oceanic) seismic event could have triggered it.

Heavy Metal Season: Approximately 4200 Before Imperial. Proximate cause: volcanic eruption. Location: Somidlats near Eastern Coastals. A volcanic eruption (believed to be Mount Yrga) caused atmospheric occlusion for ten years, exacerbated by widespread mercury contamination throughout the eastern half of the Stillness.

Season of Yellow Seas: Approximately 9200 Before Imperial. Proximate cause: unknown. Location: Eastern and Western Coastals, and coastal regions as far south as the Antarctics. This Season is only known through written accounts found in Equatorial ruins. For unknown reasons, a widespread bacterial bloom toxified nearly all sea life and caused coastal famines for several decades.

Twin Season: Approximately 9800 Beforc Imperial. Proximate cause: volcanic eruption. Location: Somidlats. Per songs and oral histories dating from the time, the eruption of one volcanic vent caused a three-year occlusion. As this began to clear, it was followed by a second eruption of a different vent, which extended the occlusion by thirty more years.

APPENDIX 2

A Glossary of Terms Commonly Used in All Quartents of the Stillness

Antarctics: The southernmost latitudes of the continent. Also refers to people from antarctic-region comms.

Arctics: The northernmost latitudes of the continent. Also refers to people from arctic-region comms.

Ashblow Hair: A distinctive Sanzed racial trait, deemed in the current guidelines of the Breeder use-caste to be advantageous and therefore given preference in selection. Ashblow hair is notably coarse and thick, generally growing in an upward flare; at length, it falls around the face and shoulders. It is acid-resistant and retains little water after immersion, and has been proven effective as an ash filter in extreme circumstances. In most comms, Breeder guidelines acknowledge texture alone; however, Equatorial Breeders generally also require natural "ash" coloration (slate gray to white, present from birth) for the coveted designation.

Bastard: A person born without a use-caste, which is only possible for boys whose fathers are unknown. Those who

distinguish themselves may be permitted to bear their mother's use-caste at comm-naming.

Blow: A volcano. Also called firemountains in some Coastal languages.

Boil: A geyser, hot spring, or steam vent.

Breeder: One of the seven common use-castes. Breeders are individuals selected for their health and desirable conformation. During a Season, they are responsible for the maintenance of healthy bloodlines and the improvement of comm or race by selective measures. Breeders born into the caste who do not meet acceptable community standards may be permitted to bear the use-caste of a close relative at comm-naming.

Cache: Stored food and supplies. Comms maintain guarded, locked storecaches at all times against the possibility of a Fifth Season. Only recognized comm members are entitled to a share of the cache, though adults may use their share to feed unrecognized children and others. Individual households often maintain their own housecaches, equally guarded against non–family members.

Cebaki: A member of the Cebaki race. Cebak was once a nation (unit of a deprecated political system, Before Imperial) in the Somidlats, though it was reorganized into the quartent system when the Old Sanze Empire conquered it centuries ago.

Coaster: A person from a coastal comm. Few coastal comms can afford to hire Imperial Orogenes to raise reefs or otherwise protect against tsunami, so coastal cities must perpetually rebuild and tend to be resource-poor as a result. People from the western coast of the continent tend to be pale, straight-haired, and sometimes have eyes with epicanthic

folds. People from the eastern coast tend to be dark, kinky-haired, and sometimes have eyes with epicanthic folds.

Comm: Community. The smallest sociopolitical unit of the Imperial governance system, generally corresponding to one city or town, although very large cities may contain several comms. Accepted members of a comm are those who have been accorded rights of cache-share and protection, and who in turn support the comm through taxes or other contributions.

Commless: Criminals and other undesirables unable to gain acceptance in any comm.

Comm Name: The third name borne by most citizens, indicating their comm allegiance and rights. This name is generally bestowed at puberty as a coming-of-age, indicating that a person has been deemed a valuable member of the community. Immigrants to a comm may request adoption into that comm; upon acceptance, they take on the adoptive comm's name as their own.

Creche: A place where children too young to work are cared for while adults carry out needed tasks for the comm. When circumstances permit, a place of learning.

Equatorials: Latitudes surrounding and including the equator, excepting coastal regions. Also refers to people from equatorial-region comms. Thanks to temperate weather and relative stability at the center of the continental plate, Equatorial comms tend to be prosperous and politically powerful. The Equatorials once formed the core of the Old Sanze Empire.

Fault: A place where breaks in the earth make frequent, severe shakes and blows more likely.

Fifth Season: An extended winter—lasting at least six months, per Imperial designation—triggered by seismic activity or other large-scale environmental alteration.

Fulcrum: A paramilitary order created by Old Sanze after the Season of Teeth (1560 Imperial). The headquarters of the Fulcrum is in Yumenes, although two satellite Fulcrums are located in the Arctic and Antarctic regions, for maximum continental coverage. Fulcrum-trained orogenes (or "Imperial Orogenes") are legally permitted to practice the otherwise-illegal craft of orogeny, under strict organizational rules and with the close supervision of the Guardian order. The Fulcrum is self-managed and self-sufficient. Imperial Orogenes are marked by their black uniforms, and colloquially known as "blackjackets."

Geneer: From "geoneer." An engineer of earthworks—geothermal energy mechanisms, tunnels, underground infrastructure, and mining.

Geomest: One who studies stone and its place in the natural world; general term for a scientist. Specifically geomests study lithology, chemistry, and geology, which are not considered separate disciplines in the Stillness. A few geomests specialize in orogenesis—the study of orogeny and its effects.

Greenland: An area of fallow ground kept within or just outside the walls of most comms as advised by stonelore. Comm greenlands may be used for agriculture or animal husbandry at all times, or may be kept as parks or fallow ground during non-Seasonal times. Individual households often maintain their own personal housegreen, or garden, as well.

Grits: In the Fulcrum, unringed orogene children who are still in basic training.

Guardian: A member of an order said to predate the Fulcrum. Guardians track, protect, protect against, and guide orogenes in the Stillness.

Imperial Road: One of the great innovations of the Old Sanze Empire, highroads (elevated highways for walking or horse traffic) connect all major comms and most large quartents to one another. Highroads are built by teams of geneers and Imperial Orogenes, with the orogenes determining the most stable path through areas of seismic activity (or quelling the activity, if there is no stable path), and the geneers routing water and other important resources near the roads to facilitate travel during Seasons.

Innovator: One of the seven common use-castes. Innovators are individuals selected for their creativity and applied intelligence, responsible for technical and logistical problem solving during a Season.

Kirkhusa: A mid-sized mammal, sometimes kept as a pet or used to guard homes or livestock. Normally herbivorous; during Seasons, carnivorous.

Knapper: A small-tools crafter, working in stone, glass, bone, or other materials. In large comms, knappers may use mechanical or mass-production techniques. Knappers who work in metal, or incompetent knappers, are colloquially called "rusters."

Lorist: One who studies stonelore and lost history.

Mela: A Midlats plant, related to the melons of Equatorial climates. Mela are vining ground plants that normally produce fruit aboveground. During a Season, the fruit grows underground as tubers. Some species of mela produce flowers that trap insects.

Metallore: Like alchemy and astronomestry, a discredited pseudoscience disavowed by the Seventh University.

Midlats: The "middle" latitudes of the continent—those between the equator and the arctic or antarctic regions. Also refers to people from midlats regions (sometimes called Midlatters). These regions are seen as the backwater of the Stillness, although they produce much of the world's food, materials, and other critical resources. There are two midlat regions: the northern (Nomidlats) and southern (Somidlats).

Newcomm: Colloquial term for comms that have arisen only since the last Season. Comms that have survived at least one Season are generally seen as more desirable places to live, having proven their efficacy and strength.

Nodes: The network of Imperially maintained stations placed throughout the Stillness in order to reduce or quell seismic events. Due to the relative rarity of Fulcrum-trained orogenes, nodes are primarily clustered in the Equatorials.

Orogene: One who possesses orogeny, whether trained or not. Derogatory: rogga.

Orogeny: The ability to manipulate thermal, kinetic, and related forms of energy to address seismic events.

Quartent: The middle level of the Imperial governance system. Four geographically adjacent comms make a quartent. Each quartent has a governor to whom individual comm heads report, and who reports in turn to a regional governor. The largest comm in a quartent is its capital; larger quartent capitals are connected to one another via the Imperial Road system.

Region: The top level of the Imperial governance system. Imperially recognized regions are the Arctics, Nomidlats, Western Coastals, Eastern Coastals, Equatorials, Somidlats, and Antarctics. Each region has a governor to whom all local quartents report. Regional governors are officially appointed by the Emperor, though in actual practice they are generally selected by and/or come from the Yumenescene Leadership.

Resistant: One of the seven common use-castes. Resistants are individuals selected for their ability to survive famine or pestilence. They are responsible for caring for the infirm and dead bodies during Seasons.

Rings: Used to denote rank among Imperial Orogenes. Unranked trainees must pass a series of tests to gain their first ring; ten rings is the highest rank an orogene may achieve. Each ring is made of polished semiprecious stone.

Roadhouse: Stations located at intervals along every Imperial Road and many lesser roads. All roadhouses contain a source of water and are located near arable land, forests, or other useful resources. Many are located in areas of minimal seismic activity.

Runny-sack: A small, easily portable cache of supplies most people keep in their homes in case of shakes or other emergencies.

Safe: A beverage traditionally served at negotiations, first encounters between potentially hostile parties, and other formal meetings. It contains a plant milk that reacts to the presence of all foreign substances.

Sanze: Originally a nation (unit of a deprecated political system, Before Imperial) in the Equatorials; origin of the Sanzed race. At the close of the Madness Season (7 Imperial), the nation of Sanze was abolished and replaced with the Sanzed Equatorial Affiliation, consisting of six predominantly Sanzed comms under the rule of Emperor Verishe Leadership Yumenes. The Affiliation expanded rapidly in the aftermath of the Season, eventually encompassing all regions of the Stillness by 800 Imperial. Around the time of the Season of Teeth, the Affiliation came to be known colloquially as the Old Sanze Empire, or simply Old Sanze. As of the Shilteen Accords of 1850 Imperial, the Affiliation officially ceased to exist, as local control (under the advisement of the Yumenescene Leadership) was deemed more efficient in the event of a Season. In practice, most comms still follow Imperial systems of governance, finance, education, and more, and most regional governors still pay taxes in tribute to Yumenes.

Sanzed: A member of the Sanzed race. Per Yumenescene Breedership standards, Sanzeds are ideally bronze-skinned and ashblow-haired, with mesomorphic or endomorphic builds and an adult height of minimum six feet.

Sanze-mat: The language spoken by the Sanze race, and the official language of the Old Sanze Empire, now the lingua franca of most of the Stillness.

Seasonal Law: Martial law, which may be declared by any comm head, quartent governor, regional governor, or recognized member of the Yumenescene Leadership. During Seasonal Law, quartent and regional governance are suspended and comms operate as sovereign sociopolitical units, though local cooperation with other comms is strongly encouraged per Imperial policy.

Seventh University: A famous college for the study of geomestry and stonelore, currently Imperially funded and located in the Equatorial city of Dibars. Prior versions of the University have been privately or collectively maintained; notably, the Third University at Am-Elat (approximately 3000 Before Imperial) was recognized at the time as a sovereign nation. Smaller regional or quartent colleges pay tribute to the University and receive expertise and resources in exchange.

Sesuna: Awareness of the movements of the earth. The sensory organs that perform this function are the sessapinae, located in the brain stem. Verb form: to sess.

Shake: A seismic movement of the earth.

Shatterland: Ground that has been disturbed by severe and/or very recent seismic activity.

Stillheads: A derogatory term used by orogenes for people lacking orogeny, usually shortened to "stills."

Stone Eaters: A rarely seen sentient humanoid species whose flesh, hair, etc., resembles stone. Little is known about them.

Strongback: One of the seven common use-castes. Strongbacks are individuals selected for their physical prowess, responsible for heavy labor and security in the event of a Season.

Use Name: The second name borne by most citizens, indicating the use-caste to which that person belongs. There are twenty recognized use-castes, although only seven in common use throughout the current and former Old Sanze Empire. A person inherits the use name of their same-sex parent, on the theory that useful traits are more readily passed this way.

Acknowledgments

Whew. That took a bit, didn't it?

The Stone Sky marks more than just the end of another trilogy, for me. For a variety of reasons, the period in which I wrote this book has turned out to be a time of tremendous change in my life. Among other things, I quit my day job and became a full-time writer in July of 2016. Now, I *liked* my day job, where I got to help people make healthy decisions—or at least survive long enough to do so—at one of the most crucial transition points of adult life. I do still help people, I think, as a writer, or at least that's the impression I get from those of you who've sent letters or online messages telling me how much my writing has touched you. But in my day job, the work was more direct, as were its agonies and rewards. I miss it a lot.

Oh, don't get me wrong; this was a good and necessary life transition to make. My writing career has exploded in all the best ways, and after all, I love being a writer, too. But it's my nature to reflect in times of change, and to acknowledge both what was lost as well as what was gained.

This change was facilitated by a Patreon (artist crowdfunding) campaign that I began in May of 2016. And on a more somber note...this Patreon funding is also what allowed me to focus wholly on my mother during the final days of her life, in late 2016 and early 2017. I don't often talk about personal things in public, but you can perhaps see how the Broken Earth trilogy is my attempt to wrestle with motherhood, among other things. Mom had a difficult last few years. I think (so many of my novels' underpinnings become clear in retrospect) that on some level I suspected her death was coming; maybe I was trying to prepare myself. Still wasn't ready when it happened...but then, no one ever is.

So I'm grateful to everyone—my family, my friends, my agent, my Patrons, the folks at Orbit, including my new editor, my former coworkers, the staff of the hospice, *everyone*—who helped me through this.

And this is why I've worked so hard to get *The Stone Sky* out on time, despite travel and hospitalizations and stress and all the thousand bureaucratic indignities of life after a parent's death. I definitely haven't been in the best place while working on this book, but I can say this much: Where there is pain in this book, it is real pain; where there is anger, it is real anger; where there is love, it is real love. You've been taking this journey with me, and you're always going to get the best of what I've got. That's what my mother would want.

extras

meet the author

Photo Credit: Laura Hanifin

N. K. Jemisin is a Brooklyn author who won the Hugo Award for Best Novel for *The Fifth Season*, which was also a *New York Times* Notable Book of 2015. She previously won the Locus Award for her first novel, *The Hundred Thousand Kingdoms*, and her short fiction and novels have been nominated multiple times for Hugo, World Fantasy, Nebula, and RT Reviewers' Choice awards, and shortlisted for the Crawford and the James Tiptree, Jr. awards. She is a science fiction and fantasy reviewer for the *New York Times*, and you can find her online at nkjemisin.com.

if you enjoyed
THE STONE SKY
look out for
THE HUNDRED THOUSAND KINGDOMS
The Inheritance Trilogy
by
N. K. Jemisin

Yeine Darr is an outcast from the barbarian north. But when her mother dies under mysterious circumstances, she is summoned to the majestic city of Sky. There, to her shock, Yeine is named an heiress to the king. But the throne of the Hundred Thousand Kingdoms is not easily won, and Yeine is thrust into a vicious power struggle with cousins she never knew she had. As she fights for her life, she draws ever closer to the secrets of her mother's death and her family's bloody history.

With the fate of the world hanging in the balance, Yeine will learn how perilous it can be when love and hate—and gods and mortals—are bound inseparably together.

1

Grandfather

I am not as I once was. They have done this to me, broken me open and torn out my heart. I do not know who I am anymore.

I must try to remember.

* * *

My people tell stories of the night I was born. They say my mother crossed her legs in the middle of labor and fought with all her strength not to release me into the world. I was born anyhow, of course; nature cannot be denied. Yet it does not surprise me that she tried.

* * *

My mother was an heiress of the Arameri. There was a ball for the lesser nobility—the sort of thing that happens once a decade as a backhanded sop to their self-esteem. My father dared ask my mother to dance; she deigned to consent. I have often wondered what he said and did that night to make her fall in love with him so powerfully, for she eventually abdicated her position to be with him. It is the stuff of great tales, yes? Very romantic. In the tales, such a couple lives happily ever after. The tales do not say what happens when the most powerful family in the world is offended in the process.

* * *

But I forget myself. Who was I, again? Ah, yes.

My name is Yeine. In my people's way I am Yeine dau she Kinneth tai wer Somem kanna Darre, which means that I am the daughter of Kinneth, and that my tribe within the Darre people is called Somem. Tribes mean little to us these days, though before the Gods' War they were more important.

I am nineteen years old. I also am, or was, the chieftain of my people, called *ennu*. In the Arameri way, which is the way of the Amn race from whom they originated, I am the Baroness Yeine Darr.

One month after my mother died, I received a message from my grandfather Dekarta Arameri, inviting me to visit the family seat. Because one does not refuse an invitation from the Arameri, I set forth. It took the better part of three months to travel from the High North continent to Senm, across the Repentance Sea. Despite Darr's relative poverty, I traveled in style the whole way, first by palanquin and ocean vessel, and finally by chauffeured horse-coach. This was not my choice. The Darre Warriors' Council, which rather desperately hoped that I might restore us to the Arameri's good graces, thought that this extravagance would help. It is well known that Amn respect displays of wealth.

Thus arrayed, I arrived at my destination on the cusp of the winter solstice. And as the driver stopped the coach on a hill outside the city, ostensibly to water the horses but more likely because he was a local and liked to watch foreigners gawk, I got my first glimpse of the Hundred Thousand Kingdoms' heart.

There is a rose that is famous in High North. (This is not a digression.) It is called the altarskirt rose. Not only do its petals unfold in a radiance of pearled white, but frequently it grows an incomplete secondary flower about the base of its stem. In its most prized form, the altarskirt grows a layer of overlarge petals that drape the ground. The two bloom in tandem, seed-bearing head and skirt, glory above and below.

This was the city called Sky. On the ground, sprawling over a small mountain or an oversize hill: a circle of high walls, mounting tiers of buildings, all resplendent in white, per Arameri decree. Above the city, smaller but brighter, the pearl of its tiers occasionally obscured by scuds of cloud, was the palace—also called Sky, and perhaps more deserving of the name. I knew the column was there, the impossibly thin column that supported such a massive structure, but from that distance I couldn't see it. Palace floated above city, linked in spirit, both so unearthly in their beauty that I held my breath at the sight.

The altarskirt rose is priceless because of the difficulty of producing it. The most famous lines are heavily inbred; it originated as a deformity that some savvy breeder deemed useful. The primary flower's scent, sweet to us, is apparently repugnant to insects; these roses must be pollinated by hand. The secondary flower saps nutrients crucial for the plant's fertility. Seeds are rare, and for every one that grows into a perfect altarskirt, ten others become plants that must be destroyed for their hideousness.

* * *

At the gates of Sky (the palace) I was turned away, though not for the reasons I'd expected. My grandfather was not present, it seemed. He had left instructions in the event of my arrival.

Sky is the Arameri's home; business is never done there. This is because, officially, they do not rule the world. The Nobles' Consortium does, with the benevolent assistance of the Order of Itempas. The Consortium meets in the Salon, a huge, stately building—white-walled, of course—that sits among a cluster of official buildings at the foot of the palace. It is very impressive, and would be more so if it did not sit squarely in Sky's elegant shadow.

I went inside and announced myself to the Consortium staff, whereupon they all looked very surprised, though politely so. One of them—a very junior aide, I gathered—was dispatched to escort me to the central chamber, where the day's session was well under way.

As a lesser noble, I had always been welcome to attend a Consortium gathering, but there had never seemed any point. Besides the expense and months of travel time required to attend, Darr was simply too small, poor, and ill-favored to have any clout, even without my mother's abdication adding to our collective stain. Most of High North is regarded as a backwater, and only the largest nations there have enough prestige or money to make their voices heard among our noble peers. So I was not surprised to find that the seat reserved for me on the Consortium floor—in a shadowed area, behind a pillar—was currently occupied by an excess delegate from one of the Senm-continent nations. It would be terribly rude, the aide stammered anxiously, to dislodge this man, who was elderly and had bad knees. Perhaps I would not mind standing? Since I had just spent many long hours cramped in a carriage, I was happy to agree.

So the aide positioned me at the side of the Consortium floor, where I actually had a good view of the goings-on. The Consortium chamber was magnificently apportioned, with white marble and rich, dark wood that had probably come from Darr's forests in better days. The nobles—three hundred or so in total—sat in comfortable chairs on the chamber's floor or along elevated tiers above. Aides, pages, and scribes occupied the periphery with me, ready to fetch documents or run errands as needed. At the head of the chamber, the Consortium Overseer stood atop an elaborate podium, pointing to members as they indicated a desire to speak. Apparently there was a dispute over water rights in a desert somewhere; five countries were involved. None of the conversation's participants spoke out of turn; no tempers were lost; there were no snide comments or veiled insults. It was all very orderly and polite, despite the size of the gathering and the fact that most of those present were accustomed to speaking however they pleased among their own people.

One reason for this extraordinary good behavior stood on a plinth behind the Overseer's podium: a life-size statue of the Skyfather in one of His most famous poses, the Appeal to Mortal Reason. Hard to speak out of turn under that stern gaze. But more repressive, I suspected, was the stern gaze of the man who sat behind the Overseer in an elevated box. I could not see him well from where I stood, but he was elderly, richly dressed, and flanked by a younger blond man and a dark-haired woman, as well as a handful of retainers.

It did not take much to guess this man's identity, though he wore no crown, had no visible guards, and neither he nor anyone in his entourage spoke throughout the meeting.

"Hello, Grandfather," I murmured to myself, and smiled at him across the chamber, though I knew he could not see me. The pages and scribes gave me the oddest looks for the rest of the afternoon.

* * *

I knelt before my grandfather with my head bowed, hearing titters of laughter.

No, wait.

* * *

There were three gods once.

Only three, I mean. Now there are dozens, perhaps hundreds. They breed like rabbits. But once there were only three, most powerful and glorious of all: the god of day, the god of night, and the goddess of twilight and dawn. Or light and darkness and the shades between. Or order, chaos, and balance. None of that is important because one of them died, the other might as well have, and the last is the only one who matters anymore.

The Arameri get their power from this remaining god. He is called the Skyfather, Bright Itempas, and the ancestors of the Arameri were His most devoted priests. He rewarded them by giving them a weapon so mighty that no army could stand against it. They used this weapon—weapons, really—to make themselves rulers of the world.

That's better. Now.

* * *

I knelt before my grandfather with my head bowed and my knife laid on the floor.

We were in Sky, having transferred there following the Consortium session, via the magic of the Vertical Gate. Immediately upon arrival I had been summoned to my grandfather's audience chamber, which felt much like a throne room. The chamber was roughly circular because circles are sacred to Itempas. The vaulted ceiling made the members of the court look taller—unnecessarily, since Amn are a tall people compared to my own. Tall and pale and endlessly poised, like statues of human beings rather than real flesh and blood.

"Most high Lord Arameri," I said. "I am honored to be in your presence."

I had heard titters of laughter when I entered the room. Now they sounded again, muffled by hands and kerchiefs and fans. I was reminded of bird flocks roosting in a forest canopy.

Before me sat Dekarta Arameri, uncrowned king of the world. He was old; perhaps the oldest man I have ever seen, though Amn usually live longer than my people, so this was not surprising. His thin hair had gone completely white, and he was so gaunt and stooped that the elevated stone chair on which he sat—it was never called a throne—seemed to swallow him whole.

"Granddaughter," he said, and the titters stopped. The silence was heavy enough to hold in my hand. He was head of the Arameri family, and his word was law. No one had expected him to acknowledge me as kin, least of all myself.

"Stand," he said. "Let me have a look at you."

I did, reclaiming my knife since no one had taken it. There was more silence. I am not very interesting to look at. It might have been different if I had gotten the traits of my two peoples in a better combination—Amn height with Darre curves, perhaps, or thick straight Darre hair colored Amn-pale. I have Amn eyes: faded green in color, more unnerving than pretty. Otherwise, I am short and flat and brown as forestwood, and my hair is a curled mess. Because I find it unmanageable otherwise, I wear it short. I am sometimes mistaken for a boy.

As the silence wore on, I saw Dekarta frown. There was an odd sort of marking on his forehead, I noticed: a perfect circle of black, as if someone had dipped a coin in ink and pressed it to his flesh. On either side of this was a thick chevron, bracketing the circle.

"You look nothing like her," he said at last. "But I suppose that is just as well. Viraine?"

This last was directed at a man who stood among the courtiers closest to the throne. For an instant I thought he was another elder, then I realized my error: though his hair was stark white, he was only somewhere in his fourth decade. He, too, bore a forehead mark, though his was less elaborate than Dekarta's: just the black circle.

"She's not hopeless," he said, folding his arms. "Nothing to be done about her looks; I doubt even makeup will help. But put her in civilized attire and she can convey…nobility, at least." His eyes narrowed, taking me apart by degrees. My best Darren clothing, a long vest of white civvetfur and calf-length leggings, earned me a sigh. (I had gotten the odd look for this outfit at the Salon, but I hadn't realized it was *that* bad.) He examined my face so long that I wondered if I should show my teeth.

Instead he smiled, showing his. "Her mother has trained her. Look how she shows no fear or resentment, even now."

"She will do, then," said Dekarta.

"Do for what, Grandfather?" I asked. The weight in the room grew heavier, expectant, though he had already named me granddaughter. There was a certain risk involved in my daring to address him the same familiar way, of course—powerful men are touchy over odd things. But my mother had indeed trained me well, and I knew it was worth the risk to establish myself in the court's eyes.

Dekarta Arameri's face did not change; I could not read it. "For my heir, Granddaughter. I intend to name you to that position today."

The silence turned to stone as hard as my grandfather's chair.

I thought he might be joking, but no one laughed. That was what made me believe him at last: the utter shock and horror on the faces of the courtiers as they stared at their lord. Except the one called Viraine. He watched me.

It came to me that some response was expected.

"You already have heirs," I said.

"Not as diplomatic as she could be," Viraine said in a dry tone.

Dekarta ignored this. "It is true, there are two other candidates," he said to me. "My niece and nephew, Scimina and Relad. Your cousins, once removed."

I had heard of them, of course; everyone had. Rumor constantly made one or the other heir, though no one knew for certain which. *Both* was something that had not occurred to me.

"If I may suggest, Grandfather," I said carefully, though it was impossible to be careful in this conversation, "I would make two heirs too many."

It was the eyes that made Dekarta seem so old, I would realize much later. I had no idea what color they had originally been; age had bleached and filmed them to near-white. There were lifetimes in those eyes, none of them happy.

"Indeed," he said. "But just enough for an interesting competition, I think."

"I don't understand, Grandfather."

He lifted his hand in a gesture that would have been graceful, once. Now his hand shook badly. "It is very simple. I have named three heirs. One of you will actually manage to succeed me. The other two will doubtless kill each other or be killed by the victor. As for which lives, and which die—" He shrugged. "That is for you to decide."

My mother had taught me never to show fear, but emotions will not be stilled so easily. I began to sweat. I have been the target of an assassination attempt only once in my life—the benefit of being heir to such a tiny, impoverished nation. No one wanted my job. But now there would be two others who did. Lord Relad and Lady Scimina were wealthy and powerful beyond my wildest dreams. They had spent their whole lives striving against each other toward the goal of ruling the world. And here came I, unknown, with no resources and few friends, into the fray.

"There will be no decision," I said. To my credit, my voice did not shake. "And no contest. They will kill me at once and turn their attention back to each other."

"That is possible," said my grandfather.

I could think of nothing to say that would save me. He was insane; that was obvious. Why else turn rulership of the world into a contest prize? If he died tomorrow, Relad and Scimina would rip the earth asunder between them. The killing might not end for decades. And for all he knew, I was an idiot. If by some impossible chance I managed to gain the throne, I could plunge the Hundred Thousand Kingdoms into a spiral of mismanagement and suffering. He had to know that.

One cannot argue with madness. But sometimes, with luck and the Skyfather's blessing, one can understand it. "Why?"

He nodded as if he had expected my question. "Your mother deprived me of an heir when she left our family. You will pay her debt."

"She is four months in the grave," I snapped. "Do you honestly want revenge against a dead woman?"

"This has nothing to do with revenge, Granddaughter. It is a matter of duty." He made a gesture with his left hand, and another courtier detached himself from the throng. Unlike the first man—indeed, unlike most of the courtiers whose faces I could see—the mark on this man's forehead was a downturned half-moon, like an exaggerated frown. He knelt before the dais that held Dekarta's chair, his waist-length red braid falling over one shoulder to curl on the floor.

"I cannot hope that your mother has taught you duty," Dekarta said to me over this man's back. "She abandoned hers to dally with her sweet-tongued savage. I allowed this—an indulgence I have often regretted. So I will assuage that regret by bringing you back into the fold, Granddaughter. Whether you live or die is irrelevant. You are Arameri, and like all of us, you will serve."

Then he waved to the red-haired man. "Prepare her as best you can."

There was nothing more. The red-haired man rose and came to me, murmuring that I should follow him. I did. Thus ended my first meeting with my grandfather, and thus began my first day as an Arameri. It was not the worst of the days to come.

if you enjoyed
THE STONE SKY
look out for
WAKE OF VULTURES
The Shadow
by
Lila Bowen

Nettie Lonesome dreams of a greater life than toiling as a slave in the sandy desert. But when a stranger attacks her, Nettie wins more than the fight.

Now she's got friends, a good horse, and a better gun. But if she can't kill the thing haunting her nightmares and stealing children across the prairie, she'll lose it all—and never find out what happened to her real family.

Wake of Vultures *is the first novel of the Shadow series featuring the fearless Nettie Lonesome.*

Chapter 1

Nettie Lonesome had two things in the world that were worth a sweet goddamn: her old boots and her one-eyed mule, Blue. Neither item actually belonged to her. But then again, nothing did. Not even the whisper-thin blanket she lay under, pretending to be asleep and wishing the black mare would get out of the water trough before things went south.

The last fourteen years of Nettie's life had passed in a shriveled corner of Durango territory under the leaking roof of this wind-chapped lean-to with Pap and Mam, not quite a slave and nowhere close to something like a daughter. Their faces, white and wobbling as new butter under a smear of prairie dirt, held no kindness. The boots and the mule had belonged to Pap, right up until the day he'd exhausted their use, a sentiment he threatened to apply to her every time she was just a little too slow with the porridge.

"Nettie! Girl, you take care of that wild filly, or I'll put one in her goddamn skull!"

Pap got in a lather when he'd been drinking, which was pretty much always. At least this time his anger was aimed at a critter instead of Nettie. When the witch-hearted black filly had first shown up on the farm, Pap had laid claim and pronounced her a fine chunk of flesh and a sign of the Creator's good graces. If Nettie broke her and sold her for a decent price, she'd be closer to paying back Pap for taking her in as a baby when nobody else had wanted her but the hungry, circling vultures. The value Pap placed on feeding and housing a half-

Injun, half-black orphan girl always seemed to go up instead of down, no matter that Nettie did most of the work around the homestead these days. Maybe that was why she'd not been taught her sums: Then she'd know her own damn worth, to the penny.

But the dainty black mare outside wouldn't be roped, much less saddled and gentled, and Nettie had failed to sell her to the cowpokes at the Double TK Ranch next door. Her idol, Monty, was a top hand and always had a kind word. But even he had put a boot on Pap's poorly kept fence, laughed through his mustache, and hollered that a horse that couldn't be caught couldn't be sold. No matter how many times Pap drove the filly away with poorly thrown bottles, stones, and bullets, the critter crept back under cover of night to ruin the water by dancing a jig in the trough, which meant another blistering trip to the creek with a leaky bucket for Nettie.

Splash, splash. Whinny.

Could a horse laugh? Nettie figured this one could.

Pap, however, was a humorless bastard who didn't get a joke that didn't involve bruises.

"Unless you wanna go live in the flats, eatin' bugs, you'd best get on, girl."

Nettie rolled off her worn-out straw tick, hoping there weren't any scorpions or centipedes on the dusty dirt floor. By the moon's scant light she shook out Pap's old boots and shoved her bare feet into into the cracked leather.

Splash, splash.

The shotgun cocked loud enough to be heard across the border, and Nettie dove into Mam's old wool cloak and ran toward the stockyard with her long, thick braids slapping against her back. Mam said nothing, just rocked in her chair by the window, a bottle cradled in her arm like a baby's corpse. Grabbing the rawhide whip from its nail by the warped door, Nettie hurried past Pap on the porch and stumbled across the yard, around two mostly roofless barns, and toward the wet black shape taunting her in the moonlight against a backdrop of stars.

"Get on, mare. Go!"

A monster in a flapping jacket with a waving whip would send any horse with sense wheeling in the opposite direction, but this horse had apparently been dancing in the creek on the day sense was handed out. The mare stood in the water trough and stared at Nettie like she was a damn strange bird, her dark eyes blinking with moonlight and her lips pulled back over long, white teeth.

Nettie slowed. She wasn't one to quirt a horse, but if the mare kept causing a ruckus, Pap would shoot her without a second or even a first thought—and he wasn't so deep in his bottle that he was sure to miss. Getting smacked with rawhide had to be better than getting shot in the head, so Nettie doubled up her shouting and prepared herself for the heartache that would accompany the smack of a whip on unmarred hide. She didn't even own the horse, much less the right to beat it. Nettie had grown up trying to be the opposite of Pap, and hurting something that didn't come with claws and a stinger went against her grain.

"Shoo, fool, or I'll have to whip you," she said, creeping closer. The horse didn't budge, and for the millionth time, Nettie swung the whip around the horse's neck like a rope, all gentle-like. But, as ever, the mare tossed her head at exactly the right moment, and the braided leather snickered against the wooden water trough instead.

"Godamighty, why won't you move on? Ain't nobody wants you, if you won't be rode or bred. Dumb mare."

At that, the horse reared up with a wild scream, spraying water as she pawed the air. Before Nettie could leap back to avoid the splatter, the mare had wheeled and galloped into the night. The starlight showed her streaking across the prairie with a speed Nettie herself would've enjoyed, especially if it meant she could turn her back on Pap's dirt-poor farm and no-good cattle company forever. Doubling over to stare at her scuffed boots while she caught her breath, Nettie felt her hope disappear with hoofbeats in the night.

A low and painfully unfamiliar laugh trembled out of the barn's shadow, and Nettie cocked the whip back so that it was ready to strike.

"Who's that? Jed?"

But it wasn't Jed, the mule-kicked, sometimes stable boy, and she already knew it.

"Looks like that black mare's giving you a spot of trouble, darlin'. If you were smart, you'd set fire to her tail."

A figure peeled away from the barn, jerky-thin and slithery in a too-short coat with buttons that glinted like extra stars. The man's hat was pulled low, his brown hair overshaggy and his lily-white hand on his gun in a manner both unfriendly and relaxed that Nettie found insulting.

"You best run off, mister. Pap don't like strangers on his land, especially when he's only a bottle in. If it's horses you want, we ain't got none worth selling. If you want work and you're dumb and blind, best come back in the morning when he's slept off the mezcal."

"I wouldn't work for that good-for-nothing piss-pot even if I needed work."

The stranger switched sides with his toothpick and looked Nettie up and down like a horse he was thinking about stealing. Her fist tightened on the whip handle, her fingers going cold. She wouldn't defend Pap or his land or his sorry excuses for cattle, but she'd defend the only thing other than Blue that mostly belonged to her. Men had been pawing at her for two years now, and nobody'd yet come close to reaching her soft parts, not even Pap.

"Then you'd best move on, mister."

The feller spit his toothpick out on the ground and took a step forward, all quiet-like because he wore no spurs. And that was Nettie's first clue that he wasn't what he seemed.

"Naw, I'll stay. Pretty little thing like you to keep me company."

That was Nettie's second clue. Nobody called her pretty unless they wanted something. She looked around the yard, but all she saw were sand, chaparral, bone-dry cow patties, and the remains of a fence that Pap hadn't seen fit to fix. Mam was surely asleep, and Pap had gone inside, or maybe around back to piss. It was just the stranger and her. And the whip.

"Bullshit," she spit.

"Put down that whip before you hurt yourself, girl."

"Don't reckon I will."

The stranger stroked his pistol and started to circle her. Nettie shook the whip out behind her as she spun in place to face him and hunched over in a crouch. He stopped circling when the barn yawned behind her, barely a shell of a thing but darker than sin in the corners. And then he took a step forward, his silver pistol out and flashing starlight. Against her will, she took a step back. Inch by inch he drove her into the barn with slow, easy steps. Her feet rattled in the big boots, her fingers numb around the whip she had forgotten how to use.

"What is it you think you're gonna do to me, mister?"

It came out breathless, god damn her tongue.

His mouth turned up like a cat in the sun. "Something nice. Something somebody probably done to you already. Your master or pappy, maybe."

She pushed air out through her nose like a bull. "Ain't got a pappy. Or a master."

"Then I guess nobody'll mind, will they?"

That was pretty much it for Nettie Lonesome. She spun on her heel and ran into the barn, right where he'd been pushing her to go. But she didn't flop down on the hay or toss down the mangy blanket that had dried into folds in the broke-down, three-wheeled rig. No, she snatched the sickle from the wall and spun to face him under the hole in the roof. Starlight fell down on her ink-black braids and glinted off the parts of the curved blade that weren't rusted up.

"I reckon I'd mind," she said.

Nettie wasn't a little thing, at least not height-wise, and she'd figured that seeing a pissed-off woman with a weapon in each hand would be enough to drive off the curious feller and send him back to the whores at the Leaping Lizard, where he apparently belonged. But the stranger just laughed and cracked his knuckles like he was glad for a fight and would take his pleasure with his fists instead of his twig.

"You wanna play first? Go on, girl. Have your fun. You think you're facin' down a coydog, but you found a timber wolf."

As he stepped into the barn, the stranger went into shadow for just a second, and that was when Nettie struck. Her whip whistled for his feet and managed to catch one ankle, yanking hard enough to pluck him off his feet and onto the back of his fancy jacket. A puff of dust went up as he thumped on the ground, but he just crossed his ankles and stared at her and laughed. Which pissed her off more. Dropping the whip handle, Nettie took the sickle in both hands and went for the stranger's legs, hoping that a good slash would keep him from chasing her but not get her sent to the hangman's noose. But her blade whistled over a patch of nothing. The man was gone, her whip with him.

Nettie stepped into the doorway to watch him run away, her heart thumping underneath the tight muslin binding she always wore over her chest. She squinted into the long, flat night, one hand on the hinge of what used to be a barn door, back before the church was willing to pay cash money for Pap's old lumber. But the stranger wasn't hightailing it across the prairie. Which meant...

"Looking for someone, darlin'?"

She spun, sickle in hand, and sliced into something that felt like a ham with the round part of the blade. Hot blood spattered over her, burning like lye.

"Goddammit, girl! What'd you do that for?"

She ripped the sickle out with a sick splash, but the man wasn't standing in the barn, much less falling to the floor. He was hanging upside-down from a cross-beam, cradling his arm. It made no goddamn sense, and Nettie couldn't stand a thing that made no sense, so she struck again while he was poking around his wound.

This time, she caught him in the neck. This time, he fell.

The stranger landed in the dirt and popped right back up into a crouch. The slice in his neck looked like the first carving in an undercooked roast, but the blood was slurry and smelled like rotten meat. And the stranger was sneering at her.

"Girl, you just made the biggest mistake of your short, useless life."

Then he sprang at her.

There was no way he should've been able to jump at her like that with those wounds, and she brought her hands straight up without thinking. Luckily, her fist still held the sickle, and the stranger took it right in the face, the point of the blade jerking into his eyeball with a moist squish. Nettie turned away and lost most of last night's meager dinner in a noisy splatter against the wall of the barn. When she spun back around, she was surprised to find that the fool hadn't fallen or died or done anything helpful to her cause. Without a word, he calmly pulled the blade out of his eye and wiped a dribble of black glop off his cheek.

His smile was a cold, dark thing that sent Nettie's feet toward Pap and the crooked house and anything but the stranger who wouldn't die, wouldn't scream, and wouldn't leave her alone. She'd never felt safe a day in her life, but now she recognized the chill hand of death, reaching for her. Her feet trembled in the too-big boots as she stumbled backward across the bumpy yard, tripping on stones and bits of trash. Turning her back on the demon man seemed intolerably stupid. She just had to get past the round pen, and then she'd be halfway to the house. Pap wouldn't be worth much by now, but he had a gun by his side. Maybe the stranger would give up if he saw a man instead of just a half-breed girl nobody cared about.

Nettie turned to run and tripped on a fallen chunk of fence, going down hard on hands and skinned knees. When she looked up, she saw butternut-brown pants stippled with blood and no-spur boots tapping.

"Pap!" she shouted. "Pap, help!"

She was gulping in a big breath to holler again when the stranger's boot caught her right under the ribs and knocked it all back out. The force of the kick flipped her over onto her back, and she scrabbled away from the stranger and toward the ramshackle round pen of old, gray branches and junk roped together, just barely enough fence to trick a colt into staying put. They'd slaughtered a pig in here, once, and now Nettie knew how he felt.

As soon as her back fetched up against the pen, the stranger crouched in front of her, one eye closed and weeping black and the other brim-full with evil over the bloody slice in his neck. He looked like a dead man, a corpse groom, and Nettie was pretty sure she was in the hell Mam kept threatening her with.

"Ain't nobody coming. Ain't nobody cares about a girl like you. Ain't nobody gonna need to, not after what you done to me."

The stranger leaned down and made like he was going to kiss her with his mouth wide open, and Nettie did the only thing that came to mind. She grabbed up a stout twig from the wall of the pen and stabbed him in the chest as hard as she damn could.

She expected the stick to break against his shirt like the time she'd seen a buggy bash apart against the general store during a twister. But the twig sunk right in like a hot knife in butter. The stranger shuddered and fell on her, his mouth working as gloppy red-black liquid bubbled out. She didn't trust blood anymore, not after the first splat had burned her, and she wasn't much for being found under a corpse, so Nettie shoved him off hard and shot to her feet, blowing air as hard as a galloping horse.

The stranger was rolling around on the ground, plucking at his chest. Thick clouds blotted out the meager starlight, and she had nothing like the view she'd have tomorrow under the white-hot, unrelenting sun. But even a girl who'd never killed a man before knew when something was wrong. She kicked him over with the toe of her boot, tit for tat, and he was light as a tumbleweed when he landed on his back.

The twig jutted up out of a black splotch in his shirt, and the slice in his neck had curled over like gone meat. His bad eye was a swamp of black, but then, everything was black at midnight. His mouth was open, the lips drawing back over too-white teeth, several of which looked like they'd come out of a panther. He wasn't breathing, and Pap wasn't coming, and Nettie's finger reached out as if it had a mind of its own and flicked one big, shiny, curved tooth.

The goddamn thing fell back into the dead man's gaping throat. Nettie jumped away, skitty as the black filly, and her boot toe brushed the dead man's shoulder, and his entire body collapsed in on itself like a puffball, thousands of sparkly motes piling up in the place he'd occupied and spilling out through his empty clothes. Utterly bewildered, she knelt and brushed the pile with trembling fingers. It was sand. Nothing but sand. A soft wind came up just then and blew some of the stranger away, revealing one of those big, curved teeth where his head had been. It didn't make a goddamn lick of sense, but it could've gone far worse.

Still wary, she stood and shook out his clothes, noting that everything was in better than fine condition, except for his white shirt, which had a twig-sized hole in the breast, surrounded by a smear of black. She knew enough of laundering and sewing to make it nice enough, and the black blood on his pants looked, to her eye, manly and tough. Even the stranger's boots were of better quality than any that had ever set foot on Pap's land, snakeskin with fancy chasing. With her own, too-big boots, she smeared the sand back into the hard, dry ground as if the stranger had never existed. All that was left was the four big panther teeth, and she put those in her pocket and tried to forget about them.

After checking the yard for anything livelier than a scorpion, she rolled up the clothes around the boots and hid them in the old rig in the barn. Knowing Pap would pester her if she left signs of a scuffle, she wiped the black glop off the sickle and hung it up, along with the whip, out of Pap's drunken reach. She didn't need any more whip scars on her back than she already had.

Out by the round pen, the sand that had once been a devil of a stranger had all blown away. There was no sign of what had almost happened, just a few more deadwood twigs pulled from the lopsided fence. On good days, Nettie spent a fair bit of time doing the dangerous work of breaking colts or doctoring cattle in here for Pap, then picking up the twigs that got knocked off and roping them back in with whatever twine she could scavenge from the town. Wood wasn't cheap, and there wasn't much of it. But Nettie's hands were twitchy still, and so she picked up the black-splattered stick and wove it back into the fence, wishing she lived in a world where her life was worth more than a mule, more than boots, more than a stranger's cold smile in the barn. She'd had her first victory, but no one would ever believe her, and if they did, she wouldn't be cheered. She'd be hanged.

That stranger—he had been all kinds of wrong. And the way that he'd wanted to touch her—that felt wrong, too. Nettie couldn't recall being touched in kindness, not in all her years with Pap and Mam. Maybe that was why she understood horses. Mustangs were wild things captured by thoughtless men, roped and branded and beaten until their heads hung low, until it took spurs and whips to move them in rage and fear. But Nettie could feel the wildness inside their hearts, beating under skin that quivered under the flat of her palm. She didn't break a horse, she gentled it. And until someone touched her with that same kindness, she would continue to shy away, to bare her teeth and lower her head.

Someone, surely, had been kind to her once, long ago. She could feel it in her bones. But Pap said she'd been tossed out like trash, left on the prairie to die. Which she almost had, tonight. Again.

Pap and Mam were asleep on the porch, snoring loud as thunder. When Nettie crept past them and into the house, she had four shiny teeth in one fist, a wad of cash from the stranger's pocket, and more questions than there were stars.